teddekker.com

DEKKER FANTASY

BOOKS OF HISTORY CHRONICLES

THE LOST BOOKS (YOUNG ADULT)
Chosen
Infidel
Renegade
Chaos
Lunatic (WITH KACI HILL)
Elyon (WITH KACI HILL)
The Lost Books Visual Edition

THE CIRCLE SERIES
Black
Red
White
Green
The Circle Series Visual Edition

THE PARADISE BOOKS
Showdown
Saint
Sinner

Immanuel's Veins
House (WITH FRANK PERETTI)

DEKKER MYSTERY

Kiss (WITH ERIN HEALY)
Burn (WITH ERIN HEALY)

THE HEAVEN TRILOGY
Heaven's Wager
When Heaven Weeps
Thunder of Heaven

The Martyr's Song

THE CALEB BOOKS
Blessed Child
A Man Called Blessed

DEKKER THRILLER

THR3E
Obsessed
Adam
Skin
Blink of an Eye

THE Heaven TRILOGY

THE Heaven TRILOGY

TED DEKKER

THOMAS NELSON
Since 1798

NASHVILLE DALLAS MEXICO CITY RIO DE JANEIRO

Published in Nashville, Tennessee, by Thomas Nelson. Thomas Nelson is a registered trademark of Thomas Nelson, Inc.

Thomas Nelson, Inc., titles may be purchased in bulk for educational, business, fund-raising, or sales promotional use. For information, please e-mail SpecialMarkets@ThomasNelson.com.

ISBN: 978-1-59554-780-4

Printed in the United States of America

10 11 12 13 14 QG 5 4 3 2 1

For LeeAnn, my wife,
without whose love I
would be only a shadow
of myself. I will never
forget the day you saw heaven.

Dear Reader;

As many of you know, all of my novels are written out of personal experience. This trilogy of novels, *Heaven's Wager*, *When Heaven Weeps*, and *Thunder of Heaven*, followed a time of terrible mourning for me. My brother, Danny, who was 33 at the time, died suddenly from Bacterial Meningitis. He left two children and a wife behind.

His death was like a gut punch to me. I reeled for weeks. Months. Unable to comprehend the pain that kept reducing me to tears. And so I turned to my muse, that gift I was given to work through my own challenges.

A novel. Which turned into three novels.

Heaven's Wager asks one question as the rather humorous story of our bank robber takes flight: Is there really life beyond the skin of this world? What does it look like?

But I wasn't entirely satisfied after penning that novel, and so I dove in again, this time with an even starker, darker tale which I appropriately titled *When Heaven Weeps.* It left some readers reeling. So then they perhaps felt the same pain I had in those darkest of moments. But it left most readers shouting with joy at my side.

I can't count how many readers swear this novel is the best—perhaps the only good—thing I've ever written. You'll have to decide.

Thunder of Heaven was a return to the jungle for me, a way to tie the death of my brother into our mutual rearing in the jungles of Indonesia.

The three novels in your hands call back to a critical chapter in my life which bore great pain and now, many years later, great satisfaction. I think I've answered those questions for the most part. I only pray that you too find your answers.

Table of Contents

Heaven's
Wager

Chapter One

Present Day

AN OVERHEAD fan swished through the afternoon heat above Padre Francis Cadione's head, squeaking once every rotation, but otherwise not a sound disturbed the silence in the small, dimly lit room. A strong smell of lemon oil mixed with pipe smoke lingered in the air. The windows on either side of the ancient desk reached tall and narrow to the ceiling and cast an amber light across the oak floor.

Some described the furnishings as gothic. Cadione preferred to think of his office as merely atmospheric. Which was fitting. He was a man of the church, and the church was all about atmosphere.

But the visitor sitting with folded hands in the burgundy guest chair had brought his own atmosphere with him. It spread like an aura of heavy perfume that dispensed with the nostrils and made straight for the spine. The man had been sitting there for less than a minute now, smiling like a banshee as though he alone knew some great secret, and already Padre Cadione felt oddly out of balance. One of the visitor's legs swung over the other like a hypnotizing pendulum. His blue eyes held their gaze on the priest's, refusing to release the connection.

The padre shifted his eyes, reached for his black pipe, and clicked its stem gently along his teeth. The small gesture of habit brought a familiar easiness. A thin tendril of tobacco smoke rose lazily past his bushy eyebrows before meeting wafts of fan-air and then scattering. He crossed his legs and realized the moment he had done so that he'd inadvertently matched the visitor's posture.

Relax, Francis. You're seeing things now. He's just a man sitting there. A man not as easily impressed as others, perhaps, but a mere man nonetheless.

"So then, my friend. You seem to be in good spirits."

"Good spirits? And what do you mean by good spirits, Padre?"

The man's gentle voice seemed to carry that strange aura with it—the one that had tingled the padre's spine. It was as though their roles had become confused. Spun around by that old ceiling fan whacking away up there.

Padre Cadione drew at the pipe and released the smoke through his lips. He spoke through the haze. Atmosphere. It was all about atmosphere.

"I only meant you seem to be pretty happy with life, despite your . . . adversity. Nothing more."

"Adversity?" The man's left brow arched. The smile below his blue eyes broadened slightly. "Adversity is a relative term, isn't it? It seems to me that if someone is *happy,* as you say, his circumstances cannot be adequately described as *adverse.* No?"

Cadione wasn't sure if the man actually wanted an answer. The question felt more like a reprimand—as if this man had risen above mere happiness and now schooled those foolish mortals who still struggled with the simple pursuit of it.

"But you are right. I am in very good spirits," the man said.

Cadione cleared his throat and smiled. "Yes, I can see that."

Thing of it was, this man was not just happy. He literally seemed thrilled with whatever had gotten under his skin. Not drugs—surely not.

The visitor sat there cross-legged, staring at him with those deep blue eyes, wearing an inviting smile. Daring him, it seemed. *Come on, Padre, do your thing. Tell me about God. Tell me about goodness and happiness and about how nothing really matters but knowing God. Tell me, tell me, tell me, baby. Tell me.*

The priest felt a small, nervous grin cross his face. That was the other thing about this man's brand of happiness. It seemed infectious, if a tad presumptuous.

Either way, the man was waiting, and Cadione could not just sit there forever contemplating matters. He owed this man something. He was, after all, a man of God, employed to shed light. Or at least to point the way to the light switch.

"Being certain of one's place in life does indeed bring one happiness," Cadione said.

"I knew you could understand, Padre! You have no idea how good it is to speak to someone who really understands. Sometimes I feel like I'm ready to burst and no one around me understands. You do understand, don't you?"

"Yes." Cadione nodded instinctively, grinning, still surprised by the man's passion.

"Exactly! People like you and I may have all the wealth in the world, but it's this other thing that is really the magic of life."

"Yes."

"Nothing compares. Nothing at all. Am I right?"

"Yes." A small chuckle escaped Cadione's lips. Goodness, he was starting to feel as though he were being led into a trap with this long string of *yeses.* There could be no doubting the man's sincerity. Or his passion, for that matter. On the other hand, the man might very well have lost his reason. Become eccentric, even senile. Cadione had seen it happen to plenty of people in the man's social strata.

The visitor leaned forward with a sparkle in his eyes. He spoke in a hushed voice now. "Have you ever seen it, Padre?"

"Seen what?" He knew he sounded far too much like a young boy sitting wide eyed at the instruction of a wise father, but Cadione was powerless to stop himself.

"The great reality behind all things." The man lifted his eyes past Cadione to a painting of God's hand reaching out to a man's on the wall behind. "The hand of God." He nodded at the painting, and the priest twisted in his seat.

"God's hand? Yes, I see it every day. Everywhere I look."

"Yes, of course. But I mean really *see,* Padre? Have you actually seen him *do* things? Not something you believe he *might* have done. Like, *Lookie there, I do believe God has opened up a parking spot near the door for us, Honey.* But have you really seen God do something before your eyes?"

The man's exuberance reignited the tingle in Cadione's spine. If the man had lost his sensibilities, perhaps he had found something better. Of course, even if God did have his fingers down here on Earth stirring the pot, people couldn't just open their eyes and *see* it. He pictured a large thumb and forefinger picking up a car and moving it to allow a van easy parking.

"Actually, I can't say that I have."

"Well, I know someone who has. I know someone who *does.*"

A silence settled. The visitor stared at him with those piercing baby blues. But the eyes were not the eyes of a madman. Padre Cadione drew on the pipe, but it had lost its fire and he was rewarded with nothing but stale air.

"You do, huh?"

"I do." The man leaned back again, smiling softly. "And I have seen. Would you like to see, Padre?"

There was a magic in the man's words. A mystery that spoke of truth. He swallowed and leaned back, once again matching the visitor's posture. It occurred to him that he had not actually responded to the man's question.

"It might change your world," the man said.

"Yes. I'm sorry, I was . . . uh . . ."

"Well then." The man drew a deep breath and crossed his legs once again. "Open your mind, my friend. Wide open. Can you do that?"

"Yes . . . Yes, I suppose."

"Good. I have a story for you."

The visitor took another deep breath, thoroughly satisfied with himself, it seemed, and he began.

CHAPTER TWO

One Year Earlier
Week One

THE CITY was Littleton, a suburb of Denver. The neighborhood was best known as Belaire, an upper-middle-class spread of homes carefully spaced along black streets that snaked between bright green lawns. The street was named Kiowa after the Indians who'd long ago called the plains their own. The home, a two-story stucco topped with a red ceramic tile roof—affectionately called the Windsor by the developer—was the most luxurious model offered in the subdivision. The man standing at the front door was Kent Anthony, the holder of the hefty mortgage on this little corner of the American dream.

In his left hand, a dozen fresh-cut red roses moved to a gentle breeze, starkly accenting the black, double-breasted suit that hung from his narrow shoulders. He stood a lanky six feet, maybe six-two with shoes. Blond hair covered his head, close cropped above the collar. His eyes sparkled blue above a sharp nose; his smooth complexion cast the illusion that he was ten years younger than his true age. Any woman might see him and think he looked like a million bucks.

But today was different. Today Kent was *feeling* like a million bucks because today Kent had actually *earned* a million bucks. Or maybe several million bucks.

The corners of his mouth lifted, and he pressed the illuminated doorbell. His heart began to race, standing right there on his front porch waiting for the large colonial door to swing open. The magnitude of his accomplishment once again rolled through his mind and sent a shudder through his bones. He, Kent Anthony, had managed what only one in ten thousand managed to achieve, according to the good people in the census bureau.

And he had done it by age thirty-six, coming from perhaps the most unlikely beginnings imaginable, starting at absolute zero. The skinny, poverty-stricken child from Botany Street who had promised his father that he would make it, no matter what the cost, had just made good on that promise. He had stretched his boundaries to the snapping point a thousand times in the last twenty years and now . . . Well, now he would stand tall and proud in the family annals. And to be truthful, he could hardly stand the pleasure of it all.

The door suddenly swung in and Kent started. Gloria stood there, her mouth parted in surprise, her hazel eyes wide. A yellow summer dress with small blue flowers settled graciously over her slender figure. A queen fit for a prince. That would be him.

"Kent!"

He spread his arms and smiled wide. Her eyes shifted to the hand holding the roses, and she caught her breath. The breeze swept past him and lifted her hair, as if invited by that gasp.

"Oh, Honey!"

He proudly offered her the bouquet and bowed slightly. In that moment, watching her strain with delight, the breeze lifting blonde strands of hair away from her slender neck, Kent felt as though his heart might burst. He did not wait for her to speak again but stepped through the threshold and embraced her. He wrapped his long arms around her waist and lifted her to meet his kiss. She returned the affection passionately and then squealed with laughter, steadying the roses behind him.

"Am I a man who keeps his word, or am I not?"

"Careful, dear! The roses. What on Earth has possessed you? It's the middle of the day!"

"*You* have possessed me," Kent growled. He set her down and pecked her cheek once more for good measure. He spun from her and bowed in mock chivalry.

She lifted the roses and studied them with sparkling eyes. "They're beautiful! Really, what's the occasion?"

Kent peeled off his coat and tossed it over the stair banister. "The occasion is you. The occasion is us. Where's Spencer? I want him to hear this."

Gloria grinned and called down the hall. "Spencer! Someone's here to see you."

A voice called from the hallway. "Who?" Spencer slid around the corner in his stocking feet. His eyes popped wide. "Dad?" The boy ran up to him.

"Hi, Tiger." Kent bent and swept Spencer from his feet in a great bear hug. "You good?"

"Sure."

Spencer wrapped his arms around his father's neck and squeezed tight. Kent set the ten-year-old down and faced them both. They stood there, picture perfect, mother and child, five-three and four-three, his flesh and blood. Behind them a dozen family pictures and as many portraits graced the entryway wall. Snapshots of the last twelve years: Spencer as a baby in powder blue; Gloria holding Spencer in front of the first apartment, lovely lime-green walls surrounded by wilting flowers; the three of them in dwelling number two's living room—a real house this time—grinning ear to ear as if the old brown sofa on which they sat was really the latest style instead of a ten-dollar afterthought purchased at some stranger's garage sale. Then the largest picture, taken two years earlier, just after they had purchased this home—house number three if you counted the apartment.

Kent saw them all in a glance, and he immediately thought a new picture would go up now. But on a different wall. A different home. A much bigger home. He glanced at Gloria and winked. Her eyes grew as if she'd guessed something.

He leaned down to his son. "Spencer, I have some very important news. Something very good has just happened to us. Do you know what it is?"

Spencer glanced at his mother with questioning eyes. He nimbly swept blond bangs from his forehead and stared up at Kent. For a moment they stood, silent.

Then his son spoke in a thin voice. "You finished?"

"And what is *finished* supposed to mean? Finished what, boy?"

"The program?"

Kent shot Gloria a wink. "Smart boy we have here. And what does that mean, Spencer?"

"Money?"

"You actually finished?" Gloria asked, stunned. "It passed?"

Kent released his son's shoulder and pumped a fist through the air. "You bet it did! This morning."

He stood tall and feigned an official announcement. "My friends, the Advanced Funds Processing System, the brainchild of one Kent Anthony, has passed all tests with flying colors. The Advanced Funds Processing System not only works, it works perfectly!"

Spencer grinned wide and whooped.

Gloria glowed proudly, reached up on her tippytoes, and kissed Kent on his chin. "Splendid job, Sir Anthony."

Kent bowed and then leapt for the living room. A catwalk spanned the two-story ceiling above; he ran under it toward the cream leather furniture. He cleared the sofa in a single bound and dropped to one knee, pumping that arm again as if he'd just caught a touchdown pass. "Yes! Yes, yes, *yes!*"

The Spanish-style interior lay immaculate about him, the way Gloria insisted it remain. Large ceramic tile ran past a breakfast bar and into the kitchen to his right. A potted palm draped over the entertainment center to his left. Directly before him, above a fireplace not yet used, stood a tall painting of Christ supporting a sagging, forsaken man holding a hammer and spikes. *Forgiven,* it was called.

He whirled to them. "Do you have any idea what this means? Let me tell you what this means."

Spencer squealed around the sofa and jumped on his knee, nearly knocking Kent to his back. Gloria vaulted the same cream leather sofa, barefooted, her yellow dress flying. She ended on her knees in the cushions, smiling wide, waiting, winking at Spencer, who had watched her make the leap.

Kent felt a fresh surge of affection seize his heart. Boy, he loved her! "This means that your father has just changed the way banks process funds." He paused, thinking about that. "Let me put it another way. Your father has just saved Niponbank millions of dollars in operating costs." He thrust a finger into the air and popped his eyes wide. "No, wait! Did I say millions of dollars? No, that would be in one year. Over the long haul, *hundreds* of millions of dollars! And do you know what big banks do for people who save them hundreds of millions of dollars?"

He stared into his son's bright eyes and answered his own question quickly before Spencer beat him to it. "They give them a few of those millions, that's what they do!"

"They've approved the bonus?" Gloria asked.

"Borst put the paperwork through this morning." He turned to the side and pumped his arm again. "Yes! Yes, yes, yes!"

Spencer slid off his knee, flopped backward on the couch, and kicked his legs into the air. "Yahoo! Does this mean we get to go to Disneyland?"

They laughed. Kent stood and stepped toward Gloria. "You bet it does." He plucked one of the roses still gripped in her hand and held it out at arm's length. "It also means we will celebrate tonight." He winked at his wife again and began to dance with the rose extended, as if it were his partner. "Wine . . ." He closed his eyes and lifted his chin. "Music . . ." He spread his arms wide and twirled once on his toes. "Exquisite food . . ."

"Lobster!" Spencer said.

"The biggest lobster you can imagine. From the tank," Kent returned and kissed the rose. Gloria laughed and wiped her eyes.

"Of course, this does mean a few small changes in our plans," Kent said, still holding up the red bud. "I have to fly to Miami this weekend. Borst wants me to make the announcement to the board at the annual meeting. It seems that my career as a celebrity has already begun."

"This weekend?" Gloria lifted an eyebrow.

"Yes, I know. Our anniversary. But not to worry, my queen. Your prince will be leaving Friday and returning Saturday. And then we will celebrate our twelfth like we have never dreamt of celebrating."

His eyes sparkled mischievously, and he turned to Spencer. "Excuse me, sire. But would Sunday or Monday suit you best for a ride on the Matterhorn?"

His son's eyes bulged. "The Matterhorn?" He gasped. "Disneyland?"

Gloria giggled. "And just how are we supposed to get to California by Sunday if you're going to Miami?"

Kent looked at Spencer, sucking a quick breath, feigning shock. "Your mother's right. It will have to be Monday, sire. Because I do fear there is no carriage that will take us to Paris in time for Sunday's games."

He let the statement stand. For a moment only the breeze sounded, flipping the kitchen curtains.

Then it came. "Paris?" Gloria's voice wavered slightly.

Kent turned his head toward her and winked. "But of course, my queen. It is, after all, the city of love. And I hear Mickey has set up shop to boot."

"You are taking us to *Paris?"* Gloria demanded, still unbelieving. The giggle had fled, chased away by true shock. "Paris, France? Can—can we *do* that?"

Kent smiled. "My dear, we can do anything now." He lifted a fist of victory into the air.

"Paris!"

Then the Anthonys let restraint fly out the window, and pandemonium broke out in the living room. Spencer hooted and unsuccessfully attempted to vault the couch as his parents had. He sprawled to a tumble. Gloria rushed Kent and shrieked, not so much in shock, but because shrieking fit the mood just now. Kent hugged his wife around the waist and swung her in circles.

It was a good day. A very good day.

Chapter Three

THEY SAT there, the three of them, Gloria, Helen, and Spencer, in Helen's living room, on overstuffed green chairs, the way they sat every Thursday morning, preparing to begin their knocking. Gloria's right leg draped over her left, swinging lightly. She held folded hands on her lap and watched grandmother and grandson engage each other with sparkling eyes.

The fact that Spencer could join them came as one of the small blessings of homeschooling. She had questioned whether a boy Spencer's age would find a prayer meeting engaging, but Helen had insisted. "Children have better spiritual vision than you might think," she'd said. It only took one meeting with Helen for Spencer to agree.

At age sixty-four, Gloria's mother, Helen Jovic, possessed one of the most sensitive spirits harbored in the souls of mankind. But even the most dimwitted soul who'd read her story would know why. It was all there, penned by her late husband, Jan Jovic—the events of that fateful day in Bosnia as told in "The Martyr's Song" and then the rest of the story written in *When Heaven Weeps.*

Gloria knew the story perhaps better than she knew her own for the simple reason that it was written and her own history wasn't. How many times had she read Janjic's story? She could clearly imagine that day when a handful of soldiers including Jan Jovic entered the small village in Bosnia and tormented the peaceloving women and children.

She could imagine the great sacrifice paid that day.

She could see the heavens opening.

And above all she could hear the song. "The Martyr's Song," penned now and sung throughout the world by many devout believers.

That day had forever changed Jan Jovic's life. But it was only the beginning.

If you knew how to listen, the Martyr's Song could be heard today, still changing lives. Helen's life, for example. And then her daughter Gloria's life. And now Spencer's life.

When Jan had died Helen was still quite young. She'd been left alone to find solace with God. And nothing seemed to bring her that solace like the hours she spent shuffling about the house, hounding heaven, drawing near to the throne. The shuffling used to be pacing, an insistent pacing that actually began many years ago while Gloria was still a child. Gloria would often kneel on the sofa, combing the knots from her doll's hair, watching her mother step across worn carpet with lifted hands, smiling to the sky.

"I am an intercessor," Helen told her young daughter. "I speak with God."

And God spoke to her, Gloria thought. More so lately, it seemed.

Helen sat flat footed, rocking slowly in the overstuffed green rocker, her hands resting on the chair's worn arms. A perpetual smile bunched soft cheeks. Her hazel eyes glistened like jewels set in her face, which was lightly dusted with powder but otherwise free of makeup. Her silver hair curled to her ears and down to her neck. She was not as thin as she had been in her early years, but she carried the additional fifteen pounds well. The dresses her mother wore were partly responsible. She could not remember ever seeing her mother wear slacks. Today the dress was a white summer shirtwaist sprinkled with light blue roses that flowed in soft pleats to her knees.

Gloria glanced at her son, who sat with his legs crossed under him the way he always sat, Indian style. He was telling his grandmother about the upcoming trip to Disneyland with wide eyes, stumbling over his words. She smiled. They had finalized the plans last evening at Antonio's while dining on steak and lobster. Kent would leave for Miami Friday morning and return Saturday in time to catch a 6 P.M. flight to Paris. The short-notice tickets had cost the world, but the fact had only put a broader smile on her husband's face. They would arrive in France on Monday, check into some classy hotel called the Lapier, catch their breath while feasting on impossibly expensive foods, and rest for the next day's adventure. Kent was finally about to live his childhood dream, and he was setting about it with a vengeance.

Of course, Kent's success did not come without its price. It required focus, and something was bound to give in favor of that focus. In Kent's case it was his faith in God, which had never been his strong suit anyway. Within three years of their marriage, Kent's faith left him. Entirely. There was no longer room in his heart for a faith in the unseen. He was too busy chasing things he *could* see. It wasn't just an apathy—Kent did not do apathy. He either did or he did not do. It was either all out or not at all. And God became not at all.

Four years ago, just after Spencer had turned six, Helen had come to Gloria, nearly frantic. "We need to begin," she'd said.

"Begin what?" Gloria had asked.

"Begin the knocking."

"Knocking?"

"Yes, knocking—on heaven's door. For Kent's soul."

For Helen it was always either knocking or hounding.

So they had begun their Thursday morning knocking sessions then. The door to Kent's heart had not opened yet, but through it all Gloria and Spencer had peeked into heaven with Helen. What they saw had them scrambling out of bed every Thursday morning, without fail, to go to Grandma's.

And now here they were again.

"Delightful!" Helen said, flashing a smile at Gloria. "That sounds positively wonderful. I had no idea there was more than one Disneyland."

"Heavens, Mother," Gloria said. "There's been more than one Disney park for years now. You really need to get out more."

"No, thank you. No, no. I get out quite enough, thank you." She said it with a grin, but her tone rang with sincerity. "My being a stranger in that world out there is just fine by me."

"I'm sure it is. But you don't have to sequester yourself."

"Who said I was sequestering myself? I don't even know what sequestering means, for goodness' sake. And what does this have to do with my not knowing about a Disneyland in Paris, anyway?"

"Nothing. You were the one who brought up being a stranger. I'm just balancing things out a bit, that's all." God knew Helen could use a little balance in her life.

Her mother's eyes sparkled. She grinned softly, taking up the challenge. "Balance? Things are already out of balance, Honey. Upside down out of balance. You take one hundred pounds of Christian meat, and I guarantee you that ninety-eight of those pounds are sucking up to the world. It's tipping the scale right over, love." She reached up and pulled at the wrinkly skin on her neck. Nasty habit.

"Maybe, but you really don't have to use words like *sucking* to describe it. That's what I'm talking about. And how many times have I told you not to pull on your neck like that?"

Dramatics aside, Helen was right, of course, and Gloria took no offense. If anything, she warmed to her mother's indictments of society.

"It's just flesh, Gloria. See?" Helen pinched the loose skin on her arms and pulled, sampling several patches. "See, just skin. Flesh for the fire. It's what's tipping the scales the wrong way."

"Yes, but as long as you live in this world, there's no need to walk around pulling your skin in public. People don't like it." If she didn't know better, she would guess her mother senile at times.

"Well, this isn't public, for one thing, dear." Helen turned to Spencer, who sat watching the discussion with an amused smile. "It's family. Isn't that right, Spencer?"

She turned back to Gloria. "And for another thing, maybe if Christians went around pulling their skin or some such thing, people would actually know they were Christians. God knows you can't tell now. Maybe we should change our name to the Skinpullers and walk around yanking on our skin in public. That would set us apart."

Silence settled around the preposterous suggestion.

Spencer was the first to laugh, as if a dam had broken in his chest. Then Gloria, shaking her head at the ridiculous image, and finally Mother, after glancing back and forth, obviously trying to understand what was so funny. Gloria could not tell if Helen's laughter was motivated by her own skin-pulling or by their infectious cackling. Either way, the three of them had a good, long hoot.

Helen brought them back to a semblance of control, still smiling. "Well, there's more to my suggestion than what you might guess, Gloria. We laugh now, but in the end it will not seem so strange. It's this ridiculous walking around pretending not to be different that will seem crazy. I suspect a lot of heads will be banging the walls of hell in regret someday."

Gloria nodded and wiped her eyes. "Yes, you're probably right, Mother. But you do have a way with images."

Helen turned to Spencer. "Yes, now where were we when your mother so delicately diverted our discussion, Spencer?"

"Disneyland. We're going to Euro Disney in Paris," Spencer answered with a smile and a sideways glance at Gloria.

"Of course. Disneyland. Now Spencer, what do you suppose would be more fun for a day, Euro Disney or heaven?"

The sincerity descended like a heavy wool blanket.

It was perhaps the way Helen said *heaven.* As if it were a cake you could eat. That's how it was with Helen. A few words, and the hush would fall. Gloria could feel her heart tighten with anticipation. Sometimes it would begin with just a look, or a lifted finger, as if to say, Okay, let us begin. Well, now it had begun again, and Gloria sighed.

Spencer's mouth drifted into a smile. "Heaven!"

Helen lifted an eyebrow. "Why heaven?"

Most children would stutter at such a question, maybe answer with repeated words learned from their parents or Sunday school teachers. Basically meaningless words for a child, like, "To worship God." Or, "'Cause Jesus died on the cross."

But not Spencer.

"In heaven . . . I think we'll be able to do . . . anything," he said.

"I think we will too," Helen said, perfectly serious. She sighed. "Well, we'll see soon enough. Today it will have to be Paris and Disneyland. Tomorrow maybe heaven. If we're so fortunate."

The room fell silent, and Helen closed her eyes slowly. Another sign.

The sound of her own breathing rose and fell in Gloria's ears. She closed her eyes and saw pinpricks in a sea of black. Her mind climbed to another consciousness. *Oh, God. Hear my son's cry. Open our eyes. Draw our hearts. Bring us into your presence.*

For a few minutes Gloria sat in the silence, displacing small thoughts and drawing her mind to the unseen. A tear gently ripped opened in heaven for her then, like a thin fracture in a wall, allowing shafts of light to filter through. In her mind's eye, she stepped into the light and let it wash warm over her chest.

The knocking started with a prayer from Helen. Gloria opened her eyes and saw that her mother had lifted her hands toward the ceiling. Her chin was raised, and her lips moved around a smile. She was asking God for Kent's soul.

For thirty minutes they prayed like that, taking turns calling on God to hear their cry, show his mercy, send word.

Near the end, Helen rose and fetched herself a glass of lemonade. She got hot, praying to heaven, she said. Being up there with all those creatures of light made her warm all over. So she invariably broke for the lemonade or ice tea at some point.

Sometimes Gloria joined her, but today she did not want to break. Today the presence was very strong, as if that crack had frozen open and continued to pour light into her chest. Which was rather unusual, because usually the tear opened and closed, allowing only bursts of light through. A thoughtful consideration by the gatekeepers, she had once decided. So as not to overwhelm the mortals with too much at once.

Thoughts of Paris had long fled, and now Gloria basked in thoughts of the unseen. Thoughts of floating, like Spencer had said. Like the pinpricks of light in the dark of her eyes. Or maybe like a bird, but in outer space, streaking through a red nebula, wide mouthed and laughing. She would give her life for it, in a heartbeat. Thinking of it now, her pulse thickened. Sweat began to bead on her forehead. Raw desire began to well up within her, as it often did. To touch *him*, to see the Creator. Watch him create. Be loved with that same power.

Helen once told her that touching God might be like touching a thick shaft of lightning, but one filled with pleasure. It might very well kill you, she said, but at least you'd die with a smile on your face. She'd chuckled and shook her head.

Her mother seated herself, slurped the lemonade for a few seconds, and set the clinking glass beside her chair. Helen sighed, and Gloria closed her eyes, thinking, *Now, where was I?*

It was then, in that moment of regularity, that the tear in heaven gaped wide, opening as it never had. They had prayed together every Thursday, every week, every month, every year for five years, and never before had Gloria even come close to feeling and seeing and hearing what she did then.

She would later think that it is when contemplating inexplicable times such as these that men say, *He is sovereign. He will do as he wills. He will come through a virgin; he will speak from a bush; he will wrestle with a man. He is God. Who can know the mind of the Lord? Amen.* And it is the end of the matter.

But it is not the end of the matter if *you* are the virgin Mary, or if *you* hear him from a bush like Moses, or if *you* wrestle with God as did Jacob. Then it is only the beginning.

It happened suddenly, without the slightest warning. As if a dam holding the light back had broken, sending volumes of the stuff cascading down in torrents. One second trickles of power, feathering just so, like lapping waves, and the next a flood that seemed to pound into the small living room and blow away the walls.

Gloria gasped and jerked upright. Two other audible heaves filled the room, and she knew that Spencer and Helen saw it as well.

The buzzing started in her feet and ran through her bones, as if her heels had been plugged into a socket and the juice cranked up. It swept up her spine, right into her skull, and hummed. She gripped the chair's padded arms to keep her hands still from their trembling.

Oh, God! she cried, only she didn't actually cry it, because her mouth had frozen wide. Her throat had seized. A soft moan came out. "Uhhhh . . ." And in that moment, with the light pouring into her skull, rattling her bones, she knew that nothing—absolutely nothing—could ever compare to this feeling.

Her heart slammed in her chest, thumping loudly in the silence, threatening to tear itself free. Tears spilled from her eyes in small rivulets before she even had time to cry. It was that kind of power.

Then Gloria began to sob. She didn't know why exactly—only that she was weeping and shaking. Terrified, yet desperate for more at once. As if her body craved more but could not contain this much pleasure in one shot. Undone.

Far away, laughter echoed. Gloria caught her breath, drawn to the sound. It came from the light, and it grew—the sound of a child's laughter. Long strings of giggles, relentlessly robbing the breath from the child. Suddenly Gloria ached to be with the child, laughing. Because there in the light, captured in a singular union of raw power and a child's unrestrained giggles, lay eternal bliss. Ecstasy. Maybe the very fabric from which energy was first conceived.

Heaven.

She knew it all in a flash.

The light vanished suddenly. Like a tractor beam pulled back into itself.

Gloria sat arched for a brief moment and then collapsed into the chair's soft cushions, her mind spinning through a lingering buzz. *Oh, God, oh, God, oh, God, I love you! Please.* She could not say the appropriate words. Perhaps there were no appropriate words. She moaned softly and went limp.

No one spoke for several long minutes. It was not until then that Gloria even remembered Helen and Spencer. When she did, it took another minute to reorient herself and begin seeing things again.

Helen sat with her face tilted to the ceiling, her hands pressed to her temples.

Gloria turned to her son. Spencer was shaking. His eyes were still closed, his hands lay on his lap, palms up, and he shook like a leaf. Giggling. With his mouth spread wide and his cheeks bunched and his face red. Giggling like that child in the light. The sight was perhaps the most perfect image she had ever witnessed.

"Jesus," her mother's soft voice groaned. "Oh, dear Jesus!"

Gloria squeezed the chair just to make sure she was not floating, because for a moment she wondered if she'd actually been taken from the chair and set on a cloud.

She looked at her mother again. Helen had clenched shut her eyes and lifted her chin so that the skin on her neck stretched taught. Her face rose ashen to the ceiling and Gloria saw then that her mother was crying. Not crying and smiling like Spencer. But crying with a face painted in horror.

"Mom?" she asked, suddenly worried.

"Oh, God! Oh, God, please. Please, no!" Helen's fingers dug deep into the chair arms. Her face grimaced as though she were enduring the extracting of a bullet without an anesthetic.

"Mother! What's wrong?" Gloria sat straight, memories of the incredible laughter dimmed by this sight before her. "Stop it, Mother!"

Helen's muscles seemed to tense at the command. She did not stop it. "Oh, please God, no! Not now. Please, please, please . . ."

From her vantage, Gloria could see the roof of her mother's mouth, surrounded by white dentures, like a pink canyon bordered by towering pearl cliffs. A groan broke from Helen's throat like moaning wind from a deep, black cavern. A chill descended Gloria's neck. She could not mistake the expression worn by Helen now—it was the face of agony.

"Nooooo!" The sound reminded Gloria of a woman in childbirth. "Noooo . . ."

"Mother! Stop it right now! You're frightening me!" She jumped up from the chair and rushed over to Helen. Up close she saw that her mother's whole face held a slight tremor. She dropped to her knee and grabbed her mother's arm.

"Mother!"

Helen's eyes snapped open, staring at the ceiling. The moan ran out of air. Her eyes skipped over the white plaster above. She mumbled softly. "What have you shown me? What have you shown me?"

She must have found herself then, because she suddenly clamped her mouth shut and dropped her head.

For a moment they stared at each other with wide eyes.

"Mom, are you okay?"

Helen swallowed and looked over to Spencer, who was now watching intently. "Yes. Yes, I am. Sit down, my dear." She shooed Gloria back to her seat. "Go sit down. You're making me nervous." Helen was obviously scrambling for reorientation, and the words came out with less than her usual authority.

Gloria stood, stunned. "Well, you scared the living daylights out of me." She retreated to her chair, trembling slightly.

When she faced Helen again, her mother was crying, her head buried in her hands. "What *is* it, Mother?"

Helen shook her head, sniffed loudly, and straightened. "Nothing, Honey. Nothing."

But it was not *nothing;* Gloria knew that.

Helen wiped her eyes and tried to smile. "Did you hear the laughter?"

Gloria glanced at her son, who was nodding already. "Yes. It was . . . it was incredible."

Spencer grinned at her. "Yeah. I heard the laughter."

They held stares, momentarily lost in the memory of that laughter, smiling silly again.

The contentment came back like a warm fog.

They sat silently for a while, numbed by what had happened. Then Helen joined them in their smiling, but she could not hide the shadows that crossed her face. Still, the laughter consumed Gloria.

At some point a small thought ran through her mind. The thought that they were leaving for Paris soon—to celebrate. But it seemed like a fleeting, inconsequential detail, like the memory that she'd brushed her teeth that morning. Too much was happening here to think of Paris.

CHAPTER FOUR

ACROSS TOWN, Kent, light-footed and as carefree as he could remember feeling, walked up the broad steps leading to Denver's main branch of the multinational banking conglomerate Niponbank. It was an old, historic building with a face-lift of gigantic proportions. Although sections of the original wood-frame structure could still be seen on the back half of the bank, the front half appeared as grand and as modern as any contemporary building. It was the bank's way of compromising with elements in the city who did not want the building torn down. The stairway flared at street level and narrowed as it ascended, funneling patrons to three wide glass doors. Behind him eight lanes of Thursday morning's traffic bustled and blared obnoxiously, but the sound came as an anchor of familiarity, and today familiarity was good.

He smiled and smacked through the glass doors.

"Morning, Kent."

He nodded to Zak, the ever present security guard who meandered about the main lobby during business hours. "Morning, Zak. Beautiful day, isn't it?"

"Yes sir. It surely is."

Kent walked across the marble floor, nodding at several tellers who caught his eye. "Morning."

"Morning."

Mornings all around. The long row of tellers readied for business to his left. A dozen offices with picture windows now sat half-staffed on his right. Hushed tones carried through the lobby. High heels clacked along the floor to his right and he turned, half expecting to see Sidney Beech. But then, she'd already left with the others for the bank's annual conference in Miami, hadn't she? Instead it was Mary, a teller he'd met once or twice. She stepped by with a smile. Her perfume followed her in musty swirls, and Kent pulled the scent into his nostrils. Gardenia blossoms.

A dozen circular pedestals stood parallel to the long banking counter, each offering a variety of forms and golden pens to fill them out. A twenty-foot brass replica of a sailing yacht hovered five feet off the floor at the foyer's center. From a distance it appeared to be supported on a single, one-inch gold pipe under its hull. But closer inspection revealed the thin steel cables running to the ceiling. Nevertheless, the effect was stunning. Any lingering thoughts of the building's historic preservation evaporated with one look around the lobby. The architects had pretty much gutted this part of the building and started over. It was a masterpiece in design.

Kent stepped forward, toward the gaping hall opposite the entrance. There the marble floor ended, and a thick teal carpet ran into the administration wing. A large sea gull hung on the wall above the hall.

Today it all came to him like a welcoming balm. The sights, the smells, the sounds all said one word: *Success.* And today success was his.

He'd come a long way from the poor-white-trash suburbs of Kansas City. It had been the worst of all worlds—bland and boring. In most neighborhoods you either had the colors of wealth or the crimes of poverty, both of which at least introduced their own variety of spice to a boy's life. But not on Botany Street. Botany Street boasted nothing but boxy manufactured homes sporting brown lawns only occasionally greened by manual sprinklers. That was it. There were never any parades on Botany Street. There were never any fights or accidents or car chases. To a household, the neighbors along Botany Street owed their humble existence to the government. The neighborhood was a prison of sorts. Not one with bars and inmates, of course. But one to which you were sentenced with the drudgery of plowing through each day, burdened with the dogged knowledge that, even though you weren't running around stealing and killing, you were about as useful to society as those who did. Your worthless state of existence meant you would have to park your rear end here on Stupid Street and hook up to the government's mighty feeding tube. And everyone knew that those on the dole were a worthless lot.

Kent had often thought that the gangs across town had it better. Never mind that their purpose in life was to wreak as much havoc as possible without going to prison; at least they had a purpose, which was more than he could say about those on Botany Street. *Stupid Street.*

His candid observations had started during the third grade, when he'd made the decision that he was going to be Jesse Owens one day. Jesse Owens didn't need a basketball court or a big business or even a soccer ball to make the big bucks. All Jesse Owens needed were his two legs, and Kent had a pair of those. It was on his runs beyond Botany Street that Kent began to see the rest of the world. Within the year he had arrived at two conclusions. First, although he enjoyed running more than anything else in his little world, he was not cut out to be Jesse Owens. He could run long, but he could not run fast or jump far or any of the other things that Jesse Owens did.

The second thing he figured out was that he had to get off Botany Street. No matter what the cost, he and his family had to get out.

But then, as a first-generation immigrant whose parents had begged their passage to America during the Second World War, his father had never had the opportunity, much less the means to leave Botany Street.

Oh, he'd talked about it enough, all the time in fact. Sitting on the shredded brown lounger after a long day shoveling coal, in front of a black-and-white television that managed one fuzzy channel. On a good day he might have a generic beer on his lap. "I tell you, Buckwheat (his dad always called him Buckwheat), I swear I'll take us out of here one day. My folks didn't come two thousand miles on a boat to live like rabbits in someone's play box. No sir." And for a while Kent had believed him.

But his dad had never managed that journey beyond Botany Street. By the time Kent was in sixth grade he knew that if he ever wanted a life remotely similar to Jesse Owens's or even the average American's, for that matter, it would be solely up to him. And from what he could see there were only two ways to acquire a ticket for the train leaving their miserable station in life. The one ticket was pure, unsolicited fortune—winning the lottery, say, or finding a bag of cash—a prospect he quickly decided was preposterous. And the other ticket was high achievement. Super high achievement. The kind of achievement that landed people Super Bowl rings, or championship belts, or in his case, scholarships.

Beginning in grade seven he divided the sum total of his time between three pursuits. Surviving—that would be eating and sleeping and washing behind the ears now and then; running, which he still did every single day; and studying. For several hours each night he read everything he could get his spindly fingers on. In tenth grade he got a library card to the Kansas City Municipal Library, a building he figured had about every book ever written about anything. Never mind that it was a five-mile run from Botany Street; he enjoyed running anyway.

It all paid off for him one afternoon, three months after his father's death, in a single white envelope sticking out of their mail slot. He'd torn the letter out with trembling fingers, and there it was: a full academic scholarship to Colorado State University. He was leaving Stupid Street!

Some came to characterize him as a genius during his six years of higher education. In reality, his success was due much more to long hard hours with his nose in the books than to overactive gray matter.

The sweet smell of success. Yes indeed, and today, finally, success was his.

Kent walked into the hall. The back foyer was empty when he entered. Normally Norma would be sitting at the switchboard, punching buttons. Beyond her station the wide hall continued to a series of administrative divisions, each housing a suite of offices. At the hall's end, an elevator rose to three additional floors of the same. Floors four through twenty were serviced by a different elevator used by the tenants.

Kent's eyes fixed on the first door, ahead to his right, shadowed in the hall's fluorescent light. Bold, white antique letters labeled the division: Information Systems Division. Behind that door lay a small reception room and four offices. The spawning ground for Advanced Funds Processing System. His life. The division could have been placed anywhere—in a basement bunker, for all that mattered. It had little to do with the Denver branch specifically and was in fact only one of a dozen similar divisions hammering out the bank's software across the globe. Part of Niponbank's decentralization policy.

Kent walked quickly down the hall and opened the door.

His four coworkers stood in the small lobby outside of their offices, waiting for him.

"Kent! It's about time you joined us, boy!" Markus Borst beamed. His boss held a champagne glass brimming with amber liquid. A large, hooked nose gave him the appearance of a penguin. A bald penguin at that.

The redhead, Todd Brice, pushed his oversized torso from the sofa and grinned wide. "It's about time, Kent." The kid was a fool.

Betty, the department secretary, and Mary Quinn held champagne glasses they now raised to him. Red and yellow crepe paper hung in ribbons from the ceiling.

He dropped his case and laughed. He could not remember the last time the five of them had celebrated. There had been the occasional birthday cake, of course, but nothing deserving of champagne—especially not at nine o'clock in the morning.

Betty winked one of those fake black lashes. "Congratulations, Kent." Her white-blonde hair was piled a little higher than usual. She handed him a glass.

"Ladies and gentlemen," Borst announced, lifting his own glass. "Now that we are all here, I would like to propose a toast, if I may."

"Here, here," Mary chimed in.

"To AFPS, then. May she live long and prosper."

A chorus of "Here, here!s" rumbled, and together they sipped.

"And to Kent," Mary said, "who we all know made this happen!"

Another chorus of "Here, here!s," and another round of sips. Kent grinned and glanced at the light glaring off Borst's balding head.

"Gee, thanks, guys. But you know I couldn't have done it without you." It was a lie, but a good lie, he thought. In reality he could have done it easily without them. In half the time, possibly. "You guys are the best. Here's to success." He lifted his glass.

"Success," they agreed.

Borst downed the rest of his drink and set it on the coffee table with a satisfied sigh. "I say we close her down at noon today," he said. "We have a big weekend coming up. I'm not sure how much sleep we'll be getting in Miami."

Todd lifted his glass again. "To knocking off at noon," he said and threw back the balance of his drink.

Mary and Betty followed suit, mumbling agreement.

"Betty has all of your plane tickets to the Miami conference," Borst stated. "And for Pete's sake, try not to be late. If you miss the flight, you're on your own. Kent will be giving the address since he obviously knows the program as well as any of us, but I want each of you to be prepared to summarize the essentials. If things go as well as we expect, you may very well be mobbed with questions this weekend. And please, leave any mention of program bugs out of your comments for now. We don't really have any to speak of at this point, and we don't need to muddy the waters yet. Make sense?"

The man was handling himself with more authority than was customary. No one responded.

"Good, then. If you have any questions, I'll be in my office." Borst nodded theatrically and retreated to the first door on the right. Kent swallowed the last of his champagne. *That's it, Borst, go to your office and do what you always do. Nothing. Do absolutely nothing.*

"Kent." He lowered his empty glass and found Mary at his elbow, smiling brightly. Most would tag Mary as chunky, but she carried her weight well. Her brown hair was rather stringy, which did not help her image, but a clear complexion saved her from a much worse characterization. In any case, she could write basic code well enough, which was why Borst had hired her. Problem was, AFPS did not consist of much ordinary code.

"Morning, Mary."

"I just wanted to thank you for bringing us all here. I know how hard you've worked for this, and I think you deserve every bit of what you have coming."

Kent smiled. *Brown-nosing, are we, Mary?* He wouldn't put it past her, despite the innocent round eyes she now flashed up at him. She went with the flow, this one.

"Well, thanks, Mary." He patted the hand at his elbow. "You're too kind. Really."

Then Todd was there at his other elbow, as if the two had held a conference and decided that he would soon hold the keys to their futures. Time to switch their attention from the bald bossman to the rising star.

"Fantastic job, Kent!" Todd lifted his glass, which was empty, and threw it back anyway. By the looks of it, Todd had a few hidden vices.

Kent's mind flashed back to the two-year stint during graduate studies when he himself had taken to nipping at the bottle during late nights hovering over the keyboard. It was an absurd dichotomy, really. A top honors student who had found his brilliance through impeccable discipline, now slowly yielding to the lure of the bottle. A near drowning on one of his late-night runs had halted his slippery slide back to Stupid Street. It had been midwinter, and unable to muscle through a programming routine, he'd gone for a jog with half a bottle of tequila sloshing in his gut. He had misjudged a pier on the lake for a jogging path and run right off it into freezing waters. The paramedics told him if he'd not been in such good shape, he would have drowned. It was the last time he'd touched the stuff.

Kent blinked and smiled at Todd. "Thanks. Well, I've got some work to finish, so I'll see you guys tomorrow, right?"

"Bright 'n' early."

"Bright 'n' early." He nodded, and they stepped aside as though on strings. Kent walked past them to the first door on the left, across from the one through which Borst had disappeared.

This was going to be all right, he thought. Very much all right.

HELEN HOBBLED along beside her daughter in the park, eyeing the ducks waddling beside the pond, nearly as graceful as she. Walking was a thing mostly of the past for her wounded legs. Oh, she could manage about fifty yards without resting up for a while, but that was definitely it. Gloria had persuaded her to see an orthopedic doctor a year earlier, and the quack had recommended surgery. A knee replacement or some such ridiculous thing. They actually wanted to cut her open!

She'd managed a few hours of sleep last night, but otherwise it was mostly praying and wondering. Wondering about that little eye-opener God had decided to grace her with.

"It is lovely here, don't you think?" Helen asked casually. But she did not feel any loveliness at all just now.

"Yes, it is." Her daughter turned to the skating bowl in time to see Spencer fly above the concrete wall, make a grab for his skateboard in some insane inverted move, and streak back down, out of sight. She shook her head and looked back at the pond.

"I swear, that boy's gonna kill himself."

"Oh lighten up, Gloria. He's a boy, for goodness' sake. Let him live life while he's young. One day he'll wake up and find that his body doesn't fly as well as it used to. Until then, let him fly. Who knows? Maybe it brings him closer to heaven."

Gloria smiled and tossed a stick toward one of the ducks swaying its way in search of easy pickings. "You have the strangest way of putting things, Mom."

"Yes, and do you find me wrong?"

"No, not often. Although some of your analogies do stretch the mind." She reached an arm around her mother and squeezed, chuckling.

"You remember that time you suggested Pastor Madison take the cross off the church wall and carry it on his back for a week? Told him if the idea sounded silly it was only because he had not seen death up close and personal. Really, Mother! Poor fellow."

Helen smiled at the memory. Fact of it was, few Christians knew the cost of discipleship. It would have been a fine object lesson. "Yes, well, Bill's a fine pastor. He knows me now. And if he doesn't, he does a fine job pretending as though he does."

She guided her daughter by the elbow down the path. "So you leave tomorrow, then?"

"No, Saturday. We leave Saturday."

"Yes, Saturday. You leave Saturday." The air seemed to have grown stuffy, and Helen drew a deliberate breath. She stopped and looked around for a bench. The closest sat twenty yards away, surrounded by white ducks.

Gloria's voice spoke softly at her elbow. "You okay, Mother?"

Suddenly Helen was not okay. The vision strung through her mind, and she closed her eyes for a moment. Her chest felt stuffed with cotton. She swallowed hard and turned away from her daughter.

"Mother?" A cool hand encircled her biceps.

Helen fought back a flood of tears and narrowly succeeded. When she spoke, her voice warbled a bit. "You know that things are not what they seem, Gloria. You know that, don't you?"

"Yes. I know that."

"We look around here, and we see all sorts of drama unfolding about us—people marrying and divorcing and getting rich and running off to Paris."

"Mother . . ."

"And all along, the drama unfolding in the spirit world is hardly noticed but no less real. In fact, it is the real story. We just tend to forget that because we cannot see it."

"Yes."

"There are a lot of opposites in life, you know. The first will be last, and the last, first." Gloria knew this well, but Helen felt compelled to say it all, just the same. To speak like this to her only daughter. "A man finds the whole world but loses his soul. A man who loses his life finds it. A seed dies, and fruit is born. It is the way of God. You know that, don't you? I've taught you that."

"Yes, you have, and yes, I do know that. What's wrong, Mother? Why are you crying?"

"I am not crying, Honey." She faced Gloria for the first time and saw her raised eyebrows. "Do you see me weeping and wailing?" But her throat was aching terribly now, and she thought she might fall apart right here on the path.

She took a few steps into the grass and cleared her throat. "Death brings life. In many ways, you and I are already dead, Gloria. You know that, don't you?"

"Mother, you *are* crying." Her daughter turned her around as if she were a child. "You're trying not to, but I can hear it in your voice. What's wrong?"

"What would you think if I were to die, Gloria?"

Gloria's mouth parted to speak, but she said nothing. Her hazel eyes stared wide. When she did find her voice, the words came shaky.

"What do you mean?"

"Well, it's a simple enough question. If I were to pass on—die—and you buried me, what would you think?"

"That's ridiculous! How can you speak to me like that? You're nowhere near dying. You shouldn't think such thoughts."

The tension provided Helen with a wave of resolve that seemed to lighten her emotion for the moment. "No, but *if,* Gloria. If a truckdriver missed his brakes and knocked my head off my shoulders—what would you think?"

"That's terrible! I would feel terrible. How can you say such a thing? Goodness! How do you think I would feel?"

She looked directly at her daughter for a few seconds. "I didn't say *feel,* Honey. I said *think.* What would you suppose had happened?"

"I would suppose that a drunken truckdriver had killed my mother, that's what I'd think."

"Well, then you would think like a child, Gloria." She turned away and feigned a little disgust. "Humor me in my old age, dear. At least pretend that you believe what I've taught you."

Her daughter did not respond. Helen cast a sideways glance and saw that she had made the connection. "Mother, there is no end to you."

"No. No, I suppose there isn't, is there. But humor me. Please, darling."

Gloria sighed, but it was not a sigh of resignation—it was a sigh that comes when the truth has settled. "All right. I would think that you had been taken from this world. I would think that in your death, you had found life. Eternal life with God."

"Yes, and you would be right." Helen turned to face Gloria and nodded. "And what might that be like?"

Gloria blinked and turned to the pond, lost in a hazy stare. "It would be . . ." She paused, and a smile curved her lips ever so slowly. ". . . like what we saw yesterday. Laughing with God." Her eyes grew wide, and she faced Helen.

"So, then, would you want me to find that?"

Her daughter's eyebrows narrowed in question for a fleeting moment, and then she nodded slowly. "Yes. Yes, I suppose I would."

"Even if finding it meant losing this life?"

"Yes. I suppose so."

Helen smiled and drew a deep, satisfied breath. "Good."

She stepped close to Gloria, put her arms around her daughter's waist, and pulled her close. "I love you, Sweetheart," she said and rested her cheek on her daughter's shoulder.

"I love you too."

They held each other for a long moment.

"Mother?"

"Yes?"

"You're not going to die, are you?"

"Someday, I hope. The sooner the better. Either way, our worlds are about to change, Gloria. Everything is turning inside out."

CHAPTER FIVE

KENT WOKE at 6 A.M. on Friday, instantly alert. His plane departed at nine, which gave them two hours to dress and make their way to the airport. He flung the sheets aside and swung his legs to the floor. Beside him, Gloria moaned softly and rolled over.

"Up and at 'em, Sweetheart. I've got a plane to catch."

Gloria grunted an acknowledgment and lay still, milking the waning seconds for the last of sleep, no doubt.

Kent walked under the arch into their spacious bathroom and doused his head under the tap. Fifteen minutes later he emerged, half dressed, expecting to make a trip to the kitchen to ask Gloria about his socks. But he was spared the jaunt downstairs—he would not find Gloria down there because she was still in bed with an arm draped over her face.

"Gloria? We have to leave, Sweetheart. I thought you were up."

She rolled toward him and sat up groggily. "Oh, goodness! I feel like a freight train hit me."

Her complexion looked rather peaked, at that. He sat beside her and ran a finger under her chin. "You look pale. Are you okay?"

She nodded. "Stomach's a bit upset."

"Maybe you have a touch of the flu," Kent offered. He rested a hand on her knee. "Why don't you take it easy. I can get to the airport alone."

"I wanted to take you."

"Don't worry about it. You rest up. We have a big trip tomorrow." He stood. "The twelve-hour flu has been making the rounds at the office. Who knows? Maybe I brought it home. Do you know where my navy silk socks are?"

Gloria motioned to the door. "In the dryer. Honestly, Honey, I'm fine. You sure you don't want me to take you?"

He turned and gave her a wink. "Yes, I'm sure. What's a trip to some lousy airport? We have Paris to think about. Get some rest—I'll be fine." Kent bounded down the steps to the laundry room and rummaged around until he found the socks. He heard the clinking in the kitchen and knew then that Gloria had followed him down.

When he rounded the refrigerator, Gloria was scooping grounds into the coffee machine, her pink housecoat swishing at her ankles. He slid up behind her and slipped his arms around her waist. "Really, Honey. I have this handled."

She dismissed the comment with a flip of her wrist. "No. I'm feeling better already. It was probably that asparagus I ate last night. You want some coffee? The least I can do is send you away with a decent breakfast."

He kissed her on the neck. "I'd love some coffee and toast. Thank you, Sweetheart."

They ate together on the dinette set, Kent neatly dressed, Spencer rubbing sleep from his eyes, Gloria looking like she had risen from her coffin for the occasion. Coffee gurgled, porcelain clinked, forks clattered. Kent eyed Gloria, ignoring the concern that whispered through his skull.

"So, you have tennis today?"

She nodded. "One o'clock. I play Betsy Maher in the quarterfinals." She lifted a white cup to her lips and sipped. "Assuming I'm feeling better."

Kent smiled gently. "You'll be fine, Honey. I can't remember the last time you missed a match. In fact, I can't remember the last time you missed anything due to illness." Kent chuckled and bit into his toast. "Man, I remember the first time we played tennis. You remember that?"

His wife smiled. "How could I forget with your reminding me every few months."

Kent turned to Spencer. "You should've seen her, Spencer. Miss Hotshot with her tennis scholarship trying to take on a runner. She might have been able to place the ball where she wanted, but I ran her into the ground. She wouldn't stop. And I knew she was getting tired after the fourth set, because I could barely stand up and she was over there wobbling on her feet. I'd never seen anybody so competitive." He glanced at Gloria. Some color had come back into her face.

"Until she puked."

"Gross, Dad!"

"Don't look at me. Look at your mother."

Gloria just smiled. "Don't forget to tell him who won, dear."

"Yes, your mother did whip me good that day—before she puked, that is. I think I fell in love with her then, while she was bent over by the far net post."

"Gross!" Spencer giggled.

"Fell in love, ha! As I remember it, you were head over heels for some other thing in a skirt at the time."

"Perhaps. But it all began between us then."

"Well, it took you long enough to come around. We didn't even date until you were out of school."

"Yes, and look at where we are today, dear." He stood, slid his dish into the sink, and returned to kiss her on the cheek. Her skin was warm. "I think it was worth the wait, don't you?"

She smiled. "If you insist."

Twenty minutes later, Kent stood by the front door and saluted them, packed bags in hand. "Okay, you guys have the itinerary, right? I'll see you at five o'clock tomorrow night. We have a plane to catch at six. And remember to pack the camera, Honey. This is one trip that's going down in Anthony family history."

Gloria walked to him, still wrapped in her pink bathrobe. "You take care of yourself, my prince," she said and kissed him gently on the cheek. "I love you." For a moment he looked into those sparkling hazel eyes and smiled.

He bent and kissed her forehead. "And I love you. More than you could possibly know, Sweetheart."

"See you, Dad," Spencer said sheepishly. He walked over and put a flimsy arm around his father's waist.

Kent ruffled his hair. "See you, Chief. You take care of Mommy, you hear?" He kissed him on the forehead.

"I will."

He left them standing at the door, his son under his wife's arm. There was a connection between those two he could never entirely grasp. A knowing glint in their eyes that sapped his power, made him blink. It had been painfully obvious yesterday around the dinner table. But he had just made them rich; it was to be expected, he supposed. They kept exchanging glances, and when he'd finally asked them about it, they'd just shrugged.

Man, he loved them.

The flight from Denver International to Miami was an eventful one. At least for Kent Anthony it was eventful, if for no other reason than because every waking moment had become eventful. He had become a new man. And now in the DC-9 cabin, even his peers recognized him in a new light. Five others from Niponbank's Denver branch were making the belated trip to Florida for the conference. He'd meandered about the aisle, talking to all of them. And all of them had looked at him with a twinkle in their eyes. A glint of jealousy, perhaps. Or a spark of hope for their own careers. *Someday, if I'm so lucky, I will be in your shoes, Kent,* they would be thinking. Of course, there was always the possibility that the glint was actually light—a reflection from the oval windows lining the fuselage.

His boss, Markus Borst, sat three rows up with his shiny bald spot poking just above the seat like an island of sand in a black sea. Borst had worn a toupee over that bald spot all last year, discarding it only after the underhanded comments had driven him to hide for long days with a DO NOT DISTURB sign on his closed door. What the superior did behind that door, Kent could not fathom. He was certainly not breaking records for coordinating software design, as his title suggested. And when he did emerge from his cave, he did little but look over Kent's shoulder and wish he'd thought of this, or mumble about how he could have done that.

And now, within the week Borst could very well be working for him. Kent ran a finger under his collar and stretched his neck. The red tie had been a good choice. It accented the navy suit well, he thought. The perfect attire for meeting the real powerhouses in the bank's upper echelon. They would have heard about him by now, of course. Young man, firm grip, broad shoulders, brilliant mind. From the western United States. He's got the stuff.

An image of a podium facing a thousand executives around dinner tables formed in his mind. He was at the microphone. *Well, it wasn't so difficult once I constructed the advanced timing paradigm. Of course, it's all a matter of perspective. Brilliance is a function more of the destination than of the journey, and let me assure you, my friends, we have arrived at a destination never before imagined, much less traveled.* The conference hall would shake under thunderous applause. He would hold up his hand then, not emphatically but as a slight gesture. It did not take much to command.

Not so long ago, a man named Gates—Bill Gates—introduced an operating system that changed the world of computing. Today Niponbank is introducing the Advanced Funds Processing System, and it will change the world of banking. Now they would be standing, pounding their hands together. Of course, he wouldn't take direct responsibility for the work. But they would understand, just the same. At least those at the top would understand.

Beside him Will Thompson cleared his throat. "Hey, Kent. You ever wonder why some people move up the ladder so quickly and others stay put their whole careers? I mean people with the same basic skills?"

Kent looked at the forty-year-old loan manager, wondering again how the man had finagled his way on this trip. Will insisted that his boss, already in Miami, needed him to explain some innovative ideas they had been working on to some higher-ups. But Kent didn't know Will to have an innovative bone in his body. His colleague's black hair was speckled with gray, and a pair of gold-rimmed glasses sat on his nose. Yellow suspenders rode over a white shirt in good East Coast fashion. If he considered anyone at the bank a friend, it was Will.

"Hmm?"

"No, really. Look at us. I still remember the first day you skipped into the bank, what, seven years ago?" He chuckled and sipped at the martini on his tray. "You were as green as they come, man. Hair all slicked back, ready to set the office on fire. Not that I was any more experienced. I think I had a whole week on you. But we came in at the bottom, and now look at us. Making triple digits, and still climbing. And then you take someone like Tony Milkins. He came six months or so after you and he's what? A teller." Will chuckled again and sipped his drink.

Kent shrugged. "Some want it more. It all comes down to the price you're willing to pay. You and I put our dues in, worked long hours, got the right education. Shoot, if I were to sit down and calculate the time and energy I've put into making it this far, it would scare most college kids right out of school and into boot camp."

"No kidding." Will sipped again. "Then there's a few like Borst. You look at them and wonder how in God's name they ever sneaked in. You'd think his old man owned the bank."

Kent smiled and looked out the window, thinking he'd have to be careful what he said now. One day it would be him that people like Will talked about. True enough, Markus Borst was misplaced in his position, but even those well suited for their positions bore the brunt of professional criticism from the lower ranks.

"So, I guess you'll be moving up now," Will said. Kent glanced at him, noting a hint of jealousy there.

Will caught the look and laughed it off. "No, well done, my friend." He lifted a finger and raised his brows. "But watch your back. I'm right behind you."

"Sure," Kent returned with a smile.

But he was thinking that even Will knew that the notion of Will doing any such thing was an absurd little piece of nonsense. The loan manager could look forward to nothing but slipping into eventual obscurity, like a million other loan managers throughout the world. Loan managers simply did not become household names like Bill Gates or Steve Jobs. Not that it was Will's fault, really. Most people were not properly equipped; they simply did not know how to work hard enough. That was Will's problem.

It suddenly occurred to Kent that he'd just come full circle on the man. He thought of Will in the same way that Will thought of Tony Milkins. A slacker. A friendly enough slacker, but a dope nonetheless. And if Will was a slouch, then people like Tony Milkins were slugs. Ham-and-eggers. Good enough to collect a few bills here and there, but never cut out to spend them.

"Just watch your back too, Will," Kent said. "Because Tony Milkins is right there."

His friend laughed and Kent joined him, wondering if the man had caught his offhanded dig. Not yet, he guessed.

The plane touched down with a squeal of rubber, and Kent's pulse accelerated a notch. They deplaned, found their luggage, and caught two cabs to the Hyatt Regency in downtown Miami.

A porter dressed in maroon, with a tall captain's hat and a nametag that read "Pedro Gonzalas" quickly loaded their bags on a cart and led them through a spacious foyer toward the front desk. To their left, a large fountain splashed over marble mermaids in a blue pool. Palm trees grew in a perfect circle around the water, their leaves rustling in the conditioned air. Most of the guests walking about had come for the conference. Left their branches across the globe to gather in dark suits and gloat over how much money they were all making. A group of Asians laughed around a smoking table, and Kent guessed by their demeanor that they might be near the top. Important men. Or at the very least, thinking themselves important. Some of his future peers, perhaps. Like the short, white-haired one drawing most of the attention, sipping an amber drink. A man of power. Filthy rich. Two hundred and fifty dollars a night for a hotel like this would come out of his tip fund.

"Now *this* place is first class," Todd said beside him.

"That's Niponbank for you," Borst agreed. "Nothing but the best. I think they took the whole hotel. What do you think *that* cost?"

"Geez. Enough. You think we'll have open access to those little refrigerators in the rooms?"

Mary turned to Todd with a raised brow. "Of course we will. What, you think they lock them up for the programming staff? Keep their minds clear?"

"No. I know they'll be open. I mean free. You think we'll have to pay for what we take?"

Borst chuckled. "Don't be a moron, Todd. They cover the entire trip, and you're worried about free booze in little bottles. I'm sure there'll be plenty to drink at the reception. Besides, you need to keep your head clear, boy. We're not here for a party. Isn't that right, Kent?"

Kent wanted to step away from the group, disassociate himself from their small talk. They sounded more like a boy scout troop than programmers who had just changed history. He glanced around, suddenly embarrassed and hoping they had not been overheard.

"That's right," he offered and drifted a few feet to his left. If he was lucky, the onlookers wouldn't put him with this group of clowns.

They'd come to the long, cherrywood check-in counter, and Kent stepped up to a Hispanic dark-haired woman, who smiled cordially. "Welcome to the Hyatt," she said. "How may I help you?"

Well, I have just become rather important, you see, and I am wondering if you have a suite . . .

He terminated the thought. *Get a grip, man.* He smiled despite himself. "Yes, my name is Kent Anthony. I believe you have a reservation for me. I'm with the Niponbank group."

She nodded and punched a few keys. Kent leaned on the counter and looked back toward the men laughing in the lounge chairs. Several were shaking hands now, as if congratulating themselves on a job well done. *Excellent year, Mr. Bridges. Stunning profits. By the way, have you caught wind of the young man from Denver? The programmer? Isn't he here somewhere? Brilliant, I've heard.*

"Excuse me, sir."

Kent blinked and turned back to the counter. It was the check-in clerk. The pretty dark-haired one. "Kent Anthony, correct?" she asked.

"Yes."

"We have a message for you, sir." She reached under the counter and pulled a red envelope out. Kent's pulse spiked. It was starting already then. Someone other than the bonehead troop under Borst's command had sent him a message. They had not sent it to Borst; they had addressed it to him.

"It's marked urgent," she said and handed it to him.

Kent took the envelope, flipped it open, and withdrew a slip of paper. He scanned the typed note.

At first the words did not create meaning in his mind. They just sat there in a long string. Then they made some sense, but he thought they had made a mistake. That they had given him the wrong message. That this was not *his* Gloria to which the note referred. Couldn't be.

His eyes were halfway through the note for the second time when the heat came, like a scalding liquid searing through his veins from the top of his head right down his spine. His jaw fell slack, and his hand began to quiver.

"Are you all right, sir?" a voice asked. Maybe the clerk's.

Kent read the note again.

KENT ANTHONY:

YOUR WIFE GLORIA ANTHONY IS IN DENVER MEMORIAL HOSPITAL STOP
COMPLICATIONS OF UNDIAGNOSED NATURE STOP
CONDITION DETERIORATING QUICKLY STOP
PLEASE RETURN IMMEDIATELY STOP
END MESSAGE

Now that quiver had become a quake, and Kent felt panic edge up his throat. He whirled around to face Borst, who had missed the moment entirely. "Markus." His voice wavered.

The man turned, smiling at something Betty had just said. His lips flattened the moment he laid eyes on Kent. "What is it?"

Yes indeed! What was it? Leave these in power about him to their excesses before he'd had a chance to help them understand who he was? Leave the party in Borst's hands? Good grief! It was a preposterous notion!

Surely Gloria would be fine. Just fine.

Please return immediately, the message read. And this was Gloria.

"I have to go. I have to return to Denver." Even as he said it, he wanted to pull the words back. How could he leave now? This was the pinnacle. The men laughing over there by the fountain were about to change his life forever. He had just flown two thousand miles to meet them. He had just worked *five years* to meet them!

"I'm sorry. You'll have to take the meeting for me." He shoved the note at his boss and stumbled past him, suddenly furious at this stroke of fate.

"Great timing, Gloria," he muttered through clenched teeth, and immediately regretted the sentiment.

His bags were still on the cart, he realized, but then he didn't care where his bags were. Besides, he would be right back. By tomorrow morning, perhaps. No, tomorrow evening was the Paris trip. Maybe on the way to Paris then.

Okay, Buckwheat. Settle down. Nothing has happened here. Just a little glitch. A bug. She's only in the hospital.

Kent boarded a Yellow Cab and left the bustle at Miami's Hyatt Regency behind. Gloria would be okay. Had to be. She was in good hands. And what was one conference? A dread fell into Kent's gut, and he swallowed.

This had not been in the plans. Not at all.

CHAPTER SIX

THE WAITING room in Denver Memorial's ICU wing was decorated in a rust color, but in Helen's mind it was red and she wondered why they would choose the color of blood.

Helen gripped pastor Bill Madison's arm at the elbow and steered the much larger man toward the window. If anybody could understand, it would be the young, dark-haired Greek who had attracted her to the Community Church in the first place ten years earlier. He had been fresh out of seminary then—not a day over twenty-five and bubbling with love for God. Somewhere in there the church bureaucracy had tempered his passion. But Pastor Madison had never been confused about his beliefs.

He had arrived in the night sometime, but she could not remember precisely when because things were fuzzy now. They were all exhausted, that much was clear, and her knees throbbed with a dull pain. She had to sit. Behind them, Spencer sat like a lump on one of the blood-rust waiting chairs.

Helen knew her strained voice betrayed her anxiety, but given the circumstances, she hardly cared. "No. I'm not telling you I *think* I've seen this. I'm telling you I *did* see this." She squeezed hard, as if that might help him understand. "You hear me?"

Bill's dark eyes widened, but she didn't know if it came from her announcement or her squeezing. "What do you mean, you *saw* this?" he asked.

"I mean I *saw* this!" She stretched a shaking arm toward the swinging doors. "I saw my daughter in there, on that bed, that's what I saw." The anger came back as she recalled her vision, and she shook with it.

He eyed her with a raised brow, skeptical to the bone, she saw. "Come on, Helen. We all have impressions now and then. This is not a time to stretch perceptions."

"You are questioning my judgment then? You think I did not see what I say I saw?"

"I'm just saying that we shouldn't rush to conclusions at times like these. This is a time for caution, wouldn't you say? I know things are difficult, but—"

"Caution? What does caution have to do with the fact that my daughter is in there spread on the table? I saw it, I'm telling you! I don't know why I saw it or what God could possibly mean by showing it to me, but I saw it, Pastor. Every last detail."

He glanced about the room and steered her toward the window. "Okay, keep your voice down, Helen." A thin trail of sweat leaked past his temple. "When did you see this?"

"Two days ago."

"You saw all of this two days ago?"

"Isn't that what I just said?" she demanded.

"Yes." He turned from her and sat on the windowsill. His hands were shaking. Helen stood by the window.

"Look, Helen. I know you see things differently than most—"

"Don't even start, Pastor. I don't want to hear it. Not now. It would be insensitive."

"Well, I'm trying to be sensitive, Helen. And I'm thinking of the boy over there. No need to bury his mother just yet."

Helen looked toward Spencer, who sat, chin on palms, legs swinging under the chair. Dark circles looped under his bloodshot eyes. Through the night he'd slept a fitful hour, at most.

"I'm not *burying* my daughter, Bill. I am confiding in you. I saw this, and it terrifies me that it is precisely what I saw."

He did not respond to that.

She stared out the window and folded her hands. "The fact is I like it even less than you. It's gnawed at me like a cancer since that first moment. I can't seem to wrap my mind around this one, Bill." A lump rose to her throat. "I can't understand why God is doing this thing. And you would think *I* should know, of all people."

His hand reached out and rested on her shoulder. The gesture brought a sliver of comfort. "And how can you be certain it is God?"

"It doesn't matter. It is God by default. What he allows, he does."

"Maybe, but only if he is truly God. Omnipotent. All powerful. And if so, it is for him to decide why he would do such a thing."

"Yes, I *know* that, Bill! But it's my daughter in there hooked up to a machine!" She lowered her head, confused and angry at the emotions boiling up within her.

"I'm very sorry, Helen." Bill's voice sounded strained.

They remained silent for a few long moments, face to face with the impossibilities of the matter. Helen wasn't sure what she expected from him. Certainly not a pithy statement of inspiration. *Now, now there, Helen. Everything will be just fine. You'll see. Just trust in the Lord.* Heavens! She really ought to know. She'd been here before, facing the threat of death like this.

"So then, you saw more?" Bill was speaking. "Did you see her die?"

She shook her head. "No, I did not see her die."

She heard him swallow. "We should pray then," he said.

Helen tried to still her emotions. "I did not see her death, but I did see more, Bill."

He didn't answer right away. When he did, his voice came haltingly. "What . . . what did you see?"

She shook her head. "I can't say, really. I . . . I don't know."

"If you saw it, how could you not know?"

She closed her eyes, suddenly wishing she had said nothing to the man. She could hardly expect him to understand. "It was . . . hazy. Even when we see we don't always see crystal clear. Humanity has managed to dim our spiritual eyesight. But you already know that, don't you, Bill?"

He did not respond immediately, possibly offended at her condescension. "Yes," he finally offered in a weak voice.

"I'm sorry, Pastor. This is rather difficult for me. She is my daughter."

"Then let's pray, Helen. We will pray to our Father."

She nodded, and he began to pray. But her head was clogged with sorrow, and she barely heard his words.

KENT BROWSED through the trinkets in the airport gift shop, passing time, relaxing for the first time since he'd read that message eight hours earlier. He'd caught a connection to Chicago and now meandered through the concourse, waiting for the 3 A.M. redeye flight that would take him to Denver.

He bent over and wound up a toy monkey wielding small gold cymbals. The primate strutted noisily across the makeshift platform, banging its instrument and grinning obnoxiously. *Clang-ka-ching, clang-ka-ching.* Kent smiled despite the foolishness of it all. Spencer would get a kick out of the creature. For all of ten minutes possibly. Then it would end up on his closet floor, hidden under a thousand other ten-minute toys. Ten minutes for twenty dollars. It was skyway robbery.

On the other hand, it was Spencer's face grinning there for ten minutes, and the image of those lips curved in delight brought a small smile to his own.

And it was not like they didn't have the money. These were the kinds of things that were purchased by either totally irresponsible people, or people who did not bother with price. People like Tom Cruise or Kevin Costner. Or Bill Gates. He would have to get used to the idea. *You wanna live a part, you'd better start playing that part. Build it, and they will come.*

Kent tucked the monkey under his arm and sauntered over to the grown-up female trinkets neatly arranged against the wall beside racks of *I love Chicago* sweaters. Where Gloria had picked up her fascination with expensive crystal, he did not know. And now it would no longer matter, either. They were going to be rich.

He picked up a beveled cross, intricately carved with roses and bearing the words "In his death we have life." It would be perfect. He imagined her lying in some hospital bed, propped up, her green eyes beaming at the sight of the gift in his hand. *I love you, Honey.*

Kent made his way to the checkout counter and purchased the gifts.

He might as well make the best of the situation. He would call Borst the minute he got home—make sure Bonehead and his troop were not blowing things down there in Miami. Meanwhile he would stay by Gloria's side in her illness. It was his place.

And soon they would be on the plane to Paris anyway. Surely she would be able to travel. A sudden spike of panic ran up his spine. And what if the illness was more serious than just some severe case of food poisoning? They would have to cancel Paris.

But that had not happened, had it? He'd read once that 99 percent of people's fears never materialize. A man who internalized that truth could add ten years to his life.

Kent eased himself into a chair and glanced at the flight board. His plane left in two hours. Might as well catch some sleep. He sank deep and closed his eyes.

SPENCER SAT next to Helen, across from the pastor, trying to be brave. But his chest and throat and eyes were not cooperating. They kept aching and knotting and leaking. His mom had gone upstairs after seeing Dad off, saying something about lying down. Two hours and an exhaustive run through his computer games later, Spencer had called through the house only to hear her weak moan from the master bedroom. His mom was still in bed at ten o'clock. He'd knocked and entered without waiting for an answer. She lay on her side, curled into a ball like a roly-poly, groaning. Her face reminded him of a mummy on the Discovery Channel—all stretched and white.

Spencer had run for the phone and called Grandma. During the fifteen minutes it took her to reach their house he had knelt by his mother's bed, begging her to answer him. Then he had cried hard. But Mother was not answering in anything more than the occasional moan. She just lay there and held her stomach.

Grandma had arrived then, rambling on about food poisoning and ordering him around as if she knew exactly what had to be done in situations like this. But no matter how she tried to seem in control, Grandma had been a basket case.

They had literally dragged his mom to the car, and Grandma had driven her to the emergency room. Dark blue blotches spotted her skin, and he wondered how food poisoning could bring out spots the size of silver dollars. Then Spencer had overheard one of the nurses talking to an aide. She said the spots were from internal bleeding. The patient's organs were bleeding.

"I'm scared," he said in a thin, wobbly voice.

Helen took his hand and lifted it to her lips. "Don't be, Spencer. Be sad, but don't be afraid," she said, but she said it with mist in her eyes, and he knew that she was terrified too.

She pulled his head to her shoulder, and he cried there for a while. Dad was supposed to be here by now. He'd called from the airport at six o'clock and told the nurse he was catching a 9 P.M. flight with an impossible interminable layover in Chicago that wouldn't put him into Denver until 6 A.M. Well, now it was seven o'clock, and he had not arrived.

They had started putting in tubes and doing other things to Mom last night. That was when he first started thinking things were not just bad. They were terrible. When he asked Grandma why Mom was puffing up like that, she'd said that the doctors were flooding her body with antibiotics. They were trying to kill the bacteria.

"What bacteria?"

"Mommy has bacterial meningitis, Honey," Grandma had said.

A boulder had lodged in his throat then. 'Cause that sounded bad. "What does that mean? Will she die?"

"Do not think of death, Spencer," Grandma said gently. "Think of life. God will give Gloria more life than she's ever had. You will see that, I promise. Your mother will be fine. I know what happens here. It is painful now, but it will soon be better. Much better."

"So she will be okay?"

His grandmother looked off to the double swinging doors behind which the doctors attended his mom, and she started to cry again.

"We will pray that she will be, Spencer," Pastor Madison said.

Then the tears burst from Spencer's eyes, and he thought his throat might tear apart. He threw his arms around Grandma and buried his face in her shoulder. For an hour he could not stop. Just couldn't. Then he remembered that his mother was not dead, and that helped a little.

When he lifted his head he saw that Grandma was talking. Muttering with eyes closed and face strained. Her cheeks were wet and streaked. She was talking to God. Only she wasn't smiling like she usually did when she talked to him.

A door slammed, and Spencer started. He lifted his head. Dad was there, standing at the door, looking white and ragged, but here.

Spencer scrambled to his feet and ran for his father, feeling suddenly very heavy. He wanted to yell out to him, but his throat was clogged again, so he just collided with him and felt himself lifted into safe arms.

Then he began to cry again.

THE MOMENT Kent slammed through the waiting room door he knew something was wrong. Very wrong.

It was in their posture, his son's and Helen's, bent over with red eyes. Spencer ran for him, and he snatched the boy to his chest.

"Everything will be all right, Spence," he muttered. But the boy's hot tears on his neck said differently, and he set him down with trembling hands.

Helen rose to her feet as he approached. "What's wrong?" he demanded.

"She has bacterial meningitis, Kent."

"Bacterial meningitis?" So that would mean what? Surgery? Or worse? Something like dialysis to grace each waking day. "How is she?" He swallowed, seeing more in those old wise eyes than he cared to see.

"Not good." She took his hand and smiled empathetically. A tear slipped down her cheek. "I'm sorry, Kent."

Now the warning bells went off—every one of them, all at once. He spun from her and ran for the swinging doors on numb legs. The sign above read "ICU." The ringing lodged in his ears, muting ordinary sounds.

Everything will be fine, Kent. Get a grip, man. His heart hammered in his ears. *Please, Gloria, please be all right. I'm here for you. I love you, Honey. Please be all right.*

He gazed around and saw white. White doors and white walls and white smocks. The smell of medicine flooded his nostrils. A penicillin-alcohol odor.

"May I help you?"

The voice came from his right, and he turned to see a figure standing behind a counter. The nurses station. She was dressed in white. His mind began to soothe his panic a bit. *See now, everything will be just fine. That's a nurse; this is a hospital. Just a hospital where they make people better. With enough technology to make your head spin.*

"May I help you?" the nurse asked again.

Kent blinked. "Yes, could you tell me where I can find Gloria Anthony? I'm her husband." He swallowed against the dryness of cotton balls seemingly stuffed in his throat.

The nurse came into better focus now, and he saw that her nametag read "Marie." She was blonde, like Gloria—about the same size. But she did not have Gloria's smile. In fact she was frowning, and Kent fought the sudden urge to reach over there and slap those lips up. *Listen lady! I'm here for my wife. Now quit looking at me like you're the Grim Reaper and take me to her!*

Marie's dark eyes looked across the hall. Kent followed the look. Two doctors bent over a hospital bed behind a large, reinforced viewing window. He made for the room without waiting for permission.

"Excuse me, sir! You cannot go in there! Sir—"

He shut her out then. Once Gloria saw him, once he looked into her beautiful hazel eyes, this madness would all end. Kent's heart rose. *Oh, Gloria . . . Sweetheart. Everything will be just fine. Please, Gloria, Honey.*

Four faces popped into his mind's eye, suddenly, simultaneously, with a brutality that made him catch himself, midstride, halfway to the room. The first was that of the wench back there with dark eyes. Grim Reaper's bride. The second was Spencer's. He saw that little face again, and it was not just worried. It was crushed. The third was Helen's sweet smiling face, but not smiling. Not at all. Wrinkled with lines of grief maybe, but not smiling. He wasn't sure he'd ever seen it that way.

One of the doctors had moved, and he saw the fourth face through the window, lying there on that bed. Only he did not recognize this face at first. It lay still, stark white under the bright lights overhead. A round, blue corrugated tube had been fed into the mouth, and an oxygen line hung from the nostrils. Purple blotches discolored the skin. The face was bloated like a pumpkin.

Kent blinked and set his foot down. But he did not move forward. Could not move forward.

Bile rose into his throat, and he swallowed hard. What this one face here could possibly have to do with the others he could not fathom. He did not know this face. Had never seen a face in such agony, so distorted in pain.

And then he did know this face. The simple truth tore through his mind like an ingot of lead crashing through his skull.

This was Gloria on the bed!

His heart was suddenly smashing against his rib cage, desperate to be out. His jaw fell slowly. A high-pitched screaming set off in his mind, denouncing this madness. Cursing this idiocy. This was no more Gloria than some body pulled from a mass grave in a war zone. How dare he be so sure? How dare he stand here frozen like some puppet when all the while everything was just fine? There had been a mistake, that was all. He should run over there and settle this.

Problem was, Kent could not move. Sweat leaked from his pores, and he began to breathe in ragged lurches. *No!* Spencer was out in the lobby, his ten-year-old boy who desperately needed Mommy. This could not be Gloria! He needed her! Sweet, innocent Gloria with a mouth that tasted of honey. Not . . . not this!

The doctor reached down and pulled the white sheet over the bloated face.

And why? Why did that fool pull that sheet like that?

A grunt echoed down the hall—his grunt.

Then Kent began to move again. In four long bounds he was at the door. Someone yelled from behind, but it meant nothing to him. He gripped the silver knob and yanked hard.

The door would not budge. *Turn, then! Turn the fool thing!* He turned the knob and pulled. Now the door swung open to him, and he staggered back. In the same moment he saw the name on a chart beside the door.

Gloria Anthony.

Kent began to moan softly.

The bed was there, and he reached it in two steps. He shoved aside a white-coated doctor. People began to shout, but he could not make out their words. Now he only wanted one thing. To pull back that white sheet and prove they had the wrong woman.

A hand grabbed his wrist, and he snarled. He twisted angrily and smashed the man into the wall. "No!" he shouted. An IV pole toppled and crashed to the floor. An amber monitor spit sparks and blinked to black, but these details occurred in the distant, dark horizon of Kent's mind. He was fixated on the still, white form on the hospital bed.

Kent gripped the sheet and ripped it from the body.

A *whoosh!* sounded as the sheet floated free and then slowly settled to the ground. Kent froze. A naked, pale body laced with purple veins and blotches the size of apples lay lifeless before him. It was bloated, like a pumped-up doll, with tubes still forcing mouth and throat open.

It was Gloria.

Like a shaft of barbed iron the certainty pierced right through him. He staggered back one step, swooning badly.

The world faded from him then. He was faintly aware that he was spinning and then running. Smashing into the door, facefirst. He could not feel the pain, but he could hear the crunch when his nose broke on impact with the wooden door. He was dead, possibly. But he couldn't be dead because his heart was on fire, sending flames right up his throat.

Then he lurched past the door somehow, pelting for the swinging ICU entry, bleeding red down his shirt, suffocating. He banged through the doors, just as the first wail broke from his throat. A cry to the Supreme Being who might have had his hand in this.

"Oh, God! Oh, Gauwwwd!"

To his right, Spencer and Helen stood wide eyed, but he barely saw them. Warm blood ran over his lips, and it gave him a strange, fleeting comfort. The gutturals blared from his spread mouth, refusing to retreat. He could not stop to breathe. Back there his wife had just died.

"Oh, God! Oh, Gauwwwd!"

Kent fled through the halls, his face white and red, wailing in long deathly moans, turning every head as he ran.

A dozen startled onlookers stood aside when he broke into the parking lot, dripping blood and slobbering and gasping. The wails had run out of air, and he managed to smother them. Cars sat, fuzzy through tears, and he staggered for them.

Kent made it all the way to his silver Lexus before the futility of his flight struck him down. He slammed his fist against the hood, maybe breaking another bone there. Then he slid down the driver's door to the hot asphalt and pulled his knees to his chest.

He hugged his legs, devastated, sobbing, muttering. "Oh, God. Oh, God. Oh, God!"

But he did not feel God.

He just felt his chest exploding.

chapter seven

Week Three

KENT ANTHONY held Spencer on his lap and gently stroked his arm. The fan whirled high above, and an old Celine Dion CD played softly, nudging the afternoon on. His son's breathing rose and fell with his own, creating a kind of cadence to help Celine in her crooning. He could not tell if Spencer was awake—they had hardly moved in over an hour. But this sitting and holding and just being alive had become the new Anthony home signature in the week or so since Gloria's sudden death.

The first day had been like a freight train smashing into his chest, over and over and over. After sobbing for some time by the Lexus he had suddenly realized that little Spencer needed him now. The poor boy would be devastated. His mother had just been snatched from him. Kent had stumbled back to the waiting room to find Helen and Spencer holding each other, crying. He'd joined them in their tears. An hour later they had driven from the hospital, dead silent and stunned.

Helen had left them in the living room and made sandwiches for lunch. The phone had rung off the hook. Gloria's church partners calling to give their condolences. None of the calls were from Kent's associates.

Kent blinked at the thought. He shifted Spencer's head so he could reach a glass of tea sitting by the couch. It was one good thing about the church, he supposed. Friends came easily. It was the *only* good thing about the church. That and their attending to the dead. Kent's mind drifted back to the funeral earlier that week. They had managed to mix some gladness into the event, and for that he was thankful, although the smiles of those around him never did spread to his own face. Still it made for a manageable ordeal. Otherwise he might have broken down, a wreck on that front pew. An image rolled through his mind: a slobbering man, dressed in black and writhing on the pew while a hundred stoic faces sang with raised hymnals. Might as well toss him in the hole as well.

A tear slipped from the corner of his right eye. They would not stop, these tears. He swallowed.

Helen and two of her old friends had sung something about the other side at the funeral. Now *there* was a religious case. Helen. After setting sandwiches before them that first day, she had excused herself and left. When she returned three hours later, she looked like a new woman. The smile had returned, her red eyes had whitened, and a buoyancy lightened her step. She had taken Spencer in her arms and hugged him dear. Then she had gripped Kent's arm and smiled warmly, knowingly. And that was it. If she experienced any more sorrow over her daughter's death, she hid it well. The fact had burned resentment into Kent's gut. Of course, he could not complain about the care she had shown them over the last ten days, busying herself with cooking and cleaning and handling the phone while Kent and Spencer floated around the house like two dead ghosts.

She was on her way to collect Spencer now. She had made the suggestion that the boy visit her for a few hours today. Kent had agreed, although the thought of being alone in the house for an afternoon brought a dread to his chest.

He ran his fingers through his son's blond hair. Now it would be him and Spencer, alone in a house that suddenly seemed too big. Too empty. Two weeks ago he had described their next house to Gloria while they dined on steak and lobster at Antonio's. The house would be twice the size of their current one, he'd told her. With gold faucets and an indoor tennis court. They could afford that now. "Imagine that, Gloria. Playing on your own air-conditioned court." His wife had smiled wide.

In his mind's eyes he saw her leaning into a forehand, her short white skirt swishing as she pivoted, and a lump rose in his throat.

He lay his head back and moaned softly. He felt trapped in an impossible nightmare. What madman had decided that it was time for his wife to die? If there was a God, he knew how to inflict pain exceptionally well. Tears blurred Kent's vision, but he held himself in check. He had to maintain some semblance of strength, for Spencer if not for himself. But it was all lunacy. How had he grown so dependent on her? Why was it that her passing had left him so dead inside?

The doctor had patiently explained bacterial meningitis to him a dozen times.

Evidently the beast lingered in over half of the population, hiding behind some cranial mucous membrane that held it at bay. Occasionally—very rarely—the stuff got past the membrane and into the bloodstream. If not caught immediately it tended to rampage its way through the body, eating up organs. In Gloria's case the disease had already set its claws into her by the time she got to the hospital. Eighteen hours later she had died.

He'd replayed that scene a thousand times. If he'd taken her to the hospital Friday morning instead of traipsing off for glory, she might be alive today.

The monkey and the cross he'd purchased as gifts still lay in his travel bag upstairs, absurd little trinkets that mocked him every time he remembered them. *"Lookie here, Spencer. Look what Daddy bought you!"*

"What is it?"

"It's a stupid monkey to help you remember Mommy's death. See, it's smiling and clapping 'cause Mom's in heaven." Gag!

And the crystal cross . . . He would smash it as soon as he built up the resolve to open that bag. The doorbell rang, and Spencer lifted his head. "Grandma?"

"Probably," Kent said, running the back of his wrist across his eyes. "Why don't you go check?"

Spencer hopped off his lap and loped for the front door. Kent shook his head and sniffed. *Get a grip, old boy. You've handled everything thrown your way for years. You can handle this.*

"Hello, Kent," Helen called, entering the room at Spencer's leading. She smiled. She was wearing a dress. A yellow dress that struck a chord of familiarity in Kent. It was the kind of dress Gloria might have worn. "How are we doing this afternoon?"

How do you think, you old kook? We've just lost our hearts, but otherwise we are just peachy. "Fine," he said.

"Yes, well I don't believe you, but it's good to see that you're making an attempt." She paused, seeing right through him, it seemed. He made no attempt to rise. Helen's eyes held his for a moment. "I'm praying for you, Kent. Things will begin to change now. In the end, they will be better. You will see."

He wanted to tell her that she could keep her prayers. That of course things would get better, because anything would be better than this. That she was an old, eccentric fossil and should keep her theories of how things would go to herself. Share them with some other cross-stitchers from the dark ages. But he hardly had the energy, much less the stomach, for the words.

"Yeah," he said. "You taking Spencer?" Of course she was. They both knew it.

"Yes." She turned to the boy and laid a hand on his shoulder. "You ready?"

Spencer glanced back at his father. "I'll see you soon, Dad. You okay?"

The question nearly had him blubbering. He did not want the boy to go. His heart swelled for his son, and he swallowed. "Sure, Spencer. I love you, son."

Spencer ran around the couch and hugged his neck. "It's okay, Dad. I'll be back soon. I promise."

"I know." He patted the boy's back. "Have fun."

A soft *clunk* signaled their departure through the front door. As if on cue, Celine ceased her crooning on the CD player.

Now it was just his breathing and the fan. He lifted the glass of ice tea, thankful for the tinkle of its ice.

He would sell the house now. Buy a new one, not so large. Scrap the tennis court. Put in a gym for Spencer instead.

The tall picture of Jesus holding a denim-clad man with blood on his hands stood to Kent's right. *Forgiven,* the artist had called it. They said that Jesus died for man. How could anyone follow a faith so obsessed with death? That was God, they said. Jesus was God, and he'd come to Earth to die. Then he'd asked his followers to climb on their crosses as well. So they'd made as their emblem a familiar symbol of execution, the cross, and in the beginning most of them died.

Today Jesus might have been put to death by lethal injection. An image of a needle reared in Kent's mind, and he cringed, thinking of all the needles Gloria must have endured. *Come die for me, Gloria.* It was insane.

And to think that Gloria had been so enraptured with Christianity, as if she actually expected to meet Christ someday. To climb up on that cross and float to the heavens with him. Well, now she had her chance, he supposed. Only she hadn't floated anywhere. She'd been lowered a good eight feet into red clay.

An empty hopelessness settled on Kent, and he sat there and let it hurt.

He would have to go back to work, of course. The office had sent him a bouquet of flowers, but they had made no other contact. He thought about the Miami meeting and the announcement of his program. Funny how something so important now seemed so distant. His pulse picked up at the thought. Why had they not called to tell him about the meeting?

Respect, he quickly decided. You don't just call a man who has lost his wife and segue into office talk. At least he had a bright career ahead of him. Although, without Gloria it hardly seemed bright. That would change with time.

Kent let the thoughts circle in his mind as they had endlessly for days now. Nothing seemed to fit. Everything felt loose. He could not latch on to anything offering that spark of hope that had propelled him so forcefully for years.

He leaned back and stared at the ceiling. For the moment his eyes were dry. Stinging dry.

SPENCER SAT in his favorite green chair across from Grandma Helen with his legs crossed Indian style. He'd pulled on his white X-Games skateboard T-shirt and his beige cargo pants that morning because he loved skateboarding and he thought Mom would want him to keep doing the things he loved most. Although he hadn't actually hopped on the board yet. It had been a long time since he'd gone more than a week without taking to the street on a board.

Then again, things had changed a week ago, hadn't they? Changed forever. His dad had lost his way, it seemed. The house had become big and quiet. Their schedule had changed, or gone away, mostly. His heart hurt most of the time now.

Spencer ran his fingers through blond curls and rested his chin on his palms. This hadn't changed though. The room smelled of fresh-baked bread. The faint scent of roses drifted by—Grandma's perfume. The brown carpet lay beneath them exactly as it had two weeks ago; the overstuffed chairs had not been moved; sparkling china with little blue flowers still lined an antique-looking cabinet on the wall. A hundred knickknacks, mostly white porcelain painted with accents of blue and red and yellow, sat in groupings around the room and on the walls.

The large case Grandma called a hutch hugged the wall leading to the kitchen. Its engraved lead-glass doors rested closed, distorting his vision of its contents, but he could see well enough. A small crystal bottle, maybe five inches high, stood in the middle of the top shelf. The contents looked almost black to him. Maybe maroon or red, although he'd never been good with all those weird names of colors. Grandma had once told him that nothing in the hutch mattered to her much, except that one crystal bottle. It, she said, symbolized the greatest power on earth. The power of love. And a tear had come to her eye as she said it. When he had asked her what was in the bottle, she had just turned her head, all choked up.

The large picture of Jesus rested quietly on the wall to their right. The Son of God was spread on a cross, a crown of thorns responsible for the thin trails of red on his cheek. He stared directly at Spencer with sad blue eyes, and at the moment, Spencer didn't know what to think about that.

"Spencer."

He turned to face Grandma, sitting across from him, smiling gently. A knowing glint shone in those hazel eyes. She held a glass of ice tea in both hands comfortably.

"Are you okay, Honey?"

Spencer nodded, suddenly feeling strangely at home. Mom wasn't here, of course, but everything else was. "I think so."

Helen tilted her head and shook it slowly, empathy rich in her eyes. "Oh, my poor child. I'm so sorry." A tear slipped down her cheek, and she let it fall. She sniffed once.

"But this will pass, son. Sooner than you know."

"Yeah, that's what everybody says." A lump rose in his throat, and he swallowed. He didn't want to cry. Not now.

"I've wanted to talk to you ever since Gloria left us," Helen said, now with a hint of authority. She had something to say, and Spencer's heart suddenly felt lighter in anticipation. When Grandma had something to say, it was best to listen.

"You know when Lazarus died, Jesus wept. In fact, right now God is weeping." She looked off to the window opened bright to the afternoon clouds. "I hear it sometimes. I heard it on that first day, after Gloria died. It about killed me to hear him weeping like that, you know, but it also gave me comfort."

"I heard laughter," Spencer said.

"Yes, laughter. But weeping too, at once. Over the souls of men. Over the pain of man. Over loss. He lost his son, you know." She looked into his eyes. "And there weren't doctors clamoring to save him, either. There was a mob beating him and spitting in his face and . . ." She didn't finish the sentence.

Spencer imagined a red-faced man with bulging veins spraying spit into that face on the painting over there. Jesus' face. The image struck him as odd.

"People don't often realize it, but God suffers more in the span of each breath than any man or woman in the worst period of history," Helen said.

Surprisingly, the notion came to Spencer like a balm. Maybe because his own hurt seemed small in the face of it. "But can't God make all that go away?" he asked.

"Sure he could, and he is, as we speak. But he allows us to choose on our own between loving him and rejecting him. As long as he gives us that choice, he will be rejected by some. By most. And that brings him pain."

"That's funny. I've never imaged God as suffering. Or as hurting."

"Read the old prophets. Read Jeremiah or Ezekiel. Images of God wailing and weeping are commonplace. We just choose to ignore that part of reality in our churches today."

She smiled again, staring out of that window. "On the other hand, some will choose to love him of their own choosing. And that love, my child, is worth the greatest suffering imaginable to God. That is why he created us, for those few of us who would love him."

She paused and directed her gaze to him again. "Like your mother."

Now a mischievous glint lit his grandmother's face. She sipped at her tea, and he saw a tremble in her hand. She leaned forward slightly. "Now, that's a sight, Spencer," she said in hushed voice.

Spencer's palms began to sweat. "What is?"

"The other side." She was grinning now like a child unable to contain a secret.

"The other side of this pain and suffering. The realm of God." She let it drop without offering more. Spencer blinked, wanting her to continue, knowing that she would—had to.

Helen hesitated only a moment before dropping the question she had brought him here to ask. "Do you want to see, son?"

Spencer's heart jumped in his chest and his fingers tingled cold. *Want to see?* He swallowed. "See?" he asked, and his voice cracked.

She gripped the arms of her chair and leaned forward. "Do you want to see what it's like on the other side?" She spoke hushed, eagerly, quickly. "Do you want to know why death has its end? Why Jesus said, 'Let the dead bury the dead'? It will help, child."

Suddenly his chest felt thick again, and an ache rose through his throat. "Yes," he said. "Can I see that?"

Grandma Helen's mouth split into a broad smile. "Yes! Actually you would've been able to see it that first day, I think, but I had to wait until after the funeral, see? I had to let you mourn some. But for some reason things have changed, Spencer. He is allowing us to see."

The room was heavy with the unseen. Spencer could feel it, and goose flesh raised on his shoulders. A tear slipped from his eye, but it was a good tear. A strangely welcomed tear. Helen held his gaze for a moment and then took a quick sip of her tea.

She looked back at him. "Are you ready?"

He wasn't sure what *ready* was, but he nodded anyway, feeling desperate now. Eager.

"Close your eyes, Spencer."

He did.

It came immediately, like a rush of wind and light. A whirlwind in his mind, or maybe not just in his mind—he didn't know. His breath left him completely, but that didn't matter, because the wind filled his chest with enough oxygen to last a lifetime. Or so it felt.

The darkness behind his eyelids was suddenly full of lights. Souls. People. Angels. Streaking brightly across the horizon. Then hovering, then streaking and looping and twisting. He gasped and felt his mouth stretch open.

It struck him that the lights were not just shooting about randomly, but they flew in a perfect symmetry. Across the whole of space, as if they were putting on a show. Then he knew they *were* putting on a show. For him!

Like a million Blue Angels jets, streaking, hair-raising, perfect, like a billion ballerinas, leaping in stunning unison. But it was their sound that made little Spencer's heart feel like exploding. Because every single one of them—one billion souls strong—were screaming.

Screaming with laughter.

Long, ecstatic peals of barely controlled laughter. And above it all, one voice laughed—soft, yet loud and unmistakably clear. It was his mom's voice. Gloria was up there with them. Beside herself with joy in this display.

Then, in a flash, her whole face filled his mind, or maybe all of space. Her head tilted back slightly, and her mouth opened. She was laughing with delight, as he had never seen anyone laugh. Tears streamed over bunched cheeks, and her eyes sparkled bright. The sight did two things to Spencer at once, with crushing finality. It washed some of that joy and desire into his own chest, so that he burst into tears and laughter. And it made him want to be there. Like he had never wanted anything in his whole life. A desperate craving to be there.

The whole vision lasted maybe two seconds.

And then it was gone.

Spencer slumped in his chair like a blubbering, laughing, raggedy doll.

When Grandma Helen finally took him home two hours later, the world seemed like a strange new place to him. As if it were a dream world and the one he'd seen in Grandma's house was the real one. But he knew with settling certainty that this world, with trees and houses and his dad's Lexus parked in the driveway, was indeed very real.

It made him sad again, because in this world his mom was dead.

CHAPTER EIGHT

Week Four

KENT PUNCHED the numbers again, hoping that this time, Borst would be in his office. In the last two weeks he'd left three messages for his supervisor, and the man had yet to return a call. He had called the first week and left word with Betty that he would be taking two or three weeks off to collect himself, put things in order.

"Of course," she'd said. "I'll pass it right on. Do what you need to do. I'm sure everyone will understand. Our hearts are with you."

"Thank you. And could you ask Borst to give me a call?"

"Sure."

That had been seventeen days ago. Goodness, it had not been *he* who'd passed on. The least they could do was return a call. His life was in enough disarray. It had taken all of two weeks for him to take the first steps back to reality. Back to the realization that aside from Spencer, and actually because of Spencer, his career was now everything.

And now Borst was avoiding him.

The phone rang three times before Betty's voice crackled in his ear. "Niponbank Information Systems; this is Betty."

"Betty. Hi. This is—"

"Kent! How are you?" She sounded normal enough. Her reaction came as a small wave of relief.

"Okay, actually. I'm doing better. Listen, I really need to speak with Borst. I know he must be busy, but do you think you could patch me through for a minute?" It was a lie, of course. He knew nothing of the kind. Borst had not had a busy day in his life.

She hesitated. "Uh, sure, Kent. Let me see if he's in." A butterfly took flight in his belly at her tone. Borst was always *in*. If not in his office then in the john, reading some Grisham novel. *Let me check?* Who did they think he was?

Betty came back on. "Just a minute, Kent. Let me put you through."

The line broke into Barry Manilow's "I Write the Songs." The music brought a cloud to Kent's heart. That was one of the problems with mourning; it came and left without regard for circumstances.

"Kent!" Borst's voice sounded forced. Kent imagined the man sitting behind that big screen in his office, overdressed in that navy three-piece he liked to wear. "How are you doing, Kent?"

"Fine."

"Good. We've been worried about you. I'm sorry about what happened. I had a niece who died once." Borst did not elaborate, possibly because he'd suddenly realized how stupid that sounded. *Don't forget your pet ferret, Monkey Brains. It died too, didn't it? Must've been devastating!*

"Yeah. It's tough," Kent said. "I'm sorry for taking so much time off here, but—"

"No, it's fine. Really. You take all the time you need. Not that we don't need you here, but we understand." He was speaking quickly. "Believe me, it's no problem."

"Thanks, but I think the best thing now is to get back to work. I'll be in on Monday." It was Friday. That gave him a weekend to set his mind in the right frame. "Besides, there are a few clarifications I need to make on the funds processing system." That should spark a comment on the Miami conference. Surely the reception to AFPS had been favorable. Why was Borst not slobbering about it?

"Sure," his supervisor said, rather anemically. "Yeah, Monday's good."

Kent could not contain his curiosity any longer. "So, what did they say to AFPS?" he asked as nonchalantly as possible.

"Oh, they loved it. It was a real smash, Kent. I wish you could have been there. It's everything we hoped for. Maybe more."

Of course! He'd known it all along. "So did the board make any mention of it?" Kent asked.

"Yes. Yes, they did. In fact, they've already implemented it. System wide."

The revelation brought Kent to his feet. His chair clattered to the floor behind him. "What? How? I should have been told. There are some things —"

"We didn't think it would be right to bother you. You know with the missis dying and all. But don't worry; it's been working exactly as we designed it to work."

We *nothing, Bucko. It was my program; you should have waited for me!* At least it was working. "So it was a big hit, huh?" He retrieved his chair and sat down.

"Very big. It was the buzz of the conference."

Kent squeezed his eyes and gripped his fist tight, exhilarated. Suddenly he wanted to be back. He imagined walking into the bank on Monday, a dozen suits thumping his back with congratulations.

"Good. Okay, I'll see you Monday, Markus. It'll be good to get back."

"Well, it'll be good to have you back too, Kent."

He thought about telling the man about the changes he'd made to the program before leaving for Miami but decided they could wait the weekend. Besides, he rather liked the idea of being the only man who really knew the inner workings of AFPS. A little power never hurt anybody.

Kent hung up, feeling decent for the first time since Gloria's death. It was settled, then. On Monday he would reenter his skyrocketing career. It would breathe new life into him.

MONDAY MORNING came slow for Kent. He and Spencer had spent the weekend at the zoo and Elitch Gardens amusement park. Both the animals and the mobs of people served to distract them from their sorrow for a time. Helen had dragged them off to church on Sunday. Actually, Spencer had not needed dragging. In fact, it might be more accurate to say that *Spencer* had dragged him off to church—with Helen's full endorsement, of course. Pastor Bill Madison had lectured them on the power of God, which only served to annoy Kent immensely. Sitting in the pew, he'd thought about the power of death. And then his mind had drifted to the bank. Monday was on his mind.

And now Monday was here.

The arrangements had gone smoothly. Helen would watch Spencer at her place on Monday and Tuesday. Linda, one of Helen's buddies from church, would watch him Wednesday morning at the house. Spencer insisted he could finish off his homeschool curriculum on his own this year. Next year he might attend the public school.

Kent rose a full hour ahead of schedule, anxious and not knowing exactly why.

He showered, dressed in navy slacks and a starched white shirt, and changed ties three times before settling on a red silk Countess Mara. He then sat at the kitchen table, drinking coffee and watching the clock. The bank opened at eight, but he would walk in at ten after. Seemed appropriate. Make a statement, although he was not sure why he needed to make a statement. Or even what that statement would be. Possibly he relished the image of walking through the bank after everyone else had arrived, nodding to their smiles of consolation; acknowledging their words of congratulations. He dismissed the notion. If anything, he felt like sneaking in and avoiding the predictable shows of sympathy. Still, some form of congratulations would be in order.

A hundred scenarios ran through his mind, followed by a healthy dose of self-correction for letting the thoughts occupy him at all. In the end he blamed it all on his stressed mental state. Some psychiatrists suggested that men bent upon success became more attached to their work than to their spouses. Married to their jobs. He doubted he'd ever gone to such extremes, but the notion seemed somewhat attractive now. After all, Gloria was gone. So then, possibly he was having first-date jitters.

Kent scoffed at the idea and stood from the table. Enough blather. Time to go.

He climbed behind the wheel of the silver Lexus and drove to the bank. The butterflies rose in his stomach when the renovated office complex, now bearing the name Niponbank, loomed on the corner of Fifth and Grand. A thousand times he'd approached the old, red-brick building in the Lexus, barely aware of the downtown maze through which he drove. Hardly noticing his stopping and starting at lights as he closed in on the twenty-story structure, sitting there like an oversized fire station.

Now every movement became acute. A newsman ran on about inflation over the stereo. Cars streamed by, completely lost to the fact that he was reentering their world after a three-week absence. Pedestrians wandered in abstract directions with intent, but otherwise aimless. He wondered if any of them had lost someone recently. If so, no one would know. The world was moving ahead, full stride, with or without him.

The light just before the bank remained red for an inordinate period. Two full minutes, at least. In that time he watched eighteen people ascend or descend the sweeping steps leading to the bank's main floor. Probably tenants from the upper stories.

The car behind him honked, and he started. The light had turned. He motored across the intersection and swung the Lexus into the side parking lot. Familiar cars sat in their customary slots. With one last look in the mirror, his pulse now drumming steadily, Kent eased out of the sedan. He snatched his briefcase from the backseat and strode for the main entry.

Like walking up to a dream date on prom night. Good grief!

Long, polished, white steps rose like piano keys to the brass-framed glass doors. The year-old face-lift suited the building. He grabbed the brass handrail and clicked up the steps. With a final tingle at the base of his spine, he pushed through the entry.

The three-story lobby loomed spacious and plush, and Kent paused just inside the doors. The tall brass yacht hovered ahead, stately and magnificent, seemingly supported by that one thin shaft. Sidney Beech, the branch's assistant vice president, clacked along the marble floor, thirty feet from Kent. She saw him, gave him a friendly nod, and continued her walk toward the glass-enclosed offices along the right wall. Two personal bankers he recognized as Ted and Maurice talked idly by the president's office door. A dozen stuffed maroon guest chairs sat in small groupings, waiting in perfect symmetry for patrons who would descend on the bank at nine.

To Kent's left, the gray-flecked floor ran up to a long row of teller stations. During peak hours, fifteen tellers would be shuffling bills across the long, hunter-green counter. Now, seven busied themselves for the opening.

Kent stepped forward toward the gaping hall opposite him where the marble floor ended and the teal carpet ran into the administration wing. The large seagull that hung on the wall above the hall seemed to be eyeing him.

Zak, the white-haired security guard, stood idly to Kent's right, looking important and doing exactly what he had done for five years now: nothing. He had seen it all a thousand times, but coming in now, it struck him as though new. Like a déjà vu. *I've been here before, haven't I? Yes, of course.* At any moment a call would come. Someone would notice that Kent Anthony had just entered the building. The man responsible for the new processing system. The man whose wife had just died. Then they would all know he had arrived.

But the call did not come.

And that bothered him a little. He stepped onto the carpet and swallowed, thinking maybe they had not seen him. And, after all, these front-lobby workers were not as close to his world as the rest. Back in the administration sections they referred to those who worked out in the large foyer as the *handlers.* But it was them, the *processors,* who really made banking work—everyone knew that.

Kent breathed deeply once, walked straight down the hall, and opened the door to his little corner of the world.

Betty Smythe was there at her desk on the left—bleached, poofy-white hair and all. She had a tube of bright red lipstick cocked and ready to apply, one inch from pursed lips already too red for Kent's taste. Immediately her face went a shade whiter, and she blinked. Which was how he supposed some people might respond to a waking of the dead. Only it was not he who had died.

"Hi, Betty," he said.

"Kent!" Now she collected herself, jerked that red stick to her lap, and squirmed on the seat. "You're back."

"Yes, Betty. I'm back."

He'd always thought that Borst's decision to hire Betty had been motivated by the size of her bra rather than the size of her brain, and looking at her now he was sure of it. He glanced about the reception area. Beyond the blue armchairs the hall sat vacant. All four oak office doors were shut. A fleeting picture of the black nameplates flashed through his mind. Borst, Anthony, Brice, Quinn. It had been the same for three years now.

"So how are things going?" he asked absently.

"Fine," she said, fiddling with the latch on her purse. "I don't know what to say about your wife. I'm so sorry."

"Don't say anything." She had not mentioned AFPS yet. He turned and smiled at her. "Really, I'll be fine." So much for the blaring reception.

Kent walked to the first door on the left and entered his office. The overhead fluorescent stuttered white over his black workstation, tidy as he had left it. He closed the door and set the briefcase down.

Well now, here he was. At home once again. Three computer monitors rested on the corner station, each displaying the same exotic-fish screensaver in unison. His high-back leather chair butted up to the keyboard.

Kent reached for his neck and loosened his collar. He slid into his chair and touched the mouse. The screens jumped to life as one. A large three-dimensional insignia reading "Advanced Funds Processing System" rolled out on the screen like a carpet inviting entry. "Welcome to the bank," the last of it read. Indeed, with this little baby, an operator had access to the bank in ways many a criminal would only dream of through fitful sleep.

He dropped into his chair, punched in his customary access code, and dropped a finger on the ENTER key. The screen went black for a moment. Then large yellow letters suddenly popped up: ACCESS DENIED.

He grunted and keyed in the password again, sure he had not forgotten his own son's name: SPENCER.

ACCESS DENIED, the screen read again. Borst must have changed the code in his absence. Of course! They had integrated the program already. In doing so, they would need to set a primary access password, which would automatically delete the old.

Kent hesitated at the door to his office, thinking again that he had been in the office for a full five minutes now and not one word of congratulations. Borst's closed door was directly across the hall. He should walk in and let the man bring him up to speed. Or perhaps he should make an appearance in Todd's or Mary's office first. The two junior programmers would know what was up.

At the last moment he decided to check in on Will Thompson in the loan department instead. Will would know the buzz, and he was disconnected.

He found Will at his desk, one floor up, bent over his monitor, adjusting the focus.

"Need any help with that?" Kent asked, grinning.

Will looked up, surprised. "Kent! You're back!" He extended a quick hand. "When did you get back? Gee, I'm sorry."

"Ten minutes ago." Kent reached down and twisted a knob behind the monitor. The menu on the screen immediately jumped into clear view.

Will smirked and sat down. "Thanks man. I always could count on you. So, you okay? I wasn't sure I'd ever see you back here."

Kent sat in a guest chair and shrugged. "I'm hanging in there. It's good to be back to work. Keep me distracted, maybe."

The loan officer lifted an eyebrow. "So, you're okay with it all?"

Kent looked at his friend, not sure what he was asking. "It's not like I have a lot of choice in the matter, Will. What's done is done."

"Yeah. You're right. I just thought that on top of your wife's death and all, you might see things differently." The room suddenly seemed deathly quiet. It struck Kent then that something was amiss. And like Betty, Will had not congratulated him. A thin chill snaked down his spine.

"See what differently?" he asked.

Will stared at him. "You . . . you've talked to Borst, right?"

Kent shook his head. Yes indeed, something was very much amiss, and it wasn't sounding good. "No."

"You're kidding, right? You haven't heard a thing?"

"About what? What are you talking about?"

"Oh, Kent . . ." His friend winced. "I'm sorry, man. You've got to talk to Borst."

That did it. Kent stood abruptly and strode from the room, ignoring a call from Will. His gut turned in lazy circles down the elevator. He stepped into the computer wing and walked right past a wide-eyed Betty to the back offices where Todd and Mary would be diligently at work.

He smacked through Todd's door first.

"Hey, Todd."

The redhead started and shoved his chair back. "Kent! You're back!"

A stranger sat in a chair to the junior programmer's right, and the sight caught Kent off guard for a moment. The man rose with Todd and smiled. He stood as tall as Kent, he wore his hair short, and his eyes were the greenest Kent had ever seen. Like two emerald marbles. A starched white shirt rested, crisp, on broad shoulders. The man stuck his hand out, and Kent removed his eyes from him without taking it.

Todd stood slack-jawed. A button on his green shirt had popped open, revealing a hairy white belly. The programmer's eyes looked at him like black holes, filled to the brim with guilt.

"I'm back. So, tell me what's up, Todd. What's happening here that I don't know about?"

"Ah, Kent, this is Cliff Monroe. I'm showing him the ropes." He motioned to the man beside him. "He's new to our staff."

"Good for you, Cliff. Answer my question, Todd. What's changed?"

"What do you mean?" The junior programmer lifted his shoulders in an attempt to look casual. The motion widened the shirt's gap at his belly, and Kent dismissed the sudden impulse to reach in there and yank some hair.

Kent swallowed. "Nothing changed while I was out, then?"

"What do you mean?" Todd shrugged again, his eyes bugging.

Kent grunted in disgust, impatient with the spineless greenhorn. He turned and stepped across the hall to Mary's office. He pushed the door open. Mary sat at her desk with her phone pressed to her ear, facing away from the door, talking. She turned around slowly, her eyes round.

As if, Honey! You knew I was coming. Probably having an important discussion with a dial tone. Fitting partner.

Kent shut the door firmly and strode for Borst's door, his spine now tingling right up to his skull. The man sat stiffly in his chair, his three-piece suit tight, sweat beading his brow. His bald spot shone as if he'd oiled it. His large, hooked nose glistened like some shiny Christmas bulb. The superior made a magnanimous effort to show shock when Kent barged in.

"Kent! You made it back!"

Of course I made it back, you witless fool, he almost replied. Instead he said, "Yes," and plopped down in one of Borst's tweed guest chairs. "I called you on Friday, remember. So who's the new employee?"

"Cliff? Yes, he's a transfer from Dallas. An excellent programmer, from what I hear." The middle-aged man flicked his tongue across thick lips and ran a hand through what hair he had. "So. How's the missis?"

The room lapsed into silence. The missis? Gloria? Borst must have realized his blunder, because a stupid grin crossed his face, and he went red.

Kent spoke before the man could cover his error, hot with anger. "The missis is dead, remember, Markus? It's why I've been gone for three weeks. You see, there's an office across the hall that has my name on it. And for five years now, I've been working there. Or had you forgotten that as well?"

Borst turned beet red now, and not from embarrassment, Kent guessed. He continued before the man could recover. "So how did the AFPS presentation go, Markus?" He forced a smile. "Are we on top?" He meant, am *I* on top, but he was sure that Borst would catch the drift.

The phone rang shrilly on the desk. Borst glared at Kent for a moment and then snatched it up, listening.

"Yes . . . yes put him through."

Kent sat back and crossed his legs, aware that his heart was pounding. The other man straightened his tie and sat upright, attentive for whoever was about to address him on the phone. He turned from Kent and spoke. "Yes, Mr. Wong . . . Yes, thank you, sir."

Mr. Wong? Borst was thanking *the* Mr. Wong?

"I'd be delighted." He turned and faced Kent purposefully. "Yes, I'm tied up with a luncheon on the East Coast Wednesday, but I could fly to Tokyo on Thursday." Kent knew that something very awful was happening here. He was now sweating badly, despite the air conditioning.

"I'd be delighted," Borst said. "Yes, it did take a lot, but I had a good crew on it as well . . . Yes, thank you. Good-bye."

He dropped the phone in its cradle and stared at Kent for a long moment. When he finally spoke, it came out rehearsed. "Come on, Kent. Surely you didn't expect all of the glory on this, did you? It's my department."

Kent swallowed, suddenly fearing the worst. But that would be virtually impossible.

"What did you do?" His voice sounded scratchy.

"Nothing. I'm just implementing the program. That's all. It is *my* program."

Kent began to tremble slightly. "Okay, let's back up here. In Miami I was set to introduce AFPS to the convention. You remember that, right?" He was sounding condescending, but he could not help himself.

Borst nodded once and frowned.

"But I got called away, right? My wife was dying. You with me here?"

This time Borst did not acknowledge.

"So I asked you to wing it for me. And I'm assuming you did. Now, surely somewhere in there you mentioned my name, right? Gave credit where credit was due?"

Borst had frozen like ice.

Kent scooted forward on his seat, steaming. "Don't tell me you stole all the credit for AFPS, Markus. Just tell me you didn't!"

The division supervisor sat with an ashen face. "This is *my* division, Kent. That means that the work out of here is *my* responsibility. You work for me." He went red as he spoke. "Or did *you* forget *that* simple fact?"

"You put the paperwork through! This has always been my bonus! We've discussed it a thousand times! You left me out?!"

"No. You're in there. So is Todd, and so is Mary."

"Todd and Mary?" Kent blurted incredulously. "You put my name in small print along with Todd's and Mary's?" And he knew Borst had done exactly that.

He shoved an arm toward the door. "They're junior programmers, Markus! They write code that I give them to write. AFPS is *my* code!" He nearly shouted now, boring down on the supervisor with a straining neck.

"I designed it from scratch. Did you tell them that? It was *my* brainchild! I wrote 80 percent of the functioning code, for Pete's sake! You yourself wrote a measly 5 percent, most of which I trashed."

That last comment pushed Borst over the edge. The veins on his neck bulged. "You hold your tongue, mister! This is my department. I was responsible for the design and implementation of AFPS. I will hire and fire who I see fit. And for your information, I have been allotted a twenty-five-thousand-dollar spiff for the design engineer of my choice. I was going to give that to you, Kent. But you are rapidly changing my mind!"

Now something deep in Kent's mind snapped, and his vision swam. For the first time in his life he felt like killing someone. He breathed deeply twice to stabilize the tremor in his bones. When he spoke, he did so through clenched teeth.

"Twenty-five thousand dollars!" he ground out. "There was a performance spiff on that program, Markus. Ten percent of the savings to the company over ten years. It's worth millions!"

Borst blinked and sat back. He knew it, of course. They had discussed it on a dozen occasions. And now he meant to claim it all as his. The man did not respond.

The rage came like a boiling volcano, right up through Kent's chest and into his skull. Blind rage. He could still see, but things were suddenly fuzzy. He knew he was erupting, knew Borst could see it all—his red face, his trembling lips, his bulging eyes.

Gripping his hands into fists, Kent suddenly knew that he would fight Borst to his death. He had just lost his wife; he was not about to give up his own livelihood. He would use every means at his disposal to claim his due. And in the process he would bury this spineless pimp before him.

The thought brought a sterling cool to his bones, and he let it filter through his body for a moment. He stood, still glaring angrily. "You're a spineless worm, Borst. And you're stealing my work for your own."

They held stares for a full ten seconds. Borst refused to speak.

"What's the new code?" Kent demanded.

Borst pursed his lips, silent.

Kent spun from the man, exited the office with a bang, and stormed down to Todd's office. He shoved the door open.

"Todd!" The junior started. "What's the new AFPS access code?"

Todd seemed to shrink into his chair. "M-B-A-O-K," he said.

Kent left without thanking him.

He needed a rest. He needed to think. He grabbed his briefcase and walked angrily past Betty's desk without acknowledging her. This time one of the tellers called a greeting to him as he rushed through the towering lobby, but he ignored the distant call and slammed through the tall glass doors.

CHAPTER NINE

THE MADNESS of it all descended upon Kent one block from the bank. It was then that a burning realization of his loss sank into his gut. If Borst pulled this off—which, judging by the call from Wong, he was doing just splendidly—he would effectively strip Kent of everything. Millions of dollars. That hook-nosed imbecile in there was casually intercepting his life's work.

Kent's chest flushed with a wave of panic. It was impossible! He'd kill anybody who tried to steal what was his. Shove a gun in the guy's mouth and blow his brains out, maybe. Good grief! What was he thinking? He could hardly shoot a prairie dog, much less another man. On the other hand, maybe Borst had just given up his right to life.

And what of Spencer? They would be virtually broke. All the boasting of Euro Disney and yachts and beachfront homes would prove him a fool. An image of that grinning monkey from the Chicago airport clapped its cymbals through his mind. *Clang-ka-ching, clang-ka-ching.*

Kent snatched up his cell phone and punched seven digits. A receptionist answered after two rings. "Warren Law Offices."

"Hi. This is Kent Anthony." His voice wavered, and he cleared his throat. "Is Dennis in?"

"Just a minute. Let me see if he's available."

The line remained silent for a minute before his old college roommate's voice filled his ear. "Hello, Kent. Goodness, it's been awhile. How you doing, man?"

"Hey, Dennis. Actually, not so good. I've got some problems. I need a good attorney. You have some time?"

"You okay, buddy? You don't sound so good."

"Well, like I said, I've got some problems. Can I meet with you?"

"Sure. Absolutely. Let's see . . ." Kent heard the faint flip of paper through the receiver. "How about Thursday afternoon?"

"No, Dennis. I mean now. Today."

Dennis held his reply for a second. "Pretty short notice, buddy. I'm booked solid. It can't wait?"

Kent did not respond. A sudden surge of emotions had taken hold of his throat.

"Hold on. Let me see if I can reschedule my lunch." The phone clicked to hold music.

Two minutes later Dennis came back on. "Okay, buddy. You owe me for this. How about Pelicans at twelve sharp? I already have reservations."

"Good. Thanks, Dennis. It means a lot."

"You mind me asking what this is about?"

"It's employment related. I just got screwed out of a major bonus. I mean major, as in millions."

Static sounded. "Millions?" Dennis Warren's voice cracked. "What kind of bonus is worth millions? I didn't know you were in that kind of money, Kent."

"Yeah, well, I won't be if we don't act quick. I'll give you the whole story at lunch."

"Twelve o'clock then. And make sure you have your employment file with you. I'll need that."

Kent pulled back into traffic, feeling a small surge of confidence. This wasn't the first time he'd faced an obstacle. He glanced at the clock on the dash. Nine o'clock. He'd have to burn three hours. He could retrieve a copy of his employment agreement from the house—that would take an hour if he stretched things.

"God, help me," he muttered. But that was stupid, because he didn't believe in God. But maybe there was a Satan and his number had come up on Satan's big spinning wheel: *Time to go after Kent. After him, lads!*

Ridiculous.

PELICANS GRILL bustled with a lunch crowd willing to pay thirty bucks for the privilege of eyeing Denver's skyline while feasting. Kent sat by the picture window, overlooking Interstate 25, and stared at his plate, thinking he really should at least finish the veal. Apart from a dip from the mashed potatoes and a corner sawed off the meat, his lunch sat untouched. And that after an hour at the table.

Dennis sat dressed smartly in a black tailored suit, cut with care to hang just so on his well-muscled frame. The jet-black mustache and deep tan fit his Greek heritage. By the Rolex on his wrist and the large emerald ring on his right forefinger, Kent's college roomy had obviously done just fine for himself. He had listened to Kent's tale with complete rapture, biting at his steak aggressively and *humphing* at all the right junctures. The man had just heard of Gloria's death for the first time, and the announcement had brought his fork clattering to his plate. He stared at Kent, frozen, his mouth slightly agape.

"You're kidding?" he stammered, wide eyed. Of course he had known Gloria. Had met her at their wedding, three years after college, when they were both just getting started. "Oh, Kent, I'm so sorry."

"Yeah. It all happened so quickly, you know. I can barely believe it's happened half the time."

Dennis wiped his mouth and swallowed. "It's hard to believe." He shook his head. "If there's anything I can do, buddy. Anything at all."

"Just help me get my money, Dennis."

His friend shook his head. "It's incredible how these things can come out of nowhere. You heard about Lacy, right?"

Lacy? A bell clanged to life in Kent's mind. "Lacy?" he asked.

"Lacy Cartwright. You dated her for two years in college. Remember her?"

Of course he remembered Lacy. They had broken up three months before graduation. She was ready for marriage, and the thought had frightened him clean out of love. Last he'd heard she had married some guy from the East Coast the same year he and Gloria had married.

"Sure," he said.

"She lost her husband a couple years ago to cancer. It was quick from what I heard. Just like that. You didn't get the announcement? Last I heard she'd moved to Boulder."

"No." Kent shook his head. Not surprising, really. After the way he'd cut her off, Lacy wouldn't dream of reintroducing herself at *any* juncture, much less at her husband's funeral. She was as principled as they came.

"So what do you think about the case?" Kent asked, shifting the conversation back to the legal matter. Dennis crossed his legs and leaned back. "Well . . ." He sucked at his teeth and let his tongue wander about his mouth for a moment, thinking. "It really depends on the employment contract you signed. You brought it with you?"

Kent nodded, withdrew the document from his briefcase, and handed it to him.

Dennis flipped through the pages, scanning the paragraphs quickly, mumbling something about boilerplate jargon. "I'll have to read this more carefully at the office but . . . Here we go: Statement of Propriety."

He read quickly, and Kent nibbled on a cold pea.

The attorney flopped the document on the table. "Pretty standard agreement. They own everything, of course. But you do have recourse. Two ways to look at this." He held up two fingers. "One, you can fight these guys regardless of this agreement. Just take them to court and claim that you signed this document without full knowledge."

"Why? Is it a bad document?" Kent interrupted.

"Depends. For you, in your situation, yes. I'd say so. By signing it you basically agreed to forfeit all natural rights to proprietary property, regardless of how it materialized. You also specifically agreed to press no claims for compensation not specifically drawn under contract. Meaning, unless you have a contract that stipulates you are due 10 percent of the savings generated by this . . . what is it?"

"AFPS."

"AFPS . . . it's up to the company to decide if you are entitled to the money."

Kent's heart began to palpitate. "And who in the company decides these things?"

"That's what I was going to ask you. Immediately, it would be your superior."

"Borst?"

Dennis nodded. "You can go over his head, of course. Who above him knows of the work you put into this thing?" Kent sat back, feeling heavy. "Price Bentley. He's the branch president. I sat in a dozen meetings with him and Borst. He has to know that the man is about as bright as mud. Can't I bring in coworkers?"

"If you want to sue, sure. But by their reactions, it sounds to me like they might be more on Borst's side than yours. Sounds like the guy was doing some fast talking while you were out. Your best bet is probably to go straight to the bank president and appeal your case. Either way you're going to need strong support from the inside. If they all side with Borst, we're going to have to prove a conspiracy, and that, my friend, is near impossible."

Kent let the words soak in slowly. "So basically either I gain favor with one of Borst's superiors and work internally, or I'm screwed. That about it?"

"Well, like I said, I really need to read this thing through, but, barring any hidden clauses, I'd say that's the bottom line. Now, we can always sue. But without someone backing up your story, you might as well throw your money to the wind."

Kent smiled courageously. But his mind was already on Price Bentley's face. He cursed himself for not taking more time to befriend upper management. Then again, they'd hired him as a programmer, not as a court jester. And program he had, the best piece of software the banking industry had seen in ten years.

"So I go back there and start making friends," he said, looking out the picture window to the cars flowing below. From the corner of his eye he saw Dennis nod. He nodded with him. Surely old Price was smart enough to know who deserved credit for AFPS. But the idea that another man held the power to grant or deny his future sat like lead in his gut.

CHAPTER TEN

KENT WALKED straight to Price Bentley's office on Tuesday morning before bothering with Borst.

He'd spent Monday afternoon and evening chewing his fingernails, which was a problem because he had no fingernails to speak of. Spencer had wanted to eat chicken in the park for dinner, but Kent had no stomach for pretending to enjoy life on a park bench. "Go ahead, son. Just stay away from any strangers."

The night had proved fitful. A sickening dread had settled on him like a human-sized sticky flysheet, and no matter what twists and turns he put his mind through, he could not shake it free. To make matters worse, he'd awakened at three in the morning, breathless with panic and then furious as thoughts of Borst filtered into his waking mind. He'd spent an hour tossing and turning only to finally throw the covers across the room and swing from bed. The next few hours had been maddening.

By the time the first light filtered through the windows, he had dressed in his best suit and downed three cups of coffee. Helen had collected Spencer at seven and had given Kent a raised eyebrow. It might have been his palms, wet with sweat. Or the black under his eyes. But knowing her, she had probably seen right into his mind and picked through the mess there.

He had nearly hit a yellow Mustang at the red light just before the bank because his eyes were on those sweeping steps ahead and not on the traffic signal. His was the first car in the lot, and he decided to park on the far row in favor of being seen early. Finally, at eight sharp, he'd climbed from the Lexus, swept his damp, blond locks back into place, and headed for the wide doors.

He ran into Sidney Beech around the corner from the president's office. "Hi, Kent," she said. Her long face, accentuated by short brown hair, now looked even longer under raised brows. "I saw you yesterday. Are you okay? I'm so sorry about what happened."

He knew Sidney only casually, but her voice now came like warm milk to his cold tremoring bones. If his mission was to win friends and influence the smug suits, a favorable word with the assistant vice president couldn't hurt. He spread his mouth in a genuine smile.

"Thank you, Sidney." He reached for her hand and grasped it, wondering how much would be too much. "Thank you so much. Yes. Yes, I'm doing better. Thank you."

An odd glint in her eye made him blink, and he released her hand. Was she single? Yes, he thought she was single. The left corner of her lip lifted a hair. "That's good to hear, Kent. If there's anything I can do, just let me know."

"Yes, I will. Listen, do you know what Mr. Bentley's schedule is today? There's a rather important issue that I—"

"Actually, you might catch him now. I know he has an eight-thirty with the board, but I just saw him walk into his office."

Kent glanced in the direction of the president's office. "Great. Thank you, Sidney. You're so kind."

He left, thinking he had overdone it with her, maybe. But then, maybe not. Politics had never been his strong suit. Either way, the exchange had given him a sensibility that took the edge off the manic craziness that had gripped him all night.

True to Sidney's words, Price Bentley sat in his office alone, sorting through a stack of mail. Rumor had it that Price weighed his salary: 250. Only his salary came in thousands of U.S. dollars, not pounds. The large man sat in a gray pin-striped suit. Despite being partially obscured by a layer of thick flesh, his collar looked crisp, possibly supported by cardboard or plastic within its folds. The man's head looked like a plump tomato atop a can. He looked up at Kent and smiled. "Kent! Kent Anthony. Come on in. Sit down. To what do I owe this pleasure?" The president did not rise but continued flipping through the stack.

If the man knew of Gloria's passing, he was not going there. Kent stepped to an overstuffed blue guest chair and sat. The room seemed warm.

"Thank you, sir. Do you have a minute?"

"Sure." The bank president leaned back, crossed his legs, and propped his chin on a hand. "I have a few minutes. How can I help you?"

The man's eyes glistened round and gray. "Well, it's about AFPS," Kent started.

"Yes. Congratulations. Fine work you guys put together back there. I'm sorry you couldn't be at the conference, but it went over with quite a splash. Excellent job!"

Kent smiled and nodded. "That's what I heard. Thank you." He hesitated. How could he say this without sounding like a whiner? *But sir, his blue ribbon was bigger than my blue ribbon.* He hated whiners with a passion. Only this was not about blue ribbons, was it? Not even close.

"Sir, it seems there's been a mistake somewhere."

Bentley's brows scrunched. "Oh? How's that?" He seemed concerned. That was good. Kent picked up steam.

"The Advanced Funds Processing System was my brainchild, sir, five years ago. In fact, I showed you my rough diagrams once. Do you remember?"

"No, I can't say that I do. But that doesn't mean you didn't. I see a thousand submissions a year. And I'm aware that you had an awful lot to do with the system's development. Excellent job."

"Thank you." So far so good. "Actually, I wrote 90 percent of the code for the program." Kent leaned back for the first time. He settled into the chair. "I put a hundred hours a week into its development for over five years. Borst oversaw parts of the process, but for the most part he let me run it."

The president sat still, not catching Kent's drift yet. Unless he was choosing to ignore it. Kent gave him a second to offer a comment and then continued when none came.

"I worked those hours for all those years with my eye set on a goal, sir. And now it seems that Borst has decided that I do not deserve that goal." There. How could he be any clearer?

The president stared at him, unblinking, impossible to read. Heat rose through Kent's back. Everything now sat on those blind scales of justice, waiting for a verdict. Only these scales were not blind at all. They possessed flat gray eyes, screwed into that tomato head across the desk.

Silence settled thick. Kent thought he should continue—throw in some lighthearted political jargon, maybe shift the subject, now having planted his seed. But his mind had gone blank. He became aware that his palms were sweating.

Bentley suddenly spread his jowls in a grin, and he chuckled once with pursed lips. Still not sure what the man could possibly be thinking, Kent chuckled once with him. It seemed natural enough.

"The savings bonus?" the president asked, and he was either very condescending or genuinely surprised. Kent begged for the latter, but now the heat was sending little tingles over his skull.

"Yes," he answered, and cleared his throat.

Bentley chuckled again, and his jowls bounced over his collar with each chuckle. "You actually thought that you had a substantial bonus coming, didn't you?"

The breath left Kent as if he'd been gut-punched.

"Those saving spiffs are hardly for non-management personnel, Kent. Surely you realized that. Management, yes. And this one will be substantial indeed. I can see why you might be slobbering over it. But you have to pay your dues. You can't just expect to be handed a million dollars because you did most of the work."

Kent might have lost his judgment there, on the spot—reached over and slapped Fat-Boy's jowls. But waves of confusion fixed him rigid except for a blinking in his eyes. Niponbank had always boasted of its Savings Bonus Program, and everyone knew that it was aimed at the ordinary worker. A dozen documents clearly stated so. Last year a teller had come up with an idea that earned him a hundred thousand dollars.

"That's not how the employment manual lays the program out," Kent said, still too shocked to be angry. Surely the president didn't think he could get away with *this* line of argument. They would fry his behind in court!

Bentley's lips fell flat. "Now, you listen to me, Anthony. I don't give a rat's tushy what you think the employment manual says. In this branch, that bonus goes to the management. You work for Borst. Borst works for me." The words came out like bullets from a silenced pistol.

The president took one hard breath. "What work you did for the bank, you did on our time, at our request, and for it we paid you well over a hundred thousand dollars a year. That's it. You hear me? You even think about fighting this, and I promise you we will bury you." The large man said it, shaking.

Kent felt his mouth drop during the diatribe. This was impossible! "You can't do that!" he protested. "You can't just rip my bonus off because . . ." And suddenly Kent knew precisely what he was up against. Bentley was in on it. He stood to receive huge sums of money from the bonus. He and Borst were in on this together. Which made it a conspiracy of sorts.

The man was glaring at him, daring him to say more. So he did.

"Listen!" He bit the word off with as much intensity as Bentley had used. "You know as well as I do that if I had been in Miami, I would have made that presentation, and I would be receiving most if not all of the bonus." A lump of self-pity rose to join the bitterness, and he trembled. "But I wasn't, was I? Because I had to rush home to tend to my wife, who was dying. So instead, you and Borst put your slimy heads together and decided to steal my bonus! What was it?" Kent wagged his head, mocking. 'Oh, poor little Anthony. His wife is dying. But at least he'll be distracted while we stab him in the back and strip him naked!' Is that about it, Bentley?"

The bank president's reaction was immediate. His eyes widened, and he drew an unsteady breath. "You speak like that to me in my own office? One more word out of you, and I'll have you on the street by day's end!"

But Kent had lost his political good sense entirely. "You have no right to do any of this, Bentley! That is my bonus you are stealing. People go to jail for theft in this country. Or is that news to you, as well?"

"Out! Get out!"

"I'll take this to the top. You understand me? And if I go down, you're going down with me. So don't even think about trying to cut me out. Everyone knew that the programming was my code."

"You might be surprised what everyone knew," Bentley shot back. He had forsaken that professional sheen, and Kent felt a spike of satisfaction for it.

"Yes, of course. You will bribe them all, I suppose?" he sneered.

The room went quiet again. When Bentley spoke again, it was low and stern, but the tremor was unmistakable. "Get out of my office, Anthony. I have a meeting in a few minutes. If it's all right with you, I need to prepare a few notes."

Kent stared the man down for a moment. "Actually, nothing is okay with me just now, sir. But then, you already know that, don't you?" He stood and walked behind the chair before turning back.

"And if you try to take my job from me I will personally sue you to the highest heaven. Your bonus may be an internal matter, but there are state laws that deal with employment. Don't even think about stripping me of my income."

He turned to the door and left Bentley sitting with big jowls and squinty eyes, like Jabba the Hut.

It was not until he heard the door close behind him that Kent fully realized how badly it had just gone for him. Then it crashed on him like a block of concrete, and a sick droning obscured his thoughts. He struck for the public restrooms across the lobby.

What had he done? He had to call Dennis. All of his worst fears had just come to life. It was a prospect he could not stomach. *Would* not stomach. Walking across the lobby, he suddenly felt like he was pushing through a steam bath. More than anything he'd ever wanted, possibly even more than the money itself, Kent wanted out of this nightmare. Go back three weeks and check back into Miami's Hyatt Regency. This time when they handed him the note it would have a different name on it. *I'm sorry, you have the wrong party,* he'd say. *I am not Ken Blatherly. My name's Kent. Kent Anthony. And I'm here to become a millionaire.*

Ignoring a young man he recognized as one of the tellers, Kent bent over the sink and threw water on his flushed face. He stood, watched the water drip down his face, and strode for the public phone in the corner, not bothering to wipe his face. Water spotted his starched shirt, but he couldn't care less. Just let Dennis be in. Please let him be in.

The young teller walked out, his eyes wide.

Kent punched the number.

"Warren Law Offices," the female voice came.

"Dennis in?" Silence. "Is Dennis in?"

"Who's calling?"

"Kent."

"May I tell him what it is regarding?"

"Just tell him it's Kent. Kent Anthony."

"Please hold."

No new thoughts formed in the silence. His mind was dipping into numbness.

"Kent! How's it going?"

Kent told him. He said it all in a long run-on sentence that ended with, "Then he threw me out."

"What do you mean, threw you out?"

"Told me to get out."

Silence again.

"Okay, buddy. Listen to me, okay?" Those were sweet words because they came from a friend. A friend who had something to say. That would be good, wouldn't it?

"I know this may sound impossible right now, but this is not over, you hear me? What he did in there, what Bentley just did, changes things. I'm not saying it hands us the case, but it gives us some pretty decent ammo. Obviously the political approach is dead. You pretty much slaughtered that. But you also managed to give us a fairly strong case."

Kent felt like crying. Just sitting down and crying.

"But I need you to do something for me, buddy. Okay? I need you to walk back to your office, sit down at your desk, and work the day out as if nothing at all happened. If we're lucky, they will fire you. And if they fire you, we'll slap the biggest unlawful discharge suit on them the state has ever seen. But if they don't fire you, I need you to continue working in good faith. We can't give them cause to release you. They might consider your confrontation this morning as insubordination, but there were no witnesses, right?"

"Right."

"So then you work as if you did nothing but go to Bentley's office and deliver some paper clips. You hear me? Can you do that?"

Kent wasn't sure he could, actually. The thought of seeing Borst and company back there made him swallow. On the other hand, he had to keep his options open. He had a mortgage and a car payment and groceries to think about. And he had Spencer.

"Yes, I can do that," he replied. "You really think we have something here?"

"It may be messy and take awhile. But yes, I do."

"Okay. Okay. Thanks, Dennis. I owe you."

"Don't worry. There'll be a bill if things go our way."

Kent tried to chuckle with his friend. It came out like a cough.

He hung up, straightened himself in front of the mirror, and let his eyes clear. Ten minutes later, he left the restroom and strode for the administrative offices, clenching his jaw. He'd been through hell already. There could be nowhere but up from here.

Nowhere but straight up.

HELEN SHUFFLED over the groove a dozen years of pacing had worn in her bedroom carpet along the length of the double French doors leading to her second-story balcony. It was her prayer closet. Her prayer groove. The place from which she most often broke through to the heavens. In better days she would think nothing of staying on her feet, pacing for hours at a stretch. But now her worn legs limited her to a plodding twenty minutes, tops. Then she would be forced to retreat to her bed or to the rocker.

She wore a long, pink housecoat that swayed around her bare feet. Her hair rested in tangles; bags darkened her eyes; her mouth had found frowning acceptable these days. Despite her understanding of a few things, the fact that her daughter was now gone did not rest easily. It was one thing to peek into the heavens and hear the laughter there. It was another thing altogether to be stuck here, yearning for that laughter. Or even the sweet reprimanding voice of her dear Gloria, instructing her on the finer points of manners.

She pulled at her skin and smiled briefly. *Skinpullers.* Gloria was right, it was a ridiculous name.

It was most often the memories that brought floods of tears to her eyes. But in the end she supposed that it was all right, this weeping. After all, Jesus himself had wept.

Five feet to the right, her white-lace-canopy bed waited with sheets already pulled back. Beside it, a clay bowl filled with red potpourri sent wafts of cinnamon across the room. The ceiling fan clicked overhead, barely moving the air in its lazy circles. Helen reached the end of her groove and turned back, eyeing that bed. Now it was on her left.

But she was not headed there just yet, despite the midnight hour. Not until she broke through here, in her groove. She could feel it in her spirit—or more accurately, her spirit *wanted* to feel something. It wanted to be spoken to. Soothed by the balm from heaven. Which usually meant that heaven wanted to soothe her. Speak to her. It was how God drew mortals, she'd decided once. He spoke desire into willing hearts. Which actually came first, the desire or the willing, was sort of like the chicken or the egg scenario. In the end a rather ridiculous exercise best left to theologians.

In either case, Helen knew to trust her senses, and her senses suggested she intercede now—intercede until she found what peace her spirit sought. If for no other reason than she knew of no other way. The problem began when her eyes had been opened to that scene in the heavens before Gloria's death. She had seen her daughter lying on the hospital bed, and that had sent her over a cliff of sorts.

Oh, she had recovered quickly enough, but it was the rest of the vision that had plagued her night and day over the last few weeks.

Helen closed her eyes and paced by feel, ignoring the dull pain in her knees, subconsciously stepping off the seven paces from end to end. Her mind drifted back to the meeting with Pastor Madison earlier that afternoon. He had said nothing more about their conversation at the hospital. But when she walked into his office today and plopped down in the guest chair facing him, he'd stared her straight through. She knew then that he had not so easily shaken her claim at having seen more.

"How you doing, Bill?" she'd asked.

He did not bother answering. "So, what's happening, Helen?"

"I don't know, Pastor. That's what I came to find out. You tell me."

He smiled and nodded at her immediate response. "Come on, Helen. You are as much a pastor to me as I am to anybody here. You made some pretty strong statements at the hospital."

"Yes. Well, it hasn't gotten any better. And you are wrong if you think that I do not need you to pastor me. I am nearly lost on this one, Bill."

"And I am *completely* lost, Helen. We can't have the blind leading the blind, now, can we?"

"No. But you have been placed in your office with a gifting that comes from God. Use it. Pastor me. And don't pretend that you are a mere clergyman without supernatural guidance—we have enough of those to fill the world's graveyards as it is."

The large Greek smiled and folded his hands on his oak desk. He presented a perfectly stately image, sitting there all dressed in black with a red tie, surrounded by bookshelves stuffed with expensive-looking books.

"Okay, Helen. But you can't expect me to see the way you see. Tell me what you saw."

"I already told you what I saw."

"You told me that you saw Gloria lying in the hospital. That's all you told me. Except that you saw more. So what did you see?"

She sighed. "I was praying with Gloria and Spencer, and we were taken to a place. In our minds or our spirits—I don't know how these things actually work. But I was given a bird's-eye view of Gloria's hospital room two days before she died. I saw everything, right down to the green pen in the attending physician's coat."

She said it with a firm jaw, steeling herself against emotion. She'd had enough sorrow to finish the year out, she thought.

Pastor Madison shook his head slowly. "It just seems incredible. I mean . . . I've never heard of such vivid precognition."

"This was not *pre* anything. This was as real as if I were there."

"Yes, but it happened *before*. That would make it *pre*. A vision of what is to happen."

"God is not bound by time, young man. You should know that. I was there. Maybe in spirit only, but I was there. It is not my job to understand how I was there; I leave that to the more learned in the church. But understanding does not necessarily change an experience. It merely explains it."

"I don't mean to argue with you, Helen. I'm not the enemy here."

Helen closed her eyes for a moment. The pastor was right, of course. He might very well be her only ally in all of this. She would be wise to choose her words with more care.

"Yes. I'm sorry. It's just . . . maddening, you know." Memories of Gloria clogged her mind, and she cleared her throat. "I'm afraid I'm not entirely myself these days."

"But you are yourself, Helen." His deep voice came soothingly. A pastor's voice. "You are a woman who has lost her daughter. If you were not frustrated and angry, I might worry."

She looked up at him and smiled. Now he was indeed pastoring her, and it felt like it should—comforting. She should have come here a week ago.

"You said you saw something else, Helen. What was the rest?"

"I can't tell you, Bill. Not because I don't want to, but because I have only seen glimpses that make no sense. And I've felt things. It is the feelings mostly that bother me, and those are hard to explain. Like God is whispering to my heart but I can't see or hear his words. Not yet."

"I see. Then tell me how it feels."

She looked past his shoulder to a long string of green books with a German-looking name stamped in gold foil across each spine: knowledge.

"Questions? Step right up! We have the answers. Yes, ma'am. You in the yellow dress."

"Yes. Why does God kill the innocent?"

"Well, now. That depends on what you mean by kill. Or by innocent—"

"I mean kill! Dead. Head against the rocks. And innocent. Plain innocent!"

"Helen?"

She looked back at Bill. "Tell you how it feels? It feels like those whispers to the heart. Like you've just walked into a dark dungeon. You've just seen one skull, and the hair on your neck stands on end, and you know there must be more. But you see, that's where it all gets fuzzy. Because I don't know if it's God's dungeon or Satan's dungeon. I mean, you would think it was Satan's. Who ever would think of God having a dungeon. But there are others peering into this dark space, as well. Angels. God himself. And there is the sound of running feet—running away. But I know that the skull there on the black earth is Gloria's. I do know that. And I know it's all part of a plan. It's all part of the running feet. That's the thing. You see, my daughter was sacrificed."

Helen paused and drew her breath carefully, noting that it had grown short. "There are some more things, but they would not make any sense right now." She looked up at him with heavy eyes.

"And this does?"

She shrugged. "You asked for it."

Pastor Madison looked at her with wide eyes. "And I don't think you can be so sure that your daughter was sacrificed. God does not work like that."

"You don't think so? Well, it's one thing to read about how God butchered a thousand nasty Amalekites long ago, but when the object of his ax is your own daughter's neck, the blindfolds go on, do they?"

Bill sat back without removing his eyes from hers. His dark brows were pulled together, creating furrows above the bridge of his nose. He'd stopped shepherding, she thought. Not that she blamed him. She had stopped bleating.

"It's okay, Bill. I don't really understand it, either. Not yet. But I would like you to pray with me. Pray *for* me. I'm a part of this, and it's not yet finished; that much I do know. It is all just beginning. Now you're a part of it. I need you, Pastor."

"Yes," he said. "Of course I will. But I want you to at least consider the possibility that you are misreading these images." He held up his hand. "I know it's not in your nature to do so, Helen. But so far all that has happened is that your daughter has died. I'm not minimizing the trauma of her death, not at all. In fact that very trauma may be initiating all of this. Can you at least understand my line of thinking?" His eyebrows lifted hopefully.

She nodded and smiled, thinking he might very well be the one who was misunderstanding here; he appeared to have missed the point entirely. "Yes, I can. Any psychiatrist in his right mind would tell me the same." She stood then. "But you are wrong, Bill. Gloria's death is not the only thing that has happened. They are rather frantic in the heavens, I think. And there is more to come. It is *this* for which I need your prayers. That and possibly my sanity. But I assure you, young man. I have not lost it yet."

She had walked out then.

He had called two hours later and told her he was praying. It was a good thing, she thought. He was a good man, and she liked him.

Helen let the memory drift away and brought her mind back to the present. Lack of understanding seemed as valuable to God as understanding. It required man to dip into the black hole of faith. But dipping into the hole was pretty much like walking through the dungeon at times.

She tilted her head back and breathed to the ceiling. "Oh God, do not keep silent; be not quiet, oh God, be not still." She quoted the Psalms as she often did in prayer. It was a kind of praying that seemed to fit her new life. "I am worn out calling for help; my throat is parched. My eyes fail looking for my God."

Yes indeed. In its own way, God's silence was as powerful as his presence. If for no reason other than it nudged you toward that hole. Taking the plunge was another matter. That took faith. Believing God was present when he felt absent.

She closed her eyes and moaned at the ceiling. "God, where have you gone?"

I have gone nowhere.

The voice spoke quietly in her spirit, but loudly enough to make her stop halfway down her groove.

Pray, daughter. Pray until it is over.

Now Helen began to tremble slightly. She sidestepped to the bed and sat heavily. "Over?" she vocalized

Pray for him and trust me.

"But it is so difficult when I cannot see."

Then remember the times when you have seen. And pray for him.

"Yes, I will."

The voice fell silent.

A wave of warmth swept through Helen's bones. She stretched her arms for the ceiling and tilted her head back. How could she have ever doubted this? This being who breathed through her now? "Oh, God, forgive me!"

Her chest swelled, and tears spilled from her eyes, unchecked. She opened her mouth and groaned—begging forgiveness, uttering words of love, trying to contain the emotions burning in her throat.

Helen sank to the mattress twenty minutes later, thoroughly content, unable to rid her face of its broad smile. How could she have possibly questioned? She would have to tell the pastor in the morning. It was all painfully obvious now.

An hour later, all of that changed.

Because an hour later, half an hour after she'd fallen into the sweetest sleep she could imagine, God spoke to her again. Showed her something new. But this time it did not feel like a soothing breath sweeping though her bones. This time it felt like a bucket of molten lead poured down her neck.

A scream woke her, filling her mind like a blaring klaxon that jerked her from the dream. It was not until she'd bolted up in bed and sat rigid that she realized the scream was coming from her own mouth.

"God, noooooo! Noooo! Noo—"

She caught her breath mid-wail. God no *what?* Why was she drenched in sweat? Why was her heart racing like a runaway locomotive?

The vision came back to her like a flood.

Then she knew why she had awakened screaming. She moaned, suddenly terrified again.

Darkness crowded her, and she glanced around the room for references, for some sense to dash this madness. Her wardrobe materialized against the far wall. The French doors glowed with moonlight. Reality settled in. But with it, the stark vision she had just witnessed.

Helen dropped to her back and breathed again, pulling in long, desperate breaths. "God, why, God? You can't!"

But she knew he could. Knew he would.

It took her three full hours to find a fitful sleep again and then only after changing her pillowcase twice. She thought it might be the wetness from her tears that kept her from sleep. But in the end she knew it was just the terror.

God was dealing in terror.

CHAPTER ELEVEN

KENT DRAGGED himself to the bank Wednesday morning, gritting his teeth in a muddle of humiliation and anger. He'd managed his way back to his office yesterday after the Bentley fiasco—fortunately without encountering a soul. For two hours he'd tried to work—and failed miserably. At eleven he'd left, brushing past Betty, mumbling something about an appointment. He had not returned.

Today he entered through the front door, but only because of his attorney's insistence that he maintain normalcy—act like nothing under the sun was bothering him when actually he was falling apart inside. He hurried through the lobby with his head down, fiddling with his third button as if something about it required his full attention. One of the tellers called out his name, but he pretended not to hear it. The button was far too consuming.

He rested his hand on the door to the Information Systems suite and closed his eyes. *Okay, Kent. Just do what needs to be done.* He pushed his way in.

Betty stared at him uncomfortably. Oversized fake black lashes shielded her eyes from the fluorescents. He had an urge to pluck one of them off. Then when she batted her eyes, there would be only one lash fanning the reception room; the room was too small for two anyway.

He nodded. "Morning."

"Morning," she returned, and her voice cracked.

"Borst in?"

"He's in Phoenix today. He'll be back tomorrow."

Thank God for small favors.

Kent walked into his office and closed himself in. Ten minutes later he came to the grinding conclusion that he could not work. Just couldn't. He could pretend to work and play Dennis Warren's game if it would reward him with a fat settlement. But with the door closed, pretending felt absurd.

He punched up a game of solitaire and found it dreadfully boring after the second hand. He tried to call Dennis but learned from the little bimbo at the law offices' front desk that he was in court.

When the knock on the door sounded at ten, it came as a relief. A kind of put-me-out-of-my-misery relief. Kent punched the dormant solitaire game off his screen. "Come in," he called and adjusted his tie knot out of habit.

The new transfer walked in and shut the door. Cliff Monroe. All crisp and clean and charged to climb the ladder. He smiled wide and stuck out his hand—the same hand that Kent had ignored two days earlier.

"Hi, Kent. It's a pleasure to meet you. I've heard a lot about you." His pineapple-eating smile covered the full spectrum—a genuine ear-to-ear grin. "Sorry about the other day."

Kent took the hand and blushed at the memory of *the other day.* "Not your fault. I should apologize. Not the best first impression, I guess."

Cliff must have taken Kent's tone as an invitation to sit, because he grabbed a chair and plopped down. His eyes flashed a brilliant green. "No, it wasn't a problem, really. From what I've picked up between the lines, if you know what I mean, you had every reason to be upset."

Kent straightened. "You know what's going on?" Cliff was still wearing that grin. His teeth seemed inordinately white, like his shirt. "Let's put it this way, I know that Kent Anthony was primarily responsible for the creation of AFPS—I knew that while I was still in Dallas. That's where I transferred in from. I guess the boys upstairs decided that you could use another decent programmer. It's not permanent yet, but believe me, I hope it becomes permanent because I love this place. Even if I don't have my own office yet." Somewhere in that long preamble Cliff had lost his grin. He pressed on before Kent could refocus him. "Yes sir, I would absolutely love to move to the mountains here in Denver. I figure I can crack code during the week, make some decent dough, and the slopes will be mine on the weekends. Do you snowboard?"

The oversized kid was a piece of work. Kent just stared at the programmer for a moment. He'd heard of this type: all brain when it came to the keyboard, and all brawn when it came to the weekends. He smiled for the first time that day.

Cliff joined him with a face-splitting grin of his own, and Kent had an inkling that the kid knew exactly what he was doing.

"I've skied a day or two in my time," he said.

"Great, we can go sometime." The new transfer's face dropped long. "Sorry about what happened to your wife. I mean, I heard about that. It must be hard."

"Uh-huh. So what do you know besides the fact that I was responsible for AFPS?"

"I know that things got a bit topsy-turvy at the convention. Your name was somehow bypassed in all the fuss. Sounds like Borst grabbed all the glory." Cliff grinned again.

Kent blinked and decided not to join him. "Yeah, well you may think that's a cheesy let's-all-have-a-grin-about-it affair, but the fact is, Borst not only got the glory, he's getting all the money as well."

The kid nodded. "Yeah, I know."

That set Kent back. The kid knew that as well? "And you don't have a problem with that?"

"Sure I do. I also have a problem with the fact that the slopes are two hours away. I came to Denver thinking the resorts are out everybody's backdoor, you know. But unless we can find a way to move mountains, I think we're both kinda stuck."

Yes, indeed, Cliff was no dummy. Probably one of those kids who started punching up computer code while they were still in diapers. "We'll see."

"Well, if you need my help, just ask." Cliff shrugged. "I know I will."

"You will what?"

"Need help. From you. My responsibility is to dig into the code and look for weaknesses. I've found the first three already."

"Look for weaknesses, huh? And what makes you think there are any weaknesses? What three?"

"Todd, Mary, and Borst." That grin wrinkled the kid's face again.

Kent could hardly help himself this time. He chuckled. Cliff was looking more and more like an ally. Another small gift from God, possibly. He'd tell Dennis about this one.

He nodded. "You're all right, Cliff. But I wouldn't be saying that too loudly around here, if I were you. You know what they say about power. It corrupts. And by the sound of things, Borst has found himself a load of power lately."

Cliff winked. "Not to worry, Kent. I'm on it already. You got my vote."

"Thanks."

"Now seriously, I do have a few questions. Do you mind running me through a few routines?"

The kid was a walking paradox. At first glance, clean cut and ready to brown-nose the closest executive, but something entirely different under the starch. A snowboarder. Spencer would get a kick out of this.

"Sure. What do you want to know?"

They spent the rest of the morning and the first afternoon hour plowing through code. Kent's instincts proved correct: Cliff was a regular programming prodigy. Not as fluent or precise as Kent, but as close to him as anybody he'd met. And likable to boot. He'd set up shop down the hall in an office that had served as the suite's overflow room before his arrival. He retreated there shortly after one.

Kent stared at the door after Cliff's departure. What now? He picked up the phone and began to dial Dennis Warren's number. But then he remembered that the attorney was in court. He dropped the phone in its cradle. Maybe he should talk to Will Thompson upstairs. Recruit the loan officer's support on the matter of the missing bonus. That would mean walking past Betty again, of course, and he could hardly stand the thought. Unless she was taking a late lunch.

Kent shut his computer down, grabbed his briefcase, and headed out.

Unfortunately, Betty was back from lunch, unwittingly transferring blush from her well-oiled face to her phone's mouthpiece while gabbing with only heaven knew who. Some other lady who had absolutely no clue about banking. Her beautician perhaps.

Kent didn't bother reporting his plans. He found Will upstairs, banging on his monitor again. "You need some help there, young man?"

Will jerked up. "Kent!" He sat back and nodded in a bouncing motion.

"You still having problems with that monitor?"

"Every time you come by, it seems. The thing keeps winking off on me. I need to inadvertently push it off the desk and requisition a new one. Maybe a twenty-one incher."

"Yeah, that'll definitely push the loans right along. The bigger the better."

Will conducted a few more of his nods and smiled. "So I heard that you had a run-in with Bentley yesterday," he said.

Kent sat calmly in the guest chair facing Will, ignoring the heat suddenly washing over his shoulders. "And how did you know that?"

"This is a small city we work in, Kent. Complete with built-in, free-flowing lines of communication. Things get around."

Good night! Who else knew? If big-mouth here knew, the whole world would soon hear. Probably already had. Kent glanced around the room and caught a pair of eyes resting on him from the far side. He shifted his eyes back to Will.

"So what did you hear?"

"I heard that you walked in there and demanded to be named employee of the month for your part in the AFPS development. They said you were screaming about it."

The heat spread right down Kent's spine. *"Employee of the month?* That lousy imbecile! I could . . ." He bit off the rest and closed his eyes. They weren't messing around, then. He had become their fool. The poor fellow in administration who wanted a bigger pat on the back.

"You didn't actually scream at—"

"You're darned right I screamed at that jerk!" Kent said. "But not about some lousy employee-of-the-month parking space." He breathed heavily and tried to calm his pulse. "People are actually buying that?"

"I don't buy it." Will sat back and glanced around. "Keep your voice down, man."

"What's everybody else saying?"

"I don't know. They're saying that anyone who screams at Bentley about employee-of-the-month status has got a screw loose, to be sure." A slight grin crossed the loan officer's face. "They're saying that if anybody should get employee of the month it should be the whole department because AFPS came from the department."

Something popped in Kent's mind, as if someone had tossed a depth charge in there and run for cover. *Kaboom!* He stood to his feet. At least he *wanted* to stand to his feet. His efforts resulted in more of a lurch. The room swam dizzily.

He had to get to Dennis! This was not good!

"I've got to go," he mumbled. "I'm late."

Will leaned forward. "Kent, sit down for heaven's sake! It's not a big deal. Everybody knows you were the real brains behind AFPS, man. Lighten up."

Kent bent for his case and strode deliberately from the desk. He only wanted one thing now. Out. Just out, out, out.

If there had been a fire escape in the hall, he might have taken it in favor of chancing a face-to-face encounter with another employee. But there was no fire escape. And there *was* another person in the elevator. She might have been Miss America, for all he knew, because he refused to make eye contact. He pressed into the corner, praying for the moments to pass quickly.

The backdoor released him to the alley, and tears blurred his vision before the latch slammed home. He bellowed angrily, instinctively. The roar echoed, and he spun his head, wondering if anyone had heard or seen this grown man carrying on. The alley lay dark and empty both ways. A large diesel engine growled nearby—an earthmover, perhaps, breaking ground on someone's dream.

Kent felt very small. Very, very, very small. Small enough to die.

WHILE KENT was dying at work, Helen was doing her best to forget the images that had visited her the previous night. But she was not doing so good.

She stirred the pitcher of ice tea slowly, listening to Spencer hum "The Martyr's Song" in the other room. All of their lives seemed to hinge on that song, she thought, remembering how Spencer's grandfather had loved to sing it in his mellow, baritone voice. From grandfather to grandson. Ice clinked in the tea, and she began to sing softly with him. "Sing oh Son of Zion . . ."

If the boy only knew.

Well, today he would know a little more. Enough for things to brighten.

She hobbled past Spencer, who sat, as usual, cross-legged on the floor, then she eased into her worn green rocker. A small glass bottle sat in the hutch, ancient and red, glaring at her with its history. It held its secrets, that glass vile, secrets that brought a chill to her spine still. She swallowed and shifted her eyes. Now the picture of the cross with Jesus spread out, dying on its beams, stared directly at her, and she kept up with the boy in a wobbly soprano. ". . . I've been waiting for the day, when at last I get to say, my child, you are finally home."

She would have to hold it together now—in front of the boy at least. She would have to trust as she had never trusted. As long as she could keep her eyes off the scales of justice that had found their way into her mind, she would do fine. As long as she could trust that God's scales were working, even though her own tipped, lopsided, in her mind, she would make it.

Funny how so many saw that cross as a bridge over the gulf between God and man—between heaven and earth—and yet how few took the time to cross it. No pun there, just a small nugget of truth. How many were busy looking for another way across? How many Christians avoided the death of God? Take up your cross daily, he'd said. Now, there was a paradox.

"Spencer."

"Yes, Grandma?" He looked up from the Legos that had held his attention for the last half-hour. He'd built a spaceship, she saw. Fitting.

She looked around the room, thinking of how best to tell him. "Did your father talk to you last night?"

Spencer nodded. "Sure."

"About his job?"

Spencer looked up at her curiously. "How did you know that?"

"I didn't know. That's why I asked. But I did know he was having . . . complications at work."

"Yeah, that's what he said. Did he tell you about it?"

"No. But I wanted to help you understand some things today about your father."

Spencer let the Lego pieces lie on the floor and sat up, interested. "He's having a hard time."

"Yes he is, isn't he?" She let silence settle for a few seconds. "Spencer, how long do you think we've been praying for your father to see the light?"

"A long time."

"Five years. Five years of beating on the brass heavens. Then they cracked. You remember that? Almost three weeks ago?"

The boy nodded, wide eyed now. "With Mom." Spencer scrambled to his feet and climbed into "his" chair opposite Grandma. The air suddenly felt charged.

"It seems that our prayers have caused quite a stir in the heavens. You should know, Spencer, that everything happening with your father is by design."

The boy tilted his head slightly, thinking that through. "Mom's death?"

The boy was not missing a beat here. "It has its purpose."

"What purpose could God have in letting Mom die?"

"Let me ask you, which is greater in regard to your mother's death? *Her* pleasure or your father's sorrow?" She suddenly wanted to throw her own grief on the scales and withdraw the question. But that was not her part here—she at least knew that.

He looked at her for a moment, thinking. The corner of his mouth twitched and then lifted to a small sheepish grin. "Mom's pleasure?" he said.

"By a long shot, Honey. You remember that. And no matter what else happens to your father, you remember that a hundred thousand eyes are peering down on him from the heavens, watching what he will do. Anything can happen at any time, and everything happens for a purpose. Can you understand that?"

Spencer nodded, his eyes round with eagerness.

"You ever hear of a man named C. S. Lewis? He once wrote, 'There is no neutral ground in the universe: every square inch, every split second, is claimed by God and counter claimed by Satan.' It's like that with your father, Spencer. Do you believe that?"

Spencer closed his mouth and swallowed. "Yes. Sometimes it's hard to know . . ."

"But you do believe it, don't you?"

"Yes. I believe it."

"And why do you believe it, Spencer?"

He looked at her, and his eyes shone like jewels. "Because I've seen heaven," he said. "And I know that things are not what people think they are."

Her feelings for the boy boiled to the surface, and she felt a lump rise in her throat. Such a tender face under those blue eyes. He had Gloria's face. *Oh, my God, my God. What could you possibly be thinking?* Her chest felt like it might explode with grief, looking at the boy.

She felt a tear slip from her eye. "Come here, Honey," she said.

The boy came and sat on the arm of her chair. She took his hand and kissed it gently then pulled him onto her lap. "I love you, my child. I love you so dearly."

He blushed and turned to kiss her forehead. "I love you too, Grandma."

She looked into his eyes. "You are blessed, Spencer. We have just begun, I think. And you have such a precious part to play. Savor it for me, will you?"

"I will, Grandma."

"Promise?"

"Promise."

For a long time, Helen held her grandson, rocking in the chair in silence. Remarkably, he let her—seemed to relish the embrace. Tears were soon flowing freely down her face and wetting her blouse. She did not want the boy to see her cry, but she could not stop herself. Her life was being shredded, for God's sake.

Quite literally.

CHAPTER TWELVE

KENT SLUMPED into a dead sleep sometime past midnight Wednesday, with visions of vultures circling lazily through his dreams. He woke late and scrambled to dress for work. The thought of returning to the den of thieves made him sick just now, but he had not seen his way past Dennis Warren's suggestion that he at least maintain his status of employment with the bank. And he had not succeeded in making contact with the attorney the previous afternoon, despite a dozen attempts. His lawyer's bimbo was developing a dislike for him, he thought.

And now it was morning. Which meant it was time to go back to the bank. Back to hell. Maybe today he would wash Borst's feet. Give him a good rubdown, perhaps. Congratulate him for making employee of the month. *Jolly good, sir.* Good grief!

"Dad."

Kent looked up from the edge of the bed, where he'd just pulled on his last sock. Spencer stood in the bedroom doorway, fully dressed. His hair lay in a tangled web, but then the boy was going nowhere today.

"Hey, Spencer."

His son walked in and sat next to him. "You're up late," the boy observed.

"Yeah. I slept in."

Spencer suddenly put an arm over his shoulder and squeezed him gently. "I love you, Dad."

The show of affection brought a heaviness to Kent's chest. "I love you too, son."

They sat together, still and quiet for a moment.

"You know that Mom is okay, don't you?" Spencer looked up. "She's in heaven, Dad. With God. She's laughing up there."

Kent blinked at that. "Sure, son. But we're down here. There's no heaven down here."

"Sometimes there is," Spencer said.

Kent ruffled the boy's hair and smiled. "Heaven on earth. You're right. Sometimes there is." He stood and fed his tie around his collar. "Like when your mother and I got married. Now *there* was some heaven. Or like when I first bought the Lexus. You remember when I came home with the Lexus, Spencer?"

"I'm not talking about that kind of heaven."

Kent walked to the mirror on the wall, not wanting this conversation now. Now he wanted to tear Borst's throat out. He saw his eyebrows furrow in the mirror. Beyond, Spencer's reflection stared back at him. This was his boy on the bed, eyes round, legs hanging limp almost to the ground.

"C'mon, Spencer. You know I don't see things the way you do. I know you want what's best for Mom, but she's just gone. Now it's you and me, buddy. And we will find our own way."

"Yeah, I know."

That's right, son. Let it go.

"But maybe we should follow Mom's way."

Kent closed his eyes and clenched his jaw. Mom's way? And what was Mom's way? Mom's way was death. *Yeah, well, why don't we all just die and go to heaven?*

He pulled his tie tight and turned back to Spencer. "We don't live in a fantasy world; we live in a real world where people actually die, and when they die it's the end. Six feet under. Game's over. And there's no use pretending otherwise."

"What about God?"

The doorbell chimed in the foyer. That would be Linda, the sitter Helen had arranged for, coming to watch Spencer for the day. Kent turned for the door.

"Why don't you just believe in God?"

Kent stopped and turned back toward Spencer. "I do believe in God. I just have a broader concept, that's all."

"But God loves you, Dad. I think he's trying to get your attention."

Kent swung around, his gut suddenly churning. He wanted to say, *Don't be so simplistic, Spencer. Don't be so stupid!* Wanted to shout that. If what was happening in his life had anything at all to do with some white-bearded scribe in the sky, then God was getting senile in his old age. It was time for someone with a little more compassion to take over.

Kent turned back to the door without responding.

"He won't let you go, Dad. He loves you too much," Spencer said softly.

Kent whirled, suddenly furious. His words came before he could stop them. "I don't care about your God, Spencer! Just shut up!"

He spun around and steamed for the front door, knowing he had crossed a line. He pulled open the door and glared at the brunette baby-sitter who stood on the front steps.

She shoved out her hand. "Mr. Anthony?"

"Yes." Kent heard Spencer pad up behind him, and he wanted to turn to the boy and beg his forgiveness. Linda was staring at him with bright gray eyes, and he diverted his gaze past her to the street. *Spencer, my dear son, I love you so much. I could never hurt a hair on your head. Never. Never, never!*

He should turn now and hold the boy. Spencer was all he had left. Kent swallowed and stepped past her. "Take care of him," he instructed without shaking her hand. "He knows the rules."

Every bone in Kent's body ached to spin and run back to Spencer. Yet he trudged forward to the Lexus waiting in the driveway. He saw his son from the corner of his eye when he slammed the door shut. The boy stood in the doorway with limp arms.

Kent roared down the street, thinking he had just stooped as low as he had ever stooped. Might as well have licked some concrete while he was down there. Why the subject of God sent him into such a tailspin he could hardly fathom. Death usually seemed to bring people to their knees, begging the man upstairs for some understanding. But Gloria's death seemed to have planted a root of bitterness in his heart. Maybe because she had died so violently despite her faith. And his mother-in-law Helen's prayers had ended where all prayers end: in her own gray matter.

He arrived at the red-brick bank filled with foreboding from its first sighting, ten blocks earlier. He would call Dennis again today—find out how quickly they could get a suit filed. Maybe then he could leave.

Kent made his way to the alley behind the bank. There was no way he would step through those fancy swinging doors up front and risk running into fat-boy Bentley. The rear entrance would do just fine for the balance of his tenure, thank you. He stepped down the dingy alley.

White fingers of steam rose from a sewer grate halfway down the narrow passage.

Garbage lay strewn beside the dumpster, as if the whole cage had been tipped and then righted again. Some homeless vagrant too eager for his own good. Kent pulled a ring of keys from his pocket and found the silver one he'd been issued for the door a year earlier after complaining he needed longer access. Since then he'd come and gone as he pleased, often working late into the night. The memory sat in his mind now, mocking.

How many hours had he given to the bank? Thousands at least. Tens of thousands, all for Borst and Fat-Boy. If Spencer's God was somehow actually involved in the world, it was as a tormentor. Let's see which of them we can get to scream the loudest today. Kent pushed the key into the slot.

A whisper rasped on the wind behind him. "You ain't seen nothin' yet, you sicko." Kent whirled.

Nothing!

His heart pumped hard. The dumpster sat still; the alley gaped on either side, empty to the streets, white strands of steam lifted lazily from the grate. But he had heard it, clear as day. *You ain't seen nothin' yet, you sicko!*

The stress was getting to him. Kent turned to the gray-steel fire door and reinserted the key with an unsteady hand.

To his left, a movement caught his eyes, and he jerked his head that way. A man wearing a torn red Hawaiian shirt and filthy slacks that had possibly once been blue leaned against the dumpster, staring at him. The sight frightened Kent badly, and his hand froze on the key. Not three seconds ago, he would have sworn the alley was empty.

"Life sucks," the man said, and then lifted a brown bag to his lips and took a slug from a hidden bottle. He did not remove his eyes from Kent's. Scattered patches of scraggly hair hung off his neck. His lumpy nose shined red and big.

"Life really *ssssucksss!*" He grinned now, and his teeth were jagged yellow. He cackled and lifted the brown bag.

Kent watched the vagrant take another slug. He yanked on the door and stepped in quickly. Something was haunting him; his mind was bending. G*et a grip, Kent. You're losing your grip.*

The door swooshed shut, and suddenly the hall was pitch dark. He groped the wall, found the switch, and flipped it up. The long fluorescent tubes stuttered to white, illuminating the empty hall. Long and empty like the prospects facing his life now. Bleak, white, long, empty.

Life sucks.

Kent forced himself to the end and out to the main corridor. Somehow he had embarked on a roller coaster, swooping up and down and around sharp curves at breakneck speed, intent on throwing him to his death. Some thrill ride from hell, and he wasn't being allowed to disembark. Each hour was rolling into the next, each day full of new twists and turns. They say that when it rains, it pours. Yes, well, it was pouring all right. Fire and brimstone.

Betty was gone when he stepped into the Information Systems suites, probably to the john to apply yet another layer of mascara to her foot-long fake lashes. She'd always fancied herself to be half her age with twice the life. Kent slipped into his office and closed the door quietly. *Here we go then.* He sat and tried to still the buzzing in his head.

For a full minute Kent stared at the exotic fish making their predictable sweeps across the three monitors. It was not until then that it occurred to him that he still gripped his briefcase. He dropped it on the floor and picked up the phone.

It took five minutes for the cranky secretary at Dennis Warren's office to finally put him through, and then only after Kent's threat to call back repeatedly every three minutes if she didn't tell Dennis this very minute that he was on the phone.

Dennis came on. "Kent. How goes it, my friend? Go easy on my girls."

"She was giving me lip. Shouldn't give lip to customers, Dennis. Bad business."

"You're not a customer. Not yet, Kent." A chuckle. "When you get a bill, you'll be a customer. So what's up?"

Kent chose to ignore the jab. "Nothing. Unless you call sitting in an office doing nothing for eight hours while everybody around you has their ear to the wall, listening for your *nothing,* something. It's falling apart here, Dennis. The whole bank knows."

"Lighten up, buddy."

"We have to move forward, Dennis! I'm not sure how long I can do this."

A long silence filled his ear, which was rather uncharacteristic of his friend, who never seemed at a loss for words. Now Dennis was suddenly silent. Breathing, actually. Breathing heavily. When he spoke his voice sounded scratchy.

"We can move forward on this as soon as you are positive, Kent."

"Positive? About what? I *am* positive! They think I've lost my mind around here! Do you understand that? They think I'm off the deep end, for goodness' sake! We're going to bury these guys, if it's the last thing we do!" He let the statement settle, wondering if his voice had carried out to the hall. "Right?"

A chuckle crackled on the phone. "Oh, we'll be doing some burying, all right. But what about you, Kent?" Now Dennis was speaking around short breaths, pausing after each phrase to pull at the air. "Are you positive about where you stand?" A breath. "You can't go soft halfway through." A breath. Another breath. Kent scrunched his eyebrows.

The attorney continued. "It's not like God's going to reach down and hand you answers, you know. You decide to go one way, you go all the way that way. Right to the end, and screw them all if they need their crutch!" A series of breaths. "Right, Kent? Isn't that right?"

Kent furrowed his brow. "What are you talking about? Who's talking about going soft halfway? I'm saying we bury them, man! Screw 'em all to the wall." He let the comment about the crutch go. Something was confused there.

"That's right, Kent," the attorney's voice rasped. "You do whatever it takes. This is life and death. You win, it's life; you lose, it's death."

"I hear you, man. And what I'm saying here is that, by the looks of things, I'm already a dead man. We have to move now."

"You do things their way and you end up getting buried. Like some fool martyr." A ragged pause. "Look at Gloria."

Gloria? Kent felt his pulse rise in agreement with his attorney. He understood what Dennis was doing now. And it was brilliant. The man was reaching out to him; connecting with him emotionally; drawing the battle lines.

"Yes," he said. And Dennis was saying that the bank and God were on the same side. They both wanted to do some burying. Only God was really fate, and fate had already done its burying with Gloria. Now the bank was having its go. With him.

The hair lifted on the nape of his neck. "Yes. Well, they're not going to bury me, Dennis. Not unless they kill me first."

The phone sat unspeaking in his palm for a few seconds before Dennis came on again. "No. Killing is against the rules. But there are other ways."

"Well, I'm not actually suggesting killing anybody, Dennis. It's just a figure of speech. But I hear you. I hear you loud and clear. And I'm ready. When can we get this ball rolling?"

This time the phone went dead for a long time.

"Dennis? Hello?"

"No," Dennis returned. His voice was distant, like an echo on the phone now. "I don't think you are ready. I don't think you are ready at all, my fine friend. Perhaps this afternoon you will be ready."

The phone clicked. Kent held it to his ear, stunned. This afternoon? What in the world did this afternoon have to do with anything? A sudden panic rose to his throat. What was going on? What in—

The phone began burping loudly in his ear. An electronic voice came on and told him in a roundabout way that holding a dead phone to the ear was a rather unbrilliant thing to do.

He dropped the receiver in its cradle.

Yes indeed, the roller coaster from hell. *After him, lads! After him!*

Now what? What was he supposed to do in this cursed place? Sit and stare at fish while Borst sat across the hall, planning how to spend his forthcoming fortune?

Cliff poked his head in once and offered a "Good morning" around that pineapple-eating grin of his. Kent forced a small smile and mumbled the same.

"You keep your nose clean, now. You hear?" Cliff said.

"Always. Clean's my middle name," he returned. He tried to find some levity in his own irony, but he could not.

"Okay. Just hang in there. Things will look up if you hang in there."

When Kent looked up, Cliff had pulled out. The door clicked shut. Now what did *he* know? Like some father offering sound wisdom. *Hang in there, son. Here, come sit on my lap.*

He tried to imagine Cliff catching air on a snowboard. The image came hard. Now Spencer, there was someone who could catch air. Only it was on a skateboard.

Kent spent an hour running through e-mail and idiotic bank memoranda. Most of it went to the trash with a click. He expected that at any moment one of the others would pop in and say something, but no one did, and the fact began to wear on him. He heard their muffled voices on several occasions, but they seemed to be ignoring him wholesale. Maybe they didn't know he'd come in. Or more likely they were embarrassed for him. *Did you hear about Kent and Bentley? Yeah, he's really flipped, huh? Poor guy. Lost his wife—that's what did it. For sure.*

Several times he contemplated calling Dennis back—asking him what he'd meant about this afternoon. But the memory of the man's voice echoing in the receiver made him postpone the call.

He called up AFPS and entered the new password: MBAOK. The familiar icon ran across the screen, and he let it cycle through a few times before entering the system. A program like this would be worth millions to any large bank. He should just download the source code and take it on the road. It was his, after all.

But that was the problem. It was not his. At least, not legally.

Kent was startled by the sudden buzz of his phone. Dennis, possibly. Calling to apologize about that ludicrous exchange. He glanced at the caller ID.

It was Betty. And he was in no mood to discuss office business. He let the phone buzz annoyingly. It finally fell silent after a dozen persistent burps. What was her problem?

A fist pounded on his door, and he swung around. Betty stood in the door frame, stricken white. "You have a call," she said, and he thought she might be ill. "It's urgent. I'll put it through again."

She pulled the door closed. Kent stared after her.

The phone blared again. This time Kent whirled and snatched up the receiver. "Hello."

"Hello, Mr. Anthony?" It was a female voice. A soft, shaky female voice.

"Yes, this is Kent Anthony."

A pause. "Mr. Anthony, I'm afraid there's been an accident. Do you have a son named Spencer Anthony?"

Kent rose to his feet. His hands went cold on the receiver. "Yes."

"He was hit by a car, Mr. Anthony. He's at Denver Memorial. You should come quickly."

Adrenaline flooded Kent's bloodstream like boiling ice. Goose flesh prickled down his shoulders. "Is . . . Is he okay?"

"He's . . ." A sick pause. "I'm sorry. I can't . . ."

"Just tell me! Is my son okay?"

"He died in the ambulance, Mr. Anthony. I'm sorry . . ."

For a moment the world stood still. He didn't know if the woman said more. If she did, he did not hear it because a buzzing had erupted in his skull again.

The phone slipped from his grasp and thudded on the carpet. Spencer? His Spencer!? Dead?

He stood rooted to the floor, his right hand still up by his ear where the receiver had been, his mouth limp and gaping. The terror came in waves then, spreading down his arms and legs like fire.

Kent whirled to the door. It was shut. Wait a minute, this could have been one of those voices! He was going mad, wasn't he? And now the voices of madness had touched him where they knew he would be hurt most. Tried to yank his heart out.

He died in the ambulance, the voice had said. An image of Spencer's blond head lying cockeyed on an ambulance gurney flashed through his mind. His boy's arms jiggled as the medical van bounced over potholes.

He staggered for the door and pulled it open, barely conscious of his movements. Betty sat at her desk, still white. And then Kent knew that it had been a real voice.

Blackness washed through his mind, and he lost his sensibilities. The days leading up to this one had weakened them badly. Now they simply fell away, like windblown chaff.

He groaned, unabashed, oblivious to the doors suddenly cracking around him for a view of the commotion. A small part of his mind knew that he was lumbering through the hall, hands hanging limp, moaning like some retarded hunchback, but the realization hung like some tiny inconsequential detail on the black horizon. Everything else was just buzzing and black.

Kent stumbled through the hall door, on autopilot now. He was halfway to the main lobby when the cruelty of it all crashed into his brain and he began to gasp in ragged pulls like a stranded fish gulping on the rocks. Spencer's sweet, innocent face hung in his mind. Then Gloria's swollen body, still blotched and purple.

He lifted his hands to his temples and fell into an unsteady jog. He wanted to stop. Stop the groaning, stop the pain, stop the madness. Just stop.

But it all came like a flood now, and instead of stopping he began to sob. Like a man possessed, Kent ran straight through the main lobby, gripping the hair at his temples, wailing loudly.

For a moment, banking stopped cold.

Twelve tellers turned as one and stared, startled. Zak, the security guard, brought his hand to the butt of his shiny new .38, for the first time, possibly.

Kent burst through the swinging doors, leapt down the concrete steps, and tore around the corner. He slammed into the car, hardly knowing it was his.

Spencer! No, no, no! Please, not Spencer!

His son's face loomed tender and grinning in Kent's mind. His blond bangs hung before his blue eyes. The boy flipped his head back, and Kent felt a wave of dizziness at the ache in his own chest.

The door to his Lexus was not opening easily, and he frantically fumbled with a wad of keys, dropping them once and banging his head on the mirror as he retrieved them. But he did not feel any pain from the gash above his left eye. It bled warm blood down his cheek, and that felt strangely comforting.

Then he was in his car and somehow screaming through the streets with his horn blaring, wiping frantically at his eyes to clear his vision.

He felt barely conscious now. All he noticed were the pain and blackness that crashed through his mind. He wove in and out of traffic, banging on the wheel, trying to dislodge the pain. But when he squealed to a stop at the hospital and met a wide-eyed paramedic head on, bent on restraining him, uttering consolations, he knew it made little difference.

Spencer was dead.

Somewhere in the confusion, a well-meaning man in a white coat told him that his son, Spencer, had been struck by a car from behind. A hit-and-run. One of the neighbors found him sprawled on the sidewalk, halfway to the park, with a broken back. Spencer couldn't have known what hit him, he said. Kent screamed back at the man, told him he should try letting a car snap *his* spine at forty miles an hour and see how that felt.

He stumbled into the room where they had left Spencer's little body lying on a gurney. He was still in his shorts, bare chested and blond. They had worked with his body, but at first glance Kent saw that his son's torso rested at an odd angle to his hips. He imagined that body snapping in two, folding over, and he threw up on the gray linoleum floor. He lurched forward to the body, hazy now. Then he touched his son's white skin and rested his cheek on his still rib cage and wept.

It felt as though a white-hot iron had been pulled from the fires of hell and stamped on his mind. No one deserved this. *No one.* That was the tattoo.

The pain burned so strongly that Kent lost himself to it. They later told him that he'd ranted and raved and cursed—mostly cursed—for over an hour. But he could remember none of it. They gave him a sedative, they said, and he went to sleep. On the floor, in the corner, curled up like a fetus.

But that was not how he remembered things. He just remembered that most of him died that day. And he remembered that branding iron burning in his skull.

CHAPTER THIRTEEN

Week Six

HELEN JOVIC piloted the ancient, pale yellow Ford Pinto through a perfectly manicured suburbia, struck by the gross facade. Like a huge plastic Barbie-doll set carefully constructed on the ground to cover a reeking cesspool beneath. Made to cover these dungeons down here.

It felt strange driving through the world. Lonely. As if she were dreaming and the houses rising above green lawns were from another planet—because she knew what was really here, and it resembled something much closer to a sewer than this picture-perfect neighborhood.

That was the problem with holing yourself up in prayer for a week and having your eyes opened. You saw things with more clarity. And God was making her see things more clearly these days, just as he'd done with Elisha's servant. Drawing her into this huge drama unfolding behind the eyes of mortals. She played the intercessor—the one mortal allowed to glimpse both worlds so that she could pray. She knew that. And pray she had, nearly nonstop for ten days now.

But it was just the beginning. She knew that just as she would know the turning of the leaves signaled the coming of autumn. More was to follow. A whole season.

She was starting to accept God's judgment in the matter. Much like a housewife might accept her husband's leadership—with a plastic smile to avoid confrontation. Of course, this was God, not some man brimming with weaknesses. Still, she could not let him so easily off the hook for what he had done. Or at the very least, allowed—which, given his power, was the same thing. Her time seemed to be divided equally between two realities. The reality in which she cried pitifully, chastising God for this mad plan, begging for relief, and the reality in which she bowed and shook and wept, humbled to have heard God's voice at all.

Chastising God was foolishness, of course. Utter nonsense. Humans had no right to blame their difficulties on God, as if he knew precisely what he was doing when he breathed galaxies into existence but was slipping now in his dealings with the beings on planet Earth.

On the other hand, it was God himself, in all of his wisdom, who had created man with such a fickle mind. Believing one day, doubting the next; loving one moment, forgetting within the hour. Mankind.

"Oh God, deliver us from ourselves," she muttered and turned the corner leading toward Kent's.

She no longer struggled with the believing, as most did. But the loving . . . Sometimes she wondered about the loving. If human nature was a magnet, then self-gratification was steel, clinging stubbornly. And loving . . . loving was like wood, refusing to stick to the magnet no matter how much pressure was applied. Well, like it or not she was still human. Even after all she had been through before this mess. Yes indeed, Kent here was a *saint* compared to what she had been.

"Why are you taking us here, Father? Where does this road end? What have you not shown me?"

In the five weeks since she'd first seen the heavens open, together with Gloria and Spencer, she had seen a glimpse of the light every day. But only on three occasions had she seen specific visions of the business up there. That first one when she had learned of this whole mess. The second showing Spencer's death. And a third, a week ago, just after Spencer had joined his mother.

Each time she had been allowed to see a little more. She had seen Gloria laughing. And she had seen Spencer as well, laughing. She didn't know if they laughed all the time—it seemed the pleasure of it would wear thin. Then again, wearing thin would require time, and there was no time in heaven, was there? And actually it had not been one big laughter up there. Not every moment was filled with laughter, if indeed there even were such things as moments on the other side. Twice in the last vision she had seen both Spencer and Gloria lying still, neither laughing nor speaking but hanging limp and quivering, their eyes fixed on something she could not see. Wallowing in pleasure. Then the laughter came again, on the tail of the moment. A laughter of delight and ecstasy, not of humor. In fact, there was nothing funny about the business her daughter and grandson were up to in the heavens.

It was the business of raw pleasure. If she had not seen that, she might very well have gone mad.

Helen blinked and turned onto Kent's street. His two-story rose like a tomb, isolated against the bleak, gray sky.

In her last vision, Helen had caught a glimpse of this thing's magnitude, and it had left her stunned. She had seen it in the distance, beyond the space occupied by Gloria and Spencer, and for only a brief moment. A million, perhaps a billion creatures were gathered there. And where was *there?* There was the whole sky, although it seemed impossible. They had come together in two halves, as though on cosmic bleachers peering down on a single field. Or was it a dungeon? It was the only way Helen could translate the vision.

An endless sea of angelic creatures shone white on the right, clamoring for a view of the field below. They appeared in many forms, indescribable and unlike anything she had imagined.

On the left, pitch blackness created a void in space filled only with the red and yellow of countless flickering eyes. The potent stench of vomit had drifted from them, and she had blanched, right there, on the green chair in her living room.

Then she saw the object of their fixed attention. It was a man on the field below, running, pumping his arms full tilt, like some kind of gladiator fleeing from a lion. Only there was no lion. There was nothing. Then the heavens faded, and she saw that it was Kent and he was sprinting through a park, crying.

She had gone to him that afternoon and offered him comfort, which he'd promptly rejected. She had also asked him where he'd been at ten that morning, the time of her vision.

"I went for a run," he'd said.

Helen pulled into the drive and parked the Pinto.

Kent answered the door after the third buzz. By the rings under his eyes the man had not been sleeping. His hair lay in blond tangles, and his normally bright blue eyes peered through drooping lids, hazed over.

"Hello, Kent," Helen offered with a smile.

"Hello." He left the door open and headed for the living room. Helen let herself in and closed the door. When she walked under the catwalk he had already seated himself in the overstuffed beige rocker.

The odor of day-old dishrags hung in the air. Perhaps week-old dishrags. The same music he had played for days crooned melancholically through the darkened living room. Celine someone-or-other, he had told her. Dion. Celine Dion, and it wasn't a tape; it was a CD, like the initials of her name. CD.

She scanned the unkempt room. The miniblinds were closed, and she blinked to adjust her eyesight. A pile of dishes rose above the breakfast bar to her right. The television throbbed silently with colors to her left. Pizza boxes lay strewn on a coffee table cluttered with beer bottles. If he permitted, she would do some cleaning before she left.

Something else had changed in the main room. Her eyes rested on the mantel above the fireplace. The large framed picture called *Forgiven* was missing. It had been of Jesus, holding a denim-clad killer who held a hammer and nails in his hand that dripped with blood. A faint, white outline showed its vacancy.

She slid onto the couch. Kent was not being so easily wooed. *Father, open his eyes. Let him feel your love.*

Kent glanced at her as if he'd heard the thought. "So, what do you want, Helen?"

"I want you to be better, Kent. You doing okay?"

"Do I look like I'm doing okay, Helen?"

"No, actually you look like you just returned from hell." She smiled genuinely, feeling a sudden surge of empathy for the man. "I know there's little I can say to comfort you, Kent. But I thought you might like some company. Just someone to be here."

He eyed her with drooping eyes and sipped at a drink in his left hand. "Well, you think wrong, Helen. If I needed company, you think I'd be in here watching silent pictures on the tube?"

She nodded. "What people need to do and what they actually do are rarely even remotely similar, Kent. And yes, I do think that even if you did need company, you would be in here watching the tube and listening to that dreadful music."

He shifted his stare, ignoring her.

"But your situation is not so unique. Most people in your position would do the same thing."

"And what do *you* know about my position?" he said. "That's asinine! How many people do you know who've lost their wife and their son in the same month? Don't talk about what you do not know!"

Helen felt her lips flatten. She suddenly wanted very much to walk over there and slap his face. Give him a dose of her own history. How dare he spout off as if he were the sole bearer of pain!

She bit her tongue and swallowed.

On the other hand, he did have a point. Not in her being clueless to loss; God knew nothing could be further from the truth. But in his assertion that few suffered so much loss in such a short time. At least in this country. In another time, in another place, such loss would not be uncommon at all. But in America today, loss was hardly in vogue.

Father, give me grace. Give me patience. Give me love for him.

"You are right. I spoke too quickly," she said. "Do you mind if I do a little cleaning in the kitchen?"

He shrugged, and she took that as a *Help yourself.* So she did. "You have any other music?" she asked, rising. "Something upbeat?"

He just *humphed.*

Helen opened the blinds and dug into the dishes, praying as she worked. He rose momentarily and put on some contemporary pop music she could not identify. She let the music play and hummed with the tunes when the choruses repeated themselves.

It took her an hour to return the kitchen to the spotless condition in which Gloria had kept it. She replaced the dishrags responsible for the mildew odor with fresh ones, wondering how long they would remain clean. A day at most.

Helen returned to the living room, thinking she should say what she had come to say and leave. He was obviously not in the mood to receive any comfort. Certainly not from her.

She glanced at the ceiling and imagined the cosmic bleachers, crowded with eager onlookers, unrestrained by time. She stood behind the couch and studied the man like one of those heavenly creatures might study him. He sat dejected. No, not dejected. Dejected would be characterized by a pouting frown, perhaps. Not this vision of death sagging on the chair before her. He looked suicidal, devastated, unraveled like a hemp rope chewed by a dog.

"I cleaned the kitchen," she said. "You can at least move around in there without knocking things over now."

He looked at her, and his Adam's apple bobbed. Maybe her voice reminded him of Gloria—she hadn't considered that.

"Anyway. Is there anything else I can do for you while I'm here?"

Kent shook his head, barely.

She started then. "You know, Kent, you remind me of someone I know who lost his son. Much like you did, actually."

He ignored her.

She considered leaving without finishing. *Are you sure, Father? Perhaps it is too soon. The poor soul looks like a worm near death.*

God did not respond. She hadn't really expected him to.

"He was crazy about that boy, you know. They were inseparable, did everything together. But the boy was not so—what shall I say—becoming. Not the best looking. Of course, it meant nothing at all to his father." She dismissed the thought with a wave. "Nothing at all. But others began to ridicule him. Then not just ridicule, but flatly reject. They grew to hate him. And the more they hated him, the more his father loved him, if that was possible."

Helen smiled sweetly. Kent looked at her with mild interest now. She continued.

"The boy was murdered by some of his own peers. It about killed the father. Reminds me of you. Anyway, they caught the one who killed his son. Caught him red-handed with the weapon in his hand. He was homeless and uncaring—headed for a life behind bars. But the father did not press charges. Said one life had been taken already. His son's. Instead, he offered love for the one who'd killed his son."

She looked at Kent's eyes for a sign of recognition. They stared into her own, blank. "The unexpected affection nearly broke the young killer's heart. He went to the father and begged his forgiveness. And do you know what the father did?"

Kent did not respond.

"The father loved the killer as his own son. Adopted him." She paused. "Can you believe that?"

Kent's lip lifted in a snarl. "I'd kill the kid." He took a swig from that drink of his.

"Actually, the father had already lost one son. To crucifixion. He wasn't about to let another be crucified."

He sat there like a lump on a log, his eyes half closed and his lower lip sagging. If he understood the meaning behind her words, he did not show it.

"God the Father, God the Son. You know how that feels, don't you? And yet you have murdered him in your own heart. Murdered the son. In fact, the last time I was in here, there was a picture of you above the fireplace." She motioned to the whitewashed wall where the picture had hung. "You were the one holding the hammer and nails. Looks like you got tired of looking at yourself."

She grinned.

"Anyway. Now he wants to adopt you. He loves you. More than you could ever know. And he knows how this all feels. He's been here. Does that make sense to you?"

Kent still did not respond. He blinked and closed his mouth, but she wasn't about to start interpreting his gestures. She simply wanted to plant this seed and leave.

For a moment she thought that he might actually be feeling sorrow. But then she saw his jaw muscles knot up, and she knew better.

"Think about it, Kent. Open your heart." Helen turned from him and walked toward the door, wondering if that was it.

It was.

"Good-bye, Kent," she said, and walked out the door.

She suddenly felt exhilarated. She realized that her heart was pounding simply from the excitement of this message she had delivered.

Her Pinto sat on the driveway, dumb and yellow. She withdrew her keys and approached the car door. But she didn't want to drive.

She wanted to walk. Really walk. An absurd notion—she had been on her feet enough already, and her knees were sore.

The notion stopped her three feet from the car, jingling the keys in her hands. She could not walk, of course. Helen glanced back to the front door. It remained closed. The sky above hung blue in its arches. A beautiful day for a walk.

She wanted to walk.

Helen turned to her left and walked to the street. She would walk. Just to the end of the block. Granted, her knees were not what they once were, but they would hold her that far if she walked slowly. She hummed to herself and eased down the sidewalk.

KENT SAW the door swing shut, and its slam rang like a gong in his mind. He did not move except to swivel his head from the entry. But his eyes stayed wide open, and his fingers were trembling.

Desperation swept in like a thick wave, and on its face rose a wall of sorrow that took his breath away. His throat tightened to an impossible ache, and he grunted to release the tension in the muscles. The wave engulfed him, refusing to sweep by alone, carrying him in its folds.

Then Kent's shoulders began to shake, and the sobs came hard. The ache worked on his chest like a vise, and he was suddenly unsure if it was sorrow or desire now squeezing the breath out of him.

Spencer was right.

Oh, God! Spencer was right!

The admission erupted from his mind, and Kent felt his mouth yawning in a breathless cry. The words came out audibly, in a strained croak.

"Oh, God!" He clenched his eyes. Had to—they were burning. "Oh, God!"

The words brought a wash of comfort, like a soothing anesthetic to his heart. He said it again. "Oh, God."

Kent sat in the wave for a long time, strangely relishing each moment of its respite, aching for more and more. Losing himself there, in the deepest sorrow, and in the balm of comfort.

He recalled a scene that played on the walls of his mind like an old, eight-millimeter film. It was Gloria and Spencer, dancing in the living room, late one evening. They held hands and twirled in circles and sang about streets that were golden. His camera eye zoomed to their faces. They gazed at each other in rapture. He had discarded the moment with a chuckle then, but now it came like the sugar of life. And he knew that somewhere in that exchange lay the purpose of living.

The memory brought a new flood of tears.

When Kent finally stood and looked about the living room, it was dusk. Spent, he trudged into the kitchen and opened the refrigerator without bothering to turn on the lights. He pulled out a day-old pizza, slid onto a barstool, and nibbled on the soggy crust for a few minutes.

A mirror glared at him from the shadowed wall. It showed a man with sagging cheeks and red eyes, his hair disheveled, wearing the face of death. He stopped his chewing and stared, wondering if that could be him. But he knew immediately that it was. There was the new Kent—a broken, discarded fool.

He turned his back to the mirror and ate part of the cold pizza before tossing it and retiring before the television. Kent fell asleep two hours later to the monotones of some Spanish soccer commentator.

The alarm clock's green analog numbers read 11 A.M. when his eyes flickered open the following morning. By noon he had managed a shower and clean clothes. He had also managed a conclusion.

It was time to move on.

Only six days had passed since Spencer's death. Four weeks to the day since Gloria's passing. Their deaths had left him with no one. But that was just it—there was no one left to mourn with. Except Helen. And Helen was from another planet. That left only him, and he could not live with himself. Not just himself.

He would have to find death quickly, or go off and find some life.

Killing himself had a certain appeal—a kind of final justice to the madness. He had mulled over the idea for long hours in recent days. If he did kill himself, it would be with an overdose of some intoxicating drug; he'd already concluded that after discarding a hundred other options. Might as well go out flying high.

On the other hand, something else was brewing in his head, something set off by Helen's words. This God business. The memory lingered like a fog in his mind, present but muddled. The emotions had nearly destroyed him. A sort of high he could not remember having felt.

He remembered thinking, just before falling asleep the night before, that it might have been his love for Spencer that triggered the emotions. Yes, that would be it. Because he was desperate for his son. Would give anything—everything—to give him life. How incredible that one little life could mean so much. Six billion people crawling over the globe, and in the end, the death of one ten-year-old boy caused him to ache so badly.

Kent left the house, squinting in the bright sunlight.

It was time to move on.

Yes, that was the conclusion.

But it was really no conclusion at all, was it? Move on to *what?* Working at the bank carried as much appeal as a barefooted trek across the Sahara. He hadn't had contact with any of his coworkers for a week now. How could he possibly face Borst? Or worse, fat-boy Bentley? They no doubt carried on, soaking in acclamations of a superb job, reaping his rewards while he sat dead in the water, surrounded by two floating bodies. If he had even a single violent bone in his body he'd take that nine-millimeter pistol his uncle had given him for his thirtieth birthday and walk on down to that bank. Play postal worker for a day. Deliver some good will.

He could sue, of course—fire a few legal projectiles their way. But the thought of suing with Dennis Warren's assistance now brought a sickness to his gut. For one thing, Dennis had gone off to lala land that last day. His attorney's words still rumbled through his mind: *I don't think you are ready. I don't think you are ready at all, my fine friend. Perhaps this afternoon you will be ready.*

This afternoon? Then Spencer had died.

No, Dennis was out of the question, Kent concluded. If he did sue the bank, it would be with another attorney.

That left finding another job, a thought that sickened him even more than the notion of suing. But at least he would be able to continue paying the bills. A lawsuit might very well suck him dry.

Either way, he should probably talk to Helen again. Go back for some of the comfort she seemed to have a handle on. God. Maybe Spencer was right after all. Kent felt a knot rise to his throat, and he cursed under his breath. He wasn't sure he could stomach too many more of these emotional surges.

The day passed in a haze, divided between the park and the house, but at least Kent was thinking again. It was a start. Yes, it was time to move on.

CHAPTER FOURTEEN

THE VISION came to Kent that night in the early morning hours, like a shaft of black through the shadows of his mind.

Or maybe it wasn't a vision. Maybe he was actually there.

He stood in the alley behind the bank. Steam rose from the grate; the dumpster lay tipped on its side, reeking foul, and Kent was watching that vagrant slurping at his bagged bottle. Only now he wasn't tipping the bag back. He was sticking a long, pink tongue down the bottle's neck and using it like a straw. It was the kind of thing you might expect in a dream. So yes, it must have been a vision. A dream.

The vagrant no longer wore faded clothes but a black tuxedo with shiny shoes and a pressed shirt. Downright respectable. Except for the straggly hairs growing off his chin and neck. It appeared as though the man was attempting to cover up a dozen red warts, but the long strands of hair only emphasized them, and that certainly was not respectable. That and the tongue trick.

The vagrant-turned-respectable-citizen was rambling on about how lucky Kent was with his fancy car and big-time job. Kent interrupted the prattling with the most obvious of points.

"I'm no better off than you, old man."

"Old man?" The vagrant licked his lips wet with that long pink tongue. "You think I'm old? How old do I look to you, fella?"

"It's just an expression."

"Well, you are right. I am old. Quite old, actually. And I have learned a few things in my time." He grinned and snaked his tongue into the bottle again without removing his eyes from Kent.

Kent furrowed his brow. "How do you do that?" he asked.

The tongue pulled out quickly. "Do what?"

"Make your tongue do that?"

The vagrant chuckled and fingered one of the warts under his chin. "It's one of the things I've learned over the years, boy. Anybody can do it. You just have to stretch your tongue for a long time. See?" He did it again, and Kent shuddered.

The man pulled his tongue back into his mouth and spoke again. "You ever see those tribal people who stretch their necks a foot high? It's like that. You just stretch things."

A chill seemed to have descended into the alley. The white steam from the grate ran along the ground, and Kent was thinking he should get on in to work. Finish up some programming.

But that was just it. He didn't want to walk through that door. In fact, now that he thought about it, something very bad had happened in there. He just couldn't quite remember what.

"So what's keeping you, boy?" The man peered at the door. "Go on in. Take your millions."

"Huh? That's what you think?" Kent replied. "You think people like me make millions slaving away for some huge bank? Not even close, old man."

The grin left the vagrant's face, and his lips twitched. "You think I am stupid? You call me old man, and yet you talk as though I know nothing? You are a blathering idiot!"

Kent stepped back, surprised by the sudden show of anger. "Relax, man. I don't remember calling you a fool."

"Might as well have, you imbecile!"

"Look, I really didn't mean to offend you. I'm no better off than you, anyway. There's no need to be offended here."

"And if you think you're no better off than me, then you're really a fool. Furthermore, the fact that you're not yet even thinking of doing what I would do in your place proves you are a moronic idiot!"

Kent furrowed his brows, taken aback by the vagrant's audacity.

"Look. I don't know what you think you would do, but people like me just don't make that kind of money."

"People *like* you? Or *you?* How much have *you* made?"

"Well that's really none of your . . ."

"Just tell me, you fool," the man said. "How much money have you rightfully made in that cement box over there?"

"How much . . . rightfully?"

"Of course. How much?"

Kent paused, thinking about that word. *Rightfully.* Rightfully he had made the bonuses due from AFPS. Millions. But that hardly counted as income. And it was certainly no business of this weirdo, anyway.

A sly grin lifted the vagrant's lips. He tilted his head slightly and narrowed his eyes. "Come on, Kent. It's really not that difficult, is it?"

Kent blinked at the man. "How do you know my name?"

"Oh, I know things. I've been around, like I said. I'm not the fool you might think. I say you've made millions, boy. And I say you take your millions."

"Millions? It's not like I can just waltz into the vault and take a few million."

"No. But you have a key, now, don't you?"

"A key? Don't be stupid, man. A key to this door has nothing to do with the vault. Besides, you obviously know nothing about security. You don't just walk into a bank and steal a penny, much less a million."

"Stop calling me stupid, you spineless idiot! Stop it, stop it, stop it!"

Kent's heart slammed in his chest.

The vagrant barely moved now. He glared at Kent, and his voice growled low. "Not that key, you fool. The key in your head. The backdoor to that software. You have the only backdoor code. They don't even know it exists."

The alley grew still. Deadly still. It occurred to Kent that he had stopped breathing.

"I won't tell. I promise," the man said through his grin. He opened his mouth wide and began to cackle. The sound of his laughter bounced off the tall brick walls.

Kent jumped back, stunned.

That mouth widened, showing a black hole at the back of the vagrant's throat. His tongue snaked like a long road leading into the darkness. It grew like a vortex and swallowed the alley in echoing chuckles.

Kent bolted upright.

Silence crashed in on him. Darkness met his wide eyes. Wet sheets stuck to his stomach. His chest thumped like an Indian war drum.

He sat in bed, wide awake, paralyzed by the thought that had awakened him so rudely. The images of the vagrant quickly dwindled to oblivion, overshadowed by the singular concept he'd dropped in Kent's mind. Not a soul had known of the backdoor he'd programmed into AFPS that last week. He'd meant to tell Borst in Miami, complete documentation on it as soon as they returned. That was before.

ROOSTER.

That was the code he'd temporarily assigned to the security entry. With it, any authorized banking official could enter the system through an untraceable handle, tackle any security issue, and leave without affecting normal operations. Of course, not just any banking official would be authorized. Only one or two, perhaps. The president and vice president, who would have to guard the code in the strictest confidence. Under lock and key.

Kent swung his legs from the bed and stared into darkness. Outlines of the room's furniture began to take vague shape. The realization of ROOSTER's significance ballooned in his mind like a mushroom cloud. If the bank had not discovered the backdoor, then it would still be open to anyone with the code.

And he had the code. The vagrant's key.

ROOSTER.

What could an operator accomplish with ROOSTER? Anything. Anything at all with the right skills. Software engineering skills. The kind of skills that he himself possessed with perhaps greater mastery than anyone he knew. Certainly within the context of AFPS. He'd *written* the code, for heaven's sake!

Kent pushed himself from the bed, quaking. He glanced at the clock: 2 A.M. The bank would be deserted, of course. He had to know if they'd found ROOSTER during the program's initial implementation. Knowing Borst, they had not.

He went for the closet and stopped at the door. What was he thinking? He couldn't go down there now. The alarm company would have a record of his entry at two in the morning. How would that look? No. Out of the question.

Kent turned for the bathroom. He had to think this through. *Slow down, boy.* Halfway to the bathroom he spun back to the bedroom. He didn't need to use the bathroom. *Get a grip, man.*

On the bed again he began to think clearly for the first time. The fact of the matter was that if they had overlooked ROOSTER, he could enter AFPS and create a link with any bank on the federal reserve system. Of course, what he could do once he was there was another matter altogether.

He couldn't very well take anything. For starters, it was a federal crime. People grew old in prison for white-collar crime. And he was no criminal. Not to mention the simple fact that banks did not just let money walk without tracing it.

Each dollar was accounted for. Accounts were balanced, transactions verified.

Kent crossed his legs on the bed and hugged a pillow. On the other hand, in implementing AFPS prematurely, without his help, Borst not only had inadvertently opened his flank but he had left the barn door open on a billion accounts throughout the world. Kent felt a chill run through his veins. Niponbank's accounts alone numbered nearly one hundred million worldwide. Personal accounts, business accounts, federal accounts—and they were all there, accessible through ROOSTER.

He could waltz right into Borst's personal account if he so desired. Leave nasty messages on his bank statements. Scare the fool right into the arms of God. Ha! Kent smiled. A thin sheen of sweat covered his upper lip, and he drew an arm over his mouth.

He imagined Bentley's eyes when he opened a statement and, instead of that hundred-thousand-dollar bonus, found a notice of an overdraft. He would stiffen like a board. Maybe go purple and keel over dead.

Kent blinked and shook the thoughts from his head. Absurd. The whole notion was absurd.

Then again, everything in his life had become absurd. He had lost his resolve to live. Why not go for a piece of glory, pull off the crime of the century, steal a wad from the bank that had screwed him? It might give him a reason to live again. He'd lost a lot in the recent past. Taking a little back had a ring of justice.

Of course, doing it without getting caught would be nearly impossible. *Nearly* impossible. But it *could* be done—given enough planning. *Imagine!*

Kent did that. He imagined. Till dawn brought shape and color to his surroundings he imagined, wide eyed, with his legs bunched and a pillow under his chin. Sleep was out of the question. Because the more he thought about it, the more he realized that if ROOSTER still lived, he could be a wealthy man. Filthy rich. Start a new life. Make some of his own justice. Risk life in prison, to be sure, but life nonetheless. The alternative of plodding along the corporate trail again struck him more like a slow death. And he'd had enough of death.

It was Wednesday. Today he would go to the bank and casually find out if the ROOSTER still lived. If it did . . .

A chill ran right through Kent's bones. It was indeed time to move on. And what of Helen's little guilt trip? This God business? It would have to wait, of course. If the mighty red ROOSTER lived, he had himself a banquet to plan.

CHAPTER FIFTEEN

KENT DROVE past the bank at eight-thirty, parked on a side street, and walked briskly toward the back alley. It occurred to him that the vagrant might be there, hiding in the dim light. The thought spiked his pulse. He pulled up at the entrance and peered around the brick wall, blinking against an image of a long pink tongue poking through the neck of a bottle. But the alley appeared empty except for that dumpster, which had been emptied. Kent made straight for the rear door and slipped into the bank. He breathed once deeply, checked his tie, and strode for the Information Systems suite.

Betty's eyes popped when he opened the door and stepped in. He smiled and dipped his head, purposefully courteous. "Morning, Betty."

Her mouth opened, but no sound come out.

"What's the matter? Cat got your tongue? Borst in?"

She nodded. "Good morning. Yes."

"Good morning," he repeated and walked for Borst's office.

He tapped on the door and stepped in at the sound of a muffled call. Borst sat behind his desk, all dressed up in a new dark brown suit. The toupee had made a comeback, covering his bald spot with slick black hair. Jet black. Bright red suspenders rounded out the look.

Borst's eyes bulged out, and he bolted from his seat as though an electrode had juiced him there. The suspenders pulled his slacks snug into his crotch when he straightened. He looked like a clown.

"Good morning, Borst." This would have to go smoothly. Easy now. Step by step. "I'm back. I assume that I do still work here, right?"

The man blinked and licked pink lips. "Good night, Kent! You scared me. I had no idea you planned on coming in this morning. We didn't hear from you." His lips twitched to a grin. "Yes. Sure you still work here. Have a seat. How are you?"

"Actually, I'd like ten minutes to get situated. That okay?"

"Sure. I leave for Phoenix at noon." The man's eyebrows lifted. "You here to stay, then?"

Kent turned from the door. "Give me a few minutes. We'll talk then." He pulled the door closed and saw that Borst was already reaching for the phone. Reporting in to Bossman, no doubt. Kent's heart pounded.

Did they know?

Of course not. How could they know of a dream? He had done nothing yet.

Kent nodded at an oogle-eyed Betty and slid into his office. He locked the door. The exotic yellow fish still grazed placidly on his screen. His fingers trembled badly when he lowered them to the keyboard, and he squeezed them into fists.

Okay, settle down, man. All you're doing is checking on a piece of your own code. Nothing wrong with that.

The plan was simple. If ROOSTER remained intact, he would go in there and suck up to Borst. Buy himself some time to think this out. If they had closed ROOSTER down, he would resign.

A touch on the mouse made the fish wink off. A dozen icons hung suspended against a deep blue underwater oceanscape. Kent drew the mouse over the red-and-blue AFPS icon to an explorer icon. Entry into the system would be tracked—at least any entry through the doors of which they were aware. And if he was lucky they had not expanded their security measures to cut off his terminal completely.

His heart thumping loudly in the room's silence, Kent flew through the menus to a hidden folder requiring his own password for entry. He punched it in. The contents sprang to life. He scrolled down and scanned for the file in which he'd placed ROOSTER. The list ran by too quickly, and he repeated the scan, reading more methodically. *Come on, baby. You have to be here.*

And then it *was* there, throbbing in his vision: MISC. He dragged the mouse over the name and double-clicked.

The screen snapped to black. Kent caught his breath, aware that his legs trembled slightly now. He was on his toes under the desk, and he lowered his heels to settle the quaking. *Come on, baby.*

The monitor flashed white, riddled with black letters and symbols. Code. Kent exhaled loudly. ROOSTER's code! A living, viable, untraceable hook into the funds processing system, right here at his fingertips.

He stared at it without moving for a minute, awash with relief that he'd had the foresight to add this final whistle to the package. It wasn't pretty. No colors or boxes yet. Just raw code. But now another question: Would it still link to the system? Kent suddenly felt the heat of panic wash down his back. What if they had found it and left the code but removed its hook into the system?

He hit a key and entered a single word: RUN. A new line immediately appeared, asking for a password. He entered the name. R-O-O-S-T-E-R.

The screen darkened for a second and then popped up with the familiar blue menu he'd worked from for so many years. Kent blinked at the screen. He was in AFPS! Beyond security. From here he could do what he wished without the knowledge of another living soul.

In the right hands, it was a security measure in itself, designed to deal with sabotage and viruses. In the wrong hands it was a way into the bank's vaults. Or worse, a way into every account tied to the bank.

Kent backed out quickly, handling the mouse with a sweating palm. He watched the menus retrace their steps to the deep blue ocean scene, then he lowered his hands to his lap. Even now, short of dusting for prints, Borst could not discover that anyone had even touched this computer, much less peeked up the bank's skirt.

He breathed deeply and stood. It was insane. These crazy thoughts of stealing money would be the end of him. Preposterous. They would bury him. He thought suddenly of Spencer and lifted a hand to his brow. It was all madness.

Either way, he now had his answer.

A fist pounded on the door, and Kent bolted a full foot off the carpet. He spun to the computer and scanned the keyboard. No, there was no trace. Relax. *Relax, relax!*

"Who is it?" he called.

"Cliff."

Cliff. Better than Borst. Kent let him in. "Sorry, I didn't know it was locked," he lied.

"What are you doing in here, Kent?" The new recruit smiled. "Anything I should know about?" He nudged Kent as if they shared an understanding.

"Yeah, right." Kent willed his heart to settle. He sat and crossed his legs. "So what can I do for you?"

"Nothing. Betty just told me you were back. I figured you needed a welcome." The grin straightened. "I heard what happened. You know . . . to your son. I can hardly imagine. Are you okay?"

"Actually, I'm not sure what okay means anymore, but I'm ready to get back to work, if that's what you mean."

"I'm sure it'll take some time. Maybe getting your mind on work is the best way to pass it. And speaking of work, I've dug pretty deep since you were last here." He smiled again. "You'd be proud of me. I've found things I'm sure only you know about."

A chill broke over Kent's crown at the words. *ROOSTER?* "Yeah? Like what?"

"Like links to the Chinese banking codes that are still inactive. Now, that's what I call foresight, man."

"Well, it *is* a global system, Cliff. So what else have you dug up with that long snout of yours?"

"A few anecdotal notes buried in the code—things like that. *Borst has the brain of sausage."* He grinned wide.

"Good night, you found *that?* That *was* buried. I should probably pull it out."

"No, leave it in. He'll never find it."

They nodded, smiling.

"Anything else?" Kent asked.

"That's it so far. Well, it's good to have you back." Cliff stood and walked to the door. "After you get settled I have some code to run by you. You up for that?"

"Sure."

The younger man slapped the wall and disappeared. Now, that was close. Or was it? Actually, the chances of Cliff or anybody finding ROOSTER would be akin to picking a particular grain of sand from a bucket full of the stuff. Either way, he'd have to keep an eye on the man.

Kent settled his nerves with a few long pulls of air and walked into Borst's office.

"Have a seat, Kent."

Kent sat.

"We weren't sure we'd see you again."

Yeah, I'll bet. You and your pal Bentley both. "Well to be honest, I wasn't so sure myself. So, how were things in my absence?" he asked, thinking the question stupid but unable to think of a better way to begin this sucking-up thing to which he had now committed himself.

"Fine, Kent. Just fine. Boy, you've been through hell, huh?"

Kent nodded. "Life can deal some pretty nasty blows." He suddenly despised being here. He should stand now and walk away from this foolishness.

"But I'm back. I need to work, Markus." *That's right, get personal with him. Appeal to his need for friendship.* "I need it bad. All I really have left is my career. I miss work here. Can you understand that?" His voice came soft and sensitive.

"Yes. Makes sense." The man had taken the bait. He paused and shifted his eyes. "Look, Kent. I'm sorry about the misunderstanding about AFPS. I just . . ."

"No. You don't need to say anything. These things happen. And I apologize for blowing up the way I did. It was totally uncalled-for." *Gag. If you only knew, you slimeball.*

Borst nodded, delighted behind that controlled smile, no doubt. "Well, we all got a bit off line, I think. Perhaps it's best we just put the incident behind us."

Kent crossed his legs. The sweat was drying cold on his neck. "You're right. Water under the bridge. So how is AFPS these days?"

Markus brightened. "In a word? Incredible. We put together a doozie, Kent. They're already saying that it will save a third of the manpower the old system used. Price has estimated the overall savings to the bank at over twenty million annually."

Price? First-name basis now. Partners in crime. Probably had dinner together every night. "Great. That's great. No bugs?"

"Sure. Plenty. But they're minor. Actually, you'd probably be best suited to start working on them." The Information Systems supervisor had honestly fooled himself into full ownership of the system, Kent thought.

The man shifted the conversation back to what was apparently his favorite topic these days: money. "Hey, I still haven't allocated that twenty-five-thousand-dollar bonus," he said with a glint in his eyes. "At least not all of it. I'm giving Betty, Todd, and Mary five thousand each. But that leaves ten thousand. You need any spare change these days, Kent?" He jerked his brows high a few times. "Hmm?"

Kent nearly lost the charade then. Came within a gnat's whisker of leaping over the cherrywood desk and strangling his boss. For a few seconds he could not respond. The other *three?* Betty was getting a five-thousand-dollar spiff too? But that was just fine, of course, because he, Kent Anthony, the creator of said program, was to get double that. Yes sir! A whopping ten grand. And Borst? What would bug-eyed Borst's cut be? Oh, well, Borst was the main man. He would get 10 percent of the savings for ten years. A mere fifteen, twenty million. Chump change.

Sounded like a good, round number. Twenty million.

"Sure," Kent said. "Who couldn't use ten thousand dollars? I could cut my Lexus payment in half." That last comment slipped out before he could reign it back. He hoped Borst did not catch his cynicism.

"Good. It's yours. I'll talk to Price this afternoon."

"I thought you were going to Phoenix today."

"Yes. We are. I'll talk to Price on the plane."

It was an unstoppable freight train with those two. Kent swallowed his anger. "Thank you." He stood. "Well, I guess I should get started. I want to talk to the others—you know, make sure there are no misunderstandings."

"Good. Splendid idea. It's good to have you back."

Kent turned at the door. "One more thing, Markus. I kind of blew it with Bentley the other day. You wouldn't mind putting in a word for me, would you? It was just a bad week." He swallowed deliberately and was surprised at the sudden emotion that accompanied it. They said the grief would last a year, gradually easing. Evidently he was still in the stage where it could be set off with a mere swallow.

"Sure, Kent. Consider it done. And don't worry. He and I are rather tight these days."

Yes, I'll bet you are, Kent thought. He left before the revulsion had him doing something silly, like throwing up on the man's carpet.

PASTOR BILL Madison parked his gray Chevy on the street and strode up to Helen's door. She had sounded different on the phone. Almost excited. At least peachy. Like someone who had just been handed some very good news. Or like someone who had flipped their lid.

Given the last few weeks' events, he feared the latter. But then this was Helen, here. With Helen you could never know. The New Testament characterized followers of Christ as peculiar. Well, Helen was just that. One of very few he would consider peculiar in their faith. Which was in itself strange when he got right down and thought about it. Perhaps they should all be rather unusual; Christ certainly was.

She had asked him to pray, and he had indeed prayed. But not simply because of her request. Something was happening here. He might not have the spiritual eyes that Helen claimed to possess, but he could sense things. Discernment, some called it. A spiritual gift. The ability to look at a situation and sense its spiritual origins. Like, *This face sends chills up my spine; it must be evil.* Not that he always operated in the most accurate mode of discernment. He had once felt chills peck at his heart, looking at a strange, alien-looking face on the television screen. To him it looked downright demonic. Then his son had informed him that it was a closeup of a friendly little creature found in the Amazon. One of God's creatures.

That had confused him a little. But this thing with Helen—it was more than just a weird face on the boob tube. It was an aura that followed her around in much the same way he imagined an aura might have followed Elisha or Elijah around.

He rang the doorbell. The door swung in immediately, as if Helen had awaited his arrival with her hand on the knob.

"Come in, Pastor." She wore a yellow dress, tube socks, and running shoes, a ridiculous sight for one who had trouble walking even around the house.

"Thank you, Helen." Bill stepped in and closed the door, glancing at her legs. The musty scent of roses hung in the air. The old lady's perfume was everywhere. She left him for the living room, smiling.

"Is everything all right?" he asked, following.

She did not respond directly but walked across the carpet humming her anthem, "The Martyr's Song." She had told him once that the song summed it all up. It made death worthwhile. Bill stopped behind her large, green easy chair, fixated on the sight of Helen walking. She was seemingly oblivious to him.

"Are you okay?"

"Shhhh." She hushed him and lifted both hands, still pacing back and forth. Her eyes rested closed. "You hear that, Bill?"

Bill cocked his head and listened, but he heard nothing. Except her faint humming. "Hear what?"

"The laughter. Do you hear that laughter?"

He tried to hear laughter, but he heard only her soprano hum. *Let me to Thy bosom fly* . . . And he smelled roses.

"You might have to open your heart a little, but it's there, Pastor—very faint, like the breeze blowing through trees."

He tried again, closing his eyes this time, feeling a little foolish. If one of the deacons knew he was over at Helen Jovic's house listening for laughter with her, they might very well begin the search for a new shepherd. After hearing nothing but Helen for a few moments, he gave up and looked at her.

Helen suddenly stopped her pacing and opened her eyes. She giggled and lowered her hands. "It's okay, Pastor. I didn't really expect you to hear anything. It's like that around here. Some days it's silent. And then some days he opens up my ears to the laughter and I want to walk around the house kissing things. Just kissing everything. Like today. Would you like some tea?"

"Yes, that would be nice."

She shuffled toward the kitchen. She had her socks pulled up to midcalf. A red Reebok logo splashed across the heel of her shoes. Bill swallowed and eased around the chair. She might very well have lost it, he thought. He sat on the green chair.

Helen emerged from the kitchen holding two glasses of tea. "So, you're thinking that my elevator is no longer climbing to the top floor, am I right?" She smiled.

"Actually, I had given it some thought." He grinned and chuckled once. "But these days, it's hard to differentiate between strangeness and craziness." He lost the grin. "They thought Jesus was crazy."

"Yes, I know." She handed him the drink and sat. "And we would think the same today."

"Tell me," Bill said, "did you see Spencer's death in all of this?"

"Yes."

"When?"

"The night after we last talked, a week or so ago. When we talked, I knew there would be more skulls in the dungeon. I could feel it in my spine. But I never really expected it to be Spencer's skull lying there on the ground. It nearly killed me, you know."

"So this is really happening, then." He said it calmly, but he found himself trembling with the thought. "This whole thing is really happening. I mean . . . orchestrated."

"You have put two people in the dirt. You should know. Looked real enough to me."

"Fine, I'll grant you that. It's just hard to swallow this business about you knowing about their deaths beforehand. Maybe if I could see into the heavens like you can, it would be easier."

"It's not everybody's place to see things so clearly, Pastor. We all have our place. If the whole world saw things clearly our churches would be flooded. The nation would flock to the cross en masse. What faith would that require? We might as well be puppets."

"Yes, well, I'm not so sure having full churches would be so bad."

"And I'm not so sure the deaths of my daughter and grandson were so necessary. But when I hear their laughter, when I'm allowed to peek to the other side, it all makes sense. That's when I want to walk around and start kissing things."

He smiled at her expression. In many ways they were very similar, he and Helen. "So then . . ." He paused, collecting his thoughts.

"Yes?"

"In my office last week you told me you'd had a vision in which you heard the sound of running feet in a dungeon. To whom do the running feet in your dungeon belong?" He glanced at her feet, clad in those white Reeboks. "You?"

She laughed. "No." She suddenly tilted her head, thinking. "At least I had not considered it. But no, I don't think so. I think the running feet belong to Kent."

"Kent?"

"He's the player in this game. I mean, we're all players, but he is the runner."

"Kent's the runner. And where is Kent running?"

"Kent is running from God."

"This is all about Kent?"

She nodded. "And about you and me and Gloria and Spencer. Who knows? This might very well be about the whole world. I don't know everything. Sometimes I know nothing. That's why I called you over today. Today I know some things."

"I see." He looked at her feet absently. "And why are you wearing running shoes, Helen? You walking more these days?"

"With my knees?" She wiggled her feet on the carpet. "No, they just feel good. I've got this itching to be young again, I guess." She stared out the window behind Bill. "It seems to ease the pain in my heart, you know."

Helen sipped quietly at the glass, and then set it down. "I've been called to intercede for Kent, Pastor."

He did not respond. She was an intercessor. It made sense.

"Intercede without ceasing. Eight hours a day."

"You spend eight hours a day praying for Kent?"

"Yes. And I will do so until it is over."

"Until *what* is over, Helen?"

She looked at him directly. "Until this game is over."

He studied her, looking for any sign of insincerity. He could see none. "So now it's a game? I'm not sure God plays games."

She shrugged. "Choose your own words, then. I have been called to pray until it is over."

Bill shook his head with disbelief. "This is unbelievable. I feel like we've been transported back to some Old Testament story."

"You think? This is nothing. You should read Revelation. Things get really strange later."

The sense of her words struck at him. He'd never thought of history in those terms. There had always been biblical history, the time of burning bushes and talking donkeys and tongues of fire. And there was the present—the time of normalcy. What if Helen's peculiar view behind the scenes was really just an unusual peek at the way things really were? And what if he was being allowed to peek into this extraordinary "normalcy" for a change?

They sat and talked for a long while after that. But Helen did not manage to shed any more light on his questions. He concluded it was because she herself knew little more. She was seeing through a glass dimly. But she was indeed seeing.

And if she was right, this drama of hers—this game—It was indeed all just beginning.

chapter sixteen

Week Seven

LACY CARTWRIGHT leaned back in the lounge chair on her balcony, drinking coffee, enjoying the cool morning breeze. It was ten o'clock. Having a day off midweek had its advantages, she thought, and one of them was the quiet, out here under a bright blue Boulder sky while everyone else worked. She glanced over her body, thankful for the warmth of sun on her skin. Just last week Jeff Duncan had called her petite. Heavens! She was thin, maybe, and not an inch over five-three, but petite? Her coworker at the bank had said it with a glint in his eye, and she had suspected then that the man had a crush on her. But it had been under two years since her husband's death. She was not ready to engage a man.

The breeze feathered her face, and she lifted a hand to sweep the blonde strands behind her ear. Her hair rested on her shoulders in lazy curls, framing hazel eyes that smiled. A thin sheen of suntan oil glistened on her pale belly between a white halter top and jean shorts. Some women seemed to relish baking in the sun—lived for it even. Goodness! A picture of a hot dog sizzling on a grill popped into her mind, and she let it hang there for a moment. Its red skin suddenly split, and the image fizzled.

Lacy turned her head and studied the distant clouds looming black toward the southeast. Denver had had its share of weather lately, and it appeared the area was in for a little more. Which was another reason she liked it up here in Boulder more than in the big city. In Denver, if you weren't dealing with weather, you were dealing with smog. Or at the very least, traffic, which was worse than either. She ought to know—she'd spent most of her life down there.

But not anymore. After John's death two years earlier she had upped and moved here. Started a new career as a teller and busied herself with the monumental task of ridding her chest of its ache. She'd done it all well, she thought. Now she could get on with the more substantive issues of starting over. Like lying out in the sun, waiting for the UV rays to split her skin like that hot dog. Goodness!

A high-pitched squeal jerked her mind from its reflections. She spun toward the sliding glass door and realized the awful sound was coming from her condo. As if a pig had gotten its snout caught in a door and was protesting. But of course there were no pigs in there, squealing or not. There was, however, a washing machine, and if she wasn't mistaken, the sound was actually coming from the laundry room, where she had started a load of whites fifteen minutes ago.

The sound suddenly jumped an octave and wailed like a siren. Lacy scrambled from the lounger and ran for the laundry room. It would be just her luck that old Mrs. Potters next door was jabbing at the oversized nine-one-one numbers on her trusty pink telephone at this very moment.

Lacy saw the soapy water before she reached the door, and her pulse spiked, midstride. Not that she'd never seen soapy water before—saw it all the time, but never bubbling under a door like some kind of monster foaming at its mouth. She felt the wet seep between her toes through the navy carpet a good five feet from the door. She let out a yelp and tiptoed to the door. This was not good.

The door swung in over an inch of gray water. The washing machine rocked madly, squealing, and Lacy dove for the control knob. Her palm smashed it in, which under normal conditions would have killed the thing right then. But evidently things were no longer normal in this room, because the boxy old machine just kept rocking and wailing.

The plug! She had to pull the plug. One of those big fat plugs behind the contraption. Water bubbled over the top of the washer and ran down to the floor in streams. Frantic now, Lacy flopped belly-down on the shaking appliance and dove for the back. The plug stuck stubbornly. She squirmed over the lid so that her feet dangled, all too aware of the water soaking her clothes. She put her full weight into the next tug. The plug came free, sending her flying backward, off the dying machine and to the floor like a fish spilled from a net.

She struggled from the floor, grateful for the ringing silence. In all the commotion her hair had attracted enough water to leave it dripping. She gazed about, and her stomach knotted at the sight. A pig stuck in the door might have been better.

Before John died this would all have been different. She would simply call the precinct and have him run by to take care of things. For her it would be a quick shower and then perhaps off to lunch.

But that was before. Before the cancer had ravaged his body and sent him to the grave exactly two months before he would have made sergeant. An image of her late husband all decked out in those navy blues and shiny brass buttons drifted through her mind. He was smiling, because he had always smiled. A good man. A perfect cop. The only man she could imagine herself with. Ever.

Lacy bent over her oak dinette table half an hour later, the phone book spread yellow before her, a paper towel protecting the phone from her blackened fingers. Her attempt at messing with gears under the machine had proved futile. A lazy voice filled her ear.

"Frank," it drawled. Frank was chewing gum by the sounds of his rhythmic smacking. He'd obviously slept through the etiquette portion of his plumber-school training.

"Hi, Frank. This is Lacy Cartwright. I'm guessing you're a certified Goldtech technician, right?"

"Yes, ma'am. What can I do for you?" *Smack, smack.* She swallowed.

"Well, I have a problem out here, Frank. The water pump on my washing machine somehow got stuck open and flooded the floor. I need it repaired."

"Stuck open, huh?" A hint of amusement rang in the man's voice. "And what model number are we talking about?"

"J-28," she said, ready for the question.

"Well, you see? Now there's a problem, because J-28s don't get stuck open. J-28s use pumps operated on a normally closed solenoid, and if anything, they get stuck closed. You hear any sounds when this machine went belly up?"

"It squealed."

"It squealed, huh? I'll bet it squealed." He chuckled. "Yes, ma'am, they sure know how to squeal, them Monroe pumps." The phone went silent. Lacy was wondering where they had found Frank. Seemed to know pumps, all right. But maybe his own pump was not reaching the wellhead.

When he did not offer any further comment, she spoke. "So what do I do?"

"Well, you need a new pump, Miss Cartwright."

Another short silence. "Can you install a new pump for me?"

"Sure, I can. It's not a question of *can,* ma'am. I've been putting in new pumps for ten years." An edge had come to his voice midsentence. She lifted her eyes and caught her reflection in the dining room mirror. Her blonde hair had dried in tangles.

"The problem is, we don't have any Monroe pumps in stock today. So you see, even if I wanted to come out there, which I couldn't do for three days anyway, I couldn't do it because I don't have anything to do it with." He chuckled again.

Lacy blinked. She suddenly wasn't sure she even *wanted* Frank to fix her washing machine. "Is it hard?"

"Is what hard?"

"Do you think I could replace the pump?"

"Any idiot could replace that pump, Miss." *Evidently.* "Three bolts and a few wires, and you're in and out before you know it. I could do it with a blindfold on. In fact, I *have* done it with a blindfold on." *Good for you, Frankie.* "But, like I said, Honey. We have no pumps."

"Where else can I get a pump?"

"Nowhere. At least nowhere in Boulder. You go to the manufacturer in Denver, they might sell you one."

Denver? She gazed out the window to those ominous clouds in the southeast. It would be an hour there, another hour in traffic regardless of where it was, and an hour back. It would blow her day completely. She glanced at the clock. Eleven. On the other hand, her day was already blown. And she couldn't very well wait a week for Frankie to come out and walk around her condo with a blindfold on while he did his thing.

"Well, lady, I can't sit here all day."

Lacy started. "I'm sorry. Yes, I think I'll try Monroe. Do you have the number?"

Thirty minutes later she was in the car, headed for the freeway, with the old J-28 pump in a box beside her. Frank had been right. Once she managed to tip the washer enough to prop it up with a footstool and slide under it, removing the little beast had not been so bad. She had even closed her eyes once while loosening a bolt, wondering what possessed a man to try such a thing.

Lacy pulled onto the freeway, struck by how easily the course of her day had changed. One minute lying in attempted bliss, the next diving into soapy gray water.

Goodness.

THE WEEK had flown past, skipping across the peaks of Kent's nerves like a windsurfer pushed by a gale-force wind. It was the wind of imagination, and it kept his eyes wide and burning. By the end of that first day Kent knew what he was going to do with a certainty that brought fire to his bones.

He was going to rob the bank blind.

Literally. He was going to take every penny he had coming. All twenty million of it. And the bank would remain as blind as a bat through it all. He sat there at his desk, exhilarated by the idea, his fingers frozen over the keyboard as his mind spun.

He tried in vain to concentrate on Cliff's questions about why he'd chosen this routine or where he could find that link. And that was a problem, because now more than ever, fitting back into the bank as Joe Smooth Employee took on significance. The way he saw it, he already had some ground to make up; some kissing up to do. Walking around the bank with a big red sign reading "Here walks the man who screamed at Bentley over employee of the month parking" would not do. He would have to concentrate on being normal again. On fitting in with the other fools who actually believed they were somehow important in this nine-to-five funny farm. There was the small matter of his having lost a wife and son, but he would just have to bite his tongue on that one, wouldn't he? Just try not to bleed all over the place. He would have to rein in his mind, control his thoughts. For the sake of ROOSTER.

But his thoughts kept sliding off to other things.

Things like what he would do with twenty million dollars. Things like how he could hide twenty million dollars. Things like how he could *steal* twenty million dollars. The details flew by, dizzying in his analytical mind. A hundred sordid details—each one spawning another hundred, it seemed.

First, he would have to decide from where to take the money. Using ROOSTER he could take it from almost anywhere. But, of course, *anywhere* would not do. It would have to come from a place where twenty million would not be quickly missed. No matter how untraceable the transaction itself might be, its net result would be nearly impossible to hide. Nearly.

Then he would have to decide where to put the money. He would never actually have the physical bills—the coin—but even a ledger balance of twenty million was enough to generate at least interest. And that kind of interest was not something he needed. If the money ever turned up missing, the FBI would be all over it like stink on sewer. He would have to find a way to lie at the bottom of that sewer.

He'd have to plan the actual execution of the theft very carefully, of course. Couldn't very well be caught downloading twenty million dollars. "What are those large balances on your screen, Kent?"

"Oh, nothing. Actually, that's my bonus from AFPS, if you must know. I'm just taking an early withdrawal."

He would also have to find a way to exit his current life. Couldn't be a millionaire and work for Borst. Had no ring of justice to him. And this whole thing was really about justice. Not just with his job but with life in general. He had climbed the ladder like a good boy for twenty years only to be dropped back on his tail in the space of thirty days. Back down to Stupid Street where the concrete was hard and the nights cold. Well, now that he had taken the time to think things through, being forced to climb that ladder again, rung by rung, made as much sense as setting up post on the local corner, bearing a sign that read "Will work for beer."

Not a chance. It took him thirty days to fall; if all went well it would take him no more than thirty to pop back on top.

The hardest part of this whole scheme might very well be the spending of the money. How could Kent Anthony, computer programmer, step into a life of wealth without raising eyebrows? He would have to divorce himself from his past somehow. Not a problem. His immediate past reeked of every imaginable offensive odor anyway. The notion of divorcing himself from that past brought a buzz to his lower spine. His past was tainted beyond redemption. He would put it as far behind him as possible. Wash it from his memory entirely. Begin a new life as a new man.

In fact, it was in this last stage of the entire plan that he would find himself again. The thought of it pushed him into the certainty that coursed through his bones like charged electrons. After weeks of empty dread, it came like a euphoric drug.

Kent looked over Cliff's shoulder at the wall—at the picture of the white yacht hanging in the shadows. An image of that same boat he'd plastered on the refrigerator at home sailed through his mind. His promise to Gloria. *I swear, Gloria, we will own that yacht one day.*

A lump rose to his throat. Not that she had cared much. She'd been too enamored with her mother's religion to appreciate the finer things. Kent had always hung on to the hope that it would change. That she would drop her silly obsessions and run after his dreams. But now she was gone.

For the first few days the thoughts whispered relentlessly, and he began to construct possible solutions to the challenges. Not too unlike debugging. A natural exercise for his mind. While Cliff busied himself with the code before them, Kent busied himself with another code altogether. This morning alone, he had apologized three times for his drifting mind. Cliff guessed it had to do with the loss of his wife and son. Kent nodded, feeling like a pimp for hiding behind the sentiment.

It was one o'clock before he shut down the Cliff machine. "Okay, Ace. I've got some errands to run over lunch. You should have enough to keep you busy for a couple of days anyway." He stood and stretched.

"I suppose you're right. Thanks for the time. I'll just keep digging. You never know what I'll come up with."

A thought crossed Kent's mind. "Actually, why don't you focus on debugging for a few days and leave the digging. I mean, be my guest, dig all you want, but wandering aimlessly through my code is not necessarily the best use for a mind like yours, pal." He shrugged. "Just my opinion, of course. But if you want to find something, just ask me. I'll save you a mountain of time."

Cliff smiled brightly. "Sure, if you're here. I think that was the concern. What happens if Kent Anthony disappears?"

"Well, a week ago that strategy made sense. But it's now obsolete. I'm here to stay. You tell that to whoever punches your buttons." Kent grinned to make the point stick.

Cliff saluted mockingly. "You got it, sir."

"Good then. Off you go, lad."

Cliff left grinning ear to ear. Kent honestly felt nearly jovial. The drug of his plotting had worked its way right through his veins. It felt as though he had stepped out of some nightmare and found himself at the gates of a new undiscovered world. And he fully intended to discover every corner of it.

He locked his office, made some comment to Betty about how much work there was, and hustled out the back. Normally he would have preferred the front doors, but now was not normally. Now he would have crawled through a trapdoor in the floor if there had been one.

He hurried down the alley to his car and slid onto the leather upholstery before considering his destination. The library. He had some books to check out. No. That would leave a trail. The bookstore, then. He had some books to purchase. With cash. The nearest Barnes and Noble was three miles down Sixth Avenue. He made a U-turn and entered the flow of traffic.

Kent was not one to stop and lend a hand to stranded vehicles. Road kill, he called them. If the morons didn't have the foresight to either have their cars properly serviced or sign up for AAA they surely didn't deserve his extended hand. The dead vehicles were usually old cars stuffed with people from Stupid Street anyway. As far as he was concerned, a little breakdown on the road in heavy traffic was a good indoctrination to responsibility, a rare commodity these days.

Which was why it struck him as strange that the white Acura sidelined ahead on the left-hand side of the divided thoroughfare even caught his attention. And even stranger was the simple fact that once it was in his eyesight, he could hardly remove his eyes from the vehicle. And no wonder. It sat like a beacon of light ahead, glowing white, as if a lightning bolt had lit it up. It suddenly occurred to him that the sky was indeed rather foreboding—in fact downright dark. But the Acura was actually glowing up there, and all the other cars just sped by as if it did not exist. Kent gripped the steering wheel, wooden.

A woman with blonde hair, dressed in jeans and a green shirt, was climbing out. She turned to face his approach, and Kent's heart bolted. He didn't know *why* his heart jumped like that, but it did. Something in her face, possibly. But that was just it; he could hardly *see* her face from this distance.

Then Kent was past the car, torn by indecision. If ever there was a soul who deserved assistance, it was this one. On the other hand, he didn't do roadkill. Thirty yards flew by before he jerked the wheel impulsively and slid to a stop, five inches from the guardrail, cars moaning by on the right.

The instant he stopped, he decided it had been a mistake. He thought about pulling back into traffic. Instead, he slid out of the seat and jogged the forty yards back to the Acura. If the glow that had surrounded the car had ever actually been there, it had taken leave. Someone had pulled the plug. The woman had lifted the hood so that it gaped, black-mouthed, at him like a steel alligator. She stood watching his approach, bouncing in his vision.

Kent was ten feet from the woman when recognition slammed into his mind like a sledge. He pulled up, stunned.

It was the same for her, he thought. Her jaw dropped to her chest, and her eyes grew wide. They stood fixed to the pavement like two deer caught in each other's headlights.

"Kent?"

"Lacy?"

They responded simultaneously. "Yes."

Her eyes were like saucers. "Kent Anthony! I can't believe it's actually you. My . . . my car died . . ."

He grinned, feeling oddly out of sorts. She was prettier than he remembered. Thinner perhaps. Her face was still rather ordinary, but those eyes. They shone like two beaming emeralds. No wonder he'd taken to her in college. And age was wearing well on her.

"Lacy Cartwright. How on Earth did you end up stranded on the side of the road?" *Her car broke down, you idiot. She told you that.*

She broke into a wide grin. "This is weird. I don't know what happened. It just stopped . . ." She chuckled. "So how in the world are you?"

"Good. Yeah, good," he said, thinking it both a downright lie and the honest truth.

He stood silent for a full ten seconds, just staring at her, at a loss for what to say next. But then she was doing the same, he thought. *Come on, man. Get a grip.*

Kent finally motioned to the car. "So, what happened?"

She gazed at the tangle of tubes under the hood. "It just died. I was lucky to pull over without hitting the rail."

The atmosphere was charged with expectancy. High above, a line of lightning crackled through black clouds. "Well, I'm not a mechanic, but why don't you get in and turn her over and I'll poke around a little."

"Good." She held his eyes for a moment as if trying to read any message there. He felt a strange tightness squeeze his chest.

Lacy jumped behind the wheel, eyeing him through the windshield. He dipped his head under the raised hood. Good grief! He was staring at a ghost from the past.

The engine turned over, and he jerked back, immediately hoping she had not seen his reaction. No sense coming off like a wuss.

The engine caught and rumbled to life.

Kent stood back, studied the running motor for a moment and, seeing nothing extraordinary, slammed the hood shut.

Lacy was out. "What did you do?"

He shrugged. "Nothing."

"You're kidding, right? This thing was dead, I swear."

"And I swear that I did nothing but breathe on it. Maybe I should've been an auto mechanic. I could fix cars by breathing on them." He grinned.

"Well, you always did have a lot of hot air." Lacy shot him a coy look and smiled slyly.

They chuckled, and Kent kicked at the pavement, suddenly shy again. He looked up. "Well, I guess you're fixed up. I heard you'd moved to Boulder."

"Yeah."

"Maybe we should get together."

The smile vanished from her face, and he wondered if she'd heard. "You heard about Gloria, right?" he asked.

"Gloria?"

"Yes. My wife died awhile back."

Her face registered shock. "I'm so sorry! I had no idea."

He nodded. "Yeah. Anyway, I should probably get going. I have to get back to work."

She nodded. "Yeah, I have to get back to Boulder. My washer broke down." She offered no further explanation.

He nodded again, feeling suddenly stranded. "Yeah." She was not moving.

"I'm really sorry about your wife, Kent. Maybe we should get some coffee and talk about it."

"I heard you lost your husband a couple years ago."

She nodded. They were nodding a lot. It was a good way to fill in the blanks after, what? Thirteen years?

"You have a card?" he asked. That sounded dumb. Sounded like he was hitting on her, and he had no intention of hitting on anyone. No desire at all.

"Sure." She reached through the window, withdrew her purse, and handed him a card. Rocky Mountain Bank and Trust. Customer Service.

"I didn't know you were in banking." He glanced up at her. "You know I'm in banking, right?"

"Someone said that. Information Systems, right?"

"Yeah. Good, I'll call you. We'll catch up."

"I'll look forward to it," she said, and he thought she meant it.

"Good." Lots of *goods* and *yeahs* and nodding. "Hope your car runs well," he said and dipped his head to her.

Then he was jogging back to his car. The horizon flashed crooked fingers of lightning, and thunder boomed. The rain was eager, he thought. When he reached his door, Lacy's white Acura sped by and honked. He waved and slipped behind the wheel. Go figure.

LACY DROVE west through a hard pour with her gut twisted in knots. The chance meeting with Kent had thrown her completely off center. She sped down the blacktop, fixated on the *whap, whap* of the windshield wipers, slowly exiting the big city. But her heart was back there, on the roadside, gazing into those lost blue eyes.

Kent looked as though he'd stepped out of some lost corner of her mind, a carbon copy of the zany college student who'd managed to capture her heart. Her first love. It had been his sincerity, she'd mused a thousand times. A man as sincere and honest as he was ambitious. The unique blend of those traits had whipped up a potion that had her swooning for the first time in her life. Well, his blue eyes and blond hair had not exactly impeded her swooning, she supposed.

He had lost his wife. Didn't he have a son as well? Poor child.

And under that haunting facade hid a man aching for comfort yet repelled by it at once. She should know. She'd been there. "God, help him," she breathed, and she meant it. She meant not only that Kent would receive help, but that *God* would help him. Because Lacy believed in God. She had fallen to his feet just over a year ago while climbing out of her own despondency, learning that she did not have the world by its tail.

"Father, comfort him," she whispered. The wipers squeaked.

Lacy fought a sudden urge to pull off, whip the car around, and chase Kent down. Of course, that was ridiculous. Even if such a thing were possible, she had no business chasing after an old flame who'd just lost his wife. And since when had she become the chasing type, anyway? *Listen to me, even thinking in terms of chasing! Heavens! I don't mean chasing like some dog in heat, but chasing as in trying to . . . help the man.*

She glanced at the new water pump in the passenger seat and remembered the broken washing machine. Now, if that machine had not broken down precisely when it had, she would have missed him entirely. If the strange service tech had not been as accommodating on the phone, if he'd had a pump in stock, if she had not driven to Denver, if her car had not lost its spark for a moment when it did—any single fluctuation in this endless string of events, and she would not have met Kent.

And on top of it all, Kent had pulled over without knowing whom he would be helping. That much was evident by his shock when he recognized her.

On the other hand, every event that ever occurred did so only after a string of other events lined up perfectly.

Lacy glanced at a brown smudge on her right sleeve, a spot of smeared grease. Had he seen it? She returned to her line of thinking. Almost anything was statistically possible. But the pull in Lacy's heart suggested that today's string of events was not just a random occurrence. It had been somehow orchestrated. Had to be.

On the other hand, stranger things had happened.

Lacy ground her teeth and dismissed the mental volleys. But they did not go so easily; within the minute they were back, nipping at her mind.

In the end she decided that none of it mattered. Kent had her card. He would either call, or he would not call. And that had nothing to do with chance. It had everything to do with his choice. Her heart jumped at the thought.

An obscure memory from her early adolescent years flashed through her mind. She was all dressed up for the prom, clad in a pink dress with white frills and her hair pulled back in a cluster of curls. It had taken her and her mother a good three hours to make everything just so. It was her first date, and Daddy had told her how proud he was of her, looking so beautiful. She sat on the living room couch, holding a white carnation for her date. Peter. But Peter was late. Ten minutes, then half an hour, then an hour. And she just sat there swinging her legs, feeling all gooey inside and trying to be brave while her father stormed on the phone. But Peter never came, and his parents knew nothing about their son's whereabouts. Her father took her out for dessert, but she could not manage eye contact with anyone that night.

A lump filled her throat at the memory. Dating had never gone well for her. Even dating with Kent, who had dropped her on her seat at the slightest hint of commitment. She would do well to remember that.

What had she been thinking, *chasing* after him? She no more needed a relationship now than she needed a bout with lupus.

On the other hand, he might call.

chapter seventeen

Week Eight

HELEN TOSSED and turned, and even in her sleep she could feel her eyes jerking behind closed lids. Slapping feet echoed through her head, sounding like a marathon runner who had taken a wrong turn and ended up running through a tunnel. A tunnel called Kent's life.

The feet beat on—*slap, slap, slap*—without pause. Heavy breathing chased the slapping. The runner pulled deliberately against the stale dark air. Maybe too deliberately, as if he or she were trying to believe that the breathing was all about flooding the lungs with air, when actually it was just as much about fighting off panic. Because steady sounds do that—they fight off uncertainty with their rhythm. But this runner seemed to be losing that battle with uncertainty. The deliberate breaths were sounding a little ragged around the edges.

The slapping feet had made frequent visits to her mind in the last week, and that bothered her because she knew they were saying something. She just hadn't been able to decipher their message. At least not all of it.

She knew they were Kent's feet. That Kent was running. Running from God. The running man. She'd heard of a movie called that once. *The Running Man.* Some gladiator type running for his life through a game show.

Pastor Madison didn't like her calling this a game, but here in her own mind she could call it whatever she wanted. And it felt like a serious game show to her. The stakes were death; the prize was life. But in a cosmic sort of way, that prize wasn't so different from winning a Kenmore refrigerator with built-in ice maker or a '64 Mustang convertible, now, was it?

She took a deep breath and tried to refocus her thoughts. *Lighten up, Helen. Goodness, you're going off the deep end. We're not playing* Wheel of Fortune *here.*

Her mind sank into the dungeon again and listened to those slapping feet.

How long could a person run like that? Another sound bounced around in the dark. A thumping sound. A pounding heart to go along with the heavy breathing and the slapping feet. Which made sense, because her heart would certainly be pounding if she ran.

She imagined herself running like that.

The thought came like a sharp jab to her solar plexus.

She caught her breath.

Now there were only two sounds in the tunnel: the beating feet—*slap, slap, slap*—and the pounding heart—*thump, thump, thump.* The breathing had stopped.

Helen bolted up in bed, suddenly awake, a single thought now whispering through her skull: *That breathing stopped when you stopped breathing, sister! That's* you *in there!*

She snatched her hands to her chest. Her heart pounded to the same cadence she had heard in her dream. In the tunnel. The only thing missing was the slapping feet. And no matter how weird things were getting, she knew that she certainly had not been running up and down her hall in her sleep.

Helen knew the point of it all, then, sitting in bed feeling her heart throb under her palm. If she was not actually in the game, she was *meant* to be. Her feet were *meant* to be slapping along the floor of that tunnel. This insane urge to walk was not just some senile thing; it was the pull of God on her spirit. *Walk, child, walk. Maybe even run. But at least walk.*

It might be Kent in there running for his life, but she was in there too, breathing down his neck! Praying for him. She was in the game too. And her part was the intercessor. That was it.

Helen threw the sheets off and stood beside her bed. It was 5 A.M. She should walk, maybe. The thought stopped her cold for a moment. She was not a walker, for heaven's sake. The doctor had wanted to put new knees in her legs less than a year ago! What on earth did she think she would do now? Hobble up and down the driveway until the neighbors called the police about the lunatic they saw out their windows? Walking back and forth on her plush carpet in running shoes was one thing. Taking a prayer trek through the streets like some prophet was another thing altogether.

And more important, why on God's green earth would he want her to walk at all? What did walking have to do with this craziness? God certainly did not need on old lady's walking to move his hand.

Then again, neither had he needed old Joshua and his cohorts traipsing around Jericho to tumble the wall, now, did he? And yet he had demanded that. This was not so different.

Well, yes, this *was* different. This was different because this was now and that was then and this was her and that was Joshua!

Helen grunted and made for the bathroom. She was up. She might as well get dressed. And there was another reason why this was different. This was different because this was mad! What would Pastor Madison say? Goodness!

She stopped midstride, halfway to the bathroom. *Yes, but what would God say? Was that God talking to you back there, telling you to walk?*

Yes.

Then walk.

Yes.

It was settled then, in that moment.

Twenty minutes later Helen stepped from her house wearing her white Reeboks and over-the-calf basketball socks below a swishing green dress with yellow sunflowers scattered in a pattern only the original designer could possible identify.

"Oh, God have mercy on my soul," she muttered and stepped from the landing to the sidewalk. She began to walk down the street with no destination in mind. She would just walk and see.

And she would pray.

KENT ROLLED through the hours with all the constancy of a yo-yo those first two weeks. One moment consumed with the audacity of his ever-clarifying plot, the next blinking against memories of Spencer or Gloria. To say that he was unstable would have brought the textbook definition into clear focus.

The ideas came like weeds, sprouting in his mind as though some mad scientist had spilled super-growth formula on them. It didn't even occur to him until the end of the first week that the twisting and turning up there did not stop when he fell asleep. In fact, his best ideas seemed to sneak their way into his mind then, when he tossed in fitful sleep. In his dreams.

Just as the vagrant had flashed his tongue about and told Kent just what he thought of the situation, other voices seemed to be suggesting other opinions. He could never quite remember their precise words or even the overall context of their suggestions, but he seemed to wake each day with an eagerness to explore a vague notion. And regardless of why his mind seemed to favor the night, Kent did not complain. It was the stuff of genius, he thought.

The meeting with Lacy nagged at him occasionally, but the growing prospects of his new life overshadowed the strange encounter. Several times he pulled her card out, intending to call. But he found things confusing once he attempted to clarify his reason for contacting her. *Oh hi, Lacy. How about a nice romantic dinner tonight? Did I tell you that my wife and son just died? Because that's important. I'm a free man, Lacy.* Gag! He was certainly in no mood for a relationship.

On the other hand, he was starving for friendship. And friendship was relationship, so in that sense he was growing slowly desperate for a relationship. Maybe even someone to tell . . . Someone to share this growing secret with. But that would be insane. Secrecy was his friend here.

Life at the office began to take on its own rhythm, not so different from the one that had once marched him through the days before his world had turned upside down. And the nights. It was the night routine that Kent began to methodically add to his work regimen. He needed his coworkers to be thoroughly accustomed to his late nights at the office again. His whole plan depended on it.

It was impossible to lock or unlock the building without triggering a signal that notified the alarm company of the event. The entries were posted on the branch manager's monitors each morning. So Kent made a point of entering and leaving through the backdoor, creating a consistent record of his work habits, and then offhandedly reporting the progress he'd made the previous night to Borst.

What they could not know was that the debugging he accomplished in those late hours while they slept took only a fraction of the time indicated. He could produce more clean code in one hour than any of the others could in a day. He not only possessed twice the gray matter any of them did, but he was working on his own code.

Not his own code as in AFPS, but his own program as in refining ROOSTER and the way ROOSTER was going to wreak its havoc on the world.

Cliff made a habit of poking his head in each day, but Kent did his best to minimize their interaction. Which simply meant knowing at all times what the zany snowboarder was working on and staying clear of his routines.

"You seem awfully well adjusted for having just gone through such loss," Cliff stated at the end of Kent's first week back.

Kent scrambled for a plausible explanation. "Denial," he said, turning away. "That's what they say, anyway."

"Who says that?"

He had not been to a shrink. "The pastor," Kent lied.

"You're kidding! I had no idea you went to church. I do too!"

Kent began to regret his lie immediately.

"So how long have you been a Christian?"

"Well, actually I'm really not that well connected."

"Sure, I can understand that. They say 80 percent of churchgoers are disconnected beyond Sunday services. So I hear that your wife was a strong believer."

Kent looked up. "Really? And who told you that?"

"I just picked it up somewhere."

"Somewhere like where? I didn't know it was common knowledge around here."

Cliff shrugged uncomfortably. "Well, from Helen, actually."

"Helen? My mother-in-law's been talking to you?"

"No. Relax, Kent. We talked once when she called in."

"And you just happened to talk about me and my wife? Well that's real sweet of you— 'Poor Kent, let's gossip about his faith, why don't we? Or should we say, his lack thereof.'"

"We're Christians, Kent. Some things are not as sacred as others. Don't worry, it goes no further than me."

Kent turned away, angry without knowing exactly why. Helen had her rights. Gloria was, after all, her daughter. He began to avoid Cliff then, at the end of his first week back to work. Although getting away from the pineapple-eating grinner was easier said than done.

It took Borst most of two weeks to buy into Kent's reformed attitude. But a daily dose of soothing accolades administered by Kent greased the wheels to the man's mind easily enough. Kent had to hold his nose while smearing the stuff on, but even that became easier as the days passed.

Borst asked him about the schedule once after Kent had handed him the fix to a bug that Borst himself had attempted and failed to remedy. It had taken Kent exactly twenty-nine minutes the previous night to locate the misplaced modifier responsible.

"You got it, huh? Gotta hand it to you, Anthony. You sure can crank this stuff out." He lifted his greasy head. "You seem to work best at night these days, don't you?"

A flare hissed white-hot in Kent's mind. His heart flinched in his chest, and he hoped desperately that Borst was not catching any of his reaction. "I've always worked best at night, Markus." He'd discovered that Borst liked to be called Markus by his friends. He lowered his eyes. "But since the deaths, I'm not crazy about being alone at night with nothing to do, you know?"

"Yeah, sure. I understand." He waved the pages in the air. "You did all of this last night, huh?"

Kent nodded.

"What time you pull out of here?"

Kent shrugged. "I came back at, oh, maybe eight or so, and left at midnight."

Borst smiled. "Four hours? Like I said, you're good. You keep working like this, and the rest of us will run out of things to do." He chuckled. "Good work." He'd winked then, and Kent swallowed an urge to poke his eye out.

Instead he smiled. "Thank you, sir."

The *sir* brought a flare of pride to Borst's nostrils, and Kent left, determined to use the expression more frequently.

He resumed his friendship with Will Thompson within the first few days. As before, their shallow talk led to nothing of substance, which was fine by Kent.

"I just can't believe you're back after what they put you through," Will told him, walking to lunch the third day. Taking time for lunch sat rancid in Kent's gut, but he was on a mission to appear as ordinary as possible, and the occasional lunch would fit the image well.

"You know, if Spencer had not passed away, I don't think I would be here. But when you lose the ones you love the most, things change, Will. Your perspectives change. I just need to work now, that's all." He looked across the street to Antonio's Italian Cuisine. "Who knows? Maybe once things have settled I'll move on. But now I need stability."

Will nodded. "Makes sense."

Touché, Will. Indeed it makes sense. Everything needs to make sense. You remember that when they question you about me.

Betty Smythe became just another office fixture again, smacking her lips at the front desk, handling all of Borst's important calls and constantly scanning her little world with the peeled eyes of a hawk. It made little difference to Kent, who simply closed his door. But when the poop hit the fan, hers would be the most active mouth, flapping nonstop, no doubt. He wanted her gabbing to favor him, not cast suspicion his way. So he began the distasteful task of working his way into her corner.

A bouquet of roses, for all of her support, started him off on the right foot. The fact that she had not lifted a single finger in support of him didn't seem to temper her appreciation. Then again, judging by the amount of acrylic hanging off the end of her fingers, lifting them would be no easy task.

"Oh, Kent! You shouldn't have!"

He had always wondered if women who carried on with wide eyes about flowers really did find them as stimulating as they let on. He could see a cow slobbering over vegetation, but women were hardly cows. Well, most women weren't. Betty came pretty close, which probably explained why she had just rolled her eyes back as if she were dying and going to heaven over the red blossoms on this particular arrangement of vegetation.

"But I should have," he replied with as much sincerity as he could muster. "I just wanted you to know how much your support has helped me."

A quick flicker in her eyes made him wonder if he had gone too far. If so, she quickly adapted. "You're so kind. It was nothing, really. Anybody would have done the same." She smiled and smelled the roses.

Kent had no idea what she could possibly be referring to, but it no longer mattered. "Well, thank you again, Betty. I owe you." *Gag!*

"Thank you, Kent." Somehow one of the petals had loosed itself and stuck on her upper lip. It looked ridiculous. She didn't seem to notice. Kent didn't bother to tell her. He smiled genuinely and turned for his office.

Todd and Mary were like two peas in a pod—both eager to please Borst and fully cognitive of the fact that they needed Kent to do it. They both trotted in and out of his office like regular pack rats. "Kent, how would you do this?" Or, "Kent, I've done such and such but it's not working quite right." Not that he particularly minded. At times it even made him feel as though nothing had really changed—he had always been at the center of their world.

It was the way they straightened when Borst walked by that brought Kent back to earth. In the end, their allegiance was for Bossman.

Todd actually apologized for his behavior at one point. "I'm sorry for . . . well, you know." He sat in Kent's office and crossed his legs, suddenly a tinge redder in the face. He pushed up his black-rimmed glasses.

"For what, Todd?"

"You know, for the way I acted that first day."

Kent did not respond. Let the boy squirm a little.

"It's hard being caught in the middle of office politics, you know. And technically speaking, Borst *is* our boss, so we don't want to cross him. Besides, he was right. It's really his thing, you know?"

A dozen voices screamed foul in Kent's head. He wanted to launch out and turn this boy. Slap some sense into him. And he could've pulled it off, too. But he only bit his lip and nodded slowly.

"Yeah, you're probably right."

Todd grinned sheepishly. "It's okay, Kent. Borst promised to take care of us."

Todd obviously told Mary about the conversation, because the next time she sat her chunky self in his guest chair, she wore a grin that balled her cheeks. She dove right into a question without referring to the incident, but Kent knew they had talked. Knew it like he knew both she and Todd were, spineless, Twinkie-eating propeller-heads.

During his second week back, Kent began leaving for lunch through the front lobby. Despite his aversion to doing so, he'd done it before so he would do it now. He walked nonchalantly, avoiding eye contact but responding to the occasional call of greeting with as much enthusiasm as he could stomach.

They were all there, like windup dolls, playing their parts. The tellers whispered about their fanciful relationships and counted the money. Zak the security guard paced and nodded and occasionally swung his stick like he'd learned from some Hollywood movie. Twice Kent saw Sidney Beech, the assistant vice president, clicking across the floor when he entered the lobby, and each time he pretended not to see her. Once he saw Porky—that would be Price Bentley—walk across the marble floor, and he immediately cut for the bathrooms. If the bank president saw him, he did not indicate so. Kent chose to believe he had not.

By the end of the second week, the routines had been reestablished and Kent's most recent altercations with the bank all but forgotten. Or so he hoped. Everything settled into a comfortable rhythm, just like the old days.

Or so they thought.

In reality, with the passing of each day, Kent's nerves wound tighter and tighter, like one of those spring-operated toys in the hands of an overeager child. At any moment the spring would break and he would snap, berserk.

But the plan was taking shape, like a beautiful woman walking out of the fog. Step by step, curves began to define themselves, and flesh took on form. The emerging image was Kent's link to sanity. It kept him from going mad during the long hours of pretending. It gave him a lover to fondle in the dark creases of his mind. It became . . . everything.

He was setting them up for one major backstab.

He was going to rob them blind.

CHAPTER EIGHTEEN

Week Nine

DAWN HAD come to Denver with a flare of red in the East. Bill Madison knew because he had watched the sun rise. From gray to red to just plain blue with a little smog thrown in to remind him where he lived.

Helen had called the previous evening and asked him to join her in the morning. They had talked twice on the phone since his last meeting with her, and each time Helen's words had rung in his mind for a good hour or two after the final click of the receiver. The prospect of seeing her again had brought a knot to his gut, but not a bad knot, he thought. More like the twisting you might expect just before the first big drop on a roller coaster.

"And why, precisely, am I joining you?" he'd asked good-naturedly.

"We've got some talking to do," she said. "Some walking and talking and praying. Bring your walking shoes. You won't be disappointed, Pastor." And he knew he wouldn't be. Although he doubted they would really be doing much walking. Not with her bad knees.

He stepped up to her porch at 6 A.M. feeling just a tad foolish with the tennis shoes on. Helen opened the door on his first ring and walked right past him and into the street without uttering a word.

Bill closed the door and scrambled after her. "Hold up, Helen. Good night! What's gotten into you?" He said it chuckling. If he didn't know her, he might guess she'd suddenly become a spring chicken by the way she moved her legs.

"Morning, Bill," she said. "Let's walk for a minute before we talk. I need to warm up."

"Sure."

That's what he said. *Sure.* As if this were just one more day in a long string of days in which they had climbed from bed in the dark to meet for an edge-of-dawn walk. But he wanted to ask her what on Earth she thought she was doing. Walking like some marathoner in a knee-length dress and socks hiked above her calves. It looked ridiculous. Which made him look ridiculous by association. And he had never seen her take such bold strides, certainly not without a noticeable limp

He shoved the thought from his mind and fell in. He was, after all, her pastor, and like she said, she needed shepherding. Although, at the moment, he was following more than shepherding. How could he be expected to feed the sheep if it was ten feet ahead of him?

Bill stumbled to catch up. Not a problem—she would begin to fade soon enough. Until then he would humor her.

They walked three blocks in silence before it began to occur to Bill that Miss Knee-Socks here was not fading. If there was any fading just now it was on his end of things. Too many hours behind the desk, too few in the gym.

"Where we going, Helen?" he asked.

"Oh, I don't know. We're just walking. Are you praying yet?"

"I didn't know I was supposed to be praying."

"I'm not sure you are. But as long as I am, you might as well."

"Uh-huh," he said. Her Reeboks were no longer shiny and white like they had been a week earlier. In fact, they were not the same pair because these were well worn and the other had been almost new. Her calf muscles, flexing with each step, were mostly hidden by a thin layer of fat that jiggled beneath the socks, which encircled her legs with red stripes just below her knees. She reminded him of a basketball player from the seventies—minus the height, of course.

Her fingers hung by her side, swinging easily with each stride.

"You ever wonder why God used a donkey to speak, Bill? Can you even imagine a donkey speaking?"

"I suppose. It is rather strange, isn't it?"

"How about a whale swallowing Jonah? Can you imagine a man living in a fish for three days? I mean, forget the story—could you imagine that happening today?"

He dropped his eyes to the sidewalk and studied the expansion cracks appearing beneath them every few feet. "Hmm. I suppose. You have a reason for asking?"

"I'm just trying to nail down your orientation, Bill. Your real beliefs. 'Cause lots of Christians read those old stories in the Bible and pretend to believe them, but when it gets right down to it, they can barely imagine them, much less believe they actually happened. And they certainly would balk at such events happening today, don't you think?"

She strode along at a healthy pace, and he found himself having to work a bit to match her. Heavens! What had gotten into her?

"Oh, I don't know, Helen. I think people are pretty accepting of God's ability to persuade a whale to swallow Jonah or make a donkey talk."

"You do, do you? So you can imagine it, then?"

"Sure."

"What does it look like, Bill?"

"What does what look like?"

"What does a whale swallowing a full-grown man whole look like? We're not talking about chomping him up and gulping down the pieces—we're talking swallowing him whole. And then that man swimming around in a stomach full of steaming acids for a few days. You can see that, Bill?"

"I'm not sure I've ever actually pictured the details. I'm not even sure it's important to picture the details."

"No? So then what happens when people start imagining these details? You tell them the details aren't important? Pretty soon they toss those stories into a massive mental bin labeled 'Things that don't really happen.'"

"Come on, Helen! You don't just jump from a few details being unimportant to throwing out the faith. There are elements of our heritage we accept by faith. This doesn't necessarily diminish our belief in God's ability to do what he will—including opening the belly of a whale for a man."

"And yet you balked when I told you about my vision of Gloria's death. That was a simple opening of the *eyes,* not some whale's mouth for a man."

"And I did come around, didn't I?"

"Yes. Yes, you did."

She let it go with a slight smile, and he wondered at the exchange. Helen walked on, swinging her arms in a steady rhythm, humming faintly now.

Jesus, Lover of My Soul . . . Her favorite hymn, evidently. "You do this every day, Helen?" he asked, knowing full well she did not. Something had changed here.

"Do what?"

"Walk? I've never known you to walk like this."

"Yes, well I picked it up recently."

"How far do you walk?"

She shrugged. "I don't know. How fast do you think we're walking?"

"Right now? Maybe three, four miles an hour."

She looked at him, surprised. "Really? Well then, what's three times eight?"

"What's eight?"

"No. What's three *times* eight?"

"Three times eight is twenty-four."

"Then I guess I walk twenty-four miles each day," Helen said and grinned satisfactorily.

Her words sounded misguided, like lost birds smashing into the windowpane of his mind, unable to gain access. "No, that's impossible. Maybe a mile a day. Or two."

"Oh, heavens! It's more than a mile or two, I know that much. Depends on how fast I'm walking, I suppose. But eight times three *is* twenty-four. You're right."

Her meaning caught up with Bill then. "You . . . you actually walk . . . eight hours?" Good heavens! that was impossible!

"Yes," she said.

He stopped dead in his tracks, his mouth gaping. "You walk *eight hours* a day like this?"

She answered without looking back. "Don't fall apart on me, Pastor. My walking is certainly easier to accept than Jonah and his whale."

Bill ran to catch up. "Helen! Slow down. Look, slow down for just a minute here. You're actually saying you walk like this for *eight hours* a day? That's over twenty miles a day! That's *impossible!*"

"Is it? Yes, it is, isn't it?"

He knew then that she was pulling no punches, and his head began to buzz. "How? How do you do it?"

"I don't, Bill. God does."

"You're saying that somehow God miraculously allows you to walk twenty miles a day on *your* legs?"

She turned and lifted an eyebrow. "I should hope I walk on my legs. I would hate to borrow yours for a day."

"That's not what I mean." He was not laughing. Bill looked at those calves again, bouncing like a stiff bowl of jelly with each step. Apart from the socks, they looked plain enough to him. And Helen was asserting that she was walking twenty-four miles a day on those damaged knees that, unless his memory had gone bad, just last week favored hobbling over walking. And now this?

"Do you doubt me?"

"No, I'm not saying I doubt you." He didn't know what he was saying. What he did know was that a hundred voices were crying foul in his mind. The voices from that bin labeled "Things that don't really happen," as Helen had put it.

"Then what are you saying?"

"I'm saying . . . Are you sure you walk a full eight hours?"

"Walk with me. We will see."

"I'm not sure I can walk eight hours."

"Well, then."

"Are you sure you don't take breaks . . ."

She lost it then, right on the sidewalk in front of Freddie's Milk Store on the corner of Kipling and Sixth. She pulled up suddenly and planted both hands on her hips. "Okay, look, mister. You're the man of God here! Your job is to lead me *to* him, not away from him. Now, forgive me if I'm wrong, but you're starting to sound as though you're not sure anymore. I'm walking, aren't I? And I've been walking for over a week—eight hours a day, three miles an hour. You don't like it, you can go ahead and put your blinders back on. Just make sure you look straight ahead when you see me coming."

He dropped his jaw at the outburst. Heat flared up his neck and burned behind his ears. It was at times like this that he should be prepared with a logical response. Problem was, this was not about the logical. This was about impossibilities, and he was staring one right in the face. Which made it a possibility. But in reality, he already knew that. His outer self was just throwing a fit, that's all.

"Helen . . ."

"Now, I also had some trouble with this at first, so I'm willing to cut you some slack. But when I give you simple facts, like *I walk eight hours a day,* I don't need you analyzing me like I'm loony tunes."

"I'm sorry, Helen. Really, I am. And for what it's worth, I believe you. It's just not every day this kind of thing happens." He immediately wondered if he did believe her. You don't just believe some old lady who claims to have found kryptonite and discovered that Superman was right all along—it does work! On the other hand, this was not just some old lady.

She studied him for a full five seconds without another word. Then she *humphed* and marched on deliberately.

Bill walked beside her in silence for a full minute, unnerved. A hundred questions coursed through his mind, but he thought it better to let things settle. Unless he had missed something here, Helen was claiming that God had empowered her with some kind of supernatural strength that allowed her to walk like a twenty-year-old. A strong twenty-year-old at that. And she was not just claiming it, she was showing him. She had insisted he come and see for himself. Well, he was seeing all right.

She strode by him, step for step, thrusting each foot out proudly like Moses strutting across the desert with cane in hand.

He glanced at her face and saw that her lips were moving. She was praying. Prayer walking. Like those mission teams that went overseas just to walk around a country and pray. Break the spiritual strongholds. Only in Helen's case, it was Kent who would presumably benefit.

This was happening. This was *really* happening! Never mind that he had never in his life even heard of, much less *seen,* such a thing, this was happening right before his eyes. Like a hundred Bible stories, but alive and well and here today.

Bill suddenly stopped on the sidewalk, aware that his mouth hung dumbly open. He closed it and swallowed.

Helen walked on, possibly not even aware he'd stopped. Her strides showed not a hint of weakness. It was as if her legs did their business beneath her without her full knowledge of why or how they operated. They just did. Her concern was praying for Kent, not understanding the physics of impossibilities. She was a walking miracle. Literally.

Doubt suddenly felt like a silly sentiment. How could you doubt what you saw?

Bill took after her again, his heart now surging with excitement. Goodness, how many men had seen something like *this?* And why was it so hard to accept? Why so far out? He was a pastor, for Pete's sake. She was right. It was his job to illuminate the truth, not doubt it.

He imagined his pews full of smiling church members. *And today, brothers and sisters, we want to remember sister Helen, who is marching around Jericho.*

His bones seemed to tingle. He skipped once to match stride with Helen, and she looked at him with a raised brow.

"You just pray while you're walking?" he asked, and then he immediately held out his hands in a defensive gesture. "I'm not doubting. I'm just asking."

She smiled and chuckled once. "Yes, I pray. I walk, and I pray."

"For Kent?"

"For this crazy duel over Kent's soul. I don't know all the whys and hows yet. I just know that Kent is running from God, and I'm walking behind him, breathing down his neck with my prayers. It's symbolic, I think. But sometimes I'm not even sure about that. Walk by faith, not by sight. Walk in the Spirit. They that wait upon the Lord shall renew their strength; they shall walk and not grow weary. It wasn't literal back then, but now it is. At least it is with me."

"Which suggests that the whole business about Kent is real as well, because now it's not just visions and things in the head but this walking," Bill said. "Do you know how unusual that is?"

"I'm not so sure it's unusual at all. I just think I'm unusual—you said so yourself. Maybe it takes a bit of unusualness for God to work the way he wants to work. And for your information, I knew it was real before this walking thing. I'm sorry to hear that you thought my visions were delusional."

"Now come on, Helen. Did I say that?" He frowned and turned sideways so she could see his expression.

"You didn't need to." She set her jaw and strode on.

"Can I touch them?" he asked.

She scrunched her brow. "Touch what? My legs? No, you can't touch my legs! Heavens, Bill!"

"Not *touch* touch them! Goodness!" He walked on, slightly embarrassed. "Are they warm or anything. I mean, can you feel anything different in them?"

"They buzz."

"Buzz, huh?" He looked at them again, wondering how God altered physics to allow for something like this. They should bring some scientists out here to prove a few things. But he knew she would never allow that.

"What do you mean by *duel?* You said this was about a crazy duel over Kent's soul. That's not exactly out of the textbooks."

"Sure it is. The books may use different words, but it all boils down to the same thing. It is war, Bill. We do not wage war against flesh and blood but against principalities and powers. We duel. And what greater prize than a man's soul?" She faced forward deliberately. "It's all there. Look it up."

Bill chuckled and shook his head. "I will. Just for you, Helen. Someone's got to make sure you don't walk right off the planet."

"So that's your idea of shepherding?" Her eyes twinkled above a smile.

"You asked for it. Like you said, it's my gift. And if God can transform your legs into bionic walkers, the least he can do for me is give me a little wisdom. To help you walk."

"That's right. Just make sure the wisdom is not your own, Pastor."

"I'll try. This is just incredible!"

"You should go back now, Bill." Helen strode forward, down the sidewalk, right down Kipling. "I've got some praying to do. Besides, we don't want to get you stranded out here, now, do we?"

"I shouldn't walk and pray with you?"

"Has God told you to walk and pray with me?"

"No."

"Then go be a pastor."

"Okay. Okay, I'll do that." Bill turned, feeling as though he should say something brilliant—something commemorative. But nothing came to mind, so he just turned and retraced his steps.

THEY SAY that a split personality develops over years of dissociative behavior. Like a railroad track encountering large, gnarly roots that slowly but inevitably heave it up and split it into two wandering rails. But the development of Kent's double life was not such a gradual thing. It was more like two high-speed locomotives thundering in opposite directions with a rope tied to the tail end of each. Kent's mind was stretched there in that high-tension rope.

The persona he presented at the bank returned him to the appearance of normalcy. But during the hours on his own, away from the puppets at work, he was slipping into a new skin. Becoming a new man altogether.

The dreams strung through his mind every night, whispering their tales of brilliance, like some kind of alter ego who'd done this a thousand times and now mentored the child prodigy. *What of the body, Kent? Bodies are evidence. You realize that they will discover the cause of death once they examine that body. And you do need the body—you can't just sink it to the bottom of a lake like they do in idiotic movies, Kent. You're no idiot, Kent.*

Kent listened to the dreams, wide eyed and fast asleep.

He ingested a steady diet of ibuprofen for the pain that had latched on to his neck. And he began to settle himself with the occasional nightcap. Only they were not so occasional after the third day. They were nightly. And they were not just nightcaps. They were shots of tequila. His taste for the juice that had nearly killed him in college came back like a soothing drug. Not enough to push him into oblivion, of course. Just enough to calm his ragged edges.

When he wasn't at work, Kent was either poring over research or thinking. A lot of thinking. Mulling the same detail over in his mind a hundred times. Thinking of every possible angle and searching for any loophole he had not considered.

The Discovery Channel had a daily show called *Forensics.* A downtown library had seen fit to catalog fifty consecutive episodes. It was a show detailing actual cases in which the FBI slowly but methodically honed in on criminals using the very latest technology in forensics. Fingerprints, bootprints, hair samples, phone records, perfume, you name it. If a person had been in a room, the FBI experts could almost always find traces.

Almost always. Kent watched the shows unblinking, his analytical mind tracking all of their weaknesses. And then he would reconsider the smallest details of his plan.

For example. He had already determined that he would have to execute the theft *at* the bank—inside the building. Which meant he would have to get *to* the bank. Question: How? He couldn't very well have a cab drop him off. Cabs kept records, and any break from routine might lead to a raised eyebrow. He had to keep those eyebrows down. So he should drive his car, of course, the way he always got to the bank. Yes, possibly. On the other hand, cars represented physical evidence. They left tracks. They could be seen by passersby or vagrants, like that one he'd seen in the back alley. Then again, did it matter? What would he do with the car afterward? Drive it away? No, he definitely could not drive off. Cars could be tracked. Torch it? Now, there was a thought. He could leave a five-gallon container of gasoline in the trunk, as if it were meant for the lawn mower at home, and rig a loose wire to detonate the fuel. *Boom!* That was ridiculous, of course. Even a beat cop would suspect the torching of a car. Maybe send it over a cliff with a full tank. Watch it burst into flames on the rocks. Of course, cars rarely actually exploded on impact.

Then again, why rid himself of the car at all?

The car detail consumed hours of drifting thought over the days. And it was the least of his challenges. But slowly, hour by hour, the solutions presented themselves to him. And when they did, when he had tested them in his mind and stripped them of ambiguity, Kent found something he never would have suspected at such discoveries. He found exhilaration. Bone-trembling euphoria. The kind of feeling that makes you squeeze your fists and grit your teeth to keep from exploding. He would pump the air with his right arm, the way he had done not so long before, with Gloria and Spencer giggling at his exuberance over the completion of AFPS.

Without exception, these occasions called for a shot of tequila.

Rarely did he stop long enough to consider the madness of his plan. He had grown obsessed. The whole thing, stealing such an enormous sum of money and then vanishing—starting over—was laced with insanity. Who had ever done such a thing? In a line of a hundred thousand children, it would not be *him* but the one whose mother had mainlined heroin throughout her pregnancy who would be most likely to one day attempt such a feat.

Or the man who had lost his wife, his son, and his fortune in the space of a month.

No, it was more, he thought. It was his savage thirst for what was due him. For a life. For revenge. But more than those things. As a simple matter of fact, there was nothing else that made sense any longer. The alternative of trudging along a new career path on his own sat like lead in his gut. In the end it was this thought that compelled him to throw back the last mouthful of tequila and discard any reservation.

Through it all, Kent maintained a plastic, white-collar grin at the bank, ignoring the knots of anxiety twisting through his gut and the anticipation bursting in his chest. Fortunately, he had never been one to sweat much. A nervous sweater in Kent's current state would walk through the days dripping on the carpet and changing identical shirts every half-hour in a futile attempt to appear relaxed and casual.

Helen, his religious whacko mother-in-law, saw fit in her eternal wisdom to leave him alone those first two weeks. Which was a small miracle in itself. Helen's God had performed his first miracle. She did call Kent once, asking if she could borrow some of Gloria's old tennis shoes. Seemed she had taken to exercise and didn't see the need to buy a brand-new pair of Reeboks for sixty bucks when Gloria's were just growing mold in the closet. Why she wanted all four pair, Kent had no clue. He just grunted agreement and told her to come by the next day. They would be on the front porch. When he returned from work, they were gone.

Happy walking, Helen. And if you don't mind, you may walk right off a cliff.

KENT FOUND his way past the confusion surrounding Lacy Cartwright on a Thursday night fifteen days after their strange meeting, almost three weeks after his decision to rob the bank.

It came at midnight during one of those exhilarating moments just after a key to the entire theft had erupted in his mind like a flare. He thought of Lacy, possibly because the solution igniting his mind's horizon brought his focus to the future. Post-theft. His new life. Not that Lacy would fit into any new life, heavens no. Still, once her image presented itself, he could not shake it free.

He dialed her listed number with an unsteady hand and sat back.

Lacy answered on the fifth ring, just as he was pulling the receiver from his ear. "Hello?"

"Lacy?"

"Who is this?" She was not sounding too pleased about being called at midnight by a stranger.

"Kent. I'm sorry. Is it too late?"

"Kent?" Her voice softened immediately. "No. I was just going to bed. Are you okay?"

"I'm fine. I just thought . . . I just needed someone to talk to." He paused, but she remained silent.

"Listen to me. Sounds stupid, I know—"

"Lighten up, Kent. I've been there, remember? You're no more *fine* than I am a porcupine."

He leaned back against the cushions on the sofa and cradled the cordless phone on his neck. "Actually, things are good. Surprisingly good. I've got no one in the world to talk to, but apart from that rather insignificant detail, I would say that I'm recuperating."

"Hmm. How long has it been?" Her voice sounded sweet and soft over the receiver.

"Couple months." Had he told her about Spencer? Suddenly it was a lump rising in his throat instead of a hard-beating heart. "My son was killed in a hit-and-run four weeks ago." He swallowed.

"Oh, Kent! I'm so sorry. That's terrible!" Her voice trembled with shock, and Kent blinked at that. She was right. It was terrible—mind numbing, really. And he was already forgetting the tragedy of it all. So quickly. That made him what? A monster? "How old was your son?"

"Ten." Maybe this was not such a good idea. She was bringing things back into clear focus.

"Kent, I'm . . . I'm so sorry."

"Yeah." His voice sounded unsteady—choked with emotion. Two thoughts slinked through his mind. The first was that this emotion was redemptive—he did care after all; he was not a monster. The second was that the emotion was actually more self-pity than mourning over loss—lamenting the notion that he was indeed a monster.

"I don't know what to say, Kent. I . . . I think I know how it feels. Have you had any counseling?"

"A therapist? No. But I have a mother-in-law, if that counts."

She chuckled nervously. "What about a pastor?"

"Religious counsel? There was plenty of that to go around at the funeral, believe me. Enough for a few hundred years, I would say." What if she was religious? "But no, not really."

The phone rested silently against his cheek. "Anyway," he continued. "Maybe we could talk sometime."

"We're talking now, Kent."

The comment caught him off guard. "Yes. We are." He felt out of control. She was stronger than he remembered. Maybe the comment about religious counsel had been misplaced.

"But we can talk more whenever you're ready," she said. "I couldn't very well turn down an old friend in need, now, could I?" Her voice was soft again. "Really, call me whenever you want to talk. I know the value of talking things through."

He waited a moment before replying. "Thank you, Lacy. I think I would like that."

They talked for another half-hour, mostly about incidentals—catching up stuff. When Kent hung up, he knew he would call again. Maybe the next day. She was right: Talking was important, and he had some things he wanted to talk about.

chapter nineteen

Week Ten

THE FIRST real bump in the road came the following Monday.

Kent sat hunched over a tiny table in the coffee lounge in Barnes and Noble Booksellers after leaving work early to run some "errands"—an activity he knew would quickly outlive its plausibility as a valid excuse for leaving the bank. After all, how many errands could a single man without a life run?

He'd scoured the shelves, found two books, and wanted to make certain they contained the data he was after before making the purchase. *The Vanishing Act* lay at an angle on the green-tiled tabletop before him. The other book, *Postmortem Forensics,* rested open between his hands, spread to a chapter on skeletal remains.

Within five minutes he knew the books were perfect. But he decided to read just a little further in one particular chapter. Like another article he'd gleaned off the Internet suggested, the editor here was confirming that a gunshot wound would not bleed after death. If the pump wasn't pumping—if the heart wasn't beating—the blood would not flow. But he already knew that. It was this bit about the effects of high heat to flesh and skeletal remains that had Kent's heart suddenly drumming steadily.

He flipped the page. Human flesh was rather unpredictable, sometimes flaming to a crisp and other times extinguishing itself midburn. Various accelerants assisted the burning of flesh, but most left a residue easily detected in postmortem forensics. Gasoline, for example, left a detectable residue, as did all petroleum products.

Kent scanned quickly down the page, tense now. What then? If he could be certain of the flesh burning . . . A sentence jumped out at him. "Magnesium is sometimes used by mortuaries to—"

"Excuse me, sir."

The voice startled Kent, and he snapped the book shut. A middle-aged man sat across from him, smiling past wire-framed glasses. His black hair was swept back neatly, glistening atop a small, pointy head. A pinhead. He was dressed not unlike Kent himself: tailored black suit, crisp white shirt, red tie held snugly by a gold tie bar.

But what had Kent's pulse spiking was the fact that the stranger now sat down at Kent's table, elbows down and smiling like he had been here first. That and the man's piercing green eyes. Like snowboarder Cliff's eyes. He sat, stunned, finding no words.

"Hello." The stranger grinned big. His voice seemed to echo low and softly, as if he'd spoken into a drum. "I couldn't help noticing that book. *Postmortem Forensics,* huh? Is that the kind of book that tells you how to carve someone up without getting caught?" He chuckled. Kent did not.

The man calmed himself. "Sorry. Actually, I've always been rather interested in what happens after death. You mind if I look at the book? I might want a copy myself." The man stretched out a big tanned hand.

Kent hesitated, taken back by the man's audacity. He held out the book. Was it possible this man was an agent, somehow on to him? *Relax, Kent. The crime is nowhere but in your mind. He fixed his jaw and said nothing, hoping the man would catch his disinterest.*

The stranger scanned through the book and stopped dead center. He flipped the book around and showed a centerfold of a spread-eagle corpse. "Now where do you suppose this man is?" he asked.

"He's dead," Kent answered, "in a grave somewhere."

"You think?" The man's eyebrow arched. "You think your son is in a grave somewhere as well, then?"

Kent blinked and stared at the man hard. "My son?" Now he was growing angry. "What do you know of my son?"

"I know that he was struck by a car a month ago. He say anything to you before he died? Something that morning before you left, perhaps?"

"Why?" Kent demanded. Then it hit him. "Are you a cop? Is this part of the investigation of my son's death?"

"In a matter of speaking, yes. Let's just say we are reviewing the implications of your son's death. I understand you were angry when you left him."

Linda! They had interviewed the baby-sitter. "I wouldn't say angry, no. Look, mister. I loved my boy more than you'll ever know. We had a disagreement, sure. But that's it." What was going on here? Kent felt his chest tighten. What was the man insinuating?

"Disagreement? Over what?"

The man's eyes stared like two green marbles with holes punched in them, dead center. It occurred to Kent that the eyes were not blinking. He blinked and wondered if the man had blinked in that split second while his own eyes flicked shut. But they did not look as if they'd blinked. They just stared, round and wet. Unless wet meant that he had indeed blinked, in which case maybe the man had blinked. If so, he was timing it pretty good.

The agent cleared his throat and repeated himself. "What was your disagreement over, Kent?"

"Why? Actually we really didn't have a disagreement. We just talked."

"Just talked, huh? So you felt pretty comfortable leaving him in the doorway like that?"

Kent flashed back. "How I felt is none of your business. I may have felt like throwing up, for all you should care. Maybe I'd just ingested a rotten apple and felt like puking on the street. Does that make me a murderer?"

The man smiled gently. His eyes were still not blinking. "Nobody called you a murderer, Kent. We just want to help you see some things."

"Do you mind if I see your credentials? What agency are you with, anyway?"

The man casually reached for his pocket. He found a wallet in his breast pocket and pulled it out.

Kent did not know where the man was headed. Didn't even know what he meant by what he'd said. He *was* aware, however, of the heat snaking up his neck and spreading over his skull. How dare this man sit here and question his motives? He had loved Spencer more than he loved life itself!

"Listen, sir, I don't know who you are, but I would die for my boy, you hear?" He didn't intend for it to come out trembly, but it did. Suddenly tears blurred his vision, but he stumbled forward. "I would lay down my life for that boy in a heartbeat, and I don't appreciate anybody questioning my love! You got that?"

The stranger pulled a card from his wallet and handed it to Kent without moving his eyes. He didn't seem affected by these emotions. "That's good, Kent."

Kent dropped his eyes to the card: "Jeremy Lawson, Seventh Precinct," it read in a gold foil. He looked up. The agent's wire glasses rode neatly on his nose above a smug smile.

"I'm just doing my job, you realize. Now, if you'd rather, I can haul you in and make this formal. Or you can answer a few questions here without coming apart at the seams on me." He shrugged. "Either way."

"No, here's just fine. But you just leave my son out of this. It takes a real sicko to even imagine that I had anything to do with his death." He trembled saying it, and for a moment he considered standing and leaving the cop.

"Fair enough, Kent. And to be straight with you, I believe that you did love your son." He offered no more but sat there, smiling at Kent, unblinking. And then he did blink, just once. Like camera shutters, snapping a shot.

"Then that's that," Kent said. "If you've done your homework, you'll know that I've been through enough these last few months as it is. So if you're finished, I really need to get back to work."

"Well, now, that's just it, Kent. Seems to me there just might be more here than meets the eye."

Kent flushed. "Meaning what?"

"Have you talked to anyone else about this?"

"Talked to anyone else about *what?*"

The agent grinned knowingly and licked his forefinger. He turned the page to the book and glanced at its contents. "Just answer the question, Kent. Have you talked to anyone else? A stranger, perhaps."

Kent felt his hands tremble, and he removed them from the table. "Look. You're speaking a foreign language here. Do you know what I'm saying? I don't have the slightest idea what you mean by any of this. You come in here harangu-ing me about my son—practically accuse me of killing him—and now you want to know if I've talked to any strangers lately? What on Earth does this have to do with me?"

The cop may very well have not even heard him by his response. "A vagrant, say. Or a homeless man in an alley? You haven't talked to anyone like that recently?"

The man pried his eyes from the book and stared at him, that ear-to-ear grin still splitting his jaw. Kent squinted, sincerely wondering if Mr. Cop here hadn't slipped over the edge. His own fear that this bizarre exchange led any-where significant melted slightly. What could a vagrant possible have anything to do with . . . ?

Then it hit him, and he stiffened. The cop noticed, because his right eyebrow immediately arched curiously.

"Yes?"

The vagrant in the alley! They had talked to the spineless vagrant!

But that was impossible! That had been his mind playing with images!

"No," Kent said. "No, I haven't talked to any vagrant." Which was true enough. You did not actually talk in your dreams. Then again he *had* seen the vagrant in the alley prior to the dream, hadn't he? The man's summary of life whispered through Kent's mind. *Life sucksssss . . .* But he hadn't actually talked to that vagrant either.

"Why don't you ask me if I've had wine and cheese with the president's wife lately? I can answer that for you, as well."

"I think you did talk to a stranger in an alley, Kent. And I think he may have told you a few things. I want to know what he told you. That's all."

"Well, you're wrong. What? Some fool said he told me a few things, and that makes me a suspect in the crime of the century?" Kent almost choked on those last few words. *Control yourself, man!*

"Crime of the century? I didn't say anything about a crime, my friend."

"It was a figure of speech. The point is, you are groping for threads that simply do not exist. You are badgering me with questions about events that have nothing at all to do with me. I lost my wife and my son in the last few months. This does not automatically place me at the top of some most-wanted list, am I right? So then, unless you have questions that actually make sense, you should leave."

The man's smile left him. He blinked again. For a few seconds the agent held him in a thoughtful stare, as if that last volley had done the trick—shown Pinhead here who he was really up against.

"You are a bright one. I'll give you that. But we know more than you realize, Kent."

Kent shook his head. "Not possible. Unless you know more than I do about me, which is rather absurd, isn't it?"

The man smiled again. He shifted his seat back, preparing to leave. Thank goodness.

He dipped his head politely and offered Kent one last morsel to chew on. "I want you to consider something, Kent. I want you to remember that eventually everything will be found out. You are indeed a brilliant man, but we are not so slow ourselves. Watch your back. Be careful whose advice you take."

With that, the agent stood and strode away. He put his hands deep into his pockets, rounded a bookcase ten yards away, and vanished.

Kent sat for a long time, calming his heart, trying to make sense of the exchange. The man's words nagged him like a burrowed tick, digging at his skull. An image of the man, sitting there with his slicked hair and cheesy grin, swallowed his mind.

Ten minutes later he left the bookstore without buying the books he'd come for.

CHAPTER TWENTY

KENT SAT in the big tan leather lounger facing the tube Monday night taking stock of things. The Forty Niners led the Broncos sixteen to ten, and Denver had the ball at the fifty yard line, but Kent barely knew it. The roar of the crowd provided little more than background static for the images roaring through his mind.

He was taking stock of things. Getting right down in the face of the facts and drawing conclusions that would stay with him until he croaked.

At least that's how his self-analysis session had started out, back when Denver led six to three. Back before he had gotten started early on his nightcap. Actually he had dispensed with the nightcap routine at the first quarter whistle and settled for the bottle instead. No use kidding around. These were serious matters here.

At the top of his list of deliberations was that cop who had interrupted his reading at Barnes and Noble. The pinhead was on the case. Granted, not *the* case, but the man was onto *him,* and he was the case. Kent took a nip of liquor. Tequila gold. It burned going down, and he sucked at his teeth.

Now what exactly did that mean, *on the case?* It meant that Kent would be a fool to go through with any robbery attempt while Detective Pinhead was around. That's what it meant. Kent took another small taste from the bottle in his hand. A roar blared through the room; someone had scored.

But then, how could anyone know anything about anything other than what had already happened? Not a soul could possibly know about his plans—he'd told no one. He had started the fine-tuning of ROOSTER, but no one else had access to the program. Certainly not some pinhead cop who probably didn't know computer code from alphabet soup.

"We know more than you think we do, Kent."

"We do? And who's we? Well I think you're wrong, Pinhead. I think you know zero.

And if you know ten times that much it's still a big fat whoppin' goose egg, isn't it?"

The simple fact was, unless Pinhead could read his mind or was employing some psychic who could read minds, he knew nothing about the planned robbery. He was bluffing. But why? Why would the cop even suspect enough to merit a bluff? Regardless of why or how, the notion of continuing, considering this latest development, rang of madness. Like a resounding gong. *Bong, bong, bong! Stupid, stupid, stupid! Get your butt back to Stupid Street, fool.*

But he could plan. And he should plan, because who was to say that Pinhead would hang around? For that matter, even with the man on the case, Kent's plan was foolproof, wasn't it? What difference would an investigation make? And there *would* be an investigation, regardless. Oh yeah, there would be one heck of an investigation, all right. You don't just kill someone and expect a round of applause. But that was just it. There would be an investigation, no matter what he did. Pinhead or no pinhead. So it really made no difference whether the cop stayed on the case or not.

An episode of *Forensics* Kent had watched on Saturday replayed through his mind. It featured a case in which some idiot had plotted the perfect murder but had one problem. He'd killed the wrong man. In the end he had attempted the murder again, this time on the right person. He had failed. He was rotting in some prison now.

That was the problem with having the cops already breathing down your neck; they would be more likely to stumble onto some misplaced tidbit that nailed you. To be done right, most crimes had to come out of the blue. Certainly not under the watchful nose of some pinhead who was stalking you.

But this was not most crimes. This was *the* perfect crime. The one all the shows could not showcase because no one knew it had even occurred.

Kent lifted the bottle and noted that it was half empty.

And the cop was not the only one breathing down his neck. Cliff, the mighty snowboarder-turned-programmer, was annoying Kent with his intrusive style of *Let's check your code, Kent.* What if Boy Wonder actually stumbled onto ROOSTER? It would be the end, of course. The whole plan rested squarely on the shoulders of ROOSTER's secrecy. If the security program was discovered, the plot would blow up. And if anybody could find it, Cliff could. Not as a result of his brilliance as much as his dogged tenacity. There was a single link buried in AFPS that led to ROOSTER: an extra "m" in the word "extremmely," itself buried in a routine not yet active. If the "m" were deleted by some spelling-bee wizard intent on setting things straight, the link automatically shifted to the second "e" in the same word. Only someone with way too much time on their hands could possibly uncover the hook.

Someone like Cliff.

Kent went for a chug on the bottle and closed his eyes to the throat burn. The game was in its second half. He'd missed the big showdown at the end of the first. Didn't matter.

"Be real," he mumbled. "Nobody's gonna find no link. No way this side of Hades."

And he knew he was right.

An image of Lacy drifted through the fog in his mind. Now, *there* was a solution to this whole mess. He could discuss the fine points of committing a federal felony with Lacy. Cut her in. An anemic little chuckle escaped his lips at the thought. It sounded more like the burp that followed it.

Fact was, even if he wanted a relationship with a woman, it was simply not feasible. Not with mistress ROOSTER in his life. It wasn't that they wouldn't both share him. It was that they *couldn't.* Assuming they wanted to. Which was yet one more problem: He was thinking of ROOSTER as if it were a real person that possessed a will worth considering. ROOSTER was a link, for heaven's sake! A plan. A program.

Either way, he still could not cohabit with both ROOSTER and any living soul. Period. ROOSTER demanded it. The plan would fall apart.

So then, what on earth did he think he was doing with Lacy?

Good question. He should cut her off.

Cut her off from what? It wasn't as if he had a relationship with her. One freak roadside encounter with a stranger and a phone call hardly made a relationship.

On the other hand, Lacy was no stranger. She stood there by her car in Kent's mind, like a ghost stepping from the pages of his past.

Still, he had no desire for a relationship that could be characterized as anything but platonic. There was Gloria to think of—in the dirt nearly three months. That long? Goodness. And mistress ROOSTER.

Get a grip, Kent. You're losing it.

He lifted the bottle, sipped at the burning liquid, and scratched his chin. Sweat wet the skin beneath two days of stubble. He looked at his shirt. It was the same Super Bowl T-shirt he'd slept in for a week. Not a problem. Now that he was doing his own laundry, changing clothes had lost its appeal. Except for underwear, of course. But he could just throw the underwear in the machine once every other week and stuff them in a drawer without all the folding and sorting mess. Which reminded him; he needed another dozen. The machine could easily hold a month's worth. Once a month was clearly better than once every two weeks.

Kent looked at the tube. The game was nearing an end. Outside, the night was pitch black. He licked the bottle and thought about Pinhead again. A needle of anxiety pricked his skin. It was madness. *When you're ready, just call me,* she'd said in the voice echoing from the past. Lacy.

He made the decision then, impulsively, with two minutes to play and the Broncos now leading twenty-one to nineteen.

He climbed out of the lounger and picked up the phone, his heart suddenly stomping through his chest. Which was absurd because he certainly had no emotions for Lacy that would set off its pounding. Except that he did want to see her. That much he could not deny. The realization only added energy to his heart's antics as he dialed her number.

LACY HAD just slipped on her bathrobe when the phone began its ringing. The caller ID showed only that the call was "out of area," and she decided to pick it up on the remote chance it was a call she actually wanted to take.

"Hello."

"Hello. Lacy?"

Kent! Her heart leapt. She would know that voice anywhere.

"Yes?"

"Hi, Lacy. Is it too late?"

"And you are . . . ?"

"Oh, I'm sorry. It's Kent. Geez, I'm sorry. Pretty stupid, huh? Call up and ask if it's too late without introducing myself. I didn't mean to sound . . ."

"What do you want, Kent?"

The phone returned only silence for a few moments. Now why had she come off so curt? And why was her breathing tight? *God, help me.*

"Maybe I should call back at a better time," Kent said.

"No. No, I'm sorry. You just took me by surprise. It's only ten. You're fine."

He chuckled on the phone, and she thought he sounded like a boy. "Actually, I was wondering if I could talk to you," he said.

"Sure. Go ahead." Lacy settled onto a chair by the dinette.

"I mean come up there and talk to you."

Now her pulse spiked. "Up here? When?"

"Well . . . tonight."

Lacy rose to her feet. "Tonight!? You want to come up here tonight?"

"I know it's a bit late, but I really need someone to talk to right now."

It was her turn to freeze in silence.

"Lacy?"

What was she to say to this? *Come on up, Lover Boy.*

His voice came again, softer. "Okay, well, maybe it's not such a good idea . . ."

"No, it's okay." It was? It was nothing of the kind.

"You sure? Maybe we could meet at the Village Inn."

"Sure."

"In an hour?"

The sum of this matter began to spread through Lacy's mind like icy waters. Kent was coming to Boulder tonight. He wanted to talk to her.

"Sure," she said.

"Good. I'll see you in an hour, then."

"Sure."

Silence filled the receiver again, and Lacy suddenly felt like a high school girl being asked out by the captain of the football team. "So, what do you want to talk about?" she asked. It struck her that the question was at once both perfectly legitimate and absurd. On one hand, their relationship should remain strictly platonic, for obvious reasons. Reasons that droned through her head like World War II bombers threatening to unload at the first sign of flak. Reasons like, this man had dropped her once before and if it had hurt then, it might kill her now. Reasons like, he had just lost his wife. He was no doubt rebounding like the world's tightest-wound super-ball.

On the other hand, since when did reasoning direct the heart?

"Nothing," he said.

It was the wrong answer, she thought. Because in matters of the heart, "nothing" was much more than "something."

"Okay, I'll see you there," she said and hung up the phone with a trembling hand.

IT TOOK Lacy forty-five of the sixty minutes to prepare herself, which was in itself nonsense because other than changing clothes she had not yet *unprepared* herself from the day's preparedness, which had taken her less than fifteen minutes just this morning. Nevertheless, it took her forty-five, due in part to the fact that the blouse she thought would best suit the occasion needed ironing. Not that this was an occasion as such.

Kent was there, at the Village Inn, sitting in a corner booth nursing a cup of coffee when she arrived. He glanced up as she slid onto the bench opposite him. His eyes brightened, which was a good thing because they appeared a bit red and blurry, as if he'd been crying in the last hour. His breath smelled strongly of mints.

"Hi, Kent."

He smiled wide and extended a hand. "Hi."

She took it hesitantly. Goodness. What was he thinking? This was not a business deal that required a handshake.

Looking at him now under the lights Lacy saw that Kent had seen some abuse lately. Dark circles cupped his eyes, which were indeed rather lethargic looking. The lines defining his smile seemed to have deepened. His hair was as blond as it had been the day he'd told her to take a hike years ago, but now it was disheveled. It was Monday—surely he had not gone to work like this. Something had been pummeling him, she thought, but then she already knew that. He had walked through the valley of death. You always got pummeled in the valley of death.

They sipped at their coffees and talked small talk for half an hour—the weather, the new stadium, the Broncos—all in all, things that neither seemed to have any interest in. Without going into their past, they really didn't have much to talk about. But it hardly mattered; just sitting there across from each other after so many years held its own power, however awkward or halting it might be.

The thought of revisiting their past brought an edginess to her heart. They could always talk about death, of course. It was their common bridge now. Death. But Kent was not thinking death. Something else was running around behind those eyes.

"I met a cop today," he said out of the blue, staring at his coffee.

"A cop?"

"Yeah. I was just sitting there in the bookstore, and this cop sits down and starts giving me the third degree about Spencer. About my boy, Spencer." His face drifted into a snarl as he talked. He looked up, and his eyes were flashing. "Can you believe the audacity of that? I mean—" He glanced out the window and lifted a hand helplessly. "I was just sitting there, minding my own business, and this pinhead cop starts accusing me."

"Accusing you of what?"

"I don't even know. That was just it. He goes on as if I had something to do with . . ." He stopped and swallowed, his Adam's apple bobbing against the emotion boiling through his chest. "With Spencer's death," he finished.

"Come on, Kent! That's absurd!"

"I know. It *is* absurd. Then he just went on, as if he knew things, you know."

"What things?"

"I don't know." He was shaking his head. The poor man sat there like someone strung together by a few brittle strands of flesh. Surely he could not have had anything to do with his own son's death! Could he? Of course not!

"It was like a scene out of *The Twilight Zone.*"

"Well, I'm sure you have nothing to worry about. The authorities do things like that as a matter of routine. It's ridiculous. You'll never hear from the man again."

"And maybe you're wrong," he said. She blinked at his tone. "Maybe I have plenty to worry about. The last thing I need is some pinhead with a badge poking his greasy head into my life! I swear I could tear his head off!"

She stared at him, unsure how to respond. "Maybe you need to lighten up, Kent. You've got nothing to hide, right? Don't let it get to you."

"Yeah, easy for you to say. It's not your neck he's breathing down."

Now she felt her face flush. "And it's not yours, either. The police are just doing their job. They should be the least of your concerns. And just in case you're confused here, I'm not one of them. I work at a bank, remember?"

Kent looked at the ceiling and sighed. "I'm sorry. You're right." He collected himself, nodding as if slowly coming to agreement. Then he closed his eyes and shook his head, gritting his teeth in frustration.

Yes indeed, he had been pummeled lately. She wondered what had really happened to bring him to this strange state.

He was smiling at her, his blue eyes suddenly soft and bright at once, like she remembered them from their previous life. "You're right, Lacy. You see, that's what I needed to hear. You always did have a way with the simple truth, you know."

She gulped and hoped immediately that he had not noticed. It was not his words but the way he had said them that bothered her, as if at that moment he was dripping with admiration for her.

She chuckled nervously. "If I remember correctly, you were never too stupid yourself."

"Well, we had our times, didn't we?"

She had to look away this time. An image of Kent leaning over her as they lay under the great cottonwood behind her dormitory filled her mind. "I love you," he was whispering, and then he touched her lips with his own. She wanted to shake the image from her head, force her heart back to its normal rhythm, but she could only sit there, pretending nothing at all was happening in her chest.

"Yes, we did," she said.

Tension hung in the air as if someone had thrown a switch somewhere and filled the room with a thick cloud of charged particles. Lacy could feel his eyes on her cheek, and she finally turned to face him. She gave him a controlled grin. This was madness! He had lost his sensibilities! Two minutes ago he was ranting about some cop and how he would like to tear the poor fellow's head off, and now he was staring at her like some honeymooner.

Death does that to people, Lacy, she reasoned quickly. *It makes them lose their sensibilities. And you're reading way too much into that look. It's not as bad as it looks.*

And then bad went to terrible. Because then Lacy felt heat swallow her face despite her best efforts to stop it. Yes indeed, she was blushing. As red as a cooked lobster. And he could see it all. She knew that because he too was suddenly blushing.

Panic flashed through her mind, and she impulsively considered fleeing. Of course that would be about as sensible as Kent's tearing a cop's head off. Instead, she did the only thing she *could* do. She smiled. And that just made it worse, she thought.

"It's good to see you again, Lacy." He shook his head, diverted his eyes. "I kept telling myself that the last thing I needed was a relationship so soon after Gloria's death. It hasn't even been three months, you know. But I realize now that I was wrong. I think I do need a relationship. A good friendship, without all the baggage that comes with romance. No strings, you know. And I see now that you can give me that friendship."

He faced her. "Don't you think?"

To be honest, she didn't know what to think. Her head was still buzzing from that last heat wave. Was he saying he wanted nothing but a platonic relationship? Yes, and that was good. Wasn't it?

"Yes. It took me six months to get over John. Not *over,* over, of course. I don't think you ever get *over,* over. But to a point where I could see clearly. Some are faster healers. They're back on their feet in three or four months; some take a year. But all of us need someone to stand by. I don't think I could have made it if I hadn't found God."

If he had been eating a cherry tomato, he might have choked on it at the comment. He coughed.

She ignored him. "Ultimately his is the only relationship that brings peace. I guess sometimes it takes a death to understand that." Kent's eyes were following the rim of his coffee cup. "But, yes, Kent. You're right. It is good to have a friendship that is completely unpretentious."

He nodded.

They talked for another hour, telling for the first time their own stories of loss. Lacy's mind kept wandering back to that heat wave that had fallen over them, but in the end she settled herself with the reasoning that these things happened to people who had walked through the valley. They lost their sensibilities at times.

By the time they shook hands and bid each other a good night, the clock's fat hand was past the midnight hour. By the time Lacy finally fell asleep, it was nudging the second morning hour. Surely it was well after Kent had arrived home and fallen comfortably asleep in his big, empty house, she thought.

She was wrong.

CHAPTER TWENTY-ONE

HELEN JOVIC lived roughly eight miles from Kent's Littleton suburban neighborhood. Depending on traffic the crosstown jaunt took anywhere between fifteen and twenty minutes in her old yellow Pinto. But today she wasn't in the Pinto. Today she was on Reeboks, and the walk stretched into a three-hour ordeal.

It was the first time her walking actually took her anywhere. The minute she'd stepped off her porch, with the sun starting to splash against the Rockies, she'd felt an urge to walk west. Just west. So she'd walked west for over an hour before realizing that Kent's house lay directly in her path.

The silent urge arose in her gut like steel drawn to a powerful magnet. If Pastor Madison had been correct, she figured her normal pace carried her along at an easy three miles per hour. But now she pushed it up to four. At least. And she felt no worse off for the wear, if indeed there was any wearing going on in these bones of hers. She certainly did not feel fatigue. Her legs tingled at times as if they were thinking of falling asleep or going numb, but they never actually slowed her down.

Three days earlier she had tried walking through her eight hours and she had finally fatigued at the ten-hour mark. The energy came like manna from heaven, daily and just enough. But she had never felt the energy directing her anywhere except along the streets of her own neighborhood.

Now she felt as a salmon must feel when it strikes out for the spawning ground. Her daughter's Reeboks fit perfectly. She had already tossed her own pair in the garbage and switched to a black pair that Gloria had favored. Now she strutted down the sidewalk sporting black shoes and white basketball socks. Once she had looked at herself in the full-length hall mirror and thought the getup looked ridiculous with a dress. But she didn't care—she was a dress person. Period. She would leave fashion statements to the fools who gave a rat's whisker about such matters.

Helen entered the street leading to Kent's home and brought her focus to the two-story house standing at the far end. Not so long ago she had referred to the home as Gloria's home. But now she knew better. Her daughter was skipping across the clouds up there, not hiding behind pulled drapes in that stack of lumber. No, that was *Kent's* house.

That's your house.

The thought made Helen miss a step. She turned her mind to praying, ignoring the little impulse.

Father, this man living in that house is a selfish, no-good hooligan when you get right down to it. The city is crawling with a hundred thousand people more worthy than this one. Why are you so bent on rescuing him?

He didn't answer. He usually didn't when she complained like that. But of course she had no reason to hide her suspicions from God. He already knew her mind.

She answered herself. *And what about you, Helen? He is a saint compared to what you once were.*

Helen turned her thoughts back to prayer. *But why have you drawn me into this? What could you possibly want from my silly walking? Not to complain, but really it is rather incredible.* She smiled. *Ingenious, really. But still, you could certainly do as well without this exercise, couldn't you?*

Again he didn't answer. She had once read C. S. Lewis's explanation for why God insists on having us do things like pray when he already knows the outcome. It is for the experience of the thing. The interaction. His whole endeavor to create man centers around desire for interaction. Love. It is an end in itself.

Her walking was like that. It was like walking with God on Earth. The very foolishness of it made it somehow significant. God seemed to enjoy foolish conventions. Like mud on the eyes, like walking around Jericho, like a virgin birth.

She mumbled her prayer now. "Okay, so he is worthy of your love. Go ahead, dump some of the stuff over him. Let's have this over with. Lay him out. Drop him. You could do that. Why don't you do that?"

He still wasn't answering.

She closed her eyes momentarily. *Father, you are holy. Jesus, you are worthy.*

Worthy to receive honor and glory and power forever. Your ways are beyond finding out. A tingle ran through her bones. This was actually happening, wasn't it? She was walking around physically empowered by some unseen hand. At times it seemed unbelievable. Like . . . like walking on water.

You are God. You are the Creator. You have the power to speak worlds into existence, and I love you with all of my heart. I love you. I really do. She opened her eyes. *I'm just confused at times about the man who lives in that house,* she thought.

That's your house, Helen.

The inner voice spoke rather clearly that time, and she stopped. The house loomed ahead, three doors down, like an abandoned mortuary, haunted with death. And it was not her house. She did not even want the house.

That's your house, Helen.

This time Helen could not mistake the voice. It was not her own mind speaking. It was God, and God was telling her that Kent's house was actually hers. Or was meant to be.

She walked forward, rather tentative now. High above, the sun shone bright. A slight breeze pressed her dress against her knees. Not a soul was in sight. The neighborhood looked deserted. But Kent was in his house, behind those pulled blinds. The silver car parked in the driveway said so.

"Is that my Lexus too?" The corner of her mouth twitched at her own humor. Of course, she did not want the Lexus, either.

This time God answered. *That's your house, Helen.*

And then she suddenly knew what he meant. She stopped two doors down, suddenly terrified. Goodness, no! I could never do that! The walking is one thing, but *that?*

Helen turned on her heels and walked away from the house. Her purpose here was over. At least for the day. An unsteadiness accompanied her strides now. *That's your house; that's your house.* That could mean anything.

But it didn't mean anything. It meant only one thing, and she had the misfortune of understanding exactly the message.

Helen walked for an hour, mumbling and begging and praying. Nothing changed. God had said his piece. Now she was saying hers, but he was not speaking anymore.

She was on her way back home, less than an hour from her house—her *real* house—before she found some peace over the matter. But even then it was only a thimbleful. She began to pray for Kent again, but it was not as easy as it had been on the first part of the trip.

Things were about to get interesting. Maybe crazy.

THE SECOND real bump in Kent's road came two days later, on Wednesday morning, on the heels of the cop-in-the-bookstore bump.

The day started out well enough. Kent had risen early and shaved clean to the bone. He smiled and nodded a greeting to several tellers on his way through the lobby. He even made eye contact with Sidney Beech on his way in, and she smiled. A sexy smile. Things were most definitely returning to normal. Kent whistled down the hall and entered the Information Systems suite.

Betty sat in typical form, tweezers in hand. "Morning, Betty." Kent forced a smile.

"Morning, Kent," she returned, beaming. If he wasn't mistaken there was some interest in her eyes. He swallowed and stepped past.

"Oh, Kent. They're meeting in the conference room down the hall. They're waiting for you."

He spun around. "There's a meeting this morning? Since when?"

"Since Markus got back from San Jose yesterday with new marching orders, he says. I don't know. Something about taking more responsibility."

Kent retraced his steps and entered the hall, trying to calm himself. This was out of the ordinary, and anything out of the ordinary was bad. His plan would work under existing circumstances, not necessarily under ones altered to meet some new marching orders.

Settle down, Buckwheat. It's just a meeting. No need to go in there and sweat all over the table. Kent took a breath and walked into the conference room as casually as possible.

The others rocked their chairs around the long table, wasting time, in good spirits. Borst had taken the head of the table and leaned back. His navy vest strained against its buttons. If one of those popped it might just poke Mary in the eye. She sat adjacent to Borst, leaning admiringly toward him. You'd think the two were best friends by their body language.

Todd sat opposite Mary, his head thrown back midhowl at some brilliant comment Borst had evidently graced them with. It was Todd's hoot that covered the sound of the door opening and closing, Kent guessed. Cliff sat two chairs down from Mary, facing Borst, grinning his usual pineapple-eater smile.

"Kent! It's about time," Borst boomed. The others thought that funny and lengthened their laugh. He had to admit, the jovial atmosphere was almost contagious. Kent smiled and pulled out a seat opposite Cliff.

"Sorry. I didn't know we were meeting," he said.

They gathered themselves and dug in. Borst started by fishing for a few compliments, which the others readily served up. Kent even tossed him one. Some ridiculous comment about how perceptive the supervisor had been to bring in Cliff.

Mostly the discussion centered on preserving control of AFPS. Evidently the main Information Systems division at the administration branch in California was talking about flexing its muscles. Or, as Borst put it, *going for a power grab.*

"That's all it is, and we know it," he said. "They have a dozen greedy engineers up there who feel left out, so now they want the whole thing. And I have no intention of giving her up."

Kent had no doubt that the words were not original with Borst. They were Bentley's. He pictured Porky and Porkier yapping up a frenzy on the flight home.

"Which means we have to run a tight ship; that's all there is to it. They're looking for weaknesses in our operation as we speak. In fact, three of them are flying down next Friday to survey the territory, so to speak."

"That's crazy!" Todd blurted out. "They can't just waltz in here and take over."

"Oh, yes they can, Todd. That's a fact. But we're not going to let them."

"How?" Mary asked, wide eyed.

"Exactly. How? That's what we're going to figure out."

"Security," Cliff said.

It was only then that the meaning of this little discussion came home to Kent. Like a flash grenade tossed into his skull. Whether the delay had been caused by tequila residue or his fascination at watching Borst's fat lips move was a tossup. But when understanding did come, Kent twitched in his chair.

"You have something to say about that, Kent?" Borst asked, and Kent knew they had all seen his little blunder. To exasperate the matter, he asked the one question only a complete fool would ask in the situation.

"What?"

Borst glanced at Cliff. "Cliff said security, and you looked like you wanted to add to that."

Security? Good grief! Kent scrambled for recovery. "Actually, I don't think they stand a chance, sir."

That got a smile from them. *That's our boy, Kent.* All of them except Cliff. Cliff scrunched his eyebrows. "How's that?" he asked.

"How's what?"

"How is it that the guys from California don't have a snowball's chance in hell of taking control of AFPS?"

Kent leaned back. "How are they going to maintain a system they know nothing about?" Of course the whole notion was ridiculous. Any good department could work its way through the program. In fact, Cliff was well on his way to doing just that. He said so.

"Really? I've been here three weeks, and I've found my way around the program well enough. The code's not even under active security measures."

The room fell to dead silence. This was not going well. Tightened security could very well bring his entire plan to its knees. Kent felt a trickle of sweat break from his hairline and snake past his temple. He casually reached up and scratched the area as if a tickle annoyed him there.

"I thought you were going to take care of restricted security," Borst said, staring directly at Kent.

"We have restricted codes at every branch. No one can enter the system without a password," he returned. "What else do you want?"

"That covers financial security, but what about security from hackers or other programmers?" Cliff asked evenly. The newcomer was becoming a real problem here.

All eyes were on Kent. They were asking about ROOSTER without knowing it, and his heart was starting to overreact. He had programmed ROOSTER precisely for this purpose.

Then Cliff threw even the *not knowing* part into question. "Actually it looks like someone started to put a system into place but never finished. I don't know; I'm still looking into it."

The kid was on to ROOSTER! He'd found something that led to the link. It was all Kent could do to stay seated. This was it, then. If he didn't stop them now, it was over!

"Yes, we did start a few things awhile back. But if I recall correctly, we discarded the code long ago. It was barely a framework."

Cliff held Kent in a steady gaze. "I'm not so sure it's gone, Kent. I may have found it."

Kent's heart felt like it might explode. He forced a nonchalant look. "Either way, it was far too clumsy to accomplish anything under the current structure." Kent shifted his gaze to Borst. "Frankly, I think you're approaching this all wrong, Markus. Sure, we can look at tightening security, but that's not going to stop a power grab, as you put it. What you need is some political clout."

Borst lifted his eyebrow, and his forehead rode up under his toupee a fraction. "Yes? And?"

"Well, you have some power now. Probably more than you know. You insist on maintaining control under the fairness doctrine. You were responsible for the program's creation as a dedicated employee. It's simply unfair for the big giant to come sweeping in and take your baby away, thereby minimizing any additional advances you might have realized had it remained under your control. I think you could get a lot of ordinary employees to back you on a position like that, don't you?"

The smile came slowly, but when Borst got it, his mouth spread from ear to ear. "My, you are not so dumb, are you, Kent?" He glanced at the others. "By golly, that's brilliant! I think you are absolutely right. The little man against the big corporation and all that."

Kent nodded. He spoke again, wanting to nail this door shut while the hammer was in his hand. "If the boys in California want AFPS, no security is going to slow them down. They'll just take the whole thing and stomp the living daylights out of anyone who stands in their way. You have to put a political obstacle in their way, Markus. It's the only way." Cliff had lost his plastic grin, and Kent wondered about that. What difference did it make to the newcomer how this went down? Unless he knew more than he was letting on.

"I'm surprised Bentley didn't think of that," Borst wondered aloud. He blinked and addressed the group. "Anyway, I think I should take this to him immediately." He was already on his feet. Like the young eager student off to find his professor. Cliff held Kent's gaze for a moment without smiling. He turned to Borst.

"May I suggest we at least handle the security issue since it has been raised?" Cliff asked.

"Yes, of course. Why don't you take the lead on that, Cliff?" he said. But his mind was already in Bentley's office. "I've got to go."

Borst left, wearing a smirk.

Cliff had found his grin again.

Kent blinked. That last exchange had effectively dropped a bucket of heat on his head. It was still leaking down his spine when the others stood and wordlessly followed Borst's lead, exiting the room.

That was it. Cliff knew something. Kent lowered his head and began to rub his temples. It was unraveling. It was coming apart. In the space of ten minutes his link to sanity had been casually snipped free by some snowboarder from Dallas who knew more than he had any business knowing.

Think! Think, think, think, boy!

Okay, this is not the end. This is just another little bump. A challenge. Nobody is better at challenges than you, boy.

Kent suddenly wanted out of the building. The thought of going back to his office and having Cliff walk in with his grin scared him silly. He wanted to see Lacy.

He wanted a drink.

CHAPTER TWENTY-TWO

KENT SPENT most of the afternoon walking through the office trying to hide the pallor of death he knew grayed his face.

He took a late lunch by himself and was about to enter Antonio's when he saw Cliff. At least he thought it looked like Cliff. The junior programmer walked toward the corner across the street, and Kent's heart began to palpitate madly. It was not the sight of the snowboarder that had him suddenly fixed to the concrete; it was the sight of the pinhead walking beside Cliff, yapping with the traitor as if they were old buddies. The cop! It was the pinhead cop with slicked-back hair and wire-frame glasses!

Or was it? And then they were gone.

Kent ordered a salad for lunch and left after eating only the two black olives that came perched on top. Imagine the cop showing up here, of all places. And talking to Cliff! Unless that hadn't been the cop *or* Cliff up there. It was for this conclusion that Kent finally angled, and he angled for it hard. He was seeing things in his anxiety. Boulders were beginning to fall from the sky; only they weren't boulders at all. They were sparrows, and they weren't falling from the sky. They were flying happily about.

Get a grip, Kent.

When he got home that night he made straight for the cabinet and pulled out a bottle of tequila. Three shots and a shower later, he still had not managed to shake the sickness in his chest. His head hurt from the day's brain twisting. Thing of it was, this particular challenge was not his challenge at all. It was Cliff's challenge. If Cliff found ROOSTER, the game was over. And there was nothing Kent could do to change that. Nothing at all.

He had just poured his fourth shot when the doorbell rang for the first time in a week. Kent jerked. The shot splashed over his hand, and he cursed. Fortunately he was near the kitchen sink, and a quick run of water washed the liquor down the drain. Who could possibly be ringing his doorbell at eight in the evening?

The answer should not have surprised him. He swung the door open to a frowning Helen. A large travel bag hung from her shoulder.

"Helen! Come in," he said. *Helen, take a hike,* he thought.

She came in without answering and set her bag on the floor. Kent looked at the black duffel bag, thinking at first that she had lost her interest in running after all and was returning the shoes. But he could see already that there was more than footwear in that bag.

"Kent," Helen said, and she smiled. He thought the smile might have been forced.

"What can I do for you?" he asked.

"Kent," She took a deep breath, and suddenly Kent knew this was not just a courtesy visit. "I need to ask you a favor, Kent."

He nodded.

"If I needed you for something—really needed—would you help me?"

"Sure, Helen. Depending on what it was you needed me for, of course. I mean, I'm not exactly the wealthiest man on the earth." He chuckled, all the while scrambling to guess her next move. She was setting him up; that much was clear. She was going to ask him to help clear out her garage or some other horrendous task he could do without.

"No, it won't cost you a penny. In fact, I don't mind paying rent. And I'll buy half the groceries. That should save you some money."

He smiled wide, wondering where this could possibly be leading. Surely she didn't expect to move in with him. She hated his guts. In a mother-in-law sort of way. No, she was angling for something else, but his mind was drawing a blank.

"What's the matter, Kent? Cat got your tongue? Oh, come on now." She walked past him into the living room, and he followed her. "It wouldn't be so bad. You and me living together."

Kent pulled up, flabbergasted. "What!"

She turned to him and looked him square in the eye. "I'm asking you if I can move in, young man. I have just lost a grandson and a daughter, and I've decided that I simply cannot live on my own in that great big house." She shifted her stare. "I need company," she said.

"You need company?" Heat washed down Kent's back. "I don't mean to be rude or anything, but I'm not exactly good company these days. I'm the devil, remember?"

"Yes. I do remember. Nonetheless, I would be so grateful if you would let me use one of your spare bedrooms downstairs here. The sewing room across from Spencer's room, perhaps."

"Helen, you can't be serious!" Kent rounded the couch and walked away from her. This was absurd! What could she possibly be thinking? She would ruin everything! An image of him sneaking to the kitchen for a drink winked through his mind. She would give him hell. "There's no way it would work."

"I'm asking you, Kent. You're not going to turn out family, are you?"

Kent turned back. "Come on. Stop this, Helen. This is crazy. Just plain stupid! You'd hate it here! We have nothing in common. I'm a *sinner,* for God's sake!"

She didn't seem to hear him. "I can do the dishes too. Goodness, just look at that kitchen. Have you even touched it since I was here last?" She waddled off toward the breakfast bar.

"Helen! No. The answer is no. You have your own home. It's yours for a reason. This is my home. It is *mine* for a reason. You can't stay here. I need my privacy."

"I'm walking every day now, Kent. Did I tell you that? So I'll be gone early in the morning for my walk. You'll be gone by the time I get back, but maybe we can have dinner together every evening. What do you think?"

Kent stared at her, at a loss for words at her insane behavior. "I don't think you're listening. I said no! N-O! No, you can't stay here."

"I know the sewing room is full of stuff right now, but I will move it myself. I don't want to put you out." She walked around the bar and turned the faucet on. "Now, you know I can't stand television. It's the box from hell, you know. But I thought you could watch the one upstairs in your sitting room." She twisted the sink tap and ran water over her wrist, testing its temperature. "And I'm not crazy about drinking, either. If you want to drink any alcohol I'd prefer you did that upstairs as well. But I like music, you know. Heavy music, light music, any music as long as the words—"

"Helen! You're not listening!"

"And you're not listening!" she said. Her eyes seemed to reach out with knives and hold him at the neck. His breathing shut down.

"I said I need a place to stay, dear son-in-law! Now, I gave you my daughter for a dozen years; she warmed your bed and ironed your shirts. The least you can do is give me a room for a few nights. Is it really too much to ask?"

Kent nearly buckled under the words. It occurred to him that his mouth was open, and he closed it quickly. The tequila was starting to speak, moaning lazily through his mind. He thought that maybe he should just pull the plug now. Go out and use that nine-millimeter on his own head. End the day with a bang. At the very least he should be screaming at this old wench who had played mother-in-law in his old life.

But he could not scream because she was holding him in some kind of spell. And it was working. It was actually making him think that she was right.

"I . . . I don't think—"

"No, stop thinking, Kent." She lowered her voice. "Start *feeling* a little. Show some kindness. Let me take a room." Then she smiled. "I won't bite. I promise."

He could think of nothing to say. Except okay. It just came out. "Okay."

"Good. I will bring the rest of my belongings in from the car tomorrow after I've had a chance to clean out the sewing room. Do you like eggs, Kent?"

The woman was incredible. "Yes," he said, but he hardly heard himself say it.

"Oh, but that's right. I will have to leave before you get up. I walk at sunrise. Well, maybe we can have an egg dish one evening."

For a minute they faced each other in silence. Then Helen spoke, her voice soft now, almost apologetic. "It'll be okay, Kent. Really. In the end you will see. It will be okay. I guess you've already learned that we can't control everything in life. Sometimes things happen that we just didn't plan on. You can only hope that in the end it will all make sense. And it will. Believe me. It will."

Kent nodded. "Maybe," he said. "You know your way around. Make yourself at home."

Then he retreated to the master bedroom upstairs, grateful that he had stashed a bottle in the sitting room. It was early; maybe he should call Lacy. Or maybe drive up to see her. The idea touched off a spark of hope. Which was good, because hope had been all but dashed today.

LACY CLEANED madly, fighting butterflies all the while and chastising herself for feeling any anxiety at all. So she was about to see Kent again. So he was coming to her condo this time. So he had brought that heat wave with him on Monday night. Her rekindled relationship with him was simply platonic, and she would keep it that way. Absolutely.

"Lacy, I need to talk," he'd said, and by the sound of his strained voice, he did need something. *Lacy, I need.* She liked the sound of that. And it was okay to like the sound of someone's platonic voice over the phone.

Indirect lighting cast a soft hue over the leather sofa angled under a vaulted ceiling. The fireplace sat black and spotless. An eight-by-ten picture of her late husband, John, stood at the hearth's center, and she considered removing it but quickly discarded the notion as absurd. Possibly even profane.

She donned jeans and a canary blouse, retouched her makeup carefully, opting for ruby lipstick and a light teal eye shadow, then made coffee. Her hand spooned the grounds with a slight quiver, and she mumbled to herself. "Lighten up, Lacy."

The doorbell chimed just as the coffee maker quit sputtering. Lacy took a deep breath and opened the door. Kent wore jeans and a white T-shirt that looked as if it might have been left in the dryer overnight. He grinned nervously and stepped in. His eyes were a little red, she thought. Maybe he was tired.

"Come in, Kent."

"Thanks."

He scanned the room, and she watched his eyes in the light. A small cut on his cheek betrayed a recent shave. They sat at the dinette and launched into small talk. How was your day? Good, and yours? Good. Good. But Kent was not looking so good. He was forcing his words, and his eyes jerked too often. He was having a bad day; that much he was not hiding. Better or worse than Monday, she did not know yet, but he was obviously still fighting his demons.

Lacy poured two cups of coffee, and they sipped through the small talk. Ten minutes passed before Kent shifted in his seat, and Lacy thought he was about to tell her why he wanted to see her again so soon. Other than maybe just wanting to see her. Unless her antenna had totally short-circuited over the last decade of marriage, there was some of that. At least some, regardless of all this platonic talk.

He stared at his black coffee, frowning. Her heart tightened. Goodness, he looked as though he might start crying. This was not just a bad-day thing. Something big had happened.

Lacy leaned forward, thinking she should reach out and take his hand or something. But he might misread her intentions. Or *she* might misread her intentions. She swallowed. "What's wrong, Kent?"

He shook his head and lowered it. "I don't know, Lacy. It's just . . ." He slid his elbow on the table and rested his forehead in his palm, looking now as if the blood had been siphoned from his face.

Now Lacy was worried. "Kent. What's going on?"

"Nothing. It's just hard, that's all. I feel like my life is unraveling."

"Your life *has* unraveled, Kent. You just lost your family, for heaven's sake. You're supposed to feel unraveled."

He nodded unconvincingly. "Yeah."

"What? You don't buy that? You think you're the man of steel who can just let these little details run off your big strong shoulders?" *Whoa, a bit strong there, Lacy. He* is *a wounded man. No need to kill him off with good intentions.*

Kent looked up slowly. There was a look in those eyes that brought a strange thought to Lacy's mind. The thought that Kent might actually be drinking. And maybe not just a little. "It isn't that. I know I'm supposed to be grieving. But I don't *want* to grieve," he growled through clenched teeth. "I want to make a new life for myself. And it's my new life that's driving me nuts. It hasn't even started, and it's already falling apart."

"Nothing's falling apart, Kent. Everything will work out; you'll see. I promise."

He paused and closed his eyes. Then, as if a spark had ignited behind his blue eyes, he suddenly leaned forward and grabbed her hand. A bolt of fire ripped through her heart. "Imagine having all this behind you, Lacy. Imagine having all the money you could dream of—starting over anywhere in the world. Don't you ever wonder what that would be like?"

He glanced at his hand around hers, and he pulled back self-consciously.

"Honestly? No," she answered.

"Well, I do. And I could do it." He gripped his right hand into a fist. "If it wasn't for all these fools who keep sticking their noses in my business . . ." Now it was more rage than anger lacing his voice, and he shook slightly.

Lacy blinked and tilted her head. He was making no sense. "Excuse me. What are we talking about here? *Who* are we talking about? You still work at the bank, right?"

"The cop at the bookstore for one thing. I can't shake him."

"You can't shake him? You've seen him again?"

"No, well yes—or maybe. I don't know if I really saw him again, but he's right there, you know. Riding along in my mind."

"Come on, Kent. You're overreacting now. For all you know, he was some kook pretending to be a cop. You don't know anything about this investigation of theirs."

He snapped his eyes to hers. "Pretending?"

"No, I don't know. I'm just saying *you* don't know. I'm not actually saying he was a kook, but there's no reason to walk around in this fear of yours when you hardly know a thing about the man. You have nothing to hide."

He blinked a few times quickly and bobbed his head. "Yeah. Hmm. Never thought of that." His glassy eyes stared at her cup now. Poor guy was upside down. "Cliff's driving me nuts. I could kill the guy."

"Cliff, the new programmer? I thought you liked him. Now you're talking about killing the kid?" Lacy stood and walked to the coffee machine. "You're sounding scary, Kent."

"Yeah, never mind. You're right. I'm okay. I'm just . . ."

But he wasn't okay. He was sitting with his back to her, rubbing his temples now. He was coming unglued. And by the sounds of it, not from his wife's death, but from matters that followed no rhyme or reason. She should walk over there and knock some sense into his head. Or maybe go over there and hold him.

Her stomach hollowed at the thought. *A woman does not hold a man in a platonic relationship, Lacy. Shake his hand, maybe. But not hold him, as in, Let me put my hands on your face and stroke your cheek and run my fingers through your hair and tell you that everything—*

Something hot burned her thumb.

"Ouch!" Lacy snatched her hand to her mouth and sucked on the thumb. She had overfilled the cup.

Kent turned to her. "You okay?"

"Yes." She smiled. "Coffee burn." She returned to her seat.

"Helen moved in with me," he said.

Lacy sat back down. "Your mother-in-law? You're kidding! I thought you two were at each other's throats."

"We were. We are. I'm not even sure how it happened—it just did. She's staying in the sewing room."

"For how long?"

"I don't know." He was shaking his head again, and this time a tear had managed to slip from his right eye. "I don't know anything anymore, Lacy." Kent suddenly dropped his head onto folded arms and started to sob quietly. The man was stretched beyond his capacities.

Lacy felt her heart contract beyond her control. If she wasn't careful the tears would be coming from her eyes as well. And then one did, and she knew she could not just watch him without offering some comfort.

She waited as long as her resolve would allow. Then she stood unsteadily from her chair and stepped to his side. She stood over him for a brief moment, her hand lifted motionlessly above his head. His wavy blond hair rested against his head just as it had years ago, halfway down a strong neck.

Lacy had one last round with the inner voice that insisted she keep this relationship purely platonic. She told the voice to stretch its definition of *platonic.*

And then she lowered her hand to his head and touched him.

She could feel the electrical impulse run through his body at her touch. Or was it running through *her* body? She knelt and put her arm around his shoulder. His sobs shook him gently.

"Shhhh." Her cheek was now wet with tears. "It will be okay," she whispered.

Kent turned into her then, and they held each other.

That's all they did. Hold each other. But they held each other for a long time, and when Kent finally left an hour later, Lacy had all but decided that *platonic* was a word best left in the textbooks. Or maybe just erased altogether. It was a silly word.

CHAPTER TWENTY-THREE

KENT DRAGGED himself to work Thursday morning, swallowing continually against the dread that churned in his gut. It reminded him of the time he'd been audited by the IRS three years earlier. He'd felt like a stranded Jew interrogated by the Gestapo. Only this time things were clearly worse. Then, he'd had nothing to hide beyond the moving deduction he'd possibly inflated. Now he had his whole life to hide.

His eyes had taken to leaking again—as they had those first few weeks after Gloria's death. The tears came without warning, blurring traffic signals and dissolving his dashboard to a sea of strange symbols. A dull ache droned through his head—a reminder of the "nightcaps" he'd indulged himself in after returning from Boulder. If it wasn't for the single thread of hope that strung through his mind, he might have stayed home. Downed some more nightcaps. Of course, he would have to tread lightly now that Helen had managed to work her way into his life. Things seemed to be coming apart at the seams again, and he had hardly begun this mad plan of his.

As it was, those words Lacy had spoken the previous evening triggered a new thought. A most desperate plan, really, but one to which he could cling for the moment. "For all you know he was some kook pretending to be a cop," Lacy had said. It was true that the cop had not shown his badge, and everyone knew that a business card could be had in half an hour at Kinko's. Still, he had known too much to be pretending. That was not it. But the comment had spawned another thought that centered around the word *kook*. And it had to do with Cliff, not the cop.

From all indications, it seemed that Cliff was on to him. Somehow that little snoop had gotten a hair up his nose and decided something needed exposing. So then why not undermine the kid? Showing him to be a kook might be a tad difficult; after all, the guy had already demonstrated his competence as a programmer. But that didn't mean he was squeaky clean. For starters, he was a snowboarder, and snowboarders were not textbook examples of conformists. There had to be some dirt out there on Cliff. Just enough to spin some doubts. Even a rumor with no basis at all. *Did you know that Cliff is the ringleader for the Satanist priesthood that murdered that guy in Naperville?* Didn't matter if there was such a priesthood or a murder or even a Naperville. Well, maybe it mattered a little.

By the time Kent got to work he knew precisely how he would spend his morning. He would spend it dragging Cliff into the dirt. And if need be, he would create the dirt himself with a few clicks of his mouse. Yes indeed, twenty years of hard study and work were gonna pay off this morning.

His ritual *Good mornings* came hard, like trying to speak with a mouthful of bile. But he managed them and rushed into his office, locking the door behind him. He made it halfway to his chair when the knock came. Kent grimaced and considered ignoring the fool—whichever fool it was. It didn't matter; they were all fools. It was probably Cliff the hound out there, sniffing at his door.

Kent opened the door. Sure enough, Cliff stood proud, wearing his ear-to-ear pineapple-eating grin.

"Hey, Kent. What are you doing this morning?"

"Work, Cliff." He could not hide his distaste. The realization that he was sneering at the man flew through his mind, but he was powerless to adjust his facial muscles.

Cliff seemed undeterred. "Mind if I come in, Kent? I've got some things you might want to look at. It's amazing what you can find if you dig deep enough." Cheese.

Kent's right hand nearly flew out and slapped that smiling face on impulse. But he held it to a tremble by his side. Things had evidently just escalated. It could very possibly all come down to this moment, couldn't it? This snowboard sniffer here may very well have the goods on him. Then a thought dropped into his mind.

"How about one o'clock? Can you hold off until then?"

Cliff hesitated and lost the grin. "I would prefer to meet now, actually."

"I'm sure you would, but I have some urgent business to attend to right now, Cliff. How about one o'clock?"

"And what kind of urgent business is that, Kent?"

They stared at each other without speaking for a full ten seconds.

"One o'clock, Cliff. I'll be right here at one."

The programmer nodded slowly and stepped back without answering. Kent closed the door, immediately breathing heavily. He scrambled for the desk, frantic, his knees weak. It was the end. If he had any sense at all he would leave now. Just walk out and leave Niponbank to its own problems. He had not broken any laws yet; his coworkers could do little but gossip. He would become "that poor man who lost his wife and son and then his mind." Too bad, too, because he showed so much promise. Borst's right-hand man. The thought made him nauseous.

This whole notion of stealing twenty million dollars had been foolishness from the beginning. Insane! You just don't think up things like that and expect to pull them off. He grabbed a tissue from a box on his desk and wiped at the sweat wetting his collar.

On the other hand, if he did leave he might very well kill himself. Drink himself to death.

Kent wiped his palms on his slacks and stabbed at the keyboard. A moment later he was into the human resources secure-data files. If anyone caught him in the files without authorization, he would be fired on the spot. He ran a query on Cliff Monroe. A small hourglass blinked lazily on his screen. This exercise now seemed like a stupid idea too. What did he expect to do? Run out into the hall, ranting and raving about the programmer who was really a werewolf? Maybe the bimbos in the lobby would believe him. *Honest, gals! He's a werewolf! Spread the word—quick, before my one o'clock meeting with him.*

A record popped on the screen, showing a home address on Platte Street in Dallas, a social security number, and some other basics. According to the record, Cliff had been employed exactly one week before his transfer to Denver in response to a request placed by Markus Borst. The reason was listed as "Replacement." So Borst had not expected to see him back. *Surprise, Baldy! Here I am!*

The rest of Cliff's record noted a basic education with high scores, and a list of previous employers. The kid had worked with the best, according to his short history. *Well, not for long, fella.*

Kent glanced back at the door quickly. *Here goes nothing.* He deleted the employment history from Cliff's record with a single keystroke. Then he quickly changed the file number so that no corresponding paper file would match this record, and he saved the modifications. In the space of ten seconds he had erased Cliff's history and lost the hard copy file. At least for a while.

He leaned back. Simple enough, if you knew what you were doing. Although the crashing of his heart belied that fact. Now the real test.

Kent picked up the phone and dialed Dallas. He was patched through to a Mary in human resources.

"Good morning, Mary. Kent Anthony here from IS in Denver. I'm checking on the qualifications of an employee. A Cliff Monroe, file number 3678B. Can you pull that up for me?"

He stared at the modified file on his screen.

"Yes, what can I help you with?"

"I'm trying to determine his employment history. Can you tell me where he worked before taking a job with us?"

"Just a second . . ." Kent heard the faint sound of keys clicking. "Hmm. Actually, it looks like he has no history. This must be his first job."

"You're kidding! Isn't that a bit odd for a high-level programmer? Can you tell me who hired him?"

Mary clicked for a minute and then flipped through some papers before answering. "Looks like Bob Malcom hired him."

"Bob? Maybe I should talk to Bob. He works there?"

"Sure. Talk to Bob. Does seem a bit odd, doesn't it?"

"Can you transfer me?"

"Sure, hold on."

It took a full five minutes of refusing to leave a message and holding to finally get the man on the phone.

"Bob Malcom."

"Bob, this is Kent Anthony from Denver. I'm looking into the employment history of a Cliff Monroe . . ." He went through the spiel again and let Bob look around a bit. But in the end it was the same.

"Hmm. You're right. It does say that I hired him, but, you know, I don't remember . . . Hold on. Let me look at my log."

Kent leaned back. He bit at his index fingernail and stared at the screen.

Bob's voice crackled again. "Yep, we hired him. So it says. How long did you say he's been working there?"

Kent scooted to the edge of his seat. "Six weeks."

"On what kind of project?"

"AFPS."

"The new processing system? And you have management control over him?" Suddenly Bob's voice rang with a note of concern.

"No, I'm not his direct supervisor; I'm just running a query to understand his qualifications for a project he's working on for me. And yes, it *is* the new processing system. Is there a problem with that?"

"Not necessarily. But you can never be too careful." He paused as if thinking things through.

It sounded too good to be true. Kent was trembling again, but now with waves of relief at this sudden turn of fortunes. "What do you mean?"

"I'm just saying you can never be too careful. It's odd we sent someone without an employment history to such a sensitive assignment. You never know. Look, I'm not ready to say that Mr. Monroe is anything but what he appears to be; I'm just saying until we know for sure, we should be careful. Corporate espionage is big business these days, and with the implementation of that system of yours up there—who knows? I'll tell you what. Why don't you have Mr. Monroe give me a call?"

No, that wouldn't do. "Actually, Bob, if there's any possibility that what you're saying proves to have merit, I'm not sure we want to tip Mr. Monroe off."

"Hmm. Yes, of course. You're right. We should begin a quiet investigation right away."

"And we may want him recalled in the meantime. I'll check with the department supervisor, but seeing as he's on temporary-replacement assignment anyway, I don't see any sense in keeping him in a sensitive position. AFPS is too valuable to risk, at any level."

"Reassign him?"

"Reassign him immediately," Kent insisted. "Today. As soon as I've talked to Borst, of course."

"Yes. Makes sense. Call me then."

"Good. In fact, maybe you could send him on an errand. Run to the bookstore or something—get him out of here while we sort this out."

"I'll call him as soon as we hang up."

"Thank you, Bob. You're a good man."

Kent hung up feeling as though the world had just been handed to him on a platter. He stood and pumped his fist. "Yesss!" He walked around his office, thinking through his next play. He would tell Borst about the possibility that they had a spy working under their noses. It was perfect! Cliff the kook, a spy.

Twenty-five minutes later it was all over. Kent talked to Borst, who nearly lost his toupee bolting from his seat. Of course, he had to call Bob himself—make sure this removing of Cliff happened immediately, barking orders like he owned the bank or something. Kent watched, biting his cheeks to keep the grin from splitting his face.

The plan proceeded flawlessly. Cliff left on some errand for Bob at eleven, after popping his head into Kent's office to remind him of the one o'clock, clueless as to his impending demise. It was the last they would see of him for at least a few days while Human Resources checked out this whole business. They would discover that Cliff's file had mistakenly been wiped out, possibly, but by then, it would not matter.

Borst changed the access codes to AFPS within the hour. Cliff Monroe was history. Just like that. Which meant that for now, all was back to a semblance of order. As long as ROOSTER had not yet been discovered, there was no reason not to continue.

Actually, there was plenty of reason not to continue. In fact, every reasonable bone in his body screamed foul at the very thought of continuing.

It was noon before Kent found the solitude he needed to check on ROOSTER's status. He virtually dove at the keyboard, punching through menus as if they did not exist. If Cliff had discovered the link, he would have left tracks.

Kent held his breath and scrolled down to the MISC folder containing ROOSTER. Then he exhaled long and slow and leaned back in his chair. The file had been opened one week earlier at 11:45 P.M. And that was good, because that had been him, last Wednesday evening.

A small ball of hope rolled up his chest, ballooning quickly. He closed his eyes and let the euphoria run through his bones. Yes, this was good. This was all he had. This was everything.

The pinhead cop's face suddenly flashed before him, and he blinked it away. The authorities had not made further contact, and he had decided that Lacy was correct about one thing—they were just doing their job. At least that's what he insisted on believing. They simply could not know about ROOSTER. And without ROOSTER, they had nothing. Nada. This bit about Spencer was absolute nonsense. Why Pinhead had even gone on about everything one day being found out, Kent had no clue. Certainly the man was not a psychic. But no other explanation fit. And psychics were nothing more than con men. Which meant that nothing fit. Pinhead simply did not fit into any reasonable picture.

Once he executed the plan, the point would be moot anyway. Cops would be crawling all over the bank.

He had to do this now, before some other menace cropped up. Before some other propeller-head walked into his life, flashing a pineapple-eating grin. And *now* meant within a week. Or next weekend. Which meant beginning now.

"YOU WHAT?"

"I moved in with him."

"You moved in with Kent?" She did not answer. "Why?"

"I had no choice in the matter. Actually, I did have a choice. I could have ignored him."

"*Kent* asked you to move in?"

"No. I meant I could have ignored God. He told me to move in. And don't think I wanted to, either. Believe me, I fought this one."

Bill Madison shook his head slowly. Helen had been walking for over two weeks now. Eight hours, twenty miles a day, without any signs of weakness. It was Jericho all over again, and Bill was not sleeping so much these days. His wife had accused him of being distracted on several occasions, and he had not bothered to deny it. Neither had he bothered to tell her about Helen's little daily ventures out into the concrete jungle. It seemed somehow profane to talk idly about the matter. And he would be less than honest to deny that a small part of him wondered whether she had somehow conjured up the whole thing. A senile intercessor suffering from delusions of walking in God's power. It was not unthinkable. Actually more plausible than believing her.

But that was the problem—he did believe her. In fact he had *seen* her.

"So how did you talk him into that?"

"It wasn't pleasant."

"I'm sure it wasn't." He paused, choosing his questions carefully. They spoke every other day, give or take, and Bill found himself begging time to skip forward to their conversations. Once on the phone, he fought for every minute. Invariably it was she who ended the discussion.

"I'm surprised he didn't flatly refuse."

"He did."

"I see. And still you're there. How is he?"

"He's no nearer the truth than he was a decade ago," she returned flatly. "If I were walking in circles and he was the wall of Jericho, I might feel like we had come to the end of the first day."

"You think it's that far off?"

"No. I'm not *thinking*. It is how I *feel.*"

He smiled. "Surely there must be a crack in that armor of his. You've been breathing down his neck as you say, for weeks. You are specifically called to intercede for the man; surely that means God will hear you. *Is* hearing you."

"You would think so, wouldn't you? On the other hand, you are specifically called to pray for *your* loved ones, Pastor. Does God hear my prayers any more than he hears your prayers?"

"I don't know. I would have said *no* a month ago, but I would also have thought you crazy a month ago."

"You still do at times, don't you, Bill?" He couldn't answer. "It's okay. So do I. But you are right; God is hearing me. We are both deriving a lot of pleasure from this little episode now that I've settled into an acceptance of the matter."

"You've always interceded for others, Helen. In many ways this is not so different."

"Yes, in many ways. You are right. But in one way it's very different. I am now walking in faith, you see. Quite literally. I am living intercession, not simply praying. The difference is like the difference between splashing through the surf and diving into the ocean."

"Hmmm. Good analogy. That's good."

"He's drinking, Bill. And he's slipping. Like a slug headed for the dark creases."

"I'm sorry, Helen. I'm sure it must be hard."

"Oh, it's not so hard anymore, Pastor. Actually the walking helps. It's . . . well, it's like a bit of heaven on Earth, maybe. It's the stretching of the mind that wears one thin. Have you been feeling thin lately, Bill?"

"Yes. Yes, I have. My wife thinks I need a break."

"Good. We have too many of the thick headed among our ranks. Maybe one of these days you'll be thin enough to hear."

"Hmm."

"Good-bye, Bill. I have to fix him dinner. I promised I would. We're having egg foo yung."

CHAPTER TWENTY-FOUR

Week Eleven

KENT SAW Helen at each evening meal, but otherwise only the spotless kitchen remained as a clue that another person shared the house. By the time he dragged himself from bed each morning, she was gone. Walking, she said, although he couldn't imagine why a woman Helen's age chose 5 A.M. for her daily walk. By the time he wandered home about six, the evening meal was either on the table or simmering on the stove.

He'd peeked into the sewing room once, just to see what she had done with it. The bed had been neatly made with a comforter he'd never seen before; a small pile of laundry rested at the foot, waiting to be put away. Otherwise there was hardly a sign that Helen occupied the spotless room. Only the nightstand beside the bed betrayed her residence there. There, her Bible lay open, slightly yellowed under the lamp. A white porcelain teacup sat nearby, emptied of its contents. But it was the crystal bottle that made him blink. She had brought this one knickknack from that hutch in her house and set it here beside her bed. Her most prized possession, Gloria had once told him. A simple bottle filled with only God knew what. Kent had closed the door without entering.

He had come home Tuesday evening to the sound of what he would have sworn was Gloria singing. He'd called her name and run to the kitchen only to find Helen bent over the sink, humming. If she'd heard him, she did not show it. He had retreated to the bedroom for a quick snip at the bottle without her knowing.

The meals themselves were a time of clinking and smacking and polite talk, but not once did Helen engage him in any of her religious dogma. She'd made a conscious decision not to, he thought. In fact, by the way she carried herself, on several occasions he found himself wondering if she had succumbed to some new drug that kept her in the clouds. Her eyes seemed to shine with confidence, and she smiled a lot. Possibly she was misreading one of her prescriptions and overdosing.

If so, she had lost neither her wit nor her analytical skills. He had engaged her about her knee-high socks once and found that out immediately.

"Those socks look silly with a dress. You *do* know that, don't you?"

"Yes, I had noticed that. But they keep my legs warm."

"And so would pants."

"No, Kent. You wear the pants in this family. I wear the dress. If you think these socks look silly, think of how a dress would look hanging off your hips."

"But it doesn't *have* to be that way," he said with a chuckle.

"You're right. But to be perfectly honest with you, it's the only way I can get men to look at my legs these days."

He drove up to the house on Thursday, eager to discover what Helen had prepared for dinner. The sentiment caused him to stop with the car door half open. The fact was, he looked forward to walking into the house, didn't he? It was the only thing he really looked forward to now besides the plan. There was always the plan, of course.

And there was Lacy.

They had steak that night.

Kent forged ahead, tiptoeing through the hours, refining his plan, calling Lacy, drinking. Quite a lot of drinking, always late at night, either in his upstairs sitting room or at the office, maintaining his pattern of late nights at work.

They all took Cliff's departure in stride, talking ad infinitum about how the competition had tried to steal AFPS and almost got away with it. The speculation only fueled their perceptions of self-importance. That anyone would go to such lengths to infiltrate their ranks came off as yet one more feather in Borst's cap. The distraction proved a perfect cover for Kent's last days among them.

Step by step, the perfect crime began to materialize with stunning clarity. And that was no illusion. He had breezed through graduate school, testing with one of the sharpest analytical minds this side of Tokyo. Not that he dwelled on the fact; he just knew it. And his mind told him a few things about his plan. It told him that what he was planning was most definitely a crime, punishable by severe penalties. If he did fail, it would be the end of him. He might as well take a cyanide capsule with him in the event things went wrong.

His mind also told him that the plan, however criminal, however heinous, was absolutely brilliant. Crime-of-the-century stuff. Enough to bring a smile to any cop's mouth; enough to boil any breathing man's blood.

And his mind told him that when it was over, if he succeeded, he would be one rich fool, living in a new skin, free to suck up whatever pleasures the world had to offer. His heart pounded at the thought.

There was simply nothing he had overlooked.

Except Lacy. He had overlooked Lacy. Well, not Lacy herself—she was becoming hard to overlook. In fact, it was the difficulty of overlooking her that he had overlooked.

They talked every evening, and he had become increasingly aware of the way his gut knotted each time he thought about picking up the phone to call her. It had been the way she touched him on his last visit, holding his head as though it might break, feeling her breath in his ear. Long-lost memories had flooded his mind.

The following evening's phone call had driven the stake further into his heart.

"You okay, Kent?"

"Yes. I'm better. I don't know how to thank you, Lacy. I just . . ." And then he had started to blubber, of all things. Cried right then on the phone, and he hardly knew why.

"Oh, Kent! It will okay. Shhh, shhh. It will be okay. I promise."

He should have dropped the phone in its cradle then and walked away from her. But he could not. The calls this whole week had been no better. No more tears. But the gentle words, though not overtly affectionate, could hardly hide the chemistry brewing between them.

And now Friday had arrived. Which was a problem, because Lacy didn't exactly fit into his plan, and his plan started tomorrow.

Helen asked him if anything was wrong during the evening meal, and he shook his head. "No, why?"

"No reason, really. You just look troubled."

It was the last she said of the matter, but her words rang annoyingly through his mind. He had expected to be ecstatic on the eve of the big weekend. Not troubled. And yet he *was* ecstatic in some ways. It was the Lacy thing that tore at his heart.

Kent retired to his room and downed three shots before working up the courage to call her.

"Kent! I'm so glad you called! You would not believe what happened to me at work today." Her voice might just as well have been a vise clamped around his heart, squeezing.

"Oh? What happened?"

"They asked me to enter management school. They want to groom me for management."

"Good. That's good, Lacy." He swallowed. It could have been him six years ago, starting his climb up the ladder. And he'd climbed right to the top . . . before they decided to push him over.

"Good? It's *great!"* She paused. "What's wrong, Kent?"

"Nothing. Really, that's great."

"You sound like you just swallowed a pickle. What's wrong?"

"I need to see you, Lacy."

Her voice softened. "Okay. When?"

"Tonight."

"Right now?"

"Yes."

"Is there a problem?"

"No." Kent was having difficulty keeping his voice steady. "Can I drive up?"

She hesitated, and for some reason that worsened the ache in his chest.

"Sure," she said. "Give me an hour."

"I'll see you in an hour, then."

Kent hung up feeling as though he had just thrown a switch to an electric chair. His own electric chair. But by the time he pulled up to her condo, he had resolved the issue. He would do what needed to be done, and he would do it the *way* it needed to be done. He took a slug of tequila from the bottle in the passenger seat and pushed his door open.

God, help me, he thought. It was a prayer.

THEY SAT at her dinette table again, opposite each other, as they had done nearly two weeks earlier. Lacy wore jeans and a white shirt advertising Cabo San Lucas in splashy red letters. Kent had come wearing faded denims and loafers. His blue eyes had not lost their red sheen. The faint, sweet smell of alcohol drifted around him. He had grinned shyly and avoided contact with her upon entering.

Not that she had expected a hug or anything. But that said something, she thought. *What* it said, she had no clue.

For ten minutes they made small talk that would have carried more grace on the phone. Then Kent settled into his chair, and she knew he wanted to tell her something.

"Do you ever feel guilty about wanting to move on?" Kent asked, staring at his coffee.

Lacy felt her heart strengthen its pulse. *Move on?* she thought. *You want to move on? I'm not sure I'm ready to move on yet. At least not in a relationship with another man.* "What do you mean?" she asked and lifted her cup to her lips.

"Move on. Get past . . . John." He nodded to the mantel. "Forget about your past and begin over. You ever feel like that?"

"In some ways, yes. I'm not sure I've ever wanted to *forget* John, though. But we do have to get on with life." She looked at those baby blues, and suddenly she wanted him to just come out and tell her that he did want to move on—and move on with her. She would hold him back, of course. But she wanted to be wanted by him.

He was nodding. "Yes. Only . . . maybe even wanting to put the past totally aside. Because as long as you have those memories you can never really be new. You ever feel like that? Even a tiny bit?"

"Probably. I just never thought about it in those terms."

"Well, now that you are, does it make you feel bad? You know, for not wanting to remember the past."

Lacy thought about the question, thinking it a tad strange. "I'm not sure. Why?"

"Because I'm thinking about starting over," he said.

"Oh? And how would you do that?"

The corners of his mouth lifted barely. His eyes brightened. "If I told you, would you swear to secrecy?"

She did not respond.

"I mean, absolute secrecy. Tell no man, ever—or woman, for that matter. Just you and I. Could you swear to that on John's grave?"

Lacy recoiled at the question. John's grave? Kent was still grinning mischievously, and Lacy sat straighter. "Why? I mean, I think so. It depends."

"No, I need a definite yes. No matter what I tell you, I want you to swear to guard it. I need that confidence in you. Can you do that?"

In any other circumstance Lacy would be telling him she couldn't put herself in that situation without knowing more. But that's not what came out of her mouth.

"Yes," she said. And she knew it was the truth. No matter what he said, she would guard it as her own.

Kent watched her carefully for a few seconds. "I believe you," he said. "And if you ever break this promise, you will be putting me in the grave, right beside my wife. I want you to understand that. Acknowledge that."

She nodded, thoroughly confused as to his direction.

"Good." He took a long drink of coffee and set the cup down carefully, dead serious. "I'm going to start over, Lacy. Completely." He waited, as if he'd just revealed a sinister secret and expected her to drop her jaw to the table.

"That's good, Kent."

Kent lowered his head and looked at her, past her arching eyebrows. His lips curled in a wicked grin. "I'm going be rich, Lacy."

She thought he might burst with this thing. And so far, it was nothing worthy of his behavior. Unless it really was about her and he was showing attraction in some strange, deluded manor. *I'm going to get rich, Honey, so you and I can live a new life together.*

"I'm going to steal twenty million dollars."

"Come on, Kent. Be serious."

"I'm as serious as a heart attack, Honey."

She heard his words the way one might see a bomb's distant mushroom cloud, but it took a second for the impact to reach in and shake her bones. Her first thought was denial. But it fled before his glare, and she knew he was just that: as serious as a heart attack.

"You're going to *steal?*"

He nodded, grinning.

"You're going to steal twenty *million?*"

He nodded, still wearing that thin grin. "That's a lot of money, isn't it? It's the amount that I stood to earn from my bonus if Borst and Bentley hadn't pilfered it." He said the names through a sudden snarl. And then, more matter-of-factly, he added, "I'm going to take it."

Lacy was flabbergasted. "But how? From them? You can't just steal twenty million dollars and not expect to get caught!"

"No? I'm not touching Borst and Bentley, at least not at first. Even if they had that kind of money, you're right—it would be suicide to take such a sum from anyone."

He lifted the cup again, slowly, staring into it, and he spoke just before the rim touched his lips. "Which is why I will take it from no one." He drank, and she watched him, caught up in his drama.

She thought he had flipped his lid—all theatrical and making no sense at all. He lowered the cup to the table, landing it without a sound. "I will take it from one hundred million accounts. Next month, one hundred million interbank ATM service fees will be slightly inflated on selected customers' statements. Not a soul will even suspect a theft has occurred."

She blinked at him several times, trying to understand. And then she did. "They will see it!"

"Service fees are not reconciled, Lacy. When was the last time you even checked on the accuracy of those little charges?" He raised an eyebrow. "Hmm?"

She shook her head. "You're crazy. Someone will notice. It's too much!"

"The banks will not know except through the odd customer who complains. When someone complains, what do they do? They run a query. A query that I will be able to detect. Any account queried, regardless of the nature of that query, will receive a correction. In the world of computing, anomalies do occur, Lacy. In this case, the anomaly will be corrected on all accounts in which it is detected. Either way, the transactions will be nontraceable."

"But that's impossible. Every transaction is traceable."

"Oh?" He let it stand at that and just stared at her, his head still angled in a rather sinister manor, she thought.

Lacy stared at Kent and began to believe him. He was, after all, no idiot. She didn't know the inner workings of a bank's finances, but she knew that Kent did. If anybody could do what he suggested, he could. Goodness! Was he actually planning on stealing twenty million dollars? It was insane! Twenty *million* dollars! Her heart thumped in her chest.

She swallowed. "Even if you could pull it off, it's . . . it's wrong. And you know how it feels to be wronged."

"Don't even begin to compare this with my loss," he shot back. "And who is being wronged here? You think losing a few cents will make anyone feel *wronged?* Like, *Oh, my stars, Gertrude! I've been robbed blind!* Besides, you have to know something in order to feel anything about it. And they will not know."

"It's the principle of it, Kent. You're stealing twenty million dollars, for heaven's sake! That's wrong."

His eyes flashed. "Wrong? Says who? What's happened to me—now, *that's* wrong. The way I'm looking at it, I'm just getting centered again."

"That doesn't make it right." So this was what he'd come to tell her. That he was about to become a world-class criminal. Mafia type. And she'd bared her soul to the man.

She frowned. "Even if you pull it off, you'll spend the rest of your life running. How are you going to explain all that money? It'll catch up to you one day."

"No. You see, actually that's what I came to tell you. Nothing will ever catch up to me, because I don't plan on being around to be caught up to. I'm leaving. Forever."

"Come on, Kent. With international laws and extradition treaties, they can track you down anywhere. What are you going to do, hide out in some tropical jungle?"

His blue eyes twinkled. She furrowed her brows.

He just smiled and crossed his legs. "We'll see, Lacy, but I wanted you to know that. Because tonight may be the last time you see me."

Then she understood why Kent had come. He had not come to ask her to share his life; he can come to say good-bye. He was tossing her out of his life as he had done once before. He had bound her to this secret of his—this crime—and now he intended to heave her overboard.

The realization spread over her like a flow of red-hot lava, searing right through to her bones. Her heart seized for a few moments. She knew it! She knew it, she knew it, she knew it! She'd been a fool to let him anywhere *near* her heart.

Kent's face suddenly fell, and she thought he had sensed her emotions. The instinct proved wrong.

"There will be a death involved, Lacy, but don't believe what you read in the papers. Things will not be what they seem. I can promise you that."

She recoiled at his admission, now stunned by the incongruity facing her. *You promise me, do you, Kent? Oh, well, that fills the cockles of my heart with delight, my strapping young monster! My blue-eyed psycho . . .*

"Lacy." Kent's voice jarred her back to the table. "You okay?"

She drew a breath and settled in the chair. It occurred to her that the time she had spent hurriedly doing her face and cleaning the condo had been wasted. Entirely. "I don't know, Kent. Am I supposed to be okay?" She eyed him pointedly, thinking to thrust a dagger there.

He sat up, aware for the first time, perhaps, that she was not taking all of this with a warm, cuddly heart. "I'm sharing something with you here, Lacy. I'm *exposing* myself. I don't just walk around flashing for the public, you know. Lighten up."

"Lighten up? You waltz into my place, swear me to secrecy, and then dump all over me! How dare you? And you just want me to lighten up?" She knew that nasty little quiver had taken to her lips, but she was powerless to stop it. "And don't assume everyone you flash will like what they see!"

Lacy felt a sudden furious urge to reach out and slap him. *Don't be an imbecile, Kent! You can't just run off and steal twenty million dollars! And you can't just run off, period! Not this time!*

And then she did. In a blinding fit of anger she just reached out and slapped him across the cheek! Hard. *Smack!* The sound echoed in the room as if someone had detonated a small firecracker. Kent reeled back, grabbing at the table for support and gasping in shock.

"Whaa—"

"Don't you *what* me, Kent Anthony!" Heat washed down Lacy's neck. Her hand was stinging. Maybe she had swung a bit hard. Goodness, she had *never* slapped a man! "You're killing me here!"

His eyes flashed with anger, and he scowled. "Look. *I'm* the one who's going out on the line here. I'm risking my neck, for Pete's sake. I'm sorry I've burdened you with my life, but at least you don't have to live it. I've lost everything!" His face throbbed red. "Everything, you hear me? It's either this or suicide, and if you don't believe me, you just watch, Honey!" He jerked away from her, and she saw that his eyes had blurred with tears.

Lacy gripped her fingers into a fist and closed her eyes. *Okay, slow down, Lacy. Relax. He's just hurt.* You're *hurt.* She put her palms flat on the table, took several long pulls of air, and finally looked up at him.

He was staring at her again with those blue eyes, searching her. For what? Maybe she had mistaken his signals all along. Maybe those baby blues were looking at her as a link to reality, a partner in crime, a simple companion. God knew he was living in a void these days. And now she knew why—he was stepping off a cliff. He was playing with death. It was why the meeting with the cop had him wringing his hands.

She should be angry with herself more than with him, she thought. He had not misled her; she had simply been on the wrong track. Thinking foolish thoughts of falling in love with Kent again, while he had his eyes on this—this crime of new beginnings. And a death. Good heavens! He was planning on killing somebody!

"I *will* have to live with it, Kent," she said gently. "Whatever happens to you, happens to me now. You see that, don't you? You've climbed back into my heart." She shrugged. "And now you've just made me an accomplice, sworn to secrecy. You can understand how that might upset me a little, can't you?"

He blinked and leaned back. She could see that the thought was running through his mind for the first time. *Goodness. Men could be such apes.*

She rescued him. "But you're right. You're going to live the brunt of it all. So I may not see you again? Ever?"

He swallowed. "Maybe not. I'm sorry, Lacy. I must sound like a fool coming here and telling you all of this. I've been insensitive."

She held up a hand. "No, it's okay. It's not something I asked for, but now that it's done, I'm sure I can handle it." She looked at him and decided not to press the issue. Enough was enough. "And I shouldn't have slapped you."

"No, I guess I had that coming."

She hesitated. "Yes, I guess you did."

He gave off a nervous *humph*, off balance now.

"So, you really think striped pajamas and a buzz cut will disguise you, Kent? Maybe a ball and chain to boot? It'll be a new life, all right. Don't worry. I'll visit you often." She allowed a small grin.

He chuckled, and the tension fell like loosened shackles. "No way, Honey. If you think I'm going to prison, you obviously don't know me like you think you do."

But that was the problem. She did know him. And she knew that one way or another, his life was about to change forever. And with it, possibly hers.

"You're right. Well, I would wish you luck, but somehow it doesn't quite feel right, if you know what I mean. And I can't very well wish you failure, because I don't really go for watching people jerk and foam in electric chairs. So, I'll just hope that you change your mind. In the meantime, my lips are sealed. Fair enough?"

He nodded and grinned.

They drank coffee and talked for another hour before Kent left. He pecked her on the cheek at the door. She did not return the kiss.

Lacy cried a lot that night.

CHAPTER TWENTY-FIVE

Saturday

STEALING TWENTY million dollars, no matter how well planned, engenders undeniable risks. Big, monstrous risks. Although Kent had rehearsed each phase of the two-day operation a thousand times in his mind, the actual execution would involve dozens of unforeseen possibilities. The least of these was probably the likelihood of a Volkswagen-sized asteroid striking downtown Denver and ending his day along with a few million others'—not much he could do about that. But somewhere between *Armageddon Two* and the real world lay the lurking monsters that seemed to ruin every crook's good intentions.

Kent let the booze knock him out late Friday night. After his little confessional with Lacy he deserved a good, long drink. Besides, with nerves strung like piano wires, he doubted sleep would come any other way. There would be no drinking for the robbery's duration, which meant he would have to lay off for a few days. Or maybe forever. The nasty stuff was beginning to show.

When consciousness returned at six o'clock Saturday morning, it came like an electric shock, and he bolted from bed.

It was Saturday! *The* Saturday. Six o'clock? He was already late! He stared around his bedroom, straining his eyes against a throbbing headache. His sheets lay in a wrinkled mess, wet from sweat.

A chill flashed down his spine. Who did he think he was, off to steal twenty million dollars? *Hello there, my name is Kent. I am a criminal. Wanted by the FBI.* The whole notion suddenly struck him as nonsense! He decided then, sitting in his bed, wet with cooling sweat at a hair past six Saturday morning, to discard the whole plan.

Seven deliberate seconds passed before he rescinded the decision and threw his sheets from his legs. Twenty million good old American greenbacks had his name on them, and he wasn't about to let them go to Borst and Tomato-Head.

The trip to Salt Lake City would take nine hours, which left him two hours to dress, confirm the order for the *fish,* and retrieve the truck.

Kent ran into the bathroom, cursing himself for the alcohol. He dipped his head under the tap, ignoring the pooling water at his beltline. No time for a shower. He wasn't planning on running into anyone who would mind anyway.

He dressed on the fly, pulling on a baggy shirt and khaki slacks. Within ten minutes of his first jolt in bed, Kent was ready to leave. For good. The thought stopped him at his bedroom door. Yes, for good. He had no plans of returning to the house again—a prospect he'd thought might bring on some nostalgia. But scanning the room now, he felt only anxious to leave.

It had to look as if he'd left with the full intention of returning, which was why he took nothing. Absolutely nothing. Not a tube of toothpaste, not an extra pair of socks, not even a comb. It was always something simple that tipped off the investigators. Truly brain-dead criminals like those from Stupid Street might empty their bank accounts the day before planning a getaway. Those with no mind at all might even run around town kissing loved ones good-bye and grinning ear to ear about some secret. *Gosh, I'm sorry, Mildred. I just can't tell you. But believe me, I'm gonna be soakin' up the sun in Hawaii while you're here workin' like an idiot for the rest of your miserable life!*

That pretty much summed up his little confessional with Lacy. Goodness! Kent shivered at the thought, wondering if his little trip to Boulder might be his undoing. If the visit had been a mistake, it would be his last. He swore it then, surveying his room for the last time.

He ran into the sitting room and turned on the television. He left his bed unmade; the toothpaste lay on the vanity, capless and dribbling. A John Grisham novel rested, dog-eared, on the nightstand, bookmarked at the ninth chapter. He ran down to the kitchen and scribbled a note to Helen.

Helen,

I'm headed for the mountains to fish—clear my head. Won't be back 'til late. Sorry about dinner. If I catch anything, we can fry it up tomorrow.

Kent

He reread the note. Good enough.

Kent left through the front door, casually opened the garage and pulled out his fishing tackle. Bart someone-or-other—Mathews, he thought, Bart Mathews—waved from his riding mower three lawns up. Kent waved back, thinking that the gods were now smiling on him. Yes, indeed, Kent Anthony left his house on Saturday with one thing on his mind. Fishing. He went fishing. Kent lifted his rod in a motion that said, *Yes sir, Bart—I'm going fishing, see? Remember that.* He smiled, but his hands were trembling. He tossed the pole in the backseat, on top of a closed box he'd loaded in the wee hours last night.

Kent backed the silver Lexus into Kiowa Street for the last time and sped from suburban Littleton, blinking his eyes against nagging whispers telling him that he was nuts. *Nuts, nuts, nuts.* Maybe he should *un*-rescind the decision to rescind the decision to abort. Now, there was some clear thinking.

On the other hand, how many would-be criminals had found themselves in precisely this situation—on some precipice overlooking the actual drop and thinking the cliff suddenly looked awfully high? And there was no bungee cord to yank him back if he went into freefall, no rip cord to pull in case he decided to bail out. It was straight down to see if you could land just right and roll out of it. The facts said that 99 percent ended up splattered on the rocks below, bird meat. The facts, the facts. The facts also said that every single one of those greenbacks was waiting to go home to Papa. And in this case, he was Papa.

Besides, at some point you suddenly realized you were already there, over the cliff, falling free, and Kent decided he'd now reached that point. He'd reached it two months earlier when all hell first broke loose.

It took him forty-five minutes to reach Front Range Meat Packers. He had selected the company ten days earlier for several reasons. At least that was the story he was telling himself these days. It might be more accurate to say that he had *chanced* upon the company, and then only because of the dreams.

The dreams. Ah, yes, the dreams. Although he could hardly remember the details of the dreams when he awoke, their general impressions lingered through the day. Brilliant general impressions, like the one that suggested he find his truck on the outskirts of town, near the Coors beer-processing plant. It was as if the alcohol delivered him to a deep sleep where things became clear and memories were bright once again. He'd awakened in the middle of a dream once and found himself shaking and sweating because it really felt like someone was in the dream with him, giving him a tour.

The dreams had played on his mind like fingers across a keyboard, stretching out tunes that resonated with his own brilliance. In fact, he'd finally concluded that they were just that: his own brilliance, shocked into high gear by the events that had pushed him. Pure logic found in the quiet of sleep.

And there were several very logical reasons why the Front Range Meat Packers plant met his needs. First, and possibly most important, it was located far off the beaten track in a large warehouse district south of 470. The metal structure evoked images of the Mafia cover operations he'd seen in a dozen movies. It was also closed on the weekends, leaving a hundred short-box refrigerated trucks parked in the sprawling lot, soaking up the sun's rays until Monday. He'd walked through the lot on Tuesday, wearing glasses and sporting a slicked-back hairdo that did a good enough job of changing his appearance, he thought. He had played a meat buyer from startup Michael's Butcher Shop in East Denver, and he'd played the part well. He'd also been given a lesson on exactly why Iveco refrigerated trucks were still the best units on the road. "No chance of the meat spoiling in here. No way," meatpacker Bob "the Cruiser" Waldorf had insisted, stroking a three-inch goatee.

Which was why he needed a truck in the first place. To keep the meat—the *fish*—from spoiling.

Kent now drove up to the warehouse complex and scanned it nervously. The grounds lay deserted. He snaked the Lexus into an alley and rolled toward the adjacent complex. Gravel crunched under tires; sweat leaked down his neck. It occurred to him that the unexpected presence of a single fool here could close down the operation. There could be no witness to his visit.

The adjacent lot housed a hundred ten-by-thirty storage cubicles, half of which were empty, their white-flecked doors rusted, dented, and tilting. It was a wonder the business found willing renters for the other half of the cubicles. That was another reason he had chosen this particular location: It offered a hiding place for the Lexus.

Kent nosed the car up to space 89 and turned the motor off. Silence rang in his ears.

This was it. Technically speaking, up until now he had not actually committed any crime. Now he was about to break into a storage bin and hide his car. Not necessarily something they would fry him for, but a crime nonetheless. His heart pounded steadily. The alley on either side lay clear.

Okay. Do this, Kent. Let's do it.

Kent pulled on leather gloves and stepped from the car. He pried the roll door up with considerable effort. Its wrenching squeal echoed through the concrete cubical, and he winced. Goodness, he could have just as easily put a flashing red light atop the thing. Kmart special. One crime being committed here! Come one, come all.

But no one came. Kent hopped back into the Lexus and pulled it into the space. He grabbed his briefcase and pulled the door closed, wincing again at its screech. Still the alley remained empty. He knelt quickly, withdrew a small rivet gun from his briefcase, popped a rivet on either side of the tin door, and replaced the gun.

He left space 89 and walked briskly for Front Range Meat Packers, scouring the compound in every direction for the one fool who would ruin everything. But the compound sat still and empty in the morning light.

Kent had run through a thousand methods for stealing a vehicle—crime number two in this long string of crimes he was about to commit. It wasn't until Cruiser had offered his explanation for the five trucks outside the main compound's security fence that Kent had landed on the current plan. "See, out of a fleet of 120, those are the only 5 that are inoperable right now."

"What? Breakdowns?" Kent had said, half kidding.

"Actually, truck 24, the one on the end, is in for a routine tune-up. We take good care of our trucks. Always have, always will."

It had been a gift. Kent stood by Cruiser, frozen for a moment, sure that he'd been here before—standing next to Cruiser while the keys to the kingdom were handed over. A déjà vu from one of those dreams, perhaps. There were other ways, of course. But in an operation strewn with complications, he had no intention of turning down the offering. He'd returned Thursday night and broken into the truck with a coat hanger. If they discovered Friday that truck 24 had been left open, they would probably move it. But it was a risk he had taken gladly. The process of breaking into the truck had taken him two full hours. He couldn't very well take two hours in broad daylight struggling on the hood with a coat hanger.

Truck 24 sat, unmoved, and Kent covered the last thirty yards over the graveled lot in a run. He grabbed the truck's door handle, held his breath, and pressed the latch. The door opened. He sighed with relief, tossed his briefcase on the bench seat, and climbed up, shaking like a leaf. A small ball of victory swelled in his chest. So far, so good. Like taking candy from a baby. He was in the cab, and the coast was clear!

One of the primary benefits of spending six years in higher learning institutions was learning how to learn. It was a skill that Kent had perfected. And one of the things he'd learned as of late was how to hot-wire a truck. Specifically an Iveco 2400 refrigerated truck. Not from a book entitled *How to Hot-Wire Your Favorite Truck,* no. But from a book on safeguarding your property, along with an engineering manual, an auto mechanic's electrical guide, and, of course, an Iveco 2400 repair manual—each source lending a few details to his collective learning experience. In the end, he knew precisely how to hot-wire an Iveco 2400. The procedure was supposed to be a thirty-second affair.

It took Kent ten minutes. The Phillips head he'd brought was a tad small and wanted to slip with every rotation. When he finally freed the panel under the dash, the wires were so far behind the steering column that he nearly ripped the skin from his fingers prying them out. But in the end his learning experience proved valid. When he touched the red wire to the white wire, the truck rumbled to life.

The sudden sound startled Kent, and he jerked up, promptly dropping the wires and hitting his head on the steering wheel in one smooth motion. The motor died.

Kent cursed and righted himself on the seat. He gazed about the compound, breathing heavily. The coast was still clear. He bent over and restarted the truck. His hands were sweating in the leather gloves, and he briefly considered pulling them free. But a dozen episodes of *Forensics* crashed into his mind at once, and he rejected the notion.

He shoved the truck into reverse, backed it into the lane, and nosed it toward the complex's exit a hundred yards off. One look and any reasonable person would have known that the driver perched behind the wheel in truck 24, sneaking toward the exit gate, was not your typical driver headed out for deliveries. For one thing, typical drivers don't sit like ice sculptures on the front edge of the seat, gripping the wheel as if it were the safety rail on a roller-coaster ride. For another, they don't jerk their heads back and forth like some windup doll gone berserk. But then, none of that mattered, because there were no reasonable people—or for that matter, *any* people—to see Kent creep from the lot in truck 24.

Within three minutes he was back on the thoroughfare, headed west, anxious and sweaty and checking the mirrors every five seconds, but undiscovered.

He studied the gauges carefully. The company had seen fit to leave truck 24 full of fuel. *Way to go, Cruiser.* Kent flipped on the cooling unit and rechecked the gauges. In fact, he rechecked the gauges fifteen times in those first ten minutes, before finally settling down for the seven-hour drive to Salt Lake City.

Only he didn't really settle down. He bit his nails and walked through every detail of his plan for the thousandth time. Now that he'd actually jumped over this cliff, the ground below was looking a little more rugged than before. In fact, having executed a brilliant plan that left absolutely nothing to chance, it occurred to him that he had virtually *depended* on chance up to this point. The chance that his alarm clock would actually work that morning. The chance that no one would be at Front Range Meat Packers on a Saturday morning, regardless of the fact that they were closed. The chance that the Iveco had not been moved into the secure compound. The chance that he could actually get the Iveco started.

And now Kent began to imagine the road ahead strewn with chances . . . with flat tires and traffic delays and power outages and routine pullovers. With boulders falling from the nearby cliffs and closing the road. Or worse, squashing his truck like a roach. That one would be God's doing—if indeed Gloria had been right and there was a God. Unless it was an earthquake's doing, in which case it would be Mother Nature reaching out to express her opinion of the matter.

Don't, son. Don't do this.

He glanced at the speedometer, saw that he exceeded the posted sixty miles-per-hour speed limit, and eased his foot from the accelerator. Getting pulled over for a speeding ticket, now, that would be a story for Stupid Street.

Kent reached the preselected dirt turnoff thirty minutes later and pulled into a grove of trees blocking the view to the interstate. It took him no more than five minutes to pull out the large magnetic signs he'd hidden in the tall grass midweek and slap them into place along each side of the truck. He studied his handiwork. For the next twenty-four hours, Front Range Meat Packers truck 24 would be known as McDaniel's Mortuary's truck 1. The signs along each side said so. In black lettering that was quaint and unobtrusive but clear and definite, so there would be no doubt.

Kent pulled back onto the highway and brought the truck up to full speed. Yes, he was most definitely over the cliff now. Falling like a stone.

CHAPTER TWENTY-SIX

FINDING THE right body, the "fish," and arranging for the pickup had taken Kent the better part of a week. He'd approached the challenge in two parts. First, setting up a plausible body pickup and second, actually finding the body itself.

Although he'd established McDaniel's Mortuary as a legitimate business only two weeks earlier, to look at the ghost company's Web site you would think it was one of the older houses in the West. Of course, local mortuaries would be the first to identify a new player that suddenly appeared in their territories, so he'd been forced to use distance as a buffer against recognition. It wasn't likely that independently owned mortuaries in Los Angeles, for example, would be familiar with funeral homes in Denver.

The company of choice also needed to be large enough to handle transfers to and from other cities on a regular basis. The request for a particular body on ice could not be an unusual occurrence. In addition, the mortuary had to be computerized, allowing Kent some kind of access to its data files.

These first three restrictions narrowed the field of eligible mortuaries from 9,873 nationally to 1,380. But it was the fourth requirement that put the breaks on eligibility for all but three unwitting participants. The mortuary had to be in possession of the right body.

The right body. A body that was six-feet-one-inch tall, male, Caucasian, with a body weight of between 170 and 200 pounds. A body that had no known surviving relatives. And a body that had no identifiable dental records outside of the FBI's main identification files.

In most cases mortuaries hold cadavers no longer than two or three days, a fact that limited the number of available bodies. For a week, Kent ran dry runs, breaking into the networks using the Web, identifying bodies that fit his requirements.

The process was one of downloading lists and cross-referencing them with the FBI's central data bank—a relatively simple process for someone in Kent's shoes. But it was arduous and sweaty and nerve-racking nonetheless. He ran the searches from his system at home, sipping at the tall bottle next to his monitor while he waited for the files to download.

On Tuesday, he'd found only one body, and it was in Michigan. That had put the jitters right though him, and it had taken nearly a full bottle of the hard drink to bring them under control.

On Wednesday, he'd found three bodies, one of which was actually in Denver. Too close to home. The other two were in California—too far. But at least there were three of them.

On Thursday, he'd found no bodies, and he had shattered his keyboard with a fist, a fit he immediately regretted. It ruined both his right pinkie—which had taken the brunt of the contact, somewhere between the letters J and U by the scattered keys—and his night. There were no twenty-four-hour keyboard stores that he was aware of.

Friday he'd found three bodies, to shuddering sighs of relief. Two on the East Coast and one in Salt Lake City. He downed two long slugs of liquor at the find. Tom Brinkley. *Thank you, Tom Brinkley. I love you, Tom Brinkley!*

Tom Brinkley had died of a gunshot wound to the stomach, and according to the records, no one seemed to have a clue about him beyond that. From all indications the man had shot himself, which also indicated to Kent that there *was* at least one other thing known about the man. He was an idiot. Only an idiot would attempt suicide with a bullet through the gut. Nevertheless, that is precisely what the authorities had concluded. Go figure.

Now poor Tom's body sat awaiting cremation in Salt Lake's largest mortuary, Peace Valley Funeral Home. Kent had tagged his "fish" then—processed an order for a transfer of the catch to McDaniel's Mortuary in Las Vegas, Nevada. Reason? Relatives had been located and wished a local burial. *Now I lay my fish to sleep.* The funeral home had informed him by e-mail that the body had already been stripped and prepared for cremation. *Not a problem. Will pick up as is.* It was in a sealed box. Did he want it in a body bag? A body bag was customary. *Not a problem. Will pick up as is.*

He scheduled a "will call" Saturday between 3 and 5 P.M. He would pick up the fish then. Only he knew it was not a fish, of course. It was just one of those interesting quirks that a mind gone over the edge tends to make. It was a dead body, as cold as a fish and possibly gray like a fish, but certainly not a fish. And hopefully not slimy like a fish.

He confirmed the order an hour later from a pay phone. The girl who answered his questions had a bad habit of snapping chewing gum while listening, but otherwise she seemed cooperative enough.

"But we close at five. You get here a minute past, and you won't find a soul around," she warned.

It had taken a mere forty-five minutes with his fingers flying nervously over the keyboard to make the changes to Tom Brinkley's FBI file. The tingles of excitement had shortened his breath for an hour following. Actually *that* had been the first crime. He'd forgotten. Breaking into the FBI files was not a laughable prank. It had not seemed so criminal, though.

Kent let the memories run through his mind and kept his eyes peeled as he negotiated I-70 west. The trip over the mountains was uneventful, unless you considered it eventful to bite your nails clean off every time a patrol car popped up in your rearview mirror. By the time Kent reached the outskirts of Salt Lake, his nerves had frayed, leaving him feeling as though he'd downed a dozen No-Doze tablets in a single sitting. He pulled in to a deserted rest stop, hurried to the back of the truck, and popped the refrigerated box open for the first time.

A cloud of trapped vapor billowed out, cold and white. The cooler worked well enough. Kent pulled himself up to the back bumper and then into the unit and waved his hand against the billows of vapor. The interior drifted into view about him. Metal shelves arose on the right. A long row of hooks hung from the ceiling on the left like claws begging for their slabs of meat. *For their fish.*

Kent shivered. It was cold. He imagined the gum-snapping gal at Peace Valley Funeral Home, clipboard in hand, staring up at those hooks.

"What are those for?"

"Those? Oh, we find that bodies are much easier to carry if you take them from their caskets and hook them up. You guys don't do that?"

No, the hooks would not do. But then, he was not some white-trash bozo from Stupid Street, was he? No sir. He had already planned for this eventuality. Cruiser had told him that all trucks carried thermal blankets to cover the meat in case of emergency. Truck 24's blankets lay in a neat stack to Kent's right. He pulled them off the shelf and strung two along the hooks like a shower curtain. A divider.

"What are those for?"

"Those? Oh, that's where we hide the really ugly ones so people don't throw up. You guys don't do that?"

Kent swallowed and climbed out of the cooler box. He left the rest stop and slowly made his way to the mark on his map that approximated the funeral home's location. To any other vehicle parked beside him at a light, he resembled a mortuary truck on a Saturday run. Right? The magnetic signs were dragging on the street, exposing the meat packer's logo, right? Because that would look obscene. So then why did he have such a hard time looking anywhere but straight ahead at stoplights?

Liberty Valley's wrought-iron gates loomed suddenly on Kent's left, bordered by long rows of pines. He caught a glimpse of the white building set back from the street, and his heart lodged firmly in his throat. He rounded the block and approached the main gate again, fighting the gut-wrenching impulse to drive on. Just keep on driving, right back to Denver. There was madness in this plan. Stealing a body. *Brilliant software engineer loses sanity and steals a body from funeral home. Why? It is yet unknown, but some have speculated that there may be other bodies, carved up, hidden.*

Then the gate was there in front of him, and Kent pulled in, clearing his throat of the knot that had been steadily growing since entering this cursed city.

The long, paved driveway rolled under him like a black snake. He followed a sign that led him to the rear, where a loading bay sat empty. A buzz droned in his head—the sound of the truck's wheels on the pavement. The steady moan of madness. He backed up to the door, pulled the parking brake, and left the engine running. He couldn't very well be seen fiddling with wires to restart it.

He set himself on autopilot now, executing the well-rehearsed plan. From his briefcase he withdrew glasses and a mustache. He fixed them quickly to his face, checked his image in the rearview mirror, and pulled out his clipboard.

A blonde-headed girl with a pug nose pushed open the rear door of the funeral home on his second ring. She was smacking gum.

"You from McDaniel's?"

He could feel the sweat breaking from his brow. He pushed his glasses back up his nose. "Yes."

She turned and headed into the dim storage area. "Good. You almost didn't make it. We close in fifteen minutes, you know."

"Yeah."

"So, you from Las Vegas?"

"Yeah."

"Never heard of McDaniel's. You ever win big money?"

Big money? His heart skipped a beat. What could she know of big money?

She sensed his hesitation and glanced over at him, smiling. "You know. Las Vegas. Gambling. Did you ever win big?"

"Uh . . . No. I don't gamble, really."

Coffins rose to the ceiling on all sides. Empty, no doubt. Hopefully. She led him to a huge side door made of steel. A cooler door.

"I don't blame you. Gambling's a sin." She popped the door open and stepped through. A dozen coffins, some shiny and elaborate, some no more than plywood boxes, rested on large shelves in the cooler. The girl walked over to one of the plain boxes, checked the tag, then slapped it.

"This is it. Grab that gurney there, and it's all yours."

Kent hesitated. The gurney, of course. He grabbed the wheeled table and pushed it parallel to the casket. Together they pulled the plywood box onto the gurney, a task made surprisingly easy by rollers on the shelf.

The girl slapped the box again. Seemed to like doing that. "There you go. Sign this, and you're all set."

Kent signed her release and offered a smile. "Thanks."

She returned the smile and opened the door for him.

Halfway back to the outer door he decided it might be best if she did not watch him load the body. "What should I do with the gurney when I'm done?" he asked.

"Oh, I'll help you."

"No. No problem, I can handle it. I should be able to—I've done this enough. I'll just shove it back through the door when I'm done."

She smiled. "It's okay. I don't mind. I need to close down anyway."

Kent thought about objecting again but decided it would only raise her curiosity. She held the door again, and he rolled the brown box into the sun. From this angle, with the truck parked below in the loading dock, he caught sight of the Iveco's roof. And it wasn't a pretty sight.

He jerked in shock and immediately covered by coughing hard. But his breathing was suddenly ragged and obvious. Large red words splashed across the roof of the Iveco's box: Front Range Meat Packers.

He flung a hand toward the bottom of the truck's roll door, hoping to draw her attention there. "Can you get the door?" If she saw the sign he might need to improvise. And he had no clue how to do that. Stealing bodies was not something he had perfected yet.

But Miss Gum-Smacker jumped to his suggestion and yanked the door up like a world-class chain-saw starter. She'd obviously done that a few times. Kent rolled the gurney down the short ramp and into the truck, gripping the ramp's aluminum railing to steady his jitters. As long as they remained down here, she would not have a chance to see the sign. Now, when he drove off . . . that would be a different story.

It occurred to him then that the casket would not fit on the shelves designed for meat. It would have to go on the floor.

"How do you lower this?" he asked.

She stepped in and looked at him with a raised brow. "You're asking me how to lower a gurney?"

"I usually carry ours—battery powered. All you do is push a button. But this is a new rig. It's not outfitted properly yet." Now, *there* was some quick thinking. Powered gurneys? There must be such a thing these days. She nodded, apparently satisfied, and lowered the contraption. Together they slid the coffin off and let it rest on the floor. Now to get her back into the warehouse without looking back.

"Here, let me help you," he said and walked right past her to the warehouse door, which he yanked open.

She wheeled the gurney up after him and pushed it through the door. "Thanks," she said and walked into the dim light.

"Thank you. Have a great weekend."

"Sure. Same to you."

Kent released the door and heard its lock engage. He glanced around and ran for the cab, trembling. What if she were to come back out? *"Hey, you forgot your clipboard."* Only he hadn't forgotten it. It was in his right hand, and he tossed it onto the bench seat. With a final glance back, he sprang into the truck, released the brake, and pulled out of the loading dock, his heart slamming in his chest.

He'd crossed the parking area and was pulling onto the long, snakelike drive before remembering the rear door. It was still open!

Kent screeched to a halt and ran to the back, beating back images of a shattered box strewn behind the truck. But not this day; this day the gods were smiling on him. The box remained where he'd left it, unmoved. He pulled the door closed, flooded with relief at small favors.

He pulled out of Liberty Valley's gates, shaking like a leaf. A full city block flew by before he realized that the jerking motion under him resulted from a fully engaged parking brake. He released it and felt the truck surge forward. Now, that was a Stupid Street trick if there ever was one. He had to get control of himself here!

Two blocks later the chills of victory began their run up and down his spine. Then Kent threw back his head and yelled out loud in the musty cabin. "Yes!"

The driver in the Cadillac beside him glanced his way. He didn't care.

"Yes, yes, yes!"

He had himself a body. A fish.

CHAPTER TWENTY-SEVEN

HELEN SCANNED the note again and knew it said more than it read. This fishing business was hogwash, because it didn't bring a smile to her face as in, *Oh, good. He's gone to catch us some trout. I love trout.* Instead, it brought a knot to her gut, as in, *Oh, my God! What's he gone and done?*

She had felt the separation all day, walking the streets of Littleton. It was a quiet day in the heavens. A sad day. The angels were mourning. She still had energy to burn, but her heart was not so light, and she found praying difficult. God seemed distracted. Or maybe *she* was distracted.

Helen had walked the same twenty-mile route five days now, stopping briefly at the hot-dog stand at Fifth and Grand each day for a drink and a quick exchange with its proprietor, Chuck. She'd suspected from the first words out of Chuck's mouth that he was a man holed up in his religion.

Today she had helped him out of his shell.

"You walk every day, Helen?"

She'd nodded.

"How far?"

"A long way. Longer than I can count."

"More than a mile?"

"I can count a mile, young man."

"Longer?"

"Longer than I can count."

He'd chuckled nervously. "Ten miles?"

She sipped at the lemonade he'd served her. "Longer."

"Twenty?" he asked incredulous.

She shrugged. "I don't know for sure."

"But that's impossible! You walk twenty miles *every* day?"

She looked right into his eyes then. "Yes, I'm an intercessor, Chuck. You know what that is, don't you? I will walk as long as he requires me to."

He glanced around quickly. "You mean you pray?"

"I pray, and I walk. And as long as I'm walking and praying I don't feel strain on my legs at all." She eyed him steadily. "How does that sound, Chuck?"

He stood there with his mouth open, possibly thinking that this kind woman he'd served over the last five days was stark-raving mad. "Sound strange? Well, there's more, Chuck. I see things too. I walk on legs that have no business walking, and I see things." It was the first time she had been so vocal about this business to a stranger, but she could hardly resist.

She pointed to the overcast sky and gave it a faraway look. "You see those clouds there? Or this air?" She swept her hand through the air. "Suppose you could tear away this air and expose what lay behind. What do you think you would find?"

Chuck the hot-dog man was stuck in the open-mouth, wide-eyes look. He did not answer.

"I'll tell you what you would find. A million beings peering over the railing at the choices of one man. You would find the real game. Because it's all about what happens on the other side, Chuck. And if you could tear the heavens apart, you would see that. All this other stuff you see with those marbles in your head are props for the real game." She flashed him a grin and let that sink in. "At least, that's one way of looking at it all. And I think there is a game over your soul as well, young man."

She had left him like that, holding a hot dog in one hand with his mouth gaping as if he were ready to shove it in.

It had been the high point of the day, actually, because she knew Chuck's life would change now. But the balance of her walk had been a somber one.

Back at home, Helen picked up the phone and called Pastor Bill at home.

"Bill Madison here."

"He's gone off the deep end, Bill."

"Helen?"

"Yes."

"What do you mean?"

"Kent's gone off the deep end, and I smell death in the air. I think he may be in trouble."

"Whoa. You think he may *die?* I didn't think he *could* die in this thing."

"I didn't either. But there's death in the air. And I think it's his death, although I don't know that. There was a lot of silence in the heavens today."

"Then maybe you should warn him. Tell him about this. You haven't been . . . you know . . . told not to, have you?"

"No. Not specifically. I've had no desire to tell him, which usually means that I shouldn't. But I think you may be right. I think I will tell him the next time I see him."

They let the phones rest silent for a moment.

"Helen, are you walking tomorrow?"

"Did you awake this morning, Bill?"

"What? Of course I did."

"The answer to your question should be as obvious, don't you think? I walk every day."

He continued after regrouping himself. "Would you mind if I walked with you for a spell tomorrow? Before church?"

"I would like that, Pastor."

"Good. Five o'clock?"

"Five-thirty. I sleep in on Sundays."

IF KENT thought he could have managed it, he would have driven straight back to Denver. But his body was in no condition to pull a twenty-four-hour shift without sleeping. He had to rest somewhere. At least, that was the way he'd planned it on paper.

He pulled into Grady's Truck Stop two hours outside of Denver, near midnight. A hundred sleeping rigs lined the graveled lot to the west of the all-night diner, and he pulled the little Iveco between two large, purring diesels. So far, so good. No flat tires, no routine pullovers, no breakdowns, no boulders from the sky. He could easily be a real driver for a mortuary, handling just one more body in a series of a hundred.

Kent locked the truck up and walked briskly toward the café. The cool night air rushed softly under the power of the towering trucks on all sides. What were the odds of being recognized in such a remote spot? He paused by the front wheel of a black International tractor-trailer and studied the diner thirty yards away. It stood there all decked out in neon like a Christmas tree. Two thoughts crossed his mind simultaneously, and they brought his pulse up to a steady thump.

The first was that the Iveco back there did not have a lock on the rear door. That had been an oversight on his part. He should have bought a padlock. A grisly wino on the prowl would find his little Iveco easy pickings. Only when the vagrant got back to his lair would he and his cohorts discover that the brown box did not contain rifles or beef or a priceless statue or any such treasure, but a cadaver. A smelly old fish. A dead body—not fit for the eating unless you were on an airplane that went down in the Andes and it was either you or the bodies.

The second thought was that entering Grady's diner, all lit up like a Christmas tree, was starting to seem like one of those stupid mistakes a criminal from Stupid Street might make. *"Yes sir, everything was going perfect until I ran into Bill at Grady's Diner, and he asked me what I was doing at one in the morning toting a cadaver around in a meat truck. Imagine, Bill at Grady's Diner! Who would have possibly thought?"*

Anybody with half a brain would have thought, that's who would have thought! He should have brought his own food. Although he *was* two hours out of Denver. Who that he knew could possibly be here at midnight? But that was just the point, wasn't it? What would *he* be doing here at midnight?

Kent slunk back into the shadows and climbed into the cab he'd made home for the last sixteen hours. He lifted a 7-Up can he'd purchased four hours earlier at the Utah border and swallowed the flat dregs in one gulp. There would be plenty of time for food and drink later. Now he needed sleep.

But sleep did not come easily. For one thing, he found himself craving a real drink. Just one quick nip to settle the nerves. Grady's could probably oblige him with at least a six-pack of beer.

"Don't be a fool," he muttered and lay down on the bench seat.

It was then, parked outside of Grady's, two hours from Denver, that the first major flaw in his plan presented itself to him like a siren in the night. He jerked upright and stared, wide eyed, out the windshield.

Helen! Helen had moved in *after* he'd laid out the timetable. When the rest of his plan was put into play, they would question her, and that questioning rang through his head now, clear and concise—and as condemning as a judge's gavel.

"You're saying he left you a note stating he's going fishing on Saturday but he never comes back? Not even on Sunday?"

"Yes, officer. As far as I can tell."

"So he goes fishing—we know that from the neighbor who saw him—and goes straight to the office in his fishing gear thirty-six hours later, without bothering to come home. No pun intended here, but doesn't that smell a little fishy?"

He had decided not to return for the simple reason that he had the body to contend with. He couldn't very well drive up to his house in the meat truck. Neither could he drive around town with a body in the trunk of the Lexus for a whole day. At some point things would be smelling more than just fishy.

But that was before Helen.

An alarm went off in his head. *Stupid, stupid, stupid!* He had to get to Denver. Get home somehow.

Kent brought the truck to life and roared back to the freeway, once again bouncing on the edge of the seat like some kind of idiot.

An hour later, rumbling into the outskirts of suburban Denver, he conceded to the only plan that made sense in the morning's wee hours. A new element of risk threatened now, but nobody ever said stealing twenty million would be light on the risk factor.

Kent slowly wound his way back to the Front Range Meat Packers compound south of 470 and entered the industrial maze of metal buildings. He killed the lights and crept forward, his eyes peeled for motion, his muscles rigid, his fingers wrapped white on the wheel.

Two minutes later, Kent eased the Iveco into its original space and pulled the ignition wires free. The engine sputtered to silence. By the watch on his right wrist, it was two o'clock in the morning.

For five minutes he sat in the silence, allowing the distant highway drone to settle his nerves. He finally climbed from the truck and walked behind. The roll door remained latched. He eased the lever up and pulled the door up. The box lay on the floor, swirling in a cold mist. He closed the door.

It took him another fifteen minutes to repair the cut wire in the steering column and return the cab to its original condition. Satisfying himself that he no longer needed access to the cab, he locked the doors and shut them quietly. Come Monday morning, if Cruiser had an inkling to pull truck 24 in for service, he would hopefully find her just as he'd left her. Now, if the truck would be kind enough to keep his body hidden and free from rot for another twelve hours without its cooling unit in operation, all would be well.

Kent had made it halfway back to the storage unit housing the Lexus before realizing he'd left the McDaniel's Mortuary signs on the truck. He hastily retreated and tore them free, cursing himself for the oversight. If he could have stopped somewhere and flogged the stupidity from his mind he would have done it without consideration. Evidently he was discovering what most criminals discover midcrime: Stupidity is something that comes upon you *during* the crime, not before. Like the rising sun, you cannot escape it. You can only hope to do your dirty deed before it fries you.

Kent headed back to the storage units, hauling his briefcase in one hand and the rolled-up signs in the other. Sweat soaked his shirt, and he let stealth slip a little. You can't very well pretend to be invisible lugging ten-foot rolls of vinyl under your arm. He plopped the load on the asphalt before the storage door, retrieved the rivet poppers from his briefcase, and made quick work of the fasteners he'd installed earlier.

The Lexus gleamed silver in the moonlight, undisturbed. Kent stuffed the signs in the trunk, tossed the briefcase into the passenger seat, and climbed into the familiar cockpit. He made it all the way to the industrial park's entrance before flipping on his lights. It was 2:38 Sunday morning when he finally entered highway 470 and headed for home, wondering what other small mistake he had made back there.

Yet he had made it, hadn't he? No, not really—not at all. Really he had not even started.

Kent left his Lexus on the street where it would be seen—right in front of the red *No Street Parking* sign by his house. The small black letters below promised that violators would be towed, but they'd never actually hauled any car off that he knew of, and he doubted they would begin on a Sunday.

He entered the house, flipped his shoes off at the front door, made a little noise in the kitchen, moved a few items around, and headed for his bedroom. The trick was to clearly show his presence without actually engaging Helen. He did not want to engage Helen. Not at all.

And, considering the old lady's walking obsession, which he assumed was an everyday affair, missing her might not be so difficult. On the other hand, today was Sunday. She might not walk on Sundays. If she did not, she would at least leave for church. He would have to be gone by noon.

Kent locked the door to the master suite, peeled off his clothes, and fell into bed. He slowly drifted into a fitful sleep.

CHAPTER TWENTY-EIGHT

HELEN SLIPPED out onto the porch after the doorbell's first ring.

"He's here, Bill."

The pastor did not respond immediately.

"Let's walk." She stepped past him and strolled to the street. The silver Lexus sat along the street beside the driveway. She turned left at the sidewalk and walked briskly past it.

"He came home last night."

"He catch any fish?" Bill asked, beside her now.

"Don't know. He's hiding something."

"Hiding what? How do you know?"

"I don't know what he's hiding, but I'm going to find out the minute I get home. They're on pins and needles up there; that's how I know. Death is in the air. I can feel it."

"You mind if we slow down a little, Helen? You're walking pretty fast here."

"We have to walk fast. I'm cutting it short today. Real short. I've got to get back there." She glanced down at her Reeboks and noted they were wearing thin in the toes.

"You want to pray, Bill?"

"Sure."

"Pray, then. Pray out loud."

KENT AWOKE with a start. Something was wrong. His chest felt as though a jackrabbit had taken up residence there and was testing its thumpers. Only this was his heart—not some bunny. Which meant he'd had another dream.

He could remember nothing—not even why he was in his own bed.

Then he remembered everything, and he leapt from the bed.

Yesterday he had stolen a truck, driven to Utah, stolen a dead body, and returned to Front Range Meat Packers, where the body now lay dead; slowly warming in the back of truck 24. He'd come back to the house because of Helen. Dear Mother-in-law Helen.

It was this last tidbit that had awakened him to the drumming of Thumper's feet—this bit about Helen. He could not allow Helen to see him. And that was a problem because Helen was close. Imminent. Maybe at the bedroom door right now, waiting for the sound of his stirring.

He grabbed the khaki slacks and shirt he'd thrown off last night and pulled them on. For the second morning in a row he faced the task of leaving the room as though he fully intended to return. He made a quick circuit, rubbing some toothpaste on his teeth with his forefinger and tossing the tube in the drawer; throwing the covers loosely over the bed, half made; moving the Grisham novel forward a few pages. And he did all of it without knowing precisely what he was doing.

No matter—Helen was coming.

Kent cracked the door and listened for the sound of movement downstairs with stilled breath. Nothing. Thank God. He slipped into the hall and flew down the steps two at a time. In a matter of sixty seconds flat he managed to pull out the orange juice, slop some peanut butter on a bagel, down half of both, and hopefully leave the general impression that he had enjoyed a leisurely breakfast on a Sunday morning. He snatched up a pen and, taking a deep breath to still his quivering hand, wrote over the note he'd left yesterday.

Hi, Helen.

Sorry I missed you. Had a great day fishing. All too small to keep. If not home by six, don't wait.

Kent

Kent laid the note on the counter and ran for the entrance. The microwave clock read 9:30. He opened the front door carefully, begging not to see Helen's smiling mug. Sunlight stung his eyes, and he squinted. His Lexus sat idle on the street. Helen's yellow Pinto was parked in the garage and a third car, a green Accord, sat in the driveway behind the Pinto.

A friend's car. In the house? No, he had not heard a sound. Helen was out walking with a friend who owned a green Accord. Which meant Helen would be walking down the street with said friend, ready to run off to church. And church started at ten, didn't it?

Kent pulled the door shut and walked for his Lexus, head down, as nonchalantly as possible. If they were down the street, he would ignore them. Had to. Why? Because he just had to. He'd awakened with that realization buzzing through his skull, and it hadn't quieted just yet.

He brought the Lexus to life without looking up. It was when he started the U-turn that he saw them—like two figures on the home stretch of the Boston Marathon, arms pumping. He knew then what it felt like to jump out of your skin, because he almost did. Right there in the tan leather seats of the Lexus. Only his frozen grip on the steering wheel kept him from hitting his head on the ceiling, which was good because they might have seen the movement. You can't just throw your arms up in surprise and then pretend not to see someone—it just doesn't come off as genuine. Kent's foot jerked a little on the accelerator, causing the car to lurch a tad, but otherwise he managed to keep the turn tight and smooth.

He had a hard time removing his eyes from Helen. She and the man were about a block off, leaning into their walk, waving at him now. She wore a yellow dress that fluttered in the breeze, clearly exposing those ridiculous knee-socks pulled up high.

Should he wave back? It was obviously a *Stop-the-car* wave by its intensity, but he could pretend he'd mistaken it for a *Have-a-good-day* wave and return it before roaring off into the sunset. No, better to pretend not to have seen at all.

Kent's foot pressed firmly on the gas pedal, and he left them just breaking into a run. His neck remained rigid. Goodness, what did they know? They pulled up and dropped their arms. *"Sorry, guys, I just didn't see you. I swear I didn't see a thing. You sure it was me?"*

But he wouldn't be asking that question anytime soon, would he? Never. He glanced at the dash clock: 9:35. He had ten hours to burn.

It took Kent a good ten minutes to calm down, nibbling on blunted fingernails, thinking. Thinking, thinking, thinking. In the mirror his face stared back unshaven and wet. He should have cleaned up a little—at least thrown on some deodorant. Only a slob or a man in a great hurry would neglect basic body care. And he was beginning to smell. Kent sniffed at his armpit. No, beginning was far too kind. He reeked. Which would not present a significant problem unless he ran into someone who took note. And even then what could they do? Call the local police and report the reeking swamp thing tooling about town in the silver Lexus? Not likely. Still, it might leave an impression in some clerk's head.

"Did he appear normal to you?"

"No sir, officer, I daresay not. Not unless you consider walking around with radishes for eyes and smelling of rotted flesh at thirty feet normal."

"That bad, huh?"

"That bad."

Kent decided he would drive to Boulder for a burger. He had the time to burn, and on further thought, he needed the miles on his car. It had just gone on a fishing trip.

Two hours later he pulled into a truck stop ten miles south of Boulder, where he managed to splash some water under his pits and purchase a dry sandwich without incident. He spent three hours on the back lot mulling over matters of life and death before pulling out and cruising back toward Denver the long way. And did he use his credit card? No, of course he didn't use his credit card. That would be brain dead. Stupid, stupid. And he was done being stupid.

Darkness had enveloped Denver by the time Kent nosed the Lexus back into the industrial park holding Tom Brinkley's dead body.

Matters were considerably simpler this time around. He shut off his lights, thankful for a three-quarter moon, and idled through the alleys to the back fence. Truck 24 sat faithfully next to its two cousins, and Kent squeezed his fist in satisfaction. "You'd better be there, baby," he whispered, staring at the truck's roll door. "You'd better be right where I left you." This, of course, was spoken to the dead body, hopefully still lying in the plywood box. And hopefully not yet rotting. Things were smelling bad enough already.

Kent backed the Lexus to within two feet of the truck, hopped out, and popped the trunk. He pulled on a pair of surgical gloves, unlatched the Iveco's door, and yanked up. A heavy musty smell filled his nostrils—musty more like wet socks than musty like a dead body, he thought, although he'd never smelled musty like a dead body before. Still, it was not the smell he'd read about.

The back of the truck opened like a yawning jaw, dark to the throat, with a tongue resting still and brown in the middle. Only the tongue was the box. Kent exhaled in relief.

He pulled a crowbar from his trunk and jumped into the truck. The coffin had been screwed shut, making the prying-open part of the plan a little noisy, but within three minutes the lid lay at an angle, daring him to topple it off.

The sensations that struck next had not been well rehearsed. In fact, not planned at all. Kent had his hand under the lid, ready to flip it casually off, when it occurred to him that he was about to stare into the face of the fish. But it wasn't a fish at all. It was a dead body. He froze. And he wasn't going to just *stare,* but he was going to touch and lift and hoist that cold, gray flesh around. A chill cooled his neck.

A few seconds tripped by in silence. He should get the plastic first.

Kent jumped from the truck and grabbed a roll of black plastic from the car's trunk. He climbed back into the truck and stood over the coffin. *Now or never, buddy. Just do it.*

He did it. He kicked the lid off and stared into the coffin.

Tom Brinkley lay gray and slightly swollen with a hole the size of a fist in his gut. His hair was blond, and his eyes were open. For a full five seconds Kent could not move. It was those two eyes staring at him like marbles—glinting with life in the moonlight, but dead. Then the scent wafted past his nostrils. Faint, oh, so very faint but reaching right through to his bones, and his stomach was not responding so happily.

By the looks of it, Tom Brinkley's stomach had not responded so happily, either. It appeared as though he'd used a bazooka to end his life, judging by the size of that hole. His message to the funeral home flashed through his mind. *Not a problem. Will pick up as is.* Now he was staring at *"as is,"* and it *was* a problem.

Kent spun away and grabbed the metal shelving. Goodness, this was not in the plan. *It's just a body, for heaven's sake! A dead thing, like a fish, with a big hole in its stomach. Get on with it!*

And what if he couldn't get on with it? What if he simply did not have the stomach to slump this body around? He stared at the gloves on his hands; they would shield him from any lingering disease. Any danger he imagined was only in his mind. Right?

The thought forced Kent into a state of bumbling overdrive. He grabbed a lungful of air, whirled back to the body, reached into the coffin, and yanked Mr. Brinkley clean out in one smooth motion.

Or so he'd intended.

Problem was, this cadaver had lain dormant for a good forty-eight hours and was not so eager to change its position. They call it rigor-mortis, and the dead man had found it already.

Kent had not aimed his hands as he dived into the casket; he'd just grabbed, and his fingers had closed around a shoulder and a side of ribs, both cold and moist. The body came halfway vertical before slipping from Kent's grip. Mr. Brinkley turned lazily and landed on the edge of the coffin. His stiff upper torso slipped clean out and landed on the truck's floor boards with a loud, skull-crushing thud. Now the body slumped over the casket, belly down and butt up in the moonlight with its hands hanging out of the rear as though paying homage to the moon.

Kent swallowed the bile creeping up his throat and leapt from the truck, grunting in near panic. If there really was a God, he was making this awfully difficult. None of the books had made mention of the clammy, slippery skin. Had he known, he would have brought towels or something. Of course the books had not featured chapters on the preferred methods of lugging around dead bodies. Usually these things stayed peacefully on their tables or in their caskets.

Standing on the ground, he glanced up at the body in the back of the truck. It was gray in the dim light, like some kind of stone statue memorializing butts. Well, if he didn't get that butt into the trunk soon, there'd be a dozen cops shining their flashlights on that monument, asking silly questions. Questions like, *"What are you doing with Mr. Brinkley, Kent?"*

He turned gruffly to the job at hand, clamped his hands around each wrist, and pulled hard. The cadaver flopped out of the box and slid easily enough, like a stiff fish being dragged along the dock. He pulled it halfway out before bending under its midsection. The thought of that hole in Mr. Brinkley's stomach made him hesitate. He should have rolled the old guy in plastic.

The plastic! He'd left it by the coffin. Dumping the body into the Lexus without covering it would most definitely be one of those idiotic things Stupid Street criminals did. If they ever had an inkling to look, forensics experts would have a field day in there. Kent shoved the body back into the truck, snatched the plastic, and spread it quickly along the trunk floor, draping it over the edges. He bent back into the truck again for the wrists and yanked Mr. Brinkley's naked body out again.

In a single motion, refusing to consider what that hole might be doing to his shirt, Kent hoisted the cadaver onto his shoulder, turned sideways, and let Mr. Brinkley drop into the trunk. The body flipped on descent and landed with a loud thump, butt down. The head might have put a dent in the metal by that sound. But it was covered with plastic, so no blood would smear on the car itself. Besides, dead bodies don't bleed.

Sweat dripped from Kent's forehead and splattered onto the plastic. He glanced around, panting as much from disgust as from exertion. The night remained cool and still; the moaning of the distant highway filtered through his throbbing ears. But there were no sirens or helicopters or cop cars with floodlights or anything at all that looked threatening. Except that body lying exposed beside him, of course.

He quickly forced the head and feet into the trunk, careful not to allow contact with the exposed car. The legs squeaked and then popped on entry, and he wondered if that was joints or solid bones. Had to be joints—bones would never break so easily.

The eyes still stared out of Tom Brinkley's skull like two gray marbles. By the looks of it, his nose might have taken the brunt of that face plant in the truck. Kent yanked the black plastic over the body and shut the trunk.

Then there was the matter of the casket. Yes indeed, and he was prepared for that little problem. He pulled a blanket from the backseat, threw it over the car, retrieved the plywood coffin from the Iveco, and strapped it onto the top of his car with a single tie-down. Not to worry—it was not going far.

He quickly tidied the truck, closed the rear door one last time, and drove off, still guided by moonlight alone. He unloaded the casket into an abandoned storage bin, two down from where he'd parked the Lexus earlier. Whoever next braved the cubicle would find nothing more than a cheap plywood casket ditched by some vagrant long ago.

By the time Kent hit the freeway, it was almost 9 P.M.

By the time he made his first pass of the bank it was closer to ten.

He told himself he made the pass to make sure the lot lay vacant. But seeing the bank looming ahead as he made his way down the street, he began reconsidering the entire business, and by the time he reached the parking lot, his arms were experiencing some rigor mortis of their own. He simply could not turn the wheel.

The white moon bore down like a spotlight in the sky, peering steadily between passing black clouds. The bank towered dark against the sky. The streets were nearly vacant, but each car that did drive by seemed somehow intent on the Lexus. Kent imagined that it was because the car's tailpipe was dragging with Mr. Brinkley hiding like a lead weight back there. Or maybe he'd left a finger poking out of the trunk. He took a deep breath to calm himself. No, the tailpipe wasn't dragging or even sagging. And the finger-in-the-trunk thing was ridiculous. The lid would not have closed with anything so thick as a finger sticking out. Hair perhaps? Kent glanced in the side mirrors but saw no hair flapping in the wind.

"Get a grip, man!" he growled. "You're acting stupid!"

Kent drove three blocks past the bank before turning onto a side street to circle around. The objections were screaming now. Taking the truck—that had been nothing. Stealing the body—child's play. This, now *this* was where it all hit the fan. Only a complete imbecile would actually attempt this. Or someone who had nothing to live for anyway. Because attempting this might very well end in death. *You know that, Kent, don't you? You might die tonight. Like Spencer.*

His palms were slippery on the leather steering wheel, and he wondered if forensics could pick that up. He would have to wipe the sweat off the seat as well. He didn't want some ambitious rookie investigator concluding he'd arrived in a state of distress, leaking buckets of sweat all over the seats. Then again, he had lost his wife and child; he had reason to be distressed.

Kent approached the bank from the rear and rolled into his parking spot at the back corner by the alley. *Okay, boy. Just chill. We're just going to walk in there and take a quick look. You come here all the time at night. Nothing unusual yet. You haven't done anything wrong yet. Not much anyway.*

Kent took a deep breath, stepped from the car, briefcase in hand, and walked for the back entrance. His hand shook badly inserting the key. What if they had changed the lock? But they hadn't. It swung open easily to the sound of a quiet chirping. The alarm.

He stepped in and punched in the deactivation code. Now the alarm company knew that Kent Anthony had entered the building through the rear door at 10:05 P.M. Sunday night. No problem—that was part of this little charade. The rear offices were not monitored by video equipment like the rest of the bank; he was a free bird back here.

Kent walked through dark halls, stepping quickly by the light of glowing exit signs. He found his office exactly as he had left it, untouched and silent except for the *whir* of his computer. The exotic fish swam lazily; red power lights winked in the darkness; his high-back leather chair sat like a black shadow before the monitors. Kent's hands trembled at his sides.

Kent flipped the light on and squinted at the brightness. He set his briefcase on the desk and cracked his knuckles absently. By his estimation, he would need five hours in the building to pull this off. The first four hours would be relatively simple. Just walk into the advanced processing system using ROOSTER, execute the little BANDIT program he'd been fine-tuning for the last three weeks, and walk away. But it was the walking away part that had his bones vibrating.

Kent made one last pass through the halls, satisfying himself as to their vacancy. And then it was suddenly now-or-never time, and he walked briskly back toward his office, knowing it had to be now.

It's okay, boy. You haven't done nothin' yet. Not yet.

He withdrew a disk from his briefcase, inserted it into the floppy drive, took one last long pull of air, and began punching at the keyboard. Menus sprang to life and then disappeared, one after the other, a slide show of reds and blues and yellows. He located ROOSTER and executed it without pausing. Then he was into AFPS, through ROOSTER's hidden link, like a ghost able to do anything at will without the mortals knowing.

He'd already determined his will. His will was to confiscate twenty million dollars. And stealing twenty million dollars all came down to a few keystrokes now.

He stared at the familiar screen of programming code for a long minute, his quivering fingertips brushing lightly on the keys, his heart pounding in his ears.

It's okay, boy. You haven't done . . .

Yeah, well, I'm about to.

He entered the command line: RUN a:\BANDIT.

Then do it. Just do it.

He swallowed and depressed the ENTER key. The floppy drive engaged, the hard drive spun up, the screen went blank for a few seconds, and Kent held his breath.

A string of numbers popped up, center screen, and began spinning by like a gas pump meter gone berserk. The search was on. Kent leaned back and folded his hands, his eyes lost to the blur of numbers.

The program's execution was simple, really. It would systematically scan the massive electronic web of banking and identify accounts in which charges had been levied for interbank ATM use. Example: Sally, a Norwest bank customer, uses her cash card at a Wells Fargo cash machine and is charged $1.20 for the use of Wells Fargo's ATM. The fee is automatically taken from her account. Sally gets her statement, sees the charge, and adds it to the line that reads "Service Charges" on her reconciliation form. Case closed. Does Sally question the charge? Not unless Sally is a kook. BANDIT would search for one hundred million such transactions, add twenty cents to the fee charged by the host bank, and then neatly skim that twenty cents off for deposit into a labyrinth of accounts Kent had already established. In Sally's case, neither Norwest nor Wells Fargo would be short in their own reconciliation. They would receive and be charged precisely what they expected: $1.20. It would be Sally who was out twenty cents, because her statement would show a service charge not of $1.20 but of $1.40. The additional twenty cents she paid would be unwittingly donated to Kent's accounts while the balance of $1.20 happily made its way to Wells Fargo. No one would be the wiser.

But say Sally *is* a kook. Say she calls the bank and reports the mistake: a $1.40 charge instead of the customary $1.20 rate advertised in the bank's brochures. The bank runs a query. BANDIT immediately identifies the query, dispatches a gunman to Sally's house, and puts a slug in her head.

Kent blinked. The numbers on the screen continued to spin in a blur.

Okay, not quite. BANDIT would just return Sally her precious hard-earned twenty cents. But it was here, in the method Kent had devised to return Sally her money, that his real brilliance shone. You see, BANDIT would not just return the money lackadaisically and apologize for the blunder. Too many blunders would raise brows, and Kent wanted to keep those eyebrows down. Instead, BANDIT acted like a self-erasing virus, one that detected the query into Sally's account, and did its dirty deed of returning the twenty cents immediately, before the query returned the details of Sally's account to the operator's screen. By the time the banker had Sally's latest bank statement on the screen, it would show that the customary bank charges of $1.20 had been levied. The computer would then spit out a comment about an internal self-correcting error, and that would be that. In reality, there would undoubtedly be some deeper probes, but they would find nothing. The transactions would be executed through the back door and their trails neatly erased, thanks to AFPS. Of course, the safeguard was AFPS itself—those who entered AFPS normally left their prints at every keystroke.

Normally. But not with ROOSTER.

Either way, it really did not matter. The last hour of this operation would neutralize everything. Meanwhile, he had a body rotting in his trunk. Kent let the computer spin while he chewed his fingernails and paced the carpet. He might have shed a full gallon of sweat in those first three hours, he did not know—he hadn't brought a milk jug along to catch it all. But it did a fine job of soaking his shirt clean through.

It took three hours and forty-three minutes for the program to find its intended victims. The clock on Kent's office wall read 1:48 when the program finally asked him if he wished to get it on—transfer this insanely huge amount of money into his accounts and enter a life on the run from the long arms of the United States justice system. Well, not in so many words. There was actually only one word on the screen: TRANSFER? Y/N. But he knew what the program was really asking by that simple word, because he had written that word.

His hand hovered over the Y that would actually alter the accounts and transfer the money into his own—a process he'd calculated to take roughly thirty minutes. He pressed it, conscious of the small click in the key. The words vanished to black, replaced by a single word blinking on and off: PROCESSING.

Kent backed from the desk and let the computer do its deed. *Yes indeed, BANDIT, rob them blind.* His heart beat at twice its customary pace, refusing to calm. And he still had that clammy body to deal with.

Kent crept out to the Lexus, glancing around nervously for the slightest sign of an intruder. Which struck him as ironic because *he* was the intruder here. He popped the trunk and quickly peeled the plastic away from Mr. Brinkley's body. He had to be quick now. It wouldn't do to have a passerby seeing him hauling a flopping body from the trunk. Backing the car into the alley would have been easier, but it also would have left tire tracks that didn't belong. One of those Stupid Street moves.

The cadaver stared up at the moon with its wide, gray eyes, and Kent shuddered. He reached in, swallowing hard, wrapped both arms around the cold torso, and yanked. The body came out like a bloated sack of grain, and Kent staggered under its weight. The head bounced off the rear bumper and came within an inch of leaving a slab of skin on the asphalt, which would have been a problem.

Move it, man! Move it!

Kent hoisted the body and flipped it into the crooks of his arms as he turned. The trunk would have to remain open for the moment. He staggered down the alley, wheezing like ancient bellows now, fighting to keep the contents of his stomach where they belonged. If he'd eaten more over the last day, it might have come up then while he staggered down the alley, eyes half closed to avoid seeing what lay across his arms. Mr. Brinkley bounced naked and gray. Butt up.

The cadaver nearly fell from his grasp once, but he recovered with a lifted knee. He lost his firm grip on the body, however, and had to run the last few yards before the fish slipped all the way out of his arms.

The rear door proved another challenge altogether. Kent stood there, bent over, straining against the dead weight, knowing that if this thing fell it would leave evidence. Dead body evidence.

Problem was, his hands were trembling in their task of keeping Mr. Brinkley from landing on his toes, and the door was closed. He would have to get the body onto his shoulder—free up a hand.

"Oh, man!" He was whispering audibly now. "Oh man, oh man!" The words echoed ghostly down the alley.

It took him three panicked attempts to heave the naked body up by his head, and by the time he finally managed to snake a shoulder under it, his breathing was chasing those words. The body's flesh felt soft on his shoulder, and visions of that hole in the cadaver's gut filled his mind. But Mr. Brinkley's spare tire was sucking up to his right ear, and the realization put him into gear.

Kent opened the door and staggered through, fighting chills of horror. The thought that he'd have to wipe that door handle managed to plant itself firmly in his mind. He had dead flesh on his hands.

He ran for his office with the body bouncing on his shoulder. Groans accompanied each breath now, but then who was listening?

He heaved the body from its precarious perch the second he lurched through his office door. It fell to the gray carpet with a sickening dead-body thump. Kent winced and pushed the door shut. His face still twisted with disgust, he paced back and forth in front of the body, trying to gather himself.

To his right, the computer screen still winked through its dirty deed.

PROCESSING, PROCESSING, PROCESSING . . .

He needed fresh air. Kent ran from the bank and walked back to the car, thankful for the cool air against his drenched shirt.

He removed a green-and-red cardboard box, which had only two weeks earlier held twelve bottles of tequila, from his rear seat and carefully cleaned out the trunk. Satisfied that the Lexus carried no physical evidence of the body, he stuffed the plastic into the box and walked to a tangle of pipes and knobs poking from the concrete halfway down the alley. The smallest of these controlled the bank's sprinkler system. He twisted a valve and shut it down.

From the tequila box Kent removed a pair of running shoes and replaced his own loafers with them. A few stomps down the alley insured they would leave a print. Evidence. He wiped the rear door handle carefully and reentered the bank.

The body lay face up, naked and pasty when he stepped into his office. He shivered. The computer screen still flashed its word: PROCESSING, PROCESSING . . .

Kent stripped off his clothes, until he stood naked except the running shoes. He started to dress Mr. Brinkley but quickly decided that he could not tolerate being naked in the same room with a naked dead man. Granted, he would put up with whatever it took to do this deed, but bending naked over a dead naked body was not in the plan. He would dress first. He snatched a pair of loose jeans and a white T-shirt from the green-and-red box and pulled them on. Then he turned back to the body.

Dressing a dead body proved to be a task best done with a vengeance—anything less had him cursing. The body's stiffness helped, but the dead weight did not. He forced his white boxers over Mr. Brinkley's midsection first, holding his breath for most of the operation. Relieved, he struggled with the slacks, rolling the body around, and tugging as best he could. He had the shirt nearly over the cadaver's chest when a blip sounded at the computer.

Kent snapped his head up. TASK COMPLETE, the screen read. $20,000,000.00 TRANSFERRED.

A tremble seized his bones. He returned to the body, tearing about it now. His watch went on the wrist, his socks and shoes on the feet.

Satisfied, he withdrew his floppy disk from the drive and exited the program. A fleeting thought skipped through his head. The thought that he had just transferred twenty million dollars into his personal accounts successfully. The thought that he was a very rich man. Goodness!

But the overpowering need to flee undetected shoved the thought from his mind. He emptied half the contents from his briefcase into the tequila box. The incriminating half. What remained in the briefcase represented the work of a dedicated programmer including a personal reminder to speak to Borst Monday morning about efficiency issues. Yes sir, show them he fully expected to return to work on Monday, the morning after a casual fishing trip and a late night at the office.

Kent yanked the cadaver, now fully dressed in his clothes, to a standing position so that it leaned against his chair like some kind of wax museum piece. Here rigor mortis was his friend. He had buttoned the shirt wrong, he saw, and the slacks were hitched up high on one side. Mr. Brinkley looked like some kind of computer nerd short the pocket protector. But none of this mattered.

The corpse stared wide eyed at the poster of the white yacht. Now that Kent thought about it, he should have closed those bug eyes like they did when someone died on television.

He backed to the door, surveyed his work, and pulled the nine-millimeter semiautomatic Uncle Jerry had given him from the box. *Okay boy, now you're gonna do this.* He lifted the pistol. Once he pulled the trigger, he would have to fly. No telling how far the report might travel.

But Mr. Brinkley was having none of it. At least not yet. He suddenly slipped to the side and toppled to the floor, stiff as a board.

Kent cursed and bounded over to the body. He jerked Mr. Brinkley upright and planted him in place. "Stay put, you old fish," he mumbled through gritted teeth. "You're dying standing up, whether you like it or not."

He crouched and squinted. The gun suddenly bucked in his hand. *Bang!* The report almost knocked him from his feet. Panicked, he fired twice more, quickly, into the body—*Bang! Bang!* The body stood tall, still staring dumbly forward, oblivious to the bullets that had just torn through its flesh.

Kent swallowed and tossed the weapon back into the box. Shaking badly now, he staggered forward and yanked a two-gallon can from the box. He gave Mr. Brinkley a nudge and let him topple to the floor. He emptied the flammable mixture onto the body and then doused the surrounding carpet. He scanned the office, picked up the box, and backed to the door.

It occurred to Kent, just before he tossed the match, that he was about to go off the deep end here. Right off into some abyss, spread-eagle. He struck the match and let it flare. What on Earth was he about to do? He was about to put the finishing touches on the perfect crime, that's what he was about to do. He was about to kill Kent Anthony. He was about to join Gloria and Spencer in the ground, six feet under. At least that was the plan, and it was a brilliant plan.

Kent backed into the hall and tossed the match.

Whoomp!

The initial ignition knocked him clear across the hall and onto his seat. He scrambled to his feet and stared, unbelieving, at the blaze. A wall of orange flames reached for the ceiling, crackling and spewing black smoke. Fire engulfed the entire office. Mr. Brinkley's body lay like a log, flaming with the rest, like Shadrach or Meshack in the fiery furnace. The accelerant mixture worked as advertised. This cadaver was going to burn. Burn, baby, burn.

Then Kent fled the bank. He burst through the back door, tequila box in hand, heart slamming. His Lexus sat parked around the corner to his left. He ran to his right. He would not need the car again. Ever.

He'd run three blocks straight down the back alleys before he heard the first siren. He slowed by a trash bin, palmed the gun, and ditched the box. Behind him a cloud of smoke billowed into the night sky. He had known the old wood-frame building would go up, but he had not expected the fire to grow so quickly.

Kent looked back four blocks later, eyes peeled and unblinking. This time an orange glow lit the sky. A small smile of wonder crossed his face. Sirens wailed on the night air.

Five minutes later he entered the bus depot on Harmon and Wilson, produced a key to locker 234, and withdrew an old, brown briefcase. The case held eleven thousand dollars in twenty-dollar bills—traveling expenses—a bus ticket, a stick of deodorant, a toothbrush with some toothpaste, and a passport under his new name. It was all he owned now.

This and a few dozen accounts holding twenty million dollars.

Then Kent walked out into the street and disappeared into the night.

CHAPTER TWENTY-NINE

Eight Days Later

HELEN BROUGHT two glasses of ice tea into her living room and handed one to Pastor Madison. Returning to her own home was the one small blessing in this latest turn in events. No need to stay at Kent's if he was gone.

"Thank you, Helen. So . . ."

"So," she repeated.

"So they've concluded the fire resulted from a freak robbery attempt. You read this story?" he asked, lifting the *Denver Post* in one hand.

"Yes, I saw that."

The pastor continued anyway. "They say evidence from the scene clearly shows a second party—presumably a robber. Evidently this guy found the rear door open and entered the bank, hoping for some easy cash. Unfortunately, Kent was there, 'working late on a Sunday night, not unusual for Kent Anthony. The thirty-six-year-old programmer was well known for working odd hours, often into the early hours of the morning.'"

"Hmmm," Helen offered.

"It says that the investigators speculate that the robber stumbled into Kent, panicked, and shot him dead. He then returned and torched the place—probably in an effort to erase evidence of his presence. He's still at large, and the search continues. The FBI has no current suspects. No actual robbery was committed . . . They estimate the fire damage to reach three million dollars, a fraction of what it could have been, thanks to the rapid response of the fire department." He lowered the paper and sipped at his tea.

"And of course, we know the rest, because it's just about the funeral."

Helen did not respond. There was not much to say anymore. Things had dropped off her plateau of understanding. She was guided by the unknown now. By the kind of faith she had never dreamed possible.

"What's happening to his belongings?" Bill asked.

"His will leaves it all to Gloria and Spencer. I suppose the state will get it now—I don't know and quite frankly, I don't care. From what I've seen, there's no use for this stuff in the next life anyway."

He nodded and sipped again. For a while they sat in silence.

"I have to tell you, Helen. This is almost too much for me."

"I know. It seems difficult, doesn't it?"

Bill cocked his head, and she knew he was letting his frustration get the better of him. "No, Helen. This does not *seem* difficult. Not everything is about *seeming* this way or that way. This *is* difficult, okay?" He shifted uncomfortably. "I mean, first Kent's wife dies of a freak disease, and that was unfortunate. I understand these things happen. But then his son is killed in a freak accident. And now we've hardly put away the funeral garb, and *he's* murdered in some freak robbery attempt. Strange enough? No, not quite. Meanwhile you, the mother, the grandmother, the mother-in-law, are walking around—quite literally—talking about some game in heaven. Some master plan beyond normal human comprehension. To what end? They're all dead! Your family is all dead, Helen!"

"Things are not always what . . ."

". . . what they seem," Bill finished. "I know. You've told me that a hundred times. But some things *are* what they seem! Gloria *seems* quite dead, and guess what? She *is* dead!"

"No need to patronize me, young man." Helen smiled gently. "And in reality, she's more alive now than dead, so even there you are less right than wrong. In practical terms, you might be right, but the kingdom of heaven is not what most humans would call practical. Quite the opposite. You ever read the teachings of Christ? 'If a man asks for your tunic, give him your cloak as well.' You ever do that, Bill? 'If your eye causes you to sin, pluck it out.' You see anybody smash their television lately, Bill? 'Anyone who does not take up his cross'—that's death, Bill—'and follow me is not worthy of me . . . Let the dead bury the dead.' And it was God speaking those words, as a guideline by which to live life."

"Well, I'm not talking about the teachings of Christ here. I'm talking about people dying without apparent reason."

Helen searched him deep with her eyes, feeling empathy and not knowing really why. He was a good man. He simply had not yet seen what was to be seen. "Well, I *am* talking about the teachings of Christ, Bill, which, whether you like it or not, include death. His own death. The death of the martyrs. The death of those on whose blood the church is built."

She looked away, and suddenly a hundred images from her own past crashed through her mind. She swallowed. "The reason you look for is here, Pastor." She waved her hand slowly through the air. "All around us. We just don't often see it clearly, and when we do, it is not often as we think it should appear. We're so bent on stuffing ourselves full of life—full of *happiness*—that we lose sight of God. Make up our own."

"God is a God of joy and peace and happiness," he offered.

"Yes. But the Teacher did not have in mind sitcoms that make you laugh or happy sermons about what a breeze the narrow road really is. Heavens, no. What is pure, Bill? Or excellent or admirable? The death of a million people in the Flood? God evidently thought so. He is incapable of acts that are not admirable, and it was he who brought about the Flood. How about the slaying of children in Jericho? There are few Bible stories that are not as terrible as they are happy. We just prefer to leave out the terrible part, but that only makes the good anemic." She turned from him and gazed at the picture of Christ in crucifixion.

"We are encouraged to *participate* in the sufferings of Christ, not to pretend they were feel-happy times. 'Take this in remembrance of me; this is my blood, this is my body,' he said. Not, find yourselves an Easter bunny and hunt for chocolate eggs in remembrance of me. We are told to *meditate* on Scripture, even the half that details the consequence of evil, the conquest of Jericho and all. Not to pretend our God has somehow changed since the time of Christ. Obviously, Paul's idea of admirable and noble is quite different from ours. God forgive us, Bill. We have mocked his victory by whitewashing the enemy for the sake of our neighbor's approval."

He blinked and drew a deep breath. "Imagine me talking like that from the pulpit. It would scare the breath out of most of them." He lowered his head, but his jaw was clenched, she saw. Suddenly those images from her past were crashing through her mind again, and she closed her eyes briefly. She should tell him, she thought.

"Let me tell you a story, Bill. A story about a man of God unlike any I have known. A soldier. He was my soldier." Now the emotions flooded her with a vengeance, and she noted her hands were trembling. "He was from Serbia, you know, before he came to the States. Fought in the war there with a small team of special forces. He served under a lieutenant, a *horrible* man." She shuddered as she said it. "A God hater who slept with the devil."

She had to stop for a few moments. The memories came too fast, with too much intensity, and she breathed a prayer. *Father, forgive me.* She glanced up at the red bottle in her hutch, sitting, calling from the past. From the corner of her eye she saw that Bill was staring at her.

"Anyway, they walked into a small town one day. The commander led them straight to the church at the center. The soldier said that he knew with one look into the lieutenant's eyes that he had come with cruel intentions. It was a gross understatement."

She swallowed and plowed on before this thing got the best of her. "The commander had them gather the townspeople, about a hundred of them, I think, and then he began his games." Helen looked up at the cross again. "The priest was a God-fearing man. For hours the commander played his game—bent upon forcing the priest to renounce Christ before the townsfolk. The horror of those hours was so reprehensible that I can hardly speak of them, Bill. To hear of them I would weep for hours."

Tears slipped from Helen's eyes and fell to her lap.

"The soldier was appalled by what he saw. He tried in vain to stop the lieutenant—almost lost his own life. But in the end the priest died. He died a martyr for the love of Christ. There is a monument to him in the town now. It is a cross rising from a green lawn bearing the inscription, 'No Greater Love Has Any Man.' The day after the priest's death, they collected some of his blood and sealed it into several small crystal bottles, so they would not forget."

She stood and walked to the hutch. She'd told no one other than her daughter of this, but it was time, wasn't it? Yes, it was time she spread this seed. Her breathing was coming thick as she pulled open the glass doors. She placed her fingers around the small bottle and pulled it out. The container was only slightly larger than her hand.

Helen returned to her seat and sat slowly, her mind swirling with the images. "The soldier went back to the village the next day to beg for their forgiveness. They gave him one of the bottles filled with the martyr's blood." Helen held the bottle out on her palm. "Never to worship or to idolize, they told him. But to remind him of the price paid for his soul."

It was not the whole story, of course. If the pastor knew the whole story he would be slobbering on the floor in a pool of his own tears, she thought. Because the whole story was as much her story as the soldier's, and it stretched the very limits of love. Perhaps she would give him the book Janjic had written before he'd died, *When Heaven Weeps.* Then he would know.

"The experience profoundly changed his life," she said, looking at Bill. His eyes were misty, staring at the floor. "And ultimately it changed my life, and Gloria's and Spencer's and even yours and countless others. And now Kent's, possibly. But you see, it all began with death. The death of Christ, the death of the priest. Without these I would not be here today. Nor would you, Pastor. It is how I see the world now."

"Yes." He nodded, gathering himself. "You do see more than most of us."

"I see only a little more than you, and most of that by faith. You think I wear the face of God?"

He blinked, obviously unsure if he was meant to answer.

"You see me walking around, disturbed, worried, with a furrowed brow. You think it's the face of God? Of course not! He is furious at sin, no doubt. And his heart aches over the rejection of his love. But above it all he rolls with laughter, beside himself with joy. I see only the hem of his garment and then only at times. The rest comes by faith. We may have different giftings, but we all have the same faith. Give or take. We are not so different, Pastor."

He stared at her. "I've never heard you say those things."

"Then maybe I should have spoken sooner. Forgive me. I can be a bit mule-headed, you know."

He smiled at her. "Don't worry, Helen. If you're a mule, may God smite our church with a thousand mules." They chuckled.

For several minutes they just sat there and thought in silence. Their glasses clinked with ice now and then, but the gravity of the moment seemed to want its own space, so they let it be. Helen hummed a few bars of "The Martyr's Song" and stared out to the field beyond her house. Autumn would come someday. What would walking be like then?

"Are you still walking?" Bill asked the question as if it had been the real reason for his visit and he was just now getting around to it.

"Yes. Yes I am."

"The full distance?"

"Yes."

"But how? I thought you were walking and praying for Kent's soul?"

"Well, that's the problem. That's where things don't seem to be what they seem. I'm still walking because I've felt no urge not to walk and because my legs still walk without tiring and because I still want to pray for Kent."

"Kent is dead, Helen."

"Yes. So it seems. But the heavens are not playing along. I walked that first day after the fire, seeking release. It was to be expected, I thought. But I found no release."

She glanced at him and saw that he'd tilted his head, unbelieving.

"And then there's the dream. Someone's still running through my head at night. I still hear his breathing, the soft pounding of feet through the tunnel. The drama is still unfolding, Pastor."

Bill gave her a small, sympathetic smile. "Come on, Helen. I talked to the lead investigator myself two days ago. He told me very specifically that the coroner clearly identified the body as belonging to Kent Anthony. Same height, same weight, same teeth, same everything. FBI's records confirmed it. That body we buried three days ago belonged to Kent. Maybe he needs help in some afterlife, but he is no longer of this earth."

"They did an autopsy, then?"

"An autopsy of what? Of charred bones?"

"DNA?"

"Come on, Helen. You can't actually believe . . . Look, I know this is hard on you. It's been a terrible tragedy. But don't you think this is going a little too far?"

Her eyes bore into his with an unmoving stare. "This has nothing to do with tragedy, young man. Am I or am I not walking eight hours a day without tiring?"

He didn't answer.

"Is it some illusion, this walking of mine? Tell me."

"Of course it's no illusion. But—"

"Of course? You sound pretty sure about that. Why is God making my legs move like this, Pastor? Is it that he has discovered a new way to make the tiny humans below move? 'Hey look, Gabriel, we can just wind them up and make them walk around forever.' No? Then why?"

"Helen . . ."

"I'm telling you, Pastor, this is not over. And I mean, not just in the heavens, but on Earth it's not over. And since Kent was the main object of this whole thing, no, I don't think he is necessarily dead."

She turned away from him. Goodness, listen to her. It was sounding absurd. She had peeked in the coffin herself and seen the blackened bones. "And if you think it makes sense to me, you are wrong. I'm not even saying he *is* necessarily alive. It is just easier to believe he's alive, given the fact that I'm still praying long days for him." She turned back to him. "Does that make sense?"

Bill Madison took a deep breath and leaned back in his chair. "Well, Helen." He shook his head. "I guess so."

They sat in silence for a few minutes, staring off in different directions, lost in thought. His voice broke the stillness.

"It's very strange, Helen. It's otherworldly. Your faith is unnerving. You're giving your life to impossibilities."

She looked up and saw that his eyes were closed. A lump rose in her throat. "It's all I have, Bill. It's all anybody really has. It's all Noah had, building his impossible little boat while they mocked him. It's all Moses had, holding his rod over the Red Sea. It's all Hosea had and Samson and Paul and Stephen and every other character of every other Bible story. Why should it be so different for us today?"

She saw his Adam's apple bob. He nodded. "Yes, I think you're right. And I fear my faith is not so strong."

He was beginning to see, she thought. Which meant his faith was stronger than he realized. It could use a nudge. She'd read somewhere that eagles would never fly if their mothers did not push them from their nests when they were ready. Even then they would free-fall in a panic before spreading their wings and finding flight.

Yes, maybe it was time the pastor got a little shove.

"Would you like to see more than you've seen, Bill?"

"See what?"

"See the other side. See what lies behind what you see now."

He stiffened a little. "What do you mean, *see?* It's not like I can just flip on a light and see—"

"It is a simple question, Bill, really. Do you want to see?"

"Yes."

"And you would be willing to let go a little?"

"I think so. Although I'm not sure how you let go of something you can't see."

"You forget about how important you are, put aside your narrow field of vision; you open your heart to one thing only. To God, in whichever way he chooses to reveal himself, regardless of how it might seem to you. You let go."

He smiled nervously. "Sounds a bit risky, actually. You can't just throw out all doctrine for some experience."

"And what if that experience is God, the creator? What is more important to you, an encounter with God or your doctrine?"

"Well, if you put it that way—"

"As opposed to which way?"

"You've made your point. And yes, I think I could let go a little."

She smiled slowly. "Then let's pray."

Helen watched him close his eyes and bow his head. She wondered how long the posture would hold. "Father in heaven," she prayed aloud and closed her own eyes, "if it would please you, open this child's eyes to see what you have called him to. May he have the power to see how wide and how deep and how high your love is for him."

She fell silent and closed her eyes to darkness. *Please Father, let him feel your presence. At least that, just a taste of you, God in heaven.*

An image of Kent filled her mind. He walked down a long, deserted street, aimless and lost. His hair was disheveled, and his eyes peered blue above dark circles. For a moment she thought it might be his spirit, like some kind of ghost wandering the streets of her mind. But then she saw that it was him, really him, bewildered by the vacancy of the street on which he walked. And he was lonely.

She forgot about the pastor for the moment. Maybe she should walk. Maybe she should just leave Bill and go for another walk—pray for Kent. Yes, at least that. Her heart swelled in her chest. *Oh God, save Kent's soul! Do not hide your face from this man you made. Open his heart to your spirit. Speak words of love to his ears, drop your fragrance in his mind, dance before his eyes, show him your splendor, wrap your arms around him, touch his cold skin with a warm touch, breathe life into his nostrils. You fashioned him, did you not? So now love him.*

But I have.

Helen dropped her head at the words and began to weep. *Oh God, I'm sorry. You have! You have loved him so much. Forgive me!*

She sat bunched in her chair for several long minutes, feeling waves of fire wash through her chest. It was a mixture of agony and desire—a common sentiment these days. The heart of God for Kent. Or at least a small piece of it. The piece he chose to reveal to her.

She suddenly remembered Bill and snapped her head up.

He sat on the green chair, head bent back like a duckling begging food. His Adam's apple stuck out prominently on his neck, his jaw lay open, his mouth gaped wide, his nostrils flared. And his body shook like a ragged old cloth doll. Something somewhere had been opened. His eyes, maybe.

Helen relaxed and leaned back into her cushions. A smile split her face wide. Now he would understand. Maybe not any details of Kent's plight, but the rest would come easier now. Faith would come easier.

Tears fell in streams down the pastor's cheeks, and she saw that his shirt was already wet. Looking at the grown man reduced to a heap of emotions made her want to scream full throated. It was that kind of joy. She wondered how it was that she had never had a heart attack. How could a mortal, like Bill there, all inside out, endure such ravaging emotion, busting up the heart, and not risk a coronary? She smiled at the thought.

On the contrary, his heart might very well be finding some youth. Her legs had, after all.

Helen began to rock gently. "Do you want to see, Bill?" she whispered.

CHAPTER THIRTY

LACY CARTWRIGHT nibbled at her fingernail, knowing it was an unseemly habit and not caring. The truth be known, she had not cared for much during the last week. She glanced at the clock: 8:48. In twelve minutes the doors of Rocky Mountain Bank and Trust would open for customers.

Jeff Duncan caught her eye from across the lobby, and she smiled politely. Now, there was a man who was maybe more her type after all. Not so impulsive as Kent, but alive and well and here. Always here, not running in and out of her life every twelve years. Not pulling some impossible disappearing trick and expecting her to just get on with life. But that was just the problem—Lacy honestly didn't know if Kent had really disappeared or not. And what she did know was giving her waking fits.

Kent had come to her two nights before the big fire in Denver; that much she had not imagined. He had sat across from her and told her that he was going to do pretty much what happened. Or at least what *could* have happened. But reading the papers, what happened was not what *could* have happened at all. In fact, what happened, according to the papers, was precisely what Kent had said would happen. A robbery attempt, a death, and most important, his disappearance. He had neglected to mention that it would be *his* death, of course, but then she doubted he'd planned that much.

Then again, what actually happened was anybody's guess, and she found herself guessing that something else entirely had happened. Maybe Kent had not been surprised by some wandering robber that night, because maybe Kent himself *was* the robber; he'd suggested as much himself. So then what seemed to have happened must not have happened at all. Which was downright confusing when she thought too much about the matter.

Either way, he had left her again. Maybe this time for good. Well, good riddance.

There was one way to determine if that charred body in the Denver bank fire belonged to Kent Anthony or to some other poor soul everyone *thought* was Kent Anthony. If Kent had actually pulled off this incredible theft of which he'd spoken, he had done it brilliantly, because as of yet, no one even suspected there *had* been a theft. On the other hand, no one knew to look, much less *where* to look. All eyes were on the fire damage and the search for a loose murderer, but no one had mentioned the possibility that a robbery *had* actually occurred. And no wonder—nothing had been taken. At least not that they knew.

But she, Lacy Cartwright, might know differently. And if she did discover that Kent was alive and well and extremely wealthy—would she be compelled to tell the authorities? It was the question that had kept her tossing at night. Yes, she thought so. She would have to turn him in.

If he was indeed alive and if he had left even the slightest of trails, she would find it on the computer screen before her, in some log of ATM transaction fees. Fortunately or unfortunately, depending on the hour, eight days of looking had shown her nothing. And slowly, her anger at him rose to a boil.

"Morning, Lacy."

Lacy started and jerked her head up. Jeff smiled broadly at her reaction. "Strung a bit tight this morning, are we?"

She ignored him.

He chuckled. "I guess. Well, welcome back to the land of the living."

The comment momentarily thrust Lacy back into the land of the dead. "Yeah," she responded politely, shifting her eyes from him. Maybe that was the problem here, she thought. Maybe this land of the living here in the bank with all the customers and meaningless talk and overstuffed maroon sitting chairs was more like death, and the land that Kent had trotted off to was more like life. In a way she was a bit jealous, if indeed he was not actually in hell but roaming the earth somewhere.

Jeff leaned on the counter. "You coming to Martha's party this weekend? It might be a good thing, considering the fact that all the top brass will be in attendance."

She pulled herself back to this reality. "And this should bring me to my knees? When is it?" Actually she had no plans to attend the affair and knew precisely when it was, but Jeff was the kind of guy who liked giving out information. It made him feel important, she guessed.

"Friday at seven. And yes, you might consider paying a little homage."

"To them or to you?"

He smiled coyly. "But of course, I'll be there as well. And I'd be disappointed if you were not."

She smiled kindly. "Well, we'll see." Maybe it would be a good idea, after all. Get her mind off this Kent madness. "I'm not crazy about parties doused in alcohol." She studied his face for reaction.

"And neither am I," he said without missing a beat. "But, like I said, the brass will be there. Think of it as a career move. Reaching out to those who determine your future. Something like that. And of course, an opportunity to see me." He winked.

Lacy stared at him, surprised by his boldness.

Jeff shifted awkwardly. "I'm sorry, I didn't mean to be so—"

"No. It's okay. I'm flattered." She recovered quickly and smiled.

"You sure?"

"Yes, I'm sure."

"Well, I'll take that as a sign of promise."

She nodded, unable to answer for the moment.

Evidently satisfied that he'd accomplished his intentions in the little exchange, Jeff stepped back. "I have to get back to work. Mary Blackley is waiting anxiously for my call, and you know Mary. If it's one penny off, she's ready to declare war." He chuckled. "I swear, the old lady does nothing but wait by her mailbox for her statement. I can't remember a month when she hasn't called, and I can't remember a single complaint that has borne true."

Lacy pictured the elderly, hook-nosed lady wobbling through the doors, leaning on her cane. She smiled. "Yeah, I know what you mean. What is it this time? A missing comma?"

"Some ATM fee. Evidently, we're robbing her blind." Jeff laughed and retreated across the floor.

The heat started at the base of Lacy's spine and flashed up through her skull as if she'd inadvertently hit a nerve. *Some ATM fee?* She watched Jeff clack along the lobby floor. The clock above his head on the far wall read 8:58. Two minutes.

Lacy dived for her keyboard, hoping absently that no one noticed her eagerness. She ran a quick search for Mary Blackley's account number, found it, and keyed it in. She ran a query on all service charges. The screen blinked to black, seemed to hesitate, and then popped up with a string of numbers. Mary Blackley's account. She scrolled quickly down to the service charges levied. She lifted a trembling finger to the screen and followed the charges . . . six ATM transactions . . . each one with a fee of $1.20. A dollar-twenty. As it should be. Mary Blackley was chasing ghosts again. Unless . . .

She straightened and ran a search on the first transaction fee. According to the record that popped up, Mary had used her card at a Diamond Shamrock convenience store and withdrawn forty dollars on August 21, 1999, at 8:04 P.M. The servicing bank, Connecticut Mutual, had charged her $1.20 for the privilege of using its system.

So then, what could have prompted Mary to call?

Lacy backed out of the account quickly and walked across the lobby to Jeff's cubicle. He was bent over the keyboard when she stuck her head in and smiled.

"Lacy!" He made no attempt to hide his pleasure at seeing her materialize in his doorway.

"Hi, Jeff. Just walking by. So, you straighten Mary out?"

"Nothing to straighten out, actually. She was not overcharged at all."

"What was her problem?"

"Don't know. Printing mistake or something. She was actually right this time. Her statement did have the wrong fee on it—$1.40 instead of $1.20." He lifted a fax from his desk. "But the statement in the computer shows the correct fee, so whatever happened didn't really happen at all. Like I said, a printer problem, maybe."

Lacy nodded, smiling, and turned away before he could see the blood drain from her face. A customer stepped through the doors, and she made her way back to the tellers' windows, stunned and lost and breathing too hard.

She knew what had happened then with a dreadful certainty. Kent had done that! The little weasel had found a way to take Mary's twenty cents and then put it back as he had said he would. And he had done it without tipping his hand.

But that was impossible—so maybe that was not what had happened at all.

Lacy returned to her station and lifted the closed sign from her window. The first customer had to address her twice before she acknowledged.

"Oh, I'm sorry. What can I do for you today?"

The older woman smiled. "No problem. I know the feeling. I would like to cash this check." She slid a check for $6.48 made out to Francine Bowls across the counter. Lacy punched it in on autopilot.

"God, help me," she muttered aloud. She glanced at Mrs. Bowls and saw her raised eyebrow.

"Sorry," she said.

Mrs. Bowls smiled.

Lacy did not.

CHAPTER THIRTY-ONE

One Month Later
Wednesday

KENT SAT on the edge of the lounge chair, staring at the Caribbean sunrise, his stomach in knots over what he was about to do.

He rested his hands on the keyboard and lifted his chin to the early morning breeze. The sweet smell of salt swept past his nostrils; a tall tumbler filled with clear liquor sparkled atop a silver platter beside the laptop. The world was his. Or at the very least this small corner of the world was.

From his perch on the villa's deck, Kent could see half of the island. Luxurious villas graced the hills on either side like white play blocks shoved into the rock. Far below, sun-bleached sand sloped into emerald seas that slapped gently at low tide. The ocean extended to a cloudless, deep-blue horizon, crystal clear in the rising sun. The Turks and Caicos Islands rose from the Caribbean Sea like brown rabbits on the blue ocean, a fitting likeness, considering the number of inhabitants there who were on the run. Whether fleeing taxes or the authorities or just plain life, there were few destinations better suited to a man on the lam.

But none of this mattered at the moment. All that mattered now was that some satellites had graced him with a clear connection. After all these weeks of lying low, he was rising from the dead to wreak just a little havoc in the lives of those two fools who'd taken him for a sucker not so long ago. Yes indeed. This was all that mattered for the moment.

Kent lowered his eyes to the laptop's screen and ran his fingers over the keys, taking the time to consider. It was a commodity he had plenty of these days. Time.

He'd paid $1.2 million cash for the villa four days earlier. How the builders had managed to erect the house in the first place remained a mystery, but nothing short of a monster sledge hammer swung from heaven would knock this small fortress from its moorings. On either side, tall palms bustled with a dozen chirping birds. He turned back to the living area. Large flagstones led to an indoor dipping pool beside the dining area. With the flip of a single switch the entire front wall could be lowered or raised, offering either privacy or exposure to the stunning scenery below. The previous owners had constructed a dozen such villas, each extravagant in its own way. He'd never met them, of course, but the broker had assured Kent that they were of the highest caliber. Arabs with oil money. They had moved on to bigger and better toys.

Which was fine by him—the villa offered more amenities than he imagined possible in a four-thousand-square-foot package. And it now belonged to him. Every stick of wood. Every brick. Every last thread of carpet. Under a different name, of course.

Kent took a deep breath. "Okay, baby. Let's see what our two porky friends are doing." He began what he called phase two of the plan, executing a series of commands that took him first into a secure site and then to Niponbank's handle. He then entered a request that took him directly into a single computer sitting idle, asleep in the dark corner of its home, as well it should be at 4 A.M. mountain time. Borst and company had moved to a different wing of the bank following the fire, but Kent had found him easily enough. Beginning within the week of the theft, he had made breaking in to both Borst's and big-boss Bentley's computers a regular routine.

There was always the off chance that someone intelligent was at one of the two computers at 4 A.M.—someone with the capability to detect the break-in in real time—but Kent lost no sleep over the possibility. For starters, he'd never known Borst to work past 6 P.M., much less in the wee morning hours. And if he would be in there, poking around his computer at four in the morning, Porky was not so stuffed with intelligence as he was with other things. Such as pure, unadulterated drivel.

Kent entered Borst's computer through a backdoor and pulled the manager's hard drive up on his screen. The directory filled his screen in vivid color. Kent chuckled and sat back, enjoying the moment. He was literally inside the man's office without the other having a clue, and he rather liked the view.

He lifted a crystal glass from the table and sipped at the tequila sunrise he'd mixed himself. A small shudder ran through his bones. A full thirty days had passed since his night of terror in the bank, lugging that ridiculous body around.

And so far every detail of his plan had fallen into place as planned. The realization still made regular passes through his mind with stunning incredulity. To say that he had pulled it off would be a rather ridiculous understatement.

Kent removed his eyes from Borst's directory and looked out at the emerald seas far below. So far he was batting a thousand, but the minute he touched these keys a whole new set of risks would raise their ugly little heads. It was why his gut still coiled in knots while he presented himself to the seascape as a man in utter tranquillity. An odd mixture of emotions to be sure. Fully pleased at himself and thoroughly anxious at once.

The events of the days leading up to this one slipped through his mind. No need to be overzealous here—he still had time to abort phase two.

He'd escaped Denver easily enough, and the bus trip to Mexico City had flown by like a surrealistic scene on the silver screen. Yet once in the massive city, a certain deadening euphoria had taken to his nerves. He'd rented a room in an obscure dump some enterprising soul had the stomach to call a hotel and immediately set about finding the plastic surgeon he'd made contact with a month earlier. Dr. Emilio Vasquez.

The surgeon readily took a thick wad of money and set about giving Kent a new look. The fact that Kent's "new look" should have required four operations instead of the one did not deter Vasquez in the least. It was, after all, his trademark—doing to a man's face in one operation what took most plastic surgeons three months. It was also why Kent had chosen the man. He simply did not have three months. The rest of his plan was begging for its execution.

Four days after the big fire Kent had his new look, hidden under a heavy mask of white gauze, but there, Dr. Vasquez promised him. Definitely there. The twinkle in the surgeon's eyes had worried him. It was the first time he'd considered the possibility that he might spend the rest of his life looking like something out of a horror comic. But done was done. He'd sequestered himself in the hotel room, willing the cuts beneath the facial bandages to heal. It was a time that both stretched his patience and settled his nerves at once.

Kent lifted the chrome platter from the table and stared at his reflection. His tanned face looked like a Kevin, he thought. Kevin Stillman, his new assumed name. The nose was fuller, but it was the jaw line and brow work that changed his face so that he hardly recognized his own reflection. The plastic surgeon had done an exceptional job—although the first time Dr. Vasquez had removed the bandages and proudly shoved a mirror to his face he'd nearly panicked. Then, the red lines around his nose and cheekbones brought to mind frightening images of Frankenstein. Oh, he looked different, all right. But then, so did a skinned plum. He started to drink heavily that night. Tequila, of course, lots of it, but never enough to knock him silly. That would be stupid, and he was over being stupid.

Besides, too much liquor made the computer screen swim before his eyes, and he'd spent a lot of time staring at the laptop those first two weeks. Whereas ROOSTER allowed him undetected access into the banking system, it was that second program, the one called BANDIT, that had actually done the deed. When he had inserted his little disk into the drive that night at the bank and executed his theft, he'd left a little gift in each target account from which he'd taken twenty cents. And by all accounts the program had executed itself flawlessly. Indeed, BANDIT worked on the same principles as a stealth virus, executing commands to hide itself at the first sign of penetration. But that was not all it did. In the event the account was even so much as queried, it would first transfer twenty cents from one of Kent's holding accounts back into the target account, and then it would immediately remove itself permanently. The entire operation took exactly one and a half seconds and was over by the time the account-information screen popped to life on the operator's monitor. In the end it meant that any queried account would show erroneous charges on printed statements but not in the accounts themselves.

Kent's little virus executed itself on 220,345 accounts in the first two weeks, refunding a total of $44,069 dollars during that time. The virus would lay dormant in the rest of the accounts, waiting until September 2000 to be opened. They would obediently delete themselves if not activated within fourteen months.

It took two full weeks before he felt comfortable enough to make his first trip to the bank in Mexico City. The lines on his face were still visible, but after applying a pound of makeup he succeeded in convincing himself that they were virtually undetectable. And he was at the point of driving himself crazy in the hotel room. It was either risk a few raised brows in the bank or hang himself with the bedsheets.

The banking official at Banco de Mexico had indeed raised his brow when Kent visited under the name Matthew Brown. It was not the way Mr. Brown looked that had him jumping, it was the five-hundred-thousand-dollar cash withdrawal he'd executed. Of course the official had almost certainly reported the unusual amount—even banks that promise discretion keep a log of such transfers.

But Kent hardly cared. The maze of accounts through which the money had traveled over the last two weeks would require pure fortune to unravel. If any man were able to track the funds back to either Kent Anthony or the fire in Denver, they deserved to see him fry.

But that just wasn't going to happen.

That first five hundred thousand dollars brought a thrill to Kent's bones that he had not felt for months. He'd popped the latches of the black case he'd purchased for just this occasion and dumped the cash onto the moth-eaten bedspread in the hotel room. Then he'd stripped the piles of their rubber bands and physically rolled through them, tossing the bills into the air and letting them float lazily to the floor while pumping his fists and hooting in victory. It was a wonder the neighbors did not come pounding on his door. Possibly because there were no neighbors foolish enough to pay five hundred pesos a night to sleep in the miserable dump. He touched every bill, he thought, counting and recounting them all in a hundred different configurations. Of course he'd had little else to do then besides monitor the computer—that was his reasoning. Then he'd discarded his reasoning and celebrated by drinking himself into a two-day stupor.

It was his first alcoholic binge.

He started his well-rehearsed withdrawal plan then, flying first to Jakarta, then to Cairo, then to Geneva, then to Hong Kong, and finally here, to the Turks and Caicos Islands. At each stop he'd traveled under false identification papers, withdrawn large sums of money, and departed quickly. After each visit to a bank he'd taken the liberty of waltzing into its system using ROOSTER and isolating the links to the closed account. Bottom line, even if the local banking officials wanted to know more about the strange man who'd emptied their daily cash reserves with his massive withdrawal, they would find nothing.

He'd arrived a week ago in the islands packing just over six million dollars. All of it in cash, every last dollar untraceable. He'd become Kevin Stillman then and bought the villa. Fourteen million dollars, give or take, still waited around the world, gathering interest.

Yes indeed, to say that he'd pulled it off might very well be the century's greatest understatement. He had *rocked!* A dead man had ripped off twenty million bucks right under the nose of the almighty United States banking system, and not a soul suspected it was even gone!

That had been phase one.

Phase two had started one week after the fire, two days after Kent had received his new face. And it was phase two that was responsible for these raging emotions of insecurity now charging in to disturb the peace.

Maybe he should have been satisfied to take the $20 million minus the $44,069 and call it even. But in reality the thought hardly even occurred to him. This was not simply a matter of his getting what was coming to him; it was also a matter of Borst and Bentley getting what was coming to *them*. Some would call it revenge. Kent thought of it as justice. Putting things back the way they were meant to be. Or at least one version of how they were meant to be.

It was why he had planted a copy of ROOSTER on both Borst's and Bentley's hard drives several nights before executing the theft. And it was why he had made that first visit to their computers one week after the fire.

They already had routine access to AFPS, of course, and now they had untraceable access as well without knowing it. Only it was Kent in there doing the accessing, using their computers from remote stations. And the stuff he was accessing was not the stuff he was supposed to be accessing. Or rather it was not the kind of stuff *they* should be accessing. Naughty, naughty.

Over the course of three weeks, Kent had helped them steal money on seven different occasions. Small amounts of money—between three and five hundred dollars per whack—just enough to establish a trail. That was his little contribution to their burgeoning wallets, although to look at their private balances they certainly needed no help from him. Their contributions had been to keep the money. So far anyway. Whether because they were exceedingly greedy or because they simply did not know, Kent neither knew nor cared.

He considered all of this, set his drink back on the silver tray, and pressed his fingers together contemplatively. It had gone so smoothly that it would slip through the most sensitive digestive system unnoticed.

So then why the jitters?

Because everything up to this point had been a warmup of sorts. And now the computer sat on his table, wanting him to push the final buttons.

Kent grunted and wiped the sweat from his palms. "Well, we didn't come all this way to weasel out in the end, did we?" Of course not. Although it would certainly not hurt. And it would certainly be the wisest course, all things considered. It would . . .

"Shut up!" he snarled at himself.

Kent leaned forward and worked quickly now. He brought up ROOSTER from Borst's hard drive and then entered AFPS. He was into the bank's records.

Now the excitement of the moment brought a quiver to his bones. He brought up Borst's personal account and scanned the dozens of transactions recorded over the last few weeks. All seven deposits accommodated by him were still present. Thank heaven for small favors! He grinned and scanned down.

There were a few other deposits there as well. Large deposits. Deposits that made Kent squint. The bank was obviously paying him for AFPS. Nothing else could possibly account for a two-hundred-thousand-dollar balance.

"Not so fast, Fat-Boy," Kent muttered.

He selected *all* of the deposits with a single click of the mouse, ten in all including his own, and removed them from Borst's account to a holding account he'd built into ROOSTER. The account balance immediately dropped to an overdrawn status. Overdrawn by the $31,223 in checks Borst had written this month. He was spending his hard-earned money quickly. Well, this would give him pause.

And *this . . . will give you a hernia!*

Kent broke into the bank's primary accounting system, selected the primary bank reserves, and transferred five hundred thousand dollars to Borst's account. Using ROOSTER of course. He didn't want the authorities to know what had happened to the money. Not yet.

He posted a flag on the federal account and retreated to Borst's account. In the morning some lucky operator at Niponbank's headquarters in Japan would bring his computer up to find a nasty flag announcing the overnight disappearance of a half-million dollars from the bank's main account. Bells would clang, horns would blow, nostrils would flare. But nobody would discover the fate of the money, because it was as of yet unfindable. That was the beauty of ROOSTER.

Kent squirmed in his chair. Borst's account now showed a very healthy balance of over four hundred thousand dollars. He stared at the figure and considered leaving it. The ultimate carrot for Mr. Borst. Go ahead. Spend it, baby.

He discarded the notion. A plan was a plan. Instead he transferred the money to the same hidden account he'd set up for the other deposits, returning Borst's account to an overdrawn status. The man was going to wake up to the shock of his life.

Kent smirked, exceedingly happy for the moment.

He retreated from Borst's account and ventured into Bentley's. There he repeated the same steps, placing all of the bank president's money into another hidden account prepared for the occasion.

The porky twins were now very, very broke.

It was time to get out. Kent pulled out of the system, broke his connection, and sat back in the lounger. Sweat ran down his chest in small rivulets, and his hands were shaking.

"See how it feels, you greedy pigs," he sneered. And then he lifted his glass and threw back the remaining liquor.

Yes indeed. It was all going exactly as planned. And to this point, not a soul knew a thing.

Except Lacy, possibly. He'd said a bit much to her that night.

Or possibly that pinhead cop.

The emotion hit him then, full force, as if a lead weight had been neatly aimed from heaven and dropped on the half-naked man lounging on the deck so smugly down there. It felt as though a hole had been punched through his chest. A vacancy. The gnawing fear that it had all gone too smoothly. That in the end this dream facing him in the eyes would not be a dream at all but some kind of nightmare dressed up in sheep's clothing. That trying to live now, surrounded by his millions but without Gloria or Spencer . . . or Lacy . . .

He shook his head to clear the thought. On the other hand, there was no evidence at all that Lacy or the cop knew anything. And someday soon, perhaps, there would be another Gloria or another Lacy. Maybe. And another Spencer.

No, never another Spencer.

Kent rose, snatched the glass, and strode for the kitchen. It was time for another drink.

Chapter Thirty-Two

TWO THOUSAND miles northwest that same evening Lacy Cartwright stood over her stove struggling to flip the massive omelet she'd concocted in the shallow frying pan. She had no idea how she was going to eat the beast, but its aroma was staging a full assault on her senses, and she swallowed her saliva.

Her mind drifted back to the party Jeff Duncan had insisted she attend. The affair had been far too telling. She'd left after an hour of the foolishness and had to fend off a dozen questions the next workday. In the end she had succumbed to a little white lie. She had gotten sick. Which was, after all, true in heart-matters. Because she was still sick over this whole robbery issue. She knew he had done it—knew it like she knew the weasel was sitting on some beach somewhere, soaking up the rays.

She ground her teeth, turned off the stove, and flopped the eight-inch egg patty on a plate. If the idiot was still alive, off living with his millions, she hated him for it. If he was dead, having attempted such a fool thing, she hated him even more. How could anybody be so insensitive?

Lacy sat at the dinette and forked her omelet. She had decided a week ago that she should go to the authorities, even though she had promised not to tell. Give the little information that she had to the lead investigator. *"Hey, FBI man, you ever consider that maybe it was Kent Anthony who was the real robber?"* That would set them on a new track. Problem was, she could not be absolutely certain, which relieved her of any obligation, she thought. So she might very well tell them, but if she did, she would take her time.

Meanwhile, she had to get back to a normal life. The last time she remembered feeling in any way similar to this was after Kent had severed their relationship the first time. For a week she had walked around with a hollow gut, trying to ignore the lump in her throat and furious all at once. This time it was going on three weeks, and that lump kept wanting to lodge itself in her windpipe.

She had loved him, Lacy thought, and lowered her lifted fork. She had actually fallen in love with the man. In fact, to get right down and honest about the matter, she had been crazy about him. Which was impossible because she really hated him.

"Oh, God, help me," she muttered, rising and crossing to the ice box. "I'm losing my mind."

She returned to her seat with a quart of milk and drank straight from the carton. Impossible habit, but seeing as there was no one to offend at the moment, she carried on anyway. Now if Kent were here—

Lacy slammed the carton on the table in a sudden fit of frustration. Milk cleared the spout a full six inches before splashing to the table. Good grief! Enough with this Kent foolishness!

She jabbed at the omelet and stuffed a piece in her mouth, chewing deliberately. For that matter, enough with men, period. Lock 'em all in a bank somewhere and burn the whole thing to the ground. Now, that might be a bit harsh really, but then maybe not.

What in the world would Kent do with twenty million dollars? The sudden chirp of the doorbell startled her. Who could be visiting her tonight? Not so long ago it might have been Kent. Heavens.

Stop it, Lacy. Just stop it!

She walked for the door and pulled it open. A dark-haired man with slicked-back hair and wire-framed spectacles stood there, grinning widely. His eyes were very green.

"May I help you?"

He flipped a card out of his breast pocket. "Jeremy Lawson, seventh precinct," he said. "Do you mind if I ask you a few questions?"

A cop? "Sure," she muttered, and stepped aside.

The middle-aged man walked in and looked around the apartment, offering no reason for his being there.

Lacy shut the door. Something about the cop's appearance suggested familiarity, but she could not place him. "How can I help you?"

"Lacy, right? Lacy Cartwright?"

"Yes. Why?"

"I just want to make sure that I have the right person before I fire away, you know." He was sill wearing the wide grin.

"Sure. Is there a problem?"

"Oh, I don't know really. I'm doing a little looking into a fire down in Denver. You hear about that blaze that burned down a bank about a month ago?"

Whether or not it showed Lacy did not know, but she felt as though her head swelled red at the question. "Yes. Yes, I did read about that. And what does it have to do with me?"

"Nothing, maybe. We're just talking to people who might have known the gentleman who was killed in the fire. Do you mind if we sit, Miss Cartwright?"

Kent! He was investigating Kent's death! "Sure." She motioned to the sofa and took a seat in the armchair opposite. What was she to say?

Now that she looked at him carefully she saw why Kent had referred to him as a pinhead. His head seemed to slope to a point covered neatly in black shiny hair.

"Just a few questions, and I'll be out of your hair," the cop said, that smile stubbornly stuck on his face. He pulled out a small notebook and flipped it open. "I understand that you knew Kent Anthony. You spent some time with him in his last few weeks. Is that right?"

"And how did you discover this?"

"Well, I can't very well spill my trade secrets, now, can I?"

Lacy settled in her chair, wondering desperately what he knew. "Yes, I saw him a few times."

"Did his death surprise you?"

She scrunched her eyebrows. "No, I was expecting it. Of *course* it surprised me! Am I a suspect in the case?"

"No. No, you're not."

"So what kind of question is that? How could I not be surprised by his death unless I somehow knew about it in advance?"

"You may have expected it, Lacy. Can I call you Lacy? He was depressed, right? He'd lost his wife and his son in the months preceding the fire. I'm just asking you if he seemed suicidal. Is that so offensive?"

She breathed deeply. *Calm down, Lacy. Just calm down.* "At times, yes, he was upset. As would be anyone who'd suffered as much as he had. Have you ever lost a wife or a son, detective . . ." She glanced at his card again. "Lawson?"

"I can't say that I have. So you think he was capable of suicide, then? Is that your position?"

"Did I say that? I don't remember saying that. I said that at times he was upset. Please don't turn my words around."

The cop seemed thoroughly undeterred. "Upset enough to commit suicide?"

"No, I wouldn't say that. Not the last time I saw him."

He lowered his voice a notch. "Hmmm. And did you know about his little difficulties at work?"

"What difficulties?"

"Well, if you knew, you would know what difficulties, now, wouldn't you?"

"Oh, you mean the bit about his boss betraying him while he was mourning the death of his wife? You mean that tiny speck of trouble?"

The cop studied her eyes for a moment. "So you did know."

She was matching him tit for tat without really knowing why. She had no reason to defend Kent. He'd dumped her, after all. Now, if Lawson came right out and asked certain questions, she didn't know what she would say. She couldn't very well lie. On the other hand, she had promised Kent her silence.

"You knew him well, Lacy. In your opinion—and I'm just asking your opinion here, so there's no need to jump up and down—do you think he was capable of suicide?"

"Do you suspect he committed suicide? I thought they concluded that a robber had murdered him."

"Yes. That's the official line. And I'm not saying it's wrong. I'm just doing my best to make sure everything fits. You know what I mean?"

"Sure."

"So then, yes or no?"

"Suicide?"

He nodded.

"Capable, yes. Did he commit suicide? No."

The cop lifted an eyebrow. "No?"

"He was a proud man, Detective Lawson. I think it would take the hand of God to bring him to his knees. Short of that, I don't think he was capable of giving up on anything, much less his life."

"I see. And from what I've heard, I would have to agree with you. Which is why I'm still on the case, see?" He stopped as if that should make everything crystal clear.

"No, actually I don't see. Not in the least."

"Well, if it were a suicide there would be no need for further investigation. Suicide might be an ugly thing, but it's usually an open-and-shut case."

She smiled despite herself. "Of course. And being murdered causes guys like you a lot more work."

He smiled. "If he was murdered there would be no need to investigate *him.* We'd be looking for the murderer, wouldn't we?"

"Then it seems to me that you're barking up the wrong tree, Detective Lawson."

"Unless, of course, your friend Kent was not murdered. Now, if he did not commit suicide and he was not murdered, then what are we left with?"

"A dead body?" Mercy, where was he headed?

Lawson shoved his little notebook back into his pocket, having written maybe two letters on the open page. "A dead body! Very good. We'll make a detective out of you yet." He stood abruptly and headed for the door. "Well, I thank you for your time, Miss Cartwright. You've answered my questions most graciously."

He was hardly making sense now, she thought. She stood with him and followed him to the door. "Sure," she muttered. What did he know? Every bone in her body screamed to ask the question. *Did you know we were in love, Officer? Did you know that?* No, not that!

He had his hand on the door before she spoke, unable to restrain herself.

"Do *you* think he's dead, Detective?"

He turned and looked her in the eyes. For a long moment they held eye contact. "We have a body, Miss Cartwright. It is burned beyond recognition, but the records show that what is left belongs to Mr. Kent Anthony. Does that sound dead to you? Seems clear enough." He flashed a grin. "On the other hand, not everything is what it seems."

"So why all the questions?"

"Never mind the questions, child. We detective types practice long and hard at asking confusing questions. It throws people off." He smiled warmly, and she thought he was sincere. She returned the smile.

He dipped his head. "Good evening, Mrs. Cartwright."

"Good night," she returned.

He turned to leave and then hesitated, turning back. "Oh, one last question,

Lacy. Kent never mentioned any plans he had, did he? Say some elaborate plan to fake his death or any such thing?"

She nearly fell over at the question. This time she knew he saw her turning red under the gills. He could hardly miss it.

And then he simply flipped a hand to the air. "Never mind. Silly question. I've bothered you enough tonight. Well, thank you for your hospitality. Coffee might have been nice—we detectives always like coffee—but otherwise you did just fine. Good night."

With that he turned and pulled the door closed behind him.

Lacy sidestepped to the chair and sat hard, heat sweeping over her. Lawson was on to him! The detective was on to Kent! He had to be! Which meant that Kent was alive!

Maybe.

KENT DROVE his new black Jeep down the hill to the town at seven, just as the orange sun sank behind the waves. The sound of calypso drums and laughter carried on the warm breeze. Brent the real-estate broker had recommended the Sea Breeze. "The finest dining south of Miami," he'd said with a twinkle in his eye. "A bit draining on the wallet but well worth it." Kent could use a little draining on his wallet. It was feeling a tad heavy.

He mounted the wooden steps and bounded up the flight. A fountain gurgled red water from a mermaid's lips just inside the door. Like some goddess drunk on the blood of sailors. He turned to the dim interior. Through a causeway a fully stocked bar already served a dozen patrons perched on tall stools. Mahogany stairs wound to the upper level to his right.

"Welcome to the Sea Breeze, sir. Do you have reservations?"

Kent faced the hostess. Her black hair lay long on bare shoulders. She smiled carefully below dark eyes, and an obscure image of red water spewing from *those* round lips slinked though his mind. Miss Mermaid in the flesh. Her nametag read "Marie."

"No. I'm sorry, I didn't realize that I needed reservations."

"Yes. Maybe you could return tomorrow night."

Tomorrow? Negative, Black Eyes. "I'd rather eat tonight, if you wouldn't mind," Kent returned.

Marie blinked at that. "I'm sorry, maybe you didn't understand. You need a reservation. We are full tonight."

"Yes, evidently. How much will a table cost me?"

"Like I said, sir, we don't—"

"A thousand?" Kent lifted his eyebrow and pulled out his wallet. "I'm sure that for a thousand dollars you could find me a table, Marie. In fact for a thousand dollars you could possibly find me the best table in the house. Am I right? It would be our secret." He smiled and watched her black eyes widen. He felt the subtle power of wealth run through his veins. In that moment he knew that for the right price, Miss Mermaid Marie here would lick the soles of his sandals.

She glanced around and smiled. Her breathing had quickened by the rise and fall of her chest. "Yes. Actually we might have an opening. I apologize, I had no idea. This way."

Marie led him up two flights of stairs to a glass-enclosed porch atop the restaurant. Three tables rounded out the room, each delicately laid with candles and flowers and crystal and silver. The musty scent of potpourri hung in the air. A party of well-groomed patrons sat around one of the tables, drinking wine and nibbling at what looked to be some sea creature's tentacles. They looked at him with interest as Marie sat him across the circular room.

"Thank you," Kent said, smiling. "I'll add it to your tip."

She winked. "You are kind, Mr. . . ."

"Kevin."

"Thank you, Kevin. Is there anything else I can do for you at this time?"

"Not at the moment, Marie, no. Thank you."

She turned with a twinkle in her eyes and left the room.

The two waitresses who served him had obviously been told of his generosity and were unabashed in their attempts to please. He ordered lobster and steak and wine, and they were delicious. As delicious as they had been three months earlier when he had ordered the same in celebration with Gloria at the completion of AFPS. He lifted his glass of wine and stared out at the dark seas, crested with moonlit waves. *Well, I did it, Honey. Every bit and more, and I wish you were here to enjoy it with me.*

It settled on him as he ate that the food, though quite good, did not taste any different than it had when he'd paid twelve dollars for it back at Red Lobster in Littleton. The Heinz 57 sauce certainly came from the same vat. In fact the wine probably came from the same winery. Like different gasoline stations selling branded gas that anyone with half a brain knew came from the same refinery.

Kent finished the meal slowly, intent on relishing each bite, and uncomfortably aware that each bite tasted just as it should. Like lobster and steak should. The wine went down warm and comforting. But when he was done he did not feel as though he'd just eaten a thousand dollars' worth of pleasure. No, he'd just filled up his tank.

In the end he tipped heavily, slipped Marie her thousand dollars, and retired to the bar, where tequila was more in order. Steve, the bartender, must have heard of his tipping, because he eased right on over and set up a glass.

"What'll it be, sir?"

"Cuervo Gold. Straight up."

Steve poured the liquor into the glass and started polishing another. "You passing through?"

"You could say that. I own a place up the hill, but yes, I'll be in and out."

The man stuck out his hand. "Name's Steve Barnes. It's good to have you on the island."

"Thanks. Kevin Stillman."

The man hung around and asked a few more questions to which Kent gave short, pert answers. Eventually Steve wandered off to the other customers, who were talking about how some tourist had fallen off a fishing boat and gotten entangled in a net. Kent smiled once, but beyond the hint of humor, he found himself odd man out, and the hole in his chest seemed to widen. Maybe if he pulled out a few hundred and waved it around them. *"Hey guys, I'm rich. Stinking rich. Yes indeed, you may come over and lick my toes if you wish. One at a time, please."*

By the time Kent pulled into his circle drive back at the villa, his mind was numbed by the alcohol. Which was a good thing, he thought. Because something inside his mind had started to hurt, watching those fools carry on down at the pub.

But there was tomorrow, and tomorrow would be a day of reckoning. Yes indeed. Never mind the fifteen hundred bucks he'd just tossed down for dinner. Never mind the foolishness of those still surrounding the bar, gabbing with Steve the bartender.

Kent fell onto the covers. Tomorrow night he would turn the screws.

Sleep came within the minute.

CHAPTER THIRTY-THREE

Thursday

MARKUS BORST ran through the bank, huffing and puffing and not caring who saw him in the state of terror that obviously shone from his face like some kind of shiny red Christmas bulb.

He was not accustomed to running, and it occurred to him halfway through the lobby that he must look like a choo-choo train with his short legs pumping from the hips and his arms churning in small circular motions. But the gravity of the situation shoved the thought from his mind before it had time to set up. A dozen eyes glared his way, and he ignored them. What if Price was not in his office? Heaven help him! Heaven *help* him!

He met Mary as he was charging around the corner leading to Price Bentley's office, and she jumped with a cry. "Oh!" A sheet of paper fluttered from her grasp, and she bolted back. "Mr. Borst!"

"Not now!" he said. He rushed past her and slammed through the bank-branch president's door without bothering to knock. There was a time to knock and there was a time not to knock, and this was the latter if there ever was a time for the latter.

Price Bentley sat behind his big cherrywood desk, his bald head shining red under the bright fluorescent tubes above. His eyes widened in shock, and he came halfway out of his seat before his thighs intersected the bottom edge of his desk, propelling him back into his black leather chair. He immediately grabbed his legs and winced.

Bentley cursed. "What in the blazes are you doing, Borst! *Man* that hurt!" He opened his eyes and blinked rapidly at Borst. "Close the door, you fool. And straighten out that thing on your head! You look ridiculous!"

Borst hardly heard him. He slammed the door shut instinctively. "The money's gone!"

"What? Lower your voice and sit down, Borst. Your wig is slipping, man. Fix it."

Borst jerked his hand up to his head and felt the toupee. It had fallen halfway down his right ear. An image of that choo-choo train pumping through the lobby with a hairpiece slipping down one cheek flashed through his mind. Perhaps he'd frightened Mary with it. A flush of embarrassment reddened his face. He yanked the thing off and stuffed it in his breast pocket.

"We have a problem," he said, still breathing hard.

"Fine. Why don't you run through the lobby tooting a horn while you're at it. Sit down and get ahold of yourself."

Borst sat on the edge of the overstuffed chair, facing Bentley.

"Now, start from the beginning."

The branch president was coming across as condescending, and Borst hated the tone. It was *he,* after all, who had brought this whole idea to Bentley in the first place. He'd never had the guts to shove some of the man's medicine back into his face, but sometimes he sure had the inkling.

"The money's gone." His voice trembled as he said it. "I went into my personal account a few minutes ago, and someone's wiped out all the deposits. I'm overdrawn thirty thousand dollars!"

"So there's been a mistake. No need to come apart at the seams over an accounting snafu."

"No, Price. I don't think you understand. This is not some simple—"

"Look, you fool. Mistakes happen all the time. I can't believe you come storming in here announcing your stupidity to the whole world just because someone put a decimal in the wrong place."

"I'm telling you, Price. This is not—"

"Don't tell me what it is!" Bentley stormed. "This is *my* bank, isn't it? Well, when it's your bank you can tell me what it is. And stop calling me Price. Show some respect, for Pete's sake!"

Borst felt the words slapping at his ears as if they had been launched from a blast furnace. Deep in his mind, where the man in him cowered, a switch was thrown, and he felt hot blood rush to his face.

"Shut up, Price! Just shut up and listen. You're an insolent, bean-brained hothead, and you're not listening. So just shut up and listen!"

The president sat back, his eyes bulging like beetles. But he did not speak, possibly from shock at Borst's accusations.

"Now, whether you like it or not, regardless of whose bank this is or is not, we have a problem." Borst swallowed. Maybe he had gone too far with that attack. He shrank back a tad and continued.

"There is no *simple* accounting mistake. I've already run the queries. The money is not misplaced. It's gone. All of it. Including the small deposits. The ones—"

"I know which ones. And you ever talk to me like that again, and we're finished." The president stared at him unblinking. "I can do to you what we did to Anthony with a few phone calls. You'd best remember that."

Borst's ears burned at the insinuation, but the man was right. And there was nothing he could do about it. "I apologize. I was out of line."

Evidently satisfied that Borst was properly chastised, Bentley turned to his terminal and punched a few keys. He squinted at the screen for a moment and then went very still. A line of sweat broke from his brow, and his breathing seemed to thicken.

"You see," Borst said, "it's just gone."

The president swallowed deliberately. "This is not your account, you fool. It's mine. And it's overdrawn too."

"See!" Borst slid to the front of his chair. "Now, what's the chance of that? Both of our accounts wiped out! Someone found the deposits and is setting us up!"

"Nonsense!" Bentley swiveled back to Borst, dropped his head, and gripped his temples. He stood and paced to the window, rubbing his jaw.

"What do you think?"

"Shut up. Let me think. I told you that keeping those small deposits was a bad idea."

"And who says we've kept them? It's been less than a month. They were put there without our knowing; we were going to report them, right? That wouldn't warrant *this,*" Borst said.

"You're right. And you ran a full query, right? There's no trace of where it went?"

"None. I'm telling you, someone took it!"

Bentley sat down, hard. His fingers flew across the keyboard. Menus popped to life and disappeared, replaced by others.

"You won't find anything. I've already looked," Borst said.

"Yeah, well now *I'm* looking," Bentley snapped back, undeterred.

"Sure. But I'm telling you, there's something wrong here. And you know we can't just report it. If there's an investigation, they'll find the other money. It won't look right, Price."

"I told you not to call me Price."

"Come on! We're each a few hundred thousand dollars upside down here, and you're bickering over what I call you?"

Bentley had finished his queries. "You're right. It's gone." He slammed his big fist on the desk. "That's impossible! How's that possible, huh? You tell me, Mr. Computer Wizard. How does someone just walk into an account and wipe it out?"

A buzz erupted at the base of Borst's skull. "You would need a pretty powerful program." He stiffened in his chair. "AFPS could do it, maybe."

"AFPS? AFPS would leave a trail as wide as I-70."

"Not necessarily. Not if you know the raw code."

"What are you saying?"

"I'm not sure. I'm not even sure how it could be done. But if there were a way, it would be through the alteration of the code itself."

"Yeah, well that's not good news, Borst. And do you know why that's not good news? I'll tell you why. Because you, my dear friend, are in charge of that code! You're the brilliant one who pieced this thing together, right? Now either you stole from yourself, and from me, or someone else is using your program to rob you blind."

"Don't be ridiculous! Those monkeys in there wouldn't have the stomach much less the experience to do anything like this. And I certainly did not mess with my own account."

"Well, somebody did. And you'd better find that somebody, or it won't go nicely for you. Do you understand me?"

Borst looked up at the president, stunned by the suggestion. "Well, if it doesn't go nicely for me, you can bet it won't go nicely for you."

"And *that,* my dear, fine-feathered friend, is where you are wrong." Bentley jabbed his desk with his finger, making a small thumping sound each time it landed. "If this goes down, you'll take the fall, the whole fall, and nothing but the fall. And don't think for a minute I can't do it."

"We will deny it," Borst said, dismissing Bentley's threats.

"Deny what?"

"We deny that we know anything about our accounts at all. We ignore all of this and come unglued when the first sign of trouble crops up."

"And like you said, if they run an investigation we could have a hard time answering their questions."

"Yes, but at least it's only an *if.* You have a better suggestion?"

"Yes. I suggest you find this imbecile and put a bullet in his brain."

They stared at each other for a full thirty seconds, and slowly, very slowly, the magnitude of what they might be facing settled on both of them. The macho stuff vacated their minds, replaced by a dawning desperation. This was not a problem that would necessarily go away at the push of a button.

When Borst emerged from the room thirty minutes later, his head was bald and his face was white. But these issues were of little concern to him now. It was the pressure on his brain that had him swallowing repeatedly as he walked back to his office. And nothing, absolutely nothing, he could think of seemed to loosen the vise that now held his mind in its grip.

KENT AWOKE midmorning and slogged out to the deck, nursing a bit of a headache. He squinted against the bright blue sky and rubbed his temples. The ocean's distant crashing carried on the wind, but otherwise silence hung heavily in the air. Not a voice, not a bird, not a motor, not a single sound of life. Then he heard the muted thud of a hammer landing on some new home's wood frame down the way. And with that thud the hole in Kent's chest opened once again. A sobering reminder that he was alone in the world.

He glanced at his watch, suddenly alert. Ten o'clock Friday morning. His lips twitched to a faint grin. By now Borst and Bentley would have discovered the little disappearing trick. Now you see it; now you don't. He imagined they'd be sweating all over their desks about now. What they didn't know was that the trick was just beginning. Act one. Strap yourselves in, ladies and gentlemen. This one will rock your socks. Or perhaps steal them right off your feet without your knowing the better.

He swallowed and thought about mixing himself a drink. Meanwhile, he was wealthy, of course. Must not forget that. How many people would give their children to have what he now had? An image of Spencer, riding his red skateboard, popped into his mind. Yes, a drink would be good.

Kent mixed himself a drink and meandered out to the deck. The soft sound of waves rushing the shore carried on the breeze. He had ten hours to burn before placing the phone call. He couldn't sit around drinking himself into a stupor this time. Not with that conversation coming on tonight. He would have to stay clear headed. Then perhaps he should clear his head out there on the waves.

An hour later Kent stood by the pier, gazing down the long row of boats, wondering how much they would bring. A small chill of excitement rippled through his gut.

"Whoa there, mate!" The voice spoke with an Australian accent.

Kent whirled to face an older seaman pushing a dolly stacked with provisions down the plank. "If you'll step aside, son, I'll be by quicker than a swordfish on a line." He grinned, splitting the bristly white hair that masked his face. Years of sun had turned the man's skin to leather, but if the shorts and tank top were any indicator, he wasn't too concerned.

"Sorry." Kent stepped aside to let the man pass and then followed him up the pier. "Excuse me."

"Hold your head, son," the man croaked without looking back. "I've got a bit of a load, as you can see. I'll be with you in a jiffy. Have yourself a beer."

Kent smiled and trailed the man to a large white boat near the end of the pier. *Marlin Mate.* She was a Roughwater, the little silver plaque on her bow said. Maybe fifty feet in length.

"This your boat?" Kent asked.

"You don't hear too well, do you? Hold your head, mate." The seaman hauled the dolly over the gangplank and into the cabin, grumbling under his breath. This time Kent lost his grin and wondered if the old man's head was out to sea. He could certainly use a little fine-tuning in the social-graces department.

"Now there," the man said, coming from the cabin. "That wasn't such a long wait, was it? Yes, this is my boat. What can I do for you?" The sailor's blue eyes sparkled with the sea.

"What does something like this go for?" Kent asked, looking her up and down.

"Much more than you would think. And I don't rent her out. If you want a day trip, Paulie has—"

"I'm not sure you're answering my question. It was quite simple, really. How much would a boat like this one cost me?"

The man hesitated, obviously distracted by the strong comeback. "What's it to you? You plan on buying her? Even if you could afford her, she's not for sale."

"And what makes you think I can't afford her?"

"She's pricey, mate. I've worked her for half my life, and I still hold a decent note on her." Leather Face smiled. He'd misplaced two of his front teeth. "You got five hundred thousand dollars hanging loose in your pocket there?"

"Five hundred, huh?" Kent studied the boat again. It looked almost new to him—if the Australian had owned it for as long as he let on, he'd cared for her well.

"She's not for sale."

Kent looked back to the old man, who had flattened his lips. "How much do you want for her? I pay cash."

The man looked at him steadily for a moment without answering, probably running through those little note balances in his mind.

"Five-fifty, then?" Kent pushed.

Leather Face's baby blues widened. For a long minute he did not speak. Then a smile spread his cracked face. "Seven hundred thousand U.S. dollars, and she's all yours, mate. If you're crazy enough to pay that kind of dough in cash, well, I guess I'll have to be crazy enough to sell her."

"I'll pay you seven hundred on one condition," Kent returned. "You agree to keep her for a year. Teach me the ropes and take care of her when I'm not around."

"I'm no steward, mate."

"And I'm not looking for a steward. You just let me tag along, learn a few things, and when I'm gone you run her all you like."

The old man studied him with piercing eyes now, judging the plausibility of the offer, Kent guessed. "You show me the cash, I'll show you the boat. If I like what I see and you like what you see, we got us a deal."

Kent was back an hour later, briefcase in hand. Leather Face—or Doug Oatridge as he called himself—liked what he saw. Kent just wanted to get out to sea, feel the breeze through his hair, drink a few beers, distract himself for a few hours. Kick back on the deck of his yacht while Borst and Bentley chewed their fingernails to the knuckles.

By midday they were trolling at twenty knots, precisely. A permanent smile had fixed itself on Doug's face as he feathered the murmuring engine through the seawater. Thinking about the cash, no doubt. They sat on cushioned chairs, eating sandwiches and drinking ice-cold beer. The sun had dipped halfway when the first fish hit. Ten minutes later they hauled a four-foot tuna over the side and shoved it into the holding tank. What they would do with such a creature, Kent had no clue—maybe carve it up and fry it on the grill, although he'd never liked tuna. Give him swordfish or salmon, disguised with chicken broth, but keep the smelly stuff. Three more of the fish's cousins joined him in the tank over the next half-hour, then they stopped taking the bait. Doug was talking about how tuna ran in schools, but Kent was thinking the fish had just grown tired of the senseless self-sacrifice.

The perfect day's only damper came on the trip home, when Kent made the mistake of asking Doug how he'd come to own the boat in the first place. The old man had evidently both grown accustomed to Kent and loosened under the influence of a six-pack, and his story ran long. He'd been married twice, he said, first to Martha, who had left him for some basketball player on a beach court in Sydney. Then to Sally, who had borne them three sons and tired of them all after ten years. It was an inheritance of a hundred thousand dollars that had brought Doug to the islands with his sons, in search of a boat with which to begin life anew. He'd purchased *Marlin Mate* then. Two of his sons had left the island within the first year—off to America to find their own lives. The youngest, his little Bobby, had been swept overboard in a storm one year later.

The old man turned away and stared misty eyed to the sea, having dropped his tale like a lead weight into Kent's mind. The beer in Kent's hand suddenly felt heavy. The afternoon grew quiet beyond the splashing wake. Kent imagined a small boy cartwheeling off the deck, screaming for Daddy. A knot rose into his throat.

They docked the boat an hour later, and Kent showed as much interest as he could muster in the procedure. He shook the old man's hand. Did he want to go out tomorrow? No, not tomorrow. Could he take the boat out tomorrow then? Yes, of course. Do what you like, Doug. He thumped the man on the back and smiled. In fact, keep the stupid boat, he thought, but immediately reined in the absurd notion.

"Hey, me and the mates are going to do some drinking tonight. You want to come? There'll be dames."

"Dames?"

Doug flashed a toothless smile. "Girls, mate. Beach bunnies in their bikinis."

"Oh yes, of course. Dames. And where are we having this party?"

"Here on the boat. But not to worry, mate. The first man to puke gets thrown overboard."

Kent smiled. "Well, that's comforting. Maybe. We'll see."

CHAPTER THIRTY-FOUR

DESPITE HIS need for a clear mind, Kent downed two stiff drinks before his eight o'clock phone call. It wouldn't do to have his teeth clattering against the receiver, either, and his nerves had tightened as the hour approached.

Darkness had settled over the island. From the villa's deck the sea looked black below, split by a long shaft of white cast by the bright moon. A spattering of lights twinkled along the hillside on either side. It was hard to imagine that across that sea the sun had already risen over a bustling city called Tokyo. He'd seen pictures of the tall, chrome building that housed Niponbank's headquarters, smack-dab in the middle of the busiest part of town, but he could hardly picture the crowded scene now. The serene one before him had lulled him into a foggy state. Or perhaps the drinks had done that.

A small bell chimed behind him, and Kent started. It was time.

He grabbed the cordless phone from the table and stared at its buttons. His heart pounded like a tom-tom in his ears. For the first time in over a month he was about to expose himself. And for what?

Kent cleared his throat and spoke with a gruff voice, the voice he had decided would be his to complete his disguise. "Hello, this is Bob." Too high. He'd done this a thousand times. "Hello, this is Bob."

Get on with it, man.

He punched the numbers in quickly.

An electronic voice answered his call. "Thank you for calling Niponbank. Please press one if you wish to be served in Japanese. Please press two if you wish to be served in English." *Please press three if you are calling to turn yourself in for grand larceny.*

Kent swallowed and pressed two.

It took all of ten minutes to find the right individual. A Mr. Hiroshito—the one banking executive Kent knew who could quickly get him to the real power mongers at the top. He knew Hiroshito because the high-level man had visited Denver once, and the bank had spent a day dancing around him like crows around fresh road kill.

"Hiroshito." The man said his name like it was an order to attack.

Chill, my friend. "Mr. Hiroshito, you don't know me, but you should. I'm—"

"I am sorry. You must have the wrong connection. I will put you through to the operator."

Kent spoke quickly before the man could pass him off. "Your bank is missing one million dollars, is it not?"

The phone filled with the soft hiss of distant static. Kent was not sure if the man had transferred him. "Hello."

"Who is this?"

"I am the person who can help you recover the million dollars that was missing from your ledgers yesterday. And please don't bother trying to trace this phone call—you will find it impossible. Do I have your attention?"

Hiroshito was whispering orders in Japanese behind a muted receiver. "Yes," he said. "Who is this? How do you know of this matter?"

"It is my business to know of such matters, sir. Now, I will lay this out for you as quickly and as plainly as possible. It would be best if you could record what I say. Do you have a recorder?"

"Yes. But I must know who you are. Surely you cannot expect—"

"If you choose to accept my terms, you will know me soon enough, Mr. Hiroshito. That I can promise you. Are you recording?"

A pause. "Yes."

Here goes nothing. Kent took a deep breath.

"Yesterday a million dollars was stolen from Niponbank's main ledger, but then, you know this already. What you don't know is how I know this. I know this because a certain party within your own bank, who shall remain nameless, tipped me off. This is relatively unimportant. What *is* important, however, is the fact that I managed to break into your system and verify the missing balance. I was also able to track the first leg of the outbound transaction. And I believe I will be able to uncover the theft in its entirety.

"Now, before you ask, let me tell you what you are going to ask. Who in the world am I to think I can track what the engineers in your own bank cannot track? I am a number: 24356758. Please write it down. It is where you will wire my fee if I successfully expose the thief and return your money. As I'm sure you can appreciate, I must protect my actual identity, but for the sake of convenience you may use a fictitious name. Say, Bob. You may call me Bob. From now on, I am Bob. I can assure you that Bob is quite proficient at electronic data manipulation. Without question one of the world's finest. You have not heard of him only because he has always insisted on working in complete anonymity. In fact, as you will see, he depends on it. But there is no man better suited to track down your money; that much I can assure you with absolute confidence. Do you understand thus far?"

Hiroshito did not expect the sudden question. "Y . . . yes."

"Good. Then here are Bob's terms. You will grant him unlimited access to any bank he deems necessary for his investigation. He will both return your money and uncover the means with which the perpetrator took your money. You obviously have a hole in your system, my fine friends. He will not only return your money; he will close that hole. If and only if he is successful, you will transfer a 25 percent recovery fee into the Cayman account I recited earlier: 24356758. You will wire the money within one hour of your own recovery. In addition, if he is successful, you will grant him immunity in connection with any charge related to this case. These are his terms. If you accept them, I can assure you he will recover your money. You have exactly twelve hours to make your decision. I will call you then for your decision. Do you understand?"

"Yes. And how is this possible? How can we be sure you are sincere, Mr. . . . uh . . . Bob?"

"You can't. And once you've had time to think about it, you'll see that it does not matter. If I am unsuccessful, you pay nothing. But you must ask yourself how I know what I know. No one knows the workings of electronic high finance like I do, Mr. Hiroshito. I am simply the best. Please take this message to your superiors immediately."

"And how do I know—?"

"You know enough already," Kent interrupted. "Play the tape for the main man. He'll agree to my terms. Good day."

Kent hung up to a stammering Hiroshito and exhaled slowly. His hands were trembling, and he pulled them into fists. Man, that had felt good! He took a long drink from his glass, slammed the tumbler onto the table, and pumped a fist in victory. "Yes!"

Of course it was not victory. Not yet. But it was the deed. It was the plan. The thrill of the hunt, as they say. Within the hour the whole snobby bunch of them would at least suspect that there existed a man who possessed the electronic wizardry to waltz into their systems and do what he willed. A lunatic who called himself Bob. Now *there* was power! Not just being able to *do* it, but being settled in the knowledge that others *believed* he could do it.

Kent made his way to the bathroom on shaky legs. In twelve hours he would have his answer. And if they said no? If they said no, he might very well go in there and take another million. Then call them back and ask them if they might reconsider. *Ha!*

Yes indeed. Now *there* was power!

KENT ATTENDED Doug's party on the *Marlin Mate* later that night for lack of appealing alternatives. Actually, the thought of standing on a swaying boat with twenty people held little appeal itself. Never mind that there would be "dames." Half-naked dames at that. Never mind that there would be booze. It was all sounding rather bleak now. But staying home alone drumming his fingers on the table held even less appeal, so he took the Jeep to the pier and boarded the swaying boat.

The Aussie knew how to party. It was perhaps the only skill he'd mastered aside from skippering. As promised, a dozen girls smelling of coconut oil slithered about the twin decks. At some point, Doug must have dropped the nugget that the blond-haired man sitting quietly on the upper deck was flush with cash, because the women began to mill about Kent with batting eyes and pouting lips.

For the first hour, Kent quite enjoyed the attention. It was sometime near midnight, however, that a thought dawned on him. He was not attracted to these bathing beauties. Maybe the booze had messed with his libido. Maybe the memory of Gloria was simply too fresh. Maybe the hole in his chest had sucked the life right out of him—neutered him. The realization fell over him like a wet blanket.

By the time he dragged himself back up the hill at two in the morning, the booze had robbed his ability to consider the matter any further. It was the last time he would party with Doug and his dames.

When Kent rejoined the land of the conscious it was to a relentless chirp sounding in his ear. A whistle blowing down the alley. He spun around, except that he couldn't spin at all because Mr. Brinkley's dead body was hanging off his shoulders, butt up, gray in the moonlight. He nearly capsized in his lumbering turn.

Tweep, tweep, tweep!

His heart pounded like a drum to that piercing alarm. They had found him! A figure ran through the shadows toward him, his hand extended accusingly, blowing his whistle.

Tweep, tweep, tweep!

He and Mr. Brinkley had been caught with their pants down behind the bank! At least Mr. Brinkley had. The rest of this nonsense about buying a villa and sailing on his yacht had been a dream. He was still back at the bank!

And then the whistle-blower's face emerged from the shadows, and Kent's heart slammed into his throat. It was the vagrant! And it wasn't with a two-dollar tin whistle that he was sounding the alarm; it was with that long tongue of his, sticking out and curled like a bamboo reed.

Kent bolted up, sticky with sweat, breathing hard.

Tweep, tweep, tweep.

He reached over and smacked the alarm beside his bed.

Eight o'clock! He sprang from the bed and splashed cool water over his face. Hiroshito and company were waiting by the phone—at least he hoped they were. Ready to deal. And if not he would go ahead and rock their world a little. Sound his own wake-up call. *Tweep, tweep!* Maybe he'd take five million next time! That would put them on their seats. Of course he'd have to give it all back—this was not like taking twenty untraceable cents from millions of unsuspecting donors; this was plain old larceny. They'd be crawling over this like ants on honey. And they'd eventually find the link. Which was why he had to get on the phone and strike a deal to find their money *his* way before they found it *their* way. Kent to the rescue.

He snatched up the phone and dialed the number. This time it took less than sixty seconds before Mr. Hiroshito's sharp voice crackled in his ear.

"Hello."

"Mr. Hiroshito. It is Bob. You remember me?"

"Yes. I have someone here who would like to speak to you."

Kent sat on the deck chair facing the blue-green sea. "Sure."

Another voice spoke into the phone, this one sly like a loan shark and definitely Caucasian. "Bob? Are you there, Bob?"

"Yes." The man's tone reminded Kent of a bossman smirking on some gangster movie.

"Okay, Bob. I don't know who you are, and frankly, I don't care. But *you* know who we are, and you should know that we don't deal with extortionists and blackmailers. So why don't you just cut the charades and talk to us straight instead of playing peekaboo, okay, pal?"

Kent ground his teeth, flooded with the sudden urge to hurl the phone over the railing. Maybe fly over to Tokyo and smack some sense into Mr. Cheese Whiz. He crossed his legs and breathed deliberately.

"I'm sorry, Mr. . . ."

A pause. "Call me Frank."

"I'm sorry, Frank, but you have this all wrong. I apologize for the mix-up. You must have been out of the room when they played the tape. Nobody as bright as you sound would have the stomach to threaten a man in my position. Listen to the tape, Frankie. I'll call back in ten minutes." Kent hung up.

His chest was thumping. What was he doing? Frank had obviously listened to the tape already—it was why he had used the term *extortion.* Because frankly, when you got right down to it, this was as close to extortion as kidnapping. He had kidnapped their system, and they knew it. And what he was really proposing was that he would turn over the key to their system (that would be ROOSTER) in exchange for immunity. That and $250,000.

Kent retreated to the kitchen and poured a drink, a tequila sunrise minus the citrus and the ice. Cuervo Gold straight up. If ever there was a time he needed a drink, it was now.

When he called ten minutes later, they put him directly through.

"Bob?" It was Frank, and he was not sounding so slick.

"Did you listen to the tape, Frank?"

"Of course I listened to the tape!" the other man yelled. "Now, you listen to me . . ."

"No, you listen to me, Buckwheat! If you think for a minute that I cannot do what I claim I can do, then simply reject my terms. Don't come at me with all this strong-arm baloney. Either you hire me for a 25 percent recovery fee and immunity, or you don't. Is this too difficult to understand?"

"And how do we know that it wasn't *you* who stole the money in the first place?"

"Not a bad idea, Frankie. Except this is no ransom. Or maybe you didn't listen to the whole tape. I've agreed to turn the perpetrators over to you, and that wouldn't be me. More important, your payment of this recovery fee is contingent upon my closing the security breach through which they were able to gain access to your million dollars. You obviously have a gaping hole somewhere in your system. It was one million this time. Who's to say that it won't be ten million the next?"

"I'm not sure whether to take that as a threat or a warning, Bob."

"Take it as a warning. Don't be a fool, Frankie. I'm not your thief. Think of me as your cybercop. I don't come cheap, granted, but then, I only charge if I deliver. Do we have a deal, or don't we? I have other clients waiting."

The phone hissed for a few long seconds. They were talking, and Kent let them talk.

When a voice spoke again, it was Hiroshito's. "We will accept your terms, Mr. . . . Bob. You have two weeks to find the security breach and recover our money. Is there anything that you require of us at this time?"

"No. I will contact you Monday morning with a list of banks to which I need free access. Until then, rest well, my friends, you have chosen wisely."

"I hope so, Bob. This is most unusual."

"We no longer live in a world of stagecoach robbers slinging Winchesters, Mr. Hiroshito. Now it's the keyboard we have to worry about." The phone sat silently in his hand, and he wondered if the Japanese banking executive made any sense of the comparison.

"Good-bye."

"Good-bye."

Kent dropped the phone on the table and breathed deep. He had done it! Hey, a life of crime might not be such a bad thing. *Stick 'em up, baby!*

Of course he would not give Mr. Hiroshito a list of banks to which he needed access, because he had no intention of visiting a list of banks. He would make one stop, and one stop only. And that bank was located in Denver, Colorado.

On Monday he would step back into his old stomping grounds. Back to Stupid Street. The audacity of the plan struck Kent then as he gazed out to the lapping waves far below. It was lunacy! Terrifying, really. Like a killer returning to the scene of the crime just to see if the cops had found anything. *"Hey guys! It's me! So what do you think? Pretty clever, huh?"*

Kent rose unsteadily and made for the bottle on the kitchen counter. This called for another drink. There was no way he was going to return to Stupid Street completely sober.

CHAPTER THIRTY-FIVE

Sunday

HELEN WALKED with Bill Madison under the swaying oaks, five miles from home and going strong. The park rustled with windblown leaves, yellowed in midfall. An overcast sky grayed the early afternoon, but the light was burning bright in her heart, she thought. Brighter by the day. Which meant that something was up.

"I really need to buy some new walking shoes," she said.

Bill strutted by her side, dressed in green sweats and a pair of running shoes he'd purchased for his afternoon walks with her. That day in her living room had changed the pastor's life. The heavens had torn open for him, and he'd become a new man. He'd announced the next morning that he would like to join her in the afternoons when his schedule permitted. In fact, he'd make sure his schedule did permit. The way he told it, if he joined her on the last leg of her journey, he'd be able to keep up just fine. And keep up he had, brimming with an enthusiasm that in fact spilled over to her.

"How many pair have you been through? How long have you been walking now, anyway? Two—three months?"

"Three. I've been walking three months, give or take. And I guess I've gone through about ten pairs of shoes. Same legs though. I haven't traded those in yet."

He chuckled. "No, I guess you haven't."

They walked on for a hundred feet before Helen told him what had been on her mind for the past few miles. "We are nearing the end, I think."

He turned, surprised. "The end? As in the end of the walking?"

"Yes." She smiled. "It's quite something, you know—having the Spirit of God filling your bones like a miracle drug. It gives the notion of walking in the Spirit new meaning."

"Yes, I can see that. You know, when I first saw that vision in your living room, I couldn't get over how clear everything was. All the questions just evaporated. *Poof,* they were gone. God is obviously God, and heaven obviously exists, and every word spoken here on Earth turns a head up there. But I have to tell you, things are not always so clear down here, even after that kind of encounter. Time dims the memory, and what was so bright only a couple of weeks ago starts to cloud a little. That make sense?"

Helen nodded. "Crystal clear."

"Well, if it wasn't for your walking—this incredible thing God has done to your legs—I might honestly think you had lost your mind, praying every day for a dead man."

"We've been over this, haven't we?"

"Yes. But not lately. You still think he's alive?"

"I'm past thinking too clearly, Pastor. There's a word from God—'Lean not on your own understanding, but trust in God'—you know it?"

"Sure."

"I've learned what that means. My own mind tells me all kinds of things that would make a grown man want to climb into a hole. You think the idea of a sixty-four-year-old lady walking in tube socks and a dress, twenty miles a day, praying for a dead man, is not strange? It is quite absurd. So absurd that whole theologies have been constructed to push such events into a different time zone. As if God woke up one day and suddenly realized that the way he'd been doing things all along, with falling walls and talking donkeys and burning bushes, was really quite childish. Men have grown too smart for that, yes?" She chuckled. "So when I get to the end of my walk each day, I still have to pinch myself. Make sure it's all real. Because my mind is not so different from yours, Bill. It wants to reject some things."

"It's good to know that you're as human as I am. Maybe that's one reason God has given you this physical sign. Helps you keep the faith."

"I'm sure it is."

"So you think Kent is still alive, then?"

"We've come back to that question, have we? Let's put it this way, Pastor. Wherever Kent is, he needs my prayers. The impulse to pray has not dimmed."

"Which basically means he must be alive."

"So it seems."

"But it's all coming to an end, you say."

She closed her eyes for a moment and considered the lightness of her spirit. Although she had not had any visions for over a week now, there was an expectancy riding in the air. A lightness. A brightness, hovering just beyond the clouds. How she knew it was all going somewhere rather quickly remained a small mystery. But she did.

"I think so, yes. How it will end, I have no clue. My spirit is light, but that may be for my sake rather than his. I just don't know. One thing I do know, however. When these legs begin to wobble with fatigue, it is the end."

The pastor did what he had often taken to doing these days. He broke into a prayer. "Jesus, we love you. Father, you are sovereign, your ways beyond finding out. Thank you for choosing to dwell in us. You are mighty, you are holy, you are awesome in your power."

No matter how this ended, Helen thought, the little Community Church on the corner of Main and Hornberry was in for a little jolt. Which was not so bad. Not so bad at all.

KENT PEERED through the oval window to the darkness. A strobe on the airliner's wingtip lit the fuselage every three seconds, and he half expected to see the vagrant clinging to the silver wing on one of those flashes. Welcome to the Twilight Zone. The engine's steady drone dropped in pitch as the lumbering jet descended through the black skies. A sea of pinpricks sparkled ten thousand feet below them. Denver was lit up like a Christmas tree in October.

Kent rattled the ice in his glass and sipped at the tequila. He'd lost count of the little bottles Sally, the first-class bombshell stewardess, had brought him over the last few hours—enough to ease the sense of dread that had lodged itself in his chest somewhere over the Atlantic. It had felt akin to being trapped between a brood of vipers and a cliff overlooking a black void. Denver would be the coiling snakes, of course. They would be hissing and snapping at his heels if he was not careful.

But it was the cliff at his back that had him calling for the small liquor bottles. The dread he'd wrestled with back there on the island, staring at the blue seas those last two days while awaiting his flight stateside. The truth be told, he was growing tired of paradise on the hill before he'd really had a chance to live the good life. A gloom had settled over the villa by midday Friday, and it had refused to budge.

The problem was quite simple, actually: Kent could find nothing that captured his fancy, sitting high on the hill, nestled in his own private Shangri-la. It was all feeling like day-old soda. No matter how often he told himself that he ought to be thrilled with the new yacht—it was a lifelong dream, for heaven's sake—he could not bring himself to crawl down the hill to take her out again. The realization prompted a slowly moving panic that had gnawed at him with building persistence. The kind of panic you might expect after reaching a coveted destination for which you had sold your firstborn only to discover that the condo on the beach was really a roach-infested shack on a muddy river.

By Saturday the villa felt more like a prison than a resort. The tropical sun seemed like a relentless blast furnace, the quiet like a desperate solitude. And all the while he could not find release, a situation that only served to fuel the growing panic. Madness. Madness in paradise: human nature's grand joke. *When you finally arrive, my friends, you will find the Joker, wearing a frown.*

In the end he'd washed it away with tequila. Lots of tequila.

Sunday came slowly, but it came. Kent packed a million dollars in cash about his body and luggage and boarded his flight, indirectly bound for Denver.

The airliner settled onto the asphalt with a squeal of rubber, and Kent closed his eyes. He was Kevin, now. Kevin Stillman. *Remember that, Buckwheat. Kevin, Kevin, Kevin.* His passport said he was Kevin, his business card said he was Kevin, and a dozen accounts scattered to the four corners, each stuffed with cash, all said he was Kevin. Except at the bank—there he would be Bob.

The huge tower clock in Denver International Airport said it was ten o'clock by the time Kent left the rental desk to collect his Lincoln Towncar. It was black, fittingly. An hour later he took a room in the downtown Hyatt Regency ten blocks from the bank, walking through the lobby on pins and needles, fighting off the fear that someone might recognize him. The sentiment was thoroughly unfounded, of course. He looked nothing like the Kent of old. In fact he was *not* the Kent of old. He was Kevin Stillman, and Kevin Stillman had a new face—broader and well tanned, topped with brown hair. He was not the lanky blond some had once known as Kent Anthony. Goodness, if the prospect of being caught in this remote hotel lobby brought sweat to his forehead, what would a walk through the bank do?

He made the call to Japan at eleven that night. Hiroshito was where all hard-working banking executives were expected to be first thing Monday morning Japan time—in his office.

"Mr. Hiroshito?"

"Yes."

"It's Bob. You do remember me?"

"Yes."

"Good, I will need access to the bank president at your main Denver branch at 9 A.M. mountain time. His name is Bentley. Mr. Price Bentley. Will there be a problem with this request?"

Hiroshito hesitated. "Nine? The bank opens at eight. It is short notice."

"Not too short, I am sure. You have the capability of transferring a million dollars in much less time. Surely you have the capability of making a phone call."

"Of course. He will be ready."

"Thank you, sir. You are very helpful." Kent hung up and made for the liquor cabinet. He managed to drift off near midnight, pretty much inebriated.

THE SOUNDS of rush hour filtered through the room's window when he awoke at seven. He was in Denver! Monday morning!

Kent bounded from the bed and showered, his spine tingling with anticipation. He donned a black double-breasted suit, the first he'd worn in six weeks, by his accounting. He'd chosen a white shirt accented by a teal tie—strictly business. Bob was about to do some business.

By the time he reached the towering bank he was sweating profusely. He pulled the Towncar into a space three down from his old parking spot and turned off the ignition. Silence engulfed the cab. To his right the alley gaped with a red brick mouth, blackened slightly. That would be his handiwork. The memories strung through his mind like Polaroids on a string. He dabbed his forehead and wiped at his neck with a napkin he'd taken from the hotel lounge. Couldn't very well go in there looking as though he'd just come from the sauna.

What if, by some strange force at work in their memories, they *did* recognize him? Something about his hairline or his vocabulary or the sound of his voice. What if it struck a bell in their empty noggins, and they actually identified him?

He cleared his throat and tried the voice. "Hello." It came out squeaky, and he tried again, intentionally lowering it. "Hello, there. I'm Bob."

Kent bit his lip, slipped on black glasses, and stepped from the car, closing his hands against a tremble that had taken over his fingers. He straightened his suit and looked up at the rising steps. Customers already streamed in and out of the revolving doors. He took three long, deep breaths and strode forward. *It's now or never, Buckwheat. Buckwheat Bob. Suck it up. Think of what they did to you.*

Kent did that. He clenched his jaw and bounded up the steps, grasping madly at the sudden surge of confidence. He stepped through the revolving doors like a rooster on the hunt and stopped dead in his tracks.

It all crashed down on him with a vengeance: Zak the security guard, pacing with sagging eyes; the long row of tellers, mechanically pushing and pulling slips of paper across the green counter; the tall sailboat suspended in the middle of the lobby; a sea of muted voices murmuring on about dollars and cents; the smell of a dozen perfumes, all mixed into a potpourri of scents.

If Kent's skin had been invisible they would have all seen his heart bounce up into his throat and stick there, a ball of quivering flesh. He suddenly knew with absolute certainty that this was all a mistake. A huge monstrous mistake. He very nearly spun on his heels for a hasty getaway then. But his muscles were not responding so quickly, and he hesitated. And by then it was too late. Because by then Sidney Beech was walking directly for him, smiling as if to welcome him back into the fold.

"May I help you?" she asked, which was not what Sidney Beech normally did with just any yahoo who wandered into the bank. It was his Blues Brothers look, he quickly decided. He still had the shades on, a good thing—if she could have seen his bulging eyes she might have called security instead of wandering over with that grin on her face.

"Excuse me, can I help you with something?"

Kent cleared his throat. *Strictly business, Bob. Don't be a wuss.*

"Yes. I'm here to see a Mr. Bentley. Price Bentley."

She cocked her head, in a polite way of course. "And you are?"

"Bob."

She waited for more.

"He's expecting me," Kent said.

"Bob?"

"Bob."

"I'll let him know you are waiting, Bob. If you'd like to have a seat in our lounge . . ."

"You may tell him that I'm on a tight schedule. I don't intend on lounging around waiting for him."

She lifted an eyebrow, unable to hide a slight grin. "Of course." Sidney motioned for the overstuffed chairs and strutted off toward Bentley's office, to tell him of the kook that had just walked in, no doubt.

Kent meandered over to the ship and studied the structure, feigning interest. Several tellers watched him curiously. Perhaps he should remove the black glasses. And maybe he should have purchased some of those colored contact lenses—his blues eyes might bare his soul.

Sidney was clacking up behind him. This was it then. He let her come.

"Bob?"

He turned and ground his teeth. *Strictly business, Bob.*

"He will see you now." She had lost the grin.

Kent strode for the office without waiting for her to show the way then realized it would be a mistake. How would he know? He turned to her. "This way?"

"Around the corner," she said.

Better. He walked for the office, tall and mean, looking like a cybercop ought to look, gaining confidence with each step.

Kent put his hand on the brass knob, took a single deep breath, pushed the door open without knocking, and stepped in. The oversized branch president sat behind his desk like a bowl of firm jelly. His oblong face had swelled, Kent thought. The man was eating well on his newfound wealth. Bentley's suit buttons still stretched as he sat. He still wore his collar tight so that it pinched off his head to resemble a tomato. His big cherrywood desk still sat neat and stately. The air still smelled of cigar smoke. Only the look in Bentley's eyes had changed from Kent's last visit. And he wasn't sure if the man's eyes bulged from fear or from offense.

"Price Bentley?"

"Yes." The man extended a hand over the desk. His face split with a manufactured grin. "And you must be Bob. I was told you would be visiting us."

"You were, were you?" Kent shut the door behind him. He removed his sunglasses with a casual flip and ignored Bentley's extended hand. "Get on the horn and call Borst," he said. "I need him here too."

That controlled grin flattened to concern. "Borst? What does he have to do with this?"

"What does he have to do with *what,* Bentley?" Kent stared into the man's eyes, and a small tremor of revulsion swept through his bones. "You don't even know why I'm here, correct? Or am I wrong?"

He did not respond.

"Pick your jaw off the table and call him," Kent said. "And tell him to hustle. I don't have all day."

Bentley called Borst and set the phone down. It missed its cradle and clattered to the president's lap. He snatched it up and clanked it in its proper place. "He's on his way."

Kent watched the pathetic man, expressionless.

"Is there anything I can get for you?"

"Do I look like I need something?" Kent placed his hands behind his back and walked past Bentley toward the far window. "What did they tell you?"

The president cleared his throat. "They said you were investigating something for them."

"Investigating, huh? And did they tell you *what* I was investigating?"

The door burst open, and Borst barged in, his face flushed. "Oh. Excuse me. I got here as soon as I could."

"Sit down, Markus." Bentley said, rising. "This is Bob . . . Bob . . . uh . . . I'm sorry, I don't know your last name."

Kent faced them. "Just Bob to you. Morning, Mr. Borst. Good of you to join us." He looked at Bentley and nodded toward the guest chair beside Borst. "You might as well have a seat over by Borst, if you don't mind."

The president lifted an eyebrow. "In the guest chair? Why?"

"Because I told you to sit there. I want you to sit down beside Borst. Is that so difficult to understand?"

Borst turned white. Bentley's face flashed red. "Look, I think you—"

"Frankly I'm not really interested in what you think. I have no intention of standing here in some jaw-flapping contest with you. Now, when I say sit, you will sit. And if I tell you to open up your shirt and expose your hairy belly, you will do just that. Is this a problem? If so, you say so now, and I'll pick up that phone. But if you're interested in keeping the grossly inflated salary you've somehow managed to wrestle out of our Japanese friends, you should do precisely what I say. Are we clear?"

Bentley's tomato head seemed to swell. Kent looked at Borst and winked. "Right, Borst?"

His old boss did not respond. He might have swallowed his tongue, Kent thought.

"Now, if you don't mind, please sit over by your partner in crime there."

Bentley hesitated a moment and then stormed around the desk to sit heavily beside Borst. The large man's expression teetered between rage and fear.

Kent continued. "Now, before I go any further I want both of you to understand a few things. First, I want you to understand that I'm just doing a job here. You two could be the king and his court jester, for all I care. It makes little difference. My job is to uncover the truth. That's it."

Kent paced across the room, keeping them in his sight as he turned.

"Second, you may not approve of my approach, but obviously the people who hired your miserable necks do, or I wouldn't be here. So keep your lips closed unless I ask you to open them. *Capisce?*"

They stared at him, obviously steaming at his audacity. "You see, now, that was a question. It is appropriate to open your lips in a response when I ask a question. Let's try it again, shall we? I say *Capisce,* which is Italian for *understand,* and you say . . ."

The fear had left Bentley's eyes, for the most part. Now it was just a snarl twisting those fat lips. Borst responded first. "Yes."

Bentley dipped his head but did not speak. It would have to do for the moment.

"Good. Now, I know that you're both big shots in this bank. You're used to having a dozen or so employees follow you around eager to shine your shoes if you are so inclined. Am I right? You don't have to answer that one. Either way, I am not one of those people. Do we have this straight, or should I start over?"

Borst nodded. Bentley's lips twitched.

"Good enough. I'm here because someone obviously suspects that you two have been involved in some hanky-panky. Have you?"

The sudden question caught them off guard. Again Borst answered first. "No! Of course not."

"Shut up, Borst!" Bentley had caught his breath. "I don't think we have to answer your questions without our attorneys present, Mister."

"Is that so?" Kent arched an eyebrow. "Has anyone ever told you that your head is rather large, Bentley? Hmm? I mean, not just figuratively, but physically. I look at you, and I think . . ." He lifted a finger to his chin and looked off to the ceiling. ". . . tomato. Yes, tomato. That's what I've been standing here thinking. My, this fellow has a head that really, really looks like a tomato. Well, you listen up, Tomato-Head. There's a little document that you signed when you agreed to your bloated salary. It's called an employment agreement. I think you will find a clause in your agreement that pretty much gives me, the bank that is, full rights to investigate any matter suspect of hanky-panky. I think the word in the agreement is actually *fraud.* Same difference. Now, if you feel at a later date that we have treated you unfairly, you are free to sue to your heart's content. But until then let's keep things in perspective, shall we? Now, please answer my question. Have or have you not, Mr. Price Bentley, been involved in hanky-panky here at the bank?"

"No." He had collected himself during that long diatribe, which was fine by Kent. A bit of a fight would not be so bad.

"No. Very good. Then I'm sure you have some exceptional explanations for my concerns. Let's start with you, Borst. By the way, please remove your toupee. I find it rather distracting."

Borst's face flushed pink, and he looked up with a sheepish smile.

Kent nodded and waved a hand toward the black toupee. "Go ahead. Rip it off, my friend."

His old boss realized then that he was serious, and his jaw fell open. "You . . . you . . . that's absurd!" he sputtered.

"Either way, please remove it. It's keeping me from concentrating on my job here."

Borst spun toward Bentley, who ignored him.

Kent pushed the point. "Hurry, man. We don't have all day. Just pull it off."

Borst reached up and pulled the hairpiece from his bald head. His face now beamed the shade of red found in a grocer's meat department.

"Good. So then, my friend, were you aware that some money is missing from the bank? Stolen electronically?"

Borst's breathing came raggedly now. "No."

"No? That's funny, because it did indeed find its way into your personal account. Odd. And you, of all people, should know that money does not just float around the system of its own accord. In fact, isn't it your job to see that it does not?"

The man did not respond.

"Now would be a good time to move your lips, Borst."

"No. I mean, yes. Sort of . . ."

"Well, which is it? Aren't you in charge of this new funds processing system everyone is raving about? AFPS?"

"Yes."

"And you designed it, did you not?"

"No. No, *that* is not true!"

Bentley spoke again, furious now. "Will you keep your trap shut, Borst!"

Kent smiled. "Fighting among friends. How tragic. Which is it, Bentley? Yes, he did design AFPS, or no, he did not?"

"I barely even knew the program!" Borst blurted. "I oversee programmers, see, so I might not be as proficient about moving money around as you think. I swear I had no idea how that money got into our accounts!"

"Shut up, Borst!" Spittle flew from Bentley's lips as he spoke. "Listen to what you're saying, Meathead!"

Kent ignored the president. "But you *did* know about the money. And you knew about the money in Tomato-Head's account as well, which means he also knew about it. But we'll come back to that. I want to pursue this line of crock you're feeding me on AFPS." He wagged a finger at them. "Didn't you two take credit for its development? Didn't you sign an affidavit claiming primary responsibility for the conception and implementation of the system? I mean, the last I checked, a lot of money was headed your way as a result of the bank's bonus program. Are you telling me there was some hanky-panky in that as well? Why don't you answer that, Bentley?"

The president looked as though he had indeed tied a noose about his neck and cinched it tight. "Of course I signed an affidavit stating I was primarily responsible for the system's development. And I was. Borst was as well. You just have him tied in knots with this dog and pony show of yours. So what do you say we get down to your real concerns, Bob? What exactly are you suggesting we did or did not do?"

"Oh, my goodness. He shows some intelligence at last. Did you hear him, Borst? Didn't that come off quite nicely? I'll tell you what I'm suggesting. I'm suggesting that you and Borst here are hiding some things. For starters, money transfers were illegally issued, neatly depositing several thousand dollars in each of your accounts, and I don't buy Borst's assertion that he had no idea where that money came from. Nobody could be such an idiot. So I guess I'm suggesting, Mr. Price Bentley, that you just got caught with your hand in the cookie jar. For starters, that is."

"And I'll tell *you* that that is the most ridiculous suggestion I've ever heard. You come walking in here, spouting these absurd accusations of fraud. How dare you!"

Kent stared Bentley down for a full ten seconds. He turned to his old boss. "Borst, will you please tell Mr. Bentley here that he's starting to get under my skin. Will you tell him that I already have enough hard evidence to have him put in the slammer for a few years, and if he doesn't back off, I might do just that. And tell him to cool down. He really is looking more and more like a tomato, and I'm afraid I might just walk over there and bite into him by mistake. Go on, tell him."

Borst blinked. He was obviously completely out of his league here. "Come on, Price. Settle down, man."

Bentley snorted, but he did not attack.

"Good." Kent turned back to the president. "Now, I'll tell you what, Bentley. I really did not come all the way from the Far East to slap your wrists over a couple thousand dollars. If that were the case it would be local security in here, not me. No sir. I'm after much bigger fish. But now you've hurt my feelings with this big talk of yours, and I'm not sure I want to bring you in on my little secret anymore. I'm tempted to just walk out of here and file a report that will nail your hide to the wall. And I could do it too."

He drilled Borst with a stare and returned to Bentley. "But I'll tell you what I'm willing to do. I'm willing to let the small deposits slip and tell you what I really need from you if you'll just apologize for your nasty attitude. How's that? You put your hands together as if you're praying and tell me you're sorry, and I'll forgive this whole mess. Both of you."

They looked at him with wide eyes and gaping mouths. Borst put his hands together and looked at Bentley. The president appeared to have frozen solid.

"Come on, Price," Borst whispered.

The humiliation of the moment was really too much for Kent himself. Two grown men, begging apologies without just cause. At least none they knew of. They had nothing to do with those small deposits, and all three of the men in the room knew that. Still, Bentley was no idiot. He could not know *what* "Bob" knew.

It took a good thirty seconds of silence before Bentley slowly clasped his hands as if in prayer and dipped his head. "I'm sorry. I spoke in haste."

"Yes. I'm sorry too," Borst echoed.

Kent smiled. "Well, that's much better. I feel so much better. Don't you?"

They were undoubtedly too stuffed with humiliation to respond.

"Good, then. And please keep this attitude of contrition about you as long as I am present. Now, let me tell you why I'm really here. Last week, someone stole one million dollars from the bank through a series of ghost transactions. Transactions similar in nature to the deposits made to your accounts. And quite frankly, I'm really quite convinced that you two did it. I think you two have a bunch of money stashed somewhere and that you've used some variation of AFPS to do it."

Their faces went white together, slowly, as the blood slowly vacated. Their mouths gaped.

Kent spoke before they could. "Now, I know what you're thinking. You're thinking that I just told you differently not two minutes ago. You're thinking that I just promised to let things slide if you made that silly apology. And you're absolutely right. But I was lying. You two are quite the liars yourselves, aren't you? You really should have seen it coming."

They sat woodenly, thoroughly seized by shock. Kent firmed his jaw and glared at them. "Somewhere in the deepest folds of cyberspace there's a lot of money hiding, and I guarantee it; I'm gonna find that money. And when I do, I'm going to find your grimy fingerprints all over it. You can bet your next twenty years on that. I figure it'll take me about two weeks. In the meantime, I'll get you a number in case your memory improves and you suddenly want to talk sense."

He walked past them to the door and turned back. Borst was moving his lips in horrified silent protest. Bentley's head had swelled like a tomato again.

Kent dipped his head. "Until then, my fat friends. And I don't mind telling you, that apology really was a special moment for me. I will remember it always."

With that Kent shut the door behind him and left, hardly able to contain himself. He slipped on the dark glasses while still in the lobby, nodding to Sidney Beech as he passed. Then he was through the revolving glass doors and facing Broadway.

Man, that had felt good. Time for a drink.

CHAPTER THIRTY-SIX

THE HOLE in Kent's chest had returned shortly after noon on Monday, just three hours after his little victory over the porky twins. He was not done with them, of course, but it would be two weeks before he walked back into their lives. Two weeks with nothing to do but wait. Two weeks of empty space.

He could return to the island and live it up with Doug and friends. But the idea felt like death warmed over. Why retreat to solitude? Why not try to shake this emptiness by filling his life with a few things here? Maybe he ought to take a drive up to Boulder.

What was he thinking?

Kent decided to catch a flight to New York. He made the decision impulsively, with a slug of tequila burning his throat. Why not? Money was no object. He could hop the *Concorde* to London if he so desired. And sitting around Denver beating back memories of his past would drive him to the grave.

He checked out of the Hyatt, paid cash for a thousand-dollar ticket to New York, and was airborne by four that afternoon.

The Big Apple was just another clogged city, but it did offer its advantages. Bars, for instance. There were pubs and lounges on virtually every corner around Kent's Manhattan hotel. Kent settled for the one in the hotel—O'Malley's Pub—and retired in a daze at 1 A.M. Tuesday morning.

He woke just before noon, lost in a dark room, wondering where he was. New York. He had flown to New York. Only God knew why. To escape Denver or some such nonsense. He rolled over and shut his eyes. He imagined there would be a dozen messages on the phone number he'd called over to Bentley's assistant before leaving Denver. The president and his cohort were probably coming apart at the seams trying to get hold of him. Yes, well he would let them sweat. Let them die a few deaths, see how it felt.

Kent forced himself out of bed at one, determined to find a distraction beyond the bottle. Goodness, he was chugging alcohol as if it were a runner's water. He had to get hold of himself here.

The bellboy told him that the opera was always a stretching experience.

He attended the opera that night. The sound of the lead vocalist's crooning nearly had him in tears. For some ungodly reason the woman became Lacy in his mind's eye, mourning the loss of her lover. That would be him. He could not follow the plot, but that the play was a story of death and sorrow could hardly be missed.

Kent woke Wednesday to a refreshing thought. Refreshing, not in the sense that he particularly enjoyed it, but refreshing in that it pulled him out of the doldrums—like a bucket of ice water tossed into a hot shower. It was a simple thought.

What if they're on to you, my friend?

He bolted up in bed and grabbed the bedspread. What if, back there in Denver, someone had put a few things together? Like that cop who'd interrupted his reading time at the bookstore. What had become of him? Or Bentley himself, sitting there wheezing like a camel, what if he'd seen something in his eyes? Even Borst, for that matter. No, not Borst. The man was too stupid.

He rolled out of bed, his stomach churning. Or what of Lacy? He had actually told her, for heaven's sake! Most of it anyway. Coming here to the United States had been idiotic. And going back to the bank, now, there was a move straight off of Stupid Street. What had he been thinking! Had to get the nasty boys, yes sir. Extract a slice of revenge.

Kent dressed with a tremor in his bones and headed for the bar. Problem was, the bar hadn't opened yet. It was only 9 A.M. Back to the hotel room to down a few of those small bottles in the cabinet. He spent the day watching golf in his hotel room, sick with anxiety and bored to death for the duration.

He managed to slap some sense into himself the next day by reviewing each and every step of his plan. The simple fact of the matter was that it had been rather brilliant. They had buried Mr. Brinkley's charred body, convinced it belonged to Kent Anthony. Unless they exhumed that body, Kent was a dead man. Dead men do not commit crimes. More important, there had been no crime. Ha! He had to remember that. No theft and no thief. No case. And he was the rich fool who had masterminded it all. A very wealthy man, dripping in the stuff.

It was that day, Thursday, in the bustling city of New York, that Kent began to understand the simple facts of a wealthy life. It all started after a two-hundred-dollar lunch down the street from the hotel, at Bon Appétit French Cuisine. The food was good; he could hardly deny that. For the price, it had better be good. But it occurred to him while stuffing some cupcake-looking pastry into his mouth, with his stomach already stretched far beyond its natural limits, that these French morsels, like most morsels, would come out in much worse shape than they went in. And in all honesty, they did not bring him much more pleasure than, say, a Twinkie at twenty cents a pop. It was a little fact, but it left the restaurant with Kent.

Another little fact: No matter how much money he carried in his wallet, individual moments did not change. Hopes and dreams might, but the string of moments that made up life did not. If he was walking down the hall, placing one foot in front of the other, he was doing just that, regardless of what his wallet packed. If he was pushing the call button for the elevator, it was just that, no more and no less, regardless of the number of bills in his back pocket.

But it was that night, approaching the midnight hour while drinking in O'Malley's Pub, that the full weight of the matter presented itself to him in one lump sum. It was as though the heavens opened and dropped this nugget on him like an ingot of lead. Only it didn't come from the skies. It came from the mouth of a fellow drinker, ready to impart his wisdom.

Kent sat next to the man who called himself Bono—after the U2 singer, he said—an ex-Orthodox priest, of all things. Said he left the Greek church because it left him dry. The man looked to be in his forties, with thick eyebrows and graying hair, but it was his bright green eyes that had Kent wondering. Since when did Greeks have green eyes? Together they knocked back the shotglasses. Actually, Kent was putting them away. Bono contented himself with sipping at a glass of wine.

"You know, the problem with those Wall Street yuppies," Bono offered after a half-dozen shots, "is that they all think there's more to life than what the average man has."

"And they'd be right," Kent returned after a pause. "Average is lazy, and lazy is not much."

"Whoa, so you are a philosopher, are you? Well, let me ask you something, Mr. Philosopher. What's better about busy than lazy?"

It was a simple question. Even awkwardly simple, because everyone knew that busy was better than lazy. But at the moment, Kent was having difficulty remembering why. It was possibly the booze, but it was just as possibly that he had never really known why busy was better than lazy.

He did what all good fools do when presented with a question they cannot answer directly. He raised his voice a tad and threw the question back. "Come on! Everybody knows that being lazy is stupid."

"That's what you said. And I asked you, why?"

Bono was no fool. He'd been here before. "Why? Because you cannot excel if you're lazy. You will go nowhere."

"Excel at what? Go where?"

"Well, now. How about life? Let's start with that. I know it's not much, but let's start with excelling at that little event."

"And tell me what that feels like. What does *excelling at life* feel like?"

"Happiness." Kent raised his shotglass and threw it back. "Pleasure. Peace. All that."

"Ahh. Yes, of course. I had forgotten about happiness, pleasure, and peace and all that. But you see, the average man has as much as the Wall Street yuppie. And in the end, they both go into the same grave. That *is* where they go, isn't it?" The man chuckled.

It was then, at the word *grave,* that the buzzing had first started again in Kent's skull. "Well, most have a good eighty years before the grave," he said quietly. "You only live once; you might as well have the best while you do it."

"But you see, that's where you and the yuppies on Wall Street are mistaken," Bono insisted. "It makes a fine fantasy, no argument there. But when you've had it all—and believe me, I have—wine still tastes like wine. You might drink it out of a gold chalice, but even then you realize one day that you could close your eyes and honestly not know whether the cold metallic object in your hand is made from gold or tin. And who decided that gold is better than tin anyway? In the end we all go to the grave. Perhaps it is beyond the grave where life begins. You know anyone who's gone to the grave lately?"

Kent swallowed and flung back another shot. Lately? His vision doubled momentarily. He leveled a rather weak objection. "You're too pessimistic. People are full of life. Like that man laughing over there." He motioned to a man in a far booth, roaring with his head tilted back. "You think he's not happy?" Kent smiled, thankful for the reprieve.

Bono gazed at the man and grinned. "Yes. Today Clark looks quite happy, doesn't he?" He turned back to Kent. "But I know Mr. Clark. He's a pig-head. Recently divorced and rather smug with the notion because he no longer has to deal with his brats. He's got three of them—six, ten, and twelve—and he can hardly stand them. Problem is, he spends most of his waking hours feeling guilty for his remarkably selfish disposition. He's been trying to wash it all away with the bottle for a year now. Trust me. He will leave this place tonight and retreat to a wet pillow, soaked in tears." Bono took a sip from his glass, evidently satisfied for having made his point. "Look under any man's sheets, and you'll find a similar story. I guarantee it, certifiable."

Kent had lost his interest in arguing the point. He was too busy trying to shake loose the fingers of heat climbing into his brain. The man had hit a nerve. Clark there could easily be him, drowning his failure in the bottle, bent upon pleasure and finding none. Except that he did not hate his son, like Pig-Head did. In fact he would have killed for his son—would've gladly given up every red cent for Spencer's life. The thought brought a sliver of light to Kent's mind.

Bono stood. He slid his glass across the counter and exhaled with satisfaction. "Yessiree. I'm telling you, this life is quite pitiful. No man can escape it." He tilted his head and lifted his brows so that his green eyes bulged down at Kent. "Unless, of course, you understand what lies beyond the grave." He smiled wide and slapped Kent on the back. "But then, I'm sure you know all about that, don't you, Kevin?" He sauntered from the pub without looking back.

The words echoed in Kent's head for an hour, and no amount of tequila quieted them. Kent drank for another hour by himself before wandering back to his hotel suite. Somewhere in that hour he began to miss Gloria. Not just *wish-she-were-sitting-with-me* missing, but *blurry-eyed-I'm-lost-without-her* missing. It was all these thoughts about the grave that the green-eyed Bono had deposited on him; they brought pictures of Gloria calling to him from some great unseen horizon. And what if there was some truth to all her babble of God? That thought shoved a fist-sized lump into his throat.

Well, Gloria was dead. Dead, buried, and beyond the grave, wherever that was. But there was Lacy—she too knew of the grave. And she knew of God. Still, Lacy could never be Gloria. Kent finally drifted off to sleep, his mind all mixed up with pictures of Gloria and Lacy.

Chapter Thirty-Seven

RATHER THAN take a room in another hotel, Kent found a furnished executive suite upon his return to Denver Friday afternoon. The agent had hesitated when Kent forked over the ten thousand security deposit in cash, but he had taken it, and Kent had moved in, an event that consisted of nothing more than stepping through the door with the keys in one hand and a single garment bag hanging from his shoulder.

The suite reminded him of the kind you see on futuristic shows, stark and shiny, decorated in black and white. The furniture was all metal, glass, or leather—rather cold for his tastes. But at least it was clean. More important, it was fully stocked, from a flat-screen entertainment center to place settings for eight.

Kent mixed himself a stiff drink, pulled an ugly-looking, black, wrought-iron chair out from under the glass table, and flipped open his laptop. The Toshiba had seen its share of activity over the last six weeks. He powered it up and logged on. Communication on the laptop was through a satellite connection—never a land line. He may have executed a few dumb moves here and there, but not when it came to computing. Here, at least, in his thieving and hiding, he had covered his tracks impeccably, thanks in large part to this baby.

The message box he'd left Bentley was indeed overflowing with messages. There were a dozen or so from Bentley, ranging from the earliest nearly a week old, insisting that he meet with them again, to the latest, left on Friday, screaming about lawsuits and counter lawsuits and what else Kent did not know because he spun quickly through the rest of the voice mail. Phase two was unfolding as planned. Let them sweat.

The last message was from an unidentified number, and Kent sat up when the voice spoke low over his speakers. A chill flashed down his spine. He knew the voice!

"Hello, Bob. You don't know me . . ." *Oh yes I do! Yes, I do.* ". . . but I would very much appreciate bending your ear for a few minutes on this case at the bank. Price Bentley told me I could reach you here. I'm a law enforcement officer working a few angles on a related matter. Please call me as soon as possible to set up a meeting. 565-8970. Thanks, pal. Oh, ask for Germy."

A cop! Pinhead? Impossible! Germy? What kind of name was *Germy?* But he could swear he'd heard that voice before. And it was a cop.

Kent placed his hands over his face and tried to think. What if the cop was indeed on to him? But he'd already decided that was impossible. No theft, no thief, no crime, no problem. Only this *was* a problem, because he was sitting alone in his new apartment, sweating like boxer.

He should pretend the message had never come through. And risk raising the cop's curiosity? No. He should call the man and weasel his way out of an appointment.

Kent snatched up the phone and dialed the number. A lady answered. "Seventh precinct, may I help you?"

Seventh precinct! "Yes . . ." His heart was thumping in his ear. "I was told to call a cop at this number. A Germy?"

"Oh, you must mean the new guy: Jeremy. Hold please."

Pinhead!

The receiver barked before Kent could do anything like slam the phone down. "Jeremy here. What can I do for you?"

"Ah . . . Yes. This is . . . Bob. You left a message for me."

"Bob! Yes, of course. Thank you for calling back so quickly. Listen, I just have a few questions about this business at the bank. Do you have any time to grab a cup of coffee? Say tomorrow morning? Ten-ish?"

What could he say? *No, not ten-ish. Ten-ish is when I start on the bottle, see? How about never-ish?*

"Sure," he said.

"Great! It won't take but a few minutes. How about at the Denny's at Broadway and Fifth? You know where that is?"

"Sure."

"Good. I'll see you at ten tomorrow morning."

"Sure."

The phone went dead. Sure? Gulp.

Kent did not sleep well Friday night.

HOW THE time managed to crawl by, Kent did not know, but it did, like a snail inching its way across a nine-foot razor blade. He awoke at five Saturday morning, although opened his eyes might be a better way to characterize the event, because he'd never really fallen asleep. A shower, a cup of coffee, a few shots of tequila for the nerves, and two miles of pacing across the black-and-white-checkered linoleum delivered him reluctantly to the appointed hour. He found himself parked outside of Denny's at ten o'clock without knowing precisely how he'd gotten there.

Kent slipped on his black shades and walked in. It might look ridiculous for a grown man to wear sunglasses indoors, but he'd decided sometime past midnight that ridiculous was better than incarcerated.

Detective Jeremy sat in a nonsmoking booth, staring at Kent as he entered. And it was indeed Pinhead. Complete with slicked black hair and wire-frame glasses. He was grinning wide. *"Hello, Kent. You* are *Kent, aren't you?"*

Kent swallowed and crossed to the booth, mustering every ounce of nonchalance remaining in his quivering bones.

"Bob?" The detective half rose and extended a hand. "Good of you to come."

Kent wiped his palm and took the hand. "Sure." He sat. Pinhead smiled at him without speaking, and Kent just sat, determined to act normal but knowing he was failing miserably. The cop's eyes were as green as he remembered them.

"So, I guess you're wondering why I've asked you to meet me?"

Kent shrugged. "Sure." He needed another word badly.

"Price Bentley tells me that you're investigating a robbery at the bank. You're a private investigator?"

"I suppose you could call me that." *Cybercop,* he almost said, but decided it would sound stupid. "At this point it's strictly an internal matter."

"Well, now, that depends, Bob. Depends on whether it's connected."

"Connected to what?"

"To my investigation."

"And what might that be, Jeremy?" That was better. Two could be condescending.

"That would be the bank fire a month or so ago."

Every muscle in Kent's body went rigid. He immediately coughed to cover. "The bank fire. Yes, I heard about that. To be honest, arson was never my thing."

"Mine neither. Actually I'm following up the murder. Do you always wear sunglasses indoors, Bob?"

Kent hesitated. "I have a light sensitivity in my left eye. It acts up on occasion."

Jeremy nodded, still grinning like a chimpanzee. "Of course. Did you know the victim?"

"What victim?" *That's it—remain cool, Buckwheat. Just play it cool.*

"The gentleman murdered in the bank robbery? You know, the fire."

"Bank robbery? I didn't know there was a robbery."

"So they say. *Attempted* robbery, then. Did you know him?"

"Should I have?"

"Just curious, Bob. No need to be defensive here. It was a simple-enough question, don't you think?"

"What exactly do you need from me, Jeremy? I agreed to meet with you because you seemed rather eager to do so. But I really don't have all morning to discuss your case with you. I have my own."

"Relax, Bob. Would you like some coffee?"

"I don't drink coffee."

"Shame. I love coffee in the morning." He poured himself a steaming cup. "For some it's the bottle; for me it's coffee." He sipped the hot, black liquid. "Ahh. Perfect."

"That's wonderful. My heart is glad for you, Jeremy. But you're starting to annoy me just a tad here. Can we get on with it?"

The detective just smiled, hardly missing a beat. "It's the possible connection that has me worried. You see, whenever you have two robberies or *attempted* robberies in one bank during the span of six weeks, you have to ask yourself about the connections."

"I hardly see the similarity between a common thief who happened upon an open door and the high-tech theft I'm investigating."

"No. It does seem rather unlikely. But I always turn over every stone. Think of yourself as one of those stones. You're just being turned over."

"Well, thank you, Jeremy. It's good to know that you're doing your job with such diligence."

The detective held up his cup as if to toast the notion. "My pleasure. So, did you know him?"

"Know him?"

"The victim, Bob. The programmer who was killed by the common thief."

"Should I have?"

"You already asked that. Yes or no would be fine."

"No, of course not. Why should I know a programmer who works in the Denver branch of Niponbank?"

"He was responsible for AFPS. Were you aware of that?"

Kent blinked behind the shades. *Watch it, Buckwheat. Tread easy.* "It was him, huh? I figured it couldn't have been Bentley or Borst. So they cheated someone for that bonus after all."

"All I know is that it was Kent Anthony who developed the system, pretty much from the ground up. And then he turns up dead. Meanwhile Bentley and company end up pulling down some pretty healthy change. Seems odd."

"You're suggesting Bentley might have had a finger in the programmer's death?" Kent asked.

"No. Not necessarily. He had nothing to gain by killing Kent. I just throw it out there 'cause it's another stone that needs turning."

"Well, I'll be sure to turn over my findings if they seem to shed any light on the fire. But unless Bentley and company are somehow implicated in the fire, I don't see how the two cases tie in."

"Yes, you're probably right." The detective downed his coffee dregs and looked out the window. "Which leaves us pretty much where we started."

Kent watched him for a moment. By the sounds of it, Pinhead was not turning out to be such a threat after all. Which made sense when you thought about it. The theft had been perfectly planned. There was no way that anyone, including Detective Pinhead here, could even suspect the truth of the matter. A small chill of victory ran up Kent's spine.

He smiled for the first time, confident now. "And where would that be? Tell me, where did we start? I'm a bit lost."

"With a crime that simply does not fit the players involved. If Bentley and Borst don't fit, then nothing fits. Because, you see, if you knew the man, you would know that Kent Anthony was not the kind of man who would leave a door unlocked for a pistol-toting thief. He was not nearly so stupid. At least not according to his friends."

"Friends?" The question slipped out before Kent could hold it back.

"Friends. I talked to his girlfriend up in Boulder. She had some interesting things to say about the man."

The heat was suddenly flashing though Kent's skull. "Anybody can make a simple mistake," he said, knowing it sounded weak. He certainly could not defend a man he supposedly did not know. "In my experience the simplest explanation is usually the correct one. You have a body; you have slugs. He may have been an Einstein, but he's still dead."

Pinhead chuckled. "You're right. Dead is dead." He mulled that over. "Unless Kent is not dead. Now, maybe that would make more sense." The man drilled Kent with those green eyes. "You know, not everything is what it seems, Bob. In fact I am not what I seem. I'm not just some dumb, lucky cop."

Kent's face flushed red; he felt panic-stricken. His chest seemed to clog. And all the while Pinhead was looking directly at him. He was suddenly having a hard time forming thoughts, much less piecing together a response. The cop removed his gaze.

"My case and your case could be connected, Bob. Maybe we're looking for the wrong guy. Maybe your high-tech phantom and my dead guy are really the same person! A bit far-fetched but possible, don't you think?"

"No. That's not possible!"

"No? And why is that not possible?"

"Because I already know who did it!"

The cop arched a brow. "Who?"

"Bentley and Borst. I'm putting the finishing touches on the evidence, but within a week I can assure you, fraud charges will be filed."

"So quickly? Excellent work, Bob! But I really think you ought to rethink the matter. With my theory in mind, of course. It would be something, wouldn't it? Kent alive and kicking with a dead man in his grave?" He dismissed the theory with his hand. "Ah, but you're probably right. The two cases are probably not connected. Just turning over every stone, you know."

At the moment Kent felt like taking one of Jeremy's stones and shoving it down the detective's throat. *Try that for a theory, Pinhead!* But he could hardly breathe, much less reach over there and wrestle the man's mouth open.

"Well, I surely do appreciate your time, Bob. Maybe we will meet again. Soon." The detective smiled.

With that he stood and left, leaving Kent soaking under the arms and frozen to his seat.

This was a problem. Not just a little challenge or a bump in the road, but the-end-of-the-world-as-we-know-it kind of problem. Coming here had been a mistake. Coming back to this *country* had been a mistake. Going to the bank—that had been idiotic!

Still, there was no evidence, was there? No, no evidence. It was Pinhead's theory. A stupid theory at that.

Then a simple little picture popped into his mind and crushed what little hope he had left. It was a picture of Lacy, sitting on her couch, hands folded, knees together, facing Pinhead. She was talking. She was telling her little secret.

Kent dropped his head into his hands and tried to still his breathing.

CHAPTER THIRTY-EIGHT

KENT STOOD by the pillar just outside Macy's in a Boulder mall on Monday evening and stared at the woman, his heart beating like a kettle drum, his palms wet with balls of sweat.

Sometime on Saturday, he'd come to a new realization about life. It was a notion so profound that most people never understood it properly. It was the kind of truth one encounters only in moments when he is stretched beyond all limits, as Kent had been after that little encounter with Pinhead. And it was simply this: When you really got right down to it, life sucked.

The problem with most people was that they never really got right down to it. They lived their lives *thinking* of getting right down to it, but did they ever actually get right down to it? No. *"Next year, Martha, I promise, next year we're gonna sell this rattrap, buy that yacht, and sail around the world. Yes sir."* People's dreams acted as a sort of barrier between life and death. Take them away—let people actually live those dreams—and you would be mopping up the suicides by the dumpster full. Just look at those few who did live their dreams, like movie stars or rock stars—the ones who really have the money to get right down to it—and you'll find a trail of brokenhearted people. Brokenhearted because they'd discovered what Kent was discovering: When you really got right down to it, life sucked.

That fact had delivered Kent to this impossible place, standing by the pillar just outside Macy's Monday evening and staring at a woman, his heart beating like a kettle drum, his palms wet with balls of sweat.

Lacy sighed, obviously unsatisfied with the discount rack's selection. She walked toward him. Kent caught his breath and turned slowly away, straining for nonchalance. In the hour that he had been tailing her, she had not recognized him, but then she had not studied him either. Twice she'd caught his eye and twice he had brushed on as though uncaring. But each time his heart had bolted to his throat, and now it was doing the same.

He bent for a *Shopper's Guide* on a bench and feigned interest in its cover. She walked by him, not three feet away. The sweet scent of lilac drifted by his nostrils, and he closed his eyes. It was all insanity, of course, this stalking. Not just because someone might notice the sweating man staring at the beautiful single woman and call security, but because he was indeed *stalking.* Like some kind of crazed loony, breathing heavily over a woman's shoulder, waiting for his chance.

He had driven to Boulder that afternoon, parked his car a hundred yards from Lacy's apartment, and waited. She had returned from work at six, and he had spent a good hour chewing at his nails, contemplating walking up to her door. Thing of it was, Gloria kept traipsing through his mind. For some reason not quite clear to him, he was feeling a strange guilt about Gloria. More so now, it seemed, than when he had spent time with Lacy before the robbery. Perhaps because then he had had no real intentions of pursuing Lacy. Now, though, faced with this crazy loneliness, he was not so sure.

She'd left the condo and driven here. His greatest regret in stalking her was the decision to leave the bottle of tequila in the car. He could have excused himself to the bathroom a dozen times for nips. But returning to retrieve the bottle from the car would take far too long; she might disappear on him, a thought suddenly more unnerving than staying dry for a few hours.

He twisted his head and watched her from the corner of his eye. Lacy wore blue jeans. She seemed to float along the shiny marble floor, her white running shoes gliding along the surface, her thighs firm beside her swinging brown purse. The lime-green sweater was perhaps a cardigan, resting loosely over her shoulders, its collar obscured by her blonde hair. Her lips seemed to pout, smiling on occasion; her hazel eyes darted over the selections; her fingers walked through the clothing carefully.

Kent watched her walk toward the food court. He wiped his forehead with the back of his hand and stepped cautiously after her. She wandered past shiny windows, casually glancing at their displays without bothering to enter. Kent stepped into a sports store, grabbed a beige flannel shirt from the sale rack, and hurriedly purchased it. He went straight to the shop's dressing room and changed into the new shirt before hurrying past a confused salesclerk to catch Lacy. The red shirt he'd worn went in the nearest trash bin. *You see, Lacy, I've learned a few tricks. Yes, sir, I'm a regular sneaky guy. You gotta be sneaky to steal twenty million, you know.*

He found her in the food court. She sat cross-legged, slowly eating an ice cream cone. He watched it all while peeking around a mannequin in Gart Brothers Sporting Goods across the lobby. There was nothing sexual in his desire—nothing perverse or strange or obsessive. Maybe obsessive. Yes, actually it was obsessive, wasn't it? He blinked at the thought and removed his eyes from her. How else could you characterize stalking a woman? This was no date. *Goodness, you're losing it, Kent.*

A wave of heat washed down Kent's back, and he left the mall then, feeling small and puny and dirty for having driven there. For having peeked at her from the shadows. What was he thinking? He could never tell her the truth, could he? She would be compelled to turn him in. It would be over—all of it.

And Gloria! What would Gloria say to this?

She's dead, *bozo!*

He drove back to Denver, wondering why he should not take his own life. Twice he crossed overpasses wondering what a plunge through the rail might feel like. Like an amusement ride, falling weightlessly for a moment, and then a wrenching crash. The grave. The end. Like Bono had said, in the end it's all for the grave anyway.

Kent shook his head and squeezed his eyes against the mist blurring his vision. He grunted to clear his throat of its knot. On the other hand, he wasn't in the grave yet. He had money, more than he could possibly spend; he had freedom from any encumbrances whatsoever. No wife, no children, no debt, no nothing. That was worth a smile at least, wasn't it? Kent smiled, but the image staring back at him from the rearview mirror looked more like a jack-o'-lantern than the face of a contented man. He lost the charade and slouched in his seat.

The evening took a turn for the better near midnight, two pints of tequila later. He lounged with glass in hand on the black-leather recliner facing a black television screen in the sleek apartment. The memory of his little stalking trip to Boulder sat like an absurd little joke on his brain.

Because of some obsession. Some pearls of wisdom from a Greek named Bono. Yes indeed, life sucked.

Well, it would be the last time he stalked anyone, he thought wryly. He would drive off one of those overpasses at a hundred miles per hour in the Lincoln before doing anything so foolish again. He had the world at his fingertips, for Pete's sake! Only an absolute loser would slink back for another peek. *"Peekaboo, I see you. My name's Kent, and I'm filthy rich. Would you like to share my life? Oh, yes, one small nugget for the hopper—my life really sucks, but not to worry, we will soon be in the grave anyway."*

Kent passed out on the leather recliner sometime before the sun rose.

CHAPTER THIRTY-NINE

LACY SAT alone in Wong Foo's Chinese Cuisine Thursday evening, nibbling at the noodles on her plate. Indirect lighting cast a dim orange glow across her table. A dozen heavy wooden carvings of dragons stared down from the low-hung ceilings. Cellulose walls lent an aura of privacy to the room. Glasses clinked with iced drinks, and voices murmured softly all about her, behind those paper partitions; somewhere a man spoke rapidly in Chinese. The smell of oriental spices circulated slowly.

A man sat alone in a booth ten meters to her right, reading the paper and sipping at noodle soup. They had noticed each other shortly after he had been seated not ten minutes earlier, and his bright blue eyes reminded her of Kent at first sight. He'd smiled politely, and she'd diverted her gaze. Freaks were everywhere these days. *You don't know that, Lacy. He may be a regular Clark Kent.* Actually, all men were pretty much looking like freaks these days.

Lacy dipped her spoon into the hot-and-sour soup and sipped at the liquid. She was having some difficulty shaking Kent's image. *Why* she could not shake his image, she could not fully understand. The first week was understandable, of course. The second, maybe even the third as well. But he had been gone for over a month now, for heaven's sake. And still he left tracks all through her thoughts every day. It was nonsense. Perhaps it was the thought of him living like a king after having the audacity to rub his plans in her face.

She peered at the man reading the newspaper and found him looking at her again. Goodness. She shot him a contemptuous grin this time. *Not too bold there, Lacy. He might get the wrong idea.* Looked like a decent-enough fellow. Blue eyes like Kent's—*See, now, there I go again*—and a face that reminded her of Kevin Costner. Not bad looking actually.

He had his head buried in that paper again, and Lacy steered her mind back to the plate in front of her. She had not heard from the detective again, and neither had she made any attempt to call him, because as the days passed, the notion began to sound somewhat misguided. She certainly had found no absolute collaborating evidence suggesting Kent's theft. And even if she had, she'd made a promise to him. Not that she *should* be bound by any promise after what he had done. There had been four incidents of mismatched bank statements, but no one seemed to give them any mind. Printer error or something. Whatever it was, it had corrected itself.

Yes indeed. The only thing that had not self-corrected was her mind. And she was beginning to think it might need some professional examination. Lacy lifted her fork and savored a bite of gingered chicken. The dragons glared down at her with glassy yellow eyes, as if they knew something she did not.

They were not the only things staring at her, she thought. The pervert was staring at her again. From the corner of her eyes she could see his face turned her way. Her pulsed spiked. Unless he wasn't really staring at her at all and it was just her imagination.

She turned slowly to him. No, it was not her imagination. He yanked his eyes away as her own zeroed in on him. What kind of guy was this? She should possibly leave before he began wagging his tongue at her.

Then his blue eyes rose to meets hers again, and they held for a long second. Lacy's heart paused for that second. And before it restarted, the man rose from his seat and walked toward her.

He's leaving, she thought. *Please tell me he's leaving!*

But he didn't leave. He walked right up to her table and placed a hand on the back of the chair opposite hers.

"I'm sorry, ma'am. I couldn't help but notice you sitting all alone." He smiled kindly, quite handsomely actually. But then Ted Bundy had been quite handsome. His voice came like honey to her mind, which surprised her. A thin sheen of sweat beaded his forehead. She imagined him breathing heavily in the corner. Lacy stared at the stranger without speaking, *unable* to speak really, considering the contradictions this man represented.

He attempted a smile, which awkwardly lifted one side of his face. "I know this may sound unusual, but do you mind if I have a seat?" he asked.

A hundred voices screamed in unison in her head: *Don't be a fool! Go wag your tongue at some streetgirl! Beat it!*

The stranger did not give her a chance to speak her thoughts. He sat quickly and folded trembling hands. She instinctively pulled back, stunned by his boldness. The man did not speak. He breathed deliberately, watching her in awe, with a slight smile curving his lips.

Goodness! What was she thinking, allowing this man to sit here? His eyes were striking enough, like blue sapphires, wide and adoring. *God, help me!*

"Can I help you?" she asked.

He blinked and sat a little straighter. "I'm sorry. This must seem awfully strange to you. But . . . does anything . . ." He fidgeted uncomfortably. "I don't know . . . strike you as odd?"

Lacy was finding her senses, and her senses were telling her that this man rang bells that echoed right through her skull, as if it were churchtime at the cathedral. They were also telling her that this man had a few loose bells himself.

"Actually, *you* strike me as odd. Maybe you should leave?"

That took the curl out of his gimpish smile. "Yeah? Well, maybe I'm not as odd as you think. Maybe I'm just trying to be friendly, and you're calling me odd. Is that what you think of friendly people? That they're odd?"

Tit for tat. He didn't seem so harmful. "People don't normally wander around Chinese restaurants looking for friendly conversation. Forgive me if I sound a bit concerned."

"People aren't usually friendly, is what you're saying. Well, maybe I'm just trying to be friendly. You consider that?"

"And maybe I don't need any new friends."

He swallowed and studied her for a moment. "And maybe you should think twice before rejecting a friendly neighbor."

"So now you're my neighbor? Look, I'm sure you're a wonderful man . . ."

"I'm just trying to be friendly, ma'am. You should never bite the hand that feeds you."

"I wasn't aware that you had fed me."

He reached over, picked up her bill, and slid it into his pocket. "You are aware now."

Lacy leaned back, struck by the absurdity of the exchange. "I don't even know you! I don't even know your *name.*"

"Call me . . . Kevin." The stranger smiled. "And honest, I'm just an ordinary guy who looked across the room and saw a woman who looked like she could use some friendship. What's your name?"

She eyed him carefully. "Lacy." The bells were still gonging in her mind, but she could not place their significance. "And you can't tell me that walking up to a woman in a Chinese restaurant and asking to sit isn't rather strange."

"Maybe. But then, they say all is fair in love and war."

"So then that makes this a war? I'm not looking for a fight, really. I've had my share," she said.

"You have? Not with men, I hope."

"You're right. Men don't fight; they just leave." The crazy discourse was suddenly feeling a bit therapeutic. "You the love-'em-and-leave-'em type, Kevin?"

The man swallowed and grew very still. A pause seemed to settle over the restaurant. "No, of course not."

"Good, Kevin. Because if you were the love-'em-and-leave-'em type, I would throw you out the door myself."

"Yes, I'll bet you would." He shifted in his seat. "So we're sworn off men, then, are we?"

"Pretty close."

He eyed her carefully. "So . . . what happened?"

She did not respond.

OF COURSE Kent knew precisely what had happened. She was speaking about him. He had courted her, earned her trust, and then dropped her on her seat. And now this.

On Monday he had sworn to kill himself rather than stalk her again. On Wednesday he had broken that promise. He had allowed himself to live despite slinking back to Boulder to sneak a peek. She had gone grocery shopping that night, and he had slipped between the aisles on the edge of panic for the duration.

But this . . . He would pay for this madness. But it no longer mattered. He no longer cared. Life had somehow lost its meaning. He had followed her to the restaurant; taken a seat in plain view, and then approached her table. It had felt like stepping out on a tightrope without a net.

And now he'd had the audacity to ask her what happened. His palms were sweating, and he wiped them on his knees. The electricity between them had his heart skipping beats.

She was not responding, and he repeated the question. "So what happened?"

"No offense, *Kevin,* but if you want to befriend a lady at a restaurant, it's not necessarily advisable to strut up and drop the old *So-what's-happened-in-your-love-life-lately?* line. Comes across like something a pervert might say."

That stung, and he flinched visibly. *Whoa boy, don't expose yourself so easily.*

"You look surprised," Lacy said with a tilt of her head. "What did you expect? That I would lie down on a couch and tell you my life history?"

"No. But you don't have to bite my head off. I just asked a simple question."

"And I just more or less told you to mind your own business."

So, she was bitter and letting it ooze from her seams. She was right; he should have expected nothing less. "Okay look, I'm sorry if my introducing myself caused such offense, but maybe—just maybe—not everyone in the world is as cynical as you think. Maybe there are a few decent people around," Kent said, building his volume. Of course the whole thing was a crock, and he knew it as he spoke. He was about as decent as a rat.

She looked at him for a moment and then nodded slowly. "You're right. I'm sorry. It's just not every day that a man walks up to me and plops down like this."

"And I'm sorry. It was probably a dumb thing to do. I just couldn't help noticing you." She was softening. That was good. "It's not every day you come across a beautiful woman sitting alone looking so lost."

Lacy looked to the side, suddenly awash with emotion. He watched it descend on her like a mist. Watched her swallow. His own vision blurred. *Lacy, Oh, Lacy! It's me! It's Kent, and I love you. I really do!* His throat burned with the thought. But he could never go so far. Never!

"I'm so sorry," he said.

She sniffed and wiped her eyes quickly. "No. Don't be sorry. Actually, I think I'm in love with another man, Kevin."

Heat flashed over Kent's skull. Another man?

"I'm not even sure I could befriend you. In fact, I'm crazy about him"

Goodness, this was impossible! "Yes," he said. But he felt like saying no. Screaming, *No, Lacy! You can't love another man! I'm right here, for Pete's sake!*

"I think you should leave now," she said. "I appreciate your concern, but I'm really not looking for a relationship. You should go."

Kent froze. He knew she was right; he should leave. But his muscles had locked up. "Who?" he asked.

She looked at him, startled. "Who?" Her eyes bore into him and for a moment he thought she might lash out at him. "A dead man, that's who. Please go," she said. "Please go now," she insisted.

"A dead man?" his voice rasped.

"Go now!" she said, leaving no doubt as to her intentions.

"But . . ."

"No! Just go!"

Kent stood shakily to his feet, his world gray and fuzzy. He walked past her toward the door, right past the cashier without thinking to pay for their meals, right out into the street, hardly knowing he'd exited the restaurant.

Lacy was still in love with him. With Kent!

And this was good? No, this was bad. Because he was indeed dead. Kent was dead. And Lacy had not shown the least morsel of interest in Kevin, with his surgically altered cheeks and larger nose and sharper chin.

The realization fell on him like a boulder rolled from a cliff. He had truly died that night at the bank! Kent was truly dead. And Lacy was on the verge of death—at least her heart was. Any lingering hopes for love between them were now lost to the grave. End of story.

Kevin would have to find his own way. But Kevin didn't want to find his own way. Kevin wanted to die. Kevin didn't even exist.

He was *Kent! Kent, Kent, Kent!*

But Kent was dead.

It was the low point of his day. It was the low point of his month. It might very well be the low point of his life—although that day Gloria had died and that day Spencer had died, those had been low as well. Which was a problem because before coming here tonight, he had already been sliding along the bottom. Now the bottom was looking like the sky, and this tunnel he was in was feeling like the grave.

Kent's mind drifted to Spencer and Gloria, rotting six foot under. He might have to join them soon, he thought. Life up here above the grass was becoming quite difficult to manage. He trudged down the street thinking of options. But the only two he could wrap his mind around were trudging and dying. For the moment he would trudge, but maybe soon he would die. Either way, that woman back there was dead.

He knew that because he had killed her. Or he might as well have.

CHAPTER FORTY

KENT STORMED up Niponbank's sweeping steps Friday morning at ten, grinding his teeth and muttering under his breath. A fury had descended upon him in the wee hours of the morning. The kind that results from stacking up circumstances on the grand scale of life and then stepping back for a bird's-eye view only to see one end of the brass contraption dragging on the concrete and the other end swinging high in the sky. How much could a man take? Sure, on the one hand there was the brilliant million-dollar larceny bit, teetering up there on one side of the scale. But it was alone, hanging cold in the wind, forced into the loft by a dozen inequities piled high on the other side.

Lacy, for example. Or, as Kent saw the image, Lacy's firm jaw, snapping at him, barking for him to go. *"Just go! Now!"* Then there was the cop, an ear-to-ear grin plastered on that pointy head. Pinhead. *"You wanna know what I think, Bob? Or is it Kent?"* And there was Bono, spouting his wisdom of the grave, and Doug the Aussie, smiling toothlessly on the yacht that had killed his last son, and Steve the bartender hovering like a vulture. The images whispered through his mind, weighing the scales heavily, slowly pushing his blood pressure to a peak.

But it was the final few tidbits that had awakened him an hour earlier, panting and sweating on the covers. The ones he'd somehow managed to bury already. Gloria, swollen and purple and dead on the hospital bed; Spencer bent like a pretzel, cold as stone. Borst and Bentley, sitting behind their desks, smiling. *Welcome back, Kent.*

Somehow, all the images distilled down to the one of the porky twins sitting there, wringing their hands in the pleasure of their *deed.*

Which was why he found himself storming up Niponbank's sweeping steps Friday morning at ten, grinding his teeth and muttering under his breath.

He pushed through the revolving door and veered immediately right, toward the management offices. No nostalgia greeted him this time, only an irrational rage pounding through his veins. Sidney was there somewhere, clacking on the marble floor. But he barely registered the sound.

Bentley's door was closed. Not for long. Kent turned the knob and shoved it open, breathing as hard now from his climb up the steps as from his anger. A dark-haired woman sat cross-legged in a guest chair, prim and proper and dressed in a bright blue suit. Both snapped their heads up at his sudden entry.

Kent glared at the woman, stepped to the side, and flung a hand toward the door. "Out! Get out!"

Her jaw fell open and she appealed to Bentley with round eyes.

Bentley shoved his seat back and clutched the edge of his desk, as though poised to leap. His face had drained of color. He moved his lips to form words, but only a rasp sounded.

The woman seemed to understand. She could not possibly know what was happening here, but she wanted no part of it. She stood and hurried from the room.

"Get Borst in here," Kent said.

"He . . . he was already coming. For a meeting." The boy in Bentley was showing, like a man caught with his pants down. But if Kent's previous encounters with him were any indication, the man would gather himself quickly.

Borst walked into the room then, unsuspecting. He saw Kent and gasped.

"Good of you to join us, Borst. Shut the door." Kent closed his eyes and settled his nerves.

His former boss shut the door quickly.

"Why didn't you return my calls?" Bentley demanded. He was finding himself.

"Shut up, Bentley. I really have no desire to subject myself to more of your nonsense. I can take my share of punishment, but I'm no sadomasochist."

"And what if I had information critical to your investigation? You can't expect to walk out of here hurling your accusations and then just leave us hanging dry!"

"I did, didn't I? And short of a signed confession, nothing you could possibly tell me would prove critical to my investigation. Take my word for it. But I'll tell you what. I'll give you a chance now, how's that?"

Bentley stared at him, flabbergasted.

"Come on, out with it, man. What was so important?"

Still nothing. He had the man off center. No sense stalling.

"I didn't think so. Now, go over there and sit next to Borst."

"I—"

"Sit!"

The man jerked from his seat and shuffled over to where Borst sat, still white as a marshmallow on a stick.

"Now, for your sakes I'm going to keep this short. And I don't want to see you two slobbering all over the chairs, so save your comments for the authorities. Fair enough?"

They sat woodenly, unbelieving.

"Let me start at the beginning. I've put my findings in writing to the men who sign your checks, but I figure we have about ten minutes to chat about it before the Japanese come screaming across that phone. You ever hear cursing in Japanese, Borst? It isn't soothing stuff."

Kent took a breath and continued quickly. "For starters, you two had very little to do with AFPS. Its actual development that is. You evidently learned how to use it well enough. But in reality you did not deserve credit for its implementation, now did you? Don't bother answering. You did not. Which is a problem because, in claiming credit for another man's work you violated your employment agreements. Not only ground for immediate dismissal, but also requiring repayment in full of any monetary gain from the misrepresentation."

"That's not true!" Bentley said.

"Shut up, Bentley. Kent Anthony was solely responsible for AFPS, and you two know it as well as you know you're in this, neck deep." He drilled them with his eyes and let the statement settle in the room. "Lucky for you Kent seemed to meet an untimely demise a month after your little trick."

"That's not true! We had nothing to do with Kent's death!" Borst protested. "Taking a little credit is one thing, but we had nothing to do with his death!"

"You take a man's livelihood, you take his pride. Might as well be dead."

"You can't make any of this stick, and you know it!" Bentley said.

"We'll let the Japanese decide what sticks and what doesn't. But I'd spend just a little more time thinking about the million-dollar problem than about the Kent Anthony problem. Pretty clever, really. It took me the better part of a week to crack your little scheme."

A quiver had taken to Bentley's face, now red like a tomato again. "What are you talking about?"

"You *know* what I'm talking about, of course. But I'll tell you anyway. The way I figure it, Borst here developed this little program called ROOSTER. It looks like a security program for AFPS. Problem is, it was never released with the rest of the code. In fact it resides on only two computers throughout the entire system. That's right, the computer on Markus Borst's desk and the one on Price Bentley's desk. Interesting, given the fact that these two yahoos are the ones who ripped off Mr. Kent Anthony of his just reward. But even more interesting when you discover what the program is capable of. It is a ghost link to AFPS. A way into the system that's virtually undetectable. But I found it. Imagine that."

"But . . . But. . . ." Borst was sputtering.

"Shut up, Borst! That ain't the half of it." Kent delivered his indictment in long staccato bursts now. "It's how the program was used that tops the cake. Actually very clever, that one. A run of small, untraceable transfers to see if anyone notices and then hit them with the big one. *Bam!*" Kent smacked his palm with a fist, and they both jumped.

"One million dollars in a single shot, and no one knows where it's gone to. Unless you peek inside the accounts hidden conveniently on Borst's and Bentley's computers! Why lookie here! A million dollars all neatly tucked away for a rainy day. Not a bad plan."

"That's impossible!" Bentley was steaming red and dripping wet. "We did none of that! You can't be serious!"

"No?" The rage Kent had felt first while stomping up the bank's steps roared to the surface. He was suddenly yelling and jabbing his finger at them, and he knew that he had no reason to yell. They were both sitting five feet from him. "No? Well you're wrong, Porky! Nothing, and I mean *nothing,* is impossible for greedy slobs like you! You confiscate another man's fortune and guess what—someday you can expect yours to be confiscated as well!" He breathed hard. *Easy, boy.*

"It's all there, you idiot." He pointed at Bentley's computer. "Every last detail. You can read it like a mystery novel. Say what you want, but the data does not lie, and they already have the data. You two are going down!"

They gawked at him, thoroughly stunned.

"Do you understand this?" Kent asked, stabbing his forehead. "Is this information sinking in, or are you madly trying to think of ways to save your miserable necks?"

They couldn't respond, by the looks of it. Borst's eyes were red and misty. He was badly unraveled. Bentley was leaking smoke out of his ears—invisible, of course, but just as apparent.

Kent lowered his voice. "And let me tell you something else. The evidence is incontrovertible. Trust me; I put it together. If you want to get out of this you're gonna have to convince the jury that some ghost from the past did it all in your place. Perhaps you could blame it on that programmer you screwed. Maybe Kent Anthony's ghost has come back to haunt you. But short of an insanity plea along those lines, you're toast."

They still were not talking. Kent felt like saying more, like slapping them both back to life. But he had said what he'd come to say. It was the card he'd dreamed of playing for many long nights, and now he'd played it.

Kent strode for the door, past Bentley and Borst who sat unmoving. He hesitated at the door, thinking to put an exclamation mark on the statement. Maybe knock their heads together. *Thump! And don't forget it either!*

He resisted the impulse and walked from the bank. It was the last time he would see them. What happened to them now would be up to someone else, but in any scenario, things would not go easy for the porky twins. Not at all.

CHAPTER FORTY-ONE

HELEN WALKED alone on Monday, beside herself with contentment, unable to settle the grin bunching her cheeks. Light was crackling around the seams of heaven. She knew that because she closed her eyes and saw it almost without ceasing now. Yesterday, even Bill had seen the phenomenon. Or felt it, really, because it wasn't about physically seeing. It was more like *knowing* God's love, which in itself took a supernatural power. She mulled over one of the apostle Paul's prayers: "And I pray that you may have the power to grasp how wide and long and high and deep is the love of Christ . . ." It was something not easily grasped, that love. Something imagined with a certain degree of confidence, really. Certainly not heard or touched or seen or tasted or smelled. Not usually, anyway.

The light was like that, not easily grasped. But Pastor Bill was getting a grip on things these days. He was getting better at imagining the world beyond what most see and touch and taste. And he was imagining with belief. Faith. Believing having not seen, as the apostle put it.

Helen hummed the Martyr's Song. It was the song of life to her. *I've been waiting for the day when at last I can say . . . you are finally home . . . Song of Zion . . . Daughter of mine . . .*

In all honesty she was not certain why the light was shining so brightly beyond the sky, but she had an idea. Things were not what they seemed. The death of her daughter, Gloria—such a devastating experience initially—was not such a bad thing at all. Neither was the death of Spencer such a bad thing. She had said so to Bill a dozen times, but now Helen was feeling the truth. Their lives were like seeds, which, having died in the ground, were now bearing a splendor unimaginable in their former puny vessels. Like the martyr who had been slain in Serbia. Somehow the seed was bearing fruit decades later in lives not yet born when that priest gave his life. How that fruit actually looked she did not know yet. She could not see as much. But the light spilling out of heaven was being pushed by peals of laughter.

"Good God, take me!" she mumbled and skipped a step. Her heart pounded with excitement. "Take me quickly. Let me join them, Father."

She had heard many times of how the martyrs walked willingly to their deaths, overjoyed and eager to find the life beyond. She herself felt the same way for the first time in her life, she thought. It was that kind of joy. A complete understanding of this life stacked up against the next life. And she would gladly jump into the next if given the opportunity.

Now this death of Kent, it was not quite so clear. He had died; he had not died. He would die; he would live; he would love; he would rot in hell. In the end she might never even know. In the end it was between Kent and God.

In the end Kent was every man. In the end the pounding feet in her dreams were the feet of every man, running from God.

She knew that now. Yes, there was this grand commotion over Kent in the heavens because of the challenge cast. Yes, a million angels and as many demons lined the sky, peering on his every move. But it was the same for every man. And it was not a game, as she had once suggested to the pastor. It was life.

"Glory!" she yelled, and immediately spun around to see if anybody had been surprised by that. She could see no one. Too bad—would've been nice to treat another human to a slice of reality. She chuckled.

Yes indeed. What was happening here in this isolated petri dish of her experience was no different from what happened in one form or another to every last human being who lived on God's green Earth. Different in the fact that she had been enabled to participate with her walkathon intercession, perhaps. Different because she saw more of the drama than most. But no different up there where it counted.

The truth of it all had descended upon her two days earlier, and now she wanted one thing like she had never wanted anything in the sixty-four years her little heart had managed to beat. She wanted to cross that finish line. She wanted to step into the winner's circle. She wanted to walk into glory. If given the choice to live and walk or to die and kneel before the throne, she would scream her answer: "the throne, the throne, the throne!" Jumping like a pogo stick. She would do it in her running shoes and tall white socks, not caring if a park full of baseball players saw her do it.

She wanted it all because now she knew without the slightest sliver of doubt that it was all about God's love—so desperate and consuming for every man. And she also knew that Gloria and Spencer were swimming in God's love and screaming with pleasure for it.

"God, take me home," she breathed. "Take me quickly."

Frankly, she didn't know how Kent could resist it all.

Maybe he wouldn't. Maybe he had.

Either way, the light was bright and crackling around the seams.

"Glory!" she chirped and skipped again.

IT STRUCK Kent that Sunday, two days after Lacy had spit him out like raw quinine, that it had been almost two months since he'd become a millionaire. Actually it didn't *strike* him at all, because the thought barely crept through his mind, like a lethargic slug hoping for safe passage. He rolled over and noted that he'd slept on top of the covers again. A dim light glowed around the room's brown drapes, and by the sounds of traffic he knew it was well past morning. Not that it mattered—day and night had lost their significance to him now.

It is said that money cannot buy happiness. It is one of those axioms often spoken but rarely believed for the simple reason that money does indeed seem to bring with it a measure of happiness. At least for a while. Bono's assertion that all paths end in the grave might be true, but in the meantime, surely money might ease the journey. It was the *meantime* part that Kent was having difficulty with. Because for Kent, the conclusion of the matter—the bit about the grave—took up early residence inside him. Like a hole in his chest.

It was all a bit unusual, possibly. Not in the least fair, it seemed. But hollow and black and sickening just the same. And this all without Pinhead the cop entering the picture. Throw his mug into the mix, and it was flogging desperation.

Kent had walked long and slow that Thursday night, away from Lacy. A limousine stuffed with squealing teenagers had nearly run him over at one point. The near-miss had nearly scared him out of his skin. He had hailed a taxi then and returned to the dungeon in Denver. The sun was already graying the eastern sky when he paid the driver.

Friday. Friday had been the big day of living dangerously, taking out his last few breaths of fury on the porky twins and then submitting his findings to the bank. They had delivered his fee as agreed. Bentley and Borst would undoubtedly find their just reward. Revenge is sweet, so they say. Kent didn't know who *they* were, but he knew now that they knew nothing. His victory was hardly more than a distant memory by two o'clock that afternoon.

He spent a good portion of the next two days—or nights, really, because he didn't roll out of bed until 5 P.M.—trying to plot a comeback. Not a comeback to Lacy; she was dead to him. But a comeback to life. He had eighteen million dollars stashed, for heaven's sake. Anybody who had eighteen million dollars stashed without knowing how to spend it was the better part of a moron. The things one could do with such wealth. Granted, Bill Gates might consider the cash chicken feed, but then Mr. Bill was in a different reality altogether. Most normal human beings would have trouble finding ways to spend even one million dollars, short of purchasing some jet or yacht or some other toy that cost the world.

Kent had considered doing just that. Buying another bigger, fancier yacht, for example, and sailing it to a deserted tropical cove. The idea actually retained some luster for the better part of a beer before he discarded it. He had already purchased one yacht, and he had left it behind. Maybe he'd buy a small jet. Fly around the world. Of course he would be landing and partying at all stops, discovering the local flavors and laughing with the natives. On the other hand, most local flavors were available at specialty restaurants around town—no need to traipse around the world. And laughter was not coming so easily these days.

Perhaps he could visit a few great sporting events. Sit in the stadium with the other rich folk who could afford to drop a few C notes for the pleasure of watching men bat, or throw, or bounce a ball around. Yes, and maybe he could take his own ball and play catch with a few celebrities. *Gag.* Thing of it was, three months ago the idea would have thrilled him. Now that he had the money, he could not remember why.

On Monday another emotion found its way into Kent's mind. Panic. An unearthly desperation at the prospect of finding no solution to this dilemma. A day later the panic settled into a dull hopelessness. He stopped feeling then and just continued his trudging through what he now saw clearly as the wastelands of life. Life without Gloria and Spencer. Life without Lacy. Life without Kent. Life without any meaning at all.

Kent climbed from bed on Wednesday and pulled the drapes aside. A light drizzle fell from a dark, gray sky. Could be morning, could be afternoon, could be evening. Looked nasty whatever time it was. He dropped the heavy curtain and trudged to the bathroom, shoulders drooping. The fluorescent bulb blinked brightly, and he squinted. Toothpaste stains ringed the sink, and he thought it might be good to clean the bathroom. He'd slept in the apartment for almost two weeks now without cleaning the kitchen or the bathroom. What would Helen say to that?

Helen, dear old Helen. A lump rose to his throat at the thought of the woman. So sincere, so steady, so sweet, so gentle. Well, not always so sweet or gentle, but sincere and truthful. She'd likely walk in here and land a loud slap on his cheek.

A tear sprang to Kent's eye. What was this? He was actually missing the old wench? Maybe, maybe not, but either way the tear felt good, because it was his first tear in five days. Which meant that his heart was still alive in its prison of bones.

But the sink and the kitchen and the rest of it could wait. Helen was not here. In fact, no one was here. Nor would anyone be here soon. He could buy the place and burn it to the ground. That would clean it up good. Yes, maybe he'd do that when this was over.

When what is over, Kent?

He looked up at the mirror and stared at his disheveled reflection. The face Lacy had rejected. Three days' stubble. Maybe four days'. The face of Kevin Stillman, still bearing scars from the surgery, if you knew where to look.

When what is over, Kent?

The lump swelled in his throat, like a balloon. Another tear slipped from his right eye. *I'm sorry, Gloria. God, I'm sorry.* His chest was aching. *I'm sorry, Spencer.*

Yes, and what would Spencer think of you now?

His shoulders shook, and the mirror dissolved in a single sob. *I'm so sorry.*

It's over, Kent.

He sucked at the air and caught his breath. The notion popped in his mind with sudden clarity. Yes, it was over, wasn't it? There was nothing left to do anymore. He had spent his life. He had drained it of meaning. Now it was time to step aside and let the others have a try.

It was time to stop trudging. It was time to die.

Yes, it's time to die, Kent.

Yes, let the other fools bloody their fingers climbing up life's cliff. Let them claw over the edge to find the wastelands stretching like a dusty graveyard. In the end it was all the same. In the end it was the grave.

Yes. You've come home, Kent. Welcome home, Kent.

It was the first touch of peace Kent had felt in weeks, and it tingled down his spine. *Now I lay me down to sleep* . . . Right beside the others who wasted their lives climbing this cliff called life and then lay down to die on barren wastelands. Salmon fighting their way up the river. Lemmings rushing to the cliff. Humans dying in the wastelands. It all made sense now.

Kent brushed his teeth. No sense dying with dirty teeth. He dropped the toothbrush half finished and spat the foam from his mouth. He didn't bother running any water to clean the mess.

The easiest way to slip into the grave would be through some sort of overdose; he'd thought so a hundred times. But thinking of it now, it seemed there ought to be more to the matter. It could be a month before they found his rotting body, maybe longer. Maybe he'd do the deed in a place that made a statement. The bank, for instance. Or in the steeple of a church. On the other hand, did he care? No, he did not care at all. He simply wanted out. Done. Over. He wanted to end. Find Bono's graveyard. Find a priest . . .

Confess.

Kent was halfway across the room, headed nowhere, when the thought dropped into his head. He pictured Bono telling him that. *"Confess, my son."* The word hollowed his chest. It seemed to carry a sense of purpose. And a suicide with purpose felt better than a senseless one. It would be something like leaning over that cliff and calling down to the million fools struggling up the stone face. *"Hey, fellas, there ain't nothin' up here but ashes and tombstones. Save yourselves the energy."*

Confess to a priest. Find a church, find a man of the collar, confess the crime, then drift off to the wasteland. Maybe meet Helen's God. The thought brought a tightness to his chest again. *I'm sorry, Helen.* Dear old Helen.

Kent sat on the bed and rested his forehead on his hands. An image of Helen filled his mind, and he swallowed against the knot in his throat. She was pointing to the bare spot above his fireplace—the spot that had once graced a painting of Christ. *"You crucified him, Kent,"* Helen was saying. Only she wasn't yelling it or stuffing it down his throat. She was crying and smiling.

"Yes," he muttered beneath his breath. A tear slipped down his cheek. "And now I'm going to crucify myself, Helen."

CHAPTER FORTY-TWO

HELEN CALLED Bill at six that morning, pacing in small circles while she waited for him to answer. "Come on, Bill."

The dream had changed last night. The sound of running had quickened; the breathing had come in gasps. She had awakened wet with sweat and rolled from bed, the fingers of panic playing on her spine.

"Get up, Bill. Pick up the phone!"

A groggy voice spoke through the receiver. "Hello."

"Something's up, Bill."

"Helen? What time is it?"

"It's already six, and I should've been walking half an hour ago, but I started praying in my kitchen and I'm telling you, I could hardly stand it."

"Whoa, slow down, Helen. Sorry, I had a late appointment last night."

She stopped her pacing and peered out the window. A fine drizzle fell from a dark gray sky. "I don't know. But it's never been like this before."

"Like what, Helen. What are you talking about?"

"There's electricity in the air. Can't you feel it?" Helen moved her arm through the air and felt her hair stand on end. "Heavens, Bill, it's everywhere. Close your eyes and calm yourself. Tell me if you feel anything."

"I'm not the one who needs calming—"

"Just do it, Pastor."

The phone went dead for a moment before he came back on. "No. I'm sorry. I see only the backs of my eyelids over here. It's raining outside."

"It feels like heaven is about to tear loose, Bill. Like it's a bag of white-hot light, bursting at the seams over here."

He didn't answer right away, and she was suddenly impatient. She should be out walking and praying. The thought brought another shiver to her bones. "Glory," she whispered. Bill's breathing suddenly went ragged in the receiver.

"Helen . . . ?" his voice warbled.

Her pulse quickened. She spun from the window. "Yes? You see something?"

"Helen, I think something is going to happen . . . Oh, my God! Oh, my God!"

"Bill!" She knew it! He was seeing something right now. Had to be! "Bill, what is it? Tell me!"

But he just mumbled on. "Oh, my God. Oh, my God." His voice wavered over the phone, and Helen fought a sudden urge to drop the receiver and rush to his house. He was over there seeing into the other side, and she was standing here on this side, holding this ridiculous phone and wanting to be *over there.*

"Come on, Bill," she suddenly blurted. "Stop mumbling and tell me something!"

That put the pause in him. But only for a moment. Then he started again. "Oh, my God! Oh, my God!" It was not anything akin to swearing. Quite the opposite. This much Helen knew with certainty: Pastor Bill Madison was peeking into the heavens this very minute. And he was desperately yearning for what he was seeing, yes sir. The truth of it oozed from his shuddering voice as he cried to his God. "Oh, my God! Oh, my God!"

He fell silent suddenly.

Helen took a deep breath and waited a few seconds before pressing again. "What was it, Pastor? What did you see?"

He was not talking. Perhaps not listening, either.

"Bill . . ."

"I . . . I don't really know," came the weak reply. "It just came like a blanket of light . . . like last time, only this time I heard laughter. Lots of laughter."

"Ha! You heard it, did you? Well, what did I tell you? You see? Have you ever in your life heard such laughter?"

He laughed a crazy little chuckle. "No. But who is it? Who's laughing? . . . Do you think it's *God?"*

Helen lifted her arm and saw that the hair stood on end. She should walk. She needed to walk *now!* "The laughter is from humans, I think. The saints. And maybe from angels as well."

"The saints are laughing? *Laughing,* huh? And what about God? Did I see him in there?"

"I don't know what you saw, Bill. I wasn't there. But God is responsible for the light, and you saw the light, right? I think he is mostly loving and being loved and laughing—yes, laughing too—and weeping."

"And why, Helen? Why are we seeing these things? It's not common."

"No, it's not common. But it's real enough. Just like in biblical times, Bill. He's nudging our stubborn minds. Like my walking—impossible yet true. Like Jericho. Like two-thirds of the Scriptures, impossible yet true and here today. He has not changed, Bill." She gazed back out the window. "He has not changed."

"Yes. You are right. He has not changed."

"I have to go, Pastor. I want to walk."

"Yes, you should walk. It's supposed to snow today, they say. First snow of the season. You dress warm, okay?"

Snow? Goodness, that would be something, walking in the snow. "I'll be fine. My legs are not so concerned with the elements these days."

"Go with God, Helen."

"I will. Thank you, Bill."

Helen grabbed a light jacket on the way out and entered the gray morning air. Streetlights glowed like halos in a long string down the glistening pavement. One of those Volkswagen bugs drove by, its lights peering through the mist. The sound of its wheels running over the pavement sounded like tearing paper. She pulled on the jacket and walked into the drizzle, mumbling, hardly aware of the wet.

Father, thank you, thank you, thank you. Her body shivered once, as a chill swept through her bones. But it was not the cold; it was that light, crackling just behind the black clouds, that set off the tremor. True enough, she could not actually see it, but it fizzled and snapped and dazzled there, just the same. Her heart ran at twice its customary clip, as if it too knew that a rare power streamed through the air, unseen but fully charged.

Perhaps the prince of this earth wanted to put a damper on things. Soak his domain with a cold, wet blanket in an attempt to mask the light behind it all. But she was not seeing the blanket at all. She was seeing that light, and it felt warm and dry and bright. *Glory.*

Helen glanced at her white running shoes, stabbing forward with each stride. They flung droplets out ahead of her, christening the sidewalk like a priest flinging water on a baby's head. *Blessed be these feet, walking by the power of God.* It might have been a good idea to pull on long pants and a sweater, but she was not following good ideas these days.

She had run out of words in this prayer-walking weeks ago. She might have prayed through the entire Bible—she didn't know. But now it was just her heart yearning and her mouth mumbling. *You made this earth, Father. It's yours. There's no way a few drops will stand in your way! Goodness, you parted a whole sea for the Israelites—surely this here is nothing. In fact, maybe it's your rain. How about that?*

Helen lifted her hands and grasped at the drops, smiling wide. For a brief moment her chest felt as though it might explode, and she skipped for a few steps. Another car with lights glaring whisked by, its tires hissing on the wet street. It honked once and sped on. And no wonder; she surely looked like a drowned rat with her matted hair and drooping wet dress. *Crazy old woman, walking in this stuff. She'll catch her death!*

Now *there* was a thought. *Take me, Father. I'll gladly come. You know that, don't you? Don't get me wrong here. I'll do whatever you wish of me. But you know I'd die to be with you. To be rid of this flesh and this old wrinkled face and this hair that keeps falling out. Not that it's so bad, really. I thank you for it; really I do. And if you'd want me to, I'd bring it with me. But I'll tell you this, my God: I would give anything to be there with you. Take me any way you choose. Strike me dead with a bolt of lightning, roll me over with a monster truck, send a disease to eat away my bones—any way, just bring me home. Like those before me.*

She jumped once and swung her arm—a grandma-style victory whoop. "Glory!" This was how the martyrs had felt, she thought. Marching to Zion!

The sky slowly but barely brightened as the hours faded. Helen walked, scarcely conscious of her route. The path took her due west along side streets. She'd been here before, numerous times, and she knew the four-hour turnaround point well. If she took a loop around the fountain at 132nd and Sixth, she would end up back at home eight hours after her morning departure. The fat Buddha-looking statue at the fountain's center would be wet today, the goldfish swimming at its feet doubly doused.

Helen groaned at the thought of rounding the fountain and heading home. It should have come as a comfort with all the rain drenching her to the bone and the dark sky foreboding a storm, but it didn't. Not today. Today the thought of heading home made her heart sink. She wanted to hike right over the distant, crackling horizon like Enoch and climb under the black clouds. She wanted to find the light and join in the laughter. *Glory!*

The traffic was light, the normal straggle of pedestrians absent, the shops eerily vacant. Helen approached Homer's Flower Shop on the corner of 120th and Sixth. The old man stood under his eaves with folded arms and raised brows as she came near.

"They say snow's coming, you know. You shouldn't be out here."

"I'm fine, old man. This is no time to stop. I'm near the end now." He squinted at the comment. Of course, he could have no idea what she referred to, but then, a little mystery now and then never hurt anybody.

"Don't say I didn't warn you, old lady," he said.

She was even with him now and kept her head turned to meet his stare. "Yes, indeed. You have warned me. Now hear the warning of God, old man. Love him always. With every last breath, love him madly."

He blinked and took a step back. She smiled and walked on past. Let him think that one through. *Love God madly. Glory!*

She'd come to a string of street merchants who'd packed it in for the day, all except for Sammy the cap man who, truth be said, was more a homeless freeloader than an actual merchant, but nobody was saying so. Those who knew him also knew that he had sincerely if unsuccessfully tried at this life's game. Sometimes the ball rolls that way. He'd left a dead wife and a bankrupt estate in his wake. No one seemed to mind forking over a ten-dollar bill for a cheap, two-dollar cap—not when it was Sammy collecting the money. He stood under the eaves beside two large crates filled with his hats.

"What on Earth are you doing out here in the rain, Helen?"

She veered under the overhang. "Morning, Sammy. I'm walking. You have a cap for me today?"

He tilted his head. "A hat. You're soaked to the skin already. You think a cap will help now? Snow's coming, you know."

"Exactly. Give me one of those green ones you had out the other day."

He eyed her carefully, trying to decide if this bit of business was meant in sincerity. "You got a ten on you?"

"No, but I'll have it tomorrow."

Sammy shrugged and dug out a green hat sporting a red-and-yellow parrot on its bill. He handed it over with a smile, playing the salesman's role now. "It'll look great with that yellow dress. Nothing quite so appealing as a woman wearing a hat—dress or pants, rain or shine, it don't matter. It's the hat that counts."

She pulled it on. "Thanks, Sammy," she said and turned up the sidewalk.

Truth be told, she did it for him. What good would a hat do her? Although now that she had stretched it over her head, the bill did keep the drizzle from her eyes. "Glory!"

The horizon fizzled and crackled with light—she could feel it more than see it with her eyes, but it was real just the same. And she knew that if she could reach up there and pull those clouds aside she'd find one giant electrical storm flooded with laughter.

Helen walked on toward the turnaround point, toward the horizon, toward that sputtering light beyond what Homer or Sammy saw. If anybody was watching her on a regular basis they would notice that today her pace was brisker than usual. Her arms swung more determinedly. On any other day she might look like a crazy old woman with outdated fashion sensibilities, out for a walk. Today she looked like an ancient bag lady who'd clearly lost her mind—maybe with a death wish, soaked to the bone, marching nowhere.

Helen walked on, humming now. She stabbed the air with her white Reeboks, stopping on occasion to pump her fist and blurt out a word.

"Glory."

Chapter Forty-Three

KENT DROVE to the liquor store at three in the afternoon, two hours after he had awakened and discovered he had only half a bottle of tequila left. He had decided it would be with booze and a bullet that his world would end, and half a bottle was not enough. He would drink himself into a state just this side of comatose, place the barrel of the nine-millimeter to his temple, and pull the trigger. It would be like pulling an aching tooth from society's jaws. Just enough anesthetic to numb the nerve endings and then rip the rotting thing out. Except it was his life decaying, not just some bony incisor.

He navigated the streets in a daze, peering lethargically past the drizzle. Sleet and the occasional snowflake mixed with the rain. The sky loomed dark and ominous. Decay was in the air.

He bought three bottles of the best tequila Tom's Liquor sold and tipped Tommy three hundred dollars.

"You sure? Three hundred dollars?" The man stood there with the bills fanned out, offering them back as if he thought they might be contagious.

"Keep it," Kent said and walked out of the store. He should have brought a couple hundred *thousand* from his mattress stash for the tip. See what Tommy would say to that. Or maybe he'd give the rest of the money to the priest. If he could *find* a priest to hear him. One final act of reconciliation for Gloria's sake. For Helen's sake.

He drove back to the apartment and pulled out the pistol. He'd shot it into the dead body at the bank a few times—three times actually, *blam, blam, blam*—so he wasn't terribly surprised to find six bullets in the nine-round clip. But it would only be one *blam* this time. He felt the cold steel and played with the safety a few times, checking the action, thinking small thoughts like, *I wonder if the guy who invented safeties is dead. Yes, he's dead and his whole family is dead. And now he's going to kill me. Sort of.*

Kent turned off all the lights and opened the drapes. The red numbers on the clock radio read 3:12. Snow now drifted silently past his window. The earth was dying slowly, begging him to join her.

It's time to lie down, Kent.

Yes, I will. As soon as I confess.

But why confess?

Because it seems decent.

You're going to blow your brains against the wall by the bed over there! What does decent have to do with that?

I want to. I want to tell a priest that I stole twenty million dollars. I want to tell him where to find it. Maybe he can use it.

You're a fool, Kent!

Yes, I know. I'm sick, I think.

You are human waste.

Yes, that's what I am. I'm human waste.

He backed to the bed and opened a bottle. The fiery liquid ran down his throat like fire, and he took a small measure of comfort in the knowledge that he was going to stop feeling soon.

He sat on the bed for an hour, trying to consider things, but the considering part of him had already gone numb. His eyes had dried of their earlier tears, like ancient abandoned wells. He was beginning to wonder if that voice that had called him human waste was right about blowing off the confession. Maybe he should stick to blowing off his head. Or maybe he should find a church—see if they even heard confessions of a dying man on dark wintry afternoons.

He dragged out the phone book and managed to find a listing of Catholic churches. Saint Peter's Cathedral. Ten blocks down Third Street.

Kent found himself on the road driving past the darkened cathedral thirty minutes later. The sign out front stated that confessions were heard until 7 P.M. each night, excluding Saturdays, but the dark stained-glass windows suggested the men of God had made an early retreat. Kent thought perhaps the sign should read, *"Confessions heard daily from 12:00 to 7:00 except on dark wintry days that depress everyone including priests who are really only men dressed in long black robes to earn their living. So give us all a break and go home, especially if you are suicidal.*

Don't bother us with your dying. Dying people are really just human waste. Priests are just ordinary people, and dying people are human waste." But that would hardly fit on the placard.

The thought drifted through his mind like wisps of fog, and it was gone almost before he realized he'd thought it. He decided he might come back later to see if the lights had been turned on.

Kent went back to his dark apartment and sat on the edge of his bed. The tequila went down smoothly now, not burning so much. It was five o'clock.

CHAPTER FORTY-FOUR

THE BUDDHA-BELLY fountain came and went, and Helen did not stop.

It was as simple as that. She had passed the fountain at 11 A.M., and every other day she had turned around at the four-hour mark, but today she didn't want to turn around. She wanted to keep walking.

She could hear the water gurgling a full block before coming up on Mr. Buddha, and the impulse struck her then.

Keep walking, Helen.

I'm four hours from home if I turn now. I should keep walking?

Just keep right on walking.

Past the fountain? To where?

Past the fountain. Straight ahead.

Until when?

Until it's time to stop.

And how will I know that?

You will know. Just walk.

So she had.

That first step beyond her regular turning point felt like a step into the deep blue. Her heart raced, and her breathing thickened, but now it was not due to light spilling from the seams. This time it was from fear. Just plain, old-fashioned fear.

Certain facts presented themselves to her with convincing authority. Like the fact that every step she took west was one more step she would have to repeat later, headed east. Like the fact that it was now starting to snow, just like the weatherman had forecasted, and she wore only a thin jacket that had been soaked before the rain turned to snow. Like the fact that she was a lady in her sixties, marching off in a storm toward a black horizon. Like the fact that she did indeed look ridiculous in these tall, red-striped socks and wet, dirtied running shoes. In general, like the simple fact that she had clearly graduated from the ridiculous to the absurd.

Still she walked on, fighting the thoughts. Her legs did not seem to mind, and that was a good thing. Although they could hardly know that she was taking them farther from their home instead of closer. The first hour of walking into the cold, wind-blown snow had been perhaps the hardest hour Helen had lived in her sixty-plus years. Actually, there was no *perhaps* about it; nothing had been so difficult. She found herself sweating despite the cold. The incredible joy she'd felt when first walking a few hours earlier had faded into the gray skies above.

Still, she had placed one foot in front of the other and plodded on.

The light returned at three. Helen was in midstride when her world turned. When her eyes snapped open and she saw clearly again. That was exactly what happened. Heaven did not open up to her—*she* opened up to heaven. Perhaps it had taken these last four hours of walking blindly without the carrots of heaven dangling out in front to set her mind straight.

Either way, her world turned, midstride, and she landed her foot and froze. A crackle of light stuttered behind the walls of gray in her mind. Tears sprang to her eyes like a swelling tide. She remained still, her legs scissored on the sidewalk like a girl playing hopscotch. Her shoulders shook with sobs.

"Oh thank you, Father! Thank you!" She moaned aloud, overcome by the relief of the moment. "I knew you were there. I knew it!" Then the joy came, like a tidal wave right up through her chest, and she squeezed her hands into fists.

Just walk, Helen. Walk on.

It's been more than eight hours. It's getting dark.

Walk.

She needed no further urging.

I will walk.

She broke into a long stride. *One, two. One, two.* For a moment she thought her heart might burst with the exhilaration that now throbbed through her chest. *One, two. One, two. I will walk on. I will walk on.*

Helen strode down the sidewalk, through the strange neighborhood, toward the ominous horizon, swinging her arms like some marching soldier on parade. Snowflakes lay like cotton on her green hat and clung in lumps to her hair. She left footprints in the light snow covering the sidewalk. *Goodness, just wait until I tell Bill about this, she thought. "I just kept going, Bill, because I knew it was what he wanted. Did I consider the possibility that I had lost my mind? Sure I did. But still I knew, and he showed me just enough to keep me knowing. I just walked."*

Helen had walked another five blocks when the first pain shot up her right thigh.

She had not felt pain during weeks of walking. Now she felt the distinct sensation of pain, sharp and fleeting but unmistakable. Like a fire streaking through the femur toward her hip and then gone.

She gasped and pulled up, clutching her thigh, terrified. "Oh, God!" It was all she could say for a moment.

Walk.

Walk? Her jaw still gaped wide in shock. She rocked back on her good leg. I just had a leg cramp. I had pain! I'm twenty miles from home, and it's ending. It's over!

Walk. The impulse came strong.

Helen closed her mouth slowly and swallowed. She gazed about, saw that the street was clear of gawkers, and gingerly placed weight back on her right leg. The pain had gone.

Helen walked again, tentatively at first but then with gaining confidence. For another five blocks she walked. And then the pain flared through her femur again, sharper this time.

She gasped aloud and pulled up. "Oh, God!" Her knee quivered with the trauma.

Walk. Just keep walking.

"This is pain I'm feeling down here!" she growled angrily. "You are pulling your hand away from me! Oh God, what's happening?"

Walk, child. Just walk. You will see.

She walked. Halting at first until she realized the pain had left, as before.

It roared back with a vengeance six blocks later. This time Helen hardly stopped. She limped for ten yards, mumbling prayers through gritted teeth, before finding sudden relief.

The pain came every five blocks or so, first in her right leg and then in her left leg, and after an hour, in both legs simultaneously. A sharp, shooting pain right up each bone for half a dozen steps and then gone for a few blocks only to return like clockwork. It was as if her legs were thawing after months in the deep freeze and a thousand miles of pain was slowly coming due. Each time she cried out to God, her face twisted in pain. Each time he spoke to her quietly. *Walk. Walk, child.* Each time she put her foot forward and walked on into the falling darkness.

Three things contributed to her relentless journey despite its apparent madness. First was that quiet voice whispering through her skull. *Walk, child.* Second was the light—it had not fled. The blackening skies crackled with light in her mind, and she could not ignore that.

The third thought that propelled her forward was the simple notion that this might very well be the end. *The* end. Maybe she *was* meant to walk right up to the horizon of heaven and enter glory. Like Enoch. There might not be a flaming chariot to whisk her away. That had been Elijah's treat. No, with Helen it would be the long walk home. And that was fine by her. *Glory!*

The sun left the city dark by five-thirty. An occasional car hissed by, but the early storm had left the streets quiet. Helen limped on into the black night, biting her lower lip, mumbling against the voices that mocked her.

Walk, child. Walk on.

And she did walk on. By six o'clock both legs were hurting without relief. The soles of her feet felt as though they might have caught fire. She could distinctly imagine, if not actually hear, the bones in her knees grinding with each step. Her hips joined in the protest soon after. What began as a dull ache around her upper thighs quickly mushroomed to sharp pangs of searing pain throughout her legs.

Walk, child. Walk on.

Still she walked. The snow fell in earnest now, like ashes from a burnt sky. Helen kept her eyes on the ground just in front of her feet mostly, concentrating on each footfall as her destination—one . . . two, one . . . two. When she did look up she saw a dizzying sea of flakes swirling around the streetlights. The night settled quietly. Biting cold now numbed her exposed knees, and she began to shiver. She tucked her hands under her arms in an attempt to keep them warm, but the new posture threw her balance off, nearly sending her to the ground, and she immediately withdrew them. Oh, God! Please, Father. I have lost my mind here. This is . . . this is madness!

Walk, child. Walk on.

So she walked, but barely now, dragging one foot at a time, inching into the night. She lost all sense of direction, fighting through the landscape of her mind, aware of the pain ravaging her bones but no longer caring. At the eighth hour, back there, she had crossed the point of no return. She had stepped off the cliff and now fell helplessly onward, resigned to follow this still small voice or die trying. Either way the crackling light waited. And there would be laughter in the light. The notion brought a smile to her face, she thought, although she could not be sure because her face had gone numb.

The last fifty yards took twenty minutes—or an eternity, depending on who was counting. But she knew they were the last when her right foot landed on a cement rise of some kind and she could not pull herself up or over it. Helen fell to one knee, collapsed facedown, and rolled to her side.

If she'd been able to feel, she might have thought she had ground her legs to bloody stumps, judging by the pain she felt, but she could feel nothing at all. She was aware of snowflakes lighting on her cheek but no longer had the strength to turn away from them.

Then her world faded to black.

CHAPTER FORTY-FIVE

DESIRE FOR death is a unique sentiment, like a migraine sufferer's impulse to twist off his head in the hopes of banishing a throbbing headache. But Kent was still craving death—and increasingly so as the minutes ticked by in his dark apartment.

It might have been some deep-seated desire to delay his death that pushed him back to the church despite the falling snow. But if it was, it did not feel like any desire he'd ever felt. Nevertheless, he would do this one last deed. He would find his priest.

Snow rushed past his headlights, and it occurred to him that coming out for a priest on a night like this was nuts. But then, so was killing himself. He was a nutcase. The church's tall spiral reached into the night sky like a shadowed hand reaching for God. *Reach on, baby. Nothin' but black up there.*

He parked the car and stared at the dark cathedral. A monument to man's search for meaning, which was a joke because even the robed ones knew, way deep inside, that there was no real meaning. In the end it was just death. A dusty graveyard on the top of a cliff.

Get on with it, Kent.

Kent pushed the door open and slogged toward the wide steps.

The lump on the first step caught his attention immediately. A body lay curled like a fetus, covered with snow. Kent stopped on the sidewalk and studied the form. The priest had fallen down on the job—closed the temple up too early and now his God had dashed him on the steps. Or possibly a vagrant had come to find God and discovered a locked door instead. Either way the body did not move. It was the second dead body he'd seen recently. Maybe he should curl up and join this one.

Kent mounted the steps and climbed to the front door. It was locked. His mouth no longer had the will to swear or speak or even breathe, but his mind swore. He slogged down the steps, his mind still swearing long strings of words that no longer had meaning. He veered to the body and shoved it with his foot. *Death becomes me.* The snow fell from the vagrant's face. An old woman, smiling to beat all. A wide grin frozen on that pale face. She'd finally found her peace. And now he was on his way to find his own peace.

Kent turned from the body and walked for the car. An old memory crawled through his mind. It was dear old Helen, smiling with moist eyes in his living room. *You crucified him, Kent.*

Yes, dear Helen. But I will make amends soon enough. Like I told you, I'm going to kill my—

The next thought exploded in his mind mid-street, like a stun grenade. *That was Helen!*

His legs locked under him, stretched out for the next step.

Kent whirled back to the body. Ridiculous! That old woman lying over there was no more Helen than he was *God!* He turned back to his car.

If that wasn't Helen, then Helen has a twin.

He stopped and blinked. *Get a grip, Kent.*

And what if that is *Helen by some freak accident, dead on the step?*

Impossible! But suddenly the impulse to know trumped the rest of it.

Kent spun back toward the form and walked quickly. He bent and rolled the dead body to its back. Only it wasn't dead; he knew that immediately because its nostrils blew a few flakes from its upper lip in a long exhale. He jerked back, startled by the ghostly face smiling under a cap. His heart crashed against the walls of his chest. It *was* Helen!

It was not the grin or the face or even the hair. It was the yellow dress with small blue flowers, all but covered in snow, that made it so. The same yellow flowered dress she had worn to Gloria's funeral. The same yellow flowered dress she had worn to his door that first night moving in. That and the socks pulled to her knees.

He was staring at Helen, crumpled on the steps of this church, wearing running shoes clotted with frozen snow, smiling like she was in some kind of warm dream instead of freezing to death on this concrete slab.

Leave her.

I can't. She's alive.

Kent glanced around, saw that they were alone, and shoved his arms under Helen's limp body. He staggered to his feet with her dead weight hanging off each arm. The last time he'd done this, the body had been naked and gray and dead. He'd forgotten how heavy these things were. Well, the paramedics could deal with the crazy old fool as they saw fit.

Kent was halfway back to his car with Helen in his arms when that last thought crossed his mind. A swell of sorrow swept through his chest, and immediately he wanted to cry. For no reason that he could think of, really. Maybe because he had called her a crazy old fool and, really, she was no such thing. He looked down at the sagging body in his arms. No, this was no fool he carried. This was . . . this was precious. Helen, in all her eccentric craziness, somehow embodied a goodness. A tear came to his eyes, and he sniffed against it.

Get ahold of yourself, fool. And if she is goodness then what does that make you? Human waste.

Yes. Worse.

Yes, worse. Get rid of her.

Kent barely managed to open the passenger door without falling. He slid Helen onto the seat, slammed the door, and climbed in behind the wheel. She had fallen against the door, and her breathing came steadily now. A knot rose to his throat, and he shook his head. Thing of it was, she brought a strange sentiment out of him. One that had his windpipe aching. He missed her. That's what it was. He actually missed the old lady.

He started the Lincoln and pulled into the deserted street. The snow had eased to a powdery mist, visible only around a row of streetlights on the right. A white blanket lay undisturbed over parked cars and bushes and pavement alike. The sedan crept quietly over the snow, and Kent felt the fingers of death curl around his mind. It was death—death everywhere. A frozen graveyard. Kent swallowed hard. "God, let me die," he growled under his breath.

"Uhh . . ."

The groan from his right slammed into his consciousness like a bullet to the brain, and he reacted instinctively. He crammed his foot on the brake and pulled hard on the wheel. The Lincoln slid for the sidewalk, bumped into the curb, and stalled. Kent gripped the wheel with both hands and breathed heavy.

He whirled to the passenger's seat. Helen sat there, leaning against the passenger door with her head resting on her shoulder, cockeyed but wide eyed, and staring ahead past snow-encrusted brows. Kent's breath seemed to freeze in his throat. She was awake! Awake from the dead like a lost soul from the cast of a cheap horror movie.

Slowly she straightened her neck and lifted a hand to brush the snow from her face. Kent stared dumbly, thoroughly confused on how to feel. She blinked a few times in succession, climbing back into the land of the living, still staring out the windshield.

A small grunt came from Kent's throat, and it was this that clued her in to the fact that she was not alone. She turned to him slowly. Now her mouth was open as well. They locked like that for several long seconds, two lost souls gaping at each other in the front seat of a car, lost in a silent snowfall.

But Helen did not remain lost for long. No, not Helen.

She blinked again and swallowed. She breathed out deliberately, like the sigh of one disappointed. Perhaps she had not intended to wake up on the front seat of a car, staring at a stranger.

"Kent? You look different. Is that you?"

Well, then, perhaps not a stranger.

Kent more guffawed than answered. "Helen! What are you doing? You could have killed us!" It was an absurd statement considering his intentions, and having said it, he swallowed hard.

"You are Kent." She said it as a matter of simple fact. Like, "The sun has gone down."

"And how do you know I'm Kent?" He caught himself. "Even if I were?" But he'd already called her Helen, hadn't he? Good grief!

Either way, Helen was not listening. She was lost; he could see that in her eyes. She turned to the windshield without blinking. "Did you see it, Kent?"

He followed her eyes. The street still lay empty and white. Condensation was beginning to gather on the windshield from the hot breath. "See what?"

"See the light. Did you see the light? It was everywhere. It was heaven, I think." She spoke in awe.

The anger flared up his spine, but he bit his tongue and closed his eyes. "Helen . . . you were out cold and hallucinating. Wake up, you old religious coot. There's nothing but cold snow and death out there." Then he turned on her and let his anger swell past his clenched teeth. "I swear, I'm *sick* of all your crazy heaven and God talk!"

If he expected her to shrink, he should have known better. She turned to him with bright eyes. She did not look like an old woman who had just been dragged, half dead, from a snowstorm. "What if there *is* life out there, Kent?" Her lips flared red. "What if, behind this veil of flesh, there is a spiritual reality crackling with light? What if it was all created for a purpose? What if, behind it all, that Creator is craving relationship?" Tears sprang to her eyes.

"What if you were made to love him? What then, Kent?" Her eyes did not blink but turned to pools of tears. One of those pools broke, and a trail of tears ran down her right cheek.

Kent had his mouth opened to retort, to put her back in her place, before he realized he had nothing to say. Not to *this.* What she suggested could not be. He tried to imagine a God desperate for love, like some huge, smiling ball of light with outstretched arms. The image refused to hold shape. And if there was truth there in those words, if somehow there was a Creator who loved him so . . . he would kill himself anyway. He would slit his wrists in agony.

Kent turned from her and clenched his jaw.

"Kent." Her voice warbled soft to him.

Shut up, Helen! Just shut up! His mind screamed obscenities, locked in torment.

"Kent." She was begging. The small, stuffy cabin of the Lincoln seemed to throb with the beating of his heart. He wanted to reach over and slap her, but his hands had frozen on the wheel.

Kent cast her a sideways glance. Helen was trembling and weeping and melting on the seat before him. His heart screamed with pain. Her lips quivered with desire. A pleading smile.

She reached a shaking hand toward him. "Kent. Do you want to see?"

He could barely hear the words from her constricted throat. *"Kent, do you want to see?"*

No! No, no, no, I don't want to see! "Don't be a fool, Helen! You don't just turn on a light to see this God of yours!"

"No. But tonight is different. Do you want to see?"

No, no, no, you old hag! There is nothing to see! Tears blurred his vision.

What was happening to him? An ache tore at his heart, and he whimpered. Time seemed to cease then, in that moment of agony. *Oh, God! Oh, God! Do I want to see? Yes! Yes, I do want to see, don't I?* Kent slowly kneaded his skull with his fingers. He heard the word from his lips like a distant whisper. "Yes."

She touched his cheek.

A strobe exploded in Kent's skull. The horizon detonated with a blinding light, and he jerked upright. Everything stopped then. His heart seized in his chest; his blood froze in his veins; his breath stalled in his lungs. The world ended with one gasp.

And then it restarted with a blur of images that slammed him back in his seat and yanked his jaw open. Torrents of light cascaded into his mind and thundered down his spine. His body convulsed there on the leather Towncar seat as if seized by death throes.

But it was not death. It was life! It was the breath of God! He knew that the moment it touched him. Helen's creator was . . . was *whispering* to him. He knew that too. This raw emotion pounding through his body was just a whisper, and it said, *I love you, my beloved.*

"Oh, God! Oh, God, God!" He was screaming. Laughter drowned out his own cry—a pealing laughter that echoed across the sky. He knew that laughter! Voices from the past—a mother laughing in pleasure; a child giggling in long, high-pitched squeals of delight. It was Gloria and Spencer, there in the light, ecstatic. Kent heard their voices echo through his skull, and he threw his hand to his face and began to writhe in shame.

"Oh, God! Oh, God. I'm sorry!" It was true! The realization pummeled him like a battering ram to the chest. God! Helen's God. Gloria's God. Spencer's God. *The* God!

And he had said, *I love you, my beloved!*

The injustice of it all twisted Kent's mind, and he wormed in agony. The anguish of a mother having smothered her child. The desperation of a husband having tossed aside his bride for the whore. A wish for death.

A new surge of Helen's heaven crashed through Kent's bones, and he trembled under its power. *I love you, my beloved.*

Kent screamed. With every fiber still intact in his throat he screamed out for death, for forgiveness—but his vocal cords had seized with the rest now. They produced nothing more than a long, drawn-out groan. "Uuuuuuhhhhh . . ."

I have died already. I forgive you.

No, no, you don't understand! I am human waste. I do not know how to love. I am death!

You are my lover.

I am your hater! Kent's body buckled, and his forehead hit the steering wheel. Tears ran down his cheeks. The gross incongruity of these words swung like a steel wrecking ball against the sides of his skull.

You are my lover!

The notion that this being of white-hot love could want to love *him!* It could not be! He arched his neck and faced the Towncar's plush ceiling, his mouth stretched wide. It was then that he found his voice again. And he used it to roar, full throated. "Nooooooooo! I caaan't!"

Please love me. The whisper thundered through his body.

You were made to love him, a small voice said. Spencer's voice. Then it giggled.

Yes, Kent. Love him. That was Gloria.

Then Kent fell apart and heaved with sobs on the front seat beside Helen. In one twisted bundle of agony and ecstasy, of deep sorrow and bubbling joy, Kent loved God.

"Yes. Yes, yes, yes." He drank the forgiveness as if an overwhelming thirst had brought him to the edge of death. He gulped at the love like a fish desperate for oxygen. Except this was God filling him with breath, and it brought an unabashed quiver to each fiber of muscle still capable of movement. He reached out with every ounce of his being, every conscious thought, and he begged to be there with him.

For a few moments he *was* there with him. Or a part of God was down here in the Lincoln with him.

And then the light vanished, leaving Kent gasping for breath, draped over the steering wheel. He fell over Helen's lap and sobbed.

She stroked his head gently. Time lost its meaning for a while.

CHAPTER FORTY-SIX

"SO YOU saw him?"

Kent sat up, dazed. He looked at Helen and then back out the front windshield, misted now with condensation. "God!"

"Yes. Words just aren't adequate, are they?"

"So that was . . . God?" He knew it was. Without the slightest question.

"Yes."

Kent turned to her slowly. "Is it that way for everybody? How come I've never heard of this?"

"You've never heard about it because you've kept your ears closed. Is it that way for everybody? Yes and no."

He stared at her, wanting her to continue.

"No, not everyone will see what you have seen here tonight. At least not in the same way. But yes, in many ways, it is the same."

She turned to the windshield. "Let me tell you a story, Kent. You remember a story in the Bible about a man named Job?"

"I heard them, Helen. I heard Gloria and Spencer. They were laughing." A smile curved his mouth.

She smiled, bright eyed. "Yes, I know. You remember this man, Job? From the Bible?"

"They're in heaven, Helen," Kent returned, still distracted by the thought. "They're actually in heaven. With *him!*"

"Yes." She nodded. "Kent. I'm asking you a question here. Do you know of Job in the Bible?"

"The man who suffered?"

"Yes. Satan lost his challenge that he could make a righteous man curse God. You remember that?"

"Job remained faithful to God. And in the end he received twice the wealth. Something like that."

"It actually happened. He lost everything. His children, his wife, his wealth."

Kent turned to her, blinking.

She faced the dark sky. "Not so long ago, Satan cast another challenge before God. A challenge of reversals. This time he insisted that he could keep an unrighteous man from responding to God's love. *"No matter how you draw him, no matter how you love him, no matter how you lure him,"* Satan said, *"I can keep this man from responding to your love."*

"You're saying this actually happened?"

"Yes." She looked at him and nodded, teary eyed now. "Yes. And God accepted the challenge. The heavens have been lined with a million creatures, intent on that man's every move for months. And today, God has won the challenge." Helen smiled.

"M . . . me?" Kent asked, stunned. *"I was this man?"*

"Yes."

The notion seemed absurd. "This was all engineered, then? How . . ."

"No, not engineered, Kent. You were drawn. In ways none of us may ever fully understand, you were drawn by the father. And you were pulled . . . in a thousand ways you were pulled by Satan. Away from God."

Kent's mind spun back over the last few months and saw a long string of events full of extremes. Death. But in death, laughter, because Gloria and Spencer were laughing up there. Wealth. But in wealth, death. Or very nearly death. A whole reality behind the stage of life.

"He must have switched strategies halfway through," Kent said absently.

"Satan?"

"Yes. Killing off my family didn't work, so he set out to make me rich."

She chuckled. "Yes, you're getting the picture."

He turned to her again. "But why me?"

She sighed and shook her head. A car drove by, its lights glaring like halos in the windshield. The dull thump of rock music for a moment and then silence once again.

"That's just it, Kent. Your case is unique because of what we were able to see. But otherwise it's not so different than the challenge made over the young man or woman behind the wheel of the car that just passed us."

"It's the same for everybody?"

"You think God loves any one man more than he loves another? Does he draw one more and another less? No. Over every man there is cast a challenge. It is as intense for every man. We just don't see it. If we could . . ." She shook her head. "My, my, my."

Kent's chest began to swell, and he thought he might be reduced to tears again. This changed everything. It seemed so obvious now. So right. The meaning of life all bundled up in a few statements and yet so few knew the truth.

"So then behind this . . . this flesh . . . this physical world, there is activity . . . enough activity to blow our minds." He shook his head, overwhelmed by the notion. "We see only the tip of it all. And then only if we open our eyes."

"We fight not against flesh and blood. And we fight a war that is fleeting. Believe me, this life will pass quickly enough, although sometimes not quickly enough, it seems. Then it will be forever. Somewhere."

"Why don't more people know this? Why has no one told me this?"

She turned to him. "You think Gloria never told you this? We prayed every Thursday morning for five years for this day. You were just too wrapped up in this world to notice."

"Yes, you are right. You are so right!"

"Today you start over, Kent."

Lacy!

He grabbed Helen's arm. "We have to get to Lacy!"

"Lacy?"

"Yes. She lives in Boulder." He started the car and pulled out into the street, sliding on the snow. "Do you mind? I need you there. She'll never believe me."

"Why not? It's a beautiful, snowy night for a drive. I was rather hoping for an entirely different destination, but I suppose Boulder will do for now."

CHAPTER FORTY-SEVEN

LACY ANSWERED the door dressed in a plaid flannel shirt that hung below her jeans. "May I help you?"

Kent stood behind Helen for the moment, his heart pounding like a locomotive in his chest. He saw Lacy's eyes shift to him, questioning at first, and then recognizing. "Hello, Lacy," Helen said. "May we come in?"

"You? Kevin, right? I met you in the restaurant. What do you want?"

Helen answered. "We are not who you might think. My name is Helen. Helen Jovic. This is my son-in-law, Kent Anthony. I believe you know each other."

Lacy's eyes grew round.

Kent stepped around Helen, steadying a tremble that had parked itself in his bones since his eyes had been opened. "Hello, Lacy."

She stepped back. "That's . . . that's impossible! Kent's dead."

"Lacy. Listen to me. It's me. Listen to my voice." He swallowed. "I know I look a bit different; I've had a few changes made, but it's me."

Lacy took another step back, blinking.

"You hear me?" Kent pushed. "I told you the whole plan on a Friday night, sitting right there," he motioned to the dinette table, "drinking your coffee. Twenty million dollars, right? Using AFPS? You slapped me."

It was too much for her to reject, he knew. She stepped aside as though in a dream. Kent took it as a sign to enter and he did so cautiously. Helen followed and sat on the sofa. Lacy closed the door and stood facing him, unblinking.

The room stilled to silence. What could he possibly say? He grinned, feeling suddenly foolish and small for coming. "So, I don't know what to say."

She did not respond.

"Lacy. I'm . . . I'm so sorry." His vision swam in fresh tears. She was searching her memory banks, trying to make ends meet, reconciling conflicting emotions. But she was not speaking. He saw her swallow and suddenly it was too much for him. *He* had caused this. *He* might have changed, but the remnants of his life lay in ruins. Gutted shells, hollow lies, broken hearts. Like this heart here, beating but broken, possibly beyond mending.

Lacy's jaw clenched, and her eyes swam in pools of tears.

Kent closed his eyes and fought his own tears. Yes, indeed, she was not so happy; that much was obvious.

Her voice came barely above a whisper. "So. It *is* you. Do you know what you've done to me?"

He opened his eyes. She was still staring at him, still clenching her jaw. But some light had come to her eyes, he thought. "Yes, it is me. And yes, I've been a complete idiot. Please . . . please forgive me."

"And you came to me at the restaurant." Her jaw relaxed.

He nodded. "Yes. I'm sorry."

"Good. You should be. You should be terrified about now."

"Yes. And I am." She was going to reject him, Kent thought. She *should* reject him.

Lacy's eyes blazed. "And why did you come? Tell me why you came."

"Because . . ." It was hard, this dealing in love. First God and now her. He blinked. No, not hard at all. Not in his new skin. Hard in his old self, but in this new skin, love was the currency of life.

He said it easily then. "Because I love you, Lacy."

The words seemed to hit her with their own physical force. A tear broke from her eye. "You love me?"

Oh, what had he done to her? "Yes. Yes, I love you," Kent said. He walked right up to her and opened his arms, desperate for her love.

She closed her eyes and let him embrace her, hesitantly at first, and then she slid her arms around his waist and pulled herself into his chest, crying. For a long time they said nothing. They held each other tightly and let their embrace speak.

When Lacy finally spoke it was in a soft, resigned voice. "And I love you, Kent. I love you too."

Chapter Forty-Eight

Present Day

PADRE CADIONE turned from the window, his face wet with tears at the tale his visitor had shared over the last two hours. They had shifted about the office, reposturing themselves as the story sped on, at times leaning against the wall, at times sitting behind the desk, but always intent. The confessor had told the story with exuberance, with many hand gestures, with tears, and often with a contagious grin splitting his face. And now the tale had ended, much to the father's dismay. But had it?

Beyond the window he could see the east guard tower, stoic against the blue sky. Cadione turned back to the man before him. His chest felt as though a vise had screwed down on his heart for the duration. The visitor sat cross-legged now, swinging one leg over the other, his hands folded on his lap.

"This is true? All of it?"

"Every word, Father."

The fan continued its swishing high above, drying the sweat gathered on Padre Cadione's neck. "You believe that God is capable of such a thing today, then?"

"I know it, Father!" The man stood to his feet and spread his hands wide. Cadione leaned back in his chair. "His love is greater than the greatest love man can imagine. The most extravagant expression of love is but a dim reflection of his own! We are made in his image, yes?"

"Yes." The padre could not help but smile with the man.

"You see, then! The greatest passion you are capable of only hints at his love."

"Yes." He nodded. "But how is it possible for a man to experience God in such a way? The experiences you speak of are . . . incredible!"

The visitor dropped his hands. "Yes, but they are real. I know."

"And how do you know?"

The light glinted off the visitor's eyes, and he smiled mischievously. "I know because I am he."

Padre Cadione did not respond immediately. He was who? The man in the story? But that was impossible! "You are *who?*"

"I am he. I am Kent Anthony."

The father's heart missed its rhythm. "Kent? Your file says your name is Kevin. Kevin Stillman."

"Yes, well, now you know the whole story, don't you? There are certain advantages to changing identities, my friend. It is the one thing they permitted me to keep when I confessed. A small consolation. And of course, I had to confess—you understand that, don't you? I *wanted* to confess. But there is no use living in the past. I am a new man. And I rather like the name."

The father's mind spun. "So then, you say that you personally glimpsed heaven? That this whole wager of Lucifer's was over your soul? You say heaven bent over backward to rescue your soul?"

"You think it is presumptuous?" the man said, smiling. "It is no less so than the challenge over your soul, Father. You just do not see it." He lifted a hand to make a point. "And I'll tell you something else. Everything is not what it seems. I knew early on that the vagrant in the alley was a man of dreams, but I did see him once, and I am not sure to this day whether he was real. But he was not an angel, I can assure you."

"You're saying he was sent from hell, then?"

"Can you think of a reason why not? Now, the others—I believe they were from heaven. I cannot be sure, of course. But the Scriptures do say that we entertain angels without knowing, do they not?"

"Others?"

"Cliff. I could find no record of him in the employment files when I looked for him at the end. And the detective. Detective Pinhead. There is no record of a Jeremy Lawson at the Seventh Precinct. I always suspected there was something with those two. Perhaps even Bono at the bar."

A knock rapped on the door.

"That seems . . ."

The man grinned wide. "Impossible? Not all things are what they seem, my friend."

"What happened to the money? To the bankers?"

"Borst and Bentley? Neither work for the bank now. I told the bank everything, of course. Last I heard they were wrapped up in court battles over the bonus money. They cannot win. And no bank will hire dishonest men. I pity them, really. As for the money, I liquidated everything and returned the money to each and every account from which it was taken, twenty cents at a time. Using ROOSTER, of course. Only the authorities and a few officials at the highest level even know what happened. The bank insisted I keep the $250,000 recovery fee. I tried to give it back, but they said I had earned it by exposing Borst and Bentley. And by developing AFPS, of course."

The rap sounded again. "Time's up, Chaplain."

"Come in," Cadione called, keeping his eyes on the man. The pieces to this puzzle locked in his mind, and he stood, frozen by them.

A uniformed guard walked through the door and stopped. "Come on. Let's go." The guard waved a night stick in Kent's direction. "Back to the cell."

The prisoner named Kevin, who was really Kent—Kent Anthony—turned to leave, still smiling at Padre Cadione.

"And what of Lacy?" Cadione asked, ignoring the guard.

Kent smiled. "I'll be up for parole in two years. If all goes well, we plan to be wed then. Maybe you could do the honors, Father."

He nodded. "Yes. And Helen?"

"Yes, Helen. You will have to meet Helen someday, Padre. She was not always the kind of woman she was in this story, you know. Her life story will make you weep. Perhaps someday when we have more time, I will tell you. It will make you see things differently. I promise."

"I would like that," the chaplain heard himself say. But his mind was spinning, and he was finding it difficult to concentrate.

The prisoner turned at the door and winked. "Remember, Father. It is true. Every last word is true. The same challenge has been cast over your soul. You should ponder that tonight before you sleep. We are all Jobs in one way or another."

They led him out, still smiling.

Padre Cadione staggered to his chair and sat hard. It had been a long time since he had prayed more than meaningless words. But that was about to change.

Everything was about to change.

When Heaven Weeps

BOOK ONE

THE PRIEST

"Christians who refuse
To look squarely into the suffering of Christ
Are not Christians at all.
They are a breed of pretenders,
Who would turn their backs on the Cross,
And shame his death.
You cannot hold up the Cross,
Nor drink of the cup
Without embracing the death.
And you cannot understand love,
Unless you first die."

The Dance of the Dead
1959

CHAPTER ONE

Atlanta, Georgia, 1964

IVENA STOOD in the small greenhouse attached to her home and frowned at the failing rosebush. The other bushes had not been affected—they flourished around her, glistening with a sprinkling of dewdrops. A bed of Darwin tulip hybrids blossomed bright red and yellow along her greenhouse's glass shell. Behind her, against the solid wall of her house, a flat of purple orchids filled the air with their sweet aroma. A dozen other species of roses grew in neat boxes, none of them infected.

But this bush had lost its leaves and shriveled in the space of five days, and that was a problem because this wasn't just another rosebush. This was Nadia's rosebush.

Ivena delicately pried through the dried thorny stems, searching for signs of disease or insects. She'd already tried a host of remedies, from pesticides to a variety of growth agents, all to no avail. It was a Serbian Red from the saxifrage family, snipped from the bush that she and Sister Flouta had planted by the cross.

When Ivena had left Bosnia for Atlanta, she'd insisted on a greenhouse; it was the one unbreakable link to her past. She made a fine little business selling the flowers to local floral shops in Atlanta, but the real purpose for the greenhouse was this one rosebush, wasn't it? Yes, she knew that as surely as she knew that blood flowed in her veins.

And now Nadia's rose was dying. Or dead.

Ivena put one hand on her hip and ran the other through her gray curls. She'd cared for a hundred species of roses over her sixty years and never, never had she seen such a thing. Each bud from Nadia's bush was priceless. If there was a graftable branch alive she would snip it off and nurse it back to health. But every branch seemed affected.

"Oh, dear Nadia, what am I going to do? What am I going to do?"

She couldn't answer herself for the simple reason that she had no clue what she would do. She had never considered the possibility that this, the crown of her flower garden, might one day die for no apparent reason at all. It was a travesty.

Ivena picked through the branches again, hoping that she was wrong. Dried dirt grayed her fingers. They weren't as young or as smooth as they once had been, but years of working delicately around thorns had kept them nimble. Graceful. She could walk her way through a rosebush blindfolded without so much as touching a thorn. But today she felt clumsy and old.

The stalk between her fingers suddenly snapped. Ivena blinked. It was as dry as tinder. How could it fail so fast? She tsked and shook her head. But then something caught her eye and she stopped.

Immediately beneath the branch that had broken, a very small shoot of green angled from the main stalk. That was odd. She lowered her head for a closer look.

The shoot grew out a mere centimeter, almost like a stalk of grass. She touched it gently, afraid to break it. And as she did she saw the tiny split in the bark along the base of that shoot.

She caught her breath. Strange! It looked like a small graft!

But she hadn't grafted anything into the plant, had she? No, of course not. She remembered every step of care she'd given this plant over the last five years and none of them included a graft.

It looked like someone had slit the base of the rosebush open and grafted in this green shoot. And it didn't look like a rose graft either. The stalk was a lighter green. So then maybe it wasn't a graft. Maybe it was a parasite of some kind.

Ivena let her breath out slowly and touched it again. It was already healed at the insertion point.

"Hmmm."

She straightened and walked to the round table where a white porcelain cup still steamed with tea. She lifted it to her lips. The rich aroma of spice warmed her nostrils and she paused, staring through the wisps of steam.

From this distance of ten feet Nadia's rosebush looked like Moses's burning bush, but consumed by the flame and burned black. Dead branches reached up from the soil like claws from a grave. Dead.

Except for that one tiny shoot of green at its base.

It was very strange indeed.

Ivena lowered herself into the old wood-spindle chair beside the table, still looking over the teacup to the rosebush. She sat here every morning, humming and sipping her tea and whispering her words to the Father. But today the sight before her was turning things on their heads.

She lowered the cup without drinking. "Father, what are you doing here?" she said softly.

Not that he was necessarily doing anything. Rosebushes died, after all. Perhaps with less encouragement than other plants. But an air of consequence had settled on Ivena, and she couldn't ignore it.

Across the beds of flourishing flowers before her sat this one dead bush—an ugly black scar on a landscape of bright color. But then from the blackened stalk that impossible graft.

"What are you saying here, Father?"

She did not hear his answer, but that didn't mean he wasn't talking. He could be yelling for all she knew. Here on Earth it might come through as a distant whisper, easily mistaken for the sound of a gentle breeze. Actually the greenhouse was dead silent. She more felt something, and it could just as easily have been a draft that tickled her hair, or a finger of emotion from the past, as the voice of God.

Still the scene before her began to massage her heart with fingers of meaning. She just didn't know what that meaning was yet.

Ivena hummed and a blanket of peace settled over her. She whispered, "Lover of my soul, I worship you. I kiss your feet. Don't ever let me forget." Her words echoed softly through the quiet greenhouse, and she smiled. *The Creator was a mischievous one,* she often thought. At least playful and easily delighted. And he was up to something, wasn't he?

A splash of red at her elbow caught her eye. It was her copy of the book. *The Dance of the Dead.* Its surreal cover showed a man's face wide open with laughter, tears leaking down his cheek.

Still smiling, Ivena set down her teacup and lifted the book from the table. She ran a hand over the tattered cover. She'd read it a hundred times, of course. But it never lost its edge. Its pages oozed with love and laughter and the heart of the Creator.

She opened the book and brushed through a few dozen dog-eared pages. He had written a masterpiece, and in some ways it was as much God's words as his. She could begin in the middle or at the beginning or the end and it wouldn't hardly matter. The meaning would not be lost. She opened to the middle and read a few sentences.

It was odd how such a story could bring this warmth to her heart. But it did, it really did, and that was because her eyes had been opened a little as well. She'd seen a few things through God's eyes.

Ivena glanced up at the dying rosebush with its impossible graft. Something new was beginning today. But everything had really started with the story in her hands, hadn't it?

A small spark of delight ran through her bones. She smoothed her dress, crossed her legs and lowered her eyes to the page.

Yes, this was how it all started.

Twenty years ago in Bosnia. At the end of the war with the Nazis.

She read.

THE SOLDIERS stood unmoving on the hill's crest, leaning on battered rifles, five dark silhouettes against a white Bosnian sky, like a row of trees razed by the war. They stared down at the small village, oblivious to the sweat caked beneath their tattered army fatigues, unaware of the dirt streaking down their faces like long black claws.

Their condition wasn't unique. Any soldier who managed to survive the brutal fighting that ravaged Yugoslavia during its liberation from the Nazis looked the same. Or worse. A severed arm perhaps. Or bloody stumps below the waist. The country was strewn with dying wounded—testaments to Bosnia's routing of the enemy.

But the scene in the valley below them was unique. The village appeared untouched by the war. If a shell had landed anywhere near it during the years of bitter conflict, there was no sign of it now.

Several dozen homes with steep cedar-shake roofs and white chimney smoke clustered neatly around the village center. Cobblestone paths ran like spokes between the homes and the large structure at the hub. There, with a sprawling courtyard, stood an ancient church with a belfry that reached to the sky like a finger pointing the way to God.

"What's the name of this village?" Karadzic asked no one in particular.

Janjic broke his stare on the village and looked at his commander. The man's lips had bent into a frown. He glanced at the others, who were still captivated by this postcard-perfect scene below.

"I don't know," Molosov said to Janjic's right. "We're less than fifty clicks from Sarajevo. I grew up in Sarajevo."

"And what is your point?"

"My point is that I grew up in Sarajevo and I don't remember this village."

Karadzic was a tall man, six foot two at least, and boxy above the waist. His bulky torso rested on spindly legs, like a bulldog born on stilts. His face was square and leathery, pitted by a collage of small scars, each marking another chapter in a violent past. Glassy gray eyes peered past thick bushy eyebrows.

Janjic shifted on his feet and looked up valley. What was left of the Partisan army waited a hard day's march north. But no one seemed eager to move. A bird's caw drifted through the air, followed by another. Two ravens circled lazily over the village.

"I don't remember seeing a church like this before. It looks wrong to me," Karadzic said.

A small tingle ran up Janjic's spine. Wrong? "We have a long march ahead of us, sir. We could make the regiment by nightfall if we leave now."

Karadzic ignored him entirely. "Puzup, have you seen an Orthodox church like this?"

Puzup blew smoke from his nose and drew deep on his cigarette. "No, I guess I haven't."

"Molosov?"

"It's standing, if that's what you mean." He grinned. "It's been a while since I've seen a church standing. Doesn't look Orthodox."

"If it isn't Orthodox, then what is it?"

"Not Jewish," Puzup said. "Isn't that right, Paul?"

"Not unless Jews have started putting crosses on their temples in my absence."

Puzup cackled in a high pitch, finding humor where apparently no one else did. Molosov reached over and slapped the younger soldier on the back of his head. Puzup's laugh stuck in his throat and he grunted in protest. No one paid them any mind. Puzup clamped his lips around his cigarette. The tobacco crackled quietly in the stillness. The man absently picked at a bleeding scab on his right forearm.

Janjic spit to the side, anxious to rejoin the main army. "If we keep to the ridges we should be able to maintain high ground and still meet the column by dark."

"It appears deserted," Molosov said, as if he had not heard Janjic.

"There's smoke. And there's a group in the courtyard," Paul said.

"Of course there's smoke. I'm not talking about smoke, I'm talking about people. You can't see if there's a group in the courtyard. We're two miles out."

"Look for movement. If you look—"

"Shut up," Karadzic snapped. "It's Franciscan." He shifted his Kalashnikov from one set of thick, gnarled fingers to the other.

A fleck of spittle rested on the commander's lower lip and he made no attempt to remove it. *Karadzic wouldn't know the difference between a Franciscan monastery and an Orthodox church if they stood side by side,* Janjic thought. But that was beside the point. They all knew about Karadzic's hatred for the Franciscans.

"Our orders are to reach the column as soon as possible," Janjic said. "Not to scour the few standing churches for monks cowering in the corner. We have a war to finish, and it's not against them." He turned to view the town, surprised by his own insolence. *It is the war. I've lost my sensibilities.*

Smoke still rose from a dozen random chimneys; the ravens still circled. An eerie quiet hovered over the morning. He could feel the commander's gaze on his face—more than one man had died for less.

Molosov glanced at Janjic and then spoke softly to Karadzic. "Sir, Janjic is right—"

"Shut up! We're going down." Karadzic hefted his rifle and snatched it from the air cleanly. He faced Janjic. "We don't enlist women in this war, but you, Janjic, you are like a woman." He headed downhill.

One by one the soldiers stepped from the crest and strode for the peaceful village below. Janjic brought up the rear, swallowing uneasiness. He had pushed it too far with the commander.

High above the two ravens cawed again. It was the only sound besides the crunching of their boots.

FATHER MICHAEL saw the soldiers when they entered the cemetery at the edge of the village. Their small shapes emerged out of the green meadow like a row of tattered scarecrows. He pulled up at the top of the church's hewn stone steps, and a chill crept down his spine. For a moment the children's laughter about him waned.

Dear God, protect us. He prayed as he had a hundred times before, but he couldn't stop the tremors that took to his fingers.

The smell of hot baked bread wafted through his nostrils. A shrill giggle echoed through the courtyard; water gurgled from the natural spring to his left. Father Michael stood, stooped, and looked past the courtyard in which the children and women celebrated Nadia's birthday, past the tall stone cross that marked the entrance to the graveyard, past the red rosebushes Claudis Flouta had so carefully planted about her home, to the lush hillside on the south.

To the four—no five—to the five soldiers approaching.

He glanced around the courtyard—they laughed and played. None of the others had seen the soldiers yet. High above ravens cawed and Michael looked up to see four of them circling.

Father, protect your children. A flutter of wings to his right caught his attention. He turned and watched a white dove settle for a landing on the vestibule's roof. The bird cocked its head and eyed him in small jerky movements.

"Father Michael?" a child's voice said.

Michael turned to face Nadia, the birthday girl. She wore a pink dress reserved for special occasions. Her lips and nose were wide and she had blotchy freckles on both cheeks. A homely girl even with the pretty pink dress. Some might even say ugly. Her mother, Ivena, was quite pretty; the coarse looks were from her father.

To make matters worse for the poor child, her left leg was two inches shorter than her right thanks to polio—a bad case when she was only three. Perhaps their handicaps united her with Michael in ways the others could not understand. She with her short leg; he with his hunched back.

Yet Nadia carried herself with a courage that defied her lack of physical beauty. At times Michael felt terribly sorry for the child, if for no other reason than that she didn't realize how her ugliness might handicap her in life. At other times his heart swelled with pride for her, for the way her love and joy shone with a brilliance that washed her skin clean of the slightest blemish.

He suppressed the urge to sweep her off her feet and swing her around in his arms. *Come unto me as little children,* the Master had said. If only the whole world were filled with the innocence of children.

"Yes?"

NADIA LOOKED into Father Michael's eyes and saw the flash of pity before he spoke. It was more of a question than a statement, that look of his. More "are you sure you're okay?" than "you look so lovely in your new dress."

None of them knew how well she could read their thoughts, perhaps because she'd long ago accepted the pity as a part of her life. Still, the realization that she limped and looked a bit plainer than most girls, regardless of what Mother told her, gnawed gently at her consciousness most of the time.

"Petrus says that since I'm thirteen now all the boys will want to marry me. I told him that he's being a foolish boy, but he insists on running around making a silly game of it. Could you please tell him to stop?"

Petrus ran up, sneering. If any of the town's forty-three children was a bully, it was this ten-year-old know-nothing brat. Oh, he had his sweet side, Mother assured her. And Father Michael repeatedly said as much to the boy's mother, who was known to run about the village with her apron flying, leaving puffs of flour in her wake, shaking her rolling pin while calling for the runt to get his little rear end home.

"Nadia loves Milus! Nadia love Milus!" Petrus chanted and skipped by, looking back, daring her to take up chase.

"You're a misguided fledgling, Petrus," Nadia said, crossing her arms. "A silly little bird, squawking too much. Why don't you find your worms somewhere else?"

Petrus pulled up, flushing red. "Oh, you with all your fancy words! You're the one eating worms. With Milus. Nadia and Milus sitting in a tree, eating all the worms they can see!" He sang the verse again and ran off with a *whoop*, obviously delighted with his victory.

Nadia placed her hands on her hips and tapped the foot of her shorter leg with a disgusted sigh. "You see. Please stop him, Father."

"Of course, darling. But you know that he's just playing." Father Michael smiled and took a seat on the top step.

He looked over the courtyard and Nadia followed his gaze. Of the village's seventy or so people, all but ten or twelve had come today for her birthday. Only the men were missing, called off to fight the Nazis. The old people sat in groups around the stone tables, grinning and chatting as they watched the children play a party game of balancing boiled eggs on spoons as they raced in a circle.

Nadia's mother, Ivena, directed the children with flapping hands, straining to be heard over their cries of delight. Three of the mothers busied themselves over a long table on which they had arranged pastries and the cake Ivena had fretted over for two days. It was perhaps the grandest cake Nadia had ever seen, a foot high, white with pink roses made from frosting.

All for her. All to cover up whatever pity they had for her and make her feel special.

Father Michael's gaze moved past the courtyard. Nadia looked up and saw a small band of soldiers approaching. The sight made her heart stop for a moment.

"Come here, Nadia."

Father Michael lifted an arm for her to sit by him, and she limped up the steps. She sat beside him and he pulled her close.

He seemed nervous. The soldiers.

She put her arm around him, rubbing his humped back.

Father Michael swallowed and kissed the top of her head. "Don't mind Petrus. But he is right, one day the men will line up to marry such a pretty girl as you."

She ignored the comment and looked back at the soldiers who were now in the graveyard not a hundred yards off. They were Partisans, she saw with some relief. Partisans were probably friendly.

High above birds cawed. Again Nadia followed the father's gaze as he looked up. Five ravens circled against the white sky. Michael looked to his right, to the vestibule roof. Nadia saw the lone dove staring on, clucking with its one eye peeled to the courtyard.

Father Michael looked back at the soldiers. "Nadia, go tell your mother to come."

Nadia hoped the soldiers wouldn't spoil her birthday party.

JANJIC JOVIC, the nineteen-year-old writer-turned-soldier, followed the others into the village, trudging with the same rhythmic cadence his marching had kept in the endless months leading up to this day. Just one foot after another. Ahead and to the right, Karadzic marched deliberately. The other three fanned out to his left.

Karadzic's war had less to do with defeating the Nazis than with restoring Serbia, and that included purging the land of anyone who wasn't a good Serb. Especially Franciscans.

Or so he said. They all knew that Karadzic killed good Serbs as easily as Franciscans. His own mother, for example, with a knife, he'd bragged, never mind that she was Serbian to the marrow. Though sure of few things, Janjic was certain the commander wasn't beyond trying to kill him one day. Janjic was a philosopher, a writer—not a killer—and the denser man despised him for it. He determined to follow Karadzic obediently regardless of the elder's folly; anything less could cost dearly.

Only when they were within a stone's throw of the village did Janjic study the scene with a careful eye. They approached from the south, through a graveyard holding fifty or sixty concrete crosses. So few graves. In most villages throughout Bosnia one could expect to find hundreds if not thousands of fresh graves, pushing into lots never intended for the dead. They were evidence of a war gone mad.

But in this village, hidden here in this lush green valley, he counted fewer than ten plots that looked recent.

He studied the neat rows of houses—fewer than fifty—also unmarked by the war. The tall church spire rose high above the houses, adorned with a white cross, brilliant against the dull sky. The rest of the structure was cut from gray stone and elegantly carved like most churches. Small castles made for God.

None in the squad cared much for God—not even the Jew, Paul. But in Bosnia, religion had little to do with God. It had to do with who was right and who was wrong, not with who loved God. If you weren't Orthodox or at least a good Serb, you weren't right. If you were a Christian but not an Orthodox Christian, you weren't right. If you were Franciscan, you were most certainly not right. Janjic wasn't sure he disagreed with Karadzic on this point—religious affiliation was more a defining line of this war than the Nazi occupation.

The Ustashe, Yugoslavia's version of the German Gestapo, had murdered hundreds of thousands of Serbs using techniques that horrified even the Nazis. Worse, they'd done it with the blessing of both the Catholic Archbishop of Sarajevo and the Franciscans, neither of whom evidently understood the love of God. But then, *no* one in this war knew much about the love of God. It was a war absent of God, if indeed there even was such a being.

A child ran past the walls that surrounded the courtyard, out toward the tall cross, not fifty feet from them now. A boy, dressed in a white shirt and black shorts, with suspenders and a bow tie. The child slid to a halt, eyes popping.

Janjic smiled at the sight. The smell of hot bread filled his nostrils.

"Petrus! You come back here!"

A woman, presumably the boy's mother, ran for the boy, grabbed his arm and yanked him back toward the churchyard. He struggled free and began marching in imitation of a soldier. *One, two! One, two!*

"Stop it, Petrus!" His mother caught his shirt and pulled him toward the courtyard.

Karadzic ignored the boy and kept his glassy gray eyes fixed ahead. Janjic was the last to enter the courtyard, following the others' clomping boots. Karadzic halted and they pulled up behind him.

A priest stood on the ancient church steps, dressed in flowing black robes. Dark hair fell to his shoulders, and a beard extended several inches past his chin. He stood with a hunch in his shoulders.

A hunchback.

To his left, a flock of children sat on the steps with their mothers who held them, some smoothing their children's hair or stroking their cheeks. Smiling. All of them seemed to be smiling.

In all, sixty or seventy pairs of eyes stared at them.

"Welcome to Vares," the priest said, bowing politely.

They had interrupted a party of some kind. The children were mostly dressed in ties and dresses. A long table adorned with pastries and a cake sat untouched. The sight was surreal—a celebration of life in this countryside of death.

"What church is this?" Karadzic asked.

"Anglican," the priest said.

Karadzic glanced at his men, then faced the church. "I've never heard of this church."

A homely looking girl in a pink dress suddenly stood from her mother's arms and walked awkwardly toward the table adorned with pastries. She hobbled.

Karadzic ignored her and twisted his fingers around the barrel of his rifle, tapping its butt on the stone. "Why is this church still standing?"

No one answered. Janjic watched the little girl place a golden brown pastry on a napkin.

"You can't speak?" Karadzic demanded. "Every church for a hundred kilometers is burned to the ground, but yours is untouched. And it makes me think that maybe you've been sleeping with the Ustashe."

"God has granted us favor," the priest said.

The commander paused. His lips twitched to a slight grin. A bead of sweat broke from the large man's forehead and ran down his flat cheek. "God has granted you favor? He's flown out of the sky and built an invisible shield over this valley to keep the bullets out, is that it?" His lips flattened. "God has allowed every Orthodox church in Yugoslavia to burn to the ground. And yet yours is standing."

Janjic watched the child limp toward a spring that gurgled in the corner and dip a mug into its waters. No one seemed to pay her attention except the woman on the steps whom she had left, probably her mother.

Paul spoke quietly. "They're Anglican, not Franciscans or Catholics. I know Anglicans. Good Serbs."

"What does a Jew know about good Serbs?"

"I'm only telling you what I've heard," Paul said with a shrug.

The girl in the pink dress approached, carrying the mug of cold water in one hand and the pastry in the other. She stopped three feet from Karadzic and lifted the food to him. None of the villagers moved.

Karadzic ignored her. "And if your God is my God, why doesn't he protect my church? The Orthodox church?"

The priest smiled gently, still staring without blinking, hunched over on the steps.

"I'm asking you a question, Priest," Karadzic said.

"I can't speak for God," the priest said. "Perhaps you should ask him. We're God-loving people with no quarrel. But I cannot speak for God on all matters."

The small girl lifted the pastry and water higher. Karadzic's eyes took on that menacing stare Janjic had seen so many times before.

Janjic moved on impulse. He stepped up to the girl and smiled. "You're very kind," he said. "Only a good Serb would offer bread and water to a tired and hungry Partisan soldier." He reached for the pastry and took it. "Thank you."

A dozen children scrambled from the stairs and ran to the table, arguing about who was to be first. They quickly gathered up food to follow the young girl's example and then rushed for the soldiers, pastries in hand. Janjic was struck by their innocence. This was just another game to them. The sudden turn in events had effectively silenced Karadzic, but Janjic couldn't look at the commander. If Molosov and the others didn't follow his cue there would be a price to pay later—this he knew with certainty.

"My name's Nadia," the young girl said, looking up at Janjic. "It's my birthday today. I'm thirteen years old."

Ordinarily Janjic would have answered the girl—told her what a brave thirteen-year-old she was, but today his mind was on his comrades. Several children now swarmed around Paul and Puzup, and Janjic saw with relief that they were accepting the pastries. With smiles in fact.

"We could use the food, sir," Molosov said.

Karadzic snatched up his hand to silence the second in command. Nadia held the cup in her hand toward him. Once again every eye turned to the commander, begging him to show some mercy. Karadzic suddenly scowled and slapped the cup aside. It clattered to the stone in a shower of water. The children froze.

Karadzic brushed angrily past Nadia. She backpedaled and fell to her bottom. The commander stormed over to the birthday table, and kicked his boot against the leading edge. The entire birthday display rose into the air and crashed onto the ground.

Nadia scrambled to her feet and limped for her mother, who drew her in. The other children scampered for the steps.

Karadzic turned to them, face red. "Now do I have your attention?"

CHAPTER TWO

IVENA PAUSED her reading and swallowed at the memory. *Dear Father, give me strength.*

She could hear the commander's voice as though he were here in the greenhouse today. She suddenly pursed her lips angrily, mimicking him. "Now do I have your attention?" Ivena relaxed her face and closed her eyes. Now do I have your attention? Well we have yours now, don't we, Mr. Big Shot Commander?

For years she'd told herself that they should have told the children to leave them then. To run back to the houses. But they hadn't. And in the end she knew there was a reason for that.

Behind her the clock ticked away on the wall, one click for every jerk of the second hand. Other than her breathing, no other sound broke the stillness. Reliving that day was not always the most pleasant thing, but always it brought her an uncanny strength and a deep-seated peace. And more important, not to remember—indeed not to participate again and again—would make a mockery of it. *Take this in remembrance of me,* Christ had said. *Participate in the suffering of Christ,* Paul had said.

And yet Americans turned forgetting into a kind of spiritual badge, refusing to look at suffering for fear they might catch it like a disease. They turned the death of Christ into soft fuzzy Sunday-school pictures and refused to let those pictures get off the page and walk bloody into their minds. They stripped Christ of his dignity by ignoring the brutality of his death. It was no different from turning away from a puffy-faced leper in horror. The epitome of rejection.

Some would even close the book here in a huff and return to their knitting. Perhaps they would knit nice soft images of a cross.

It occurred to her that every muscle in her body had tensed.

She relaxed and chuckled. "What are you, the messiah for America, Ivena?" she mumbled. "You speak of Christ's love; where is yours?"

Ivena shook her head and opened the pages again.

"Give me grace, Father."

She read again.

"NOW DO I have your attention?"

Father Michael's heart seemed to stick midstroke. He mumbled his prayer now, loud enough for the women nearest him to hear.

"Protect your children, Father."

The leader was possessed of the devil. Michael had known so from the moment the big man had entered the courtyard. *Yea, though I walk through the valley of the shadow of death, I will fear no evil.*

He barely heard the flutter of wings to his right. The dove had taken flight. The commander glared at him. *Now do I have your attention?*

The dove's wings beat through the air. *Yes, you have my attention, commander. You had my attention before you began this insanity.* But he did not say it because the dove had stopped above him and was flapping noisily. The commander's eyes rose to the bird. Michael leaned back to compensate for his humped back and looked up.

In that moment the world fell to a silent slow motion.

Michael could see the commander standing, legs spread. Above him, the white dove swept gracefully at the air, fanning a slight wind to him, like an angel breathing five feet over his head.

The breath moved through his hair, through his beard, cool at first and then suddenly warm. High above the dove, a hole appeared in the clouds, allowing the sun to send its rays of warmth. Michael could see that the ravens still circled, more of them now—seven or eight.

This he saw in that first glance, as the world slowed to a crawl. Then he felt the music on the wind. At least that was how he thought of it, because the music didn't sound in his ears, but in his mind and in his chest.

Though only a few notes, they spread an uncanny warmth. A whisper that seemed to say, "My beloved."

Just that. Just, *My beloved.* The warmth suddenly rushed through him like water, past his loins, right down to the soles of his feet.

Father Michael gasped.

The dove took flight.

A chill of delight rippled up his back. Goodness! Nothing even remotely similar had happened to him in all of his years. *My beloved.* Like the anointing of Jesus at his baptism. *This is my beloved Son, in whom I am well pleased.*

He'd always taught that Christ's power was as real for the believer today as it was two thousand years earlier.

Now Michael had heard these words of love. *My beloved!* God was going to protect them.

It occurred to him that he was still bent back awkwardly and that his mouth had fallen open, like a man who'd been shot. He clamped it shut and jerked forward.

The rest hadn't heard the voice. Their eyes were on him, not on the dove, which had landed on the nearest roof—Sister Flauta's house surrounded by those red rosebushes. The flowers' scent reached up into his sinuses, thick and sweet. Which was odd. He should be fighting a panic just now, terrified of these men with guns. Instead his mind was taking time to smell Sister Flauta's rosebushes. And pausing to hear the watery gurgle of the spring to his left.

A dumb grin lifted the corners of his mouth. He knew it was dumb because he had no business facing this monster before him wearing a snappy little grin. But he could hardly control it, and he quickly lifted a hand to cover his mouth. The gesture must look like a child hiding a giggle. It would infuriate the man.

And so it did.

"Wipe that idiotic grin off your face!"

The commander strode toward him. Except for the ravens cawing overhead and the spring's insistent gurgle, Father Michael could only hear his own heart, pounding like a boot against a hollow drum. His head still buzzed from the dove's words, but another thought slowly took form in his mind. It was the realization that he'd heard the music for a reason. It wasn't every day, or even every year, that heaven reached down so deliberately to man.

Karadzic stopped and glared at the women and children. "So. You claim to be people of faith?"

He asked as if he expected an answer. Ivena looked at Father Michael.

"Are you all mutes?" Karadzic demanded, red-faced.

Still no one spoke.

Karadzic planted his legs wide. "No. I don't think you *are* people of faith. I think that your God has abandoned you, perhaps when you and your murdering priests burned the Orthodox church in Glina after stuffing a thousand women and children into it."

Karadzic's lips twisted around the words. "Perhaps the smell of their charred bodies rose to the heavens and sent your God to hell."

"It was a horrible massacre," Father Michael heard himself say. "But it wasn't us, my friend. We abhor the brutality of the Ustashe. No God-fearing man could possibly take the life of another with such cruelty."

"I shot a man in the knees just a week ago before killing him. It was quite brutal. Are you saying that *I* am not a God-fearing man?"

"I believe that God loves all men, Commander. Me no more than you."

"Shut up! You sit back in your fancy church singing pretty songs of love, while your men roam the countryside, seeking a Serb to cut open."

"If you were to search the battlefields, you would find our men stitching up the wounds of soldiers, not killing them."

Karadzic squinted briefly at the claim. For a moment he just stared. He suddenly smiled, but it wasn't a kind smile.

"Then surely true faith can be proven." He spun to one of the soldiers. "Molosov, bring me one of the crosses from the graveyard."

The soldier looked at his commander with a raised brow.

"Are you deaf? Bring me a gravestone."

"They're in the ground, sir."

"Then pull it *out* of the ground!"

"Yes, sir." Molosov jogged across the courtyard and into the adjacent cemetery.

Father Michael watched the soldier kick at the nearest headstone, a cross like all the others, two feet in height, made of concrete. He knew the name of the deceased well. It was old man Haris Zecavic, planted in the ground more than twenty years ago.

"What's the teaching of your Christ?"

Michael looked back at Karadzic, who still wore a twisted grin.

"Hmm? Carry your cross?" Karadzic said. "Isn't that what your God commanded you to do? 'Pick up your cross and follow me'?"

"Yes."

Molosov hauled the cross he'd freed into the courtyard. The villagers watched, stunned.

Karadzic gestured at them with his rifle. "Exactly. As you see, I'm not as stupid in matters of faith as you think. My own mother was a devout Christian. Then again, she was also a whore, which is why I know that not all Christians are necessarily right in the head."

The soldier dropped the stone at Karadzic's feet. It landed with a loud *thunk* and toppled flat. One of the women made a squeaking sound—Marie Zecavic, the old man's thirty-year-old daughter, mourning the destruction of her father's grave, possibly. The commander glanced at Marie.

"We're in luck today," Karadzic said, keeping his eyes on Marie. "Today we actually have a cross for you to bear. We will give you an opportunity to prove your faith. Come here."

Marie had a knuckle in her mouth, biting off her cry. She looked up with fear-fired eyes.

"Yes, you. Come here, please."

Father Michael took a step toward the commander. "Please—"

"Stay!"

Michael stopped. Fingers of dread tickled his spine. He nodded and tried to smile with warmth.

Marie stepped hesitantly toward the commander.

"Put the cross on her back," Karadzic said.

Father Michael stepped forward, instinctively raising his right hand in protest.

Karadzic whirled to him, lips twisted. "Stay!" His voice thundered across the courtyard.

Molosov bent for the cross, which could not weigh less than thirty kilos. Marie's face wrinkled in fear. Tears streaked silently down her cheeks.

Karadzic sneered. "Don't cry, child. You're simply going to carry a cross for your Christ. It's a noble thing, isn't it?"

He nodded and his man hoisted the gravestone to Marie's back. Her body began to tremble and Michael felt his heart expand.

"Don't just stand there, woman, hold it!" Karadzic snapped.

Marie leaned tentatively forward and reached back for the stone. Molosov released his grip. Her back sagged momentarily, and she staggered forward with one foot before steadying herself.

"Good. You see, it's not so bad." Karadzic stood back, pleased with himself. He turned to Father Michael. "Not so bad at all. But I tell you, Priest—if she drops the cross then we will have a problem."

Michael's heart accelerated. Heat surged up his neck and flared around his ears. *Oh, God, give us strength!*

"Yes, of course. If she drops the cross it will mean that you are an impostor, and that your church is unholy. We will be forced to remove some of your skin with a beating." The commander's twisted smile broadened.

Father Michael looked at Marie and tried to still his thumping heart. He nodded, mustering reserves of courage. "Don't be afraid, Marie. God's love will save us."

Karadzic stepped forward and swung his hand. A loud crack echoed from the walls, and Michael's head snapped back. The blow brought stinging tears to his eyes and blood to his mouth. He looked up at Sister Flouta's roof; the dove still perched on the peak, tilting its head to view the scene below. *Peace, my son.* Had he really heard that music? Yes. Yes, he had. God had actually spoken to him. God would protect them.

Father, spare us. I beg you, spare us!

"March, woman!" Karadzic pointed toward the far end of the courtyard. Marie stepped forward. The children looked on with bulging eyes. Stifled cries rippled through the courtyard.

They watched her heave the burden across the concrete, her feet straining with bulging veins at each footfall. Marie wasn't the strongest of them. Oh, God, why couldn't it have been another—Ivena or even one of the older boys. But Marie? She would stumble at any moment!

Michael could not hold his tongue. "Why do you test her? It's me—"

Smack!

The hand landed flat and hard enough to send him reeling back a step this time. A balloon of pain spread from his right cheek.

"Next time it'll be the stock of a rifle," the commander said.

Marie reached the far wall and turned back. She staggered by, searching Father Michael's eyes for help. Everyone watched her quietly, first one way and then the other, bent under the load, eyes darting in fear, slogging back and forth. Most of the soldiers seemed amused. They had undoubtedly seen atrocities that made this seem like a game in comparison. *Go on, prove your faith in Christ. Follow his teaching. Carry this cross. And if you drop it before we tire of watching, we will beat your priest to a bloody pulp.*

Michael prayed. *Father, I beg you. I truly beg you to spare us. I beg you!*

Chapter Three

IT WAS Nadia who refused to stay silent.

The homely birthday girl with her pigtails and her yellow hair clips stood, limped down the steps, and faced the soldiers, arms dangling by her side. Father Michael swallowed. *Father, please!* He could not speak it, but his heart cried it out. *Please, Father!*

"Nadia!" Ivena whispered harshly.

But Nadia didn't even look her mother's way. Her voice carried across the courtyard clear and soft and sweet. "Father Michael has told us that people filled with Christ's love do not hurt other people. Why are you hurting Marie? She's done nothing wrong."

In that moment Father Michael wished he had not taught them so well.

Karadzic looked at her, his gray eyes wide, his mouth slightly agape, obviously stunned.

"Nadia!" Ivena called out in a hushed cry. "Sit down!"

"Shut up!" Karadzic came to life. He stormed toward the girl, livid and red. "Shut up, shut up!" He shook his rifle at her. "Sit down, you ugly little runt!"

Nadia sat.

Karadzic stalked back and forth before the steps, his knuckles white on his gun, his lips flecked with spittle.

"You feel bad for your pitiful Marie, is that it? Because she's carrying this tiny cross on her back?"

He stopped in front of a group of three women huddling on the stairs and leaned toward them. "What is happening to Marie is nothing! Say it! Nothing!"

No one spoke.

Karadzic suddenly flipped his rifle to his shoulder and peered down its barrel at Sister Flouta. "Say it!"

A hard knot lodged in Father Michael's throat. His vision blurred with tears. God, this could not be happening! They were a peaceful, loving people who served a risen God. *Father, do not abandon us! Do not! Do not!*

The commander cocked the rifled to the sky with his right hand. His lips pressed white. "To the graveyard then! All of you! All the women."

They only stared at him, unbelieving.

He shoved a thick, dirty finger toward the large cross at the cemetery's entrance and fired into the air. "Go!"

They went. Like a flock of geese, pattering down the steps and across the courtyard, some whimpering, others setting their jaws firm. Marie kept slogging across the stone yard. She was slowing, Michael thought.

The commander turned to his men. "Load a cross on every woman and bring them back."

The thin soldier with bright hazel eyes stepped forward in protest. "Sir—"

"Shut up!"

The soldiers jogged for the graveyard. Father Michael's vision swam. *Father, you are abandoning us! They are playing with your children!*

Several children moved close to him, tugging at his robe, embracing his leg. Blurred forms in uniform kicked at the headstone crosses and hoisted them to the backs of the women. They staggered back to the courtyard, bearing their heavy loads. It was impossible!

Father Michael watched his flock reduced to animals, bending under the weight of concrete crosses. He clenched his teeth. These were women, like Mary and Martha, with tender hearts full of love. Sweet, sweet women, who'd toiled in childbirth and nursed their babies through cold winters. He should rush the commander and smash his head against the rock! He should protect his sheep!

Michael saw the dove in his peripheral vision clucking on the roofline, stepping from one foot to the other. The comforting words seemed distant now, so very abstract. *Peace, my son.* But this was not peace! This was barbarism!

The twisted smile found Karadzic's quivering lips again. "March," he ordered. "March, you pathetic slugs! We'll see how you like Christ's cross. And the first one to drop the cross will be beaten with the Father!"

They walked with Marie, twenty-three of them, bowed under their loads, silent except for heavy breathing and padding feet, staggering.

Every bone in Michael's body screamed in protest now. *Stop this! Stop this immediately! It's insanity! Take me, you spineless cowards! I will carry their crosses. I will carry all of their crosses. You may bury me under their crosses if you wish, but leave these dear women alone! For the love of God!* His whole body trembled as the words rushed through his head.

But they did not reach his lips. They could not because his throat had seized shut in anguish. And either way, the insane commander might very well take the butt of his gun to one of them if he spoke.

A child whimpered at Michael's knee. He bit his lower lip, closed his eyes, and rested a hand on the boy's head. *Father, please.* His bones shook with the inward groan. Tears spilled down his cheeks now, and he felt one land on his hand, wet and warm. His humped shoulders begged to shake—to sob—to cry out for relief, but he refused to disintegrate before all of them. He was their shepherd, for heaven's sake! He was not one of the women or one of the children, he was a man. God's chosen vessel for this little village in a land savaged by war.

He breathed deep and closed his eyes. *Dearest Jesus . . . My dearest Jesus . . .*

The world changed then, for the second time that day. A brilliant flash ignited in his mind, as if someone had taken a picture with one of those bulbs that popped and burned out. Father Michael's body jerked and he snapped his eyes open. He might have gasped—he wasn't sure because this world with all of its soldiers and trudging women was too distant to judge accurately.

In its place stretched a white horizon, flooded with streaming light.

And music.

Faint, but clear. Long, pure notes, the same as he'd heard earlier. *My beloved.* A song of love.

Michael shifted his gaze to the horizon and squinted. The landscape was endless and flat like a sprawling desert, but covered with white flowers. The light streamed several hundred feet above the ground toward him from the distant horizon.

A tiny wedge of alarm struck Michael. He was alone in this white field. Except for the light, of course. The light and the music.

He could suddenly hear more in the music. At first he thought it might be the spring, bubbling near the courtyard. But it wasn't water. It was a sound made by a child. It was a child's laughter, distant, but rushing toward him from that far horizon, carried on the swelling notes of music.

Gooseflesh rippled over Michael's skin. He suddenly felt as thought he might be floating, swept off his feet by a deep note that resounded in his bones.

The music grew, and with it the children's laughter. High peals of laughter and giggles, not from one child, but from a hundred children. Maybe a thousand children, or a million, swirling around him now from every direction. Laughter of delight, as though from a small boy being mercilessly tickled by his father. Then reprieves followed by sighs of contentment as others took up the laughing.

Michael could not help the giggle that bubbled in his own chest and slipped out in short bursts. The sound was thoroughly intoxicating. But where were the children?

A single melody reached through the music. A man's voice, pure and clear, with the power to melt whatever it touched. Michael stared out at the field where the sound came from.

A man was walking his way, a shimmering figure, still only an inch tall on the horizon. The voice was his. He hummed a simple melody, but it flowed over Michael with intoxicating power. The melody started low and rose through the scale and then paused. Immediately the children's laughter swelled, responding directly to the man's song. He began again, and the giggles quieted a little and then swelled at the end of this simple refrain. It was like a game.

Michael couldn't hold back his own laughter. *Oh, my God, what is happening to me? I'm losing my mind.* Who was this minstrel walking toward him? And what kind of song was this that made him want to fly with all those children he could not see?

Michael lifted his head and searched the skies. Come out, come out wherever you are, my children. Were they his children? He had no children.

But now he craved them. *These* children, laughing hysterically around him. He wanted these children—to hold them, to kiss them, to run his fingers through their hair and roll on the ground, laughing with them. To sing this song to them. Come out, my dear . . .

The flashbulb ignited again. *Pop!*

The laughter evaporated. The song was gone.

It took only a moment for Father Michael to register the simple, undeniable fact that he was once again standing on the steps of his church, facing a courtyard filled with women who slumped under heavy crosses over cold, flat concrete. His mouth lay open, and he seemed to have forgotten how to use the muscles in his jaw.

The soldiers stood against the far wall, smirking at the women, except for the tall skinny man. He seemed awkward in his role. The commander looked on with a glint in his eyes. And Michael realized that they had not seen his awkward display of laughter then.

Above them the dove perched on Sister Flouta's roof, still eyeing the scene below. To Michael's right, the elderly still sat, as though dead in their seats, unbelieving of this nightmare unfolding before them. And at his fingertips, a head of hair. He quickly closed his mouth and looked down. Children. His children.

But these were not laughing. These were seated, or standing against his legs, some staring quietly to their mothers, others whimpering. Nadia the birthday girl sat stoically on the end, her jaw clenched, her hands on her knees.

When Father Michael looked up his eyes met Ivena's as she trudged under her cross. They were bright and sorrowful at once. She seemed to understand something, but he could not know what. Perhaps she too had heard the song. Either way, he smiled, somehow less afraid than he had been just a minute ago.

Because he knew something now.

He knew there were two worlds in motion here.

He knew that behind the skin of this world, there was another. And in that world a man was singing and the children were laughing.

JANJIC LOOKED at the women shuffling across the courtyard and bit back his growing anger with this demented game of Karadzic's.

He'd dutifully kicked over three gravestones and hefted them to the backs of terrified women. One of them was the birthday girl's mother. Ivena, he heard someone call her.

Janjic could see that she'd taken care to dress for her daughter's special day. Imitation pearls hung around her neck. She wore her hair in a meticulous bun and the dress she'd chosen was neatly pressed; a light pink dress with tiny yellow flowers so that she matched her daughter.

How long had they planned for this party? A week? A month? The thought brought nausea to his gut. These souls were innocent of anything deserving such humiliation. There was something obscene about forcing mothers to lug the ungainly religious symbols while their children looked on.

Ivena could easily be his own mother, holding him after his father's death ten years earlier. Mother, dear Mother—Father's death nearly killed her as well. At ten, Janjic became the man of the house. It was a tall calling. His mother died three days after his eighteenth birthday, leaving him with nothing but the war to join.

The women's dresses were darkened with sweat now, their faces wrinkled with pain, their eyes casting furtive glances at their frightened children on the steps. Still they plodded, back and forth like old mules. Yes, it was obscene.

But then the whole war was obscene.

The priest stood still in his long black robe, hunched over. A dumb look of wonder had captured his face for a moment, then passed. Perhaps he had already fallen into the abyss, watching the women slog their way past him. *Pray to your God, Priest. Tell him to stop this madness before one of your women drops her cross. We have a march to make.*

To his right the sound came, like the sickening crunch of bones, jerking Janjic out of his reverie. He turned his head. One of the women was on her knees, trembling, her hands limp on the ground, her face knotted in distress around clenched eyes.

Marie had dropped her cross.

Movement in the courtyard froze. The women stopped in their tracks as one. Every eye stared at the cement cross lying facedown on the stone beside the woman. Karadzic's face lit up as though the contact of cross with ground completed a circuit that flooded his skull with electricity. A quiver had taken to his lower lip.

Janjic swallowed. The commander snorted once and took three long steps toward Marie. The priest also took a step toward his fallen sheep but stopped when Karadzic spun back to him.

"When your backs are up against the wall, you can no more follow the teachings of Christ than any of us. Perhaps that's why the Jews butchered the man, eh, Paul? Maybe his teachings really were the rantings of a lunatic, impossible for any sane man."

The priest's head snapped up. "It's *God* you speak of!"

Karadzic turned slowly to him. "*God* you say? The Jews killed *God* on a cross, then? You may not be a Franciscan, but you're as stupid."

Father Michael's face flushed red. His eyes shone in shock. "It was for *love* that Christ walked to his death," he said.

Janjic shifted on his feet and felt his pulse quicken. The man of cloth had found his backbone.

"Christ was a fool. Now he's a dead fool," Karadzic said. The words echoed through the courtyard. He paced before Father Michael, his face frozen in a frown.

"Christ lives. He is not dead," the priest said.

"Then let him save you."

The burly commander glared at the priest, who stood tall, soaking in the insults for his God. The sight unnerved Janjic.

Father Michael drew a deep breath. "Christ lives in me, sir. His spirit rages through my body. I feel it now. I can hear it. The only reason that you can't is because your eyes and ears are clogged by this world. But there's another world at work here. It's Christ's kingdom and it bristles with his power."

Karadzic took a step back, blinking at the priest's audacity. He suddenly ran for Marie, who was still crumpled on the cement. A dull thump resounded with each boot-fall. In seven long strides he reached her. He swung his rifle like a bat, slamming the wooden butt down on the woman's shoulder. She grunted and fell to her belly.

Sharp gasps filled the air. Karadzic poised his rifle for another blow and twisted to face the priest. "You say you have power? Show me, then!" He landed another blow and the woman moaned.

"Please!" The priest took two steps forward and fell to his knees, his face wrinkled with grief. Tears streamed from his eyes. "Please, it's me you said you would beat!" He clasped his hands together as if in prayer. "Leave her, I beg you. She's innocent."

The rifle butt landed twice on the woman's head, and her body relaxed. Several children began to cry; a chorus of women groaned in shock, still bent under their own heavy loads. The sound grated on Janjic's ears.

"Please . . . please," Father Michael begged.

"Shut up! Janjic, beat him!"

Janjic barely heard the words. His eyes were fixed on the priest.

"Janjic! Beat him." Karadzic pointed with an extended arm. "Ten blows!"

Janjic turned to the commander, still not fully grasping the order. This wasn't his quarrel. It was Karadzic's game. "Beat him? Me? I—"

"You question me?" The commander took a threatening step toward Janjic. "You'll do as I say. Now take your rifle and lay it across this traitor's back or I'll have *you* shot!"

Janjic felt his mouth open.

"Now!"

Two emotions crashed through Janjic's chest. The first was simple revulsion at the prospect of swinging a fifteen-pound rifle at this priest's deformed back. The second was the fear at the realization that he felt any revulsion at all. He was a soldier who'd sworn to follow orders. And he had followed orders always. It was his only way to survive the war. But this . . .

He swallowed and took a step toward the figure, bent now in an attitude of prayer. The children stared at him—thirty sets of round, white-rimmed eyes, swimming in tears, all crying a single question. *Why?*

He glanced at Karadzic's red face. The commander's neck bulged like a bull-frog's and his eyes bored into Janjic. *Because he told me to,* Janjic answered. *Because this man is my superior and he told me to.*

Janjic raised his rifle and stared at the man's hunched back. It was trembling now, he saw. A hard blow might break that back. A knot rose to Janjic's throat. How could he do this? It was lunacy! He lowered the rifle, his mind scrambling for reason.

"Sir, should I make him stand?"

"Should you *what?*"

"Should I make him stand? I could handle the rifle better if he would stand. It would give me a greater attitude to target—"

"Make him stand, then!"

"Yes, sir. I just thought—"

"Move!"

"Yes, sir."

A slight quiver had taken to Janjic's hands. His arms ached under the rifle's weight. He nudged the kneeling priest with his boot.

"Stand, please."

The priest stood slowly and turned to face him. He cast a side glance to the crumpled form near the commander. His tears were for the woman, Janjic realized. There was no fear in his eyes, only remorse over the abuse of one of his own.

He couldn't strike this man! It would be the death of his own soul to do so!

"Beat him!"

Janjic flinched.

"Turn please," he instructed.

The Father turned sideways.

Janjic had no choice. At least that was what he told himself as he drew his rifle back. *It's an order. This is a war. I swore to obey all orders. It's an order. I'm a soldier at war. I have an obligation.*

He swung the rifle by the barrel, aiming for the man's lower back. The sound of sliced air preceded a fleshy *thump* and a grunt from the priest. The man staggered forward and barely caught his fall.

Heat flared up Janjic's back, tingling at the base of his head. Nausea swept through his gut.

The father stood straight again. He looked strong enough, but Janjic knew he might very well have lost a kidney to that blow. A tear stung the corner of his eye. Good God, he was going to *cry!* Janjic panicked.

I'm a soldier, for the love of country! I'm a Partisan! I'm not a coward!

He swung again, with fury this time. The blow went wild and struck the priest on his shoulder. Something gave way with a loud snap—the butt of his rifle. Janjic pulled the gun back, surprised that he could break the wood stock so easily.

But the rifle was not broken.

He jerked his eyes to the priest's shoulder. It hung limp. Janjic felt the blood drain from his head. He saw Father Michael's face then. The priest was expressionless, as if he'd lost consciousness while on his feet.

Janjic lost his sensibilities then. He landed a blow as much to silence the voices screaming foul through his brain as to carry out his orders. He struck again, like a man possessed with the devil, frantic to club the black form before him into silence. He was not aware of the loud moan that broke from his throat until he'd landed six of the blows. His seventh missed, not because he had lost his aim, but because the priest had fallen.

Janjic spun, carried by the swing. The world came back to him then. His comrades standing by the wall, eyes wide with astonishment; the women still bent under stone crosses; the children whimpering and crying and burying their heads in each others' bosoms.

The priest knelt on the concrete, heaving, still expressionless. Blood began to pool on the floor below his face. Some bones had shattered there.

Janjic felt the rifle slip from his hands. It clattered to the concrete.

"Finish it!" Karadzic's voice echoed in the back of Janjic's head, but he did not consider the matter. His legs were shaking and he backed unsteadily from the black form huddled at his feet.

To his right, boots thudded on the concrete and Janjic turned just in time to see his commander rushing at him with a raised rifle. He instinctively threw his arms up to cover his face. But the blows did not come. At least not to him.

They landed with a sickening finality on the priest's back. Three blows in quick succession, accompanied by another snap. The thought that one of the women may have stepped on a twig stuttered through Janjic's mind. But he knew that the snap had come from the father's ribs. He staggered back to the wall and crashed against it.

"You will pay for this, Janjic," Molosov muttered.

Janjic's mind reeled, desperate to correct his spinning world. *Get a hold of yourself, Janjic! You're a soldier! Yes indeed, a soldier who defied his superior's orders. What kind of madness has come over you?*

He straightened. His comrades were turned from him, watching Karadzic, who was yanking the priest to his feet. Janjic looked at the soldiers and saw that a line of sweat ran down the Jew's cheek. Puzup blinked repeatedly.

The priest suddenly gasped. *Uhhh!* The sound echoed in the silence.

Karadzic hardly seemed to notice the odd sound. "March!" he thundered. "The next one to drop a cross will receive twenty blows with the priest. We'll see what kind of faith he has taught you."

The women tottered—gaping, sagging.

The commander gripped his hands into fists. Cords of muscle stood out on his neck. "Maaarch!"

They marched.

IVENA SLOWLY lowered the book with a quiver in her hands. An ache swelled into her throat, threatening to burst out. After so many years the pain seemed no less. She leaned back and drew a deep breath. *Dear Nadia, forgive me.*

Ivena suddenly leaped from her chair. "March!" she mimicked, and she strutted across the cement floor, the book flapping in her right hand. "Maaarch! One, two. One, two." She did it with indignation and fury, and she did it without hardly thinking what she was doing. If any poor soul saw her, marching through her greenhouse like an overstuffed peacock in a dress, they might think her mad.

The thought stopped her midmarch. But she wasn't mad. Merely enlightened. She had the right to march; after all, she was there. She had staggered under her own concrete cross along with the other women, and in the end it had liberated her. And now there was a kind of redemption in remembering; there was a power in participating few could understand.

"Maaarch!" she bellowed, and struck out down the aisle by the tulips. She made the return trip to her chair, smoothed her dress to regain composure, glanced about once just to be sure no one was peeking through the glass, and sat back down.

Now where was I?

You were marching through your greenhouse like an idiot, she thought.

"No, I was putting the power of darkness back in its place. I know the ending."

She cracked the book, flipped a few pages to find where she had left off and began to read.

Chapter Four

FATHER MICHAEL remembered arguing with the commander; remembered Karadzic's rifle butt smashing down on Sister Marie's skull; remembered the other soldier, the skinny one, making him stand and then raising the rifle to strike him. He even remembered closing his eyes against that first blow to his kidneys. But that blow ignited the strobe in his mind.

Poof!

The courtyard vanished in a flash of light.

The white desert crashed into his world. Fingers of light streaked from the horizon. The ground was covered with the white flowers. And the music!

Oh, the music. The children's laughter rode the skies, playing off the man's song. His volume had grown, intensified, compelling Michael to join in the laughter. The same simple tune, but now others seemed to have joined in to form a chorus. Or maybe it just sounded like a chorus but was really just laughter.

Sing O son of Zion; Shout O child of mine

Rejoice with all your heart and soul and mind

Michael was vaguely aware of a crashing on the edge of his world. It was as if he lived in a Christmas ornament and a child had taken a stick to it. But it wasn't a stick, he knew that. It wasn't a child either. It was the soldier with a rifle, beating his bones.

He heard a loud snap. *I've got to hurry up before the roof caves in about me! I've got to hurry! My bones are breaking.*

Hurry? Hurry where?

Hurry to meet this man. Hurry to find the children, of course. Problem was, he still couldn't see them. He could hear them, all right. Their laughter rippled over the field in long, uncontrolled strings that forced a smile to his mouth.

The figure was still far away, a foot high on the horizon now, walking straight toward Michael, singing his incredible song. He would have expected music to reach him through his ears, but this song didn't bother with the detour. It seemed to reach right through his chest and squeeze his heart. Love and hope and sorrow and laughter all rolled up in one.

He opened his mouth without thinking and sang a couple of the words. *O child of mine . . .* A silly grin spread his cheeks. What did he think he was doing? But he felt a growing desperation to sing with the man, to match the chorus with his own. *La da da, da la!* Mozart! An angel with the purest melody known to man. To God!

And he wanted to laugh! He almost did. He almost threw his head back and cackled. His chest felt as though it might explode with the desire. But he could not see the children. And that stick was making an awful racket about his bones.

Without ceremony, the world with all of its color and light and music was jerked from him. He was back in the village.

He heard himself gasp. *Uhhh!* It was like having a bucket of cold water thrown at him while taking a warm shower. He was standing now, facing Marie's fallen body. The spring gurgled on as if nothing at all had happened. The women were frozen in place. The children were crying.

And pain was spreading through his flesh like leaking acid.

Oh, God. What is happening? What are you doing to your children?

His shoulder did not feel right. Neither did his cheek.

He wanted to be back in the laughing world with the children. Marie stirred on the ground. The commander was screaming and now the women started to move, like ghosts in a dream.

No. The colors of Father Michael's world brightened. *No, I do not belong with the laughing children. I belong here with my own children. These whom God has given me charge over. They need me.*

But he didn't know what he should do. He wasn't even sure he could talk. So he prayed. He cried out to God to save them from this wicked man.

THE COURTYARD *had become a wasteland,* Janjic thought. A wasteland filled with frozen guards and whimpering children and moaning women. The ravens soared in an unbroken circle now, a dozen strong. A lone dove watched the scene from its perch on the house to his right.

Janjic swallowed, thinking that he might cry. But he would swallow his tongue before he allowed tears. He had humiliated himself enough.

Molosov and the others stood expressionless, drawing shallow breaths, waiting for Karadzic's next move in this absurd game. An hour ago Janjic was bored with the distraction of the village. Ten minutes ago, he found himself horrified at beating the priest. And now . . . now he was slipping into an odd state of anger and apathy drummed home by the plodding footfalls about him.

The girl with a flat face and freckles—the birthday girl dressed in pink—suddenly stood up.

She stood on the third step and stared at the commander for a few moments, as if gathering her resolve. She was going to do something. What had come over this girl? She was a *child*, for heaven's sake. A war child, not so innocent as most at such a tender age, but a child nonetheless. He'd never seen a young girl as brave as this one looked now, standing with arms at her side, staring at the commander across the courtyard.

"Nadia!" a woman called breathlessly. Her mother, Ivena, who had stopped beneath her heavy cross.

Without removing her eyes from the commander, the girl walked down the steps and limped for Karadzic.

"Nadia! Go back! Get back on the steps this minute!" Ivena cried.

The girl ignored her mother's order and walked right up to the commander. She stopped five feet from him and looked up at his face. Karadzic didn't return her wide stare, but kept his eyes fixed on some unseen point directly ahead. Nadia's eyes were misty, Janjic saw, but she wasn't crying.

It occurred to Janjic that he had stopped breathing. Sound and motion had been sucked from the courtyard as if by a vacuum. The children's whimpers fell silent. The women froze in their tracks. Not an eye blinked.

The girl spoke. "Father Michael has taught us that in the end only love matters. Love is giving, not taking. My friends were giving me gifts today because they love me. Now you've taken everything. Do you hate us?"

The commander spit at her. "Shut up, you ugly little wench! You have no respect?"

"I mean no disrespect, sir. But I can't stand to see you hurt our village."

"Please, Nadia," Ivena said.

The priest stood quivering, his face half off, his shoulders grotesquely slumped, staring at Nadia with his one good eye.

Karadzic blinked. Nadia turned to face her mother and spoke very quietly. "I'm sorry, Mother."

She looked Karadzic in the eyes. "If you're good, sir, why are you hurting us? Father Michael has taught us that religion without God is foolishness. And God is love. But how is this love? Love is—"

"Shut your hole!" Karadzic lifted a hand to strike her. "Shut your tiny hole, you insolent—"

"Stop! Please stop!" Ivena staggered forward three steps from the far side, uttering little panicky guttural sounds.

Karadzic glared at Nadia, but he did not swing his hand.

Nadia never took her round blue eyes off the commander. Her lower lip quivered for a moment. Tears leaked down her cheek in long, silent streams. "But sir, how can I shut up if you make my mother carry that load on her back? She has only so much strength. She will drop the cross and then you'll beat her. I can't stand to watch this."

Karadzic ignored the girl and looked around at the scattered women, bent, unmoving, staring at him. "March! Did I tell you to stop? March!"

But they did not. *Something had changed,* Janjic thought. They looked at Karadzic, their gazes fixed. Except for Ivena. She was bent like a pack mule, shaking, but slowly, ever so slowly, she began to straighten with the cross on her back.

Janjic wanted to scream out. *Stop, woman! Stop, you fool! Stay down!*

Nadia spoke in a wavering tone now. "I beg you, sir. Please let these mothers put down their crosses. Please leave us. This would not please our Lord Jesus. It's not his love."

"Shut up!" Karadzic thundered. He took a step toward Nadia, grabbed one of her pigtails and yanked.

She winced and stumbled after him, nearly falling except for his grip on her hair. Karadzic pulled the girl to the father, who looked on, tears running down his cheek now.

Ivena's cross slipped from her back then.

Janjic alone watched it, and he felt its impact through his boot when it landed.

Nadia's mother ran for Karadzic. She'd already taken three long strides when the dull thump jerked the commander's heads toward her. She took two more, half the distance to the commander, head bent and eyes fixed, before uttering a sound. And then her mouth snapped wide and she shrieked in fury. A full-throated roaring scream that met Janjic's mind like a dentist's drill meeting a raw nerve.

Karadzic whipped the girl behind him like a rag doll. He stepped forward and met the rushing woman's face with his fist. The blow sent her reeling, bleeding profusely from the nose. She slumped to her knees, silenced to a moan.

And then another cross fell.

And another, and another until they were slamming to the concrete in a rain of stone. The women struggled to stand tall, all of them.

A streak of fear crossed Karadzic's gray eyes, Janjic realized. But he wasn't thinking too clearly just now. He was trembling under the weight of the atmosphere. A thick air of insanity laced by the crazy notion that *he* should stop this. That he should scream out in protest, or maybe put a bullet in Karadzic's head—anything to end this madness.

The commander jerked his pistol from his belt and shoved it against the priest's forehead. He spun the girl toward the priest and released her. "You think your dead Christ will save your priest now?"

"Sir . . ." The objection came from Janjic's throat before he could stop it.

Stop, Janjic! Shut up! Sit back!

But he did not. He took a single step forward. "Sir, please. This is enough. Please, we should leave these people alone."

Karadzic shot him a furious stare, and Janjic saw hatred in those deep-set eyes. The commander looked back at the girl, who was staring up at the priest through the pools of tears that rimmed her eyes.

"I think I'll shoot your priest. Yes?"

Father Michael gazed into the little girl's face. There was a connection between their eyes, shafts of invisible energy. *The priest and the girl were speaking,* Janjic thought. Speaking with this look of love. Tears streamed down their cheeks.

Janjic felt a wedge of panic rise to his throat. "Please, sir. Please, show them kindness. They have done nothing."

"Sometimes love is best spoken with a bullet," Karadzic said.

The girl stared into the eyes of her priest, and her look gripped Janjic with terror. He wanted to tear his gaze away from the girl's face, but he couldn't. It was a look of love in its purest form, Janjic knew, a love he had never seen before.

Nadia spoke softly, still staring at the priest. "Don't kill my priest." Her voice whispered across the courtyard. "If you have to kill someone, then kill me instead."

A murmur ran though the crowd. The girl's mother clambered to unsteady legs, gulping for air. Her face twisted in anguish. "Oh, God! Nadia! Nadia!"

Nadia held up a hand, stopping her mother. "No, Mother. It will be okay. You will see. It's what Father Michael has taught us. Shh. It's okay. Don't cry."

Oh, such words! From a child! Janjic felt hot tears on his cheek. He took another step forward. "Please, sir, I beg you!" It came out like a sob, but he no longer cared.

Karadzic's lips twitched once. Then again, to a grin. He lowered his gun from the priest. It hung by his waist.

He lifted it suddenly and pressed the barrel to the girl's head.

The mother's restraint snapped and she launched herself at the commander, arms forward, fingernails extended like claws, shrieking. This time the second in command, Molosov, anticipated her move. He was running from his position behind Janjic as soon as Ivena moved, and he landed a kick to her midsection before she reached Karadzic. She doubled over and retched. Molosov jerked the woman's arms behind her and dragged her back.

Nadia closed her eyes and her shoulders began to shake in a silent sob.

"Since your flock has failed to prove its faith, you will renounce your faith, Priest. Do that and I will let this little one live." Karadzic's voice cut through the panic. He looked around at the women. "Renounce your dead Christ and I will leave you all."

Ivena began to whimper with short squeaky sounds that forced their way past white lips. For a moment the rest seemed not to have heard. Father Michael stiffened. For several long seconds his face registered nothing.

And then it registered everything, knotting up impossibly around his shattered cheekbone. His tall frame began to shake with sobs and his limp arm bounced loosely.

"Speak, Priest! Renounce Christ!"

THE PHONE rang, and Ivena jerked upright. Her heart slammed in her chest. *Oh, Nadia! Oh, dear Nadia.* A teardrop darkened the page by her thumb. She closed her eyes and let the book close on one finger.

The phone rang again, from the kitchen.

Oh, Nadia, I love you so much. You were so brave. So very, very brave!

Ivena began to cry then; she just could not help it. Didn't want to help it. She bowed her head and sobbed.

She had done this a hundred times; a thousand times, and each time she reached this point it was the same. The hardest part of remembering. But it was also the most rewarding part. Because in moments like this she knew that her heart was breaking with her Father's, looking down at miserable man; at the leper; the whore; the common pedestrian in Atlanta; Nadia. The ache in her heart now was no different from the ache in God's heart for his stray creation. It was there only because of love.

And she did love Nadia. She really did.

The phone rang incessantly.

Ivena sniffed, twisted to stand, and then thought better of it. Whoever it was could wait. It was only ten o'clock and she had no deliveries today. They could call back. She was nearly finished here anyway; no use running off prematurely. Nothing mattered as much as remembering. Except for following.

Ivena took a gulp of cool tea and let the phone ring out. When it did, she adjusted herself on the chair, sniffed again, and then began to read.

FATHER MICHAEL'S world kept blinking on and off, alternating like intermittent static between this ghastly scene here and the white-flowered field there. He was jerked back and forth with such intensity that he hardly knew which scene was real and which was a figment of his imagination.

But that was just it. Neither world came from his imagination. He knew that now with certainty. He was simply being allowed to see and hear both worlds. His spiritual eyes and ears were being opened in increments, and he could hardly stand the contrast. One second this terrifying evil in the courtyard, and the next the music.

Oh the music! Impossible to describe. Raw energy stripping him of all but pleasure. The man was only a few hundred meters distant now, arms spread so that his cloak draped wide. An image of Saint Francis, but more. Yes, much more. Michael imagined a wide, mischievous grin on the man, but he couldn't see it for the distance. The man walked toward him steadily, purposefully, still singing. The giggling children sang with him in perfect harmony now. A symphony slowly swelling. The melody begged him to join. To leap into the field and throw his arms up and dance with laughter along with the hidden children.

Across the courtyard, the tall cross leading to the cemetery stood bold against the other world's gray sky. He had pointed to that very cross a thousand times, teaching his children the truth of God. And he had taught them well.

"You may look at that cross and think of it as a gothic decoration, engraved with roses and carved with style, but do not forget that it represents life and death. It represents the scales on which all of our lives will be weighed. It's an instrument of torture and death—the symbol of our faith. They butchered God on a cross. And Christ emphasized none of his teachings so adamantly as our need to take up our own crosses and follow him."

Nadia had looked up to him, squinting in the sun—he saw it clearly in his mind's eye now. "Does this mean that we should die for him?"

"If need be, of course, Nadia. We will all die, yes? So then if we have worn out our bodies in service to him, then we are dying for him, yes? Like a battery that expends its power."

"But what if the battery is still young when it dies?" That had silenced those gathered.

He reached down and stroked her chin. "Then you would be fortunate enough to pass this plain world quickly. What waits beyond is the prize, Nadia. This"—he looked up and drew a hand across the horizon—"this fleeting world may look like the garden of Eden to us, but it's nothing more than a taste. Tell me," and he looked at the adults gathered now, "at a wedding feast you receive gifts, yes? Beautiful, lovely gifts . . . vases and perfumes and scarves . . . all delightful in our eyes. We all gather around the gifts and show our pleasure. *What a glorious scarf, Ivena.*"

A chuckle ran through the crowd.

"But do you think that Ivena's mind is on the scarf?" A run of giggles. "No, I think not. Ivena's mind is on her groom, waiting breathlessly in the next room. The man whom she will wed in sweet union. Yes?"

"I don't recall seeing a cross at the last wedding," Ivena had said.

"No, not at our weddings. But death is like a wedding." The crowd hushed. "And the crucifixion of Christ was a grand wedding announcement. This world we now live in may indeed be a beautiful gift from God, but do not forget that we wait with breathless anticipation for our union with him beyond this life." He let the truth finger its way through their minds for a moment. "And how do you suppose we arrive at the wedding?"

Nadia answered. "We die."

He looked down into her smiling blue eyes. "Yes, child. We die."

"Then why shouldn't we just die now?" Nadia asked.

"Heaven forbid, child! What bride do you know who would take her own life before the wedding? No one who understands how beautiful the bride is could possibly take her life before the wedding! It is perhaps the ugliest thing of all. We will all cross the threshold when the groom calls. Until then, we wait with breathless anticipation."

One of the women had sighed with approval.

Somehow, looking at the large concrete cross now did not engender any such mirth. He looked down at the child and felt as though a shaft had been run through his heart.

Nadia, oh, my dear Nadia, what are you doing? I love you so, young child. I love you as though you were my own. And you are my own. You know that, don't you, Nadia?

She looked at him with deep blue eyes. *I love you, Father.* Her eyes were speaking to him, as clearly as any words. And he wept.

"Don't kill my priest. If you have to kill someone, then kill me instead," a voice said.

He heard the words like a distant echo . . . words! She had actually said that? *Don't be foolish, Nadia!*

A flash of light sputtered to life about him. The white field again!

The music flooded his mind and he suddenly wanted to laugh with it. It felt so . . . consequential here, and the silly little game back in the courtyard so . . . petty. Like a game of marbles with all the neighborhood children gathered, sporting stern faces as if the outcome might very well determine the fate of the world. If they only knew that their little game felt so small here, in this immense white landscape that rippled with laughter. Ha! If they only knew! Kill us! Kill us all! Put an end to this silly game of marbles and let us get on with life, with laughing and music in the white field.

The white world blinked off. But now the commander had the gun pushed against Nadia's forehead. "Renounce your faith, Priest, and I will let this little one live! Renounce your dead Christ and I will leave you all."

It took a moment for him to switch worlds—for the words to present their meaning to him.

And then they did, with the force of a sledge to his head.

Renounce Christ?

Never! He could never renounce Christ!

Then Nadia will die.

This realization cut through his bones like a dagger. She would die because of him! His face throbbed with pain; the muscles there had gone taut like bowstrings. But never! Never could he renounce his love for Christ!

Father Michael had never before felt the torment that descended upon him in that moment. It was as if some molten hand had reached into his chest and grabbed hold, searing frayed nerves so that he could not draw breath. His throat pulled for air to no avail.

Nadia! Nadia! I can't!

"Speak, Priest! Renounce Christ!"

She was crying. Oh, the dear girl was crying! The courtyard waited.

The music filled his mind.

Fresh air flooded his lungs. Relief, such sweet relief! The white field ran to the horizon; the children laughed incessantly.

"I will count to three, Priest!"

The commander's voice jerked him back to the courtyard.

Nadia was looking at him. She had stopped her crying. Sorrow overcame him again.

"One!" Karadzic barked.

"Nadia," Father Michael croaked. "Nadia, I—"

"Don't, Father," she said softly. Her small pinks lips clearly formed the words. *Don't, Father.* Don't what? This from a child! Nadia, dear Nadia!

"Two!"

A wail rose over the crowd. It was Ivena. Poor Ivena. She strained against the large soldier, who held her arms pinned behind her back. She clenched her eyes and dropped her jaw and now screamed her protest from the back of her throat. The solider clamped a hand around her face, stifling her cry.

Oh God, have mercy on her soul! Oh God . . . "Nadia . . ." Father Michael could barely speak, so great was the pressure in his chest. His legs wobbled beneath him and suddenly they collapsed. He landed on his knees and lifted his one good arm to the girl. "Nadia—"

"I heard the song, Father." She spoke quietly. Light sparkled through her eyes. A faint smile softened her features. The girl had lost her fear. Entirely!

Nadia hummed, faint, high-pitched, clear for all to hear. *"Hm hm hm hmhmm . . ."* The melody! Dear God, she had heard it too!

"Three!" Karadzic barked.

"I saw you there," she said. And she winked.

Her eyes were wide open, an otherworldly blue penetrating his, when the gun bucked in the commander's thick, gnarled hand.

Boom!

Her head snapped back. She stood in the echoing silence for an endless moment, her chin pointed to sky, baring that tender pale neck. And then she crumpled to the ground like a sack of potatoes. A small one, wrapped in a pink dress.

Father Michael's mind began to explode. His own voice joined a hundred others in a long epitaph of distress. "Aaaaahhhhhh . . ." It screamed past his throat until the last whisper of breath had left his lungs. Then it began again, and Michael wanted desperately to die. He wanted absolutely nothing but to die.

Ivena's mouth lay wide open, but no sound came out. Only a breath of terror that seemed to strike Michael on his chest.

The priest's world began to spin and he lost his orientation. He fell forward, face first, swallowed by the horror of the moment. His head struck the concrete and his mind began to fade. Maybe he was in hell.

CHAPTER FIVE

IVENA WAS reading through tears now. Wiping at her eyes with the back of her hand and sniffing and trying to keep the page clear enough to read. The sorrow felt like a deep healing balm as it washed through her chest in relentless waves.

It felt that way because she knew what was coming next and she could hardly wait to get there! Her fingers held a slight tremble as she turned these few pages. They were worn ragged on the corners. The book stated elsewhere that you could not find mountains without going through valleys. In all honesty she didn't know whether her Nadia's death was a mountain or a valley. It really depended on perspective.

And truly, the perspective was about to change.

JANJIC STARED, his eyes wide and stinging. All about him voices of torment screamed; pandemonium erupted on the courtyard floor. Father Michael lay face-down, his head not five inches from the girl's shiny white birthday shoes.

Karadzic reached out and snatched another child by the collar. The boy's mother wailed in protest, started forward, and then stopped when Karadzic shoved the gun toward her. "Shut up! Shut up! Everyone!" he thundered.

Janjic was running before his mind processed the order to run. Straight for the priest. Or perhaps straight for Karadzic, he didn't know which until the last possible second. The man had to be stopped.

How the commander managed to get his pistol around so quickly Janjic had no clue, but the black Luger whipped around and met him with a jarring blow to his cheek.

Pain shot over his skull. It felt like he'd run into a swinging bat. His head jerked back and his legs flew forward, throwing him from his feet. Janjic landed heavily on his back and rolled over, moaning. What was he doing? Stopping Karadzic—that's what he was doing.

Janjic dragged himself from the commander, urged by a boot kick to his thigh. His mind swam. The world seemed to slow. Five feet away on the ground lay a girl who'd just given her life for her priest. For her God. For Christ's love. And Janjic had seen in her eyes a look of absolute certainty. He had seen her smile at the priest. He had seen the wink. A *wink*, for goodness sake! Something had changed with that wink. He was not sure what it meant, except that something had changed.

Dear God, she had hummed! She had *winked!*

"Puzup, get him to his feet," Karadzic ordered above the din.

Puzup stormed past Janjic and yanked the priest to his feet. Paul gaped at the scene, his expression impossible to interpret. Janjic pushed himself to his knees, ignoring the pain that throbbed through his skull. Blood dripped to the concrete from a wound behind his ear. He turned back to the commander and stood shakily. Ten feet separated them now.

The priest wavered on his feet, facing Karadzic. If the father had passed out from his fall, they had awakened him. The little boy the commander had hauled from the steps stood shaking and bawling. Karadzic pressed his pistol against the boy's ear.

"What do you say, Priest? What's this love of yours worth? Should I put another one of your children out of their misery?" Karadzic's eyes were rocks behind bushy brows, dull gray tombstones. He was grinning. "Or will you renounce your stupid faith?"

"Kill me," Father Michael's voice quavered.

Janjic stopped trying to understand the madness that had gripped this priest and his flock of sheep. It was beyond the reaches of his mind. Yet it reached out to him with long fingers of desire.

"Take my life, sir. Please leave the boy."

The smile vanished from commander's face. "Then renounce your faith, you blithering idiot! They are words! Just words! Say them. Say them!"

"They are words of Christ. He is my redeemer. He is my Savior. He is my Creator. How can I deny my own Creator? Please, sir—"

"He is your redeemer? He is her redeemer too?" He motioned to the girl on the ground. "She is dead, you fool."

The priest stood trembling for a few moments before responding. "She sees you now. She is laughing."

Karadzic stared at Father Michael.

The women had stopped their cries and the children sat still, faces buried in their mothers' skirts.

"If you must have another death, let it be mine," the priest said.

And then the rules of the game changed once more.

The girl's mother, Ivena, who had grown eerily calm, suddenly wrested herself free from Molosov but did not rush the commander again. Molosov grabbed one arm but let her stand on her own. "No," she said softly, "let it be mine. Kill me in the boy's place." She stood unflinching, like a stone statue.

Karadzic now stood with the pistol to the whimpering boy's ear, between a man and a woman each asking for death in the boy's place. He shifted on his feet, unsure how much power he truly held over this scene.

Another woman stepped forward, her face twisted in pity. "No. No, kill me instead. I will die for the boy. The priest has already suffered too much. And Ivena has lost her only child. I am childless. Take my life. I will join Nadia."

"No, I will," another said, taking two steps forward. "You are young, Kota. I am old. Please, this world holds no appeal to me. It would be good for me to pass on to be with our Lord." The woman looked to be in her fifties.

Karadzic slashed the air with his pistol. "Silence! Perhaps I should kill *all* of you! I am killing here, not playing a game. You want me to kill you all?" Janjic had known the man long enough to recognize his faltering. But there was something else there as well. A glimmer of excitement that flashed through his gray eyes. Like a dog in heat.

"But it really should be me," a voice said. Janjic looked to the steps where another girl stood facing them with her heels together. "Nadia was my best friend," she said. "I should join her. Is there really music there, Father?"

The priest could not answer. He was weeping uncontrollably. Torn to shreds by this display of love.

The gun boomed and Janjic flinched.

Karadzic held the weapon above his head. He'd fired into the air. "Stop! Stop!" He shoved the boy sprawling to his seat. His thick lips glistened with spittle. The gun shook in his thick fingers, and above it all his eyes sparkled with rising excitement.

He stepped back and turned the pistol on Nadia's mother. She simply closed her eyes. Janjic understood her motivation to some degree: The woman's only child lay at her feet. She was stepping up to the bullet with a grief-ravaged mind.

He held his breath in anticipation of a shot.

Karadzic licked his wet lips and jerked the weapon to the younger woman who'd stepped forward. She too closed her eyes. But Karadzic did not shoot. He swiveled it to the older woman. Looking at them all now, Janjic thought that any one of the women might give their lives for the boy. It was a moment that could not be understood in the context of normal human experience. A great spiritual love had settled on them all. Karadzic was more than capable of killing; he was in fact eager for it. And yet the women stood square-shouldered now, daring him to pull the trigger.

Janjic swayed on weak legs, overcome by the display of self-sacrifice. The ravens cawed overhead and he glanced skyward, as much for a reprieve as in response to the bird's call. At first he thought the ravens had flown off; that a black cloud had drifted over the valley in their place. But then he saw the cloud ebb and flow and he knew it was a singular ring of birds—a hundred or more, gliding overhead making their odd call. What was happening here? He lowered his eyes to the courtyard and blinked against the buzz that had overtaken the pounding in his skull.

For a long, silent minute Karadzic weighed his decision, his muscles strung to the snapping point, sweating profusely, breathing heavily.

The villagers did not move; they drilled him with steady stares. The priest seemed to float in and out of consciousness, swaying on his feet, opening and closing his eyes periodically. His face drifted through a range of expressions—one moment his eyes open and his mouth sagged with grief, the next his eyes closed and his mouth opened in wonder. Janjic studied him, and his heart broke for the man. He wanted to take the gentle priest to a bed and dress his wounds. Bathe him in hot water and soothe his battered shoulder. His face would never be the same; the damage looked far too severe. He would probably be blind in his right eye, and eating would prove difficult for some time. Poor priest. *My poor, poor priest. I swear that I will care for you, my priest. I will come and serve . . .*

What was this? What was he thinking? Janjic stopped himself. But it was true. He knew it then as much as he had known anything. He loved this man. He cherished this man. His heart felt sick over this man.

I will come and serve you, my priest. A knot rose to Janjic's throat, suffocating him. *In you I have seen love, Priest. In you and your children and your women I have seen God. I will . . .*

A chuckle interrupted his thoughts. The commander was chuckling. Looking around and chuckling. The sound engendered terror. The man was completely mad! He suddenly lowered his gun and studied the crowd, nodding slightly, tasting a new plan on his thick tongue.

"Haul this priest to the large cross," he said. No one moved. Not even Molosov, who stood behind Ivena.

"Are you deaf, Molosov? Take him. Puzup, Paul, help Molosov." He stared at the large stone cross facing the cemetery. "We will give them what they desire."

FATHER MICHAEL remembered stumbling across the concrete, shoved from behind, tripping to his knees once and then being hauled up under his arms. He remembered the pain shooting through his shoulder and thinking someone had pulled his arm off. But it still swung ungainly by his side.

He remembered the cries of protest from the women. "Leave the Father! I beg you . . . He's a good man . . . Take one of us. We beg you!"

The world twisted topsy-turvy as they approached the cross. They left the girl lying on the concrete in pool of blood. *Nadia . . . Nadia, sweet child.* Ivena knelt by her daughter, weeping bitterly again, but a soldier jabbed her with his rifle, forcing her to follow the crowd to the cemetery.

The tall stone cross leaned against a white sky, gray and pitted. It had been erected one hundred years earlier. They called it stone, but the twelve-foot cross was actually cast of concrete, with etchings of rosebuds at the top and at the beams' intersection. Each end flared like a clover leaf, giving the instrument of death an incongruous sense of delicacy.

The pain on his right side reached to his bones. Some had been broken. *Oh, Father. Dear Father, give me strength.* The dove still sat on the roof peak and eyed them carefully. The spring bubbled without pause, oblivious of this treachery.

They reached the cross, and a sudden brutal pain shot through Michael's spine. His world faded.

When his mind crawled back into consciousness, a wailing greeted him. His head hung low, bowed from his shoulders, facing the dirt. His ribs stuck out like sticks beneath stretched skin. He was naked except for white boxer shorts, now stained in sweat and blood.

Michael blinked and struggled for orientation. He tried to lift his head, but pain sliced through his muscles. The women were singing, long mournful wails without tune. Mourning for whom? *For you. They're mourning you!*

But why? It came back to him then. He had been marched to the cross. They had lashed him to the cross with a hemp rope around the midsection and shoulders, leaving his feet to dangle free.

He lifted his chin slowly and craned for a view, ignoring the shafts of pain down his right side. The commander stood to his left, the barrel of his pistol confronting Michael like a small black tunnel. The man looked at the women, most of whom had fallen to their knees, pleading with him.

A woman's words came to Michael. "He's our priest. He's a servant of God. You cannot kill him! You can not." It was Ivena.

Oh, dear Ivena! Your heart is spun of gold!

The priest felt his body quiver as he slowly straightened his heavy head. He managed to lift it upright and let it flop backward. It struck the concrete cross with a dull thump.

The wailing ceased. They had heard. But now he stared up at the darkened sky. A white, overcast sky filled with black birds. *Goodness, there must be hundreds of birds flying around up there.* He tilted his head to his left and let it loll so that it rested on his good shoulder.

Now he saw them all. The kneeling women, the children staring with bulging eyes, the soldiers. The commander looked up at him and smiled. He was breathing heavily; his gray eyes were bloodshot. A long thin trail of spittle ran down his chin and hung suspended from a wet chin. He was certifiably mad, this one. Mad or possessed.

The lunatic turned back to the women. "One of you. That's all! One, one, one! A single stray sheep. If *one* of you will renounce Christ, I will leave you all!"

Father Michael felt his heart swell in his chest. He looked at the women and silently pleaded for them to remain quiet, yet he doubted his dismay showed—his muscles had lost most of their control.

Do not renounce our Lord! Don't you dare speak out for me! You cannot take this from me!

He tried to speak, but only a faint groan came out. That and a string of saliva, which dripped to his chest. He moved his eyes to Ivena. *Don't let them, Ivena. I beg you!*

"What's wrong with you? You can't hear? I said *one* of you! Surely you have a sinner in your pretty little town, willing to speak out to save your precious priest's miserable neck! Speak!"

Bright light filled Michael's mind, blinding him to the cemetery.

The field! But something had changed. Silence!

Absolute silence.

The man had stopped, thirty meters off, legs planted in the flowers, hands on his hips, dressed in a robe like a monk. Above his head the light still streaked in from the horizon. And silence.

Michael blinked. What . . .

Sing O son of Zion; Shout O child of mine

Rejoice with all your heart and soul and mind

The man's words echoed over the field.

Child of mine! Michael's lips twitched to a slight grin. Rejoice with all . . .

The man suddenly threw his arms out to either side lifted his head to the sky and sang.

Every tear you cried dried in the palm of my hand

Every lonely hour was by my side

Every loved one lost, every river crossed

Every moment, every hour was pointing to this day

Longing for this day . . .

For you are finally home

Michael felt as though he might faint for the sheer power of the melody. He wanted to run to the man. He wanted to throw out his own arms and tilt his head back and wail the same song from the bottom of his chest. A few notes dribbled past Michael's lips, uncontrolled. La da da da la . . .

A faint giggling sound came from his left. He turned.

She was skipping toward him in long bounds. Michael caught his breath. He could not see her face because the girl's chin was tilted back so that she stared at the sky. She leaped through the air, landing barefoot on the white petals every ten yards, her fists pumping with each footfall. Her pink dress fluttered in the wind.

She was echoing the man's melody now, not like Michael had done, but perfectly in tune and then in harmony.

Father Michael knew then that this girl hurtling toward him was Nadia. And in her wake followed a thousand others, bubbling with a laughter that swelled with the music.

The song swallowed him whole now. They were all singing it, led by the man. It was impossible to discern the laughter from the music—they were one and the same.

Nadia lowered her head and shot him a piercing stare as she flew by. Her blue eyes sparkled mischievously, as though daring him to give chase.

But there was a difference about Nadia. Something so startling that Michael's heart skipped a beat.

Nadia was beautiful!

She looked exactly as she had before her death. Same freckles, same pigtails, same plump facial features. But in this reality he found that those freckles and that thick face and all that had made her homely before, now looked . . .

Beautiful. Nearly intoxicating. His own perspective had changed!

He took an involuntary step forward, dumbfounded. And he knew in that moment that his pity for both Nadia's appearance and her death had been badly misplaced.

Nadia was beautiful all along. Physically beautiful. And her death held its own beauty as well.

Oh death, where is thy sting?

For the first time his eyes saw her as she truly was. Before, his sight had been masked by a preoccupation for the reality that now seemed foolish and distant by comparison. Like mud pies next to delicious mounds of ice cream.

A wind rushed by, filled with the laughter of a thousand souls. The white flower petals swirled in their wake. Michael couldn't hold back his chuckles now. They shook his chest.

"Nadia!" he called. "Nadia."

She disappeared over the horizon. He looked out to the man.

Gone!

But the voice still filled the sky. Michael's bones felt like putty. Nothing else mattered now. Nothing.

They suddenly came at him again, streaking in from the left, led by this beautiful child he'd once thought was ugly. This time she had her head down. She drilled him with sparkling, mischievous eyes while she was still far off.

He wanted to join her train this time. To leap out in its wake and fly with her. He was planning to do just that. His whole body was quivering for this intoxicating ride that she was daring him to take. The desire flooded his veins and he staggered forward a step.

He staggered! He did not fly as she flew!

Nadia rushed up to him, then veered skyward with a single leap. His mouth dropped open. She shot for the streaking light above. Her giggles rose to a shrieking laughter and he heard her call, crystal clear.

"Come on, Father Michael! Come on! You think this is neat? This is *nothing!*"

It reverberated across the desert. *This is nothing!*

Nothing!

Desperation filled Michael. He took another step forward, but his foot seemed filled with lead. His heart slammed in his chest, flooding his veins with fear. "Nadia! Nadia!"

The white field turned off as if someone had pulled a plug.

Michael realized that he was crying. He was back in the village, hanging on a cross before his parishioners . . . crying like a baby.

CHAPTER SIX

JANJIC WATCHED the priest's body heaving with sobs up on that cross, and he pushed himself unsteadily to his feet. Nothing mattered to him now except that the priest be set free. If need be, he would die or kill or renounce Christ himself.

But with a single look into the priest's eyes, Janjic knew the priest wanted to die now. He'd found something of greater value than life. He had found this love for Christ.

Karadzic was shaking his gun at the priest, glaring at the villagers, trying to force apostasy and carrying on as if he thought the whole thing was some delicious joke. But the priest had led his flock well. They didn't seem capable of speaking out against their Christ, regardless of what it meant to the priest.

"Speak now or I'll kill him!" Karadzic screamed.

"I will speak."

Janjic lifted his head. Who'd said that? A man. The priest? No, the priest did not possess the strength.

"I will speak for my children." It *was* the priest! It was the priest, lifting his head and looking squarely at Karadzic, as if he'd received a transfusion of energy.

"Your threat of death doesn't frighten us, soldier." He spoke gently, without anger, through tears that still ran down his face. "We've been purchased by blood, we live by the power of that blood, we will die for that blood. And we would never, never, renounce our beloved Christ." His voice croaked. "He is our Creator, sir."

The priest turned his eyes to the women, and slowly a smile formed on his lips. "My children, please. Please . . ." His face wrinkled with despair. His beard was matted with blood and he could hardly speak for all the tears now.

"Please." The priest's voice came soft now. "Let me go. Don't hold me back . . . Love all those who cross your path, they are all beautiful. So . . . so very beautiful."

Not a soul moved.

A cockeyed, distant smile crossed the priest's lips. He lowered his head, exhausted. A flutter of wings beat through the air. It was the white dove, flapping toward them. It hovered above the father, then settled quietly to the cross, eyeing the bloodied man three feet under its stick feet.

The sound came quiet at first, like a distant train struggling up a hill. But it was no locomotive; it was the priest and he was laughing. His head hung and his body shook.

Janjic instinctively took a step backward.

The sound grew louder. Maybe the man had gone mad. But Janjic knew that nothing could be further from the truth. The priest was perhaps the sanest man he had ever known.

He suddenly lifted his head and spoke . . . no, he didn't speak, he sang. With mucus leaking from his nostrils and tears wetting his bloodied cheeks, wearing a face of unearthly delight, he threw his head back and sang in a rough, strained voice.

"Sing, o child of mine . . . "

And then he began to laugh.

The picture of contrasts slammed into Janjic's chest and took his breath away. Heat broke over his skull and swept down his back.

The laughter echoed over the graveyard now. Karadzic trembled, rooted to the earth. Ivena was looking up at the priest, weeping with the rest of the women. But it was not terror or even sorrow that gripped her; it was something else entirely. Something akin to desire. Something . . .

A gunshot boomed around Janjic's ears and he jumped. A coil of smoke rose from Karadzic's waving pistol.

The resounding report left absolute silence in its wake, snuffing out the laughter. Father Michael slumped on the cross. If he wasn't dead, he would be soon enough.

Then Janjic ran. He whirled around, aware only of the heat crashing through his body. He did not think to run, he just ran. On legs no stronger than puffs of cotton, he fled the village.

When his mind caught up to him, it told him that he also had just died.

JANJIC DIDN'T know how long he ran, only that the horizon had already dimmed when he fell to the ground, wasted, nearly dead. When moments of clarity came to him, he reminded himself that his flight from the village would mean his death. The Partisans did not deal kindly with deserters and Karadzic would take pleasure in enforcing the point. He had drawn a line in the sand back there with the commander. There was no avoiding Karadzic's wrath.

But then he remembered that he was already dead—a walking ghost. That was what he had learned in the village watching the priest laughing on the cross.

And what about the fact that his heart was pumping blood through his veins? What about these thoughts, bouncing around his skull like ricocheting pellets? Didn't they avow life? In some mundane, banal reality perhaps. But not in the same way he'd just witnessed. Not like the life that belonged to the villagers. In spite of the child cut down in cold blood; in spite of the priest's martyrdom, the villagers possessed life. Perhaps because of it. And what life! Laughing in the face of death. He had never even heard of such faith! Never!

Which was why he had to go back there.

Janjic spent the night huddled in the cold without a fire. His neck throbbed where Karadzic's pistol had cut a deep gash from a spot just behind his right ear to his shoulder. Images of the village came at him from the dark, whispers from the other side. A young girl in a pink dress falling to the concrete, wearing yellow hair clips and a neat little hole through her temple. A priest suspended from a cement cross, laughing. Did you hear me laughing? the girl had asked the priest. Laughter. It seemed to have possessed them both. The currency of life beyond. It was the laughter that had made the killing a truly horrifying event. *Face it, Jan, you have seen worse before and left with a shrug.* But this. This had reached into his chest and set off a grenade!

He had a dream in his drifting. He was in a dark dungeon, strapped to a beam. Perhaps a cross. He could see nothing, but his own breathing echoed about him, impossibly loud in the black space. It terrified him. And then the world lit with a flash and he stared at a great white field.

He'd awoken then, sweating and panting.

Sometime past midnight, Janjic stood and headed the way he'd come. He had no idea what he would do once there, but he knew that in fleeing he had committed himself to returning.

He reached the village at daybreak, stumbling over the same hill from which they had first gazed into this tranquil valley. He pulled up, breathing steadily through his nostrils. High above, gray clouds ran to the horizon, an unbroken blanket. The air lay still and silent except for the twittering of a sparrow nearby. The church rose like a huge tombstone below, surrounded by carefully placed houses. A thin fog drifted through the northern perimeter. Several homes spawned trails of smoke from their chimneys. On any other day Janjic might have come upon the scene and imagined the warmth of the fires that crackled in the bosom of those houses.

But today Janjic could not imagine fire. Today he thought only of cold death. A knot rose to his throat. The cemetery was shrouded by a dozen large poplars. Behind those drooping leaves stood a tall cross. And on that cross . . .

Janjic descended the hill, his heart beating like a tom. Now the unseen forces that had driven him from the village reached into his bones, raising gooseflesh along his arms. He'd heard an Orthodox priest pray for protection once. "Yea, though I walk through the valley of the shadow of death, I will fear no evil." Janjic whispered the prayer three times as he approached the tall trees.

Then he was beside them, and he stopped.

The gray cross stood tall beyond dozens of smaller crosses. A black dog nuzzled the earth at its base. But the body . . . The body was gone. Of course. What had he expected? Certainly they would not have left his body for the birds. But then where had they laid his body? And the child's?

Janjic stumbled forward, suddenly eager to find the priest. Tears blurred his vision and he ran his wrists across his eyes. *Where are you, Father? Where are you, my priest?*

The earth had been disturbed at the foot of the cross; heaped into a smooth mound roughly the length of a body. A tall body. And next to it a smaller mound. They had buried the priest and Nadia at the foot of the cross.

Janjic ran for the graves, suddenly overcome by it all. By the war and the monsters it had spawned; by images of peaceful women and delighted children; by a picture of the little girl falling and the priest hanging. By the echoes of that laughter and that final resounding boom!

The tears were so thick in his eyes he could not see the last few yards except for vague shapes. The dog fled and Janjic let his body fall when his boots first felt the ground rising with fresh dirt. He fell facedown on the priest's grave, sobbing from his gut now, clutching at the soil.

He wanted to beg forgiveness. He wanted to somehow undo what he had done by visiting this peaceful village. But he could not form the words. He gasped deeply, barely aware of the dirt in his mouth now. Every muscle in his body contracted taut, and he brought his knees up under him. It felt like death and he welcomed it, completely oblivious to the world now. He slammed his fist on the earth and sobbed.

Forgive me, forgive me! Oh, God, forgive me!

Janjic lay there for long minutes, his eyes clenched against an assault of images. And he begged. He begged God to forgive him.

"Janjic."

His name? Someone was speaking his name.

"Janjic."

He lifted his head. They'd gathered in a semicircle at the entrance to the courtyard, ten meters off, the women and the children. All of them.

Nadia's mother stood before him. "Hello, Janjic." She smiled with ashen lips.

He pushed himself to his knees, raising up on shaky legs. The world was still swimming.

"So you have come back," Ivena said. Her smile had left. "Why?"

Janjic glanced about the villagers. Children gripped their mothers' hands, looking at him with round eyes. The women stared without moving.

"I . . ." Janjic cleared his throat. "I . . ." He reached his hands out, palms up. "Please . . ."

Ivena walked forward. "The priest didn't die right away," she said. "He lived for a while after the other soldiers left. And he told us some things that helped us understand."

A ball of sorrow rolled up Janjic's throat.

"We can't condemn you," she said, but she was starting to cry.

Janjic thought his chest might explode. "Forgive me. Forgive me. Please forgive me," he said.

She opened her arms and he stepped into them, weeping like a baby now. Nadia's mother held him and patted his back, comforting him and crying on his shoulder. A dozen others came around them and rested their hands on them, hushing quietly in sympathy and praying with sweet voices. "Lord Jesus, heal your children. Comfort us in this hour of darkness. Bathe us in your love."

And their Lord Jesus did bathe them in his love, Janjic thought. He continued to shake and sob, a tall man surrounded by a sea of women, but now his tears were mixed with warmth.

When they had collected themselves enough to stop the crying they talked in short scattered sentences, decrying what had happened, consoling each other with talk of love. Nadia's love; Father Michael's love; Christ's love.

When they had stopped talking, Janjic walked over to the cross. Bloodstains darkened the gray concrete. He gripped it with both hands and kissed it.

"I swear this day to follow your Christ," he said and kissed the cross again. "I swear it on my own life."

"Then he will have to be your Christ," Ivena said. She took a small bottle the size of her fist from Marie. A perfume bottle, perhaps, with a pointed top and a flared base.

"Yes. He will be my Christ," Janjic said

She held the bottle out to him. It was dark red, sealed with wax. Janjic took it gingerly and studied it.

"Take it in remembrance of Christ's blood, which purchased your soul," she said.

"What is it?"

"It's the priest's blood."

Janjic nearly dropped the vial. "The priest's blood?"

"Don't worry," another spoke. "It's sealed off; it won't bite. It holds no value but to remind us. Think of it as a cross—a symbol of death. Please accept it and remember well."

Janjic closed his fingers around the glass. "I will. I will never forget. I swear it." A great comfort swept through his body. He lifted his hands wide and faced the sky. "I swear it! And I too will give my life for you. I will remember your love shown this day through these, your children. And I will return that love as long as I live."

His prayer echoed through the courtyard like a bell rung from the towers. The villagers looked on in silence.

Then somewhere, behind one of the mothers' skirts or under sister Flouta's rosebushes, perhaps, a small child giggled. It was an absurd sound, foreign in the heavy moment. It was an innocent sound that danced on strings from heaven. It was a beautiful, lovely, divine sound that sent a tremor of pleasure through the bones.

It was a sound that Janjic would never, never forget.

IVENA CLOSED the book and smiled. Glory!

For the third time that hour, the phone rang in the kitchen, and this time she walked to get it. She plucked the receiver from the wall on its fifth ring.

"Yes?"

"Ivena. Are you all right?"

"Of course I am."

"I've been calling for an hour."

"Because I don't answer my phone you think I am dead, Janjic?"

"No. Just concerned. Would you like me to pick you up?"

"Why would you pick me up?"

"The reception," Janjic said. "Don't tell me you forgot."

"That's tonight?" she asked.

"At five-thirty."

"And tell me again why I must attend. You know I'm not crazy about—"

"It's in your honor as much as mine, Ivena. It's your story as well. And I have a surprise I would like you to share in."

"A surprise? You can't tell me?"

"Then it would no longer be a surprise."

She let that go.

"And please, Ivena, make the best of it. Some of those there will be quite important."

"Yes. You've already told me. Don't worry, Janjic; what could an old woman like me possibly say to upset important men?"

"The fact that you even ask the question should be enough."

"Pick me up, then."

"You're sure?"

"Of course."

"Five o'clock?"

"Five is fine. Good-bye, Janjic."

"Good-bye."

She hung up.

Yes indeed, Janjic Jovic had written a brilliant book.

BOOK TWO

THE SINNER

"I tell you that in the same way there
will be more rejoicing in heaven over
one sinner who repents
than over ninety-nine
righteous persons
who do not need
to repent."

LUKE 15:7 NIV

chapter seven

"What a terrible thing it is for children to see death, you say.
We have it all wrong. If you make a child terrified of death, he won't
embrace it so easily. And death must be embraced if you wish to
follow Christ. Listen to his teaching. 'Unless you become like a
child . . . and unless you take up your cross daily, you cannot
enter the kingdom of heaven.'
One is not valuable without the other."

The Dance of the Dead, 1959

JAN PICKED Ivena up in his limousine at five and it quickly became obvious that she was in one of her moods.

"I'm not sure I'm in the spirit for silly surprises, Janjic."

"Silly? I hope you don't feel that way when you've seen it."

She gave his black suit a look-over, not entirely approving. "So. The famous author is honored again."

"Not entirely. You'll have to wait." He grinned, thinking of what he'd planned. In reality the event was more like two rolled into one. Roald's idea. The leaders wanted to honor them and he had this surprise for them. It would be perfect.

"I read the part of Nadia's death again this morning," Ivena said, staring forward.

There was nothing to say to that. He shook his head. "It's still hard to imagine my part in—"

"Nonsense. Your part is now the book."

They rode in silence then.

The war had ended within two months of that most sobering date. The history books read that Tito's Partisans liberated Sarajevo from Nazi occupation in April of 1945, but the war left Yugoslavia more bloodied than any other country engaged in the brutal struggle. One million, seven hundred thousand of her fellow citizens found death; one million of those at the hands of other Yugoslavs. Yugoslavs like Karadzic and Molosov and, yes, Yugoslavs like him.

Janjic spent five torturous years in prison for his defiance of Karadzic. His imprisonment had proved more life-threatening than the war. But he did survive, and he'd emerged a man transformed from the inside out.

It was then that he began to write. He had always been a writer, but now the words came out with gut-wrenching clarity. Within three years he had a three-inch stack of double-spaced pages beside his typewriter, and he'd confidently told Ivena that no one would publish them. They were simply too spiritual for most publishers. And if not too spiritual then certainly too Christian. For those publishers who did publish Christian material the pages were far too bloody. But they did contain the truth, even if the truth was not terribly popular in many religious circles. At least not this part of the truth. The part that suggested you must die if you wanted to live. He doubted anyone would ever publish the work.

But he wrote on. And that was a good thing because he was wrong.

He finished the book in June of 1956.

It was published in 1959.

It topped the *New York Times* bestseller list in April of 1960.

"There are times to forget, Ivena. Times like today. Times when love tells us that it's worth even death."

She turned to him. "So your surprise today has to do with love? Don't tell me you're going to ask her?"

Janjic grinned, suddenly embarrassed. "I'm not saying a thing. It wouldn't be a surprise then, would it?"

She *humphed,* but her lips curved with a small grin. "So love is in the air, is it? My, my. We can't seem to escape it."

"Love has always been in the air, Ivena. From that first day. Today I begin a new journey of love."

She smiled now. "You have much to learn about love, Janjic. We all do."

THE HOTEL'S grand ballroom was crowded with well-wishers, sipping punch and smiling in small groups an hour later. Seven tables with white embroidered tablecloths and tall red candles hosted enough shrimp and artichoke hearts to feed a convention. Three large crystal chandeliers hung from the burgundy domed ceiling, but it was Karen who shone brightly tonight, Jan thought. If not now then in a few minutes.

He watched her work the guests as only the best publicists could—gentle and sweet, yet so very persuasive. She wore an elegant red dress that flattered her trim figure. Her lips parted in a smile at something Barney Givens had said. She was with the leaders in the group—she always gravitated toward the power players, dazzling them with her intelligence. The twinkle in her brown eyes didn't hurt, of course. The subtle curve of her soft neck, stretched in laughter as it was now, did not impede her influence either. Not at all.

Working as the publicist for one of New York's largest publishing houses, Karen had come to one of his appearances at the ABC studios, more out of curiosity than anything, she'd said. The image of the pretty brunette sitting on the front row stayed with Jan for weeks, perhaps because hers were the most intelligent questions asked of him that night. Evidently the experience had impacted her deeply and she'd read his entire book late into that night. Exactly one month later they met again, at a lecture upstate, and this time Roald's scheming had come into play. Three months later she'd left New York for Atlanta, intent on igniting a new fire under *The Dance of the Dead.* They'd hired her as both agent and publicist, on a freelance basis. The brilliant publicist five years his junior had sparked a second wind to a waning message that launched the book into its third printing. Then its fourth, and its fifth and its sixth printing, each one expanding to meet the demand she had almost single-handedly created for his story.

Ivena might be right when she suggested that Karen was *a highbrow woman,* as she put it, but in many respects Jan owed his career to her *highbrow* brilliance.

Karen suddenly turned her head and caught his stare. He blushed and smiled. She winked and addressed Barney without missing a beat. This time Barney and Frank beside him both threw back their heads in laughter.

Jan leaned against the head table, admiring her. At times like this she could make his knees weak, he thought.

Ivena stood across the room talking to the ministry's accountant, Lorna. She wore a simple yellow-flowered dress that accented her grandmotherly look. But Jan was deceived by neither her white hair nor her gentle smile. They weren't talking cross-stitching over there—Ivena never talked of such trifles. *Drink her words deep, Lorna.*

To his right, a camera crew scanned the audience; Roald had invited them when Jan confessed his idea. His surprise.

"It's perfect publicity. They'll love it," he'd said.

"Now *you're* the publicist?"

"No, but we can't very well consult Karen, can we?"

"The whole world will know," Jan protested.

"Exactly. That's the point. You're the voice of love. Now you show some love of your own. It's perfect!"

"Who then?"

"ABC. I can talk to John Mathews about getting it on the news."

Jan couldn't have talked Roald out of it if he'd wanted to. The ABC crew was filming, and adding their commentary at leisure. It was now or never.

He picked up a fork, took a deep breath, and struck the side of his glass. The chime cut through the scattered conversation. He struck it again, and the din died down.

The camera had already swung to face him.

"Thank you. It's a pleasure to see you all here tonight. Thank you for coming." Jan's heart stomped through his chest. Roald was right: The world's eyes were on him.

He turned to face Karen, who smiled unsuspectingly beside Frank and Roald. "Most of you probably think my book, *The Dance of the Dead,* has forever changed my life. And you would be right. You might think that it's a culmination of a life, but there you would be wrong. It's only a beginning. I am, after all, still a young man."

Chuckles rippled through the room. Jan caught Ivena's eye.

"Ivena tells me that I have much to learn of love." He winked at her and she graciously dipped her head. "And she's right. I stand before you—before all of my friends, before the world—with the hopes of beginning a new journey into the heart of love tonight. A journey that will complete me."

Betty, their correspondence manager, gave a motherly smile and cast a look toward Karen. Some of them had guessed already, of course. His affections for Karen were hardly a secret.

"She came to us three years ago. She's brilliant and kind. She is breathtaking and she is stunning. But more than any of those, Karen makes me a man, I think. And I make her a woman."

Jan's coworkers had all but begged for this moment for over a year now. He could see their eyes brighten in the periphery of his vision. He stretched an inviting hand toward Karen. She moved through the crowd without removing her eyes from his. They were misted now, he thought. She reached him and took his hand. He bent and kissed it lightly.

Over her shoulder, he saw that even Ivena smiled wide.

"I can't believe you're doing this," Karen said in a low voice.

"Believe it," he returned quietly.

When he straightened, the small black box was in his hand, withdrawn from his pocket while bent. He snapped it open. A three-carat diamond solitaire sparkled in its black velvet perch. Someone gasped nearby—perhaps Lorna, who stood not five feet from them. Yes, it was rather extravagant. But then so was Karen.

She was smiling unabashedly now.

He held the box out to her and looked in her eyes. "Karen, will you take a journey with me? Will you give me your hand in marriage?"

A heavy silence gripped the room. The sound of ABC's camera hummed steadily.

A twinkle lit her eyes. "You're asking me to marry you?"

"Yes."

"You want to spend your life with me?"

"Yes." He swallowed.

She dropped her eyes to the box and reached for it. Her hand held a slight tremble, Jan saw. *She's going to . . .*

Suddenly he didn't know *what* she was going to do. You never quite knew with Karen. She ignored the ring, uttered a little shriek and threw herself at him. Her arms wrapped around his neck and she pulled him tight.

"Yes! Yes, I will."

He nearly dropped the box, but managed to snap it closed in his palm. Karen kissed him pointedly on the lips—more of a ceremonious display than an expression of passion. She drew back and winked at him. Then she immediately took the ring box from him, turned to face the camera and held it up proudly. The hall erupted with applause, nicely accented with catcalls and hoots of approval.

The next half-hour wandered by in a hazy dream for Jan. They all congratulated him and Karen, one by one. Interviews were held and camera bulbs flashed. Karen was glowing.

Roald approached them, smiling wide as the rounds of congratulations died down. "I couldn't offer more joy, my friends." He put a hand on each of their shoulders. "It's a perfect day for the perfect couple."

"Thank you, Roald," Karen said, dipping her head. She glanced at Jan with a twinkle in her eye. "I couldn't imagine more myself."

Roald chuckled. "Well, if you wouldn't mind entertaining the guests for a few minutes, Karen, the leaders would like to speak with Jan. We won't take him for long, I promise."

"Don't leave me stranded too long."

"You? Stranded? The cameras are still here, Karen. I'm sure you'll find a way to make use of them."

"I'll be right with you, Roald," Jan said.

The man hesitated and then stepped back. "Take your time." He walked from them.

"So we're really doing this, are we?" Karen asked.

Jan faced her, grinning. "Evidently. How does it feel?"

"It feels like it should, I think. Having the cameras here was a perfect touch. Your idea?"

"Roald's."

"I thought so. Good man."

"Yes." He glanced around and saw that the company was mostly engaged. He leaned forward and kissed her lightly on the lips. "Congratulations," he said.

For a moment they stood in silence. She reached up and straightened his tie, a small habit she performed too routinely. "You're such a handsome man. I'm so proud of you."

"I meant what I said, you know? Every word."

She kissed him on the cheek. "Yes, I do know, Mr. Jovic. And I meant what I said."

"What did you say?"

"I said yes."

He smiled and nodded. "Yes you did. Now if you'll excuse me for a few minutes while I take care of Roald and his friends."

"Take your time," she said.

He left her and angled for the meeting room across the hall. Roald intercepted him. They walked past a dozen guests, nodding graciously. "They're waiting already," Roald said. "I didn't mean to interrupt the moment but Barney has a flight in two hours and Bob promised his grandson a trip to the theater tonight."

"Ivena?"

"She's waiting as well," Roald said with grin.

"Good," Jan said. They entered the meeting room and closed the door on the noisy hall.

IVENA SAT adjacent to Janjic, listening to the scene unfold with a hubbub of monotony before her. They sat around the oval table, seven gray-haired evangelical icons from all corners of the country, sober yet delighted at once, staring at Janjic, their prize, who sat awkwardly at the head. They'd spent the first round congratulating him on the engagement and were getting down to the real meat. At least that was how Ivena saw the setting.

Janjic held himself in a distinguished manner—he could slip into the perfect professional sheen when the occasion demanded it. But beneath his new American skin the Serbian she had known could hardly hide. At least not from her. She saw the way he nonchalantly smoothed his right eyebrow when he was impatient, as he did now. And the way his mouth curved in a gentle but set grin when he politely disagreed. As it did now.

He'd filled out over the years and he'd always stood much taller than her, but under the commanding facade he was still a young man, looking for escape. His face was well aged for thirty-eight years—the war and five years in prison were mostly responsible. It didn't matter, he was still strikingly handsome. Crow's-feet already wrinkled the skin around his eyes from his constant smiling. His dark blond hair swept back, graying above his ears and curled at his collar. The white American shirts with their ties always looked a little silly on him, she thought. For all her fussing over him, Karen obviously disagreed.

Ivena watched Janjic shift his hazel eyes around the table, taking in their stares. Roald Barns, the president of the North American Evangelical Association, and the man who had brought them to this country five years earlier, sat opposite him.

"I think what Frank means," Roald said, motioning to the boxy man next to him, "is that we have an obligation to excellence. *The Dance of the Dead* has sold more than any religious book in this century. Excluding the Bible, of course. And that means it's become an extension of Christianity, so to speak. A voice to the lost world. It's important to keep that voice pure. I'm sure Jan would agree to that."

"Yes, of course," Jan said.

These evangelical leaders had come to honor him and to judge him in one fell swoop, Ivena thought—all dressed in starched white shirts and black ties. God forbid Janjic ever become a carbon copy of these men.

Ivena had held her tongue long enough while these men spoke their rounds of wisdom. She decided it was time to speak. "It really depends on what voice you're trying to keep pure, doesn't it, Frank?" she asked.

All heads turned to face her. "The message of the book," Frank said. "The message of the book needs to remain pure. And the lives of we who proclaim that message, of course."

"And what is the message of the book?" Ivena returned.

"Well, I think we already know the message of the book."

"Yes, but indulge me. Janjic tells me that it's my story as well as his. So then what does this story tell you about God's relationship with man?"

The leaders exchanged glances, off balance by her sudden challenge.

"It's the story of innocent bloodshed," Bob Story said to her left. The short, round evangelical leader shifted in his seat. "The death of martyrs, choosing death instead of renouncing Christ. Wouldn't you say?"

"In part, yes, that summarizes some of what happened. But what did the story *teach* you gentlemen? Hmm? I want to know because, unless I'm missing the tone of the past ten minutes, you are more concerned with protecting the image of the church than spreading the message of the martyrs. I believe you think that you have a flawed spokesman in Janjic, and it terrifies you."

The room suddenly felt hollowed of air. Janjic looked at her as if she'd lost her senses. But then she was right, and they all knew it. They loved the success of his book, but they did take exception to him now and then.

"True, yes? Janjic has written a magnificent book called *The Dance of the Dead* and he's been embraced by a world hungering for the unadulterated truth. But Janjic's just an ordinary man. An excellent writer, obviously, but a man with his share of flaws. Perhaps a man with *more* than his share of flaws, considering the scars the war has left on his heart. And now that he's been chosen by the world as a spokesman for your Christianity, you're quite nervous. Am I wrong?"

They stared at her unblinking.

A hotel waiter entered the conference room, perhaps to offer desserts, but with one look around the table, he thought better of it and turned on his heels. The air conditioner hummed behind Ivena, spilling cool air over her neck.

Roald was the first to recover. "I think I can speak for the group when I say that we have complete confidence in Jan. But you're right, Ivena. He has been chosen by the world, as you say. Although not without our help, I might add." They chuckled. "And he is a spokesperson for the church. Frank's correct—by virtue of his own success Jan has a unique set of standards, I would say. Not unlike any other role model—a sports hero, for example. To whom much is given, much is required."

Barney Givens cleared his throat. "I think Roald's right. We're not questioning God's work in either of your lives. It's a wonderful thing, more than any one of us could ask for. Your book, Jan, has done as much for this country's spiritual health as Billy Graham's crusades are doing. Don't take us wrong. But you have to remember that you do represent the church, son. The eyes of the world are on you. You have our honor, but you also have our caution."

"I didn't ask to represent the church," Janjic said. "I had God in mind when I wrote the book. Have I caused a specific offense, or are we just playing with words? I'm feeling schooled here."

"Nonsense," Frank said. "We're simply cautioning you to watch your step, Jan. You have a wonderful personality, young man, but you do tend to fly off the handle at times. I understand how difficult it must be to live with the memories of the war; I survived the battlefields of World War I myself. But that doesn't change our responsibility to hold the highest standard. Now's the time to consider pitfalls—not after you've stumbled into them."

"And how many women or children did you see butchered in your war? How many years did you spend in prison?"

"I'm not referring to stress from the war, and you know it. I'm talking about moral pitfalls, Jan. Any questionable appearance. It would reflect badly on the church."

"We're just cautioning you," Ted Rund said. "You've been known to be rather unorthodox. I, for one, couldn't be more pleased over what's happened, my friend. But you're speaking for the church now. You've been on virtually every television show in the country. We're in times of upheaval. The moral state of our country is under a full-throttled assault and the church is being scrutinized under a new light. You're one of our most effective spokesmen. We're simply holding you accountable."

Jan leaned back and tapped his fingers on the table. They were obviously not telling him everything.

"What did I do? Tell me how I offended you," Jan said.

Roald and Frank looked at each other, but it was Frank who answered.

"What you did was call our character into question last week in front of two million viewers."

"*Your* character? You mean with Walter Cronkite?" Jan asked incredulously. "He asked if the church today understands the love of Christ. I said no. You found that offensive?"

"I believe 'not at all' were the words you chose. And yes, *our* character. We represent the church; the church represents Christ's love, and you have the gall to say on a national show that we don't understand that love. You don't think that undermines the leadership?"

Ivena interrupted them quietly. "You still haven't answered my question, gentlemen. What is the real message of Janjic's book?"

They looked at her dumbly, as if her mind were not functioning properly.

"Let me tell you then," she said. "The message is that God loves man passionately. That one moment with God is worth death. He gave his own life for nothing less. I'm not sure any of you has learned the nature of God's love yet."

Except for the sound of Bob Story's spoon clinking through his coffee the room fell to silence. They had come from all over the country for a conference in Atlanta and carved out a few hours in Janjic's honor; surely they had not expected this. Jan looked at Roald and offered that set grin of his, as if to say, *"She's right—you know she is."* Roald held Jan's eyes for a full second and then looked at Ivena.

"I think that Ivena's right," he said. "We're all learning about God's love. Ivena has simply expressed this truth in a way that's as unique as Jan's story. And please do not misunderstand us; we are thrilled at the work God has done with *The Dance of the Dead.* I think my own effort speaks for itself. We just ask you to be cautious, Jan. You've risen among the ranks, so to speak. A lot of people look to your example. Just watch your step, that's all. What do they say? 'Don't bite the hand that feeds you'?"

Several of them chuckled. Ivena thought about telling them that Janjic did not need their hands, but she thought better of it.

Jan nodded. "Good enough. Point taken." That seemed to satisfy them.

"I propose a toast," Roald said. He pushed his spectacles up on his nose. "To *The Dance of the Dead.* May she live forever."

They drank to a chorus of "Amens." Surely they must know that in reality, the life of Janjic's bestseller was nearing an end. It had soared high and far, but the story had run its course over the last five years, a fact that brought Ivena pause in light of their conversation. Why were Roald and this conservative bunch so concerned about Jan's image now?

The meeting disbursed ten minutes later with firm handshakes and one last round of affirmations. The leaders were off, leaving Jan alone with Ivena in the empty room. The sounds of laughter swept in through the open door; the party was winding down.

"I should be leaving now, Janjic."

"So soon? And you haven't even congratulated me yet."

Ivena reached a hand to his cheek. "Congratulations, my dear Serb." She smiled. "I'm sure she will make you very happy."

"Thank you. Would you like Steve to take you home?"

"I'll take a cab."

"Then I'll walk you."

JAN SKIRTED the party and walked Ivena to the street. Not until they were outside did Janjic confront her about the exchange in the room. "You really think that was the best time to question their spiritual sensibilities, Ivena?"

"It was perhaps the *only* time. I don't run with them every day."

"Of course, but you were pretty direct. Actually I shouldn't complain—I think it played in my favor."

"And how is that, Janjic?"

"Compared to you they see that I'm a gentle breeze. I may have brief periods of disorientation and grab the nearest telephone pole at the sound of a car's backfire, but at least I don't line the country's top religious leaders up and school them in the love of Christ." He chuckled and then cleared his throat.

"When we return to Bosnia they will be a distant memory," she said.

"I'm happy in America. You're happy in America. Why do you cling to this silly notion of returning to the land that nearly killed us both?"

"It's a notion that won't fade. We will see, Janjic."

She wasn't sure if the hunch they would one day return to see her daughter's grave one last time came from her own latent desires or if there was more at work there, and she'd given up trying to discern three years ago.

"I'm not sure Karadzic would take my return too kindly. I've turned him into an infamous monster."

"A reputation well deserved," she said.

They walked for the curb.

"I had the dream again last night," he said. "It was so vivid."

She glanced up at him. He'd had the same dream every few nights for twenty years now—the nightmare the psychiatrists liked to blame on the war. But she had her own ideas. She stopped and turned to him.

"Tell it to me."

"You know it. There's nothing new."

"Tell it to me again. It will help you."

He swallowed. "Okay. I'm in a pitch-black room, strapped to a wooden beam behind me. It's the same: I can't see anything, but I can feel everything—the ropes digging in, the sweat leaking down my naked body. I think I am being crucified."

He stopped and breathed deep. Then he continued. "I can hear my own breathing, in long ragged pulls, echoing as if I'm in a chamber. That's all I can hear, and it terrifies me. It stays like that for a long time, as if I'm suspended between life and death." He blinked. "And then the lights are thrown on. And I'm not in a dungeon; I'm staring at a white field." He stopped and looked down at her.

"And that's where it always ends." She stated it rather than asked it.

"Yes. And it means nothing to me."

She reached up and rubbed his arm. He nervously ran his fingers through his hair. "The doctors may be right; maybe it's only my mind playing tricks, pretending to be Father Micheal on the cross."

"Those doctors are full of nonsense. Take it from me; the dream has meaning beyond this world. I'm sorry I can't tell you what that is, but one day we will know. I'm certain of it."

"Maybe you're right."

"Perhaps the dream speaks more to what you have *not* experienced than to what you have, hmmm?"

"Meaning what?"

"Meaning that there's still more to learn about love, Janjic. Meaning that *The Dance of the Dead* only tells part of the story. God knows you have more to learn of love."

He looked at her with mild surprise. "As do we all. But now you're suggesting that I haven't learned the lesson of the priest, right alongside of Roald?"

"Not necessarily. But I do worry for you at times, Janjic. Sometimes I wonder if you've become more like those around you than they've become like you. You defend the truth with vigorous words, but your life is changing."

Now his mild surprise was accompanied by a blink. "You really think so?"

"Come on, Janjic. Is it really such a secret?"

"I don't know. But changing a few things on the surface doesn't remake the man."

"No. I wasn't referring to your skin. I mean your heart. Where do your affections lie, Janjic?"

"My affections are with God. And my affections are with Karen. You may not approve, but it's me, not you, who'll marry her."

"What I'm saying has nothing to do with Karen! I'm speaking of Christ."

"You're too strong, Ivena. I've written a book on the affections of Christ, for heaven's sake! Give me some credit."

"You witnessed a dramatic expression of affection between God and man, and you've committed your observations to a book. Just because you saw the love of the priest does not mean that you've learned how to love in the same way." She paused. "Perhaps the fact that you have been unable to write since the book tells us something."

She'd never spoken quite so plainly about the matter, and he looked at her with shock. "You say that with such conviction! I also spent five years in prison for opposing Karadzic. Still you question my love for God? That it has given me writer's block?"

"You understand the love in ways most do not. But still, have you loved him that way? Loved Christ? Or have I, for that matter? And I'll tell you something else: Until we do, we'll never find peace. You've seen too much, my dear Serb."

Traffic hummed by on the street. Janjic waved at a yellow cab that veered toward them. "Yes, maybe I have seen too much. And you as well." He faced her. "You're right, one day we'll find our way through this. In the meantime, please don't rob me of the love I have for Karen." He smiled and opened her door. "Give me at least that much."

"Don't be so sure that I don't approve. You mustn't confuse caution with disapproval, my dear Serb." She climbed into the cab. "Call me soon, Janjic. Come for supper when you can."

"I will. Thank you for coming."

"It was my pleasure." She shut the door.

She left him standing there alone, watching her go. All dressed up in the wrong clothes, but so handsome nonetheless. Famous and now engaged to be married. So very wise and so very tender, yet in his own way lost without knowing it.

Her Janjic.

CHAPTER EIGHT

IVENA'S WORDS burned a hole in Janjic's soul that night. He was newly engaged, for goodness' sake—singing the song of true love—and Ivena had the audacity to suggest that his words were louder than his life. The ringing truth of her suggestion tempered him.

The next day started no better, and he decided to take an hour to sort out his mind at the park before Karen returned to the office after her morning meeting. She was evidently neck-deep in discussions with their publisher over the next edition, and as always she preferred to handle the details on her own. This time the publisher had come to Atlanta and Jan didn't even bother to suggest he attend the meeting. He was a writer, not a businessman.

It was then, sitting on a bench in Piedmont Park, that he first saw her. She was still a shimmering figure at the park's perimeter, a faceless ghost in the midday heat. She looked small and frail under the massive weeping willows that swayed with the wind. He didn't know why his eyes were drawn to her—his mind certainly wasn't. It was busy grappling with the growing dilemmas that seemed to have infected his soul since Ivena had graced him with her words. Maybe it was the woman's direct approach that drew him; or perhaps it was the intensity with which she walked, swinging her arms barely, but hustling along at a good clip nonetheless.

Jan shifted his mind back to Ivena's words.

The people had bought *The Dance of the Dead* in a feeding frenzy, desperate for meaning in a changing world. It was as if a generation had decided en masse to reflect on its past sins and had chosen this one book in which to look for absolution. The story of the young Serbian soldier who had found meaning through the brutality of war and his imprisonment following that war. There was a soul to his story that drew them. Like curious onlookers at a Big Foot exhibit.

He'd told them in bold terms at every university campus and every book signing and every radio show that *The Dance of the Dead* was a story first and foremost about the martyr's desperate love for Christ, not Jan Jovic's redemption. They would mostly nod their heads with glazed looks and ask about the girl or his ordeal in war crimes prison after that fateful day. He would tell them and tears would come to their eyes. But they were not falling to their knees and begging forgiveness as he had. They weren't throwing away their lives for Christ as Nadia had done. They weren't climbing on their crosses and laughing in delight as the priest had.

Therein lay part of the problem, he thought. His life had become a spectacle. An exhibit. But in the end they all walked away from the exhibit, shaking their heads in wonder, unwilling to climb in to join Big Foot in his lonely search for identity.

And now Ivena's little tidbit of truth: Perhaps he himself had peered at the exhibit without climbing in. Maybe he himself hadn't learned as well as he expected his audience to learn.

The woman still approached steadily. An American woman hustling her way through a park, dressed in black pants and a white shirt, going nowhere fast, as the cliché had it. He leaned back and watched her absently.

The Dance of the Dead. In the priest's village it had been a dance of rapture, begging to be joined by those who watched. A great awakening to the other side. But here in America it was inevitably different. They were more interested in having their ears tickled than their hearts changed. Perhaps he could write another book after all, one that characterized these new steps taught in the churches here. He could call it *The Death of the Dance.* That would have the publishers scrambling.

Jan leaned over and rested his elbows on his knees. His mind fell back to that day. It had been the love of Christ that had pierced his soul in the village. The sentiment swelled in his chest and rose to his throat. Dear, precious Nadia. And *Ivena!* He still couldn't imagine the grief of her loss. It was a part of his insistence that she come to America with him and he supposed it was a good thing. She alone really understood.

"Hi, there."

He jerked upright, startled by the voice. It was the woman! In his quandary she had walked right up to him and now stood not five feet away, trying to smile.

"Yes?"

She glanced behind her shoulder and he followed her look. Nothing but empty park and an old couple walking a dog. She sniffed and turned back to him.

A small shiver seemed to work its way over her body and she tried to smile again. A flat grin pulled at her pale lips. Her eyes twinkled bright blue, but otherwise her face appeared void of life. Dark circles hung under each eye and her cheeks looked powdered white though he could see that she wore no makeup. Her blond hair lay in short, stringy tangles.

Jan couldn't help his slow gaze over the woman. The plain white T-shirt rode up her arms, too small even for her delicate frame. Her blue jeans hung past flip-flops to the ground where they were frayed.

She lifted a hand to her lips and bit at a worn nail. Now, half hidden by her hand, her smile took up life. "I'm sorry. I hope I'm not too much of a shock for you," she said. "If I am, I could go. Do you want me to go?"

She said it with a tease in her voice. If he wasn't thoroughly confused, she was a junkie, strung out or coming down or doing whatever drug addicts did. He almost told her to leave then. To get lost. To find her pimp or her pusher or whomever she was looking for someplace else. He was a writer, not a pusher. He almost told her that.

Almost.

"Ah . . . No. No it's all right. Are you okay?"

"Why? Don't I look okay?"

"Actually no. You look . . . strung out."

"And you have a cute accent, mister. How old are you?"

He glanced around. The park was still empty. "I'm thirty-eight."

She reached out a hand and he took it. "Glad to meet you, Thirty-eight. I'm Twenty-nine."

He smiled. "Actually, my name is Jan. Jan Jovic."

"And mine's Helen."

"It's a pleasure to meet you."

"The same, Jan Jovic." She shot a quick look behind her again, and Jan saw concern flash through her eyes. But she recovered on the fly and looked at him, wearing that deliberate smile again. She tilted her head back, closed her eyes and ran fingers through her hair. It struck him then, while her chin pointed to the sky, that Helen was a pretty woman. Even in this anemic state she bore a faint angelic quality. She walked a few steps to the left and then returned to the spot directly before him, as if pondering some deep question.

"Are you sure you're okay?"

She eyed him, still wearing her mysterious grin.

Jan shrugged. "You look like you have something on your mind. And you keep looking back."

"Well, to be honest, I am in a bit of pinch. But it's got nothing to do with you. Boyfriend problems." She shrugged apologetically. "You know how love is—one day on, the next day off. So today it's off." She sniffed and glanced behind.

"I wasn't aware that love turned on and off so easily," he said. "So why did you come over to me?"

"Then you haven't had a lover lately, Jan. And I came over because you looked like a decent man. You have a problem with that?"

"No. But women like you usually don't walk over to men like me because we look decent."

"Women like me? And what kind of woman's that?"

She had a quick mind—the drugs hadn't destroyed that yet. "Women who are having boyfriend problems," he said.

"Hmm. You haven't, have you?"

"I haven't what?"

"You haven't had a lover lately."

He felt heat wash over his face and he hoped it didn't show as a blush. "Actually I've never been married. But I am—"

"And no lovers?"

"I'm a minister of sorts. I don't just take lovers. If there's a lover in my life it is Christ."

Her eyebrows arched. "Oh? A minister. A reverend, huh?"

"No. Actually I'm a writer and a lecturer who speaks on the love of God."

"Well, holy cripes. The pope himself!"

Jan smiled. "I'm not Catholic. And what do *you* do, Helen? I take it you aren't a nun."

"Pretty observant, Reverend."

"I'm not a reverend. I told you, I'm a writer."

"Either way, Reverend, you are a man seeking to save lost souls, am I right?"

"I suppose so. Yes. Or at least to lead them to safety. So what do you do?"

She took a deep breath. "I'm . . . I am a lover." She smiled wide.

"You're a lover. A lover who throws love on with a switch and flees her boyfriends? You are a . . . What do you call it? A woman of the str—"

"No, I'm *not* a hooker! I'd never stoop that low." Her eyes flashed. "Do I look like a hooker to you?"

He didn't answer.

"You probably wouldn't know a hooker if one crawled up on your lap, would you? No, because you're a man who peddles the love of God. Of course, how silly of me."

"I'm sorry. I didn't mean to offend you."

"No offense taken, Reverend." She used the title deliberately, with a slight smile, and Jan thought that if she'd been offended, she had already let it go. "You're as pure as the driven snow, aren't you? Probably never had so much as dirt under your nails."

"If you knew my life story you would not say that," he said.

She blinked, not quite sure what to make of that comment. The air of defense deflated about her. He shifted his gaze past her. Two figures entered the park from the direction she had come, walking fast. Helen saw his look and turned. She spun back and clenched her jaw.

"You know, maybe you could help me." She bit her lip and a shadow of fear flashed through her eyes. Jan looked at the men again. They strode together, dressed in dark suits, clearly intent on crossing the park.

"What's wrong? Who are they?"

"Nothing. No one. I mean, I don't want to involve you." She looked back to them quickly. Her fear was rising, he thought.

Jan shifted to the front of the park bench. They were after her. He could see it in the attitude of their heads and the length of their strides. He'd seen men brimming with ill intent a thousand times in his homeland; had come to recognize them with a casual glance. These two now approaching with long strides meant Helen harm.

She spun back to him and this time her resolve broke. Helen dropped to one knee, in a proposal posture; her eyes wrinkled, pleading. She grabbed his right hand with both of hers. "I'm sorry! You have to help me! Glenn swore he'd kill me the next time I left. They've been following me all day. I swear they'll kill me! Do you have a car?"

Her hands were cool on his and her face begged. Hers was the face of a victim—he'd seen a hundred thousand of them in the war and they haunted him still.

"Glenn?" he muttered, standing. But his mind was not asking about this Glenn of hers. It was weighing the world in the scales of justice, balancing the touch of this lowlife against an obscure sense of correctness that had taken up residence in his mind.

He could hear Karen at the office now. *You did what?*

He blinked. *I rescued a junkie from two hoodlums today.*

"Glenn Lutz," Helen said. "Please! I've got nowhere to go." She twisted to see the approaching men. The snappy, confident woman had dissolved into desperation.

They were no more than thirty yards off now, angling directly for them.

You did what?

I rescued a junkie from two hoodlums today, and it made me feel alive.

Jan bolted from the bench, pulling Helen stumbling behind him. "Come on! Are they armed?"

"You have a car?"

He glanced back. The men had dispensed with their professional facade and tore after them. They both held handguns, jerking in their sprint.

Jan uttered a surprised cry. "Hurry! Around the corner!" The men were closing and suddenly Jan was thinking he'd made a mistake. His heart pounded as much from the rush of adrenaline as from the run.

She raced beside him now, matching his pace with two steps for each of his, but as fast nonetheless.

But the men behind were still gaining. And the car was still out of sight.

The next time he saw Karen might very well be from a hospital bed, speaking past a bandaged face.

You did what?

Well, I tried to rescue this junkie . . .

"Where's the car?" Helen panted in near panic.

They were on the sidewalk now. He flung a hand forward, pointing. Behind him shoes clacked onto the concrete. And then one stopped. Kneeling to fire?

"Where is it?"

A white Cadillac suddenly pulled away from the curb and roared full-throttle toward them, flashing its lights. Helen pulled up beside him and Jan snatched her hand.

"Come on!"

The Cadillac squealed to a stop alongside them.

Jan yanked the door open, spun Helen around and shoved her into the backseat. He cast one last glance to the side and saw that both men had pulled up and hid their weapons. He clambered in after Helen.

"This is your car?" She was staring through the tinted window at their pursuers, panting and exuberant.

"Yes. Thank God, Steve!"

Steve pulled a squealing U-turn and punched the accelerator to the floor. "Good night, Jan! What on earth was *that?*"

Jan didn't answer directly. "You okay?" he asked Helen.

"Yes."

"What was that, Jan?" the driver asked again, glancing repeatedly in the rearview mirror. "What on *earth* was that?"

Jan gripped his hands to fists to still their tremble and he giggled.

It was a short chuckle-like giggle, but it was the first time he'd giggled in a long time. "Whoooeee!" he hooted. "We made it!"

Steve grinned wide, infected by Jan's relief. Helen let out a cry of victory. "Yeehaaa! Boy, did we!" She slapped Jan's thigh in an elemental gesture of congratulations. "Boy, did we!"

They sped around a corner. "Jan, *what* on earth was that?" Steve demanded again.

Jan looked at Helen with a raised brow. "I don't know, Steve. I really don't know."

chapter nine

GLENN LUTZ peered past the smoke glass wall on the thirtieth floor of Atlanta's Twin Towers to the crawling city below, ignoring the sweat that snaked down his nose.

It was green and gray down there, a hundred thousand bushy trees deadlocked with the concrete in a slow battle over the territory. The gray was slowly winning. Pedestrians crawled along the streets, like ants scampering to and fro in their senseless rush. If one of them were to look up and see past the reflective glass surrounding Glenn they might see the city's best-known city councilman frowning down, hands on hips, feet planted wide, dressed in white slacks and a Hawaiian shirt, and think he was gloating over his power.

But Glenn Lutz did not feel any of wealth's pleasures just now. In fact he felt buck naked, stripped of his power, robbed of his heart. Like a man just learning that his accountant had made a mistake. That he wasn't the city's wealthiest man after all. That in fact he was quite decidedly broke. That he could no longer afford the hefty lease payment on the top three floors of Atlanta's most prestigious towers and must be out in twenty-four hours.

Glenn pulled his lips back over crooked teeth, bit down and closed his eyes for a moment. He lifted thick fingers to his chin and pulled at his prickly jaw. Sweat darkened his shirt in large fans under each arm—he hadn't showered in two days and this pointless pursuit of Helen had left him frantic. He hadn't brushed his teeth either, and he was reminded of the fact with a blast of his own breath. Two days of alcohol had not entirely weakened the heavy odors of dental decay.

Glenn turned from the window and glared at the wall opposite him. It was solid mirror from black tile to ceiling and now his image stared back at him. It showed a tall man, six foot five and thick like a bull. The flesh was firm. Bone-white, hairy, and layered in cellulite maybe, but solid. His stomach could use some trimming. Helen had told him so just three days ago and he had slapped her face with an open palm. The memory sent a chill through his arms. Never mind that she'd had her arms wrapped *around* his stomach when she'd made the remark.

His mind softened. *Helen, dear Helen. How could you do this to me? How could you leave me so empty? We had a deal, baby. We're knit from the same cloth, you and I. What can you possibly be thinking?*

Glenn ground his molars. Indirect lighting cast a soft atmospheric hue over the mirrored walls. His eyes stared back at him, vacant, like two holes drilled through his head. It was his most remarkable trait, he thought. His driver's license said they were dark brown, but beyond ten feet any reasonable soul would cross themselves and swear those eyes were black. Jet black. He had started dyeing his hair light blond to accent the eyes a week after high school graduation. Now his hair hung nearly white around stubbled jowls.

Glenn lifted his chin and frowned. Truth be told, slip a black robe over his shoulders and he would look more like a warlock than some business tycoon. Now *that* would do wonders with the women. On the other hand, forget the coat; the image in the mirror was enough to terrify most women as it was.

Most. Not Helen. Helen was special. Helen was his goddess.

He glanced around the office. Over here in the business tower there was nothing to show but a single bare oak desk set on the shiny black tile. The decorator's idea had been to create a stark impression, but Glenn had fired her before she'd completed the job. Thankfully the foulmouthed wench had finished the suite on the adjacent tower; the Palace he called it. That had been three months ago, just before he'd met Helen, and to say that the Palace had delivered would be an absurd understatement. It was either pleasure to the bone or raw pain over there. Ecstasy or agony. The chambers of exotic delights. Which was appropriate considering the fact that he ran one of the country's largest drug rings out of the suite.

The phone on his desk rang and he started. He swore and strode for the black object. He snatched up the receiver. "What?"

"Sir, we really do have to talk. You have calls stacking up and—"

"And I told you not to bother me with this junk!"

"Some of them look important."

"And what could be so important? I'm occupied here, if you didn't notice."

"Yes, of course I noticed. Who wouldn't notice? And meanwhile you have legitimate business piling up around you."

Glenn felt heat flush his neck. Only she could say such a thing. He took a deep breath. "Get in here," he said, and slammed the receiver onto its cradle.

Beatrice strutted in with her chin leveled. Her black hair was piled high in a bun and her lips curved downward, matching the arc of her large nose. She was fifty pounds overweight and her cinched belt exaggerated the folds of fat at her belly. It was a symbiotic relationship with her. If she didn't know so much he might have ditched her long ago.

"What's so important?"

She slid into a burgundy guest chair and lifted a yellow steno pad. "For starters, you missed the council meeting last night."

"Immaterial. Give me something that matters."

"Okay. The renovations on the lower floors of the Bancroft Building are running into a snag. The contractor's screaming about—"

"What does this have to do with me?"

"You *own* the building."

"That's right. I *own* it. I don't build them, I buy them."

"They're saying it'll go over budget in excess of a million dollars."

"I don't care if it goes over budget two million. Right now I don't care if it goes over five million!"

She blinked at the outburst. "Fine. Then I guess you won't be interested in the rest of these matters either. What's a few million?" She was trying to bait him.

"That's right, Beatrice. And if anybody does anything stupid, I'll deal with them later. But not now."

She unfolded her legs as if to stand. "Yes, not now. Now you're taking care of more important business."

"Don't step over this line, Beatrice."

"She'll ruin you, Glenn."

"She's my life."

"And she'll be your death. What's come over you with this woman?"

Glenn didn't respond. It was a good question.

Beatrice looked at him and shook her head. "I've seen them come and go, Glenn, but never like this one. She's controlling you."

Shut up, you witch! He remained silent while her words spun through his mind. She was right in a small way. He could hardly understand his obsession with Helen himself. Helen had waltzed into his life only a few short months ago, a ghost from his past, and now she had possessed him. But Helen . . . Helen wasn't so easily possessed. She held that power over him, and his desire for her ran like fire through his blood, in spite of—or maybe because of—her refusal to be possessed.

"You want her only because you can't have her," Beatrice said. "She's nothing but a piece of trash, and you're slobbering over her like a dog. Come on, Glenn. You're neglecting your own interests. Look at you; you look like a pig."

"Out," he snarled, trembling now.

She stood with a *humph* and walked for the door. She was the only being on the planet who would dare make such statements. Glenn watched her bulging profile and fought an urge to leap after her and pound her into the tile. Beatrice turned at the door. "When was the last time you took a bath?"

"Out! Out, out!" he thundered.

She drilled him with a sharp stare and then strutted off with her chin level and proud, as if she'd somehow set him straight.

Glenn slammed a fist onto the desk and stormed for the far wall. He hit the glass with both palms and it shuddered under the blow. One of these days it would break and send him tumbling to his death. He pressed his forehead against it and peered at Atlanta, stretched out like a toy city. Nothing down there seemed to have changed in the last few minutes. It was still gray and green and scampering with ants.

"Where are you, Helen?" he muttered. "Where are you?"

THE CADILLAC rolled through Atlanta's western business district, silent except for the air conditioner's cool blast. They passed a large shiny Woolworth's storefront on their right; pedestrians strode along the sidewalk smartly dressed in dark business suits and dresses. Jan collected his thoughts before turning to Helen.

"So. Who were they?"

She looked out her window. "Do preachers always drive such expensive cars?"

"I'm not a preacher. I'm a writer. I wrote a book that did well."

"I suppose you take it any way you can get it. Not that I don't approve; I do. I just didn't expect your shiny white ride to fly in just when it did, that's all."

"I'm glad I could be of service. Which leads us back to my first question. Who were those two men?"

She shifted her eyes back to the passing road. "Where are we going?"

"To a friend's house. If I'm not mistaken, I just risked my neck back there for you. The least you can do is tell me what for."

"They were two of Glenn's men."

"And Glenn? Tell me about Glenn."

"You don't want to know about Glenn, Reverend."

"Please don't call me Reverend anymore. And again, I think I've earned the right to know about Glenn."

She smiled at him, a tad condescending. "Yes, I suppose you have, haven't you? But trust me, you don't *want* to know about Glenn. He's like a prison—just because you've earned a stay doesn't mean you *want* to go. But then you've probably never been to prison, have you?"

The notion to wallop her upside the head with one of his books crossed his mind. And then another thought: that even a year ago the impulse wouldn't have entered his mind at all. He stared at a hardcover copy of his book that peered at them from the seatpocket netting. Its surrealistic image of a man's bloodstained face stretched in laughter against a bright red sky even now seemed to mock him. Ivena was right, he'd seen too much.

Jan spoke without removing his eyes from the book. "Actually, I have spent time in prison. Five years."

Her grin softened slowly. Jan spoke while he had the advantage. "And yes, I do want to know about any man who threatens my life, regardless of the situation."

"What prison?"

"Tell me."

She turned away. "I told you. Glenn Lutz."

Now they were getting somewhere. "Yes, but you didn't tell me *who* Glenn Lutz is."

She looked at him with a raised eyebrow. "I can't believe you've never heard of Glenn Lutz. The developer? He's even on the city council, although God knows he's got no business there."

"And he's the kind of man that would have henchmen?"

"He's got money, doesn't he? When you've got money, you've always got something going on the side. In Glenn's case he's got a whole ton of money. And if people knew what he had going on the side . . ." She let the statement go. "Trust me, Preacher, you don't *ever* want to know him."

She flipped her stringy tangles back and ran her fingers through them in a futile combing attempt. Her pale skin was smooth; her jawline sloping back to a fair neck, like a delicate wishbone. She closed her eyes, suddenly sobered by her account of Glenn Lutz.

If this young woman was a junkie, which she surely was, she wasn't meant to be a junkie, Jan thought.

"And what does this man have to do with you?" he asked.

"I really don't want to talk about him, if you don't mind. He wants to kill me; isn't that enough?" Her voice wavered and suddenly Jan felt regret for having asked the question at all.

"He's your boyfriend?" Jan asked.

"No."

He nodded and looked through the front windshield. They were winding through an industrial part of town now, not so far from Ivena's house. Red-brick buildings passed on either side. Steve's reflection smiled at him in the mirror. He nodded and returned the man's gesture of support.

You did what?

I rescued a junkie from two goons in the park, but she really has no business being a junkie. Really she is quite witty.

And if not a junkie, what should she be?

I don't know.

Jan turned back to Helen. "You said Glenn wanted to—"

"Actually, I thought I said I didn't want to talk about the pig." She looked at him apologetically. "Didn't I say that? I mean, it wasn't two minutes ago and I could swear I asked you not to speak about the man."

Jan glanced to the front. Steve had lost his smile.

"Look, Reverend. I know you don't run into my type every day. I'm sure this is quite a shock to you—riding in your white Cadillac beside some lowlife running for her life. But in my world you can't just go around talking about every deal that goes down or you might find yourself on the wrong end of one of those deals." Her voice had softened. "If you knew what I'd been through in the last twenty-four hours, you might not be so critical."

He turned to her. "And if you knew what I had been through in the last twenty-four years you would not be so defensive."

They looked at each other for a long moment, each caught in the other's direct stare. Her eyes brimmed with tears and she turned. *Easy, Jan. She's a wounded one. You know about wounding, don't you? Perhaps she's not so different from you.* He cleared his throat and sat back.

They rode in an awkward silence for a few minutes.

"So," he finally said. "Now that I've saved your neck, is there any particular place you would like to go?"

The brick buildings had evolved into a heavily treed suburban neighborhood and Helen studied the homes. "He's got eyes everywhere."

"Glenn?"

She nodded.

"Then perhaps my friend can help until you decide what to do."

Helen looked at him. "Is he as kind as you?"

"He is a she. And yes, she is very kind."

"Girlfriend?"

"No." Jan smiled. "Heavens no. We're just very close."

"Then I think that would be okay."

"Good." Ivena would know what to do. Jan would drop Helen off at Ivena's house and ask her to set the girl on a course that removed her from any immediate danger. Perhaps call the authorities if Helen would allow it. He breathed deep. It was a thing to think about, this strange encounter. Something to think about, indeed.

CHAPTER TEN

Q: "You've been criticized by some for your attention to detail in the suffering of the martyrs. They say it's not decent for a Christian writer to dwell on such pain. Do you cross the line between realistic description and voyeurism?"

A: "Of course not. Realism allows us to participate in one's suffering and voyeurism takes pleasure from it. The two are like white and black. But many Christians would shut the suffering of the saints from their minds; it's not what Christ had in mind. He knew his disciples would want to forget, so he asked them to drink his blood and eat his body in remembrance. The writer of Hebrews tells us to imagine we are there, with those in suffering. I ask you, why is the church so eager to run from it?"

Jan Jovic, author of bestseller The Dance of the Dead
Interview with Walter Cronkite, 1961

THE TINY green shoot at the base of Nadia's dying rosebush had grown two inches overnight. Two inches of growth was too much for one night. Unless her memory of the previous morning was a bit fuzzy and it had already been two inches then.

Ivena bent over the blackened plant and blinked at the strange sight. The small shoot curled slightly upward, like a relaxed finger. The texture of its skin was different from any rose stem she knew of. Not as dark either.

She gently stroked the base of the shoot. By all appearances it was a graft, which could only mean one thing: She had grafted this shoot into Nadia's rosebush.

And then promptly forgotten it.

It was possible, wasn't it? She could've been so distressed over the prospect of Nadia's bush dying that her mind had wiped out a whole sequence of events. It could've been a week ago, for that matter, and judging by the growth it had been a week ago. At least.

The doorbell chimed and Ivena jerked up, startled. It was a delivery, perhaps. The bulbs she'd ordered last week. She pulled off her gloves, wiped her hands on her apron and wound her way through the small house to the front door.

She peeked through the viewer and saw two forms on the porch, one of which was . . . *Janjic! What a pleasant surprise!* She opened the door.

"Janjic! Come in, come in!" She leaned forward and allowed him to kiss each cheek. He was dressed in a well-worn beige shirt without a collar, Bosnian style, and his cologne smelled spicy when he bent for her kiss.

"Ivena, I would like you to meet Helen."

The dark lines around Janjic's eyes wrinkled with a nervous smile. He ran a hand through his hair. Ivena looked at the young woman beside Janjic. Any friend of Jan's would be a friend of hers, but this one was odd to be sure. For starters, the blue-eyed girl looked as though someone had drained the blood from her face. She smiled nicely enough, but even her lips were pale. And her hair hadn't been washed in several days at the least. The T-shirt and jeans made her look very young. Gracious, what was Janjic up to?

"Hello, my dear. My name is Ivena. Come in. Please, come in. And what of Steve?" she asked, looking to the Cadillac. "Will he join us?"

"No, I can't stay long," Janjic said, smoothing his brow.

They entered the house and followed her to the small dining room. She had bread in the oven and its warm scent wafted through the house. Why Americans purchased their bread when they could make it easily enough Ivena could not appreciate. Bread was to smell and to feel; it was to make, not just eat.

"Would you like a drink, Janjic?"

"I'm not sure—"

"Of course you would. We must have a drink together while you tell me of your new friend." She turned and winked at Jan.

"Yes. Yes, all right." Jan pulled a chair from the table, and Ivena could see that his cheeks had reddened slightly. Helen did not respond. Her eyes darted nervously about the house. She looked like a wild bird newly caged. A dove, maybe, with her soft white skin, but skittish and uncomfortable just the same.

"Sit, my dear. It's okay. I'll get us some tea."

Five minutes later they sat around a small blue pot and three porcelain cups of steaming tea, sipping the hot liquid. But really, only Jan and Ivena sipped. The girl picked hers up once and brought it to her lips, but she replaced it on the saucer without drinking. Ivena smiled politely and waited, wondering at the presence of this strange woman sitting between them.

Jan looked as though he wasn't quite sure how to begin so Ivena helped him out. "Just tell me, Jan. What would you like me to know about Helen?"

"Yes. Well, we have a problem here. Helen's in some trouble. She needs help."

Ivena looked at Helen and smiled. "But of course you do, my dear. I could see this much the moment I opened the door."

"That bad, huh?"

Ivena nodded. "I'm afraid so. What is the problem, child? You're hurting, I see."

Helen blinked.

"No offense, dear. But you look as though you just crawled from a sewer," Ivena said.

The skin around Jan's hazel eyes wrinkled with an apologetic smile. "You'll have to forgive Ivena, she doesn't really like to mince words."

"And would you *rather* I minced words, Janjic?"

"Of course not. But Helen might prefer some discretion."

Ivena tilted her head. "I may have passed my fiftieth year, but honestly, it hasn't yet affected my sight." She faced Helen. "And my sight tells me that the last thing your dear Helen needs is the mincing of words. She might very well need a bath and some hot food, but she's seen enough of wordsmithing, I'm sure."

Helen watched them with wide eyes, turning from one to the other.

"What do you say, dear?" Ivena asked.

"Wha . . . About what?"

"Would you like me to speak directly or mince my words?"

Helen glanced at Jan, then gathered herself. "Speak directly."

"Yes. I thought as much. So where did my famous author find you?"

"Actually, Jan may have saved my life," Helen said.

Ivena raised her eyebrows. "Saved your life? You did this, Janjic?"

"She was being chased in the park and I had the Cadillac. It was the least I could do."

"So now you have brought her here for safekeeping, is that it?"

"It wasn't my idea, I swear," Helen said quickly. "He could've dropped me off on a corner. Really."

Ivena looked at the girl carefully. For all the dirt and grime hovering about her, she possessed a refreshing look in her face. A certain lack of presumption. "Well, I would certainly agree with him, my dear. I can see that the corner is no place for you. He was right in bringing you here, I think. Did Janjic tell you how I came to be his friend?"

"No. He said that you were as kind as he."

"Indeed? And do you find him a kind man?"

"Sure. Yes, I do," Helen said, looking at Jan, who smiled awkwardly.

"Then I suppose that there's hope for everyone," Ivena said. "That includes you, my dear."

"You're saying I need help? Like I said, the corner would've been fine. I'm not askin' for your help here."

"Maybe not. But you would like it, wouldn't you?"

Helen held Ivena's gaze for a moment and then shifted her eyes and shrugged. "I can manage."

"Manage what?"

"Manage like I always managed."

Ivena lifted an eyebrow, but she held her tongue. Perhaps this little ragged junkie had been led to them. Perhaps Helen played a part.

"What do you think, Janjic?"

"I don't know," he answered.

Helen gazed from one to the other.

Ivena nodded. "And you want me to keep her?"

"Maybe."

"Wait a minute," Helen said, glancing between them. "I don't think—"

"Well, she certainly can't stay at the office," Ivena interrupted. "Karen would have none of it, I can promise you that."

"Karen?" Helen asked.

"Janjic's agent," Ivena said with a small grin. "His fiancée."

Helen looked at him with a raised eyebrow. "Have you considered the possibility that I might not want to stay here?"

"And you would go where?" Ivena asked. "Back to whoever put that bruise on your neck?"

Helen blinked. "No." She obviously hadn't expected that.

"Then where else?"

"I don't know. But I can't stay here! You people have no idea what my life's like."

"You don't think so? Actually, it seems pretty plain. You've never understood love and so in your search for it you've managed to mix with the wrong people. You have abused your body with drugs and unbecoming behavior and now you are fleeing that life. And perhaps most importantly you are now sitting between two souls who understand suffering."

Helen stared at Ivena as if she had just reached a hand across the table and slapped her. Ivena spoke softly. "You are fleeing, aren't you?"

"I don't know," Helen said.

"You despise your past, don't you? In moments of clarity, Helen, you hate what has happened to you and now you would do anything to get away, wouldn't you? You would risk your own life to escape this monster breathing down your back."

A heavy blanket seemed to fall over them. Their breathing thickened. It was her simple way with the truth. Yes, of course she'd managed to offend some in her time. But truth-seekers always welcomed her direct approach as they might welcome a spring of water in the hot desert. And *she* certainly didn't have the stomach to handle the truth with kid gloves; it seemed rather profane when held next to her own schooling in Bosnia. When stood up next to Nadia's death.

"You have been badly wounded, dear child. I see it in your eyes. I feel it in my spirit. It's something we share, you and I. We've both had our hearts torn out."

A mist covered Helen's eyes. She blinked, obviously uncomfortable, perhaps panicked at the emotion sweeping through her.

A knot rose to Ivena's throat and she swallowed. In that moment she knew that a child screamed to be free before her. Deep behind those blue eyes wailed a soul, confused and terrified.

She looked over to Janjic. He was staring at Helen, his mouth slightly agape. He too had seen something within her. His Adam's apple bobbed. Ivena turned back to the girl. A tear snaked down her right cheek.

"You'll be safe with me, Helen."

Helen looked quickly about the room, scrambling for control now. She wasn't used to showing her emotions, that much was obvious. She cleared her throat.

"It's okay. You may cry here," Ivena said.

It proved to be the last straw. Helen lowered her head into her hands, stifling a soft sob. Ivena rested a hand on her shoulder and rubbed it gently. "Shhhh . . . It's okay, dear."

Helen cried and shook her head. Veins stood out on her neck and she struggled to breathe.

"Jesus, lover of our souls, love this child," Ivena whispered. She let her own emotions roll with the moment. This sweet, sweet sorrow that grew out of the pit of her stomach and flowered in her throat.

She looked at Janjic.

His eyes stared wide in shock.

It occurred to Ivena that he was not necessarily seeing or feeling what she was seeing and feeling. Ivena inquired with raised brows. *What is it, Janjic? What is the matter?*

Janjic swallowed and cleared his throat. He pushed his chair back and rose unsteadily, gathering himself. "Maybe I should leave you two," he said. "I have a meeting with Karen that I should get to." He nodded at Ivena. "I will call you later."

Helen did not lift her head. Ivena continued to rub her shoulders, wondering at Janjic's odd behavior. Or perhaps she was reading more into it than was warranted. Men often felt uncomfortable around weeping women. But Janjic was not usually such a man.

"Thank you, Janjic. We will be fine."

He took one more look at Helen and then walked out.

Ivena heard the front door open, then close. She let Janjic's oddity leave her for the moment and addressed the young woman bent over her table. "There's nothing to fear, dear child. Hmmm?" She ran a finger along Helen's cheek. "We will talk. I will tell you some things that will make you feel better, I promise you. Then you may tell me whatever you like."

Helen sniffed.

A fleeting image of her dead rosebush with its strange new graft flew through Ivena's mind but she dismissed it quickly. Perhaps she would show Helen her garden later.

GLENN LUTZ paced the black tile floor, running his fingers along his stubble, feeling as though his stomach had been cinched to a knot. Waiting for any news at all. He should call up Charlie and have him put his police cruisers on the street looking for her, that's what he should do. But he'd never asked the detective and his cronies to go that far before, not for a girl. Charlie would never understand. Nobody would understand—not this.

But men had died for love before. Glenn thought he understood why

Shakespeare had written *Romeo and Juliet* now. He felt the same kind of love. This feeling that nothing in the world mattered if he couldn't take possession of the love he wanted.

And when he did haul Helen in he would have to teach her some gratitude. Yes, she needed to understand how destructive this crazy game of hers really was. If what Beatrice said about his business interests suffering was true—and of course it was—then it was really Helen's doing, not his. It was her doing because she had possessed him. And if she had not possessed him, then Satan himself had possessed him.

A rap sounded. Glenn jerked his head toward the double doors. "Come." He took a deep breath, gripped his hands behind his back, and spread his legs.

Buck and Sparks walked in. They were already back—alone. Which could only mean one thing. Glenn swallowed an urge to scream at them, now, before they spoke—he knew what they would say already. Fresh beads of sweat budded on his forehead.

The men stepped lightly on the tile, though walking lightly was not an ordinary thing for men weighing over two hundred and fifty pounds. They reminded him of two buffaloes dressed in ridiculous black suits, tiptoeing through a bed of tulips, and again he suppressed his rising fury. Of course they were nothing of the kind, and he knew it well. He employed only the best, and these two were that and more. Either one of these two could crush him with a few solid blows, and he was not a small man. Still, he would think of them as he liked. It was how he warded off intimidation, and it worked well.

They came to a stop across the room and faced him, still wearing their sunglasses.

"Get those ridiculous things off your faces. You look like two schoolchildren caught smoking in the can."

They obliged him, but they still didn't offer a reason for their unsolicited appearance. For a few moments Glenn just stared at them, thinking he really should go over there and bang their heads together. He turned his head slowly to the side, keeping his eyes on them. He cleared his throat and spat on the floor. A glob of spit splattered on the tile. Still they said nothing.

"You're afraid to tell me that she's gone, is that it?" Of course that was it and their silence sent heat up his neck. "You're standing there petrified because you've allowed a single girl, weighing no more than one of your legs, to get away from you, is that it?" He squinted at them.

But they still didn't speak.

"Speak!" Glenn yelled. "Say something!"

"Yes," Buck said.

"Yes? Yes?"

A thought rudely interrupted his intended barrage—*She's gone, Glenn.*

He held his tongue, breathing in shallow pulls. They'd let her go and for that they would have to pay. But what did that mean? *That means that Helen's gone. Gone!* A streak of panic ripped up his spine. A deep terror that brought a quiver to his hands.

It was followed immediately by another fear that these two pigs had seen his dread.

"Where?" he snapped.

"In the park, sir. A man took her in his car."

Now the heat mushroomed in his skull. He dropped his hands to his sides. A man? He could not steady the tremor in his voice. "What do you mean, a man? *What* man?"

"We don't know, sir."

"He drove a white Cadillac," Sparks interjected.

"You're telling me that she left in another man's car?"

"Yes."

Glenn fought a wave of nausea. The room drifted out of focus for a brief moment. "And you followed them? Tell me you followed them."

Sparks glanced at Buck. It was all Glenn needed to know. "But you did get a license plate number?" His voice sounded desperate, but for the moment he no longer cared.

"Well, sir, we tried, but it all happened very quickly."

"You tried?" Glenn whined mockingly, frowning deep. "You tried!" he screamed. He was slipping over a black cliff in his mind—he realized that even as he lashed out. "I didn't pay you to *try.* I paid you to bring her back! Instead she's escaped you three times in two days. And you've got the gall to walk into my office and tell me you didn't even have the sense to take down a license number?"

They stared at him, frozen.

He had killed a few men and it was always in this state of mind that he'd pulled the trigger. This kind of blinding fury that made the world swim in a black fog. Glenn closed his eyes and stood there shaking, speechless, unable to think except to know that this was all a mistake. It was an impossible nightmare. He hadn't just happened upon Helen—he'd been led to her. The hand of fate had rewarded him with this one gift, this one morsel of bliss. He had rescued her from the pit of hell and he wasn't about to lose her. Never!

There are people here, Glenn. These two buffaloes are watching you go berserk. Get a hold of yourself!

He breathed once very deep and opened his eyes. Sweat stung his eyeballs. He stepped toward them. Perhaps a little taste of insanity would be good for them. It would put the fear of God in them, at the very least. He walked briskly for the desk, retrieved a black semiautomatic pistol from the top drawer and strode for the men. Their eyes widened.

He lifted the gun and shot them quickly, each in the arm, *blam, blam,* before even he had a chance to think it through. The detonations thundered in the room. Actually, he shot Sparks in the arm; his shot went high on Buck and clipped his shoulder. Sparks moaned and muttered a long string of curses but Buck merely placed a hand over the torn hole in his shirt. His eyes watered, but he refused to show pain. For a brief moment Glenn thought they might come after him and he reacted quickly.

"Shut up! Shut up!"

Sparks stilled, gritting his teeth.

Glenn wagged the gun at them. "If she's not in this office within three days you're both dead. Now get off my floor!"

They stared at him with red faces.

He clenched his eyes and took a deliberate breath. "Go!"

They turned and strode from the room.

Glenn walked to his desk and sat heavily. If this didn't turn out right he might very well use the gun on himself, he thought. Of course there were other ways to track her down. He would employ every resource at his means to find her. A white Cadillac. How many white Cadillacs could there be registered in this city? Twenty? Fifty? The fool who'd picked her up had just made the biggest mistake of his life. *Oh, yeah, you'd better start packin' heat, baby, because Lutz is gunnin' for you.*

He dropped his head to the desk and moaned.

chapter eleven

THE IMAGE of Helen, leaning over the table crying, had softened as Steve drove Jan across the city, but it still left its imprint and he couldn't wrap his mind around the terrifying sorrow that had accompanied that image.

"So, Steve," he asked with a thin smile. "What do you make of our daring rescue?"

The chauffeur chuckled. "She's a feisty one, sir; that's for sure."

"You think she's sincere?"

"I think she's hurting. Hurting people tend to be sincere. It was good of you, sir."

"Don't call me sir, Steve. You're my elder; maybe I should call *you* sir."

"Yes, sir."

Jan smiled and let the statement stand. It was a small game they played and he doubted it would ever change. The chauffeur pulled up to the ministry and parked.

Jan stepped from the Cadillac and walked toward the towering office complex, trying to shake the annoying little buzz that droned on in his skull. The city was hot and muggy. An old black Ford with whitewall tires moaned by. The sound of beating wings drew his attention to the roofline where two gray pigeons flapped noisily for better footing. It occurred to him halfway up the steps that he'd neglected to close the door. He turned and jogged for the car, grinning apologetically to Steve, who'd already opened the driver's door to come around and shut it.

"Sorry, Steve. I'll get it."

"No problem, Mr. Jovic."

"*Jan*, Steve. It's Jan." He shut the door and headed back. At times he was embarrassed to have a driver. True, in the beginning he could not drive in a country where everyone drove at double speeds, but that had been five years ago. Somehow the driver thing had just stuck. It came with the position, he supposed.

A large illuminated sign featuring a white dove hung over the brick entrance. *On Wings of Doves*, it read in golden letters. The name of his ministry. And what was his ministry? To quicken within the world's heart the deep love of God—the same love shown by a little child named Nadia, the same love of Father Micheal. The same love Ivena suggested Jan didn't really possess at all. Ivena, now, she had lost her daughter and the love poured out of her in rivers. He wasn't sure exactly how he was to show the love of the priest anymore.

Father, show me your love again, he prayed. *Do not allow this world to swallow the fire of your love. Never. Teach me to love.*

An image of the woman, Helen, riding beside him in the car flashed through his mind. *"Do preachers always drive such expensive cars?"* she had asked.

He pushed into the office building and made his way to the elevators. Betty, the correspondence coordinator, was on the elevator, on her way to the mailroom to "set John straight," she said.

"And what are we setting John straight about today?" Jan asked.

Betty grinned softly, bunching her round cheeks into balls. She was nearing sixty and John was half her age; it was a ritual, a mothering thing for Betty, Jan often thought. She had adopted the mailroom manager as her son. She, the short, heavyset, gray-haired wise one, and John, the tall bodybuilder with jet-black hair—mother and son.

"He's gotten the crazy notion up his sleeve that we really can't answer three hundred letters a day, and so he's telling his people to send no more than two hundred letters down to our department on any given day." She waved at the air. "Nonsense!" Betty leaned forward as if to tell Jan a secret. "I think he likes flexing his muscles, if you know what I mean."

"Yes, John does enough of that, doesn't he? But be easy with him, Betty. He's young, you know."

She sighed as the bell for the sixth floor rang. "I suppose you're right. But these young ones need some guidance."

"Yes, Betty. Guide him well."

She clucked a short laugh. "And congratulations again, Jan."

"Thank you, Betty."

She stepped off and Jan rode on, grinning wide. The thought that all those letters in dispute were requests rather than checks ran through his mind. The ministry was slowly being sucked dry by them. My, my . . . where had all the money gone?

They rented the five lower floors to tenants and ran the ministry from the top three, an arrangement that gave them office space at virtually no cost. It had been another one of Roald's brilliant touches. Of course, they didn't really need all three floors, but the space allowed Jan and Karen to occupy the whole top floor as well as providing Roald a spacious if temporary office for his frequent visits. The mailroom occupied the sixth floor and the administrative offices occupied the seventh.

Jan walked in and smiled at the office secretary, Nicki, who was filling her cup with fresh coffee. "Afternoon, Nicki. They say too much of that stuff will kill you, you know."

She turned to him, flashing a broad smile. "Sure, and so'll hamburgers and soda and everything else that makes this country great."

"Touché. Any messages?"

"On your desk. Roald and Karen are waiting in the conference room." She shot him a wink and he knew it was because of Karen. Their engagement would be a hit around the office for at least another week. The thought of seeing Karen again suddenly set free a few butterflies in his stomach. He smiled sheepishly and walked into his office.

Jan glanced over the large oak desk, empty except for the small stack of messages Nicki had referred to, and headed back out. The ministry's administration was handled almost entirely by the staff now. And with Karen at the helm of public relations, he was relegated to showing up and dazzling the crowds, giving his lectures, but not much more. That and worrying about how to sustain this monster he'd created.

He opened the door to the conference room. "Hello, my friends. Mind if I join in?"

Karen stood from the conference table and walked toward him, brown eyes sparkling above a soft smile. Her hair rested delicately on a bright blue dress. Goodness, she was beautiful.

"Hello, Jan."

"Hello, Karen. Welcome back." She reached him and he kissed her cheek. The thought of an openly romantic relationship in the office still felt awkward. Although it hardly should; she was going to be his wife. "I missed you."

"And I missed you," she said quietly. She glanced over his choice of clothing and smiled, a tad disingenuous, he thought. "So I take it you've been playing today."

"I guess you could call it that. I was at the park."

She mouthed a silent, *Ahhh*, as if that put the puzzle together for her.

Roald Barnes grinned a pleasant smile with all the maturity and grace expected of a graying elder statesman. He wore a black tie cinched tight around a starched collar. "Hello, Jan," he said.

Jan looked at Karen. "How was the meeting this morning? Still on speaking terms with our publisher?"

"The meetings, plural, were . . . how should I put it? Interesting." She was slipping into her professional skin now. She could do it at a moment's notice—one second the beautiful woman, the next a sharp negotiator leveling a rare authority. At times it was intimidating.

"Bracken and Holmes refused the seventh printing."

"They did, huh? My, my. And what does this mean?" He crossed his legs and sat back.

She took a breath and exhaled deliberately. "It means we have to face some facts. Sales have faded to a trickle."

He looked at Roald. The older man's grin had all but vanished. "She's right, Jan. Things have slowed considerably."

"You think I don't know this? What are you saying?"

"We are saying that *The Dance of the Dead* is nearly dead."

"Dead?"

The word seemed to throw a switch somewhere in Jan's mind. He buried an urge to snap at the man and immediately wondered at the anger he felt. The man's choice of words could have been better, but he was only speaking the same truth that had lurked in these halls for weeks now.

"What happened to *May she live forever?* Things of this nature don't just die, Roald. They have a life of their own."

"Not in this country, they don't. If people aren't buying—"

"It's not simply a matter of people buying. I've said so a thousand times. I say it at every interview."

Jan was suddenly feeling very hot in this small room without really knowing why. Roald knew well Jan's basic resentment with characterizing the success of the book in mere numbers. After all, the book was about God. Between every page there was the voice of God, screaming out to the reader; insisting that he was real and interested and desperate to be known. How could such a message be reduced to numbers?

"I think what Roald's trying to say," Karen interjected with a firm glance over to Roald, "is that on the business end of things our income's drying up. Another printing would have helped."

"You know very well, Jan, that what's hot one year may be cold the next," Roald said. "We've enjoyed five enlightening years. But enlightenment doesn't pay the mortgage. And the last time I checked, your mortgage was rather significant."

"I'm aware of the costs, my friend. Perhaps you forget that this story was bought with blood. With blood and five years in a prison that might leave you dead within a week. You may say what you like, but be careful how you say it!" Heat washed over his collar. *Easy, Jan. You have no right to be so defensive.*

Roald became very still. "I stand corrected. But you also should remember that this world's filled with people who don't share your sentiments toward God. People who *committed* the very atrocities you've written about. And don't forget, it was I who made this book possible in the first place. I'm not your enemy here. In fact, I've bent over backward to help you succeed. It was I who convinced you to publish your book in the United States. It was I who first persuaded the publisher to put some marketing muscle behind the book. It was even I who brought Karen on board."

"Yes indeed, you did. But it wasn't just you, Roald. It was the book. It was the priest's blood. It was my torture. It was God, and you should never forget that!"

"Of course it was God. But you can't just throw your own responsibility on God. We each play our part."

"Yes, and my part was to rot for five years in a prison, begging God to forgive me for beating a priest. What was your part?"

"I don't hear any complaints about the house. Or the car, or the rest of it, for that matter. You seem pretty comfortable now, Jan, and for that you may thank me and Karen."

"And I'd give it up in a word if it mocked the lives that purchased it." *Would you, Jan?* "If you don't understand that, then you don't know me as well as you once thought. This mountain of metal and mortar is an abstraction to me. It's the love of God that I seek, not the sale of my books." *At least for the most part.*

"If you drift off to obscurity, what becomes of your message then? We live in a real world, my friend, with real people who read real books and need real love."

They sat staring at each other, silent in the wake of their outbursts. It wasn't so uncommon, really, although rarely with this intensity. Jan wanted to tell Roald that he wouldn't know real love if it bit his heart out, but he knew they'd gone far enough. Perhaps too far.

"Well, well," Karen said softly. "Last time I checked we were all on the same side here." She wore a thin smile, and Jan thought she might actually be proud of him for standing so firmly. It *was* inspiring, wasn't it? In a very small way it was like Nadia standing tall in Karadzic's face. In a very tiny way.

The heat of the moment dissipated like steam into the night.

"Now, like I was saying before this train derailed itself," Karen said, "the meetings were *interesting.* I didn't say they were disastrous. Maybe I should've been a little clearer; we might have avoided this robust philosophical exchange." She stared Jan in the eye with those beautiful brown eyes and winked. "Bracken and Holmes may have turned us down, but there are other players in this big bad world of ours. And as it turns out, I just may have found a new life for *The Dance of the Dead,* after all. No pun intended, of course."

"Which would be?" Jan asked.

She looked at Roald, who was now smiling. So he knew it as well. Jan stared at her. "What? You've been turned down by the publisher, so what was this other meeting? You've set up another speaking tour?"

"Speaking tour? Oh, I think there will be speaking tours, my dear." She was playing it out, and in the echoes of Jan's exchange with Roald it was playing like a sonnet.

"Then say it. You obviously know as well, Roald, so stop this nonsense and tell me."

"Well, what would you suppose is the most ambitious way to present your book to the masses?"

"Television? You have another television appearance."

"Yes, I'm sure there'll be more of those as well." She leaned back and smiled. "Think big, Jan. Think as big as you can."

He thought. He was about to tell them to get on with it when it came to him. "Film?"

"Not just film, Janjic. Feature film. A Hollywood movie."

"A movie?" The idea spun through his head, still not connecting. What did he know of movies?

"And if we play our cards right," Roald said, "the deal will be ours within the week."

"And what is the deal?"

Karen lifted her pen to her mouth and tapped it on her chin. "I met with Delmont Pictures this morning—the fourth meeting, actually. They've offered to buy the movie rights to the book for five million dollars."

"Delmont Pictures?"

"A subsidiary of Paramount. Very aggressive and loaded with cash."

Jan sat back and looked from one to the other. If he wasn't mistaken here, they were telling him that Delmont Pictures was offering five million dollars to make a movie of the book.

"When?"

Roald chuckled. "Deal first, Jan. Schedules will come after a deal's made. Actually, it's a wonder we still have the movie rights at all. Most publishers take the rights when they first contract. There was a piece of divine intervention."

"When did you negotiate this?"

"Over the last few weeks."

Jan nodded, still unsure. "So you're telling me that they want to make a movie of *The Dance of the Dead.*"

Karen exchanged a quick glance with Roald. "In a matter of speaking. They want to make a movie about *you,*" Karen said, biting her pen and speaking around it. "About your whole life. From your days as a child in Sarajevo through the publishing of your book. A sort of rags-to-riches story. It's perfect! Imagine it! You couldn't fictionalize this stuff if you tried!"

The Dance of the Dead contained his life story to some degree, of course. But it was much more a story of spiritual awakening. "Rags to riches? My story's not a rags-to-riches story."

Roald cleared his throat and now Jan knew why the older man had taken him to task earlier. He had known this would be a sticking point—this *rags-to-riches* take on Jan's life—and now he'd already aggressively argued his position in a preemptive strike. The man was no idiot.

"Now you listen, Jan. Listen carefully. This is a deal you want to take. This is a deal that'll place your story on the hearts of untold millions who would never dream of reading your book. The kind of people who probably could use the story the most—people too busy with their own lives to take the time to read; people so thoroughly involved in mediocrity that they've never even thought about living for a cause, much less dying for one. Now"—he placed both hands on the table before him—"I realize that they want this spin of theirs on the story, but you must accept this proposal. It will save your ministry."

"I wasn't aware that my ministry needed saving, Roald."

"Well it does. It's doomed."

It is the souls of men that are doomed, not buildings and ministries, Jan wanted to say, but he decided against it. He'd challenged Roald enough for one day. Besides, there was a ring of truth to what the elder statesman said.

"He's right, Jan," Karen said. "You know he's right." It was half statement, half question.

He looked at her and saw that she was begging him. *Please, Jan, you know that there are times to play tough and there are times to trust and accept. And you can trust me, Jan, because you're more than a business partner to me. You are a man to me. Say yes.*

A thought occurred to him then, looking at her. The thought that she was desperate for this deal. Perhaps as desperate for the deal as for him.

"Yes," he said, gazing deep into her eyes. She was beautiful. She was striking and gentle and brilliant. "Maybe you're right."

She smiled and a moment passed between them.

"You are amazing," he said, shaking his head.

She smiled and her eyes twinkled with another statement. *We're perfect together, Jan Jovic.*

Roald lifted his coffee cup for a toast. "Now then, I'll say it again, and this time you'll understand. *The Dance of the Dead:* May she live forever."

Jan grinned at the man and lifted his own cup. The entire meeting with the leaders now made sense. "May she live forever," he repeated.

They laughed then. They hauled Nicki in and told her about the Delmont Pictures deal and talked through the afternoon about the new possibilities this would open up for the ministry. They even sent Steve out for some sparkling apple cider, and asked Betty, John, and Lorna to gather all the employees in the mailroom where they announced the deal. A hundred toasts and twice as many congratulations were thrown around despite Karen's caution that it wasn't finalized. Not yet. *But will it be?* Well, yes. *There you go then! Congrats! And congrats on the engagement as well. You two were born for each other.*

Betty hugged John, nearly twice her size; Steve tossed his driver's cap into the air with a holler; even Lorna, the skinny conservative finance manager, surprised them all by pretending to dance with her teacup before turning beet red at their laughter.

The execution of the contract was set to move forward at breakneck speed. Assuming they could come to terms with the scope of the project as it related to Jan's life, they would sign documents in the Big Apple on Friday. Their first payment would come at signing—a clean million dollars.

"We'll have to celebrate with dinner," Jan told Karen in a quiet moment alone.

"Yes, we will. And we have a lot to celebrate." She winked. Every look between them seemed to drip with honey, he thought. Karen sighed. "Unfortunately I have a conference call with the New York studio at six-thirty our time. How about a late dinner or dessert?"

"I'll settle for dessert. Eight o'clock?"

"Eight it is." She stroked his cheek with the back of her finger. "I love you, Jan Jovic."

"And I love you, Karen."

CHAPTER TWELVE

IT WASN'T until five that Jan remembered the young blonde he'd left in Ivena's care. He called Ivena on the phone.

"Hello." The sound of her baritone voice brought the morning's events crashing in on Jan.

"Hello, Ivena. It's Janjic."

"Well, Janjic. Nice of you to call."

"I have some news," he said, but suddenly he wasn't thinking of the news. He was thinking of the woman. "How is she?"

"Helen? You wish to know how Helen is? Perhaps you should join us for dinner and see for yourself. She was your catch, after all."

"I wasn't aware I was fishing. But dinner may not work. I'm meeting Karen at eight." He paused. "Is she okay?"

"You will have to see for yourself, Janjic. What is the news?"

"They want to make a movie of the story."

The phone went silent.

"It won't be made without your consent, of course. But it would be a wonderful opportunity to bring our story to many who'd never read it. And it'll pay well."

"The money is nothing. You remember that, Janjic. Never think of the money."

"Of course."

"When you left this afternoon, Janjic. There was a look about you."

Suddenly the phone felt heavy in his hand.

"You saw something?" she asked.

He swallowed. "Not really, no. I . . . I don't know what it was."

"Then perhaps you should come to an early dinner, Janjic." She said it as a command. Funny thing, it was now precisely what he wanted to do. He could eat with Ivena and meet Karen for dessert at eight.

"Come, Janjic. We will wait."

"Okay. I'll be there at six."

"We will have the kraut ready."

And that was that.

JAN GAVE Steve the night off and drove the Cadillac himself. Maybe it was time to stop the chauffeuring altogether. Of course, he'd have to find another position for Steve; he couldn't just let the man go. But being driven around was feeling silly today.

He drove to the Sandy Springs district where both he and Ivena now lived, though on opposite ends. It was an upper-middle-class neighborhood, neatly cut into perfect squares, each heavily laden with large trees and manicured flowering bushes. Roald had recommended the area when they had first arrived and it had seemed far too extravagant for Jan. But then most things in America had seemed extravagant to him during those early days. Now the old custom homes and the driveways lined with their expensive cars and boats hardly made an impression at all.

For the second time that day Jan walked up the path to Ivena's small house, surrounded by sweet-smelling rosebushes in full red bloom. He rang the doorbell and stood back. His palms suddenly felt clammy. Something had happened this morning when Helen caved in on herself at Ivena's table—a shock of emotion had lit right through him. He could hardly explain it, but it had struck a chord in his mind. Like a tuning fork smacked too hard and left to quiver off key. The note had filled him with sorrow.

Jan pushed the bell again and the door swung in. Ivena stepped aside and invited him with an open arm. "Come in, Jan. It's good of you to come."

He stepped in. A kettle sang in the kitchen; the smell of sausage and kraut hung in the warm room. Dinner in Bosnia. Jan smiled and kissed Ivena on each cheek. "Of course, I would come." He straightened and looked about the living room. "So where's Helen?"

"In the kitchen."

Then suddenly she was in the doorway that led to the kitchen, and Jan blinked at the sight of her. She stood in bare feet, it was the first thing he saw. The second was her bright blue eyes, piercing right through him; those hadn't changed. But everything else had. For starters she wore a dress, one of Ivena's dresses; Jan recognized it immediately. It was the blue one with yellow flowers, a dress Ivena hadn't worn for some time, complaining that it was too small. It fit Helen's thin frame remarkably well, certainly a bit large, but not ridiculously so.

It wasn't the only change; Helen had showered as well. Her hair lay slightly unkempt, short and very blond. He couldn't tell if she wore makeup; her face shone with its own brightness.

Jan smiled wide, unable to hide his amusement. Helen and Ivena giggled together as one, as if they had just shared this secret with him and expected him to be pleased with it.

Helen lifted both arms and curtsied. "You like?" She turned slowly, unabashed, posing with an arm cocked to her hairline, as if this were a fashion runway on which she stood instead of a checkered vinyl kitchen floor. Ivena rocked back and laughed. The levity was infectious. Jan stared at them, stunned, wondering what they'd gotten into over the afternoon.

"So, you like, Janjic?" Ivena asked.

You like? Since when did Ivena use such words? "Yes, I like," he said.

Helen twirled around and let the dress rise up until it showed well-tanned thighs. "First dress I've had on in ten years. I guess I'll just have to get me some of these."

Jan chuckled.

"You see, I clean up pretty good, don't you think? Of course, I had some help from Ivena."

He was at a loss for words.

She walked toward him now, one hand on her hip, strutting for show and lifting her chin just so . . . Goodness, she was quite beautiful. She moved without a hint of presumption, as if he and Ivena were children and she the baby-sitter showing them how it was really done out in the big world. She walked right up to him and presented her hand to him. "Then let me show you your seat, good sire." A twinkle skipped through her eyes and she grinned.

Jan looked over at Ivena, hoping for rescue, but she only smiled, quite pleased to watch, it seemed. He felt his jaw gape slightly, but felt powerless to pull it shut. *Don't be silly, Jan. It's a harmless game!*

He reached out and took her hand.

Now, up to this point in the day, Jan had taken everything pretty much in stride. It wasn't the most usual day to be sure. Not with rescuing Helen and the odd emotions he'd felt at seeing her cry. Not with seeing Karen again or the announcement from her that his book was about to sell to Delmont Pictures for an ungodly amount of money. It wasn't a usual day at all. But he had taken it all in stride, if for no other reason than his life had been filled with unusual days.

But now his stride faltered; because now, when his fingers made contact with Helen's, his world erupted.

Pain surged through his chest, igniting a flash of light in his mind. It happened so suddenly and with so much force that he couldn't contain a gasp. His vision filled with a white field, flowered as far as the eye could see; a flowered desert. A sound carried across the desert—the sound of crying. The sound of weeping. A chorus of voices crying and weeping in dreadful sorrow.

Jan stood there, holding her hand, and he gasped, unable to move forward. Immediately a part of him began to back-pedal, scolding him to collect himself. But that part of him consisted of nothing more than a distant wailing, smothered by the raw emotion that seemed to reach into his chest and give his heart a good squeeze. It was an *ache* that surged through his chest at the vision. A profound sorrow. Like the emotion he'd felt at seeing her cry, amplified ten times.

And then it was gone, as quickly as it had come.

He bent over and coughed, hitting his chest as he did so. "Oh, boy. I'm sorry. Something caught in my chest."

"You okay?" Helen asked with a furrowed brow.

"Yes." He straightened. "Yes."

She turned for the dining room. "Then follow me."

He followed, pulled by her small hand. Had they seen his face? It must have turned white. He couldn't bring himself to look at Ivena; surely she'd seen.

The table was set with Ivena's china and three crystal glasses. A large red candle cast flickering light over the silverware; a bouquet of roses from Ivena's garden stood as a centerpiece; steam rose lazily from the sausages. Helen ushered him to the seat at the table's head and then slid gracefully into her own on his left.

"Ivena and I decided that the least we could do was to prepare your favorite dish," Helen said. "Seeing as how you rescued me with all that bravery." She grinned.

Jan's heart still hammered in his chest. He'd had a waking dream or a flashback to the war, but not of any setting he could remember. Still, something felt vaguely familiar about it.

Ivena's voice came distant. "Janjic?"

"I'm sorry. Yes, thank you. It reminds me of home," he said. The tension he felt was in his own mind, he thought. Helen at least seemed oblivious to it.

Ivena asked him to bless the meal, which he did and they dished food onto their plates. Much to Jan's relief, Ivena launched into a discussion about flowers. About how well the rosebushes were doing this year, all but one. Apparently the rosebush she'd brought with her to America was suddenly dying.

Jan nodded with the conversation, but his mind was occupied with the electricity that still hung in the air, with the unusually loud clinking of their forks on china, with the flickering of the flame. With that white, weeping desert that had paralyzed him at her touch. At Helen's touch.

And what would Karen think of this little dinner at Ivena's? What would *he* think, for that matter. But he already was thinking, and he was thinking that Helen was an enigma. A beautiful enigma. Which was something he had no business thinking.

He ate the sausage slowly, trying to focus on the discussion and entering it as he saw fit. Helen's hands held the utensils delicately; her short fingernails were no longer rimmed with dirt. She was a junkie, that much he could now see by a tiny pockmark on her arm. Heroin, most likely. It was a wonder she wasn't thinner. She chewed the food with small bites, often smiling and laughing at Ivena's antics over the differences between America and Bosnia. In some odd way they were like two peas in a pod, these two. This most unlikely pair. The mother from Bosnia and the junkie from Atlanta.

Slowly a deep sense that he'd been here before settled over him. He'd seen this somewhere. All of it. This mother and this daughter and this sorrow—he had seen it in Bosnia. It was in part the reason behind that bolt of lightning. It had to be. God was opening his mind.

". . . this movie of yours, Janjic?"

He'd missed the question. "I'm sorry, what?"

"Ivena says that they're making a movie of your life," Helen said. "So when are they making it?"

"Yes, well we don't know yet."

"And how can they show a film of a life that is not yet lived?" Ivena asked. "Your life's not finished, Janjic."

Jan looked at her, tempted to ignore the comment. "Of course my life isn't over, but the story's finished. We have a book of it."

"No, the book explains some events, not your entire life. You've seen the finger of God in your youth, but that hardly means it is gone."

"Ivena seems to think that I'm still Moses," Jan said. "It's not enough for me to see the burning bush; there's still a Red Sea to cross."

Helen chuckled nervously. "Moses?"

Jan glanced at Ivena. "Moses. He was a man in the Bible." He wiped his mouth with his napkin. "It was also a name given to me in prison. Did Ivena tell you about the village?"

She stared at him with round eyes and he knew that she had. "Some."

Jan nodded. "Yes. And when I returned to Sarajevo I was arrested for war crimes. Did she tell you?"

"No."

"Hmm. Karadzic persuaded the council to throw me in prison for five years. The warden was a relative of Karadzic's. He called me Moses. The deliverer." Jan took another bite of sausage, trying now to ignore the weight of the moment. "I'm surprised I survived the experience. But it was there that I first read the words of God in a Testament smuggled in by one of the other prisoners. It was after prison that I began to write my story. And now Ivena seems to think it's not finished." He put another bite of sausage in his mouth.

"Yes, we've all had difficult lives, Janjic," Ivena said. "You don't possess the rights to suffering. Even dear Helen has seen her grief."

Jan looked at Helen. Twenty-nine, she'd said. "Is that so? What's your story?"

Helen looked at him and her eyes squinted very briefly. She looked away and took a bite of sausage. "My story? You mean you're wondering how a person ends up like me, is that it?"

"No, I didn't say that."

"But you meant it."

Ivena spoke quietly. "Don't be defensive, child. Just tell him what you told me. We all have our stories. Believe me, Jan's is no prettier than yours."

She seemed to consider that for a moment. "Well, my dad was an idiot and my mom was a vegetable and I became a junkie. How's that?"

Jan let her stew.

After a few seconds she spoke again. "I was born here, in the city. My dad disappeared before I really knew him. But he was pretty well off and he left us some money; enough to last me and my mom for the rest of our lives. We were okay, you know. I went to a normal school and we were just . . . normal people." She smiled in retrospect. "I even won an eighth-grade beauty pageant down at O'Keefe Middle School—that's where I went."

She sipped her tea and the smile faded. "There was this kid at my school two years ahead of me, white trash we used to call them, poor and from the dirtiest part of town back then, down by the old industry district. At least that's where everyone said he was from, but I don't think anyone really knew for sure. His name was Peter. He used to watch me a lot. Ugly kid too. Mean and fat and ugly. Used to just stare at me across the schoolyard with these big black eyes. I mean, I was pretty, I suppose, but this sicko had an obsession. Everyone hated Peter."

Helen shuddered. "Even thinking about it now makes me sick. He used to follow me home, sneaking around behind me, but I knew he was there. Some of the other kids said he used to kill animals for the fun of it. I don't know, but it scared me to death back then."

Jan just nodded and listened to her, wondering what this childhood fright had to do with the woman sitting before him now.

"That was when my mom got sick. The doctors never could figure out what it was, but one day she was just sick. At first it was just throwing up and being weak, so that I had to take care of her. And then she started acting really strange. I didn't know it then, but she'd started using acid. Acid and heroin. And the stuff wasn't everywhere back then. You know where she got it? Peter! The creep from my school! Peter was supplying my mother with drugs!"

"Peter. The one who was following you home," Jan said. "How did you know it was him?"

"I came in one afternoon—I was out getting some groceries—and he was there, in the house, selling her dope."

"What did he do?"

"Nothing. I think he wanted to get caught. I threw him out, of course. But by then my mom was a zombie. If she didn't have drugs in her system, she was puking from her sickness, and if she did have drugs, she was out to lunch. And the kid wouldn't go away. He was always there, feeding my mom her drugs and staring at me. I started using within a few months, after I pulled out of school. We ran out of money about a year later. It all went for the drugs."

"You lost it all? Just like that?" She had cared for her mother too, Janjic thought. Just as Jan had cared for his own mother before the war in Sarajevo.

"Peter was robbing us blind. I never gave in to him; I want you to know that. The whole thing was about his demented obsession to make me his girl." Helen shifted her eyes to the wall. "My mom died from an overdose. The way I figure it, Peter killed her with his drugs. The day after my mom's burial he and I had a huge blowup. I hit him over the head with a two-by-four and took off. Never went back. We were dead broke anyway. Honestly, I think I might've killed him." She grinned and shrugged her shoulders.

"Killed him?" Jan said. "You never saw him again?"

"Never. I hitched a ride to New York that same day. Never heard a thing. Either way, if I did kill him, I figured he had it coming. One way or another he'd killed my mom and trashed my life."

She looked up at them with her deep blue eyes, searching for a nod of approval. But it wasn't approval that Jan felt sweeping through his bones. It was pity. It was a biting empathy for this poor child. He couldn't understand the emotions in their entirety, but he couldn't deny them either.

"How old were you?"

"Fifteen."

"You see, Janjic," Ivena said, "she's a child of the war as well."

"You're right. I'm so sorry, Helen. I had no idea."

Helen shifted in her seat. "Relax. It's not so bad. It could be a lot worse."

"Poor child," Ivena said. "You have never been loved properly."

Helen straightened. "Sure I have. Love is the only thing I've had my fill of. They love me and they leave me. Or I leave them. Honestly, I do *not* need your sympathy." She held up a hand. "Please, I don't do sympathy well."

Neither Jan nor Ivena responded. They'd both seen enough of the wounded to know that they all needed sympathy. Especially those who had persuaded themselves they did *not* need it. But it wasn't a gift that could be forced.

"So how did you return to Atlanta?" Jan asked.

"I came back six months ago. But that's another story. Drugs and love don't always mix so well, trust me. Let's just say I needed to get out of New York, and Atlanta seemed as good a choice as any."

"And Glenn?" Jan asked.

Helen set her glass down and turned it slowly. "Glenn. Yeah, well, I met Glenn a while back at a party. He likes to throw these big bashes. Glenn is . . . bad." She swallowed. "I mean he's really bad. People think of him as the powerful city councilman; that his money comes from real estate . . ." She shook her head. "Not really. It comes from drugs. Problem is, anybody who crosses him ends up hurt. Or dead."

"And have I crossed him already?" Jan asked.

"No. I don't think so. This was my choice. I left him. It had nothing to do with you. Besides, he's got no clue who you are."

"Except that you came in my car. Except that you're now in Ivena's house."

She looked at him but didn't offer an opinion.

"And he's your . . . boyfriend, right?"

Her eyes widened briefly. "No, I wouldn't put it that way. He puts me up in this place of his. But no. I mean no, not anymore. Absolutely not. Nobody's gonna hit me and think they can get away with it."

"No," Jan said. "Of course you're right." Heat flared up his back. Who could strike such a person?

Karadzic could, a small voice snickered. He shook his head at the thought.

"Helen would like to stay with me for a while," Ivena said. "I have told her"—she looked at Jan—"that I would accept nothing less. If there's any danger, then God will help us. And we're no strangers to danger."

"Of course. Yes, you should stay here where it's safe. And perhaps Ivena can buy you some new clothes tomorrow. I'll pay, of course. It's the least I can do. We will put our ministry funds to good use."

"You will trust two women with your bank account?" Ivena asked with a raised brow.

"I would trust you with my life, Ivena."

"Yes, of course. But your money?"

"Money's nothing. You've said so a thousand times, dear."

Ivena turned to Helen with a sly smile. "There is my first insight, young woman. Always downplay the value of money; it will make it much easier for him to hand it over."

They laughed, glad for the reprieve.

Jan left the house an hour later, his head buzzing from the day.

God had touched his heart for Helen's sake, he decided. Maybe because she was an outcast as he himself once was. His odd enchantment with her certainly couldn't be natural.

It had been God, although God had never touched him in such a specific way before. If only his whole ministry were filled with such direct impressions. He could touch a contract, say, and wait for a surge of current to fill his arms. If it didn't, he would not sign. *Ha!* He could pick up a phone and know if the person on the other end was to bode well for the ministry. He could take Karen's hand and . . . Goodness, now there was a thought.

Maybe he'd imagined the whole thing. Perhaps his emotions had gotten the best of him and caused some kind of hallucinogenic reaction, tripping him back to the weeping in Bosnia; another kind of war-trauma flashback.

But no, it had been too clear. Too real.

He drove the Cadillac toward Antoine's where he'd agreed to meet Karen for dessert. And what should he tell her of this day? Of Helen? Nothing. Not yet. He would sleep on this business of Helen. There was plenty to talk about without muddying the waters with a strange, beautiful junkie named Helen. There was the engagement and the wedding date. There was talk of love and children. The movie deal, the book, the television appearances—all of it was enough to fill hours of talk by Antoine's soft lights.

CHAPTER THIRTEEN

"What is love? Love is kind and patient and always enduring.
Love is kisses and smiles. It is warmth and ecstasy.
Love is laughter and joy.
But the greatest part of love is found in death.
No greater love hath any man."

The Dance of the Dead, 1959

IVENA MEANDERED through her kitchen at nine the next morning, humming the tune from "Jesus, Lover of My Soul." Helen still slept in the tiny sewing room down the hall. Poor girl must have been exhausted. What a sweet treasure she was, though. Abused and dragged down life's roughest paths to be sure, but so very sweet. Today she would take Janjic's signed checks—he'd given them five—and shower Helen with a little love.

Ivena turned one of four taps by the greenhouse door and the overhead misters hissed inside. She opened the door. The musty smell of dirt mixed with flower scent always seemed to strengthen with the first wetting.

She'd shown Helen the garden yesterday evening and the flowers seemed to have calmed her. Ivena had known then, seeing the spindly gray stalks of her daughter's rosebush, that it was for all practical purposes dead, despite the strange green shoot at its base. She was still having difficulty remembering if she had—

"Huh?" Ivena caught her breath and stared at the dead bush.

But it wasn't dead! Or was it? Green snaked up through the branches; vines wrapped around the rose stalks and spread over the plant.

Ivena stepped forward, barely breathing. It looked as though a weed had literally sprung up overnight and taken over the rosebush! But that was impossible!

The bush had seven main branches, each one as black and lifeless as they'd been yesterday. But now the green vines ran around each one in eerie symmetry. And they all came from the base of the plant; from the one shoot that had been grafted in.

But you did not graft that shoot, Ivena.

Yes, I must have. I just don't remember it.

Ivena reached her hand out to the strange new plant and ran a finger along its stalk. How had it grown so quickly? It had appeared yesterday, no more than four inches in length and now it ran the height of the plant! The skin was very similar to that of a healthy rose stalk, but without thorns. A woody vine.

"My goodness, what on earth do we have here?" Ivena whispered to herself. Maybe it was this vine that had killed her rosebush. A parasite. Perhaps she should cut it off in the hopes of saving the rose.

No, the rose was already dead.

"Ivena."

She whirled around. Helen stood in the doorway, her hair tangled, still dressed in her pajamas.

"Well good morning, my dear." Ivena walked toward her, shielding the bush. "I would ask you how you slept, but I think I have my answer already."

"Very good, thank you."

"Wonderful." They stepped into the kitchen and Ivena closed the door to the greenhouse behind her. "Now you'll need some food. You can't shop properly on an empty stomach."

HELEN WATCHED Ivena with an odd mixture of amusement and admiration. The Bosnian woman wore her gray hair quite shaggy. She held her head confidently but gently, like her words. Both she and Janjic shared one stunning trait, Helen thought. They both had eyes that smiled without letting up, bringing on pre-mature wrinkles around their sockets. If there were other human beings with Ivena's unique blend of quirks and sincerity, Helen had never met them. It was impossible not to like her. In the woman's presence the small voice that called Helen back to the drugs sounded very faint. Although it was still there—yes it was, like a whisper in a hollow chamber.

They ate eggs for breakfast, and then readied themselves for a few hours of American indulgence, as Ivena put it. She seemed amused by the five checks she waved about. When Helen asked her why, she just smiled. "It's Janjic's money," she said. "He has far too much."

Helen insisted Ivena take her far from the central city district—with Glenn's men on the prowl, anything within a five-mile radius of the Twin Towers was out of the question. Even here it took Helen a good hour to satisfy herself that the chances of Glenn finding her were nearly nonexistent.

Ivena drove them to a quaint shopping district on the east side, where most of the merchants spoke with heavy European accents. They parked Ivena's Volkswagen Bug on one end of the district and made their way through the shops on either side of the street.

"Honestly, Ivena, I really love the halter top. It's so . . . fitting, don't you think?" *Glenn will love it.*

"Yes, Helen. Perhaps," Ivena returned with a raised brow. "But the red blouse, it is a lady's choice."

"I don't know, it looks a little old for me, don't you think?" *He'd kill me if I wore that thing!*

"Nonsense, dear. It's fabulous!"

They held the choices up to Helen's neckline, each arguing their case; trying not to be too forceful. A moment of silence ended the debate. It was then that Ivena, the final judge, issued her verdict. "We'll get both."

"Thank you, Ivena. I swear I'll wear them both." *Glenn . . .*

Get a grip, Helen. Glenn's history.

"Yes, I'm sure you will, dear."

And so the day went, from shop to shop. With halters and blouses; with jeans and skirts; with T-shirts and dresses; with tennis shoes and pumps; with everything except for lingerie. In the end they spent a thousand dollars. But it was just money, Ivena said, and Jan had altogether too much of the stuff. They walked and they laughed and then they spent another hundred dollars on accessories.

The beauty salon presented a challenge because two choices simply couldn't be made without resorting to wigs, and Helen would have nothing to do with wigs, despite Ivena's urging. Helen favored the short sporty look. It was sexy, she said. "Sexy? And you think a full-bodied woman's look is not sexy?" Ivena countered. The beautician tried to interject her opinion, but Ivena kept cutting her short. "It's Helen's hair," she finally announced. "Do as she wishes." And she retreated to a waiting chair. Helen walked out wearing a big smile and her hair just below the ears in a cropped style that even Ivena had to admit was "quite attractive."

Three times Helen thought about the life she'd left, and each time she concluded that this time she would stay straight if it killed her. She couldn't ignore the feeling of butterflies that accompanied the brief memories—a yearning for the drug's surge of pleasure—but watching Ivena carry on about a dress, she could not imagine crawling back to her old life.

It was three o'clock by the time they returned to Ivena's flower-laden home. It was four by the time Helen had wrapped up her fashion show, displaying every possible combination their purchases allowed and then some. Ivena looked on, sipping at her iced tea and boldly proclaiming how beautiful Helen was with each new outfit.

It was five when Helen began to come unglued.

Ivena had gone out to deliver a batch of orchids to a floral shop. "Make yourself at home—smell some flowers, warm up some sausage," she'd said. "I'll be back by six." Helen retreated to her tiny room, Ivena's sewing room actually, and sat on the bed, running her hand through the clothes piled beside her. She wore a dress, the one Ivena had proclaimed the winner of the bunch before leaving—a pink dress, much like the one Ivena had loaned her yesterday, but without all the frills.

She sat on the yellow bedspread in a sudden silence, with her legs swinging just off the floor like a little girl, feeling the fabric between her fingers, when her eyes settled on the blue vein that ran through the fold in her right arm. The room was dim but she could not miss the small mark hovering there. She pulled her hand from the clothes, opening and closing it slowly. The muscles along her forearm flexed like a writhing snake. It had been some time since she'd used the vein. Heroin was too strong, Glenn insisted. It ruined her. He couldn't stomach a rag doll sapped of passion. With Glenn it was all the new rich man's drug. Cocaine.

Glenn.

She blinked in the dim light and felt butterflies take flight in her belly again. She let familiar images crash through her mind. Images of the Palace, as he called it, where she'd lived for the last three months, on and off, but mostly on. Images of the parties, teeming with people under colored lights; images of mirrors mounded with cocaine and dishes with needles; images of bodies strewn across the floor, wasted in the wee morning hours. They were images that seemed ridiculous sitting here in the old lady's sewing room. She'd heard of sewing rooms, but she'd never expected to actually see one. And now here she was, *sitting* in one, surrounded by a pile of clothes that were presumably hers.

What do you expect to do, Helen? Use these people the way you've used the rest?

Suddenly the whole thing felt not just silly but completely stupid. And just as suddenly a craving for the mound of white powder ran through her body. An ache rose to her throat and she swallowed against it. She closed her eyes and shook her head. What was she doing?

Helen lifted a hand to her neck and rubbed the bruised muscles near the spine. She had put up with her share of abuse no doubt, and she could give it as well as she took it. A slap here and little punch there; it was all business as usual. But this strangling business—Glenn had nearly killed her! She'd had no choice but to run.

Here where there were no people she let tears fill her eyes. Now what? Now she was a little girl sitting on the bed, swinging her legs, wanting to be rescued.

Wanting a hit . . .

And she had been rescued, hadn't she? By a preacher, of all things. And his crazy old friend.

No, Helen, don't think of them like that. These are good people. Precious.

"Precious? And what would *you* know of precious?" she growled. The tears began to slip down her cheeks and she wiped them angrily with her wrist.

Helen stood to her feet, and the sudden movement left her dizzy. She blinked away the tears and paced the room. Face it, honey, this is not your world. This life with the flowers and the sausage and the strange accents and the old woman's crazy talk of love, like it was something Helen knew nothing of. All the hugs and the tears . . .

. . . and Jan . . .

. . . you'd think the world was turning inside out or something. Helen cleared her throat. Truth be told, she couldn't see why Ivena's daughter's death was such a huge deal anyway. Sure it was bad enough, but when you got right down to it, a bullet to the head wasn't so crazy. Not the big monstrous deal Ivena seemed to make of it. Like it was some new revelation of love or something. These two . . . weirdos . . . these two weirdos were just different, that was all there was to it. She was a fish; they were birds. And she was suddenly feeling short of breath up here with the weird birds. She needed to get back to her pond. After all, a fish could not live on the beach forever.

He's what they call a gentleman, Helen. A real man. The kind you've never seen. And don't pretend you don't know what I'm talking about, girl.

"Shut up!" Goodness, he was a preacher! She felt heat flare on her cheeks. *He's not even American.*

No, but he's god-awful handsome and his accent's pretty cute.

Helen hit her forehead with her palm. "You're being an idiot!"

The truth of her own words struck her and she halted her pacing mid-stride. The images of the Palace mounded with Glenn's drugs slid through her mind, whispering the promise of pleasure. Of heaven here on earth. The sound of her breathing filled the small room. Like that fish gulping up on the shore. She had no business here. This was a mistake, a stupid mistake.

Which meant she had to leave. And she *wanted* to leave, because now that she was allowing good sense to prevail, she knew that she had to have a hit. In fact, she wanted a hit as badly as she could ever remember wanting one.

It came roaring back. The urge rose through her chest with such force that for a moment she lost her orientation. She was in Ivena's sewing room of all places, a crazy place to be. She didn't belong here. She'd lost her mind!

Helen snatched a pair of Nikes, pulled them over her bare feet, and ran out to the living room. It would be best to leave out the back, in case the old woman . . .

. . . *Ivena, Helen. Her name is Ivena and she's not old . . .*

. . . drove up front. Helen hurried to the attached greenhouse, suddenly eager to be free. Desperate to get back into the water. She ran out to the backyard. But there were no gates in the tall fence surrounding the lawn. She gave up and ran right through the house and out the front door. It occurred to her only then that she had no ride. She should call Glenn. He would send a car. He'd be in a stew—the thought made her shiver. You pay your dues, baby. We all pay our dues. It was one of Glenn's favorite sayings. His idea of *dues* was a bit extreme.

She raced back into the house, snatched up Ivena's phone and called Glenn's private number. His secretary, the old hooknosed witch Beatrice, answered and demanded to know where she was. Helen gave her the nearest cross street and hung up. *Take a flying leap from the top story, Beatrice. And don't forget your broom.*

Now she ran with the butterflies that fluttered through her belly. She took a turn at the sidewalk and did not stop for two blocks, thinking only once that she should've ditched the dress—she must look like some kind of pink butterfly in the stupid thing. But her craving for the Palace washed the thought away.

Helen sucked in the warm southern air and settled into a walk. It was going to be a good night. Not at first, of course. At first it might not be so good at all, but that would pass. It always did. A picture of all those clothes piled on that bed back there flashed through her mind. *Sorry, Ivena. At least I left them. At least I didn't take them.*

Sorry, Jan.

Don't be stupid.

A long white limousine was already waiting at the corner of Grand and Mason, drawing the stares of stiff-lipped pedestrians in all directions. Yes indeed, it was going to be a good night.

BEATRICE WAS waiting for Helen when the elevator doors opened at the top of the West Tower, her nose hooked and her chin lifted like a snotty schoolmaster. She looked Helen's dress over and her lips twisted to a wrinkled frown. "So, the slug has crawled home wearing a dress. You think that's supposed to impress him?"

"Shut up, Witch. I'm not trying to impress anybody."

Beatrice's eyes grew round and then squeezed to slits. "He's gonna tan your hide when he sees you in that ridiculous getup." She turned on her heels and marched for the double doors leading to the Palace.

Helen hesitated, staring at those wide black doors. Her stomach seemed to have lifted into her throat. Glenn was in there, doing only God knew what, but in reality doing only one thing: waiting for her. Yes, and in truth she was waiting for him as well, right? Or at least for what he could offer. Which was bliss. Yes, indeed, Glenn could definitely offer her bliss.

She swallowed and stepped onto the thick black carpet after the witch, chills now running the length of her spine. *You're a fool, Helen. You have a death wish?* She thought about that and the chill was quickly replaced by a tingle. *No, honey, not death. Sweet life. Sweet, sweet mind-numbing life!*

Beatrice walked in without knocking; she was the only one who could survive such boldness. Helen followed, stepping lightly, as if doing so would somehow make her entrance less obvious. The sprawling room reminded Helen of a casino she'd been in once; lots of mirrors, lots of colored light, none of it natural. Glenn was not in sight.

Beatrice retreated with a *humph* and pulled the doors shut behind her. Helen peered about the room, her heart now thumping in the silence. To her right, one of those large mirrored balls rotated above a dance floor, slowly spinning a thousand tiny white dots through the room. Otherwise the Palace lay absolutely still. When she'd left the party three nights earlier, a dozen bodies twisted slowly on the pink marble dance floor. Directly ahead, a large lion head roared down to a red leather couch. A couple had been sprawled on that sofa, wasted to the world that night. Other guests had passed out on a dozen similar couches, each under beasts that glared down at them. There were a hyena and a rhinoceros and a buffalo—all within her sight. The others wound about the suite. To her left a long bar sparkled with a hundred colored bottles, each hosting its own intoxicant.

The last time she'd seen Glenn, he'd been leaning on that bar, talking to some huge black man with his back toward her. He was not there now.

"So . . ."

Her heart seized and she spun to his voice. Glenn stood ten yards to her right with his arms to his sides, in the shadow of a Greek pillar, huge and thick like the stonework beside him. A red-and-yellow Hawaiian shirt hung loosely over his torso; white slacks ran to the floor where they met his bare feet. He took a step forward then stopped, spread his legs, and clasped his hands together like a soldier at ease. From this distance his eyes looked like holes drilled through his skull; as black as midnight. His chin was stubbled and his hair unkempt.

Helen gulped and fought the overwhelming urge to flee. This had been a mistake. A terrible error on her part—coming here, back to this monster. He liked things dirty, he said, because he *could.* Weaker men had to stay clean to impress those in power. But not he. On several occasions she had suspected that he'd gone a week or more without bathing. When she was high the fact somehow held its own appeal, but now with a clear mind the very sight of him brought bile to her throat.

"So. Where have you been?" he asked.

"Hi, Glenn." She said it straight, but her voice wavered slightly. "I've been around."

"Around, huh? Why did you leave me?"

She smiled as best she could. *You can't be weak, Helen. He despises weakness.* "I didn't leave you, Glenn. I'm here, aren't I? Nobody forced me to come here." She wanted to say, *You think you own me, you pig?* but she held her tongue.

Glenn walked toward her. He did not stop until he towered over her, within arm's reach, drilling her with those dark eyes. He lifted a hand and touched her cheek with a knotted finger, rolling it back and forth, intent on the feel of her flesh. "You look so much like your mother, you know."

Her mother? Glenn knew her mother? Helen blinked. "You knew my mother?"

"Just an expression, dear," he said, gazing with a cocked head at his fingers touching her. His body odor hit her nostrils and she turned her head, trying not to show her disgust.

"What is it, darling?" he said in a soft, labored voice. "Do I frighten you?"

His breath smelled of dead flesh. Helen felt the pressure of tears fill her sinuses. "Are you *trying* to frighten me?" she asked. *Be strong, Helen. You know how he likes that.*

A soft moan ran past his lips. "Do you have any idea how much I've missed you? I was worried sick." His finger trembled on her cheek. "I feel lost without you, you know that, don't you? Look at me."

She held her breath and clenched her jaw and looked at his face. His unshaven jaw rested open and he ran his fat tongue over those crooked teeth. "Do you love me?" he asked.

A thousand sirens of protest raged through her mind. "Yes. Of course I love you." She had to get some dope into her system. She had to before she threw up on the man's smelly shirt. "You have some snort for me, honey?"

His lips peeled back over yellowed teeth in a smile of sorts and a string of spittle bridged his open mouth. He was enjoying his power over her. "Where did you get the dress, Helen?"

"The dress?" She looked down at the pink dress, wishing she would have had the sense to leave it at Ivena's. She chuckled. "Oh, this? Goodness, nowhere. I stole it. I—"

Crack! A blow struck her cheek and spun her around to the door. She gasped and instinctively jerked a hand to her mouth. It came away red and wet. Tears stung her eyes. Behind her Glenn was breathing heavy. She had to walk the line carefully now—this line between his anger and his desire to play. She turned back to him.

"What's the matter, Glenn?" she asked, forcing a grin. "Your little treasure disappears for three days and you come unglued, is that it?"

He blinked, unsure how to take the indictment. "You look like a schoolgirl," he said. "Your hair's different."

"Yeah, and you prefer the street girl look. Then give me what I want and I'll give you your street girl."

He brought each foot forward one step. "And what is it that you want, Helen?"

She'd meant the drugs, of course. They both knew that. But now he was daring her to say anything but him. "I want you, of course," she said.

She hoped it would appease him. It did not. His hand flashed from his hip and across her head before she could react. The blow sent her staggering to her right. This time she cried out and sprawled to the floor. It felt as though her ear had been ripped off by the blow, but she knew better. She gritted her teeth and pushed herself to her knees. She could kill the monster! If she had a knife now she would rush him and stuff it into the folds of his belly.

"You want me, do you? And that's why you were off with another man?" he thundered. He was red in the face now.

"That was nothing," she returned, standing unsteadily. "You sent two men after me, what do you expect?"

"I expect you to stay home, is what I expect! I expect you to at least try to stay alive, which means staying away from other men." His hands were balled into fists at his sides.

"Well, if you'd quit hitting me I might want to stay home!"

He grunted like a bull and swung again, but this time she stepped out of the blow's path and skipped back. "You fat pig!" She had entered his game now. "I came back, didn't I?" That was it. That was her ace. The fact that his men had not caught her and still she was here of her own will.

She sidestepped and ran across the room. *Come on, baby. Play the game. Just play the game and it'll be okay.*

Glenn lumbered after her. "I swear, if you ever, and I mean *ever*, leave me again, I swear I'll kill you!" he said. Someday he might actually make good on that promise to kill her, she thought.

She leaped behind a large couch and faced him. "Unless you die of *heartbreak* first!" She said it with a grin and tore out of his way just as he crashed into the sofa. "Give me some dope, Glenn."

Glenn pulled up in the center of the room, threw his fists to either side and roared at the ceiling. She spun around, the first genuine smile now spreading her mouth. *Now* he was playing. Now he was definitely playing. And that was good. That was really good. Adrenaline rushed through her veins.

"Give me some snort, Glenn. I'll be your girl."

He ripped his shirt open, popping the buttons with a single pull. His flabby belly bulged white. She couldn't stand to touch him without the drugs in her system. "Give me the drugs, Glenn!" She called out frantically now. "Where did you stash them?"

He taunted her with an ear-to-ear grin. "Drugs? Drugs are illegal, dear. You want to be illegal in my palace? You want some dope?"

"Yes. Yes I do."

"Then beg. Drop to your knees and beg, you dirty pig."

She did. She dropped to her knees, clasped her hands and begged. "Please! Please, tell me . . ."

He grinned like a kid. "In your bedroom."

Of course! Helen twisted to the door leading to the apartment he referred to as hers. She clambered to her feet and ran for the door. Glenn pounded across the room in pursuit. She slammed through the door and scanned the room for the dope. Her bed lay exactly as she'd left it—a comforter strewn cockeyed across it, three pillows bunched at the head. When he'd first presented the hidden apartment to her, its psychedelic yellow decor had taken her breath away. Now it made her head spin. She only wanted the stuff.

And then she saw it; a small pile of white powder on the mirrored end table across the room. Glenn's hot breath approached from behind and she bolted for the stash. She stumbled forward and fell to her knees just out of the stand's reach.

His big hand landed on her shoulder. "Come here, precious."

She clawed her way to the end table, desperate now. She had to have the stuff in her system. Had to. She swung her elbow back hard and landed it on his bare chest. He grunted.

The blow stalled him enough for Helen to reach the powder, shove her nose into the mound and inhale hard. Her nostrils filled with the suffocating drug, and she fought the urge to cough. A bitter pain burned at the back of her throat and through her lungs.

Then three hundred pounds fell on her back and rolled off to the floor, squealing like a stuck pig. Glenn squirmed on the carpet and giggled. *You are a sick man,* Helen thought. *A very sick man.* But the drug had already started to numb her mind and she thought it with a twist of irony. Like, *I am with a sick man. With a smelly pig and I'm feeling good. And that's because I'm sick too. We're just two sick pigs in a blanket. Glenn and me.*

She dived on top of him, slapping his fat and squealing along with him. Suddenly he wasn't a pig at all. Unless pigs could fly. 'Cause they were flying and Helen thought that maybe she was in heaven and he was her angel. Maybe.

Then Helen just let herself go and held on to her angel tight. Yes, she decided, she was in heaven. She was definitely in heaven.

CHAPTER FOURTEEN

JAN'S MANSION, as Ivena called it, lay at the end of a street, its arched entrance bordered by tall spruce trees, its front door bearing a simple greeting etched on a cross. *In living we die; In dying we live.* Behind the house a scattering of maple leaves drifted across a blue swimming pool nestled in a manicured lawn—an absolute necessity in this heat, Roald had told him. Jan had yet to use it. The house was of Southwestern decor, inside and out, from its ceramic shingle roof to the large rust tiles that covered the kitchen floor.

In all honesty, Jan felt awkward in the large house. He used the master bedroom, the kitchen, and the living room, which left four other rooms untouched. The exercise room sat collecting dust down the hall and the dining room had seen use only once—when Karen and Roald had first come to christen the house. The whole thing had been Karen's idea—give Jan an elegant house that completed the rags-to-riches image she was building around him. Roald had jumped on the idea and found the house.

Jan and Ivena sat in the living room under the indirect lighting of two amber floor lamps, staring past a large picture window at the shimmering pool late that night.

"So then," Jan said. "She's gone. What can I say?"

"We have to find her. Don't you see, she's doomed."

"Perhaps, Ivena, but so are a million other women in this country."

"Yes, but that doesn't mean you can ignore the one that comes begging for help. Where's your heart, Janjic?"

"My heart's where it should be: with Karen."

"That's not what I meant. This has nothing to do with her. I'm talking about Helen."

"And Helen's an adult. It was her decision to leave."

Jan had battled conflicting emotions from the moment he'd heard of her disappearance. He'd come home to an answering machine stuffed with messages from a distraught Ivena. Helen had disappeared. At first a chill of concern had spread through his bones, but after collecting himself he realized that they should hardly have expected differently. Helen had come into their lives like a whirlwind and sent their minds reeling. So now she had gone as quickly and it was just as well, he thought.

And the vision he'd had upon their touch? He had responded already. Just because his eyes had been opened for her didn't mean he now carried a responsibility for her. Besides, the day with Karen had all but washed the vision from his mind.

"What did you expect?" he continued. "You can't adopt her."

Ivena stiffened beside him. "And why not? Is it so unwise to take in a wounded soul?"

"She's twenty-nine, Ivena. A full-grown woman, not some child. You don't just spend a thousand dollars on a full-grown woman and expect her to change."

The reference to the money fell on deaf ears. "Twenty-nine. Nadia would have turned twenty-nine this year, Janjic. Did you know that?" Her eyes misted.

"No. I'm sorry, Ivena, I had forgotten."

"Well, *I* have not forgotten my daughter."

"That's not what I meant."

Ivena turned to face the pool outside. "She could be her, you know. Blond hair, blue eyes, so frail. Like a child."

So, Ivena had seen her own child in Helen. "I am so sorry, Ivena. I wasn't thinking about—"

"You are not remembering so well these days, Janjic. You speak of it all the time, to so many men all puffed up in their white shirts, feeling so important. But do you *remember?"* She turned to him. "Do you remember what it *felt* like to see Nadia die?"

He stared at her, blinking. "But Helen is not Nadia."

"No, she isn't. But then she is, isn't she? It's why you wrote your book, isn't it? So that others could feel Father Micheal's and Nadia's love the way you felt it twenty years ago? So that they could show that love, not for Nadia or Father Micheal, but for others. For people desperately needing a touch from God. For street girls like Helen. Isn't that why you wrote your book? Or have you forgotten that as well?"

"Don't patronize me, Ivena. I may not have lost my daughter, but I did lose my innocence and five years of my life. I was there as well."

"Then perhaps your memory isn't so sharp. Is Helen really so different from my Nadia?"

"Of course she is! Nadia sacrificed her life, like a lamb. She was pure and holy and she embraced death for the love of Christ. Helen . . . Helen doesn't know the *meaning* of sacrifice."

"No. But what about you, Janjic? You couldn't stop the slaying of my child, but can you stop the destruction of this child?"

Jan stood to his feet. "I tried to stop the slaying of Nadia. You shouldn't rub that in my face! You have no right to heap this burden on my head. It's one thing to suggest I look into my heart for the love of Christ, but it's another thing to suggest I lay down my life for every vagrant who crosses my door."

"And you have no right to assume that just because it is I who *speak* the truth, it is also I who *make* that truth. I can't change the fact that you were at the village when my daughter was killed, no more than I can change the fact that it was *you* who showed up on my doorstep yesterday with a stray girl who was in desperate need. So I'm simply telling you, we all know about the love of Nadia—the whole world knows about the love of Nadia; you have written of it well. But what about the love of Jan?"

He wanted to tear into her; to tell her to hold her tongue. She was consumed with this resurgent focus on love. And now, because he'd made the mistake of bringing Helen to her, she had in her hands a tangible example of that love. He collapsed on the overstuffed chair and stared out at the swimming pool without seeing it. "You think that lowly of my capacity to love?"

She sighed. "I don't know what I think, Janjic. I'm simply struck by a deep desire to help Helen. Because she reminds me of Nadia? Perhaps. Because we spent a day and a night together and I grew to like the child? Yes. But also because she's desperate for love, yet she does not even know it. What good is our love if we do not *use* it?"

She was right. So very right! This wasn't some vagrant who'd waltzed across his doorstep. Helen was a woman; a grown Nadia, suffering and lost.

Ivena spoke quietly now. "You felt something, Janjic. Both times in my house with her you felt some things. Tell me what you saw."

The request took him off balance. Thinking of it now, his objections over the past hours seemed absurd. He had felt God's heart for Helen, hadn't he? And if Ivena knew how clearly . . .

He sighed. "I told you, it was strange."

"Yes, you did. So then, tell me what strange looks like."

"Sorrow. I looked at her and I felt the pain of sorrow. And I heard crying.

White light and weeping." Yes indeed, she would tell him straight now. And he deserved it. He shook his head. "It was so vivid at the time. Goodness."

They sat in silence for a moment. "So, you feel this breath of God on your heart and still you argue with me about whether Helen needs our help?"

He closed his eyes and sighed. Yes, she was right about that too, wasn't she? And yet he didn't necessarily *want* to feel the breath of God when it came to Helen.

"Why do you resist?" she asked.

"Maybe the idea of playing nursemaid to this street girl scares me."

"Scares you? And what you saw in her presence does not scare you?"

"Yes, Ivena. It all scares me! I'm not saying it's right, I'm simply telling you how I feel. I have a full plate already and I don't need a tramp camping out on my doorstep right now. I have a trip to New York in a couple days, I have wedding details to work out with Karen; I have the movie—"

"Oh yes, the movie. I had forgotten. How silly of me! You have a movie to make about what love really looks like. God forbid you take time out to try loving a poor soul yourself."

She is right, you know.

"Ivena!"

"No, you are right. It all makes perfect sense now. Christ has already died for the world's pain; there is no need for the rest of us to suffer unduly. A small girl here, perhaps. A priest there. But certainly not we who live in our fancy palaces here in God's backyard."

She is right! She is so right.

"Ivena, stop it!"

They sat in silence again. It was a thing with them; they either spoke with meaning or they did not speak.

"You know, Janjic, there are very few who have witnessed the unconditional love Father Micheal taught in the years before his death. He spoke of it often, about the hope of glory as if it were a thing he could actually taste." She smiled reflectively. "He would speak and we would listen, imagining what it would be like, wanting to go there. American Christians may not have hope for anything beyond what they can put their fingers around in this life, but we hoped for the *afterlife*, I tell you. '*When you have a desperate love for God*,' Father Micheal would say, '*the comforts of this world feel like paper flowers. They are easily put aside. If you really have God's love.*'" She paused. "Have you thought about our discussion the other day, Janjic?"

"Yes," he said. "Yes, I have."

"Perhaps God brings people like young Helen into our lives to teach us something of his love."

Jan leaned back and closed his eyes. "You're right." He rubbed his face with his hands. How could he have been so callous? *Has my heart grown so callous? God, have mercy on me.* "I had the dream again last night. Same thing. If you're right and the dream's somehow of God, I wouldn't be upset if he would speed up his clock just a little."

But Ivena wasn't listening. "Father Micheal taught Nadia well, you know," Ivena said, her voice distant. "Sometimes I think he taught her too well."

Her mouth quivered to a frown despite her best efforts to stay strong. He slipped from his chair and knelt beside her. She began to cry and he placed his arm around her shoulders. "No, Ivena. Not too well."

It happened very rarely, this free flow of sorrows, and neither tried to stop it. Tears slid from Ivena's clenched eyes and quickly ran in streams. Jan pulled her to his chest and let her cry, choking on his own emotion. "Shhh, it's okay. She waits for you, Ivena," he said. "Shhhh."

For several long minutes they held each other like that and then Jan brought her a drink of water and sat in his own seat again. She sniffed and commented about how soft she was getting in her old age and he insisted that her tender heart had nothing to do with age.

"So then," he said after some time. "If it's true that God has brought Helen into our lives to teach us of his love, who's taken her *out* of our lives?"

"She has taken herself out," Ivena responded.

"And how do you propose we find her?"

"We don't. If it is indeed God's will, he will lead her back to us."

Jan nodded. "You know, for all of my complaining about her, I must say that I did enjoy her company. She was something, wasn't she?"

"Yes. Just watch yourself, my young Serb. You are, after all, engaged to be married."

Jan blushed. "Don't be ridiculous!"

"If *I* suspected a *pitter* in your heart, do you think she did not?"

"Please. Not everyone's as thorough a romantic as you!"

"Me? A romantic? Ha! Not too many would accuse me of that."

"That's because few know you as well as I, dear."

"I'm not judging, Janjic. I'm only telling you what I see."

"And maybe it's why I'm not so eager to have Helen walk back into our lives," he said plainly. "I'm at a delicate stage of my life, you know. I have responsibilities; I have a ministry; I'm going to be married. All of this love talk is making me dizzy."

"Never mind the responsibilities Roald and the other church leaders place on you. Just guard your love for Christ and your other affections will follow."

He nodded. "You're truly a romantic at heart, aren't you, Ivena? All this talk of love is your cup of tea."

"And yours, my dear. And yours."

JAN PARKED the Cadillac and rode the elevator to the eighth floor at nine the following morning. He was back in crisp form—a starched white shirt, trim black slacks, and a narrow black satin tie.

Nicki chirped a bright-eyed *Good morning!* and brought him coffee. He should get his own coffee, he thought. Drive his own car, get his own coffee, and love as Christ had loved. What would Karen say to that?

Karen came in half an hour later, wearing a bright blue dress and a brilliant smile. "Good morning, Jan." She leaned against his doorframe and folded her arms. "You sleep well?"

"I slept well." The glint in her eyes brought a surge of adrenaline to his blood.

"Good. I did too. So, I hear you're driving yourself these days."

"Yes."

"You really think that's a good idea?"

"Yes."

She nodded and smiled. "Okay." But he knew she didn't really mean okay.

They held each other's gaze for a full second before she slipped out of his sight toward her own office.

What was it with the heart? What madness that a simple look from a woman could prove so distracting? Jan cleared his throat. He had a decent stack of calls to return, but suddenly the thought of making them seemed so utterly mundane that he pushed them aside and stood from the desk. He could return to them later. He needed to talk to Karen.

Jan walked into her office and sat across from her.

She lifted an eyebrow. "Well now. What's on your mind?"

That feeling swept through him again. A few words from her and his stomach was floating. "So, we leave for New York tomorrow. Everything's set?"

"It's all set up. But you know that from our meeting yesterday."

"Yes. I also know that with you things happen so quickly that I can't rest on yesterday's news," he said with a gentle smile.

"Nothing has changed. We fly at nine, meet Roald in New York at one, and sign the deal the following day. God willing."

"Yes, God willing."

They talked then of details already covered, but worth another pass considering the gravity of the deal they were about to sign. They also talked wedding plans. It would be a Christmas wedding—they had decided that much last night. A big wedding with a thousand guests. She would plan it, of course. She'd been born to plan this wedding. It would have to be in a park—a Southern belle affair—with enough glamour to attract national coverage. She thought she might be able to talk Billy Graham into doing the honors.

Jan finally excused himself to make some calls, he said. By the stack of messages on her own desk, Karen needed to make many more calls than he.

She came into his office late morning with some updates. Delmont Pictures was definitely on track, she said. They wanted to launch a fresh round of book interviews within the month, with a broader audience.

"So how does it feel, Jan?" Karen asked with a smile.

"How does what feel?"

"Please, don't pretend you don't know. You're going to become a star, my dearest."

He grinned slightly. "Oh? And here I thought I was already a star."

"Not like this, you aren't. Strap in, Jan, because you're going to be a household name. Just don't forget that your lovely wife played a part in it when they're scrambling for your autograph."

He laughed. "Ha! *My* autograph? Never. Even if they wanted it, I would have to sign Father Micheal's name. Or Nadia's."

"Hmmm," she said. "You'll see. We're entering brand-new territory here. I don't think you have a clue."

"Maybe. But we can never forget the price paid."

And paid for what, Jan? Your wealth and honor?

He looked away from her, sobered by the thought.

"What is it, Jan?"

"Do you ever wonder if the story has changed people, Karen? I mean really *changed* them?"

"Of course it has! Don't be ridiculous, it's changed thousands of lives."

"And how?"

She paused. "Jan, I know what you're thinking, and it's the prerogative of every artist to want to know that his work has somehow made a difference in the world. But believe me, your work, like none other I've known, has made an impact on the hearts of men. I came here because I believed in the book, and I've known from the beginning that it was the right choice."

He nodded. "Yes. And I'm not saying you're wrong, but tell me how it has changed a man's heart. Tell me about *one* man."

Karen eased around the desk and sat in the guest chair next to him. She placed a hand on his shoulder. "Jan, look at me."

He did and her eyes were round and gentle.

She lifted a finger to his cheek and stroked it very lightly. "You have no reason to feel this way," she said. "We're impacting hundreds of thousands with this ministry. You can't reach into the hearts of men and personally change them, but you can tell them the truth. And you have. You've done it well. And trust me, Jan, the movie will do even more."

What part was she playing now? The comforting agent, talking to her client, protecting her investment? Or the loving fiancée? Perhaps both. Yes, both. But why did he even question her motives?

"Look at me," she said. "I had no intention of loving God before meeting you. You think I haven't changed?" She smiled and winked. "And it's touched my heart in other ways as well."

"Yes?"

"Yes. It's not every day you'll find my hand on a man's cheek."

His face grew red beneath her touch—he couldn't see it, but he could feel the heat sweep over his skin. He lifted his hand and took hers. "And it's not every day that you'll find me holding such a delicate hand as yours."

She blushed pink. They sat silenced by their own admissions for a moment.

"And you . . . we can't forget you, Jan. The story has transformed your life."

"Has it?" he asked. "I wonder at times if my love for myself isn't greater than my love for others." He paused and shifted his gaze to the far window facing a blue sky. "Just two days ago, for example, I met this woman . . . a tramp really. A junkie. Her name was Helen." The memory of the vision he'd had at her touch suddenly skipped through his mind. *Choose your words carefully, Janjic.*

"Yes?"

Jan told Karen about rescuing Helen and taking her to Ivena's. And then he told her about how she'd disappeared. He left out the strange emotions he'd felt in her presence, but explained his fear of caring for such a wayward soul. How it might taint his perfect world. Somewhere in there Karen removed her hand from his and sat back to listen.

"So you see, if I've changed so much, why does the thought of showing compassion to this simple desperate girl scare me? Even repel me?"

"I don't know. You tell me." It struck him that her tone was not completely friendly.

"I'm not talking about any kind of romantic attraction, Karen. Helen's a poor lost soul. What would Father Micheal say? He would say that I should give her what is mine. That if she asked for my shirt, I should give her my coat as well. That if she wanted a lift for one mile, I should offer to take her two."

"Yes, he might. And you've done that, haven't you? A thousand dollars of clothes? What did the woman think she needed?"

"Well, that was actually Ivena's doing. They had differing ideas of what to buy so they evidently bought everything, just to be sure."

Ordinarily Karen would have laughed, but now she only smiled, and thinly at that. "So then you've done what you should have and she's gone. If you're concerned about not doing enough, I would think you're going a bit far." She said it and waited a moment before adding, "Don't you think?"

"Maybe." He nodded. Karen seemed impatient with the conversation and he could see that she wasn't the one to discuss Helen with. "Yes, you may be right." He smiled and turned the discussion to the coming trip. It took Karen a few minutes but she seemed to forget about Helen, and after a few minutes the twinkle in her eye returned.

Or so Jan thought, until he stood to leave for the night.

"Jan."

He turned back. "Yes?"

She stood and put her hand on his arm. "I think you were right about Helen. Okay? It's easy to lose sight of what love means these days, but I didn't mean to discourage you."

"No, and you didn't. But thank you, Karen. Thank you."

"So then, New York tomorrow?"

He lifted her hand and kissed it gently. "New York tomorrow."

Chapter Fifteen

GLENN LUTZ was back in his game. He conducted business over lunch—a shipment of hash from Jamaica—and by his rough count, the deal would put over five hundred thousand dollars in his bank over the next month. He would have to shove that morsel up Beatrice's nose.

The limousine took him back to the Twin Towers where he took the elevator up to his perch atop the East Tower. Memories of his reunion with Helen brought a smirk to his face. They were made for each other, he thought. Carved from the same stone as children and presented to each other only now, when they were old enough to play properly. Helen had gone sky-high last night and he'd joined her there. He had left her at two in the morning, curled semicomatose on the bed, gone to the house, showered, and regained his desire for her.

It had been a good morning, he thought. Everything was back in its place. He'd even seen the wife and kids, although he hadn't spoken to the kids—they were off to school by the time he emerged from the shower. His wife on the other hand had sulked about the kitchen, asking every question except the one he knew blared in her mind: *Where have you been for the past three days, Glenn?*

Never mind where I've been, meat brains. I own this house, don't I? Mind your own business or you'll be out on the street before you have the time to blink. And your kids with you. She was really no longer much of a wife anyway. A live-in mother, taken care of nicely enough, and they both knew it.

He spent the rest of the afternoon catching up on phone calls, slowly building an appetite for the woman. It wasn't the same kind of desire as when she left him—no, nothing could be so strong. It was a desire that came and went with the day's passing and now it was coming.

Glenn left his empty, mirrored office at six o'clock and entered the enclosed walkway that spanned the eighty-foot gap to the West Tower. Only he used the private passage. It was one of the Tower's features that had attracted him in the first place. He did not own the entire building, but he did own a twenty-year lease on the stories that mattered, including the walkway that conveniently separated his two lives.

He entered the Palace. "Helen?" The room lay in the dim late-day light. "Helen?" She was here, of course. He had called just an hour ago, received no answer, and sent Beatrice in to check. She had come back to the phone and informed him that she was still sprawled on the bed, dead to the world.

"Helen!" He strode for her door and shoved it open.

At first he thought she was in the shower because the bed sat empty; a tangle of sheets half torn from the mattress. He grinned and tiptoed across to the bathroom. It too was empty. Steamy from a recent shower, but vacant. The kitchen, maybe.

Unless . . . The thought that she might have fled again first crossed his mind then. A flash of panic ripped up his spine. He grunted, whirled from the bathroom and lumbered across the floor to the third room in the small apartment. He grabbed the corner and spun onto the kitchen floor. It was empty!

Impossible! The witch had just checked!

Glenn turned back to the main room and fixed his gaze on the wastebasket where he'd thrown her pink dress, muttering obscenities. But the basket gaped empty. The dress was gone. He knew it then with certainty; Helen had fled.

Unless she really hadn't fled but was hiding somewhere, to play. "Helen!" He ran back to the main room, screaming her name. "Helen! Listen you dope, this is *not* funny! You get yourself out here right now or I swear I'm gonna tan you good, you hear?"

The room's silence seemed to thicken around him; he wheezed, pulling at the air as if it would run out at any minute. "Helen!" He ran to the double doors and yanked on the handles, only to discover they were locked as he'd instructed. Then how? He bounded for the drawer under the bar, pulled it open and grabbed at the contents.

But the key was missing! The wench had taken the key and fled!

A red cloud filled Glenn's vision. He would kill her! The next time he laid hands on that puke he would skin her alive! Nobody . . . *nobody* did this and survived. His limbs were shaking and he grabbed the bar to steady himself.

Easy, boy, you're gonna pop your cork here.

As if it had heard, his heart seemed to stutter. A small shaft of pain spiked across his chest and he clutched at his left breast. *Easy, boy.* He breathed steadily and tried to calm himself. The pain did not repeat.

Glenn staggered over to the wall phone, wiping the sweat from his brow. He punched the witch's number. She picked up the interoffice line on the tenth ring.

"Mr. Lutz has gone home for the day. Please call back—"

"Beatrice, it's me, you idiot! And what were you doing while our little pigeon was busy flying the coop?"

"She . . . she's gone?" she stammered in response.

"Now you listen to me, you fat witch. You get me Buck now. Not in five minutes, not in three minutes, but now! You hear? And tell me you ran that reverse trace I told you to yesterday."

"I have the address."

"You'd better hope she shows up there. Now get over here and unlock this cursed door!" He slammed the phone into its cradle. This time he'd make sure things got done right, if he had to do them himself.

Glenn lifted his hands and covered his face. *Helen, Helen. What have you done?* The ungrateful dope would learn her lesson this time. He would not bear this nonsense any longer.

Could not.

THE STRANGE vine in Ivena's greenhouse had grown wild, adding a foot to its length in each of the last two days. She'd continued thinking it might be a weed of some kind, overtaking the rosebush in Amazonian fashion. But today she knew that something had changed.

It was the smell that greeted her when she first cracked the door to the greenhouse. The poignant aroma of rose blossoms, but sweeter than any of her flowers had ever offered.

She pushed the door open and looked in. To the right, the tall orchids glistened yellow after their misting. Three rows of pink roses lined the opposite wall. The red tulips were nearing full maturity along the kitchen wall. But these all registered with the vagueness of a gray backdrop.

It was the bush at the center of the left wall that captured Ivena's attention. Nadia's rosebush, which was hardly a rosebush at all now. A single flower perched above the green vines. A flower the size of a grapefruit and Ivena knew that the sweet scent came from this one bloom.

She stepped into the greenhouse and walked halfway to the plant before stopping. "My, my." The sight before her was an impossibility. She swallowed and searched her memory for a flower that resembled this one. A white flower with each petal edged in red, round like a rose but large like a trumpet lily.

"My, my." *Dear God, what have we here?*

The aroma was strong enough to have been distilled from flowers, as in a perfume. Too strong to be natural. Ivena stepped lightly forward and bent over to view the vines beneath the flower. They hadn't grown so much since yesterday, but they had yielded this stunning flower.

Ivena turned and hurried from the room, retrieved a thick book of horticulture from her living room and returned, flipping through the same pages she'd scanned three times already in as many days. She simply had to identify this fast-growing plant. And now that it had flowered it should not be so difficult. A flower was a plant's most striking signature.

She'd run through the pages of roses without a match. She turned the last page of roses without finding any similar. So, then, a lily. Perhaps even an orchid, or a tulip, somehow cross-pollinated from her own, which was impossible. Nevertheless, she was out of her realm of knowledge.

It took her three quarters of an hour to exhaust the reference book. In the end she could find nothing that even remotely resembled the strange flower.

She closed the book and leaned on the frame that housed the plant. "What are you, my dear flower?" she whispered. She would have to bring Joey in for a look. He would offer an explanation. You didn't become a master of botanical gardens without knowing your flowers.

Ivena lowered her nose to the petals. The aroma drew right into her lungs; she thought she could actually feel it. It was more than a scent—it was as if an aura was being emitted by the petals, something so sweet and delightful that she found herself not wanting to leave the room.

"My, my!"

She lingered for another ten minutes, mesmerized by the unlikely invasion into her world.

HELEN APPROACHED Ivena's house from the north, sprinting down the sidewalk in the dress, oblivious to her appearance. She had to get in that house; it was all that mattered now. Ivena and Jan would know what to do; she had spent the last few hours convincing herself so.

The plan, if she could call it a plan, had proceeded like clockwork. Of course the plan was only an hour old and it would end in less than thirty seconds when she knocked on Ivena's door. Beyond that she had no idea what to do. What she did know was that she had woken from her night of indulgence at 1:00 P.M. with the absolute knowledge that she had to leave Glenn's pigsty.

She had felt the same way before, of course, and she'd left. But this time . . . maybe this time it was for good. Images of Jan and Ivena wandered about her mind, calling to her. It had been good, hadn't it? Sitting like a real lady, eating sausage and kraut and discussing issues with such a real man. Such a sophisticated, kind man. And when had she ever spent a day with someone so wise as Ivena? Despite her ancient tastes, the woman had a mind books were written from.

Helen had spent four hours lying on the bed feeling sick and lonely and impossibly useless. She'd climbed out twice to throw up, once after allowing her mind to recall the way Glenn had slobbered over her during the night, and once from the drugs. She was in bed when the witch came to check her at five, and she decided to play dead. It was then, when Beatrice left, that she conceived of her plan. The trick was to throw herself together, get out using his key, and put as much distance as possible between herself and the Palace before the pig came back. She figured she would have an hour; Glenn wouldn't have sent Beatrice if he was on the way.

Helen had hit the street and boarded a bus before the possibility that Ivena might not welcome her with open arms even crossed her mind. Ivena did not strike her as the kind who would extend a second chance so easily. On the other hand, she and Jan were the kind who would forgive and forget. Or at least forgive.

She cast a quick look back down the street one last time, saw no cars, and ran up to the door. Breathing as steadily as possible, she lifted a trembling hand to the doorbell and pushed it. The bell's faint chime sounded beyond the door. She smoothed her dress—the dress Ivena had insisted she buy—and waited, wanting very badly to step into the warm safety of this house.

The door swung in and Ivena stood there, wearing a light blue dress. "Hello, Helen," she said as though nothing at all was strange about her reappearance. She might have continued with a question, like, *Did you get the milk I asked for?* Instead she stepped aside. "Come in, dear."

Helen moved past Ivena.

"Come into the kitchen; I'm making supper." Ivena strolled ahead. "You can help me, if you like."

"Ivena. I'm sorry. I just—"

"Nonsense, Helen. We can speak of it later. You're not hurt?"

Helen shook her head. "No. I'm fine."

"Well you do have a nasty bruise on your cheek. From this Glenn character, yes?"

"Yes."

"We should put some cream on it."

Helen looked at the older lady and felt a pleasure she had rarely known, an unconditional acceptance of sorts. It swept through her chest and clamped down on her heart for a moment. She couldn't help the dumb drop of her jaw. "So then, you aren't angry?"

"I was, child. But I released it last night. You were hoping for anger?"

"No! Of course not! I just . . . I'm not used to being . . ." She let her voice trail off, at a loss for words.

"You're not used to being loved? Yes, I know. Now, why don't you see how the stew is doing while I make a quick phone call."

"Sure." Ivena simply welcomed her back as if she *had* just run down to the corner for some milk. "You like?" Helen asked, curtseying in the dress.

Ivena grinned. "You wore the best for your little trip, I see. Yes, I like."

Helen let Ivena make her phone call while she peeked under the pot of simmering stew. The smell brought a rumble to her belly; she had not eaten since leaving yesterday. Ivena was speaking in excited tones now. To Jan! Meaning what? Meaning they were celebrating the return of their little project? Or meaning that Jan disapproved of Ivena's—

"Helen?" Ivena called.

"Yes."

"Did you use the phone yesterday?"

To call Glenn; she'd forgotten. "Yes," she said.

There was another moment of conversation before Ivena hung up and bustled into the kitchen, turning off the burner and placing the warm pot in the refrigerator. "Come along, dear. We must leave," Ivena said.

"Leave? Why?"

"Jan says that it's too risky. If Glenn is as powerful as you say, he may have traced your call. Do you know, would he do such a thing?"

Helen swallowed. "Yes."

"And there would be a problem if he came looking for you?"

"Yes. Good night, yes!" Helen spun around, panicked by the thought. It was true! He was probably on his way at this moment. "We have to get out, Ivena! If he finds me here . . ."

Ivena was already pushing her to the front. "Get in my car quickly." She snatched a ring of keys from the wall and gently nudged Helen out the door. They stopped and peered both ways before running across the lawn and piling into an old gray Volkswagen Bug with rusted quarter panels. Ivena didn't so much pile as climb and Helen urged her on. "Hurry, Ivena!"

"I am hurrying! I'm not a spring chicken."

Ivena fired the car up and pulled out with a squeal. "Thankfully I drive faster than I run," she said and roared down the street.

Helen chuckled, relieved. "Pedal to the metal, mama. So where to?"

"To Janjic's," Ivena said. "We will go to Janjic's mansion."

GLENN SAT in the town car's rear seat, fussing and fuming, screaming long strings of obscenities while Buck steered the car with his one good arm and used the other as a guide. Sparks hadn't been so lucky; it would be a month before the man would have use of his arm. But Buck's bullet had done nothing more than slice into his shoulder. A few inches lower and it would've drilled a hole through his heart; the fact hadn't been lost on him.

"Up ahead, sir," Buck said.

"Where?" Glenn leaned forward. The light was already failing.

"Should be one of these houses up on the left."

A car peeled from a driveway ahead; an old gray Bug. Some lowlife teenager showing off his new ride. They slowed and followed the numbers. 115 Benedict, Beatrice had said. 111 . . . 113 . . . 115. "Stop!" It was a small house surrounded by a hundred bushes blooming with white flowers. And if he was right, there would be one flower in that house ripe for the picking. Or squashing, depending on how it all came off.

"Isn't this the driveway that Bug came from?" Buck said.

Bug? The gray Bug! Glenn spun to the street. "Yes!" It couldn't be far. Had it turned left or right at the end? "Move, you fool! Don't just sit here, get after it!"

They squealed into pursuit and caught it thirty seconds later, cruising west. Glenn leaned over the seat, breathing heavy beside Buck and peering through the dusk. He recognized her head, immediately—that light blond head he had held just last night. If he could reach her now he would take a handful of that hair and shake her like a rag doll, he thought. And he would do that soon enough now, because he had *found* her! He'd found the tramp. Sweet, sweet Helen. It now made little difference whether she intended to hide back at the house of flowers or at the Bug's current destination. This time he would take care of things right. It would have to be a plan that lasted. One that took her completely off balance and thoroughly persuaded her to stay in her cage. Or better still, a plan that lured her back of her own choosing. Because she loved him. Yes, she did love him. *Here, kitty, kitty.*

It occurred to Glenn that his mouth hung open over the leather seat before him. A string of drool had fallen to the back of the seat. He swallowed and sat straight.

"Back off!" he snapped. "Back off and follow that car until it stops. You lose it and I swear I'll put a bullet through your other arm."

CHAPTER SIXTEEN

Q: "What does this kind of love feel like?"
A: "The love of the priest? Imagine mad desperation. Imagine a deep yearning that burns in your throat. Imagine begging to be with your lover in death. King Solomon characterized the feeling as a sickness in his songs. Shakespeare envisioned it as Romeo's death. But Christ . . . Christ actually died for his love. And the priest followed him gladly."

Q: "And why do so few Christians associate love with death?"
A: "Just because they're Christians does not mean they are necessarily followers of Christ. Followers of Christ would characterize love this way because Christ himself did."

Jan Jovic, author of bestseller The Dance of the Dead
Interview with New York Times, *1960*

JAN PACED the entryway and padded across the polished rust tile in stocking feet, feeling screwed into a knot without knowing exactly why. Ivena was on her way, bringing Helen with her. So the woman had come back after all. Ivena was right; they should show her Christian love. Christ had dined with the vagrants of his day; he had befriended the most unseemly characters; he'd even encouraged the prostitute to wash his feet.

So then, why was Jan reluctant to embrace Helen?

Father, what is happening here? You touch me with this woman; you give me this mad sorrow for her, but for what reason? Unless it was not you but me, conjuring those feelings in my own mind.

Perhaps it wasn't reluctance he felt at all, but fear. Fear for what the woman did to him both times he'd seen her. Karen's face flashed through his mind, smiling warmly. Even she had concluded that he ought to show friendship to Helen, although the conclusion had not come so easily.

Jan stopped his pacing and breathed deeply through his nose. The strong odor of vanilla from the three lit candles filled his nostrils. He'd turned the lights down, a habit ingrained during Sarajevo's siege. Turn the lights down and stay low. Of course, this wasn't Sarajevo and there was no siege. But this was Helen, and he had not imagined those two men chasing her in the park. She was in more danger than she let on.

The doorbell chimed and he started. Here already!

Jan stepped to the door and pulled it open. Ivena bustled in with Helen in tow. "Are you quite sure this is necessary, Janjic?" Ivena asked.

Jan closed the door, turned the deadbolt, and faced them. "Maybe not, but we can't take the chance of being wrong." He turned to Helen, who stood in the shadows. "Hello, Helen. So what do you think? Is this necessary?"

She stepped forward into the yellow light; the petite woman with short blond hair and deep blue eyes, dressed in a wrinkled pink dress. It was hard to imagine that she was the cause of all this commotion. She was just a junkie. She wore no shoes and her feet were dirty—that gave her away. On closer inspection so did the round bruise on her left cheek. She'd been hit very hard there. Jan's heart was suddenly thumping in his chest.

"It could be," she said.

"And what kind of danger are we talking about?" He swallowed, acutely aware that she was affecting him already; afraid that she might drown him with his own compassion. *Father, please.*

"I don't know . . . anything. You saw the men that chased us."

"Then we should call the police."

"No."

"Why not? This man has abused you. You're in danger."

"No. No police."

Ivena turned for the living room. "Standing here will do us no good. Come in, Helen, and tell us what has happened."

Helen kept her eyes on Jan for a moment before turning and following Ivena. Jan watched them go. Ivena had indeed adopted Helen, he thought. They sat in a triangle—Helen on the couch, Ivena on the love seat, and Jan in his customary leather armchair—and for a moment no one spoke. Then Helen twisted her hands together, pulled them close as if to hold herself, and smiled. "Boy, it smells good in here. Is that vanilla, Jan?"

Her voice played over his mind as if it possessed life. Goodness! It was happening again! And she had said what? *Is that vanilla, Jan?* Yet those words—the simple sound of her voice—and the image of her huddled on the couch played like fingers on the chords of his mind.

"Yes," he answered. "From the candle."

She was looking around. "So this is the mansion Ivena keeps talking about. It's nice."

"It's too much," Jan said.

"You live here alone?"

"Yes."

"Then you're right; it's too much."

Ivena *humphed.* "I've always told him the same. He needs a good woman to make this a home. Now tell us, Helen. Why did you leave yesterday?"

There it was; Ivena had opted for the direct approach, like a good mother.

And Helen did not seem to mind this time. "I don't know. I was lonely, I guess," she said.

"Lonely? Lonely for this fellow who put that bruise on your cheek?"

She shrugged and bit her lip.

Ivena glanced at Jan. "And why did you come back?" she asked.

Again Helen shrugged. She stared at one of the floor lamps, and Jan saw her eyes glisten in the amber light. She was as confused and desperate as they came, he thought. A child so categorically lost that she did not even know she was lost. A woman strung out by an impossible childhood and left to dangle by a single thread. In her case it might be a thread of pleasure. Give her pleasure, any form of pleasure, and she would cling to you. But give her love and she might fly away, confused by the foreign notions of trust and loyalty. Her leaving and coming were as much a matter of habit as desire.

Jan stared at her and felt his heart ache. *Helen, Helen. Sweet Helen.* He wiped a thin sheen of sweat from his palms. "You don't need to be afraid, Helen. You will be safe, here. I promise."

She lifted her blue eyes. "I hope so."

"But we should know more about Glenn, I think. We're involved now; we should know more."

Helen nodded slowly and then she told them about Glenn. The simple truth, from her own eyes, of course, but honesty hung in her voice. Slowly she unveiled the ugly truth about her relationship with the demented drug dealer. And slowly, as she talked, Jan felt his ache for her increase. He arose once to check the street, but came back reporting nothing unusual.

Glenn was a man who lived for control, and beneath the city's layers he pulled a lot of strings . . . Helen believed him. She'd heard him—seen him—manipulate men much more powerful in the public eye. But really it was Glenn who pulled the strings with his huge fistfuls of money. It was a power as intoxicating as the drugs. It was a give-and-take relationship—they both gave and they both took.

Her voice droned sweetly through Jan's mind, like an airborne drug—playing on his emotions as no voice had ever played. He listened to her and his heart seemed to physically swell. It grew and ached with every new sentence she spoke. So much so that toward the end of her story, he stopped hearing her altogether.

It wasn't the way she looked. It was more, far more. It was her voice; the look beyond her eyes. A fire deep in her pupils that mesmerized him. It was her sloppy English and her giggle and her plain way with the truth. There was not a shred of plastic about her.

But more even. It was the fact that her heart was beating. She was sitting there on his couch and her heart was beating and somehow his own heart was beating with it. The thought made his palms wet.

He imagined telling Karen about this. *Oh, Karen. This woman is so wounded. She's in such need of love. The love of God. Christ's love.*

Helen, sweet Helen, was no ordinary woman, he knew that now. And the realization began to soak the back of his shirt with sweat.

". . . will I stay?" Helen asked.

She had asked the question of him. "What? I'm sorry, what?"

"What do we do now? Have you been listening, Jan? Because you do look distracted. Doesn't he look distracted, Ivena?"

"Of course, I've been listening," he said and blushed. Helen was smiling slyly as if she'd caught him, and he suddenly felt very self-conscious. *She is beautiful,* he thought. *Wrinkled pink dress, scraggly blond hair and all. Quite beautiful. Stunning actually. Even with her bare feet. They are tender feet.*

Stop it, Jan! Stop it! This is absurd! You are nearly married and here you are ogling a young woman.

He faced Ivena and heard his voice as if at a distance. "What would you say, Ivena?"

She had lowered her head and was looking at him past her eyebrows. "I would say that I detect a *pitter*, Janjic."

She was referring to his heart! Good heavens, she was accusing him right here before Helen! "Good enough. You will stay the night then. It could be dangerous to return to your house alone. Use the apartment."

"Apartment?" Helen asked.

"There's a fully equipped suite in the basement. Old guest quarters. Actually no one's used it since Ivena occupied it for a few weeks while we found her house. It has its own entrance but it's well locked. Ivena knows the ropes."

Jan glanced at Ivena and saw that she held a raised eyebrow.

The shrill ring of the phone saved Jan from any further comment. He stood quickly and strode for the kitchen. Ivena had gone too far this time. He would speak to her about this *pitter* nonsense.

But she is right, Janjic.

He grabbed the receiver from the wall. "Hello." *She could not be right.*

"Jan Jovic?" a low voice asked.

"Yes?"

The man on the phone took a deep breath, but did not speak. Jan's heart spiked. "May I help you?"

"Listen to me, you little punk. You think you can keep her?" A few pulls of heavy breathing filled the receiver and Jan spun away from the women. A small strobe ignited in his mind and suddenly he was there, again. Facing Karadzic's venomous stare in a distant landscape.

"She's a dog in heat. You know how to keep other dogs away from a dog in heat?" It was Karadzic! It was him!

"You kill them," the voice said. "Now you've been warned, preacher pimp. If she's not back in her kennel within forty-eight hours you'll pray to God that you never laid eyes on her." Heavy breathing again.

Jan's mind spun, gripped by panic.

A soft click sounded. And a dial tone.

For a moment Jan could not move. Had he just been threatened? Of course he had! But it was not Karadzic, was it? It was Glenn Lutz.

He breathed deliberately and blinked several times to regain clear vision. The women had stopped talking. He forced the phone back onto its hook.

"Is there a problem, Janjic?" Ivena called.

"No," he said, and immediately thought, *That was a lie.* But what else could he say? *Don't mind me, I'm just losing my mind over here. I do that once a month. Helps me stay in touch with my past.*

Jan considered excusing himself and walking for the bedroom. Instead he opened the refrigerator and stared at the contents for a few moments. He reached for the pitcher of tea with a shaking hand, thought better of it and grabbed a small bottle of soda water instead. Slowly the tremble worked its way out of his limbs.

This was all far too much. He had a life to attend to, for heaven's sake. He was bound for New York in the morning. With Karen! His fiancée! He really should walk in there and tell Ivena that she should take Helen to a church shelter or another place properly staffed to help women in need. This was his home, not some church. And now his life was being threatened by her crazed lover!

But when he entered the room and saw Helen sitting on the couch, his heart swelled once again, despite the odd look she cast his way. His stomach hovered for a moment.

Dear God, this was madness!

Perhaps, but Jan knew then for the first time, looking at the young woman on his couch, that he did not *want* her to leave. In fact, the thought of her leaving brought a feeling not unlike panic to his chest.

Which was a problem, wasn't it? A very big problem.

JAN BARELY slept that night. He mumbled prayers to his Father, begging for understanding, but no understanding came. If God had indeed ignited his heart for this woman, what kind of switch had he thrown? And why? And what would Karen make of Ivena's *pitter*? Which was maybe more than a *pitter*.

She would never understand. Neither would Roald. How could they? *Jan* didn't even understand!

He rose half a dozen times and peeked through the windows for any sign of intruders, then finally drifted off near 3:00 A.M.

He left the house at six, before either Ivena or Helen had emerged from their rooms. They'd agreed that if anyone needed to leave the house, it would be Ivena, alone. Helen would not leave for any reason. And under no condition were they to open the door for a stranger. There was easily enough food in the icebox to tide them over. He would think things through and come back from New York with a plan, he promised.

Karen gave him several strange looks during their drive to the airport. "What?" he asked once.

"Nothing. You just seem distracted," she replied.

He almost told her about the crazy threat, but decided she didn't need the worry hanging over her.

"I have a lot on my mind," he told her with a smile. It seemed to satisfy her. An hour later the jet leveled off at thirty thousand feet. Slowly the images that had kept him awake during the night began to fade.

They sat side by side in the first-class cabin, fingers intertwined, talking of everything and nothing, flying high in their own private world. The musky perfume she wore smelled delicate and womanly, like Karen herself, he thought. Dinner was served: lobster tails with buttered potatoes and a red wine sauce he'd never tasted before—certainly not with lobster. It was heavenly. Although, Karen did advise the stewardess that the beans hadn't been properly stringed and Jan felt awkward for her saying it.

Roald had arranged to meet them with an entourage of Christian leaders and human rights activists who strongly supported the making of the movie. Some of Delmont's people would be there as well, Karen told him. They wanted to make an event out of the occasion. Trust Roald and Karen to come up with any excuse to publicize. He told her as much and she giggled, biting her tongue between her front teeth. She didn't laugh—that would have been expected. But she giggled like a little girl and she bit her tongue and she squinted her eyes as if she'd done something especially tricky, although they both knew it was nothing unusual at all. She did that because she was with him. She did that because she was in love.

Jan leaned back and smiled. *This is where you belong, Janjic.* "You know, it's amazing to consider God's faithfulness," he said.

"How so?"

"Look at me. What do you see?"

"I see a strong man on top of the world."

He tried not to blush. "I'm a boy who grew up in the slums of Sarajevo and who lost his family to war and illness. A young man who roamed Bosnia, killing along with the rest. And then once, in a small village I did something decent; something right. I stood up for the truth. I defended one of God's children and was immediately thrown into prison for five years. But now look at me, Karen. Now God has granted me this incredible blessing of living." He grinned with her. "Now I'm flying in first class, eating lobster with my wife to be. Wouldn't you say that God is faithful?"

"Yes. And that faithfulness is now in my favor," she said, smiling. "Because I'm seated next to you." She took his hand and kissed it gently. He looked at her and his desire surged. It was a mad moment; one in which he thought they should move the wedding up. December felt like another lifetime. *Let's elope, Karen.*

And why not?

"Do you love me, Jan?"

The question sent a ball of heat down his spine. "How could I not love you, Karen? You're brilliant, you're ravishing, and, yes, I love you."

She smiled at the words. "Fine. I'll settle for that."

Jan kissed her to seal the words. He needed the reassurance more than she, he thought.

When they landed in New York, a long white car took them to the downtown Hilton where they were ushered into the main reception room. A gathering of thirty or so waited under a huge crystal chandelier with Roald at their center. Frank and Barney stood by his side, both grinning wide—they must have come up from Dallas with him.

Karen turned him to her just inside the entrance and she quickly tightened his tie. "What would you do without me, huh? Remember to smile for the cameras. Not too big. Be confident. Remember, they pay for confidence."

He felt too awkward to respond, so he just cleared his throat.

The pattering of hands echoed through the hall and for a moment the hotel's bustle seemed to stall. Jan was suddenly aware that every eye watched him.

He nodded politely and let the applause die. Roald held up his hand. "Ladies and gentlemen, I'm proud to announce that we are entering into an agreement with Delmont Pictures to produce a movie of *The Dance of the Dead* for theatrical release." Immediately the room filled with applause. It was all unnecessary, of course, but Roald had his ways.

He wasn't finished. "This is Jan Jovic's story; a story that reaches out to all those suffering for the sake of the Cross; a film that will take a message of hope to millions who need to hear of God's love and of those still suffering throughout the world." Again they applauded. A TV camera caught the event on video. Jan dipped his head and they clapped yet again, beaming proudly at him. They had all gathered for their own causes; some for the sake of a profitable movie, others for amnesty groups, perhaps hoping to ride the coattails of this film to bolster their own coffers. Some for the church.

They wanted a word from Jan and he gave them a brief one, publicly thanking

Roald and Karen for their undying support and service to which they all owed this opportunity. Then it was a mingling affair with all present taking turns shaking his hand and discussing their particular appreciation or concern. He took a dozen questions from reporters holding bulging microphones. He was well practiced with the media, of course, and he gave them all their time while the rest talked in small groups, eating cheese and shrimp and sipping beverages. Karen made the rounds, pitching the deal as only she could. Several times he caught her eye. Once she winked and he lost the question just asked of him by a reporter.

Night had fallen by the time the last guest left. Roald and Karen insisted that they go out to dinner, the finest. An hour later they sat around a table at Delmonico's on Broadway, reviewing the day. Everything was set for the meeting with Delmont in the morning. It would be nothing more than a formality—that and the collecting of a check, of course. One million at execution, four million within thirty days. They lifted their glasses and toasted their success. It seemed appropriate.

"So," Roald said as they cut into their steaks. "Karen tells me that you ran into a drug addict the other day. She spent the night at Ivena's and then left with a thousand dollars from the ministry fund?"

Jan glanced at Karen. "Well no, she didn't actually take a thousand dollars. Ivena bought her some clothes on my suggestion."

"That's good, Jan." He smiled and Jan could not gauge the man's sincerity. "So somewhere there's a junkie wandering around wearing a mink coat and laughing about how she socked it to some sorry sucker."

Jan recoiled at the cynicism. "No. No mink coat. And she left the clothes, except for a pink dress."

"A pink dress?" Karen asked.

"It was one Ivena made her buy," Jan said with a grin. She didn't return the smile.

Roald stuffed another bite of meat into his mouth. "Well, she's gone. After tomorrow a thousand dollars will seem like loose change."

Jan dropped his eyes and sawed into his steak. "Actually, she's not gone," he said. "She came back last night."

Karen froze for a moment. "She's back?"

"Yes. She showed up at Ivena's house and I made them come to mine."

Roald looked at Karen and then back. "You mean this woman is in *your* house? Now?"

"Yes, with Ivena. Is that a problem?"

"Why your house?" Karen asked. A cube of steak remained poised on her fork. Her eyes were wide.

"She's being chased. I didn't think she'd be safe at Ivena's."

"So let me get this straight." It was Roald's turn again. They were not taking this so well, Jan thought. "A female drug addict comes to you on the run, runs off with a thousand bucks, comes back the next day with a flock of mobsters on her tail and you take her into your house? You don't take her to the cops or the shelter, but you leave her in your house while you take off for New York? Is that it?"

"Maybe I should've called the police, but—"

"You didn't even *call* the cops?"

"She insisted that I not. Look, she was in danger, okay? So maybe I should've called the police. But I couldn't just tell her to get lost, now, could I? You forget that I run a ministry that stands for embracing those who suffer. It's not only in Bosnia that people suffer."

The exchange left them silent for a moment. "We should watch *who* we embrace," Roald said. "This is the exact sort of thing we talked about at—"

"Why does it concern you?" Jan asked. "I help one woman desperate for her life and it's a problem?"

"No, Jan. But you have to understand—we're in sensitive times now. This movie deal depends on your reputation. Do you understand that?"

"And what does my helping one junkie have to do with my reputation?"

"She's in your *house*, Jan. You keep a young junkie in your house and that could definitely look off-color to some people."

"You can't be serious. You really think someone would question that?"

"That's exactly what I'm suggesting! You're in a new league now, my friend. Any sign of impropriety and the walls could come crashing down. To whom much is given, much is required. Remember? Or have you forgotten our discussion altogether? Frank would choke if he knew you were entertaining a young woman. Especially now that you're engaged."

"Stop it!" Karen said. "You've made your point, Roald. Don't be asinine about it. It's *my* engagement, not just Jan's you're talking so flippantly about. Have some decency."

Roald and Jan stared at their plates and went back to work on their steaks.

"Now, while it's true that a young woman staying with Jan could look off-color, we're talking about a fluid situation here. I doubt if even your most conservative partners would come unglued about Jan helping a drug addict for a few days, woman or not. Let's not make this more than it is."

"Thank you, Karen," Jan said. "I couldn't have said it better."

Roald didn't respond immediately. Jan caught Karen's eye and winked. "And don't worry, Roald. She won't be staying there long. As soon as I return I'll get her the help she needs."

"I'm sorry. Perhaps I spoke too quickly." Roald smiled. "You're right." He lifted his glass for a toast. "Just looking out for you, my friend. No offense intended."

Jan lifted his glass and clinked Roald's. "None taken." They drank.

"That's better," Karen said with a smile. "You do what needs to be done, Jan. Just remember that your big mansion there, as Ivena calls it, has room for only one woman." She winked and joined them in the toast. "You just make sure she's gone when we get back."

"Of course."

"Send her to the Presbyterian shelter on Crescent Avenue—give her to the Salvation Army—take your pick. But she can't stay at the house," she said.

"No. No of course not."

They looked at each other in silence for a few moments.

"Well, then," Roald cut in. "That's settled."

All three of them lifted bites to their mouths at the same time, and dinner resumed. It was a small caveat in an otherwise perfect trip, Jan thought. And Karen was right. He should settle the matter the minute he returned. He really should.

chapter seventeen

WHILE JAN sat in the expensive atmosphere of Delmonico's in New York Friday night, Glenn Lutz sat alone at his own Palace bar, stewing. The room was mostly dark except the backlit bar itself. A half-empty bottle of rum stood next to his glass. It was his second for the day and it might not be his last. The bar had been carved from mahogany and stained a very dark brown. The decorator had wanted to paint it bright yellow, of all colors. That was before he'd fired her. He'd fired her, all right. Yes sir, he had fired that little freak, right after he'd bitten her lip. Now *that* had been a night.

Glenn remembered the occasion and tried to smile, but his face did not cooperate. The plan he'd settled on was a good plan, but it didn't feel good just now. It had come on the dawning notion that he could cage *any* woman. Women as pretty as Helen, women who wouldn't be missed. It wasn't the caging of Helen that he really wanted, was it? No, it was her free spirit that attracted him most. The very fact that she *did* resist him with a tenacity that most wouldn't dream of. Even the fact that she'd fled half a dozen times now. Each time his desire for her had swelled until now he could hardly stand it all.

So then, as much as he relished the idea of caging her or forcing her to return, he'd decided that he had to allow her to return on her own. He needed her to want him. It was the next step in this madness he'd given himself to.

The decision to let her free of her choosing was one he now doubted perhaps more than any he'd made in his life. Because there was always the chance that she would *not* come back, wasn't there? If that happened he would go out with a machine gun and cut her and anybody near her down in one long staccato burst. Or maybe he'd just revert to the caging approach.

The plan didn't prohibit him from removing obstacles that stood in the path between them, of course. Preacher-man, for instance. Good God, a *preacher* of all things. The house Helen had entered belonged to a Jan Jovic, he learned from Charlie down at the precinct that same night. And Charlie had heard about the man. He'd seen a news story about the man sometime back—a preacher who'd escaped from prison or something. A preacher? A *preacher* was trying to steal his Helen? Glenn had thrown the phone across the room when Charlie had told him.

As it turned out he was one of those foreigners who'd written a book about the war and made a bundle. *The Dance of the Dead.* Glenn's first impulse was to make *him* dead. He'd learned all of this within thirty minutes of his return. It was then, after deciding that a preacher couldn't be a threat to him, that he'd settled on the plan. He'd made one phone call to the preacher, and then he'd drowned himself in several bottles of rum.

He had spent the entire day pacing and sweating and yelling, completely immobilized from conducting any business. He'd forced himself to keep a lunch appointment with Dan Burkhouse, his banker and friend of ten years. It was Dan who'd lent him his first million, in exchange for some muscle on a nonperforming loan. Well, he'd killed the nonperforming loan, thereby implicating Dan, and making him a confidant by necessity. Besides Beatrice, only Dan knew the dirty secrets that made Glenn Lutz the man that he was. Of course, not even they knew the truth about his youth.

He had gone still dressed in his smelly Hawaiian shirt and between bites of snapper at the Florentine told Dan about his decision to let Helen come and go. If not for the private dining room his agitated tone would've raised some eyebrows for sure. The banker had shaken his head. "You're losing perspective, Glenn. This is crazy."

"She's possessed me, Dan. I feel like I'm falling apart when she's not with me."

"Then you should get some help. The wrong woman can bring a man down, you know. You're going too far with this."

Glenn had not responded.

"How can one woman do this to you?" his friend pressed. "There's a hundred women waiting for you out there."

Glenn had glared at the man and effectively cut him off.

Now he lifted the bottle and chugged at its mouth. The liquid burned down his throat but he didn't flinch. He would suck it dry, he thought. Tilt it up and suck at the bottle until it imploded. Or just stuff the whole thing into his throat. No pain, no gain. And what was paining now? His chest was paining because Helen had driven a stake through his heart, and regardless of what that old witch

Beatrice told him, he did still have a heart. It was as big as the sky and it was burning like hell.

He yanked the bottle from his mouth and hurled it against the mirrored wall. It shattered with a splintering crash. *Don't be such a melodramatic lush, Lutz.*

The phone shrilled in the dead silence and he bolted upright. He scrambled for it, grasping for the tiniest thread that it might be Helen.

"Lutz."

"Glenn." It was the witch. Glenn slumped on the bar.

"I've got a phone call for you. You may want to take it."

"I'm not taking phone calls." The phone clicked in his ear before he could slam it in the witch's ear. She'd disconnected him. That was it! He was going to walk over there right now and—

"Hello?"

The voice spoke softly in the receiver and Glenn's heart slammed up into his throat. He jerked upright.

"Hello?"

His voice wavered. "Helen?"

"Hi, Glenn."

Helen! Glenn's heart was now kicking against the walls of his chest. Tears flooded his eyes. Oh, God, it was Helen! He wanted to scream at her. He wanted to beg for her.

"You're mad at me?" she said quietly.

Glenn squeezed his eyes and fought for control. "Mad? Why did you leave? Why do you keep leaving?"

"I don't know, Glenn." She paused. By the sound of her voice she was near tears. "Listen, I want some stuff."

"Who are you with?"

"No one. I'm staying in this man's house with the lady I told you about, but she went home to water some flowers or something. She'll be gone for a few hours."

"You think I don't know? You think I'm useless here, waiting for you to come crawling home!" *Easy, boy. Play her. Lure her.*

He took a deep breath and lowered his voice. "I miss you, Helen. I really miss you."

She remained silent.

"What did I do to make you leave? Just tell me," he begged.

"You hit me."

"You don't like that? You don't like being hit like that? I'm sorry. I swear, I'm sorry. I thought you liked it, Helen. Do you?"

"No." Her voice was very soft now.

"Then, I'm sorry. I swear I won't do it again. Please, Helen, you're killing me here. I miss you, sweety."

"I miss you too, Glenn."

Really? Dear Helen, really? Tears slipped down his cheek.

"I want to come, Glenn. But I want you to promise me some things, okay?"

"Yes, anything. I'll promise you anything, Helen. Please just come home."

"You have to promise me that you'll let me come whenever I want."

"Yes. Yes, I swear."

"And you've got to promise me that I can leave whenever I want. Promise that, Glenn. You can't force me to stay. I want to stay, but not if you force me."

He hesitated, finding the words difficult. On the other hand, she already had the power. And what was in a promise but words? "I promise. I swear you can leave whenever you wish."

"And I don't want you to hit me, Glenn. Anything else, but no hitting."

This time everything within him raged against the absurdity of her request. Letting her go was one thing, but she wanted to castrate him as well? He was slipping, he thought. "I promise, Helen."

"You promise all of those things, Glenn. Otherwise I don't think I can come."

"I said I promise! What else do you want? You want me to cut off my fingers?" *Easy, easy.* He lowered his voice. "Yes, I promise, Helen."

She hesitated and he wondered if he'd lost her on that last one. He felt panic swell in his chest.

"Can you send a car?" she asked.

"I'll have a car there in two minutes. I have one just down the street." She didn't respond. "Okay, Helen?"

"Okay."

"Okay. You won't be sorry, Helen. I swear you won't be sorry."

"Okay. Bye." The phone clicked off.

Glenn set the receiver in its cradle with a shaking hand. Exhilaration coursed through his veins and he gasped for breath. He uttered a small squeaking sound and skipped out to the middle of the room and back. When he went for the phone to call Buck, his hands were shaking so badly he could barely dial the number.

She would be here in fifteen minutes! Oh, so many preparations to make. So many, so many he could hardly stand it.

THERE WERE three flowers now, each the size of small melons, brilliant white and edged in red, twice as large as any other flower in the greenhouse. Joey inspected each part of the plant with delicate fingers. He'd always reminded Ivena of a jockey, very lean and short, hardly the type you might figure for a renowned horticulturist. He looked more the average gardener than the scientist with his frumpy slacks and cotton shirt.

"What do you make of them?" Ivena asked.

The small man pried through the petals and grunted. "Boy they sure do put off their aroma, don't they?"

"Yes. Have you seen anything like them?"

"And you're saying that you didn't make this graft? 'Cause this is definitely a graft."

"Not that I remember. Heavens, I'm not that forgetful."

"No, of course not. Has anybody else had access to this greenhouse?"

"No."

"Then, we'll assume that you made this graft."

"I'm telling you—"

"For the sake of argument, Ivena. It certainly didn't just appear on its own. Either way, I've never seen a graft like this. We're looking at several weeks' worth of growth here and—"

"No. Less than a week."

He dipped his head and looked at her over his wire-frame glasses. "This from the woman who doesn't even remember grafting the plant? I'm just telling you what my eyes see, Ivena. You decide what you want to believe."

She nodded. He was wrong, of course, but she let it go.

"Even with a few weeks' growth, these flowers are extraordinary. You see there the stamen reminds of the lily, but these white petals lined in red—I've never seen them."

"Could they be tropical?"

"We're in Atlanta, not the tropics. I did my thesis on tropical aberrations in subtropical zones, and I've never come across anything like this."

He touched and squeezed and *humphed* for a few minutes without offering any further comment. She let him examine the bush at his pace and searched her memory again for the grafting he'd insisted she must have done. But still she knew that he was wrong. She'd no more grafted the vine into the rosebush than she'd won the Pulitzer recently.

Joey finally straightened and pulled off his glasses. "Hmm. Incredible. Would you mind me taking one of these flowers to the Botanical Gardens Lab? It has to exist. I'm just not placing it here. But with some analysis I think we can. May take a couple weeks." He shook his head. "I've never even heard of a vine like this taking off from a rosebush."

"You want to cut one off?"

"Just one. You have plenty more coming along behind these. They are flowers, not children."

"No, of course they aren't. Yes, you may. Just one," she said.

chapter eighteen

THE LONELINESS had struck Helen after two hours with Glenn while Ivena was off attending her flowers. Thing of it was, she was even high at the moment, but the emotion still swept through her bones like an unquenchable tide. Sorrow.

Somehow things had gotten turned around in her mind. This wasn't the Palace as Glenn liked to call it. This was feeling like a dungeon next to Jan's house. She had left the white palace for the dirty dungeon—that's how it felt and it was making her sick. Worse, she had left a prince for this monster.

She'd rolled on the bed and thought about that. The preacher wasn't her prince. He couldn't be. They were like dirt and vanilla pudding; you just don't mix the two. And it was clear who was who.

Not that Jan wasn't a prince—he was; just not her prince. He could never be her lover. Imagine that. What would they say to that? Helen winning the heart of a famous writer who drove around in a white Cadillac. A shy, handsome man with hazel eyes and wavy hair and a real brain under those curls. A real man.

Given just the two of them without all this mess around them, she might even have a shot with him. She might not be Miss Socialite, but she was a woman, and one who had no problem reading the look in a man's eyes. Jan's looks were not the roving kind she was used to, but there was light there, wasn't there? At times she thought it might be pain. Empathy. But at other times it had made her heart beat a little faster. Either way, each time they had been together his looks had come often and long. That much was enough, wasn't it?

He likes you, Helen.

He's married.

No, he's not. He's engaged.

Goodness, just imagine having a man like that on your arm! Or imagine someone like that actually loving you. That last thought felt absurd, like the drugs were talking, and she pushed the nonsense from her mind.

But the sorrow wouldn't budge, and the thoughts returned five minutes later. *But what if, Helen.*

What if? I would die for a man like that! I'd be happy to just sit with him and hold his hand and cry on his shoulder. And I would love him until the day I died, that's what if. And not just a man like that, but Jan.

But then again, she was the dirt and he was the vanilla. She'd never deserve a man like that. There was no mixing the two.

She'd stayed another hour and then left the big pig facedown on the floor, passed out next to a small pool of his own vomit.

She'd returned still intoxicated, and to her relief Ivena was still gone. She climbed under clean sheets and passed out without removing her clothes.

Ivena was upstairs cooking breakfast when she awoke. It gave her time to shower and change before presenting herself with as much confidence as she could muster. If Ivena knew anything about her little escapade to the dungeon, she didn't show it.

Helen spent most of the day walking around the house in a daze and for the most part Ivena let her be. Jan's home really did feel like a palace, and in a strange way she felt like dirt on its floor. But she could clean up, couldn't she? The notion brought a buzz to her mind. *What if?*

And Jan was coming home tonight.

JAN PARKED the Cadillac on the street and walked up the path to his home two days later, on Sunday evening. Darkness had quieted the city, bringing with it a cool breeze. The cicadas were in full chorus, chirping without pause, ever-present but invisible in the night. The oak cross hung undisturbed above his door. *In living we die; In dying we live.*

The trip to New York had come off as well as they had planned in most regards and better than they had imagined in others. They'd signed the deal on Saturday, deposited the million dollars with some fanfare, and decided to stay in the Big Apple through Sunday. Jan had called Ivena and been informed that nothing had happened. At least nothing that he should concern himself about. Ivena had not elaborated. She'd made some flower deliveries on Friday evening—a few late customers to catch before the weekend—but otherwise she and Helen had mostly sat around talking and growing tired of remaining in a house that was not her own.

He withdrew his key and opened the front door. Dim light glowed from the far hall leading to the bedrooms, but the rest of the house lay in darkness. He flipped the switch that controlled the entryway lights. They stuttered to life.

"Hello."

Silence.

"Ivena!"

Jan walked into the living room, still holding his overnight bag. Had they left? He flipped another switch and the room stuttered to life. No sign of the women. "Ivena!"

"Hello, Jan."

He whirled to the voice. Helen stood, arms crossed, leaning on the wall in the hall's soft light with one leg cocked like a stork. Immediately his knees felt weak, as if she'd injected him with a drug that had gone for his joints.

"Good night! You scared me," he said.

"I'm sorry," Helen returned. But she was smiling.

"Where . . . where's Ivena?"

"She left an hour ago. Said she couldn't spend the rest of her life here while her flowers died at home. She's pretty excited about some flowers that she says are going nuts over there. We haven't heard a peep from anyone so we figured it would be safe enough."

"She just left? Is she coming back?" Helen lowered her arms and walked into the light. He saw the difference immediately and his heart jumped. She wore a strapless white evening dress with a sheen, and it flowed with her small frame like a fluid cream. She wore sandals and a pearl necklace that sparkled in the kitchen light. But it was her face that had pricked his heart. She was smiling and staring at him. The bruises had vanished, either under the hand of God or with the careful application of makeup, and honestly he thought it must have been the hand of God, because her complexion appeared as smooth as new ivory. Her hair lay just below her ears, bending in delicate curls.

Jan's hand released the travel bag he'd carried in. It landed with a distant *thump.* Goodness, he'd all but forgotten about the madness.

Helen stared at him with those impossibly blue eyes, smiling. She turned for the kitchen but her eyes lingered on him for a moment. She swayed naturally as if born to wear that dress. Jan's mind began to scramble. *You dropped your bag, you big oaf. You stood here like an idiot, gaping at her, and you dropped your bag!*

"Yep, she left," Helen said. "She wants you to call her when you get back, which I guess is now." She picked an apple out of the fruit bowl and took a small bite from it.

"So she said nothing about coming back?" Jan asked, opening the icebox.

"She said she didn't think that was necessary."

"No?"

"No." Helen looked at him from behind the apple and she winked. "She said you should take us out for dinner."

"She said that? Take you and Ivena out?"

"Yes. What do you say, Jan? Want to take me out to dinner? I didn't get all dressed up for nothin', you know." She took another bite, her teeth crunching through the brittle fruit.

There now, he was cornered. Cornered with a pounding heart and weak knees, like a teenager on his first date. The icebox was open and he'd retrieved nothing from it. He closed the door.

"Well, I guess that would be—"

"I knew it!" She tossed the apple into the sink and rushed over to him. Before he could move, she had her hands around his own, pulling him back down the hall. "I want to show you something," she said. Jan stumbled after her, too stunned to speak, very aware of her hands on his.

"What about Ivena?"

"I'll call her while you get ready."

She led him to his own bedroom. "I hope you aren't mad, but I just couldn't resist," she said, glancing back with a smile. His door was open and she pulled him through. On his bed lay his best black suit. A white shirt and his red tie were arranged neatly with the jacket. The slacks draped to the floor and his shoes rested at their cuffs. "Will you wear this?"

She had been in here. Helen had done this.

"I found them in your closet. They're perfect."

"You found these in my closet?"

"Yes. They're yours. Don't you recognize them?"

"Yes, of course I do. I just . . ." He chuckled. "It's not every day that I have my clothes laid out for me."

"You're upset?"

"No. No. So you want me to wear this suit and take you to dinner, right?"

She stared at him without responding.

He laughed. "Okay, madam." He dipped his head. "Your wish is my command. If you will please step outside, I'll get dressed and we'll be off. Did Ivena suggest where we dine?"

"The Orchid."

"The Orchid, then."

She tilted her head, as if surprised that he'd taken her up so suddenly. A mischievous grin lit her face and she curtsied in return. "I will be waiting." She left and pulled the door closed behind her.

Jan showered quickly, his mind busily scolding himself for playing along. It wasn't that he didn't want to take her to dinner, or even that he shouldn't take her to dinner. It was that his knees had gone weak at the sight of her. It was that he *did* want to take her to dinner. It was the madness of it all. It was the voice that had started speaking to him while the hot water cascaded over his skull. *You like her, Jan. You really like her, don't you?*

Yes, I like Helen. She's a refreshing person with charm and . . .

No, you really like her, don't you? You like her so much you can hardly stand it.

Don't be absurd! I'm engaged to Karen. What of Karen? Oh, dear Karen!

He forced his mind to a new line of thought. They were going to the Orchid, the finest restaurant in town. A romantic . . .

Stop it! He shook his head and stepped from the shower. Goodness, he was not an undisciplined schoolboy. These matters of the heart were best left to careful thought.

Jan grunted and dressed quickly.

You aren't married. Ivena will be there, of course. It's only dinner. A farewell dinner—you will tell her that she must leave at dinner.

A tremble had taken to his fingers and he had some trouble with the buttons, but he managed after a few more lines of scolding. He examined himself one last time in the mirror. His wavy hair lay combed back and wet, darker than Helen's but still blond. His eyes were nearly as bright, hazel not blue, but as bright. Now his jaw, it was square and strong while hers was so . . . delicate. He smacked his cheek lightly with his right hand. *Stop it!*

She was waiting in his chair, one leg folded over the other, a copy of *The Dance of the Dead* spread open in her hands. Her eyes looked up as she closed the book.

"My, we are quite handsome." She set the book on the coffee table and walked toward him with an extended hand, sliding gracefully in that dress.

"What about Ivena?"

"She's going to meet us there. Shall we, then?"

"Yes," he said, and he took her elbow and led her from the house.

Dear God, help me, he prayed.

JAN SLAMMED through the men's room door and stepped inside. Ivena was late! And her absence was becoming a very big problem.

The bathroom was empty. He slumped against the wash counter and leaned on his hands. His mind spun in crazy circles, confused, buzzing. His breath came in short pulls. It was as if he'd ingested some hallucinogenic drug that now raged through his blood stream. But he hadn't, he was sure of it. He had done nothing but bring her here, order his food, and engage her in small talk. *Get a grip, Janjic. Control yourself.*

He twisted the faucet and splashed cold water on his face. It was the girl. It was Helen. She had bewitched him. Her voice was the drug, her breath an intoxicant that made straight for his spine and spread like a fire through his bones. It was why he had excused himself and come here not five minutes into the meal—because he was losing his mind out there, watching her bite into her salmon and drink her water. Watching her jaw move with each word.

Jan patted his face with a towel and straightened to stare at his image in the mirror. "My God, what are you doing to me?" he muttered, and he said it as a prayer. "What's the meaning of this?"

You are falling for her, Janjic.

He didn't answer the charge. It just sat in his mind, awkward and misguided, like a belch in the middle of careful speech.

If you're not careful, you'll have fallen for this girl.

But why? Why, why, why? I don't want *to fall for her! There's no reason to it.*

He had to find some control somewhere, because he simply could not afford to give his heart to someone as unlikely as this woman sitting wide-eyed and so very delicate and . . .

Oh, God . . . it was the most ridiculous thing he could imagine. Ask him to tell a fanciful tale and his imagination would not wander this far. He'd just asked Karen for her hand in marriage before the entire world, just a few days ago. Now he was in Atlanta's most extravagant restaurant, sharing dinner with another woman. With Helen.

With such a beautiful, sweet, genuine woman who seemed to have the power to melt his heart with a single innocent look.

Karen's face wandered through his mind and Jan moaned. He fell back to the counter. *Karen, dear Karen! What am I doing. Rescue me!* If she could only see him now, playing teenager with the sexy little hippie. He ground his teeth and struck the side of his head with his palm.

"Stop it, Janjic! Just stop this nonsense!" he said aloud. And then to himself, *Coming here was a terrible mistake, and now you're going to have to go out there and straighten this mess out. You've gone over the edge on this.*

"Excuse me."

Jan spun around. A stranger stood by the door looking at him curiously. "Are you all right?"

Jan blinked. "Yes." How long had the man watched him? "Yes, I'm fine." He straightened his coat and hurried from the room. *You're losing it, Jan.*

Jan walked back to the table on weak legs. He saw her when he was still twenty paces off, sitting frail and alone against the Orchid's twenty-story view of Atlanta's skyline. A tall white candle cast a yellow hue across her neck. She was looking away from him, at the city lights below. Her left hand was cocked delicately over her glass; she drew circles around its rim with her forefinger. Her hair rested delicately against her cheek, touching her silky skin.

It was details such as these that screamed out at him. And he wasn't seeing them because they were exceptional; he was seeing them because *she* was exceptional. She could be scraping the mud from her soles over there and his knees would go weak.

A tingle ran up Jan's spine and flared at the base of his neck. The air thickened about him, forcing him to pull at it deliberately in order to breathe. He pulled up behind the salad bar.

You're acting like a schoolboy, Jan. Control yourself!

He straightened his tie and walked on. Then he was there, and he slid into his chair. Actually, he *attempted* to slide into his chair; it came off more like a collapse. *Collect yourself, you oaf.*

"Oh, hi. You're back."

"Yes." *Now, Janjic. You must tell her now that this has all been a terrible mistake and that you should leave immediately.*

"I was just thinking about how wonderful you've been to me," she said. He looked up and saw that she was innocently forking a piece of pink salmon into her mouth. Innocent because it didn't seem as though she was deliberately tempting him or intoxicating him or any such thing. She was simply eating a piece of fresh salmon. But it wasn't looking so innocent to him. It flooded him with a dizzying shower of images. Images that set off crazy vibrations in his bones.

She lifted her eyes and the candle's flame flickered in her pupils. "I can't remember anyone being so kind to me."

"It's nothing, really," he said. "You're a person who should be . . . that it is good to be kind to."

"Why?"

"Why?"

"Why am I a person who should be loved? That is what you meant, isn't it?"

Good God! Heaven help me! "Yes. Everybody should be loved."

"You're very kind."

"Thank you. I try to be kind."

"I read some of your book this afternoon. You had a tough time when you were a kid."

"Not unlike you," he said. *You are delaying, Janjic.* He cut into his own salmon and took a bite. The meat was tender and sweet. "Did you read about the village?" he asked.

"Yes."

"And what did you think?"

She shrugged. "It seemed . . ." She hesitated.

"Say what you like. It seemed what?"

"Well, it just seemed a bit, I'm not sure . . . crazy maybe. What Ivena's daughter did—what was her name?"

"Nadia."

"That was crazy. I can't imagine anyone dying like that. Or the priest for that matter. Really, I could never do anything so dumb. Don't get me wrong, I'm sure it was hard for Ivena to see her girl killed. I just don't really understand how she could do something so pointless. Does that make sense?"

"And what would you have done?"

"I would have told them whatever they wanted to hear. Why die over a few words?"

Jan stared at her, struck at her lack of comprehension in the matter. She really didn't understand love, did she? *And do you, Jan?* More than she. Far more than she.

"Then you've never felt the kind of love that Nadia or the priest felt," Jan said.

"I guess not. And have you?"

"Yes," he said. "I think so."

Jan went for another bite. *There you have it, Romeo. How many times have you asked that same question of yourself? How many times has Ivena asked? And now it comes from Helen.*

She said nothing. Her fork clinked on the china; her lips made a very soft popping sound as they took in another bite.

"You write very well, Jan," she said in a soft voice. He looked up. She was throwing her magic at him again. Her eyes, her voice, her hair, her smile—it all smothered him and made his heart feel as though it were trying to beat in molasses.

"Thank you. I started writing when I was a boy."

"Your words are very beautiful. The way you describe things."

"And you are very beautiful," he said.

Goodness, what had he just said?

His first instinct was to take it back. To beg insanity and tell her that they should leave now because he had just flown in from New York and was very tired. Tired enough to say that she was beautiful, which, although true enough—so very, *very* true—had no business coming from his mouth. He was engaged to another woman. Did she know that? Of course she knew that.

He ignored the impulse entirely.

"You know that, don't you? You are very beautiful, Helen. Not just in the way you look, but in your spirit. You. Helen. You're a beautiful person."

She blinked slowly, as if caught in a surrealistic dream. Her eyes drifted for a moment, as if sheltering something, and then she gazed at him. "Thank you, Jan. And I think you're very handsome."

Jan felt his hands go numb. They were staring at each other, locked in a visual embrace. Everything inside of him wanted to reach across the table and stroke her chin. To leap from his seat and take her in his arms and hold her and kiss her lips. He managed to find some deep reservoir of control and remain seated.

Please, Father! Why do I feel so strongly? These are new feelings.

Heat rushed through his ears. It was madness, still. But for the time he embraced the madness and it raged through his body like a ferocious lion. *This cannot be of my own doing*, he thought. *It is beyond me.* There was a physical bond between them now, like a chord of electricity.

"Is it warm in here, or is it just me?" she said softly.

"Perhaps it's just us," he said, and he knew that later he would regret saying that. Complimenting someone for their beauty was one thing. Telling a woman that she was making you warm was another matter altogether. But the moment demanded it, he thought. Absolutely demanded it.

"Yes, maybe," she said, and she smiled.

Jan broke off and took up his water glass. He drank quickly, suddenly feeling panic biting at his mind. What was he doing? What in God's name did he think he was doing?

"I have a confession to make," Helen said. "I lied. Ivena didn't say a word about you taking us to dinner. I made that up."

He set the glass down. "You did?"

"I wanted to be alone with you."

"She's not coming?"

"No. I didn't call her."

He began to shovel salad into his mouth, acutely aware of the heat that flushed his face. But it wasn't anger.

She followed his lead and picked at her own salad. They ate in silence for a full minute, pondering the exchange. It did Jan very little good—his mind had ceased to function with any meaning. Something had happened to him, and he couldn't corner it with any understanding. First the vision and now this.

"What about Glenn?" he asked. The question sounded like something an adolescent might ask in a state of hurt jealousy. Jan shoveled the salad quickly.

Helen shifted her eyes. "I told you, we're through."

"Yes, but you did return to him after saying that. And he's quite obsessive, isn't he? He may not be through with *you*."

"Yeah well, I *am* through with him. And he may be obsessive, but it cuts both ways. If I leave, it's over. It was stupid of me to go back, but I hardly knew you then, you know."

Jan lost his focus on the line of questioning and went back to his salad. He'd said enough already.

Helen shifted the topic by talking about the book again. Asking him questions about what Serbian prison was like. It was a welcome segue and Jan plunged after it. Anything to distract him from the madness. But there was a twinkle in her eye from that moment—one that told him she'd seen his heart. One he feared was flashing in his own eye as well. It didn't matter, he was powerless to change it.

They sat at the table for another hour, talking of their pasts and staying away from the present. After all, the present had already done a fine job of presenting itself.

Jan took Helen home, to Ivena's. She would stay with her at least for the night, until they developed a more adequate plan. Like what? she asked. Like he didn't know. Maybe Ivena had some ideas. But he couldn't go in and talk to Ivena now. No, horrors no! It was too late. He should really get to bed.

Jan left Helen at the curb, watched her walk to the door, and left without looking back to see how Ivena might react. His palms were wet, his shirt was sticky, and his mind felt as though a blender had made a pass or two while he was busy fighting off the butterflies with Helen.

He cried out to God then, in the silence of the car. *Father, you have created me, but have you created me to feel this? What kind of emotions are these running through my heart? And for whom? This woman I hardly know? Please, I beg you, possess my spirit! I am feeling undone.*

And what of Karen. Oh, dear God, what of Karen?

Jan no longer held the presence of mind to pray. He just drove home and slowly shut down.

CHAPTER NINETEEN

KAREN HAD been scheduled to fly to Hollywood at ten on Monday morning. Jan didn't come in until ten-thirty. For starters, his sleep had been interrupted by the dream again. The encounter with Helen hadn't helped his sleep either. But in all honesty, his coming late was as much motivated by Karen's schedule as his sleeping habits. He was certainly in no condition to look Karen in the eye, much less explain the rings under his own. To his relief she'd departed on time. Appointments with a dozen contacts would keep her tied up for three days. He would not see her until Thursday, which was fine by him. He needed to clear the voices that ran circles through his head.

He sauntered in, determined to return his mind to a semblance of reason. Billy Jenkins, a skinny mailroom clerk, congratulated him in the elevator. "Boy, Mr. Jovic. It's really cool about the movie, huh?"

Jan mumbled an awkward, "Uh-huh," and smiled as best he could. But his heart was not well.

All hope for a clear head disappeared at eleven, while Jan sat at his desk, feet propped on the writing surface. Because that was when Ivena called him and told him of her idea. She had seen some car loitering on her street and she didn't feel Helen was safe in her little cottage. So she and Helen would stay in Janjic's basement suite for a few more days. That was her idea. There were no other alternatives. They would be safe in that huge apartment under Janjic's house; God knew that security system he'd gotten was useful for something.

"What?"

"It's either that or send her to a shelter, and you know very well that sending her to a shelter would be no better than cutting her loose on the street. She would be back in that beast's hands by nightfall. And we can't have that."

Jan didn't respond.

"Janjic? Did you hear me?"

"She can't stay at my place, Ivena."

"Nonsense, dear. I will be there." She paused. "And there is something strange going on at my house, Janjic."

"She's acting strange?"

"No, no. Nadia's rosebush has died."

"Please, Ivena. Forgive me for sounding uncaring, but there's more at stake here than your garden. She can't stay at my house."

Ivena exhaled into the phone. "Janjic, please now. Think beyond yourself. It's not only about you this time. You'll hardly be aware of us."

He wanted to tell her some things. Like the fact that he was quite sure he would hardly be aware of anything *but* them. Like the fact that the little *pitter* she'd detected had now grown to a steady *thump.*

But he didn't. And she was right, he thought; this was more than just himself. Sweat broke from his brow. He knew Ivena sensed his heart already. And yet she suggested this? What was she plotting?

"Anyway, you don't mind us. Now I must leave; we have some shopping to do."

"More shopping?"

"Food. Your selection is quite dreadful. Good-bye, Janjic."

"Good-bye, Ivena."

She had not asked about the previous night, and Jan hadn't offered any details. But surely she knew that something was up.

And what *was* up? His heart was up. Unless he was sorely mistaken, his heart had attached itself to her. To Helen. Every cell of gray matter objected with vigor, of course, but it seemed to have little impact on the emotions that ran through his veins.

He spent a good portion of the day arguing with himself. Telling himself that he'd been a fool for taking her to dinner. For allowing himself to even look at such a young woman.

On the other hand, she was only nine years younger than him. And she was a woman. An unmarried woman. And he an unmarried man.

But you are engaged, Janjic! You've made a promise!

But I am not married. And I've done nothing to betray Karen. Can I help this madness? Did I ask for it?

You're in love with her, Jan.

He was no longer arguing so strenuously against that voice. It had repeated itself a dozen times, and he'd been unable to persuade it differently. He could only spin through all the reasons why he should not love her—at least not love her in *that* way. Reasons such as the fact that she was a junkie, for heaven's sake! Or like the fact that she was another man's lover. This madman Glenn's lover. Or had been. Goodness, what was he thinking? Karen was perfect in every respect, and she too made his heart beat with a steady rhythm.

Yes, but not like Helen, Jan. You're in love with Helen, Jan.

Nonsense! And what about Roald and *The Dance of the Dead*? What of Frank Malter and Barney Givens and Bob Story? The church leaders' ears would likely steam if they knew what was broiling here. They'd warned against the appearance of evil—this madness with Helen would be nothing less.

And the movie deal—what would Hollywood care what he did? They weren't the most moral lot, those movie people. They wouldn't have any problems.

See now, the very fact that he thought in terms of Hollywood's lack of morality in connection with this Helen business proved that she had to go!

It was Karen who was being trampled on with this foolishness. This betrayal in his heart.

By the end of that first day Jan had managed maybe an hour's work. Ivena called him at four and informed him that she and Helen were concocting supper. At his place.

"What?" he stammered, leaping to his feet.

She hesitated. "There is a problem, Janjic? I'll pay for the groceries if—"

"No, no, no." Pay for the groceries? What was she talking about? He proceeded to insist that in the wake of the big movie deal he had to work late. Go on without him. She reluctantly agreed, and Jan breathed a sigh of relief. Not that he didn't want to see Helen. Not that he did not want to sit across from her and look into those deep blue pools of love. In fact, the very thought of sitting under her spell made his palms break out in sweat. But he could not! Not with Ivena there! Not *without* Ivena there! Not until he made some sense of this madness.

When Jan drove up to the house at ten, Ivena's Bug sat on the street. He left the Cadillac on the front apron, careful not to alert them by opening the garage door. He peeked through the mail slot and saw that the lights had been turned down. If Helen was here, she had retreated to the basement suite. Unless she was waiting for him in the hall again. He wouldn't put it past her. The thought sent a chill down his spine and suddenly he hoped desperately that she'd done just that. He fumbled with the key and let himself in quietly.

But Helen wasn't in the hall tonight. In fact, he couldn't be sure that she was even in the house. And he wasn't about to go knocking on her door. He tiptoed down the hall, set the alarm for 5:00 A.M., and fell into bed.

Tuesday ended up being a mixed day. On one hand it was busy, which was good. On the other hand, he discovered that his little secret was not such a secret.

Lorna and John both came by his office and asked him if everything was all right, to which he answered, of course, and promptly steered the conversation to operational details.

But Betty was not so easily put off. She was concerned; he was not himself these days.

"Nonsense."

"This wouldn't have anything to do with the girl, would it?"

"What girl?"

"The one you rescued in the park."

He felt the blood leave his face.

"Oh, come on, Jan, everyone's whispering about it. They say that this girl stayed in your apartment for a few days."

"Who told you that?"

"I heard it from John. Is it true, then?"

"Yes. Just for a few days. With Ivena, of course."

"And what about you, Jan? What do you make of this girl?"

"Wha . . . Nothing. What do you mean? I'm just giving her a place to stay while this blows over. What do you mean?" It occurred to him that he might have given himself away with that delivery.

"You can't hide your feelings from me, Jan," she said with a tilted head, her eyes fixed on his. "And what would Karen make of this?"

"Karen knows. Helen's a mess, for crying out loud. We can't throw her out on the street for the sake of appearances."

"Maybe. I'm not judging you; I'm only asking. Someone needs to keep you in line. Anyway, I just wanted you to know that there's some talk—you know how these things go."

"Well, kindly tell all the chatterboxes that I don't take kindly to their prying."

Her eyebrow arched. "No one's accused you of anything. Karen's such a lovely lady, you can understand how she has the employees' sympathies."

"That's absurd! There's nothing to sympathize about!"

"I didn't say I disapproved, Jan. I'm only advising you that others might."

"What are they doing down there? Placing bets over the matter? This is ridiculous. Helen's just a woman, for heaven's sake. Just because she's using my flat doesn't mean I have any feelings for her."

"Do you?"

"Of course not. As a person, yes, but . . . Please, Betty. It's been a very difficult day."

"Then I will pray for you, Jan. We certainly can't have our movie star falling apart at the seams on us, now can we?" She winked at him and then left.

Jan spent the next half-hour trying desperately to dismiss the revelation that he'd become a walking wager. Was his insanity that obvious?

Roald called at ten and wanted Jan to meet the director of Amnesty International, Tom Jameson, who was flying in to Atlanta at noon. Jan spent three hours with the man and eagerly agreed to meet him for dinner at seven. By four that afternoon, he'd recaptured a semblance of reason, he thought.

He called Ivena at five and informed her that he would not be joining them for dinner again. She did not object. In fact she seemed distracted.

"Is everything okay, Ivena?"

"Yes, of course. It could not be better."

"You heard me then; I won't be home until late tonight. Please don't wait up for me."

"Something is happening, Janjic." She sounded eager. Even excited.

"Meaning what? Helen has done something?"

"No. But I feel it in my bones. Something very unique is going on, don't you feel it? The sky seems brighter, my feet feel lighter. My garden is in full bloom."

"I thought Nadia's rosebush was dead."

"Yes."

"Hmm. Well, you sound in good spirits. That's good. Just don't leave her alone too much."

"Helen? She's fine, Janjic."

"Yes, but it's still my house. We can't have a stranger just wandering around all alone."

"She's not a stranger. Let go, Janjic."

Let go?

He wasn't sure he'd heard right. "What?"

"You must relax, Janjic. Something is happening."

"Of course something's happening. I'm getting married. We're making a movie."

"Much more, I think."

"And I have no idea what you're talking about."

Silence settled between them for a few moments. She wasn't telling him everything, but he wasn't sure he wanted to hear everything right now.

"Has she seen a counselor?" Jan asked.

"She saw Father Stevens this afternoon. She liked him."

"Good. That's good. Maybe he can find her new accommodations."

"Perhaps."

They left it at that, and Jan spent the next two hours shaking the conversation from his head.

Let go. Something is up, Janjic.

The dinner with Tom Jameson was a welcome distraction. The man's enthusiasm for the movie deal and its possibilities dwarfed this Helen business. By eleven that night, Jan had recovered himself sufficiently to whistle lightheartedly as he drove himself home. The madness had left him.

But that all changed on Wednesday.

He rose at five and showered, thinking about the conference call Nicki had arranged between him, Roald, and Karen at nine. Karen had some news she wanted to share with both of them.

Only when he left his room dressed and ready for the office did he once again think of Helen, sleeping in the suite below. Butterflies lifted his stomach. He rounded the corner for the kitchen and stopped mid-stride.

Suddenly those butterflies were huge and monstrous and doing backflips, because suddenly she was there, leaning over the coffeepot, dressed in an oversize white shirt that hung to her knees.

Jan took one step back on the chance she had not seen him.

"Morning, Jan."

He swallowed, replaced his foot and walked in. "Morning, Helen." She had not looked up at him yet. "Where's Ivena?"

"She's still in bed. Sleep well?" she asked, and now she turned her head, still fiddling with the coffee machine.

"Yes," he thought he said, but he couldn't be sure with all the commotion streaming through his head. He said it again, just to be sure. "Yes." She was looking at him with those blue eyes, smiling innocently. Nothing more; he could see that.

But he *did* see more. She was throwing her magic at him. His knees felt weak and his breathing stopped. Waves of heat washed down his back. He instinctively reached a hand to the refrigerator to steady himself.

You are in love with her.

"I can't seem to get the water . . . Do you know how this thing works?"

"Yes."

She waited for him to say more. But he just stood there stupidly. He wasn't thinking so quickly. "Could you show me how?" she prompted.

"Yes." He walked over to her and bent over the coffee maker, absolutely clueless as to what she wanted him to do. She moved over a foot maybe, certainly no more. Not beyond the reach of his elbow, which bumped up against her stomach. The touch sent a wave of hot air through his mind and he lost what little concentration he'd had.

You are in love with her, Jan.

He almost straightened and told the voice to shut up. But the thought of doing even that swam away with the rest of his reason. Instead he just fumbled cluelessly with the buttons and the pot and the plug, still wondering what he was supposed to do here.

She stood beside him, looking over his shoulder, her hot, sweet breath playing with the hairs on his neck. Or maybe not; maybe that was a breeze from the window. But it lifted the hairs on his neck just the same, and he was struck by a sudden panic that she might notice her effect on him.

Jan straightened, but too quickly and without aim; his head hit the cupboard above the counter. *Thump.*

Helen giggled. "Are you okay? Actually, I just need it turned on."

"On?" He bent over the machine. Maybe she hadn't noticed his stiffness. The power button was suddenly there, big and bold on the right and he wondered how she could have missed it. He pressed it, heard a soft hiss, and extracted himself from the workspace. "There."

"Thank you, Jan."

"Sure. No problem." He backed away and took a banana from the fruit basket. "So everything's working for you downstairs?" he asked.

"Perfect. The television doesn't work but at least the coffee maker is a simple affair." She smiled, and he laughed as if it were a truly humorous comment.

"Well, if there's anything you need, please let me know."

"Jan?"

"Yes." He took a bite from the banana.

"How long can I stay here?"

"Well, how long do you think you need to stay?"

"I think that depends on you." Her eyes! Dear God, her eyes were drowning him! *Look away. Look away, Jan!*

"You think?"

She nodded, not moving her eyes from his. "It *is* your house."

"Yes, I guess it is that." He took another bite from the banana. "Well, let's just say that you can stay until you need to go," he said.

"Really?"

"How long are you thinking?" he asked.

"I don't know." She smiled and he thought she might have winked, but he quickly decided she had not. "Like I said, that's up to you."

"Okay." For an impossible moment they held eye contact, and then he turned. "Well, I have to get to the office for a conference call." Jan started for the front door, still gripping the banana in his right hand.

"Jan."

He reached for the door with a sweaty palm and turned to face her.

"Maybe we could have dinner tonight," she said.

His knees would not stay still. She stood there smiling at him, and every fiber in his body cried to run over there and fall to his knees and beg for her forgiveness for even considering that she was anything less than an angel.

You are in love with her, Jan. You are hopelessly in love with her.

He didn't bother putting up a defense this time.

"Yes. I would like that," he said. His voice wavered but he didn't try to steady it. "I would like that very much."

Jan opened the door and walked out into the fresh morning air, barely able to breathe. He'd already made the turn down the sidewalk that paralleled the street when he remembered the car and turned back. It occurred to him that he had a half-eaten banana in his hand when he tried to open the car door. He hated bananas with a passion. Ivena must have bought them. He grunted and laid it in the flower bed, thinking to throw it away when he returned.

When he returned to take Helen to dinner.

GLENN LUTZ sat at his desk at a quarter to four that same afternoon, sweating profusely. He'd taken the last five impossible days without Helen as well as any sane man could. But what sanity he still possessed was wearing unbearably thin.

She'd come last Friday night, snorted a fistful of his drugs and then teased him the way only Helen could tease. She'd played cat and mouse with him for an hour, running and laughing hysterically, before he could finally take it no longer and broke his promise not to hit her. It had been a blow with his fist, on top of her head, and it had dropped her like a sack of potatoes. When she'd come around fifteen minutes later, she proved much more cooperative.

He had let her go as promised, swearing the blow to her head had been a mistake. When would she be back? Soon, she'd said. The next day? Maybe. But only if he promised not to hit her.

But she hadn't come back the next day. Or the next, or the next, or the next. And now Glenn knew that he wouldn't be able to keep his promise to give her the freedom she demanded. He'd initially persuaded himself that going without would only elevate the pleasure when it did come. Like crossing a desert without water and then plunging into a pool at an oasis. Well, that was fine for a day or two, but now the desert was killing him and it was time to call in the marines. Either that or lie down and die.

Glenn glanced at the clock in his office. It was now 5:00 P.M. He hadn't been home in four days. It was a new vow he'd fallen into: He would only go home to shower on days after seeing Helen. The rest of the time he could conduct business on his terms, caking on the deodorants if a meeting necessitated, but otherwise staying pure until her return. It occurred to him in moments of clarity that he had become a demented man over time; that any man on the street who knew how Glenn Lutz lived his life would go white as a sheet. But they were not him, were they? They didn't possess the power he did, the self-control. They did not have his past with Helen. And so they could go drown themselves in their holy water, for all he cared. There was a time to conquer the world and there was a time to conquer a woman. He'd had his fill of conquering the world; it was a woman who begged to be conquered now. Truth be told, a far nobler task.

It was time to fetch Helen. He wouldn't break into the preacher's house, of course. Breaking and entering involved neighbors and alarms and physical evidence that proved risky. It was always better to snatch a person outside of their home.

Glenn stood, wiped the sweat from his face and flung his fingers out, dotting his desk with droplets of moisture. This time . . . this time he would have to deposit a greater reservoir of motivation in her. If she expected him to sit and wait in death, then she would have to give a little of her life to sustain him. He smiled at the thought. Clever. Very clever.

A knock sounded on the door and he started. That would be either Buck or Beatrice. No one else would dare, even if they could get to the top floor. "Come."

Beatrice walked in. She'd stacked her hair a foot high and it looked absurd, exaggerating her sloping forehead. She was clearly a witch.

"What?" he asked.

"I have a surprise for you." Her teeth seemed large for her mouth, but that too could've been an illusion cast by the hairdo.

"What?"

"She's in the Palace."

"She . . ." The meaning of her words hit him then and he lost his voice.

"Helen's in the Palace," she said.

"Helen?" His voice came out scratchy. Impossible! He spun to the door that led across to the West Tower. "She . . . Helen?"

The witch refused to smile. "She's waiting."

The relief washed over him like a wave of warm water. Immediately his entire body began to tremble. *Helen!* His flower had returned!

Glenn was breathing heavily already. His face drained and his lips quivered. He broke from his stance and lumbered for the door that would lead him to her.

HELEN SAT on the edge of the dance floor in the Palace, fidgeting with her hands, terrified for having come. After nearly five days without him she'd come back, powerless to stop herself, it seemed. And powerless because her legs were trembling and her body was convulsing from withdrawals. It made her stomach float and her mouth salivate. If she wasn't physically addicted, then she was addicted in a worse way, from the soul up.

But she had to return by five-thirty. Yes, she had to get back to Jan, she couldn't go crazy here—it would ruin her. She'd spent the day a nervous wreck, fighting desperately for control until she finally decided that one hit would not hurt. One dip back into the waters. She was, after all, still a fish, and fish could not stay up on the shore forever. One taste of . . . this.

That priest Ivena had sent her to had talked about stability in terms of loyalty and trust. But what could he possibly know of her? *This* was her loyalty and trust; the drugs. And Glenn. The beast. Beauty and the Beast.

The door to her right slammed open and she leaped to her feet. He stood there with his arms spread like a gunslinger, panting and sweating.

Helen stood. "Glenn." She should go now, she thought. Or she should run to him and throw her arms around him. Helen smiled, partly with seduction, partly in amusement at herself. "I missed you, Glenn."

He dropped to his knees and started to cry. "Oh, I missed you too, baby. I missed you so much."

She felt an odd blend of empathy and disgust, but it did not stop her. She went for him, and when she reached him, knelt down and kissed his forehead. He smelled of sick flesh, but she was growing accustomed to his peculiarities.

Then Helen put her arms around his huge frame and together they toppled over backward.

CHAPTER TWENTY

"The love that I saw in the priest and in Nadia was a sentiment that destroyed desire for anything less than union with Christ. If you say you love Christ, but are not driven to throw away everything for that pearl of great price, you deceive yourself. This is what Christ said."

The Dance of the Dead, 1959

JAN THREW safety to the wind and roared toward Ivena's house. Put a man who'd relied too heavily on a chauffeur for most of his driving career behind the wheel and stir his heart into panic and you'd better warn the public. A car blared its horn to his right, and Jan punched the accelerator. The Cadillac shot through the intersection safely. He'd just run a stop sign. He braked hard and heard a squeal; those were *his* tires! *Settle down, Janjic!* Ivena's was just around the corner.

It was jealousy that raged through his blood, he thought. And he really had no business courting jealousy. Especially over Helen. Not so soon. Not ever! Goodness, listen to him.

But there it was: jealousy. An irrational fear of loss that had sent him into this tailspin. Because Helen was missing. Helen was gone.

It had been a good day, too. The conference call with Karen could have been awkward, but Roald's ever-present booming voice had preempted any opportunity for private talk. Karen announced her news: In light of the movie deal, their publisher, Bracken and Holmes, had agreed to publish another edition of *The Dance of the Dead,* with updates that tied into the movie. And they were underwriting a twenty-city tour! What does this mean? Jan wanted to know. "It means, dear Jan, more money, I'd say," Roald had boomed. Karen then told them that the publisher had arranged a dinner with Delmont Pictures Saturday evening. They wanted Jan there. Where? New York, of course. New York again? Yes, New York again. It would be huge, better than anything she could have wished for.

Jan had joined them in their enthusiasm and then hung up, feeling stretched at the seams. His mind had become a rope, pulled at by two women. Karen the lovely one, deserving of his love; Helen the unseemly one, suffocating him with her spells of passion. The craziness was enough to send any man to a psychiatrist's couch, he thought.

But that had been the least of it.

Jan had rushed home at five-thirty, found Helen gone and a note from Ivena on his fridge. She would be back in a couple of hours. But there was no word of Helen. He quickly showered while he waited for her return.

He'd dressed in the same black suit he'd worn on their last outing, but with a yellow tie this time. An hour had ticked by. Then two, while he paced the floor. And then he knew that she would not return, and his world began to crumble. He'd called Ivena, swallowing back the tears so that she couldn't hear.

Helen was missing. Helen was gone.

He brought the Cadillac to a halt in front of her house and climbed out. He still wore the black suit, less the tie. His shiny leather shoes crunched up Ivena's sidewalk, loud in the night. He would have to tell her everything—he could no longer walk around carrying these absurd emotions alone.

She greeted him quietly. "Hello, Jan. Please come in."

He stepped past her, sat on the sofa, crossed his legs and lowered his head into his hands. A strong scent of flowers filled the room—perfume or potpourri perhaps. It was nearly suffocating.

"Ivena—"

"Why don't I get us some tea, Janjic. Make yourself comfortable."

Ivena walked straight for the kitchen and returned with two cups of steaming tea. She put his on the lamp table at his elbow and sat in her favorite chair.

He looked white in the face and he ignored his tea. "Thank you. Ivena, there is something that I have to tell you. I really—"

"So, Janjic, I was not wrong about the *pitter*?"

He looked up, surprised. "No, you weren't." He stood and paced three steps and then returned to his chair. "I don't know what's happening to me. This crazy idea for Helen to stay in my house wasn't the best."

"You're upset, I can see. But don't take your frustration out on me. And if you must know, I approve."

"You approve?"

"I do approve. I didn't at first, of course, when I first saw you looking at her, I thought you must be mad, being engaged to Karen as you are."

He stared at her, unbelieving.

"But no, you weren't mad. You were simply falling for a woman and doing so rather hard." She sipped her tea and set the saucer on the table. "So now you are in love with Helen."

"I can't believe you're talking this way. It's not that simple, Ivena. I'm not just *in love* with Helen. How can I suddenly be *in love* with a woman? Much less this . . . this . . ."

"This improper woman? This tramp?"

"How could this possibly happen to me? I'm engaged to Karen!"

"I've been asking myself that same question, Janjic. For three days now I've asked it. But I believe it's beyond you. Not entirely, of course. But it is more than your making. You care for Karen, but do you love her?"

"Yes! Yes, I love Karen!"

"But do you love her the way you love Helen?"

"I'm not even sure I *do* love Helen. And what do you mean 'the way'? Now there are different ways to love?" He immediately lifted a hand. "Don't bother answering. Yes, of course there are. But I'm no judge between them."

Ivena sat quietly.

"You should be outraged," he said, and truly *he* felt outraged. Outraged at his confusion and angry at Helen's disappearance. "And how do you suppose that I love Helen?"

"With passion, Janjic. She takes your breath away, no?"

The words sounded absurd, spoken out loud like that. It was the first time the matter had been presented so plainly. But there was no doubting the matter. "Yes. Yes, that's right. And what kind of love is that?"

Ivena smiled. "Well, she's quite a stunning woman, under all the dirt. It's not so confusing really."

He just looked at her for a minute. "I'm saying things that I shouldn't be saying, and you are counseling me as if this were a high school crush."

Ivena didn't respond.

"She had an impossible grip on my heart from the first, you know. I didn't look for it," Jan said.

Ivena only nodded, as if to say, *I know, Janjic. I know.*

"And there's something else you should know. I took her out. Before I brought her here on Sunday night we went to the Orchid for dinner. I didn't ask, mind you. She asked *me!* She'd laid out my suit—this suit." He jabbed his breast, suddenly grinning at the memory. "It was incredible. I could hardly eat."

"I know."

"You know?"

"She told me," Ivena said with a slight smile.

"She did? She told you that I could hardly eat?"

Ivena nodded. "And she said that you excused yourself to the rest room to gather yourself because you were—how did she put it—coming apart at the seams, I think."

"She told you *that?*"

"It's true?" she asked with a raised brow.

"Maybe, but I can't believe she would tell you that. She picked that up?"

"She's a woman. You're a man. The love between you carries its own language. Love is impossible to hide, Janjic. And Helen is far more intelligent than you seem to realize."

"You're right, she is." Jan sat back and cradled his face with both hands. "So you know everything then. You know that I'm madly in love with her." He said it and it felt good to say. He lowered his hands and leaned forward. "That I've never loved another creature with so much passion. That I can hardly think of anything but her. That every time I look into her eyes, my knees grow weak and my tongue feels thick. I can't breathe properly when she's in the room, Ivena." He suddenly felt that way now, he thought. "My heart aches and fills my chest. I am—"

"I think I get the point, my young Serb."

"And now she's gone back to him."

Ivena lifted her porcelain cup and drank slowly, as if tasting her tea for the first time. She set the cup in her lap. "Yes. And it's not the first time."

"What do you mean?"

"She went back the night you left for New York. Only for a few hours, but I could see it in her eyes."

What was she saying? "You could see *what* in her eyes?"

"I could *smell* it. And she held her head in pain the next morning. I'm not an idiot, Janjic."

Rage mushroomed in Jan's skull. He stood from his chair. "I swear if I ever . . . I'll kill that devil!"

"Sit, Janjic."

"He's beating her, isn't he?" His face flushed with blood. "He's abusing her! How could she go back to him!"

"Sit, Janjic. Please sit down. I am not the enemy."

He sat and buried his head in his hands. It was madness. It was more than madness now. It was horror. "And who *is* the enemy?" he asked.

"The thief who comes to steal and destroy," she said.

Yes, of course. He knew that, but it made nothing easier.

"Do you think Father Micheal's love came out of his own heart?" Ivena asked.

"No."

"Of course you don't, Janjic. You've told the whole world the same. Do you forget your own words?"

Jan looked at her. "No, I don't forget my own words. We're speaking of Helen here, not the priest. This isn't about fighting for our lives against some madman named Karadzic. This is about ridiculous emotions that are driving *me* insane!"

"And these emotions that are driving you insane, they are the same sentiments that put Father Micheal on the cross. They are the same that Christ himself showed. For God so loved the world, Janjic. Is this the love with which you love Helen?"

He stared at her stupidly.

"I swear, Janjic, you can be thickheaded at times. You are feeling the love of the priest; the love of Christ. It's not coming from your own heart. Have you ever considered the likelihood that you aren't meant to marry Karen? Then I'll tell you now, you can't marry Karen."

"Because of this minor inconsistency with Helen? Don't be—"

"No! Because God wouldn't want you to marry Karen. It's better to break off now before you have a covenant with her. Or do you consider an engagement the same as a covenant marriage?"

"No."

"Well then. You must follow this love God has placed in your heart for Helen. And you must do so without any offense to Karen."

"How on earth can I pursue a relationship with an unbeliever?"

"Did God command Hosea to take Gomar? I'm not suggesting you marry the girl, anyway. But there is more here than meets the eye, Janjic. Consider it a word from God."

It struck him as clearly as the mountain air in that moment. Could it be? He'd seen that brief vision of the flowered field and heard the weeping. Perhaps it was more than a casual act of God's grace to reveal it. Perhaps it was God's *intent* that he love Helen! And not just as a poor lost soul, but as someone his heart ached for.

The notion flooded Jan with a sudden sense of ease. It took the craziness out of his turmoil, lent him validity. Ivena must have seen the change in him because she was smiling.

"You think Helen is *meant* to be loved by me," he said. "It's why you approve."

"In as much as Christ loves the church, I think so."

"And Christ loves the church with this mad, passionate emotion?"

Ivena stood and walked to the bookcase on the opposite wall. "Would you like to see something, Janjic?"

A blue vase holding a single flower rested on the third shelf. A brilliant white bloom with red-trimmed petals, the span of Jan's hand. She pulled the flower from the base and faced him like a schoolgirl presenting her carnation.

"Do you smell it?"

It was the strong fragrance he'd smelled walking in. "I smell something. Your perfume, I thought."

"But I'm not wearing any perfume, Janjic."

Jan stood and walked toward the flower. Immediately the scent strengthened in his nostrils.

"Now you smell it," she said, smiling.

"That's impossible."

"But true. It is a lovely scent, isn't it?"

"And it all comes from the one flower? Naturally?"

"Yes."

Jan studied the petals. They seemed oddly familiar. She handed it to him and he held it up to the light.

"Where did you find this?"

"I'm growing them, actually. You like it?"

"It's stunning."

"Yes. I think I may have stumbled across a new species. I've already given Joey one for analysis."

"You don't know the name?" he asked, turning the flower in his hand. The petals were like satin. The scent reminded him of a very strong rose.

"No. They're the result of a rose graft."

"Amazing."

Ivena smiled wide, like a proud child. "Yes. The aroma is like love, Janjic. Unless a seed dies and falls to the ground it cannot bear fruit. But look at where it all leads. It's a sweet scent begging to be taken in. Not something you can just ignore, is it?"

Jan placed his nose near a petal and sniffed again. The flower's fragrance was so strong it brought water to his eyes. He returned it to the vase and retreated to his chair.

"So you think I should love Helen?"

He shook his head. "They'll blow their tops."

"Who will?"

"Karen, for one. Roald, the leaders, the employees—everyone."

"But you can't pretend. That would be worse."

Then he remembered why he'd come here in the first place. "She's gone."

Ivena turned. "She'll come back."

"You're sure? How can you know that?"

"I can't. But she's a woman and I'm telling you, she'll be back."

They sat and talked about what they should do then. Should they call the police? And tell them what? Jan said. That this girl named Helen had returned to her lover, which was not a good thing because Jan Jovic—yes, the famous author Jan Jovic—had a crush on her. But it wasn't a crush because it was God's love, which both was and wasn't like a crush. The same but different. Maybe. Yes, that would go over nicely.

In the end they agreed that they could do nothing else themselves. Not tonight at least. They would pray that God would protect Helen and reveal his love to her. And that Jan would hear God's voice and not run amok in his own emotions. Actually that last prayer was Ivena's, but Jan found himself agreeing with it. God knew that he was walking on new ground here. The grounds of love.

JAN NEARLY called in sick Thursday morning. Helen hadn't returned and he'd slept only three hours, half of it on the couch. In all honesty, he was sick, but it wasn't the kind of illness Karen would understand. At least not while it was directed at another woman. He finally dragged himself in at ten, if for no other reason than to save himself the agony of waiting.

The employees were looking at him with questioning eyes, he thought. They knew, they all knew. Their soft smiles and gentle frowns were saying so. The frowns he may have imagined, but then again maybe not. According to Betty's admission—which he was still trying to dismiss—they were practically laying odds on his sanity.

Karen bounded into his office within five minutes of his arrival, humming and moving to her tune. Thank goodness she was not so well connected with the gossip on the lower floors. He smiled with her as best he could, and listened patiently as she talked about her trip.

It had been a smashing success, by her telling; one to put in her portfolio. It was not only the reprint agreement with the publisher, it was eight—count them, eight—television appearances in the next two months and that was not including the tour to kick off the new edition. Jan was happy for her, and the news did distract him slightly. He found enough resolve to keep Karen in a state of general ambivalence about him, he thought.

But his thinking proved incorrect.

She flashed two tickets in her hand. "It's all set, Jan. We have first-class tickets to New York on the five-thirty flight tomorrow."

New York! He'd forgotten. "I thought the dinner was Saturday."

"It is, but I thought we could make a weekend of it. Roald won't be there, you know."

Suddenly it was all too much. He did smile; he did do that, but evidently not with enough muster to fool her. In fact, he couldn't be sure it didn't come off as a frown, if his heart was any judge. Karen dropped the hand holding the tickets to her side, and he knew that she'd seen through his facade.

She closed the door and slid into one of the guest chairs. "Okay, Jan Jovic. What's wrong?"

"What do you mean?" *She means why is your face sagging, dummkopf.*

"Something's up," she said, staring straight at him. "All day you've been wearing this plastic smile. I could walk in here and tell you that Martians have just landed on Peachtree Street and you'd smile and tell me how nice that was. You are as distracted as I've seen you. So what's up?"

Jan looked out the window and sighed. *Father, what am I doing? I do not want this.* He faced her again. She looked at him with her head tilted, beautiful in the morning rays that streamed through the window. Karen was a treasure. He could not imagine a woman as lovely as her. Except Helen. But that was absurd! Helen was off with another man! For that matter she might not even return. And if she did return, how could he possibly entertain thoughts of love for such a woman?

Father, I beg you! Deliver me from this madness.

"Jan, tell me." Karen was pleading with a woman's knowing voice now. She knew something already, by intuition.

He looked into her eyes, and suddenly he wanted to cry. For her, for him, for love. For all it was said to be, love had turned him into a worm this week. His eyes stung, but he refused to cry in front of her. Not now.

"Helen's gone again," he said.

She sat back and crossed her legs. "Sure, we agreed she would go. And that's a problem?"

"Yes. Actually it is." He could not look at her directly.

"Jan . . . She's just one girl." Her voice was soft and soothing. "Lost, wandering, hurt, sure. I can understand that. But our ministry goes way beyond this one person." She leaned forward and put her open palm on the desk for his hand. He took it. "It'll be okay, I promise."

He could not carry on any longer. He could not. "She's not just one girl, Karen."

The room fell to a terrible silence. "And what does that mean?"

He looked into her eyes and tried to tell her. "She means more to me. She . . ."

Karen removed her hand and sat straight. "You've fallen for her, haven't you?" Her eyes misted over.

"I . . . Yes."

"I knew it!"

"Karen, I . . ."

Now she was red. "How *dare* you?" She said it trembling and Jan recoiled. "How could you slobber all over a tramp like that?"

"I'm not slob—"

"How dare you do this to me!"

"Karen, I—"

"I *love* you, you big oaf! I've loved you for three years!" Now she had slipped into rage and he knew he'd made a very big mistake in telling her. "We're engaged, for God's sake! We went on television and promised our love in front of half the world and now you're telling me that you've fallen for the first bimbo that struts in front of you? Is that it?"

"No, Karen! That's not it! It was beyond me."

"Oh, yes, of course. How silly of me. You couldn't help it, could you? Did she crawl up at the bottom of your bed to keep you company at night?" Tears ran from her eyes now. "And what do you suppose this means for our engagement?" she demanded.

"I had to tell you the truth."

"What am I supposed to tell the studio? Did you even think of that before inviting this pathetic bimbo into your house? What should I tell them, Jan? Oh, yes, well Jan is no longer speaking on the martyrs. He's writing a new book; a personal guide to live-in bimbos. In fact, he's living with one now. *That* will go over huge, I can assure you! Roald will fry you!"

Jan was too stunned for clear thoughts, much less words. He only felt like curling up and dying. *I do not mean to harm you, Karen! I am so very sorry. Karen, please . . .*

"You think you can make this movie without me? You're a fool to throw it all away!"

She suddenly stood. Her hand came across the desk and landed with a loud *smack* on his cheek. His head jerked to the side. Without saying another word Karen spun around, pulled the door open, and walked from the office.

"Karen! Please, I . . ." Nothing else came. *You love her, tell her that. You do love her! Don't you?*

He heard the loud slam of the suite's front door.

For a full ten seconds Jan could not move. Nicki ran in, glared at him, and then ran out after Karen. To tell the world.

His face stung, but he barely felt it. He just sat there in a daze, looking with a blank, watery stare. Then he lowered his head to the desk and let the tears come. He was dying, he thought. Life could not be worse. Nothing, absolutely nothing could possibly feel as sickening.

But he was wrong.

Chapter Twenty-One

"We all have some of Karadzic swimming under the surface. We have all spit on the face of our Creator. Thinking that we have not is self-righteous arrogance—which is itself a form of spitting."

The Dance of the Dead, 1959

JAN PULLED into his driveway at seven, just as dusk darkened the sky over Atlanta. Helen had been gone for one day now and his world had caved in on itself.

He'd already shut the car door when it occurred to him that he could have pulled into the garage. There was no longer anyone to sneak past. He turned and walked for the front door.

He saw the white paper pegged to his door when he rounded the corner and it made him stop. A note? His heart bolted in his chest. A note!

Jan dropped his briefcase, bounded up and ripped the paper from the tack that had been shoved into the post. It was a full sheet with faint lines, the kind found in any full-size notebook. He tilted the sheet into the moonlight and dropped his eyes to the bottom.

Helen.

It was signed by Helen! His fingers trembled.

Help me please.
I'm so sorry. Please come. I need you.
The top of the west tower. Hurry, please.

Helen.

A drum took to Jan's chest. Dear God! Helen! He ran for the car, threw the door open, and fired the engine.

It took Jan ten minutes to reach the Towers—enough time for him to wet his steering wheel with sweat and spin through a dozen reasons why coming here was a bad idea, not the least of which was Glenn Lutz. The man had threatened Jan directly on the phone, and there was no guarantee that the note hadn't been written by him rather than Helen.

But she was almost certainly in trouble. He could have taken the note to the police, but he'd never quite lost his skepticism of the authorities, not since Bosnia. And going to the police would make this a public affair; he was quite sure he wasn't ready for that. Not with Helen.

In the end it was his heart that kept his foot on the pedal. He *wanted* to go. He had to go. Helen was there, and the thought of it made him throw reason to the wind.

Jan pulled the Cadillac under the first towering building—the West Tower—and inched to a stop in a space adjacent to the elevators. The underground structure was nearly vacant in the after hours.

A tall man dressed in black stood with his hands clasped behind his back near the elevator. Jan sat still for a moment. Maybe going to the police would have been a better idea after all. He climbed out and walked for the stranger.

The man ignored Jan until the doors had slid open and he'd stepped into the car. Then the Mafia type dropped his arms, walked in, turned around, and punched a code into a small panel. The doors slid closed.

Jan searched for the top floor button and was about to push the highest number on the panel when the man held out his hand. Message clear. The man was his escort.

A trail of sweat crept over Jan's temple. Helen hadn't arranged this. He couldn't shake the notion that he'd just stepped off a cliff. The elevator car rose past the last lighted number and jerked to a halt. It opened to a hallway and after hesitating, Jan followed the man down the passage and then to a set of massive copper doors. His host nodded and Jan pushed past them, swallowing at a knot that had risen to his throat.

He stepped into what appeared to be a plush penthouse suite, complete with a bar to his left and a dance floor to his left. But it was the large man standing next to a white pillar at the room's center that arrested his attention.

The doors shut behind him.

He was huge and pale, nearly albino in the dim light. His hair was blond, almost platinum, and his eyes were black. He wore a Hawaiian shirt and booted feet poked out from white cotton slacks. The man's lips twisted into a smile and Jan knew that this freak before him was Glenn Lutz.

"Well, well, well. The lover boy has come to force my hand," Glenn said. He lowered his head and peered at Jan past his eyebrows. "You do realize that you are trespassing on my ground, don't you? You do realize what that means, don't you?"

Jan quickly scanned the room for Helen. She wasn't here. This was not good. Jan took an involuntary step backward.

Glenn chuckled. "You'd like to kill me, wouldn't you, Preacher? That's why you came. But we can't have that. I have a surprise for you."

A shadow suddenly shifted to Jan's right. He'd only just begun to turn when the side of his head exploded.

A flashback.

But it wasn't feeling like a flashback. His world swam in darkness. He staggered to his right and instinctively threw out his arms for balance. And then finding it, he grabbed at his head, half expecting to feel a great hole there. His fingers felt a full head of hair, wet above his left ear, but intact.

The pain struck him as he tried to straighten, a deep ache that throbbed over his skull. He'd been hit on the head. Then a blow landed on the other side.

Thirty years of life in Bosnia roared to the surface. He was a writer and lecturer, but he was a survivor first, albeit a survivor who hadn't practiced surviving for a long time. Either way, his mind knew the drill well.

He staggered back two steps, groping for consciousness, blind to the world from that last blow. He nearly fainted then. If he didn't move quickly he might not move again. Jan gathered every last reserve of strength and he rushed straight forward, right past his attackers and out onto the floor. Grunts of objection sounded behind him and he lumbered forward, like a bull struck by a sledge.

He couldn't fight—not in this state—that much screamed through his mind. But it was all that screamed through his mind, because the rest of it had shut down, cowering from those two cracks to the head. He could not see; he could only run. The condition proved unfortunate.

Jan had covered less than ten yards when his knees smacked into a piece of furniture. He cried out and pitched headfirst onto a cushioned object. A couch. His head swam and he rolled off, landing on his side with a dull *thump* that took his breath away.

They were on him then, like two hyenas pouncing for the kill. Hands jerked him to his knees and held him still. It was as if they carefully lined up the last blow;

one, two, three . . . Crack! It landed on the crown of his skull, and he collapsed in a sea of black.

TWILIGHT LAPPED the edges of Jan's mind, tempting him to awaken, but he thought he would sleep a while longer. An annoying bell had crashed through his ears one too many times already, like a huge mallet swung for a gong.

The sound invaded his dead sleep relentlessly and he rolled . . .

But that was where the gong show ended. Because he couldn't roll.

His eye cracked and he saw nothing but black. A monster pounded on his skull, sending shafts of pain right down his spine. He tried to lift his head, but it refused to budge. Slowly his focus returned.

He knew then that he wasn't in his bed. He lay on his side in a corner, with his back to a wall. He was naked except for his underwear. Dark stains ran down his belly and dyed his white briefs red. Blood.

He'd been beaten badly by those two shadows. Jan tried to lift his head again, and this time it came up for a full second before falling back down to the carpet with a dull thump. He paid for the effort with a spike through the brain, and he clenched his eyes against the pain.

He was still in the nightclub, he'd seen that much. Mirrored walls and a dark dance floor. Colored lights cast eerie hues of red and green and yellow across the black carpet.

A voice sounded to his left. "He's waking, sir."

Hands grabbed his arm and pulled him into a sitting position. He wavered there for a moment and then lifted his head. This time he got it all the way up and rested it on the wall behind him. A figure stood by the bar to his right, replacing a phone in its cradle. The man had a bandage around his shoulder. Jan hadn't done that, had he? Not that he could remember.

The black-suited man seated himself in a folding chair and looked at him without expression. Jan's reflection stared back at him from the mirrored wall. Blood ran in long fingers down his neck and chest from red-matted hair. *What are you doing here, Jan? And where in the devil are you?*

He answered his own question. *You are in a place owned by Glenn Lutz because Helen asked you to come.*

A door to his left smacked open and he turned only his eyes, favoring his aching head. It was Glenn. The man seemed to glide more than walk. His hands hung huge with thick fingers that curled like stubby roots. Jan looked into his eyes. They were nothing more than black holes, he thought. A chill spiked down his spine. The man was smiling and his crooked teeth looked too large for his mouth.

"Well, well. So the preacher has decided to join us again. You've been here for nearly a day and finally you have the courtesy to show your face." He stared at Jan, obviously relishing the moment. "I apologize for the blood, but I wasn't sure you'd want to cooperate without the right persuasion. And stripping you . . . I hate to humiliate you but . . ." He paused. "Actually, that's not true. None of that's true. I love the blood. Even if you'd agreed to everything up front I'd have beat you bloody."

Helen was right. This man was evil. Possessed maybe. Jan uttered a silent prayer. *Heavenly Father, please save me.*

"But you know that already, don't you, Preacher?" Glenn tilted his head forward and grinned like a jack-o'-lantern. "You've touched our tender flower, haven't you? Hmm? Felt her bruises?"

"No," Jan said hoarsely.

Glenn stepped forward and swung his arm in a wide arc. His hand crashed against Jan's head like a club. If he hadn't already been sitting, the blow would have taken him from his feet. As it was, it nearly broke his neck. A white ball of pain swallowed him and sent him over a cliff of blackness.

HE DIDN'T even know he'd passed out until he struggled back into consciousness. It must've been some time, because Glenn was leaning over the bar with a drink in one hand. His belly hung low, bared like an albino watermelon beneath his Hawaiian shirt hitched up by the bar. He looked back, saw that Jan had stirred, pushed himself off and strode across the floor

"Back again? Thoughtful of you."

Hands jerked Jan to a seated position. He let his head slip and closed his eyes. A finger rested under his nose and pushed it back. "You look at me when I'm talking to you." Lutz stepped back and Jan steadied his head.

"That's better. Now we're going to do this once, Preacher. Only once. Because you know I don't have all day, right? You do know that I'm Satan, don't you? To you I'm Satan. I would just as soon cut your tongue off as listen to you talk. But you caught me on a good day. I have my precious flower back, and that makes me feel generous, so we're going to do it differently. But we're only going to do it once; I want you to be very clear about that. Are you understanding this?"

Jan's head slowly cleared. He gave the man a shallow nod.

"Speak to me when I ask you a question, Preacher."

"Yeth," Jan said around a swollen tongue. That last blow had done some damage to his mouth.

"Okay." He turned and nodded to the man sitting in the folding chair by the bar. "Bring her."

The man walked to a door and knocked. Two came from the other room; another thug first, and then a woman.

Helen.

It was an odd moment. Jan wasn't even fully conscious; he was still in a fog; his life hung over a cliff, suspended by a thin thread it seemed. And all of this *because* of Helen.

Yet when his eyes focused and he became certain that it was her, everything else became useless information. Because she was here and he was here, and he was watching her wide blue eyes emerge from the shadows, flowers of delicate beauty. His pulse surged and his knees suddenly felt weak. He wanted to beg for her forgiveness and that terrified him. She should be begging for *his* forgiveness. And how could his knees feel weak at the sight of her? They'd been cut from under him already.

His body was too weak to show any of this—too weak to move. He sat like a side of beef against the wall, unmoving, but his heart began to do backflips when Helen looked at him.

"Thank you, my dear, for joining us," Glenn said. "Come, stand in front of him."

She walked to a point five feet from Jan, all the while looking at him with those fawn eyes. *Listen to me, Helen. Listen to me, it's all right. I love you, my dear. I love you madly.* His mind spoke it, but he knew she couldn't possibly gather any such thing from his sagging face.

"Stand him up!" Glenn said.

The two men walked over, each took an arm, and they hoisted Jan to his feet. His head throbbed and he could not support his own weight. They held him under the arms.

"Now we have the two lovers together." Glenn stood to one side, like a minister wedding a bride and groom. "It is a lovely sight, isn't it? What do you make of him, my dear?" This to Helen.

She stood frozen with her mouth slightly agape. Perhaps he'd doped her. Or perhaps she'd doped herself.

"Helen?" Glenn said.

"Yes?" she responded, breathy and quiet.

"I asked you what you thought of him."

"He looks hurt."

Glenn chuckled. "Good. That's good. Doesn't it make you want to spit on him?"

She didn't respond.

"Helen, remember our little chat earlier? Hmm? Do you remember that, honey?"

"Yes."

"Good. Now, I know that it may not feel natural at first, but it will later. So I want you to do what we talked about. Okay?"

The room seemed vacated of air. Nobody moved. Jan hung limp. Helen looked as if she were in another world altogether. A moment of reckoning. But Jan didn't know what was being reckoned.

Glenn spoke very softly now. "Helen."

Nothing.

"Helen, if you don't do what we talked about I'll break some of your bones. Do you hear me, princess?"

Helen hesitated and then took a step forward. She swallowed hard and closed her eyes. The sound of her shallow breaths worked like billows in the room. But she made no other move.

Glenn's threat came very quietly. "Helen, I swear I will break some bones, dear."

Her nostrils flared and she pursed her lips. Then she leaned forward and spit into Jan's face.

Jan blinked, shocked, staring at her wounded expression, hardly aware of the spittle on his cheek.

"Good," Glenn cooed. "Good. Now hit him, Helen. Hit him and tell him that he makes you sick."

Helen shifted on her feet, and Jan saw the terror in her eyes. She stood still.

Glenn took one long stride toward Jan and swung his fist like a mallet from his hip. "Hit him!" he screamed. The knuckles struck the left side of Jan's chest and a pain stabbed through his heart. The room swam, and for a moment Jan thought he might pass out again.

Glenn stepped back and looked at Helen. Sweat glistened on his face. He smiled. "You hit him or I hit you. That's the game, Helen."

It struck Jan then that Glenn meant to ruin him. This was all about Helen, not him. He was only the prop. Jan felt the first real shafts of fear run through his mind.

Don't do it, Helen! Don't do it! This is madness!

This couldn't be happening. At any moment the police would crash through the door with drawn weapons. He was a well-known man. He was on the verge of becoming a household name, and here he was in some absurd lovers' quarrel between two twisted souls. He had no business being here!

Karen's face flashed through his mind. *Dear, God! What have I done?*

Helen's body began to tremble—Jan saw it and he wondered if Glenn saw it. She looked small and puny standing next to him. Ugly. Jan blinked.

She's my enemy, he thought. A small wave of revulsion swept through Jan's gut. He felt inhuman in that moment. Like a pile of waste stepped on by a passing parade. Not the celebrity writer at all.

Oh Karen, dear Karen, what have I done?

Helen's face began to wrinkle. Tears ran down her cheek. Her hands began to quake badly, and Jan thought she was building her rage. But Glenn's face was suddenly white; he'd seen something else in her.

"You do it, you pig!" he growled. "You do it or I'll pound you to a pulp, you hear me?"

Her mouth suddenly cracked to a frown and a high, squeaking sound escaped her throat. Her eyes closed and her hand balled into a fist. Her cry wasn't a wail of rage. It was a cry of anguish. She was being torn to shreds.

Helen suddenly moaned loudly and she swung her hand in a wide arc.

The blow may have landed, Jan didn't know, because in that moment the nightclub vanished.

With a brilliant flash of light, it was gone.

He wasn't in the colored light, propped up like a side of beef. He was standing on the edge of an endless flowered field. The same white desert he'd seen once before, when he'd first touched Helen.

And then suddenly he knew that he'd seen this scene more than just once. He'd seen it a thousand times! This was the scene from his dreams! The white field that flashed into his dreams! How had he not recognized it?

It lay absolutely still.

Still except for the weeping.

He noticed her then. There was more than the field of flowers before him: There was a figure wearing a pink dress, lying on the petals not fifteen feet from him, looking at him. It was Helen.

Helen!

Only Helen hardly looked like Helen because her face was as white as cotton and her eyes were gray. She looked as though she'd been in a grave for a while before they'd dug her out and placed her here, on the bed of strange flowers.

Her chest rose and fell slowly, and she stared at him. But if she recognized him her blank look did not show it.

The weeping was for her.

He knew that because it came sweeping out of the sky on the lips of invisible mourners. Like a Requiem Mass for the dead. Such sadness, such anguish over Helen.

Still she gazed at him with flat, pale lips and dead eyes, breathing slowly while the sky filled with a million baying voices. Then the voices suddenly descended upon him, drowning him in their sorrow.

He was weeping immediately. Without warning. The pressure of grief fell so strongly on his chest that he couldn't breathe. He could only expel his breath in a long moan. He began to panic under the pain. He was dying! This was surely death flowing through his veins. He fell forward, unable to stand.

Jan collapsed among the white petals, prone at her feet. At Helen's feet. He gasped and rolled onto his back. The sky sustained a long howl; the mourners' undying grief. And Jan wept bitterly with them. He held himself tight to keep from falling apart and he wept.

Jan's eyes were closed when the sky went black and silent. Only his own weeping sounded. His eyes snapped open. He was back in the nightclub, hanging limp between the two men and blubbering like a baby.

Glenn was yelling. ". . . you hear me, you piece of trash!" He was towering over Helen, who had fallen to her knees, cowering and sobbing. "You make me sick!" Glenn spat at her. "Sick!"

Jan strained against the hands that held him, but succeeded only in inviting a new surge of pain through his head. *Helen, dear Helen!* His face twisted in empathy. *Oh, God, please save her! I love her.*

Tell her that, Jan. Tell her!

She sagged on the floor, heaving with sobs, her face white and her lips peeled back in desperation. Jan spoke to her. "Helen." It came out more like a moan, but he didn't care now. "Helen, I love you."

She heard and opened her eyes. They were blue. Deep blue. Swimming in tears and red around the edges and stricken with grief, but blue.

"Helen." They were both crying hard then. Looking at each other with twisted faces and weeping without words.

Glenn took a step back and glanced between them. For a moment his eyes widened. Then his face flashed red and screwed to a knot. He leaped forward and swung his foot like a place-kicker. The black boot struck Jan in his ribs. Something snapped and Jan's world began to fade.

Helen had stretched her arms out to him; her fingers spread and taut, like desperate claws. Glenn whirled and swung his foot at her. The blow knocked her to her side and she quieted to a quivering lump, but her eyes did not leave Jan's.

The brutes dropped him and he collapsed onto his face. Another blow landed on his back. And another.

He lost consciousness then, thinking the world was ending.

THEY LEFT Jan tied in the corner for another day, alone and without water. During that time he saw no one. He drifted in and out, through fields of white flowers and chambers that echoed with the sound of weeping. Heaven was weeping. Heaven was weeping for Helen.

He could only guess what the beast had done to her. But he could hardly bear to guess and so mostly he didn't. New wounds on his chest had soaked the carpet at his feet with blood before finally coagulating. Glenn had kicked him twice; he remembered that. But the aches and bruises were all over. They had beat him after he'd passed out.

They came for him at night—two thugs and Glenn. The monster was wearing a grin and he looked freshly showered. If Jan had been in working order he might have thrown himself at the man and choked him.

"Dump him in his backyard," Glenn said with satisfaction. "And tell him the next time he messes with my woman, he won't be so lucky." He chuckled and the men hoisted Jan to his feet. His world faded with the pain.

When he awoke he was in his backyard by the pool, staring at the stars.

CHAPTER TWENTY-TWO

"If you were to put all of the world's pain in one fifty-five-gallon drum, it would look silly next to the mountains of gold and silver found in each moment with God. Our problem is that we rarely see past the drum."

The Dance of the Dead, 1959

SUNDAY PULLED Jan along a hazy road of reawakening with fits and starts.

Evidently he'd pulled himself into the house and passed out on the carpet by the couch. It was light out when an incessant ringing had awakened him again. He remembered thinking that he must get to that phone; he needed help. He hauled himself to his feet and answered. It was Ivena. The sound of her voice brought tears to his eyes. Ivena had been trying to reach him for two days now, and what in the world did he think he was doing not answering his phone? "I don't care if you have woman problems or not, you don't ignore me! I nearly called Roald looking for you."

"I was beaten, Ivena," he'd said. And she was at his door five minutes later.

She took one look at him, appalled, all that dried blood from head to foot, and she was immediately the war mother. No time to bemoan the injustice of it all; this one needed attending. He actually thought he was feeling much better and insisted that he could shower and eat and everything would be fine. But she would have none of it. They were going to the hospital and that was final.

In the end, he acquiesced. He hobbled out to the Cadillac, his arm over Ivena's shoulder, and she drove him to St. Joseph's Hospital. Everything started going blurry again when they turned the first corner.

When he awoke again, an IV tube snaked out of his arm, chilling it to the shoulder. A doctor hovered over him and pulled at his chest with strings. They were stitching up some cuts there. This time consciousness came and stayed; the

IV's hydrating solution was primarily responsible, the doctor told him. He was as dry as a cracked riverbed. Another day and he would've been dead. And how did all this happen anyway?

Jan told him and an hour later there was a cop standing by the hospital bed, asking questions and taking notes. Ivena heard it all then for the first time as well, sitting in the corner, his concerned mother. They asked her to leave once but she wouldn't, and Jan insisted that she stay. The policeman seemed to hurry the interview along just a bit when he learned that this was all supposedly done at the hands of Glenn Lutz. *The* Glenn Lutz? he'd asked. Jan presumed so, although he'd never met *the* Glenn Lutz before. The description certainly fit. The cop left soon after, assuring Jan that the proper authorities would pursue the matter.

All told, Jan had a mild concussion, two deep cuts—one above his right ear and one on his chest—two broken ribs, a half dozen smaller cuts and bruises, and a severe case of dehydration. By early afternoon they had him fully rehydrated, sewn up, and adequately medicated to get about. He asked to be released and the doctor agreed only after Ivena assured him in the strongest terms that she would care for him. She had cared for worse. Anyway, his concussion was already three days old, his cuts had been bandaged and his veins flooded; what else could they do but observe? She could observe.

Once home, it took Ivena an hour to arrange him on the couch and satisfy herself that he was settled. She would make supper, she announced. It didn't matter that it was only four o'clock, he needed some real food in his system, not some hospital Jell-O. So they ate a meaty cabbage soup with fresh bread and they talked about what had happened.

"I know what you told the police, Janjic, but what else happened?" Ivena asked.

He remained quiet for a few moments, looking out the window now. Yes indeed, what did really happen? And where was Helen now?

"This is beyond me, Ivena."

"Of course it is."

"I told Karen."

"Hmm."

"She wasn't happy."

"You broke your engagement?"

"No."

They sat quietly for a moment.

"I had another vision."

"Yes?"

He watched the swaying willow beyond the pool. "I was tied there waiting for Helen to strike me. He forced her to hit me, you know. I didn't tell the policeman that, but he did. He made her spit on me . . ." A lump rose to Jan's throat and he swallowed. "She didn't want to, I know she didn't want to. And when she swung, I went into a vision."

They had stopped eating for the moment. "Tell me," Ivena said. "Tell me the vision."

Jan told her what he remembered, every detail. And as he told her, the emotions of it came back. Heaven was weeping for Helen. He too was there for Helen, weeping at her feet. It was so vivid! So very vivid, paling the beating in comparison. By the end, Ivena had set her bowl aside and was wiping tears from her eyes.

"Describe the flowers on the field again."

He did. "And there's something else, Ivena. It's the same field that I've seen in my dreams for twenty years now. I saw that."

"You're sure? The same field?"

"Yes, without question. Not the dungeon, just the very end of the dream. The white field."

"Hmm. My goodness. And where is Helen now, Janjic?"

"She's with him." He sat up and pushed the pillows aside, wincing. "Dear God, she's with him and I can't stand it! We should go up there and throw the man out!"

"You're in no shape to play soldier. Besides, you've told the police everything. This is America, not Bosnia. They don't tolerate kidnapping and beating so easily here. They'll arrest the man."

"Maybe, but I did go there on my own. He made a point of mentioning that. Said I was trespassing." Jan stood and paced to the window. "I'm telling you, Ivena, there's more here; I can feel it."

"And I agree, my dear. But this battle is not yours to pursue. It's one to receive."

"Meaning exactly what? Just let things happen? It wouldn't surprise me if she were dead already."

"You mustn't speak like that! Don't speak that way!"

"And yet you're suggesting that we just sit by and allow the police to deal with Glenn? When they do launch their investigation, you think a powerful man like this will have nothing to say in his defense? I'm telling you he will say it was me who went to threaten him. At the very least it will be days, weeks before anything is done."

She scrunched her brow. "I'm not saying we should do nothing. Simply that the police will do something, and we should wait until we see what they do. And I'm saying that you're in no condition to run around."

She took up her bowl and dipped into it again, but her soup must have been cold because she set it down. "Then again, I may be wrong. I could easily be wrong. I wouldn't have suggested that Nadia do what she did, and yet it was the right thing. It was beyond her."

"It *was* the right thing. And if this madman were to kill Helen, I think I would kill him."

Ivena sat in her armchair, glassy-eyed. Neither of them was seeing things too clearly, Jan thought. Yes, he had seen the vision clearly enough, but it gave him no clues how to save Helen. And that was the one thing they both did see: Helen *did* need saving. Not just from the monster, but from her own prison.

"I wanted to, you know," Ivena said.

"You wanted to what?"

"I wanted to kill Karadzic." A tear left its wet trail down her cheek. "I tried, I think."

"And so did I."

"But Nadia didn't. She didn't even *want* to kill him. And neither did the priest. They chose to die instead."

Jan turned back to the fading light. What could he say to that? His head was hurting. "Yes, they did." He returned to the couch, suddenly exhausted.

Ivena stood and took their dishes to the kitchen and just like that the conversation was over. They did not return to the subject until late that night. "So I guess we just sit tight and see what the police do for now?" Jan asked after Ivena had announced her intentions to retire.

"Yes, I guess so."

"And we'll deal with the ministry tomorrow. The employees will be concerned about my absence."

"Fine."

And that was that. She made sure that he was in good shape, fed him a painkiller, and left him to sleep.

JAN DIDN'T sleep quickly. He'd spent half the day in sleep and it didn't return so easily now. Instead he began to think about what the others would say to this.

Or at least what they would say to what *he* would tell them about this, because he wasn't sure he could tell Roald and Karen all the details.

In fact, he wasn't sure he would be telling Karen *anything* soon. He didn't even know if she was still working for him. Did she know what had happened to him? He hadn't shown up for work Friday, but that was not unheard of. And the dinner! He'd missed the dinner in New York!

Suddenly Jan was wide awake. He tried to put the concerns out of his mind. Tomorrow was Monday; he would find out then. But the thoughts chased about his mind like a rat on a running wheel. Karen's face—her sweet smiling face—and then her angry slap. Perhaps he'd been a fool to tell her about Helen. He could hardly even imagine what would become of his relationship with Helen. They would . . .

He didn't know what they would do. If indeed she came out of this in one piece. And yet he had sacrificed his relationship with Karen already. Hadn't he?

Jan finally threw the sheets from his legs in a fit of frustration and walked for the phone.

He called Roald. The man's gruff voice filled the phone on the tenth ring. "Hello."

"Roald, this is Jan."

"Jan. What time is it?"

"It's late, I know. I'm sorry—"

"Everything okay?"

So. The man had not heard. "Yes. Have you talked to Karen?"

"Not since our conference call. Why? Weren't you with her in New York yesterday?"

"No, we had a problem with that. Listen I have something I need to talk to you about. Can you come by my house tomorrow?"

"Your *house?* I suppose I could. What's up?"

"It's nothing, really. Just something I'd like your input on."

They agreed to meet at ten.

It took Jan another hour to shake the mental mice and drift into sleep.

THE MORNING came quickly, to the sound of Ivena's singing in the kitchen—"Jesus, Lover of My Soul." She was in there cooking something that flooded the house with a delicious smell. "Let me to Thy bosom fly," her voice warbled.

Jan lifted himself to his elbows and fell back with the aches of stiff sleep. By the time he'd loosened enough to walk out to the kitchen, she was already setting the table. She saw him, still dressed in his pajamas, and she chuckled. "Oh my, my, look at yourself."

He glanced at his reflection in the chrome oven-hood and saw that she referred to his hair; it stood straight up past the white bandages. He flattened it. "I am a sick man, Ivena. Don't cross me."

"Not sick enough to stay in bed, I see."

"And did you expect less?" he asked, motioning to the two place settings.

"No. I have had a wonderful sleep, Janjic."

He hobbled for the chair. "That's more than I can say. I feel like a steamroller ran over me." He then told Ivena about his call to Roald. "They don't know. Karen doesn't know. I don't know if she's even on board any longer."

"No?"

"How can she work for me? This isn't good."

"You'll be fine."

"She's the backbone of the ministry."

"No, the testimony's the backbone, Janjic. *The Dance of the Dead.* The martyr's song. The testimony you've been waving about like a flag for five years; *that* is the backbone of the ministry."

"Yes, and it's been Karen who's done most of the waving. I'm nothing but the flagpole. Without her . . . I can't imagine what it would be."

She chuckled. "So then choose your women carefully, Janjic. They all want my handsome Serb. So many women . . ."

"Stop your nonsense. It's more serious than you think," he said, and ordinarily he would have grinned, but his heart was sick. "Do you know that I missed a dinner engagement in New York on Saturday night?"

She cast him a side glance. "Am I hearing some anger in this voice of yours, Janjic?"

He sipped at the steaming coffee. "Maybe. I'm not sure I've done the right thing with Karen. I feel like I've cut off one leg to save the other and now I may lose both."

"Don't worry, you will find your way. And I'm sure that missing one meal with Karen won't have any bearing on the path you end up taking."

"The dinner was with the movie people."

"Yes, and I'm not sure about this movie business anyway."

"Well, it's too late. It's finished."

"What is finished? Your life is finished, so now they will make a movie of it? I don't think so. We will see what happens to your movie deal, Janjic."

"That's ridiculous."

"Still, we will see." She said it smiling. "Roald will be here soon enough. It's already nine-thirty."

Nine-thirty! He hadn't realized it was so late. Jan excused himself and hurried off to dress.

Roald arrived fifteen minutes later while Jan was still in his room, struggling to get his socks on without ripping his stitches. "Where is he?" the elder statesman's voice boomed.

"Take a breath, my friend. May I get you something to drink?" Ivena returned.

Jan shook his head at her condescending tone. He entered the living room behind Roald, who'd taken a seat. The man was wearing a black tailored double-breasted suit familiar to Jan. "Good morning, Roald."

The man did not turn. "Jan I hope you have more sense than I think you have, partner. What in tarnation did you do to Karen?"

Roald turned, saw Jan's head, and came out of his chair. "What on earth happened to you?"

"Nothing," Jan said, sitting. He wore a navy shirt that covered his chest wounds. "Sit. So, I take it you talked to Karen."

"Doesn't look like nothing. Goodness, what happened? Are you okay? You look like you've been trampled by a herd." He sat.

"Not quite. Tell me about Karen first."

"Karen? Well, Karen's in New York, did you know that?"

"We had a dinner engagement there Saturday night. I couldn't make it."

"And you didn't have the decency to at least call? They had the dinner without you, you know."

"Honestly, Roald. I was quite tied up." He said it without humor. "So Karen attended?"

"No. And frankly that's a problem. What happened to you?" he asked for the third time.

Ivena interrupted them when she brought drinks, and then excused herself. She had some flowers that needed tending, she said. They would have to conquer the world on their own. She gave Jan a wink and left.

"So, *no one* from the ministry attended the dinner, then?" Jan asked.

"No one. It was a handful of executives from Delmont Pictures and the publisher."

"Goodness, what a mess. I'm sure Karen's upset about that."

Roald leaned back and picked up the coffee Ivena had placed by his chair. "Actually, she seems to care less about all that. She's directed her anger to you, my friend."

"Me?"

"You. She seems to think there may be a problem. There are greater concerns at hand now, and I told her as much. We're on the verge of breaking new ground; you realize that, don't you? No one's ever done what we'll do with this film. It's unprecedented. Already the whole evangelical community is talking about it. I'm out there talking you two up to the world—speaking about how the 'Jan and Karen show' will change the way Christianity is seen in the broader realms of arts and entertainment—and unbeknownst to me, the two of you are home having a world-class spat. It's embarrassing to say the least."

"And you shouldn't be embarrassed. You're mistaken—we're not having a fight. We had a talk. Karen took it badly. That's all." That was not all, of course, and Jan knew it well.

"Then maybe you can explain to me why she's talking about moving her things out of the office."

"She's leaving?"

"Not yet. But she seems to think the engagement's in some sort of jeopardy, and I told her that was nonsense. There's far too much at stake."

Jan cringed. "I didn't break off the engagement."

Roald nodded. "I told her that you cared for her, you know. She went on about this Helen character that you've helped, and I told her there was no way on God's green earth that you—after all that you've been through and with all that lies ahead of you—would do something so foolish as fall for a hooker. The church would throw you out on your ear! I think Karen somehow got the idea that you were actually losing interest in her, Jan. You have to watch your words, my friend. Women'll take what you say farther than you intend."

"Helen's not a hooker." He could see a glint cross the man's eyes.

"Hooker, junkie, tramp . . . what's the difference? She's not the kind of woman you can be seen with. It would be a problem. Especially with Karen in your life. You do see that, don't you? We warned you as much."

Jan nodded. This was not going as planned. Roald was somehow moving him along a path of reason he didn't want to travel.

"Do you know what a rare woman Karen is?" Roald asked. "Yes, of course you do. That's what I told her just an hour ago. And do you know what she told me?"

"No."

"She told me that matters of the heart have nothing to do with what's rare or common, or right or wrong. The heart follows its own leading. And you know she's right. So I guess I have to ask you, Jan, where is your heart leading you?"

Jan swallowed. "I don't know. I mean I do know. But the direction seems to change."

Roald blinked a few times. "It does, does it? In case you hadn't realized it, Jan, my boy, you're not some adolescent teenager; you're a full-grown man with the trust of the church. And you're engaged to be married, for heaven's sake! Don't you think sticking your nose in the air to sniff out where the winds of love are blowing on any particular day is a bit preposterous for a man of your standing?"

"Don't lecture me, Roald. Did I say that I was sticking my nose in the air? Not that I can remember. You asked about my heart, not my will. If you want me to be straight with you, then give me some respect."

Roald took a deep breath. "Fine. I only hope that your will doesn't flip-flop like your heart. You do know if you don't find a way to reconcile with Karen, we stand to lose everything. Millions."

Jan stared at him, angry now. "Millions? This isn't about money!"

"No, but it is about a whole lot of basic issues that seem to have escaped your reason more frequently lately. We're changing the world with this, Jan! We're moving the church forward." He grasped his hand to a fist as he said it. "And you want to throw that all away over a woman?" Roald leaned forward. "Never! If you were to jeopardize this project by taking to this tramp of yours, the board would undoubtedly remove its endorsement of you. I can hardly imagine Bob's or Barney's reaction. Frank Malter would do backflips. I would have to consider leaving myself."

Jan leaned back, stunned by the statement. He sat speechless.

Roald tilted his head. "I know that's not going to happen, because I know you're not that stupid. But I want to be absolutely clear here: I will tie neither my name nor my goodwill to a man who betrays the trust of the church by taking up with a freak."

"She's not—"

"I don't care what she is, she's out!" he thundered. "You hear? She's out, or I'm out! And without Karen and me, your world'll come crashing down around your ears, my friend. I can promise you that."

This couldn't be happening! Roald was gambling, of course, positive that Jan had no real intention of continuing any relationship with Helen.

Roald sat back and crossed his legs and let his breath out slowly. "Now, I'm not saying that you have to resolve this all by day's end. I'm not saying you have to kick her out on the street, but there are places that care for women like her. Where is she anyway?"

"She's not here."

"Good. That's a start." Roald paused. "Jan, I know this may sound rather harsh, but you have to understand that I'm protecting a much larger interest. An interest which has bearing on not only you and me and Karen, but on the whole church. *The Dance of the Dead* has and must continue to impact the church at large."

"But not at the expense of its own message," Jan said thickly.

"No, of course not."

"And yet you are meddling with God's love."

"God's love. What's God's love without purity? I'm rescuing you from dipping into deception, my friend."

For a while they sat in silence—Jan because he had nothing to say; Roald probably for effect. "You agree then?" Roald said.

"I'll think on it," Jan said.

"And you'll give Karen a call?"

Jan didn't answer that one. His head was still spinning. Spinning and aching.

Roald evidently took his silence for a positive sign. "Now, tell me how you managed to bump your head. My goodness, it looks horrible."

He wasn't about to tell Roald the grim details now. "It was nothing. Rather embarrassing really. I was jumped by a couple of hoodlums," he said.

"Hoodlums? You were robbed? Good night! You filed a report?"

"Yes."

"Good. When will the bandage come off?"

"It'll be off in a few days, I guess. It happened Friday, and I ended up in the hospital. That's why I missed the New York trip."

"You were in the hospital? I had no idea! Well that explains a lot. Karen's due back today." He patted Jan's knee and gave him a wink. "You let me handle this,

Jan. I'll call her for you. You know how women love to care for the wounded. She'll be doting on you before you know it."

Jan wanted to slug him then. It was the first time he'd felt quite so offended by the man's audacity, and it swept over him with a vengeance.

Roald stood and set down his glass. "I'm just looking out for you, buddy." He stretched out his hand and Jan took it. "I'll see you soon. Call me when you have things straightened out." He started for the door and paused.

"By the way, Betty wanted me to tell you that she would call this afternoon. They are concerned, naturally. And she said she's praying. And that all bets are off—she said you'd know what that meant." He lifted an eyebrow.

Jan nodded.

Roald left then and Jan steamed through his house, tending to his errands, which amounted to little more than getting himself another drink and finishing some cold breakfast. The visit had made a bad day impossible, he thought. Not only was he sick about Helen, he was now forced to feel sick about feeling sick. Roald was robbing him of his true purpose. He was a thief. One who pulled many strings in the evangelical church, and one who made some pretty compelling arguments, but a thief just the same.

And Helen? *Father, rescue me from this pit,* he prayed. *Lead me out.*

CHAPTER TWENTY-THREE

IVENA STOOD in the greenhouse, blinking at the sight, breathing, but barely. There was a new feel in the air.

To her left Nadia's rosebush had died, but you would never know it without digging through the swarming green vines to the dried branches beneath. No fewer than fifty vines now ran from the bush along the wall, reaching at least twenty feet toward the rose beds along the adjacent wall. Bright green leaves dominated the heavy foliage, but they paled under the dozens of large flowers that flourished along each vine, each as crisp and white as the day they first bloomed.

And all of this in two weeks.

Joey hadn't finished his analysis, but Ivena hardly cared. She knew now that he'd find nothing. This was a new species.

She stepped forward and stopped. The strong, sweet scent flooded her lungs like a medicinal balm. The orchids to her right were looking soft due to her neglect. So be it; she'd lost her interest in any but these new flowers. And today there was something new in here; she just couldn't put her mind to it.

A strand of her hair tickled Ivena's cheek and she brushed it aside. She glanced at the window, expecting to see it open. But it wasn't. The door then. No. The kitchen door? No. But there was movement of air in here, wasn't there?

The flowers' aroma seemed to sweep into her nostrils. And her hair whispered ever so gently along her neck. She'd put a swamp cooler in two years ago precisely because of the room's complete lack of ventilation, but it sat quietly on the far wall.

She walked to the vines and touched some of the flowers. *What are you doing, Father? Am I going mad? Janjic knows, doesn't he? You showed him that vision.* But she wasn't sure he did.

She waited, numb in the silence. But very much alive; she always felt thoroughly awake with these flowers. A very faint sound drifted through her ears. The sound of a chime off in the distance. The neighbors, perhaps.

Ivena stood still for another twenty minutes, swimming in the impossible notion that something significant had changed in the room but unable to understand what, or even verify if anything was different. It would be her secret. Other than Joey, she had decided to share the greenhouse itself with no one until she herself fully understood what was happening here. And something was definitely happening.

HELEN CRAWLED out of bed late afternoon on Tuesday. She had been in the Palace since Thursday evening, when she'd come for the quick visit before her big date with Jan. Funny, it didn't feel like five days. And five days of her own choosing, for the most part. She would have left when Glenn had first told her about his plans with Jan. Oh yeah, she would've flown the coop then, but he'd drugged her and swore to break every finger on both hands if she didn't do precisely what he asked. And then they'd brought her out and there Jan was, crumpled on the floor, beaten to a pulp. She was still partly drugged at the time or she might have bolted then. Instead she'd done it. She had actually done it.

The moment her hand first struck his flesh, she knew she couldn't continue. She could not because she *did* love this man she'd just spit on. And although she had not attacked Jan as Glenn had insisted, she *had* technically fulfilled his demands: She'd spat on him and she'd hit him. Glenn stopped short of breaking her fingers, and she'd stayed there with him, hiding in the drugs, feeling sick of herself. She could have gone at any time, but to where? Definitely not back to Jan.

She could never go back to Jan.

Tears came to her eyes every time she thought about him. She'd never known the meaning of shame as she knew it now. The thought of Jan made her feel small and puny—he was too good for her. And not just too good, but beautiful and lovely, and she was sick and ugly in front of him, leaning forward and spitting in his face.

Helen showered slowly, washing three days of grime from her skin, letting the hot water soak deep into her bones. She pulled that dress on, the white one she'd worn for Jan when they went to dinner, the one that made her look beautiful. She cried as it came over her shoulders. She just could not stop these tears.

Helen tore the dress off, threw it in the corner and fell onto the bed, weeping. She was a fool. That much was an inescapable fact. A useless piece of flesh walking around pretending to be alive. Dead meat. Her tears wet the sheets. And that was how it was meant to be because she was a fish who belonged in water. This pool of tears was her home. Never mind that she could not manage more than a few days in the environment before disgust overtook her—it was no better on dry land. There she was only a fish *out* of water.

Thirty minutes later, she pushed herself from the bed, plodded over to the corner, and picked up the dress. She pulled it on without thinking now, afraid that if she did think, she would end up in a pool of tears again. And what if Glenn walked through those doors right now? He might break her fingers anyway, just for wearing this thing. She'd snuck it in, intending to change into it for her big date with Jan that night . . .

Stop it, Helen! Please. Just go.

She didn't bother with the makeup. She combed her hair and left the Palace the back way, looking like an overdressed tramp, she thought. But she did not know what else to wear. Not for this.

The westbound bus lumbered up ten minutes later, and she climbed aboard, avoiding eye contact with the dozen other passengers who were undoubtedly gawking at her. Undoubtedly.

The bus motored through the city, stopping every block to exchange riders with the street, and Helen took the ride staring blankly out the window. She couldn't afford to break down right here in front of strangers. It was only when she stepped off at Blaylock Street and started the one-block trek to the house that she started fighting misgivings again.

She plowed on, most definitely feeling like a fish out of water now. She had no business doing this. None at all. For one thing, Glenn *would* break her fingers despite his guarantee that she could go as she liked. For another, she had hit him. She had spat in his face.

Then Helen was there, standing in front of the door. She read the sign above: *In living we die; In dying we live. I am dying,* she thought. She stood swaying on her feet for a full minute before walking forward. She tapped lightly and then stepped back.

The door opened. Jan stood there, a white bandage around his head. He looked at her, dumbfounded, eyes growing. He was not speaking. It was a terrible moment, Helen thought. Her gut was twisting and her chest felt like it might explode. She wanted to turn around and run. She had no business being here. None at all! Her fingers trembled at her side.

"Helen?"

She spoke, but no words came. She meant to say, "*Yes,*" but only a breathy rasp came out.

"Oh, dear God!" He suddenly leaped into motion and waved her forward. "Come in! Come in!"

Helen hesitated and then stepped across the door's threshold, compelled by his hand. Her skin was burning. She hung her head and looked at the floor while he closed the door and locked it. From her peripheral vision she saw him hurry over to the window, pull the curtain aside, and peer outside. Satisfied, he quickly crossed the room, looked out another window and pulled the drape tight. Then he hurried back and stopped in front of her. She could hear his breathing, hear him swallow. She almost expected his hand to swing for her face. She'd already decided to expect some measure of displeasure. Some harsh words at the very least.

"Helen." His voice wavered. "Helen." His hand reached for her face. He touched her chin. Helen closed her eyes and lifted her head slowly, thinking that she should flee now, before it was too late. She opened her eyes.

The skin around his misted eyes wrinkled with grief. "Helen." He lifted his other hand and took her face in both hands. Oh, the pain in those eyes! Tears slid down his cheeks as he held hers tenderly.

Then suddenly, without warning, his arms were around her neck, and he stepped forward, pulling her to him. He rested his hand behind her head. "Oh, thank you, Father! Oh, my dear, you are safe!" he sobbed. Her nose pressed into his shoulder and she stood there, stunned.

He swayed back and forth, heaving with sobs and blubbering about her coming home. He was not angry? Her mind screamed foul. It couldn't be! She should be punished! It was a trick—at any moment he would throw her against the wall and glare at her.

But he didn't. He just held her tight, lost in his own tears, and he told her that he loved her. He was moaning that now. That she was beautiful and that he loved her.

Helen lifted her hands and placed them slowly around his waist.

The sorrow and relief came like a flood, rising right through her chest and rushing out of her eyes. "I'm so sorry!" she cried. "I'm sorry, Jan." She kept repeating that and she cinched her arms around his waist.

They held each other for a long time there on the entry tile.

Then they stepped back and her eyes widened at the sight of his shirt. "Oh, my goodness!" she said, lifting a hand to her lips. "You're bleeding!"

He wiped his eyes and looked at his white T-shirt, now stained with red streaks. "So I am." Then he chuckled and spread his hands as if they were wet, still looking down. "I was just changing my bandages when you came."

She didn't see the humor but she chuckled with him. It seemed to fuel his own humor and he started laughing. Then they were laughing together. Looking at his bloodstained shirt and laughing together, out of pure, sweet relief.

Helen looked at his face—at his dark skin wrinkled around laughing hazel eyes; his teeth white in his delight, his hair swept back to his collar—and she knew she did not deserve him. Not this wildly handsome man giddy with joy at her return. She swallowed a lump that had gathered in her throat.

She helped him into the bathroom where together they finished changing his bandages. She winced at seeing the cuts and felt tears coming again. They slipped down her cheeks like a cleansing oil and he let her cry softly.

They didn't talk about Glenn that night. They did not talk about what had happened or about what they would do. They each had their own problems, that much needed no voicing. Instead they talked about the fact that the pool needed to be cleaned, and about Ivena's roses, and about why Cadillacs were really no better than Fords, a subject about which both were undeniably clueless.

And they laughed. They laughed until Jan insisted that he would split a stitch if they didn't control themselves.

THE NEXT morning drifted by like a dream for Helen. She'd slept in the suite downstairs and risen to the smell of bacon. Ivena was busy over the stove, smiling and humming her song. That song she'd said was the priest's favorite. Ivena had placed three settings about the table.

"Hello, Ivena," she said, coming up behind.

Ivena whirled around, incidentally flinging grease across the kitchen. "Helen! Oh, come here, child!" She waved her forward. "It is so good to have you home."

Helen stepped forward, unable to suppress a wide grin. "Good to be home," she said. They hugged each other and Helen helped by mixing up some orange juice. They ate breakfast together and laughed about things Helen could not remember, but they were certainly funny at the time.

She wandered about most of the morning, slowly disconnecting herself from the past, spending time with Jan and Ivena, pinching herself from time to time to make sure this was not some long hallucinogenic trip she'd taken. But it was not.

It was all real. The rose Ivena had brought smelled like a real rose, the ice clinked in the afternoon stillness, the tea tasted sweet to her tongue, the leather furniture felt cool to the touch, and the light sparkled in Jan's hazel eyes whenever he looked at her, which was at every possible opportunity. In all respects it proved to be a perfect morning.

They ate lunch together, the three of them, suspended by an air of unbelief at being together. And Jan could not seem to keep his eyes from her. When she finally excused herself for a nap, a shadow passed across his face, as if it were a great disappointment. She was falling in love with him, she thought. Not just loving, but falling. She couldn't remember feeling so strongly for one man. It was a good emotion.

HELEN'S RETURN came like a breath of life to Jan. He thought of it as her homecoming, even though this was obviously not her home. Actually, it felt like it should be her home. He had spent the night in peaceful sleep, wondering at the effect this one woman had on him. She had gone back to Lutz, yes. And she had spit on Jan, but none of that seemed to bear any weight in his mind. Instead he found himself dizzy over her choice to return here. She had chosen to come back!

Helen was now in *his* house, wandering around on those bare feet, shy, yet curious, spreading an air of expectancy wherever she stepped. And he was wondering why he should be so lucky to have her in his house. *Father, Father, what are you doing? What on earth have you done with this meddling of yours?*

They talked only once of Glenn Lutz, and then only in the context of the danger he might pose. Jan wanted to call for police protection, but Helen would still have none of it. Glenn would not be a problem, she insisted. She'd come to tears when Jan had pressed for her reasoning and left it at that. Poor Helen! Poor, poor dear! Ivena held her for a few minutes and brought comfort. It would be all right—the police already knew of the attack and not even Lutz would be so mad as to try a repeat. So Jan told himself. But he did check the window every hour just to be sure.

Thoughts of the movie deal came only sporadically. He had talked to Roald midday and the man seemed pleased with himself. Everything was back on track. Just get better, Jan. We miss you.

After lunch Helen excused herself to the apartment for a nap. Ivena announced that she too must leave for a few hours. Her flowers needed her touch. Jan found himself alone in the house, reading through parts of *The Dance of the Dead*, trying to guess what Helen thought as she read.

The doorbell suddenly echoed through the house, startling Jan. A salesman, perhaps. He set the book down, walked to the door, and pulled it open. Karen stood there. Karen! Dressed in a pure white blouse and a navy skirt, stunning and more beautiful than ever.

Jan felt his jaw drop and he barely had the presence of mind to close it before speaking. "Karen!"

"Hi, Jan. May I come in?"

Come in? Jan glanced back into the house instinctively. "Are you okay? Is there a problem?" she asked.

"No. No, of course you can come in." He stepped aside. "You just . . . I just . . . Come in, please."

She held his eyes for a moment and then stepped past the threshold and into the living room. Jan closed the door. "Roald told me what happened. I'm so sorry. Are you okay?"

"I'm fine, really."

She reached up and touched the head wrap very gently. "How bad is it? Shouldn't you be lying down?"

"Just a surface wound. I'll be fine, really."

"You sure?" She searched his eyes, genuinely caring, he thought.

"Yes. Would you like a drink?"

"Yes, that would be nice."

Yes, that would be nice, she said, and her voice carried sweet and lovely and terrible to Jan. He cut straight for the kitchen and pulled out a glass. *Yes, that would be nice.* Four years of affection were carried by that voice. He poured her a drink of iced tea and returned to the living room.

"Here you are," he said, handing the glass to her. They sat—he on his chair, she on the adjacent couch. Her brown hair rested on her shoulders, curling delicately around soft cheeks. Her eyes avoided him in the silence, but they were speaking already, saying that she wanted to make amends. That she was sorry for her outburst and that her life was miserable without him.

Then they were looking at each other, frozen in the heaviness. *She's thinking that I'm fixed by her beauty*, Jan thought. *She's thinking that I'm speechless because of my deep love for her.* Her perfume was musky and strong.

"Jan." Her eyes were moist. "Jan, I'm sorry. I am so sorry."

"No, Karen. No, it's I who should be sorry. I had no right. I don't know what to say—"

"Shhh." She put a finger to her lips and smiled. "Not now. And just know that if my imagination went wild it was because of my love for you. I would never hurt you. I don't want to hurt you."

Jan sat still, immobilized by her words. What had Roald told her? That Jan had sent Helen away? Yes, that's what he'd told her. Anything less and Karen would be demanding to know where Helen was. She was not a weak woman.

But he could see that she'd been deceived yet again. And she deserved far more. He had to tell her now. But the words were not flowing so easily.

"You were being mugged and here I was imagining that you were off with this woman." She laughed. "I should've known you better—forgive me. You were in the hospital and I was off steaming like a silly schoolgirl."

Roald had made the situation impossible. Now she was making it unbearable. And to make matters worse, Jan just smiled. He should have frowned and told her some things. Instead, he was sitting there smiling like a gimp. *Yuk, yuk, how silly of you, Karen.*

"I called the studio and explained what happened to you. They extend their best wishes."

He nodded. "Thank you. I . . . Thank you." *Now, Jan! Now.* "Maybe you should tell that to Roald. I'm not sure he's so understanding."

"Oh, I don't know. He's just concerned for you. The logical one, you know. For him it's a simple matter of mathematics. Deals like this come to the church only once every decade or so—you can't blame him for overreacting when something looks like it might interfere."

"He threatened to withdraw his support," Jan said.

"He did, did he? You see, he is overreacting. And maybe I had something to do with that. I think I convinced him that you had gone off the deep end with this woman." She smiled apologetically. "It was plain silly."

Now, Jan. You must tell her now! "Yes, but it still concerns me. Am I supposed to think that every time Roald doesn't agree with something, he'll threaten to withhold his support?"

"No."

"So then why would he make such a statement?"

"I'll talk to him about it." She paused. "But he *was* faced with this nonsense that I fed him. You shouldn't be so hard on him."

"Perhaps. But I don't see his right to threaten me. What if it were true? What if I had fallen for . . . well, for a woman like Helen, for example? Am I to assume that if I step over the wrong line I will be punished like a child?"

"No." Karen had tightened slightly. Or maybe it was just his imagination. "No, you're right. Like I said, I'll talk to him." She lifted her glass and let the liquid flow past her lips. She was lovely; he could not deny the fact. And she was a strong woman, though not strong enough to let his comment about Helen pass, hypothetical or not.

She spoke, smoothing her skirt, looking down. "It isn't true though, is it, Jan?"

"What isn't true?" he asked. He knew of course, and his heart was hammering in his chest.

"You're not in love with this woman." She looked at him. "With this Helen."

He would have answered. Sure he would have. What he would have said he'd never know, because suddenly it was neither his voice nor Karen's speaking in the stillness. It was another.

"Hello."

They looked toward the basement entrance together. She stood there with her blond hair in tangles, smiling innocently. Helen.

Helen! Heat washed down Jan's back. He shot a quick glance at Karen, who was staring, stunned. She'd never met Helen so she could not know . . .

Then Helen changed that as well. She walked forward and extended her hand to Karen. "Hi, I'm Helen."

Karen stood and mechanically reached out her hand. "This is Karen," Jan said.

"Hi, Karen."

"Hello, Helen," Karen returned. But she wasn't smiling. Jan rose from his seat and they stood there awkwardly, Karen to his right and Helen to his left, staring at each other in very different ways. Helen as if wondering what the big deal was, and Karen as if she'd just been stabbed in the back with a ten-inch bowie. It was an impossible moment, but Jan knew that there was no chance of rescuing it.

And then he knew something else, staring at these two women side by side. He knew that he loved the woman on the left. He loved Helen. Somehow seeing them side by side, there was simply no question of it. It was the first time that he'd held both in his mind and seen their places in his heart. To Helen he was even now giving his love, and to Karen his empathy.

He cleared his throat. "Helen's staying with me for a few days while she gets back on her feet. I'm sorry, I should have told you."

Karen glared at him. "Back on her feet? And here I thought it was you who was receiving all the attention. Or is that bandage something you picked up at the dime store?"

"Karen . . ." He shook his head. "No, it's not like that—"

"Then what is it like, Jan? You take me for a fool?" The daggers from her eyes tore at his heart. *No, Karen! It's not like that! I do care for you!*

But you love Helen.

"Please—"

"Save your breath." She was already walking for the front door. "If you need me, do us both a favor and call Roald." Then, with a slam of the door, she was gone.

For a long moment Jan and Helen just stared at that closed door in silence. "Maybe I should go," Helen finally said.

"No! No, please don't leave me."

"She seemed so . . . hurt."

"But it's not you. It's me. It's my love for you."

She thought about that for a few moments, and then she came to him and put her head on his chest. "I'm sorry," she said.

"No, don't be." He stroked her hair. "Please don't be."

NEVER BEFORE had Helen felt so chosen. It was how she came to see the meeting with Karen. She'd been chosen by Jan. Not chosen as Jan's girl, necessarily, or even as the woman who belonged in this crazy scenario. Just . . . chosen. To think of it beyond that led only to confusion. And whom had *she* chosen? Glenn or Jan?

Jan.

On Thursday, Jan emerged without the head wrap. It had been a week since his attack; four days since his hospital visit; three days since Helen's return. The two-inch cut above his right ear was healing remarkably well. He carried himself like someone who'd just discovered a great secret, and Helen caught him looking at her strangely on occasion, as if there was something in her eyes that threw him for a loop. At times he seemed to have difficulty keeping his gaze from her. Not that she minded. Goodness, no! She didn't know what to do with it, but she certainly didn't mind.

He made mention of a man named Roald a few times, a man associated with his work. Something about the fact that Roald would just have to adjust. They seemed busier that day, eager for the day to run its course. Several times she heard Jan and Ivena talking in soft tones, and she let them have their space. If the talk concerned her, she didn't care. Actually, it probably did concern her—what else would they be discussing concerning the police and Glenn? But hearing this she wanted to interfere even less.

She continued her reading of *The Dance of the Dead*, and it struck her that the central character in the book was perhaps the most profound person she'd heard of or read about. The fact that his name was Jan Jovic and that he was in the next room talking to Ivena, the mother of the daughter, Nadia, was difficult to believe. The fact that he had winked at her no less than three times that very day was mind numbing. She had winked back, of course, and he'd turned red each time.

Ivena left at five o'clock, after a long talk with Jan in the backyard. They were up to no good, those two. "I will see you tomorrow, Helen," she announced wearing a grand grin. "Behave yourself and don't let Janjic out of your sight. He is trouble-prone, you know." She winked.

"I wouldn't dream of it, Ivena."

Jan walked up behind her. "We're not children, Ivena."

"I know. And this is supposed to comfort me?"

They laughed and Ivena was off in her little gray Bug.

She'd been gone for less than ten minutes before Jan entered the living room and made his grand announcement. "Helen, I think that you owe me a date. Am I right?"

She laughed nervously. "I guess."

"You guess? Either I am right or I'm not, my dear. Which is it?"

"You're right. I did stand you up, didn't I?"

"Well then, shall we?"

"Now?"

"Yes, now."

"To where?"

"Ah, but that would ruin my surprise."

"Wearing this?" she asked, indicating her jeans and T-shirt.

"You look lovely."

She stood, smiling nervously. "You're saying that you want to take me on a date now? Right now?"

"Yes. That's what I'm saying."

"You're sure?"

"I insist. Have I given you any other impression since you first came back?"

"No."

He smiled very wide. "Okay, then." He stretched out his hand.

Helen touched it . . . then took it. "Okay, then."

CHAPTER TWENTY-FOUR

IT HAD been a bad week for Glenn Lutz. A very bad week indeed.

Homicide detective Charlie Wilks and another cop, Parsons, sat across from him in black suede guest chairs, the only furniture in the office other than his desk. They sat with crossed legs, their hands in their laps, avoiding his direct glare, isolated in the top story of the East Tower. They, like the Atlanta sky beyond the great glass wall to their left, wore a gray pallor of death.

Glenn was losing his patience with them. In fact, he'd lost his patience long before their arrival, when Beatrice had first informed him that Charlie needed to see him. It meant that the slime-ball preacher had whined like some two-bit hooker.

"So you receive one call from some lowlife preacher and you come whimpering to me? Is that all the esteemed Atlanta police force is good for these days? Can't you go find yourselves a cat to haul from a tree or something?"

"If we were talking about one call from some lowlife preacher, we wouldn't be here and you know it, Glenn," Charlie returned. "We interviewed him in the hospital and we checked the guy out. He's one of the most popular religious figures in America." The detective nodded to a copy of *The Dance of the Dead* sitting on Glenn's desk. "A fact you seem to have familiarized yourself with already."

"Yeah, so the guy's a writer. Does that make his word better than mine? I thought we had an understanding."

"We do have an understanding. You keep your habits out of the public, and I won't throw any fits. This Jan character is definitely a public man."

"Actually, as I recall, the understanding was you keep your hands off and I get you elected."

Wilks smiled uneasily and turned pink around the collar. "Come on, Glenn. I'm not a magician. You can't expect me to keep my hands in my pockets every time you haul some upstanding citizen in and beat him up. Who's next, the mayor?"

"This punk's not the mayor, and I'm not saying that I did beat him. And as far as Mayor Burkhouse is concerned, he may be the mayor today, but you just remind him that he *is* up for re-election in nine months."

Charlie scowled briefly. "Come on, Glenn. Come on, man, we all go way back. All I'm saying is that there are ways and there are ways, you know what I mean? Not everyone's attention is best arrested by a club to the head. I don't need you upsetting the balance we have by making a public display of people like this Jan fellow."

Glenn looked at the detective and thought about reaching into the desk drawer for his revolver. Put a hole in that forehead. That was absurd, of course. He might have this city by the short hairs, but that was *because of,* not in spite of, men like Charlie here.

He glanced at the book on his desk. Jan Jovic was no louse. He'd been through more than most; had to hand him credit there. There was as of yet no conclusive evidence that Helen had gone back to him, but if it surfaced that she had, Glenn would have to kill the preacher, that much he knew with certainty. It was one thing for a man to stumble onto your possession and mistakenly think it his for a time. It was another thing for that man to be schooled in the matter for a couple of days and then still have the gall to take what was not his.

Glenn placed his hand on the book and tapped its red cover lightly. "This man isn't doing me any favors, Charlie. If he touches my girl, I'm gonna have to kill him. She's been gone for two days now, and if it turns out that she even went near him, I'm gonna have to put a slug in his head. You know that, don't you?"

Charlie lifted his hands in resignation. "No, I don't know that, Glenn. This guy made a complaint, for crying out loud! He turns up dead and I'm supposed to say what? 'Oh, well, let's never mind that one'?"

"He came here to threaten me. I defended myself. That's the story. And you watch your tone in my office! Do something useful—go find Helen. You should be turning this punk's house inside out but instead you're here telling me how to run my business."

Charlie shook his head slowly. "I can't cover up everything. Some things have a life of their own, and I'm telling you this is one of them."

The man needed a lesson in respect, Glenn thought bitterly.

"Did you know that Delmont Pictures just announced a movie deal with this guy?" Charlie asked. "That book there is slated to be on the silver screen soon, and you're sitting here talking about taking out its main character. You think I can cover that up?"

Glenn squinted. "Delmont Pictures? Delmont Pictures is making a film about *this* guy?"

"That's right. News to you, I take it. Maybe if you took a bath and got your head out of that powder now and then, you'd know what—"

"Shut up!" Glenn shoved a huge hand toward the door. "Get out!"

They stood to their feet. Detective Parsons was wide-eyed, but Charlie was not as easily influenced as he once was. He'd seen this all before—one too many times, it appeared.

"Out, out, out!" Glenn jabbed his forefinger at the door.

"We're getting out, Glenn. But you remember what I said. I can only do so much. Don't cut your own throat."

"Out!" Glenn thundered.

They left.

It had been a bad week. A very bad week indeed.

JAN DROVE the Cadillac in silence, his stomach floating with anticipation, exchanging amused glances with Helen and generally ignoring her questions as to their destination.

She had brought the magic into his house with those blue eyes, Jan thought. She had appeared at his doorstep dressed in her wrinkled dress, trying so hard to find acceptance, feeling despondent and puny, when all the while it was *she* who carried the power. *She!* It was a power to intoxicate with a single look. The magic to send him to the ground, weak-kneed, with a casual glance. The ability to squeeze his heart with the delicate shift of her hand. She could move her chin, just so, to ask for some more bacon or another glass of tea, and his breathing might thicken right there at the table. It was a raw power, maddening and exhilarating at once. And it was she who possessed it. *Helen.*

If she only knew this—if she could only grasp her hold over his thoughts, if she too could feel, actually *feel* this same love for him—they could rule the world together. Never mind that she was from the street, it was nothing in the face of these emotions that swept through him.

But she didn't know her own power, he thought. Not the way he knew it. Well, tonight that might change. And the thought of it made Jan's stomach rise to his chest as he pulled the Cadillac along the deserted drive, toward the dead end.

"This is it?" Helen asked.

"What time is it?"

"Almost seven."

"Let's hope we are not late."

A round white moon cast a perpetual twilight over a wall directly ahead, perhaps twelve feet in height, extending each way as far as Jan could see. Vines covered the barrier, thick and dark but still green by the bright moonlight. No other structures were in sight, only this tall fence. Jan stopped the car and turned off the ignition.

"This is it?"

He looked at her and winked. "Follow me, my dear."

They climbed out. "This way." He led her to a small gate buried in vines, cut from the wall, no more than five feet tall. Jan looked back and saw that she stepped lightly, her eyes wide and casting their spell without even looking at him. His heart was bucking already. *Father, this is what you mean. Yes?*

He rapped on a section of wood bared from vines. He glanced back and winked. "Jan Jovic is not a man without friends, my dear."

A muffled call answered and the gate swung in. Jan stooped and walked through the entrance, followed by a hesitant Helen. The man who'd opened the gate stood to Jan's shoulder and wore a smile that could have been stolen from a happy-face sticker. "Thank you, my friend. I won't forget this." He turned to Helen. "Helen, meet Joey, Atlanta's premier expert on botany. He's the gardener here. A friend of mine."

She took his hand and gazed about. "Where *are* we?"

They stood at the edge of a sprawling garden—a botanical garden with flowering trees and rosebushes and perfectly groomed hedges as far as they could see. Flagstones surrounded by tiny white flowers led deeper and then branched in three directions within twenty paces. Tall shaped trees stood like guardians over the prize below them; gazebos spotted the paths, each laden with red and blue and yellow flowers glowing by moonlight. It was a paradise.

"You ever hear of the Garden of Eden?" Joey asked. "This is the closest you'll find on earth today. Welcome to the Twelve Oaks Botanical Gardens, my friends. A gift from God with a little help from the taxpayers."

They looked about without responding. They could not respond, Jan thought. It was a breathtaking sight in the moon's surreal hue.

"You kids enjoy," Joey said with a wink. "Lock up when you leave." He walked down the path, around a bush and disappeared from their sight.

Jan stood there in the quiet and suddenly his heart was sounding loud in his ears. This was it. He prayed a silent prayer—*Father, if it is your desire, make it so.*

Then he grabbed her hand and ran onto the path. "Come on!" he cried breathlessly.

Giggling, she ran behind him. Her hand felt cool and soft in his. He was feeling everything. The breeze against his face, the flagstone underfoot, the sweet smell of flowers lifting through his nostrils. He released her hand and ran between two tall trees shaped like rockets poised for launch. A thick lawn opened before him and he veered to the right.

She chased him, squealing with delight now. "Jan! Don't lose me. Where are we going?"

"Come on!" he cried. "Come on!"

They raced through the garden; he without direction, only acutely aware of her breathing just behind and to his left; she gaining on him and that was good. *Catch me, my darling. Catch me and touch me.*

Then she did. She reached out and touched his side, still giggling. Her finger sent a chill through his skin. Jan pulled up and swung to her. Helen ran full into his arms. He held her and twirled around as if they were on a dance floor and this was an embrace in motion. She laughed and threw her head back.

It was the first time he had held her without tears and he thought his heart would burst from the joy of it. He wanted to say something—something smart or romantic, but he forgot how to speak in that moment. The moon shone on her neck, and her small Adam's apple bobbed barely as she laughed—it was this he saw and he couldn't stand its power over him.

It is only a whisper of what I feel, Jan.

The voice spoke in his mind and he nearly stumbled, mid-twirl. So then Ivena was right. It was beyond him. But then he knew that already. *I love you, Father.*

Jan broke away, laughing with Helen now, feeling more alive than he thought possible. He jumped into the air like a child. *I love you, Father! I love you, I love you, I love you!* Then he faced Helen and his love for her and the Father were nearly the same.

He winked at her and ran farther into the garden.

She flew after him; they were two birds frolicking in flight. They tore through the garden, falling into a sort of hide-and-seek on the run. It was the finding that attracted them, and they did it as frequently as possible, at nearly every bush large enough to conceal whoever led the chase until the other caught up for an embrace.

Jan plucked a yellow flower and placed it in her hair above her ear. She found it funny and picked another for his hair. Time was lost. Man had been created for this. It was the kind of thing a man might sell everything he owned for, Jan thought. But it could not be bought.

Spare me, Father, or I will die looking at her. You've put a fire in my heart and I cannot tame it. But no, don't quench it! Feed it. Feed it until it consumes me.

Robbed of breath from the run and aware for the first time that his wounds sent a slight ache through his chest, Jan swung into a gazebo and crashed back into a bench. She hopped into the seat opposite him and they sat sprawled, panting and laughing and looking at each other.

This is it, Jan thought. *This is what I have waited my whole life for. This madness called love.* He put his head back on the latticework, looked to the sky and groaned. "Oh, my dear God, it's too much."

He looked back at Helen. She was staring at him with a wide smile, catching her breath. "This is what I call a date, Jan Jovic."

"You like?" he asked, mimicking her customary verbiage.

"I like. I most definitely like."

"I couldn't think of a place more suited for you."

She sat up and leaned on both arms. "Meaning what, Wordsmith?"

"The flowers, the smell of sweet honey, the rich green grass, the moon—they're nearly as beautiful as you."

She blushed and turned to face the lawn. Goodness, that had been rather forward, hadn't it! He followed her gaze. He had not noticed before, but the lawn sloped to a fountain, surrounded by a glimmering pool. It was a warm night and a breeze drifted over the water to cool them. The rich smell of a thousand musky flowers lining the gazebo filled the air. In this very private garden they had found a secret place, hidden from the bright moon's direct glare but washed in its light.

"We're not so different, you and I," Jan said.

"We are very different. I could never measure up to you." She had grown sober.

"Nor I you."

"Don't be silly. You're a rich man," she said. "A good man."

"And your grace could not be bought with the wealth of kings."

She turned to him, grinning. "My, we *are* a wordsmith, aren't we?"

"There aren't words for you, Helen. Not ones which tell with any clarity what should be told."

Helen was staring at him now, her blue eyes swimming in the moonlight. She held him in her gaze for a long time before standing and walking to the gazebo's arching entrance to face the moon with her back to him. "This can't happen," she said softly. "We're from different worlds, Jan. You've got no idea who I am."

"But I do. You're a woman. A precious woman for whom all of heaven weeps. And my heart has joined them."

"Don't be crazy! It's too much. I have no business being here with you." The strain of tears had entered her voice. "I'm a drug addict."

He stood and approached her from behind. "And I am desperate for you." He couldn't help himself. He could not bear to hear her speak like this. His heart was pounding in his chest and he wanted only to hold her. The madness was so very heavy.

"I'm sick," she bit off bitterly. "I . . ."

And then she ran. She ran from the gazebo and around a row of short pines, crying in the night.

Oh, dear Father, no! This can't happen! Jan bolted after her. "Helen!" His voice rang in the night, desperate, as if braying in death.

"Helen, please!" He caught sight of her fleeing around a bush ahead and he tore after her. "Helen, I beg you, stop! You must stop, I beg you. Please!" He was near panic. How could she have swung in his arms one moment and now fled so quickly?

He saw her ahead, running fast in the moonlight and then disappearing around a billowing hydrangea. "Helen!"

Jan reached the bush, but she was not in sight. He ran on, looking in all directions for her, but she had vanished. "Helen! Please, Helen!"

The night echoed his call and fell silent. Jan pulled up, panting hard. He clutched his gut against a sharp pain that had speared him there. His vision blurred with tears, and he mumbled, "Oh, God, my God, my God, what have you done?"

The sound of a soft cry drifted to him and he spun to a row of gardenia bushes. He released his stomach, the pain forgotten, and he stumbled forward. The sound carried on the night, a soft gulping sob.

He rounded the flowers and stopped. She sat on a bench, head planted in her hands, crying. Jan walked to the bench on shaking legs. He sat and swallowed.

"I am so sorry for your pain, Helen. I am so very sorry."

"You don't understand. I'm no good for you," she said softly.

"I will decide what is good for me. *You* are good for me. You are perfect for me!" He placed a hand on her shoulder.

She pulled back. "I'm dirty. I'm—"

"You are clean and you have stolen my heart!" he blurted. "Helen, please look at me. Look into my eyes." He shifted around and lifted a hand to her chin.

She looked up, her face wrinkled in shame, her eyes swimming in tears.

"What do you see, Helen?"

For a moment she didn't speak.

"What do you see?"

She spoke very softly. "I see your eyes."

"And what do they say to you?"

She wiped her face, breathing steadily, catching her breath. "They say you're hurting."

"And why? Why am I hurting?"

She hesitated. "Because your heart aches."

He held her eyes in his stare, begging her to say more. To see more. A knot rose to his throat. *My poor Helen, you are so wounded.*

She had settled and she blinked. "Your heart aches for me," she said.

Jan nodded. "Put your hand on mine," he said, reaching his right hand out, palm up. She did so gently, without removing her gaze from his. Her touch seemed to run right up his bones and lock itself around his heart.

"Do you feel that?"

She didn't respond, but she moved her hand slightly. Their breathing sounded loud in the night.

"What do you feel?"

She swallowed and he noted that both of their hands were trembling with the touch. Her eyes were pooling with tears again.

"How does it feel?"

"It feels nice."

"And when I speak to you, when I say, '*I am mad about you,*' what do you feel, Helen?" He was having difficulty speaking for the pounding of his own heart.

"I feel mad about you," she said. He couldn't be certain, but he thought she might have leaned forward slightly, and that made him dizzy.

Jan reached his free hand to her cheek and stroked it gently. He slid his other hand up her arm now, and every nerve in his body screamed out for her love. She *was* leaning forward! She was leaning forward and the tears were slipping silently down her cheek.

Jan could not hold himself any longer. He slid his arms around her shoulders and drew her against him. The tears flooded his eyes then. She pushed him back and for one terrible moment he wondered what she was doing. But her lips found his and they kissed. They held each other tenderly and they kissed deep.

It was as though he had been created for this moment, he thought. As though he were a man parched bone-dry in a desert, and now he had fallen upon a pool of sweet water. He drank deep from that pool, from her lips. From this deep reservoir of love. The moments stretched, but time had lost itself in their passion.

It is only a whisper of how I feel, Jan.

The voice again. Softly. Gently.

Jan released her and they played with each other's fingers, lightheaded, shy. "It feels too good to be true," Helen said. "I've never felt this kind of love."

He did not respond but reached for her and kissed her lightly on her lips again. His heart was kicking madly against his chest; if he wasn't careful he might fall over dead right here in Joey's Garden of Eden.

Jan rose to his feet and pulled her up. "Come."

They walked through the hedges, hand in hand, lovers numb from each other's touch. Everything they saw now had a heavenly glow. The flowers seemed unnaturally bright by the moon's light. Their senses ran sharp edges, feeling and tasting and smelling the air as if it were laden with a potion concocted to squeeze their hearts.

They walked laughing and giggling, stunned that such care had been taken for their benefit. Anyone watching might very well see them and think them drunk. And truth be told they *were* drunk. They had sipped from each other's lips and were inebriated beyond their reason. It was a consuming love that swept them through the garden. They might have tried walking on the pond had it come to mind.

And yet for Jan, it was all just beginning. He had not brought her to the garden for this alone. Not at all. They reached a white metal pillar at the end of a long flowered archway and he knew it was time. If it was not now it might be never, and it definitely could not be never.

He gripped the pole and swung himself around to face her. She pulled up, surprised, with not an inch to spare between them. Her musky breath covered his nostrils. Her eyes flashed blue, and her lips impulsively reached forward and touched his. "I love you, Jan Jovic," she whispered. "I love you."

"Then marry me," he said.

She froze and pulled back. Their eyes held each other, round and glazed. Jan pushed a strand of hair from her cheek with his thumb. "Marry me, Helen. We are meant to be one."

Her mouth opened in shock, but she could not hide the smile. "Are you serious?"

"I'm madly in love with you. I've been madly in love with you from the time you walked up to me at the park. I can't imagine spending my days without you. I am meant to be with you. Anything less would destroy me."

She blinked and looked into his eyes. "I . . . I don't know what to say."

"Say yes."

"Yes."

He kissed her. His world began to explode then, and he knew he could not contain the passion that racked his bones. He had to do something, so he stepped back and leaped into the air. He whooped and beat the air with his fist. Helen laughed and hopped on his back. He cried out in surprise and not a little pain, and then collapsed to the sod. They lay there panting, smiling up at the stars and then at each other.

It was the end of a long journey, Jan thought. A very long journey that began with the priest's departure to heaven and now deposited him here, in a heaven of his own.

But it was also just the beginning. He knew that too, and a fleeting terror sliced through his mind. But the intoxicating lips of his new bride-to-be smothered him with a kiss, and the terror was lost.

For now, the terror was lost.

THE PHONE rang five times before Ivena picked it up. "Hello."

"Morning, Ivena."

"Good morning, Joey."

"How's the garden?"

"Good. Very good."

"And the flowers?"

"Growing."

"The tests came back today, Ivena."

She didn't respond.

"It's an unknown species."

"Yes."

"They're . . . extraordinary, you know." He cleared his throat. "I mean very unusual."

"Yes, I know."

"My flower has taken root."

Silence filled the phone.

"Ivena?"

"Then guard it well, Joey. It's not for everyone to see."

"Yes, I think you're right. Do you want to hear what I found?"

She hesitated. "Not now. Come over and explain it to me sometime. I have to go now, Joey."

"You okay, Ivena?"

"I've never been better. Never."

BOOK THREE

The Lover

"As a bridegroom rejoices over his bride,
so will your God rejoice over you."

Isaiah 62:5 NIV

"I remember the devotion of your youth,
how as a bride you loved me . . ."

Jeremiah 2:2 NIV

CHAPTER TWENTY-FIVE

Three Months later

GLENN LUTZ stormed through the walkway between the Twin Towers like a bull, panting from the exertion, his hands red with blood. The passage was not air-conditioned and Atlanta's late-day heat pressed through his skin. He was slipping into the boiling waters of madness and there was no life preserver in sight. Even the violence he periodically delivered to some unsuspecting soul who crossed him no longer eased his fury. Detective Charlie Wilks had approached him three times in the last month, begging him to ease up. Well now he could expect another call, just as soon as the detective learned of the whipping he'd just administered. Beating the mayor's third cousin to a pulp had a ring of absurdity to it, which was perhaps why Glenn had not been able to resist.

Maybe one day he would take his whip to old Charlie—now there would be a smart move. His relationship with the man wasn't as cozy as it once had been. One of these days Charlie might forget their past altogether and send in a hit squad. Which was why Glenn *had* gone easy. Which was why he had left the preacher alone. Which was why he hadn't gone out with a Tommy gun and sawed through Jan.

Glenn slammed through the door to his office. "Beatrice!" She wasn't here. He swore, crossed to his desk and punched the intercom. "Beatrice, get in here. Bring a towel."

He held his hands up, careful not to make too much of a mess. His knuckles glistened red; half of the blood was probably his own.

Beatrice walked in, took one look at his hands, and *tsked.* "You really should stop this nonsense, you know. Let her go." She tossed him the white towel. "You have a luncheon tomorrow; you think people won't notice skinned knuckles?"

He wiped his hands without answering her. Beatrice was growing as bold as Charlie. She sat in one of the guest chairs across from his desk and studied him condescendingly, as if she were his mother. He slid into his chair. It was an odd relationship, this depending so completely on someone you detested so much. And in truth, besides Helen, she was his dearest friend. It was a horrible thought.

"But I take it you aren't going to let her go her way, are you?" Beatrice said.

"Her way is my way."

"On occasion, obviously, or she wouldn't keep coming. But she is married to another man now. She's been married to him for two months, and I don't see divorce papers floating around anywhere. She's chosen him."

Glenn crashed his fist on the desk. "She has *not* chosen him! He's a witch!"

"He's a religious man," she corrected. "And I thought I was the witch."

"Same thing. No one could have swept her off her feet like that."

"Maybe it would be best if she was faithful to him. Best for you, that is."

He stared at her and scowled.

They sat in silence for a few moments, she swinging one leg over the other with hands folded; he mulling over a mental image of his fists smashing into that long face.

"You should find yourself another woman, Glenn," Beatrice said.

"And you should find yourself some sense, Beatrice. There is no replacement for Helen. You know that."

"Why? Because of something that happened twenty years ago? Because you were called Peter then and were possessed by an adolescent obsession for her? You're no longer fifteen, Glenn. And Helen is no longer the prom queen. I could find you a dozen girls far better than her."

"Uhhh!" He grunted and slammed both fists on the desk top once. Then twice. He frowned at her. "Do you know why I make in a single day what you'll never make in your entire life, Beatrice? I'll tell you why. Because I know how to get what I want, and you don't even *know* what you want! Because I *am* obsessed! And you are possessed. *I* own you. You remember that."

She blinked at the reprimand.

He leaned back and closed his eyes, furious with her. In fact he did feel possessed at times, unable to function for the voices in his head. But it had been the same for as long as he could remember. When he first caught sight of Helen across the hall in junior high, for example, wearing her navy skirt and sucking on a lollipop.

Her image danced over the rope in his mind's eyes, blue skirt flapping in slow motion. *One, two, buckle my shoe; three, four, close the door; five, six, peek-a-boo, guess who I am; that's right, and you ain't seen nothing yet.*

"I'm going to help her out," Glenn said, shifting his eyes toward the glass wall on his left. It had been two months coming and now it was time. Charlie could go suck on a tailpipe. He'd played by the fool's rules long enough.

"You're going to help her out? And how are you going to help Helen out?"

Glenn did not look at her. "I'm going to give her a little motivation."

"The movie deal?"

"Yes. But . . . more."

He could hear her breathing in the stillness now. It was the way he said *more*, he thought. As in, much more. As in terribly much more. He faced Beatrice now, pleased that she had kept silent.

"They say that the path to some women's hearts runs through the skull," he said quietly.

"They say that?"

"I say that."

"Charlie won't sit by if you hurt the preacher."

"Who said anything about the preacher?"

She shifted in her seat, all two hundred pounds of her, squirming. Glenn smiled and spoke softly before she could ask another question. "I'm telling you this so that you'll quit flapping your jaw, Beatrice. Soon this'll all be over. I'm going to force the issue. So you can shut your hole, and be a good witch."

She stared him down, but not with her usual backbone. His power had softened her some, he thought. She still wasn't speaking.

"But yes, the movie deal. I want the movie deal done this week. Can we do that?"

"Maybe. Yes," she said.

"I don't care what it takes, Beatrice. Anything, you understand?"

"Yes. This does not sound especially smart, Glenn."

His hands trembled on the desk, but he said nothing.

"Does she know who you really are?"

Shut up, Beatrice! Shut up, you fat weasel! Glenn bit his tongue to keep the thoughts from blurting out. "No. No, she doesn't know anything. And in truth, neither do you. Not even close."

Beatrice stared at him for a full five seconds and then stood and left the room, waddling like a black duck.

Glenn exhaled slowly and rested his head back on the chair, thoughts of Beatrice already dismissed. It was Helen who filled his mind again. Helen, who had evaded him for so long. Helen, who was about to learn who her lover really was. Helen, that two-timing sick worm. Helen, sweet, sweet Helen.

HELEN SET the breakfast table carefully, humming absently. Outside, the morning birds chirped and skittered about the large willow's branches. It had rained in the night, leaving the air cool and the shrubs glistening, washed of the summer dust. A scattering of leaves drifted on the pool's glassy surface. *I'm home,* Helen thought. *This is my home.*

It struck her that the tune she'd been humming was the old hymn Ivena often sang: "Jesus, Lover of My Soul." Antique lyrics but a rather catchy tune once you let it set in. To think that two months ago she'd never even heard the tune. And now here she was, bouncing around Jan's kitchen—her kitchen—wearing a pink house robe, arranging place settings and orange juice for two.

She had heard of whirlwind romances before but hers and Jan's had been a tornado. A storybook affair, scripted perfectly with everything except the glass slippers. Even the wedding had been fanciful, under a bright sun in that very garden—Joey's Garden of Eden—with a minister and thirty or so witnesses, exactly four weeks to the day after Jan had asked for her hand. And these first seven weeks had drifted by in a hazy bliss. Nearly perfect.

Nearly.

"Good morning, dear." Helen started and spun to his voice. Jan stood less than a step from her, smiling warmly, dressed to kill in a crisp white shirt and a red tie. A dusting of gray swept along the sides of his wavy dark blond hair, disheveled above those bright hazel eyes. Her handsome Serb.

He stepped forward and kissed her forehead. "How's my peach tree?"

She chuckled and kissed his chest without answering. He was like this always—loving and warm and saturated with passion for her. His love leaked from every pore of his body. And she was not worthy of it. Not she.

"Good morning. Sleep well?"

"Like a baby. You know I still haven't had the dream—not once in three months. Twenty years like clockwork, and then you walk into my life and the dreams end. Now tell me you're not a gift from God himself."

"What can I say? Some of us have it and some of us don't. I made us some breakfast," she said, grinning. He slid onto his chair at the table's head and lifted his glass of orange juice with a wink. "And you most definitely have it." He took a long drink and set the glass down with obvious ceremony and a long sigh.

"Perfect," he said. "It's the perfect drink for the occasion."

"Occasion? What occasion?"

"It's been seven weeks. Seven. The number of perfection, you know. They say that if your first seven weeks go without a hitch, you're in for another seven years without a single conflict."

She smiled. "I've never heard any such thing," she said.

"Hmm. Maybe because I made it up. But it's a good saying, don't you think?"

She joined him, laughing now despite herself. "You see things too simplistically, honey." *Honey.* She was calling this man such an endearing term and it suddenly struck her as odd, in light of what he did not know. But he was that and more. Far more. A perfect man. He was looking at her now, across the table as he often did, obviously pleased at the sight of her. She tried not to notice, but failed with a blush.

She directed the conversation to more rote matters. "So what do you have on your plate today?"

"Today. Today it's business as usual, but I have to fly to New York on Friday."

Helen blinked. "Again? You were just there three days ago." Her heart quickened at the revelation.

"Yes, I was. And I'm sorry to leave you alone in the house again so soon. But Delmont Pictures called last night and insisted we make this meeting. I'm sure it's nothing. You know these movie people; everything's always urgent." He grinned as if she should find some amusement in that. But her mind was already nibbling at the notion of having another weekend alone.

"Perhaps Ivena could come and stay the weekend with you," Jan suggested, biting into his cereal.

"No. No, I'll be okay." Helen returned his smile. "I might as well get used to it. It comes with marrying a star, I suppose," she teased.

He tossed his head back and laughed. "Nonsense. And if you married a star, then I married a queen."

She giggled with him and picked at her breakfast. *Oh, dear Jan, please do not leave me alone!*

"Besides," she said, "I'm not sure Ivena would cotton to being torn away from her garden for a whole weekend. Is it just me or is she obsessive?"

Jan chuckled. "She is taken with it, isn't she? You know, since our marriage I don't think I've even been in her greenhouse. In fact I've only been in her house once or twice. We really should visit her more often."

"She visits us all the time. I think she likes it that way. But still, she seems to have changed."

"In what way?"

"I don't know. She always seems to be in a hurry to get home. Preoccupied."

"I haven't noticed. But then my mind's been on another woman these past few months."

"Well, at least you've got that right." They laughed and picked at their breakfast.

"You're all right when I leave you, aren't you, Helen?" Jan asked.

"Yes, of course. Sure, of course. Why wouldn't I be?"

He grinned. "A beautiful woman like you? If another man even glances in your direction while passing on the street, you tell me. I will discipline him, I promise. With my belt or a paddle."

"Don't be silly. You'll do no such thing." He was such a lovely man. In moments like this he could take her breath away with those crazy comments.

"Still, you are a beautiful woman. Please be careful."

"Don't worry, my ever-protective lover. I will behave." Helen said it and then diverted the discourse again. "Roald will be there?"

"In New York? Roald and Karen both."

"Karen?"

"Yes, Karen."

"So you'll see her again."

"In a matter of speaking. At a meeting. She *is* still the agent of record on this picture, and she stands to gain or lose a tremendous amount of money, depending on how well it does. Not that money was ever Karen's primary motivation."

"No, you were," Helen said with a smile. "Or maybe your status was."

"Perhaps. Betty tells me that she's seeing someone in New York. A producer. It was just as well she moved back."

"Well, you don't need her in the office anyway. You have Betty and the others."

"It's still a bit quiet. Roald's been to the office only twice since . . ."

"Since you married the tramp," Helen filled in.

"Nonsense!"

"You know that's how he feels. Don't worry, I'm used to it."

"And you shouldn't be used to it." His face was suddenly red. "Ever!"

"Okay, Jan." She couldn't help her smile.

He exhaled and continued. "Anyway, you're right: the others have been very supportive. It's nearly like the old days, only without Roald and Karen. And actually, you'd never know anything had changed by the flow of money. I'll tell you, Helen, I've never seen so much money. When you deal in millions, the world changes. Speaking of which, your Mustang is due in at the dealership today. Should I have it picked up?"

"Serious?"

"It is what you asked for, isn't it? A red convertible?"

"Yes."

"Then it's in. I'll have Steve pick it up."

She looked at him with a sense of wonder. It was hard to believe that she actually owned half of what he did, which was a lot now. And it wasn't bothering him one bit. The Mustang was the least of it. They had spent the first week in Jamaica and there Jan had begun with the gifts, each given as if it were but a small token of his love. A diamond necklace over a candlelight lobster dinner, a pair of sparkling emerald earrings on a moonlit beach, impossibly expensive perfume under her pillow. A dozen others. But it was the new home he had conceived for her—the castle, he liked to call it—that often lit his eyes. A home twice the size of this meager cottage. One fit for his bride, nothing less would do. He'd already purchased the forty acres on which construction was slated to begin in one week. Two months ago the expense would have been unthinkable. But to hear Jan speak of it, now anything less would be beneath them. It consumed most of his energies these days. The book, the movie, the money; they were the fruits of love. And there seemed to be no reasonable limits to his desire to express his love. She was his obsession.

And not his alone.

Jan looked out the window. "You know, if it wasn't for all this money, I wonder if Roald would have carried out his threats. I think he and his boys are still fuming under their collars, but the money has silenced them. Not that I'm complaining; they've done well to keep the matter private. Karen too. But I wonder where they would be without the money."

"You question their belief in you?"

"I never would have thought so, but I don't know now. Not everyone is as understanding or noble as you, my dear."

Noble? *No, Jan. I may have captured your heart, but I am not noble.*

"Money is the glue that holds us all together now," he said. "The ministry, the movie, the book—it all seems to have boiled down to a few million dollars."

"Wars have been fought for less," she said.

"True enough. But I think that when this movie is over, both Roald and Karen will be out of our lives. Of course, we won't need them, will we? We have enough now to live our lives out in comfort in our new home. I will be free to travel at leisure, speaking as I like. Not even their rumors will affect us."

"Sounds good to me." She stopped. "What rumors?"

He blinked. "Rumors. They're nothing."

"They're about me?"

He hesitated.

"They're about me. Tell me."

He sighed. "An article was written in a leading evangelical periodical, casting suspicion on any religious leader that would marry a woman with . . . how did they say it . . . questionable morals. You see, that is what they say. But they don't know you. And they certainly don't know me. And besides, like I said, as soon as the movie is made, it won't matter."

Heat washed over Helen's face. They were asinine! Hypocrites! When had one of them ever reached out to her with Christ's love? Even after she'd publicly prayed for forgiveness in Jan's church. And she had done it with complete sincerity, yet now these leaders were turning on her, openly questioning her morals? Men were such pigs. Churched or unchurched, they were evidently all the same. Except Jan, of course. Guilt nipped at her.

And if he were to discover the truth she might have to slit her wrists!

"You're right," Jan said to her silence. "It's absurd. It means nothing. Helen, look at me."

She did, feeling small and dumb at his table, but she did look at him. His eyes were sad and his mouth held a slight smile. "You must know one thing, my dear Helen. You are more precious to me than anything I could possibly imagine. Do you understand? You are everything to me."

She nodded. "Yes, I know that. But the world obviously doesn't share your feelings. It's a bit awkward being the hated half of a celebrity known for his love."

"No, no, no. Don't say that. Some love my book; some hate my book. It's not me they love or hate. And just because a few religious men take exception to you doesn't mean the whole world hates you." He grinned mischievously. "In fact, sometimes I think my own staff prefers you to me."

"Yeah, well that's Betty and John and Steve. But I swear, the church people . . ." She shook her head.

"And the church leaders are not the church, Helen. We are all the church. You and I. The bride of Christ. And you, my dear, are my bride."

His smile was infectious and she returned it. Jan threw his napkin on the table. "I have to go." He rounded the table and took her face in both of his hands. They were large, tender hands that had been brutalized by war and now took nothing for granted. "I love you, Helen," he said.

"I love you, Jan."

"More than words," he said, and he bent down.

She closed her eyes and let him kiss her lightly on her lips.

If you only knew, Jan.

He released her face and when she opened her eyes, he was already at the front door. He turned there. "Helen, when I am gone, be careful. Guard your heart. I could not bear to lose it," he said. Then he smiled and left without waiting for a response.

Helen was not so accustomed to praying, but she prayed now. "Oh, dear God, help us. Please, please, help us. Please help me."

CHAPTER TWENTY-SIX

IVENA STEPPED from her home Friday evening and took a long pull of fresh air into her lungs. The heat had been tempered by rains over the past few days, and looking at the boiling skies, she thought it would rain again tonight. Janjic had gone off to some meeting in New York again. Perhaps she would call Helen and ask her if she would like to come for a visit later. She was a bottle of heaven, Janjic's girl. And in some ways she was Ivena's girl too.

Ivena locked the door and stepped past her rosebushes onto the sidewalk. A black car rolled by slowly, headed in the same direction as she, toward the park three blocks west. A man looked absently at her from the side window. Thunder rumbled on the far horizon. The breeze swept through a row of huge leafy spruce trees across the street, like a green wave. Yes, it would rain soon but she wanted to walk for at least a few minutes.

Her mind buzzed with the awareness that he was near. That God was near. In fact, not since the days following Nadia's death so many years ago had God been so close. And when God was near, the human heart did not fare so well, she thought. It tended to turn to mush.

Ivena looked back to her small house with its greenhouse hidden behind the tall white fence. He was certainly in there, crawling all over his jungle of love. She stopped and faced the house, tempted to return to the garden. To the flowers and the aroma that could no longer be contained by the glass walls. The green vines had taken over not only the garden but her own heart, she thought. To step into the room was like entering the inner court, the bosom of God. She'd smelled the flowers a block from home once and feared someone had broken in. She'd run all the way only to find them swaying in the light breeze that sometimes moved through the room. She never had found its source.

Ivena turned and continued on her walk; she needed the exercise.

She could not be gone from the garden too long without being overcome by a yearning to return. And she had noticed something else. She was remembering things very clearly for some reason. Remembering the expression on her daughter's face when that beast Karadzic had pulled the trigger. Remembering the even drawing of Nadia's breath. And the slight smile. "I heard the laughter," Nadia had said.

"Oh, Father, show me your laughter," she mumbled quietly, walking with her arms wrapped around herself now.

Boom!

Ivena flinched. It was thunder, but it might as well have been the bullet to Nadia's head.

She sighed. "You know that I love you, Father. It still does not seem right that you've taken Nadia before me. Why must I wait?"

One day she would join her daughter and that day could not possibly come quickly enough. But it would not be today. For one thing, her body was showing no signs of slowing down. It might be another fifty years before natural causes took her. For another thing, she had a part to play in this drama about her. This passion play. She knew that like she knew that blood flowed through her veins, unseen but surging with life.

Nadia had heard the laughter of heaven, and the priest had *laughed* the laughter of heaven, right there on the cross, begging to go. Now Janjic had heard the heavens weeping.

And then Christ had planted his love for Helen in Janjic's heart.

Once Ivena understood that, she'd known that she was in a passion play. They were walking through Solomon's Song. Solomon's garden, more likely. A sprinkling of love from heaven, for the benefit of the mortals who wandered about, oblivious to the desperate longing of their Creator.

"And what of me, Father? When will I hear so clearly?"

Nothing but distant rumbles answered her. She reached the park's entrance and decided to walk once around before returning home, hopefully before the rain.

This drama unfolding behind man's eyes was a great thing. Much greater than the building of grand cities or towering pyramids. Greater than the winning of wars. It had a feel of far loftier purpose. As if the destiny of a million souls hung in the balance of these few lives. Of Janjic's story, *The Dance of the Dead.* Father Micheal, Nadia, Ivena, Janjic, Helen, Glenn Lutz—they were the main players here on earth. And the masses lived in ignorance of the struggle, while their own future was being decided.

The how and why were lost on Ivena. Only this vivid sense of purpose. But one thing she did know: This passion play was not over. Janjic may make his movie, but the story was not yet complete. And now she was being called to play a larger role. She did have the benefit of the garden, but as astounding as that was, she yearned for more. For a glimpse of heaven itself.

"Show me, Father. You cannot show me? You showed Nadia and Father Micheal and Janjic. Now show me. Don't leave me out here in the wind by myself."

The park was vacant except for her, she saw. That car she'd seen drive by sat parked near the outbuildings to her right, but she saw no people. It was a warm wind that blew through her hair, carrying the smell of freshly mowed grass. It reminded her of the smells from the garden in which Janjic and Helen were wed. A smile bunched her cheeks at the memory. Janjic had invited some of his closest friends and all of his employees to a dinner party, explained his heart and then presented his fiancée.

They were a conservative lot for the most part, and they had gawked at dear Helen as if she were from a newly discovered culture. But Betty, the motherly one, had given a rousing speech in the defense of love. It had quelled their doubts, she thought. At least some of their doubts. The rest had slowly faded in the weeks following. It was not every day that a man as respectable as Janjic reversed his engagement for another woman. Especially after only two weeks.

The ceremony had been simple and stunning. The setting was idyllic, yes, with all those flowers and perfectly manicured bushes, but it was the sight of Janjic and Helen together that turned the event into an unforgettable day. Her dear Serb simply could not keep his eyes from his bride. He stumbled through the day grinning from ear to ear, responding slowly when spoken to, terribly shy and thoroughly smitten. It was enough to keep the entire party in a perpetual blush. If only they knew the truth—that this display was nothing less than a clumsy mortal's attempt to contain a few cells from God's heart in his own.

Their love hadn't stopped there, of course. The two were inseparable. Yet, regardless of Janjic's love, he was still human. As human as ever and sometimes more, Ivena thought.

And Helen . . . Helen was categorically human.

A shadow shifted to her left and Ivena turned. Two men approached her, large men dressed in black cotton pants, looking past her at something. They had appeared rather suddenly, she thought. A moment ago the park was empty, and now these two strode toward her, now less then ten feet off. How was that possible?

She continued to walk and turned to her right to see what had caught their attention. But there was nothing.

Ivena had just started to turn back when a hand clamped around her face. They had come right to her! "Hey!" Her cry was stifled by a piece of cloth. The man was suffocating her! *Oh, dear God, these men are attacking me!*

"Hey!" she cried again, both arms flailing. Her voice was completely muffled by the hand this time, but she did manage to hit something soft and she heard a grunt.

A sharp metallic smell stung her nostrils, right through her sinuses. They were drugging her! Ivena's mind began to swim. Thunder rolled again, louder this time, unless that was how it felt to be drugged. Black clouds obscured her vision. She screamed at them then, but she knew that nothing was coming out. It was a wail in her own dim world.

Am I dying? Am I dying? she asked.

But Ivena did not know, because her question stopped in a pool of darkness. She slumped in her attacker's arms.

THE RAIN crashed down in sheets, bringing twilight an hour early to Atlanta. Helen stood by the sliding door to the backyard and watched droplets dance furiously on the pool's surface. Behind her the house lay in dim shadows, silent except for the dull roar of rain. She should really turn on the lights, but she lacked the motivation to move just now.

Jan had left for New York. He would be up to his eyeballs in meetings right now, being important. Being the star. *I need you, Jan. I need . . .*

You need what, Helen? Jan? Or the feelings he will bring you? Call Ivena.

She ground her teeth. The urges had started at noon, a muddled mix of desire and horror stuffed in her chest. She wasn't physically addicted, she knew that because she'd broken her addiction in those first four weeks of abstinence, with the help of a drug counselor, as Jan called him. Still, her mind was craving; her *heart* seemed hooked. She didn't understand how all of that worked, but she did know that her mind was hooked. She couldn't break the mad desperation that raged through her veins. Physical dependence would've been easier, she thought. At least with it, she would have an excuse people might understand.

But this craving was maybe worse. It was through her whole being.

Yet it was more than just the drug. Helen wanted the Palace. That horrible, terrible, evil place. That wonderful place. It was this realization that made her cringe.

You should call Ivena, Helen.

No! Helen spun from the door. She made her decision in that moment, and the shackles of her desperation fell away. She ran for the phone and snatched it from the wall. Now it was only desire that flooded her mind, and it felt good. God, she had missed that feeling. No, not God . . . She sealed the thought from her mind.

The witch answered the phone. "Beatrice. It's Helen."

Glenn's assistant drew a breath. "Yes?"

"Can you send a car?"

"The wench wants to return, is that it? And what if Glenn's not here?"

"Is he?"

Silence. The woman obviously wanted to say no. But her silence had answered already. "You don't know what you're messing with, honey."

"Shut up, you old witch. Just get me a car. And don't take all day."

She heard a few mumbled expletives. The phone went dead.

Helen hung up and retreated to the window, biting at her nails. Her heart thumped in anticipation now. The rain pelted in sheets, covering the concrete in a thick mist of its own splatter. It was like a shield, this dark rain. What happened now would be gone when the sun came out.

She ran about the house, turning on lights with trembling hands. She changed quickly into jeans and a yellow T-shirt. When the car pulled up fifteen minutes later, Helen bolted from the house, yanked the rear car door open, and plowed in. The driver was Buck. She leaned back in the safety of the dark cabin and breathed deep. The rich smell of cigarette smoke filled the car.

"Got a cigarette I can bum, Buck?"

He handed a pack of Camels back without answering. She lit one and drew on the tobacco. Rain thundered on the roof. The smoke filled her lungs and she smiled. She was going home, she thought. Just for a visit, but she was definitely going home.

They parked in the Tower's garage ten minutes later and rode the private elevator. It clanged to a stop at the top floor, and Helen stepped in the causeway that led to the Palace. "Go on in," Buck said. "He's waiting for you."

He was waiting? Of course he was waiting! Glenn would be waiting on his knees. And Jan . . . She snuffed out the thought.

She crept down the empty hall, expecting to see the witch at any time. But Beatrice wasn't here to greet her. Helen stopped at the entry door and tried to calm herself. But her pulse was having none of it. *This is insane, Helen. This is death.* It was the last thought before the door swung in under the pressure of her hand.

Helen entered the Palace.

Music greeted her. A soft rhythmic saxophone; the sound of Bert Kampfort, Glenn's choice of sensual tunes. The lights glowed in hues of red and yellow. It was hard to believe that she'd been here just last weekend and still the atmosphere was crashing in on her like a long-lost wave of pleasure. The dance floor reflected slowly turning pinpoints of light from the overhead mirrored ball.

"Helen."

Glenn! She spun toward the voice. He stood by the couch under the lion's head.

"Hi, Glenn." Helen stepped onto the floor. He wore his white polyester slacks, barefoot on the thick carpet. A yellow Hawaiian shirt hung loosely on his torso. His sweaty lips were peeled back in a wide grin, revealing his crooked teeth. This part of him—this dirty smelly part—had not stayed in her memory so well, but it came raging to the surface now. She needed the drugs. They would dull the edges.

Helen stopped three paces from him and saw for the first time the wet streaks on his cheeks. He had been crying. And it was not a grin but a grimace that twisted his face. His legs were shaking.

"Glenn? What's wrong? Are you okay?"

He sat heavily to the couch, crying openly now.

"Why are you crying?"

"You're killing me, Helen," he growled through clenched teeth. And then like a lost boy, "I can't stand it when you're gone. I miss you so much."

He was sick, she thought, and she wasn't sure whether to feel sorrow or revulsion for him. Large sweat stains darkened the pits of his shirt and she smelled the stench from his underarms. "I'm sorry, Glenn . . ."

He grunted like a hog and shot out of the seat in a blur of rage. His fist slammed into her solar plexus and she folded over his arm. Pain speared through her stomach. His fist crashed down on the crown of her head and she fell flat to the floor.

"You are killing me!" he screamed. "Don't you know that, Helen? You're killing me here!"

She curled into a ball, trying desperately to breathe.

"Helen? Do you hear me? Answer me." He knelt over her, breathing hard.

"Are you okay, dear?" He leaned close, so that his breath washed over her face. She caught a snatch of air and moaned.

A hot wet tongue slid up her cheek. He was licking her. Licking her face. She squelched a sudden urge to turn and bite his tongue off. It would be her death.

"Helen, my dear, I missed you so much."

She could breathe now and she feigned a giggle. "Glenn, dear. Give me some dope. Please."

"You want some dope, honey?" he asked, as if she were his baby.

"Yes."

"Beg."

"Please, Glenn." She kissed him.

He leaped from the floor like a child now. "I have a surprise for you, Helen. What do you want first, the dope or the surprise?" She pushed herself to her knees. His eyes glinted with delight.

She ran a finger along his arm seductively. "You have to ask? You know how much I like to fly, honey."

He threw his head back and howled with laughter. He was mad, she thought. He had actually lost his senses. Glenn led her to the bar where he produced a pile of powder and within the minute Helen was feeling better.

"Now the surprise," he insisted with a crackerjack grin.

"Yes, the surprise," Helen cried, raising her fist. She was feeling so much better. "Lead me on, my king."

His eyes flashed mischievously and he loped for the apartment. She followed, giggling now. "What is it? What is it, Glenn?"

"You'll see! You're gonna love it!"

He crashed through the door and pulled up. She stumbled in and peered about the apartment. "Where? What is it?"

Glenn's eyes glistened, round, eager. He kept his eyes on her and crept to the bathroom door. "Is it here?" he asked in play, and opened the door. She looked in. Nothing.

"No. Stop playing, you big oaf."

"Is it here?" he asked, lifting the bedspread.

"Come on, Glenn, you're driving me crazy. Show me."

He stepped to the closet, eyes wide, a gaping smile splitting his face. "Is it here?" he asked.

"What are you playing at, you silly—"

Her words caught in her throat. The closet was open. A person stood, bound like a mummy and propped in the corner. A woman.

Ivena!

At first Helen did not comprehend what she was seeing. Why was Ivena here? And wasn't it odd that she was tied up like that? The woman's eyes were open, looking at her, crying tears that wet the gag in her mouth.

Realization crept over Helen like a hot lava flow, searing her mind despite its state of numbness. Glenn had brought Ivena to the Palace! And he had hurt her, badly enough to produce a bloody nose and a bruised face.

Those soft brown eyes stared at Helen, and she felt her heart begin to break. "Ivena?" she croaked.

"Do you like my surprise, Helen?" Glenn asked. He was no longer smiling.

"Oh, Ivena. Oh, God, Ivena!" Helen sank to her knees. Her world began to swim. Maybe this was one of those bad trips.

Glenn was laughing now. He was enjoying this. His whole body shook like a bowl of jelly and that struck Helen as odd. The door to the closet was shut now, and she wondered what she had seen in there. She'd dreamed that Glenn had bound and gagged Ivena, of all people, and propped her up in the closet. Goodness, she was hallucinating badly.

Helen giggled with Glenn, testing the waters at first. But when he howled with humor, she let restraint fly out the window and joined him, laughing until she could hardly kneel, much less stand.

The world drifted into a safe place of fuzzy edges and warm feelings. She was home, wasn't she? Hands hauled her up onto the bed.

Yes, Helen had come home.

chapter twenty-seven

THE MASSIVE storm that pounded Atlanta stretched right up the eastern coast and dumped rain on New York that dark night as well. But in the delicate ambiance of Brazario's Fine Dining, the party from Delmont Pictures was oblivious to it. Here the light was soft, the smell of coffee rich, and the laughter gentle. Jan picked at his soft-shell crab and nodded at Tony Berhart's assertion that if a movie could make the women cry, it was destined for success. Well, *The Dance of the Dead* would make most men cry as well, he said, and that would make it unstoppable. The studio's VP of acquisitions lifted a toast to accent his point.

"Here, here," agreed Roald, who lifted his own glass in acknowledgment. They had arrived on different planes, he, Karen and Roald, all from separate states, brought together by the good folks at Delmont Pictures.

Karen sat across the table to Jan's right. Three tall red candles burned between them, casting an orange glow over her face. She laughed with Roald. She had perfected the art of socializing like few Jan knew, laughing at precisely the right moment but knowing when to stand up and be heard as well.

Jan thought back to their encounter just an hour earlier. The wind was blowing when he reached the restaurant, and he held the door for a woman approaching to his left. She was less than five feet away before they recognized each other.

Karen.

She pulled up as if slapped.

"Hello, Karen."

She recovered quickly. "Hello, Jan." She walked past him and he entered behind her.

"So, here we are then," he said. "We meet after all."

"Yes." She cast him a quick glance, then scanned the foyer for a sign of their hosts. "They should be here. Have you seen Roald?"

"No. No, I just arrived. Are you okay, Karen?"

"What do you mean?"

"You know what I mean."

"I'm fine, Jan. Let's just get this movie out of the way. We can do that, can't we?"

"Yes . . . I heard you were seeing someone. I'm glad."

"And so am I. Let's not talk about it. You do what you need to do, and let me do what I need to do. Okay? Where's Roald?" She crooked her neck for view.

"I really had no choice, Karen. You do realize that, don't you?"

"I don't know, Jan. Did you?"

"I don't know what you've heard, and I don't expect you to understand, but what happened between Helen and me, it was beyond us. God is not finished with this story."

"And what happens to the rest of us poor sad sacks while God finishes your story? We just get trampled for the greater good, is that it?"

"No. But this love for Helen, it did come from him. The attraction between you and me was somewhat misplaced. Surely you see that now."

"Oh come on, Jan. Don't cast this off on God. You know how pathetic that sounds? You dumped me for another woman because God told you to?"

"Then forget how it happened. Were we really right for each other? You're already with another man. And I'm with another woman."

She stopped her searching and looked into Jan's eyes without responding.

"We were caught up in the momentum of it," Jan said. "Perhaps you were as interested in *The Dance of the Dead*—in the Jan Jovic franchise—as in me."

Finally she responded. "Maybe. And what would that make your attraction to me?"

"A strong infatuation with the woman who made me a star." He smiled.

They held stares. "A month ago I would've slapped you for saying that."

Roald had walked in then and effectively ended the conversation.

Now she looked at him from across the table, and smiled, proud of her pet project. Professionally delighted to be with the author of *The Dance of the Dead* if not his fiancée.

"Well, I'm sure you're wondering why we called you all here so suddenly," Tony said. "We appreciate your understanding."

The table grew quiet. The Delmont executive glanced around at them and settled his eyes on Jan. "I'm sure Karen has told you there's been a change." He smiled. "This is how we in the world of entertainment like to introduce changes. We entertain first, and then we discuss business." A few chuckles. "But let me assure you, you'll be pleased with what I have to say. Your contract with Delmont Pictures allows for the studio to sell the movie rights at our discretion as long as it does not materially affect you. It's something we would do only if it were clear that the sale would make fiscal sense for all parties. We have received and accepted such an offer."

Meaning what? Jan glanced at Karen.

"You're selling the movie. Why?" she asked.

"Yes, we're selling the movie. The deal both guarantees us a good profit and offers you higher payment. An additional three million upon completion."

They sat stunned. It was Karen again who pressed for details. "Forgive my ignorance here, Tony. But why?"

"They're an upstart studio, you've heard of them, I'm sure. Dreamscape Pictures?"

She nodded. "They have that kind of money?"

"Yes. Point is, they want full assurances that you will fulfill your contract, so they threw in the three-million incentive. They're obviously extending themselves on this deal and they can't afford any missteps. And, if you want to know, I think it was a smart move on their part. This movie will make a bundle. A new company like Dreamscape could use that."

"And why not you?" Jan asked.

"Because ten million in the bank is always going to trump a hundred million on the table." Tony shrugged. "If it means anything to you, I voted against the deal."

Roald spoke up for the first time. "So bottom line is, we lose nothing. And all things remaining equal, we gain three million dollars. What about production and distribution? These guys know their business?"

"They have solid partners. And with the amount of money they're putting on the deal, you can bet they won't settle for a home movie. You'll get what you want."

"What kind of contract?" Karen asked.

"Virtually identical to the existing one. Like I said, they're just interested in protecting their investment."

Karen nodded. "Well. Then I guess congratulations are in order, Tony. You've done us well."

The executive looked at Jan. "What do you think, Jan?"

"I think Karen's right. If they want to pay us three million dollars for what we would've done anyway, I won't turn down their money. So we're now at an eight-million-dollar deal? Isn't that rather much?"

"That, Jan," Roald said, "is exceptional. And Karen's right: Tony, you have done us very well. I think this calls for celebration."

Tony laughed. "We are celebrating, Roald. Can't you tell?"

It did become a celebration then, for another two hours, drinking and laughing and enjoying the benefits of wealth. In many ways the evening was like a mountain peak for Jan. Not only had God given him Helen, he had returned Jan's favor with the world, it seemed. With Karen and Roald and *The Dance of the Dead*. Everything was going to return to normal now. And normal as a millionaire was something he was getting to like. Very much.

HELEN PRIED her eyes open and stared at the clock by the bed. It was 10:00 A.M. Hazy memories from the night drifted through her mind. She'd called Glenn . . .

Helen jerked up. She was in the Palace! And Jan . . . Jan was in New York. She collapsed, flooded with relief. But the sentiment left her within the minute.

She rolled to her back and groaned. Rain still splattered on the window. Jan wasn't scheduled to return until the next day, Sunday, but he would have called, no doubt. She would have to concoct a reasonable story for not answering the phone.

Oh, dear Jan! What have I done? What have I gone and done? Helen put a hand over her eyes and fought the waves of desperation crashing through her chest. One of these days she would have to end this madness. Or maybe Glenn would do it for her. A notion to call out to God crossed her mind, but she dismissed it. This wasn't some fanciful world filled with visions and martyrs and a God who spoke in the darkness. This was not Jan's *Dance of the Dead*. This was the real world. Glenn's world. Jan had grown up in a different land altogether. Jan and Ivena both—her husband and her mother. Mother Ivena . . .

Ivena.

Ivena!

A chill spiked through her spine. Helen scrambled from the bed, squinting against a throbbing headache. She had imagined seeing the dear woman bound and gagged. Helen threw the closet door open.

It was empty. *Oh, thank you, God! Thank you!* So then she had imagined it all. Drugs could do that easily enough. She wandered into the bathroom, splashed water on her face and brushed her teeth. She had to get home—to Jan's home. To her home. It was crazy coming here! *This is the last time.*

She stopped her brushing and stared at the mirror, her mouth foaming white. *This is the last time, you understand? You understand that, Helen? Never again.* She suddenly spit at the mirror, spraying it with toothpaste.

"You make me sick!" she muttered and rinsed her mouth.

Helen pulled on a pair of blue jeans and slunk from the apartment, headed for the bar and a cigarette. Maybe a drink. The large room lay in shadows, lightless except for the foreboding gray that made its way through the far windows. The room's pillars stood like ghosts in the silence. She veered to her right and made for the bar.

Helen had reached the counter and was bending over it when she heard the sound. A soft grunt. Or a moan of wind. No, a soft grunt!

She spun around and faced the shadows.

A form sat there, its white eyes staring at her from the gloom.

Helen jumped, terrified. The form was human, bound to a chair, gagged. Helen could not move. She could only stare for the moment while her heart pounded in her ears and the woman drilled her with those white eyes.

It was Ivena. Of course, it was Ivena, and that hadn't been a dream last night. Glenn had taken the woman and . . .

The horror of it brought a sudden nausea to Helen's gut. She brought her hand to her mouth and fought for her composure. The injustice of it, the sickness of it—how could any human do this? And then in that moment Helen knew that she was staring at a mirror. Not a real mirror, because that was Ivena bound to the chair twenty feet off. But a mirror because she was no less bound than Ivena. Helen was looking at herself and the sight was making her nauseous. But unlike Ivena, she came here willingly. With desire, like a dog to its own vomit.

A groan broke from Helen's mouth and she stumbled forward, gripping her stomach with one hand. She couldn't read Ivena's expression because of the gag, but her eyes were wide. The ropes pressed into her flesh—the pink dress she wore was torn, Helen could see that as she neared. And yes, her face was badly bruised.

A knot wedged in Helen's throat, allowing only a soft moan. Tears blurred her vision. She had to get that gag off. Panicked, she rushed right up to Ivena and tore at the strip of sheet wrapped around her mouth. It took some wrenching, and Ivena winced in pain, but the gag came free, exposing Ivena's face. The woman was crying with an open mouth and quivering lips.

Helen grasped for the knots that held Ivena. She found one at her waist and tugged at it, whimpering in panic. "Are you hurt? Did he hurt you?"

Of course she was hurt.

"Leave them, Helen," Ivena said softly. "He'll only hurt me more."

Helen yanked at the ropes, desperate to free her.

"Helen, please. Please don't."

Helen grunted in frustration and hit the chair with her palm. She sank to her knees, lowered her head to Ivena's shoulder, and wept bitterly.

For a full minute they did not speak. They shook with sobs and wet their faces with tears, Ivena bound to the chair and Helen kneeling beside her. Ivena was right: she couldn't untie her; Glenn would kill them both.

"Shshshshshsh . . . ," Ivena whispered, gathering herself. "Be still, child."

"I'm sorry, Ivena! I'm so sorry." There were no words for this.

"I know, Helen. It will be all right."

Helen straightened and looked at the older woman. The gag made of sheet was still in her hand and she gently wiped Ivena's face with it. "He's a monster, Ivena." Then she was crying again.

"I know. He's a beast."

"How long have you been here?"

"Yesterday, I was attacked . . ." Ivena turned her face away.

If I had called her to spend the weekend as Jan suggested, she would be safe, Helen thought. *I've done this to her!*

Ivena seemed to gain some resolve. She set her chin and swallowed. "And why are you here, Helen?"

Ivena didn't know? She had not suspected! Helen lifted both hands to her face and hid her face, utterly shamed. She turned away and wept silently.

"Come here, child."

Helen stood frozen.

"Yes, it's a terrible thing. But it's done. Now you will be forgiven."

Helen turned to her. "How can you say that? How can anyone say that? Look at you. You're tied to a chair, beaten and bloody, and you're talking to me about forgiveness? That's not right!"

"No dear, you are wrong. Forgiveness is love; love takes us past the death. You must know something, Helen. You must listen to me and remember what I now tell you. Are you listening?"

Helen nodded.

"Blood is at the very center of man's history. The shedding of blood, the giving of blood, the taking of blood. Without the shedding of blood there is no forgiveness. Without the shedding of blood there is no *need* for forgiveness. It's all about life and death, but the path to life runs through death. Does this make any sense?"

"I don't know."

"Whoever will find his life must lose his life. If you want to live, you must die. It was what Christ did. He shed his blood. It sounds absurd, I know. But it's only when you decide to give up yourself—to die—that you yourself will understand love. Hear this, Helen. You will never understand the love of Christ; you will never return Janjic's love until you die."

"That doesn't make sense."

"No. Trying to love without dying doesn't make sense."

Helen looked at Ivena's body, still bound like a hog. She fought to hold back the tears.

"I've heard the laughter, Helen."

The door to their right suddenly thumped open and they stared at it as one. It was Glenn, standing in the light, hands on hips, grinning. He walked toward them, still dressed in those white polyester slacks, now smudged with dirt.

"I see you've found your gift, Helen? You didn't seem too interested last night so I wrapped her for you here."

Helen fought to contain her rage, but it boiled over. She shrieked and swung her right fist at Glenn. He caught her wrist easily. "Easy, princess."

"I hate this! I hate this, you pig!"

Glenn twisted her arm until she winced with pain. "You watch your tongue, you filthy slug!"

"She means nothing to you!"

"She means everything to me. She's going to work some magic for me, aren't you, old woman?" He shoved Helen off and she held her arm, still glaring at him.

"Yes, she is," Glenn said.

"What can you hope to gain by this?" Helen asked.

"I hope to gain a little cooperation, princess." His upper lip bunched up, revealing his large crooked teeth. "This bag of bones here will provide some motivation for you and your preacher."

Helen tensed. "Meaning what?"

"It means that since you've had difficulty with your loyalty, I'm going to help you out a little, that's what it means. That's my gift to you. You might even think of it as a wedding present."

He was headed into dangerous waters with this tone of his, and Helen decided not to push him.

"Don't you want to know how it works, dear? Hmm? Operating instructions? Okay, let me tell you. First, you let this bag of bones free on the street. Let it wander back home or go shopping or whatever it does. Maybe clean it up a little first." He took a deep breath and paced theatrically.

"The point is to try to keep the bag of bones alive. A game really. If you and your preacher friend agree to separate, the bag of bones lives. If not, she dies. That's the only rule. You like it?"

Separate? Glenn was demanding that she and Jan separate?

"Oh, and one more thing. You've got three days. Sort of like a resurrection thing. If you do the right thing, the tomb will be empty in three days. The tomb being the preacher's house. Empty of you, Helen."

He couldn't be serious, of course. It was insane! "Come on, Glenn. Don't fool around. She's not—"

"I'm *not* fooling around!" he screamed.

Helen jumped. Glenn's face scowled, red.

"I'm as serious as a heart attack, baby! You have three days, and if you want this bag of bones here to live through our little game, you'd better do some thinking."

Helen's knees suddenly felt weak. He was insane! She spun her head to Ivena. The woman was looking at Glenn, her eyes still soft, absent of fear. Maybe smiling.

"Now cut her ropes and turn her loose," Glenn said. He flashed a smile. "Time to play."

With that he turned on his heels and strode from the room.

CHAPTER TWENTY-EIGHT

"Suffering is an oxymoron. There is unfathomable peace and satisfaction in suffering for Christ. It is as though you have searched endlessly for your purpose in life, and now found it in the most unexpected place: in the death of your flesh. It is certainly a moment worthy of laughter and dance. And in the end it is not suffering at all. The apostle Paul recommended that we find joy in it. Was he mad?"

The Dance of the Dead, 1959

JAN APPROACHED his home's entryway midafternoon Monday with a sense of déjà vu raging through his mind. He'd been here before: walking up to the sign that read *In living we die; In dying we live*, on a hot summer afternoon, surrounded by stifling silence, wondering what waited behind those doors.

Helen had not answered his calls from New York.

Father, you must save her, he prayed for the hundredth time since leaving her on Friday. *You must protect her.* He prayed it because she was slipping—he could feel it more than deduce it. Helen was in a fight for her life and the fact that he'd left her for three days now played like a horn in his mind. It was killing him.

Jan unlocked the door and stepped in. The lights were off; the house appeared vacant. "Helen! Helen, dear, I'm home!"

He set down his garment bag and tossed the keys on the entry table. "Helen!" Jan hurried into the kitchen. "Helen, are you here?" Only the ringing of silence answered his call. Where was she? Ivena! She would be with Ivena.

"Hi, Jan."

He whirled to the hall. Helen stood by the basement stairs, dressed in jeans and a white T-shirt, trying to smile and managing barely. Jan's pulse spiked. He reached her and took her into his arms. There was something wrong here, but at least it was *here,* not there; not in some place of wickedness.

"I missed you, Helen." Her musky smell filled his senses and he closed his eyes. "Are you okay? I tried to call."

"Yes," she said thinly. "Yes, I'm all right. How was your trip?"

Jan stepped back. "Terrific. Correction, the meeting was terrific, the trip itself was dreadful. These trips are getting more difficult every time I take them. Maybe you should come with me next time."

"Jan, there's been a . . . a problem." If she'd even heard his last comment she didn't show it. "Something's happened."

"What is it? What problem?"

She turned and walked into the living room, not responding. It was serious then. Serious enough to make Helen balk, which was not so easily accomplished

"Helen, tell me."

"It's Ivena." She turned and her eyes glistened wet. "She's . . . she's not so good."

"What do you mean? What happened?" His tone was panicked and he swallowed. "What happened to Ivena, Helen?"

She lowered her head into her hands and started to cry. Jan stepped up to her and smoothed her hair. "Shhh, it's okay, dear. Everything will be okay. You're more precious to me than anything I know. You remember that, don't you?"

The comment only added to her tears, he thought. "Tell me, Helen. Just tell me what's happened."

"She's hurt, Jan."

Now he stepped back in alarm. "Hurt? Where? Where is she?"

"At home."

"Well . . . How did she get hurt?" he demanded, aware that he'd taken a harsh tone now. "Did she have a car accident?" A picture of that crazy gray Bug stuttered through his mind. He'd told her a hundred times to get something larger.

"No. She was hurt."

"Yes, but how? How was she hurt?"

"I think you should ask her that."

"You can't tell me?" Now Jan was worried. She was making no sense. This was more than an accident. "Okay, then, if you won't tell me, we'll go there."

"No, Jan. You go."

"Don't be ridiculous! You'll come with me. I'm not leaving here without you."

She shook her head and the tears were flowing free now. "No. I can't. You have to go alone."

"Why? You're my wife. How can I—"

"Go, Jan! Just go," she said. Then, with closed eyes, "I'll be here when you return, I promise. Just go."

He stared at her, stunned. Something very bad had happened to Ivena. That much was now obvious. Not as clear was Helen's behavior.

"I'll be right back," he said. He kissed her on the cheek and ran for his car.

JAN FOUND Ivena's house unlocked and he stormed in, not thinking to knock. His imagination had already pushed him past such formalities.

"Ivena . . ." He pulled up.

She sat in her brown overstuffed chair, humming and smiling and slowly rocking. The heavy scent of her roses filled the room; she must have strewn them everywhere. The distant sound of children laughing carried on the air.

"Hello, Jan." Her head rested on the cushion—making no effort to look at him.

Jan shoved the door closed behind him. At first he didn't see the bruising. But the discoloration beneath her makeup became obvious—black and blue at the base of her nose and on her right cheek.

"Did you have a good trip?" she asked.

"What happened?"

She straightened her head. "My, we are demanding. Did you speak to Helen?"

"Yes."

"And? She told you what?"

"That you'd been hurt. That's all. She refused to come. What's going on?"

She leaned her head back. "Sit, Janjic." He sat opposite her. "First you tell me how your trip was, and then I'll tell you why my head hurts."

"My trip was fine. They're paying us more money. Now stop this nonsense and tell me what's going on."

"More money? Goodness, you will be floating in the stuff."

"Ivena!"

Ivena's body ached, but her spirit was light. She might not be floating in money like Janjic, but she was still floating. "Okay, my dear Serb. Calm your voice; it hurts my head."

"Then tell me why your head hurts and why my wife will not come here with me."

Ivena took a deep breath and told him. Not everything, not yet. She told him how the big oaf, Glenn . . . how his men had taken her in the park, using chloroform, she thought. When she'd awoken she'd met the man behind Helen's fears. Nothing less than a monster, ugly and smelly and no less brutal than the worst in Bosnia. He had bound her and spit on her and clubbed her with his huge fist.

Janjic was out of his chair then, red in his face. "That's . . . insane! We should call the police! Did you call the police?"

"Yes, Janjic. Please sit."

He sat. "And what did they say?"

"They asked me if I wanted to press charges."

"And?"

"I said I would have to think about it. I wanted to talk to you first."

"That's absurd! Of course you want to press charges. This man's not someone to play with!"

"You think I do not know? You weren't the only one who spent some time in his chambers. But there's more to this than what the eye sees."

Jan shoved a hand toward her. "Of course there is! There's a monster who first tried to destroy Helen and who's now trying to destroy my . . ." He swallowed. "My mother."

It was the first time he'd called her that. "I am flattered, Janjic. And if I had a son, I could only hope for one as kind as you. But there's still more. You're not asking *why* Glenn took me."

"Why?" he asked.

"As a threat." Ivena pushed herself slowly from her chair and hobbled for the kitchen. "Do you want a drink, Janjic?"

He followed her, but did not answer her question. "This has to do with Helen." His voice had stiffened. "Look at you. You can hardly walk and yet you're playing this as if it were some kind of game. What does Helen have to do with this?" he demanded.

She stopped in the middle of the kitchen and faced him. "But it *is* a game, you see? And it seems that Helen is the prize." She left him staring and retrieved two glasses.

"What game?"

"What game? It is the game of life, a testing to see where the player's loyalties really do lie. Like Christ's temptation in the desert—bow to me and I will give you the world. But with Glenn it is, 'come to me and I will extend my mercy.'" She poured the lemonade, knowing Jan couldn't understand yet.

"Ivena—"

"Leave Jan, Glenn told Helen, and I will allow this bag of bones to live." She handed him the drink.

For a long moment, the kitchen was quiet except for the sound of those children laughing down the street. Ivena took a sip of her drink and then walked for the living room again, smiling. She had nearly reached the chair when he spoke.

"He said that? Glenn said that if Helen didn't leave me he would kill you? He actually threatened your life?"

"Yes, Janjic. He said that."

He marched into the room and set his glass down without drinking from it. "He can't do that! He can't just threaten like that and hope to get away with it! We have to call the police immediately!"

She eased into her chair and sighed.

"Ivena! Listen to me! This is madness! He's not one to fool with!"

"You know, I have had an incredible peace these last few weeks. And do you know what has accompanied that peace?"

Jan sat down without answering.

"A desire to join Christ. To join Nadia. To see, with my own eyes, my Father in heaven."

"But you're not saying that you want to die! That's why you haven't called the police? Because you actually want this creep to end your life? That's suicide!"

"Please!" she chided. He blinked. "I have no death wish. I said that I wish to join Christ. I did not say that I wish to die. There is a difference. Even Paul the apostle saw joining Christ as gain. Do not mock my sentiment!"

"I'm sorry. But you seem to take this all too lightly. Goodness, your life has been threatened and you've been beaten up! Did he give a time frame?"

"Three days."

"He said that if Helen does not leave me in three days, he will kill you?"

"Am I not speaking clearly, Janjic?"

"It's impossible! Who does he think he is?"

"He is a man obsessed with destroying your union with Helen. With stealing her love. And he's doing it by threatening death. Love and death. They seem to intersect often, have you noticed?"

"Perhaps too often. I'm going to call the police." He started to walk for the phone. "This is utter nonsense."

"There is more, Janjic." She guessed it was her tone that stopped him.

He hesitated and then turned to face her.

She looked at him, unable to hide a smile, wanting him to ask her. He only stared at her, still distracted.

"I saw the field."

"The field?"

"The vision."

His eyes widened and he blinked. "Of Helen? You heard heaven weeping?"

Her face took on a wide grin. "Not the weeping. But I heard the laughter."

"You saw the field of flowers?" Jan asked.

She nodded. "Tell me again what the flowers in your vision looked like, Janjic."

"White."

"Yes, but describe them."

"Well, I wasn't looking too closely . . . they were large . . . I don't know."

Ivena stood and walked for the bookcase behind him. She pulled the single red-rimmed flower from a crystal vase and turned to him. "Were they like this?"

He stepped toward her. "Maybe. Yes, as a matter of fact I think they were. It's the same flower you showed me before. What is it?"

"I'll show you." She took his hand and pulled him through the kitchen, excited now. "You will like this, Janjic. I promise you."

"Ivena—"

"Hush now. You will see. I know you will like this."

She reached the greenhouse door and paused, thinking that such an occasion needed an introduction. But there was nothing that could prepare him. She turned the knob and shoved the door open.

A soft breeze greeted their faces, pushing the hair from their foreheads. Ivena stepped in and spread her arms in the wind, drawing the air into her lungs. The delicate aroma rose through her nostrils, stinging but sweet. Oh, so very sweet. She faced the rosebushes and for a moment she forgot about Janjic stepping in behind her. Hundreds of vines covered the walls and ceiling in emerald green. A thousand brilliant white flowers trimmed in red swayed gently, bowing with the breeze. The vine's leaves rustled delicately against each other, filling the room with a cacophony of soft rustling. It all swept over Ivena's senses like a drug. She could almost taste honey on the air.

The door shut behind her, and Ivena turned to see Janjic standing wide-eyed, mouth agape.

"They came from Nadia's rosebush," she said. She ran for the bush and rustled her hand through the leaves. "You see it was a graft, but I didn't make it."

"A graft?" He stepped gingerly, as though anything less might break something. "What . . . ? This is amazing, Ivena! How did you grow this?"

"I didn't. It's beyond me. It began the day Helen came into our lives."

He shot her a glance, and then looked about, blinking.

"And there is more," Ivena said. "I can't find a source for the breeze. I think it comes from the flowers themselves."

"'Let your wind blow through my garden,'" he quoted from the Song of Solomon. "It's impossible!" He spun around to face her. "Who else have you told?"

"Only Joey."

Jan couldn't stop his turning and staring. "And you knew about this all along? Why didn't you tell me? How did it grow?"

He looked closer at the graft and then she retraced the plant's growth for him, first along one wall, then another and another until the whole greenhouse was covered with vines and leaves and flowers.

She watched him walk around the small garden for thirty minutes, amazed.

"I should go to Helen," he finally said.

"Yes. And now you know the truth."

He shook his head. "I'll do anything to keep her love. Anything."

"Then promise me one thing. Promise me that no matter what happens in the days to come you won't become distracted by hate or revenge or any other notion that seizes your heart."

They'd stepped into the kitchen and he looked back at her, surprised. "Of course. You say that as if you know something I don't. And you'll still press charges. This changes nothing. We should call the police immediately."

"Yes, I will press charges, but know that this could all become very public."

"Public? We're talking about your safety, for heaven's sake! What do you mean?"

"She's been back to him, Jan. More than once," Ivena said.

He was halfway across her living room and he froze mid-stride. "What?"

"She has been to Glenn four times already. All in the last month."

His face drained white. "That can't be! How's that possible? I've been with her constantly! We've just been wed! How can you say this?"

"Glenn told me."

"And he's a liar!"

"Helen was there, Janjic. She came to Glenn the same night he took me."

He's stopped breathing, Ivena thought.

"She saw me bound and gagged, and she removed my gag. We talked and she was very sorry. But she was there, Janjic. By her own choice."

He started to shake his head and then stopped. Slowly his face filled with blood; his neck bulged with fury. A tremble took to his lips and he stood enraged.

He spoke in a low, bitter voice. "How dare she? I have given her everything! How can she even think of wallowing back to that pig!?"

A chill of fear swept through Ivena's back at his tone. "It's no different than what most men do with Christ," she said. "No different from Israel turning her back on God. Helen is no different than the church, worshiping at the altar one day and blundering back into sin the next. She's doing nothing more than what you yourself have done."

His eyes were glazed. "I don't care! I'll kill him!"

"Janjic—"

"No!" The muscles in his jaw flexed. "No man will do this to my wife! No man! I can't sit by while he plays his games."

"You must. Janjic—"

He whirled for the door.

"Where are you going?"

He didn't answer.

She knew then that she might not see him again. Not if he was going to the Towers. "Janjic! Please!"

The door slammed shut and he was gone.

Ivena rose from her chair and watched him through her front window. He pulled the Cadillac out of her driveway and roared down the road. A single tear snaked from the corner of her eye.

Father, you will protect him, won't you? You must. It is not finished for him. His story is not yet complete.

And what about your story, Ivena? Is it complete?

She answered aloud. "Yes, I am finished now. If you give me a choice I will join the laughter up there."

Ivena sighed again and walked to the telephone. She should call the police. Yes, she would do that.

chapter twenty-nine

JAN DROVE straight for the Towers, his vision clouded red with fury. He knew that he had snapped back there. The fact loitered in his mind like a fly, slightly annoying but small enough to disregard for the moment.

It was the image of Helen slinking back to that pig, lying on his bed, that drove Jan mad. Or it was three months of images, all hidden in a reservoir deep in his mind, building to this day when they had broken past their dam and now drove him like a lunatic toward the pig's house. Toward Atlanta's Twin Towers, visible from five miles out, rising tall against the blue sky.

He had no plan; no idea what he would do when he arrived or how he would get to Glenn. He only knew that he had to face that beast now.

And what about Helen, Janjic? Will you knock some sense into her as well?

Yes.

No! Oh dear God, no! The image of the garden flooded his mind. No, he could never harm her. He loved Helen desperately.

She would not be this way if it weren't for Glenn. The man's evil touch was still running through her veins. And now the madman had taken his fight to Ivena. Dear Ivena was the innocent bystander in this, as she'd been twenty years ago. Nadia had died then; there was no way he would allow any harm to come to Ivena now.

The thoughts battered his mind, occupying what space he should have given to reason. To a plan. It occurred to Jan that he was stopped at a red light not two blocks from the Towers, and he had better start thinking about what he was going to do here. He was going to ride to the top floor and he was going to take a tire iron with him. That's what he was going to do.

A horn blared and he saw that other cars had already crossed the intersection. He punched the accelerator and shot through. Helen had said that Glenn's office was in the second tower—the East Tower. He sped past the first building with which he was already familiar and approached the second.

Jan whipped the Cadillac into the underground parking and screeched to a stop in a restricted space beside the elevators. It had been twenty years since he had set his mind on harming another man, but the memory of it came to him now with a surge of adrenaline.

He grunted, popped the trunk and jumped from the car. He yanked the car's tire iron from the repair kit, slammed the trunk and slid the rod up his shirt. A parking attendant walked toward him from the entry gate. Jan ran to the elevators without acknowledging the man. One of three elevator doors slid open and he entered quickly. Thank God for small favors. *God?*

Jan stabbed the top floor button and rode the humming car to its peak without stopping. Maybe he should have called the police before leaving Ivena's. But then she would. Either way, the police didn't seem too interested in bringing this powerful man under their thumb. These Karadzics of the world seemed to have their way too often. But not with his wife!

The arrival bell clanged and he entered the thirtieth floor, his nerves strung tight. A receptionist looked up at him from her station behind a counter that hid all but her head. A huge brass sculpture of the Twin Towers hung on the wall behind her.

"May I help you?"

Jan walked for the counter. "Yes, I'm here to see Glenn Lutz."

"Do you have an appointment?"

"Yes. Yes, of course I have an appointment."

The receptionist glanced to Jan's right, toward a tall cherry door, and picked up the telephone.

Jan turned and strode for the door without waiting for her to let him in. "Excuse me, sir. Sir!" He ignored the call and pushed through, gripping the iron under his shirt.

A black-haired woman looked up from her desk sharply. Jan took in the room with a glance. Beyond her, wide-paneled doors led to what would be the man's office. This would be his secretary, then. An ugly wench with a hooked nose. He had to move while she was still off balance.

She stood as he moved forward. "Excuse me."

"Not now, miss," he snapped.

Her eyes widened suddenly, as if she recognized him. As well she might—he'd been here before. She stepped out from her desk quickly, blocking his way with lifted hands. "Where do you think you're going?"

"Out of my way," he grunted. And he slapped her hands aside. She made a high squeaking sound, protesting like a mother hen. But Jan wasn't interested in this woman. His mind was now thoroughly taken by getting through the door. He didn't stop to think clearly about what might be waiting behind the doors; he simply barged ahead.

The woman charged him from behind. She dived onto his back with a wild shriek. Janjic dropped instinctively. It had been twenty years since his special forces training, but his reflexes had not forgotten. He dropped to one knee and threw his right shoulder down. The wench's momentum carried her over his back and she sailed through the air, landing with a loud crash against the wall. Her black bun had unraveled in the flight and now drooped past white cheeks.

Jan sprang for the doors and yanked them open, his heart now slamming into his throat. *You want a war, baby? You want to threaten my family? You will feel a touch of Bosnia today.*

Glenn's bulky frame stood across the room, by a windowed wall, hands on hips, gazing to the city beyond. He spun around, snarling at the sudden intrusion. But when he saw that it was Jan, the snarl vanished. He gawked for a moment.

Jan whipped out the iron, slammed the door shut behind him, locked it, and angled for the desk to his right.

Isolate and minimize. The training came like a haunting memory now, dulling the edge of fear. Isolate the man from any potential weapon and minimize his ability to take the offensive.

Glenn had regrouped already and now a wicked grin split his face. "So the preacher wants to get serious. Is that—"

"Shut up!" Jan yelled. Glenn blinked. "Just shut up!"

The millionaire's face turned red.

Jan held the iron out and felt the desk at the back of his knees. He reached for the drawers behind him, found the one closest and pulled it open. An assortment of pens and notepads crashed to the floor.

"You still think of me as a preacher? But you know me better now, don't you? I'm the man Helen loves. That's me. But before I became that man; before I came to your land I was what? I was a killer. How many men have you killed with your own hands, Glenn Lutz? Ten? Twenty? You're a novice."

He glanced back, found another drawer and ripped it out. More junk, but not the weapon he looked for. *Keep speaking, Jan. Keep him distracted.*

"You think you can throw terror around as if you own it?" He yanked another drawer out and papers spilled to the black tile floor. "Have you ever felt terror, Glenn Lutz?"

The man stood there huge and ugly, his arms spread like a gunslinger. But the smile had gone, replaced by flat lips. From this distance his eyes looked like black holes. The man was large enough to crush Janjic. Surely a man like this would have a weapon of some kind in his desk. Jan jerked a fourth drawer open, keeping his eyes on the man.

"No, you have not felt terror!" Jan's breathing came heavily now. Seeing the monster's thick face filled his gut with revulsion. He wanted only to kill the pig.

Glenn's eyes shifted to the drawer Jan had just opened. Suddenly the man snapped out of his trance. His lips pulled back and he bolted forward like a charging bull.

For a fleeting second, Jan knew that coming here had been a very bad idea. Panicked, he blindly snatched at the drawer behind him. His hand closed around cold steel.

Glenn came in, roaring now, his face bulging. Fury rose through Jan's veins and he whipped what he now knew was a gun around to face the charging man.

Glenn thundered forward, undaunted.

Jan sprang to his left at the last moment, narrowly avoiding the huge body. He spun around and swung the tire iron down on the man's blond skull. Glenn grunted and slammed into his desk, facedown on the polished wood grain. It was the first time Jan had struck a man in twenty years, and now the horror of it seeped through his bones.

A fleeting image of himself standing over the priest with a bloodied rifle filled his mind.

Still, this was the man who had molested his wife! Who now threatened to kill Ivena! He begged for a beating!

Jan jerked the iron back and swung again, this time hitting the man's back. Glenn grunted. Jan swung again, this time with all of his weight. The blow landed on his shoulder with a sick crunch. It should have immobilized the monster.

It did not.

Glenn growled, rolled to his back and stood. He faced Jan, his eyes flashing red, his neck bulging with veins. His right arm hung limply, but Glenn didn't seem to notice. His eyes glared, bloodshot above twisted lips. He growled and took a step forward. Jan knew then that if he did not stop the man, it would be his own death.

He jerked the gun up and pulled the trigger.

Boom! The report thundered in the enclosed room.

Glenn's right arm flew back, like a tether ball on a string. The room fell to a surreal slowness. Glenn seemed oblivious to his pain, but his eyes snapped wide in shock.

Yes, that's it, you pig. Yes, I do have your gun and it is loaded isn't it? That one was through your hand, the next will be through your head!

"Don't move!" Jan screamed.

Glenn's arm dropped to his side. The right corner of the man's mouth twitched. They stood rooted to the floor, facing each other down, Jan with the extended pistol and Glenn with a sick grin.

"You've just signed your own death warrant. You know that, don't you?" Glenn said. His right shoulder had broken under the tire iron, Jan saw, and the bullet had torn a gaping hole through his hand.

Glenn looked at it slowly. He measured the damage and then seemed to accept it with a blink. He looked up at Jan and closed his eyes. "You will die along with the old hag now."

"I don't think you understand the situation here," Jan snapped back. "You see, I have the gun. One small pull from my finger and you will die. If you don't at least pretend to understand that, then I will be forced to demonstrate my resolve. Are we clear?"

Glenn opened his eyes. "You talk big for a preacher."

Pounding sounded on the locked door.

"Pick up the phone and tell your friend out there to leave us alone," Jan instructed.

Glenn snarled angrily. "You're dead meat!"

A wave of heat washed over Jan's back. He wanted to shoot the man in his bulging belly. He trembled in restraint. "You really should have more respect, but obviously you don't know the meaning of the word, do you?" He was a pig who wouldn't think twice about smashing those big fists over Helen's ears. How could she come to this man! Jan's gun hand shook.

"You aren't going to do anything I ask?"

Glenn only stared at him.

"Lift your left hand," Jan ordered.

Glenn did not move.

"Lift your hand!" Jan screamed. "Now!"

The man had the audacity to stand there without flinching. Jan lowered the gun, lined up its sight on Glenn's left hand, and pulled the trigger. *Boom!* The slug took off the end of his index finger. The pounding on the door intensified.

Glenn's face drained white and then immediately flushed red. He gaped at his finger and began to roar in pain. He fumbled with his shirt in an attempt to stop the flow of blood but succeeded only in drenching it.

"Next time it will be your knee and you will use a crutch the rest of your life," Jan said. "Do you understand? Take your shirt off."

"What?"

"I said take your shirt off, you oaf. Take it off and wrap it around your hand. The flow of blood will distract me."

This time Glenn followed the suggestion quickly. He eased his flabby torso out of the shirt and crudely wrapped it around both hands. Sweat glistened on his white flesh.

"Tell them to shut up," Jan ordered, waving the gun toward the door.

"Shut up!" Glenn screamed at the door.

The pounding stopped.

"Good. Now I want you to listen and listen very carefully. You may be a wealthy man with the power to squash weak women, but today this power will not extend to my world. Not to me or to Ivena or to Helen. Helen has chosen to accept my love and now you will let her have her choice. You will not bully her. Do you understand?"

"I didn't bully her into coming back," Glenn said. "We all make our own choices."

"And you'll stop manipulating hers," Jan shouted.

"Manipulating? How? By providing a little motivation? That's nothing less than what you did when you took her away. You show her a carrot. I show her a stick. In the end she makes the choice."

"You think I keep her caged in my house? She's free to come and go as she wants and I don't see her running to you every day. She would stay with me except for your drugs. And if you think this pointless game with Ivena will somehow persuade her to come crawling back against her own will, then you're wrong. Even if she did, what would you have? Someone you pressured against their will?"

"We all apply pressure. Even your God applies pressure. It's either the carrot or the stick. Heaven or hell."

Jan blinked at the man's logic. It was an odd place to argue these matters, Jan holding the gun and Glenn bleeding into his shirt. "But love can't be bought with heaven or hell. It's given freely. Did she ever *love* you? No. She loves me."

Glenn's lips twisted to a grin. "She loves you but she comes begging to me, is that it? You're as stupid as she is. Call it what you like, when she's here she's loving me!"

"With your threats and your violence you'll gain nothing."

"I will gain Helen!" Glenn growled.

"No, you have already *lost* Helen."

"She'll come crawling back, don't kid yourself. We both know it. You'll lose her. *And* the old bag of bones."

"Silence! This is all nonsense! Helen will *not* come back to you! Never!"

"And that choice is hers," Glenn said. "You said so yourself." He shuddered. "I need a doctor."

"Yes, and so did I when I last left this building," Jan said. "Do you think the police will just stand by and let you threaten whoever you like? You have no sense of yourself."

"The police? You walk into my property and assault me and you think you can run to the police? You are naive, Preacher. You don't even know the truth about your precious wife."

For the first time Jan saw the true mistake in coming here. The police. "She loves me, it's all the truth I need," Jan said. There was something about the man's tone, though. "What truth?"

"I knew your precious lover when she was a child, you know," Glenn said, still smiling.

What was he talking about? He knew *Helen?*

"Only I wasn't Glenn back then. I was Peter. She tell you about Peter?"

Peter! The boy who'd trailed Helen home from school and supplied her mother with drugs! The revelation whirled about in Jan's mind. Glenn wasn't confessing; he was twisting the knife. Jan suddenly felt sick, standing here in this man's tower, playing his game. He was beyond this. And what had he gained by coming here? An image of the garden swept through Jan's mind and he suddenly wanted out. *Oh Helen! Dear Helen, if you only knew.* But she didn't know and he would not tell her.

"You're a sick man," Jan said.

"You think I'm sick?" Glenn licked his lips. "Then what will you think when I tell you that the reason Helen's mother got sick in the first place was because I poisoned her?" He grinned wide, showing his crooked teeth.

"You poisoned her?"

"That's right. I made Mommy sick and then I eased her pain with drugs." Glenn began to giggle. He stood there with bloodied hands, thrilled with himself, giggling insanely.

Jan backed up, revolted. Evil possessed this man's soul to the very core. Glenn Lutz was no less than Karadzic, but in a new skin.

It was time to leave.

"Pick up the phone and tell your men to give me safe passage out," Jan said.

Glenn just smiled with parted lips.

Jan waved the gun. "Do it!"

"What's the matter, Preacher? I'm not quite what you bargained for, am I?"

"You just leave us alone, do you understand? You hurt a single hair on Ivena's head and your world will crumble around you. I promise you that much. Now tell your men, before you bleed to death."

Glenn hesitated, but he went for the phone after glancing at his blood-soaked shirt.

Jan left then, keeping his gun trained on Glenn. He stepped past the glaring assistant he'd sent flying and ran for the elevator. Behind him he could hear Glenn cursing at her. If he took the man's roaring as any indication, this wasn't over. Coming here might have been a terrible mistake. He had just blown a man's hand off.

Jan roared from the parking structure, his hands trembling on the steering wheel. Yes indeed, this hadn't been such a bright idea. Not at all.

GLENN SLUMPED in his chair and held his hands up as best he could to keep the blood flow in check. It was the first time anyone had marched into his own building and demanded anything, much less waved a gun at him and uttered vile threats. Jan Jovic had shifted the balance in the game.

Of course, the preacher had also just handed him the leverage he needed with Charlie. He had been assaulted. This meant open war.

"Where's that doctor?" Glenn demanded.

"On his way," Beatrice returned, pulling loose strands of hair behind her ears. "So is Charlie."

Glenn hardly heard her for the pain in his arms. He couldn't keep them from shaking.

Buck appeared in the door. "You called, sir?" His eyes shifted to the wrapped hand and widened. "Are you okay?"

"No, I'm not okay. I've been shot!"

"The preacher shot you?"

Glenn didn't answer and Buck just stared at him.

"I want the old bag dead," Glenn said matter-of-factly.

He refused to look at Beatrice, who was no doubt glaring at him. It wasn't often he conducted business of this nature in front of her. She liked to pretend that it was beneath her, although they both knew differently.

Buck glanced at her. "Yes, sir." He dipped his head without expression and left.

"You have a problem with that, Beatrice?"

She hesitated. "No. But you'll lose your advantage."

"My leverage is with Dreamscape Pictures. I own him! And now he's just handed his life over to me. Our preacher's about to get more than he bargained for."

Glenn's shoulder ached. His hands burned with pain and a shiver worked its way through his bones.

"Find the old man. Roald. It's time I introduced myself."

Chapter Thirty

IT WAS 5:00 P.M. when Jan swung the Cadillac into his driveway and turned off the ignition. The drive through the city had cleared his mind some, enough for him to know that he'd slipped back into his war skin back there and it hadn't paid any dividends.

He had shot Glenn Lutz. Goodness, he'd just shot a man through the hands! Jan shoved the door open and stepped out of the car.

A surge of anger rose through his chest. But now it was directed toward Helen, not Glenn. It had been flaring at the base of his spine from the moment Ivena had told him about Helen's infidelity. And now Helen waited for him past that door and Jan wasn't sure he could walk through it.

In living we die; In dying we live, the sign above the door read. *You are killing me, Father.* How could anyone betray him as Helen had? He had loved her in every way he knew how, and still she'd betrayed him! Ivena's suggestion that her rejection of him was no different from his own rejection of Christ was well and fine, but it did not ease the whirlwind of emotions whipping through his mind.

Jan felt a tremor take to his bones. He stood on the sidewalk and balled his hands into tight fists. "Why?" he muttered through clenched teeth. There could be no pain worse than this ache of rejection, he thought. It was a living death.

A sudden image of Helen standing, smiling innocently, came to him. In his mind's eye he snatched the image by the throat and strangled her. The image struggled briefly in terror and then fell limp in his hands. He grunted and dropped her.

Jan shut his eyes and shook his head. "Father, please! Please help me." Ivena's words strung through his mind. *She is no different than you, Jan.* The rage and the sorrow and the horror all rolled into a searing ball of emotion. He dropped to one knee and stared up at the sky. "Forgive me, Father. Forgive me, I have sinned."

Another thought filled his mind. *The police will come for you, Jan.*

The tears came freely now, streaming down his cheeks. He lifted both fists above his head and opened his hands. "Oh, God, forgive me. If you have grafted this love of yours into my heart, then let it possess me."

He didn't know how long he remained on his knees facing the house before standing and making sense of himself. He had just leaped off a cliff back at the Towers, he thought, and he had no business loitering around for the impact. But there was Helen —it was all about Helen. He could not continue without resolving this madness.

In living we die; In dying we live. He was living and he was dying and he was not entirely sure which was which.

JAN'S GOING, even for these two hours, had dumped Helen back into a deep pool of depression. It was a strange brew of shame and sorrow and a desperate longing to be held in someone's strong arms. In Jan's strong arms. She'd distilled the emotions to one: loneliness. The kind that felt like a living death.

She imagined throwing herself at him when he returned, but her shame dismissed the image. Instead she paced away the minutes, making the trip to the front window to peek for his return a hundred times, while a terrible agony gripped her heart. It was a pain that overshadowed all the pleasure of a thousand nights in the Palace. Dear God, she was a pig!

The sound of the latch froze her to the carpet on the far side of the room. She was gripped by the sudden impulse to hide. *God, help me!*

"Helen."

Oh, the sound of his voice! *Forgive me, please forgive me!* A lump rose to her throat and she swallowed it quickly.

"Yes?"

He closed the door and walked across through the shadows toward her. She shivered once. He emerged from the darkness, his eyes soft and lost. But there was no anger in them.

Helen sat on the couch. *You see, Helen? He loves you deeply! Look at his eyes, swimming in love.*

How could anyone dare to love her with such intensity, knowing what he now surely knew? Surely Ivena had told him everything. Helen felt the tears rising but was powerless to stop them. She dropped her head into her arms and began to weep.

He stepped forward, dropped to his knees and gently placed both arms around her shoulders. His hands were trembling. "It's okay, Helen. Please, don't cry." His voice was strained. She dissolved now, gushing with sorrow that had welled up in her chest.

"I'm so sorry!" She wept, shaking her head. "I'm so sorry."

"I know you are." So he did know. "Please, Helen. Please stop crying. I can't bear it!" And then he was crying with her. Not just sniffling, but crying hard and shaking.

She draped one arm over his shoulder and they buried their faces in each other's necks and wept. Neither spoke for a long time. For Helen the relief of his love came like water to a bone-dry soul, parched by his absence. By her own folly. *Forgive me! You've given me this man, this love, and I've rejected it! Oh, God, forgive me!* She squeezed Jan tighter. *I'll never let him go! Forgive me, I beg you!*

Jan lifted her face with gentle hands and wiped at her tears with his thumbs. "I love you, Helen. You know that, don't you? I would never reject you. Never. I could not; you are my life. I would die without you."

"I'm sorry."

"Yes. But no more. No more tears. We are together, that's all that matters."

"I don't know why I go back, Jan. I . . ."

He pulled her into his shoulder and shook with another sob. "No, no! It's okay." He held her tight, like a vise. It was the first time she fully understood his pain—that he was screaming inside, fighting to hold his sorrow from crushing her.

The realization was numbing, shocking her into a dumb stare as he fought for control. *Oh, God, what have I done? What have I done?*

And she knew then that her own tears—her loneliness and her heartache—it was all for herself. Not for Jan. *She* missed him. *She* felt lonely. *She* wanted to be forgiven.

But this man in her arms, his emotions were directed toward her. He wanted to comfort *her*. He wanted to forgive *her*. It was the difference between them, she thought. A gulf as wide as the Grand Canyon. Her selfish love and his selflessness. That was the message of his book, *The Dance of the Dead*. He had died to a piece of himself for her. Even now in her arms he was dying to a piece of himself for her sake.

And what death was she willing to give for him? Not even the death of her own self-gratifying pleasures. She clenched her jaw and swore to herself then that she would never, never go back to Glenn. Never!

Helen kissed Jan's mouth, and she wiped his tears away. He returned the kiss and they held each other for a long minute.

"Helen, listen to me," Jan finally said.

"I'm so sorry—"

"No, no. Not that. We have another problem. I've made a mistake. I think we might have to leave." He suddenly stood and strode quickly for the kitchen.

Helen sat up. "Jan? What mistake?"

"I went to the Towers," he said with his back to her. "I shot Glenn Lutz."

She sprang to her feet. "You shot him? You killed Glenn?"

"No. I shot his hands." He lifted the receiver from the wall and faced her. "I'll explain in the car, but right now I think we should get Ivena and find a safe place while we work this out."

Helen stared at him, stunned. "A safe place?"

"Yes." He quickly dialed Ivena's number. "You could grab a few items, but we need to leave."

"How long?"

"I don't know. A day. Two." He leaned into the phone. "Ivena? Thank God you're safe."

Jan had shot Glenn's hands? The truth of it struck her as she stood in the living room, staring dumbly at Jan's back while he talked to Ivena. Heat suddenly rushed over her skull. She spun to the front door, half expecting to see Buck or Stark in the frame. But the door rested shut. Either way, Glenn would've undoubtedly dispatched them by now.

Helen ran for the bedroom, panicked. She stuffed a toothbrush and a tube of toothpaste along with a few other toiletries and some underwear into Jan's overnight bag. Where could they possibly go?

Jan had shot Glenn. Did he know what that meant?

She ran out to the living room. Jan was locking the sliding door to the backyard. "We've gotta move, Jan. Do you have any idea where we're going?"

"To safety," he said.

"And where will you be safe from Glenn? He has ears—"

"I know, Helen. And I'm not a stranger to danger. I've seen my share."

Jan quickly pulled the drapes. He shot her a fleeting smile, grabbed her hand, and hurried for the door. "If there is danger it will likely be at Ivena's house, not here."

"He said three days," Helen said. The street was clear and they walked briskly for the car.

"That was while he still had two good hands. I may have changed his mind."

Helen uttered a small nervous laugh and climbed into the Cadillac. But there was no humor in her voice. They sped from the house and Helen demanded Jan tell her exactly what had happened at the Towers.

He did.

Helen knew then that someone would die. That much was now a certainty. The only question was who.

CHARLIE WILKS stood in Glenn's office, stunned by the bloodied floor before him. Glenn sat limply in his chair, weakened by the ordeal. It was an unusual sight to be sure; not because Charlie was unaccustomed to bullet wounds or puddles of blood, but because it was Glenn's blood. The strong man had been visited by his match.

A doctor Glenn called Klowawski had already fixed his shoulder in a temporary sling and bound his hands in white strips of gauze like a boxer. The repair work would be done in the clinic, but not until Glenn had had his say with Charlie.

"You're sure it was Jan Jovic who did this?" Charlie asked. "Not someone who looks—"

"It was the preacher, you idiot! He stood here for ten minutes waving my own gun at me. You think I imagined the whole thing?"

Charlie glanced at the bloodied shirt glistening in a heap on the floor. "Of course not." Someone had tried to mop some of the blood from the floor with the white cotton shirt and succeeded only in smearing circles on the tile. Glenn had this coming to him, and for that Charlie felt no sympathy. But the law did prohibit citizens from storming into other people's offices and blowing holes in their hands. Jan Jovic had just found himself a heap of trouble and Glenn would play it to his advantage.

"This gives me what I need," Glenn said. "You do realize that."

"Yes it does. It gives you the right to have Mr. Jovic apprehended. But nothing more."

"That's not what I'm talking about."

"And what are you talking about, Glenn?" Charlie knew, of course.

"This muddies the waters. It gives you a good cover."

"Gives me cover? And why would I need cover? I'll get your man, throw him in the slammer for a few days, prosecute him like the law requires—"

"That's not what I want. It's not enough."

"What then? You want him dead?"

"No." Glenn wore a small smirk. "Not him—he's too valuable alive. I just paid ten million for his backside. I need him alive but I also need him willing. The old hag, on the other hand . . ."

"The woman?"

"I'm going to kill the old woman and I want you to stay out of my way. Help me if I need it."

Charlie took a breath and let it out slowly. It wasn't the first time, of course. But Glenn was messing with decent people, not the regular scum he mixed with.

"I'll make it worth your while, of course."

Charlie sat in a guest chair. "So let me get this straight. You want to kill an old defenseless woman who's known by half the country as an icon for motherly love and you want me to cover up the murder? That about it?"

Glenn's lips flattened. "Yes. That's exactly what I want. You haul the preacher in and let me deal with him up close, and you use the distraction of this whole mess as a smoke screen when they find the old woman's body."

"They are two different people—"

"I don't care if they're ten different people!" Glenn yelled, red in the face. "I'm going to kill the old hag, and you're going to see that no one looks my way! Is that too much to ask? He's a criminal, for crying out loud. He shot an unarmed man."

Charlie drummed his fingers on the chair's armrests and pursed his lips. It could be done, this cover-up of Glenn's. But it could also blow up.

"There's fifty thousand in it for you," Glenn said. "One hundred if we need your help."

Charlie felt his pulse quicken. "Fifty? Five-O?"

"Fifty."

"Help in what way?"

"Setting her up." He waved a bandaged hand in a dismissal. "It won't come to that."

"You'll make it look like an accident?" Charlie said.

"Of course."

"Okay. But if this goes sour, this discussion never happened. You remember that." Charlie stood. "I'll put out an APB on the preacher; you go ahead and create your little accident. But for God's sake, keep it clean."

Glenn smiled past crooked teeth. "It's already done, my friend. It's already done."

CHAPTER THIRTY-ONE

JAN SAW the black Lincoln parked across the street from Ivena's house the moment he entered her block. He jerked the Cadillac's steering wheel and plowed into the curb sixty yards from the house.

"What are you doing?" Helen demanded. "You just drove off—"

She saw the car and froze.

Jan clawed at the handle and shoved the door open. "Stay here."

"Jan, wait . . ."

But he didn't hear the rest because he was already sprinting for the house. The black Lincoln had been in the Towers' parking garage. It had no business here. He muttered under his breath and veered for Ivena's backyard.

A tall wooden fence bordered Ivena's heavily vegetated yard. Purple hydrangea and white gardenia flowers spilled over the white pickets. Jan slid to a stop at the fence, peered through two slats, and seeing nothing but an empty lawn past the vines, clambered over. He dropped to a crouch, his heart now pounding in his ears. Behind him, a car door thumped shut—Helen was following. Too late to stop her now.

The greenhouse's glass walls were too crowded with vines to see past at this distance. A steady breeze whispered through the leaves overhead, but otherwise the air lay quiet. Jan rushed for the back door.

Images of Ivena's body, crumpled and bleeding, filled his mind. If he was right she would be in the greenhouse with the flowers. It was a preoccupation for her.

Jan grabbed the knob and threw the door open.

Ivena stood there in the middle of the room, her face raised to the ceiling, her eyes closed. The breeze swept her hair back from her neck. If she'd heard him, she did not show any sign of it.

Jan scanned the room. The doorway to the house gaped to a dim interior. The assailant, if there was one, would be in there, waiting.

"Ivena," he whispered, keeping his eyes on the kitchen doorway.

"Hello, Janjic. You are back, I see," she said loudly.

He started and snatched his finger to his mouth, but she hadn't moved her head to him.

"Come in, Janjic."

"Ivena!" he whispered harshly. "Shhh. Quickly! You must come!"

She faced him. "What's wrong?"

"Come now! Shhhh!"

He looked through the door to the house and Ivena followed his gaze. She hurried over to him, wide-eyed. "What is it?"

Jan didn't respond. He grabbed her hand and yanked her through the door. Such a relief swept through his bones at her stumbling safely into the backyard, that he hardly noticed the tall man materialize in the inner door's shadows.

But then he did notice, and his heart lodged firmly in his throat. His muscles locked up. The man stepped from the shadows, a gun leveled. Behind Jan, Ivena crowded his back. "Janjic Jovic, you tell me the meaning of this immediately or I will—"

Jan threw himself backward, into Ivena.

She cried out, but managed to stay upright.

Boom!

The gun's detonation sounded obscenely loud in the small room. Ivena needed no further encouragement. Jan snatched her hand and they ran together nearly step for step toward the back fence.

Helen had one leg draped on each side of the pickets. "Back, Helen!" Jan shouted. "Get back!" He spun around, grabbed Ivena around the waist, and hoisted her the full height of the fence with a grunt. "Pull her over!"

Helen complied and Ivena disappeared. Jan threw himself over without waiting. He glanced back in time to see the black-clad gunman slide to a stop at the corner of the greenhouse. The man was no idiot; he was powerless outside with a noisy gun.

Jan dropped to the ground. Helen had Ivena's hand and they were running for the car already.

Winded and panting like billows in chorus they piled into the Cadillac. Jan fired the engine and threw the car into drive. Jan squealed through a U-turn and sped down the street.

JAN SWERVED through suburban Atlanta a good five minutes before easing his foot from the accelerator and slowing the Cadillac to the posted speed limit. It took a full ten minutes for the flood of questions and explanations to subside into silence. Ivena seemed more horrified with Jan's attack at the Towers than with the fact that a gunman had nearly put a bullet through her skull in her own home.

"It was foolish, Janjic. Now you've endangered yourself."

"And I wasn't endangered before? He's a beast. I couldn't just stand by while an animal rampages through our lives."

"And now he will rampage less? I don't think so."

Jan ground his teeth but didn't respond directly.

"Where are we going?" Helen asked beside him.

"To Joey's cottage," Jan said.

"The gardener?" Helen asked.

"Yes. He lives in a small house on the property, bordering the gardens."

"You think it's safe there? What makes you think Glenn's men aren't already there waiting?"

"Glenn may be a monster, but he's not omniscient. No one knows of the place. It's pretty secluded."

Ivena spoke from the backseat. "My, my, I see we are in a pickle, Janjic. What are you up to now?" This from a woman who'd been kidnapped and beaten not forty-eight hours earlier.

They sped toward Joey's Garden of Eden rehashing their predicament. Ivena was right, Jan thought: They were in a pickle. Jan took a deep breath and breathed a prayer. *I beg you to see us out of this madness, Father. It was your meddling that started it.*

But it was not God who'd blown holes through Lutz's hands, was it? No. On the contrary, not so long ago someone had driven holes through *God's* hands. So what did that make Jan? The devil? Now there was a thought.

They approached Joey's cottage unseen as far as Jan could tell. Overgrowth crowded the dirt driveway that snaked along the property's bordering twelve-foot hedge. Tall oaks surrounded the small wooden structure, foreboding in the failing light. A yellow Ford Pinto sat on a gravel bed beside a house shrouded in foliage. The shades were pulled, but light glowed beyond them. It was six o'clock; Joey would be home from his day in the garden.

They climbed from the car, unspeaking. Vines crawled over the red brick. Green vines with large white flowers. They stood still and gazed at the sight. Ivena's flowers covered the side of the house; Jan could not mistake them.

Ivena walked for them without a word. She touched a blossom and turned back, her eyes round. Jan led Helen up the steps. Joey opened the door before their first knock. "Jan? Well, my goodness. I wasn't expecting company."

"Forgive me, Joey. We—"

"Come in, come in." The short man swept a thin arm into his home. "I didn't say I didn't *want* company. Only that I wasn't expecting it."

They walked in and Joey closed the door.

"Can I get you something to drink?"

"Actually, Joey, this isn't exactly a social visit. I mean it is, but not like you might expect. I'm afraid we're in a bit of trouble."

"The flowers have done well, I see," Ivena said.

Joey smiled. "Yes. Yes they have." They looked at each other but said no more.

Joey turned back to Jan and Helen. "Well, well, please sit down." He hurried around the small living room, straightening rust-colored cushions on a green rattan couch and a matching chair. A stone fireplace ate up half the floor space, but the decor was surprisingly colorful and cozy. Then again, Joey was a gardener—he would favor beauty.

He sat on the washed stone mantel. "So you are in some trouble. Tell me."

He listened while they spun their story, hearing it from beginning to end in one sitting, Saying it aloud, Jan was struck by its absurdity. This tale of love and horror, it sounded impossible in this land of peace. And to think, not four miles away construction was already in progress on the castle he was building for his bride. He looked at Helen—at the amber light shining in her glassy eyes—and a hand seemed to squeeze his heart. God's hand, he thought.

Joey kept looking at him as if checking to make sure it was really him, the author he knew. He could only nod. But in the end Joey insisted that they would be safe here. At least for a day while they decided what to do. Although they would have to manage with two bedrooms. Joey would take the couch.

He offered them bowls of a beef stew and they talked over a dozen options, none of which made any sense to Jan. The situation seemed impossible. Walking into a man's place of business and shooting him wasn't exactly self-defense. At the very least Jan needed to contact an attorney. In fact, why not drive to the police station right then and turn himself in? Yes indeed, why not? It seemed their only option.

Jan finally set his bowl on the coffee table and sighed. "I think there's only one thing that makes sense. But it's not Helen who's angered Glenn now. It's me. And he's made a direct threat against you, Ivena. There's only one way to ensure your safety."

"And what of you?"

"Please hear me out. If I were to contact the police and demand protective custody for you I believe they'd give it. You've already lodged a complaint. They can't ignore you now."

"So you want them to put *me* in jail?"

"You've done nothing wrong; they wouldn't put you in jail."

"But you have, Janjic. You have assaulted this man. They will put *you* in jail for that."

"Maybe. But then a prison may be the safest place for me. Until they unravel the truth."

"The truth is you shot a man," Helen said. "Regardless of what Glenn has done, they won't let that slide."

They looked at each other. "Either way I'll face consequences. If I can bring a detective here to hear our story we'll at least buy protection for Ivena. Do you have any doubt that Glenn will hurt Ivena?"

"No. But you're putting a lot of confidence in the police, aren't you? We're safe from him here."

"And how long do you think we can stay here? I have business expected of me. By midday tomorrow they'll be scouring the country for my whereabouts. I see no alternative. In the morning I'll call the detective who took Ivena's statement. What was his name?"

"Mr. Wilks," Ivena said. "Charlie Wilks."

"I wouldn't trust a soul," Helen said. "I'm telling you, if you think turning yourself in to the police is the way to go on this, then you don't know Glenn. He's got connections. You should call an attorney."

"I will. But first I will use my own contacts," Jan said. He stood and walked to the black telephone that hung on the wall.

"Who?"

He picked up the receiver. "Roald. Perhaps my estranged friend can pull a trick from his hat yet."

DETECTIVE CHARLIE Wilks was at his office desk at nine o'clock Tuesday morning when the third light on his phone lit to an annoying buzz. He punched the flashing cube. "Wilks."

"Detective Wilks, this is Jan Jovic."

Charlie sat up. "Jovic?" He glanced through the open door of his office. A dozen desks filled the gap, occupied by other detectives with lessor seniority.

"Yes. I have something—"

"Hold on. Could you hold on?"

"Yes."

Charlie rose from his desk, closed the door and returned. "Sorry about that. Where are you, Mr. Jovic?"

"I'm safe, if that's what you mean."

The man's voice carried a foreign accent. *Safe?* "You do realize that I have a citywide APB on you as we speak. I'm not sure what the laws are like back in your country, but here in America shooting a man's hands off is a crime. Are the others with you?"

The man hesitated a moment. "Others?"

"We have Helen and this Ivena who are also missing. I'm assuming they're with you."

"Yes. And Ivena reported her complaint to you yesterday, is that right?"

"Of course. But surely you understand that until I've had a chance to examine her claims, my hands are tied. In the meantime, I have seen Mr. Lutz's hands with my own eyes."

"All in good time, my friend. I want you to guarantee Ivena and Helen protective custody. When you hear their stories you will see that it is Glenn Lutz, not I, you should be searching for."

"I know where Glenn Lutz is. In fact I spoke to him this morning. You, on the other hand, I do not. You're only making things worse for yourself. Just tell me where you are and I'll hear you out."

"I will. But not until tomorrow morning. Until then, please do not make more of this than is absolutely necessary. I'm not a man without influence, Mr. Wilks. You may expect a call tomorrow."

The phone went abruptly dead.

Charlie's pulse spiked. He immediately punched up another line and dialed a string of numbers. Who would've guessed that a man with the backbone to shoot Glenn Lutz would cave so easily. Then again, Jovic had no reason to mistrust the police.

His friend's familiar voice spoke over the receiver. "Yes?"

"Hello, Glenn. I have some news."

"You do, do you? For your sake, Charlie, it better be good."

"See now, why are you always so hostile?" Charlie leaned back in his chair, confident. "He called."

Glenn's heavy breathing cut short. "The preacher called?"

"He wants to meet with me tomorrow morning. Ivena and Helen are with him."

"Where?"

"He wouldn't tell me. But he will."

The sound of Lutz's breathing filled the earpiece again. "And you'll tell me, won't you?" A few more loud breaths. "Won't you, Charlie?"

The man was clearly sick. "A hundred grand? That's what you said you'd pay if you need my help, right? I'd call this helping."

"That's what I said."

"You'll be my first call," Charlie said, grinning. "I'll even give you an hour head start."

"You just call me."

CHAPTER THIRTY-TWO

THE SKIES boiled black over Atlanta that evening, threatening rain before the traffic ended its rush. Jan parked the Cadillac in an alley two blocks from the ministry and climbed out. He was counting on his call to Detective Wilks buying him some time. If there was a police car watching the building for his return, this visit might backfire.

Jan scanned the street, saw no sign of the police, and stepped onto the sidewalk. He buried his hands in his pockets and walked with his head lowered. The employees should all have gone home by now, but there was always a chance that someone from the neighborhood would recognize him.

Jan had left Helen and Ivena at Joey's cottage nearly three hours ago. He'd made a pass by his street, hoping to retrieve a fresh change of clothes for he and Helen, but the police cruiser parked across the road had changed his mind. Ivena's house was also being watched. He'd opted for Woolworth's instead. Helen would have to live with the white dress he'd selected. It was a size five and the salesclerk had assured him that five was a good size for a small woman. He bought himself nothing.

He glanced up. The street was clear of cars. Evidently the police were more concerned with the houses than the ministry. Or perhaps it was the late hour.

Jan veered into the alley adjacent to the ministry building and walked for a steel fire door. "Don't let me down, Roald," he muttered. "Please not now."

He pulled the handle and the door swung out. A chill of relief washed down his back. He entered the dark hall, felt his way to the stairwell, and took the stairs two at a time. Red exit signs showed the way, but eight floors winded him and he paused at the top landing to catch his breath.

He pushed his way into the familiar office suite. He heard the voices immediately and knew that Roald had come through. He had not seen their cars, which meant they'd parked on the back street as he'd requested.

The conference room door was open and Jan walked in.

They were all there, and they looked at him as one. Roald, Karen, and Betty. Frank and Barney Givens, as well. He'd asked Roald for the council's attendance if possible; whether Frank and Barney had flown in or happened to be in the city, Jan did not know. Two of the four were here. And Betty was here as a representative from the ministry. The employees would want to know the truth once it hit the street, and he intended they receive it through Betty.

"Good evening, my friends," Jan said with a slight smile.

Roald sat at the head of the long table, frowning, his glasses riding the end of his nose. Beside him Karen leaned back with folded arms. Frank and Barney sat stoically to the left and Betty smiled warmly on his right.

"You'd better sit, Jan," Roald said.

"Hello, Roald. It's a pleasure to see you as well." A voice of caution whispered through Jan's mind. They were not reacting with the concern he'd imagined. Betty was smiling, but the others were not even cordial. "I was under the impression that I called this meeting. Why do I feel like I've walked into a snake pit here?" Jan asked, still standing.

"Oh, no, Jan," Betty said. She glanced around nervously. "How could you say—"

"You have something to say, say your piece," Roald interrupted.

Jan glared at him. "Thanks, Betty. Okay, Roald, I will." He pulled a chair out on Betty's side and sat. "Thank you for coming, Frank and Barney. Karen." They nodded in turn but offered no formal greeting.

"By your stiff lips I gather you've heard about the incident yesterday."

No reaction.

"I'll take that as a yes. I also know that from the beginning you haven't understood my relationship with Helen. No, let me rephrase that—from the beginning most of you have detested my relationship with Helen. Well, now the balance has shifted, because now I've been forced to do some things I'm not proud of. Something you may think will tarnish my image. But if you will just open your minds for a few minutes, I sincerely believe that you'll see things differently."

They sat and stared at him without responding.

Jan shifted his eyes from Roald. "Frank, three months ago you and Barney and the others from the council warned me about the delicate nature of my image as a church spokesman, and I will say that I questioned your judgment at the time. But I see some truth in your assessment now. 'To whom much is given, much is required,' I believe that was your quote. There were greater concerns at stake besides my own issues, you said. Concerns of the church. The ministry, for example. *The Dance of the Dead.* An opportunity to reach millions with a message of God's love. You wanted me to subordinate my own needs to the greater good of the church, isn't that right?"

Frank's eyes flickered and Jan spoke on.

"Well now perhaps there is an opportunity for you, all of you"—he glanced about the table—"to subordinate your own issues to the greater concerns of the church. To *The Dance of the Dead.* Perhaps now it's time for you to support me and my ministry, because, believe me, no one else will. What you've heard is true. I shot this madman Glenn Lutz in his hands, with his own gun, but only because he threatened to kill Ivena. Only because he's a monster of unearthly magnitude. And if you really knew—"

"We know more than you think we know," Roald interrupted.

"Meaning what?" A spike of anger rode Jan's spine.

"Are you finished?"

This was not going as planned. He had intended on laying out the whole scenario as he knew it to be. He'd come confident that they would hear him out and rally to his defense. But Roald did not seem to possess a soft bone in his body. Which seemed beyond even Jan. Karen had hardly moved since his entrance. Not that he expected any huge favors from her. Betty was the only one who showed a sympathetic spirit, but Betty did not possess the power these others did.

"No, I'm not finished. But you're obviously not understanding my point here, so why don't you go ahead and tell me what's on your mind, Roald." He bit down hard and suppressed an urge to walk over there and knock his head against the wall.

"Fine, I will. While you've been busy hiding from the police, which is the most ridiculous thing I've ever heard of, we've been busy trying to salvage your career. This goes much deeper than you realize, my naive friend. You have some problems, and now by association we have some problems."

"You think I don't know this? What—"

"The contract we signed with Dreamscape has some problems."

"The contract? What does the contract have to do with this? I thought they said it was virtually identical to the old one."

"Virtually, yes. But not exactly. It has a clause relating to morality that has come to our attention."

"Morality. And how does morality affect us in this contract?"

"That depends. It contains a clause that gives Dreamscape the right to pull the plug in the event that the moral character of the story's subject comes under question at any time before the movie's release date. The subject of the picture is you, Jan."

The statement dropped in Jan's mind like a small bomb. He blinked. "*My* moral integrity? What does that mean? They're already taking exception to my mistake yesterday? Or is it you, who are making more—"

"Not the shooting, you idiot! Stupid as that was—"

"Please don't interrupt me, Roald!" Jan said. "At least give me that courtesy."

"Of course."

"And if it's not the shooting, then what?"

Roald didn't respond. Frank did. "It's the woman, Jan. You were warned about her, weren't you?"

Jan's mind swam, too stunned to piece their reason together.

"I told you she was a risk," Roald snapped. Karen still hadn't spoken. She simply rocked back in her chair, arms still folded. Roald continued. "The studio is putting millions on the table, producing a picture that views the world through an exceptional lens—the eye of Jan Jovic, a man who has learned of love through the brutal lessons of war. And now they discover their *hero* is living with a . . . an unseemly woman. I told you she was a bad idea, didn't I? I sat right here and told you that this junkie of yours could ruin everything. And did you listen? No. Instead you go off and marry her, of all things!"

"And you know nothing, Roald!"

"No, of course I don't. That's why you ignored my advice to begin with. Because I know nothing. And you, the white crusader, know everything."

"Okay, guys," Karen said. "We're still on the same side here."

"Are we?" Roald shot back. "I'm on the side of getting this movie made, of getting this message out. And frankly I don't know what side Jan's on anymore."

"I'm on the side of love," Jan said. "The same side you were on at one time. It's the heart and soul of my story."

"Well, now your love is going to get *The Dance of the Dead* canceled. Your relationship with Helen undermines your moral authority."

The notion felt like a sick joke to Jan. "We're married, for heaven's sake! How could morality be an issue in marriage?"

Roald shook his head. "You really should have listened to me. It's the appearance of evil that matters, Jan. How are they going to sell a movie about one man's discovery of God and morality when his morals are in question? Isn't that what I told you?"

"And I'm asking you how my morality is in question!"

"Because appearances do matter, Jan. And your . . . *wife* does not give off the best appearances!"

Jan wanted to strike the man with his fist. He rose and stood against the conference table, shaking with rage.

"Now you want to shoot me like you did Mr. Lutz?" Roald asked.

"Okay, Roald," Karen said. "You've made your point." She turned to Jan and her eyes were emotionless. "Sit down, Jan."

Jan forced himself back into his chair. Frank and Barney sat side by side, like a jury studying the cross-examination.

"Dreamscape has given us a condition for continuance," she said. "They won't make the movie with a questionable moral dilemma hanging over your head."

"That's utterly ridiculous! And what's 'questionable' supposed to mean anyway?"

"It means," Roald said, "that either the woman goes or the movie goes. That's what it means."

"That's absurd! They want me to divorce? And they see that as moral? No studio could be so stupid! Someone else will buy the movie rights!"

"No they won't. Dreamscape has already made it clear that they won't sell the rights. Not as long as there's an adulterous relationship in the mix."

"I am *not* in an adulterous relationship! Who would make such a claim?"

Karen spoke. "They didn't say you were committing adultery—they claim that Helen's still seeing Glenn Lutz."

The room fell to silence. A sweat broke out on Jan's forehead. "The movie is about me, not Helen. And how would Dreamscape know of Glenn?"

"You are married to Helen. It looks bad," Roald answered, holding his eyes on Jan. "And Dreamscape would know about Glenn because for all practical purposes, Dreamscape is Glenn."

Dreamscape was Glenn? But how?

Then Jan knew how. Glenn had set this up for one purpose and one purpose only. The man would stop at nothing to get Helen back!

"So, Glenn acquires *The Dance of the Dead* through Dreamscape and he tells you that unless I end my relationship with Helen, *his* lover, then he won't make the picture. Is that about it?" Jan knew that a tremble accompanied his words, but he no longer cared. "And that doesn't sound odd to you? This pig is the devil himself and you don't see it, do you? It seems that I have grounds to sue him for manipulating the terms of the contract!"

"It doesn't matter how it sounds to us, Jan," Karen said. "He paid for the rights to the movie and we signed a contract that gives him the technical right to cancel the movie on these grounds. And now that you've assaulted him, he no doubt has other grounds."

"And he assaulted me. When the world discovers that, Glenn won't have a leg to stand on."

"So you say, but he has a voice as well. And either way he'll probably sue for all moneys already paid. Am I right, Roald?"

"Yes. That's right."

Jan faced the man. "So you talked to him yourself, Roald? You plotted behind my back with this devil?"

"Yes, I spoke to him. He called me. What did you want me to do? Refuse a call from the man behind our futures?"

"Your future, perhaps, but not mine. I'll *never* give in to a monster like Glenn."

"You will refuse, then? You'll kiss off seven million dollars and this entire ministry and everything you've lived for? Over this one lousy woman?"

Jan slammed his hand on the table and they all jumped. "She is *not* one lousy woman! She is everything! I have lived my life preparing to love her. And nothing—not seven million dollars, not a hundred million dollars—nothing will come between us! Do you understand this, or do I need to stamp it on your forehead?"

Roald's face flushed red. "You're throwing everything away! Everything!"

"Not Helen. I will not throw Helen away. *She* is everything! Nothing else matters!" Jan sat back and breathed heavily. "How can you sit there and suggest that I divorce my wife so that you can line your pockets with gold?"

Roald's face turned red and for a moment Jan thought he might leap over the table and attempt to remove his head.

"I don't think that's what Roald had in mind," Karen said with an apologetic smile. "I think he's genuinely concerned with the bigger picture here—"

"Is that what you think?" Jan interrupted. "And what did you have in mind, Karen? That somehow in this mess you would be vindicated?"

She appeared to have been slapped. Karen pulled herself up to the table. "Now you listen to me, you meathead. First of all, you must know that if this deal falls through it will be the end of the ministry. You ever think of that? The book will be canceled, the tours, everything will go away without the movie. A million lives will be impacted. You must see that. And the fact that you're living with—or married to—a woman who's in an adulterous affair with another man does give you right of divorce, doesn't it? In many circles it would be the only moral thing to do. What Roald's suggesting isn't that unreasonable."

Jan stared at Karen, wondering what other motive lay behind her sudden plea for reason. "Then, you don't understand either, Karen. The world doesn't turn on reason alone. It's a matter of love. I love her. Desperately. Surely *you*, of all people, can understand that."

He saw a flicker of surprise in her eyes. She did not answer.

Barney cleared his throat and spoke for the first time. "You can't always follow your heart," he said. "Not when it defies reason. God's given man a mind for good reason. We all know the pull of love. Love is blind and full of passion and, yes, reason hardly stands a chance. But it must, don't you see? All that is good and decent depends on it. You cannot just leave your mind to follow your heart's whims. There are greater issues at stake."

Jan felt anger rise again. "Such pretty words from a great lover, I am sure. But let me tell you, Father Micheal's love for God was not born of his mind alone. No, it came first from his heart. He was desperate for God and glad to die for him. Your words of reason will drain the heart of its power."

He turned to the others, leaning forward now. "I'll tell you, I've been given a very small slice of God's love for Helen and it makes my knees weak in her presence. You're suggesting I face God and tell him to keep his heart? Because a leader in the church said it was *unreasonable?* That's your position on this matter?"

"Of course not!" Frank said. "We're telling you to do what is right! But I can see that you're too selfish with this love of yours to consider what consequences your decision might have on the rest of the church. This is not simply about you and your feelings for one woman. The greater good of the church must be considered."

"The greater good of the church, you say. And the church is the Bride of Christ. So what is the greatest good for the Bride?"

"You're twisting my words to suit your own means! The Bride is not this one woman. The Bride is the church, millions strong. It is she you must consider."

"Love for the masses outweighs love for the few, is that it? Then let me suggest that God would quickly choose the true love—the unbridled, passionate love—of one soul over the acknowledgment of his deity from a hundred million churchgoing souls!"

"You demean the church?" Roald challenged.

"No, Roald, *you* demean the church. You mock the Bride. You undermine the value of love. The universe was created in the hopes of distilling a portion of genuine love. And now you suggest ignoring such love in favor of creating a moving picture for a profit. Nothing will ever compare to love, brother. Not all the devices man's mind can conceive, not a hundred thousand bulls slaughtered on the Day of Atonement. Nothing!"

Roald frowned. "And you have the spiritual pride to assume that you alone now possess God's love in your own heart? This love for an adulterous woman?"

"No, not me alone. But it's no different than God's love for an adulterous nation. For Israel. No different than his deep love for the church. His bride. You."

The leader found nothing to say. For a moment Jan thought he might see the light. But after blinking a few times, Roald set his jaw and pushed his chair back. "This is crazy. I can't believe we're even thinking of throwing this away because of one . . . The way you speak smells of heresy." He stood. "Well, Jan Jovic, I told you this once, but I'll tell you now for the last time. If the woman stays, then we go." As if on cue Frank and Barney stood with Roald.

"We've had enough of this nonsense. I assume you called us here to ask for our support. And now you have our conditions. I only hope that God speaks some sense to your heart."

"Yes, well you may pray for me, Roald. You do remember how to do that, don't you?"

Roald glared at Jan then huffed from the room with Frank and Barney.

Karen blew out some air and crossed her legs. "Well, *that* was quite a speech."

"Perhaps I expressed myself too strongly."

Betty spoke quietly. "I don't think so. I think you said what you needed to say. I've never heard such wonderful words." Her kind eyes smiled, and Jan thought that asking for her attendance was perhaps the only part of the meeting that had come off as planned.

"Thank you, Betty. You're very kind."

Karen grinned. "You certainly left no doubt as to where you stand. You're really going out on a limb this time, aren't you, Jan?"

He sighed and closed his eyes. What was happening? *Father, what have you done to me? You're stripping me of all you've given me.*

And now Glenn was threatening worse. How had he managed this impossible turn of events? He pictured the heavy man standing with bloodied hands in his office just yesterday, and now seeing the man's twisted smile, fear lapped at Jan's mind. The man was capable of anything.

"Jan."

He opened his eyes. Karen studied him. "You know on one level I can understand what you're doing."

"Yes? What am I doing, Karen? *I* don't even know what I'm doing."

"You're staying by the side of an unfaithful woman, that's what you're doing. And in staying by her side, you're throwing away the kind of life that most people can only dream about."

"Maybe." Jan looked at the chalkboard to their left. The figures of the new edition's intended distribution sprawled in white numbers, still vivid from the planning meeting during which they'd been drawn three weeks ago. "Or perhaps I've found the kind of love that most people only dream about. Anything less would be meaningless."

"Perhaps. That's the level I can understand. I look at you, and I find it hard to believe that you actually love her that way. It tears me up, you know. That could have been me you were speaking about." She shifted her gaze. "It's your sticking by her when she doesn't deserve you that I can't understand. That you love an unfaithful woman so much."

It was the first time they had spoken so candidly of Helen. Betty's eyes shone with understanding. Jan looked at Karen. "I'm sorry, Karen. I didn't mean to hurt you. Please tell me you know that."

"Maybe," she said. She was barely smiling and that was a good thing.

"I swear, Karen. I'm not sure I even understand it myself."

"This could change your life, you know? You could lose everything."

"The studio won't back down?"

"I don't know. It does seem crazy, doesn't it?" She shook her head. "This is all happening too quickly. You don't actually think Lutz would hurt Ivena, do you?"

"Of course he would! You don't know the man."

"Then you should go to the police," Betty said. "You hurt a man who threatened you. It may not be the act of a saint, but it's not the end of the world."

"She's right," Karen agreed. "That may be your only hope now. *Our* only hope; you're not the only one who stands to lose on this."

"I came here hoping that Roald could pull some strings. Either way, I've already arranged to meet the police in the morning."

"Good." Karen stood and Betty followed suit.

"And what if Glenn isn't bluffing?" Jan asked.

Karen walked to the door and shrugged. She faced him. "I think you're doing the right thing, Jan. I want you to know that. Your love for her is a good thing. I see that now."

"Thank you, Karen."

She smiled. "We've pulled through some bad times before."

"None this bad," he said.

"No, none this bad."

Then she left.

Betty patted him lightly on the shoulder. "I will pray for you, son. And in the end, you'll see. This will all make sense."

"Thank you, Betty."

She too left him, now all alone.

Jan lowered his head to the table and he cried.

CHAPTER THIRTY-THREE

"The day of death [is] better than the day of birth.
It is better to go to a house of mourning than
to go to a house of feasting."

Ecclesiastes 7:1–2 NIV

JAN PULLED the Cadillac onto the overrun driveway leading to Joey's cottage. He drove slowly, listening to the crunch of gravel under the car's tires. *Father, you have abandoned me. You have given me everything only to strip it away.*

Joey's Pinto was missing. Perhaps the gardener had gone for supplies.

Jan parked the Cadillac and walked to the house. He'd reached the first step up to the porch when the door flew open. It was Ivena. She stared at him with wide eyes.

"Hello, Ivena."

Suddenly Joey pushed past her.

"Hello, Joey. I—"

A buzz erupted in his mind. He instinctively turned to where the Pinto should have been. But of course it was not there.

"Where's Helen?"

"Janjic. Janjic, please come in. We were worried."

He spun to her. "Where is Helen?" he shouted.

"We think she took the car," Joey said.

Jan closed his mouth and swallowed. He stared at Ivena and she looked back, her eyes misted with anguish. He wanted to ask her how long Helen had been gone, but that didn't matter, did it?

No, nothing really mattered. Not anymore. She had gone back. His bride had gone back.

Jan suddenly felt such a shame that he thought he might break into a wail right there on the front step. He whirled from them and fled down the path leading into the garden. Overhead, thunder boomed and he stumbled forward, through the hedge, and now a growling sound escaped his throat. It was a moan that he felt powerless to stop. His chest was exploding and he could not contain himself.

He plunged through the garden without thinking of where his feet carried him; he only wanted to leave this place. It was a place of treachery and mockery and the worst kind of pain. It was not what he wanted. Now he only wanted death.

"SHOULD WE go after him?" Joey asked.

"No. It is something he must face on his own," Ivena said. Tears glistened on her cheeks.

"Are you sure he'll be okay?"

"He is walking through hell, my friend. He is dying inside. I don't know what will happen. All I know is that we are witnessing something the world has rarely seen in such a plain way. It makes you want to throw yourself at the foot of the cross and beg for forgiveness."

Joey looked at her, a puzzled look on his face.

She turned to him and smiled. "You will understand soon enough. Now we should pray that our Father will visit Janjic." Then she walked into the cottage.

HELEN TOLD herself that her decision to go was for Jan's sake. She told herself that a hundred times.

As a matter of fact, it had been her first thought. That first seed that had taken root in her mind. *Maybe you can talk some sense into him. Maybe Glenn will listen to you.* That had been around noon, before she really had time to mull the possibilities through her mind.

By midafternoon her thoughts had become as stormy as the skies rumbling overhead. No matter how strenuously she tried to convince herself otherwise, she knew then that she actually wanted to go back. That she *had* to go back. And not just to tell Glenn that he was being a baby about this whole mess, but because butterflies were flapping wildly in her stomach and her throat was craving a taste.

By late afternoon a perpetual tremor rode her bones. The possibility of pleasure had taken up residence and was growing at an obscene rate. Her reason began to leave her at four. Questions like, *How could you even think of doing this again?* or *Who in God's name would stoop so low?* became vague oddities, worth noting, but hardly worth considering. At five her reason was totally gone. She stopped trying to convince herself of anything and began planning her escape.

The fact that Joey left the keys in the yellow Pinto made leaving that much easier. She would have the car back before they knew it was missing. Ivena was off talking to Joey in the garden about some new species of rose; they wouldn't know if a meteor struck the house.

By the time Helen pulled into the underground parking structure at the Towers, she was sweating. She very nearly turned the car around then in a last-minute flash of sense. But she didn't. She stepped onto the concrete and suddenly she was desperate to be upstairs, high on the thirtieth floor.

To tell Glenn what a baby he was being about this whole mess, of course.

Just that. Just to step in for Jan and call the pig off Ivena and save the day. And to take a tiny snort. Or maybe two snorts.

JAN CLIPPED his foot on a small shrub rounding a corner and sprawled face first to the cool sod. He lay there numb for a few moments. Then it all gushed out of him in uncontrollable sobs. He lay there and shook and wet the grass with his tears.

Time seemed to lose itself, but at some point Jan hauled himself from the ground and settled into a heavily flowered gazebo. Thunder continued to rumble, but farther away now.

Jan slumped on the gazebo bench and stared at the black shapes of bushes lining the lawn before him like tombstones. Slowly his mind pieced together his predicament. He was hiding from the police, but that was the least of it. The price his imprudence would extract from him would be relatively small compared to what he'd lost with Helen's leaving.

The rug was being pulled from beneath his feet, he thought. *The Dance of the Dead* was finding its death. And not mercifully, but with savage brutality. Karen was right: Everything would change if they canceled the movie. The ministry, his notoriety, the castle he was building for his bride. It would all be snatched away—leaving him with what?

His bride.

Ha!

His bride! Jan trembled with fury in the small shelter. For the first time since entering the garden he spoke aloud.

"Father, I want you to take this from me. I cannot live with this!" His voice came in a soft growl and then grew in volume. "You hear me? I hate this! Take her from me. I beg you. You have given me a curse. She's a curse."

"Good evening."

Jan jerked upright at the voice. A man stood in the moonlight, leaning against the gazebo's arch.

"Beautiful night, isn't it?"

Jan ran a hand across his eyes to clear his vision. Here was a man, tall and blond, smiling as if meeting another person after dark in this garden was an everyday occurrence.

"Who . . . who are you?" Jan asked. "The garden's closed."

"No. I mean yes, the garden is closed. But I'm not anyone to be afraid of. And if you don't mind my asking, how did you get in?"

"My friend is the gardener. He let me in."

"Joey?" The man chuckled. "Good old Joey. So what brings you here so late at night? And looking so forlorn."

Jan stood. Who did this man think he was, questioning him like this? "I guess I could ask the same of you. Do you have permission to be here?"

"But of course. I have come to speak with you."

"You have?"

"Do you still love her, Jan?"

Jan's heart quickened. "How do you know my name? Who sent you?"

"Please. Who I am isn't important. My question is, Do you still love her?"

"Who?"

"Helen."

There it was then. Helen. "And what do you know about Helen?"

"I know that she is no more extraordinary and no less ordinary than every man. Every woman," the man said.

The answer sounded absurd and it made Jan wonder again who he could be, knowing Helen and Joey and speaking so craftily. "Then you don't know Helen. Nothing could be farther from the truth."

"Tell me why she is so different."

"Why should I tell you anything?" Jan paused. Then he gave the man his answer. "She's stolen my heart."

The man smiled. "Well, then that would make her extraordinary. And what makes her less?"

"She has broken my heart."

"Does she love you?"

"Well, now that's the big question, isn't it? Yes, she loves me. No, she hates me. Which side of her mouth would you like the answer to come from? The side that whispers in my ear late at night or the side that licks from Glenn's hand?"

The man suddenly grew very still. The smile that had curved his lips flattened. "Yes, it hurts, doesn't it?" He swallowed—Jan saw it because the moon had broken through the clouds and now lighted one side of a chiseled face. His Adam's apple bobbed. The man turned to face the shadows, and lifted a finger to his chin. The anger in Jan's heart faded.

The stranger cleared his throat. "It does hurt. I won't dispute you." He faced Jan again and spoke with some force. "That doesn't make her more or less extraordinary, my friend. She is predictably common in her treachery. So utterly predictable."

Jan blinked, unable to respond.

"But how you respond to her, now that could be far less common." The man's words hung on a delicate string. "You could love her."

"I do love her."

"You do love her, do you? Really love her?"

"Yes. You have no idea how I have loved her."

"No? She is desperate for your love."

"She cannot even *accept* my love!"

"No, she can't. Not yet. And that's why she's so desperate for it."

Jan paused, removing his gaze from the man. "This is absurd, I don't even know you. Now you expect to engage me about this madness without telling me who you are? What gives you that right?"

"Ivena once said that God has grafted his love for Helen into your heart. Do you believe that?"

"And how do you know what Ivena has told me?"

"I know Ivena well. Do you believe what she said?"

"I don't know, honestly. I no longer know."

"Still, you must have an opinion on the matter. Was Ivena mistaken?"

"No. No, she was not mistaken. It started that way, but it doesn't mean I still have any part of God's heart. A man can only live with so much."

"A man can only *live* with so much. True enough. At some point he will have to *die* for something. If not now, then for an eternity."

Jan stilled at the words, surprised. How much truth was in those few words? *At some point he will have to die for something.* They could easily be from his own book, and yet spoken here by this stranger they sounded . . . magical.

"I love her, yes," Jan said, and a lump rose to his throat. "But she does not love me. And I'm afraid she will never love me. It's too much. Now I feel nothing but regret."

The stranger did not move. "Do you know that even the Creator was filled with regret? It's not such an unusual sentiment. He was sorry he'd ever made man, and in fact he sent a flood to destroy them. A million men and women and children suffocated under water. Your frustration is not so unique. Perhaps you are feeling what he felt."

"You're saying that God felt this anger? It certainly doesn't seem to fit with this love he gave me."

"You are made in his image, aren't you? You think he's beyond anger? The emotions of rejection are a powerful sentiment, Jan. God or man. And yet still he died willingly, despite the rejection. As did the priest and Nadia. As will others. So perhaps it's time for you to die."

"Die? How would I die?"

"Forgive. Love her without condition. Climb up on your cross, my friend. Unless a seed fall to the ground and die, it cannot bear fruit. Somehow the church has forgotten the Master's teachings."

A buzz droned through Jan's mind. They were his own words thrown back into his face. "The teaching's figurative," he argued.

"Is the death of the will any less painful than the death of the body? Call it figurative if it makes you comfortable, but in reality the death of the will is far more traumatic than the death of the body."

"Yes. Yes, you are right. In the death of the body the nerve endings soon stop feeling. In the death of the will the heart doesn't stop its bleeding so quickly. Those were my own words."

"Perhaps you've forgotten," the man said. "Now you're tasting that same death."

"*She* is causing my death. Helen is forcing me to die," Jan said.

"No more than you have caused the death of Christ. Yet he loved you no less." A wide smile spread across the stranger's face and the moonlight glinted off his eyes. "But the fruits of love are worth death, my friend. A thousand deaths."

"The fruits?"

"Joy. But for the joy set before him, Christ endured the Cross. Unspeakable joy. A million angels kissing one's feet could not compare to the rapture found in the tender words of one human."

Jan swallowed. This stranger would know, he thought, although he wasn't sure why. He stood and paced the floor of the gazebo, thinking of these words. He turned his back to the man and stared out at the round white moon. The man was no ordinary friend of Ivena, surely. Not with this insight.

The edge is gone from my pain already, he thought. *I have spoken to this man for no more than a few minutes and my heart is feeling hope again.*

"And what of Helen?" Jan asked without looking back. "How will she learn to love? She must *die?"*

It was a backward way of looking at the universe, he thought. He'd always understood the place of death, as it related to life. A seed must fall to the ground and die before giving life to the tree. But he'd never associated death with *love.* Yet it was in love—in the death of self required by love—that it made the clearest sense. The man hadn't answered his question.

"You're saying that she too"—he turned to the man—"must find—"

He caught himself mid-sentence. The man was gone. Jan spun around, found no one and stepped from the gazebo. The stranger was not in sight! He had said his piece and then left.

Jan called into the night, "Hello. Is anybody there? Hello." But the garden remained still except for his own voice.

The stranger's words echoed through his mind. *She is desperate for your love.*

What was he doing? His whole life—all of eternity—seemed to be in the balance for this one woman. For Helen. And he had all but cursed her. *Oh, dear Helen. Forgive me!*

Jan tore for the path and angled for the east wall that hid Joey's cottage. A panic fluttered through his stomach.

Oh, Father, forgive me!

THE PINTO was still missing when Jan burst through the hedge. He slid to a stop on the gravel, his heart thumping in his chest. She had come back and left already, perhaps.

He bounded up the cottage steps and flung the door open. A dim lamp glowed by the single rattan chair, casting light over Ivena's face.

"She hasn't come yet, Janjic." She'd been crying, he could hear it in her voice. Ivena walked toward him without waiting for him to close the door. She placed her arms around him and laid her head against his chest. "I am sorry, dear. I am very sorry."

Jan put his hand on her head. "So am I, Ivena. But we aren't finished. There's more to this story. Isn't that what you've been saying?"

"Yes." Ivena stepped back and sniffed. "I have been praying for your understanding, Janjic."

He stepped into the cottage and closed the door. "And God has answered your prayer."

She smiled. "Then I will retire now."

"And I will wait for her."

Ivena and Joey each slept in the bedrooms, leaving the living room to Jan, a gracious gesture considering the circumstances. The night rested eerily quiet. Crickets chirped in the forest, but no traffic sounds reached the cottage. Jan suddenly felt a return of the pain that had flooded his bones earlier. He sank to his knees by the amber lamp, feeling destitute.

What if Helen did not return? Silence rang in his ears, high-pitched and piercing. He gripped his hands into fists. How could the stranger in the garden possibly know of this dread that rushed through his veins? It was death. His heart was being torn to shreds by a death no less real than Father Micheal's. At least the priest had gone to the grave with a smile.

He gritted his teeth, biting back a shaft of fury.

No, Janjic. If you die, it will be for love.

I am dying for love and it is killing me. He should brand that on his forehead. He slumped to his haunches, overcome by grief. The night blurred in his vision.

For a long time Jan knelt like a lump of clay, feeling lifeless. He got up once and poured himself a glass of tea, but he left it full on the counter after a single sip. He walked to the fireplace and slid along the wall to his seat.

The noise came to his ears then. It was a slight grating and it was at the front door. He had not heard a car approach.

He looked up, thinking it was the wind—it would cease any moment. But it didn't. In fact, if he wasn't mistaken, it was the front latch and it was being poked and scratched. Jan came halfway to his feet, his heart pounding.

And then the door swung in, open to the night, and Jan froze. She stood there. Helen stood there, wavering on her feet, taking in the room as if she were trying to understand it.

It occurred to Jan in that moment that he should scream at her. He should slap her and send her packing, because she was standing in the doorway, obviously stoned, slinking back from that beast.

But he could do no such thing. Never.

Helen took two steps forward and stopped again in a wedge of light from the moon, orienting herself in the darkness.

Jan stood up in the darkness and she faced him, perhaps not even knowing precisely who he was. "Helen?"

She looked at him with blank eyes glistening in the dim light.

Jan stepped toward her. "Helen, are you okay?"

She stood still, unresponsive.

"Helen, I'm so sorry!" He reached her and saw that she was trembling. He swept her from her feet, and she felt like a rag doll. A limp doll shaking and now whimpering with tears. "Oh, my dear. I'm so sorry," he said.

You are sorry for precisely what, Janjic? It is she, not you, who has betrayed.

But it is I who love, he answered himself.

Jan took her to the couch and laid her down. "Sleep, darling. Sleep." He pulled an afghan over her body. "It's okay. I'm here now." He knelt beside her and tucked the blanket around her carefully. Tears were streaming down her face, he saw. And his. His heart was breaking for her. Weeping. Like heaven, his heart was weeping for Helen.

She didn't speak to him for a long time, but he knew from her drooping eyes and sweet mouth, wrinkled with anguish, that she felt so much shame. So much that she could not speak it. It was this as much as any lingering intoxication that immobilized her.

Jan laid his head on her breast and he held her gently. They wept together for long minutes. Then she pushed herself up and buried her wet face in his neck.

"I'm sorry . . . ," she whispered. A sob choked her off.

"Shhhh." He pulled her tight.

She groaned. "No. I'm so sorry. Oh, God, I'm sorry. I'm so sorry . . ." Her words were loud enough to wake the house.

But Jan couldn't speak for the fist in his throat. He only wept with her and she kept groaning her remorse. It was a union of their spirits and it was sweet. The fruit of love. The stranger was right; his death in forgiveness was nothing compared to this joy.

Slowly she quieted, and he held her against his chest. Her body eventually stopped its shaking and then her breathing fell into a deep steady rhythm. She was asleep. His wife was asleep.

CHAPTER THIRTY-FOUR

HELEN KEPT to herself the following morning, nursing a cup of coffee and looking as if she would have chosen to remain hidden under the covers given a choice. Fortunately the hours leading up to Jan's phone call to the police were too mixed with speculation about their futures to give any space to the previous evening's debacle. Now more than ever, it seemed that a meeting with Detective Charlie Wilks was their only hope to save Jan and keep Ivena safe. One thing they all agreed on: Lutz had to be stopped. Regardless of how they felt about it, he quite literally held their lives in his hands. And now that Roald and the council had refused to help, there was no one but the authorities to whom they could appeal.

Jan put an overdue call in to Bill Waldon, an attorney the ministry had used on occasion, but Bill was no defense counsel. He put Jan in touch with a Mike Nortrop who was. Nortrop heard the short version of the story and then announced that there was nothing he could really do until the police charged Jan with a crime. The minute they did, Nortrop would be at the station. In the meantime, *Yes!* Jan must absolutely turn himself in. Running had been a "cockamamie" idea in the first place, he said. He hung up with the insistence Jan call him the minute they had any word.

Helen still didn't like the idea, but Jan saw no alternatives.

He made the call.

"Detective Wilks, please."

"One moment."

Ivena, Helen, and Joey all sat around the table, watching Jan in silence.

"Wilks here."

Jan took a breath and spoke calmly. "Good morning, Mr. Wilks. This is Jan Jovic."

"Jan. Well, Jan, it's good that you called. We were getting worried down here. Is everything all right?"

"Everything's fine. You're ready to meet?"

"Yes, of course we are," Wilks said. "I've been waiting for your phone call. Just tell me where you are."

Helen suddenly leaned forward and waved her hand frantically, whispering words Jan could not understand.

"Hold the phone a second." He covered the mouthpiece with his palm. "What?"

"Tell him to meet you alone, first. Not here."

"I thought our point was to secure protection for Ivena," he whispered.

"Just ask him. Please, it can't hurt."

Jan lifted the phone. "Hello?"

"I'm waiting, Jovic."

"I would like to meet you alone," he said. "Without Ivena."

"Alone? That wasn't the deal."

The detective's voice had tightened, and it triggered an alarm in Jan's spine. Why would the man care? He glanced at Helen. "It's me you want."

"We had a deal, Mr. Jovic. Now you're backing out of that deal, is that it?"

"Why are you interested in seeing Ivena? She's done nothing."

"That was *your* deal, mister."

"Yes, and now I'm changing it. Do you have a problem with that?"

"Yes, I have a problem . . ." He heard the man take a deep breath. Jan knew then that Helen was right. He could not trust the police. Heat washed over his shoulders.

"Look, Mr. Jovic, let's be reasonable—"

"I am trying to be reasonable. But I don't understand *your* reason. What crime has Ivena committed that you need to see her?"

"Please, Jan. Okay to call you Jan?"

"Sure."

"Okay, Jan. You've broken the law, do you understand that? I can book you on a dozen counts as we speak. Now you don't turn yourself in like we agreed and I swear I'll put you away as a felon, you hear me?"

"Yes, but why *Ivena?*"

"Because that was the deal! I need to verify her story," the detective snapped. "And don't think I can protect you if you don't play ball, buster. Glenn may be the victim on this one, but believe me, he knows how to play both sides."

"That sounds like a threat."

"You just tell me where you are."

"I will call you back, Detective Wilks. Good-bye."

Jan dropped the phone in its cradle, his head buzzing from the exchange.

"What did he say?" Helen blurted. "He went weird on you, didn't he? I told you he was in Glenn's hands. I knew it!"

Jan shook his head, unbelieving.

"The police are corrupted by Glenn, then?" Ivena asked.

"And I'll tell you something else," Helen said. "We won't be safe here forever."

They all turned to her. "Why?" Joey asked.

"They know we're north of town. They followed me that far before I lost them."

Silence settled around Joey's kitchen table. No one knew quite how to deal with the revelation.

"Which basically means we've got a problem," Jan said. "A very big problem. We have no one to turn to."

"Karen?" Ivena asked.

"She has no political clout. She might be help in a courtroom, as a witness, but not with the police now. What does it matter if we're in the right if Glenn kills Ivena? What we need is protection now." He shook his head. "I can hardly believe it's come to this. It's a free country, for heaven's sake!"

"Can the ministry help?"

"No."

"What about other friends? Surely you have well-placed friends," Joey said.

"I've been in the country for five years. Apart from Roald and Karen and their circle I'm only a passing face. And what does it matter? Glenn owns the rights to the movie. He owns me!"

"No one owns you, Janjic. What is this movie? I told you—"

"The movie is the future of the ministry, Ivena. Say what you like, but it's the gateway to a million hearts. And it's a livelihood."

"Not if Glenn Lutz owns it."

She was right. She could not be more right.

"Then what?" Joey asked. "I'm not hearing too many options that make sense."

No one responded.

"It's not safe here. What do we do?" Joey asked quietly, his eyes wide.

Jan knew then what they had to do. He'd known deep inside from the moment Roald walked out of the conference room last night. But it was suddenly very clear. He glanced at Helen and wondered how she would respond.

He snatched up the phone and punched in a number. The others only stared at him. It rang four times before someone picked up.

"Hello?"

"Betty?"

"Jan! Jan what on earth's happening? The police are—"

"Thank God you're there. Listen to me carefully, Betty. I need you to hear me very carefully. Is anyone else in the room?"

"No."

"Good. Please don't tell anyone that I called. It's very important, do you understand? What I'm going to say to you has to remain absolutely confidential. You can't tell the police anything. Can you do that?"

"Yes. I think so."

"No, you need to be certain. My life may depend on it."

"Yes, Jan. I can do that."

"Good. I need you to do a couple things for me. First you must go to my house. It'll be watched by the police, but ignore them. If they question you, tell them that you're retrieving mail as you always do when I'm absent on trips. If they ask where I am, you tell them that I'm in New York, of course. You have that? New York."

"Yes."

"Under my bed you'll find a small metal box. It's locked. Take it with you. Can you do that? It should fit under your dress." Jan glanced at Ivena, who'd raised her eyebrows. He ignored her.

"Yes," Betty said.

"Good. And I need to meet with some of the employees tonight. John and Lorna and Nicki. Some of the group leaders. Not at the ministry."

"My place?"

Jan hesitated. Betty's house would be perfect. She lived on a small farm on the west side of town. "Yes, that would be good. Be sure that no one knows. I can't overstress the need for secrecy."

"I understand. Really. What about Karen?"

The question took Jan by surprise. "If she's still in town, perhaps. Yes. There's one more thing. I need ten thousand dollars in cash. You'll have to convince Lorna to cash a check, but do it discretely. She may give you some trouble, you know how she is—"

"I can handle Lorna. Are you okay, Jan? This isn't sounding good."

"We're fine, Betty. I'll see you at nine o'clock tonight. If there are any problems, please leave your porch light off. I'll know not to come then."

Betty told him that she'd pray for him, and not to worry, she hadn't been born yesterday. That much he knew. He wondered if sending her to the house to smuggle his safe out under the nose of the police had been so wise. He hung up and exhaled.

"And what was the meaning of that?" Ivena asked.

"That, Ivena, was our ticket out of this mess. Our only way now. And it's your dream come true."

JAN TURNED the Cadillac's headlamps off before entering the long dirt drive to Betty's house at nine that evening.

"Light's on," Helen said.

The porch light was on. "I see that." He flipped the car's lights back on and drove to the ranch house. A white picket fence bordered the small neat lawn. Jan recognized the cars parked along the drive, Karen's blue Fairlane among them, straddling the grass to their right. He turned off the ignition and they got out.

"You're sure about this, Jan?" Helen asked, standing before the white farmhouse.

Jan took her hand and kissed her knuckles. "It's the only way."

"He's right," Ivena said. "It feels right."

"You're not sure, Helen?" Jan asked.

"It's not me. I like the idea, but I'm not the one jumping off a cliff."

Jan pulled her hand and they walked up the sidewalk. "We eagles like the cliffs," he said with a grin.

Betty answered his tap on the door. "Jan. Come in." He ushered Helen and Ivena inside and they stood gazing at nearly a dozen familiar faces, now crowded in Betty's living room. Silence swallowed whatever speculation the staff harbored about the meeting's purpose.

Betty smiled and nodded at Jan. John sat beside Lorna, both intent on him. Steve wiggled nervously to their left. Karen stood at the back with folded arms.

"Good evening, my friends," Jan said, smiling.

"Good evening."

Helen and Ivena took seats that Betty had set out facing the couch. Jan stood behind his chair. "Thank you for coming on such short notice. And thank you, Betty, for getting everyone here."

He took a deep breath. "So then, I'll be as brief as possible." They hung on his words already. Such a devoted group, so many friends. "You've all met my wife, Helen." A string of acknowledgments. "Most, if not all of you, were at our wedding." He paused and looked at Helen. She'd agreed to his plan wholeheartedly, but now she blushed.

"Some of you know the circumstances surrounding our marriage. But today you will all become participants in a dilemma that is changing our lives." *Move on, Janjic. Tell them.* "What you hear may sound . . . unusual to some of you. It may even sound impossible, but please hear me out. For your own sakes, hear me out."

No one moved. He glanced at Betty and saw her head dip slightly. Not even she knew what he'd come to tell them.

"Twenty years ago a priest named Father Micheal discovered a love for God, and he died for that love. Little Nadia died for the same love; you all know the story well—it is *The Dance of the Dead.* That love changed my life. It introduced me to the Creator."

He cleared his throat and took a deep breath. "Today, it seems that love has been born in me as well. I who saw the martyr's death, I who saw the love of Nadia am myself learning their love. We all are, I suppose. But to feel the love of the Father, it is something that will undo a man."

Jan fell silent for a few moments, judging their response. But they just stared at him with round eyes, eager for him to continue.

"I tell you this to help you understand what I will say now. I am taking my bride back to Bosnia."

The room suddenly felt evacuated of air.

"I won't be returning to America. Ivena, Helen, and myself are leaving for Bosnia to live. In Sarajevo."

They sat like mannequins, unmoving. Perhaps they didn't understand what he was saying. "But . . . but what about the movie?" John asked.

"The movie is gone."

Now a gasp ran through the gathering. "What? Why? That's impossible!"

"No, I'm afraid it's not impossible, my friends. You see, I was given a choice. The producer doesn't think my marriage . . . benefits the movie."

"But that's ridiculous," John said. "What does your marriage have to do with the movie?"

Choose your words, Janjic. "Nothing. Nothing at all. And yet they disagree. They seem to think that my character is in question." He put his hand behind Helen's head and she blushed.

"I would like to wring their necks personally!" It was Betty again.

Jan did not laugh. "Believe me, I understand the sentiment."

"So they can do that?" John demanded. "They can insist that?"

"They can and they have."

Lorna spoke the question undoubtedly on all of their minds. "And what does that mean for the ministry?"

"I'm afraid we'll have to return what we've been paid to the movie studio. It means that we have no choice but to close the ministry."

The cry of outrage came immediately from every corner of the room. "No! They can't do that! Never!" Even Karen looked stunned. Yet surely she knew this was coming.

"Can't we fight this?" Steve demanded. "Can't we get a lawyer or something?"

Jan looked at the wiry old man. The ministry had become his life. Helen lowered her head as if she was beginning to understand the price being paid for her.

"We could, but I am told that technically the producers are within their rights. It comes down to a choice that I must make. And I've made that choice. The ministry must close its doors. I'm sorry. The time has come for me to return to my homeland."

"What about Roald?" John asked. "Can't he do something?"

"Actually, I'm afraid even the council is deserting us this time. Not everyone sees the church in the same way, and now they see it differently than I do."

"I never did like that stuffed shirt!" John said.

"Please understand me, my friends. I don't want to leave you. But it's the call God has put in my heart. My story isn't finished, as Ivena has insisted for some time now, and the next chapter does not occur on American soil."

"And what will happen in Bosnia?"

"We will be free to love each other." He glanced at Helen.

Jan stated it simply and firmly, but they did not swallow it so quickly or easily. They went back and forth for another full hour, the more outspoken employees speaking their minds repeatedly, some arguing that Jan was right, others questioning what they saw as a preposterous suggestion. How could a whole ministry just shut down because of one deal gone bad?

In the end it was Lorna, biding her time for most of the debate, who brought the room to stillness once again. She simply outlined the financial state of the ministry. Without the movie deal, they would be lucky to get out of their lease without legal action. They were flat broke. Payroll was out of the question—even the one coming this Friday. And Jan? Jan would have to give up his house and his car, not to mention possibly being forced into bankruptcy. They might all be losing their jobs, but Jan was losing his life.

That silenced them all.

They stared at Jan with sad eyes now, finally understanding the full purpose of the meeting. For five long years they had given their lives to *The Dance of the Dead.* And now the dance was over.

They cried and they hugged and in the end they smiled. Because Jan could not hide the glint in his eyes. He was sure that they finally did believe him: It was indeed God who had placed this new tune in his heart. So he would dance a new dance—a dance of life, a dance of love.

And now that he thought about it, Jan could hardly stand to remain on American soil a second longer. It was time to go home.

Chapter Thirty-Five

GLENN SAT cross-legged like a brooding beast on top of his desk. A dull pain throbbed relentlessly under the sling that held his right arm. A single white bandage sufficed for the finger on his left hand, but at times its pain overshadowed that of his shoulder.

They had scoured the northern outskirts of Atlanta for nearly two days without finding a sign of Helen following her disappearance. She'd come to him, and that had been a slice of heaven. But she had also left, and then lost the tail he'd put on her. Worse, the preacher had not followed through with his promise to meet Charlie. Charlie had tipped his hand, and Glenn had nearly taken his head off telling him so.

But they couldn't hide forever. Now it would be better to kill them all. One way or another he would at least kill the preacher and the bag of bones. And the next time he laid hands on Helen, he would maim her. At least.

The door suddenly cracked and Beatrice stepped in. "Sir, I have some news."

"Well, give it to me. You don't have to be so theatrical," he growled.

She ignored him and made her way to the guest chair. Only when she'd seated herself and smoothed out her black skirt did she speak. "They've left the country," she said.

Glenn sat, speechless. What was the wench telling him? They had fled to Canada? Or Mexico?

"The preacher has signed ownership of everything over to a manager for liquidation and he's taken the women out of the country."

A panic washed over his back. *He's taken her? He's taken her for good?* Glenn shoved himself off his desk, hardly aware of the pain that shot through his bones. His phone crashed to the tile. "He can't do that! He can't do that, can he? Where? When?"

Beatrice shrank back. "To Yugoslavia. Yesterday."

"Yugoslavia? Bosnia?" Glenn strode quickly to his left and then doubled back to his right. The preacher had taken Helen back to Bosnia! It was impossible! "He can't just leave! He owes me over a million dollars. Don't they know that?" He was having difficulty breathing, and he stopped to pull air into his lungs. "Doesn't that imbecile Charlie have any control at all?" He swore. *Think. Think!* "We have to stop them."

"I'm not even sure Detective Wilks knows it's happened. I received a call from the man in charge of the liquidation. He told me not to bother suing; he's already been instructed to funnel all proceeds from the sale to satisfy your debt."

"But she went with him?"

"Relax, Glenn. It's not the end of the world. You stand to lose a lot of money on the movie deal. That should concern you more."

He whirled to her. "And you know nothing, you witch!" He spit savagely to his right. "I'm losing her!"

She did not respond.

Glenn suddenly pulled up. "They are in Bosnia?"

"That's what I—"

"Shut up! Maybe it's better this way. I'll have them killed in Bosnia! They can't touch me!" *But that was not true.* Nothing *could be better this way!*

Beatrice sat back. "Killed in Bosnia? All of them?"

"If I can't have her, I have no choice but to kill her. You know that."

A thin smile crossed her mouth. She stared at him over her horn-rimmed glasses. "Who do you know in Eastern Europe?" she asked.

Glenn closed his eyes and desperately tried to settle himself. How could this have possibly happened? He groaned and exhaled a lungful of stale breath. He walked to the desk and ran his hand along its high-gloss finish. He would see her again, he swore it to himself. Dead or alive he would see her again.

His hand came to rest beside a notepad. He lifted it. The preacher's book stared up at him, its red cover mocking him in full-throated laughter. *The Dance of the Dead.* He picked it up. To think that this maniac had actually made a fortune from his tale of death. They were not so different, he and the preacher. And the other pig, the one who had butchered—

Glenn froze. A chill snaked down his spine. The notion exploded in his mind like a white-hot strobe and he stood with a limp mouth.

"Glenn?"

"I want you to do something, Beatrice," he said softly and turned to face her. "I want you to find someone for me. Someone in Bosnia."

"Who? I have no idea how to find anyone in Bosnia," she said.

Glenn smiled as the idea set in. "You will, Beatrice. You will find him. And you will learn about him in this book." He held it toward her with a shaking hand.

"Who?" she asked again, taking the book.

"Karadzic," Glenn said. "His name is Karadzic."

BOOK FOUR

THE BELOVED

"Love is as strong as death,
its jealousy unyielding as the grave.
It burns like blazing fire,
like a mighty flame.
Many waters cannot quench love;
rivers cannot wash it away.
If one were to give all the wealth of his house for love
it would be utterly scorned."

SONG OF SONGS 8:6–7 NIV

CHAPTER THIRTY-SIX

Sarajevo, Bosnia
Four Weeks Later

IVENA STOOD at the graves where they'd buried Father Micheal's and Nadia's bodies. She stared up at the pitted concrete cross. It was her third visit in as many weeks since their return. Already the vine she'd brought from Joey's garden curled around the graves and wound up the lower half of the cross in a delicate embrace. The large white flowers seemed totally natural now, reacting as she had expected to the rain and the sun that spurred their growth.

The small village had faded over the years, now hardly more than a collection of vagrants who eked out an existence off the land and lived in the crumbling houses. The church's blackened spire stretched against the sky, a burned-out backdrop to the overgrown graveyard she stood in. Most towns had managed to recover after the war's atrocities. Most.

Some of the others who had been there that day still visited regularly, but they could not keep the grounds up. The locals couldn't care for the grave of an old dead priest, no matter how horrible the tale of his death. The country was simply littered with a hundred thousand stories as terrible.

Ivena sank to her knees and gripped the foot-high grass in both hands. The dirt felt cool under her knees. *Father, are you taking care of my beloved? Is she keeping you company?*

She looked up at the cross, still stained with the priest's faded blood. Their bones were under the dirt, but they themselves were laughing up there somewhere. Ivena let the images from that day string through her mind now, and they obliged with utmost clarity. The priest's face beaten to a bloody pulp by Janjic; her Nadia standing and staring into the commander's face without a trace of fear; the marching of women under their crosses; Karadzic's furious snarl; the boom of his gun; the priest hanging from this cross, begging to die. His laughter echoing through the cemetery and then his death.

A tear crawled down Ivena's cheek. "I miss you, Nadia. I miss you so much, my darling." She sniffed and closed her eyes. *Why did you take her and not me, Father? Why? I would go now. What kind of cruelty is it to leave me here while my daughter's allowed this frolic of hers? I beg you to take me.*

She'd nearly found her way there a month ago, in those Twin Towers of Lutz's. But it had not been God's timing, so it seemed. She wasn't finished in this desert yet. Still, she could not escape the hope that her time would come soon. If nothing else, that she would die of old age.

Now she lived with her brother on the very edge of Sarajevo, not so far away from her little village, really. She'd lost everything in Atlanta, but the quick departure felt more like a cleansing than a loss. In her mind it was more good riddance. Janjic and Helen had taken an apartment downtown where he had sequestered himself to write. Ivena saw them every few days now, when she went to visit. By all appearances God still had a firm grip on Janjic's heart. It seemed that the extraordinary play of God's wasn't over yet, and knowing it made Ivena long for heaven even more.

Ivena sat on her knees and began to hum. Americans did not understand death, she thought. They were not eager to follow the footsteps of Christ. In reality, joining Christ was a terrifying notion for most churchgoing Americans. Oh, they would quickly snatch up the trinkets he tossed down from heaven—the cars and the houses and such gifts. But talk to them about joining Christ beyond the grave and you would be rewarded by a furrowed brow or blank eyes at best.

Even Helen, after her incredible encounter with Christ's love, was still confused. Even after being on the receiving end of Jan's love she still did not know how to return that love for the simple reason that she wasn't yet willing to die to her own longings.

Love is found in death. Love is found only in death.

They had come to Bosnia and all seemed well enough; Helen had not gone back to her ways. But she was not a transformed woman either. Not really. She had made it about as far at the average believer, Ivena supposed. But you would think that after such an overt display of love, she would be clambering for Jan. When else in history had Christ actually placed his love for the church in a man? When else had a woman been the recipient of that love in such a unique way?

Ivena sighed and opened her eyes. "Well, I will join you, Father. Call me home now and I will come gladly." She smiled. "I love you, Christ. I dearly love you. I love you more than life."

The sun was dipping in the west when she stood. "Good-bye, Nadia. I will visit next week."

She walked for her brother's old black Peugeot. The town lay in a dusky silence found only in the country. A dog was barking incessantly across the village. At a squawking chicken by the sound of it. "Ah, my Bosnia, it is good to be home."

Ivena climbed into the car, shut the door and reached for the key. The faint odor of petrol filled the cab. Half the cars in Bosnia were either parked on their axles or patched with twine and wire. Blasco's was no exception. At least it ran. Though with gas or whatever caused this terrible smell leaking it was a wonder it didn't blow sky—

A hand suddenly clamped over her mouth and yanked her head back into the seat. Her fingernail caught on the key ring and tore. She cried out but the sound was muffled by the rag the perpetrator was trying to jam past her teeth. She instinctively bit down hard and heard a grunt of pain.

The strong hand shoved the rag into her mouth and she felt she might gag. Another hand gripped her hair and pulled her head backward. She stared at the bare metal ceiling and screamed from her throat. Blackness covered her eyes—a blindfold, strapped tightly to her skull.

Hands shoved her onto her belly and then bound her wrists behind her back. It was only then, blinded and tied facedown, that Ivena stopped reacting and scrambled for some reason.

Her kidnapper had climbed over the seat and now he fired the car. The Peugeot lurched forward.

Suddenly the sentiments that had preoccupied her mind over the past hour were gone. Another took their place. The desire to live. The desperate hope that nothing would harm her. She cried out to God again, but this time the words were different.

Save me, my Father, she prayed. *Don't let me die, I beg you!*

HELEN WALKED over the concrete slab in bare feet, holding a cup of tea close to her chest. She approached the square window in the tenth-story flat and peered out to the sprawling city of Sarajevo, dimmed by the late-day overcast. Behind her, the living room clacked with Jan's incessant typing.

Clack, clack, clack . . .

Square houses bordered thin streets in the Novi Grad district in which she and Jan now lived. The frequent rains made the trees green enough, but the cold that accompanied them could hardly be in greater contrast to Atlanta's smothering heat. And it was not the only contrast. Her whole existence here was one giant contrast.

For starters, the flat. Janjic's uncle Ermin had offered the place to them for a pittance, a thousand dollars for the year, paid up-front of course. Jan had brought the ten thousand dollars in cash with them and given three thousand to Ivena. The remaining seven thousand was enough to live comfortably in Sarajevo for a year, he'd said. They had spent three thousand already, most of it on the rent and outfitting the top-floor apartment with amenities that helped Helen feel more at home. A toaster oven, stuffed furniture, a real refrigerator, rugs to warm the floors. A typewriter, of course. Jan was a writer once again; they had to have the typewriter. By Sarajevo standards they had done well with the place.

But it wasn't America. Not at all. What was first-class in these hills would do well to pass for middle-class back home.

This is home, Helen. This is your new home.

She sipped at her hot tea. Behind her Jan sat at the kitchen table, a pair of old glasses hanging off his nose. He'd started working on his new book the very day they'd taken the apartment.

Clack, clack, clack . . .

They saw Ivena once, maybe twice a week now, but she had already fit back into her beloved homeland, with greater ease than Jan—no surprise considering what each had given up to come here. The days Ivena came were Helen's favorite. She was family now. Besides Jan, her only family.

Helen looked to the street below; the market across the way bustled with a late-day rush. Which reminded her, she needed some potatoes for dinner. Helen turned around and leaned on the window sill. "Jan?"

He smiled and pried his eyes over those silly black-rimmed glasses. "Yes, dear?"

"I think I'll go down and buy some potatoes for supper. I was going to try that potato soup again. Maybe this time I can get it right."

He chuckled. "It was fine last time. A bit crisp, perhaps, but in my mouth it was deliciously crisp."

"Stop it. Not only am I learning to cook, I'm learning to cook strange foods. Maybe you'd like to cook tonight."

"You're doing wonderfully, dear."

Helen drank the rest of her tea in one gulp and set the cup on the tile counter with a clink. Every surface seemed harsh to her. If it wasn't cement, it was tile. If it wasn't tile it was brick or hard wood. Carpet was hardly known on this side of the world. She didn't care how upscale this flat was in Sarajevo, it still reminded her of the projects back home.

Clack, clack, clack . . .

Jan was intent over the machine again.

"I'll be going then. Do you need anything?" *Listen to me, "I'll be going then." That's how a European would say, "I'm outta here."* This land was changing her already.

"Not that I can think of," Jan said.

She walked over to him and kissed his forehead. "I'll be back."

"Make some friends," he said with a grin.

"Yes, of course. The whole world is my friend."

"I'm mad about you, you know?"

"And I love you too, Jan," she said smiling, and she slipped out the door.

The steep stairs were enough to discourage more than one or two ascents each day, and the thought that she would be coming back up with a bag full of potatoes brought a frown to her face. They hadn't heard of elevators in this corner of Europe yet.

Helen walked briskly for the market, keeping her head down. A bicycle careened by, splashing water from the morning's shower onto the sidewalk just ahead of her. Horns beeped on the street. They didn't *honk* here; they beeped, a high tone expected of tiny cars. *Beep, Beep.*

Clack, clack, clack . . .

Jan could work for twelve hours straight without a break on that book. Well, he did take breaks, every hour in fact. To smother her with kisses and words of love. She smiled. But otherwise it was only the book. Her and the book.

It was really *The Dance of the Dead*, but written from a whole new point of view. Ivena was right; the story wasn't finished, he said. It wasn't even that well told. And so he was up there clacking away, engrossed in a world even more foreign than this wacky world below.

Helen entered the open marketplace and nodded at a woman she'd seen shopping here before. One of the neighbors, evidently. Some of them spoke English, but she was growing tired of discovering which ones did not. A nod would have to do. The tin roof over her head began to tick softly. It was sprinkling again.

The market was crowded for late in the day. Helen passed a shop brimming with bolts of colored cloth. The owner was checking some plastic he'd strung across the back where the tin gaped above. A small kiosk selling snacks made on the spot filled her nostrils with the smell of frying pastries.

Helen made her way to the fresh vegetable stand and bought four large potatoes from a big man named Darko. He smiled wide and winked and Helen thought she'd made herself a friend as Janjic suggested. Perhaps not what he'd imagined.

She left the market and crossed the street. It was then that the deep male voice spoke behind her, like a distant rumble of thunder that pricked her heart. "Excuse me, miss." Helen glanced back, saw the tall man keeping stride with her ten feet behind, but she immediately dismissed his comment as misdirected. She certainly did not know him.

"You are an American?"

Helen stopped. He was speaking to her. And then he was beside her, a very large man, square and wearing black cotton pants. His shirt was white with silver-and-pearl buttons, like those cowboy shirts she'd seen in the shops back home. She looked into his eyes. They were black, like his pants. Like Glenn's eyes.

"Yes?" she asked.

A crooked smile split the man's boxy jaw. "You are American, yes?"

He spoke with a heavy accent, but his English was good. "Yes. Can I help you?"

"Well, miss, actually I was going to ask you the same thing. I saw you in the market and I thought, now there is a pretty woman who looks like she could use some help."

"Thank you, but I think I can handle four potatoes. Really."

He tilted his head up and laughed. "An American with humor. So then humor me. What is your name?"

A bell of caution rang through Helen's bones. "My name? And who are you?" she asked.

"My name is Anton. You see, Anton? Is that such a bad name? And yours?"

"I'm not in the habit of giving my name to strangers, actually. I really should be going." She turned to go. But did she really want to go? She stunned herself by answering the question quickly. No.

"You don't want to do that," the man said. She looked at his face. White teeth flashed through his grin. "Really, you want to know me. I have what you're looking for."

Helen stared at him. "You do, do you? And what is it that I'm looking for?"

"For a destination. For a place to go. A place that feels like home; that swims in your mind the way you like."

She blinked. "I'm sorry, I need to leave."

"No. No you shouldn't do that. You're American. I know a part of Sarajevo that's very . . . what should I say? Friendly to Americans. Do you like to fly, American?"

What was he talking about?

You know what he's talking about, Helen. You know, you know.

"What's your name?" the man asked again. The sky was still spitting the odd raindrops. Pedestrians had cleared the streets for the most part. To Helen's left, an alley ran between two gray buildings, dark and dingy.

"Why are you talking so strangely to me? Do I look like I have 'fool' stamped on my forehead?"

He found the remark funny. "No. And that's precisely why I'm speaking strangely to you. Because you're not a fool. You know precisely what I'm talking about. You really should join us."

Helen's blood was pumping steadily now. A thousand days from her past screamed through her spine. She should leave this man now. He was the devil himself—she should know, she'd shared the devil's bed many a night.

But her feet were not moving. Instead they were tingling, and it had been a while since her feet had tingled like this. She wet her lips, and then immediately hoped he did not read her too clearly.

"There are other Americans here?"

"Did I say that? No. There are others like you."

She hesitated. Her breathing was coming harder now. *Run, Helen, Run!* "How do I know who you are?" Her ears were hot.

"I am Anton, and you must ask yourself another question; how do I know what I know? Unless I am who I say I am?"

"And who are you, Anton?"

"Tell me your name and I will tell you who I am."

She cleared her throat. "Helen."

He grinned wide and nodded his head once. "And I'm the one who will help you fly."

She swallowed, looking up into his eyes.

"May I see your hand?" Anton asked

She opened her hand and glanced down at it. His large hand suddenly held hers gently. She tried to pull it free, but the man held her firmly and she saw that his eyes were not threatening. They were deep and dark and smiling. She let him take her hand. But he was not interested in her hand; his eyes followed her arm to the tiny pockmark from her old days on the needle.

Then the man who called himself Anton did a very strange thing. He leaned over and he kissed that tiny scar very gently. And Helen let him do it. His lips sent a shiver right up her arm and through her skull.

There was suddenly a small black card in his hand and Helen had no clue where it had come from. She took it. He held her eyes in his own for what seemed an eternity. Then he turned and left without another word.

It occurred to Helen that she had stopped breathing. Her heart was slamming in her chest. She looked at the card. It had an address on it—this man's address—and a simple map. The den of iniquity. She should throw it to the ground and stamp her feet on it, she thought.

Instead she shoved it into her pocket and walked numbly for the flat.

HELEN HAD calmed herself before entering the apartment, but a tingle rode her spine and she was powerless to dismiss it.

"Did you find the potatoes?" Jan asked without looking up. He continued his typing, reached the end of a section and slapped the carriage back. *Ding!* He lowered his hands and looked at her. She held up the four large spuds.

"They'll make a fine soup," he said and clapped his hands together once. "I'll give you a tip, my dear. Use a low flame. It may take a few minutes longer, but we'll be using ladles instead of forks if you do."

She *humphed,* feigning disgust at him. "Come over here and I'll use a ladle on you, Jan Jovic."

He threw his head back, delighted. Then he clambered out of his chair and padded over to her. "Have I told you recently that you're the light of my world?" he said, taking her head in his hands. He kissed her cheek. When he withdrew his eyes were on fire. No, his passion for her hadn't dimmed, not even a little, she thought.

"I love you, Jan," she said.

Do you? I mean really, like he loves you?

He winked and returned to the table.

Helen slid into the kitchen and dumped the potatoes into the sink for cleaning.

Clack, clack, clack . . .

The day fell to darkness as Helen prepared their supper. Outside, the cars beeped on through the evening. Inside, the room kept time to Jan's clacking. But

Helen was not hearing the sounds. She was still hearing the stranger's voice, soft and soothing.

And I am the one who will help you fly.

The card lay in her pocket. God forbid if Jan should find it! She eased into the bedroom and placed it under the mattress. He stopped his clacking and she rushed out, but he was only reading a page he'd written.

Do you want to fly, Helen?

The soup spoon slipped from her hand and splashed the hot liquid onto her arm. "Ouch!"

"You okay?"

"Fine."

She dug out the spoon and chided herself. *Stop this nonsense! Stop it! You are not an adolescent. You are the wife of Jan Jovic.*

Yes, but do you want to fly, wife of Jan Jovic?

In the end she butchered the soup. It was not crispy; it was not even too thick. But it tasted bland and not until Jan mentioned salt near the end of their meal, did she remember that she'd forgotten the spice altogether. She apologized profusely.

"Nonsense," he said. "Too much salt's bad for the heart. It's much better this way, Helen."

She retired at nine, leaving Jan to finish his chapter. But she could not sleep. Her mind settled into a dream of sorts, wide awake but lost in the stranger's world, in recounting every detail of their meeting. And then it slipped into Glenn's Palace and a mound of powder and she gave up trying to fight the thoughts. Instead she let them run rampant through her mind, even embellishing them.

She pretended to be asleep when Jan came to bed, but in reality she dozed for another two hours. The card lay under her mattress, and at one point she was sure she could feel it. And if Jan rolled over here, he would feel it! She started and sat.

"What is it?" Jan asked, suddenly awake.

She gazed about in the darkness. "Nothing," she said, and collapsed to her back.

Sleep finally overtook her near midnight. But even then she could not shake that man's haunting face.

Do you want to fly, Helen?

Yes, of course. Don't be silly. I would love to fly. I'm dying to fly.

Do you want to die, Helen?

I want to fly. I don't want to die.

I want to sleep.

CHAPTER THIRTY-SEVEN

JAN AMBLED down the avenue the following afternoon, stretching his legs, whistling into a light breeze. He'd asked Helen to walk with him but she seemed content to stay home. Perhaps even a little preoccupied with staying home.

The sights and sounds of Sarajevo came to him like a rich, soothing balm as they did every morning, healing wounds long forgotten. When he'd walked these streets five years earlier, the war's scars still mocked the city on every corner; blasted buildings and pitted roads.

But now . . . now his city was brimming with new life and a people fanatical about reestablishing their identity. There was some dissatisfaction with Tito and his government, of course—talk of an independent Bosnia. And there were occasional words between the Serbs and the Croats, even the Muslims. That had become a staple of the people; a prerequisite the land seemed to extract from its inhabitants. But the country was nothing like the war-torn shamble he'd left.

"Hello, Mira," he called, passing the bakery where the plump baker swept clouds of flour through her doorway. "Nice day?"

She looked up, startled. "Oh, Janjic, there was a gentleman looking for you. I sent him down the street."

"Oh? And did this gentleman have a name?"

"Molosov," she said.

The name rang through Jan's mind like a manic rat. Molosov was looking for him? So the soldier from Sarajevo had heard that he'd returned. They'd discussed the possibility a hundred times and now it was happening.

"Hmm," Jan finally managed.

"You send your wife down, and I will sell her something special, just for you," the baker said.

He chuckled. "Good enough."

Jan glanced up and down the street; it was empty. He left Mira and walked on, but with a stiff step now. Molosov. The name sounded strange after such a long time. And if Molosov had heard of his return, what of Karadzic?

The sun was out today. In Atlanta he would have been sweating like a pig. Here the warmth was like a smile from heaven. It had only been a month, and yet it felt like a year. He'd heard from Lorna, who had sent him the settlement statement from the ministry last week. She'd managed to pay off all of their debts and come away with nearly five thousand dollars. What should he do with it? Lorna wanted to know.

Give it to Karen, he'd written back. *She deserves it and more.*

As for himself and Helen, they had four thousand dollars still, which was barely enough to carry them through the year. Then they would see. Honestly, he had no clue.

Helen wanted to return to America, he knew that much. But then she was young and it was her first time leaving the country. She would adjust. He prayed she would adjust.

"Janjic."

He turned toward the voice. A man stood on the curb, staring at him. The street suddenly appeared vacant except for this one man. Jan stopped and looked at the figure. There were others striding in his peripheral vision, but one look at this man and they ceased to exist.

Janjic's pulse spiked. It was Molosov! The soldier he'd roamed Yugoslavia with, finding enemies to kill. One of the soldiers who had crucified the priest.

Now Molosov was here, grinning at him from the street.

"Janjic." The man strode to him, and a smile suddenly split his face. "That is you, Janjic?"

"Yes. Molosov."

The man thrust his hand out and Janjic took it. "You're back on the streets of Sarajevo," Molosov said. "I'd heard you'd gone to America."

"I'm back." In any other place this man would be his mortal enemy. They had never gotten along well. But they had been through a war together, and they were both Serbs. That was the bond between them.

Molosov slapped him on the shoulder and Jan nearly lost his balance. "You are looking good. You've put some meat on your bones. I see America has been good to you."

"I suppose," Jan said. "And you? You are good?"

"Yes, good. Alive still. If you're alive in Bosnia, you are good." He chuckled at his remark.

"You were looking for me?" Jan asked.

"Yes. My friend in the market told me about you a week ago, and I have watched for you. I am planning to go to America." He said it proudly, as if he expected immediate affirmation for the disclosure.

"You are? Very good. I am not."

Molosov wasn't put off. "This place is no longer for me. I was thinking you could help me. Just with information, of course."

Jan nodded, but his mind was elsewhere. "Have you heard from the others?" Jan asked. "Puzup, Paul?"

"Puzup? He's dead. Paul left the country, I think. To his new homeland, Israel."

"They were good men." He wasn't sure why he said that. There was some goodness under everyone's skin, but Puzup and Paul were not especially well endowed with it and Jan had concluded as much in his book.

Molosov withdrew a cigarette. "And you, Janjic, you have a wife now?"

"Yes. Yes, I'm married."

"A fat lady from America?"

Jan smiled with him. "As a matter of fact, she's from America. The loveliest woman I've ever known."

He chuckled, pleased. "American women are the best, yes? Well, let me give you some advice, comrade," Molosov said in good humor. "Keep her away from Karadzic. The beast will devour her!"

A spike drove down Jan's spine at the words. His feet felt suddenly rooted to the concrete. "Karadzic?"

The man's smile faded. "You two were not so close. Forgive me—it's been a long time."

"Karadzic is . . . he's in Sarajevo?"

"He's always been in Sarajevo."

Of course, Jan already knew that if the man were still alive, he would live somewhere near Sarajevo. But hearing it now sent a buzz through his skull. "And what's Karadzic up to these days?"

"The same. I worked for him, you know. For three years, until I couldn't stomach his nonsense. Karadzic was born to kill. He doesn't do well without a war, so he makes his own."

"And how does he do that?"

"In the underground, of course. He's Sarajevo's prince of darkness." The man laughed and drew on his cigarette.

"So Bosnia has its own Mob, is that it?"

"Mob? Ah, the American gangsters. Yes, but here it's all done with threads of nationalism. It legitimizes the business, you see."

"But his business is illegitimate?"

"Are you joking?" He looked around to be certain they weren't overheard. "Karadzic doesn't have a legitimate bone in his body. If you're looking for drugs in Bosnia, his dirty fingers will have touched them somewhere along the line, no question."

The heat started at the crown of Jan's head and washed over his face. Drugs! His mind flashed to Helen. It was the association alone, he knew, but still he was suddenly thrust to the verge of panic, standing there on the sidewalk beside Molosov. *Dear God, help us!* A dreadful sense of foreboding washed through him.

And Helen.

"Just stay out of his way. Or better, go back to America; this place isn't safe for people like you and me." He jabbed Janjic playfully with the hand holding his cigarette. "At the very least, if your wife is as beautiful as you say, keep her out of his sight. He makes pretty women ugly very quickly." The man chuckled again.

But Jan didn't find any humor in his words. None at all. He was barely hiding his terror. Or perhaps he wasn't.

"I . . . I have to go now," Jan said and began to turn.

Molosov's voice lost its humor. "Hold on. You weren't easy to find. We have a lot to discuss. I'm very serious, Janjic. I am planning on going to America."

"I live in the flats on the west side of the market. Top floor, 532." Jan suddenly thought better of giving out the address, and he turned to his old comrade. "But keep this to yourself."

Molosov grinned again. "I will. Good to see you. I live on the east end of the Novi Grad. Welcome back home."

Jan turned back and took the man's extended hand. "Yes, good. Good to be home."

He left then, striding evenly for half a block. And then seeing Molosov disappear around the corner, he broke into a jog.

She has been acting strangely, Janjic. Helen has not been herself.

Nonsense! He was just piecing together impossible strings of coincidence.

She didn't come on this walk with you, Janjic. She did not want to.

Shut up! You're being a child!

Still he had to get back to see her. If anything happened to Helen now he would die. He would throw himself from their window and let the street take him home.

Jan reached their building and swung into the atrium. He took the stairs two at a time and had to pause after five flights to catch his breath. By the time he reached the tenth-floor flat his chest burned. He crashed into the apartment.

She was not in sight!

"Helen!"

His black typewriter sat alone at the table. "Helen!" he screamed.

"Hello, Jan." He spun toward the bedroom. She walked out, wide-eyed. "What's wrong?"

Jan doubled over to his knees and panted. *Thank you, Father!* "Nothing. Nothing."

"Then why were you screaming like that?"

He straightened, smiling wide. "Nothing. It was nothing. I ran up the stairs. You should try it sometime; excellent exercise."

She grinned. "You scared me. Don't smash in here screaming the next time you decide to exercise, if you don't mind."

"I won't," he said. He pulled her to his chest and stroked her hair. "I promise I will not."

Chapter Thirty-Eight

THE DAY seemed to keep time to the *clacking* of Jan's typewriter, but it all came to a silent halt late that afternoon, when Jan clapped his hands with satisfaction, stood from the table, and proudly announced that he was leaving. His uncle Ermin had a car he wanted to sell them. An old bucket of bolts, Jan said, but the old man had fixed it up—given it a new coat of blue paint and tweaked the carburetor so that it actually ran. Perhaps having a car wouldn't be such a bad idea. They could drive out into the country and see the real Bosnia. Even Ivena had access to a car.

He said he would be gone for a couple of hours. Helen's heart was pounding already.

He kissed her on the nose, then again on the cheek, and after a short pause, again on the head. Then he slipped out the door with a wink, leaving her alone in the kitchen staring after him. The old wooden wall-clock with painted ivy leaves read five o'clock.

Horns honked through the open window to her right. She closed her eyes and swallowed, trying to shake the voice that suddenly whispered through her mind. And then it wasn't whispering—it was buzzing, like an annoying fly that refused to go away.

Helen leaned back on the kitchen counter. *You know that if you pull that card out you won't stop. You know you'll go.*

Of course, I won't go! Going would be suicide! Her heart thumped in her chest. How could she possibly be having these thoughts after a month of freedom? That's what her time in Jan's strange country had been: freedom. No Glenn, no drugs, no chains. And now a stranger who called himself Anton had walked out of the shadows and offered her chains once again. What a fool the man was to think he could just waltz into her life and expect her to follow.

Helen ground her teeth. What a fool she was to think she would *not* follow!

"God, please . . ."

She ditched the feeble attempt at prayer and let her mind play with the card. *If I leave now I could see this place in the Rajlovac district and be back before Jan returns. I would just walk there and then walk back. Is it a sin to walk?*

But you won't just walk.

Don't be stupid, of course I'll just walk! That's all I'll do. A rush of desire flooded her veins, and she pushed off the counter toward the bedroom.

You want the chains, Helen?

She pulled the black card from beneath her mattress and straightened the covers quickly. Her hand trembled before her eyes. "Rajlovac," it read.

Don't be a fool.

But suddenly the impulse to at least walk toward the place hammered through her mind. She walked straight for the front door and eased into the staircase, thinking that she *was* being a fool. But her spine tingled at the thought of flying. And she was already hating herself for having come this far. Why would she even dare to think about any of this?!

Her feet padded quickly down the stairs. She cracked the door to the street and slipped into the dying light. She would walk east. Just walk.

Voices of caution whispered through Helen's mind, casting their inevitable arguments as her feet carried her east. But within ten minutes, she'd shoved the debate aside, preoccupied instead with the eyes that seemed to watch her progress. They were just strangers, of course, watching the Western woman—was it that obvious?—walk briskly with her head down. But to Helen it seemed as though every eye was focused on her. She picked up her pace.

The streets ran narrow, bordered by square tan buildings. Rajlovac—she'd heard that there was money in the Rajlovac. A short boxy car snorted past, spewing gray smoke that smelled strangely comforting. The structures were thinning. She was headed away from home and every step she took would have to be retraced, in the dark.

She should be home, peeling the potatoes for tonight's meal, listening to music, reading a novel. Being loved by Janjic. Helen grunted and watched her feet shuffle over the ground. No, she did not want to do this, but she *was* doing this and she *did* want to do this.

She pulled the black card out a dozen times and glanced at the sketched map on the fly. It wasn't until she had entered the Rajlovac district that she began thinking that coming here had been a terrible mistake. The sun sat on the western horizon, casting long shadows where the buildings did not block it all together. If there was money in Rajlovac, it wasn't wasted on the buildings, she thought. At least not in this industrial section where the card had led her. Here the old gray structures appeared vacant and unattended. The occasional blown-out window gaped square and black to the darkness within. A newspaper floated by, whipped by the wind. Its cover picture of a man shouting angrily had been all but washed out by the weather. Three men stood across the street, arms folded against the cool, wool caps on their heads. They watched her pass with mild interest.

You should be back with Jan, Helen. How long have you been gone? Less than an hour. If you turn back now he'll never know.

But her feet kept their pace, shuffling forward as if pulled by habit. Right into the falling darkness, ignoring the fear that now snaked down her spine. This was not right. A large building suddenly rose at the end of the dead-end street she'd entered, ominous against the charcoal sky.

Helen stopped. This was it. She stood alone on the asphalt and faced the ten-story blackened building. Gray cement towered on either side, chipped and pocked by years of abuse and war. The sound of water trickled faintly along the curb, sewer water by the musty smell. She took a hesitant step forward and then stopped again.

Thirty meters ahead a flag waved above a large door; a dirtied white flag with a black object on either side, but she couldn't make out the shapes at this distance. She took a breath to still a tremor that ran through her bones, and she walked forward.

You have to turn around, Helen. You've had your walk. It's time to go home and prepare the evening meal. Go and let Jan hold you. He'll do that, you know. He will hold you and he will love you.

Her feet ignored the plea and stepped forward.

If night had not fallen over the rest of Sarajevo yet, it had come here first. She wondered absently if this was how it felt to walk into your own grave. Other than the trickle of sewer water the night lay still. Perhaps she'd gotten it wrong.

A chill suddenly streaked down her spine. The markings on the flag were skulls, she saw. Black skulls waving in the breeze. A human form clothed in dark wool lay in the gutter to her right, evidently dead to the world. Helen stopped for the third time, blinking against the warning bells that rang in her head. Another body was propped in the far corner, barely visible.

Helen stood before the metal door and stared at the brown paint, peeling like scabs from a rusted surface. A throbbing beat came from deep within the building, barely audible, but somehow comforting.

You aren't walking any longer, Helen. Now you're going in. That wasn't the deal.

She reached a trembling hand forward and pushed gently on the door.

Do you want to fly, baby?

The door swung in quickly, startling her. But it had not given on its own—a man stood in the shadows looking at her with dark eyes. At first he said nothing, and then, "Who invited you?"

"A . . . Anton," Helen said.

A faint smile crossed the man's face. "Yes, of course. Who else would find such a beautiful woman. You know what we do here?"

Helen's heart skipped a beat. *Do you want to fly? Or do you want to die? We do both here.* "Yes," she said, but her voice held a tremor.

"Then follow me." The man turned and walked into the building. Helen crossed the threshold, her mind screaming foul. But still her legs seemed to control her movements, as if they possessed a mind of their own. That was foolishness, of course; she was telling her legs to move because she wanted desperately to move forward. Into this dungeon.

The hall was very dim, dressed in the same peeling paint that covered the outer door. They passed several limp bodies, strung out on the floor. He led her into a stairwell where he stepped aside and pointed down a flight of steps. Helen glanced up the stairs that ascended to her right, but he stabbed his index finger into the darkness below.

"Down," he said.

She swallowed and began her descent. The door banged behind her and she turned to see that the man had left her. She was alone, surrounded by silence. A dull consistent thump came from the walls—the sound of heavy pulsating music. Or the sound of her heart.

She lowered her foot to the next step, and then the next, until the steps ended in a landing before another door. She knew at a glance that the heart of the building lay here. Anton was here, beyond this fortified entry, sealed into thick concrete. A small window on the door grated open, exposed a pair of bloodshot eyes for a couple of seconds, and then snapped shut. The door swung in.

This is it, Helen. If you enter now you won't be able to make it back in time to peel the potatoes.

She stepped inside and stopped.

Helen stood in a tunnel roughly hewn from the rock beyond the building. Red and amber bulbs strung along the ceiling not three feet over her head cast an eerie light down the passage. Wet concrete ran underfoot, curving to the right twenty feet ahead. The dusty odor of mildew mixed with the smell of burning hair filled her nose. Her senses tingled with anticipation.

"Hello, Helen."

She spun to her right where another smaller tunnel gaped in the shadows. The man who called himself Anton stepped from the dark, smiling with a square jaw. He wore a black robe over the white shirt now, like some kind of vampire. The orange light glinted off his round eyes.

"I did not expect you to come so quickly." He reached a hand out to her. Behind him, tiny feet scurried along the tunnel. Rats. The tinkle of water was louder here too, she noted. That sewer water was making its way down somehow.

Helen hesitated and then took his hand.

He chuckled and the sound of his voice carried down the hall. "I promise you that I will not disappoint you, my dear." Anton kissed her hand with thick red lips. "Come."

She walked forward on soles tingling numb. The sound of her own heart thumped with the faint music. He led her along the dimly lit passage to a door made of wood with heavy cross members. He gripped the wooden latch, winked at her, and shoved the door open. "After you, my dear."

Helen stepped past the large man into a smoke-filled room. The sweet smell of hashish wafted through her nostrils. Here the yellow lights peered through a haze of the stuff, casting a soft glow about the room. The ceiling hung low, seemingly hewn from sheer rock and supported by a half dozen pillars. Bright red-and-yellow rugs covered the stone floor, nearly wall to wall. Thick white candles blazed on old wooden end tables. Tall earthen pots filled with purple and green feathers stood by each of the pillars; brass and silver plates adorned the walls, reflecting the myriad of flickering flames. It was a gothic kind of psychedelia.

A dozen bodies reclined on stuffed pillows and chairs, unmoving to fuzzy throbbing music, but fixated on her. Helen gazed at them and immediately felt a kinship—their eyes swam with a language she knew well.

She felt a hand on her shoulder, and she twisted her head to meet Anton's black stare. He smiled thinly but did not speak. His eyes lowered to her arm and he traced it lightly with a thick finger. Something about the way those eyes sparkled sent a shiver down her spine and she shifted her gaze from him.

One of the figures—a man—rose and walked slowly toward her, grinning dumbly.

"What's your price?" Helen asked.

Anton chuckled softly. But he didn't answer.

The other man walked up to her and lifted a hand to her cheek. His finger felt hot. *You're in this now, Helen. You're home. Whether you like it or not, you are home.*

"You want to know what the price is?" the man said. A large scar ran across his right cheek and it bunched up in a knot when he smiled. "I am Kuzup. I am your price, princess." He bit the tip of his tongue.

Anton seemed to find humor in the man's statement. "This one's beyond you, Kuzup. She's too rich for your blood."

Helen smiled with them, but her skin tingled with fear. "And even if you could afford me, I'm not for sale," she said.

They both laughed. "Down here we're all for sale," Kuzup said.

A small prick flashed up Helen's arm and she jerked. Anton's big hand closed over her mouth from behind. "Shhhhh. Let it go, princess."

He'd put a needle into her arm. His hand was not rough, only coaxing, and she let herself go.

"Shhh." His hot breath washed over her ear. It smelled like medicine. "Do you feel it?"

The warmth ran through her body in comforting waves. "Yes," she whispered. She didn't know what Anton had given her, but the drug quickened her pulse. This was good. She was into this. *I'm flying now, baby.*

He released her and the room swam. Kuzup was giggling. Anton held a small syringe, which he tossed into a pot to his right.

Helen sauntered out onto the floor and eased herself onto a thick cushion. The music worked its way through her body like a massage. An obscure thought occurred to her, the thought that Jan would like this. Not seeing her with strangers like this, but feeling the euphoria that drifted through her bones now.

"How much?" she heard Kuzup asking.

"Are you made of gold? Because you'll need a mountain of it to match what I've been offered for this one."

"Bah!"

Helen lost interest in their babbling. To her right, a woman lay on her back, staring wide at the ceiling. Mucus ran from her nose and for some reason Helen found some humor in the sight. The woman was beautiful, with golden hair and brown eyes, but she'd been reduced to a stiff board, gawking at the low-hung black stone. Did she know how absurd she looked, sweating on the floor?

And you, Helen? You're less foolish? She rolled into a ball, feeling suddenly euphoric and sick at once. Like a self-conscious dog, lapping at some vomit—such a comforting treat, as long as no one knew. But he would be home soon, wouldn't he? Jan would be home to tell her about the blue car his uncle had sold him. They could take romantic trips to the countryside now.

A high-pitched cackle cut through Helen's thoughts. She saw a woman dressed in red with her arms entwined about Anton's neck. Her hair was long and black. She was kissing him on the nose, and then on the forehead and down his cheek, whispering words through pursed lips. The woman threw her head back and laughed at the ceiling. They both looked at Helen, pleased with themselves.

"So she has come without a fight, our American beauty," the woman said, loudly enough for Helen to hear. Then the woman turned to Anton and licked his right cheek with a wet tongue. He did not flinch. He only smiled and watched Helen. The lady in red was speaking to him, calling him names. Names that made no sense to Helen.

Except one name. She cooed it in a low voice.

Karadzic.

She called him Karadzic and that name rang a bell deep in Helen's mind. Perhaps an endearing term Janjic had called her once. Yes, Janjic Jovic, her lover.

Karadzic.

chapter thirty-nine

SHE WAS gone when Jan burst into the flat to announce his smart dealing over the car. He'd struck a deal with his uncle Ermin: no money for thirty days, and if the car still ran, he would pay one hundred a month for six months. It was a good trade, given the unavoidable fear that the rattling deathtrap might fly apart at any moment.

But Helen wasn't in the flat. His breast-beating would have to wait until she returned from the market. Darkness was falling outside, and she didn't often go down to the street after sunset. She hadn't cooked yet either.

Jan sat at the table and picked away at his typewriter. He was nearing the end of the book. One more chapter and it would be ready for the editor. Not that he had an editor. No publisher, no editor, not even a reader. But this time the book was for him—for the writing. It was a purging of his mind, a cleansing of his soul. And it all came down to this last chapter. Ivena would have to live with the fact that his story was now done. Not his full life, of course, but this ravishing love story of his was now over. It had found its fulfillment back here in Bosnia.

He glanced at the pile of completed pages, stacked neatly beside the typewriter. The title smiled across the cover page. *When Heaven Weeps.* It was a good name.

If there was a real caveat, it was in the simple realization that he didn't know what he would write in this last chapter. Up to this point the book had fairly written itself. It had rushed from his mind and his fingers had hardly kept pace.

Helen isn't back, Jan.

Jan stood from the table and walked to the window. The market closed at eight, but the shoppers had thinned already. *Where are you, dear Helen?* He glanced at the watch on his hand. It was ten past seven.

And what if she's gone, Jan?

His pulse quickened at the thought. No. We are beyond that. And where would she go? *Father, please, I beg you for her safety. I beg you, don't allow harm to come to her.*

It occurred to him that he was sweating despite the cool breeze. He spun from the window and rushed from the flat. He would go to the market and find her.

Jan entered the open-air market three minutes later, quelling memories that brought a mutter to his lips. He strode quickly through the street, craning for a view of her. Of her unmistakable blond hair. *Please, God, let me see her.*

But he did not see her.

He approached Darko's vegetable kiosk, where the big man was busy filling boxes with squashes for the night.

"Darko, have you seen Helen?"

The man looked up. "No. Not tonight."

"Earlier, then? At dusk?"

He shook his head. "Not today."

"You are sure?"

"Not today, Janjic."

Jan nodded and glanced around. "She was home three hours ago."

"Don't worry, my friend. She will return. She is a beautiful woman. Beautiful women always seem to find distractions in Sarajevo, yes? But, don't worry, she is lost without you. I have seen it in her eyes."

A distant voice snickered in Jan's mind. *And if she is beautiful, keep her away from him.* It was Molosov, and he was suddenly laughing. Heat washed down Jan's back. He fought off a surge of panic. He spun to Darko, whose grin softened under his glare.

"You know Molosov?" he demanded.

"Molosov? It's a common name."

"A big man," Jan said impatiently. "Brown hair. From the east side of Novi Grad. He was here yesterday. He said he had a friend in the market."

"No."

Jan slammed his palm on the merchant's table and grunted. Darko looked at him with surprise. Jan dipped his head apologetically and ran from the kiosk. *Please, Father. Not again, please! I cannot take it.*

He stopped at the next kiosk and questioned vigorously of Helen and Molosov to no avail. But that small voice in his head kept snickering. He ran through the market, fighting to retain control of his reason, desperate now to find either Helen or Molosov. Of course it was just a hunch, he kept telling himself. But the hunch burrowed like a tick in his skull.

If anyone knew Molosov, they weren't talking easily. Until he spoke to the beggar at the west side of the market.

"You know Molosov? A big man with dark hair from the east end of—"

"Yes, yes. Of course I know Molosov." A smile came to his ratty face.

"Tell me where to find him."

"I can't—"

"You think I'm playing? Tell me, man!"

The beggar pushed Jan's hand aside. "Perhaps a little money will loosen my memory."

Jan shoved his hand into his pocket and snatched a fistful of bills. He held them in front of the beggar's growing eyes. "Take me to him and this will be yours."

Twenty minutes later, Jan stood before Molosov in a small tin shack with a dozen men betting on a game of cards. A bare bulb burned above them. At first mention of Karadzic's name, Molosov ushered Jan outside by the arm. "You're trying to have me killed?" he demanded.

"I have to know where he is! You know—you must tell me!"

"Lower your voice! What's this about?"

Jan told him, but Molosov wasn't forthcoming. Karadzic's place was not common knowledge. He tried repeatedly to dismiss Jan's fears, but the quick shifting of his eyes told of his own fears. In the end, it took the thousand dollars Jan had pocketed for the car to persuade the big soldier. Jan withdrew the wad and offered it to the man. "Take it. It will buy your passage to America. Tell me where he is."

Molosov looked at the money and glanced around nervously again. "And what if she's not there?"

"It's a risk I'm willing to take. Hurry, man!"

Molosov took the bills and told him, swearing him to tell no one.

Jan turned then and ran into the night, east toward the Rajlovac.

And what if Molosov is right? What if Helen isn't there? What then, Jan?

Then I will weep for joy.

But dread pounded through his chest. He didn't expect to be weeping for joy. Weeping, perhaps, but not for joy.

THE DEAD-END street Molosov had directed Jan to was pitch black when he swung into it thirty minutes later. He pulled up and flattened his palms on his chest as if by gripping it he could ease the burning of his lungs. His breathing sounded like bellows echoing from the concrete walls.

A flag, Molosov had said. With skulls. Jan could see nothing but foreboding black. He stumbled forward and then stopped when the dim outline of the banner materialized over a door, thirty yards ahead. Three bundled bodies lay on the sidewalk, he saw. Another in the gutter, either dead or wasted.

A picture of Karadzic filled his mind, square and ferocious, screaming at Father Micheal. He had fought that image for twenty years now. The notion that Helen was in there with the beast suddenly struck him as preposterous.

Jan walked forward. *And if he is inhuman, what is Helen?*

He grunted and rushed forward. Lights flashed in his peripheral vision; the war was coming to his mind again and he blinked against it. Jan shoved the door open and stepped into a dark hall. The faint beat of music carried through the walls. He stood and willed his eyes to adjust; his breathing to slow.

At the end of the hall stairs rose to his right and descended to his left. Down. With Karadzic it would be down. He crept down the steps and ran into another entry. The music sounded louder, keeping beat with his heart. He tried the door. It was locked.

A small window suddenly grated open, casting a shaft of yellow light over his chest. Jan stepped back. The door swung open.

You don't belong here, Janjic.

No one appeared. Ahead a tunnel had been carved from the rock, lit by colored lights. Whoever had opened the door probably stood behind it, waiting. Jan stepped through. The music thudded now.

You really have no sense in coming here, Janjic.

The door slammed behind him and he whirled around. He could see no one. Another door led into the wall behind the entrance and he tried it quickly. It was locked.

"Lover boy has come for his woman?"

The voice echoed in the chamber and Jan spun around. *Father, please! Give me strength.*

"Janjic. After so long the savior has returned home. And to save another poor soul, no less."

This time he could not mistake the familiar rumbling voice; it was tattooed on his memory. Karadzic! *Steady, Jan. Hold yourself.* He took a deliberate breath and let it out slowly. He stood and gripped his hands into fists.

Feet crunched faintly and then stopped directly in front of him. He took a step backward in the darkness. Pale yellow light suddenly flooded the tunnel.

The figure stood before him, an apparition from a lost nightmare. He was tall and boxy, balanced on long legs and dressed in black, with a wicked grin splitting a square jaw. It was Karadzic.

Two distinct urges collided in Jan's mind. The first was to launch himself at the larger man; to kill him if possible. The second urge was to flee. He had faced Karadzic once and lived to tell the story. This time he might not be so lucky.

Jan moved his foot a few inches and then stood rooted to the earth, tensed like a bowstring.

"So good to see you again, my friend," Karadzic said softly. "And you have come so quickly. I had expected to force your hand, but now you have jumped into my lap."

Jan couldn't speak. He could only stare at this incarnation of terror. The man had lured him here. He'd used Helen against her will to bring him in, he thought.

Jan spoke quietly. "You always had your way with women. You prey on the weak because you yourself are only half a man."

"And you still have a tongue, do you?" Karadzic said. "I did not bring your woman here, you poor fool. She came to me, perhaps in search of a man. I can see why she left you."

"You lie! She did not come on her own."

"No? Actually I had planned on luring her with the old woman, but it wasn't necessary."

The old woman?

An arm suddenly clamped over Jan's mouth and yanked his head back. He swung his elbow back and was rewarded with a grunt. A hand punched his kidneys and he relaxed to the pain.

"Perhaps you would like to see your Helen?"

The arms from behind jerked his hands behind him and lashed his wrists together with rope. They shoved a rag in his mouth and ran a wide strip of tape over it. Karadzic walked slowly up to him. His old commander breathed heavily, his lips parted and wet. Sweat glistened on his forehead. Without warning his arm lashed out and he struck Jan on his ear. He gasped in pain.

"You would do well to remember who's in charge," Karadzic said quietly. "You always were confused about the power of command, weren't you?" He thrust his face up to Jan's, his smile now gone. The man's breath smelled sweet of liquor. "This time you'll wish you were already dead."

Jan winced. Karadzic struck again, on Jan's cheek.

The man spun and marched down the tunnel. "Bring him," he said.

The hands behind shoved Jan and he stumbled forward. They propelled him quickly down the dim passage, to a steel door beyond which Karadzic had stopped. Then the door opened and Jan was pushed roughly into the room. He scanned the interior, breathing shallow, fearing what he might see here.

A dozen sets of eyes stared at him, blank in their state of stupor. Candles flickered amber through the white haze. The music seemed to resonate with the black rock walls, as if they were its source.

Then Jan saw the body moving slowly on the floor not ten feet from where he stood and he knew immediately that it was Helen.

Helen!

Oh, dear God! What have you done?

He screamed despite the rags in his mouth, but the weak sound was lost to the music's dull thump. He threw himself forward against the hands that held him, struggling frantically to free himself. *Oh, dear Helen, what have you done? What have they done to you?* His vision blurred with tears and in a sudden fury he flailed back and forth. She needed help, couldn't they see that? She was lying on the ground moving like a maimed animal. What kind of demon would do this to his wife?

Angry shouts sounded behind him and a rope flopped around Jan's neck. They dragged him back, straining against the rope. The door crashed shut and he was shoved down the corridor. Jan tripped and sprawled to his knees. *She was smiling, Janjic. Writhing in ecstasy and smiling with the pleasure of it.*

They pulled him to his feet and kicked him forward. *Helen, dear Helen! What have they done to you?*

They've done to her what she deserves, you pathetic fool. They have given her what she has wanted all along.

He was forced down a long tunnel, and then another that branched to the right. The passage ended in a cell hewn out of solid black rock. By the light of torches they strapped his arms to a twelve-inch-wide horizontal beam bolted to the wall. Two men restrained him while Karadzic looked on. But the fight had left Jan and he let them jerk his limbs about as they pleased.

His mind was on Helen. She had fallen again. He'd brought her two thousand miles to escape the horrors of Glenn Lutz, and now she had found worse. A death sentence for both of them. And why? Because he hadn't loved her dearly enough? Or because she herself was possessed with evil?

Ivena's words came back to him. "Helen's not so different from every man," she'd said. But Jan could not picture *any* man, much less *every* man doing this. And if Ivena was right and this was a play motivated by God himself, then perhaps God had lost his sense of humor.

They suddenly ripped the tape from Jan's mouth and pulled the rag free. His lips felt on fire.

"You really shouldn't have tried to stop me twenty years ago," Karadzic said. "See what it's cost you? All for an old priest and a gaggle of old ladies."

"I've paid for my insubordination," Jan said. "You took five years from me."

"Five years? Now you'll pay with your life."

"My life. And what do you hope to gain by taking my life? It wasn't enough to kill an innocent priest? Blowing the head from a small child's shoulders didn't satisfy your blood thirst?"

"Shut up!" Even in the dim light he could see Karadzic's face bulged red. "You've never understood power."

"The real war is against evil, Karadzic. And it seems you don't recognize evil, even when it crawls up inside of you. Perhaps it's you who don't understand power."

Karadzic didn't answer, at least not with words. His eyes flashed angrily.

"You don't have the courage to take your anger out on me, face to face," Jan said. "You hide behind a woman!"

The commander looked at Jan for a moment and then placed his hands on his hips and smiled. "So. Our valiant soldier will fight for his lover's life. He realizes that I'm going to kill her, and now he'll use whatever means at his disposal to persuade me otherwise." Karadzic leaned forward. "Let me tell you, I don't bow to humiliation so easily, Janjic."

"No? But the priest humiliated you, didn't he? You marched into the village intent on sowing some horror and instead you received laughter. You've never lived it down, have you? The whole world looks at you as a coward!"

"Nonsense!"

"Then prove yourself. Let the woman free."

"And now the soldier attempts manipulation. I told you, your woman's here of her own choosing. Your *mother,* Ivena, I took by force. But not dear Helen."

"Ivena? You have Ivena? What could you possibly want with an innocent woman?" Nausea swept through Jan's gut.

"She was to lure your lover, my friend. But now she'll serve another purpose."

"You have me. Release them, I beg you. Release Ivena; release Helen."

Karadzic grinned. "Your Helen is far too valuable to release, Preacher."

Preacher? "You have no complaint against her. You have me. I beg you to let her go."

Now the big man chuckled. "Yes, I have you, Janjic. But I was offered a hundred thousand dollars for the death of the preacher *and* his lover. That would be your Helen. I do intend to collect this money."

A hundred thousand dollars? Jan was too shocked to respond. Then he knew it all in a flash.

Lutz!

Somehow Glenn Lutz had his finger in this madness.

"Lutz . . ."

"Yes. Lutz. You know him, I see."

A growl formed in Jan's stomach and rose through his throat. His blood felt hot and thick in his veins. Then he lost his reason and began screaming, but the words came out in a meaningless jumble. His heart was breaking; his heart was raging. He wanted to kill; he wanted to die. He suddenly threw himself against the restraints, thinking that he had to stop the man.

Karadzic was going to kill his mother and his wife.

A blow crashed against his head. Karadzic's fist. Jan shuddered and settled back, silent. A balloon of pain swelled between his temples.

Another fist smashed into his jaw and stars dotted his vision. Jan slumped forward and lost his mind to the darkness.

CHAPTER FORTY

JAN COULDN'T tell if he'd regained consciousness or if the black before his eyes was still the darkness of his mind. He thought he blinked a few times, but even then he couldn't be sure. Then he heard ragged pulls of breath and he knew that he was hearing himself.

He was still strapped to the beam, hands spread wide. His shoulders ached badly and he made a feeble attempt to shift his weight back from them. An immediate surge of pain changed his mind. He sagged on the beam and fought to clear his mind.

The room echoed with his own heaves of breath. The sound brought a chill to his bones, a déjà vu that suddenly had the hair on his neck standing.

He had been here.

When?

It came back to him like a fist from the darkness: He was in the dungeon from his dreams!

For twenty years he had dreamed of this very place—he knew it was the same. The same sound, the same beam at his back, the same pitch-blackness. The details had sunk to obscure depths during these last dreamless months, but they came raging to the surface now. The dreams had been a premonition of his own end.

Death awaited at the end of this mad journey. He'd been given love—a graft of God's heart, Ivena had said. And now he'd found death. The price of love was death. Jan's chest tightened with remorse. What a fool he'd been to bring Helen to Bosnia. To Karadzic! *Oh, dear Helen, forgive me! Oh, God, help me.*

A soft voice whispered in the darkness. *"It is a only a shadow of what I feel."*

Jan caught his breath and lifted his head.

"No more than a faint whisper."

The voice was audible! Jan held his breath and scanned the darkness but saw nothing. He was hallucinating.

"You feel this pain?

"Your worst pain is like a distant echo. Mine is a scream."

This was not a hallucination! It couldn't be! *Oh, my God! You're speaking! I'm hearing the voice of God!* A tear slipped down his cheek. He stilled and listened to the loud inhaling and exhaling of his breath. He could see nothing but blackness. Then he spoke in a whisper.

"And my love for Helen?"

"A small taste. You could hardly survive more. Do you like it?"

Then it was true! "Yes! Yes, I like it! I love it!"

A small voice began to giggle behind the other. A child who laughed, unable to contain his delight. It fell like a balm of contentment over Jan. God and this child were seeing things differently, and it wasn't a sad thing they were seeing. Tears fell from Jan's eyes in streams. He began to shake, smothered in these words whispered to his mind.

His world suddenly flashed white and he gasped. At first he thought it might be the war memories, but he saw immediately that it wasn't. The field of white flowers stretched out before him, ending in a brilliant emerald ocean. The sky rushed toward the distant water, in rivers of red and blue and orange.

He shifted his feet and looked down. A thick carpet of grass squeezed between his toes, so rich and lush that it appeared aqua. Within three meters, the bed of red-and-white flowers began, swaying ever so gently with a light breeze. They were the flowers from Ivena's greenhouse. The sweet odor of rose blossoms swept through his nose.

Still the sky fled to the horizon, like a sunset photographed in time-lapse but never ending. Jan stared at the surreal scene and let his jaw fall open. It was not of this world. It was of the other. And it was part of his dream.

He heard a faint note on the air, like the distant drone of a huge wind. He was thinking that the sound might be coming from the field when he saw it, a single black line on the horizon moving toward him.

The line stretched as far as he could see in either direction. Slowly it grew, moving in with increasing speed. Jan caught his breath. Tiny shapes emerged from the faceless line. They flew toward him, below the streaming sky, against the tide, as though riding an airborne tsunami.

Jan jerked back a step and froze, unsure what to do. Then the sea of figures was upon him, rushing a hundred feet over his head, silent except for an aerodynamic moan, like a mighty rushing wind. He yelped and crouched low, thinking they might clip his head. But they were a good hundred feet up. It was the sheer volume of them that cast the illusion of proximity.

He stared, dumbstruck. They were children, mostly. He could see their blurred bodies streaking over him in hues of blue and red. A faint bubbling sound suddenly erupted from the children, running up and down the scales, as if magical chimes were moving with them. Only it wasn't a chime; it was laughter. A hundred thousand children giggling, as if their sweep down upon him was a great joke they now delighted in.

Jan's mouth spread in a smile. A chuckle escaped his mouth.

The laughter grew in response. And then Jan was laughing with them.

The line suddenly ended and he saw that the leaders had looped up into the sky, like a wave curling back on itself. They screamed in for another pass. A man with long hair led the flight, and at his right a smaller figure clung to his hand, squealing in fits of laughter; he saw them both clearly this time. They looked at him directly and their eyes sparkled with delight. When it seemed they were close enough to touch, Jan recognized them.

It was Father Micheal and Nadia!

Suddenly Jan wanted to leap up and join them. He stood to his feet. He was laughing with them, right there in the stone room; he knew that because his shoulders were feeling the pain from his body's jostling. But in his mind—in this other world—he jumped and flung his hands up futiley. He *had* to join them!

They looped back again, but this time they stopped high above and hovered like a cloud that covered the sky. The sound fell silent.

Jan pulled up, astonished. What was happening?

Then a thin wail cut through the air. And another, and another until the sky moaned with the sound of weeping. Jan stepped back, stunned. What had happened?

He lowered his eyes to the meadow. And he saw what they saw. A body lay on the flowers, ten feet from him, and he knew. It was Helen, and heaven was weeping for her.

Two emotions collided. Delight and grief. Love and death.

Jan's world snapped back to black, and he inhaled quickly. He was back in the dark room. The vision of heaven was gone.

THAT WAS *your dream, Jan. The dungeon and then the field. It was this. You have somehow waited for this moment since the day you saw Father Micheal and Nadia die. You were meant for this. This is your story.*

"God?" His voice echoed in the chamber. He was speaking as if God were physically in the room.

Yes, and so he was. Is.

"God?"

But only silence answered him.

A sense of desperation welled up in his chest. A yearning for the laughter, for the voice of God, for the smell of the flowers from Ivena's garden. But they were gone, leaving only the lingering memory of Helen, lying on the grass. She was not laughing. Was she dead?

And what if she was? What if that was the meaning of this vision? Karadzic had killed her and now heaven was weeping. He straightened in his straps, suddenly panicked. In that moment he knew what he would do.

"Karadzic!" he screamed. His head ached with the exertion. "Karaaadzic!"

Fire burned at his shoulders. But he had to do this, didn't he? It was the thinnest of threads, but it might be Helen's only hope. "Karaaaadzic!"

A fist pounded on the door. "Shut up in there."

"Tell Karadzic to come. I have something to tell him."

A moment of silence. "He wants nothing from you," the voice said.

"And if you're wrong? This will mean everything to him."

A grunt sounded, followed by a long period of silence. Jan called out twice more, but the guard didn't answer.

The door suddenly rattled with keys and then swung in. Shafts of yellow light fell across Jan's body, and he lifted his head.

Karadzic stood in the doorway, slapping keys in his right hand like a baton, legs spread. "So, you wish to beg me for your life after all?" He chuckled and his voice echoed in the chamber.

"I'm no longer interested in my life. Only Helen's."

"Then you're a fool and I pity you," Karadzic said.

"Helen was always the prize. That's why Lutz offered you money for her death. If he can't have her, then he'll kill her. But believe me, if that dirty pig thought for a moment that he could have her as his own, willingly, he'd never kill her."

Karadzic's lips twisted to a grin. "Is that it, Lover Boy?"

"Lutz would pay much more for Helen alive. I'm sure of it."

The smile softened on Karadzic's face. "Don't try tricks with me, soldier."

"Don't take my word. Ask Lutz himself. If he's paying you a hundred thousand dollars for our deaths, then he'll pay two hundred thousand for Helen's heart. I promise you."

"And I'm not interested in your promises. You think your sly tongue will play to your favor?"

"I'm not speaking of my promises, you idiot," Jan said. Karadzic's eyes narrowed. "I'm telling you what Lutz will say when you talk to him."

"And what makes you think I'll talk to him?"

"Your greed will see to it."

"And your stupidity will see to your death."

"You would be a fool not to call Lutz. Demand double for Helen's willing return and he'll agree to pay you."

"Even if you're right, how do you propose I force the woman to return to Lutz? You say he's a pig."

Jan gathered himself and straightened against the beams. His shoulders throbbed, as if needles had been run through his joints.

"You persuade Helen to openly renounce her love for me." Saying it made Jan sick.

Karadzic stared dumbly. "Renounce her love? You're talking women's talk."

"If she were to renounce her love, it would break her spirit. That's why the priest wouldn't renounce his love for Christ. Haven't you understood that yet? It wasn't only words he was refusing to give you; it was his heart. If Helen renounces her love for me, she won't be able to live with the shame. She'll go eagerly back to America. And in America there is only Lutz for her." How could he even say such words? Living with Lutz would be a death of its own. But then God could still woo her, couldn't he?

Karadzic was no fool in the art of bending minds; the war had taught him well. His eyes darted back and forth. "So you propose I break her heart by forcing her to renounce you? You think I am so naive?"

Jan took a deep breath. "No, you can't force her. She must do it willingly. So play one of your games, Karadzic. The same game you played with the priest. Perhaps you'll recover the shame he heaped on your head."

Karadzic blinked rapidly. Jan had struck a chord there.

Jan continued quickly. "You can't force her, but you can motivate her. Tell her that if she doesn't renounce her love for me, you'll kill her." He swallowed hard.

Karadzic licked his lips, understanding already. Jan went on.

"You tell her that, but if she chooses to die rather than renounce her love for me you do *not* kill her. You release her. And if she does renounce her love, then you release her to Lutz. Either way she lives. Either way you may kill me." Jan forced a smile. "It's a game of ultimate stakes. She chooses to live and you become very rich; she chooses to die and you still get your ransom, but not for her. Only the half paid for me. She is free."

"Her choice to die for you will set her free," Karadzic stated with a glint in his eyes. "But her choice to live will hand her over to Lutz. Or I could just kill you both and collect the money already offered."

"You could."

Karadzic stared at him for several long seconds. Then he backed out of the room. "We will see," he said, and he was gone.

The door closed and Jan slumped against his straps.

KARADZIC ENTERED the dimly lit quarters beneath the earth and stared at the large American seated cross-legged in his leather chair. The man stood to his feet and faced him. He looked albino in the yellow light; very white from his blond hair to his pale skin, this pig. Karadzic had never suspected that another man could send a chill down his spine, but Glenn Lutz did, every time he turned those black eyes his way. He did not like that.

"Well?" Lutz asked.

"He has a proposal for you," Karadzic said, walking for his liquor cabinet.

"He knows that I'm here?"

"No. Of course not. He thinks I will call you."

"He's not exactly in a position to give proposals, is he? What's his proposal?" Lutz demanded.

"He says that you will pay me double for the woman's heart."

Glenn breathed loudly in the chamber. "I didn't make a thirty-hour trip to cut out her heart. I came to kill her. Straight and simple. Once she's dead, I don't care what you do with her. He's ranting."

"He's not suggesting that I cut her heart out. He's suggesting that I play a game with her." Karadzic poured scotch into a glass and faced the bulky American. "The same game that I played with the priest in the village."

Lutz stared dumbly. He wasn't connecting. "I paid you to bring them in. Fifty thousand American dollars for each. Now I'm going to kill them both. I'm not interested in games."

"And what if the game gave you Helen back? Hmm? What if she came willingly to you as yours and yours alone? What would you pay for that?"

Glenn pulled and pushed the stale air through his nostrils as if they were old bellows. His eyelids fell over those black eyes like shutters and then snapped open. The man had lost a part of himself somewhere, Karadzic thought.

Karadzic spoke again. "He says that you will pay me two hundred thousand dollars if I'm able to persuade her to renounce her love for Janjic. He says that if she renounces her love for him in the face of death, she'll lose her will to love him and return willingly to you."

Glenn stared at Karadzic for a long time without moving his eyes. Finally he spoke. "And if she refuses?"

"Then we set her free. We kill only Janjic." He took a sip from the glass.

"I came to kill them both," Glenn said, but his conviction seemed tempered.

"Janjic is right. If the woman renounces her love for him, her spirit will be broken. She will be yours for the taking." Karadzic smiled. "But either way I will kill him. You will have her alive or dead. Either way you will win."

"I thought the game was to set her free if she chooses to die."

"That was Janjic's request. But if she chooses to die rather than renounce her pathetic love for one man, then we will give her that wish." It really was like the priest, wasn't it? Karadzic felt his pulse thump through his veins. A sort of vindication.

"And why should I pay you—"

"Because you could not do it," Karadzic interrupted, suddenly angry. "She would never renounce her love with you standing there." He had no idea if that was true or not, but suddenly the money was sounding very attractive. And playing the game again carried a poetic justice that was starting to gnaw at his skull. "I will kill Janjic regardless. And I am offering you the chance to have your woman alive and willing. It's your choice. One hundred thousand for both dead, or two hundred thousand for Janjic dead and Helen in your arms."

Glenn turned from him and put his hands on his hips. The man wasn't beyond trying to kill *him*, Karadzic thought. Lutz would pull the trigger without a thought. But this was Bosnia, not America. Here the American would play by his rules. Or die. If it wasn't for the promise of the money Karadzic would have killed the fat slob already. It would be a pleasure to watch the pig die.

"I'll double my payment for Helen," Glenn said, turning. "One hundred thousand for her if you can make her curse the preacher. I'll pay you our agreed fee of fifty thousand for the preacher. That's one hundred fifty thousand. No more."

He said it all as a man used to authority, and Karadzic almost told him to swallow his money. But he didn't. He might do that later.

"Fine," he said, and walked for the door. "I will expect you to keep your promise." Lutz was boring into him with those black eyes when he turned back to him. "Do not leave this room," Karadzic said. He left and a chill of fury ripped down his spine.

Maybe he would just kill them all. When it was over and he had his money. But now he would play. The thought brought a grin to his lips.

Poetic justice.

CHAPTER FORTY-ONE

HELEN FELT hands moving her, jostling her around, but her mind still drifted in lazy circles. They had changed her position, she knew that much, and now she grasped for threads to the real world. The room with all of its colored lights and feathers wasn't easily distinguished from her dreams.

She was standing, or lying on her back. No, standing, with her arms thrown to either side, immobile. Odd. Helen turned her head slowly and closed her eyes against the tiny flames of light. The candles looked like fireflies skittering across her horizon. She moaned. When the pinpricks behind her eyes cleared, she looked again and the room came into soft focus.

The black walls glistened with the glow from several dozen white candles staggered at various heights, their flames flickering like jerky dancers. A couple of figures moved in the shadows but most of the others she'd seen were no longer present. Helen tried to shift her feet to rid a tingling there, but she found she couldn't. She lowered her head and studied her bare feet. Yes, they were bare. And pressed side by side, hanging limply. Off the ground.

The last detail cleared her mind and she blinked. Her feet were bound together, suspended off the floor! Her arms . . . She lifted her head quickly and looked at her right arm. Half-inch rope had been wrapped around her forearm and a huge crossbeam. She turned her head. Her left arm was bound to the same beam.

A chill ran up her spine. What was happening to her? She pulled against the restraints, but they didn't give, and her head throbbed with pain for the effort. They'd ripped her tan cotton slacks at the knees, baring her calves. The white of her blouse was smudged with dirt, and the sleeves shredded to her armpits.

What is happening? Helen began to whimper, not because she wanted to whimper, but because she wanted to ask and nothing else would come from her mouth. She desperately searched the room and caught the looks of the two men, but they only stared, unblinking.

"H . . . help." Her cry squeaked like a pathetic little toy, and she began to weep softly through trembling lips. "Please help." But the room was empty except for these two men calmly looking at her.

She knew then that her life was about to end. There was a feel to the air unlike any she'd ever known. A biting chill but hot, so that her skin glistened with sweat. She shivered. The room smelled like rotten meat, but tinged with a medicinal odor she recognized as heroin. Evil filled this dungeon, dark and lurking, but very much alive. And she had come here eagerly.

Helen's body shook with fear and shame. *Oh, Jan, dear Jan, what have I done? I am so sorry.*

How many times had she said that?

She bit her lip, hard enough to draw the tangy taste of blood.

The door opened to her left and a large figure stood in the frame, backlit by the hall's orange light. Karadzic.

Suddenly she knew who this man was. He was Karadzic! *The* Karadzic! He was Jan's commander in the book!

A woman was shoved past him, stumbling to her knees. Her dress was ripped up one side, but it looked vaguely familiar. The two men who'd been in the room stepped forward and hauled the woman to her feet.

Helen saw her face, streaked with blood so that it looked torn along a jagged line. She caught her breath.

It was Ivena! Ivena was here!

"Ivena!"

Ivena turned her head slowly and looked at Helen. Then her eyes widened and immediately wrinkled with empathy. Ivena's mouth parted in a silent cry. "Dear Helen . . . Oh, dear Helen, I am so sorry."

Helen turned to the door where Karadzic still stood in shadows. "What are you doing to her? She's an old woman. You can't—"

"Don't be afraid for me," Ivena said, now with a soft voice. Helen faced her. There was a glint in Ivena's eyes and it wasn't from the firelight. "I fear for you, dear Helen. For your soul, not for your body. Don't let them take your soul."

A white light flooded Helen's mind with that last word, as if a strobe had been ignited. She jerked her head up.

The room had vanished. She gasped.

A field of white flowers stretched out before her, surrounded by a brilliant blue sky.

Her vision snapped back to the room, where the big man, Karadzic, was stepping in, followed by the woman in red. They both wore clown grins.

But Helen remained here less than a second, before the white world popped back to life like a flashbulb. The flowers swayed, delicate in the breeze, bowing to a prone figure not ten feet away. She heard what sounded like a child sobbing quietly, and Helen quickly scanned the surreal sky. It was turquoise now and it flowed like a river toward the horizon.

Helen dropped her eyes. The woman on the ground was dressed in a pink dress with little flowers and . . .

It was *her!* It was her, *Helen!*

The soft sobbing halted for a brief second, leaving only deathly silence. The world had frozen with Helen in it, standing agape, lying near death.

And then the screaming started. A hundred thousand voices wailed at once, desperate in their agony. In her mind's eye Helen covered her ears and doubled over. The sound ripped through her nerves like a razor. They were weeping for that prone figure. For *her.*

"God, dear God, forgive me!"

Instantly she was back in the dim room, with her last cry echoing around her. Karadzic and his black-haired woman stared at her, their smiles gone. They had heard her.

"God can't hear you, fool!" The big man was dressed in a black robe with the lady in red at his arm. Two others had followed them in and now took their posts to Helen's right. Then Karadzic stepped to the center of the room and faced her. "You think calling out to God will save you? It didn't save the priest, and he was better than you."

The two men who'd waited near the back had Ivena by her arms now. They jerked her to the side where they stood her up facing Helen. But the glint in Ivena's eyes did not fade.

The candles flickered silently. Helen sagged from the cross, heaving with emotion. But it really wasn't from the madness in this room, was it? It was from that vision. It had left her sight, but the weeping still crashed through her heart.

Karadzic approached Helen, wearing a twisted grin again. He was very tall, so that his face came level with Helen's. He lifted a thick hand and ran his fingers down Helen's cheek.

"Such soft skin. It's a shame, really." Karadzic spoke very softly, and he wiped the tears from Helen's cheek. It made little difference; fresh tears spilled in silent streams. He leaned closer, and Helen could smell the musty odor of his breath.

"Today you will die. You know that, don't you?" he whispered.

Karadzic's eyes were no more than six inches from Helen's; they roved in their sockets, searching Helen's face. He ran a thick tongue delicately over his teeth; sweat glistened on his upper lip. "In one hour you will be dead. After we've had our fun. But you can save yourself. You're going to decide whether or not you want to stay alive now. Do you understand?"

He looked into Helen's eyes, waiting.

Helen nodded. A squeak of air escaped her throat. Fear spread through her bones, replacing the sorrow brought on by the vision. She glanced over at Ivena, who stared at her with that fire in her eyes.

"Helen," Karadzic whispered. His mouth popped lightly with the parting of his lips and tongue. "Such a pretty name. Do you want to stay alive, Helen? Hmm? Do you want to go back to your lover?"

Helen nodded. She glanced over Karadzic's shoulder and saw that the others hadn't moved. The faint hiss of burning candlewicks played over her mind. The man was breathing deliberately through his nostrils.

"Say it, my darling. Tell me you want to stay alive."

"Yes," Helen said. But it came out like a whimper.

Karadzic smiled. "Yes. Then you remember that, because if you don't, I'm going to let Vahda break your fingers off, one by one. It will sound very loud in this room. You will think that you're being shot, but it will only be your bones snapping loudly." Somewhere in there his smile had vanished.

Helen realized that she was no longer breathing.

Karadzic turned and walked back. A pistol was shoved in his belt, large and black. Helen's breath came in sudden short pants. Chills swept over her skull. *Oh, God! Please save me. I'll do anything!*

Karadzic turned around by the woman, Vahda, and for a long moment they stared at Helen, unmoving. Shadows flickered with the candle flames, dancing across their faces.

Karadzic reached out to the guard on his right and took a revolver from him.

Helen's heart crashed into her throat. Her breathing shortened—she was hyperventilating. Glenn's eyes were black. No, it was Karadzic, and his eyes were like holes. Why were they doing this? What had she done to anger them?

"Now, Helen, we brought you here to kill you. And we're going to do that." He spoke very softly, very matter-of-factly. "But since your husband was kind enough to tell my story to the world and bring me such fame, I've decided to give you a choice. You did read his book, didn't you?"

She didn't respond. Couldn't.

"Good. Then you'll remember that I gave the priest a choice. You do remember that?"

Karadzic took a step forward. "Look at me, Helen." She did, still trembling. "Here is your choice. It's quite simple. If you renounce your love for Janjic, I will set you free."

She blinked at the man. Renounce her love? For Janjic! She could do that easily—they were just words.

"Do you understand? Tell me that you don't love him—that you would curse him if he were here—and I'll set you free. Do you understand?"

She nodded impulsively.

You can't renounce your love, Helen.

Of course I can. I have to! She refused to look at Ivena, but she could feel the woman's eyes on her.

"Very good."

"You . . . you won't hurt him?" Helen asked.

"Hurt him? If you reject him, what will it matter? He'll be dead to you anyway."

Her head began to throb. She closed her eyes, desperate to wake up from this nightmare.

"Helen."

She opened her eyes. Karadzic had lifted the gun and rested its barrel on his cheek. He tilted his head, and looked past his bushy eyebrows at her.

"You know what happened to the priest. I know you do. I killed him."

She didn't move. The air felt very still.

"But I want you to be sure that I will do what I say. I want you to know that when I say I'm going to kill someone, I will kill them." His mouth was open in a slight smile.

"Look at Ivena, Helen."

Helen turned toward Ivena. The older woman looked directly at Helen with an eagerness in her eyes and the hint of a smile on her lips. There was no fear; there was only this absurd confidence that glowed about her. A fresh surge of tears spilled from Helen's eyes.

The guards stepped aside and Ivena stood on her own feet, wavering.

"Do not weep for me, Helen. The weeping is for you," Ivena said.

From the corner of her eye Helen saw Karadzic lift his arm to Ivena. A *boom!* crashed through Helen's skull and she jerked back. Ivena's neck folded back. The side of her head was gone. She fell to the floor like a sack of flour.

Then Helen's mind began to explode with panic. There was laughter, but she couldn't remove her eyes from Ivena's limp body to see where it came from—maybe from Karadzic and his woman. Maybe it was from her.

Ivena! Dear God, Ivena was dead!

Oh, God, please save me! I please beg you to save me! Please, please!

JAN STRAINED against the ropes, ignoring the pain that throbbed in his joints. It had begun, he knew that much. He could feel the tension in his gut, and it made him nauseous.

Dear Father, I beg you, save her. I beg you!

He heard a distant report: a gunshot far away. Had they shot her? Jan dropped his chin to his chest and groaned aloud. Bile filled his throat and he threw up. He spit the bitter taste from his mouth and groaned again. It was too much.

Karadzic would do whatever possible to encourage Helen's denouncement of love, even if it meant harming her. And Ivena, what would he do to Ivena? The thought of that bullhead touching Helen revolted Jan, actually made his body quiver on its moorings.

He let his head loll and begged God for the moments to pass quickly. If she renounced her love, she would be gone forever and Jan thought he might as well die without her. Which was precisely what would happen. Karadzic would butcher him.

But if Helen chose death instead? Karadzic might break his word and kill her. But there were no other options. At least they would die as one, in love.

Father, you cannot allow her to die. She is your Israel; she is your church; she is your bride.

A picture from the Psalms, of a giant eagle screaming from the sky to protect its young, spun through his mind. *You have cast this madness, Father. Now save us. You have made me Solomon, desperate for the maiden; you have made me Hosea, loving with your heart. Now show me your hand.*

Silence.

Jan hung from his restraints, wanting death. He could hardly think for the pain. If Karadzic would free his hands, he would claw the man's eyes out! Jan ground his teeth. He would pummel that thick face! *How dare he touch—*

The world abruptly stuttered to white.

The vision!

Laughter crashed in on him from all sides. The field of flowers and this hilarious laughter. A wave of relief swept over his chest and he chuckled suddenly. Then the sentiment thundered through his body and he could not contain it. It was pleasure. Raw pleasure and it boiled from his bones in bubbles of joy!

Jan doubled over, as far as his bound arms allowed, and he laughed. The room echoed with the sounds of a madman, and he couldn't help thinking that he'd finally lost his sanity. But he knew at once that he could not be more sensible. He was drinking life and it was making him laugh.

Every fiber in his body begged to die in that moment; to join that laughter forever. To roll through the field and rush through the blue sky with Father Micheal and Nadia.

The vision vanished.

He blinked in the darkness. *You know Nadia spoke of laughter, Janjic. You know Father Micheal laughed. And then they both died. The laughing precedes death.*

Then let me die, Father.

But save Helen. I beg you.

THEY HAD left the room for a while, to give her time to think things through, the woman said. Ivena's body lay in a pool of blood to Helen's right, her eyes open and dead. The candles cast wavering shadows across the room. And Helen stared with round eyes, a sheen of sweat glistening on her skin, breathing in ragged lurches.

She had passed out once, from hyperventilation, she thought. When she came to, she wondered if the whole thing had been a bad dream, but then she saw the body and she started crying again.

The problem was quite simple. She didn't want to renounce her love for Jan. Her mind revisited his incredible kindness and his passion. Renouncing his love could very well be death in and of itself. At the very least she could never face him again.

But then she didn't want to die. No, she would never allow them to kill her.

The door banged open, and Karadzic walked in with the woman and two guards. One of the guards walked to Ivena's body and began pulling it to the side.

"Leave it!" Karadzic said.

The guard released the body and joined his comrade on Helen's left.

Karadzic took up his position before her, like an executioner eager to get on with it. Vahda was biting at a fingernail, obviously excited. They stared at her in silence for a moment.

Karadzic spoke in a low rumble. "Now, Helen. We're going to begin breaking your fingers. I prefer the knife and we might get to that, but Vahda has persuaded me that a woman will do anything to keep her fingers."

Helen began to shake again. The nails in the beam at her back were squeaking with her trembling: an obscene sound that sent chills down her legs.

"Oh, God!" she moaned. "Please, God!"

Karadzic lifted his eyebrows. "God? I told you, God isn't listening. I think your God—"

It was all she heard. Because the world exploded again. It flashed white.

She was back in the vision!

Only this time, the field of white flowers was swimming in the laughter of children. Helen caught her breath. There was another sound there with the children—she recognized it immediately. It was Ivena! Laughing with the children. Hysterical.

And the prone figure had vanished. And that was funny, she thought. No, that was delightful. That was perfectly incredible! That was better than anything she could ever have imagined.

She heard her own laughter, joining the chorus. Not because it was so funny, in fact funny was a terrible word to describe this emotion erupting from her belly. She felt as though she'd been yanked from an acid bath and plunged into a pool of ecstasy. This intoxicating world of intense pleasure.

This is heaven.

"Stop it!"

The voice snapped Helen back to the room.

"STOP IT!" Karadzic stood trembling. "You think it's funny?"

Helen was chuckling. The woman hung from his cross covered in her own sweat, shaking like a leaf. A moment before, it had been terror twitching those muscles; now it was laughter.

The scene ran through Karadzic's mind like a sick joke. He had seen this before. In a small village not so far away, twenty years ago.

"Shut up!"

She stopped and looked around like an idiot, as if unsure of where she was. The absurdity of this sudden turn in her demeanor brought a chill to Karadzic's bones. What in God's name did she think she was doing?

"You laugh like that again, I'll put a bullet in your stomach! Do you hear me?"

Helen nodded. But her eyes were no longer round and wide. They looked at him with mere curiosity. He would have to put the fear back into her. He would break two fingers, one on each hand. Her index fingers.

Karadzic took a step forward, noting that his own hands still trembled. He closed them into fists. "We will see how you feel after—"

"I've made my decision," she interrupted calmly.

He blinked. "You have, have you?"

"Yes."

"Not so fast." This was not sounding good. "I have Janjic. Do you know that?" The pitch of his voice had elevated, but he didn't care.

"You . . . you have Jan?" She swallowed, and for a second he thought she might burst into tears again. "I love him," the woman said.

"You're a fool," Karadzic muttered through clenched teeth.

"I will die rather than renounce my love for Jan."

This was impossible! "You won't just die! You'll have all of your bones broken, one by one, you little coward!"

Her eyes stared at him without moving. Tears spilled from each, leaving fresh trails down her cheeks. But she did not blink.

"If you think you'll find some perverted satisfaction from hurting an innocent woman, then do it," Helen said.

"You think you're innocent? Did I drag you here? You've killed your own lover by coming here."

Her cheeks sagged.

Karadzic continued quickly. "Janjic will die and only you can save him. Renounce him, you fool. They're only words! Don't be an imbecile."

"No!" she screamed. "No." She began to cry again. She was going to break.

Her face wrinkled with pain. Karadzic could smell the change in her and he encouraged her gently.

"Save yourself," he said. "Renounce him."

She inhaled sharply and settled slowly against the ropes. She looked directly into his eyes and Karadzic swallowed. There was a new woman behind those eyes and she was stronger than he'd thought.

"You know I can't do that," she said quietly. "Kill me. I'll die for him—it's long overdue."

The tremble started at Karadzic's head and worked its way down to his heels. If he hadn't been immobilized on the spot, he might have lifted his pistol and shot her then.

Vahda was not so paralyzed. She shrieked and flew past Karadzic with claws extended. Her fingers dug into Helen's neck and she raked them down her chest, leaving trails of blood.

Karadzic stepped forward and brought a heavy hand across Vahda's head. The woman sprawled to the floor. "She's mine!" he shouted. "Did I tell you to do this?"

He stepped back, trying desperately to gather himself. He was losing control of the situation, the one thing no good commander could allow. His breathing came thick and slow. White spots floated in his vision. Vahda pushed herself to her feet.

Karadzic faced Helen. "So. You think you are smart. Choosing your death. Well, I *will* kill you. And I will allow Vahda to break your bones. But you won't die until you've witnessed the death of your lover. Would you like that?"

The woman did not react.

He screamed it. "I said, would you like that?"

She blinked. But otherwise she only peered at him. Her neck was bleeding badly from Vahda's fingernails.

"Get the prisoner," Karadzic snapped.

Two guards quickly left the room for Janjic.

"Vahda, dear. Remember, this is my game, not yours. You must remember that." She didn't acknowledge him. "So now you may break two of her fingers, but only two," he said.

She turned to him with a glint in her eyes.

"Yes, darling. You may. And her knees."

Chapter Forty-Two

THE FIRST thing Jan saw when the two guards dragged him into the room was a tall woman in red with long black hair. She was facing the wall. He saw Karadzic to the left, wearing a sinister grin by candlelight. Then the woman moved aside and he saw Helen.

She'd been tied to a thick wooden cross. Her head lolled to one side, and she stared out into the room, expressionless. She hadn't seen him.

There was blood on her neck. And her knees . . . *Oh, dear God!* Her knees were a bloody mess. Jan panicked then. He growled and flung himself forward.

His attempt was rewarded with a stiff blow to the side of his head. He slumped between the guards and Helen's image swam in his vision. She was looking at him now. Slowly a thin smile formed on her mouth. *Dear Helen! My poor Helen!*

Her index fingers were oddly disjointed. Nausea swept through his stomach. He turned from her and saw the body folded over itself in the shadows. It was a woman, lifeless, dressed in . . .

It was Ivena! That was Ivena lying in the corner with her head bloodied. *Oh, dear God! Dear God!*

Jan closed his eyes and lowered his head. The sorrow rose through his chest and rushed from his eyes, as if a dam had broken deep in him. He hung from his arms between the guards and he wept.

"Do you like what you see, Janjic?" Karadzic asked quietly.

Shut up! Shut up, you devil from hell!

"Don't listen to him, Jan. Listen to me." It was Helen's voice!

He lifted his head and blinked.

"Shut up!" Karadzic said.

But Jan was looking into Helen's eyes, and he saw something there. Something new. Something that reached into his chest and squeezed his heart. It was the way he'd felt in the restaurant on their first date, the same feeling that had given him weak knees in the garden under a full moon. It was the same beating of his heart that had pounded in his ears while she leaned over his shoulder looking at the coffee machine.

And yet it was coming from her heart, not just his. He could see the love in her eyes and in the lines around her lips. She seemed hardly aware of her broken bones. She was swimming in a new dimension.

He began to cry, and the guards shifted awkwardly on their feet.

"Jan." It was Helen again, weak yet speaking his name. His body trembled.

"Jan, I love you."

He lifted his head to the ceiling and began to wail out loud. Waves of joy washed through his bones.

The guards released him suddenly and he crashed to the ground. He hardly felt the force of the fall. She loved him! Dear God, Helen was loving him!

He wanted to look up at her and tell her that he loved her too. That he would give anything to hear her say those words again! That he would die for her.

Jan's lips pressed against the stone ground and his tears pooled. He rolled to his side and tried to push himself up. He couldn't. But he had to. He had to stand and rush over to Helen and kiss her face and her feet and her wounded knees and tell her how terribly much he loved her.

Karadzic was screaming something. Jan opened his eyes and saw that the man had thrust a pistol in Helen's cheek. But Helen's eyes were on Jan.

She didn't seem to care about the gun. And it occurred to Jan that he didn't either. In fact, it all seemed rather absurd; this big man shoving his black weapon at Helen, as if doing so should bring her to her knees. She was tied up, how could she possibly fall to her knees? She was strapped to the cross, bleeding, and she was smiling.

A bubble of laughter escaped Jan's lips.

For a long, awkward moment the room fell to silence. Karadzic and his woman stood shaking, glaring at Jan, at a loss. Helen looked into Jan's eyes.

Karadzic suddenly spun, gripped the pistol in both hands, and squeezed the trigger. A deafening report boomed through the room.

The slug tore into Jan's side, burning as if someone had jabbed him with a branding iron. He gasped and clutched his side.

"Dear Father, save us," Helen's trembling voice whispered. Her chin rested on her chest. "Love us. Let us hear your laughter."

"Silence!" Karadzic screamed.

The door suddenly banged open and a ghost from the past stood there, huge and white and round-eyed. It was Glenn. And a moment later Jan knew that he was in the flesh. Glenn Lutz was *here!*

Helen had looked up and was staring directly at Glenn. "Show your hand. Show the power of your love. Let us hear your laughter. We've died already, now let us live." She was praying for the laughter.

Karadzic had spun to Glenn, who stood dumbfounded, glaring at Helen on the cross.

The room fell to an eerie silence.

"Kill her," Glenn said in a breathy voice. His face suddenly contorted with hate, and he stepped up between Karadzic and Vahda. "Kill her." His voice rose in pitch and he began to shake. "Kill her!" he screamed.

Karadzic stood rooted to the ground.

The sound came like bubbling spring, gushing from the rock. It was laughter. It was the same laughter from the vision. But it wasn't from the vision. It was from Helen. Helen had lifted her head and was laughing open-mouthed.

"He, he, he, he, he, ha, ha ha ha ha ha!"

Jan held his breath with the suddenness of it. It was the picture from the cover of *The Dance of the Dead*, only here, painted on Helen.

If Glenn's senses hadn't already snapped, they did in that moment. He roared and swung a huge fist at Karadzic's face. Bone smashed bone with a sickening thud and Karadzic staggered backward. Like an unleashed tiger, Glenn sprang at Karadzic while the commander was still off balance. But Karadzic set himself and the two large men collided.

Glenn shook like a leaf now, his lips pressed white with desperation. With a thundering roar, he ripped the gun from Karadzic's grasp and jumped back.

Helen's laughter echoed through the room, and Glenn jerked the pistol toward her in a blind fury.

The reprieve was what Karadzic needed. He snatched another gun from behind his back and jerked it up in line with Glenn. But the American's gun was already steadied.

A boom crashed through the room. Jan's heart stopped its beating. *Oh, God!* He clenched his eyes shut. *Oh, dear God!*

Laughter pealed about him. Helen's laughter. In death? She had joined Ivena and—

Jan snapped his eyes open and stared at Helen. Her eyes were closed and her mouth was open and she was still laughing.

Then Glenn's huge body fell, like a side of beef. His head bounced off the concrete a foot from Jan's. His eyes were open and there was a hole in his right temple.

Helen was still laughing, seemingly oblivious to the struggle around her. Her mouth was open with delight and tears wet her cheeks.

Karadzic faced her, sweat pouring from his skin. He took a step back and his eyes skipped around. It occurred to Jan that he was terrified. The big man opened his mouth in a moan.

Jan looked at Glenn's torso again, and this time he saw the black handle wedged under his shoulder. The gun!

Jan glanced up at Karadzic. The man trained his wavering gun forward, as if struggling against an unseen force. They had been here before. Only this time it wasn't the priest's laughter Karadzic would silence. This time it was Jan's wife's. The realization passed through his mind and he thought his chest would explode. Still Helen did not stop her laughing.

Jan reached out his right hand and grabbed for the gun under Lutz's body, keeping his eyes on Karadzic all the while. The man was transfixed by the sight of Helen. At any instant the gun in his hand would buck.

Cold steel filled Jan's hand. His world swam. He found the trigger and pulled the pistol out in one quick motion. A groan broke from his throat and he heaved the gun up in Karadzic's direction. He yanked the trigger.

Boom!

The slug hit his old commander somewhere below the waist, but Jan kept jerking on the trigger. *Boom! Boom! Boom! Boom! Boom!*

Click. The gun was empty.

Karadzic staggered back, wide-eyed, his own weapon unfired. He stared at Jan, wavering on his feet. Several blotches of red spread on his shirt. His nose was twisted and bleeding.

The man fell face forward on the concrete and lay still.

The room grew quiet.

Karadzic's woman had gone white. She eased toward the door, glanced one last time at Karadzic's lifeless form, and ran from the room. One of the guards ran out behind her, blinking in disbelief.

Only then, with Helen hanging from the cross, Jan lying in a pool of his own blood, and the last guard cowering against the far wall, did it occur to Jan that they were alive.

He dropped the gun and pushed himself to an elbow. He saw Helen looking at him in silence, and immediately collapsed to his side. Pain shot up his spine and he groaned.

Helen looked at the remaining guard, who still stood trembling. "Please, please," she begged. "Please help us."

The guard suddenly rushed across the room with a drawn knife and Jan's pulse spiked with alarm. The man ran to the cross and his blade flashed. It severed the cords. Helen fell free. The guard caught her, quickly lowered her to the ground, and ran from the room.

Jan's world began to drift. The universe had been created for moments like these, he thought. It was an odd thought.

Jan felt his head being lifted and he opened his eyes. She'd managed to crawl to him and lift his head in her arms. She was sobbing.

"Forgive me! I'm so sorry, Jan. Forgive me! Forgive me, forgive me, forgive me. I was so wrong. I was so, so wrong."

Her words floated in and out. She'd never said such things, but then she'd never been who she was now. Jan's body trembled, but this time with an unspeakable joy. The fruits of love. The universe was indeed created for moments like these.

He stared up at her, a dumb smile spreading across his face.

Helen leaned over his face. He felt her hot tears fall on his cheek. Then her warm lips on his own. And on his nose.

"I love you, Janjic."

She kissed him again, around his eyes.

"I love you, Jan Jovic. I will love you forever. With Christ's love, I love you."

She began to cry again and Jan lost consciousness, in the arms of an angel. In the embrace of true love.

CHAPTER FORTY-THREE

Six Months Later

A LIGHT New England breeze swept over the tall black cliffs that held the Atlantic Ocean at bay, and lifted Helen's hair from her shoulders. Before her, as far as she could see, whitecaps dotted the blue sea. In either direction, green grass rolled with the hills. It was the ideal setting to convalesce, she thought. Beautiful and healthy and perfectly peaceful.

She sat in the gazebo across the small glass table from Jan and breathed the salty air deep into her lungs. He sat in his wheelchair and stared at the ocean, wearing a loose cotton shirt and looking stunningly handsome.

Fifty yards behind them, their white colonial house sat stoically on the lawn. She would be in there preparing supper for them about now if it weren't for her knees. But they'd hired Emily to do more than nurse them to health, Jan insisted. On a day as bright as today Emily would probably serve them on the sprawling veranda.

Helen faced Janjic. "I love you, Jan."

He turned to her and his hazel eyes reflected the sea's green, smiling in their wrinkles. "And I'm mad about you, my dear." He extended a hand and rubbed her pregnant stomach. "And you, Gloria."

They'd already decided it would be a girl and they would call her Gloria, because of the glory that had set them free.

Helen smiled. "Thank you for bringing me back."

"What, to America?" He chuckled. "Did I have a choice?"

"Sure. We could have stuck it out in Bosnia." She looked out to sea. "Of course, you wouldn't have gotten the new book deal for *When Heaven Weeps.* Nor the movie." She smiled.

"And I wouldn't have the luxury of living my life in peace with my bride and my child," he added. "Like I said; did I have a choice?"

"No, I guess not."

"My only regret is that you're not well enough to serve me hand and foot." He smiled wide. "A celebrity deserves no less, don't you think?"

"Jan Jovic, how could you say such a thing? Don't worry, my knees are better by the day. I'll be at your beck and call before you know it." They laughed.

Helen stood and walked behind him. Ivena's red-and-white flowers cascaded over the thatchwork, spreading their sweet, musky scent. They'd brought a shoot with them six months ago and planted it along the south wall of the house and here, by the gazebo. Only Joey's Garden of Eden also featured the new species of lily and there it had nearly taken over the botanical garden's east wall.

Helen drew Jan's hair back, bent over and kissed behind his ear. "It's you I worry about, my dear. I don't know what I would do without you."

"Then let's make sure you don't have to live without me," he said. "I've lived through worse. You think a hole in my liver will hold me back?"

He said it with courage and she smiled.

Helen leaned over and kissed his other ear. "Well, I promise that I will love my wounded solider until the day that I die. And I have no intention of going anytime soon."

She laid her head on his hair and closed her eyes. How could she have possibly betrayed this man? The memory of her treachery sat like a distant pain at the back of her mind—always there but incomprehensible. An insatiable love for this man had replaced her addiction in whole.

The details of the last few months were written in black-and-white for the world to read in Jan's new book. The fact that Glenn's estate owned the legal rights to *The Dance of the Dead* was now irrelevant. His old book wasn't the complete story—he'd told them clearly enough at the news conference. *When Heaven Weeps* was. And as a new property it wasn't under the restrictions of the old contract he'd signed with Glenn's company.

Neither Roald nor the council could argue with that. Jan had graciously omitted their most ugly moments from the story. But not the woman that they had scorned. Not Helen. Jan had put her on nearly every page, both her ugliness and her beauty. Mostly her beauty, Helen thought.

She kissed the crown of his head.

He pulled her hand. "Come here."

She walked around the chair and sat in his lap.

He took her chin and looked into her eyes. "You're everything to me. You're my bride. You make my heart pitter and my knees weak. You think I would leave that for the grave?"

"No. But maybe for the laughter."

"I have the laughter already. I carry it in my heart, and it's for you."

Helen smiled and leaned forward. "You're very sweet, my prince." She kissed him lightly on the lips and then pulled back. His eyes were on fire with love.

"I love you. More than life," he said.

"And I love you. More than death."

She kissed his lips once again. She could not help herself. This love of theirs—this love of Christ's—was that kind of love.

THUNDER OF HEAVEN

PROLOGUE

Eight Years Ago

"It's starting again, Bill."

"Again? These things start every time we turn around."

She ignored the pastor. "I had another vision."

The line was silent for a moment.

"You're walking again?"

"No. But I'm praying. I want you to join me."

"What was the vision?"

Helen paused. "I'm not sure."

"You had a vision but you're not sure what it was?"

"Something terrible is happening, and somehow its outcome rests in my hands. In our hands."

"Our hands? God can't deal with this on his own?"

"Please don't be smart. I'm too old for games."

"Forgive me." He let out a long breath. "I'm not sure I'm ready for another round, Helen."

"I don't think anyone is this time." A tremor laced her voice. "He who is faithful in little will be given much. This feels like much. And, frankly, I'm a little scared."

The line was silent.

"Who is it?" Bill finally asked.

"Tanya," Helen said.

CHAPTER ONE

THOSE WHO know call that part of the jungle the hellhole of creation for good reason. And they call the Indians who live there the fiercest humans on earth for even better reason. It's why no one wants to go there. It's why no one *does* go there. It's why those who do rarely come out alive.

Which is also why the lone American girl who ran through the jungle really had no business being there. At least according to those who know.

Tanya Vandervan jogged to a halt atop a cleared knoll and tried to still her heavy breathing. She'd run most of the way from her parents' mission station, hidden by trees a mile behind, and in this heat, a mile's run tended to stretch the lungs.

She stood still, her chest rising and falling, hands on hips, her deep blue eyes sparkling like sapphires through long blond hair. The rugged hiking boots she wore rose to clearly defined calves. Today she had donned denim shorts and a red tank top that brightened her tanned skin.

Still drawing hard but through her nose now, she lifted her eyes to the screeching calls of red-and-blue parrots flapping from the trees to her left. Long trunks rose from the forest floor to the canopy, like dark Greek columns supporting tangled wads of foliage. Vines dripped from the canopy—the jungle's version of silly string. Tanya watched a howler monkey swing suspended by a single arm, whether provoking or protesting the parrots' sudden departure, she could not tell. She smiled as the brown mammal reached a flimsy arm out and nabbed a purple passionfruit from a vine before arching back into the branches above.

A gunshot suddenly echoed through the valley and she jerked toward the plantation. Shannon!

An image of him filled Tanya's mind and she ran down the knoll, her heart thumping steady again.

To her right, the clearing butted against hills that rose to a black cliff, looming a mile to the plantation's north. The Richtersons' large two-story white house sat still in the midday air, white like a marshmallow on a sea of green.

On Tanya's left grew fifty acres of the plantation's exotic crop: *Cavash* coffee beans, commonly regarded among connoisseurs as the finest coffee in the world. Shannon could be there working the fields, but she doubted it—he'd never taken much interest in his father's farming.

His father, Jergen, had fled Denmark and carved out this living because of his hatred toward the West. *The West is trampling out the earth's soul,* he would say in his booming voice. *And Washington's leading the charge. One of these days America will wake up and their world will be different. Someone will teach them a lesson and then they might listen.* They were just words, nothing else. Jergen was a coffee farmer, not a revolutionary.

Shannon spouted his father's rhetoric on occasion, but really, it was love, not hate, that drove his world. Love for the jungle.

And love for Tanya.

The thunder of gunfire boomed again. Tanya smiled and broke to her left, sprinting around the fields toward the firing range.

Tanya saw them when she cleared the last coffee bush—three blond Scandinavian heads bent over a rifle with their backs to her. Shannon's father, Jergen, stood on the left, dressed in khaki green. The visiting uncle, Christian, stood to the right, a brother look-alike.

The bare-chested young man between them was Shannon.

Tanya's heart jumped at the sight and she pulled up, stepping lightly.

Shannon stood tall for eighteen, over six feet, and wrapped in muscles that seemed to grow larger each day. Countless hours in the sun had darkened his skin and lightened his long blond hair. She often teased him, suggesting he take a comb to his head, but in reality she rather liked the way those loose strands fell down his neck and into those bright emerald eyes. It meant she could sweep his hair aside with her fingers, and she liked touching his face that way. His pectoral muscles flared from a rippling stomach and met broad shoulders. Today he wore only loose black shorts—no shoes on this man.

Tanya smiled at the image of being carried on those shoulders, down the mountain, while Shannon insisted she was as light as a feather.

His carefree voice drifted to her. "Yeah, the Kalashnikov's good up to a few hundred yards. But it's no good for long range. I like the Browning Eclipse," he said, motioning to another rifle on the ground. "It's good out to a thousand."

"A thousand?" his uncle said. "You can hit targets that far?"

Shannon's father spoke softly. "He can hit a quarter at eight hundred yards. He's championship material, I'm telling you. In the States he'd win anything in his class."

Tanya stopped twenty paces behind the three men and crossed her arms. For all of their manly prowess, they hadn't noticed that she was watching them from the brush. She'd see how long a woman could stand behind them without being noticed. Ten to one when they did notice her, it would be Shannon's doing. But the wind blew in her face—he wouldn't be smelling her so quickly today. She smiled and stilled her breathing.

"Show him, Shannon," his father said, holding the rifle out to him.

"Show him? Where?" Shannon took the rifle. "The targets are only two hundred yards out."

Jergen looked past his brother to the plantation's far end. "Yes, but the shed's a good way off. How far would you say that is, Christian?"

All three faced the distant structure, sitting against the tall forest. "Must be a good thousand yards. Maybe more."

"Twelve hundred," Jergen said, still looking at the small barn. "And that weather vane propped on top, do you see it?"

Christian lifted his field glasses from his chest and peered north. "That rooster? You can't expect Shannon to hit that from this distance."

"No, not just the rooster, Christian. The rooster's head."

"Impossible." He lowered the glasses. "There's no way. The best marksman in the world would have trouble putting a round there."

"*A* round? Who said anything about *a* round? That rooster there's been rusted in place for years now. I'll place money on the boy placing *three* rounds in its head from this distance."

Shannon gazed stoically at the distant target. Tanya knew he could shoot, of course. Anything to do with hunting and sport he did well. But she had to use her imagination to even see the rooster's head. There was no way this side of Jupiter a professional marksman, much less Shannon, could hit a target so far away.

The three men faced away from her, still unaware that she watched.

Shannon suddenly cocked his head over his shoulder, smiled, and winked at her.

She smiled and returned the wink. For a moment they held stares, and then Shannon returned his gaze to the rooster. Tanya took a step closer, swallowing.

"Show him, Shannon," Jergen said, glasses still at his eyes.

Shannon flipped the rifle in his hands, gripped the bolt, and chambered a round in a single smooth motion. *Kachink!*

He dropped to one knee and brought the gun to his shoulder, squeezing his eye to the scope. His bronzed cheek bunched on the wood stock. Tanya held her breath, anticipating the first detonation.

Shannon adjusted his grip on the rifle once and sank slowly to his haunches. For several long seconds nothing happened. Father and uncle stared ahead, each through their own binoculars. Tanya breathed, but barely. The air grew deathly still.

The first shot came suddenly, *Crack!* and Tanya started.

Shannon flinched with the recoil, chambered another round—*Kachink*—steadied himself briefly, and squeezed off another shot. And then a third, so close to the tail of the second that they chased each other to the target. Echoes reverberated across the valley; father and uncle stood frozen, binoculars plastered to their eyes like generals on the battlefield.

Without lowering his rifle, Shannon twisted his head and drilled Tanya with his bright green gaze. A broad smile split his face. He winked again and stood.

His uncle grunted. "My dear goodness! He's done it! He's really done it!"

Tanya walked forward and laid a hand on his arm. The breeze lifted his shoulder-length hair, and she noted the thin sheen of sweat that covered his neck and chest. He bent and kissed her lightly on the forehead.

Tanya took his hand and pulled him while his father and uncle still gazed through their binoculars. "Let's go for a swim," she whispered.

He laid the rifle against a bale and took after her.

He caught her within ten paces and together they plunged into the trees, laughing. The shrieks of howler monkeys echoed through the canopy like wailing clarinets.

"You know what the natives say?" Shannon said, slowing to a walk.

"What do they say?" she asked, panting.

"That in the jungle if you move, they will see you. Unless they're downwind, in which case they see you anyway, with their noses. Like I saw you sneaking up behind us back there."

"No you didn't!" She swung around and faced him on the path. He pulled up, pretending to study the branches. But she saw the sparkle in his emerald eyes.

Her heart swelled for him and she grabbed his head and pulled him to her mouth, kissing him deeply. The heat from his bare chest rose to her neck. She released him and glared mockingly.

"The wind was full in my face! There was no way you smelled me. Admit it, the first you knew I was behind you was when you turned around!"

He shrugged and winked. "If you insist."

She held him, wanting to kiss him again, but resisting for the moment. "Okay, that's more like it," she said, smiling, and they walked again.

"The Kalashnikov," Shannon said.

"What?"

"The Kalashnikov," he repeated, grinning slyly. "It's what I was talking about when you walked up behind us."

She stopped on the path, recalling the discussion. "Come on, you oaf." She grinned mischievously. "Beat me to the pool."

She ran past him, springing on the path ahead of him, placing each footfall on the squarest surface possible with each stride as he'd taught her. He could have passed her easily; could've probably taken to the trees and still reached the pool ahead of her. But he remained behind, breathing down her neck, silently pushing her to her limit. The path quickly entered thick, shadowed underbrush, perpetually damp under the canopy, forcing her to skip over the occasional stubborn puddle. Thick roots encroached on the muddy trail.

She veered to a smaller path—scarcely an indentation in the brush. The sound of crashing water grew in her ears and a haunting image flashed through her mind: Shannon standing next to the falls by the black cliffs, over a year ago. His arms had been spread and his eyes were closed and he was listening to the witch doctor's mutterings before the old bat *Sula's* death.

"Shannon!" she'd cried.

Their eyes flickered open as one—Shannon's bright green, Sula's piercing black. Shannon smiled. Sula glared.

"What are you doing?" she'd asked.

At first neither replied. Then the old bat's lips screwed into a smirk as he said, "We are talking to the spirits, my flower of the forest."

"Spirits." She shot Shannon an angry glance. "And what spirits are you talking to?"

"What is my name?" the old witch doctor asked.

"Sula."

"And where does my name come from?"

She hesitated. "I'm not sure I care."

"Sula is the name of the god of death," the old man said past his twisted grin. He waited, as if that should bring her horror. "Sula is the most powerful spirit on earth. All the witches before me took his power and his name. And I, too, have. That is why I am called Sula."

Shannon had stepped aside and was watching the man with something that hovered between intrigue and humor. He looked at Tanya and winked.

"You might think it's funny," she'd snapped at Shannon. "But I don't!" She faced the witch doctor, suppressing an urge to pick up a rock and throw it at him.

His eyes had narrowed to slits and he'd simply slipped into the forest.

She'd never told her father about the episode—a good thing because he might have come unglued over it. The *Yanamamo* tribe was known as "the Fierce Ones" for good reason—they were perhaps the most violent people on earth. And the source of their obsession with death was clearly spiritual. So her father insisted, and she believed him.

One month after the incident, Sula had died, and with him, Shannon's curiosity of his power. The tribe had buried him in the forbidden cave to three days of wailing. None in the tribe had yet worked up the courage to become Sula. To take on the spirit of death. To take on Satan himself, as her father put it. The tribe had been without a witch doctor for one year now, and as far as Tanya and her parents were concerned, that was good.

Tanya shook the memory off. It was over. Shannon was back to his old self. With Shannon still at her heels, Tanya broke from the jungle and pulled up at the cliff's edge, overlooking a waterfall that plunged twenty feet into a deep aqua pool below. Their pool.

She spun, panting. His body rushed by her, stretched out parallel, and soared over the cliff. She caught her breath and watched him fall in a swan dive before he could even see the water. If he ever miscalculated, he'd break every bone in his body on the rocks below. Her heart rose to her throat.

But he did not miscalculate. His body broke the surface silently and disappeared. For a while he didn't reemerge, and then he shot from the water and threw his long locks back with a flick of his neck.

Without a word, Tanya spread her arms and fell toward him. She broke the surface and felt the welcome chill of mountain water wash up her legs.

In that moment, free-falling into the pool's deep, she thought she had indeed come to paradise. She had been taken by her God, plucked at a young age from the suburbs of Detroit, and deposited in a jungle haven where all her dreams would come true.

She broke the surface beside Shannon. He kissed her while she still drew breath and then they struck for a sunny rock on the far side. She watched him pull himself effortlessly from the water and sit facing her, his legs dangling into the pool.

Tanya reached him and drew herself up to his knees. "Are all plantation boys as full of themselves as you?"

He suddenly reached in and lifted her from the water.

Tanya laughed and fell forward, knocking him onto his back. He put his arms over his head and lay on the warm rock. The sun glistened off tiny beads of water on his chest. She propped herself up beside him and traced the droplets with her finger.

There was nothing she could imagine as lovely as Shannon. This stunning specimen of a man with whom she was madly in love. God had brought her into the jungle seven years ago for this, she thought. To find the man she would spend her life loving. To one day marry him and bear his sons. He swallowed and she watched his Adam's apple rise and fall in his throat.

"I love you, Tanya," Shannon said.

She kissed his cheek. He drew her down and kissed her lips. "I think . . ." He kissed her again. "I really think I'm madly in love with you," he said.

"Always?" she asked.

"Always."

"Till death do us part?"

"Till death do us part," he said.

"Swear it."

"I swear it."

Tanya kissed his nose lightly.

"And I love you, Shannon," she said.

And she did. With every living cell she loved this boy. This man. Yes indeed, she thought. This was paradise.

It was the last day she would ever think it.

CHAPTER TWO

TANYA LEFT Shannon near the pool, just after the heat's peak. She jogged most of the mile home, smothered by such contentment that she wondered if the warmth she felt came from the Venezuelan skies or her own heart.

She ran toward her parents' small mission station, and the image of a cool tumbler filled with iced lemonade filled her mind. The heat had parched her. Ahead, the tin-roofed house her father had built seven years earlier flashed with the dipping sun. Tanya had helped him paint the hardwood siding green. To blend, he'd said.

Her parents, Jonathan and Heidi Vandervan, had responded to the call of God seven years earlier when Tanya was ten. She could still see her father seated at the dinner table announcing his decision to take them to the jungle.

Her father's family lived in Germany and her mother really didn't have any family to speak of. A brother named Kent Anthony lived in Denver, but they hadn't spoken in over fifteen years. Last they heard, Kent was in jail.

Either way, leaving the United States presented no great loss for either of her parents. A year later they had landed here, in the heart of Venezuela, among the Yanamamo.

Tanya passed several buildings to her left—the radio house, a small school, a generator shed, a utility shack—and jogged to the porch.

The distant sound carried to her then, just as she stepped through the front door, a faint beating hum. She looked toward the sky to see what it was, but all she could see was the bright blue sky and a flock of birds lifting from a nearby tree. She closed the door.

Her father was leaning over a radio he'd disassembled on the kitchen table; her mother was cracking eggs into a bowl on the counter. Tanya strode straight to the refrigerator. The latent odor of kerosene fuel drifted through the kitchen, but she'd grown accustomed to the smell after so many years. It was the aroma of home, the scent of technology in a jungle hothouse.

"Hi, honey," her father called. "Want to help me put this thing back together?" He studied a coil in his right hand.

"Sorry, they don't offer electronics in my curriculum. Looks like a mess. I thought you built the toolshed for this kind of thing," Tanya said, smiling. She opened the refrigerator.

"Exactly," her mother said. "You hear that, Jonathan? The kitchen table is no place for mechanics."

"Yes, well, this isn't some lawn mower or generator here. This is a radio and radios have hundreds of very small, sensitive parts. Half of which I can't seem to find just now."

Tanya chuckled and withdrew the pitcher of lemonade.

"But they *are* here," he said. "Somewhere in this pile. If I'd torn into this mess in that shed, there's no telling where they'd run off to. You'll have your table before supper. I promise."

"Sure I will." Her mother winked at Tanya and feigned disgust.

A muffled beating flickered in the back of Tanya's mind, that same hum she'd heard just before entering. Like a moth caught in the window. She poured the yellow drink into her glass. A breeze lifted the curtain from the kitchen window, carrying with it that moth sound.

But it wasn't a moth, was it? Not at all, and that fact occurred to Tanya when the tumbler touched her lips, before she'd drunk any of the lemonade. The sound came from large blades beating at the air. She froze there, her arm cocked. Jonathan lifted his head from the radio pieces.

"What is it?" Tanya asked.

"A helicopter," her father answered. He turned to his wife. "Were we expecting a helicopter this afternoon?"

Tanya sipped at the liquid, feeling the cool juice flow down her throat.

"Not that I was aware of," Heidi said and leaned to the window, pushing the curtain aside.

It occurred to Tanya that the helicopter sounded somehow different, a higher pitch than the Hughes she'd grown accustomed to. A layered *whit, whit, whit.* Maybe two helicopters. Or more.

She lowered the tumbler to her waist, imagining five or six of the things hovering to a landing on their back lawn. Now that would be something different.

The glass in her hand suddenly shattered and she jerked. She dropped her eyes and saw that it had just crumbled like a piece of old dried lace. Glass speckled the wood floor and she thought it would have to be swept before anyone stepped there.

Then every motion fell into a surreal slowness, unfolding like dream fragments. The room shuddered, surrounding her with a rapid thumping sound as if a giant had mistaken the house for a drum set and decided to execute a long roll.

Tha-da-dump, tha-da-dump.

The counter splintered at her elbow and her father leapt from his chair. Tanya's heart slammed in her chest.

She jerked her head up and watched white holes punch through the ceiling in long ragged strings. She heard the roar of machinery scream overhead and it occurred to her that these were bullet holes in the ceiling. That bullets had slammed into the counter, ripping it apart. That a bullet had smashed her glass.

The realization fell into her mind like an anvil dropped from a high-rise crashing into concrete. She turned toward the window, stunned. An arm grabbed her midsection, throwing her to the wood floor. Her father's voice yelled above the din, but she couldn't make out his words. Her mother was screaming.

Tanya sucked at the air and found her lungs suddenly stubborn. She wondered if she'd been hit. It was as if she could see everything from an outsider's perspective and the scene struck her as absurd. She lowered her eyes to her stomach, feeling gut-punched. Father's hand was there.

"Quickly!" he was yelling. He tugged at her arm. Blood seeped from his shoulder. He'd been hit!

"Get in the cellar! Get into the cellar!" His face twisted like crow's-feet around watery eyes.

He's hurting, she thought as he shoved her toward the hall. The hall closet had a trapdoor built into its floor. He was motioning for her to climb down the trapdoor and into the cellar, as he called it. Then adrenaline reached her muscles and she bolted.

Tanya yanked the door open and shoved aside a dozen shoes littering the floor. Using her forefinger, she frantically dug at the ring her father had attached to its lip, hooked it with her fingernail, and pulled. The door pried up.

Tears ran down her father's face, past his parted lips. The chopper's engines had retreated for a moment but now they drew near once again. They were returning.

Behind Jonathan, Tanya's mother scooted along the floor toward them, her face ashen white and streaked wet. Blood dripped to the floor from a large hole in her right arm.

Tanya spun back to the trapdoor and thrust it to one side. A thought careened through her skull, suggesting that she had broken her nail while yanking on the trapdoor. Ripped it right off, maybe. Hurt bad enough. She swung her legs into the hole and dropped into darkness.

The cellar was tiny, a box really—a crate large enough to hide a few chickens for a few hours. Tanya squeezed to one side, allowing room for her father or mother to drop in beside her. The guns were tearing at the roof again, like a gas-powered chain saw.

"Father, hurry!" Tanya yelled, panic straining her throat.

But Father did not hurry. Father dropped the lid back onto the crate, *Clump,* and pitch-blackness stabbed Tanya's wide eyes.

Above, the bullets were cutting the house up like firewood. Tanya sucked at the black air and threw her arms about to orient herself, suddenly terrified that she'd come down here alone. Above, she could hear her mother screaming and Tanya whimpered below the clamor.

"Mother?"

Her father's muted voice came to her urgently, insisting something, but she could make out only her name.

"Tanya! Ta . . . ugh!"

A faint thud reached into the crate.

Tanya cried out. "Father!"

Her mother had fallen silent too. A numbing chill ripped through Tanya's spine, like one of those chain guns blasting, only along her vertebrae.

And then the hammering stopped. Echoes rang in her ears. Echoes of thumping bullets. Above her only silence. The attack had been from the air—no soldiers on the ground. Yet.

"Fatherrrrr!" Tanya screamed it, a full-throated, raw scream that bounced back in her face and left her in silence again.

She panted and heard only those echoes. Her chest felt as though it were rupturing, like a submarine hull fallen too deep.

Tanya suddenly knew that she had to get out of this box. She stood from her crouch and her back collided with wood. She reached above her head and shoved upward. It refused to budge. The door had somehow been locked!

Tanya fell back, gasping for air, stretching her eyes in the darkness. But she saw only black, as if it were thick tar instead of emptiness around her. Her right elbow pressed against a wooden slat, her left shoulder bumped a wall, and she began to tremble in the corner like a trapped rat. The musty smell of damp earth swarmed her nostrils.

Tanya lost it then, as if an animal had risen up within her—the beast of panic. She growled and launched herself elbows first toward the space through which she'd descended. Her arms crashed abruptly into rigid wood and she dropped to her knees, barely feeling the deep gash midpoint between her wrist and elbow.

Trembling, she swung her fists against the wood, dully aware of how little it hurt to smack her knuckles into the hard surface. Impulsively, as a course of reflex alone, she sprang every responding muscle and stood, willing her head to break from the grave.

But her father had built the box from hardwood and she might as well have slammed her crown into a wall of cement. Stars blinded her night and she collapsed to the floor, dead to the world.

CHAPTER THREE

SHANNON RICHTERSON had watched Tanya down the path, fighting the urge to run after her and insist she stay. She'd glanced back with those bright blue eyes twice, nearly destroying him with each look, and then she'd disappeared from sight.

She'd been gone for an hour when the distant fluttering caught his ears. He lowered the knife he'd been aimlessly whittling with and turned first one ear and then the other to the south, testing the sound carried among a thousand jungle noises. But that was just it; this beating didn't come from the jungle. It was driven by an engine. A helicopter.

Shannon rose to his feet, slipped the knife into the sheath at his waist, and jogged down the path toward the plantation, a mile south. He hadn't noticed a chopper on today's schedule, but that didn't mean anything. His father had probably drummed up something special for Uncle Christian.

Shannon covered the first half-mile at a fast run, taking time to judge his footing with each long stride. Another, harsher sound joined the beating blades and Shannon slid to a stop, a hairline chill nipping at his spine. The sound came again—a whine punctuated with a hundred blitzing detonations. Machine-gun fire!

A chill erupted and blew down Shannon's spine like an arctic wind. His heart froze and then launched him into overdrive. His legs carried him from standstill to a blind sprint in the space of three strides. He streaked over the path and covered the last quarter mile in well under a minute.

Shannon burst from the jungle fifty yards from the two-story Victorian house his father had built fifteen years earlier when they'd first fled Denmark for this remote valley. Two images burned into his mind, like red-hot irons branding a hide.

The first was the two adults who stood in the front lawn, their hands lifted to the clouds—his father and Uncle Christian. The image threw abstract details his way. His father wore khakis, as always, but his shirt was untucked. And he wore no shoes, which was also uncommon. They stood there like two children caught at play, facing west, wide-eyed.

The second image stood in the sky to his right. An attack helicopter hovered fifty feet from the earth, a stone's throw before his father, motionless except for the blur of blades on its crown. A round cannon jutted from its nose, stilled for the moment. The thing hung undecided, maybe searching the ground for a landing point, Shannon thought, immediately rejecting the notion. The whole lawn below was a landing pad.

Warning klaxons blared in Shannon's skull—the kind that go off an instant before impact, the kind that usually render muscles immobile. In Shannon's case his tendons drew him into a crouch. He stood on the edge of the jungle, his arms spread at his hips.

And then the helicopter fired.

Its first burst shifted it to the rear a yard or two. The stream of bullets cut into his father's abdomen, sawing him in two with that first volley. Shannon watched his father's upper torso fold at the waist, before his legs crumpled below him.

A high-pitched scream split the air, and Shannon realized it was a woman's scream—his mother screaming from the house—but then everything was screaming around him. The engine hanging in the sky, screaming; that nose-mounted chain gun, screaming; the jungle to his rear, screaming; and above it all his own mind, screaming.

His uncle whirled and ran for the house.

The helicopter turned on its axis and spit a second burst. The slugs slammed into Uncle Christian's back and threw him through the air, forcing his arms wide like a man being readied for the cross. He sailed though the air, propelled by the stream of lead—twenty feet at least—and landed in a heap, broken.

The entire scene unfolded in a few impossible moments, as though stolen from a distant nightmare and replayed here, before Shannon in his own backyard. Only a small terrified wedge in his mind functioned now, and it was having difficulty keeping his heart going, much less properly processing cohesive thoughts.

Shannon stood nailed to the earth, his tendons still frozen in that crouch. His breathing had stopped at some point, maybe when his father had folded. His heart galloped and sweat streamed into his bulging eyes.

Some thoughts slurred through his mind. *Mom? Where are you? Dad, are you gonna help Mom?*

No, Dad's hurt.

And then a hundred voices began to yell at him, screaming for him to move. The helicopter suddenly sank to the ground and he watched four men roll to the ground. They came to their feet, gripping rifles. One of them was dark, he saw that. Maybe Hispanic. The other was . . . white.

The latter saw him and yelled. "The kid . . ."

It was all Shannon heard. *The kid.* In an American accent.

Something in Shannon's skull snapped then, just as the khaki-clad American lifted his rifle. He stared into that man's eyes and two simultaneous instincts flooded his mind. The first was to rush toward the bullet that AK-47 would hurl his way—speed its collision with his front teeth. He had no use for life now.

Shannon blinked.

The second instinct blasted down his spine in streams of molten fire, screaming for this man's death before his own. Shannon's muscles responded in the same instant he blinked.

He jerked to his left, snatching his knife from his belt as he moved. He lunged forward in a crouch, snarling, muttering in barely audible gutturals.

Shannon sidestepped midstride and felt the whip of slugs whirl past his right ear.

The soldier dropped to a knee and shifted his sights. Shannon dove to his left and decided there, midair and parallel to the ground, with bullets buffeting the air to his right, that it would have to be now.

At the last moment, he tucked his shoulder under, rolled topsy-turvy twice, and came to his feet with his knife already cocked. He slung the blade sidearm, carrying the momentum of his rise into the delivery.

Everything fell to slow motion then. The man's rifle still fired, following Shannon's tumble, kicking up dust just behind and below, overcompensating for Shannon's forward motion and undercompensating for his lateral movement. The knife spun, butt over blade, crossing the path of bullets, flashing once in the late sun, halfway to the man.

Then the blade buried itself in the man's chest. The soldier staggered back and struck the helicopter's opened door. The gun fell from his hands and Shannon was rolling again.

A second soldier lifted his weapon and Shannon bolted for the corner of the house—survival instincts were shouting above the other voices. He pelted full tilt, arms and legs pumping. Slugs tore into the siding an instant after he crossed into the house's shadow. Without pausing, Shannon veered to his left and raced for the jungle, keeping the house between himself and the helicopter.

Behind him a second airborne chopper began firing, its slugs tearing through the foliage ahead of him. He shifted course once, then twice, knowing that at any second one of those projectiles would smack into his back—like that, *Smack!*—and fill his spine with burning steel.

A tree just ahead and to his left trembled and splintered under a barrage of lead. He dove to his right and rolled into the forest before the gunner corrected his aim. Then Shannon was under the heavy jungle canopy, his heart slamming in his chest, sweat running down his face, but out of their reach.

Mom's in the house.

He spun back to the colonial beyond the trees. A figure inside suddenly ran past one of the rear windows, was gone for a moment, and then reappeared. It was his mother and she was wearing her favorite dress, the one with yellow daisies. Another obscure detail.

His mother's face was wrinkled with panic, lips down turned, eyes clenched. She was fumbling with the window latch.

Shannon ran four steps toward the edge of the forest and pulled up. "Mom!" he screamed.

His voice was lost in the helicopter's whine overhead.

Shannon bolted for the house.

CHAPTER FOUR

TANYA QUAKED in the corner of the box, her mind slowly crawling from a dark dream about chain saws chewing through a bed surrounded by all of her stuffed animals, scattering white cotton fibers as it sawed. But then her parents were among the animals leaking red.

She was having difficulty knowing if her eyes were open or closed—either way she saw nothing but blackness. The memories fell into her mind, like Polaroids suspended by threads. Her glass of lemonade shattering in her hand; holes popping in the ceiling; her father crouched in the hall; her mother crawling behind on her belly; the trapdoor descending overhead.

Then darkness.

She was here, in the crate where her father had led her. He and Mother were—

Tanya snapped upright and immediately regretted it. Pain throbbed over her crown. She ignored it for a moment and reached for the ceiling. She felt the trapdoor and she shoved, but it refused to budge. It had been bolted, or something very heavy held it in place.

"Father?" she said, but the crate seemed to swallow the sound. She tried again, screaming this time. "Dad!" A breath. "Mom!"

Nothing. Then she remembered the sounds out there, before she had torpedoed into the ceiling. Smacking bullets, her mother's scream, her father's grunt.

Tanya slumped back, sucking at the stale air. "Oh, God!" she groaned. "Please, please, God."

She started breathing hard, sucking rapidly in and out like an accordion gone berserk. She clenched her eyes even tighter against the thoughts. Mucus ran from her nostrils—she could feel the trail. Tears mingled and fell on her folded forearms. Something else was wet there too, on her right arm.

She began to whisper, repeating words that seemed to still the panic. "Get a grip, Tanya. Get a grip. Get a grip."

She suddenly shivered, from her head down through her spine. And then it became too much once again and she started screaming. She arched her neck and shoved the air from her lungs, past taut vocal cords. "Help! Help!"

But nobody was listening up there because everybody was dead up there. She knew it. She groaned loudly, only it sounded more like a snort. She scrambled to her knees, gathered what strength she had, and launched herself toward the trapdoor again.

Her muscles were already thickening and she slammed into the hard wood like a sack of rocks. Tanya collapsed onto her belly.

Things went dark again.

SHANNON CLEARED the tree line, headed pell-mell for his mother who had just smashed the glass with her elbow in a frenzied attempt to escape the house. She was a bloody mess.

Shannon's vision blurred and he groaned with panic. His foot caught something—a rock—and he sprawled on the edge of the lawn.

The tree at the forest edge just behind him splintered with a hail of bullets. But it didn't matter—he was down now and they could pick him off easily.

He clambered to his knees and looked skyward. The helicopter's cannon was lined up on him, ready to shoot.

But it didn't shoot. It hung there facing him.

Shannon stood slowly, quaking. Fifty meters to his right, his mom had one leg out the window, but she had stopped dead and was staring at him.

"Shannon!"

Her voice sounded inhuman—half groan, half bawl—and the sound of it sent a chill down Shannon's back. "Run, Shannon! Run!"

"Mom?"

The helicopter turned slowly in the air, like a spider on a string. Fire filled Shannon's throat. He'd seen the thing do this trick with his father and uncle. His feet wouldn't move.

He had to save his mother—pull her from that window, but his feet wouldn't move.

A streak suddenly left the helicopter. The wall above Mom's head imploded for a split second. And then the room behind his mother erupted in a thundering ball of flame.

A wave of heat from the detonation struck Shannon broadside. He stared in the face of the blast, unbelieving. The window his mom had been in was gone. Half of the house was gone; the rest of it was on fire.

Shannon whirled around and ran for the jungle, barely aware of his own movement. He ran into a tree and his world spun in lazy circles, but he managed to get back up and run on. This time he made it without a single shot. But this time he didn't care.

SHANNON RAN under the canopy, his mind numb, every sense tuned to raw instinct now. He leapt over fallen logs, dodging thorn-encrusted vines, planting each foot on the surest available footing despite his pace. He cut sharply to his right within a hundred meters. In his mind's eye, Tanya called to him from the mission, her lips screaming, stricken and pale.

Behind him, shouts rang through the trees. A sapling suddenly split in two and he jerked to the left, ducking. The staccato reports of automatic-weapon fire echoed through the jungle and he ran forward, toward the south—toward Tanya.

What if they had taken the mission out as well? How could Americans do that? CIA, DEA. His father's words about America's evils echoed through his mind. But Father was dead.

To his right, beyond the jungle's border, voices carried to him and he realized his pursuers were running along the edge of the forest, following him on even ground. They were yelling in Spanish.

Whoever they were, they were well organized. Military or paramilitary. Guerrillas possibly. They'd come intent on killing everyone on the plantation. And now he had escaped. He should turn into the jungle and run for the black cliffs. From there he could get to the Orinoco River, which snaked to the Atlantic. But he couldn't leave Tanya behind.

Then the realization struck him again—his mother and father were dead!

Tears leaked past his eyes. His vision swam and he drew a palm across his wet cheeks as he ran, barely missing a stump jutting from the forest floor. He shook his head and steeled himself against the tears.

To his right, the voices fell away and then grew again. A shot snapped through the canopy and he realized that running parallel with them was stupid. He veered to his right, leapt over a large log, threw himself to the earth, and rolled into the log's crease until his face was plastered with rotting wood and earth.

Ten seconds later they rushed by, breathing heavily. These were jungle-trained soldiers, Shannon thought, swallowing. He stood to his feet and cut straight for the mission clearing. He ran to the jungle's edge, knelt by a towering palm, and wiped his eyes again.

The mission house lay a hundred yards directly ahead. Soldiers skirted the perimeter to his far left, yelling back and forth to the others who crashed through the underbrush. He rose, intent on running across the open field to the house when he saw them: soldiers hauling several bodies through the door.

Shannon froze. He couldn't see the faces of the victims dragged to the porch, but he knew their identities already.

Shannon moved forward slowly, aware that a buzz droned between his ears. His vision blurred and he took another step.

The tree beside him smacked, and he jerked his head to the left. A slug had splintered the bark. Shouts filled the air and Shannon spun to see soldiers along the perimeter running toward him. One had dropped to his knee and was firing.

Shannon leapt back into the trees, looked back to the house once, and ground his molars. A lump filled his throat and for another brief moment he thought it might be better if they just killed him.

CHAPTER FIVE

ABDULLAH AMIR stood in what was left of the Richtersons' plantation house and stared at the smoldering hole where the bedrooms had been a few minutes earlier. He picked up a blue-and-white china bell from an end table and shook it delicately. It chimed above the crackling flames—*ding, ding, ding.* So pretty and yet so delicate.

He hurled it against the wall, shattering it.

"The Americans have no shame."

"These were not American. They are from Denmark."

He turned to see his brother, Mudah, walk through the front door. His brother had made the trip from Iran for this occasion. It made sense—the future of the Brotherhood rested in this one plan they had hatched. "God's Thunder," they had dubbed it. And it was by all measurements a plan worth a thousand such trips.

"They might say the same about you. You've just destroyed one of their trinkets without reason," Mudah said.

"And you've just killed *them*," Abdullah said.

"Yes, but for *good* reason. For Allah."

Abdullah's lips lifted in a small grin. In many ways, they were different, he and his brother. Mudah was happily married, with five children—the youngest, a two-year-old daughter, and the eldest, an eighteen-year-old son. Abdullah had never married, which was one reason he had been chosen to spearhead this mission into South America. He wasn't as devout as his brother. Mudah lived for Allah, while Abdullah lived for political reasons. Either way, they had their common enemy. An enemy both would give their lives to destroy. Materialism. Imperialism. Christianity. America.

"Yes, of course. For Allah." He looked out the window. "So now this jungle will be my home."

"For a while, yes."

"A while. And how long is a while?"

"As long as it takes. Five years. No more than ten. Worth every day."

"If it doesn't kill me first. Believe me, this jungle can drive a man mad."

Mudah smiled. "I do believe you. What I have more difficulty believing is that the CIA actually cooperated with us."

"You don't know the drug trade. I gave them enough information to indict two drug cartels in Colombia in exchange for this one small plantation. It's not so hard to believe."

Mudah was silent for a moment. "One day *they* will find it hard to believe."

Abdullah let the comment pass. They would indeed.

"Have they found the other one?" Mudah asked.

The question brought Abdullah back to their immediate concern. "If not, they will. He killed one man. And if they don't find him, I will. We can't afford survivors. It wouldn't serve any of us."

Mudah paused and looked at Abdullah. "You make Father proud, Brother. You will make all of Islam proud."

WHEN TANYA found consciousness again, it was to the sound of *clunking* above her. She sat up groggily, thinking the night had ended with morning—the nightmare passed. But when she opened her eyes, darkness remained and she knew with a sinking dread that she had dreamt nothing.

The clunking though, that was new. She opened her mouth to scream out when muffled voices drifted into her box. Strange voices muttering foreign words. Her heart bolted and she closed her mouth.

Her body began to quake again. She grabbed her knees and willed it to stop.

The boots paused very near, maybe in the hall, and then they dragged something away, into the living room. She shuddered at the images the sound evoked and began to sob under her breath.

For long minutes she crouched, still, drifting between abstract thoughts. At one point the ache on her skull grew like a boulder in her mind, and she put her fingers into a gash along her crown. A sticky wetness she thought must be blood drenched her hair. She wondered what would happen if a spider laid its eggs in that gash up there. Mother had warned her a hundred times, "An insect's eggs can be much more dangerous than its bite, Tanya. You be careful in those rivers, you hear?"

Yes, Mom, I hear. But now I don't hear. I don't hear a thing 'cause you're dead, aren't you, Mother? They killed you, didn't they? She cried after that thought.

Her mind cleared slowly. A pain gnawed in her arm, and she ran her fingertips down to a deep cut below her elbow. Now the spiders would have two places to plant their eggs. Tanya sucked deep, suddenly aware that the air in her hole was stuffy, maybe recycled already. She could suffocate—drown in her own carbon dioxide.

She reached for the ceiling again and pushed. It might as well have been a brick wall.

Her head ballooned with pain. If she had to die, a quick death would be good. But she wasn't ready to die, and the thought of dying slowly in this black box made her cry again.

A voice called from her memory—her father in his deep, confident way, "Tanya! Tanya, where are you, honey? Come to the hall; I want to show you something." It was her first week in the jungle. She'd been ten then. Father had come ahead of her and Mother to build the house. Now, after three months they'd joined him. Three months of waiting and explaining to her American friends that yes, she was leaving them for a very long time, but not to worry, she would write. She'd written three times.

"Come here, honey." She found her father looking into the hall closet and smiling proudly.

"What is it, Papa?" He'd ushered her to the spot and squatted next to her.

"It is a secret storage place," he'd said, beaming. "Think of it as a place we can hide things."

She had peered into the dark square and shuddered. "It's so dark. Why do you want to hide things?"

Her mother had intervened then. "Oh, you never mind your father, Tanya. He's just playing out his childhood fantasies. You are not to go in there. It's not safe. You understand? Never."

Jonathan had chuckled and Tanya had skipped away, giggling. There were many more interesting things in her new surroundings than a box in the ground. In fact, her father had never actually used the hiding place, at least to her knowledge.

Except now. Now he had led his daughter down in there and left her to die. The thought stung and Tanya widened her eyes despite their blindness. All right, she had to think this through or she might do just that. She might die.

For starters, she had to find a way to move in this tiny space. If she didn't stretch her joints, they would lock. Her knees were already cramping. She sniffed at the wetness covering her upper lip and ran her wrist under her nose. The walls on either side rose a mere six inches from each shoulder, and she'd established the ceiling's proximity as maybe eighteen inches above her head. She stretched her legs out. They encountered no wall and she found her first sliver of relief. She sat like an *L* with her back against one end.

Tanya reached farther with her feet, but they struck the far end of the box. She swore. Lying down straight was out. All right think. *Think!*

Heavens, listen to me. I'm stuck down in this box and I'm swearing. I don't swear. Especially when the only person who can possibly get me out of this is God. Help me, dear Father. Please, help me!

Okay, all right. What do I do? Tanya stilled and forced her mind to work logically, one step at a time.

Father, if you will let me live, I swear . . .

You'll swear what to God? As if that would make a difference.

Just let me live and I'll do anything. Anything. I swear.

The side walls were set in dirt or concrete—she didn't know which, but either way they were going nowhere. The end walls would be the same as the side walls. The floor beneath her led to even more dirt.

It was a grave.

The ceiling had already proved uncompromising, although she had only tried force. Maybe finesse would do better. Yes, finesse.

Tanya sat up and blinked in the pitch-darkness. She should explore the entire box with her fingers. Especially the ceiling—maybe she would find a lock or a crack or some simple way out of this box.

A sliver of hope brought some light to Tanya's mind. What she needed was light in her eyes, but this was a start, she thought, and she needed a start badly. She lifted her arms above her head and began walking the rough-hewn wood with careful fingertips as if she were pretending to read Braille.

"God, help me," she breathed. "I'll do anything, if you help me. Anything."

THE THUNDER of a gathering storm cracked overhead as Shannon fled for his life. Less than a hundred meters to his rear, the shouts of men were drowned by the sky's booming voice.

The rain came quickly, in sheets, just as Shannon approached the steeper grades ascending to the cliffs. Now would be a good time to return home, he thought. Mother had said they were having seven-bean soup for supper and he loved seven-bean soup.

The thought struck him like a wedge to the forehead and ignited a string of images. His heart leapt to his throat and he sobbed, but quickly cut off his breath. Not now. Not now.

Shannon had run under these trees many times, often ignoring the path and scrambling through the jungle, laughing with Yanamamo Indians chasing his heels. Of course, those times had been times of play. The sun had been shining then, the jungle floor visible, and the foliage dry. Now the rain carried rivulets of mud down the steep slopes.

He glanced down the mountain and saw blurred figures no more than seventy meters behind. He veered off the path and lunged for the steep incline to his left. Through the steady downpour, he heard muffled shouts followed by a *Pop!* The weapons' fire came in close succession then, ripping through the air like a string of firecrackers.

His foot dug into the soft embankment and found a root. With the greenery around him crackling at the sound of flying bullets, he leapt into the jungle and began clawing his way up the incline. He crested the slope and launched himself forward, panting hard and shaking from exertion. The black cliffs rose above the canopy.

Heavy pounding drifted through the leaves behind him—the sound of helicopters. So they had joined in the pursuit! They would cut off the cliffs.

Shannon came to a full stop in a clearing at the base of the cliffs. The stark contrast between heavy green jungle and the sheer black shale towering above sparked an image of a tombstone rising from a cemetery lawn. The cliffs couldn't be climbed except in two well-marked passes.

He rested his hands on his knees and gasped for breath in the thin mountain air, thankful that for the moment the rain had ceased. The beating of blades warned of the heavy pursuit.

Shannon turned his tear-streaked face to the jungle below. He'd left them for the moment, but they would find him quickly. He had to think. His heart thumped in his chest like an overworked pump bleeding through blown seals.

The pond! He hadn't been to the water hole in over a year, but maybe he could hide there.

Shannon grabbed a handful of grass and quickly wiped the mud from his soles. Keeping his eyes on the trees, he ran parallel to the forest, leaping from rock to rock.

He had managed two hundred meters before the sound of chopping rotors pushed him back into the jungle. He jogged through the trees along the black cliffs without breaking pace, occasionally catching glimpses of the helicopters unloading men onto the cliffs.

He reached a small, muddy pond, dropped to his belly, pried his eyes to the sky, and then snaked out of the jungle. A clump of brush consisting of little more than twisted, broken reeds floated in the middle of the pond. Shannon slipped into the stagnant water, submerged himself, and swam for the clump. He surfaced in a small cavern formed by the brush and grasped a root.

Thin shafts of light filtered through the mass of broken reeds above. He spat at a large *Durukuli* lizard, closed his eyes, and shook his head at the swelling of tears in his eyes.

Voices barked around the water's perimeter. He held his breath and forced his muscles to relax. The feet padded by and passed into the brush. For the moment he was safe.

He swallowed hard as he stared past the unmoving lizard that sat flicking its tongue. The sound of sweat dripping from his chin and into the water echoed through his ears, like the passing of seconds leading nowhere. *Drip, drip, drip.*

Then images of the attack began to draw gauze over his mind again. He just wanted to go home, now. It was over, wasn't it? It was all over. He should go home before darkness drew the snakes.

But he couldn't move. He let more tears—streams of them—run over his face and he found some comfort in those tears. Nobody could see him. Soon though, he would have to do something.

Soon.

TANYA COLLAPSED to her rear end, thoroughly stuffed with dread. She'd spent long chunks of time walking the box with her fingertips. The minutes faded into hours, but they could actually have been only seconds. It was that kind of feeling: a strange confusion staring relentlessly into midnight, but knowing morning must have come. And gone.

She had found no way out.

Besides the small crack around the trapdoor, her fingers had felt only parallel lines separating exactly eight stacked boards on all four sides of this crate. She'd estimated each board at eight inches in height. That would make the box just over five feet deep and roughly the same in length. Five by five by three, she thought. A good size for a grave. Big, actually. Now the Egyptian tombs—there were some serious graves.

But this couldn't be her grave. Not really. She was only seventeen! And her father had meant to *save* her, not bury her alive! She began to cry in steady streams. Her shoulders shook with the emotion as she wept.

Oh, God. Why? What have I or my father or my mother ever done to deserve this? Why would you allow them to die? Just tell me that, if you are so loving and so kind.

She lifted a dirt-packed nail to her lips and chewed. The dirt ground between her incisors, like tiny pieces of glass that sent shivers down her back. They were so innocent, her parents. So loving and patient. They gave their lives for others. For her.

Please, Father, save me. I will do anything.

Tanya's mind began to crumble. She had come to the end of her senses. There were no more meaningful tasks to occupy her fingers. Her nostrils were stuffed with the musty smell of decay; her ears heard only weak sobs; she could taste nothing but her own leaking mucus.

A thousand pinpricks of light flashed in her forehead, like star bursts on the Fourth of July and she thought it might be because her brain was tearing loose from its moorings. Her hands trembled like those of a very old man in desperate prayer and her eyes began to ache. They hurt because they had rolled back into her skull, from where they had a better seat for the fireworks. Her mouth yawned, exhaling stale air.

Then she heard the screaming.

It started low and distant like an approaching train blowing its horn, but quickly grew to a shrill screech, as if the train had thrown on its brakes and slid uncontrollably forward.

It occurred to her that the sound was hurting her throat and she realized that the scream came from her.

She was screaming. It wasn't a yawn at all—it *was* a scream. Sometime during that scream she fell asleep. Or passed out. They were the same down here in the box.

It was then, as she lay dead to the world, that the first vision came, like a bolt out of heaven. In a single white flash, bright sky blossomed above her. The darkness was gone. And there, huddled in the box, Tanya gasped.

She was like a bird high in the sky, circling a clearing in the jungle far below. Such relief, such contentment washed through her that she shuddered in pleasure. Silent wind rushed past her; bright sky made her squint; the smell of jungle rose wet and sweet. She smiled and twisted her head.

This is real, she thought. *I've become a bird or an angel flying high over the trees.*

A yellow bulldozer snorted gray smoke as it carved a swath of trees leading to a large square field to the north. The plantation. Shannon's plantation. And directly below, the mission.

She dipped her wings for a closer look. A stick house was being built in the center of the clearing. The tall blond-headed man working there leaned judiciously over a table saw and Tanya recognized her father immediately. His bright blue eyes glanced to the sky, smiling. He lifted a hand, as if he wanted her to come to him, and then he leaned over the saw once again.

But this was all very strange. She had never seen the mission or the house before its completion. And now through a bird's eye she saw each detail. She saw that he had carefully placed the roof joists with eighteen-inch centers for added strength; she saw that one of the windows lay cracked on the floor, waiting replacement. She saw that he had rested several large timbers against the corner and now one of those timbers slipped toward him.

With sudden alarm, she realized that the timber would smash into her father, and she screeched a warning. Jonathan pried his eyes to the sky, saw the falling timber, and dove from its path with scarcely an inch to spare. Wide eyed, he rolled to his feet. For a moment he stared at the timber in disbelief, obviously shaken badly. He lifted his eyes to the bird hovering above—to Tanya—and he smiled.

"Thank you, Father," he whispered.

And then, as if speaking directly to her, he said, "Remember, always look past your own eyes."

The sky suddenly went black, as if someone had flipped a switch.

Only no one had turned out the lights. She had just opened her own eyes. And in the box there was no light.

Tanya breathed raggedly and curled up into a ball, wishing desperately that she could slip back into the bright sky where she could look past her own eyes.

CHAPTER SIX

THE SMALL cavity under the clump grew dark as dusk settled over the mountain jungle. Relentless chopper blades passed back and forth, low over the trees. Twice he heard men arguing over how to proceed. Twice they had skirted the pond, cursing.

For the past twenty minutes the air had remained quiet. Shannon had decided that he had to get over the cliff to the river beyond, and he knew where he could climb it along a narrow crack. But another image had taken up residence in his mind. It was the old shaman, eyes black and piercing, a black jaguar's fur draped over his head, tapping a crooked cane. He was mumbling in low gutturals—reciting the old legend of how man had been formed from the blood of a wounded spirit as it fled skyward, mortally wounded.

"From blood to blood," the old man's voice croaked. "Man was born to kill. It is why the spirit of death is the strongest. Sula."

A chill ran along Shannon's spine. *You were right, Sula,* he whispered.

Then go.

Shannon blinked in the darkness. *Go?*

To the grave.

His fingers trembled and he wasn't sure if it came from the cold or from this thought whispering through his mind. The grave was strictly forbidden. It could mean death. Or it could mean power, to the next witch doctor. None of his friends had ever dared venture within a thousand meters of the cave where the tribe had buried, not only Sula, but a whole line of witch doctors before him.

Shannon swallowed. But what if he could take that power and avenge his parents' deaths? Another voice whispered through his mind. Tanya's. And it was telling him not to be a fool.

But Tanya was dead, wasn't she? Everybody was dead. He began to cry again, desperate and shaking in the cold water.

He made the decision on impulse, as much out of fear and destitution as anything else. He would go to the cave.

Shannon sucked a lungful of air, submerged into the cold water, and swam for the bank. The perimeter was clear when he surfaced and stood on the grass. He ran toward the black cliffs, pushed by a numbing determination now—a singular desire to dive into the Sula's power. For comfort or for revenge or just for his own sanity, he wasn't sure, but he ran faster as he neared the old cave.

Large fruit bats beat their huge wings in near silence overhead. Insects screeched. The looming black rock cast a foreboding shadow, even in the dark, hiding the moon.

He broke out into the clearing, thirty yards before the cave, and stopped. A human skull hung over the entrance—Sula's first victim. They had retold the story at his burial amid cries that wailed through the jungle like forlorn trumpets. The skull belonged to a woman who had wandered too far from her own tribe. Sula said she had come to cast a spell on their village and he'd taken a rock to the back of her head. He'd been fourteen.

Shannon stared into the cave and fought a sudden panic crashing around his ears. He took an involuntary step back, swallowing.

"Sula," he whispered. "Sula."

A cold breeze rustled the leaves over his head, sending a chill deep into his bones. The cave looked like a dark throat. Like the cliff was actually a face and the hanging skull was its one eye, and the cave was its yawning mouth. The natives said that the cave reached an endless abyss of black space where the spirits had first lived. Hell itself.

An image flashed in Shannon's mind, and he blinked. It was Mother, screaming past the window of the house. Begging him to run for his life.

Shannon swallowed and walked for the cave. Tears filled his vision and he marched on. He felt as though he were walking over a cliff.

"Kill me." He ground the words out past clenched teeth.

And then he was stumbling forward, his head thumping with blood.

"Kill me!" he screamed. He ran for the hole, gripped by a maniacal frenzy. He scooped up a handful of rocks and hurled them into the cave.

"Kill me! Kill me!"

Shannon stopped, legs spread. He was in the face of the cave, five feet from the mound of dirt that covered Sula. The shaman's crooked cane stuck up at the grave's head, like a dagger. A bleached jaguar's skull hung on the cane—fangs white, eyeholes black.

Shannon's muscles began to twitch with horror. It was the kind that starts deep in the marrow and spreads out to the bones and burns the flesh from the inside. He knew then that coming here had been a mistake. He was going to die.

Cold wind blew past his face, lifting his long hair. A low moan pushed it through the opening, out into the silent jungle. His legs quaked and he dropped to his knees, breathing heavy now.

"Sula . . ."

Touch the grave.

He began to sob.

Touch the cane.

Shannon spread his arms wide and lifted his face to the cave's rock ceiling. His body heaved with torturous sobs that rang through the chamber.

The cane, you spineless worm! Touch the cane!

With a final cry that sounded more like a long groan, Shannon threw himself at the grave. He scrambled over the mound and dove for the cane. His hands seized the crooked pole and he fell flat, facedown, his torso hitching in soft sobs.

The power came like an electric current, silent but unmerciful.

A wave of raw energy ripped down his back, contracting it with rapid pulses that seized his lungs and bent his spine backward like a bow. His head and his feet jerked a foot off the ground, straining to reach back and complete an impossible arc. For a full five seconds, his body convulsed, threatening to snap his back in two. He could not breathe; he could not utter a single sound; he could only drown in the power that swallowed him.

And for a moment he was sure that he was indeed drowning.

With a soft popping sound, it released him and his face thudded to the dirt. His mouth was open, and he could taste the earth, but as far as he was concerned, he was dead.

TANYA SHRIVELED in the corner, unraveling. Twice now the lights had stuttered to life in her mind, each time revealing the same blue sky and the same clearing below. The images came suddenly, like the flash of a bulb hung buzzing in her brain for a minute or two and then vanishing. She imagined a monk in a monastery cellar pulling a huge switch, like on a Frankenstein movie she'd seen once at Shannon's house. Maybe that was her, Lady Frankenstein, only when the switch was pulled, her body didn't rise from the table. Instead she saw visions.

Now they came again.

Her father was down there again, working diligently, this time setting those beams that had almost fallen on him. Otherwise the scene appeared the same as the two previous episodes. A bulldozer chugged in surreal silence, the hammer swung by her father, the spinning of a saw—none with sound. And always bright blue skies and vivid green jungle. Flocks of parrots drifted above the canopy.

A voice rose to her. "Remember, always look past your own eyes." She looked down and saw that her father had lifted his chin to her. *Well, what does that mean, Father?* But she couldn't ask, because she wasn't really there with him. She was a bird or something, flying around.

But the scene had a sense of truth with it, as if she were looking at her father, months before she'd come to Venezuela. As if what she saw in the framed house was actually how he'd built it.

Now a memory joined her thoughts. She was sitting at the table of their newly constructed home and Father was telling them about how God had kept him safe those three months. And more specifically, he was telling them a story of how he'd almost been smashed by a falling beam. But a dove from the sky had screeched and he'd looked up just in time to see the beam.

It was the voice of God, he'd said.

Tanya twitched in the corner of the box and pulled her knees closer. *Heavens! That really happened,* she thought. *That wasn't part of my dream—Father told us that story. And now I'm hallucinating that it was me in the form of some bird—maybe a dove—that warned him.*

Maybe the mind played these kinds of tricks just before it died. Or maybe she was actually there, watching.

Either way, Father was telling her to *look past her own eyes.*

chapter seven

SHANNON CAME to his senses ten minutes later. But they weren't really his senses at all, were they? Well, yes, they were his, but his senses had changed, hadn't they?

He pushed himself to his knees, and then to his feet. The taste of copper filled his mouth—blood from the fall. He swallowed and shivered with a sudden passion. At first he didn't know what had changed—he only knew that he couldn't stand waiting any longer. He had to get out of this cave and up the cliffs.

The cane still stuck out of the grave, like a big toothpick. The wind still sailed past his cheeks and his breathing still echoed in the dark chamber. But somehow it all seemed a bit simple to him. He turned around and faced the jungle.

"Sula," he whispered. It was time to go. Shannon ground his molars, spit blood to the side, and ran into the night, unable to contain the hot rage that boiled through his veins.

That was it—his sorrow had given way to a bitter fury. That was the difference in him. He stopped and looked around at the dark jungle. An image of the old witch doctor, grinning with twisted lips, flashed through his mind. It was true, then. Sula lived.

Shannon felt a finger of fear crawl up his back.

A sudden dark fog crowded his mind and he blinked in the night, disorientated. Where was he going?

Oh, yes. He was going to the cliffs. He was running away. But that hardly made sense. He should go back to the plantation and do something!

No, he should escape. Then he would do something. What, he had no idea. He was only eighteen. A mere boy. A boy with Sula.

Shannon reached the black cliff, spit into his hands, and started to climb. It rose two hundred meters into the dark sky, lighted occasionally by the moon, which peered through passing clouds. Night creatures chirped in disjointed, overlapping chorus, millions strong.

Despite the cool night air, the climb quickly coaxed streams of sweat from Shannon's pores. The thin crack he'd often studied as a possible ascent path rose like a dark scar in the dim light. Using his hands as a wedge in the thin crack, he picked his way up the rock surface. With proper climbing shoes the task would have been tricky. Only because his bare feet were calloused did he manage it now.

"Sulaaaa . . ."

He'd climbed a full hundred meters without any major problems when the crack began to thin. He paused, blinked the sweat from his eyes, and pressed on.

Within another ten meters the gap closed to a paper-thin seam that stopped at a small ledge jutting from the smooth surface above. Another hundred meters of cliff loomed above him. He couldn't back down now, not without rope. A chill ran down his spine, and he breathed deep to steady his nerves.

He walked the face of the cliff with his fingers.

Nothing.

Shannon stared again at the ledge above, his heart now pounding like a piston engine. It was one foot, maybe eighteen inches beyond the nearest handhold. Reaching it would require him to release the hold securing him to the face. Missing it would send him plummeting to his death.

An image stilled his breathing: a man free-falling with his arms and legs stretched to the sky, screaming. Then a sickening *thud*—a large boulder at the base breaking the fall like a fist to the back.

The image brought a twitch to his lip. He grinned softly.

"Sulaaaaa . . ." *You're a sicko, Shannon. Sicko.*

He looked at the ledge above him. He lunged upward with every last muscle sprung taut and his toes digging against the rock. He slapped his right hand against the cliff face above him.

Nothing.

He felt only flat stone. No ledge.

His body slid down the smooth cliff surface, his fingers digging hopelessly for a grip. His fingertips lost contact with the stone surface altogether. He was free-falling and his heart ran clear up into the roof of his mouth.

Then the ledge filled his hand and he locked onto it, shaking violently. Trembling so bad that he knew he would shake loose unless he found a better hold. Dangling from three fingers, he swung his left hand up as high as he could and managed to grip the same ledge.

He hung for a few moments and then edged his way along the shelf. There had to be a way up somewhere.

He inched his way farther. Again nothing. The ledge narrowed. His fingertips crowded the cliff surface. If the edge played out . . . well, if the edge played out he would die, wouldn't he? Smashed for the vultures on the rocks below. Panic spiked up his neck, threatening to erupt in his skull. He hung totally helpless. He could not go back; he couldn't descend; he couldn't climb. His life hung on this one ledge and this time the realization started his bones quaking.

Stretched to the right as far as his arm allowed, his fingers crossed a fissure and he froze. The crack? He inched his fingers a little farther and the break deepened—deep enough for him to work his hand into.

Shannon took a deep halting breath, thrust his hand into the rift, clenched his knuckles to make a wedge, and swung out into the dark abyss before him, dangling from his right fist. His hand held.

He looked down at the bottomless drop below his feet and thrust his left hand into the opening over his right to create another wedge. He hung like that for a full minute, gasping at the night air for breath. His knuckles stung and his lungs refused to fill, stretched as he was. He began hauling himself up, hand over hand.

His knuckles were bare and his hands were slippery with blood when he pulled himself over the top. Catching his breath, he rolled to his back behind a group of boulders. Pain throbbed up his arms. He lay still, numb and confused.

Muffled voices suddenly carried on the wind. Shannon bolted upright and caught his breath.

Again, a man calling and then laughing.

Shannon crept to the boulders and edged his head over its rim for a vantage point. The night scene ran into his mind in one long stream of images. A fire bending in the breeze a hundred meters ahead, west. Two dozen faces glowing in its light. Behind them, a helicopter—no, two choppers, like buffaloes feeding on the rock. Supply packs sat scattered about the camp, propping up weapons. A single man stood on guard, hands on hips, twenty meters off.

Shannon breathed deep, knowing immediately what he would do as if his whole life in the jungle had prepared him for this one moment.

A strange beckoning called. A desire, whispering in the night, urging him forward. He swallowed, still scanning the scene before him, his blood now surging through his veins. Not so much in anger, he noted with mild surprise. A craving.

A new picture rolled through his brain, slow motion. A scene of him flying parallel to the ground, hurling his knife sidearm.

The steel flashing through the air while he was still airborne.

Bet you were surprised, huh, boy? And here you thought you were going to plug me with a bullet or two. A faint smile drifted across Shannon's lips.

Sula . . .

Then the image was gone, leaving only black sky in his eyes. He pulled his head back and blinked. He scrambled across the small clearing and soundlessly leapt over its rim. He ran around the boulders, staying low to the ground. The guard stood with his back to him, bent over cupped hands, a rifle slung on his right shoulder. The outline of a knife hung loosely at his hip.

The man turned his back to the wind, facing Shannon, his head still bowed to his hands. Shannon held his breath. A flame flashed once unsuccessfully, lighting the guard's browned lips pursed around a fresh cigarette. He would later wonder what could have possibly possessed him to go then, so suddenly, with hardly a thought. But Shannon went then, just before another flame lit the man's face.

He sprinted on his toes, directly toward the glowing face, knowing the light would blind the man momentarily, knowing the wind carried away what little sound he made. He covered the twenty yards in the time it took the guard to light his cigarette and draw deep once, with his head tilted back.

Carrying his full momentum at the man, Shannon slammed his left palm under the raised chin and snatched the man's knife from its sheath in one abrupt motion. He lunged forward after the back-pedaling man, stepped into the reeling body, flipped the blade in his hand, and jerked it across the exposed neck before the man had gathered his senses for a cry.

He hadn't planned the steps to the attack—he'd simply seen the opportunity and gone. Blood flowed from the guard's jugular, spilling to the stone. The dangling cigarette momentarily lit the man's bulging eyes and then tumbled from his lips. The guard crumpled in a heap and then flopped to his back, his boots twitching between Shannon's spread legs.

What's happened to you, man? You're a sicko.

Yeah, a sicko.

Shannon reached for the man's rifle, wrenched it free, snatched an extra clip from his belt, and ran for a large boulder ten meters to his right. He slid to his knees, panting.

No sounds of pursuit carried in the night. He quickly checked the weapon in his hands, found a round chambered, and snapped the firing selection to single shot. It was an AK-47; he'd fired a thousand rounds through one like it down on the range. From long distances the weapon could only scatter hopeful fire, but within a couple hundred meters, Shannon could place a slug wherever he wanted.

He slid up the boulder and studied the camp, no more than seventy meters away. The men still talked around the fire. The helicopters were old Bell machines, identical to the one Steve Smith used to shuttle supplies to the plantation.

A spark ignited in Shannon's mind. "You know why they never used the Bell in conflict?" Steve's voice came. "Because of the fuel tank," and he'd pointed to the pod hanging on the tail boom, just under the main engine. "That there tank's made of steel." He'd smiled. "You know why steel's no good?"

Shannon had shaken his head.

"Because steel gives off sparks. It had better stop a bullet, 'cause if the bullet goes through you're gonna have one heck of an explosion. *Kaboom!*" Steve had laughed.

Shannon drew a deep breath and lined his sights up with the exposed fuel tank under the tail boom of the old Bell. He could easily place a bullet into that skin. *Kaboom!* And what if it didn't explode? They would be over him like a swarm of bees.

You just killed a man back there, didn't you? Yeah, and you still have his blood on your fingers. You're definitely a sicko.

Shannon fought a sudden surge of nausea. He closed his eyes and fought for control. The black fog swarmed his mind. For a moment he felt disoriented, and then he was okay. He glanced around in the night. Yeah, he was okay.

He snugged his finger on the trigger, but it shook badly and he took another deep breath. He applied a little pressure to the trigger.

The Kalashnikov suddenly jerked in his arms, crackling in the calm night air.

A thundering detonation lit the dark sky, mushrooming with fire. The helicopter's tail section bucked ten feet into the air, flipped once as it rose, reached its apex, and slowly fell. He removed the rifle's butt from his cheek and gazed, open mouthed, at the sight. Then the flaming wreckage crashed to the ground, and pandemonium erupted in the camp.

Shannon quickly pressed his eye back to the sights and swung the weapon to his left. Black silhouettes jumped about, scrambling for the rifles. Shannon exhaled, lined the sights with one figure, and pulled the trigger.

The gun jerked against his shoulder. The man fell to his knees and threw his arms to his face, shrieking.

Then Shannon began to shoot on count—one, two, three, four—each time pulling the trigger, as if the dancing silhouettes were clay pigeons and he in a head-to-head contest with his father. Five, six, seven, eight . . . On all counts but one—count six, he thought—a man staggered.

When he reached the twelfth count, the firing pin clicked on an empty chamber. The guerrillas fled toward the jungle now. Shannon yanked out the spent magazine, slammed another into the rifle, chambered the first round, and swung the weapon to bear on the fleeing men. He squeezed off shots in succession, barely shifting the rifle to acquire each new target. All but one lurched forward midstride and fell to the ground short of the jungle. Only one escaped, number seventeen. Two, counting number six.

Shannon's heart hammered in his chest. Adrenaline flogged at his muscles and he staggered to his feet, his eyes peeled in the night, his fingers trembling.

He blinked. Where was he? For a horrible moment he didn't know. He was on the top.

A voice groaned near the burning, twisted wreck that had been a helicopter, and it all came back like a flood. He'd killed them, hadn't he? *Sicko Sula.*

He threw the weapon down and tore for the trees. He would go now, he thought. To the river. To safety. And then he didn't know to what.

FOR THE fourth time the switch to the strange visions had been thrown, and Tanya was floating above her house. Each time, her father had worked alone down there. Each time, his voice was the only sound she heard. Each time, it said, *"Look beyond your own eyes,"* as if it was information she needed.

Well now, what exactly could that mean? For starters, she could not *look* anywhere—she was trapped in her black box, dying. She could most definitely not look *beyond,* because there was no getting beyond the box. That was the whole problem. Father was saying look beyond, but he had locked the box. And as for the *own eyes* bit, well, she wasn't positive she had eyes any longer.

So the dream was nonsense. Unless it wasn't a dream. What if she were really seeing her father down there and he was really telling her to look? Imagine that! Now, what would that be? A vision, maybe?

Tanya heard a thumping below her, down on the ground near the house. Then it occurred to her that the sound came from her own chest, not from the dream or vision. Her breathing thickened and she might have shifted, but she'd lost touch with most of her body so she couldn't be certain. The parts she could feel moaned in protest. Her throbbing arm, her aching head, her bent spine.

If this were a vision or some episode of reality, then she should follow her father's suggestions, shouldn't she? She should look beyond her own eyes. Maybe look through the dove's eyes, if indeed this was a dove through which she peered. And what could she see? The clearing, her father, the house with all its framework.

Look *beyond.*

A thought struck her and she dove toward the house. Her heart now filled her ears. Why hadn't she thought of this earlier? If this were real, then she should be able to see the closet that Father had built. And the crate below. Her crate. Maybe she was already in the crate!

She swooped low and flew between the rafters—through the living room to the framed hall. The stick closet looked tiny without siding. The box rested in the floor, minus its trapdoor. Sure enough. There it was. Her box. Or an image of her box. Either way it didn't matter—she didn't see anything new here. Only a box that should have been labeled *The box in which I will lock up my only daughter until she dies.*

She hovered for a moment and then fluttered down into the closet—into the box. She might as well see the thing well lit. Knowing what kind of box sealed her fate might be a juicy tidbit, a welcome morsel in her last moments.

The box looked very much like the one her fingers had helped her imagine. Except one small detail. There was a hole in one end. *Father has not yet covered this one end,* she thought. *He'd better cover it. It won't do to have snakes crawling through that there tunnel, 'cause someday I'm gonna be in this box.*

Tunnel.

The image of a tunnel hit her head on, like a sledge to the forehead. Her head rang like a gong, setting off a vibration that hurt her teeth and buzzed down her spine.

Instantly Tanya awoke, wide eyed, gasping raggedly. For a brief moment she stared into darkness, trying to remember what had woken her. Then she jerked upright and spun to the wall at her back. The episode had revealed this wall as a door leading into a tunnel—she knew that now. It was the kind of door that snugged in place. She would have to pull at it, the one thing she had not attempted in her despairing hours.

Tanya whimpered and scratched at the stubborn wall. And what if the whole dream had been just that? Hallucinations spun by a despondent mind. She dug at the wood, willing her nails to find purchase. A long sliver ran under her right index fingernail and she gasped. Suddenly furious, she shifted back and slammed her right heel into the base of the wall.

It caved.

Warm, stale air filled her nostrils. It *was* a tunnel!

Quaking with anticipation, she ignored the passing thought that creatures might have taken up residence in the passage. She yanked at the twisted wall, slid it behind her, and scrambled into the earthen hole.

Like a wounded dog, she dragged herself on all fours away from the box. Away from that death crate. Where the passage led she lacked the strength to imagine, but her father had laid it in before the house had been completed. He wouldn't end it in a pit of snakes.

Tanya slopped through the muddy tunnel for a long time. A very long time, it seemed. Three times she encountered furry things that scurried off. Many times she heard tiny feet retreat before she reached them. But she was far past caring about minor details. Life waited at the end of this tunnel and she would reach it or die trying.

And then she did reach it, so suddenly that she thought someone had flipped that switch in Frankenstein's cellar again and initiated another episode. But the fresh air pouring over her head suggested that this was no vision. Night had fallen, the crickets screeched, howler moneys cackled, a jaguar screamed—she had reached the outside!

Tanya spilled from the tunnel, past wadded brush, ten paces from a river. The *Caura,* she thought. A small dock confirmed her guess. The tunnel had surfaced south of the mission, near their dock. Tanya stood slowly, forcing her crippled muscles to stretch past their newly memorized limits. Then she stumbled forward, to the pier, to a canoe still swaying in the water. The Caura River fed within ten miles into the Orinoco, which then ran toward the ocean. Toward people.

She rolled into the wood craft, nearly tipping the whole contraption over, and ripped the tie-knot free. The river drew her out into its current slowly and she flopped to her belly.

Then Tanya surrendered to the darkness lapping at her mind.

SHANNON RAN all night. Up from the cliffs to the top of the mountain, and then down toward the river that would take him to the sea and to safety. The Orinoco, ten miles downriver, over the mountain from the plantation.

The jungle lay heavy and the night dark, making his progress slow. But then it would also slow down any pursuit. He ran in silence, lost in the fog of the last day. His bones ached and his muscles felt shredded by the miles of savage terrain. The cruel ground had bruised his already calloused feet. But one thought pushed him forward: the thought that he would come back one day and kill them all. Every last one of them and any living soul that had anything even remotely to do with them. Shove a bomb down their throats maybe.

The sun already climbed the eastern sky when he finally burst into the clearing that bordered the gorge. The sound of thundering water exploded in his ears. He approached the deep valley and peered down at the torrential river as he placed a hand on the rope bridge to steady himself.

The Orinoco River had cut a two-hundred-foot swath into the valley floor. An old trail on the opposite side switched back and forth to the river below. The only way across was on the old rope bridge that swung precariously over the two-hundred-foot gap. He'd decided he was going to cross the swinging bridge, descend to the river, pick his way past the rapids, and then find something—a canoe, a large log, anything—to sail down the river.

He looked at the boards strapped together on the bridge. The wood appeared rotten—the hemp rope frayed. The whole contraption looked as though it might go into the water at any moment.

In fact, even as he looked a piece of wood split and sent a small fragment tumbling lazily to the river.

He watched it fall. He would have to watch his footing as he crossed. Then another board bucked, splitting to its pale core, as if an invisible ax had attacked the wood.

A chill flashed up Shannon's spine. It all sprang to his mind in a brief instant: the fact that the wood wasn't crumbling but being hit. By bullets!

He spun around.

The helicopter fired from a long distance—too far for accuracy—but it bore in quickly. The sound of its whirling blades was swallowed by the rapids, but Shannon couldn't mistake the flashes erupting from its nose.

For a moment Shannon stood shocked by disbelief, unable to move. In that moment another board fell to pieces, two meters from his planted feet. Two options streamed through his mind: He could retreat to the forest or he could race forward, across the bridge.

With a sudden roar the gunship spun overhead, climbed sharply, and kicked its tail around. It was lining up for a second pass.

Shannon leapt to the bridge. He grabbed the rope and scrambled down the sagging span, but the sudden movement caused the bridge to lurch wildly under his feet. In a moment of panic he almost missed the rope entirely and then found it quickly. To his right the attacking craft lined up on the bridge for another pass.

Crossing had been the wrong choice—he knew it then, when the first bullets took a chunk from the board at his feet. He should have run back to the forest. Now he stood in the open, helpless, with a cannon playing the planks like invisible fingers on a keyboard.

He was going to die!

The thought immobilized him.

THE PILOT watched the boards disintegrate before the boy and he eased the stream of lead to the right, knowing now that he could hardly miss.

"Finish him!" Abdullah said beside him.

The pilot quickly refocused his fire. The young man suddenly jerked back as if a huge hand had slammed into his chest. A spray of red blood glistened through sunlight. They had him!

He flipped backward over the rope that supported the bridge and tumbled lazily through the air, his hands limp like a puppet's. The fall alone would have been enough to kill a man, but neither of them could miss the gaping, bloody hole in the boy's side.

Abdullah groaned and the pilot blinked at the sound.

And then, far below, the body splashed into the current and disappeared.

"Around," Abdullah ordered. Sweat poured from his face. His black hair with its distinctive white wedge lay plastered against his skull. "Around. We have to be certain."

The pilot guided the helicopter around to look for the boy. But the pilot knew he was wasting his time.

The boy was dead.

CHAPTER EIGHT

Eight Years Later
Monday

"GOOD MORNING, BILL."

"Good morning, Helen. You sound good."

"I have news."

That made the pastor pause. "What kind of news?"

"It's starting," Helen said. She paused. "Evil is thick in the air and it's about to take this country by storm."

"I'm pretty sure those were your exact words eight years ago."

"I told you then and I've told you a hundred times since that the death of Tanya's parents was only the beginning."

"Yes, Helen, you did tell me. And I've prayed with you. For eight years. That's a long time."

"Eight years is nothing. God's playing his pieces in this chess match and really I think it began fifty years ago. They've been moving and countermoving for decades up there on this one."

"A chess match? I hardly think we're pawns in some game."

"Not a game, Bill. A match. The same match cast over each of our hearts. And you're right—we're not simply pawns. We have a mind of our own, but that doesn't mean God isn't telling us to move two spaces to the right or one space forward. Actually, it's more like a whisper to our hearts, but it's the thunder of heaven. It's up to us whether we will listen to that thunder, but make no mistake, he moves the match. In this case, the match started way back. And one of the moves was for Tanya's parents to go as missionaries to Venezuela. To bring truth to the Indians, yes, but perhaps even more, to bring Tanya there, so that she could become who she is."

"You honestly believe that Tanya's parents were called to the jungle, left their church with great hopes and prayers, struck off for Venezuela, lived among the Indians for ten years, and then were murdered for the effect it would have on their daughter? Who, incidentally, is not looking like a great prophet or any such thing these days."

"Yes, Bill. I do think that was one of the primary purposes in all of this. Yes, that is how God works. A missionary is called to Indonesia perhaps as much for a young boy they talk to in the airport in New York on their way out of the country, than for all the people they preach to in the next twenty years in the foreign land. Perhaps that boy is a Billy Graham or a Bill Bright. God is quite brilliant, don't you think?"

Her pastor was silent on the phone.

"But Tanya's time is coming, Bill. You will see. It's coming soon."

TANYA VANDERVAN sat flatfooted in the wooden chair, aware that her palms were sweating despite the cool air spilling from the vents mounted above. She shifted her gaze to the room's single window overlooking Denver's skyline from ten stories up, thinking that even here, within the whitewashed walls of Denver Memorial, she hadn't managed to escape the jungle. Eight years earlier she had fled a heavy jumble of green, only to be led into a tangled web of confusion in her own mind. And now she had found another jungle—these concrete structures outside her window, built up around her like a prison.

Thank God for Helen.

She moved her eyes back to the older men sitting like a panel of judges behind the long table. The medical review board of Denver Memorial Hospital consisted of these three dressed in white smocks. They knew her as Sherry. Sherry Blake. Dr. Sherry Blake, six months and counting in the hospital's intern program.

And by their frowns, six months too long, and counting far too slow. Most in the medical profession had emerged out of the stuffiness that had characterized hospitals in the seventies—these men had somehow missed the boat.

Sherry crossed her legs and nervously ran a hand behind her neck. Her hair fell in soft curls to her shoulders now—no longer blond, but brown. It swept across her forehead, above eyes no longer blue but darkened to a hazel color. The idea had been her own, five or six years ago, based on the notion that if she changed her name and her appearance, maybe then, with a new identity, she could escape her mental turmoil. Maybe then she could escape haunting memories of Shannon. The psychobabble quacks had tried to discourage her, but she'd lost confidence in them long before.

The idea had grown on her, until she'd become obsessed with altering her identity. She legally changed her name, dyed her hair, and wore hazel contact lenses. The change was so dramatic that even Helen had hardly recognized her. Comparing her high-school graduation picture to her new image in the mirror, even Tanya—Sherry—could barely see the similarities.

"What I think Dr. Park is suggesting, Miss Blake, is that there's a certain behavior becoming of doctors and other behavior that doesn't fit the image very well." Ottis Piper removed his eyes from her and peered through his glasses to the paper before him. "At least the image Denver Memorial considers acceptable. Boots and T-shirts are not part of that image."

Sherry raised an eyebrow, teetering precariously on the fence between total submission to these in white coats and bull-frank honesty.

She knew submission would bode well for her career. *Suck it up, baby. Swallow all their nasty foolishness with a yawning gullet. Tell them what they want to hear and get on with your life.*

Whatever's left of it.

Bull-frank honesty, on the other hand, might give momentary satisfaction but would most probably leave her wishing she had swallowed their nonsense after all. Unfortunately, the chill now washing over her head seemed to have frozen her mouth, and no matter how desperately part of her wanted to apologize, she could not.

"Oh? Are you dissatisfied with my work, Dr. Piper? Or is it just this image thing that has you in stitches?"

That set the gray-haired British import back a few inches. His eyes expanded.

"I'm not sure you understand the nature of this review, Miss Blake. We're here to discuss *your* behavior, not ours." His accent bit off each word precisely and Sherry found herself wanting to reach out and shove something into that mouth. A sock, maybe.

Her mind was urgently suggesting she retract herself from this insane course. After all, interns sucked up. It was a skill learned in med school. Suck-up 101.

"I apologize, Mr. Piper. I spoke too soon." She attempted a polite smile, wondering if it looked more like a snarl. "I will pay more attention to the way I dress, although in my defense, I've worn boots and T-shirts only once, last week, on my day off. I came to visit a patient who needed a hand to hold."

Director Moreland watched like an eagle from his side perch, not unfriendly necessarily, but not friendly either. Park, the last of the trio, spoke. "Just watch your dress, Miss Blake. We run a professional institution here, not a recreational park."

"Professional? Or militant? Dress isn't an issue in most hospitals anymore. Maybe you should get out a bit more."

Piper peered over the bifocals he'd mounted on his nose and cleared his throat. "It seems we have a matter of slightly greater importance to discuss. In the past two weeks you've fallen asleep three times while on duty. One of those times you missed a patient call." He paused.

"Yes," Sherry said, "I'm sorry about that."

"Oh, I don't think it's as simple as sleep, Miss Blake. I think it has more to do with the *lack* of sleep." Sherry's fingers felt suddenly cool, drained of blood. Where was the Brit headed with this?

"You see, lack of sleep is a problem with our profession. Tired doctors make mistakes. Sometimes big ones—the kind of mistakes that kill people. And we don't want to kill people, do we now?"

"What happens to me out of this place is none of your business," she said.

"Oh? You're denying you have a problem, Miss Blake?" Piper queried smugly.

She swallowed. "We all have trouble sleeping now and then."

"I'm not speaking of now and then. I'm speaking of every night, my lady."

"I'm not *your lady*, Piper. Where did you hear about this?"

"Just answer the question."

"I don't think it's any of your business whether or not I have trouble sleeping. What I do in my home is my problem, not yours."

"Oh? I see. So if you come to work sloshed, we should just turn an eye as well?"

"I'm not coming to work sloshed, am I? I intend on finishing my internship with full honors. Someday people like you will report to people like me."

"You are out of line!" Piper whispered harshly. "Answer my questions! Isn't it true, Miss Blake, that you depend on medication to keep you awake at work? For all practical purposes, you're a drug addict!"

Sherry sat speechless, trembling behind her calm facade.

"Is this true, Sherry?" the director asked from her left.

She looked past him, through the window. A horn blared in the parking lot—some patient on edge. "I'm not a drug addict. And I resent the suggestion. I've had my problems with insomnia," she said, swallowing again. For a moment she thought her eyes might water. That would be a disaster.

"But it hasn't kept me from getting this far," she said evenly.

"How long have you had this condition?"

"A while. A few years. About eight, I suppose."

"Eight years?" Park spoke again.

"How bad are the episodes?" Moreland asked.

"By what standards?"

"By any standard. How much sleep did you get last night?"

She blinked, thinking back to the restless night. An easy night, all things considering. But they wouldn't think so.

"Two hours."

"And the night before?"

"Maybe two."

He paused. "And that's normal?"

She shifted her eyes to him now. "Yes, I guess it's fairly normal."

"For seven years of medical school you've averaged two hours of sleep a night?"

She nodded. "Pretty much."

"How?"

"A lot of coffee . . . And medication when it becomes unbearable."

"So how did all this begin?" Moreland asked.

His sympathy would be her only hope now, she thought. But she'd never done sympathy well. The realization that she was lowering herself into those waters with these sharks made her swallow.

On the other hand her boat was about to capsize anyway.

"When I was seventeen, my parents were killed," she said, looking back out the window. "They were missionaries in Venezuela, among the Yanamamo. Guerrillas wiped out the mission and a plantation nearby. I was the only one who survived. They killed my mother, my father, a good friend, and his parents." She cleared her throat.

"I spent a few days locked in an underground box without realizing that it opened to a tunnel that I managed to escape through. I think I may have slept through two or three nights since." She shrugged and looked at Moreland. "The memories keep me awake. Posttraumatic stress disorder."

"I'm sorry," Moreland said. "Have you had any progress?"

"For short periods, yes. But never without relapse." Memories of therapy drifted through her mind—hundreds of hours of the stuff. Each hour spent carefully retracing her past, searching for that switch they hoped would turn all this off. They had managed to pull the shades a time or two, but never a switch.

Sherry looked at Piper and saw that his lips no longer pressed together. His eyes had softened. Maybe the human being in him was surfacing. She looked away, not wanting to see his pity.

"You lived with family after that?" Moreland asked.

"I lived with my adopted grandmother, Helen Jovic, until I went to med school. My uncle's mother-in-law, if that makes any sense. She was the most helpful despite all her antics. More helpful than all the quacks since then."

"But none of this has helped?" Moreland pressed.

"No," Sherry answered. She suddenly wondered if telling them would be her undoing. The whole hospital would be buzzing with rumors about the intern who woke up screaming each night because her parents were slaughtered when she was a kid. Poor girl. Poor, poor Sherry.

She shifted in her seat. "And if you wouldn't mind, I'd really appreciate you keeping all this to yourselves. I'm sure you understand."

"I'm afraid it isn't quite that simple." Piper, the Brit, was speaking. "I'm afraid you have more to fear from yourself than from others." Sherry faced him and saw the dispassionate look in his eyes. Heat flared up her back.

"Meaning what?" she asked.

"Meaning, irrespective of what others think or say of you, Miss Blake, the fact remains that you are a danger to your own career. And to others. A condition as severe as yours that depends on a regular dose of *uppers* will one day kill a patient, and we simply cannot have that at Denver Memorial."

"I've given my life to becoming a doctor. You're not actually suggesting—"

"I'm suggesting that you need a rest, Sherry. At least three months. We're talking about the lives of patients here, not your precious little ego. You missed a call last week, for goodness' sakes!"

Sherry felt a chill wash over her skin. Three months for what? To see one more quack? She stared at the man for a full ten seconds, thinking she was losing her mind. When she spoke, her voice held a tremor.

"Do you have any idea how many hours of study it takes to finish at the top of the class, Mr. Piper? No, I suppose you wouldn't because you finished near the bottom, didn't you?"

A twitch in his right eyebrow indicated she had struck a chord there. But it didn't matter now. She had gone too far. Sherry stood to her feet and turned to Moreland. Every bone in her body wanted her to scream, "I quit!"

But she couldn't, not after seven years in the books.

She drilled him with flashing eyes, spun on her heels, and strode from the room, leaving all three doctors blinking.

CHAPTER NINE

THERE WAS only one living soul who knew of Shannon Richterson's true fate. Only one man who knew how he'd really died eight years earlier. He knew because he, too, had come from Venezuela, farther down the same river that Shannon had fallen into after being shot. What he knew about the killers who had attacked the jungle that fateful day might have done wonders for Sherry Blake.

There was only one problem. Even if he had known about Sherry, he was not exactly the sensitive kind of guy who cared. In fact, he himself was a killer.

His name was Casius, and while Sherry was stomping out of Denver Memorial, he was standing at the end of a CIA conference table in Langley, Virginia, glaring at three seated men, suppressing a sudden urge to slit their throats.

For a brief moment, Casius saw a familiar black fog wash into his vision, but he blinked and it vanished. If they'd noticed, they hadn't shown it.

They deserved to die, and one day they *would* die, and maybe, just maybe if things fell his way, he would do the killing. But not today. He was still playing their game today.

That was all going to change soon.

He turned away from them. "Let me tell you a story," he said, walking toward the window. The thin one, Friberg, was the director of the CIA. He wore thin lips under a bald head. His eyes were dark.

Casius faced the group. "Do you mind if I tell you a story?"

"Go ahead," Mark Ingersol said. Ingersol, the director of Special Operations, was a heavyset man with slick, black hair. David Lunow, Casius's handler, just stared at him with an amused glint in his eye.

Casius met Ingersol's gaze. "Last week you sent me to kill a man in Iran. Mudah Amir. He lived in a rural house and spent most of his time with his wife and children, which made the task a challenge, but—"

"He was a monster," Ingersol said. "That's why we sent you."

Heat flashed up Casius's spine. Ingersol was right, of course, but he had no right to be right. Ingersol himself was a monster. They were the worst kind of monsters, the kind who killed without bloodying their hands. "Excuse the observation, but I don't think you know what a monster is."

"Anyone who blows up one of our embassies is a monster, in my book. Get on with it."

"You send me to kill. Does that make you a monster?"

"We don't send you to kill innocent—"

"The innocent always die. That's the nature of evil. But it doesn't take a man foaming at the mouth to fly a plane into a building. It takes a man dedicated to his war. An evil man, maybe, or a godly man. But evil is not exclusive to the Mideast. The monsters are everywhere. Maybe in this room."

"And *I'm* a monster?" Ingersol said.

Casius ignored him. He turned from them and closed his eyes. "I had to wait two days for the wife and children to leave before I killed Mudah Amir, but that wasn't the point."

He took another deep breath, calming himself. In truth if Mudah was a monster, then so was he. Yes, a monster.

"Mudah didn't die quickly." He turned back and stared at them for a few seconds. "Do you know how easily a man can be made to talk when you've removed a finger or two?" Casius asked.

"Mudah told me of a man. An Abdullah Amir—his brother, in fact. He spit in my face and told me that his brother, Abdullah, would strike out at America. And he would do it sooner than anyone might suspect. Not an unusual threat from a man about to die. But what he told me next did catch my attention. Mudah insisted that his brother will strike at American soil from the south. From Venezuela."

Director Friberg's eyes flickered, but he held his tongue.

Casius walked back to the table and rested a hand on the back of his chair. "I wouldn't bother you with the sole confession of a man about to die. But I have more."

Casius took a settling breath. "You know of a man named Jamal Abin, I'm sure."

The name seemed to still the room. For a moment they replied only with their breathing.

"It's our business to know about men like Jamal," Ingersol finally said. "There's not much to know about him. He's a financier of terrorism. What does he have to do with this?"

David spoke for the first time. "I believe Casius is referring to the reports circulated that Jamal was behind the killing of his father in Caracas."

"Your father was killed in Venezuela?" Ingersol asked. It hardly surprised Casius that the man didn't know. His history was known only by David, who'd first recruited him.

"My father was a mercenary employed in the drug wars in South America. His throat was slit in a Caracas nightclub, and yes, I believe Jamal was ultimately responsible for his death. Not personally, of course. Jamal isn't one to show his face much less kill someone himself. But now he's left a trail."

They sat there, not comprehending.

"After I killed Mudah, I searched his flat. I found a safe stashed under the bed in his room with evidence that ties Jamal to him and his brother, Abdullah." Casius pulled a folded sheet of paper from his pocket, unfolded it carefully, and slid it across the table.

"What's this?" Ingersol asked.

"A receipt for a million dollars delivered to Mudah, earmarked for Venezuela."

They studied the wrinkled sheet and passed it around. "And you're saying this *J* is Jamal's signature."

"Yes. It ties Jamal, the 'financier of terrorism' as you call him, to Mudah's brother, Abdullah. I would say that this lends some credibility to our dying man's confession, wouldn't you?"

No one responded.

"It's not really that complicated," Casius said. "Jamal is a known terrorist. I'm holding evidence that ties Jamal to Abdullah, who evidently has a base in Venezuela. I say that's a pretty strong case."

Ingersol frowned and nodded. "Reasonable."

"There's more. The safe also contained a document that detailed the location of Abdullah's base. Interesting enough by itself. But the location in question, an old plantation, was overrun by an unidentified force roughly eight years ago. A Danish coffee farmer, Jergen Richterson, and his family were killed along with some neighboring missionaries." Casius fed them the classified details and watched Friberg's eyes narrow barely.

"According to your own records, there was no formal investigation into the attack. Of course there were no survivors to push the matter either. Unusual, don't you think? I believe the information I have leads to Abdullah Amir, and I believe that Abdullah will lead me to Jamal."

Casius paused. "I want Jamal."

"Do you snoop around our files on a regular basis?" Friberg asked quietly. "Where's this document that supposedly shows Abdullah's base?"

"I have it."

"You'll turn it over."

"Will I? I want the mission."

"I'm afraid that's out of the question," Friberg said. "The fact that Jamal may have been involved in your father's death creates a personal link that precludes your involvement."

"Yes, that's your policy. Still, it's what I'm demanding. You either assign me to run a reconnaissance mission to the region, or I do my own."

"You do nothing on your own, boy." Friberg's neck flushed red. "You do what we tell you or you do nothing. Is that clear?"

"Crystal. Unfortunately, it's also unacceptable."

Casius faced Friberg down. He'd thought that it might come to this and a part of him welcomed it. He had hoped they would let him go—Jamal was a high-profile threat. But if they refused he would go anyway. That was the plan. That had always been the plan.

"Do you have the location with you?" Friberg asked.

Casius smiled, but he said nothing.

"Then you have twenty-four hours to turn it in. And don't push us."

"Is that a threat?"

"That's an order."

He had done well up until now, playing by their rules. But suddenly the heat in his head was mushrooming and the black fog was swarming. Casius felt a small tremor race through his bones.

"Good. Then I won't threaten you either." His voice was shaky and his face had grown red—he could feel it. "Just a word of caution. Don't push me, Director. I don't do well when pushed."

Silence engulfed them like hot steam. David glanced nervously at Ingersol and Friberg. Ingersol looked stunned. Friberg glared.

Casius turned and headed for the door.

"Twenty-four hours," Friberg said.

Casius walked out without responding.

It had started. Yes, it had definitely started.

CHAPTER TEN

Tuesday

ON MOST nights, Sherry read until one or two in the morning, depending on the book, depending on her mood. She would then nibble on some morsel from the kitchen and climb into bed, prepared to endure the last waking hour before sleep introduced the evening's haunting dream—the same one that had presented itself to her every night for the past eight months. The beach one.

But not tonight.

Sherry's roommate, Marisa, had come home at eight and heard an earful about Sherry's review before the board. After storming out of the hospital, Sherry had roamed the park, trying to make sense of this last wrench thrown into her cogs. She'd nearly called her adopted grandmother, Helen, but then she discarded the idea. There was no living soul wiser than Helen, but Sherry wasn't sure she was ready for a dose of wisdom.

All in all, the day had been a disaster, but then so were most of her days.

Marisa had gone to bed at ten and Sherry had curled up with a novel just after that. But that was where the familiar ended and things started going topsy-turvy.

The room lay quiet below her. That was the first topsy-turvy thing. Not that it lay quiet, but that it lay *below* her.

The second topsy-turvy thing was the figure sprawled on the armchair, with arms and legs flopping over the sides like some couch potato who'd passed out after one too many beers. But the figure was no couch potato. It was her. She was sleeping on the armchair, her chest rising and falling in long draws, her mind lost to the world. A blue blanket lay across her waist. She didn't remember anything about getting herself a blue blanket.

The third topsy-turvy thing was the clock. Because it read eleven o'clock and that figure there on the couch—Sherry—was indeed asleep. At eleven o'clock. Which was impossible.

Then another tidbit struck Sherry: She was floating above it all, like a drifting angel looking down on herself, like a bird soaring overhead. Like a dove.

Like eight years ago in the box!

A warm glow surged through her belly at the thought. If she really was sleeping and not dead from a heart attack, then this episode must be a vivid dream of some kind. Most definitely not a nightmare, which was another topsy-turvy thing, because she didn't know how to dream without having a nightmare.

And yet here she was, floating like a dove over her slumbering body at eleven o'clock in the evening!

Topsy-turvy.

Then suddenly she wasn't floating like a dove over her slumbering body. She was soaring through a bright blue sky high above an endless forest like a bat out of hell. No, like an angel from heaven. Most definitely an angel.

Wind streamed past her eyes. She heard nothing, not her own breathing, not the wind. Then she was above a jungle paradise. Flocks of parrots flapped silently, several hundred meters below.

Parrots. Jungle. And then Sherry knew that she was in Venezuela again, flying over the tropical rain forest. Her heart rose to her throat and she dipped closer to the trees. Memories flashed through her mind. Images of jogging through this forest, of swimming in the rivers and running hand in hand with Shannon over the plantation. A warm contentment rushed through her veins and she smiled.

Below her, the jungle yielded to fields and she pulled up, startled. It *was* the plantation! She recognized the rows of coffee plants as if they were still there, a week before harvest, beaded red under the sun. To her right the old mansion rose white from the fields; as she swooped to the left, she could see the mission station resting in the afternoon sun, undisturbed. Neither clearing showed any signs of life.

The sight made her tremble, hanging in the air like a dove on a string. What was this? The beginning of a nightmare after all? But even her nightmares had never played this vividly.

Then a sign of life twitched at the corner of her vision and she turned toward the shed topped by the rooster Shannon had shot. The weather vane still graced the metal building, pierced head and all. But it wasn't the rooster that had moved; it was the door that now swung open, pushed by a young man who stepped out into the sun.

Sherry spun to him and immediately drew back, stunned. It was Shannon! An adolescent with long blond hair, a reincarnation of the boy she'd lost in the jungle eight years earlier. Her heart hammered in her chest and she drew shallow breaths, afraid to disturb the scene below. Afraid he might see her and turn those green eyes skyward. She didn't know if she could manage that without breaking down.

And then suddenly Shannon did turn those green eyes skyward. He smiled at her!

Her heart stopped; her breathing ceased. Whatever body she possessed quaked in the sky. A thousand voices collided in her mind. The nerve endings in her fingers and toes rattled madly.

Then the forest rolled up beneath her, like a canvas prepared for the tube.

Sherry bolted up in the armchair, her eyes wide open, her breath now coming in quick short gasps. She jerked her head about the room.

Her mind began to connect scattered dots into an image. She was in her apartment again; drool edged down her cheek; Marisa stood over the sink in the kitchen; daylight streamed through the windows; the clock on the wall now read seven o'clock. Those were the dots, and together they said she'd just slept through the night!

And she'd had another vision. Like the one that she'd had in the box eight years ago.

Sherry stood to her feet, still trembling. The blue blanket fell to the floor. What could be the meaning of such a vision, anyway?

"Marisa?"

"Good morning," her roommate called politely from the kitchen.

Sherry staggered over to the kitchen, running her hand over her head as if that might clear her thoughts.

Marisa turned and studied her with a raised brow. "You okay?"

Sherry ran her eyes about the room, still collecting herself. "I slept through the night," she said as much to herself as to her roommate. "Without a nightmare."

Her roommate stilled her hands in the sink.

Sherry continued, as though still in her dream. "And I had a vision, I think."

Now Marisa turned to face her, quickly drying her hands on a towel. "A vision? You mean you dreamt something."

"Maybe, but it was different from the ones on the beach. It was like the dream I had in the box when my parents were killed. I was floating above all this stuff and seeing things that were real, in real time. Like the clock, it read eleven, and I was sleeping on the chair. Did you cover me with a blanket?"

"I came out to get a drink at about eleven and saw you asleep. I didn't want to wake you, so I just pulled it over you."

"Yeah, well I saw the afghan on me."

The dream came back to Sherry in full color now. She remembered the boy and she felt her heart lift. Shannon! Only that couldn't have been real time, because he looked unchanged from the last day she'd seen him.

"I saw Shannon," she said and her voice trembled slightly.

"You always see Shannon," her roommate said.

"No. I've *thought* about him a lot, but this is the first time I've seen him." Sherry sat on a stool, her mind abuzz. "And I slept through the night—without a nightmare. That says something."

"Well, I can't argue with that. Maybe standing up to Piper yesterday did some good after all."

"That's not it. Although I think I just might agree to their three-month medical leave—somehow I can't see working with them now."

Marisa dipped her hands back into the dishwater. "So you're saying this was an actual vision. Like the kind your grandmother supposedly has."

"I don't know. But this wasn't just a dream."

Her roommate raised a brow and wiped a green plate. "You actually saw Shannon this time. Really saw him, huh?"

"He was younger than he would be now. But it felt so real."

"You never saw his body . . ."

"That's what I'm saying. I actually saw him—"

"No. I mean after he was killed. You never saw Shannon physically dead."

"Please, we've been over this a dozen times. He's dead. Period. I'm not going to open up old wounds." She'd said the same many times, but the argument didn't feel as strong in light of her dream. He had been alive there, hadn't he?

"You say that, but I'm telling you, you don't have closure. How do you know he was actually killed back there, if you didn't see his body?"

"Don't be stupid." Sherry turned to the window, remembering. It had been some government man who'd told her the plantation had been overrun, the Richtersons killed. Drug infighting. "Everyone knows that he was killed."

"Then verify it again. Track it down again. Official knowledge of his death. People have been tormented for years by lingering doubts, and from what I can see, you fall into that group. You're still having dreams about him, for crying out loud!"

"I *do* have official knowledge," Sherry said.

She clenched her eyes and tried to think reasonably. The very idea that he might still be alive cut at her like a knife. A thousand hours of therapy had placed him in a small corner of her mind—always there, always vivid, but small. Now he was suddenly coming back to the surface, and she could not allow a dead past to retake her mind. It would be worse than her nightmares.

A lump the size of a boulder pressed painfully in her throat and she cleared it. "I don't want to go there again."

But suddenly she knew that she did have to go there again. If for no other reason than the fact that she'd had this crazy dream. She had to at least verify his death again. Now that the issue had risen from the grave, she would either have to live with its haunting or bury it once again. The realization blared loud like a horn.

Sherry swallowed and steeled herself against further sentimentality. God knew she had been through worse than this. Much worse.

"How would I verify it?"

"Call the government. Living relatives."

"Most of his family came from Denmark."

"Then living relatives in Denmark. Your mother was American, right? We can find an agency who tracks foreign deaths. Can't hurt."

Sherry nodded. They would only confirm his death.

chapter eleven

THE TWENTY-FOUR hours Director Friberg had given Casius to turn over his findings had come and gone. Casius had only gone. That was the problem. But then it really wasn't such an unusual problem—not with Casius.

David Lunow sat across from Mark Ingersol, gazing through the tinted window at the CIA complex, suddenly wishing he'd brought the car after all instead of riding his bicycle. An ominous black sky dumped rain over the hills of Virginia, masking the skyline. Ingersol sat stoically with greased hair and furrowed brow. The door suddenly opened and Friberg walked in. He didn't bother to apologize for keeping them waiting. He simply strode to the head of the table, sat carefully, and pulled his sleeves down, one at a time.

"So, we have a problem, I take it," he said and then looked up at David.

"It appears so."

Friberg glanced at the assassin's red portfolio that lay square in front of Ingersol.

"Suggestions?"

Ingersol spoke, "Maybe he's outlived his usefulness."

"Sir, if I may," David said, "Casius is the most active operative we have."

"*Active* is not synonymous with *useful,* David. An operative is only useful if he can follow simple directions. It appears your man has a problem with that. He's beyond control. Perhaps it's time we put him aside."

A chill spiked at the base of David's skull. *Put him aside?* They all knew you didn't just "put aside" assassins. You didn't just give killers lunch money and drop them off at the next bus stop. You eliminated killers. Otherwise they might very well end up in your own backyard, killing someone you didn't want killed.

David cleared his throat. "He's on the edge, but I wouldn't characterize him as out of control."

Ingersol and Friberg both stared at him without responding.

"I really don't see a reason to terminate him."

"I think the man has outlived his invitation at the agency," Friberg said.

David blinked. "If you'll pardon me, sir, I don't see it that way. A man who does what Casius does *needs* a kind of reckless confidence. We've lived with it for seven years."

Ingersol cast a questioning glance at Friberg and it occurred to David that in all likelihood neither of these men knew the facts about Casius. He reached for the red folder and opened it.

"We know who we're dealing with," Friberg said.

"And I know him better," David continued before they could stop him. "I knew of Casius's father—went by the name Micha. A sniper for hire who was best known for picking off half a dozen cartel bosses. When his father was killed in that nightclub, Casius was eighteen. He had his father's touch, to say the least. He came to us one year later. He had no living relatives, no property—nothing. Wanted a job. We put him through our training regimen, but believe me, Casius didn't need our training. We might have taught him a trick or two, but he was born to kill."

"He's unstable," Friberg said. It sounded more like a command. Like saying, *The trash is full,* when you really mean, *Take the trash out.*

"Actually, he's very much in control of his decisions."

"The man doesn't even distinguish between us and the people we pay him to kill. You heard him. In his mind we're all monsters."

"He's a killer. You accuse another killer of being a monster and you're accusing him of being a monster. That's understandable." David paused. "Look, very few agents have the ability to operate at his level. And with that come a few unavoidable consequences, I agree. But you don't just replace a man like this every day. We could go ten years without finding his equal."

"I don't care if it takes twenty years to find his equal—we can't afford a rogue agent digging around where he has no business digging." Friberg glared at him. "If Casius becomes a liability, we have no choice but to unplug him. I'm surprised that concerns you."

"If he becomes a liability, maybe. But I don't think we've reached that point. What if he does take Jamal out? Do we have a problem with that?"

"That's not the point. His motivation is personal and he's out of control."

"I disagree," David said.

The director turned to Ingersol. As the head of Special Operations the decision would ultimately be Ingersol's. "And you?" Friberg asked.

Ingersol pulled the red folder toward him. An eight-by-ten photo of Casius, with short black hair and bright blue eyes, was paper-clipped to the left flap. Ingersol studied the photo.

"You think you can draw him in?" he asked David.

"I can always draw him in. I'm his handler."

"Then bring him in again."

"And if he won't come in?" Friberg asked.

No one answered.

Friberg stood. "You've got another twenty-four hours," he said and walked from the room.

THE ROOM was beneath the earth, shrouded in blackness. Only one man knew its location and in reality no one knew that man. His name was Jamal. They hated him or loved him, but they did not know him.

Well, yes, there were those who knew his face and his voice and his money. But they didn't know *him*. They didn't know his loves and his desires and all the reasons why he did what he did. If they knew his passion, it was only the passion to strike out. To exact his revenge.

But then Jamal could not imagine life any other way.

A small ticking sound echoed softly through the darkness. He'd sunk the ten-by-twenty room into the earth and the water sometimes found its way through the rocks. In a way the sound was comforting. A sort of gentle reminder that the clock was winding down. The time was so close now. So very close.

The smell of musty dirt crowded his nostrils. A twenty-watt bulb glowed under a copper shade on his desk, casting a rust-colored light over the ancient wood. To his right a large cockroach skittered across the wall and stopped. Jamal stared at it for a full ten seconds, thinking that a cockroach had the best of all lives, living in its own darkness without thought for more.

He walked to the wall, snatched up the insect before it could move, and quickly pinched off its head. Jamal returned to the desk and set the roach on top of the hot copper shade. Its headless body twitched once and then stilled.

Jamal pulled on his headset and punched a phone number into the pad before him. The electronics along the wall to his right were the kind one would expect in a submarine perhaps, not here in this dungeon. But there was more than one way to remain hidden from the world and Jamal possessed no desire to sink beneath the waves every time he wanted to pull his strings. Of course, bringing the electronics here, of all places, had not proved a simple matter. It had taken him a full year to pull it off without raising suspicions.

The protected signal took thirty seconds to find its mark. The voice that spoke into his earpiece sounded as though it came from the bottom of a well. "Hello?"

"Hello, my friend."

The man's breath stilled. Jamal's voice had that strange effect on men.

A shiver rippled through Jamal's bones. "It is ready?"

It took a few seconds for the man to respond. "Yes."

"Good. Because the time has come. You will begin immediately. You can do this?"

"Yes."

"Listen very carefully, my friend. We can't turn back now. No matter what happens we cannot turn back. If anything happens that might threaten our plans, you will accelerate them, do you understand?"

"Yes."

Jamal held the man in silence for a moment. He picked the roach from the shade and pulled its wings off. The body had been slightly baked and a smell similar to burnt hair rose to his nostrils. He bit the thorax in two and rolled the one half in his mouth, allowing saliva to gather. He put the other half back on the hot shade. Only breathing sounded in his earpiece.

"Perhaps you're forgetting who you're speaking to, Abdullah," Jamal said, and then spit out the bug. "If you cease to please me, I will unmake you as easily as I made you."

"You did not make me. I did not need your interference. I could have done this without you."

A swell of black rage swept over Jamal. He blinked. "You will die, for that, my friend."

More breathing in the earpiece.

"Forgive me . . . I am anxious."

Abdullah had finally said what he had always felt, from the first day Jamal had approached the Brotherhood to give him logistical control over their plans in Venezuela. He had not come from their circles and they had questioned not only his loyalty, but his usefulness. It had taken him three months to gain their confidence and persuade them that his involvement was critical to the success of the plan. It *wasn't* critical, of course—Abdullah would have pulled it off without him. But they knew as well as he that Jamal knew too much and was too powerful to ignore. And in all reality, Jamal had altered the plan to meet his objectives. As such it was a better plan. Infinitely better.

"Please forgive me." Abdullah's voice was raspy over the line.

Jamal abruptly cut the connection.

For a few seconds he sat there, silent under the significance of what they had accomplished. A wave of heat washed through his chest. He peeled off his headset and put his face into his hands.

A mixture of relief and hatred rolled through his mind. But really it was more like sorrow, wasn't it? Deep, bitter sorrow. The emotions surprised him, and they were joined by another: fear.

Fear for allowing such emotion. He began to shake.

Jamal lowered his head and suddenly he was sobbing. He sat alone in his dungeon, trembling like a leaf and crying like a baby.

CHAPTER TWELVE

Wednesday

SHERRY'S EYES slammed open and she bolted up, her chest thumping loudly in the still morning. The sheets about her lay soaked with sweat.

For a few endless seconds the world seemed to have frozen and she wasn't sure how to make things move again. Half of her mind was still back there, in the jungle, where she'd just died.

"Marisa!"

Sherry threw the linens from her legs and swung to the floor.

"Marisa!"

The apartment echoed vacant. Marisa had already left for the university. The analog clock by her bed read 8:15, but it felt like midnight, and in all honesty, Sherry wasn't positive she was actually awake yet.

Panic swarmed around her mind. She'd come face to face with . . . what? What had she just seen?

"Dear God . . ." The prayer sounded like a groan. She ran for the kitchen and threw water on her face. "Oh, God . . ."

She had been back in the box. After eight years of nightmares, she had actually gone back. And her fingers trembled with the stunning reality of it.

Helen.

Sherry jerked up and caught her breath. Yes, of course! She had to talk to Helen!

She paced the kitchen. "Okay . . . Okay, slow down." She gripped her trembling fingers into fists and breathed deliberately. "You're awake. This is not a dream. It's morning." No, this wasn't a dream, but neither was what she had just seen. Not a dream. She wasn't sure what it was, but it was real. As real as anything she had ever experienced. As real as the box.

Sherry ran for her bedroom and pulled on a pair of jeans. Helen would know, wouldn't she? She'd had visions. *Dear God, what are you doing to me?*

Only when she pulled her Mustang into that old familiar driveway in front of Helen's two-story home did she think of calling first.

She walked to the front door and rang the bell.

No one answered. She rang again. Sherry was about to pound when the door swung open. Helen stood leaning on a cane, yellow dress swaying at her knees.

"Well, well, speak of the devil," Helen said.

"Hello, Grandma."

"You've finally decided to come."

Sherry smiled, suddenly off balance. "I'm sorry. I know it's been a while. But—"

"Nonsense. Timing is everything."

Sherry blinked. "I have to talk to you."

"Of course you do. Come, come." She shuffled back and Sherry entered. The house smelled of gardenias and the white roses Helen claimed came from Bosnia.

Sherry followed the older woman into the living room. Helen had taken her in and loved her like a daughter. But she hadn't been ready for love at first.

"Tea?"

"No, thank you."

"Do you know why I frighten you at times, Tanya?"

"Frighten me? You don't frighten me." Sherry sat and watched Helen settle into her overstuffed rocker. "And it's Sherry, remember? It was hard enough changing my name once; I have no intention of doing it again."

"Yes. Sherry. Forgive me." Helen picked up her own glass of iced tea and sipped. She set it down and looked into Sherry's eyes. A knot rose slowly up her throat. It was like that with Helen. She hadn't even said what she'd come to say, and already Sherry was feeling the significance of her presence.

"Let's not kid each other. I do frighten you at times. But then if I were in your place, I might be frightened as well."

"What place is that?"

"You're running. I ran once, you know. When I was about your age. It was a terrifying experience."

"I don't think that I'm running. I may not be as spiritual as you, Grandma, but I love God and I understand that he has his ways."

"No, you're running," Helen said. "You've been running ever since your mother and father died. But now something has happened and you're thinking twice about running."

Sherry looked at her. It was like speaking to a mirror—there was no fooling the woman. She smiled, suddenly unsure of what to say.

"I've been waiting for you," Helen said. "It's not often that God gives us visions, and when he does, they mean something."

"You know about my dream?" Sherry asked, surprised.

"So you *have* had a vision."

Sherry sat forward, excited now. "I always dream. I guess you'd call them nightmares. But now in the last two nights—"

"Tell me your vision," Helen said.

Sherry blinked. "Tell you what I saw?"

"Yes, dear. Tell me. I've been waiting a long time for this moment—I really don't want to wait any longer. You've been chosen for this and I've been chosen to hear this. So please, tell me."

A long time for this moment? Sherry looked away and settled in her chair, seeing in her mind's eye the vision as if it had just happened. A tremor took to her bones and she closed her eyes.

"I fell asleep, but then I was wide awake, in another world as bright as day. Exactly like what happened in the box. The first vision I had was two nights ago. I saw Shannon . . ."

"So he's alive."

"No. I don't think so. That's not why I came. I came about the second vision. The one last night."

She thought very briefly about the search she and Marisa had made for Shannon yesterday. Marisa had identified the International Liaison for Missing

Persons as their starting point for finding records on the Richtersons' deaths. The agency had sent them on a goose chase that had ended three hours later, on the phone with a public relations officer named Sally Blitchner. Sherry learned for the first time that, yes, there was a record of the Richtersons in Venezuela. Then she gave her a number for a man in Denmark.

The man had a heavy accent. Yes, of course he knew the Richtersons, he'd announced over the line. After all, he *was* a Richterson. The eighty-year-old man claimed his nephew had gone to the States twenty years earlier with his wife and son, Shannon. Then he'd decided that America was no longer a free country and he'd gone into the jungles of Venezuela, to grow coffee. Yes, that had been tragic, hadn't it? Should never have gone in the first place, the man said. And no, he had not heard of any living relative. They had all died. There were no survivors.

The words settled in her mind with welcomed finality. *There were no survivors.* So. Shannon hadn't survived. She'd known that all along and yet her bubble of hope had popped and her heart had dropped to her gut.

"Sherry . . ."

Sherry opened her eyes to see Helen resting, her head leaned back, eyes staring at the ceiling. Sherry took a deep breath and let the vision flood her mind.

"It was what happened last night that . . . scared me. It's not like real sleep—even though I'm asleep. I'm on a long white beach between the towering trees and the ocean's blue waters." She felt the pressure of panic rise through her throat at the vivid image, and she closed her eyes. "It's just me, standing on this long wide white beach."

She stopped.

"Please go on," Helen encouraged.

"I can actually feel the sand with my hands." Sherry lifted her right hand and rubbed her fingers together. "I could swear I was really there, smelling the salty breeze, hearing sea gulls cry overhead and the waves splashing every few seconds. It was incredible. And then I see this man walking toward me, over the water. *On* the water, like he was Jesus in that one story. Only I know he's not Jesus because he's dressed in black, with jet-black hair to his shoulders. And his eyes glow red." Sherry breathed deliberately now, feeling her pulse build momentum.

"I run behind a wide-leaf palm, shaking. I know that I'm shaking because I'm gripping the palm and its leaves are moving and I'm afraid the man might see the tree on the beach. Of course, that's ridiculous because all the trees are swaying in the breeze."

Helen remained speechless, and Sherry continued, "So, I watch the man walk right onto the beach, about fifty meters from my tree, and he begins to dig a hole in the sand with his hands, like a dog burying a bone. I watch him throwing that sand between his legs, wondering why a man who could walk on water would dig like that. And then I hear children laughing, and I think, *Yes, that's how children would dig a hole.* But as soon as I think it, real children, not just their laughter, are running onto the beach. I can't even tell you where they come from, but they're suddenly everywhere—and then adults too, thousands of them crowding the white sand, tossing balls, talking, laughing.

"But the man's still there, in the middle of all these people, digging that hole. They don't see him. And if he sees them, he doesn't show any sign of it. Then the man drops an object, like a coconut, into the hole; covers it with sand; and walks off the beach, onto the water, and over the horizon."

She continued quickly, aware that her heart now pounded steadily in her ears.

"At first nothing else happens. The people are just out there running over the sand, right over that spot. But then suddenly a plant pokes through the sand. I can actually see it grow. It just grows and the people are walking around it as if this is some everyday occurrence. They're walking around it so I know they must see the plant, or else they would step on it, right?"

Sherry paused, not really expecting Helen to answer.

Sherry felt her lips twitch and it occurred to her that most people sitting in Helen's chair would be narrowing their diagnosis to schizophrenia about now.

Her fingers were trembling and she closed them. "It grows like a mushroom. A giant mushroom that keeps growing. And as it grows, I sink to my knees. I remember that because a sharp shell dug into my right knee. The mushroom towers over the whole beach, like a giant umbrella blocking the sun."

Sherry swallowed.

"Then the rain falls. Large drops of flaming liquid, like an acid that smokes wherever it lands, pouring down in torrents from the mushroom above us." Her voice was wavering a bit. She folded her hands and struggled to sound sane.

"The drops . . . melt . . . they melt everything they touch. People are trying to leave the beach in a panic, but they can't. They just . . . they just run around in circles being pelted by these large drops—acid drops that melt their flesh. It's the most horrible sight. You know, I'm yelling at the people to leave the beach, but I don't think they can hear me. They just run through the rain and then fall in a heap of bones."

Sherry closed her eyes.

"Then I see that the acid is on my skin . . ."

Her throat seized for a few seconds.

"I begin to scream . . ."

"And that's the end?" Helen asked.

"And then I hear a voice echo around me. *Find him.*" Sherry swallowed at the lump in her throat. "That's what I think I heard. *Find him.*"

They sat in silence for a few seconds, when Sherry heard a creaking. She opened her eyes to see Helen rise slowly to her feet and hobble to the window.

Helen looked out for some time. When she finally spoke, it was without turning.

"You know, Sherry, I look out of this window often and I see an ordinary world." Sherry followed her gaze. "Ordinary trees, ordinary grass, ordinary blue sky, sometimes snow, coming and going, hardly changing from one year to the next. And yet, even though most never see it, those of us with any sense know that an extraordinary force began all of this. We know that even now that same force fills the space we can't see. But sometimes, once in a great while, an ordinary person is allowed to see that extraordinary force."

Helen turned to her now, smiling. "I'm one of those people, Sherry. I have seen beyond. And now I know that you have as well."

Sherry sat up. "I'm not a prophet."

"Surprising, isn't it? Neither was Rahab, in the Old Testament. In fact, she was a prostitute—chosen by God to save the Israeli spies. Or what about the donkey who spoke to Balaam? We can't always understand why God chooses the vessels he chooses. God knows it makes no sense to me. But when he does choose a vessel, we'd better listen to the message. He wants you to go back, dear."

"Go back?" Sherry shook her head. "To Venezuela?"

Helen nodded.

"I can't go back!" Sherry said. "I don't want to be a vessel. I don't want to have these visions or whatever they are. I'm not even sure I *believe* in visions!"

Helen returned to her chair and sat without responding.

"What even makes you think that's what this is about?" Sherry asked.

"I have this gut feeling I've learned not to ignore."

"I'm finally sleeping for the first time that I can remember," Sherry said. "I just want things to be normal."

"But you're running. You have to go."

"I'm not running! That's stupid! I want to *sleep,* not run!"

"Then sleep, Tanya." Helen was smiling gently. "Sleep and see what happens. But I have seen some things too, and I don't mind telling you that this is far beyond you or me, dear. It began long before you were trapped in a box. You were chosen before your parents went down there."

"I'm not *interested* in being chosen!"

"Neither was Jonah. But at one time, you must have agreed to this, Tanya."

Sherry swallowed. The words she had spoken in the box eight years earlier suddenly skipped through her mind—*I'll do anything.*

"It's Sherry, not Tanya," she said. "And what you're saying is crazy! I can't go back to the jungle!" Coming here had been a mistake. She wanted to walk out then. Run.

"You've been swallowed by this thing. Sleep won't be easy in its stomach. Bile doesn't sit well with the human condition. By all means, if you can stand it, sleep forever. But if it were me, I'd go."

CHAPTER THIRTEEN

Thursday

CASIUS STOOD in the blue phone booth and cracked his neck nonchalantly. "I realize you think my leaving was a mistake. Is that a threat?" Of course it was, and Casius knew it well. But the verbal sparring seemed to carry its own weight in this world of theirs. He ran his hand over bunched jaw muscles and eyed the busy street outside.

"Your not coming in is obviously a problem for them," David's voice said over the phone.

"Is it?"

"Of course it is. You can't spit in their faces and just expect to walk away."

"And why are they so eager for me to come in, David? Have you asked yourself that?"

The agent hesitated. "You have proprietary information obtained on a classified mission. You're threatening to go after Jamal on your own, using that information. I see their point."

"That's right. Jamal. The man who killed my father in a nightclub. The man who has reportedly been a funding source for some of this decade's most aggressive terrorist attacks. Who has a price of $250,000 on his head. Jamal. And now I discover that he's tied to an operation in Venezuela and you expect me to ignore it? I'm going to find Jamal and then I'm going to kill him. Unless Friberg *is* Jamal, I'm not sure I see his problem."

"You don't even know if Jamal is down there. All you know is that there's a man named Abdullah down there who may or may not have ties to Jamal. Either way, it's the principle behind it," David said. "I understand why you would want to go after Jamal, but the agency has asked you to cooperate. You're breaking rank."

"Open your eyes, David. I'll tell you this because you've always been good to me. Things aren't always what they seem. They could go badly for you in the coming weeks."

"Meaning exactly what?"

"Meaning maybe your superiors don't have your best interest in mind this time. Meaning maybe you should consider going away for a few weeks. Far away." He let the statement stand.

"What are you saying?"

"I've said it." Casius eased up on his tone. "Call it a hunch. Either way, don't try to defend me. I have to leave now."

"Does this mean you're refusing to come in?"

"Good-bye, David."

THE SUBURBAN home had been built in the fifties, a two-story farmhouse crowded by an expanding city. He'd purchased it five years ago and it had functioned as well as he'd expected.

Casius ran through the inventory quickly. He estimated the value of the contents alone at over half a million dollars. Most of it he would leave behind for the wolves. He could only afford to take what would fit in a large sports bag. The rest he would have to leave and risk losing to their searches. It didn't matter. He had millions stashed in banks around the world, most of it taken from one of his very first hits—an obscenely wealthy militant.

Casius strapped each of three canvas cash-packed straps tightly to his waist. The $700,000 would be his only weapon now. He pulled a loose black shirt over his head and examined himself in a full-length mirror, pleased with his new appearance. His hair hugged his skull in a close-cropped sandy brown matting—a far cry from the black curls he'd sported just ten hours earlier. His eyes stared a dark menacing brown rather than blue. It wouldn't be enough to throw off a professional, but the ordinary person would have a hard time identifying him as the man in the CIA profile. The money belts bulged slightly at his waist. He would have to wear his trench coat.

Casius glanced around the house one final time and lifted the bag. In an ironic sort of way, leaving so much brought a warmth to his gut. It had all come from them, and now he was giving it back. Like flushing the toilet. The system that had spawned men like Friberg was no better than Friberg himself. He wasn't sure which he hated more, Friberg or the sewer he had crawled from.

But that was all going to change, wasn't it?

Casius left the house, tossed the bag in the rear of his black Volvo, and slid behind the wheel. The dash clock read 6 P.M.—nearly twelve hours had passed since his call with David. They would be coming soon. Once the CIA discovered his absence, they would follow him carefully, knowing full well that he would kill whoever got in his way.

And kill he would. In a heartbeat. He glanced in the rearview mirror and turned the ignition key. The car rumbled to life. Killing David Lunow might be a problem—he had actually grown to like the man. If there was anyone on the globe he might call a friend, it would be him. But they wouldn't send David. It had been five years since the man had seen the killing end of any weapon. No, it would be contract killers. By leaving he was practically screaming for a bullet to the head. A chill ran up his spine and he grinned softly.

Casius shoved the stick shift forward and eased the car out of the long driveway, scanning for surveillance as he left the three-acre lot behind. Of course they knew where he was headed—but they would not know his route.

He reached the lake twenty minutes later. A deserted pier stuck over the water like a rickety old xylophone. The moon lit a thin multicolored sheen of oil that rested on the surface. Casius quickly removed heavy wire cutters from the trunk, snipped the chain strapping the gates together, and eased the black car onto the pier. He withdrew the black sports bag and started the car toward the polluted water.

The last bubbles popped through the surface three minutes after the car's plunge. Only a wide hole in the water's oily film showed for the vehicle's passage. Satisfied, Casius slung the bag to his shoulder and jogged toward the city—toward the crowded streets.

Within half an hour he'd hailed a yellow cab. "Airport," he instructed, climbing behind an Asian driver.

"Which airline?" the man asked, pulling into the street.

"Just the main terminal," Casius answered. He pulled the bag against his leg and gazed out the window. He had covered his bases. There was no way for them to trace him now. They would scour his house of course, but they would find nothing.

He was going down into the jungle and one way or another he would put Jamal to death.

CHAPTER FOURTEEN

Friday

THE GOOD news was that Sherry slept long and hard that night.

The bad news was that her sleep was filled with a hollow scream that could only have been shaped in hell itself.

Sherry doubled over on the sandy beach, throat raw and wailing.

Oh, God! Oh, God, save me! Oh . . .

She was running out of breath and panicking and unable to stop her shrieking. She was dying—a slow death caused by the acid that sizzled on her skin. The pain raged to her bones, as if they had been opened and molten lead had been poured into them. All around her the people were crying and toppling onto the sand, skeletons.

Sherry bolted upright in bed, still screaming. The room echoed with her hoarse voice and she clamped a hand over her mouth. She breathed heavily through her nostrils, eyes peeled at the soaked bed.

She wasn't dead.

The vision had come back. Stronger this time. Much stronger.

"Oh, God," she whimpered. "Oh, God, this is worse than the box . . . Please . . ."

Helen!

Sherry didn't bother brushing her teeth or dressing. She threw her bathrobe on and ran for the car.

Helen answered on the second knock, as if she'd been waiting.

"Hello, Tanya."

Sherry walked in, still trembling.

"You look a bit ragged, my dear." Helen looked her over and then walked for the living room. "Come on, then. Tell me again."

She walked in and sat.

"You did not like the bile, I take it," Helen said.

The bile?

Helen must have seen her expression. "The stomach of the whale. Jonah. The acid."

"The bile," Sherry said. She dropped her head and began to cry.

"I'm sorry, my dear," Helen said gently. "Really, I am. It must be painful. But I can assure you that it won't end. Not until you go."

"I don't *want* this!" Sherry cried.

"No. But you're not sweating blood yet, so I suppose you're all right."

Sherry stared at her through blurred vision, at a loss for what she could possibly mean. "I can't go through another night like that, Grandmother. I mean . . . I really don't think I can. Physically."

"Exactly."

"This is *mad!*"

"Yes."

Sherry lowered her head and shook it. Helen began to hum an old hymn and after a while it had a settling effect on Sherry.

Wiping her eyes, she lifted her head and studied the older woman.

"Okay. So what you're saying is that God has chosen me for some . . . some purpose. I have to go back to the jungle. And if I don't he'll torment me with these . . . these . . ."

"Pretty much, yes. I doubt he's the one doing the tormenting, but he isn't getting in the way. It seems that you're needed."

"Do you have any idea how absolutely stupid this all sounds?"

Helen looked at her for a few seconds. "Not really, no. But I've been through a bit."

"Yeah." Sherry's mind swam at the thought of returning to her past.

"I don't see how that would be possible," Sherry said.

"Why not?"

"For one thing, the place was overrun by soldiers! Who knows what's there now."

Helen nodded. "Father Petrus Teuwen is there. Petrus. Not where your parents were, but in Venezuela, on a mission station farther south, I believe. My husband knew him well when he was a boy. I talked with Petrus yesterday. He's an exceptional man, Tanya. And he would welcome you."

A small buzz erupted between her ears. "You talked to him? He knows about this?"

"He knows some things. And he knew of your parents."

"So you're really suggesting I pick up and go down there?" Sherry asked incredulously.

"I thought I said that yesterday. You weren't listening?"

"For how long?"

"Until you have had enough. A week, a day, a month," Helen said.

"Just up and fly all the way to South America for a day? It takes a full day just to get down there."

Was she serious? Of course she was serious! Maybe God was calling her as he had called her parents nearly twenty years ago.

But the irony of the thought. Helen was right. Sherry *had* spent eight years running from her past and now she was suggesting Sherry just step back there. Like it was some kind of booth at a fair she could walk in and out of at will. But it wasn't some booth—it was the house of horrors and the last time she'd gone in there the lid had locked shut.

But then that was Tanya Vandervan. She was Sherry Blake. The changing of her identity suddenly struck her as absurd. Goodness, her mind couldn't see what her hair or eyes looked like. The mind was on the wrong side of the skull, where the visions and nightmares wandered around at night.

The silence was stretching.

"You're free to go now that you've left the hospital," Helen said. "Do you think this is by chance? Think about it, Sherry."

She did. She thought about it, and the thought that returning might bring justification to her leave of absence from the hospital felt strangely warm. "So just buy a ticket and show up on Father Teuwen's doorstep?"

"Actually, I'd get word to him. But basically, yes."

Sherry sat for a long time and tried to wrap her mind around this call of God's. But the more she thought about it, the more its madness faded.

She spent most of the day with Helen, who took it upon herself to make some phone calls. Sherry mostly sat in the big armchair, crying and asking questions and slowly, ever so slowly, warming to the idea that something very, very strange was happening. God had his purposes, and somehow, she had been pulled into the middle of them all.

DAVID LUNOW sat in the director's office with legs crossed and palms wet. He had been brought in to discuss Casius, of that he was sure. The large desk Friberg sat behind was made of a wood that reminded him of oak. Of course, it couldn't be oak—oak was too cheap. Probably some imported wood from one of the Arab countries. Two high-backed chairs faced the desk. Mark Ingersol sat in one, David in the other. He couldn't remember spending so much time with the brass.

Friberg dropped the phone in its cradle and stared at them without expression. He stood up and walked to the tall window behind the desk.

"No word?" Friberg asked.

"No," Ingersol said.

"Then we move. Quickly," Friberg said, facing them. His jaw muscles flexed. "Under no circumstances can we allow this man to live."

David blinked. "Sir, I'm not sure I understand why he poses such a threat. He's off on his own, and I can understand your frustration with his pigheaded attitude, but—"

"Shut up, Lunow," Friberg said quietly. "The only reason you're sitting where you are now is because you know the man better than anyone else. You played a part in his leaving and now you'll play a part in his elimination. You're not here to express your reservations."

Heat flared up David's neck. The warning Casius had spoken on the phone rang through his head.

"Of course, sir. But without knowing more, I'm not sure I can be effective. It seems he knows more than I do about what's going on."

"He's after Jamal," Friberg said. "And to get to Jamal he's going through Abdullah Amir. That's all he knows and it's all you need to know."

"I'm not sure that's all he knows. He at least suspects more."

"Then we have even more reason to take him out."

David sat quietly now. He'd stepped into deep waters, that much was now clear.

"Perhaps it would help if we knew your concerns," Ingersol said. "I'm just as much in the dark here as David. Casius has become a liability, but I'm not sure either of us understands just how much of one."

Friberg turned back to the window and leaned on the ledge. He spoke out to the lawn. "I don't have to tell you that this is 'need to know' only. And as far as I'm concerned, you're the only two who need to know." He ran a hand over his balding head. "Casius has inadvertently stumbled into an operation we were involved in eight years ago." He turned back to them. "We know about Abdullah Amir. We know about his compound, and suffice it to say we can't allow Casius to compromise our position in Venezuela because he has some hairbrained notion that Jamal is involved."

Ingersol shifted in his seat. "We have an operation involving Abdullah Amir?"

"It was before your time, but yes. Let's leave it at that. Under no circumstance is Casius to reach that compound. Am I making myself clear? We pursue him at all costs."

David sat stunned. He wasn't sure they knew what they were getting into with Casius. He'd never known a more dangerous man. The man was born to kill. "I'm not sure pursuing him is the best option, sir."

"Because?"

"He may do more damage defensively than he would otherwise."

"It's a risk we'll have to take. This man of yours may be good, but he's not God. And now that you've blown our chances of dealing with him cleanly I need your recommendations for bringing him in."

David ignored the comment and considered the request.

"I'm not sure you can bring him in, sir. At least not alive." He lifted his eyes to Ingersol. "And there certainly aren't any operatives I'm aware of who could kill the man easily."

"That's ridiculous," Ingersol said. "No man is that good."

"You can try," David said. "But you better take the cavalry with you, because there's no way a single man will have a chance against Casius in his own backyard."

Ingersol turned to Friberg. "I've already alerted all our agents south of the border. We have eyes in every major town in the region. Why can't we insert two or three teams of snipers?"

David answered, "You could, but I doubt he'd ever give them a shot. You have to remember, the guy grew up in the region. He knows the jungle down there. His father was jungle trained, a sniper himself. Trust me, Casius would put his father to shame." David shook his head. "I still think going after him will be a mistake. You'd have a better chance taking him once he reemerges."

"No. We waited once; we won't wait again!" Friberg's face blotched red. "I want Casius dead! I don't care what we have to send in there after him; we send it all. I want some strategic options for a takeout here, not this quibbling over snipers. You just tell me how we can get to this guy and let me worry about the execution."

"What about sending troops, David?" Ingersol asked softly. "If you don't think snipers can reach him—what about cutting him off?"

"Troops? Since when does the CIA order troops around?" David asked and immediately regretted the question. Ingersol's left eye twitched below that slicked-back hairline, as if to say, *"Get off it, David. Just answer the question."*

"Yes, well supposing you could get troops, they would have to be Special Forces. Jungle trained with combat experience. You insert them in a perimeter around this plantation Casius is presumably headed for and you might have a shot at him."

"We can do that," Friberg stated flatly. "How many do you think it will take?"

"Maybe three teams," he replied uncomfortably. "Provided they're jungle trained. I think he'd have a hard time getting around three Ranger teams. But it won't be pretty."

A new light of hope seemed to have ignited behind Friberg's eyes. "Good. I want specifics on my desk in three hours. That's all."

It took a moment for Ingersol and David to realize they had been dismissed. David left with words buzzing through his head. They weren't Friberg's words. They were the words spoken by Casius a day earlier and they were suggesting he go away for a while.

Far away.

CHAPTER FIFTEEN

"HELLO, MARISA. Sorry to wake you. I missed you last night and I woke early."

"It's okay. I just got up. Where are you?"

Sherry hesitated and shifted the receiver. "I had the . . . vision again last night—" Her voice broke and she cleared her throat.

The phone sat silent at her ear.

"I'm leaving for a few days. Maybe a week. Maybe longer, I don't know."

"*Leaving?* Where are you now?"

"Well, that's just it. I'm at the airport. I'm going to Venezuela, Marisa."

"You're doing *what?*"

"I know. It sounds crazy. Like going back into the snake pit. But I had this talk with Helen, and . . . well, there's a flight that leaves at eight. I have to be on it."

"What about passports or visas? You can't just hop on a plane and take off, can you? Who are you staying with?"

"My parents got me dual citizenship, so actually, yes—I can just hop on a plane. I'll be there in twenty-four hours. It's just a trip, Marisa. I'll be back."

The phone went silent again.

"Marisa?"

"I can't believe you're actually doing this! It's so sudden."

"I know. But I'm going. Something's . . . going on, you know? I mean, I don't know what, but I've got to go. For my own sanity, if nothing else. Anyway, I wanted you to know. So you don't worry."

"Don't worry? Sure, okay. You're going back into the jungle to look for a boyfriend who's been dead for ten years, but hey—"

"This isn't about Shannon. I know he's dead. This is different. Anyway, I've gotta get to the gate."

Marisa sighed. "Watch yourself then, okay? Really."

"I will." Sherry smiled. "Hey, I'll be back before you know it. No big deal."

"Sure you will."

CHAPTER SIXTEEN

Sunday

"I DON'T *know, but I don't think it's about the boy," Helen said.*

"It never was about the boy," Bill replied. "Besides, I thought he was dead."

"Yes. So they say. But it's not about Tanya, either. Not really."

"So you've said. Tanya is a Jonah, and it's really about Nineveh."

"I know, but I'm not sure it's about Nineveh anymore either."

"So now we don't even know who the players are in this chess match of yours?"

"We know who the players are. They are God and they are the forces of darkness. The white side and the black side. What we don't know is which players they are prodding and whether those players will actually move. But I have this feeling, Bill. The black side doesn't have a clue about what's really happening. This is an end run."

"As long as the players cooperate."

Helen was silent for a moment.

"Have you ever wondered what kind of man embraces evil, Bill?"

"What kind of man? Every man. What do you mean?"

"I mean, what kind of man would kill others?"

"Many men have killed others. I'm not sure I follow."

"It's just something that's been gnawing at me. One way or another Tanya is going back to confront the same evil that killed her parents. I was just thinking about what kind of evil that was. That drove those men. And I think you're right . . . I think it's the same kind of evil that's in every man. But not every man embraces it."

"And the death of Christ destroys it."
"Yes. The death of Christ. Love."

THE VALLEY would have looked like any other valley in Venezuela's Guyana Highlands, except for the black cliffs jutting to the sky. As it was, the stark contrast between the green jungle and the sheer rock served as a reminder to the Indians that the men occupying the valley were men with black souls. Death Valley, that's what they now called the region that had only eight years ago been occupied by messengers of God.

In a fortified complex within the mountain at the plantation's northern border, Abdullah Amir sat with folded arms, like a sentinel overseeing his brood. A shock of white split his black hair at the crown, accentuating a sharp nose that jutted from a naturally dark face. His eyes glistened black, casting the illusion that no iris, only pupil, had formed there. His right cheek blistered with a long scar rising from the corner of his mouth.

The room he occupied was nearly dark, plain, with stained concrete walls. But mostly it was damp and smelly. The smell came from the large black insects in the room. He had long ago given up with the bugs, and now hundreds of them occupied all four corners, climbing over each other to form small mounds, like hanging wasp nests. Not that he minded them. In fact, they had become like companions to him. No, he didn't really mind them at all.

What he did mind was Jamal. Or more pointedly, Jamal's orders—he had never actually met the man. As far as he was concerned, Jamal had hijacked his plan and was taking the glory for it. Yes, Jamal had made improvements, but they were not critical. It hardly mattered that he was a highly respected militant in the Mideast. He was not here, in the jungle where the plan was hatched. He had no business controlling anything.

Abdullah sat in a metal folding chair and gazed through a picture window to blazing lights illuminating the processing plant one story below. Three large vats used for cocaine refinement stood like swimming pools against a backdrop of five chemical tanks strung along the far wall. Beyond the concrete wall, two helicopters sat idle in the hangar. The operation ran like a well-oiled machine now, he thought. Here in the jungle where the days ticked by with only cicadas keeping cadence.

Sweat leaked down his temple, and he let it run. His life had been a living hell here in the jungle, but by Jamal's tone, that would soon change.

A fly crawled lethargically across his forearm. He ignored it and let his mind fall back to the first time Jamal had made contact.

Abdullah had come to this coffee plantation as part of a well-conceived plan the Brotherhood had plotted years before his arrival—a plan that would eventually change history, they were sure of it. It was brilliant for its simplicity as much as its extravagance. They would develop links within the drug trade south of the United States and exploit the traffic routes for terrorism. South America was certainly much closer to the United States than Iran. And for the kind of acts they had in mind, close was critical. The whole world had set its focus on North Africa and the Middle East after Osama bin Laden's rampage anyway. South America was a far safer home for such an extraordinary plan.

After spending two years in Cali, Colombia, Abdullah had struck his deal with the CIA to occupy this valley.

And three years after that, Jamal had entered his world. Jamal, an unknown name then, had somehow persuaded the Brotherhood to let him take control of the plan. He had the money; he had the contacts; he had a better plan.

It was then that Abdullah had begun the construction of the underground fortress, at Jamal's insistence, of course. Abdullah had already built a perfectly sufficient building, yet he had been forced to scrap it in favor of Jamal's plan.

Hollowing the caverns from the mountain near the plantation had been a harrowing experience in the terrible heat and humidity. And keeping the operation undercover meant they had to get rid of the rock without alerting air or satellite surveillance. The CIA had agreed to allow them a modest drug operation—not one that necessitated the hollowing of a mountain. The CIA had no clue what they were really up to.

They'd moved 200,000 tons of rock. They had done it by drilling a three-foot tunnel right through the mountain and depositing the dirt in the Orinoco River far below in the adjacent valley.

Using the same tunnels to deliver the logs to the river had been Jamal's idea as well. Everything, always, Jamal's. It wasn't the plan itself that bore into Abdullah's skull; it was the way Jamal held him by the neck. The way he toyed with him, demanding this and questioning that. One day Abdullah would have to kill the pig. Of course, he would have to find him first, and finding him might be harder than killing him.

A knock sounded on the door.

Abdullah answered without moving. "Come in."

A Hispanic man with an eye patch entered and closed the door. "Excuse me, sir."

"Yes?"

"The shipment is under way successfully. Three logs bound for Miami."

Abdullah turned his head slowly and looked at the man. He'd put the man's eye out for insubordination—questioning his orders about how long the men should work harvesting down in the fields. Jamal had called earlier that morning—it had been a bad day.

Abdullah turned back to the window without responding.

"We will ship again in two days," Ramón said.

"Keep an eye out, Ramón," Abdullah said.

The man hesitated. "Sir?"

Abdullah faced him quickly. "I said keep an eye out, Ramón. The spiders may try to eat us soon."

From the corner of his eyes Abdullah saw Ramón glance at the wall. After a moment of silence the man spoke again. "Jamal made contact?"

Was it so obvious? "We will send them soon. Many people will die. Let us pray that Jamal is among them."

"Yes, sir."

Abdullah resumed his stare out the window. For several long minutes they remained silent, looking down at the idle cocaine plant. It was like that out here in the cursed jungle, Abdullah thought. The world was an empty place. Damp and hot and crawling with spiders, but as empty as a deep hole. Like this prison of his.

At times he even forgot about Yuri's little toys far beneath their feet. "You may go, Ramón."

"Yes, sir."

The man left, and Abdullah sat still.

FIVE HOURS later and one hundred miles to the east, a cool wind whipped around the bow of a seven-thousand-ton lumber carrier pushing through choppy waters with powerful twin Doxford diesels. As far as the eye could see, whitecaps covered the sea.

Moses Catura, captain of the *Lumber Lord*, strained his eyes through the misty windows that surrounded the pilothouse. They should have been in sight by now. The evening pickups were always the worst. And in choppy waters they were nearly impossible.

"Andrew. Where the heck are the buggers?" Moses yelled through an ancient-looking intercom mounted on the wall beside him.

For three years they had guided the massive Highland Lumber transporter across the Caribbean Sea to the southern ports of the United States—over a hundred trips in all. Andrew burst through the door of the pilothouse. "One mile to port, sir. It's going to be a tough one. Wind's picking up and the tide is heading back in. I'd say if we don't get to her within half an hour, she'll be pulled back."

"Right. Twenty degrees to port." Moses barked the command into the ear of the pilot beside him, then turned and yelled down the tube, "Full steam ahead." He turned to Andrew. "Get the crane ready. How many are there?"

"Three, all grouped together so they look like one blip on the receiver." Andrew smiled. "Nothin' like a little lumber on the side, eh, sir?"

"Get going, Andrew, or you won't see a dime." Andrew slammed the door and dropped to the deck below.

The captain turned on the fog lights and gazed ahead as the huge ship slowly turned. The frequencies for the transmitters on each log had been received eight hours earlier and programmed into the homing screen that Andrew kept in his cabin. Only he and Andrew knew the stray logs contained shipments of cocaine. To the rest, the logs were just valuable lumber that they were paid handsomely to keep their mouths shut about. Most of the crew were old-timers who figured the captain deserved a few extra dollars from the smuggled lumber. Of course they didn't mind taking their share either.

Moses spoke into the intercom. "How close?"

"Two hundred meters, sir. Five degrees should do it."

"Five degrees port," Moses yelled into the pipe.

"Seventy-five yards. Just a hair starboard," Andrew barked.

"Full stop. Two degrees starboard."

The large cargo vessel shuddered as its massive twin screws thrashed in reverse. Andrew plucked each log from the ocean with the large crane and swung them carefully to the aft hold where uncut logs were transported.

Fourteen minutes later the *Lumber Lord* steamed at full power north, leaving the gray coastline of South America in its wake. Moses smiled and turned toward the comfort of his cabin. Just a few more trips and he would retire.

chapter seventeen

CASIUS HAD left New York under the alias Jason Mckormic and arrived twenty-nine hours later in Georgetown, Guyana.

Except for a single black bag, he carried nothing. He'd deposited $400,000 in a safe-deposit box at the Mail Boxes Etc. on the corner of Washington and Elwood—three miles from the airport in New York. Another $300,000 rested in the watertight money belts that clung to his waist under a suffocating coat. Thirty-seven hours had droned by since he'd abandoned his car to the lake, most of it crammed into window seats aboard four separate jetliners.

The yellow taxi he'd hailed at the airport slid to a stop on the gravel road by the pier. His mind hummed as if it remained at thirty thousand feet.

Casius tossed two hundred pesos over the seat and climbed out. Two cargo boats hugged the dock a hundred meters off, each loading for departure to the northern port of Tobago. From Tobago, their fruit cargo would be sold throughout the Lesser Antilles within the week. Passage would take either boat within two miles of Venezuela's coastline just north of the Guyana—on the Venezuela border.

An old man with crooked black teeth squinted at him lazily. Casius nodded and smiled gently. "Señor."

The man grunted and looked on.

Casius's deeply tanned skin favored him in this environment, as did his khakis. But the crowd serving these boats was a rough one. He spent an hour roaming the pier, mixing in and passing by the ships as if he belonged.

He boarded the larger of the cargo boats on his third pass, during an especially boisterous argument over a spilled load of bananas, found a deserted cabin belowdecks that looked by the mess as though it had been used for the drying out of frequent drunks, locked the door, and slid under the bunk.

Midafternoon, the boat left the harbor under full power. Twice in the night men tried to open the door to the cabin. Twice they retreated mumbling angrily. By midnight, the boat ran just off the borders of Venezuela.

Casius peered from the window into a dark, pouring rain. He focused his eyes through the rain but couldn't see the coastline. The thought of swimming in the dark now made his stomach turn.

He flipped the latch that secured the porthole window and pushed out. Layers of hardened varnish gave way with a snap. The window swung out to sea, immediately inviting gusts of wet sea air through the opening. He checked the gear he'd strapped to his bare body one last time—the money belts were cinched around his waist and one change of clothes was sealed in the black bag. The coat, the khakis, the shirt, and the shoes he'd worn on the flight would go out the window before him. Didn't need them.

He stepped up onto a chair, tossed the bundled clothes out into the wind, and eased his body through the opening, headfirst, facing the stars. He pushed himself out until he hung only by the backs of his calves. With one last look into the sea, he kicked his legs free of the porthole and flipped backward into the cold, dark water.

The water crashed about his ears and then he heard only the churning screws from the ship. Blackness hung in the depths below him like deep space and visions of sharks whipped through his mind. He clawed for the surface and shook his head against a sudden panic. The ship ran into the night, leaving him in the white foam of its wake. Casius struck out westward.

He swam for two hours. Three different times, when the rain thinned, he found himself swimming parallel to the distant shore instead of toward it. The waves were high and the rain annoying but the land steadily approached and Casius swam steadily toward it. When the beach finally came, it was a welcome relief.

Casius slogged from the water and sank to the sand twenty meters from the jungle wall. Trees with long vines towered along the perimeter, their menacing arms stretching out in the predawn light. He stood to his feet, adjusted the wet money belts, and walked to the edge of the black forest. He took a deep breath through his nostrils, spit to his right, and stepped once again into the jungle.

If he was right, the CIA would be waiting for him already.

SHERRY BLAKE watched the helicopter twirl toward the sky, shoving gusts of wind in wide dusty circles. Her hair whipped about her face and she lowered her head until the air settled. To her left a jungle airstrip ran along the barren valley floor, carved by a freak of nature itself, not by human hands. The location was a natural choice for the station. Had it not been for the Richtersons' plantation twenty miles north, her father might have chosen this spot fifteen years earlier.

When she looked up, Father Petrus Teuwen was smiling broadly and looking at her with raised eyebrows. She liked him immediately. Bright white teeth filled his mouth like piano keys. His black hair rested long on his cleric's collar. Sherry doubted he'd been to a barber in four months.

"Welcome back to the jungle," he said. "I'm sure you must be tired."

Sherry let her eyes wander over the jungle line a hundred meters off. "Yes," she replied absently.

The trees stood tall with moss-covered vines stringing below the canopy. Green. So much dark, rich green. As the chopper's beating dwindled, the jungle noises came to her. A background of cicadas screeching nonstop, parrots calling against songs of a dozen louder hooters. The branches of a towering tree shook. She watched a furry, brown howler monkey poke its head out and study the mission.

The scene streamed through her mind, pulling her heart to her throat, and for a brief instant she wondered if she was in one of her nightmares, only in three dimensions.

"Boy, this brings back memories," she said, bending for her bag.

"I'm sure it does. Here, let me take that."

Sherry followed him toward a long structure she assumed was the station house, although it reminded her more of a dormitory. A simple tin roof covered the creosote-darkened building. The father turned to her. "I don't get much farther north, actually. Most of my work is with the southern Indians. Your parents worked among the Yanamamo up north, Helen tells me. I heard what happened. I'm so sorry."

She glanced at him and saw that he was indeed sorry. She smiled. The noises about her still rapped at her memories, and for the hundredth time since leaving the Denver airport, she wondered if this whole idea had been misguided. What could she possibly do in the jungle? Oh, yes, the vision. She had come because of the vision.

But the vision seemed a thousand miles away. It struck her as an absurd whisper barely remembered. Flying over the endless forest in the helicopter, she had decided she would leave when the chopper returned to the station again in three days. She would give this whole dream thing three days. And only because she had no choice in the matter. She could not very well step from the cockpit, glance about the mission, and climb back in, could she? That would look ridiculous. No, she would have to wait until the next trip.

She swallowed and willed her heart to lower from her throat. "And what did you hear, Father?"

"I heard that drug bandits attacked your mission. And if what the Indians say is correct, the valley is still occupied."

She looked up, surprised. "Now? You mean these people have never been brought to justice? I was told that they were!"

"It's not necessarily occupied by the same people who destroyed the mission compound, but drug merchants work in the area. The law isn't exactly swift in the jungle. Neither is the government. Half of them are partners with the drug lords. It's a sizable portion of the economy. I imagine the church raised some noise in the beginning, but memories pass quickly. Some battles are hardly worth fighting."

They came to the house and the father veered to the door on the far right. "Here we are." He went in ahead of her and set the bag in the room. "This is where you'll stay. It's not much, but it's all we have, I'm afraid."

Sherry glanced through the door and saw that it contained a single cot and a bathroom. "This will be fine. You wouldn't happen to have a drink, would you? I'd forgotten how hot this place gets." She waved her hand against her throat like a fan.

"Of course. Follow me." He led her to the middle door, which opened to a sizable living room and a kitchen beyond. The smell of kerosene filled her nostrils. Like her home eight years earlier. *God, what are you doing to me?* She plopped in a chair and waited for the father to bring her the glass of lemonade. Like the glass that had crumbled in her own hand eight years earlier. *Dear God.*

Afternoon cicadas were singing outside. It sounded like a death mass. She smiled at the priest and drew the cool drink past her lips.

"Thank you."

He sat across from her and said, "My pleasure."

She crossed her legs. "So, who told you about the attack on our mission?"

He shrugged. "The mission board, I suppose—five years ago when I first arrived."

"Did they mention the plantation next to the mission?"

He nodded, his smile now softening so she could barely see his white teeth. "They said the bandits were most likely after the fields there. The way I understood it, the mission was simply in the way." He looked out the window with a faraway stare. "From what the Indians have told me, I think that must be right. They wanted the plantation for their drugs and took the mission with it. That's what happened from man's perspective anyway. It's hard to know what God had in mind."

"And what have you heard about the plantation owners?" she asked, feeling sweat run down her blouse. "The Richtersons."

"They were killed." He looked at her. "As far as I was told, no one survived. In fact, I only learned of your survival from Helen, several years ago. I knew Helen's husband. He was with some soldiers who came to our village in

World War II. His leader killed a girl I knew very well. Nadia. Perhaps Helen told you about Nadia."

"Yes, she's told me the story."

"I was there," the father said. "Nadia was my friend."

"I'm sorry." Helen had asked her to read the book her husband had written about the episode, but she never had. "So the Indians told you Shannon was killed?" she asked. "They saw his body?"

"Most of what I have heard is hearsay. But, as far as I know, yes." He smiled apologetically. "But I'm sure I don't need to tell you that. Again, I'm terribly sorry."

"It's all right, Father. I've come to terms with my parents' death."

Father Teuwen eyed her carefully. "So if you don't mind me asking, Sherry. Why *have* you come to the jungle after all these years?"

Sherry lowered her eyes to the floor. The sound of a barking dog filtered through the thin walls. And then the dog was yelping as if it had been hit by a hurled stone or the flat of a hand maybe.

"It may sound strange, but actually Helen convinced me that I should come. Because God called me." She nodded, thinking about that. "Yes, because God called me."

She lifted her eyes to his and saw that he had both eyebrows raised—whether in eagerness or in doubt she could not tell. "Do you believe God speaks, Father?"

"Of course God speaks." He lifted a finger and cocked his ear. "Listen." She listened and she knew he meant the jungle sounds. "You hear that? That's God speaking now."

She smiled and nodded. "But do you believe he speaks specifically to people today?"

"Yes. I do. I've seen too much of the supernatural out here"—he motioned outside—"to doubt that it flies about us every day. I'm sure he speaks to the willing ear now and then."

She nodded approvingly. He was a wise man, she decided.

"Well, it feels very strange to me, I can assure you. Not only am I being peppered with memories that frankly scare me to death, but I'm supposed to find answers in the midst of them all." She shook her head. "I don't feel very spiritual, Father."

"And if you felt very spiritual, my dear, I might worry for you. It's not your duty to feel predisposed to any clear message. Think of yourself as a vessel. A cup. Don't try to guess what the Master will pour into you before he pours. Only pray it is the Master who pours. Then be willing to accept whatever message he wishes to fill you with. It's his to fill, Sherry. You only receive."

The words came like honey and she found herself wanting more. She uncrossed her legs and shifted back in her seat. "You're right." She looked away. "That makes so much sense. God knows I need things to make sense now."

"Yes. Well that's both good and bad. If your life made too much sense to you, you might forget about God altogether. It is man's most prolific sin—to be full of himself. But your tormenting has left you soft, like a sponge for his words. It's your greatest blessing."

"Suffering a blessing? I've suffered a lot."

"Yes, I can see that. Christ was once asked why a blind man had been born blind. Do you know how he answered? He said the man had been born blind so that God would one day be glorified through it. We see only the terrible tragedy; he sees more. He sees the ultimate glory." He let that sink in for a bit, but she wasn't sure how far it was sinking.

"When you're finished, Sherry, you will see that many were affected for the good because of your suffering. And because of your parents' death. I'm sure of that."

Now the words washed through her chest with warmth and she felt her heart rise. Somehow she knew that a volume of truth had just entered her mind.

She dropped her eyes, hoping he would not see the moisture there. "Sherry," he said. "Sherry Blake. I thought your last name was Vandervan."

"It used to be."

"And you changed it?"

She nodded.

He waited for a moment, regarding her with those kind eyes. "I think that when this is through, Sherry, you will embrace your past. Every part of it. You have done the right thing in coming here. A part of history rests on your shoulders."

For a few long moments neither spoke. It sounded absurd. What could this lost corner of the jungle have to do with history? Sherry sipped her lemonade without looking directly at him, and the father studied her. Then he smiled and clapped his hands, startling her.

"Now, young lady, it's growing late and I'm sure you have a lot to think about. I have some supper to fix. Feel free to rest or wander about the station—whatever suits your fancy. We will eat in an hour."

He turned to the kitchen and pulled up his sleeves.

Yes, she liked the father very much, she thought.

chapter eighteen

Monday

THE JUNGLE came back to Casius like thick honey—slow at first but then with sudden volume.

The roots tore at his feet until he found his rhythm, jogging with a certainty that allowed him to place his feet where he wanted. Vines slapped at his face until his eyes adjusted to the shadows of the night. The creatures screamed about him, pricking at his nerves until he managed to shove them to the bottom of his mind. When daylight streamed through the canopy, he picked his pace up considerably, and he lost his thoughts to memories of the past.

He had lived a lifetime in the years since leaving this land, and in truth he hadn't escaped it. He had lived for this day. A hundred missions had led to this one. He would live or he would die, but in the end, those responsible for his father's death would die with him.

The thoughts pounded through his mind with the cadence of his footfalls. He knew more than anyone at the CIA, including Friberg, could possibly suspect. In fact, he knew more than Friberg himself knew. And knowing what he knew, he would be surprised if they didn't hunt him down with Special Forces. The stakes were too high to rely on agents. They would take no chances, and David would tell them that meant sending in jungle-trained forces.

It was midmorning before Casius emerged from the jungle on a rise that fell slowly to the Orinoco Delta. A village below housed a small population of fishermen who also ran cargo and passenger boats up and down the river for extra income. Casius carefully wiped the calf-high mud from his legs with wet leaves and unstrapped the bag still lashed to his back. He donned a pair of shorts, and over them, slacks. Then he slipped into a pair of light brown loafers, put on a large loose-fitting, wrinkle-free shirt, and covered his head with a baseball cap. He shoved a pair of sunglasses into his shirt pocket, buried the plastic bag that had kept the clothes dry, and headed for the small village in the distance.

Casius approached a pontoon boat tended by a fisherman who sat scrubbing its hull. "Excuse me. Can you tell me how I might find a fare to Soledad?" he asked.

The man stood from the boat and regarded him. "You are a tourist, no? You like feeshing? I catch a very large feesh for you."

"No fish, my friend. I need a ride up the river."

"Si, señor. Two hundred pesos. I tek good care of you."

"You've got a deal," Casius said.

The fisherman ordered two quickly appearing sons around as if he had just been appointed the general of an army, and readied the boat in five minutes flat. Ten minutes later he piloted the screaming forty-horse Evinrude upriver toward the small but relatively modern town of Soledad. Casius sat near the rear, studying the passing jungle, arms crossed, his gaze fixed, a thousand thoughts spinning circles through his mind.

ABDULLAH WALKED into the concrete shipping room and saw Ramón bent over one of the logs prepared for the night's delivery. The Hispanic man caught his look and nodded, still speaking to the worker who stuffed the hollowed log with cocaine bags. Across the room, conveyor chains ran into the mountain toward the large pipe that would deliver the log into the river far below. Abdullah walked up behind the two men and peered at their work.

The shipping method had been Jamal's idea and thus far they had lost fewer than ten logs to stray currents. The logistics were simple: Fill the buoyant Yevaro logs with sealed cocaine, shoot the lumber through a long, three-foot pipe that ran through the mountain to the Orinoco River, and collect the logs when they spewed into the ocean, two hundred miles east. The river delivered with unwavering consistency, spewing its littered waters into the ocean unceasingly. Homing beacons attached to each log assisted the pickup. The logs had passed into American lumberyards without incident for five years now. The tree's thick bark hid the panel cuts exceptionally well, rendering detection virtually impossible.

"How many tonight?" Abdullah asked, and the worker started at the sound of his voice.

"Three, sir."

Abdullah nodded in approval. "Follow me, Ramón." He walked for the elevator, inserted a key for the lower floor, and stepped back. The car ground down to the restricted basement.

"You know our world will change now?"

"Yes."

"And you are prepared for whatever changes this might bring?"

"What changes do you anticipate?" the soldier asked carefully.

"Well, for one I suspect this place will soon cease to exist. We can't expect them to sit by idly. The world will come apart, I think."

Ramón nodded. His one good eye blinked. "Yes, I think you are right."

The bell clanged and Abdullah stepped from the elevator. The laboratory door was closed at the end of the hall. He eyed it without approaching.

"We must clear the surrounding jungle of any possible threat," he said absently. "There is only one base within a hundred-mile radius of the plantation. I want it occupied immediately."

"The Catholic mission."

"Yes. I want it under our control. Send a team to neutralize the compound. And I want it done cleanly. You will attack the station tomorrow night."

"Yes, sir."

"Leave me."

Ramón retreated into the elevator and the door closed.

APART FROM Ramón and Abdullah, only Yuri Harsanyi even knew of the lower floor's existence. And Yuri knew it intimately, like a mouse would know its hole in the wall.

He wore a white lab coat, starkly contrasting with his jet-black hair that rested raggedly above his otherwise plump, pale face. "Stocky" was a word he'd decided appropriately described his build. Stocky and large. Six foot three, to be exact. It was why he tended to bend over the tables, and now his body seemed to have taken a liking to the posture.

The nature of his mission demanded he remain hidden in the basement at all times, wandering hunchbacked between the white laboratory and his adjoining living quarters. The floor housed several other rooms, but Yuri had been out to the perimeter rooms only twice. His own quarters provided all the comfort he could expect here. Besides, as far as he was concerned, the more time he spent in the laboratory, the sooner he would finish his task. And the sooner he finished his task, the sooner he would be off to begin his new life, wealthy this time.

The walls about him were white. Four workbenches holding two lathes and two molding devices lined the walls. To Yuri's right, a door led to his living quarters, and next to the door, Plexiglas sealed off a ten-by-ten room. A single chrome refrigerator-sized safe stood in the room's center, facing a single table loaded with computers.

But Yuri's focus rested on one of two steel tables dead center on the lab's concrete floor. Brackets on each table gripped oblong objects—one the size of a football, the other twice that size. Both sat with opened panels, staring dumbly at the ceiling. Bombs.

Nuclear bombs.

Yuri stood with his arms crossed as he gazed at the shiny steel objects. He felt a buzz of contentment ring through his chest. They would work. He knew without a doubt that the bombs would work. A simple collection of exotic materials fashioned in perfect harmony. He had transformed them into one of the most powerful forces on earth. To find a party who would pay a hundred million for the smaller device would not be so difficult. Yuri had thought of little else in the last six months, and with the completion of the project at hand, the pressure he felt to make a decision seemed unbearable.

The skimpy salary Russia had driveled his way for so many years would be tip money. Socialism had its price, he had decided. Not even the Politburo should expect to breed the world's most brilliant nuclear scientists without rewarding them adequately. And now it was time to pay up. He smiled at the thought.

A fly took flight from the overhead light and buzzed past Yuri's ear before settling on the larger sphere.

For him the phone call almost seven years ago had been the voice of an angel. Why the Russian Mafia had chosen him he hadn't cared to ask. All he knew was that they had offered one hundred thousand dollars up front, in cash, an additional ten thousand each month, with a million-dollar bonus upon the completion of the project. That and the small detail that the project was for the Brotherhood, a militant Islamic group. Others had talked of getting jobs in the free world, but no other nuclear scientist could hope to make even one-hundredth of the offer. He had accepted unreservedly.

Securing the basic elements had taken three years, years during which, in all honesty, Yuri felt more like a captive than a scientist. But filling his shopping list, as he referred to it, took time in the new world.

Although their timing was right; if the Brotherhood had waited until after Bush had gone after Al qaeda and clamped down on proliferation as his administration had, the task would have been much more difficult. The Clinton years had been the right time.

The list was simple enough: Krytron triggering devices, high-grade detonators, high-yield explosives, uranium, plutonium, beryllium, and polonium. Along with scores of hardware items, of course.

Clinton years or not, one didn't walk into a hardware store and pick up initiators filled with beryllium and polonium. Weapons inspectors' discovery of Iraq's extensive nuclear program had brought about the tightening of the reporting required by the Nuclear Nonproliferation Treaty. And it wasn't just the plutonium and uranium that were carefully guarded, it was any component required for a nuclear device.

Case in point, a nuclear detonation requires absolutely perfect timing between the shaped charges surrounding the plutonium. Forty perfectly timed explosions, to be exact. If even one of the forty was off by the tiniest fraction of a second, the bomb would fizzle. Only one very rare triggering device could offer such precision: a Krytron device. And only two companies in the world manufactured Krytron triggering devices. Yuri needed eighty of them. Unfortunately, each was reported to a governing body and carefully tracked.

He could have gone for a new triggering mechanism, but the chances for failure would have increased considerably. No, he needed the Krytron devices and they alone took two years to secure, and then only because of the former Soviet Union's black market, which had its share of disgruntled officers willing to turn a blind eye for $100,000. The world's supplies of beryllium and polonium were as tightly monitored. The focus was always on the radioactive elements, like plutonium, but in reality the plutonium had been the easiest. There was a lot of it around and with his contacts in the Russian Mafia, he had secured it in less than six months.

Bottom line, all of the necessary elements could be obtained, assuming money was no object. Yuri wasn't sure where these men got their money—drug trade, oil, who knew—but they obviously had what it took. All the items he'd requested eventually made it into the jungle.

And now it was time to take them out of the jungle.

Of course, there was the small matter of Abdullah, and Abdullah was no one to play with. His heart was the color of his eyes, Yuri thought. Black.

Yuri walked over to the larger of the two weapons, a fission device roughly three times the yield of the Nagasaki device. To modern standards the design itself was basic, very similar to that of the first bomb. But there was nothing simple about the sixty-kiloton explosion it would create.

A black sphere rested in the opened panel, measuring thirty-five centimeters in diameter. It was dotted with forty precisely spaced red circuits with a wire protruding from each, giving it the appearance of a hairy fruit. To the front of the sphere sat a white receiver and a small collector. The outer housing shone silver—polished aluminum—no more than an expensive case for the black bomb inside. The large fly crawled over that shiny surface and Yuri reached a hand out to chase the insect off.

Four years and untold millions and now the prize: two shiny spheres with enough power to level a very large city. Yuri walked over to the supply cabinet and stepped into it. A wide range of small tools lined three of its walls. He knelt down, pulled out a brown wooden chest, and opened its lid. There lay his ticket to $100 million—two black spherical objects, identical in appearance to those in the nuclear devices. If he proceeded now, his fate would be sealed. He would either become a very wealthy man or a very dead man.

Yuri swallowed and willed his hammering heart to be still. One of those cursed flies lighted on his hair and he impulsively smacked at it, stinging his ear badly. He wiped his sweaty palms on his thighs, lowered trembling hands into the box and withdrew the smaller sphere. "Please, God," he whispered faintly. "Let this one last thing go in my favor." Of course that was ridiculous, because he no more believed in God than he believed he would live if Abdullah discovered him.

Yuri stood, shoved the door shut with his foot, and carefully carried the black ball to the metal table on which the smaller device sat. With a final glance toward the entrance, he began the swap.

The idea was simple, really. He would take the nuclear explosives out of their casings and replace them with identical-looking explosives that contained only air. When Abdullah did get around to exploding his little toys, they would not even spark. The nuclear explosive would be safe with Yuri. It was his creation—he should reap the rewards. Let the man deploy his imitation bomb. By the time Abdullah discovered the malfunction, Yuri would be halfway around the world with two very valuable devices for sale.

He completed the swap in under five minutes. Holding the volleyball-sized nuclear sphere in sweaty fingers, he returned to the closet and eased the orb into the brown crate. Then he repeated the entire procedure with the second sphere. He sealed the lid and stood as a shiver snaked up his spine. So far so good.

He took a mop and rested it on the lid, thinking the crate might not draw as much attention in such an attitude. On the other hand, the mop normally rested on the floor like any mop. Seeing it propped up so high might actually draw Abdullah's attention. Yuri returned the mop to the floor and chided himself for being overcautious. Wiping the sweat from his brow, he closed the closet door and stepped back into the lab. He would transfer the spheres to his suitcase later that night and take it with him to Caracas on his leave in the morning.

Yuri stood with his hands hanging loosely at his sides, breathing deeply, calming himself, and looking at the tables before him. The two aluminum cases looked as much like nuclear weapons as they had thirty minutes earlier. Only a trained eye would notice the small variations. So then. He had committed himself.

The bookcase to his left suddenly scraped along the floor and Yuri started. Abdullah? He leapt over to the tables and quickly scanned for any forgotten screw, a loose bolt—anything that might alert the Arab. He brought his sleeve across his face and picked up an idle voltage meter.

Abdullah entered the laboratory frowning, his jaw jutting below gleaming black eyes. He wore a pointed frown that seemed to ask, "So what have you been up to, my friend?" A chill washed through Yuri's skull.

"They are finished?" Abdullah asked.

"Yes, sir," Yuri answered. He cleared his throat.

The Arab stared at him without changing his expression for a few long seconds and Yuri felt his palms grow sweaty. Abdullah stepped forward. "Show me the remote detonation procedure again." He walked over to the table and glared over Yuri's shoulder. "Show me everything again," he said.

"Yes," Yuri answered and hoped the man could not feel the slight tremble in his bones. "Of course, sir."

chapter nineteen

SCATTERED LIGHT bulbs lit the darkening coast when the pilot finally cut the outboard to a gurgle and coasted the small boat to a rickety dock bordering the river town of Soledad. Casius paid the man his two-hundred-peso fare and made his way into the town toward the Hotel Melia Caribe. From a dozen trips downriver with his father, he knew it was one of three hotels in which one could expect to see tourists venturing this deep into the land.

The moment Casius stepped into the lobby his eyes rested on a pale, lanky man studying a newspaper in the corner. The man's eyes lifted and met his own. They held for a moment and then returned to the paper. Casius glanced about the room and quickly decided the man was the most likely prospect for a CIA agent. He returned his gaze to the man, willing him to look up again. If the man was an observer, fingering Casius with short brown hair and dark eyes might prove a challenge. But any man with his profile would be reported, and Casius wanted Friberg to know that he had spotted them as well. The man's eyes had grown still; he was no longer reading.

The man glanced up again and met his gaze. Casius nodded and winked. Recognition passed between them. His jaw firm, Casius turned and walked to the front desk, keeping the man in his peripheral vision. So Friberg had reacted quickly as expected. Forty-eight hours and they already had men in place.

He took a room on the second floor. He ruffled the bed, cracked a few drawers, tested the shower—leaving the shower curtain pulled—and wet a towel. Satisfied that the room looked used, he slipped into the hall. The back stairs led into the lobby below, but an old wooden fire escape led into an alley behind the hotel. Casius climbed through the fire escape, dropped into the alley, and made his way down the dark passage. No sign of the agent.

He walked through alleys to a small shop on the south side of the city. The gray cinder blocks splashed with dirty white paint looked unchanged from his last visit to this alley. Casius stepped up to the shop's back entry door, found it unlocked, and stepped into Samuel Bonila's gun shop.

He paused in the entryway, letting his eyesight adjust to the dim light.

"María?" a gruff voice called.

Casius stepped into the lighted shop and eyed Samuel evenly. The man blinked and returned the gaze.

"What are you doing?" Samuel demanded. "We do have a front door for customers. And we are closed."

"You are Samuel Bonila?" Casius asked, knowing the answer.

The man hesitated.

"I'm not going to hurt you," Casius assured him.

"Yes, that is my name. And who are you?"

"My father was known to you, Mr. Bonila. A foreigner who knew how to shoot. Perhaps you remember him?"

"A foreigner who—"

Samuel suddenly stopped and stared at Casius, searching. "You are . . . ?"

"Yes."

The storekeeper blinked and took a step forward. "But I can't see the resemblance. You've changed. You're nothing like the boy I remember."

"Time changes some people. I need you to keep my coming here to yourself, Mr. Bonila. And I need to purchase a few knives."

"Yes, of course." He glanced to the door. "You have my full confidence." He smiled, suddenly pleased. "And you will be needing a gun? I have some very fine imports."

"I'm sure you do. But not this time. I need two knives."

"Yes, yes." He took one more long look at Casius and then hurried to a case behind him.

Casius left the shop five minutes later with Samuel mumbling behind him. Ten minutes later he checked into a cockroach-infested joint that had the gall to call itself a hotel and took a room on the third floor. He shed the money belts, withdrew five thousand dollars, and hid the rest in the ceiling above the bathroom mirror. It had been over twenty-four hours since his last sleep. Exhausted, he fell onto the bed and slept.

He awoke six hours later to the sound of insects shrieking in the nearby forest as the city slept in silence. Without lighting the room, Casius splashed water on his face and stripped to his black shorts. The jaguar tattoo blackening his thigh would give him away in the jungle so he covered it with a wide band of medical tape. He withdrew a tube of camouflage paint from his pouch and applied the green oil to his face in broad strokes. It was a habit of stealth that successfully masked his face beyond possible recognition.

He shoved the bowie knife he'd purchased from the gun shop into the back of his waistband and strapped the Arkansas Slider around his neck. The waist pouch and the rest of his clothes he shoved under the bed.

Dawn broke over Casius's shoulder as he left the city on foot and entered the towering jungle. The plantation lay thirty miles due west. It would take him a day and a half to circle the valley and make an approach from the south. The route would add another thirty miles to the journey, but he'd decided the strategic advantage of the longer course outweighed the inconvenience. For starters, the CIA would expect him to take the quickest route now that he had been spotted. But more importantly, the cliffs would be relatively easy to guard. A southern approach, on the other hand, consisted of a hundred thousand acres of heavy jungle inhabited mostly by Indians. It would be more difficult to protect.

As he passed their nests, macaws and herons took flight—squawking at his intrusion into their world. Twice he stopped in his tracks as thousands of brightly colored parrots scattered to the skies, for a moment blacking out the rising sun. Spider monkeys gazed down, screeching at him. The air felt clean; the vegetation glistened with dew. Everything was untouched by human hands here. His bare feet were quickly covered with surface cuts but his pace remained unbroken. During the next thirty-six hours he would sleep only once, for a few hours. Otherwise he would stop for food—mostly fruits and nuts. Maybe some raw meat.

He grunted and cracked his neck as he ran. It felt good to be in the jungle.

CHAPTER TWENTY

Tuesday

SHERRY BLAKE awoke from her first night of sleep in the jungle with a start. The vision had reoccurred. In terrifying colors and screaming sound.

It took her a few seconds to understand that she was in the mission house, alive and well—not on a beach trying to dig a hole in the sand to escape the acid. She ripped the damp sheet from her legs and reached the door before realizing she wore only a loose, oversize T-shirt. She wasn't in her apartment with Marisa, for heaven's sake. She was in the jungle with the priest. She returned for a pair of shorts and her shoes.

Outside, the jungle was shrieking its way into another day, but the noise in Sherry's mind came mostly from the people on the beach, as the acid rain fell from the mushroom, like brown globs of searing molasses. She shook her head and pulled on the boots.

When Sherry entered the common room adjacent to her sleeping quarters, Father Teuwen had already perked coffee and fried eggs for breakfast. "Good morning," he said, beaming a smile. "I thought you might enjoy—" He saw her face and stopped. "Are you all right?"

She lifted a hand to her hair, wondering what he saw. "Yes. I think so. Why?"

"You look like you saw a ghost. You didn't sleep well?"

"Like a baby. At least my body slept like a baby. My mind decided to revisit this crazy vision I keep having." She plopped onto the couch and sighed.

The father brought a steaming cup to her and she thanked him. "Yes, Helen mentioned them," he said.

She sipped at the hot coffee and nodded. "I think I might prefer a whale to this."

Father Teuwen smiled and sat opposite her in an armchair. "Even Jonah eventually decided that speaking the truth was better than the whale."

"And if I *knew* that word, I'd be all mouth. Here we are talking about messages from God and yet I don't have a message, do I? Not even close. All I have is some dreadful vision that plagues me every night. Like a game show in the heavens, daring the guest to crack some absurd riddle."

"Patience, my dear." His voice was soothing and understanding. "In the end, you will see. Your path will lead to understanding."

She leaned back and stared at him. "And maybe I don't *want* to go down this path. God is love—so where's all the love?"

He crossed his legs and spoke deliberately. "The path between the natural and the supernatural—between evil and good—is not such an easy path, Sherry. It's usually accomplished with things like death. With tormenting. Why do you suppose Christianity waves a cross on its flag? Do you know how cruel the cross was? You would think there might be a simpler, more humane means for God to bring about the death of his Son. But before fruit can grow, a seed must die. Before a child is born, a mother must wail. I don't see how a few sleepless nights is such an impossible price," he said, still smiling.

Sherry set the cup down, spilling a splash of coffee on her thumb. "A few sleepless nights? No, I don't think so, Father. I wouldn't call being locked in a box while your parents are butchered above you and then living through eight years of nightmares a few restless nights!"

The priest didn't flinch at the words. "Let me tell you a story, Sherry. I think it may bring this into perspective for you.

"One day not too many years ago, near the end of World War II, a common man—a doctor—was detained and brought to a detention camp with his wife. His twelve-year-old son was in the safekeeping of his grandmother, or so the doctor thought. In reality his captor, an obsessed man named Karadzic, had also found the boy. Bent upon breaking the doctor's spirit, they placed the man in a cell adjacent to two other cells—one holding his wife and the other holding his son. Of course he did not know his son was in captivity—he still thought he was safe with his grandmother.

"The wife's and son's mouths were strapped shut and each day all three were brutally tortured. The doctor was told that the screams from the cell on his left were his wife's screams, and those on his right were the screams of a vagrant child, picked from the streets. He was told that if he ordered the child's death, both he and his wife would be spared, and if he refused, they would both be killed on the eve of the seventh day.

"The doctor wept continually, agonizing over the groans of pain from his wife's cell. He knew he could spare her with the death of one stray child. Karadzic intended on dragging the son's body in after the doctor had ordered his execution, in the hopes of breaking his mind.

"But the doctor could not order the child's death. On the seventh day both he and his wife received a bullet to the head, and the boy was released." The priest paused and swallowed. "So the doctor gave his and his wife's lives for another, not even knowing it was that of his own son. Does this seem fair to you, Sherry?"

Sherry's head swam in the horror of the tale. Another emotion muddied the waters of her mind—confusion. She didn't respond.

"We don't always understand why God allows one to die for another's life. We don't easily fathom God's Son's death. But in the end"—he swallowed again—"in the end, Sherry, we will understand what Christ meant when he said that in order to save your life you must lose it."

Petrus looked away and shrugged. "Who knows? Maybe my parents' death saved me for this day—so that I might speak these words to you."

Sherry dropped her jaw. Father Petrus was the boy? "You were—"

The priest looked back to her and nodded, smiling again. "I was the boy." Tears wet his cheeks and Sherry's world spun. Her own eyes blurred.

"One day I will join my parents," the father said. "Soon, I hope. As soon as I have played my role in this chess match."

"They both died for you."

He turned away and swallowed.

Her chest felt as though it might explode for him. For her. She had lived through the same, hadn't she? Her father had died for her above that box.

The father had found love. Love for Christ. In some ways, she had as well.

"What is it with death? Why is the world filled with so much violence? Everywhere you turn there is blood."

He turned back to her. "In living we *all* eventually die. In dying we live. He has asked us to die. *Take up your cross and follow me.* Not a physical death necessarily, but to be perfectly honest, we of the West are far too enamored with our own flesh. Christ did not die to save us from a physical death."

"That doesn't remove the horror of death."

"No. But our obsession with life is as evil. Who is the greater monster, the one who kills or the one who is obsessed with their own life? A good strategy by the dark side, don't you think? How can a people terrified of death climb up on the cross willingly?"

The statement sounded absurd and Sherry wasn't sure what to make of it.

"In the great match for the hearts of men, it isn't who lives or dies that matters," Petrus said. "It's who wins the match. Who loves God. We each have our part to play. Do you know what the moral of my parents' story is?"

She looked at him.

"The moral of the story is that only true, selfless love will prevail. No greater love hath a man than to lay down his life for a friend. Or a son. Or a stranger in a cell next to you."

"Your parents *died.*"

"We *all* die. My parents defeated Karadzic. Their love set me free to do what it is I must do."

"So do you think I've been brought to the jungle to die?" she asked.

He tilted his head down slightly. "Are you *ready* to die, Sherry?"

A ball of heat washed over her skull and swept down her spine. It was the way he asked the question.

Are you ready to die, Sherry?

No.

It all swam through her mind—her parents' deaths, the father's story, her own nightmares—they all swirled together to form this lump that swelled in her throat.

She stood and walked into the kitchen. "What's there to eat?"

DAVID LUNOW handled the paper cup gingerly. Someone had told him that coffee grew acidic once its temperature fell below 170 degrees. He supposed real connoisseurs could gauge this with the dip of their tongue. All he ever managed was a blister and a curse. Either way, in his opinion, good coffee was always piping hot.

Mark Ingersol stood next to him on the arching park bridge and stared at the brown water below. "I know you hold some reservations about going after Casius, and frankly, I share them. But that doesn't mean we don't follow our orders. Neither does it mean we slack off. If the director wants us to take Casius out, then we take him out. Period."

"In my opinion, you're begging for problems," David said. "This is the kind of thing that blows up in your face." He felt Ingersol's stare, but he refused to look. "We've been at this two days and already Casius has walked in and out of our fingers, stopping just long enough to let us know that he was fully aware of our pursuit. We're lucky he didn't lure our man into some alley and kill him."

"Maybe, but that doesn't change our objective here. And that objective is to kill Casius."

Ingersol picked up a pebble that rested on the railing and flicked it into the water. It landed with a *plunk* and disappeared. "Well, we'll find out soon enough. The Rangers will be inserted before nightfall."

David leaned on the railing. "If they fail, I suppose you could always carpet bomb the jungle. You might get lucky." If Ingersol saw any humor in the statement, he showed no reaction. "Actually, if the teams fail, you wait for Casius to come out and hope to catch him on the rebound. Like I initially suggested."

"What are the Rangers' chances?" Ingersol asked.

David turned to Ingersol. "You mean chances of walking out of that jungle alive, or chances of killing Casius?"

Ingersol looked up at him blankly.

"Either way, some people are going to die. The only question is how many," David finally offered, and then added for Ingersol's benefit, "and who ends up taking the fall for it all."

CAPTAIN RICK Parlier blinked at the sweat snaking into his eyes. His square jaw sported three days of stubble, efficiently covered by a healthy layer of green camouflage paint, accentuating the whites of his eyes. His right hand gripped a fully loaded M-16. His left hand vibrated loosely to the thumping Pratt and Whitney above them. His last cigar protruded from curled lips. He was going back in, and he wasn't sure how he felt about that.

Parlier glanced at the others sitting expressionless in the dimming light and turned his head to the trees rushing below. The blades of the DEA troop carrier beat persistently above him as the helicopter carried his team farther and farther into the uncharted jungle. He'd taken Ranger teams into the jungle three times before, each time successfully accomplishing the objective laid before him. It was why he'd been selected, he knew. He could count the number of men with active jungle combat on a few hands. Now desert, that was different—a whole flock of them had tasted battle in the desert. Not that they'd actually fought much, but at least there had been real bullets flying around. Neither environment was what most would call a blast. But then, except in literal terms, war never was. He preferred the jungle anyway. More cover.

He'd thought the use of three teams to take out one man a bit hyperactive at first. But the more he read up on Casius, the more his appreciation for the two helicopters chopping in the sky behind them grew.

Three teams: Alpha, Beta, and Gamma, he'd dubbed them. Eighteen of the best jungle fighters in the Rangers' arsenal. The plan was simple enough. They would be dropped off on the summit of a mountain overlooking the valley Casius was supposedly headed for. The teams would set up observation posts and send scouts into the valley. Once positive identification had been made, they were to terminate the target at the earliest possible opportunity. Until then, it would be a game of waiting.

Only one restriction hampered their movement. Under no circumstances were they to pass the cliffs. Why? Why did the bureaucrats place any of their nonsensical constraints on them?

He glanced over his men, who sat unmoving. Behind those closed eyelids lives were being lived, memories recalled, procedures rehearsed. His first lieutenant, Tim Graham, looked up. "Piece of cake, Cap'n."

Parlier nodded once. Graham was their communications man. Give him a diode and a few capacitors and Tim could find a way to talk to the moon. He could also wield a knife like no man Parlier had ever seen, which was probably the single greatest reason the army had managed to steal the boy away from eager electronics firms.

The rest of the team consisted of his demolition expert, Dave Hoffman; his sniper, Ben Giblet; and two other light-fighters like himself: Phil Crossley and Mark Nelson. The team had trained and fought together for two years. There could hardly be a tighter fit.

His mind wandered to the target's portfolio. Casius was an assassin with "numerous" confirmed kills, the report said. Not ten or sixteen, but "numerous," as though it was a secret number. A sharpshooter who favored a knife, which meant he had the nerves of a rhino. Anybody who had the skill to take out a target at a thousand yards yet chose to get up close, eyeball to eyeball, had a few screws loose above them eyeballs. The worst of it was the man's apparent adaptability to the terrain. Evidently he had grown up in this jungle.

"What odds you put on this guy lasting the day?" Graham asked.

Phil scoffed. "As far as we know the guy's back in Caracas smokin' a joint and laughing his head off at the Rangers streaking off to pop some white man in leech country."

Someone chuckled. Hoffman eyed Phil. "They wouldn't send three teams to a drop point unless they had it on good intel this guy would show up."

"You don't get good intel this deep, my friend."

"Ready the drop line," Parlier barked as the helicopter feathered near the summit of their drop zone. The troop carrier hovered over a break in the canopy. Hoffman threw the two-hundred-foot rope overboard. Parlier nodded and he dropped into the trees, disappearing below the canopy. One by one the Rangers lowered themselves into the trees.

DEEP WITHIN the mountain, Yuri Harsanyi sat shivering with excitement. In less than an hour a helicopter would take him away to safety. And with him, the large black suitcase that held his future: two thermonuclear weapons.

He had carefully stored the devices in his case the night before and then secured the straps tightly around the leather bag. The replacement bombs sat powerless in Abdullah's casings. When he tried to detonate his bombs, he would get nothing but silence. By then Yuri would be far removed, living a new life, squandering away his newfound wealth. He had rehearsed the plan a thousand times in the last three days alone.

Yuri saw that the left strap had loosened slightly in the humid heat. He cinched it tight and hoisted the suitcase from the floor. If they decided to inspect him now, he would have a problem, of course. But they'd never checked his bags before. He glanced around the room he'd lived in for so long and stepped away for the last time.

An hour later, precisely on schedule, the helicopter wound up and took off with Yuri sweating on its rear bench.

CHAPTER TWENTY-ONE

CASIUS PLUNGED through the dense foliage, sweating bare chested, with mud plastered up his legs and streaking his chest, his black shorts now clinging wet and torn down the right thigh. He'd covered forty miles in the twenty-four hours since entering the jungle, tracking by the sun during the day and by the stars at night. He'd slept once, eight hours earlier. His father would have been proud of him.

But then his father was dead.

Casius halted at the edge of a twenty-foot swath cut from the forest floor, surprised to see the wide scar so deep in the jungle. The canopy above had survived and now grew together, creating the appearance of a large tunnel through the underbrush.

He pulled out a wrinkled topographical map. The compound lay ten miles to the east, in the direction of this wide overgrown path. Casius crossed into the jungle and resumed his jog.

Since his departure from the city, he'd eaten only papaya and yie palm cut on the run, but hunger pains now slowed his progress. Without a bow and arrow, killing a heron or a monkey would be difficult, but he needed the protein.

Ten minutes later he spotted the root that would give him red meat. Casius took his knife from his belt, cut deep into a twisted *mamucori* vine, and let the poisonous sap run over his blade. Under normal conditions the Indians dissolved the poison in boiling water, which would evaporate from any dipped surface, leaving only deadly residue. But he had neither the time nor the fire necessary for the application.

Finding the howler monkeys was like finding a traffic light in the city. Approaching them undetected wasn't nearly as simple. The small animals had an uncanny sense of danger. Casius slipped behind a tree and eyed a group of five or six howlers shaking branches fifty meters away, high in a Skilter tree. He slid into the open and crept toward them. The approach was painstakingly slow, and for fifteen full minutes he inched forward, until he came to rest behind a large palm. Four monkeys now sat chattering unsuspecting on the end of a branch that hung low, no more than twenty meters from his position. Casius slipped from behind the tree and hurled his knife into the group.

They scattered in terror as the knife flipped toward them. The blade clanged into the branches, grazing one of the monkeys. It was two minutes before the poison reached the monkey's nervous system and sent it plummeting from its perch high in the tree, unconscious. He picked it up, snapped its neck with a quick twist, and resumed his push south. The poison would be harmless to him, and the meat would replenish his depleted energy. He had always preferred meat cooked but he had learned to eat it however it came. Today a fire was out of the question, so the meat would remain raw.

The sun had already dipped behind the horizon by the time Casius reached the rock outcropping overlooking the Catholic mission station, twenty miles south of his destination by the map. A scattering of buildings rose from the valley floor—it was inhabited then. Once the valley had been vacant. Now, even from this distance, a mile above, Casius could see a cross at the base of an airstrip flying a limp windsock.

A slow river wound its way past the end of the airstrip and then lazily wandered through the flat valley toward the south. If there was one thing Casius needed now it was information, and the mission might give him at least that.

He dropped from the cropping and began the descent. He'd seen no one on the station. Odd. Where were the Indians? He'd think they'd be loitering all over the place looking for whatever the missionaries might give them in exchange for their souls.

Half an hour later, he stepped from the jungle under a black sky and jogged for a long house lit with pressure lamps from the interior. The night sang with overlapping insect choruses, and the memory of it all brought a chill to Casius's spine.

Casius ran up to the house in a crouch and flattened himself next to a window. He looked through and saw two people seated at a wooden table, dipping spoons into their evening meal. A priest and a woman. The priest's collar was missing, but there was no mistaking his black-and-white attire. The woman wore a white T-shirt, the sleeves rolled once or twice baring her upper arms. Her dark hair fell shoulder length and for a moment he thought she reminded him of a singer whose music he had once purchased. Shania Twain. He had put the CD through his sound system only twice, but her image had made an impression. Or was it that actress . . . Demi Moore? Either way she brought images of a soft-souled American to his mind. Somehow misplaced in this jungle.

He watched the two eat and listened to their indistinguishable murmur for a full minute before deciding they were alone. He slipped around the house.

SHERRY STARTED when a knock sounded on the door. *Rap-rap-rap.*

The evening had been quiet. There were the comforting sounds normal to jungle living: the forest's song, a pressure lamp's monotonous hissing, clinking silverware. Following the father's confession of his parents' sacrifice, the day had floated by like a dream. Perhaps the most peaceful day she'd experienced in eight years. They talked of what it meant to lose life and what it meant to gain it. They talked of real love, the kind of love that gave everything, including life. Like her father had given, and according to Father Teuwen, the kind they were all asked to give. She let herself go with him, remembering the passionate words of her own father—reliving the best of her own spiritual journey, before the box.

It brought her peace.

For the last twenty minutes her mind had come full circle, to the box, to suffering. She had cried, but it wasn't a cry of remorse. It was the cry of a heavy meaning. A head cold was coming on, she thought. Unless it was only the day's crying that stuffed her sinuses.

And suddenly this *rap-rap-rap* on the door.

She glanced at Father Teuwen and swiveled in her seat to see the door swing open. A well-muscled stranger stood in the frame, his arms hanging loosely to his sides, his legs parted slightly, his shoulders squared. But this simple realization quickly made way for the dawning that the man wore only shorts. And torn shorts at that.

Sherry felt her jaw part slightly. His face was painted in strokes of green and black that swept back from his nose, casting the odd illusion that his head belonged on a movie screen, not here on a mission station. Brown eyes peered from the paint. A sheen of moisture glistened on the intruder's dirtied chest, as if he'd worked up a good sweat and then tumbled to the dust. Short-cropped, dark wet hair covered his head. If she didn't know better, she would have sworn that this man had just come from the jungle. But she did know better. He was a white man. And white men didn't come from the jungle during the night. It was too dangerous.

The stranger stepped into the room and pulled the door closed behind him. Now other details filled her mind. The sharp edges to his clenched jaw, the hardened muscles, the muddied legs, the wide band of browned tape around his thigh, the bare feet.

He was dripping on their floor.

"Good evening," he said, speaking evenly as if they should have expected this visit.

The father spoke behind her. "My goodness, man. Are you all right?"

The man shifted his eyes from Sherry to the priest. "I'm fine, Father. I hope I'm not intruding, but I saw the lights and hoped I could ask you a few questions."

Sherry stood. His voice moaned through her skull like a howling wind. She saw that Father Teuwen was already on his feet, gripping his chair with one hand. "Ask a few questions? Heavens, you sound like the jungle patrol or something, popping in to ask a few questions. Where on earth did you come from?"

The man shifted his dark gaze to Sherry for a moment, and then back to the priest. He looked suddenly lost, she thought. As if he'd crossed over from another dimension and mistakenly opened their door. She noted that her pulse raced and she assured herself that the man meant no harm.

"I'm sorry, perhaps I should leave," he said.

"No. You cannot leave, man!" the priest objected quickly. "Look at you.

It's night out there! A bit dangerous, don't you think?" He paused, catching himself. "But then I suppose you already know that. You look like you've just spent the day in the jungle."

For a moment the man did not respond and Sherry thought he had indeed made a mistake and was now looking for a graceful exit. A hunter perhaps. But what would a hunter be doing running around barefoot at night? The whole thing was preposterous.

"Perhaps I've made a mistake by coming here," the man said. "I should leave."

The father stepped up beside Sherry now. "This is a Catholic mission," the priest said evenly. "I'm sure you know that. I'm the priest here—I think I have the right to know the identity of a man who calls on my door in the middle of the night, don't you?"

The man's arms still hung loosely at his sides, and Sherry noted that the knuckles on his right hand were red with blood. Perhaps he was a drug runner, or a mercenary. Her pulse quickened.

"I'm sorry. I should leave." He shifted his feet.

"And why do you insist on withholding your identity, sir?" Father Teuwen asked. "I will have to report this, of course."

That stopped the man. He eyed the priest long and hard. "And if I tell you who I am, you won't report me?"

So the man was on the run! A fugitive. Sherry's pulse quickened again. She glanced at Father Teuwen and saw that he was grinning knowingly.

"That would depend on what you tell me, young man. But right now I can tell you that I'm imagining the worst. And if you tell me nothing, I will report what I imagine."

The stranger slowly smiled.

THE MOMENT the priest stood, Casius knew coming here had been a mistake and he cursed himself.

He had wanted to leave then, before the father asked any questions. Perhaps a missionary would hold his curiosity. But the priest had proved otherwise. And now he had no choice but to either kill them or take them into some kind of confidence. And killing them wasn't really an option either, was it? They had done nothing; they were innocent.

The woman's eyes were ringed in red, as if she'd been crying recently. He smiled at the father. "You're a persistent man. You don't give me much choice. But trust me, you may wish you'd let me go."

"Is that a threat? I suppose that goes for the sister as well."

He noted the woman's quick glance at the priest. So she was a nun then. Or at least she was being cast as a nun by the father. "Did I threaten your life, Father?"

The father glanced at the nun. "You don't have anything to fear from us."

Casius decided he would give them a bone, a herring—just enough to draw out their knowledge of the region. Sooner or later they would call on the radio, of course. But by then it would no longer matter.

"I work for the DEA. You know the agency?"

"Of course. Drug enforcement."

"We suspect a significant operation south of here. I'm on a reconnaissance mission. I was inserted a mile from here, at the top of the western ridge."

The priest nodded.

Casius paused, searching their eyes. "I'm planning to take the Caura River south tonight." In reality he was headed north, of course. "As for my dress, I realize it's not every day you see a westerner traipsing through the brush near naked. But then I'm Brazilian, from Caracas."

"You don't sound so Brazilian," the father said.

Casius ran out a long sentence of fluid Portuguese, telling him he was wrong before switching back to English. "I attended university in the United States. Now, if you don't mind, I have a few questions of my own."

"And your name?" the father asked.

"You may call me Casius. Anything else, Father? My GPA perhaps? My ancestry?"

The woman chuckled and then launched into a cough. Casius smiled at her.

"You're quite bold, Sister. Not many women would willingly choose the jungle as a place to live."

She nodded slowly and spoke for the first time. "Well, I suppose I'm not most women, then. And not many men, Brazilian or not, would run through the jungle, half naked, in bare feet."

She sounded as if she had a cold from her husky tone. He ignored the comment. "Have you heard rumors of any drugs south?" he asked, turning back to the father.

"To the south? Actually no. Which is surprising, because most of the Indians we serve are from the south. How far did you say?"

"Thirty miles, along the Caura River."

The father shook his head. "Not that I am aware of. They must be well concealed."

"Possibly. But I suppose that's why they pay me. To find the difficult ones," Casius responded.

"What about up north?" the nun asked.

He blinked. "Up north? Caracas?"

"Not the city. The jungle up north."

Casius glanced at the father. So they had their suspicions of the north.

"We've heard occasional rumors of drug running farther north. I think the sister refers to those rumors," the priest said.

Casius felt his pulse surge. "How long ago did you hear these rumors?" he asked, trying to sound casual.

"How long? They come sporadically." The father turned to the woman. "Wouldn't you say, Sister? Every few months or so." She nodded, her eyes a bit too wide, Casius thought.

"Interesting. Farther north, huh? How far north?"

"Twenty miles or so. Wouldn't you say, Father Teuwen?" the woman said.

"Yes."

Casius looked from one to the other. "Well, I'll definitely report it. Any unique details?"

They both shook their heads.

"I'm sorry, but what are your names?"

"Forgive me. Petrus Teuwen. And this is Sherry Blake. Sister Sherry Blake."

Casius nodded. "It's a pleasure meeting you," he said. He turned and reached for the door.

SHERRY THOUGHT the man who called himself Casius knew more than he admitted and she thought to ask him about the assault on their mission. But the incident at the plantation occurred eight years earlier, and judging his age, he would have been too young to be involved with any agency at the time.

The longer she looked at him, the more she thought he resembled some outrageous drugstore action figure. Or one of those Wrestlemania wrestlers, snarling at the television cameras and flexing their muscles for the kids. Either way she had seen his kind before, and they had always made her cringe.

She saw the knife at his back as he turned. A large bowie shoved into his waistband. Casius could do more than observe, she decided. His image couldn't have stood in greater contrast to the day's discussion with Father Teuwen. A small knot of disgust churned in her belly.

The man suddenly turned back. "I'm sure you can understand my need for your silence," he said evenly. "At least for the next day or two. Drug merchants aren't well-bred men. They would think nothing of slitting your throats."

He said it so casually, so evenly, that Sherry wondered again if he himself were a drug runner, lying to gain their confidence and planning to return later and do just that. Slit their throats. But that made no sense. He could have done it already.

Casius turned from them, stepped through the door, and was gone into the night. She let out a breath of relief.

"Do you believe him?" the father asked to her left.

"I don't know. He smells like death to me," she replied, still staring at the closed door. Muddy water spotted the floor where the man had stood.

"Yes, he does," Father Teuwen agreed quietly. "Yes indeed, he does."

CHAPTER TWENTY-TWO

CASIUS LEFT the mission house feeling a surge of blood lust pull at his pulse. He cut northeast through the jungle, his thoughts suddenly full of the woman. A nun possibly, but more likely a visitor by her wide eyes, posing as a nun for her own protection. If so, it had been the father's doing. Strong man, the father, worthy of his post. Hardship had visited the priest often, he guessed. The woman might not have the father's weathered soul, but her own soul wasn't as soft as Casius had initially guessed. Odd for such a feminine-looking woman. He pushed the thought from his mind and pressed forward.

A faint sound suddenly registered in his mind—a distant, abstract contradiction in the jungle. He caught himself midstride and stilled his breathing. A cough, perhaps? It didn't repeat itself, but now a rhythmic thumping drifted through the trees, from the direction of the mission.

Boots! Running for the compound!

Casius cursed under his breath. This deep in the jungle the heavy clodding of boots on the run was a sound rarely heard. Definitely military. He stood still and spun through his options. He was too close to his objective to ignore an attack.

He swore again and cut back through the jungle toward the mission station. The father and the nun had their own lives to live and defend—they weren't his concern. But those boots, they came from men who had no business in this part of the jungle—that made the priest and nun his concern.

Casius leapt over a log and sprinted down the jungle path, withdrawing the bowie as he ran. The mission clearing came abruptly, and he pulled up behind a wide tree on the compound's edge.

His pulse settled quickly and he slid around the tree, knowing the dark trunks at his back would keep him concealed.

A bright moon drifted between clouds, revealing two groups of men, clearly paramilitary by their khaki dungarees. A band of three or four ran doubled over for the utility shack at the airstrip's turnaround, possibly headed for the radio. Four others ran directly toward the mission house.

Without thinking through his options, his heart now pounding in his ears, Casius crouched low and ran for the mission house. They clutched rifles that jerked in cadence to their run. The sound of spare clips rattled with each footfall. They had come to kill.

Worse still, he was running after them. Racing right across this wide-open field in plain sight now, jeopardizing his whole mission for the sake of two missionaries he hardly knew. No, he was protecting *his* mission. Yes, protecting his mission.

Two of the soldiers veered toward the living quarters on the left; two ran for the far right. Keeping those on his right cleanly in his peripheral vision, Casius cut left, wielding his knife wide, underhanded. The lead soldier smashed his rifle butt against the door with a loud *crack!* that split the night air. The door snapped open.

Casius reached them then, just as the first man lifted his leg to step inside. He crashed full tilt into the second man's back, propelling him chin first into the doorjamb. The soldier's jaw snapped with a crunch. The other man disappeared inside, unaware of his partner's troubles.

Casius saw the others to his right spin toward him. He operated solely on instinct, from the gut, where killing was born.

With his left arm he caught the man who'd crashed into the doorjamb under his arm before the man slumped to the ground. With his right he slashed his blade across the soldier's neck. He swiveled him like a shield to face the other two now fumbling with their weapons. One had his rifle at his cheek, the other at his waist. Casius slung his knife at the first man and released the man in his arms. He snatched the rifle from the dead soldier's hands and threw himself to his right.

Two sounds registered then: The first came from his bowie, drilling that first man in the neck. He knew that because he glimpsed it as he rolled not once but twice, chambering a round as he tumbled. The second sound came from within the building. It was a single gunshot. He knew immediately that someone had died inside.

Another boom crashed on his ears—that second man across the yard, next to the one with a knife in his neck, was firing at him. Casius came to his knee with the rifle at his shoulder, pumped two slugs into the soldier's chest, and spun to the first door again. To his right, both soldiers crumbled to the earth.

The night fell eerily silent and Casius knelt frozen, the rifle against his shoulder, trained on the dark doorway through which the first solider had disappeared. On the lawn, three of the man's compadres lay in heaps. Casius felt his heart thump against the wooden stock and he breathed deep, keeping that black doorway in focus.

Across the compound shouting came now. The other men had secured their objective and were coming. Casius watched the steel barrel sway with each breath, a throbbing cannon begging for a target.

But the target was taking its time, in there feeling for a pulse, gloating over spilt blood, no doubt. Heat flashed up his spine at the thought. Saving lives never seemed to come easy to him. Killing, on the other hand, was second nature. He was a killer. Slayer. Not savior. He should just waste them all and get on with it!

The door to his right suddenly burst open. At the same moment the dark doorway in his barrel sights filled with a beaming Hispanic male. He squeezed the trigger three times in rapid succession, slamming the man back in a silent scream.

The yelling rushed closer now.

Casius spun to his right and saw the woman standing there wide-eyed and gaping. Which meant the father had probably been shot.

"Wait there!"

He bounded across the lawn and into the living quarters. A figure ran out of the back room—Father Petrus, white-faced and haggard, but somehow alive.

"What . . . ?" the father began.

"Not now! Run!" Casius snapped.

The priest ran past him and Casius followed.

The woman hadn't moved. A glance told him that she'd been coherent enough to pull on work boots. She wore the same white T-shirt and shorts she'd worn earlier.

Casius crossed the lawn in four long strides and snatched the woman's hand. "Follow me if you want to live! Quickly," he said and tugged at her arm.

She refused to budge for a moment, her eyes scanning the dead bodies. A small guttural sound came from her throat. A moan. Her cold hand trembled badly in his own.

"Move!" Casius snapped.

"Sherry!" Petrus had spun back.

She sprang over the bodies, staggered once, nearly planting herself face-down, and then regained her balance.

They ran like that, Casius leading, pulling Sherry by an outstretched arm toward the looming jungle ahead and Father Petrus to their side. Voices began shouting behind, but at each other. Casius remembered the woman's white shirt. It would be an easy target. He ran faster, now literally dragging her behind. But honestly, he wasn't thinking of her. He wasn't thinking of himself either. He was thinking of that dark jungle just ahead. Once he reached that dark mass of brush he could resume his mission.

They plunged past the first trees, pell-mell. No shots rang out behind and he glanced back. No pursuit. Casius slowed to a quick walk.

A soft sob filtered into his ears. He blinked. For the first time a strange notion took shape in his mind. He had a woman in tow, didn't he? A woman and a priest. A small buzz droned between his ears.

He realized he still held the woman's hand. He dropped it and instinctively wiped his sweaty palms on his shorts.

He couldn't take them with him. The sob came again, just behind, through clenched teeth, as if she fought a losing battle to keep her emotions in check. A haunting from America, trailing him into the jungle like his own personal ghost, he thought.

Casius swallowed hard, refusing to look back. He could set them in the direction of a nearby village and send them packing with a slap on the back. But he might as well be sending them to their deaths.

And there's a problem with that?

No, of course not.

Yes.

Heat flushed his face at the thought and he veered from the path into the jungle. The men behind weren't pursuing, but there was no telling what else might show up on a marked path.

He mounted a large log bordering the trail and dropped beyond it. The woman's boots scuffed the log's bark. They were following without protesting. Fingers of panic raked his mind.

Casius spun around. The black canopy masked the moon high above. Sherry froze ten feet behind as if she were his shadow, staring at him with white eyes in the dark. Petrus stopped beside her. For a few long moments neither moved.

His options spun through his mind, calculated for the first time. On one hand he was tempted to leave them. Just bolt now while they stood like mummies, leaving them to crawl back to the path and survive on their own. Back to the mission perhaps. The men might have left.

On the other hand, she was a woman. And he was a priest.

Then again, that was why he *should* leave them. He could hardly make the plantation, much less penetrate it with them stumbling behind.

They still hadn't moved, a fact that now dawned on him with a glimmer of hope. Maybe the woman wasn't some soft-souled talker, but one of those athletic types. She'd kept up with him easily enough, it seemed. And she had just witnessed him shoot a man in the throat while the blood from two others flowed under her boots. Yes, she'd cried, but she hadn't screamed or wailed as some would.

In reality, leaving her would be killing her. His shoulders settled and he closed his eyes briefly.

When he opened them, he saw that the woman had taken a step toward him. The priest followed.

"Sherry and Petrus, right?" His voice sounded as though he'd just swallowed a handful of tacks.

"Yes," the priest said, voice steady.

He exhaled and squeezed his hands into fists. "Okay. Sherry and Petrus. Here's the way it is. You want to live? You do exactly as I say. No talking, no questions. Out here it could mean life or death. You take all those feelings in your chest and you stuff them. When we get to safety, you can do what you want. I'm sorry if that sounds harsh, but we're just trying to survive here. Not save souls."

"I'm not a nun," she said.

"Fine. Follow me as close as possible. Watch where I place my feet; it'll help. Father, you follow her. If you become too tired, tell me quietly." He turned from them and waded into the brush. Sherry followed immediately.

He slid over another waist-high log, thinking she might need help over. But from his sideways glance he saw that she mounted the log quickly and followed in step with Petrus right behind.

He would take them to the plantation's perimeter, stash them safely, and return after a quick penetration.

Chapter Twenty-Three

ABDULLAH AMIR leaned over his desk, picking a scab that had formed over an infected mosquito bite on his upper lip. White miniblinds covered the window that overlooked the processing plant. Behind him a dilapidated bookcase housed a dozen books, haphazardly inserted.

Abdullah sucked blood from his lip and returned his attention to the Polaroids spread on the desk. He had taken them of the bombs in the lab below, their panels opened like two spacecraft waiting to be boarded while the Russian scientist slept. Beside the photographs, a hardcover book titled *Nuclear Proliferation: The Challenge of the Twenty-first Century* lay open.

It had been nearly a week since Jamal had made contact. He'd simply said that it was time and then vanished. The thought that the man might be on his way here to the compound had not escaped Abdullah. The thought both terrified and delighted him. He'd decided that if Jamal came, he would kill him.

A knock startled him. Abdullah shoved the photographs into the book and dropped the evidence into his top drawer. "Come."

Ramón opened the door and guided the captain of the guards, Manuel Bonilla, into the room.

The captain's eyes skirted him and beads of sweat covered Manuel's forehead.

"Yes?" Abdullah said.

"We successfully took the compound, sir."

But there was more. Abdullah could see it in the man's tight lip. "And?"

"We suffered four casualties, sir."

It took a moment for Abdullah to understand the words clearly. When he did, heat surged up his spine and washed through his head. "What do you mean, you suffered casualties?" Abdullah felt his voice tremble.

The man stared directly ahead now, not making eye contact. "It was highly unusual," Manuel replied awkwardly. "There was a woman . . . She escaped with the priest."

Abdullah stood slowly. A wave of dizziness washed through his head. The infection on his lip stung. Not so long ago he would have lashed out in a moment like this, but now he only felt sick. What he was about to do loomed like a giant in his mind.

"I am sorry—"

"Shut up!" Abdullah screamed. "Shut up!"

He sat, aware that he was trembling. Where was Jamal?

"Find her," he said. "When you find her, you will kill her. And until then, you will double the guard in the valley."

Manuel nodded with an ashen face, sweat now running in small rivulets down his cheeks. He turned to leave.

Abdullah stopped him. "And if you think they are alone, you are an idiot."

Manuel nodded again, turned, and left the room.

"Have you heard from Jamal?" Abdullah asked Ramón.

"No, sir."

"Leave."

PARLIER LIFTED his hand and peered over the rim with the night-vision goggles sticking from his eyes like Coke bottles. The valley dipped below him several miles before breaking abruptly at a formation he thought might be the cliffs they had been warned about. But in the jungle night, the formation was difficult to make out clearly.

Graham dropped to his belly next to him. "You see it?" he asked in a hushed voice.

"Not sure. I think so. We got us a valley and some kind of rock formation halfway down there." He pulled away the glasses and swiveled to Phil. "What do we have on the GPS, Phil?"

"That's gotta be it. We're 5.2 clicks north, northeast of the compound."

Parlier twisted back on his elbows. The others joined him along the rock outcropping. He peered through the glasses again. "Then that has to be it. We have, say, a couple miles to the cliff and then another couple to the bottom of the valley. There must be a clearing in there somewhere, but I'm not seeing it with these things. Anyone else see a clearing?"

They peered ahead, some through goggles, others dumbly into the night. A mile behind them Beta and Gamma teams waited for their first intel report before taking up their positions. By the look of things, the airdrop had put them on the money.

"Nothing," Phil said. Someone slapped an insect from his skin.

"So our man is supposed to come out of this valley?" Graham asked. "He'll have to cross those cliffs. That's where we nail him."

Phil grunted. "And we're supposed to sit and wait for this guy up here? I say we cover the top of the cliffs."

"Can't," Parlier said. "We have orders to stay back. Graham, get on the horn and tell Beta to make for a position one mile due east. And Gamma one mile west. I want twenty-four-hour surveillance on that cliff, starting now." He turned to his sniper. "Giblet, you think you could put a round where it needs to go from this distance?"

Ben Giblet studied the jungle below them. "It would be tight. Yeah."

Graham looked at Parlier with skepticism. "We gotta get down there, Rick, and you know it. What's the big deal? We got us a compound with a bunch of druggies down in the valley. I don't see the danger in taking the cliffs."

"That's not the point. We have our orders."

Parlier peered into the dim light below. Graham was right, of course. But the orders had been to stay away from the cliffs. Meaning what? Meaning the *face* of the cliffs or the *lip* of the cliffs? If it came down to it, he might do some interpreting of his own on this one, he thought.

THE *PRINCESS* cruise ship rested in the green harbor waters under a black sky. The ship bustled with passengers who scurried up and down her planks like ants to and from their nest. Yuri Harsanyi boarded the luxury cruiser bound north for San Juan and headed quickly for his cabin. The short-notice fare had cost him three thousand dollars and he had barely made the ship before its scheduled departure at 10 P.M. But he was safe. And the suitcase was with him.

He glanced nervously down the narrow hall before opening the door to his assigned cabin on the third level: #303. There was no way anyone would find him here. He fumbled with his key, unlocked the cabin door, picked up the heavy bag, and entered his room. He boosted the case onto one of the double beds and walked across the cabin to the small bathroom. He looked in the mirror and stretched his neck, thinking he should shower, shave, and then go for dinner. He stepped from the cramped room and removed his shirt.

He shed his slacks and eyed the black case. It contained enough power to vaporize the ship in less than two-thousandths of a second. One minute here, the next—*poof*—gone. Six inches of steel hull disintegrated like the sides of a soap bubble. That man had ever discovered how to harness this incredible power was a miracle. He wondered briefly if any damage had come to the devices during the trip out of the jungle. But the suitcase hadn't left his side.

Yuri reached into the shower and turned the hot water on. His dirty clothes lay strewn on the floor. After testing the water, he stepped into the shower.

But his shaving kit was still in the suitcase.

Yuri stepped from the shower and walked quickly over to the suitcase. He hesitated, watching water drip from his wet face onto the hard case. Then he reached down, released the straps, sprung the latches, and opened it.

For a brief moment Yuri's eyebrows scrunched at the sight within. The two spheres he had placed in the case were gone. Instead a square box rested among the clothes. And then his eyes sprang wide. Abdullah had found him out! Taken his bombs and put this . . .

In that moment, two tungsten contacts fell together, sending a surge of DC current into a detonator that ignited C-4 explosive. An explosion shredded the room precisely three seconds after Yuri opened his case. No nuclear explosion—just plastic explosive that had been substituted for Yuri's bombs.

Even then the explosion was no laughing matter. Ten pounds of high explosive incinerated the cabin in a single white-hot flash. The explosion rocked the port side of the ship. Fire, smoke, and debris spewed out of the porthole that had erupted under the impact of the blast. Amazingly the flame-resistant mattresses, although gutted of their stuffing, did not burn.

But then Yuri Harsanyi could not be aware of these small details. His life had already ended.

CHAPTER TWENTY-FOUR

SHERRY KEPT to the painted man's heels, depending on his movements to guide her through the brush. What sight they did have in the dark seemed more instinctive than a function of sensory perception. An instinct the man had obviously developed. An instinct that neither she nor Petrus had. The father was strong and he kept up, but at this pace, he was hardly better than she.

She was a medical intern from Denver, Colorado, who should be following a doctor on his rounds through whitewashed halls right now. Not running through a nightmare, behind some crazed lunatic. Maybe it was just that—another nightmare grabbing at her boots and slapping at her face instead of real tree roots and leaves clawing at her. She prayed she would bolt up in bed soon.

Actually the dream idea made some sense. She couldn't remember waking, which could mean she still slept. She'd gone to her room to retire; she remembered that. And then the gunshots and the images of killing and now this man leading her like a rabbit through the jungle. The thoughts careened through her skull as she struggled to keep him in sight.

Hadn't he said something about going south on the river? She had no idea where they headed, but this was no river. An image of Father Petrus popped into her mind. *Living is about dying.* His words echoed in her mind. *We all live to die.*

"So do you think I have been brought to the jungle to die?" she'd asked, barely serious.

"Are you ready to die, Sherry?" The words suddenly struck her with clarity. Was she ready to die? No, she wasn't. Right now all she felt was a strong urgency to survive. *God, save us. Please save us.*

Casius had killed with the ease of a man shooting pool, she thought. Which made him what?

On the other hand, he had saved them. Without Casius she would be back in that yard now, lying in her own blood. Which made him her angel in the night. But could an angel kill the way this man had killed?

She suddenly slipped hard to her seat and grunted. Mud oozed through her denim shorts. She scrambled to her feet before Petrus reached her. She ran forward, realizing that Casius hadn't even paused to see if she was okay. He was there, not ten feet ahead, his back still rising and falling like a shadow. A branch smacked her face and she threw an arm against it, tempted to rip it off the tree and stomp it underfoot. She swallowed the frustration growing like a knot in her throat and pushed forward.

Sherry followed relentlessly, stumbling quite regularly, several times to her seat. Twice she lost Casius and was forced to call out. Each time Petrus ran into her and muttered apologies. When it happened, the man had been no more than five yards from them. If he made more noise, it would have been much easier, but he seemed to glide like a ghost. Tracking both him and the ground proved nearly impossible.

She explained the problem to him defensively the second time. He stared at her through the dark for a few seconds, as if trying to comprehend. Then he turned and continued, but this time awkwardly brushing his hands against the foliage to make some noise as he passed. That helped her. But then the rain came, and what had seemed nearly impossible became downright ridiculous.

Sherry let the tears come to her eyes again, wiping constantly to clear her vision. But she would not let the man hear her silent sobs as she pushed on.

Oh, God, please let me wake up.

THE JOURNEY had been an easy one until the rains began. And even that wouldn't have been such a problem if it hadn't come as they began a sharp descent into a valley. The dark, steep jungle, now wet, proved to be the limit.

Their pace slowed to a crawl. Casius stopped frequently and waited for the woman to catch up, slipping and sliding her way down the mountain.

He pitied her, after a fashion. Poor woman had come to the jungle probably thrilled to visit, and now she had been thrust into this impossible world. And led by him of all people. He was no ladies' man. If she didn't already know it, she would soon enough.

Her strength surprised him. She might not have developed the skills to navigate through the foliage with ease, but she had the will of a jaguar.

Midpoint down the descent, Casius admitted bitterly that reaching the plantation before dawn would not be possible with the two. Fortunately, the rain would wash most of their tracks away, which was good considering the jungle would certainly be searched at first light. The attack had been no random pillaging. On his own he would press on, night or day, search or no search. But not with this woman and priest crashing through the brush behind him. They would be spotted from the sky, smashing into trees and shaking their limbs.

Which meant they would have to hide out during the day. With a woman. And a priest.

"All right, mister," the woman suddenly snapped through the darkness. "*This* is too much. We're cut, we're bruised, and we're exhausted. Will you stop for just a minute and let me rest?"

He spun. "Why don't you hoist a flag above the trees while you're at it? Just in case they missed your voice." She peered at him angrily through the darkness. "We will rest soon," he said and turned back down the hill.

They had traveled seven or eight miles from the mission when Casius found the cave. Overgrown vines coated with moss covered its mouth but the lay of the rock clearly suggested a break. He walked past it twice before pulling the matted brush aside enough to make out a small cavern. He pried the covering aside to create a hole for them to crawl through. "Crawl in," he said, waving them forward.

The woman came close, her mouth wide, gazing into the damp darkness. "In there?" she asked.

"You wanted to rest. You can't just flop on the ground and fall asleep.

They'd find you for sure. We'll be safe in there." He jabbed a finger into the blackness.

"It'll be safe? What if something else is in there?" Her voice came ragged and breathy; her cold was worsening.

"Just don't threaten it. Go in slow," he said.

She pulled back and shifted her hazel eyes to his.

Father Petrus stepped up, looked up at him, and slid into the cave without a word.

"You go," Sherry said. "I'll hold this for you." She slid behind him and grabbed the tangle of vines at his hand, gripping his forefinger with them.

He pulled himself free and shrugged. "Suit yourself," he returned and slipped through the opening. The cave immediately opened up to a small enclave, perhaps seven feet square. A damp moss blanketed the ground, providing for a fairly comfortable bed. The sound of critters scurrying confirmed that they were not alone—spiders by their light ticking. But most spiders would scatter, not attack. They would be safe enough. He could barely see her outline against the dark sky as she entered haltingly.

"As long as we're stopped, we should sleep," he said matter-of-factly. "In the morning I'll try to get you something to eat. As soon as we're sure the jungle is clear, we'll leave."

"I want to thank you for what you did back there," Father Petrus said.

"I wouldn't thank me just yet, Father. We're not exactly in the Hilton yet."

"Actually, I'm not thinking of my own comfort. But God—"

"This has nothing to do with God."

That shut the man up. Casius found himself wishing he'd left the priest in his bungalow.

"Get some sleep," he said.

Sherry sat cross-legged, quiet for a moment, peering around in the darkness. "I'm not sure I can sleep," she finally rasped. "I said I was tired and bruised, not sleepy. I'm not sure if you happened to notice with all of that testosterone floating through your veins, but we've been just a bit traumatized here."

No, not soft-souled at all. Not this one. "Suit yourself," he said as calmly as possible. He patted the moss with his open palm and turned his back to her, as though she were already the furthest thing from his mind. He dropped to his side and closed his eyes without the slightest interest in sleep now.

The priest followed his example, whispering encouragement to the woman. For several minutes the cave remained quiet behind him. And then the woman lay down, but by her ragged breathing, he knew she was not acclimating well. In fact, she now seemed at her worst. Surely, at some point exhaustion would take her.

Casius ground his teeth and forced his mind to run through his options for the hundredth time.

SHERRY WOKE to the smell of burning wood. She started and pushed herself to her arms. Three feet away a small fire managed to burn through damp wood, filling the cave with smoke.

The vision had come again and raged with its intensity, soaking her with sweat. And now she had awakened. Which clearly meant that the rest of this was not a vision or a nightmare or any other such supernatural episode. The attack, the escape, and now this cave—they were all real. Sherry swallowed and sat all the way up.

Father Petrus slept on one side, head facing the wall away from her.

How Casius had managed a fire of all things, she didn't know, but he bent over it now, blowing into the coals as rising white ash filtered through his hair. A single small flame flickered lazily over red embers. Smoke drifted past him, bent at the cave's ceiling, and then wandered out the small opening through which they had crawled in the night. The tiny firelight flickered amber on the rough stone walls, highlighting a dozen plum-sized insects fixed to the cave's interior. Sherry swallowed again and turned her eyes to a dead lizard lying limp next to the man.

"Good morning," he said without looking up from the flame. "The fog is thick outside, so I lit a small fire. It will mask the smoke. You need some food, and I didn't think you'd want to eat it raw. We'll wait here until the search parties have come and gone."

"What search parties?"

"They know we escaped. They will send out search parties."

Made sense. "Where are we going?" she asked.

"I'm taking you to safety," he replied.

"Yes, but to where?"

"The Caura River. We'll find a boat that can take you to Soledad."

His voice tweaked a raw nerve in Sherry's spine, reminding her that she had decided she did not like him. She stared at the wide yellow strip running from the creature's snout to its tail. If she had woken hungry, her appetite had already made a hasty retreat. She looked up at the man as he quickly skinned the lizard with a large knife and lay strips of its flesh in the coals.

The firelight danced off broad, muscled shoulders. He knelt over the coals and she thought his calves must be twice the size of her own. The broad band of tape still clung to his thick thigh. A makeshift Band-Aid perhaps. Dark hair lay close to his head. His eyes glimmered brown in the dim light. Camo paint was still plastered on his face, unwashed by the rain.

Whoever he was, she doubted he was simply a DEA scout who'd grown up in Caracas. In another world he could easily bear the title "the Destroyer" or "the Emancipator" or some other such stage name. The likeness resonated.

Smoke stung her eyes. "Is there a way to get rid of the smoke?" she asked. Her cold had worsened through last evening's rain. She cleared her sore throat.

He looked at her and blinked once. "No." He returned to the preparation over the fire, and she realized he would probably insist she eat the meat.

She unfolded her cramped legs and stretched them before her, leaning back on her hands. Mud had dried on her shins and thighs, no doubt covering a dozen cuts and bruises. She rested one boot over the other and edged close to the fire, watching the man's face. He glanced at her legs quickly and then back to the lizard meat now simmering in the red coals.

"Look, Casius." She cleared her throat again, thinking she sounded like a husky man with the cold. Her chest felt as though a vise had moved in over night. "I realize this is all a terrible inconvenience for you. We've crashed some terribly important mission you were dying to complete. Life-and-death stuff, right?" She flashed a grin, but he merely glanced at her without responding. A wedge of heat rose behind her neck.

"The fact is, we are together. We might as well be civilized."

He pulled the meat from the fire, laid it on the moss, and sat back to his haunches. "You've thrown a kink in my plans." He lifted his eyes and studied her for a moment.

Sherry shoved herself up and crossed her legs. "Is that how you see us? A kink?"

He dropped his eyes to the fire and she saw his jaw muscles clench. *Now that was good, Sherry. Go ahead, alienate the man. He's obviously a brute with the social skills of an ape. No need to enrage him. Just toss him a banana and he'll be fine. He saved your life, didn't he?*

Then again, she wasn't exactly the queen of social graces either. "You know, the thing of it is, I didn't choose this. And I don't mean just *this,* as in running through the jungle with some . . . Tarzan, but coming to the jungle in the first place."

He didn't respond.

"A week ago I was a medical intern, studying with top honors. And then my grandmother convinces me that I have to get to this mission station two hundred miles southwest of Caracas. Something terrible is about to happen, you see. And I'm somehow a part of it. I'm having terrible nightmares about something that's going to happen. So I rush down here, only to be thrown into a bloodbath. Do you know how many men you killed back there or don't you count?"

He looked up at her. "Some men need to be killed."

"Some?"

He held her eyes for a few seconds. "Most."

The word seemed to fill the enclave with a thick silence. *Most?* It was the way he said it, as if he really meant it. As if in his opinion, most people had no business living.

"You are right," Father Petrus said. Sherry turned to see that he'd awoken and faced them. "In fact, all men need to be killed—one way or another. But not by you they don't. You are the hand of God?"

The corner of Casius's mouth lifted. "We are all the hands of God. God deals in death as well as life," he said.

"And to whom do you deal death?" Father Petrus asked.

Casius looked as though he might break off the conversation. He dropped his eyes and stirred the coals. But then he looked up.

"I deal death to who he tells me to kill."

The fire crackled.

"*Who* tells you to kill?"

Casius stared, eyes blank. "Your God, as you call him, doesn't appear to be so discriminating. He slaughtered whole nations."

"Are you directed by God?"

No response.

"Then, you are against him," Petrus said. "And in the grand scheme of things, that's not such a good place to be. But still, we are grateful for what you did. Now, what's for breakfast?"

Casius glared at him. Looking at the man, a small portion of sorrow spread through Sherry's chest. There was a whole history there that neither she nor Petrus could possibly know.

She dropped her eyes to the fire, suddenly feeling heavy. "I was told yesterday that life comes through dying." She lifted her eyes and saw that Casius stared at her. "Are you ready to die, Casius?"

She had no idea why she asked the question. Really she was asking it of herself. A knot rose to her throat and the flames suddenly swam. She swallowed.

Casius tossed a stick onto the fire, sending a shower of sparks to the ceiling. "I'll be ready to die when death defeats me."

"So . . ." She was speaking again, and she still wasn't sure why. "Death hasn't put its claws into you yet? You yourself haven't felt the effects of death—you're too busy killing."

"You speak too much," he said.

This was all wrong. She didn't mean to insult this man. On the other hand, he reminded her of everything she'd come to believe was offensive. Men like Casius had killed her parents.

"I'm sorry. It's not that I'm not grateful for your help—I am. You just bring back some pretty . . . awful memories. I've seen enough killing." She looked at Petrus. "The father told me that for every killing, there is a dying. There were two sides to the crucifixion of Christ—a killing and a dying. Like in some grand chess match, there are the black players who are the killers, and there are the white, who are the die-ers. One kills for hate, while others die for love. I was just coming to understand that . . ."

"You show me someone—anyone—who dies for love, and I'll listen to you. Until then, I will kill whom I have to. And you should learn to keep your mouth closed."

"You are CIA?" Father Petrus asked.

He pulled back into himself then and breathed deliberately. "I've said too much already. I'll be back as soon as I check the perimeter." He stood abruptly, walked to the entrance, and slid out, leaving Father Petrus and Sherry alone with the fire.

And the lizard.

CHAPTER TWENTY-FIVE

Wednesday

THEY SPENT the rest of the morning in an odd silence, waiting for signs of a search, huddled speechless in the small cavern. Several times the woman made comments in hushed tones, but Casius immediately lifted a finger to his lips. As long as they were in the cave, they wouldn't have the advantage of being able to hear an approach. Their own silence became critical. He was glad for the restriction.

Casius made the fifth perimeter sweep of the day, stepping lightly from tree to tree, eager to confirm the direction of any search party and resume their journey north. Eager to step beyond the strange dichotomy that seemed to rear its head as the day progressed.

He decided that the priest's and woman's presence was simply an inconvenience. A *kink,* as he'd said. As long as he ignored them, they wouldn't be much of a threat to his mission. He'd soon dump them in the arms of safety and continue. He pulled into the shadow of a large Yevaro tree and scanned the slope before him. Several times helicopters had beat low over the trees, possibly carrying men to the search. So far, none had ventured this deep.

He leaned on the tree and thought about the woman. Sherry. She was an enigma. For reasons out of his grasp, ignoring her was more difficult than he had imagined. She kept popping into his mind like one of those spring-loaded puppets. Only she was no more a spring-loaded puppet than he was her monster. The talk had put a spur in his chest. A small ache. *And what about you, Miss Sherry Blake? You and your mission from God, come to the jungle to die with your priest. What kind of heart do* you *have?*

A good heart. He knew that and it gnawed at his mind. She'd surprised him with the questions earlier and he had surprised himself even more by engaging her. An image of her leaning back in the dim firelight rose in his mind's eye. Her dark hair lay on her shoulders; her hazel eyes glistened like marbles in the flickering flame. The white T-shirt was no longer white, but muddy brown. She had well-muscled legs and a silky smooth complexion under the dirt. Her cold had turned her voice husky and her eyes a little red. She'd slept again—stretched on her side, her head resting on her arm. Sherry Blake.

He'd seen someone who looked like her before. Not Shania Twain or Demi Moore, but someone from his past. Someone from Caracas maybe. But he had shut out his past. He couldn't even remember what his father or mother looked like. They said the stress of the killing had done that. Washed out portions of his mind.

Casius left the tree and scaled the hill to his right quickly. He paused at its crest and listened carefully. Far off, possibly as far as the mission, another helicopter whacked at the sky.

The snap of a twig interrupted his thoughts and he shrank back into the tree's shadow. Down the slope, slogging away from them, three men headed back toward the mission. So they had come and gone then. He watched them step carefully through the brush, dressed in khakis and a mismatch of paramilitary garb. They held their course and disappeared through the jungle.

Casius turned and retreated to the cave quickly. He found Sherry on her side and the priest poking a stick at the ashes, attempting to revive the dead fire. Light streamed in through the vines at the entrance now.

"I'm sorry, but I had to extinguish the fire when the fog lifted," he said, dropping to one knee. "They're gone. We'll go now."

He slid through the opening, followed by the woman and then Father Petrus. It dawned on him that if a guard had been waiting in the open he would have hardly noticed. He swore under his breath. For all their talk of killing, the pair might be the death of him.

He looked at Sherry, suddenly struck by her beauty in the full light. "Let's go," he said.

"WHERE DID you last have them in sight?" Abdullah asked. It was late and he was tired. Tired from the lack of sleep, tired of incompetent men, tired of waiting endlessly for Jamal's call.

Ramón leaned over the map in the security room. Other than the laboratory below, this room contained the only real sophistication in the compound. There was the processing plant, of course, and the conveyors that took the logs to the chute through the mountain, but those were relatively basic operations. Security, on the other hand, was always a matter of the highest regard in Abdullah's mind. Not even Jamal knew what he had here.

The map showed the boundaries of the perimeter security system, a sensitive wire buried several inches under the forest floor. Using radio waves, the system showed the mass of any object that crossed over, allowing them to distinguish animals of smaller mass from humans.

"They crossed here." Ramón pointed to an area south of the compound. "Three persons. Traveling fast, I think."

Abdullah blinked, letting the last statement settle. Who could possibly be in the jungle so close to the compound? Hunters maybe. The infection on his lip throbbed and he ran his tongue over it gently. "How can you know they are traveling fast?" he asked.

"They crossed the perimeter here and then exited here, ten minutes later. At first we thought they had left, but within a few minutes they reappeared here."

Heat spread down Abdullah's neck. Hunters? Yes, hunters might move about like that. But so deep in the jungle? It could just as easily be a sniper with his spotter. Or a reconnaissance mission, launched by some suspecting party. The Russians, perhaps, somehow tipped off as to Yuri's location after all these years. Or the CIA.

Or Jamal.

"And what have you done?" he asked.

"I have ordered Manuel to pick them up."

Abdullah whirled to the man, his eyes glaring. "Pick them up? And what if it's a sniper? How do you plan on picking up a trained sniper? You don't just pick up trained men; you take them out!"

Ramón stepped back. "If we kill them and they are in contact with some authority, then their absence will be a warning. I thought they should be taken alive."

Abdullah considered that, turning from the man as he recognized the validity of the man's point. "But you don't just pick them up as if they were stray dogs. You saw how well Manuel did with the mission compound. How can you possibly—"

A rap suddenly sounded on the door and Ramón opened it.

Manual stood, winded and breathing hard. "We have spotted them, sir. Two men and a woman."

"Good!" Ramón said. "Take them with the tranquilizers."

Manuel turned to leave. "And Manuel," Abdullah said. "If you let these three escape again, you will die. Do you understand?"

The guard stared wide-eyed for a moment and then dipped his head.

CASIUS LED them through the jungle at a punishing pace. To make a statement, Sherry thought. The statement that he wanted to leave her and her big mouth for the animals. They moved steadily through the trees, down one slope, over the next, up a cliff, through a creek, only to begin the cycle again.

The man dragging her through the brush was a killer many times over, that much was now painfully obvious. Like the men who had killed her parents. Killers for some abstract cause, ignoring the simple fact that for every one they killed, someone else was sentenced to live with that death. A brother, a sister, a wife, a child. No telling how many nightmares Casius had spawned in his years. She detested the man.

On the other hand, he had saved her life. And every time he spoke she found herself chasing away an absurd sentimentality. As if he were her guardian.

God forbid.

But true enough. It was why she had become so angry at him, she decided. It was as if her parents' killer had stepped out of her nightmares and come to save her with a flashing smile. One last twist of the knife.

The muscles in his calves balled and flexed with each stride. His bare feet moved effortlessly over the forest floor. Sweat glistened on his broad shoulders. At one point she found herself wondering what it would feel like to run a finger over such insanely massive muscle. She quickly dismissed the thought.

Father Petrus took up the rear, and Sherry thought about his suggestion that she was now on God's path, waiting for God to reveal truth as he saw fit. And if so, then this man was also a part of God's grand plan. Maybe somehow connected to the vision. Yes, the vision that came around each night like the falling of a pole-driver. That mushroom growing huge, night after night.

Casius had paused three times in the last fifteen minutes, surveying the land ahead carefully. Now he stopped a fourth time and raised his hand for silence.

A flock of parrots squawked into flight above them. Sherry held a hand to her chest, feeling her thumping heart beneath her fingers. "What is it?" she whispered.

He jerked a finger to his lips, listening.

CASIUS HAD felt it four times now—that hair-raising sense of prying eyes. They had progressed to within two miles of the compound, the last three hours under cover of darkness. He would leave Sherry and the father there under the shadow of several large boulders, scout the plantation quickly, and return for them within a few hours. He would then take them to the Caura River and return depending on what he found at the compound.

At least that had been in his mind. But now this tickle at the base of his brain unnerved him.

He had seen no sign of men. And yet that fourth sense—as if they'd been monitored by invisible eyes for the past fifteen minutes. In the dark, the man who used surprise wielded the biggest weapon. As an assassin he had relied heavily on sudden surprise in darkness. Losing it now with the woman and the priest would force him to abort his plan until he could get rid of them.

On the other hand he had been careful, staying under the heaviest canopy and avoiding ridges. Only a lucky observer could have picked them out and then only with powerful scopes. If there had been men stationed on the ground, he would have discovered them; he was confident of that.

Casius lowered his hand and stepped forward. Behind him, Sherry and Petrus followed. Although they hadn't talked, Sherry's disposition toward him had changed in the last few hours, he thought. Less animosity. Sharing the struggles of life and death united even enemies, it was said. Maybe that accounted for his own growing apprehension over leaving her alone while he scouted the plantation. In fact, it could have been her presence that brought that tickle to his neck.

Within ten minutes, they came to the edge of a clearing. Twenty yards out a small pond shone with the moon's reflection. Three large boulders jutted from the ground at one end. He turned to them and nodded. "All right. See those boulders? I want you to wait under them for a few hours while I scout ahead."

Sherry stepped next to him, breathing steadily from exertion. He could smell her breath, like only a woman's breath could smell, although he could not imagine why—she hadn't worn lipstick or gloss for at least twenty-four hours. She peered ahead, her lips slightly parted, apprehension clear in her round eyes. Her shoulder touched his arm and it startled him.

She faced him and he shifted away as casually as possible. "A few hours? For what?" she asked.

Casius opened his mouth, not sure what he intended to say. It was then, with his mouth gaping and she looking like a puppy up at him that the faint coughs carried to him on the wind.

The instant before the darts reached them, he knew they were coming. And then they struck, *whap, whap*, the first in his arm, the second in his thigh. Thin and hairy and buried to their hilts.

Tranquilizer darts!

Whap, whap! Sherry was hit!

His first thought was of Friberg's face, grinning back in Langley. His second was of the woman. He had to save Sherry.

He slung an arm around her waist and pulled her back, deeper into the jungle's cover. She was saying something. He could smell her breath, but he could not make out her words. He faced her and saw her wide eyes, inches from his face.

Casius staggered back as the drug swept through his veins. He fell, still holding the woman, breaking her fall with his own. Far away a shout rang out. Spanish, he thought. So he had been followed. But how? Something heavy rested on his chest.

Then his world went black.

CHAPTER TWENTY-SIX

Thursday

RICK PARLIER stood over Tim Graham, who fiddled with the tuning dials on the satellite transmitter. They had been in the jungle one night, and already the insects were taking their toll. The satellite dish had been set up in the canopy within minutes of their securing a base on the mountain's crest. Contact had been established with Uncle, Rick's designation for their U.S. link, and Graham had confidently settled down next to his toys. The receiver was left on at all times, and the frequency altered every thirty minutes to a schedule followed by all three parties.

It had been an hour since the receiver had first started sputtering, refusing either transmission or reception.

"There it is." Graham withdrew what looked like a giant winged ant from the opened receiver. "Bugger chewed right through the variable volume resistor. Made a mess. Should be all right now."

Five minutes later, Tim Graham hit the power switch and handed the mike to Parlier. "Should work now."

Parlier took the mike and depressed the transmission lever. "Uncle, this is Alpha, Uncle, this is Alpha. Do you copy? Over."

Static sounded over the speaker for a moment before the response came: "Alpha, this is Uncle. Read you loud and clear. Where the heck you been?"

"Sorry. We had a little problem with our radio. Over."

There was a pause and the voice came back on. "Copy, Alpha. What is the status of the target? Over."

Parlier looked out into the jungle. Uncle had reported a disturbance at some mission station twenty-five miles south and had speculated that it might be connected with their target. Then nothing. No action, no word, no nothing.

He pressed the toggle. "No activity on this side. Beta and Gamma report no movement. Will advise, over."

"Roger, Alpha. Keep to the schedule. Over and out."

Give me equipment that works in the jungle and I will, Parlier thought as he handed the mike back to Graham. "Good work, Graham. Keep this radio clean. We can't afford another break like that."

"Yes, sir."

Parlier stood, walked to the boulders cropping from the crest, and glanced over his men. Phil and Nelson were on glass duty, peering diligently through the high-powered field glasses to the cliff lip below. Next to them, Giblet rested on his back, shooing away various flying insects with his hands. His sniper rifle sat propped on a tripod beside him, readied for a shot. Of course, even if they did spot the man, it was highly unlikely that Giblet would have the time to get a shot off. And even if he did, it would be a quick one—he could miss.

Graham's recommendation that they descend to the cliffs had gnawed in his gut all night. Beta and Gamma had established similar observation posts from which they studied the forests in the valley below. In addition to the cliff, they watched the canopy, looking for anything unusual that might indicate the passage of humans below them. So far they had observed nothing.

Except for insects, of course. They had observed plenty of those.

Parlier walked back to his radioman. "All right, Graham. Tell Beta and Gamma to hold tight. I'm taking this team to the cliff."

Tim Graham grinned and snatched the mike from its cradle. "Immediately, sir."

"Make sure you explain that we're not going *to* the cliffs. We're just going *near* the cliffs. You got that? And tell them I want them on the horn if they hear so much as a monkey fart."

"Yes, sir. Anything else?" The radioman grinned.

"Pack up. We're headed down."

DAVID LUNOW knocked once and walked into Ingersol's office without waiting for a response. The man looked up, staring past bushy black eyebrows. His hair slicked back nicely, David thought, the kind of hairdo he could wear without washing it for a week.

David walked up and eased into a wing-backed chair facing Ingersol's desk. He stroked his mustache and crossed his legs.

"If you don't mind, I have to express my concerns. In the fifteen years I've been at the agency, I don't remember a single occasion when we've gone after anyone like we're going after Casius. Except in situations where we had full knowledge of a specific intent to damage. Now, correct me if I'm wrong here, but Casius isn't exactly on a course to inflict any real damage. He may take out some rogue drug operation, but so what? Explain to me what I'm missing."

"He broke ranks. A killer who breaks ranks is a dangerous man."

"Yes. But there's more, isn't there?"

"You're his handler, David. Someone suggests taking out your man and you have a problem. I can understand that. Haven't we covered this?"

"It's more than that. Casius can take care of himself. Actually, that's its own problem. We're gonna end up with blood on our hands whether we like it or not. But it's this dogmatic insistence that we take him out instead of considering other alternatives, alternatives that seem much more reasonable to me, that has me baffled."

Ingersol stared at him judiciously. "Not all issues of national security are put out in broad distribution memos."

David flashed a smile at the man. "Look, all I'm saying is that nobody knows Casius like I do. Going after him this way is liable to create precisely the kind of problem we're trying to avoid by killing him. And the director must know that."

He studied Ingersol's face at the first mention of the director. Nothing. He continued, "Evidently someone figures that risk is warranted, given what Casius might uncover down there. I think they're trying to protect something."

"Pretty strong words for a man in your position," Ingersol said. "You wanna rethink that?"

"I have. A hundred times. I think Casius is headed for a deep-cover operation, and I think someone wants him dead before he discovers whatever's being hidden down there in that jungle."

"The world's full of deep-cover operations, Lunow. And if they weren't worth protecting, they wouldn't be deep cover, would they? It's not your position to question whether there is or isn't something to hide. It's your job to follow orders. We've been over this."

"You're trying to take him out. I just wanted to make my position clear for when this thing hits the fan. And you know it will, don't you?"

"Actually, no, I don't."

"If I'm right, it will. Because whatever is down there, it's about to be exposed."

"All right. You've made your point. Finished. And, for the record, I think you're overreacting because it's *your* man down there breaking ranks. Go have a drink on me, but don't come waltzing into my office accusing the agency of negligence."

David felt his cheeks flush. A trickle of sweat broke from his hairline.

"Are we clear?" Ingersol asked.

CHAPTER TWENTY-SEVEN

SHERRY'S EYELIDS felt heavy, as if they had been coated with lead while she slept. She applied pressure to them, wanting light to fill her eyes, but they weren't cooperating because the darkness did not roll back.

An image of Casius running barebacked through the brush filled her mind. Muscle rippled across his shoulder blades with each footfall.

She should open her eyes. And then another thought struck her: What if her eyes were already open?

She shoved herself to her elbow, lifted a finger to her eye, and recoiled when it contacted her eyeball. A chill broke over her head and she threw her arms out. They collided with cold stone. Or cement.

She was in a dark cement room—a holding cell. She must have been thrown here after the dart.

Sherry turned and extended an arm, afraid it would contact another wall. But it swished harmlessly through the stuffy air. She leaned forward and it touched the opposite wall. Five feet.

She was in a holding cell. Blacker than tar. It all came crashing in on her like a wave hitting the beach. In that instant Sherry became a girl again, trapped in her father's box with no way out.

Panic surged through her mind. She whirled about, whimpering, lurching in all directions, feeling the air and cold cement surfaces. The whimper rose to a wail and she fought to her knees, shaking.

Oh, God, please!

The blackness felt like syrup over her face. A heavy, suffocating syrup. Waves of dread slammed into her mind, and she thought that she might be dying. Again. Dying again like she had in the box.

Her wail changed into a dreadful moan that lingered on and on. She knelt there in the dark, moaning, crumbling, dying.

Oh, God, please, I'll do anything.

She suddenly froze. Maybe this wasn't a cell! It could be a dream. One of her recurring nightmares. That had to be it! And if she just opened her eyes, it would all be gone.

But her eyes were already open, weren't they?

Sherry pulled her legs up and hugged them. An ache filled her throat. "Oh, God, please."

Her words whispered in the small chamber. She bobbed back and forth, groaning. "Please, God . . ."

Are you ready to die, Sherry?

The father's words rolled through her mind, and she answered quickly, "No." Then rocking, feeling the terror freeze her bones, she suddenly wished for death to come. She swallowed again. "Yes."

But she didn't die. For an hour she sat trembling and rocking in the cold, damp space, mumbling, "Please, God." She had no idea what lay above her. She had no desire to find out. Her body had shut down except for this rocking.

It occurred to her through the fog that she had come full circle. Eight years ago she had been trapped like this. She had made a vow, and now God was testing her resolve. She was in the black belly of a whale and the vision was her acid.

Will you die for him, Sherry?

For who?

The light lit her mind abruptly, without warning, while she was still rocking. Her first thought was that a strobe light had been dropped into the cell, but then she saw the beach and she knew she was in the other world.

Sherry stood shaking to her feet and sucked hard at the fresh sea breeze. A smile spread her mouth wide and she wanted to scream. Not with terror, but with relief and joy and the pleasure of life.

The waves lapped against the beach and then hissed in retreat. She lifted her eyes and felt the wind cool against her neck as the palm branches swayed above. She spread her arms wide, turned slowly on the soft sand, and laughed aloud.

On the third twirl she saw the black-cloaked man walking over the water, and she knew he was coming to plant his seed in the beach, but she didn't stop. Let him do his deed. She would enjoy the sun and the wind while she could. When the acid rains came, she would stop. And die.

Are you ready to die, Sherry?

Yes.

The familiar vision rolled forward in stunning reality.

But one thing changed this time. Not in the vision, but in her understanding of it. This time when the mushroom grew, she saw that it wasn't a mushroom at all. No, of course not! How could she have missed it? It was a cloud.

The kind of cloud that grew out of a bomb blast.

Chapter Twenty-Eight

CASIUS AWOKE on a cot and slowly sat upright. The events of the night came to him haltingly as he lifted his hand to the bruise on his right shoulder. His captors had used a tranquilizer dart. And they'd also shot the woman and the priest. They held them elsewhere.

Sherry.

A small ache burned in his chest at the thought. He'd led the woman into the jungle; she was now his to deal with. It was a wrinkle to this whole operation he could do without. But a wrinkle that was beginning to haunt him.

Casius swept his eyes around the prison. The room was ten by ten—cinder block. Empty except for this one bed. No windows, one door, all white. A brazen bulb glared on the ceiling. The bare mattress he sat on looked like something they'd found in an alley, grayed with age and stained with brown rings. It smelled of urine.

He carefully checked his body for wounds or breaks but didn't find any. They had taken him easily. They had either been exceptionally lucky or they possessed a security system far more advanced than he would have expected.

Casius leaned against the wall and rested his head back.

His wait ended within the minute. A scraping sounded at the door.

So now the game would begin in earnest. He settled his stiffened muscles and let them come.

The soldier who entered came in gripping a nine-millimeter Browning revolver in both hands. An eye patch rested like a hole over his right eye. He was Hispanic.

Another man stepped past the door and Casius felt his chest tighten. Short-cropped, black hair with a streak of white topped the man's hollow face. He was looking at Abdullah Amir. The man bore a surprising similarity to his brother. Casius's hand twitched instinctively on his lap and he calmly closed his fingers.

The man stood with his arms limp at his sides, eyeing Casius with drooping eyes. He wore a white cotton shirt with short sleeves and tight maroon pants that ended an inch above black leather shoes. Casius felt a thin chill break down his spine, and he suddenly wondered if he could pull this off. The whole thing.

A corner of his mind had expected this, of course. But now looking at Abdullah, the truth of it all hit his head like a sledge and he wondered if he'd overestimated his mental strength and patience.

By Abdullah's raised eyebrow, he saw Casius's fear. "You think I'm a ghost?" he asked.

Casius swallowed and regained composure, his mind still reeling. The man could have no clear fix on his identity. At least not yet.

Abdullah stared, unwavering. "Who are you?"

Casius suppressed the instinct to launch himself into the man now and be done with it. He glared at the man without answering, gathering his resolve to play his cards as planned.

"Abdullah," Casius growled softly.

The Arab's eyes registered a flicker of doubt. For a moment he looked nonplussed.

Casius spoke before the man could utter a word. "Your name is Abdullah Amir. I killed your brother ten days ago. You look very much like him. Your brother was an effective terrorist—you should be proud."

Casius smiled and the man blinked, stunned to silence. Every muscle in his thin body went taut, baring veins at his neck and forearms.

"You killed . . . Mudah is dead?" Abdullah sputtered. For a moment Casius thought Abdullah might shoot him there, on the spot. Instead he regained his composure slowly as if he could flick it on and off between those ears. It spoke well of his strength, Casius thought.

"CIA." Abdullah spoke as if he'd just swallowed a bitter pill. Now a different glint flashed through the man's eyes. "And what is your agency doing so deep in the jungle?" he demanded.

"We're looking for a killer," Casius said. "Perhaps you, Abdullah. Are you a killer?"

The man found no humor in the question. He looked at Casius carefully. "What is your name?"

"Your family is in Iran. In the desert. What brings you to the jungle?"

The Hispanic guard shifted his one good eye to Abdullah, his gun still leveled unwavering at Casius's head.

"Why did you kill my brother?" Abdullah asked.

Casius considered the question. "Because he was a terrorist. I despise terrorists. You're monsters who kill to feed a blind lust."

"He had a wife and five children."

"Don't they all? Sometimes wives and children die too."

Moisture beaded the Arab's upper lip and glistened under the ceiling bulb. Casius felt his own sweat trickle past his right temple. His vision clouded with that familiar black fog and then cleared.

"You yourself are a killer," Abdullah said. A fleck of spittle stuck to his curled pink lip. "The world seems to be full of monsters. Some of them kill for God. Others drop bombs from ten thousand feet and kill for oil. Both kill women and children. Which kind are you?"

A small voice whispered in his mind. *You are the same as he,* it said. *You are both monsters.*

Casius said the name slowly, before he realized he was saying it. He felt a tremor take to his bones, and he fought for control.

When he spoke, he could not stop the anger that tightened his voice. "You,

Abdullah Amir, are a monster of the worst kind. How many have you killed in your eight years on this plantation?"

A SMALL warning bell was ringing in the dark, Abdullah thought. Set off by the agent's last statement. But he could not place it. What he could place was the simple fact that the CIA must now suspect his extracurricular activities. It was why they had sent this reconnaissance. Maybe his brother had talked under this assassin's knife. Either way, the operation was now in jeopardy.

Jamal's order had new meaning now.

The dark-haired man reminded him of a warrior, displaced in time, stripped of his clothing for some ungodly reason, still covered in his war paint. They had found only a knife on him. Well, then, he would have this man killed with a blade. Across the neck, perhaps. Then he would have his gut ripped out. Or maybe in the reverse order.

"According to the CIA's records you put a few people down, coming to this valley," the man said to Abdullah. "This was once a coffee plantation and there was a mission station nearby—both of which had to go. But it seems that fact bothered the CIA as little as it did you."

The last statement made Abdullah blink. This agent knew about the CIA's involvement? And by the flicker of the man's eye, he obviously did not approve.

"But that's not my concern," the assassin said, holding his gaze. "Jamal, on the other hand, is my concern."

Jamal? This man knew of Jamal! "What is your name?" Abdullah asked again.

"Casius. You know of Jamal."

Abdullah felt his pulse pound. He did not respond.

"I'm not sure you realize what kind of trouble has just landed on your doorstep, my friend, but trust me—your world is about to change."

"Perhaps," Abdullah said evenly. "But if so, then yours as well."

"Tell me what you know about Jamal, and I'll walk out of this jungle without a word. You realize my absence alone will raise red flags."

Abdullah felt a smile form slowly on his lips. The man's audacity struck him as absurd. He was here, under a gun, and yet he seemed comfortable issuing threats? "If I could give you Jamal's location right now, believe me, I'd do it eagerly," Abdullah said. "Unfortunately, Jamal is thinner than a ghost. But then I'm sure you know that, or you wouldn't be chasing him through this godforsaken jungle. He is not here, I can assure you. He has never been here. You, on the other hand, are. A fact you don't seem to appreciate."

"Jamal may not be here, but he *is* your puppeteer, Abdullah, isn't he? Only an idiot would think differently."

Heat flared up Abdullah's neck. What did the man *know?*

Casius shifted his gaze. "Your brother spoke quite freely before I cut him. Evidently your competence was of some concern to him. But really, if you read between the lines, I think it was more Jamal who regarded you as stupid." The man looked back into Abdullah's eyes. "Why would Jamal feel obligated to take over an operation you had perfectly under control? This was all your idea, wasn't it? Why did he take over?"

But Abdullah could not dismiss the words easily. In fact, he knew this to be true. Jamal *did* think of him as stupid—every communiqué dripped with his condescension. And now this assassin had forced the same information out of his own brother before slicing him open.

A tremble ran through Abdullah's bones. He had to think. This man would die—that much was now certain—but not before he told Abdullah what he knew.

The fool was staring at him as if he were the one doing the interrogating. His eyes glinted fierce, not in the least cautious. He obviously knew more than he was saying.

"I want Jamal," Casius said. "His offense of me dates back eight years and has nothing to do with you. You tell me how Jamal makes contact with you, and I will make sure your operations stay well covered."

Abdullah raised an eyebrow. "If it's true that this operation is really under Jamal's thumb, why would I give a killer information that might lead to him?" he asked.

Casius drilled him with an unblinking stare. "Because if *Jamal* isn't killed, I'm quite sure he'll kill you. In fact, if I were a betting man, I might say you were already dead. Your usefulness is finished. You're now a liability."

Abdullah came very near to grabbing Ramón's gun and shooting Casius then. Only the man's arrogance kept him alive. That and the tiny voice that whispered in his ear. Something was amiss.

His face twisted with contempt. He turned his back on the man and left without another word. If Casius had any useful information, it was now immaterial. The man was dead already.

Abdullah spoke as soon as the door slammed shut. "Prepare the bombs. Have them ready to ship," he said, and his voice held a tremor.

"So soon?"

"Immediately! Jamal is right; we cannot wait."

"Send them to detonate?"

"Of course, you idiot. Both. We send both and then tell their government they can stop their detonation by complying with our demands, as planned. But we will detonate them anyway, after the Americans have had a chance to wet themselves. Injury to insult—the best kind of terror. Release our people or we will blow a hole in your side." He grinned. "We will shove in the knife and then turn it. Just as planned."

"And the others?"

Abdullah hesitated. He'd nearly forgotten about the woman and the priest. "Kill them," he said. "Kill them all."

CHAPTER TWENTY-NINE

CASIUS NEEDED a distraction.

As soon as the door had closed, he was pressed against it, willing his heart still so he could hear unobstructed. They had clicked off ten paces before pausing at what could only be the elevator by the faint whir that started just after their final step.

It took him ten minutes to settle on his course of action. His cell probably lay beneath the ground, on the basement level. The steel door had been bolted, leaving him hopelessly penned in. The only movable objects in the room were the wooden bed, the thin mattress, and the glaring light bulb. Otherwise the cell provided nothing usable.

An hour after Abdullah and Ramón left, two others that Casius assumed must be guards descended on the elevator and took up positions in the hall—one opposite his cell and one next to the door.

He knew he had very little time. As long as Abdullah thought he worked for the CIA, the Arab might hold him alive, hoping for leverage. But the minute the man learned that he was on the run from the CIA, Abdullah would kill him. And Casius doubted the CIA would have any problem forwarding the truth.

Working very quietly, Casius removed the mattress from the bed and propped the wooden frame on its end, directly under the light, so that anyone entering the room would see only the frame at first look. He then ripped strips of cloth from the mattress and mounted the frame under the light. He unscrewed the white-hot bulb until the light blinked off and let it cool before removing it completely.

Working by feel in the darkness, Casius wrapped the bulb in the cloth strips and then squeezed the glass in his palm. It imploded with a snap, slicing into his forefinger. He bit his tongue and carefully removed the cloth, taking the broken glass with it. He felt for the tungsten wire. It remained intact. Good.

Casius reached for the ceiling, found the light fixture, and guided the bulb into its socket. The tungsten wire glowed a dull red without the vacuum.

He tore another strip from the mattress and wound it around his bleeding forefinger. He took a deep breath and mounted the frame again. He grabbed a handful of stuffing from the mattress and lifted it to the glowing wire. The dry material smoldered for only a moment before catching fire.

Casius dropped to the concrete, shoved the flaming material into the mattress, and set it against the far wall. He retreated to the wall behind the door and watched the fire grow until the room blazed orange. Waiting until the last possible moment, he drew a last deep breath of clean air from the room and waited.

So now he would either live or die, he thought. If the guards did not respond, the smoke would suffocate him. His heart began to pound like a piston in a freightliner. His temples throbbed and he squelched the fleeting temptation to run over to the mattress and extinguish the deadly flame.

Within seconds the room billowed with thick smoke. The guard's alarm came then, when the gray clouds seeped past the door. It took them another full minute to decide on a course of action, most of it spent calling to him for a response. When none came, a muffled voice argued that the prisoner must be dead and they would be too if Ramón thought they had allowed it.

The keys scraped against the metal lock and the door swung open, but Casius remained crouched behind, his lungs now bursting in his chest. The guards called into the smoke for a full thirty seconds before deciding to enter.

Casius sprang then, with every remaining ounce of strength. He crashed into the door, slamming the first guard against the doorframe and shoved his palm up under the man's jaw, snapping his head back into the wall. The guard crumpled to the ground. Casius snatched his rifle from his limp hands, slid behind the wall, and gasped for breath. Smoke filled his lungs with the draw, but he bit against a cough.

Gunfire thundered in the hall. Holes punched through the wall above him. Casius shoved the AK-47 around the corner and shot off six scattered rounds. The gunfire ceased. Casius slid into the doorway on one knee, lifted the rifle to his shoulder, and put a bullet through the other guard's forehead, smashing him to the ground with a single shot.

Adrenaline throbbed through his veins. He coughed hard now, bent over, ridding his lungs of the smoke. He scanned the hall, saw there were four other doors, and then ran for the steel elevator at the end.

It took him five seconds to understand that the car would go nowhere without a key. The other doors then—and quickly. An alarm had been raised.

Casius ran to the first door, found it locked, and fired a slug through its lock. He kicked it in, hit a light switch, and stepped into the room under stuttering fluorescent tubes. The room lay bare except for a single table and three chairs. Charts lined the walls. There was no exit from here.

Blueprints, darkening purple with age, were taped to the wall on his left. The architectural drawing nearest him showed a cross section of the black cliffs. And nestled in the hill between the plantation and the cliffs, a cross section of a three-story structure. This structure. Casius shifted his eyes to another blueprint, next to the first. This one showed an expanded view of the underground construction, complete with an elevator at one end.

No less than twenty drawings lined the walls, detailing the complex. Long blue lines shaped a passage that ran through the mountain. Red-dotted rectangles showed the tunnel's purpose. Cocaine was refined in a large plant on the second floor and then loaded into logs that were shot through the mountain into the Orinoco River and carried out to sea.

Casius left the room and closed the door.

The next door opened easily with a turn of its knob and revealed a utility closet. He snatched a machete from the corner and ran back to the elevator.

Surprisingly, the red indicator still had not lit, which caused him pause. Either they hadn't bothered to install any alarms in the lower level—figuring that any threats would come from above—or they waited for him, knowing that the elevator was the only way out.

But they were wrong.

With the *clank* of steel against steel, Casius shoved the blade between the doors and leaned into the machete. The doors resisted for a moment and then yielded. He surveyed an empty shaft that fell to another basement level and rose to the bottom of the car, one story above.

He had to find the woman. Sherry. It was ironic—he had stalked a terrorist like Abdullah for years and he had planned for the fall of the CIA nearly as long. And yet here was a woman and he knew he had to save her. She was somehow different.

Or was she?

The black fog lapped at his mind.

He grunted and dropped down to the bottom of the shaft. He pried open the dormant elevator door and entered a dark, damp hallway formed in concrete, empty except for a single doorway on the left. Like a root cellar, although in the jungle there was no need for a root cellar.

A faint cry echoed above him, far away. An alarm! His heart bolted and he leapt into the hallway.

A picture of Sherry filled his mind—her gentle features, her bright eyes, her curved lips. She was the antithesis of everything he had lived for. He was driven by death, she by . . . what? Love?

The door was concrete and he found it bolted. But no lock. He jerked the bolt out and shoved the slab. It grated open to a pitch-black room.

His breathing echoed back at him from the emptiness.

"Sherry?"

Nothing.

Casius spun around. He had to get out before the place swarmed with Abdullah's men. He'd taken a step back toward the elevator shaft when he heard a groan behind him.

"Hel . . . hello?"

Casius whirled around. A strange rush surged through his veins.

"Sherry?" His heart was hammering and it wasn't from fear.

"Casius?"

SHERRY SAW the silhouette standing in the open doorway like a gunslinger and she wondered what Shannon was doing in her dream. Shannon was dead, of course. Or maybe it was her captor, the terrorist with the bomb, if the vision of the mushroom was right. Abdullah. He'd visited her a few hours ago—now he'd come back.

She felt sluggish and she knew that she was waking. The figure turned to leave and it struck her that maybe this *was* someone real.

"Hello?"

The figure spun. Was it Casius? Had Casius come to save her? She climbed out of her dead sleep.

"Sherry?"

It *was* Casius!

"Casius?"

She pushed herself up and Casius swept in. He dropped to one knee and placed an arm under her back. He lifted her up like a rag doll and ducked out of the cell.

He smelled like sweat, which was no surprise—he was wet with it. His face was still green from the paint.

"Where's the priest?" he asked quietly.

He was still holding her. "I don't know. What happened?"

It must have occurred to him that he was holding her because he dropped his left arm and let her stand on her own.

"Come on. We don't have much time."

Casius ran for a set of steel doors at the end of the hall and pressed his ear against them. It was an elevator, resting closed.

He stepped back and lifted the machete. "It's clear. Stand back," he said in a hushed voice.

The assassin jammed the blade into the crack and pried the doors open. A cable ran up the dark elevator shaft. He wedged the machete kitty-corner in the doors and stepped into the shaft. Without speaking to her, he hauled himself up the cable, right past the doors where Sherry peered in with wide eyes.

"Where are you going?" she asked. Sherry looked up and saw the bottom of the car twenty feet higher. Casius was now parallel to a large opening on the opposite side of the shaft, ten feet up. He swung into the causeway without answering her, but she had her answer already. He dropped to his belly and reached down the shaft for her.

She edged forward and, clasping the pried elevator door with her left hand, she stretched her right hand up for his arm, wondering if she had the strength to hang on.

But he seized her wrist like an iron claw and the question fell away. She gripped nothing but thin air. He literally snatched her from her feet and hauled her up to the opening. She threw her leg over the lip and rolled into him.

He repeated the process, taking them another floor higher, just below the elevator itself. And then they were standing and scanning the tunnel they had entered.

A long line of lights hung from an earthen ceiling stretching both ways several hundred feet, maybe longer. To their right the tunnel ended in a glowing light; to their left the tunnel dimmed to darkness. An idle conveyor belt ran waist high the length of the passage.

A shout suddenly echoed down the tunnel and the sound of boots thudding onto packed earth reverberated past them. Casius grabbed her wrist and pulled her into a stumbling run toward the dark end of the tunnel. She pulled her hand free and tore after him, pumping her fists in panic.

"The priest!" she panted.

"Just run!" he said.

Cries of alarm suddenly filled the air. A shot crashed around her ears. Casius slid to a stop and Sherry almost ran through him. She threw her arms up and felt her palms collide with his wet back. Her hands slipped to either side and she smacked into his wet flesh. But neither seemed to notice.

They had reached a steel platform, she saw, and Casius had managed to unlatch its gate. He leapt over the threshold and yanked her through. When he punched something on the wall, the whole contraption trembled to life and began to rise. They were on a freight elevator of some kind. Flashes of fire erupted down the tunnel, chased by shouts of anger. Sherry instinctively crouched.

Then they were past the earth ceiling and rising through a vertical shaft lit by a string of bulbs along one wall.

Casius was madly searching the floor with wide eyes. Something about his jerking movements sent a chill down Sherry's spine. He was afraid, she thought. And not just afraid of the guns below. He knew something she did not, and it was sending him scampering about in fits.

She grabbed the rail and watched him, too stunned to ask what he was doing. He rounded the floor twice and evidently found nothing, because he ended with wide eyes raised to her.

He glanced above and she followed his gaze. A dark hole yawned ten feet higher. And above it—dirt. The end.

"Take your shirt off!" he snapped frantically.

"Wha . . . ! Take my what?"

"Quick! If you want to live through this, take your shirt off. Now!"

Sherry clawed at the T-shirt and pulled it over her head. She wore only a sports bra. Casius snatched the shirt before it had cleared her head and pulled it over his own. He'd lost his mind, she thought.

"You're gonna have to trust me. Okay?" Her shirt barely stretched over his chest, and one shoulder ripped at its seam. He had lost his mind.

"We're going for a ride. You just let go and let me carry you. Understand?"

She didn't answer. What could he possibly . . . ?

"You understand?" His face was white.

"Yes."

And then the gears ground to a halt and the floor began to tilt toward a hole waiting like an open mouth. It was a steel tube maybe three feet in diameter, disappearing into blackness.

Casius swung an arm around her waist and threw himself to the floor, pulling her with him so that she lay on top of him, faceup. Their heads were pointed into the gaping steel tube. He was taking her into the shaft, headfirst!

Sherry closed her eyes and began to whimper then. "Please, please, please, God." The smacking of steel colliding with steel suddenly crashed in her ears. Bullets! Like heavy hail on a tin roof. The men below were firing their guns up the elevator shaft and their bullets were slamming into the steel floor. She clenched her eyes and began to scream.

And then they were falling.

It was why he'd searched the floor frantically, she realized. It was why he insisted on taking her shirt when he'd found nothing else. Because his back was sliding against steel. She didn't know how long this ride would last or where it would take them, but she imagined that her thin cotton shirt was already giving way. His skin would be next.

Like breakaway tobogganers, they gained speed. Sherry pried her eyes open and lifted her head. Far away now, the dwindling entrance glowed between her jerking feet. Below her, the man suddenly tensed and squeezed her like a vise. His arms were wrapped around her midsection, coiled like a boa constrictor.

He grunted and she knew the T-shirt had given way. His forearms wound tight, forcing the air from her lungs. She grabbed at them in panic—but to no avail. And then he was screaming and white-hot terror streaked up her spine. She opened her mouth, wanting to join him. But she had no wind for a scream.

He went suddenly limp; his scream fell to a soft groan and she knew he'd lost consciousness. She sucked a lungful of air and then another. Casius's arms bounced limp. She imagined a long smear of blood trailing them. Oh, God, please!

And then the mountain spit them out, like discarded sewage. Sherry heard the rushing water below them and it occurred to her that they were headed for a river. And under her, Casius was unconscious. She instinctively reached for the sky with both arms. Her scream echoed off the towering canyon walls above.

Cold water engulfed her and sucked the breath from her lungs as if it were a vacuum. Sound fell to murmuring gurgles and she clenched her eyes tight. *Oh, God, help me. I'm going to die!* She instinctively clutched the assassin's arm.

He came to life then, shocked by the water, disoriented and flailing like a drowning man. Sherry opened her eyes and struck for the lighter shade of brown, hoping she would find the surface there. She tugged at his arm once and then released him, hoping he would find his own way. Her lungs were caving in.

She nearly inhaled water before her head cleared the surface. But she held on and gasped desperately before her bottom teeth broke water. Casius shot through the surface next to her and she felt a rush of relief wash over her.

Sherry looked about, still pulling hard at the air. They were in a fast-flowing river, deep and smooth where they were, and crashing over rocks on the far side. She felt a hand grip her shoulder and propel her toward the nearest bank. They landed on a sand bar two hundred meters downriver, like two grounded porpoises, belly down, heaving on the shore. Sherry flopped her head to one side, and she saw Casius with his face in the mud. His shoulder blades oozed red through her T-shirt and her heart rose to her throat.

She tried to go to him, but a black cloud settled over her eyes. *God please,* she thought. *Please.* Then the black cloud swallowed her.

CHAPTER THIRTY

ABDULLAH BOLTED from his chair, sending it clattering to the wall. Heat rose through his chest in one suffocating wave, and he felt his face flush red.

"Both? Impossible!" How could they escape? Even if the agent had found another way out of his cell, the lower level was sealed!

Ramón shook his head. A dark ring of sweat soaked into his black patch. His voice quivered when he spoke. "They're gone. The priest is still in his cell."

Abdullah's head spun. "I thought I told you to kill them!"

"Yes. I was going to. But considering—"

"This changes everything. The Americans will try to destroy us now."

"But what about our agreement with them? How can they destroy us with the agreement?"

"The *agreement*, as you call it, is worthless now. They've never known the extent of our operation, you idiot. Now they will." He hesitated and turned his back. "They will turn on us. It's their nature."

Abdullah suddenly slammed his fist on his desk and clenched his teeth against the pain that shot up his arm. Ramón stood still and stared past him. Abdullah closed his eyes and bowed his head into his other hand, gripping his temples. A haze seemed to be drifting over his mind. *There now, there now, my friend. Think.*

For a moment Abdullah thought he might actually burst out in tears, right there in front of the Hispanic fool. He took a deep breath and cocked his head to the ceiling, keeping his eyes closed.

There, there. He wagged his head, as if to crack it. *It is nothing more than a chess match. I've made a move and now they have made a move.* He ground his teeth.

A CIA agent has penetrated my operation and escaped to tell. The same agent who killed my brother.

Heat flared up his neck again and he shook his head against it, pursing his lips and breathing hard through his nostrils.

It had been a mistake not to kill the man immediately. Maybe the fall had killed them.

"Sir?" He heard the voice, knew it was Ramón's, but chose to ignore it. He was thinking. *There, there. Think.*

An image of a thousand marching boys, all under the age of thirteen, suddenly popped to mind. Good Muslim boys on the Iraqi border, chanting a song of worship, dressed in colors. Going to meet Allah. He'd watched the scene through field glasses fifteen years earlier with a lump the size of a boulder lodged in his throat. The mines began erupting like fireworks, *pop! pop!* and the children's frail brown bodies began flipping like sprung mousetraps. And the rest walked on, marching into the arms of death. He remembered thinking then that this was the sole fault of the West. The West had armed the Iraqis. The West had spawned infidelity, so that when he saw an example of purity, such as these young boys marching to Allah, he cringed instead of leaping for joy.

So then, think. Ramón was calling him again. "Sir."

Shut up, Ramón. Can't you see that I am thinking? He thought it, maybe said it. He wasn't sure. Ramón was saying something about the agent not knowing about the bombs. *Yes? Says who? Says you, Ramón? You're a blind fool.*

A buzz droned above him and he opened his eyes. The black bugs in the corner were crawling over each other in a writhing mass. One small firecracker in that ball would decorate the wall nicely. He dropped his head to Ramón. The fool *was* actually saying something.

Abdullah cut him off midsentence. "Ship the bombs immediately." Ramón's mouth hung open slightly, but he didn't respond. His good eye was round like a saucer.

Abdullah stepped forward, a quiver in his bones. The agent's escape could well be the hand of Allah forcing him forward. If Jamal was coming, the bombs would be gone when he got here. It would be he, not Jamal, who ended this game.

"Tonight, Ramón. Do you understand? I want both bombs sent tonight. Pack them in the logs as if they were drugs. And do it yourself—no one else can know of their existence. Are you hearing me?"

Ramón nodded. A trail of sweat now split his eye patch and hung off the corner of his lip.

Abdullah continued, noting that he would have to watch the man. He snatched a pointer and stepped up to a dirtied map of the country and the surrounding seas. His voice came ragged.

"There will be three ships. They will pick up the logs tonight, just outside the delta." Abdullah followed the map with the pointer as he talked, but it only ran in jagged circles from his taut nerves and he dropped it to his side. "The fastest of the three ships will carry the larger device to our drop point at Annapolis near Washington, D.C. The second will take the inoperable device to the lumberyards in Miami, just like any other shipment of cocaine." He paused, still breathing heavy. "The freightliner will carry the smaller device to a new drop point there"—he stabbed with the pointer again—"near Savannah, Georgia." He turned to face Ramón.

"Tell the captains of these vessels that it is an experimental shipment and that they will be paid double the normal rates. No, tell them they will be paid ten times the normal rate. The shipments must arrive at the destinations as planned, before the Americans have a chance to react to the news they will receive from this agent."

"Yes, sir. And the priest?"

"Keep him alive. A hostage could be useful now." He grinned. "As for the agent, we will use him as our demand instead of the release of prisoners as Jamal planned. Either way the bombs will go off, but perhaps they will deliver this animal to us." Abdullah felt a calm settle over him.

"I want the logs in the river by nightfall," he said. He suddenly felt strangely euphoric. And if Jamal appeared before then? Then he would kill Jamal.

Ramón still stood, watching him. Abdullah sat and looked at him. "You have something to say, Ramón? Do you think we have lived in this hellhole for nothing?" Abdullah smiled.

For a brief moment he pitied the man standing before him as if he were a part of something important. In the end he, too, would die.

"Do not disappoint me. You are dismissed."

"Yes, sir," Ramón said. He spun on his heels and strode from the room.

SHERRY AWOKE on the riverbank with the vision once again stinging her mind. Casius glanced up at her from a rock where he worked over a palm leaf, twisting a root. He motioned beside her. "Your shirt's right there." Two holes had been worn through to his shoulder blades. She pulled it on and walked over to him.

"That stuff on your face doesn't come off very easily," she said, noting the camo paint had survived the river.

"Waterproof."

She looked at a small puddle of salve he'd forced from the root onto the palm leaf.

"And what is that?"

"It's a natural antibiotic," Casius said.

She winced, remembering the slide. "For your back?"

He nodded.

"Can I see?"

He twisted his back to her. His shoulder blades were worn to glistening red flesh.

"Here." He handed the palm leaf back to her. "This will help. I've seen this stuff work miracles."

She took the palm. "Just wipe it on?"

"You're the doctor. It has a mild antiseptic in it as well. It'll help with the pain."

He flinched when she touched the seared flesh. Sherry smeared it on, tentative at first, but then using the whole palm leaf as a brush. He groaned once, and she let up with an apology. A sense of déjà vu hit her like a sledge when he winced, and for a moment she felt as though she were in a hospital working with a patient in the emergency ward—not here in the jungle bent over the assassin.

But then she was seeing things strangely these days. *Everything* was one big déjà vu. Casius just fell into the pot with the rest.

They left the river with Casius insisting they get to a town as soon as possible. He had to get her to safety and return for the priest, he told her. He took to the jungle as if he knew exactly where they were. A hundred questions burned through her mind then.

They had just escaped some terrorist who planned to do something with a bomb, if she understood the vision now. She was supposed to *die* for this? No, that was only Father Petrus's talk.

An image of a nuclear weapon detonating filled her mind and suddenly she wanted to tell Casius everything. She had to—even if there was only the smallest chance of it all being true.

She swallowed at her dry mouth and held her tongue. What if he was part of this? But of course, he *was* part of this. So then, which side was he on?

They walked for a long time, in a dumb silence. When they did talk, it was her doing. She asked small questions, mostly, pulling short but polite answers out of him. Answers that seemed pointless.

"So you work for the CIA, right?" she finally asked.

"Yes."

"And you said that they were after you? Or are you after Abdullah?"

He glanced at her. "Abdullah?"

"Back at the compound. I could be wrong, but I think he's a terrorist. He's got a bomb, I think."

Casius walked on, mumbling something about everyone having a bomb.

He led her to a small village while the sun still stood overhead. Despite the availability of phones in the town, he insisted that she not contact anyone yet. He would call and alert the right people to Abdullah's operation, he said.

He made his call and then convinced a fisherman to lend them a small pontoon boat. They were soon rushing downriver, accompanied by a whining twenty-horse outboard and a backdrop of birds squawking in the treetops.

"Thank you for what you did back there," Sherry said, breaking a long stretch of silence. "I guess I owe my life to you."

Casius glanced at her and shrugged. He stared off to the jungle. "So what makes you think this Abdullah character has a bomb?"

She considered the question for a moment and decided she should tell him. "Do you believe in visions?" she asked.

He looked at her without responding.

"I mean supernatural visions. From God," she said.

"We've been over this. Man is God. How can I believe in visions from man?"

"On the contrary, God is Creator of man. He also is known to give visions." It sounded stupid—something she was just really believing for the first time herself. She could almost hear him mocking now. *Sure, honey. God speaks to me too. All the time. He told me just this morning that I really need to floss more regularly.*

She plunged ahead anyway. "That's how I know Abdullah has a bomb."

"You saw that in a vision?" He spoke in a voice that might as well have said, *Yeah right, lady.*

"How else?" she said.

He shrugged. "You saw something at their compound and pieced it together."

"Maybe brilliance isn't something that comes with seven years of higher education. But then neither is stupidity. If I say I had a vision, I had a vision."

He blinked and turned his head downriver.

"I had a vision about a man planting something in the sand that killed thousands of people. That's the reason I'm here in this jungle instead of back in Denver. The only reason." She swallowed and pressed on, hot in the neck now. "Did you know that building is built on an old mission site? Missionaries used to live there."

She waited for a response. She didn't get one.

"If there is a bomb . . . I mean like a nuclear bomb, it would make sense that he's planning on using it against the United States, right? You think that's possible?"

Casius turned and studied her for a long moment. "No," he said. "The facility is a cocaine processing plant. He's a drug runner. I think nuclear weapons are a bit beyond his scope."

"You may be a pretty resourceful killer, but you're not listening to me, are you? I saw this man in my dreams and now I've met him personally. That means nothing to you?"

"You can't actually expect me to believe you were drawn to the jungle to save mankind from some diabolical plot to detonate a nuclear weapon on U.S. soil." He looked back at her and forced a smile. "You don't find that just a bit fantastic?"

"Yes," Sherry said. "I do. But it doesn't change the fact that every time I close these eyes this Arab keeps popping back onto the stage and planting his bomb."

"Well, I'll tell you what. As it turns out, I'm going back into that jungle to kill that Arab of yours. Maybe that will stop him from popping into your mind."

"That's insane. You'll never make it."

"Isn't that what you want? To stop him?"

How could he go back in there knowing they would be waiting for him? Could God use an assassin? No, she didn't think so. Then she knew what she had to do and she said it without thinking.

"You have to get Father Petrus out. I have to go with you."

"That's out of the question."

"Father Petrus—"

"I'll get the priest. But you're not coming."

"It's me, not you who—" Sherry pulled up short, realizing how stupid it was all sounding.

"Who has been guided by visions?" he finished for her. "Trust me, I'm guided by my own reasons. They would make your head spin."

"Killing never solved anything," she said. "My parents were killed by men like you."

The revelation took the wind out of him. It was fifteen minutes of silence before they spoke again.

"I'm sorry about your parents," he said.

"It's okay."

It was the way that he said, "I'm sorry," that made her think a good man might be hiding under that brutal skin. A lump came to her throat and she wasn't sure why.

CHAPTER THIRTY-ONE

CIA DIRECTOR Torrey Friberg stood in the east wing of the White House, staring out the window at the black D.C. sky. It was a dark day and he knew, without a question, that it would only get darker. Twenty-two years in the service of this country, and now it all threatened to blow up in his face. All on the account of one agent.

He turned away from the window and glanced at his watch. In less than five minutes they would brief the president. It was insane. Less than a week ago it had been business as usual. Now, because of one man, his career teetered on the edge of disaster.

He glanced over at Mark Ingersol, sitting with crossed legs. The man had pretty much figured things out, he assumed. With David Lunow's help he could hardly not. But his new appointment to Special Operations would ensure that he keep this one to himself—he had too much to lose.

The door suddenly banged open and the national security advisor, Robert Masters, walked into the room with Myles Bancroft, director of Homeland Security. Bancroft held the door for the president, who walked in ahead of two aides.

Friberg stepped past Ingersol and extended his hand to the president, who took it cordially but without greeting. His gray eyes didn't sparkle as they did for the cameras. They peered past a sharp nose—all business today. He swept a hand through his graying hair.

The president seated himself at the head of the oval table and they followed suit. "Okay, gentlemen, let's skip the formalities. Tell me what's going on."

Friberg cleared his throat. "Well, sir, it appears that we have another threat on our hands. This one's a little different. Two hours ago—"

"I know about the threat we received," the president interrupted. "And I wouldn't be here if I didn't think it held some water. The question is how much water."

Friberg hesitated and glanced at Bancroft. The president caught the glance. "What can you tell me about this, Myles?"

Bancroft sat forward in his seat and placed his arms on the table. "The message we received two hours ago was from a group claiming to be the Brotherhood, which, as I'm sure you know, is a terrorist organization. They originate out of Iran, but they've been largely inactive over the past few years—since our crackdown on Afghanistan. They're a splinter group outside Al qaeda gone underground. They're reportedly giving us seventy-two hours to deliver a recently defected agent to the Hotel Melia Caribe in Carabelleda, Venezuela. If within seventy-two hours the agent isn't delivered, then the group threatens to detonate a nuclear device that it claims to have hidden in the country."

The president waited for more, but none came. "Is this a real threat?"

Friberg answered, "We have no evidence whatsoever of any nuclear activity in the region. We've handled dozens of threats, which, to use your words, hold more water than this one. The chances that the Brotherhood has anything resembling a bomb is highly unlikely. And if they did, a threat like this would make no sense."

The president turned to Bancroft. "Myles?"

"Frankly, I agree. My guess is that they don't have it, but I'm basing that on nothing more than my gut. Nonproliferation has had nuclear components under the highest scrutiny since the Gulf War. Despite all the experts who insist suitcase bombs are available on any black market street corner, assembling all the components to actually build a bomb is, as you know, nearly impossible. I can't see it, especially not in South America."

"But it still involves a weapon of mass destruction," the president said. "We treat them all the same. What were the chances of Iraq getting the bomb? Tell me about the man who issued the threat. This Abdullah Amir."

Friberg answered, "We have no idea how Abdullah Amir came to be in South America, or whether in fact he *is* in South America."

The president just looked at him.

"It's more likely that the threat came from one of the drug cartels in the region." Friberg made a decision then, hoping desperately that Ingersol would follow his lead. Sweat wet his brow and he took a deliberate breath.

"We recently sent an agent operating under the name Casius into the jungle to take out a powerful drug cartel in the region. A black operation. Our information is a bit sketchy, but we believe that the agent attempted an assassination and failed. We believe the cartel is responding with this threat. But it's important to remember what Bancroft said, sir. It's highly improbable that the cartel has anything resembling a bomb at their disposal."

"But it is possible."

Friberg nodded. "Anything is possible."

"So, what you're saying is that you initiated black operations against a drug cartel and your guy, this Casius, missed his target. So now the cartel is threatening to blow up the country?"

Friberg glanced at Ingersol and caught the glint in his eye. "Isn't that pretty much your assessment, Mark?" His nerves ran taut. Ingersol's next few words would cast his position. Not to mention Friberg's future.

Ingersol nodded. "Basically, yes."

"And this Brotherhood threat is just to throw us off? We're not dealing with Islamic militants at all but some drug runners?"

"That's our assessment," Ingersol answered.

The president looked at his security advisor, Masters. "Make sense to you, Robert?"

"Could be." He looked at Friberg. "DEA involved in this?"

"No."

"If this agent of yours failed in his assassination attempt, why is the cartel so uptight? Seems like an unusual reaction, doesn't it?"

Friberg had to get them off this analysis until he and Ingersol had time to talk. "Based on our information, which I should reiterate is still sketchy, Casius took out some innocents in his attempt. He has a history of high collateral damage."

Friberg threw the lies out, knowing he had now committed himself to a far more involved cover-up than he'd imagined. His mind was already isolating the potential leaks. David Lunow topped the list of potential snitches. He would have to be silenced.

And as for the Rangers, they were puppets without political agendas—even if they stumbled into something down there, they wouldn't talk. Mark Ingersol had just committed himself to going along for the ride. It could be done. It had to be done—as soon as this bomb foolishness passed.

It dawned on Friberg that the other three were staring at him. "I really think it's as simple as that, sir. They know how excited we get over things like nuclear threats. They're playing us."

"Let's hope you're right. In the meantime, we treat this thing like any other threat of terror. So let's hear your recommendations."

Friberg took a deep breath. "We deliver Casius and defuse the demand."

"Beyond that. Myles?"

"We activate full Homeland Security measures and put all law enforcement on alert. And we look for a device, particularly in the path of recognized drug routes. Despite the unlikelihood of there actually being a bomb, we follow full protocol."

Friberg wanted to get past this foolishness. Seventy-two hours would come and go and there would be no bomb. He'd seen it a hundred times, and each time they'd had to run through this nonsense. A year ago in the wake of the big attack it had been one thing. But getting all worked up every time some nut yelled *Boo* was getting old.

Myles Bancroft continued, "We've already made a preliminary search plan that starts with the southeast coast and the West Coast and expands to all major shipping points in the country. The Coast Guard will bear the heaviest burden. If the cartel did manage to land a bomb in our borders, it was most probably through a seaport."

The president frowned and shook his head. "It's like trying to find a needle in a haystack. Let's pray to God we never actually have to face a real nuclear bomb."

"No system's perfect," Masters said.

"And if they have managed to get a device through, you honestly think we have a chance of finding it?" the president asked, turning back to the director of the CIA.

"Personally?" Friberg asked.

The president nodded.

"Personally, sir, I don't think we have a bomb to find. But if there is a bomb, finding it in seventy-two hours will be extremely difficult. Every bill of lading identifying merchandise which entered our country from South America during the past three months will be reviewed, and those that indicate merchandise which could possibly harbor a bomb will be traced. Merchandise will be tracked to its final destination and searched. It can be done, but not in seventy-two hours. That's why we start with southeastern and western seaports."

"Why not just take the cartel out?" Masters asked.

Friberg nodded. "We're also recommending positioning to move on the cartel's base of operations. But as you say, if the threat is legitimate, all it would take is a flip of a switch somewhere and we could have a catastrophe on our hands. You bomb them, and you'd better be sure that first salvo will kill them or they might twitch their finger and detonate. You don't play strongman with someone who has a nuclear weapon hidden somewhere."

"No? And how do you play?"

He paused. "Never been there."

The president stared at a window across the room. "Then let's hope we aren't there now."

No one spoke. Finally the president stood from the table. "Issue the appropriate orders and have them on my desk right away. You'd better be right about this, Friberg." The president turned and walked toward the door.

"This is only a threat. We *have* been here before, sir," Friberg said.

"Keep this sealed. No press. No leaks," the president said. "God knows the last thing we need is media involvement."

He turned and left the room, and Friberg released a long, slow breath.

CHAPTER THIRTY-TWO

SHERRY FOLLOWED Casius up a long flight of stairs behind the hotel he'd taken earlier on a weekly basis. She was certain the assassin's mind had left him during the trip.

On the river they had talked only once about their captivity. A riveting conversation in which he mostly stared off to the passing jungle, grunting short replies. He had shut her out. She had once again become baggage.

Now his eyes remained open only as a matter of courtesy to his brain, which was thoroughly engrossed with what he would do next. And what he would do was return and kill Abdullah. Destroy the compound and slit Abdullah's throat. When she asked him why, he had simply drilled her with those dark eyes and told her the man was a drug runner. But the explanation hardly made sense.

She asked him again what he thought she should do if there actually was a nuclear weapon in the jungle. But he dismissed the notion outright, so strongly that she began to question her own memory of the vision.

In the end it all came down to their beliefs. He'd come to the jungle to kill. Nothing more complicated than that. Just kill. Like the skull-man in her visions, like a demoniac. She, on the other hand, had come to die—if not literally, as Father Teuwen seemed to suggest, then to die to her past. To find life through a symbolic death of some kind. Maybe she had found it already in the prison back there. A reliving of her death as a child.

They talked about the jungle, finally. It seemed like a common bridge that did not lead to some allusion to life or death. Casius seemed more knowledgeable about the local jungle than anyone she could imagine. If she didn't know better, she might assume the man had grown up here, in this jungle instead of the ones north by Caracas.

For a terrifying moment she even imagined that if Shannon had lived, he might have become a man like this—tall, rugged, and handsome. Shannon would be a gentler, kinder man, of course. A lover, not a killer. She shoved the comparison from her mind.

At some point floating over the brown waters, she had finally decided that he struck a chord of familiarity with her because he was meant to play this part in her mission. He, too, had been drawn by God and the fact resonated with her like a memory.

Maybe he had been right in saying their worlds were not so far apart. Like heaven and hell kissing up against each other, but separated by some impenetrable steel plate. Maybe that explained the growing ache in her heart as they approached the sleepy town of Soledad in the afternoon.

They walked into a grungy room on the third floor. He shut the door.

"This is your room?" she asked, looking about the dimly lit hotel pad. Other than a queen bed and a single dresser, the room was bare. Soledad had a dozen hotels with far better accommodations than this, but at least the dresser had a mirror.

"It's not exactly the Hilton, but it has a bed," he said, fumbling for something in the bathroom. "I've paid through tonight. You probably want to find something a little cleaner."

Casius stepped out of the bathroom and tossed two well-stuffed money belts onto the bed. Evidently killing paid well. He dropped to his knees, pulled some folded clothes and a waist pouch hidden under the bed, and tossed them next to the money belts.

"Travel light, do we?" Sherry asked, grinning at the small pile of possessions.

The assassin looked at her without smiling. "I'm not exactly on a vacation."

"I could use some clean clothes and a shower," Sherry said.

Casius motioned to the pile of clothes on the bed. "You'll find those a bit large, but they'll do until we can get some clothes from the market. Go ahead, clean up. The water's hot and there are towels in the bathroom."

Sherry nodded and took the clothes. A bit big indeed. She would float in his clothes. On the other hand, the white T-shirt hanging from her own body was literally falling apart. Her denim shorts had survived in remarkable condition, considering the jungle. A good wash and they would do. She tossed his pants back onto the bed and turned, holding his white cotton shirt.

"Thank you," she said and stepped into the bathroom.

Sherry took a long shower, relishing the steaming water, scrubbing the dirt from her pores. She washed and wrung out the jeans, donned his shirt, and ran her fingers through her hair. Not exactly fit for a prom, but at least she was clean. She debated removing her colored contacts. They normally stayed in place for a month at a time, but the journey through the jungle had worn on her eyes and she decided to remove them despite the questions a sudden change in eye color might draw from the man.

"Thank God for hot water," she said, stepping from the bathroom.

Casius kneeled at the dresser, writing on a tablet. "Good," he said without looking up. His mind was obviously buried in that tablet. She plopped onto the bed and lay back, closing her eyes.

"I'm going to shower," he said, and when she looked up, he was already gone.

Sherry lay back down and rested for a while. At the moment the man planting his little silver sphere in the sand seemed far away. Like a dream fogged by reality.

What was she to do now? Contact the authorities with her version of what had happened? Tell them that she had been captured by a *terrorist* holed up in the jungle? *And there's more*, she'd say.

Really? And what would that be, miss?

He's got a nuclear bomb that he's going to blow up in the United States, she'd say.

A nuclear bomb, you say? Oh, heavens! We'll activate the bat-signal right quick, miss. What did you say your address was?

She rolled to her side and groaned. Maybe she had read too much into the dream. Other than being taken hostage for a day, nothing concrete had happened to lead her to the conclusion that anything remotely similar to a bomb was involved. Only her dream. And really, it could mean that her life was about to blow up, rather than a real bomb.

Get a grip, Sherry.

Father Teuwen's face filled her mind. He was still back there. She swallowed. That had been real. The father's words came to her. *Think of yourself as a vessel. A cup. Do not try to guess what the Master will pour into you before he pours,* he had said. *Your life of torment has left you soft, like a sponge for his words.*

But you have poured, Father. Every night you pour, filling me with this vision.

Are you ready to die, Sherry?

Sherry sat upright on the bed, half expecting to see Father Teuwen standing there. But the room was empty. The sound of splashing water ceased—Casius was finishing his shower.

Helen had said she was gifted. That she played some part in God's plan. Like a piece in some cosmic chess match. Heavens, she felt no more like a knight or a bishop than she felt like Father Teuwen's sponge.

She pushed herself from the bed and walked to the dresser. Her image stared back from the mirror. She scratched at her hair, trying to make some order out of it. Her eyes stared back at her, bright blue again. It struck her that with wet hair she looked like her old self—like Tanya. The door to the bathroom opened and she looked up to the mirror, her hair forgotten. In the reflection, the bathroom door opened and Casius stepped out.

Only it wasn't Casius she was seeing. It was a blond-haired man, still shirtless, still wearing the black shorts, but clean.

Something clicked in her memory then—something painful and buried deep. A déjà vu in three dimensions that made her blink. Sherry whirled around. He stood, ruffling his hair.

He saw her stricken face and froze.

"What?" he said. "What's wrong?" He looked quickly around the room, saw no danger, and returned his questioning eyes to her.

Sherry looked from his hair to his face, cleaned of the camo paint for the first time. His eyes were green. Her knees began to quake. Her throat froze shut, and she felt suddenly dizzy. His likeness crashed in her mind like a ten-ton boulder.

But it was an impossibility and her mind refused to wrap itself around this image. A thousand pictures from her early years streaked across her mind's eye. Her Shannon grinning above the falls; her Shannon shooting from beneath the surface to smother her with kisses; her Shannon popping a shot off at that rooster above the shed and then turning to her with a sparkle in his eye.

A reincarnation of that image stood before her now. Taller, broader, older, but otherwise the same.

She found her voice. "Shannon?"

SHANNON STOOD staring at Sherry. Her mouth gaped as if she were looking at a ghost. And he had already opened his mouth to tell her to get a grip when he saw the change in her eyes. They were blue. They were not hazel.

The words stuck in his throat. He could not place the significance of the change in her eye color, but the detail spun crazily through his mind. She was now clearly a dead ringer for someone he knew. Problem was, his mind had misplaced the identity. For three days her image had whispered to him; now it had tired of its suggestions and it began to wail. *You know this person! You really do know her!* Another assassin? CIA? The warning bells blared through his skull.

Then she called him. "Shannon?" she said. As if it was a question.

The way she said his name, "Shannon," threw a face up in his mind. It was Tanya's face. His legs went weak. But it had to be the wrong face, because this could not be Tanya. Tanya was dead.

She said it again. "Shannon?"

Heat surged up his neck and burned at his ears. He dropped his hand and swallowed, feeling that if he did not sit, he might fall. "Yes?" he answered, sounding like a child, he thought.

She wavered and what color remained in her face drained. "You—you're Shannon? Shannon Richterson?"

This time he barely heard the question because a notion was growing like a weed in his head. Sherry had known the jungle too well for an American. Her eyes were bright blue. Could it possibly be?

"Tanya?" he said.

Two large tears fell from each of her blue eyes and her lips quivered. Then Shannon knew that he was looking at Tanya Vandervan.

Alive.

His heart lifted to his throat and the room shifted out of focus.

Tanya was alive!

TANYA FELT the tears fall down her cheek. She grabbed at the chair beside her. It was either that or fall.

It was Shannon! "Tanya?" The voice soared in from a thousand memories and she suddenly wanted to throw her arms around him and flee all at once. Casius. The assassin! Shannon? This man who had dragged her through the jungle on a mission of death was really Shannon. After all these years. How was it possible?

"Yes," she answered. "What's happening?" The question echoed through the room. It was him! She stepped to the bed as if on a cloud and sat down, numb.

Shannon wavered on his feet. "I . . . I thought you were dead," he said. She could see small pools of tears in the wells of his eyes.

"They told me that you were killed," she said and swallowed against the stubborn lump in her throat.

"I came to the mission and saw the bodies. I . . . I thought you were dead." He backed up a step and ran into the wall. She saw his Adam's apple bob. He was hardly in control of himself, she realized.

"How did you . . . get out?"

"I . . . I killed some of them and escaped over the cliffs," he said. "What . . ."

She stood and stepped toward him, hardly realizing she was doing so. This man had become someone new. Someone from her dreams.

"Shannon . . ."

He rushed toward her. His arms spread clumsily before he reached her. She felt as though her chest might explode if she did not touch him now. Their bodies came together. Tanya embraced his broad chest and she began to weep. Shannon held her carefully with trembling arms.

They swayed, holding each other tight. For a few moments, he became the boy under the waterfall once again, strapping and young with a heart as big as the jungle. He was falling in a swan dive, arms spread wide, long blond hair streaming behind. Then they were tumbling under the water and laughing, laughing because he had come back for her.

She buried her face in his neck and smelled his skin and let her tears run down his chest.

The next thought fell into her mind like a stun grenade, obliterating the images with a blinding flash.

This wasn't Shannon holding her with his flesh pressed against her. This was . . . this was Casius. The killer. The demoniac.

Her eyes opened. Her arms froze, still encircling him. A panic ripped up her spine. *God, what have you done to him?*

She pushed herself away slowly, carefully, suddenly terrified. He had gone rigid. He stood there and faced her, his thick muscles winding their way around his torso like vines. Angry scars bulged over his chest, like slugs under his skin.

This wasn't Shannon.

This was some beast who had taken over the body of the boy she had once loved and transformed it into . . . this! A sick joke. With her at its brunt. *Oh, dear Tanya, we have decided to answer your prayers after all. Here is your precious Shannon. Never mind that he is twisted and spewing bile from the mouth. You asked for him. Take him.*

"No," she said aloud, and her voice trembled.

Shannon's eyes flashed questioning.

She took a deep breath and tried to settle herself. She still couldn't believe that this was happening. That this killer, Casius, was somehow connected to her Shannon. *Was* Shannon!

"You . . . you've changed."

He stood and she watched his chest expand with heavy breathing. But he did not respond. He seemed suddenly as confused as she.

"What *happened* to you?" She didn't mean them to, but the words came out accusing. Bitter.

His upper lip curled to an angry snarl. Like a wounded animal. But he recovered immediately. "I escaped . . . to Caracas. I took the identity of a boy who was killed with his father, the same year my parents were."

"No! I mean what happened to *you?* You've become . . . them!"

The words somehow reached in and flipped a switch in him. His eyes dimmed and his jaw flexed. She took another step back, thinking she should turn and run away. Leave this nightmare.

"Them? I *kill* them!" he said.

"And who's them?"

"The people who killed my mother!" He said it with twisted lips, bitter beyond himself. "Do you know the CIA ordered it? To give that man in the jungle a place to grow his drugs?"

"But you don't just kill! That's why we have laws. You've become like them."

He spoke quietly now, trembling all over. "My law is Sula."

The name echoed through her mind. *Sula.* The god of death. The spirit of the witch doctor.

"I will do *anything* to destroy them. Anything! You have no idea how long I've planned this." Spittle flecked his lip. "And you have no idea how sick they are."

She blinked. "What are you saying? How can you say that? You're insane!"

"They killed my . . . our parents!" His face was twisted into an ugly, terrifying scowl.

"How could you do this to me?" she whispered.

"I've done nothing to you!" Shannon said. He turned from her and strode for the door. Without looking back, still wearing only his pants, he stepped from the room and shut the door.

Tanya backed to the bed in shock. She sat heavily, hardly able to form coherent thoughts now. When one did string through her head, it said that this was madness. That the world had gone berserk and she along with it.

She lay back, acutely aware of the afternoon silence. Outside, horns honked and pedestrians yelled muted words. She was alone. Maybe even God had deserted her.

Father, what's happening to me? I'm losing my mind.

Then Tanya began to cry softly on the bed. She felt as abandoned and destitute as she had those first weeks after her parents had been killed.

Will you die for him, Tanya?

For him? Shannon.

She curled up in a ball and let the grief swallow her.

CHAPTER THIRTY-THREE

"YES, THAT'S *right, Bill; we don't have a clue what's going on down there. But whatever it is, it's changing the world."*

"I'm preparing for my Wednesday evening teaching at the church, my son is at soccer practice, and Tanya is down in the jungle changing the world."

"Yes. She's loving and she's dying and she's changing the world."

"And who's she loving?"

"The boy."

"Shannon. So he is alive?"

"I think so. I think that she was called down there to love him."

"How does that change the world?"

"I don't know. But it's all I get now. To pray for her to love the boy. In fact, I really think that's what this is all about. Tanya loving Shannon. I really do think maybe Tanya's parents were called down there twenty years ago so that Tanya could fall in love with the boy."

The line was silent.

"And I think Father Petrus was brought to the jungle years ago for this day."

"Important day," he said.

SIX HOURS after Shannon and Tanya fell through the tube into the Orinoco River, three large Yevaro logs followed them. The mountain spit them out like torpedoes and they rushed through muddy waters toward the coast. They reached the Orinoco Delta and bobbed out to sea.

A clipper bearing the name *Angel of the Sea* plucked the first log from the ocean at eight that evening. The log sat snug, among twenty other similar exotic logs bound for the coastal port of Annapolis, twenty miles from Washington, D.C., thirty miles from the CIA headquarters in Langley. *Angel of the Sea* cut north at a steady forty-knot clip. Barring any unforeseen storms, she would arrive at her destination within thirty hours.

Marlin Watch, bound for Miami, hauled the second log from the waters an hour later. This log contained a silver sphere that consisted of nothing more than a small ball of plutonium. Enough to set off a Geiger counter if one were run along the log's surface, but otherwise it was harmless.

Two miles behind her, the *Lumber Lord* stowed the third log in its forward hold and steamed north behind the other two ships. Captain Moses Catura leaned over his map in the pilothouse and spoke to Andrew, who stood beside him.

"Two degrees to port, Andrew. That should compensate for the winds." He looked up into the darkness ahead and swore under his breath. It was the first time he had taken the freighter north on such short notice, but Ramón had insisted. And for a single log! They must have a million dollars of cocaine packed into the tree.

"All set, Captain," Andrew said. "We should make good time if the weather holds."

Moses nodded. "Let's hope so. I don't like the feel of this one. The sooner we get these logs off-loaded the better."

"They're paying well. More than we make in a year. It's one log—what could go wrong with a single log?" Andrew referred to the $100,000 they were being paid for the run. In Senegal where his family waited, his share would make him a wealthy man.

"Maybe, Andrew. Did you know that the Coast Guard is larger than South Africa's entire navy? They're not friendly to drug runners."

Andrew chuckled. "We're not drug runners. We have no idea how that log got on board. We're stupid sailors." He turned to face the darkness ahead with the captain. "Besides, this will be our last run. It's fitting that we make so much on our last run."

Moses nodded at the thought.

Below him the Yevaro log they had plucked from the water slowly dried. In its belly a silver sphere sat dormant, housing a black ball cradling enough force to vaporize the seven-thousand-ton ship with a single cough.

JAMAL TURNED his back on the busy street and spoke into the phone. "Hello, Abdullah."

Silence.

"Do you have anything to report, my dear jungle bunny?"

"I have followed your directions."

"Good. They are on their way, then?"

He could almost hear Abdullah's mind spinning on the other end. "I was told to prepare them," Abdullah said. "Not to send them."

"Unless there was a problem. Isn't that what I told you? Hmm?"

"What problem—"

"Don't be an imbecile!" Jamal spit into the phone. "You don't think I know when you eat and when you sleep and when you pass gas?"

His hand was shaking and he took a breath to still himself. He had two men in the compound who reported to him regularly. Not that he needed them often—he knew Abdullah's moves before the fool did.

"I am on my way, my friend. If you have not done precisely as I have said—"

"The bombs are on the way," Abdullah said tightly.

Jamal blinked. "They are." The words stopped him cold.

"Good."

He slammed the phone down and walked from the phone booth.

SWEAT GLISTENED on Abdullah's face under the fluorescent lights. He set the phone down, poured another splash of tequila into his shot glass, dipped a quivering tongue into the burning liquid, and then tilted his head slowly back until it drained empty into his mouth. Although he'd never been a drinking man, the last twenty-four hours had changed that. He and Ramón had done little except sit at his desk and wait. And drink.

The alcohol made him perspire, he thought. Like a pig. "Where are the ships now?" he asked again.

"Coming to Cuba maybe," Ramón answered.

So, Jamal was coming. And when he did arrive, he would die. Abdullah felt a chill tickle his shoulders. He honestly wasn't sure which thought gave him more pleasure, killing Jamal, or detonating a thermonuclear weapon on American soil.

He ran a finger along the edge of the transmitter lying on the bar beside him. It was a simple 2.4 gigahertz transmitting device, impossible to isolate quickly. But it tied into a far more sophisticated transmitter hidden one mile away, secured in the jungle canopy in a protective housing. From there a tiny burst masquerading as a television signal would be simultaneously relayed through commercial communication satellites. Not all would fail. Not all could be stopped.

And by the time the authorities detected the burst, which they would, it would be too late. The detonation of the first bomb would automatically send a signal to set the second bomb on a twenty-four-hour countdown to detonation. Two green buttons rose from the black plastic like two peas. He circled first one button and then the other. Below the buttons, nine numbers made up a small keypad. Only he and Jamal had the codes to stop the inevitable.

Abdullah spoke without lifting his head. "You are sure the logs arrived at the boats intact?" He waved the question off with a nod of his head. "Yes, of course, you have said so."

"Do you think they will give us the agent?" Ramón asked.

Abdullah thought about Casius and blinked. A widening thought in his mind suggested it might be best if they did not deliver the agent. Then his hand would be forced—it would be Allah's doing.

Abdullah glanced at the clock ticking on the wall opposite them. It had been twenty-four hours and not even a breath from the fools. A chill suddenly spiked at the base of his skull. What if they had ignored the message entirely, thinking him a madman? What if they hadn't even received the message? It had been relayed through the same relays he would use for the bombs. Five million dollars of technology—all from Jamal, of course.

Abdullah grunted and shoved himself back from the bar. "Something isn't right. We'll send another message."

He walked for the door with Ramón on his heels. His fingers were shaking badly. Power was its own drug, he thought, and it was coursing through his veins. At the moment he might very well be the most powerful man in the world.

FRIBERG JERKED in his seat when the knock came on his door. He lifted his head, but the door opened before he could say anything. Mark stepped in.

Ingersol's greased hair flopped to the right side. He threw it back with a hurried hand and rushed forward. "We received another message!"

Friberg stood and snatched the message from the man. "Settle down, Ingersol." But he was already reading the typed communiqué in his fingers.

Ingersol sat in one of the chairs facing his desk. "This guy's dead serious. He's adamant that he has a bomb. I thought you said—"

"Shut up!"

Friberg slowly sat. "Forty-eight hours," he read. "He's cutting the time from seventy-two hours to forty-eight hours because we have been *insufficiently responsive?"* He lowered the paper. "That's absurd! This guy can't be serious."

Ingersol's greasy black hair had fallen to his cheek again. "This isn't the kind of communiqué a man who's bluffing sends, sir. He's either a total imbecile or he *does* have a bomb. And the fact that he's survived Casius this long does not bode well for the imbecile theory." Ingersol stopped and took a long pull through his nostrils.

The director felt a ball of heat spread over his skull. And what if Ingersol were correct? What if . . . ?

The note was signed Abdullah Amir. Disconnected fragments of information fell together in his mind and he blinked. Jamal. Casius was after Jamal.

What if Casius had actually stumbled onto more than the cocaine plant?

"What's going on?" Ingersol repeated. "It seems to me that I've stuck my neck out with you. I deserve to know what I've gotten into, don't you think?"

Friberg eyed the man. Ingersol was a wreck. If he didn't pull him in, he would destroy them both.

"You and me, Mark. It goes no further than this room, you understand?"

Ingersol didn't respond.

"All right. You want to know? Ten years ago Abdullah Amir approached us with a plan to infiltrate the Colombian cartels in exchange for his own piece of the operation. We agreed. He disappeared into their networks. Two years later he reappeared, this time with enough information to wipe out two drug cartels. In exchange, he wanted our cooperation, allowing him to establish and operate a small cocaine plant next-door in Venezuela. We agreed. We pointed him to a coffee plantation and gave him some assistance in taking it over. Nothing major—minor casualties. He's been operating there ever since. Small stuff. We got the DEA to sign off on the deal, but I was the agent who put it together. It was highly successful, all told. We shut down nearly a hundred thousand acres of production in exchange for a hundred."

Ingersol blinked. "That's it?"

Friberg nodded.

"And what does that have to do with this bomb?"

"Nothing. Unless Casius was right and Jamal is connected with Abdullah Amir. Or unless Abdullah isn't who we think he is. South America would make a good base for a strike against America." The sense of it occurred to Friberg even as he spoke it.

"And none of Abdullah's money has found its way into your retirement account, right?"

Friberg didn't respond.

Ingersol shook his head and stared off to the window. He had no choice, Friberg realized. He had already committed himself in front of the president. The money was only dressing.

"I've been suckered into this," Ingersol said and Friberg did not object. "I wasn't looking for this. It's not what I do."

"Maybe, Mark. But we all face the choice at some time. You've already made yours."

Ingersol's eyes fell to the note and Friberg lifted it up. Yes, there was the matter of the bomb, wasn't there? That could be a real spoiler. "So you think we're dealing with a madman who actually has a bomb?" Friberg asked.

"I don't know anymore," Ingersol returned.

"I don't either. But if we are, we now have twenty-four hours to deliver Casius and defuse the situation. Or find this bomb." The idea of it sounded absurd. A suicide mission or even a biological attack was one thing—they had all seen it. But a nuclear bomb? In Hollywood movies, maybe.

"Who else knows about this?" Friberg asked, lifting the transcript.

"No one. It just came over the wire less than ten minutes ago."

"And what's the current status of the search?"

"The Office of Homeland Security is working through its protocol. Law enforcement's on full alert. They're looking—the import documents in question have been identified, and traces are being done now. But it's only been twenty-four hours. We're nowhere near the discovery phase in this thing. In twelve hours we may have traces complete, but very few searches, if any." Ingersol bit his lower lip.

"No one hears about this last message, you understand?"

Ingersol nodded and flipped his hair back again.

"Good. Give the Rangers the clearance to sweep the valley. We go for anything that lives in that compound. If Abdullah does have a bomb, we're risking him detonating it the minute we attack, but I don't see our choice at this point. Anything from the satellites yet?"

"Nothing except cocaine fields. If they have anything else down there, it's hidden."

"And no word of Casius?"

"None."

"Then we go for Abdullah Amir or whoever is sending these crazy messages. I'm going to recommend that all southern ports be closed until we get a better feel for the situation. We'll call it a drill or something. We've got to shake something loose." He lost himself in thought for a moment. They all knew it was simply a matter of time before a terrorist finally found a way to get a nuclear bomb into the United States. The World Trade Center collapse would look like a warm-up exercise.

Ingersol stood. "I'll get on this. I hope you know what you're doing."

CHAPTER THIRTY-FOUR

SHANNON RICHTERSON ran through the jungle barefoot, under a black fog of confusion. Above the canopy, the sun shone in a blue sky, but in his mind light barely reached his thoughts.

Sherry was Tanya. Tanya was alive. He could hardly manage the notion. Tanya Vandervan alive. And filled with anger at him. Couldn't she see that he was doing what so few in the world had the stomach to do?

What would she have him do? Kneel beside Abdullah and pray that he lie down and kill himself. Shannon grunted at the thought.

She only knew the half of it. If she really knew what was happening here, she might kill Abdullah herself. Or kill Jamal.

Jamal had to die. If he did nothing else here in the jungle, he would put Jamal to death.

Shannon pulled up near the edge of Soledad, breathing heavy, hands on hips.

In reality it was *he* who made the difference in the real world. The world was filled with treachery and the only way to face such an evil was with treachery itself. It had been one of the first lessons he'd learned from the natives as a boy. Fight violence with violence.

But Tanya . . .

Tanya had come up with this nonsense about dying.

Shannon spit into the dirt and jogged on. Eight years had come down to this moment, and no person—no woman—would have a say now. Not even

Tanya. He had held her and kissed her and at one time would gladly have given his life for her—but she'd changed. And she hated him.

Shannon's mind grew dark and he groaned above the pounding of his feet. He closed his eyes.

He would show her.

He pulled up at the thought. She wasn't Tanya any longer. Not really. She'd become Sherry.

He doubled back and ran for the town.

And now he would show Sherry how things worked in the real world. Why he was doing this. How to deal with a world gone sick. Maybe then she would understand.

He would return to the jungle and finish what he had started, and he would let Sherry see for herself.

GRAHAM KEYED the radio. "Roger, go ahead."

"The mission has changed. Sweep the valley compound and eliminate any unfriendlies you encounter. Copy?"

Graham looked up at Parlier. Parlier nodded. "Ask him what he means by unfriendlies," he said.

Graham depressed the transmit toggle. "Roger, sir. Request you clarify unfriendlies."

Static sounded for a moment.

"If you don't know their name, then they're unfriendly. Understood? You take out anything that walks."

Parlier nodded at Graham. "What about the agent?"

"Copy that. What about the agent?" Graham asked into the mike.

"Take him out."

"Copy. Alpha out."

Parlier was already walking toward the other men stationed on the cliff. He turned back to Graham. "Get Beta and Gamma on the horn and tell them to follow our lead. I want to be at the base of the cliffs by morning. There Beta spreads east and Gamma spreads west."

He swung back to the cliff. "Pack up, boys. We're going down."

TANYA HAD drifted for over three hours, lying on the hotel bed. Her thoughts spun lazy circles around the notion that she had really lost her mind this time. That this whole thing might well be an extended dream episode in which she had flown the coup and revisited South America only to find Shannon a mad killer instead of her innocent love. After eight years of nightmares a mind could imagine that, couldn't it? She'd read somewhere that if all the power of the brain were harnessed, it could rearrange molecules to allow a person's passage through walls. Well if it could walk through solid objects, surely it could conjure up this madness.

A knock on the door about launched her into orbit. She sat up and nearly slipped from the bed.

He walked in then. Shannon. Or Casius, or whoever he really was. The tall, rugged killer with green eyes and firm muscles. She wanted to shrivel into the corner.

He walked to the dresser, snatched a small backpack from it, and fastened it around his waist. "Okay, lady," he said. "Pull yourself together. We're taking a walk."

"A walk? To where?"

"A walk to hell. What does it matter? We both survived, fine. Now you're going to see how things work in this screwed-up world of ours. Get up."

He walked over, grabbed her by the arm, and yanked her to her feet roughly, eyes flashing.

Tanya felt a stab of pain rip up her arm and she gasped. He relaxed his grip and pulled her toward the door. She stumbled after him.

"I've *seen* your world. Let go of me!"

"And now you're going to see why I do what I do. I owe you at least that much, don't you think?"

"You don't have to hurt me. Let me go!"

This time he did. She followed. She would play his absurd game for the moment. She wasn't sure why. But she had to find out what had caused the love of her life to be transformed into this . . . creature. Shannon led her from the hotel. She stopped at the street, but he continued walking. He shot her an angry glare and she followed.

They walked to the outskirts of Soledad. She expected him to turn into a side street and show her his "screwed-up world" at any moment. But he didn't. He walked past the last road and turned onto a thin path snaking into the jungle.

"Wait a minute," she objected. "I'm not about to go back into the jungle with you. Are you nuts? You think you—"

He spun back, grabbed her by the arm, and propelled her before him.

She fought an urge to whirl around and slap him. "Okay!"

Then she lost comprehension of what his intentions might be. He passed her once they entered the forest and she followed, thinking she would turn back at any moment and return to the town.

But she didn't. For one thing they had switched paths several times and she quickly realized that she could hardly navigate her way back. For another thing, she was drawn by the bare-chested man ahead of her, leading her like a wild savage. Not drawn *to* him, of course, but *by* him, like a homing beacon faintly red in the distance.

That it was Shannon leading her into the jungle and not Casius made her think that she might follow him to hell if he asked her to. Deep in her heart, Shannon was still her lost love.

But she hardly considered the notion before replacing it with the notion that *he* deserved to be sent to hell.

Dear God, help me!

She was panting within the hour. Shannon didn't bother looking back to check on her. If anything he walked faster, more deliberately, intent on punishing her maybe. She determined then not to give him the satisfaction. She had kept up with him once—she could do it again. As long as he let her, of course.

Tanya walked behind him, watching his muscles roll over his bones with each footfall. To think she had once loved this man so passionately. Shannon. How had he grown so strong? Not that he wasn't strong before, but this . . . this man ripping through the jungle ahead of her was as powerful as they came in the human species.

And she hated him for it because those once tender fingers had been replaced by claws. Those emerald eyes she had once gazed into with a weak heart now slashed and cut with an unquenched fury.

And what would you expect from a boy traumatized by his parents' slaughtering? Eight years of nightmares?

No. That would be you, Tanya.

Tanya gritted her teeth and rebuked the sentiment. He had become one of them. Walking the world seeking whom he might destroy. This demoniac now leading her into hell.

The thoughts whirled unchecked.

The moon rose behind them and highlighted his glistening back. Still he refused to look at her. He could smell her perhaps, like some ruthless animal who knew when it was being followed. And she could smell his sweat—musky and sweet in the humid night.

She stopped in the trail and spoke for the first time since entering the jungle. "Where are you leading me? It's dark."

He walked on, ignoring her.

"Excuse me!" Anger flashed up her spine. "Excuse me, it's dark, if you hadn't noticed."

His voice drifted back amid the screaming of cicadas. "I suggest you stay close if you don't want me to leave you here."

She mumbled angrily under her breath and ran to catch up. He had led her into danger without consideration for her safety and now he was threatening to leave her behind.

Tanya caught him and pounded on his shoulder. "Stop it!" she shrieked. "What are you trying to prove? This is crazy!"

He swung around, fists clenched. "You think so? You think *this* is crazy? Then listen to me, Tanya. *This* is nothing!" She could see that he was trembling. "This is two people walking along a path in the real world. I'll tell you what's crazy. Watching a bunch of men shoot holes into your mother and father while you stand by powerless. *That* is crazy. And that's the real world. But then you're not used to the real world, are you? You're too busy running from your nightmares, I suppose. Explaining away the death of Mommy and Daddy. Trying to make sense of it all? There's only one thing that makes sense now and it's got nothing to do with your God."

He turned around and left her standing, her mouth agape. *Running from my nightmares?* She followed quickly, fearing the dark alone.

And he had called her Tanya.

He's wounded, Tanya.

He's an animal.

He's a wounded animal, then. But he needs my love.

They walked in silence for hours, stopping only periodically for rest and water. Even then they did not talk. Tanya let her mind slip into a numb rhythm that followed the steady cadence of her feet.

In the end it was only prayer that soothed her frazzled spirit.

Father . . . dear God, I'm lost down here. Forgive me. I'm lost and lonely and confused. I hate this man and I hate that I hate him. And I don't even know if that's possible! What are you doing? What is your purpose here?

She stepped without caution on the path behind Shannon now, trusting his leading.

I hate this man.

But you must love this man.

Never!

Then, you would be like him.

Yes, and I'm a fool either way.

A picture of Jesus spread on the cross hung in her mind. *Forgive them, Father, for they know not what they do.* The image brought a knot to Tanya's throat.

Then her mind returned to the vision. What significance her life now played in this insanity was far beyond her. The thought of a bomb's mushroom cloud barely registered out here in the heavy forest. For all she knew the whole notion was absurd. Shannon certainly thought so.

Her mind returned to him. *God, help me.*

With each step, she resigned herself to the knowledge that this was indeed a part of some symphony conducted by God himself. In some absurd way it did make sense. In the end she would see that. The realization gave her strength.

CHAPTER THIRTY-FIVE

Saturday

THEY HAD come far in the eight hours—farther than Shannon would have guessed the woman would last. He stopped by the Caura, five miles downriver from the plantation, and stood in the morning sun with a clenched jaw. The river was only twenty feet wide here and it curled around this meadow. It would be the safest place to leave her. She would have greater visibility of any approaching animals, and if he failed to return, she could find her way to safety down the river. It would also give him a way to reach her quickly once he'd finished.

Tanya.

She hardly registered as Tanya any longer. She was "that woman." It was what his mind called her now. And then on occasion the other part of his mind would call her "Tanya," and his heart would break a little. The voices pushed him at a relentless pace.

Ahead, the mountain rose and then fell over the cliff to the plantation. A *Year* bird cawed long and sober above him, and Shannon lifted his gaze to the canopy. The black bird's foot-long beak rested open. A yellow eye studied him. Shannon lowered his head and looked at the trees cresting the rise ahead. Abdullah waited there. A killing waited there—a throat begging for the blade. He imagined the thick brown cords of Abdullah's neck, parting under the edge of his knife. The man's eyes were smiling.

Shannon's breathing thickened. The plan was well laid and ticking along like a clock. Friberg would be moving by now. A chill flashed up his spine. He wanted to be there, facing the man who'd killed his mother and father, feeling the pounding of his heart, tasting his blood.

"Can we rest?" The sound of the woman's voice jerked him back to the river. Yes, that woman. Tanya. He could hardly remember why he had brought her. To share this part of his life with her, of course. To bring her into a holy union with death. To hate her so that she could love him. It was something that made no sense to weak minds, but to others it made perfect sense.

In the black fog.

You've lost your sanity, Shannon.

Have I? The world is insane.

He turned to her. She stood twenty feet off, haggard and dripping wet and looking near collapse. She gazed at him steadily. Her mind wasn't as weak as her body, he thought.

"You'll wait here," he said. "If I don't return, take the river east to Soledad."

He heard his voice from a distance, as if he were floating over his own body, and it sounded strange. Like the words of some dark priest summoning a body for sacrifice.

"Why are you doing this?" she asked softly.

"To help you understand," he said.

"Understand what? That you're a tortured soul?"

Shannon forced a grin. The fog swam in his mind.

"You see? Even now you insist on berating me," he said. "Don't you want to understand how your beloved Shannon turned out to be so wicked? I'm going to show you how."

"Shannon . . ." She stopped.

She called you Shannon.

"You're showing me only one thing," she continued. "You're showing me that you need help. I'll admit that I may have overreacted back there, but you've gone over the edge. You need help."

"Maybe it's you who need help. Have you considered that possibility? Or is your mind too full of nightmares to consider that?"

He saw her swallow. "Be careful what you say. My name's Sherry. Or Tanya. You remember that name, don't you?"

"And my name is what?"

"Shannon," she said softly. "We've both had a difficult time with things. I'll give you that. I've spent eight years reliving the nightmare of those three days, trapped in the box. But now there's only one right way. You think our meeting out here in the jungle is purely chance? You think my dreams are stupid?" She paused. "I suppose you do. But that doesn't change what we should do."

"And what should we do?"

"I don't know. But not this."

"*This?* You don't even know what *this* is," he said. "This, *Tanya,* is the shedding of blood. This, *Tanya,* is the bull and I hold the sword. Without the shedding of blood there can be no forgiveness of sin. Isn't that in your Bible? Half the world sits on padded pews singing pretty songs about the blood of Christ. Well, now you will see what it means to shed blood in the real world."

As he spoke, threads of confusion wrestled in his mind. He should not talk to her like this. She was extending a hand of peace. Maybe more. And what was he offering her? Only anger. Hatred.

"You've given yourself to Satan, Shannon. Can't you see that?" Her voice sounded deeply saddened. "I was wrong to be angry with you. Forgive me. I pity you."

Pity? Any illusion he harbored about her offering him peace shattered with her words. Revulsion swept through his gut like a wave crashing to shore.

He knew he couldn't allow her the satisfaction of seeing the impact of her words, but his hands were shaking already. Surely she could see that. The knife was at his waist—he could flip it out to her in the space of a single breath—pin her to the tree behind.

He blinked. What was he thinking? It was *Tanya* there!

Shannon lifted a trembling finger. "We'll see who should pity whom. I don't have time for this. Stay here by the river. I'll be back tonight."

He spun away and broke into a jog, knowing he should tell her how to avoid the crocodiles, but too furious to bring himself to it. She would have to depend on her God.

THOUGHTS CRASHED through Shannon's mind as he ran under the trees, confused and furious. Slowly the images of the woman were replaced by images of Abdullah. Slowly the lust for his blood crept through his mind, like an antiseptic numbing this other pain. Slowly Shannon climbed back into his old skin and prepared himself for the end of this long journey.

The first indication that he wasn't alone on the mountain came at the base of the black cliffs. A flock of parrots took to the air down valley, squawking loudly. He immediately pulled up and changed direction.

Shannon eased his way through the bush to the right of the disturbance. He moved from tree to tree, carefully measuring the jungle before him. The wind shifted and a light breeze brushed his face. He dropped to the ground as the strong smell of fish—tuna fish—filled his nostrils.

Humans. Whites.

Then he saw the soldier. Through the brush, still about fifty yards off, to his left, a single man dressed in the stripped-down military garb typical of the Special Forces. Close-cropped hair topped the man's camouflage-painted head. An automatic rifle crossed at his waist.

Shannon stared through the foliage at the hidden warrior and quickly considered his options. This was probably the perimeter guard of a post farther ahead. The cliff likely.

He studied the man carefully for a full five minutes before moving forward. He slowly edged his way closer to the shifting guard. For Shannon, armed with only a knife, stalking a trained killer armed with an automatic weapon, stealth would be the difference between life and death.

He stopped, crouched low behind the foliage, and studied the husky man. Regardless of their confidence, most of these white boys didn't belong in the jungle—at least not *this* jungle.

Shannon drew back his knife, held it for a second, and then hurled it at the man's exposed head. The startled soldier had barely started his turn when the butt of the knife smashed into his temple and dropped him. Shannon waited for a few moments, allowing the adrenaline in his veins to ease. Confident that no alarm had been raised, he slid next to the unconscious Ranger, retrieved his knife, and quickly removed a nine-millimeter revolver from the man's waist. He left the man on his back and slipped through the trees toward the cliff pass.

Laying the Ranger out hadn't been necessary, of course. He could've just as easily made his way past the team unnoticed. But since the CIA had gone as far as inserting Ranger forces to stop him, the least he could do was let them know he appreciated the gesture.

He thought of the woman briefly, like a distant memory now. *No, you can't change what I am, Tanya. And I am a killer. It's what I do. I kill. I do not die. There has been enough dying. Dying is for fools.*

CHAPTER THIRTY-SIX

LUMBER LOADING dock D on the southern tip of Miami Harbor received the order to close six hours after the director drafted the recommendation. Three of those hours had been spent chasing down the proper naval authorities, who were evidently indisposed at a convention in Las Vegas. It had taken the port authorities another two hours to implement the orders. In sum total, the ports along the southern tip of Miami closed their doors to business eight hours after the decision had been made to do so.

Not bad for a monolithic bureaucracy. Too slow, considering the stated operational goals of Homeland Security.

During the last two hours of operation at loading dock D, a large converted fishing vessel bearing the name *Marlin Watch* unloaded the last of her cargo and pulled back out to sea for its return voyage to Panama. No one paid much attention to the unmilled Yevaro log set among the others. It was, after all, just a log.

Thirty minutes after it had been unloaded from the ship, the mid-size log was put aboard an eighteen-wheeled lumber rig with six other imports and transported to the Hayward Lumberyard on the outskirts of Miami proper.

Six hours later, an eighteen-wheel International rumbled into the yard, loaded the log, and left without filing any paperwork.

Farther north a clipper named *Angel of the Sea* moved steadily up the northeastern coastline of the United States.

Farther south, just entering U.S. waters, another ship, a larger one called the *Lumber Lord,* steamed up Florida's eastern coastline.

"HOW MANY?" Abdullah demanded, dropping his empty glass on the desk.

"Eighteen. The men passed the perimeter security line at the base of the cliffs three minutes ago, three groups in single file."

Abdullah whirled around and slammed his fist onto the desk. "They don't believe me? They're attacking?" He glared at the wall map. "Eighteen men, single file—they are professional soldiers. How long until they reach us?"

"An hour, if they move quickly. An hour and a half if they are careful," Ramón responded.

So then, they were coming for him. Eight years of waiting and now it was happening. The Americans weren't taking him seriously.

He shuddered, as if a nerve had been touched in his back. But then a nerve had been touched by the heat that rose through his spine. Maybe it was better this way. They would have their guard down and the blasts would rock their smug little world. Even if they did bring him down in the process, they would still feel a little heat.

He turned to Ramón, who stood waiting anxiously. "Tell Manuel to take his six best men and position them for surveillance near the northern edge of the compound. They are not to engage the soldiers unless they reach us." He twisted his head and looked at the map that outlined the perimeter's defense system. The old Claymore mines were buried just beneath the surface of the jungle floor in a three-meter band that circled the entire complex. It had taken them over two months to lay the three thousand mines, and for three years now, they had remained undisturbed.

"Activate the compound mines and inform the men to stay clear." He swung to Ramón. "Do it!"

Ramón left quickly.

Abdullah rounded his desk and sat carefully. The room was silent except for a slight scraping sound that came from the bugs in each corner. They were hard-shelled species that clung to each other's backs with long bipeds.

It was time to send another message. The Americans had never felt terror, not really. Not lately. They had never had their limbs severed or their wives raped or their children killed. So now he would change that.

Where was Jamal?

What if Yuri's bomb did not detonate? Abdullah shuddered and closed his eyes. Sweat soaked his collar, and he ran a hand across his neck.

Someone walked into his office and Abdullah opened his eyes. The room seemed to shift off center before him. Everything doubled—two doors, two Ramóns. He twisted his head and blinked. Now there was one. He lifted wet palms to the desk and set them before him. A fly settled on his knuckle but he did not bother it.

"Where are the bombs?" he asked.

"The boat with the larger device should be entering Chesapeake Bay now. It will be in place with time to spare." Ramón's voice quaked—he was afraid, Abdullah thought. Imagine that, afraid.

"The *Lumber Lord* is still off Florida's coast, going north."

Abdullah nodded. At his right hand the black transmitter sat facing the ceiling.

"Send a message to the Americans," he said quietly. "Tell them that they have thirty minutes to withdraw their men from the valley."

He ran a finger over the green knobs. His world had slowed. A drug had entered his body, he thought. But even the thought was slow. As if he had slipped into a higher consciousness. Or possibly a lower consciousness. No, no. It would have to be a higher state of mind, one that approached greatness. Like those boys marching off to their death on the minefields.

"Tell them that if they do not withdraw the soldiers, then we will detonate a small bomb. Don't tell them it will trigger the countdown for the larger one," he said, and his fingers trembled on the box.

MARK INGERSOL stood with his arms dangling, sweating as though it were a sauna and not a situation room he and Friberg had retreated to.

They had received a third message.

A thousand books lined oak bookcases, wall to wall, surrounding the long conference table. But no amount of book learning would help them now. The crisis had gone critical and Friberg should have gone ballistic. The tall leather chairs around the wood table should be occupied with a dozen high-ranking strategists. Instead, there sat only one man and he slouched, numb, barely able to move.

"Do we tell him or not?" Ingersol asked.

Friberg lifted his eyes, looking more like a puppy than top shop man. "Tell who?"

"The president! You can't just sit on something like this. That madman down there has given us thirty minutes—"

"I know what that madman down there has given us. I'm just not sure I believe it."

"Believe it? If you don't mind me pointing out the obvious, we're way past believing here. We'll find out soon enough whether or not they have the bomb. In the meantime, we should be briefing the president."

"I've been in this game long enough to know what is obvious, *Ingersol.* What's obvious here is that you and I are in a hot spot if this idiot has the bomb. You think there's anything anyone can do about this in thirty minutes? How about putting out an all-points bulletin, flood the news channels with the message—'Get out, 'cause a nuclear bomb is about to explode down the street from you!' We'd lose more to the panic than to the bomb."

"Either way, the president should know."

"The president is the *last* person who should know!" Friberg had come back to life. His face twisted in a red snarl. "The less he knows the better. If there is a detonation, we have a problem. Agreed. But we don't need to draw attention to the issue now. There's been a threat and we're handling it—that's all he needs to know. I updated him less than three hours ago. We're proceeding systematically. Just a routine threat, that's all. Get it through your head."

Ingersol blinked and took a step back. "And how will it look if this thing goes off and it's discovered that you withheld information?"

"We, Ingersol. *We* withheld information. And it won't be discovered—that's the whole point. Not if you pull yourself together here."

A chill descended Ingersol's spine. "We should at least pull the Rangers back. Sending them in now is crazy. Abdullah will detonate!"

The director nodded. "You're right. Pull them back immediately."

Ingersol lingered a moment, thinking he should say something else. Something that would diffuse this madness, make his heart ease up. But his mind had gone gray.

He turned from the table and left the room. They should have sent the message to the Rangers ten minutes ago. As it was, the men would have less than fifteen minutes to retreat before Abdullah did his thing.

Whatever that was.

Chapter Thirty-Seven

TANYA COLLAPSED under a tree at the perimeter of the river clearing within minutes of Shannon's hasty departure. It occurred to her that there might be creatures in the brown water a hundred feet off, but she'd lost interest in her own safety.

The madness of eight years was slowly unwinding in her mind; she could feel it as though it were a snake uncoiling. She did not know how just yet, but somehow this was all forming a collage with meaning. The notes were beginning to make music. The words were carrying a message. And it was all flowing through her.

She spent the first few hours in a haze, barely aware of the curious birds squeaking above or the parade of insects crawling over her shoes and legs.

The words she had spoken to Shannon were not her own. Oh, they had come from her own mouth and even her own mind, but her spirit had handed them off to her mind. She knew that because a warmth had started to glow in her spirit and it wasn't her own.

God was warming her. He was holding her and breathing his words of comfort into her like a father whispering to a crying baby.

And with his breath came a new understanding of Shannon. An ache for him that burned in her bones. He had been tormented for years, she saw, much like she had been. But his tormentor had been from hell, grinding him into the ground. Her torment had been a gift from heaven, a seasoning to soften her spirit, as Father Teuwen had suggested. A thorn in her flesh, preparing her for this day. This colliding of worlds. This crescendo of clashing cymbals, like the finale in a grand symphony.

There was the matter of the dream and the bomb and all that, but in reality none of it seemed important to her anymore. Now it was all about Shannon.

Tanya lay her head on her forearm and closed her eyes. "Shannon, poor Shannon," she whispered. Tears immediately flooded her eyes. That ache in her heart swelled for him. It wasn't love as in the classical sense of romantic love, she thought. It was more like empathy.

"I'm so sorry, Shannon." The sound of his name coming softly from her lips threw her mind back to a time when they spoke in hushed tones to each other. I love you, Shannon. I love you, Tanya.

What's happening, Father? Speak to me.

Then Tanya tumbled into an exhausted sleep.

SHANNON KNELT on the edge of the jungle, breathing hard from the run. Before him the old plantation sprawled with awful familiarity, like a landscape pulled from an old nightmare and shoved before his eyes. He caught his breath and swallowed. The mansion had deteriorated to flaking boards several hundred meters to his right. The once manicured lawn on which his mother and father had been ripped apart now swayed with waist-high grass.

Tanya's voice whispered in his ear. *Are you ready to die, Shannon*? An absurd question. A wedge of heat ripped through his skull.

Are you ready to kill, Shannon?

Yes.

He jerked his gaze to the left, where the entrance into the mountain processing plant sat closed off by a large hangar door. Apart from two guards standing on either side of the overhead door, no other humans were in sight. The field hands probably lived in the old mansion, he thought. God only knew what they had done in there, who had slept in his bed all these years. He should burn it as well. To the ground.

Shannon stepped back into the forest and ran along the perimeter toward the hangar. He had encountered another set of guards earlier and found them incompetent—lazy from years of facing no trained adversaries. They might be able to butcher natives in their sleep, but today he would advance their training. He dropped to his knees now thirty meters from the nearest guard.

A single entry door opened, and Shannon pulled back into the shadows. A man dressed in a white lab coat stepped out briefly, talked to the guard, and then retreated back inside.

The grass between the jungle and the hangar stood two feet high, uncut in recent months—a foolish oversight. Shannon slid the green backpack loaded with explosives to his chest and lowered himself so that the bag dragged on the earth. He snaked from the tree line, keeping just below the grass.

He'd covered half the distance to the two guards before he stopped and eyed them carefully. Using the gun he'd taken off the Ranger would be like waltzing in with a marching band, but then he'd always preferred the knife anyway. Both guards leaned against the tin siding, their rifles propped within easy reach.

Shannon rubbed a small stone he'd brought from the jungle and waited. A full five minutes passed in sweltering stillness before the guards both faced away.

Shannon hurled the rock to the far side of the hangar door, in the direction they faced but to the tin eaves. The stone clattered and they jerked.

He came from the grass then, while their senses were taken by the initial start. Before the stone thumped harmlessly to the ground twenty yards past the guards, Shannon was halfway to them, a knife in each hand. The bowie he hurled at the closest guard, while he ran; the Arkansas Slider he flipped to his right hand while the bowie was still in flight.

From his peripheral vision Shannon saw the bowie take the first guard in his temple. The second guard whirled then, but Shannon's throwing arm already swept forward with the Slider. It flew through the air and buried itself in the man's chest, to the right of his breastbone. Neither man had cried in alarm; both gasped and sank to their seats.

Shannon veered for the single door, snatched the bowie from the closest guard, and flattened himself against the wall, adrenaline pounding through his veins. The euphoric buzzing that always accompanied his killing tingled up his spine. He swung the pack at his chest onto his back, gripped the doorknob, and pulled out the Ranger's nine-millimeter Browning.

One of two things would happen when he opened the door. They might spot him, in which case he would find himself in a full-scale firefight. Or he would slip in unnoticed. He couldn't remember the last time he'd left the success of a mission to such poor odds, and he ground his teeth thinking of it now. Either way he was committed.

Shannon twisted the knob and pushed very slowly. Sweat dripped from the end of his nose and splashed onto his knee. The door opened a crack and he held still.

No response.

He stretched his neck and peered into the slit. His heart thumped in his chest like a basketball being dribbled in an empty gym. A single helicopter rested in his narrow view. He pushed the door wider. Two helicopters. And beyond, a door that led to the processing plant.

But the dimly lit hangar was still, unguarded. Shannon drew a breath of the humid air, slipped through the door, and eased it shut behind him. Without pausing, he ran to the cover of a tall, red tool chest and crouched behind. Working quickly now, he pulled the pack off his chest and withdrew three charges. He set each timer to thirty minutes and slung the bag over his shoulder.

Shannon peered around the tool chest, saw that no one had entered the hangar, and eased over to the nearest helicopter. He shoved a bundle of C-4 under the fuel tank and went for the other one. The third bundle he tossed behind a large fuel tank at the hangar's rear. When the explosive detonated in twenty-eight minutes, the hangar would come down. If they managed to get one of these birds airborne, it would go off like a bomb in the air. Shannon shook the sweat from bangs hanging like claws over his forehead.

The door leading into the processing plant rested closed. Shannon ignored it and ran for the corner beams that arched to the ceiling. His luck so far had been good.

Maybe too good.

THE RANGER teams penetrated the jungle in a conventional three-pronged fork foray. Rick Parlier led his team up the center, stepping through the brush light-footed. A dozen insects droned around him, but only those honing in on his neck bothered him and then only after an hour of high-stepping through the valley and finding nothing. He would have preferred to move much faster—take the team in on the run. But three self-repeating facts kept tumbling through his mind.

One, they didn't know the geography. This wasn't like picking a point over a few sand dunes and racing on over. It was more like crawling through a thicket of thorns. At night.

Two, although they knew that the valley was occupied, they didn't know precisely how many others hid beneath the canopy.

And three, the agent was still at large, running about these trees like some kind of maniac. Best they could figure, he'd laid Phil out cold back there a few hours ago. Nothing else made any sense.

Parlier slipped behind a large palm and slapped at his neck, thinking it was time to speed things up when Mark snatched his fist to the air behind him, motioning a full stop. He dropped to his knees and waited for Graham to reach them from the rear of the file.

Graham slid in beside Parlier. "We got a problem, sir. Uncle has ordered us back."

Parlier stared at the communications man. "Are they nuts?"

"You got me. They refuse to give an explanation. Just get out and get out fast. We got five minutes to get back to the cliffs."

"What did you tell them?"

"I told them that was impossible."

Parlier stood and snatched the transmitter from Graham's hand. "We've got some imbecile ordering us around! I'm—"

An explosion suddenly shattered the air no more than a hundred meters to their right. Parlier whirled toward the sound.

The jungle shrieked with the response of a thousand creatures. "That was Gamma!" Graham snatched the transmitter back. He fingered the mike and spoke quickly into it. "Come in, James. What was that?"

The radio hissed its silence.

Graham's hand trembled, and he depressed the transmission lever again. "Gamma, Gamma, this is Alpha. Come in!"

The receiver shrieked to life. "Alpha, we got trouble here! We got a man down. Tony's down. I repeat, we got a man down from some kind of mine!"

Parlier grabbed the microphone from Tim. "James, this is Parlier. Now listen carefully. Get your man and get back to the cliffs. Do not, I repeat, do not proceed forward. Do you copy?"

"Copy that. Retreating now." The radio fell silent.

A land mine? To protect what? "Beta, you copy that last transmission?"

"Copy, Alpha. Standing by."

"Get the heck out of there, Beta. Get back to the cliffs, you copy?"

"Copy, sir."

Parlier tossed the mike back to Tim and signaled a retreat to Mark, who passed the signal back to Ben and Dave in the rear file.

"Go." Graham slung the radio over his arm and moved out quickly.

Parlier turned and took one last look at the jungle that descended into the valley. Four days in the jungle and they'd seen only one other human being—and him for a brief moment before being cold-cocked. Now they had a man down. If they didn't get some clarification by nightfall, he was coming back to finish this job on his own. Maybe bring Graham.

Parlier turned and retreated toward the cliffs.

ABDULLAH SAT at his desk and watched the clock. He'd never noticed its faint ticking before, but now it was louder than the soft clicking of the bugs.

Sweat trickled slowly down his chin and dripped onto a white sheet of paper on which he'd scrawled his first transmission. Several flies sat unmoving on his knuckles, but he hardly noticed them. His eyes remained fixed on that clock as his mind crawled through a fog.

He breathed steadily, in long pulls, blinking only when his eyes stung badly. Ramón sat cross-legged, staring at Abdullah through his one good eye, breathing, but otherwise motionless.

Something had changed. Yesterday the notion of detonating a nuclear weapon in the United States had been exhilarating, to be sure. But it had been a project. A plan. Even an obsession. But always more Jamal's obsession than his.

Now it had become his own. A desperate craving—like a gulp of air after two minutes under water. He felt as if *not* pushing this little plastic button might suck the life from his bones.

The effect seemed surreal. Impossible, actually. His mind skipped through the chain of events as Yuri had described them so many times.

Who was he to change the world? Abdullah Amir. A tremor ran through him at the thought. He almost pushed the button then. A high ringing sound popped to life in his head and the clock shifted out of focus for a moment. Then his vision was back.

The Rangers now had five minutes to pass the perimeter defense wire. Abdullah mumbled a word of prayer for their failure. It was in Allah's hands now.

CHAPTER THIRTY-EIGHT

RAMÓN WATCHED Abdullah and felt a new kind of fear overtake his soul. His right leg had fallen asleep fifteen minutes ago and his back ached from his static posture.

Abdullah sat there sweating profusely, dripping on his desk, unmoving. His reddening eyes slowly shifted from the clock on the wall to the transmitter at his hand. His right cheek twitched every few seconds, as if a fly had lighted there. His lips twisted in an odd grimace, one that might just as easily be fashioned from delight as bitterness.

Ramón glanced up at the wall clock and saw the second hand pass through the bottom of its arc to the top. He swallowed, suddenly struck by the absurdity of it all. It would not just be this plastic button pushed in thirty seconds; it would be a fist down the throat of an unsuspecting world. Not one but two atomic weapons detonated twenty-four hours apart. In the name of God no less.

The second hand climbed, and Ramón suddenly thought that he should stop the man. He should lift his pistol and shoot him through that wet forehead. The thought screamed through his mind, but Ramón couldn't get the message out there, to his extremities where frozen muscles waited.

Then the red hand was at the top.

It occurred to Ramón that he had stopped breathing. He jerked his eyes to the Arab. Abdullah's face quivered, shaking a final drop of sweat free of his upper lip. His eyes bulged at the clock like two black marbles.

But he hadn't pushed that green button.

Ramón pried his eyes to the wall. The second hand was falling, past the large five, then the ten. Then he heard a loud exhale and he jerked his eyes back.

Abdullah sat slumped in his chair, his eyes closed, expressionless. Ramón dropped his gaze to the man's hand. The Arab's forefinger still rested on the green button.

It was depressed.

DAYTONA BEACH had always been known for its beaches and worshiped for its sun. On most Saturdays the sky stretched blue. But today clouds had swept in from the west on cool winds, shielding the tourists from the rays. Consequently the beach lay gray and nearly empty. Where thousands of tourists normally slouched on the white sand or splashed in the surf, only the bravest slogged along the beach.

Twenty miles out to sea, the *Lumber Lord* steamed steadily north, up the coast of Florida. A flock of sea gulls fluttered over the ship, snatching up whatever morsel they could find. A dozen crew members were engaged in an enthusiastic water fight led by Andrew. Captain Moses Catura had assumed his typical position in the pilothouse and watched the men below drench each other. He smiled to himself. It was the kind of moment that made him glad to be alive.

It was also his last moment.

A single signal, invisible to the human eye, boosted and relayed from the coast of Venezuela to the southeastern coast of Cuba, found the *Lumber Lord* then. It penetrated her hull, located the small black receiver resting in one of the logs, and triggered it.

The detonation in the *Lumber Lord* started innocently enough. Krytron triggering devices released their four-thousand-volt charges into forty detonators that surrounded the core of the silver sphere. The detonators simultaneously fired the fifteen kilograms of shaped charges that Yuri had meticulously positioned around the uranium tamper. With absolute precision, just as the Russian had designed them to perform, the shaped charges crushed the natural uranium tamper into an orange-sized ball of plutonium.

It was an implosion rather than an explosion at this particular point.

The implosion compressed the plutonium core so forcefully that an atom at its core split and released a neutron. At exactly the same moment, the shock from the initial implosion broke the initiator housed within the center of the plutonium. When the initiator was crushed, beryllium and polonium contained in its core combined and released a flood of neutrons into the surrounding plutonium.

Within three-millionths of a second, the first neutron split from its parent atom—generation one.

In fifty-five generations the mass of plutonium reached a supercritical state and the little plutonium sphere shredded the boundaries of nature.

The entire episode lasted for less than one-thousandth of a second.

Suddenly the little orange-sized sphere of plutonium was no longer a sphere at all, but a 300 million degree sun, reaching out at over a thousand miles per second. Twenty miles off the coast of Daytona Beach, history's third offensive nuclear explosion had been detonated.

In one moment the *Lumber Lord*'s massive steel hull was lumbering through calm seas, and in the next, a blinding ball of light had vaporized the ship as though it were made only of crepe paper.

The explosion lit up the horizon like a sputter of the sun. A huge fireball rose from the sea and stared the unsuspecting bathers in the face. In the first millisecond, a thermal pulse of light reached to the beach, effectively giving nearly a thousand onlookers what amounted to a bad sunburn. A dozen fires ignited along the coast.

An electromagnetic pulse from the blast cut off electricity and communications in the city. A huge mushroom cloud rose over the ocean and rumbled for several long seconds.

Then all went silent.

After an endless pause, the city slowly began to fill with sounds once again. Police sirens wailing up and down the streets, aimless and desperate without radio contact. People running helter-skelter, screaming.

The tidal wave rippling in was a small one by tidal standards, but enough to surge a hundred yards inland. The water spread past the beaches roughly ten minutes after the blast.

Then the vacuum created by the blast caved in on itself and the winds, which had earlier brought the clouds, resumed their push out to sea. The radiation fallout drifted away from the land, for the moment.

The detonation was a mere sniff of the destruction within the grasp of the much larger sister device, now already in a countdown to its own detonation.

Twenty-three hours, forty-eight minutes and counting.

TANYA SLEPT beneath the towering trees, ignorant of the passing jaguar, unaware that not one but three crocodiles eyed her from the far shore; oblivious to the little sun that had lit the sky off of Florida's coast. For her it was darkness. The sweet darkness of sleep.

Until the sky opened up suddenly, like a tear in space. The beach lay before her and the surf lapped at sandy shores. The vision was back. Only this time Shannon was there calling for her to come.

Shannon. Sweet Shannon. I love you, Shannon.

She flinched in her sleep. I love what he was.

Come, Tanya. The boy was calling to her. *Please save me.*

The sky in her mind erupted then, like a flash grenade. The wind was sucked from her lungs by a white-hot fire and the world returned to black.

Tanya bolted upright, panting under the towering tree. Sweat streamed down her neck. The bomb had gone off!

The bomb had just gone off!

CHAPTER THIRTY-NINE

MARK INGERSOL stood in the basement room among the computers and teletype machines with one arm across his belly and the other lifted to his chin. He had never been the type of man to bite his nails, but for the last twenty minutes he had managed to draw blood from his right forefinger. He had spoken directly to the Ranger team this time, bypassing the regular communication channels. A soldier named Graham had told him they couldn't withdraw in time.

"What do you mean you can't withdraw in time? You're a Ranger! Hightail it, man!"

Twice he'd been tempted to call back—check on their progress. But in the end he just paced. The operator on duty had come over once and asked if he could be of help. Ingersol had sent the man packing.

And now the clock on the wall had ticked off two minutes past the deadline and nothing had happened. That was good. That was real good. Ingersol felt this shoulders ease.

Ingersol blew some air from his lungs and walked for the bathroom.

Regardless of this crazy bomb threat, a few annoying loose ends still dangled in his mind. David Lunow for instance. He relieved himself, thinking already of what it would feel like to take out someone like David. A rogue agent was one thing, but David? He was a friend.

He pushed through the bathroom door, turned for the exit, and glanced at the teletype machine. White paper rose past its roller like a tongue. A chill fell down Ingersol's back.

The message could have come from a hundred different sources. A thousand sources. He veered to his right and leaned over the machine.

At first the words didn't place clear meaning in his mind. They read quite simply:

> *If you do not deliver the agent as requested, then another bomb will detonate. In Miami. A much larger device, which is already triggered. You have precisely twenty-four hours.*
>
> *The Brotherhood*

It was that word—*another*—that suddenly came to life like a siren in Ingersol's skull. His knees went weak and that chill washed right down to his heels. He reached trembling fingers for the white sheet and ripped it from the teletype. He whirled about and ran from the room.

Ingersol reached the director's office four stories higher in twenty-five seconds. Friberg was on the phone, his face white, his eyes wide. He did not look up when Ingersol shook the message at him. His mind wasn't in the room.

". . . Yes, sir. I understand, sir. But that was under different pretenses. Things have obviously changed."

He's talking to the president, Ingersol thought. *It's happened!*

Friberg spoke again. "Well, if he had one, yes he could have more."

"He does," Ingersol said. Friberg's face was still white. Ingersol swallowed and lowered the message.

Friberg listened for a moment. "Yes, sir." He then hung up.

They stared at each other for a few seconds, silent.

Friberg's face suddenly settled before he said, "NORAD recorded a twenty-kiloton blast two miles off of Daytona Beach five minutes ago."

Ingersol blinked rapidly several times. He sat in the guest chair, numb.

Friberg looked out the window, still white but otherwise expressionless. "Fortunately it was a bad beach day; no reported casualties yet. They've reported heavy structural damage on the beachfront."

"This wasn't supposed to happen."

"It happened. Get used to it."

"What is the president doing?"

Friberg faced him. "What do you expect he's doing? He's going ballistic. Calling in the troops. He's ordered the closing of all airports. The Europeans are already screaming about the fallout headed their way. They've got a squadron of F-16s on the tarmac and they're screaming for a target, and now I suppose they'll begin the evacuation of southern Florida. Like I said, they're going ballistic."

"You gave the F-16s a target?"

"No."

Ingersol shoved the message to Friberg. "Well, you'd better. We've got another bomb."

Friberg took the communiqué and glanced over the message. "You see, this is precisely why we can't give the Air Force their target."

"What do you mean? This changes everything! I'm not going to just sit by and watch—"

"Shut up, Ingersol! Think, man! That device was remote detonated. We can't just sweep in and carpet bomb the jungle. Anybody crazy enough to set off one bomb because we didn't deliver someone's head on a platter is crazy enough to detonate a second at the first sniff of an attack!"

"The second bomb is already triggered."

"So he says. Could be a bluff. If it is, we're pretty much done."

"We should suppress any signals coming from the region."

"We're on it."

That set Ingersol back. So the man was thinking beyond his own problems finally. "Can't they drop a smart weapon on the compound? Something that hits them before they know it's on its way?"

"And accomplish exactly what? If he *has* already triggered the second device, killing him now would only remove any chance of terminating this twenty-four-hour countdown of his. If he hasn't triggered it, we can't afford to set him off."

"So what, then?"

Friberg glanced at the message again. "We evacuate southern Florida. We look for the bomb in every nook and cranny surrounding Miami. We curse the day we allowed Casius to live. We locate Abdullah Amir using whatever resources exist and we hope we can isolate any signal he's using for the detonation."

A thought dropped into Ingersol's mind. The thought that a highly skilled operative dropped into that jungle might be their best bet.

"Then we should send Casius after him."

Friberg blinked. "Casius?"

"He's the best operative we have, he knows the lay of the land, and he's already there."

"He's also AWOL. We have no way of contacting him." Friberg stood. "Forget Casius. We've got some briefings to run. We'll give the president an update from the car."

He headed for the door.

"Where are you going?" Ingersol asked, still short on breath.

"*We,* Ingersol. We are going to Miami."

THE SIMPLE fact that very few United States residents had ever seen the effects of a nuclear blast rendered the news that a detonation had just occurred off the coast of Florida at first impossible to believe. The terrorist activities in New York had been horrifying; this was simply incomprehensible. When the pictures finally flashed on the tube, the nation came to a literal standstill.

The first live images came from a jetliner flying high enough to avoid the electromagnetic pulse. They showed a coastline dotted by a thousand small trails of smoke that news commentator Gary Reese of CBS said were scattered fires. By the time the first helicopter flew over the region against specific orders to clear the air space, 90 percent of the country hovered around television sets, gawking at images of fires and gutted buildings.

A hand-held video taken from a hotel room in Daytona Beach was first played by a local ABC affiliate. But within minutes the networks had picked it up and the simple image of the eastern horizon lighting up, midday, replayed itself a thousand times on every television set across America.

The largest freeways ran bare through silent cities. Bars with televisions were crowded with customers, their necks cocked to the sets.

All regular programming was canceled and the talking heads began their analysis to a gaping public. The president begged the country's patience and vowed swift retribution. It was a terrorist attack, everyone quickly agreed. Some analysts suggested responding with nuclear weapons immediately and overwhelmingly. Others insisted on a surgical strike. Against whom or where seemed almost beside the point.

Then news of another kind came and a new terror spread through the nation like a raging fire. Residents of south Florida were being asked to evacuate their homes. In a calm manner, of course, controlled by the National Guard along five selected routes running north. But leave quickly and take nothing. Why? Well, there could only be one reason regardless of what the official word insisted.

There was another bomb.

And if there was another bomb in Florida, then who was to say that the same terrorists hadn't hidden one in Chicago or Los Angeles or any other city? Wouldn't it make more sense to spread the weapons for greater impact?

Within three hours of the detonation, the nation ran amuck in panic. The truth settled in like a gut punch—the impossible had just happened and no one knew what to do.

CHAPTER FORTY

SHANNON DROPPED into the processing plant behind one of the five large white tanks, each marked respectively with the chemical that it held: calcium bi-carbonate, sulfuric acid, ammonium hydroxide, potassium permanganate, and gasoline. Chemicals used to refine cocaine. He peered around the tank marked "gasoline" and scanned the room. Pipes fed from the tanks to the mixing vats clustered in the room's center. The vast operation was controlled from the glass room that hugged the east wall opposite the tanks.

Two armed guards loitered by the door leading from the lab. An additional eight to ten men worked in the lab. As things now stood, crossing the room without raising an alarm would be impossible. He had roughly twenty-four minutes before the first helicopter exploded.

Shannon slipped the pack from his back, set a timer to twenty-two minutes, and wedged the plastic explosive under the gasoline tank. He slipped to the ammonium hydroxide tank on the far left, laid a small bundle of C-4 on the cement floor behind it, set the timer for one minute, and retreated back to the right side.

He crouched and waited. Directly across the room from him, the tunnel through which he and the woman had escaped ran into the mountain. Tanya. Her name was Tanya, come back from the dead to speak to him about her God. She was as beautiful as he remembered. Possibly more. His heart pounded steadily.

And the priest? It was too late for the priest.

The air shattered with an explosion. Immediately all heads jerked to the far corner and Shannon bolted from his cover. Steams of ammonium hydroxide jetted from the ruptured tank to his far left. Yells of alarm filled the air as pipes hissed the potent gas. Before any of the men had fully registered the nature of the accident, Shannon was across the room and in the tunnel, sprinting down the earth floor toward the elevator shaft he and Tanya had used.

He tossed a single bundle of C-4 under the conveyor track as he ran. It would close the tunnel. Then he was at the gaping elevator shaft—clear to the bottom with the car resting above him. He looked back toward the processing lab from where the ruckus now carried. If he'd been spotted, they weren't pursuing.

He reached into the shaft, grabbed the thick steel cable, and lowered himself to the basement level, ten feet above rock bottom. He withdrew the bowie knife, jammed it between the elevator doors, and wrenched hard. The steel doors gaped and he shoved his foot through the opening. Five seconds later Shannon tumbled into the hall that had sealed him in just two days ago.

ABDULLAH STOOD slightly hunched in the upper room, drenched in sweat, his facial muscles twitching spastically.

He considered calling the coast for confirmation of his blast but the fidgeting Hispanic before him was right. They couldn't trust anyone now. In fact, they should leave, before a fighter jet dropped one of those bombs on them that drilled through mountains. Before Jamal arrived by helicopter.

"But they can't attack us. They know the second device is already on a countdown. They will assume that only I can stop it. You see, that's the power of true terror." He couldn't remember such a feeling of satisfaction.

The room suddenly shook under the rumble of an explosion and Ramón bolted from his chair, terrified.

Abdullah sprang to the window. A dozen men scrambled about below, fleeing what appeared to be the contents of a ruptured tank. An accident? It was too coincidental. The seconds slogged off in his mind with the surreal pace of a huge pendulum.

And then he saw the half-naked man disappear into the tunnel to his far left and he swallowed.

The agent. Casius!

He spun to Ramón. "It's the agent!" For a moment he couldn't think. He stared at Ramón, who'd already drawn his gun.

"Casius?" Ramón said.

The Americans had sent the killer after him again! Instead of withdrawing, the CIA was going for the jugular.

It was time to leave. "Bring me the priest!"

He leapt over to the desk and snatched up the transmitter.

"The priest?"

"The priest, you idiot! The hostage! I need a hostage!"

SHANNON PLACED four charges in the basement where they'd held him before swinging back into the elevator shaft and climbing hand over hand to the second level.

Using the bowie again he pried his way into the middle floor, gun in hand. Apart from three closed doors, the hall lay empty.

Shannon slid up to the two doors on his left, listened for a brief moment with his ear pressed to the wood, and cracked them open only to find each empty. The men had probably rushed to the explosion in the lab. A barroom and a mess hall each received a timed explosive.

He ran back to the elevator and pressed the call button, ignoring the third door, which he knew must lead to the large processing lab. Only the third floor remained above him. Abdullah would be there.

The elevator whirred to life behind the door. Shannon blinked at the sweat leaking into his right eye and took a deep breath. He would go up there and kill Abdullah as he had always planned. And then he would leave the jungle forever. A picture of Tanya flashed through his mind and his head twitched.

Are you ready to die, Shannon?

Soon. I will be soon.

He flattened himself on the wall, leveled his gun at the elevator doors, and exhaled.

RAMÓN PRESSED himself into the elevator car's corner, squatting low. He'd taken the priest up to Abdullah and then he'd been sent to deal with Casius. The agent had eluded him once, but he wouldn't escape again. The elevator bell rang loudly and he shrank farther down.

The elevator jerked to a stop and the doors parted. Ramón's gun hand wavered before his eyes. Nothing. He held his breath and waited, straining for the first glimpse of movement.

But there was nothing. The doors slid closed and the elevator sat still, waiting further instructions.

Now what? If Ramón pressed any button, he might very well give himself away. Unless the agent was on the basement level. But then why didn't the car descend? Someone else had called the car, not he.

For a few moments Ramón remained crouched in the corner waiting, undecided. Meanwhile the agent was no doubt below or above. He wouldn't be on this floor. The thought finally prompted him to lean forward and press the "open" button.

The doors spread again and Ramón trained his gun on the opening. Still nothing. He stood and eased to the door's edge.

SHANNON SMELLED the musty scent of sweat the moment the doors opened and he was back-pedaling to the corner before they stopped. He sighted down the wall and waited.

The doors closed on the occupant, but the elevator sat still. He waited with his gun arm extended. The charges in the hangar would explode in less than five minutes. He didn't have all day.

The door opened again and after a moment a gun poked past the wall. Still he waited, his patience wearing thin.

A hand followed the gun. Shannon shot then, into the hand. The slug took it off at the knuckles and he ran forward. The hall filled with the gunman's wail.

Shannon's mind echoed with another wail—a wail suggesting that he didn't have the time for this. He stepped into the elevator just as the doors began to close. The man he'd wounded knelt in a gathering pool of blood. It was the one-eyed man. Shannon shot him through the forehead and had a hand on his collar before the head lolled back. The man's eyes remained open. He angrily jerked the body from the car, leapt over it, and stabbed the third-floor button.

Too slow. Any minute the mountain would begin its collapse under heavy explosions.

The elevator groaned upward. Shannon cursed the heat flashing along his spine. Anger blurred his thinking. What if Abdullah waited in ambush on the third floor? Had he thought *that* through? No. He only wanted to kill the man, a blind desire that ran through his blood like molten lead. Eight years of plotting had finally come to this moment.

And what if Abdullah wasn't up there at all?

Shannon ground his teeth. The bell sounded and the door slid open before his extended gun.

The hall was empty.

He stepped from the car, thinking even as his foot cleared the threshold that he was in a fool's game now. Acting before thinking.

The hall lay vacant and white-walled excepting two brown doors. Shannon ran for the first, tossing the Browning to his left hand midstride. The door was locked. Any minute now that C-4 would start blowing the helicopters. Grunting against a surge of panic, he stepped back, pumped a single slug through the handle, and smashed his foot against the door. It snapped open and he jumped through, gun extended.

The contents of the room barely registered. Some kind of storage. What did register was that they did not include Abdullah.

Shannon spun around and ran for the second door. This time he didn't bother trying the handle. He simply shot through the lock and crashed it open with the sole of his foot. He leapt through and fell to a crouch, swinging his weapon in a quick arc.

A desk strewn with papers was on one end of the office; a tall bookcase stood against the other. The office was empty! Impossible!

Shannon stood, at a loss, his mind spinning. This could mean only one thing: Abdullah had escaped! A growl started in his throat and rose past his gaping mouth in a ferocious snarl. A red surge swept through his mind, momentarily blinding him.

He looked back to the desk. A book on nuclear proliferation lay facedown. The bomb.

Yes, the bomb.

Across the room a glass picture window was shaking and it occurred to him that the explosions had started. Then the sound came, deep-throated booms that shook the floor under his feet.

Shannon's mind snapped then as instinct took control of his body. He bent low, snatched a thin rug from the wood floor, and ran from the room. When the gasoline tank went, the main complex would collapse. Screams drifted over another detonation, still in the hangar, he thought. Those helicopters were popping.

He punched the call button and the elevator doors sprang open. The car suddenly quaked badly and he knew one of the basement explosives had detonated early. If the one in the tunnel went, he would be finished.

The elevator ground down a floor and opened to the tunnel that housed the conveyor. Shannon sprang from the car and sprinted away from the processing lab. The ground suddenly shook with a string of explosions and the overhead lights winked to black. The gasoline tank had gone! The caverns would come down around his ears!

He pelted forward. The freight elevator waited in darkness thirty yards ahead, powerless now. But he could still take the shaft up to the tube.

It was suddenly there, barely lit by the flames raging in the lab far behind. He vaulted over the rail and grabbed at the framework built into the vertical shaft. He flung the rug over his shoulder and clawed his way up, knowing that at any moment the explosives in the tunnel below would blow.

And then they did, with a steel-wrenching thunder. Stone crumbled and fell past him. Shannon slung the rug into the tube and scrambled over the lip for the second time in as many days. This time it would be belly down—he had no time to adjust his position. The rug slid forward and the elevator framework behind him tore loose from the rockface.

Shannon gripped the rug with both hands and fell toward the river far below.

CHAPTER FORTY-ONE

"IT APPEARS that we might, and I want to stress the word *might,* have another device located somewhere in southern Florida." The president's face looked white on the tube, despite the makeup CNN had hurriedly applied, David thought.

It was happening. And he was learning about it with the rest of the department—heck, with the rest of the country. He had suspected something, but never this. The briefing room was silent.

"It is very important that any residents within a fifty-mile radius of the pier head north using the recommended routes as quickly and as calmly as possible. This is only a precaution, mind you, and we can't afford panic. I cannot tell you how important it is for you not to panic. Everything in the realm of possibilities is being done to search the area with highly specialized sensors. If another nuclear device is located near Miami, we will find it. But we must take the precautions the Office of Homeland Security has laid out."

The president was talking, but another voice was whispering in David's mind as well. It was Casius, and he was telling David to leave town for a while. Far away. Which meant that Casius knew, or at least suspected more than any of them.

WHILE AMERICA glued its eyes on Miami, a U.S. registered clipper bearing the name *Angel of the Sea* slipped up the Intracoastal Waterway best known as Chesapeake Bay. It was one of hundreds of boats on the water that day. The small cargo vessel had made the trip from the Bahamas to Curtis Point—just south of Annapolis and a stone's throw from Washington, D.C.—dozens of times, each time with a variety of imported goods on board, usually with at least a partial load of exclusive lumbers that sold by the pound rather than by the foot.

The small business had made its owner—best known as John Boy in the local bars—quite wealthy. Or more accurately, the *extracurricular* business he conducted with *Angel of the Sea* had made him well off.

For every week John Boy spent traipsing back and forth to the Bahamas, he spent two dealing the coke. His price from Abdullah was half what every other dealer paid to get their hands on the white powder—the benefits of establishing this new route.

Fine by him. The less he paid, the more he made and, judging by the ease of his trips, this route could hardly be safer. Jamal had done his homework. Heck, on more than one occasion he had waved to the Coast Guard while steaming through the bay. They all knew John Boy.

John Boy had been nursing a beer behind the wheel when news of the nuclear blast off Florida's coast reached him. He stared dumbfounded at the tube for half an hour and his beer had gone warm. He had just cut through those waters himself, less than twenty-four hours earlier. If he'd stopped off in Freeport as was his custom, he might be . . . toast. Literally. But Ramón had insisted on making the trip a straight shot this time.

"You see, you can never tell, John Boy," he muttered to himself at the wheel. "You live and let live, and you die when it's your time." That's the way he'd always lived his life.

"Holy Moses." Next you know, some mad man'll be wheeling a bomb up to the Capital. Maybe it was time he thought about moving west.

He glanced at the chart spread out before him. If the weather held, he'd make Curtis Point in four hours, anchor in the bay, and head home. The log with the goods would have to wait this time. He always waited until all eyes were firmly off the ship before unloading that last log—forty-eight hours at least. But now with this Florida thing . . .

"Holy Moses."

ABDULLAH HAD just stepped from the underground passage, dragging a blindfolded priest, when the mountain began its trembling. Around him the jungle came to life with fleeing creatures and Abdullah crouched low. The escape passage behind the bookcase had been his idea from the beginning, but he'd always imagined using it to flee his own men, or Jamal, not some assassin from the CIA. Either way, he had chosen well in sending Ramón down in the elevator to deal with Casius.

The Caura River's current waited half a mile to the south. He had pushed the button on Yuri's transmitter and if all had gone well, the bomb aboard the *Lumber Lord* had detonated. But had it? He ground his molars, desperate to know this one detail.

Nothing here mattered now. The second bomb would soon detonate and nothing would make him stop it.

Actually, nothing *could* stop him.

Yes, that was right, wasn't it? He had the codes, but he hadn't memorized them. And now they had just gone up in smoke because of the American's own foolishness. So no one could stop the second bomb. Other than Jamal, of course. But Jamal wasn't here to stop it. He had only to make his way out of the jungle now.

He shivered and suppressed the urge to send the second signal, detonate the second bomb, in case the first had failed.

Abdullah closed his eyes. It was the second bomb that would make history—not this little firecracker he'd sent them. The second bomb was now close enough to Washington, D.C., to destroy the CIA. And the Capital. The thought pushed a soft groan through his chest.

He considered shooting the priest and leaving him here—it would be much simpler than taking him. But another thought stopped him. There were others out there, the ones who'd crossed the perimeter sensors. American soldiers. A hostage would be wise. He would kill him downriver, after the Caura joined the Orinoco.

CHAPTER FORTY-TWO

Sunday

AT TEN thousand feet, peering from a military transport's bubble, David Lunow thought metro Miami looked like an octopus with long tentacles of creeping automobiles reaching out from the bloated city. The lines stretched north two hundred miles along five major routes that had hemorrhaged into several hundred smaller escape routes.

Based on reports from the National Guard, the scene on the ground brought new clarity to the meaning of "chaos." Driven from their homes at the president's urging and by relentless television images of a blackened Daytona Beach, twenty million city dwellers scurried like rats from a rising tide. Honking cars clogged the streets within hours. Bicycles wobbled in and out of stalled vehicles. Some of the more fit jogged. In the end the runners led the exodus. No mode of transportation moved as fast as they.

And where were they all going?

North. Just north.

David glanced at his watch. Ten hours. Across the aisle, Friberg gazed out another window with Mark Ingersol. David caught Ingersol's attention and thumbed outside. "There's no way they're going to get away in time. You know that."

The man's eyebrow lifted. "They're doing better than I imagined. If they had any brains, they'd just leave the cars and walk."

"For the record, sir, I want to make it clear that I believe we're going about this wrong. We should be looking north as well."

"You've said that. We don't have the time to check Miami and you want us to spread ourselves even thinner? You have a hunch. We have a threat on paper that puts a bomb in Miami. I'm not sure we have any choice."

He had a point, of course. But David's hunch was making his skin crawl. The plane dipped a wing and began a quick descent to Miami International. They were the only plane on pattern and within ten minutes they were down.

The air seemed thicker than David remembered and he couldn't help but wonder if the detonation out to sea had affected the weather. They were ushered into the terminal where a solemn gray-haired Lieutenant John Bird met them with an outstretched hand.

"I hope you have some information for us," Bird said, taking each hand quickly. "I've got a thousand men scattered over southern Florida and we don't even know what we're looking for. A picture or a description wouldn't hurt." He spoke without smiling. By the rings under his eyes, he hadn't slept for a while, David thought.

"If we knew what you were looking for, you would know by now, wouldn't you?" Friberg's tone earned a hard stare from the National Guard officer.

"Tell me what you've got," Friberg demanded.

Bird hesitated only a second before spitting out his report in staccato fashion. "We're sweeping every port south of the blast site in ten-man teams with Geiger counters. So far, nothing has turned up. We're manually picking through every storage bin waiting for customs inspection, but like I said, without a specific description the process is slow. We've isolated every shipment received in the last three days and are currently searching their deliveries, but again, we're shooting in the dark. If we at least had a size on this thing—"

"But we *don't* have a size on this thing. What about the DEA leads? Have you traced the suspected trafficking routes?"

"Not yet, sir. We—"

"Not yet? I thought the DEA gave that top priority. These terrorists are operating out of drug country, Lieutenant. Don't you think it would make sense for them to use trafficking routes?" The director's face flushed red. "Bring me the DEA intelligence."

"Yes, sir." Bird eyed Friberg for a moment.

"Now, Lieutenant."

Bird turned and strode for the door.

"Excuse me, sir," David interjected. "But have we established contact with Casius?"

Friberg faced him. "What would Casius have to do with this, Lunow? If we'd made contact with him, he'd be dead, wouldn't he?"

"Maybe. Maybe not."

Friberg's nostrils flared.

"But I was referring to his knowledge of the situation, not his elimination. You put the word out to him?"

"He's a rogue agent. Our intentions are to kill him, not court him. And we don't exactly have a direct line to the man's head."

"He's been in contact with these terrorists, for crying out loud! He may have information you need," David said. "And if you wanted to get word to him, I would think a few well-placed helicopters with loudspeakers might be a start. But you're not interested in bringing him in, are you?"

Friberg trembled when he spoke. "You are out of line, Lunow! But I don't have the time to address your obvious lack of understanding right now. We've got a deadline here."

The director turned his back on David and strode for the window.

"Ingersol!" he snapped.

Ingersol flashed David an angry stare and followed the director over to the window. Bird burst through the doors, gripping the DEA report. He joined the men at the window.

David swallowed. "We're toast," he mumbled. "We're toast and they know it."

SHANNON CRAWLED from the Orinoco River, feeling a deep desperation he'd rarely felt. It was the same vacuum that had sucked at his chest eight years earlier. The emptiness he thought might precede suicide.

His back stung badly and he wondered if the skin was drawing infection. He was a good ten miles from where he'd left Tanya on the banks of the Caura River.

Shannon stood for a moment on the shore, his hands dripping limp at his sides. For the first time in eight years he had failed to kill a man he'd pursued. Abdullah had escaped.

He gripped his hands to fists, glanced up the mountain, and lumbered forward. He would finish this. It was all he knew, this drive to kill. And it wasn't just about Abdullah, was it? He was showing them all.

The feeling couldn't be too different from what a trapped animal felt, pounding relentlessly into a concrete wall, oblivious to the blood seeping from its head.

Shannon blinked the sweat from his eyes and crashed through the underbrush, not caring who heard him now. If this was his last mission, so be it. It would be a fitting end—to die having killed the one who had taken the life of his mother on the lawn.

Are you ready to die, Shannon?

Tanya.

Her face rose up in his mind, out of the black fog. A seventeen-year-old blonde, diving from the cliff into his arms. A twenty-five-year-old woman, running through the jungle at his heels. His vision blurred and he grunted.

You're a fool, Shannon.

He pulled up and gripped his head, suddenly terrified. For a few long breaths he shook on the path. What was he doing? What had he *done?*

The black fog settled into his mind slowly.

A thought stuttered through his mind. An image of his blade crossing Abdullah's neck. He shook again, this time with a familiar eagerness.

Shannon dropped his arms and ran. He would kill Abdullah and then he would kill Jamal.

Chapter Forty-Three

TANYA WAS sleeping dreamlessly when the blow caught her midsection. She instinctively coiled up, coughing. A voice screamed above her.

"Get up!"

Another blow slammed into her back and she scrambled to her knees. Above her, a figure slowly shifted into focus, backlit by the afternoon sun. Her head spun, and she thought she was going to faint. But the feeling passed, and she blinked at the man.

A man with the white wedge through his hair still stood over her, grinning with twitching lips. Abdullah. She knew him immediately.

He held a silver pistol in his right hand. A small aluminum skiff tied to a muddy stump bobbed on the current behind him. The man's white shirt had been browned by river muck and his black shoes were caked with mud. He'd saved his pants by rolling them up above his socks to hairy, bony shins that looked as though they hadn't seen the sun in years. The angry scar on his cheek curled with his grin. He'd come down the river from the plantation, which meant Shannon had failed to find him.

"Well. What a surprise. It's the assassin's woman," Abdullah said. His tongue seemed dark in his mouth when he spoke, like an eel hiding in its black cave. His wet lips quivered spastically.

"It appears that you'll die after all." The Arab's eyes glistened black and bulging, and Tanya thought that he had lost himself. She stood slowly.

She saw Father Petrus then, kneeling in the mud by the skiff, blindfolded, hands tied behind his back.

"Father Petrus!" She instinctively moved toward him.

"Shut up!" Abdullah struck her shoulder, and she fell back to her seat.

She scrambled around. "What have you done to him?"

"It's okay, Tanya." The priest's voice was hoarse.

Tanya? He knew her real name?

Abdullah smiled, amused. "You want your priest, don't you? Yes, of course, you are about to die and you want your priest." He turned to the river. "Priest, come here."

Petrus did not move.

"Come here!" Abdullah screamed. "Are you deaf?"

Father Petrus got his legs under him and staggered toward them. The Arab stepped out impatiently and shoved him the last few yards. Petrus collapsed beside Tanya.

She ripped his blindfold off and threw it to one side. Petrus blinked in the light, and she helped him to his seat.

Abdullah looked at them, an amused expression on his face, momentarily lost, it seemed. He lifted his black eyes and studied the tree line above the clearing. "Where is your man now? He's not here, is he? No. He couldn't have come this far so quickly. But he'll come. He'll come for his lover."

Please, God . . . Tanya started the prayer but didn't know where to go with it.

Abdullah rested his eyes on her again. He motioned to her with the pistol. "Do you know what I've done?"

His face held such a look of pure evil that Tanya instantly knew. The bomb. He had detonated the bomb in her vision. Fear squeezed at her heart.

"Yes?" A twisted grin lifted his left cheek, the one without a scar. Sweat snaked from his temples. "Do you know?"

"You're the devil," she said.

His lips snapped shut. His eyes glared round. "Shut up!" Spittle flecked on his lower lip.

She looked at Father Petrus seated beside her. Their eyes met and his were bright. His face sagged and his clothes were torn but his eyes were bright. A smile tugged gently at his mouth. She blinked. A lump rose in her throat.

She looked up at Abdullah. "You're the hand of Satan."

The Arab's gun hand began to tremble and she spoke again, gaining confidence now, "Yes, I do know what you've done. You've detonated a nuclear bomb."

He stopped, surprised. "It worked?"

He didn't know? "Yes, I think so."

"And how would you know this?"

"I saw it," she said simply. "In a dream."

He cocked his head slightly and examined her face carefully. "You saw it, did you? And what else did you see?" His lips twisted. "Do you see what will happen now?"

She hesitated. She only knew that it would be good for Shannon to come through the trees now. And she didn't necessarily want him to save her, although that seemed reasonable enough, but she wanted him to be here. Shannon.

"I'm sure you want to kill," she said.

He blinked. "And will I succeed?"

"I don't know."

"Then you don't know anything."

"I know that you're death."

"Shut up!" he screamed. His voice echoed about the trees.

She looked past him to the tree line. *Shannon, do you hear that, my love? Come quickly. Please, there isn't much time.*

My love?

"If you speak again, I'll kill him," Abdullah said, pointing the gun at Petrus.

She looked back at him. "You can't kill him."

Abdullah's face quivered with anger.

"He would hear the gunshot. My Shannon would hear it," Tanya said.

The Arab's black eyes seemed to hollow with hate. Like two holes drilled through that skull of his.

"Lie down on your stomach."

Petrus protested. "Please, I must—"

"Shut up!"

Tanya hesitated and then did as he asked. His knee dropped into her back and she waited for something to happen. The fear returned then, as she lay on her stomach. A panicking terror that ripped through her bones like white-hot lead. Nausea swept through her and she imagined his blade reaching forward and slicing through her neck.

Oh, God, please! Please save me! Her heart crashed in her chest and her muscles strung tight. Behind her Abdullah's breathing thickened.

And then Abdullah simply stood and walked away.

TANYA LAY on her stomach for a long minute before moving. Petrus was still seated beside her, staring at the river. She followed his eyes. Abdullah squatted on the muddy bank, twenty meters off. He stared at them, rocking, gun limp in his right hand.

Tanya pushed herself up to her seat and faced Abdullah.

"Father Petrus?"

He answered without turning. "Yes, Tanya?"

"I'm . . . I'm very sorry, Father."

He turned his head and raised a brow. "Sorry? Don't be sorry for me, my dear. We are winning. Can't you see that?"

"Winning? We're sitting on a river a thousand miles from anywhere with a madman staring us down. I'm not sure I'm following."

"And to be honest, I'm not necessarily following either. But I do know a few things. I know that your parents were drawn to this jungle twenty years ago so that you could be here today. I know that a young girl named Nadia died in my homeland of Bosnia forty years ago so that I could be here today." He offered a smile. "This is far beyond us, my dear."

"My parents were *killed,* Father."

Father Petrus looked up to the canopy to his left and sighed. "So were mine. And I think we may be as well. As were all the disciples and Christ himself."

Tanya's mind spun. Something in her belly told her that his words were spun of gold. Her vision swam.

"God's chess match," she said.

She expected him to comfort her. To reason with her or something. But he didn't.

"Yes."

For a full minute they just stared out to the trees, hearing a sea of cicadas, watching Abdullah's glazed-over stare from across the way. He was squatting and waiting for something. He was insane.

"You're saying that my parents died so that I would end up in a box and pledge my life to God to come back here and lay on a riverbank and die myself."

"Perhaps. Or so that you could do something only you can do." He looked at her. "Do you know what that might be?"

She considered the question. "It sounds crazy, but maybe to love . . . Shannon."

"The boy."

"Yes, the boy. You know him better as Casius. The assassin."

The father's eyes widened with the realization. "Casius." A smile tugged at his lips. "Of course."

A tear pooled in her eye. "It may not make any sense to you, but my heart is crying for him."

"So then he is a part of this too."

"He was the man I loved."

"Yes, but more."

"What?"

"I don't know. But nothing is without a purpose. For all we know *his* parents were somehow drawn to the jungle so that he could become who he has become."

"An assassin? Doesn't sound like God to me."

"And the man who killed Hitler, was he raised up by God?"

"You're saying that one of the reasons God brought our parents to the jungle was so that Shannon and I could fall in love and become who we are today for some reason somehow connected with this . . . this attack on America by these terrorists."

"The chess match. I'm saying that the black side has had something up its sleeve and God has known for a long time. Yes. It happens a thousand times a day."

"We are hardly pawns. What if my parents had not responded to God's call?"

"Then you wouldn't have fallen in love with Shannon, would you?"

"And what if Helen hadn't persuaded me to come back?"

"Then . . . then you wouldn't be able to love Shannon again."

"And?"

He paused. "And I don't know."

A knot rose in her throat and she swallowed against it. "Part of me does still love him. But he's changed. I'm not sure I know how to love him."

"Love him the same way you are loved," he said.

She looked at Petrus and he held her gaze for a long time. His brow lifted mischievously. "I knew a priest who died for a village once. He was crucified. Would you like to feel the love he felt, Tanya?"

Feel love? The silky voice of B. J. Thomas crooned through her ear, *Hooked on a feeling.*

"Yes," she said.

Petrus smiled and closed his eyes.

Tanya looked away. Abdullah still sat across the way, staring at them. The birds still called in the afternoon heat. A warm breeze swept over her—a breeze laced heavily with the odor of sweet gardenia flowers. Like the gardenias around Helen's house. The ones from Bosnia.

Tanya's heart hammered. She felt the scent caress her nostrils and then sink into her lungs. Heat surged through her bones, like an electric shock.

She gasped and fell back to the grass.

The euphoria followed almost immediately, swallowing her whole. An ecstasy unlike any she had ever felt. As if her nerves had been injected with this drug—God's love flowing through her.

But it wasn't simply her nerves or her bones or her flesh. It was her heart. No, not her heart, because her heart was just flesh and it was more than a drug that wrapped itself around flesh.

It was her soul. That thing in her chest that had long ago taken to hiding in her bowels. Her soul was doing backflips. It was leaping and twirling and screaming with pleasure.

She threw her arms wide on the grass and laughed out loud, thoroughly intoxicated by the love. She felt hot tears run down her cheek as if a tap had been turned on. But they were tears of ecstasy. She would give her life to swim in a lake of these tears.

In that moment she wanted to explode. She wanted to find a lost orphan and hug him tight for a whole day. She wanted to take her tears and sprinkle them on the world. She wanted to give. Give everything so that someone else might have this feeling. It was that kind of love.

Then an image of a cross stuttered through her skull and she caught her breath. Her arms were still spread wide in laughter, but her chest had frozen. A man bled on the towering wooden beams. It was a priest. No, it was Christ! It was God. He was loving. All of this came from him. These tears of joy, this euphoria that had raged through her bones, her soul doing backflips—all because of his death on those beams.

The image burned into her mind like a red-hot branding iron.

And then it was gone.

Tanya lay prostrate, shaking in sobs. She wept because for the first time in memory everything was starting to clear. The purpose of life lay before her, crystal and breathtakingly beautiful. It all made sense. It not only made sense; it made lovely sense. And she was reduced to this . . . this blubbering lump in the face of it all.

Yes, something terrible had happened. But God was taking care of that. It wasn't her concern now. What mattered now was that she had been loved. That she was loved.

That she had been called to love.

Shannon, oh Shannon! How her heart ached for him. It was as though this breath flowing through her body had given her a transfusion of love. Love for Shannon.

Tanya lay on her back and stared past tears at the sun. She was barely aware that Father Petrus was crying softly beside her. The jungle slept in the noon heat. To think that history lay cradled in the bosom of a young woman lost here in the deepest of jungles while the rest of the world went mad seemed absurd. High above, a macaw flapped lazily through the blue sky. It showed no concern for the humans by the river. Maybe it didn't even see them.

Tanya closed her eyes, once again consumed with an image of the tall, muscular man who had dragged her here. Shannon Richterson.

Father, I will do as you will. I will do anything. I will love him. Please bring him back to me.

Will you die for him, Tanya?

Tanya heard a rustle and opened her eyes just in time to see Abdullah grinning, swinging his gun down. Its butt struck her head and her world exploded with stars and then went black.

BY THE time David Lunow followed his superiors into the final transport out of Miami International, less than three hours remained until the Brotherhood's twenty-four hours expired. And Bird's men had found nothing.

The Bell helicopter rose slowly and then skimmed north over deserted streets. Stragglers could be seen wandering the main streets of the downtown districts and farther north the highways were clogged, effectively shutting down any retreat for the millions of stranded motorists. One thing became crystal clear as the helicopter wound its way out of danger's way: If another bomb did detonate inland, a lot of U.S. citizens would die despite the evacuation. A million. Maybe more. And if the bomb went off in another city, then many more.

David turned to Ingersol and noted that the man had been watching him with a hazed stare. "If this thing goes, you're toast; you know that, don't you?"

For the first time in many days, Ingersol did not respond.

"In fact, regardless of what happens, you're toast."

Still no response.

"If you would have listened to me a week ago, we might not have had the first blast and we probably wouldn't be running for cover now. Someone's gonna take the fall."

When he received no response to his third charge, David turned back to the window.

"God help us," he mumbled. "God help us all."

OF THE nearly three hundred million people living in the United States of America, the only ones *not* awake and watching the real-time satellite picture of southern Florida were those fleeing southern Florida.

It was an event that shut down the world. The cities near Miami had been deserted, the hospitals had been evacuated, and the air space had been cleared. It was a looter's paradise down there and nobody cared. Not even the looters. They were too busy trucking north.

The talking heads hosted an endless lineup of experts who stammered their way through hours of speculation. In the end, nobody looked good; nobody looked bad. They all pretty much looked desperate.

Someone in the White House had leaked the twenty-four-hour detail and every station now had a clock on-screen, ticking down the time from the last blast. Give or take a few seconds, the clocks now read one hour, thirty-eight minutes.

John Boy sat eating a sandwich in his home in Shady Side, watching NBC's coverage of the nation's meltdown, shaking his head. All seaports had been closed, but not before he'd lowered anchor in the bay. The terrorists had finally done it.

John Boy's boat, *Angel of the Sea,* sat in silent waters, and if anybody had been listening with a highly specialized listening device, they might have heard the faint electronic ticking in the bowels of her hull. But nobody was listening to *Angel of the Sea.* Nobody was even thinking of her.

Except Abdullah, of course.

And Jamal.

CHAPTER FORTY-FOUR

LOST IN the madness, barely aware of himself, Shannon came upon the bank where he'd left the woman.

The sun was dipping in the west. Ahead lay an endless sea of foliage, rolling and climbing and falling and plunging. And under it somewhere crept a single man running from him. The Arab Abdullah. It was madness. They both were mad.

But deep in his mind, beyond the madness, an image replayed itself in an endless loop, drawing Shannon forward despite it all. An image of a thick green lawn, and on the lawn his father. And beside his father, his mother. Father was cut in two; Mother's head was missing. And in the machine hovering over them, Abdullah was grinning. And beside the Arab, a thousand men in brown suits, with plastic grins.

The miles passed underfoot steadily, with pounding monotony. But the thoughts were anything but monotonous—they were hell.

As his feet ate up the miles, a few new frames joined that clip running through his brain. They showed a young woman trapped screaming in a box while her own father soaked up the bullets above her.

Tanya.

She had latched her claws into him. He couldn't shake the images. In fact, they seemed to work their way deeper into him with each footfall, like barbed spurs.

She was as beautiful as the day he'd last seen her, swimming in the waters beneath the waterfall. His mind drifted to old memories. To tender moments that seemed grossly out of place in his mind. Snapshots from a fairy tale of happy endings. Pages filled with laughter and gentle embraces. Sweet delicate kisses. Windblown hair across a fair neck. Soft words whispered in his ear.

I love you, Shannon.

Tears blurred his eyes and he gave a grunt before clenching his teeth and shoving them back.

Abdullah, Abdullah, Shannon. Think of Jamal. Think of the plan.

Tanya, oh, Tanya. What has happened? We had paradise.

But Abdullah had snatched it away, hadn't he? And the CIA. They would all die. All of them.

Shannon ran under the canopy, desperately fighting the terrible ache lodged in his throat. Then years of discipline began to win him over to his mission. He had come to this jungle to kill. He had waited eight slow, agonizing years for the perfect timing, and now it was here.

Sula . . .

He lowered his head and replayed the brutal slaying of his parents, isolating each bullet as it spun through the air and landed into flesh. With each slap of his feet, another bullet bit deep. With each breath, the helicopter's rotors rushed through the air. A knife to the throat would be too good for Abdullah. His death would have to be slow—the blood would have to flow long.

When Shannon came upon the bank where he'd left Tanya, he was barely aware of himself. He swam through a black fog.

He entered from the south, through tall trees and scarce brush. The murmur of flowing water carried in the stillness. A gentle breeze played over the grass.

Tanya lay in the grass.

Shannon pulled up.

She was on her back in the middle of the grass. Not that he expected her up and working, but she lay folded with one leg under her torso—odd for sleep.

Shannon scanned the tree line quickly. He tested the air but the wind was at his back. She could be sleeping, still exhausted from the long trek.

He watched her chest rise and fall with each breath. For a long time, he watched her and the ache in his throat returned.

Dear Tanya, what have I done? What have I done to you? He closed his eyes. When he opened them, his vision was blurred.

You are wounded, my dear Tanya. Thinking like that—using those words, *dear Tanya*—released a flood of emotion in his chest. *A stake was driven into your heart when you were a tender woman. And now I have pushed it deeper. I just wanted to show you, Tanya. Can you understand that? Killing is all I have. It is what Sula gave me. I meant to show you that. I didn't mean to hurt you.*

Shannon leaned against the tall Yevaro tree beside him and let the pain roll through him. The jungle sounds fell away and he allowed himself to wallow in the strange sentiments. The field before him lay in surreal stillness, peaceful with Tanya resting on the grass. He stood at the perimeter, wreaking of blood. Like a foul monster peering from the shadows at a sleeping innocent beauty.

He clung to the bark and felt his torso buck with a dry sob.

It was the first time he'd ever felt such ravaging sorrow. She lay out there so innocent, breathing like a child, and he . . . he had nearly killed her.

Kill her, Shannon.

He blinked. The fog was washing through his mind and for a moment he thought he might be dying. Kill her? How could he even think of killing her?

Sula . . .

Shannon closed his eyes and swallowed hard. He stepped out into the clearing and then saw the dark stain in her hair when he was halfway across the clearing.

His instincts took over midstride, before he formed the clear thought that this was blood on her head. He dove and had the knife from his belt before he hit the grass.

"Stand up, you fool!" a voice sneered across the clearing.

That voice. A chill flashed down Shannon's spine.

Tanya was still breathing—the wound hadn't been fatal. A blow to the head had left her unconscious. And now Abdullah was screaming at him.

"Stand up or I will shoot your woman!"

Abdullah had found his way here! In a thousand square miles of jungle he had stumbled upon Tanya. It was the river, of course. He had taken the river as most would. The crocodiles hadn't gotten to her, but Abdullah had.

Shannon's mind had already climbed back into its killing skin. Now he would kill Abdullah. And he would do it in front of Tanya.

He stood slowly and saw Abdullah step from the trees, dragging a man by the collar. The priest! He had Father Petrus.

Shannon cursed his own carelessness. He had given Abdullah the upper hand. It was the insanity plaguing him, the voices screaming in his skull, the foolish sentiments—they had made him weak. Now he faced a man bearing a gun at a distance of twenty meters without the least element of stealth in his favor.

The terrorist's white teeth flashed through a wicked grin and he forced the priest to kneel. Father Petrus's head lolled—he was barely coherent.

He shifted his gun to cover Tanya. "Throw your knives down. Slowly. Very slowly. And don't think that I won't kill her. If you even flinch, I will kill her, do you understand?" He held the gun three feet from Tanya's prone body, which still rose and fell in deep sleep.

Shannon ground his teeth. If he moved quickly enough, he could flip the knife backhanded and stick Abdullah in the throat. From this distance he could kill the man easily. Bleed him like a pig.

But Abdullah would have time to squeeze the trigger. If the gun had been trained on him, he might avoid the bullet, but Abdullah had the gun on Tanya.

"Throw them down!"

Every muscle in Shannon's body begged to hurl the knife now. He hesitated one last second and then tossed the knife. It landed with a soft thud. He clenched his jaw.

"The other one. Or are there two others?" Again that grin.

Shannon bent slowly and withdrew the Arkansas Slider from an ankle sheath. He threw it aside. It landed on the bowie and clanked.

"Turn around slowly."

Shannon glanced about the perimeter, his mind racing for alternatives, but they came slow just now. He turned as Abdullah asked. If he could coax the man into arm's reach, he could kill him without risking the woman. Quickly, before the butcher had time to know he'd been outwitted. Or slowly to give him time to feel his death.

"Turn around."

When Shannon turned back, Abdullah was kicking Tanya in the ribs.

Shannon flinched.

"Back!" Abdullah screamed. Spittle frothed on his lips. Bulging veins wrapped his taut neck.

"I told you to move slowly. Next time I will put a bullet in her thigh."

The Arab was quick. Very quick. He had anticipated—possibly even provoked—the reaction from Shannon and snapped back with amazing speed. Like a snake.

Tanya stirred on the next kick to her midsection. She moaned and pushed herself to her knees. A thin trail of dried blood stained her temple.

Kill him, Shannon. Kill them both. Kill them all.

He hated the thought.

Tanya stood and faced Abdullah. She hadn't seen Shannon yet. The priest still knelt, between them, eyes closed.

"Turn and greet your visitor." Abdullah grinned with childish pleasure at his cleverness.

Tanya turned. Very slowly. As if she were in a dream.

Their eyes met. Hers were blue and round, the eyes he remembered from the pool. Her lips sprang open. The same lips that had kissed him, dripping wet on the rocks. Something had changed in her face since he'd left her here. He saw more there than a cry for help. Actually, it wasn't a cry for help at all.

Shannon's heart stopped beating for a few long moments. She was pulling him back to the pool and he wanted to go.

The Arab stepped to the side and smiled at them. "You are reunited, yes?" He shoved a coil of fishing string at Tanya. "Hogtie him! Do you know what a hogtie is?"

She shook her head.

"Of course not. It's a tie for pigs." He jerked his pistol toward Shannon. "Tie him."

Shannon looked at Abdullah and saw that his eyes danced with fire.

He looked back at Tanya. She walked toward him, holding his eyes with her own. She stared at him like a child looking upon a magician performing an illusion—with utter awe. As if the last eight years were nothing more than one of her vivid dreams, and she was looking at him for the first time after finally waking.

A slight smile lifted the corners of her lips.

"Shannon," she said, and her soft voice echoed through his mind.

"Shut up!" Abdullah screamed. His voice rang about the perimeter and a flock of startled parrots took flight with screeches of protest. Abdullah kept his gun trained on her, sidestepping to match her pace.

"Did I tell you to talk to him? No, I told you to tie him!" He made a crazy circular motion with his free hand. "Tie his hands behind his back, to his ankles."

Stunned, Shannon watched her approach. She was hardly hearing the Arab—he knew that now. He had studied a hundred men under extreme trauma, more often than not trauma provoked by him. And he knew this: Tanya was barely aware of the man to her right. She was thoroughly engrossed with *him*, with Shannon.

The realization made him dizzy.

She had reached him and was gazing up at his face now. She lowered her eyes to his neck, his shoulders, his chest, studying each muscle as though for the first time. Tenderly, like a lover.

"Tie him!"

A voice was screaming in Shannon's mind, way back where his ears could barely hear it, but his mind was bending over in pain.

"Tie my hands behind my back and then to my ankles when I kneel down," Shannon said, his voice trembling. He suddenly wanted to cry. As he had cried just a few minutes earlier. What was happening to him?

Tanya.

Sula. Both names took hold of his thoughts, warring for dominance.

He was no longer thinking as clearly as he had a week ago.

Tanya pulled her eyes from him, still smiling softly. She slid around him and took his hands in hers. Spikes of heat ripped up his bones and he felt his fingertips quiver.

She was touching them gently; feeling his fingers, his palms. She ran her fingers down his arms. She was speaking to him with her tender touch. His heart raced.

Tie me, Tanya. Please, just tie me.

She wrapped the string around his wrists loosely, still touching his hands lightly, tracing his palms. She cinched her knots and he knelt. She knelt behind him and passed the line under his ankles.

He could feel her hot breath on his shoulders as she worked, leaning over him. The heavy aroma of flowers—gardenias—caressed his nostrils and he trembled once.

What's happening to me?

Kill her, Shannon! Kill her, you spineless worm!

He let his head loll to one side. Stillness settled over the clearing. Even the wind seemed to pause. Tanya's chin approached and then lightly touched his back, and his flesh quivered at her nearness.

A lump swelled in his throat, and for a terrible moment he thought he might burst into tears. For no reason at all.

Dear Tanya, what have I done to you? I am so sorry.

Kill her! Kill—

"Shannon," she whispered.

He froze.

She whispered it again, barely audible yet tender. "Shannon. I love you." Her breath played over his shoulder, and he could smell it. Musky and sweet. Gardenias.

The last of his control left when the scent of her reached his lungs. She was breathing love into him. He went limp—all but his heart, which was slamming against his chest desperately.

And then she was done with her tying.

"Step away from him," Abdullah said.

Tanya did not move. Maybe she hadn't heard him.

Abdullah shrieked this time. "Get back!"

Tanya stood slowly and stepped aside. Abdullah swept in and yanked the ties tight. Shannon bit his lip against the pain and gathered his senses. Any illusion he'd harbored of freeing himself from Tanya's loose bonds fell away.

Abdullah jumped back and cackled like a hyena. "There, you pig. You won't be so difficult to kill now, will you?"

He grabbed Tanya and shoved her back toward the center of the clearing. She stumbled forward and spun to him, flashing a vicious glare. For a second, Shannon thought she might yell at Abdullah. But the moment passed and she returned her gaze to him.

Abdullah stood halfway between them and stepped back to study his victims. He spread his legs and grinned wide.

He licked the spittle from his lips and shifted the gun to his left hand and then back to his right. "Well, well." He glanced at his watch. "We have time. Do you know what I have done, assassin?"

Tanya was staring at Shannon again, oblivious of Abdullah. Her figure distorted in the tears that hung in his eyes.

"I have detonated a nuclear device in your country, gringo. And another is set to go off soon. It's on a countdown that will end in less than an hour. A countdown that can only be stopped by me now."

Shannon stared at the man without expression.

"I have the power, and the world can do nothing." He tapped his temple. "The only code to stop it is locked in my mind."

"Shannon." It was Tanya, speaking in that soft, milky voice again. "Forgive me. I'm so sorry."

Abdullah jerked his head toward her. "Shut up!"

Shannon blinked the mist from his eyes, feeling as though he might crumble from the insanity of her words.

Tanya ignored Abdullah. "I know some things now, Shannon. I know that I was made to love you. I know that you need me to love you. I know that I always have loved you, and that I love you desperately now."

Abdullah took three leaping steps to her and brought a heavy hand across her bare cheek. The air resounded with the sound of flesh smacking flesh.

Crack!

Heat flared up Shannon's neck. He grunted and jerked against the bindings in sudden rage. Tanya's face turned a bright red. But her smile didn't waver.

"Leave her alone!" Shannon screamed. "You touch her and I'll rip your heart out!"

Pain shot down his spine and his head swam, and he knew now that it was Sula's doing. He closed his eyes against the agony.

"Shannon." She was speaking again and her words flowed like a balm flows. "Shannon, do you remember when we used to swim together, in the pool?"

He opened his eyes.

The Arab stood, dumbstruck.

Shannon remembered.

"Do you remember how I fell into your arms? And how you kissed my lips?" Her deep blue eyes held him.

The Arab spun his head to Shannon, off balance now.

Tanya ignored him. "Do you know that it was for today that we loved each other then? It was beyond us, Shannon. Our parents—they died for this day."

The words made no sense to him, but her eyes and her lips and her voice—they all crashed in on him at once. Her breath seemed to flow to him again.

She was loving him with an intensity he did not know could possibly exist. The blood drained from his head, and he let her words wash over him.

Something she had said made Abdullah step back.

"We're a part of God's plan, Shannon. You are. Like Rahab. God's trump card."

Shannon's mind spun in wild circles.

"Those bonds of love have never been broken. Tell me that you love me, Shannon. Please, tell me."

The pressure on his chest felt like a dam set to burst. Tears ran down his cheeks. Blood roared through his ears, and his face twisted in anguish.

"I love you desperately, Shannon."

I love you, Tanya.

A ball of anguish rolled up his chest, swelling as it rose.

Kill her—

"No!"

The pain roared in his ears, and for a moment he thought he was passing out. Tears spilled from his eyes and his face contorted in agony.

"Nooooo!" He let the cry run out and he gasped. "No, you sick spineless worm. I *love* her!" Sobs robbed his breath. He sucked in a lungful of air, tilted his head back, and screamed full throated at the sky.

"I love her!"

His cry echoed, silencing the jungle.

And then the ball of pain ripped up through his skull. His muscles tensed in a seizure and then released him. He groaned and sagged to a huddle.

For an endless moment, the world was blank to him. The river stopped rushing by, the ground no longer pressed into his knees, the breeze seemed to freeze. And then slowly his mind began to crawl out of its hole.

" . . . when I say something, I mean what I say!" The Arab was screaming and his face was red. Shannon turned to Tanya beyond him.

Tanya? He felt oddly as though he had stepped into a new world. Or out of one.

Tanya! What was she doing? She was smiling at him.

He began to sob softly. "I . . . I love you, Tanya," he said. He knelt there lost, like a child. "I love you. I love you so much. I'm sorry. I'm so sorry."

"Shut up!" Abdullah screamed.

She began to cry. "Shh . . . no, don't cry, Shannon. We're together again. It's okay now. Everything will be okay now."

"Tanya," he sobbed. The forest echoed with his cry. "Oh, God!" he wailed. "Forgive me. I've been so wrong. Oh, God, help me!"

And what have you done, Shannon? What have you gone and done? Panic skirted through his mind. *I've got to stop—*

Boom!

The gunshot echoed through the trees and Shannon snapped his eyes open. Father Petrus lay on his side, blood leaking from a head wound. *Oh, dear God, what have I done?*

Tanya was crying.

"Shut up!" Abdullah said as his face twisted with rage, and he leapt for Shannon. A knife glistened in his right hand. He slashed forcefully, slicing Shannon's chest to the ribs.

Shannon sat back to his haunches. His head swam.

The Arab trembled from head to foot. His eyes shone black and eager. He stood like a rabid dog over a rabbit. He reached down and cut again—across Shannon's shoulder.

Shannon moaned. Nausea swept through his gut. He looked at Tanya, pleading. Not for her help. For her love.

"I love you, Tanya," he said.

Tears streamed silently down her face as she mouthed her answer. *I love you, Shannon.*

The Arab slashed again, spittle flying from his lips. The blade flashed across Shannon's chest, forming a cross of sorts. He brought his arm back for another thrust.

"Sula!" Tanya's voice cut across the clearing.

The Arab spun, arm still cocked. Shannon's mind was only half here, at the river. The other half was thinking that he had to stop something. Something only he could stop.

Tanya was staring at Abdullah. She'd called him *Sula.* The corners of her mouth slowly rose. "I know you. We've met. Remember? You're called Sula and it means death."

Yes, death. Known as Sula to some. Lucifer to others. They were the same. Abdullah was frozen, holding the gun in his left hand and the knife now dripping with blood in his right. His face went white.

Tanya stood with her arms at her side, a new boldness in her posture. "And how are you stopped, Sula?"

The Arab slogged forward three steps. He stared dumbstruck at Tanya.

"You know that I can't let you kill him," Tanya said softly.

The world began to slow down. Things were going topsy-turvy. He had to stop something. Something much worse than this. And she was going to make sure that he did it.

Abdullah shook like a leaf now. Somehow this strange encounter between him and Tanya had flipped a switch.

Tanya spread her arms, still barely smiling. "You've done this before, haven't you?"

Shannon screamed then. "Abdullah! Take me! Leave her." He strained against the line, feeling it cut into his flesh. Blood from his chest and shoulder wounds ran down his belly.

The Arab looked at him, his facial muscles quivering. He held the gun at his side.

"No. Take me instead," Tanya said. She had lifted her arms to form a cross.

The Arab swiveled his head and lifted the pistol to her head in one smooth motion. The world fell to blurred images. Tanya shifted wide blue eyes to Shannon and they poured love into him.

She was giving her life for him!

Shannon's mind lost coherence then. He roared to his feet, snapping the line as he did so. The jungle was screaming.

His head hit Abdullah's back and the man's gun bucked. *Boom!*

From the corner of his eye, Shannon saw Tanya standing, her arms spread wide, her head tilted back. Abdullah had shot her! He'd shot Tanya!

The jungle was still screaming, long wails of desperation screeching around his ears.

And then the Arab hit the ground and Shannon crashed down on top of him. He shoved his knees forward, so that he straddled the man's chest. His left hand had found Abdullah's black hair. He snatched his bowie from Abdullah's belt.

Then it occurred to him that the screaming came from his own throat, not the jungle.

For a moment Shannon thought that he had died as well. His soul had been sucked clean of his body, leaving only a vast empty hole. But he knew that couldn't be true, because he was still screaming. "Noooo! Noooo!" Just that, over and over.

Only then did he realize that Tanya wasn't falling. The realization snatched the wind from him and he pulled up.

For a moment Abdullah shifted out of his focus. He jerked his head up and he stared into Tanya's blue eyes. She lowered her arms.

She was alive. Shannon's arms began to shake.

"Don't kill him, Shannon."

The Arab coughed beneath him.

Shannon breathed heavy, his lungs burned. His worlds were colliding. For a few moments no one moved.

He released his grip on Abdullah's hair. He would follow this woman over a cliff if she suggested it.

You have to stop it, Shannon. Only you can stop it.

He snatched up Abdullah's gun and scrambled to his feet. "Tanya! There's a bomb!" He was frozen by this strange panic that swept through him. He felt oddly vacant. *Tanya, there's a bomb?* What was he saying?

She looked at him dumbly. "It went off already—"

"No. Another bomb!"

Dear God, what had he done!

Abdullah struggled to his elbows, coughing again. The man should be dead already. But Shannon had changed somehow. The fog was gone and that realization was dizzying.

Abdullah stood and backed up slowly, staring. Then he turned and stumbled toward the skiff.

"Stop!" Shannon lifted the gun and fired it into the air. "The next one won't miss."

The Arab halted.

Shannon ran for him. He wasn't sure how much time he had, but that no longer mattered. Either he would make it or he wouldn't.

The Arab turned around and Shannon shoved the gun under his chin. "Give me the transmitter!"

The Arab didn't flinch. "It's useless without the code, you fool. I don't even know the code—"

"Give it to me!" Shannon screamed.

Abdullah dug in his pants pocket and pulled out the black transmitter. Shannon grabbed it and shoved the man away. He turned it on end, activated it with a familiar flip of the power switch, and stared at the number pad.

He lifted an unsteady hand, entered a five-digit code, pushed the green button on the left, and waited. In less than three seconds the red light on the top blipped once.

Transmission confirmed.

Tanya had come up and stood with her arms limp at her sides. The Arab stared at him white faced.

"Only Jamal—"

"I am Jamal."

Abdullah's face slowly went white. His lips suddenly twisted to a snarl and he launched himself with a scream. Shannon reacted without thinking. He stepped into the charge and brought his right palm across the man's head. The impact dropped Abdullah like a sack of grain.

For a long moment Shannon just stood there, staring at the fallen terrorist.

"You are Jamal?" Tanya asked. "Who is *Jamal?*"

The strength left Shannon's legs. He backed away from them then, suddenly horrified. "Jamal," he said.

She took a step toward him. "Yes, who is Jamal, Shannon?"

A desperate urge to run rushed through his head. His limbs began to shake.

"Shannon . . . Nothing Jamal has done will change my love for you." She smiled.

It was too much. Shannon dropped his head and sobbed.

She came at him and placed a hand on his shoulder. "It's okay—"

"No!" He spun away.

"Please . . ."

Shannon turned back and flung both arms wide. "I am Jamal! Don't you see? The bombs are mine!"

She blinked. Her face turned white.

He took a breath. "I made a vow, Tanya . . . Everyone who had a part in the killing of . . . our parents. The terrorists, the CIA." He paused . . . it was sounding absurd.

She stared at him for a long second. "A nuclear bomb?"

He looked at her desperately. "Sula . . ." was his only explanation.

"He took you."

Sorrow boiled over, and he turned from her, sobbing again. "Oh, God . . . Oh, God," he prayed. He caught his breath. He sat hard to his seat and put his head between his knees.

Her hands were suddenly on his shoulders, and he wanted to pull away.

"Tell me what you did," she said.

He closed his eyes.

"Tell me."

How could he tell her?

He lifted his head and swallowed. He spoke, only half hearing himself. "I found out that the Brotherhood had sent Abdullah to South America for the purpose of building and smuggling a bomb into the United States. That's why they established the drug routes. And the CIA helped them, without knowing about the bomb. They wanted Abdullah out of Colombia, so they suggested Venezuela. That's why my parents were killed. Your parents."

"And how did you become Jamal?"

"I decided the best way to destroy them was to take over their plan. Hijack it and use it to destroy the CIA. I persuaded the Brotherhood to let me coordinate parts of the plan. I took a good plan and made it better."

"A bomb wouldn't have killed just the CIA," she said softly.

"I know. I don't know. It didn't matter." He could hardly remember why he had done it now.

The Arab had stopped his groaning and lay still, perhaps unconscious. The jungle screamed about them, oblivious to all of this. They sat still for a while. She was stunned; he was numb.

"But it's okay now," Tanya said softly. "If you hadn't become Jamal, the second bomb would have gone off." She paused and her fingers began to work on his shoulders.

He turned to her.

"And if I hadn't loved you," she continued, "the bomb would have gone off. Father Petrus was right. If my parents hadn't come to the jungle, or if we hadn't fallen in love, or if Abdullah had chosen a different location, the bomb would have gone off. It was all God's leading, his turning evil to good."

Shannon understood what she was driving at, but the notion seemed impossible.

"If our parents hadn't been killed?"

She nodded. "Yes, if our parents hadn't been killed, the bomb would have gone off. They would have done it without you and today three million people would have died around Washington."

Movement caught the corner of his eye, and he jerked his head.

Abdullah was halfway to them, face snarled and black, a bowie knife in his right hand. His scream began then, when he was only ten feet away.

Shannon rolled to his right, away from Tanya, palmed the pistol he'd taken from the man, and came up on one knee, gun leveled. Killing had been like breathing for the last eight years. He'd lived to kill as much as he'd lived to breathe. He'd hunted and he'd slaughtered and always he'd relished each death. Sula.

But now Sula had been overcome by love, and with Abdullah tearing at him like a rabid dog, pulling the trigger came hard. At the last moment, he inched the barrel down. The gun bucked in his hand.

Boom!

The slug took Abdullah in the hip.

The force of the impact spun him into the air and he landed with a thump to his back.

Shannon dropped the gun and slumped to his seat. He closed his eyes and moaned. *Father died for this? Mother died for this, so that I could become the one man who could stop the bomb?*

He had fallen madly in love with a seventeen-year-old woman in the jungle for this?

Tanya's arms slipped around his neck and her hot breath brushed his cheek. She was crying very softly.

"I love you, Shannon. And God loves you desperately."

He draped his arms over her as she buried her face in his neck.

Then they were crying together, swept back to the pool, lost in each other's embrace, lost in love reborn.

epilogue

One Month Later

TANYA STOOD by the square oak table fidgeting nervously, watching the door through which she assumed they would bring Shannon. It was her first visit to the Canyon City Correctional Facility and she hoped it would be her last.

Helen eased herself into a chair with a sigh. "Not bad for a prison."

Tanya shifted on her feet. Yes, but it was still a prison.

"Don't worry, dear," Helen said softly. "From what you've told me, Shannon will have no problem handling himself here. Besides, he's practically a national hero. He stopped the bomb, for goodness' sakes. He won't be in here long."

"He's not who he used to be," Tanya said. "I'm not sure what he can handle anymore."

Tanya had remained by Shannon's side during the indictment and the subsequent grand jury hearing. It was a strange case to be sure. The media had a field day with the CIA agent who was really Jamal, the terrorist, who was really a boy from the jungle who had watched his parents die at the hands of terrorists *and* the CIA. Would the real Shannon Richterson please stand up?

If you asked the man on the street, the real Shannon was the man who saved America from the most horrific terrorist plot ever to be conceived. Driven mad by his parents' deaths, he had become complicit in the plot, true enough. But once he had come to his senses, he had also stopped that very plot. Without him, the plan would have been executed successfully. That's what the man on the street would say. In fact, the whole county was saying it.

But technically, Shannon had assisted terrorists. All of those he himself had killed over the years, he'd killed in the service of the United States. But thirteen people had died on the *Lumber Lord* as a result of the nuclear detonation in which Shannon had participated. They were mostly a criminal lot themselves. But that did not excuse the man most Americans wanted to see set free.

An armed guard walked past the window across the room and Tanya's heart leapt. The man who followed the guard was dressed in orange prison clothes like every other convict in the high-security building. But she hardly saw the bright color; she was looking at Shannon's face. At his hair, at his jaw line—

And then Shannon was out of sight again—for a moment. The door swung open and Shannon stepped through it. His green eyes lifted, focused on her, and held steady. He stopped just inside the door, which closed with a hush behind him.

Tanya's heart thumped and for a moment they stared at each other. She wanted to rush up to him and throw her arms around him and smother him with kisses, but somehow the moment seemed too heavy for lighthearted kisses. This was Shannon, the man whom she had been led into the jungle to love. The man she had always loved. The man who was wrapped in muscle and hardened like steel and yet as gentle as a dove.

Her Shannon.

A sheepish smile nudged his lips, and it occurred to Tanya that he was embarrassed.

"Hi, Shannon," she said softly.

"Hi, Tanya." He broke into a wide grin and walked toward them. Yes, the sight of her did that to him, didn't it? It melted him.

She stepped out to meet him. Sorrow swelled through her chest and she knew she was going to cry. He took her into his arms and she buried her head into his shoulder and slipped her arms around his waist.

"It's okay, Tanya. I'm okay."

Tanya sniffed once and swallowed hard. "I miss you."

They held each other and Tanya wanted to spend the whole hour just holding him. Behind them, Helen shifted in her chair. Shannon kissed Tanya's hair and they sat across the table from each other.

"Well, young man, you look larger in person than on the tube," Helen said. "And easily as handsome."

Shannon blushed through a smile and glanced at Tanya.

"I'm sorry, I should have introduced you. This is Helen."

Shannon looked at Tanya's grandmother. "So you are Helen. I've heard a lot about you. All good, of course. It's a pleasure meeting you." He dipped his head.

"And you." Helen grinned approvingly.

They exchanged some news and talked lightly about prison life. Tanya told Shannon about the latest positive spin on *Larry King Live* that was gathering steam. Shannon joked about the food and talked kindly about the guards. Within ten minutes they began to run out of small talk, and an awkward silence engulfed them.

Looking at the shy, gentle man across from her now, Tanya's heart ached.

"You are still confused, Shannon," Helen said.

"Grandmother," Tanya objected, "I'm not sure this is the time."

Shannon looked at Tanya and then lowered his eyes to the table.

"I can hardly remember who I was," Shannon said. The room felt charged with electricity. *You don't have to do this, Shannon.*

He closed his eyes and took a deep breath. "Actually I feel more lost than confused." He looked up at Helen, who wore a faint smile. They seemed to look into each other's souls.

"Then tell me what you remember," Helen said.

Shannon hesitated and looked away.

"I remember what happened. It just seems like a whole different person did those things." He paused. When he spoke, it was introspectively.

"When my parents were killed by the Brotherhood, something snapped. I went to the cave . . ."

"Sula," Tanya said after another pause. "The witch doctor's grave."

"Yes. And I . . . I changed there."

"What changed?" Helen asked.

"Things went fuzzy. I could hardly remember what Tanya looked like, or what my parents looked like. I became obsessed with death. With killing. Mostly with killing whoever had ruined my life."

"Abdullah and the CIA," Tanya said. He'd told her everything already, but hearing him tell Helen, it sounded new. Somehow different.

"Yes. But more than that." He shook his head and his eyes went moist. "Things got cloudy. I hated everything. When I learned about the CIA's involvement, I just began to hate everything that had anything to do with the CIA."

"But if you were driven by evil, why would you want to destroy Abdullah, who was also evil?" Tanya asked.

He shrugged. "Evil isn't so discriminating. I went back into the jungle within a year of my parents' death, intent on killing Abdullah. But while I was there, I learned that the CIA had done it as much as Abdullah had. Then I learned about the Brotherhood's plan to take a bomb into the U.S. I decided then to become Jamal and destroy both of them in one blow."

"Why didn't you just kill them and then expose the CIA?" Tanya asked.

He looked at her. "That wasn't enough. I think I could have blown up the whole world and not thought it was enough." He swallowed. "You have to understand, I was very . . . I was consumed with this thing."

"He was possessed," Helen said.

The simple declaration silenced them.

"But the powers of darkness forgot something," Helen said. "Or perhaps they've never really understood it. The Creator is the ultimate chess master, isn't he? Why he allows evil to wreak havoc, we can hardly understand. But in the end, it always plays into his hands." She paused. "As it did this time."

"It's hard for me to accept," Shannon said. There was a deep sadness in his eyes, and Tanya reached her hand out to him. "I did so much . . . damage. It feels impossible now."

"I've been there myself, Shannon," Helen said. "Believe me, I've been there. Evil is great, but not as great as God's love and forgiveness. You are freed, child. And you are loved."

Tears pooled in Shannon's eyes and one broke down his right cheek.

Tanya leaned forward and cupped his hand in both of hers. "Listen to me,

Shannon. I am madly in love with you. I have always been madly in love with you. God brought my parents to the jungle so that I could fall madly in love with you. And he did it all for a purpose. You think any of that was a mistake?"

He shook his head, but the tears were slipping down his face now.

"And the love I have for you is only a fraction of the love he has for you."

His shoulders began to shake and suddenly he was sobbing silently. Tanya looked at Helen in desperation. She smiled, but there were tears in her eyes as well.

Tanya looked back at Shannon, and it struck her then that there was more than sorrow in those tears. There was gratitude and relief and there was love.

She pushed her chair back, stepped around to him, and put her arms around his shoulders. His head rested on her shoulder and he shook like a leaf as he cried. He suddenly reached over and encircled her with his arms.

"I love you, Tanya."

"I know. I know. And I love you."

They held each other and wept. But it was most definitely a good cry. The kind that cleansed the soul and bound hearts as one. The kind that healed deep wounds. Tears of love.

At some point Tanya saw that Helen had left them. She could see the older woman standing by a large window, staring out to the blue sky. She was smiling. And if Tanya wasn't mistaken, she was humming. It was an old tune she had heard a hundred times before.

Jesus, Lover of my soul.

In the end it was always about love, wasn't it?

An Excerpt from *Immanuel's Veins*

My name is Toma Nicolescu and I was a warrior, a servant of Her Majesty, the empress of Russia, Catherine the Great, who by her own hand and tender heart sent me on that mission at the urging of her most trusted adviser, Grigory Potyomkin, in the year of our Lord 1772.

It was a year of war, this one the Russo-Turkish War, one of so many with the Ottoman Empire. I had slain the enemy with more ambition than most in the humble service of the empress, or so it has been said, and having earned Her Majesty's complete trust in my loyalty and skill, I was dispatched by her to the south and east, through Ukraine to the principality of Moldavia, just north of the Black Sea and west of Transylvania, to the country estate of the Cantemir family nestled up against the base of the Carpathian Mountains.

To my understanding, the family descendants of Dimitrie Cantemir, the late prince of Moldavia, were owed a debt for his loyalty to Russia. Indeed, it was said that the path to the heart of Moldavia ran through the Cantemir crest, but that was all politics—none of my business.

On that day my business was to travel to this remote, lush green valley in western Moldavia and give protection to this most important family who retreated to the estate every summer.

Russia had occupied Moldavia. Enemies were about with sharp knives and blunt intentions. The black plague had mercilessly taken the lives of many in the cities. A ruler loyal to Catherine the Great would soon be selected to take the reins of this important principality, and the Cantemir family would play a critical role in that decision as they held such a lofty position of respect among all Moldavians.

My charge was simple: No harm could come to this family. These Cantemirs.

The sun was sinking over the Carpathian peaks to our left as my friend in arms, Alek Cardei, and I sat atop our mounts and stared down at the valley. The great white castle with its twin spires stood on emerald grasses an hour's ride down the twisted path. A tall stone wall ran the length of the southern side where the road ran into the property. Green lawns and gardens surrounded the estate, encompassing ten times the ground as the house itself. The estate had been commissioned by Dimitrie Cantemir in 1711, when he was prince of Moldavia for a brief time before retreating to Turkey.

"I see the twin peaks, but I see no gowns," Alek said, squinting down the valley. His gloved hand was on his gold-busted sword. Leather armor wrapped his chest and thighs, same as mine. A goatee cupped his chin and joined his mustache but he'd shaved the rest of his face in the creek earlier, anticipating his ride into the estate, the arriving hero from abroad.

Alek, the lover.

Toma, the warrior.

I looked down at the golden ring on my finger, which bore the empress's insignia, and I chuckled. Alek's wit and charm were always good friends on a long journey, and he wielded both with the same ease and precision with which I swung my sword.

I nodded at my fair-headed friend as he turned his pale blue eyes toward me. "We're here to protect the sisters and their family, not wed them."

"So then you cannot deny it: the sisters are on your mind. Not the mother, not the father, not the family, but the sisters. These two female frolickers who are the talk of Ukraine." Alek turned his mirth-twisted face back to the valley. "Heat has come to the dog at last."

To the contrary, though Alek could not know, I had taken a vow to Her Majesty not to entangle myself while here in Moldavia. She was all too aware of the sisters' reputations, and she suggested I keep my head clear on this long assignment that might too easily give us much idle time.

"One favor, Toma," she said.

"Of course, Your Majesty."

"Stay clear of the sisters, please. At least one of you ought to have a clear mind."

"Of course, Your Majesty."

But Alek was a different matter, and there was hardly any reason to deny him his jesting. It always lifted my spirits.

If I were a woman, I would have loved Alek. If I were a king, I would have hired him to remain in my courts. If I were an enemy, I would have run and hid, because wherever you found Alek you would find Toma, and you would surely die unless you swore allegiance to the empress.

But I was the furthest thing from a woman, I had never aspired to be a king, and I had no mortal enemies save myself.

My vice was honor: chivalry when it was appropriate, but loyalty to my duty first. I was Alek's closest and most trusted friend, and I would have died for him without a care in the world.

He blew out some air in exasperation. "I have gone to the ends of the earth with you, Toma, and I would still. But this mission of ours is a fool's errand. We come here to sit with babies while the armies dine on conquest?"

"So you've made abundantly clear for a week now," I returned. "What happened to your yearning for these sisters? As you've said, they are rumored to be beautiful."

"Rumors! For all we know they are spoiled fat poodles. What can this valley possibly offer that the nights in Moscow can't? I'm doomed, I tell you. I would rather run a sword through myself now than suffer a month in that dungeon below."

I could see through his play already. "From frolicking sisters to suicide so quickly? You're outdoing yourself, Alek."

"I'm utterly serious!" His face flashed, indignant. "When have you known me to sit on my hands for weeks on end with nothing but a single family to occupy me? I'm telling you, this is going to be my death."

He was still playing me, and I him. "So now you expect me to give you leave to exhaust your fun here, then go gallivanting about the countryside seeking out mistresses in the other estates? Or would you rather slip out at night and slit a few evil throats so you can feel like a man?"

He shrugged. "Honestly, the former sounds more appealing." His gloved finger stabbed skyward. "But I know my duty and would die by your side fulfilling it." He lowered his hand. "Still, as God is my witness, I will not tolerate a month of picking my teeth with straw while the rest of the world fights for glory and chases skirts."

"Don't be a fool, man. Boredom could not catch you if it chased you like a wolf. We'll establish a simple protocol to limit all access to the estate, post the sentries, and mind the women—I understand that the father will be gone most of the time. As long as our duties are in no way compromised, I will not stand in the way of your courting. But as you say, they may be fat poodles."

A sound came from behind us. "Who has business with the Cantemirs? Eh?"

I spun to the soft, gravelly voice. An old shriveled man stood there, grasping a tall cane with both hands. His eyes were slits, his face was wrinkled like a dried-out prune, and his long stringy gray hair was so thin that a good wind would surely leave him bald. I wasn't sure he could actually see through those black cracks below his brow.

Alek *humphed* and deferred to me. How had this ancient man walked up on us without a sound? He was gumming his lips, toothless. Silent.

I held my hand up to Alek and drew my pale mount about to face the man. "Who asks?"

A bird flew in from the west, a large black crow. As I watched, somewhat stunned, it alighted on the old man's shoulder, steadied itself with a single flap of its wings, and came to rest. The man didn't react, not even when the crow's thick wing slapped his ear.

"I don't have a name," the old man said. "You may call me an angel if you like."

Alek chuckled, but I was sure it was a nervous reaction without a lick of humor.

"Who inquires of the Cantemir estate?" he asked again.

"Toma Nicolescu, in the service of Her Majesty, the empress of Russia, Catherine the Great, who now rules Moldavia. And if you are an angel, then you may vanish as all angels vanish, into the air of superstition."

"Toma?" the old man croaked.

"What business do you have with this estate?"

"Eh, that is you? Toma Nicolescu?"

His demeanor now bothered me more than I cared to admit. Was this my elder, whom I should honor, or a wandering lunatic?

"Watch your tongue, old man," Alek snapped.

The crow cocked its head and lined up one of its beady eyes for a hard look at Alek; the old man did the same.

"Eh? Is that you too, Toma?"

Alek's brow furrowed. "Stop playing the buffoon. And get rid of that cursed bird."

"State your business, old man," I demanded.

He lifted a bony, scarcely fleshed hand and pointed to the west. "There is evil in the wind. Beware, Toma. Beware the evil."

"Don't be a loon . . ."

I held up my hand to stop Alek, interested in the oddity before us, this ancient blind prune and his all-seeing crow.

"What makes you think there is evil to beware?" I asked.

"Eh? The crow saw it."

"The crow told you that, did he? And does your crow speak as well?" Alek's voice wrung mockery from each word.

Lightning stabbed at the plains in the east. I hadn't noticed the clouds on the horizon until now. A muted peal of thunder growled at us, as if in warning I thought, and I wasn't given to superstition. The devil wasn't my enemy and God wasn't my friend. Nothing I'd experienced in my twenty-eight years had moved me to believe in either.

The old wizard with his crow was staring at me through slits, silent. I wanted to know why the man seemed to sense the threat—it was my job to know. So I dismounted, walked up to him, and dipped my head, an easy thing to do considering his age, for I had always been given to respecting the aged.

The black bird was only three feet from me, jerking its head for a better look, sizing me up, deciding whether he should pluck my eyes out.

I spoke kindly, in a low voice. "Please, if you feel it wise, tell me why your crow would warn us of evil."

He smiled a toothless grin, all gums and lips. "This is Peter the Great. I can't see so well, but they tell me he's a magnificent bird. I think he likes me."

"I would say he looks like a devil. So why would a devil tell an angel that evil is near?"

"I'm not the devil, Toma Nicolescu. He is far more beautiful than I."

I was sure I could hear Alek snickering, and I had half a mind to shut him up with a glare.

"And who is this beautiful devil?"

"A man with a voice like honey who flies through the night." The old man removed his right hand from the staff and used it like a wing. "But God was the one who told me to tell Toma Nicolescu that evil is in contest with you. He said you would come here, to the Brasca Pass. I've been waiting for three days, and I do think one more day might have claimed my life."

"So the crow saw it, and then God told you, his angel, to warn us," Alek scoffed. "How is that possible when we didn't even know which route we would take until yesterday?"

"Perhaps God can read your minds."

"*Our* minds didn't even know!"

"But God did. And here you are. And now I have done my thing and can live a little longer with my crow. I should go now." He started to turn.

"Please, kind sir." I put my hand on his. "Our mission is only to protect the estate. Is there anything else you can tell us? I don't see how a warning of evil given by a crow is much use to us."

The man's gentle face slowly sagged and became a picture of foreboding. "I can hardly advise you, who thinks the devil is only hot air, now can I?"

I was surprised that the old man knew this about me. But it could as easily have been a lucky guess.

"As for your oversexed friend, you may tell him that this valley will certainly exhaust his feral impulses. I suspect that you are both in for a rather stimulating time. Now, I must be going. I have a long way to travel and the night is coming fast."

With that he turned and walked away, a slow shuffle that made me wonder how he expected to reach the path, much less the nearest town, Crysk, a full ten miles south.

Cheryl Muhr

Ted Dekker is the *New York Times* bestselling author of more than 25 novels. He is known for stories that combine adrenaline-laced plots with incredible confrontations between good and evil. He lives in Texas with his wife and children.